THE TELEVISION COMPANION

The Unofficial and Unauthorised Guide to DOCTOR WHO

THE TELEVISION COMPANION

The Unofficial
and Unauthorised Guide
to DOCTOR WHO

By David J Howe
& Stephen James Walker

First published in England in 2003 by

Telos Publishing Ltd
61 Elgar Avenue, Tolworth, Surrey, KT5 9JP, England
www.telos.co.uk

Previously published in a different form by BBC Worldwide Ltd, 1998.

ISBN: 1-903889-51-0 (paperback)
Text ©1998/2003 David J Howe and Stephen James Walker.

ISBN: 1-903889-52-9 (deluxe hardback)
Text ©1998/2003 David J Howe and Stephen James Walker.

The moral rights of the authors have been asserted.

Internal design, typesetting and layout
by Arnold T Blumberg
www.atbpublishing.com

Printed in India by
Brilliant Printers Pvt. Ltd., #18 & 19, Lottegollahalli,
RMV II Stage, Bangalore 560 094 India

2 3 4 5 6 7 8 9 10 11 12 13 14 15

British Library Cataloguing in Publication Data.
A catalogue record for this book is available from the British Library.

For those who paved the way.
Especially for Malcolm Hulke, Terrance Dicks
and Jean-Marc Lofficier – DJH.

For Josh, Elliott and Gregory – SJW.

ACKNOWLEDGEMENTS

For help in preparing this guide we are indebted to a number of others who share our enthusiasm for *Doctor Who* and who have made useful comments and suggestions at many stages along the way.

We are grateful to our then editor, Steve Cole, for having the confidence to commission the original version of the book, and for all his friendly advice and comments in shaping it for its first publication, by BBC Worldwide, in 1998.

Andrew Pixley as always added his encyclopaedic knowledge and insightful comments to the mix. We remain grateful to Paul Scoones and Robert Franks for their advance reading and helpful comments on the first edition, and also to Bruce Robinson, Graham Strong, David Holman, David Butler, Steve Roberts, Paul Vanezis, Richard Molesworth, Mark Ayres and everyone else who has been involved in audio and video preservation and restoration work on episodes no longer held in their original form in the BBC's archives. Thanks also to Keith Topping for some 'popular myths' suggestions.

For this second, revised edition – which we have endeavoured to make even more comprehensive than the first, for instance by incorporating a considerable amount of additional production information, much of which originally appeared in our series of *Doctor Who* Handbooks published by Virgin in the 1990s – our thanks go to Richard Bignell for his sterling work in tracking down and verifying all the locations used in the making of *Doctor Who*. His book *Doctor Who On Location* (Reynolds & Hearn, 2001) is the definitive reference work on that subject. Also to David Brunt and, again, Andrew Pixley, whose *Doctor Who Production Guide* series (Nine Travellers/Global Productions 1997) has proved invaluable to us for double checking details. For further information on the 1996 television movie, we would recommend that readers seek out *Doctor Who: Regeneration* (HarperCollins 2000) by Philip Segal with Gary Russell.

Thanks to the participants of the *Outpost Gallifrey* (www.gallifreyone.com) forums for various suggestions regarding this revised edition, all of which were valuable to us, and also to Simon Simmons and Martin Wiggins.

Finally, our appreciation goes to everyone who has ever reviewed or commented on any *Doctor Who* story, whether we have managed to include an extract here or not.

FOREWORD

The Television Companion is exactly what its title implies. It is a source of information and opinion to be enjoyed while watching what is, in our view, the best television series of its kind ever to be produced. It is not an attempt to present an exhaustive behind-the-scenes account of the making of the series; there have been other titles covering that ground. Nor does it contain minutely detailed lists of technical and production information; again, such information has been published elsewhere, for those who wish to seek it out.

Our aim in writing this book was to make available for fans and general viewers alike, for the first time, an accessible yet authoritative 'armchair guide' to *Doctor Who*, covering the entire series as originally broadcast in the UK by BBC television. We arranged the material chronologically so that the book would be suitable not only for dipping into but also for reading from cover to cover to obtain a comprehensive overview of the development of the series.

Inspired in part by the numerous and ever-popular film guides that occupy living room shelves the length and breadth of the country, we decided to focus in particular on the series' artistic merits, presenting a subjective assessment and critical appraisal of the good Doctor's televised adventures – an aspect very much glossed over in previous books about the series. Where did the stories succeed, and where did they fail? What special qualities did *Doctor Who* possess to account for its incredible longevity? Was it actually any good? These are some of the questions that we hope this book will help to answer.

Like most critics, we have no desire to impose our views on others. We have no monopoly on wisdom. Although we have written very much from our own individual perspectives – and we offer no apology for that – we have also made a point of incorporating a large number of other people's opinions and observations, quoted from a wide variety of different and in many cases contemporary sources. No other book has ever attempted to gather together and make generally accessible in this way some of the enormous quantity of critical comment and considered analysis to which *Doctor Who* has been subjected over the years, and we hope that it makes for interesting, illuminating and entertaining reading.

This is by no means all that the book contains, however. Amongst other things, the pages that follow give full details of every one of *Doctor Who*'s wonderful cliffhanger episode endings (something else that, perhaps surprisingly, has never been done in any previous book about the series); attempt to dispel a cornucopia of popular myths; highlight some particular points to watch out for in the episodes; and recall some of the series' most memorable lines of dialogue. We also of course reveal details of the plots – and now is perhaps the best point to give the 'spoiler alert' that if readers want to be surprised by the stories, they should watch them before reading this book!

The Television Companion is by no means the last word on *Doctor Who*, but we hope it is a book that will continue to stand the test of time and remain useful and entertaining for as long as the series itself is still watched and enjoyed, whether it be on video or DVD or on repeat cable, satellite or terrestrial screenings. Who knows, maybe one of these days there will be some new episodes produced, and we will find ourselves faced with the very welcome task of having to prepare a further, updated edition …

In the meantime … let us be your guides through the many worlds of *Doctor Who*.

David J Howe and Stephen James Walker

AUTHORS' NOTE

As mentioned in the Foreword, a major aspect of this book is its extensive critical appraisal of the Doctor's televised adventures. We have attempted in these sections of the text to present as fair and as balanced a picture as possible, drawing attention to both the pros and the cons of each story as we see them (and naturally enough we do not always agree on these!).

The numerous other sources of opinion and reaction from which we have quoted include contemporary newspaper reviews, the BBC's own Audience Research Reports, viewers' letters and internet postings. By far the most important source of such material, however, has been fanzines – that is, generally small print-run amateur publications produced by fans of the series for love rather than money.

There have, over the years, been literally hundreds of such fanzines produced, with a wide variety of weird and wonderful titles from *Ark in Space* to *Zygon* (in fact, some titles have been used more than once – there have, for example, been at least two different fanzines called *Matrix*). Many of these have lasted only one or two issues, while others have had much longer runs and built up loyal readerships.

Reviews have always been a staple ingredient of fanzines and, far from being full of gushing praise as those unfamiliar with them might perhaps expect, they are frequently very well-considered and insightful and sometimes reach a level of erudition more commonly to be found in university text books. On occasion, in fact, they are far more highly critical than would ever be considered acceptable in any mainstream publication! We have attempted to draw on the best and most interesting of all these earlier analyses and, although we have included only brief extracts in direct quotes from any particular review (quite apart from anything else, this is the most that we are permitted to do under the 'fair dealing' provisions of copyright law), we have been greatly inspired by everything that we have read. We owe a great debt of gratitude to all the many fanzine editors and writers to whose work we have referred in the preparation of this book, whether quoted or not. Those whose names are cited in the pages that follow constitute a veritable 'who's who' of *Doctor Who* fandom past and present, and many have since gone on to greater achievements in the world of journalism or in other careers.

The other items of information included for each individual story are largely self-explanatory, but there are perhaps a few points that we ought to make. As the first twenty-five *Doctor Who* stories had no overall title on screen (each episode had an individual title), we have adopted the title that (according to the best evidence available, including scripts and internal BBC documentation) was used by the production team themselves at the time the story was actually transmitted. In a few instances where stories are popularly known by other titles we have noted this as well. The production credits given are not exhaustive (we have had to draw the line somewhere), but they cover some of the main behind-the-scenes contributors to each story. The cast listings cover only those artistes actually credited on the transmitted episodes. In this case we have attempted, with two exceptions made for the sake of consistency, to replicate exactly what was seen on screen – although where this would otherwise result in a major error or omission we have also included additional information in a footnote. The first exception is that we have spelt the character Brigadier Lethbridge-Stewart's surname with a (grammatically correct) hyphen in all instances, although it appeared that way on screen for only five of the stories in which he featured – *The Web of Fear*, *The Invasion*, *Spearhead from Space*, *Day of the Daleks* and *Battlefield* – and was otherwise unhyphenated. The second is that we have invariably referred to the fourth Doctor's robot dog as 'K9', although the spelling was given as 'K.9' on the closing credits of *Meglos*, *Full Circle* and Parts Three and Four of *Warriors' Gate* in season eighteen and as 'K·9' on those of the *K·9 and Company* spin-off. The superscript figures that appear after the names of production crew, characters and cast members indicate the episodes to which they contributed or on which they were credited, as the case may be. Where no such numbers are given, it should be assumed that the individual in question contributed to or was credited on every episode of the story, or that the nature of their contribution to the production means that it cannot be readily subdivided between episodes in this way.

In researching the episodes currently missing from the BBC's archives and not therefore available for viewing in their original form we have used the best sources of information at our disposal, including soundtrack recordings, scripts and off-screen photographs (otherwise known as telesnaps) taken at the time of transmission.

The remainder of the text – such as the short pieces introducing each of the eight Doctors and explaining the creation of the Daleks and the Cybermen – is included with the aim of ensuring that the book gives a rounded overview of the series' development. We have tried where possible to give a new slant to these pieces, but should mention that the one entitled *The Genesis of* Doctor Who, about the series' creation, is adapted from a feature written by Stephen James Walker, with input from Andrew Pixley, for Marvel Comics' *Doctor Who* Yearbook 1996, published in 1995.

In the following contents listing, the internal story codes used by the BBC to identify the stories are included in brackets following the title. The 1996 television movie had no such code. These codes give the production order of the stories and it can be seen that, in some cases, their transmission order was different. For example, *Four to Doomsday* was the first story made featuring Peter Davison as the Doctor, but his debut on screen came in *Castrovalva*.

CONTENTS

The First Doctor
[William Hartnell]
1963-1966

THE GENESIS OF DOCTOR WHO

Doctor Who was born out of conflict. Specifically, this was a conflict between the go-ahead, commercial-minded style of programming brought to the BBC in 1963 by new Head of Drama Sydney Newman, and the traditional, more high-brow approach favoured by the old guard, as personified in particular by BBC1's Chief of Programmes Donald Baverstock. Fortunately, Newman was a man who thrived on conflict. As the series' second producer John Wiles would later disapprovingly recall: 'He liked nothing better than to hear that two producers had had a punch up in the Gents. "Great!" he would say. "That's creative conflict, man!"'

The idea of mounting a science-fiction series had been mooted some time prior to Newman's arrival at the BBC. Between April and July 1962, the staff of the Script Department, headed by Donald Wilson, had produced two reports on science-fiction, investigating the possibility of identifying some published stories that would be suitable for TV adaptation. Although well-received, these reports had indicated only a limited understanding of the genre on the researchers' part, and had surprisingly failed to give any consideration to a number of such programmes already produced by the BBC. Little more work was done in this area until after Newman took up his post at the end of the year.

It was in March 1963 that Baverstock raised with Newman the need for a new Saturday evening serial to fill the slot between the sports programme *Grandstand* and the pop music show *Juke Box Jury*. After he had considered a number of other possibilities, including one involving the exploits of two pupils in a boys' school, it was the science-fiction idea that Newman decreed should be taken forward.

At the end of March, Wilson convened a meeting with three of his staff members, Alice Frick, John Braybon and C E 'Bunny' Webber, to get the ball rolling on development of the new series. Taking as their starting point the two 1962 reports (which Frick and Braybon had been involved in preparing), they came up with a number of concepts that they thought could be suitable, including – at Wilson's suggestion – that of a time machine. Webber subsequently prepared a note on 'Characters and Setup', proposing that the three leads should be a 'Handsome Young Man Hero', a 'Handsome Well-Dressed Heroine' and a 'Maturer Man, 35-40, With Some "Character" Twist'.

Although he liked the idea of a time machine, Newman's general reaction to these proposals was that they were rather old-fashioned. He insisted that the regular line up should include a youngster to act as the focus for the series' intended educational aspect, and in place of Webber's 'Maturer Man' he devised Doctor Who, a frail and grumpy old man who has absconded with the time machine from his own civilisation on a far-distant planet.

While Wilson and Webber continued to work on the concepts and characters, May 1963 saw the appointment of the highly experienced staff producer/director Rex Tucker to take charge of the production. At this time, internal restructuring meant that the old producer/director role was being phased out and the Script Department abolished. Wilson was being transferred to become Head of Serials – the newly-created Department that would make *Doctor Who* (as the series had now been named). Tucker's job was therefore essentially that of a 'caretaker', until a new-style production team could be set up to take over.

By the end of May, Wilson, Webber and Newman had agreed an initial format document, which contained brief descriptions of the four lead characters – schoolteachers Cliff and Miss McGovern, their pupil Sue and the mysterious Doctor Who – and an outline of the first story, Webber's *The Giants*. Recording was due to get underway at the beginning of August, with the first episode pencilled in for transmission later the same month. Tucker had even asked composer Tristram Cary if he would provide the series' theme and incidental music, and had unsuccessfully sounded out actor Hugh David about playing the Doctor. Another staff writer, Anthony Coburn, had meanwhile started work on ideas for the second story. The production team had also gained Mervyn Pinfield, who as associate producer would be primarily responsible for the series' technical aspects.

Webber's *The Giants*, the first two episodes of which had by early June been completed in draft script form, received only a luke-warm reception from Newman. It had then to be abandoned altogether, mainly because the story's extensive visual effects requirements (for scenes in which the four travellers arrived in miniaturised form in the school laboratory) could not now be met as *Doctor Who* had been allocated the relatively primitive recording facilities of Lime Grove Studio D. Coburn's story, set in the Stone Age, was moved to first in the running order and the opening episode amended to incorporate the introduction of the four lead characters along the lines previously worked out by Webber.

Mid-June saw the arrival of the series' new producer, Verity Lambert, and the appointment of its story editor, David Whitaker. Lambert, a former production assistant of Newman's from his days at ABC TV, had been given the job after at least two others, Don Taylor and Shaun Sutton, had turned it down. Whitaker had previously been on staff at the Script Department for seven years.

It had by this point become clear that the planned first transmission date in late August would be impossible to meet. Whitaker and Lambert both had serious reservations about Coburn's story, *The Tribe of Gum*, but eventually realised that there was insufficient time left for a further rethink.

At the end of June, Tucker carried out auditions for the series' female leads and selected an unknown Australian actress to play Susan. A further postponement in production meant that he would no longer be able to direct the first story, as he would be on holiday on the relevant dates. He would in fact play little further part in the setting up of the series. His casting ideas were subsequently overturned by the production team who, during July, set about making their own choices.

The role of the Doctor was accepted, after initial reluctance, by well-known character actor William Hartnell. William Russell, popular for his starring role in the Sapphire Films series *The Adventures of Sir Lancelot*, won the part of the male teacher, now renamed Ian Chesterton, while that of the female teacher, Lola McGovern, went to Jacqueline Hill, whose husband was a friend of Lambert's. Carole Ann Ford was cast as Susan after Waris Hussein, the new director assigned to handle the first story, saw her performance in another programme on a TV monitor at Television Centre and drew her to Lambert's attention.

By mid-July, David Whitaker had produced a writers' guide for the freelancers being approached to contribute stories. In this, the four leads were given their final names – Ian Chesterton, Barbara Wright, Susan Foreman and Doctor Who – and an up-to-date description was included of the Doctor's ship, which at Coburn's suggestion was to have the exterior appearance of a police box. Coburn was now due to write not only the first story but also the second – a six-parter with the working title *The Robots* – while freelancer John Lucarotti had agreed to supply a historical story, *A Journey to Cathay*.

By the beginning of August, preparations were in hand to publicise the new series. Also, having previously considered commissioning the *avant-garde* French group Les Structures Sonores, Lambert decided at this point to ask the BBC's Radiophonic Workshop to collaborate with top television composer Ron Grainer to create the series' theme music. Graphic designer Bernard Lodge was given the task of coming up with a title sequence. Inspired by the work of another designer, Ben Palmer, he put together a sequence using a technique known as howl-around, which was realised in the studio by electronic effects specialist Norman Taylor when shooting for the sequence took place on Tuesday 20 August at the BBC's Television Film Studios in Ealing. This was the first material put 'in the can' for *Doctor Who*.

Early September saw the series' first transmission date postponed again to late November. Whitaker's plans for the fifty-two-week run were now beginning to come together, the intention being that the stories should fall into three distinct categories – 'past', 'future' and 'sideways' (the latter placing the time travellers in alternative dimensions or unfamiliar physical states). The provisional running order for the early part of the season was now: *The Tribe of Gum* (later retitled *100,000 BC*); *The Robots* (later retitled *The Masters of Luxor*); *A Journey to Cathay* (later retitled *Marco Polo*); a submission by Robert Gould reviving the 'miniscules' idea used in *The Giants*; Terry Nation's *The Mutants* (also known during the course of its development as *The Survivors* and *Beyond the Sun*), which featured creatures called the Daleks; and a story by Malcolm Hulke about Roman-occupied Britain around 400 AD. A little later in the month, *The Robots* and *The Mutants* were swapped around in the order, as the production team still felt dissatisfied with Coburn's scripts. Around the same time, Nation was commissioned to provide a historical adventure entitled *The Red Fort*.

On Thursday 19 September the first filming for *The Tribe of Gum* was carried out at Ealing. On Friday 27 September there then followed the first videotape recording of an episode in Lime Grove Studio D. This opening instalment was accorded the status of a pilot, the intention being that it could be transmitted if it proved successful or remade if not. On viewing the tape, Newman expressed a number of reservations and decided that the latter course of action should be taken. The new version was recorded on Friday 18 October.

During this period there remained serious concerns within the BBC about the resources needed to meet *Doctor Who*'s visual effects requirements. Matters came to a head at the end of October when Baverstock was informed that cost estimates for the pilot episode showed it to have gone way over budget. By the end of October, however, a round of intensive discussions involving Wilson, Lambert and others had agreed a financial basis on which the series could be made, and Baverstock agreed to sanction a run of at least thirteen episodes.

One upshot of all this was that Whitaker had to write a low-budget two-part story, *Inside the Spaceship*, to be slotted in after *100,000 BC* and *The Mutants*, just in case the series was then cancelled. Prior to this, the provisional running order had been amended to: *100,000 BC/ The Tribe of Gum*; *The Mutants/ Beyond the Sun*; *Marco Polo/ A Journey*

to Cathay, the 'miniscules' story by Robert Gould; *The Robots/ The Masters of Luxor*, an untitled seven-part historical story by David Whitaker; *The Hidden Planet*, a new Malcolm Hulke idea; *The Red Fort*, and a four-part futuristic story still to be decided. (As things transpired, *Marco Polo* was the last of these stories to reach fruition; all those intended to follow it were ultimately abandoned at the scripting stage and replaced by others.)

During the course of the following month, further episodes of the series began to be recorded on a regular weekly basis; and on Friday 22 November – the day of President Kennedy's assassination – Baverstock agreed to extend the run to twenty-six episodes. The following day, an important landmark was reached when *An Unearthly Child*, the opening instalment of *100,000 BC*, was finally transmitted, the start of the new series having been publicised by way of TV and radio trailers and an article in the BBC's listings magazine *Radio Times*. A widespread power failure prevented many viewers from seeing the episode, and a decision was taken to repeat it the following week, immediately prior to the next one. Wilson was sufficiently pleased, however, to cable Newman (who was visiting the USA) and inform him that *Doctor Who* had got off to a great start.

WILLIAM HARTNELL IS THE FIRST DOCTOR

William Hartnell revelled in the opportunity that *Doctor Who* gave him to break free of the 'tough guy' typecasting that had dogged him for the previous two decades. He loved appearing in a more fantastical role in a family series and becoming a hero to millions of children. 'I think I represent a cross between the Wizard of Oz and Father Christmas,' he once told the *Daily Express*. 'Yet I am always adding fragments to the part, always trying to expand on it.'

The actor had been born in the King's Cross area of London in 1908, the child of an unmarried mother, and had had a less than happy childhood growing up during a time of war and social deprivation. (So ashamed was he of his background that throughout his later life he deliberately concealed it, claiming that he came from a farming family in the village of Seaton in Devon.) He developed an early ambition to become an actor (inspired in part by his admiration for Charlie Chaplin in the silent films he saw at his local cinemas) and in 1926, with the assistance of the philanthropist art critic Hugh Blaker, was lucky enough to get a job touring with Sir Frank Benson's Shakespearian Company. Further theatre work followed, and from 1929 he started playing small roles in 'quota quickie' films.

Ill health brought a premature end to his national service in the armed forces, but his film career really took off in 1943 when, ironically, he landed the role of an indomitable army officer in the Carol Reed film *The Way Ahead*. Many other film roles followed, including some for which he received star billing, but he was continually frustrated by the fact that he was offered only 'tough guy' parts, having preferred the light comedy and farce work in which he had specialised earlier in his career.

It was Hartnell's appearances in the Granada TV comedy series *The Army Game* and the 1963 Lindsay Anderson film *This Sporting Life* that brought him to the attention of Verity Lambert when she was considering who to cast as the central character in *Doctor Who*. After a number of meetings, she became convinced that she had found her Doctor.

During his three years in the role, Hartnell crafted a highly memorable character: a wonderfully eccentric grandfather figure whose crusty facade only thinly conceals a heart of gold; an apparently doddery old man whose intellect is really as sharp as a knife; a concerned and compassionate man who, despite frequent warnings to his companions about the dangers of interfering, just cannot stop himself from getting involved, to challenge injustice and stand up for the oppressed against the oppressors. For those who grew up with *Doctor Who* in the early sixties, Hartnell *was* the Doctor – their hero of space and time.

THE PILOT EPISODE

Producer: Verity Lambert.
Associate Producer: Mervyn Pinfield.
Story Editor: David Whitaker.
Title Music: Ron Grainer and the BBC Radiophonic Workshop, arranged by Delia Derbyshire.
Special Sounds: Brian Hodgson.

Writer: Anthony Coburn. **Director:** Waris Hussein. **Designer:** Peter Brachacki, Barry Newbery. **Costumes:** Maureen Heneghan. **Make-Up:** Elizabeth Blattner. **Incidental Music:** Norman Kay. **Visual Effects:** Visual Effects Department of the BBC. **Film Cameraman:** Robert Sleigh. **Film Editor:** John Griffiths, Valerie Best, John House. **Studio Lighting:** Sam Barclay. **Studio Sound:** Jack Clayton. **Production Assistant:** Douglas Camfield. **Assistant Floor Manager:** Catherine Childs.

	First UK TX	Scheduled TX	Actual TX	Duration	Viewers
An Unearthly Child	26/08/91	14.15	14.19	25'55"	1.6

Plot: Schoolteachers Barbara Wright and Ian Chesterton become intrigued by one of their pupils, Susan Foreman, and visit her home address – a junkyard at 76 Totter's Lane – where they meet her grandfather, the Doctor. The Doctor and Susan are aliens who travel through time and space in their ship, TARDIS, which looks like an ordinary police box but actually houses a huge gleaming control room.

Episode endings:
1. The TARDIS arrives on a Palaeolithic landscape, over which falls the shadow of a man.

IT WAS MADE WHERE...?
Ealing filming: 20.08.63, 19.09.63 on Stage 3A
Studio Filming: 31.08.63 in TC5
Studio recording: 27.09.63 in Lime Grove D

CREDITED CAST
Dr. Who (William Hartnell), Ian Chesterton (William Russell), Barbara Wright (Jacqueline Hill), Susan Foreman (Carole Ann Ford).

THINGS TO WATCH OUT FOR

- A number of aspects of the pilot were changed for the transmitted version of the episode:
  - The opening theme music features a loud thuderclap noise at the beginning. (No such noise is present in the transmitted version.)
  - As the policeman does his rounds in the first scene, the air in Totter's Lane is clear. (In the transmitted version it is foggy.)
  - After saying goodnight to Ian and Barbara in the classroom, Susan splashes ink on a piece of paper, makes a Rorschach blot from it and then draws a hexagonal design before screwing up the paper. (In the transmitted version she reads a book about the French Revolution and spots a mistake.)
  - After putting his key in the TARDIS lock, the Doctor starts to withdraw the entire mechanism from the door. (In the transmitted version, he simply turns the key.)
  - Susan wears different clothes in the TARDIS. (In the transmitted version she wears the same clothes as in the school scenes.)
  - The Doctor wears an ordinary suit and tie. (This was superseded by what would become his familiar costume.)
  - As the Doctor activates the ship toward the end of the episode, Ian, Barbara and Susan try to pull him away from the controls. (In the transmitted version only Susan realises what is happening and tries to pull him away.)
  - The TARDIS's dematerialisation sound is a random selection of bleeps and tones intermixed with snatches of what would eventually become the standard effect. (In the episode as transmitted, the standard effect is heard.)
- In addition, much of the dialogue, particularly in the junkyard and TARDIS scenes, was amended for the transmitted version.

THINGS YOU MIGHT NOT HAVE KNOWN

- The pilot was first transmitted on BBC2 almost twenty-eight years after it was made, as a part of a special day's programming to mark the closure of the Lime Grove studios.

QUOTE, UNQUOTE

- **Barbara Wright:** 'But you are one of us. You look like us, you sound like us.' **Susan Foreman:** 'I was born in the 49th Century.'
- **Ian Chesterton:** 'I know that free movement in the fourth dimension of space and time is a scientific dream I don't expect to find solved in a junkyard!' **The Doctor:** 'For your science, school-master. Not for ours. I tell you before your ancestors had turned the first wheel, the people of my world had reduced movement through the farthest reaches of space to a game for children.'
- **The Doctor:** 'I cannot let you go, school-master. Whether you believe what you have been told is of no importance. You and your companion would be footprints in a time where you were not supposed to walk.'

ANALYSIS

It was always intended that *Doctor Who*'s first recorded episode could be accorded the status of a pilot – in other words, a trial run – if it failed to live up to the expectations of Sydney Newman. The making of pilots for new series was (and remains) fairly common practice in the television industry and the BBC actually had at the time a special budget allocated to finance such programmes.

After viewing the episode, Newman decided that it should indeed be remade. The pilot was somewhat rough around the edges in terms of production (for example, the doors in the TARDIS control room refused to close properly); there were a couple of line fluffs by cast members (for example, Carole Ann Ford got the chart movements of John Smith and the Common Men – a pop group that Susan was listening to on her radio – the wrong way round and hastily corrected herself); and Newman felt that the character of the Doctor, who appeared cold and unlikeable in the pilot, should be lightened, and that Susan, who came over a little too 'alien', should be made more like an ordinary human schoolgirl.

Uniquely for a sixties *Doctor Who* episode, all the material recorded for the pilot has been preserved (as a film transcription) in its raw, unedited state. It consists of a single take of all the scenes leading up to the recording break at the point where Barbara and Ian push their way into the TARDIS; a first take of all the scenes following the recording break; a brief 'false start' to a second take of the latter; and a complete second take of the latter. It is unknown what sections of this material would have been edited together to form the finished version of the episode had it been given the go-ahead for transmission at the time.

A version of the pilot was eventually shown on BBC2 in 1991 as a part of *The Lime Grove Story* – a collection of programmes marking the closure of the BBC's Lime Grove studios, where they had all been recorded. This consisted of the first section of the episode edited together with the first take of the second section. A different version was included on the BBC video *The Hartnell Years*, released in 1991; this time the complete second take of the second section was used. A later BBC video release, in 2000, of the series' third story *Inside the Spaceship*, under the title *The Edge of Destruction*, included as a 'bonus feature' all the recorded material from the pilot.

DOCTOR WHO SEASON ONE [1963-1964]

Regular Cast:
Dr. Who (William Hartnell)
Ian Chesterton (William Russell)
Barbara Wright (Jacqueline Hill)
Susan Foreman (Carole Ann Ford)

Regular Crew:
Producer: Verity Lambert
Associate Producer: Mervyn Pinfield
Story Editor: David Whitaker.
Title Music: Ron Grainer and the BBC Radiophonic Workshop, arranged by Delia Derbyshire.
Special Sounds: Brian Hodgson.

The first episode introduces us to the Doctor, his ship TARDIS, his granddaughter Susan, and Ian and Barbara, two of Susan's school teachers. From there the audience, together with Ian and Barbara, are plunged into the unknown.

The season follows a rough pattern of futuristic stories alternating with stories set in Earth's past. The fact that the series was originally intended to be partly educational is readily apparent, and is reflected in Ian's profession as a science teacher and Barbara's as a history teacher – which means that, especially in the historical adventures, explanations can come just as easily from them as from the Doctor.

100,000 BC

Note: Also known as *An Unearthly Child*.

Writer: Anthony Coburn. **Director:** Waris Hussein. **Designer:** Peter Brachacki[1] and Barry Newbery. **Costumes:** Maureen Heneghan. **Make-Up:** Elizabeth Blattner. **Incidental Music:** Norman Kay. **Special Effects:** Visual Effects Department of the BBC. **Fight Arranger:** Derek Ware. **Film Cameraman:** Robert Sleigh. **Film Editor:** unknown. **Studio Lighting:** Geoff Shaw. **Studio Sound:** Jack Clayton. **Production Assistant:** Douglas Camfield, Tony Lightley. **Assistant Floor Manager:** Catherine Childs.

	First UK TX	Scheduled TX	Actual TX	Duration	Viewers	Chart Pos.
An Unearthly Child	23/11/63	17.15	17.16	23'10"	4.4	114
The Cave of Skulls	30/11/63	17.15*	17.30	24'35"	5.9	85
The Forest of Fear	07/12/63	17.15	17.16	23'38"	6.9	61
The Firemaker	14/12/63	17.15	17.15	24'23"	6.4	70

* This episode was actually transmitted approximately fifteen minutes late as a repeat of *An Unearthly Child* had been slotted into the schedule before it for the benefit of those viewers who missed it on its original transmission due to a widespread power failure.

Plot: Schoolteachers Barbara Wright and Ian Chesterton become intrigued by one of their pupils, Susan Foreman, and visit her home address – a junkyard at 76 Totter's Lane – where they meet her grandfather, the Doctor. The Doctor and Susan are aliens who travel through time and space in their ship, TARDIS, which looks like an ordinary police box but actually houses a huge gleaming control room. The TARDIS takes them all to a Palaeolithic landscape where they encounter a tribe that has lost the secret of fire.

Episode endings:
1. The TARDIS arrives on a Palaeolithic landscape, over which falls the shadow of a man.
2. The four travellers are sealed in the tribe's Cave of Skulls with the bones of many previous prisoners, and the Doctor notices that the skulls have all been split open.
3. An escape attempt by the four travellers is foiled when they find the tribesmen lying in wait for them outside the TARDIS.
4. The TARDIS's next point of arrival is a strange alien planet. Unseen by the occupants, its radiation detector registers 'Danger'.

IT WAS MADE WHERE...?

Ealing filming: 09.10.63-11.10.63.
Studio recording: 18.10.63, 25.10.63, 1.11.63, 8.11.63, all in Lime Grove D.

ADDITIONAL CREDITED CAST

Za (Derek Newark[2-4]), Hur (Alethea Charlton[2-4]), Old Mother (Eileen Way[2,3]), Kal (Jeremy Young[2-4]), Horg (Howard Lang[2-4]).

POPULAR MYTHS

- *100,000 BC: An Unearthly Child* was transmitted ten minutes late owing to rescheduling as a result of the assassination of US President John F Kennedy the previous day. (It was transmitted only eighty seconds later than the scheduled 5.15 p.m.)
- BBC staff writer C E Webber co-scripted *100,000 BC: An Unearthly Child* with Anthony Coburn. (Webber was responsible for a story, *The Giants*, that was originally intended to open the series but was eventually rejected. Coburn drew some inspiration for *100,000 BC: An Unearthly Child* from the draft script for Webber's first episode.)
- The Stone Age episodes are set on Earth. (This *may* be the case, but it is never explicitly stated here. It could be the Stone Age of some other planet.)
- *Doctor Who* was originally transmitted 'live'. (It was always pre-recorded.)
- Actress Jackie Lane, later to play the Doctor's companion Dodo, was offered the role of Susan before Carole Ann Ford. (Lane went to an interview for the role, but withdrew when she discovered that a one year contract was involved; she was never offered the job.)
- The programme in which Waris Hussein spotted Carole Ann Ford when looking for someone to play Susan was the BBC *Suspense* play entitled *The Man on a Bicycle*. (*The*

Man on a Bicycle was transmitted some months before Hussein became involved with *Doctor Who*; it was probably therefore in another programme that her performance impressed him.)
- Jacqueline Hill once worked as a model in Paris. (She didn't.)
- The original police box seen in *Doctor Who* was a prop left over from *Dixon of Dock Green*. (It was specially made for *Doctor Who*.)

THINGS TO WATCH OUT FOR

- There is a dummy with a crushed head in the junkyard, perhaps foreshadowing the caved-in skulls that the time travellers later see in the Palaeolithic era.
- The Doctor and Susan show surprise when the TARDIS remains stuck as a police box, and Susan explains that it is supposed to change its appearance to blend in with its surroundings (an idea seriously considered by the series' creators but ruled out on grounds of cost).
- The Doctor is apparently put off smoking for life when he is attacked by Kal while about to light a large, ornate pipe.

THINGS YOU MIGHT NOT HAVE KNOWN

- Working title: *The Tribe of Gum*.
- The working title of the second individual episode was *The Fire-Maker*, that of the third was *The Cave of Skulls*, and that of the fourth was *The Dawn of Knowledge*.
- 'TARDIS' was originally intended to be the name of the Doctor's ship (in the same way as one might name a sailing boat) rather than purely a descriptive acronym.
- The bones used in the Cave of Skulls scenes were obtained by designer Barry Newbery from an abattoir; the smell they gave off under the hot studio lights was extremely unpleasant.
- William Hartnell recorded a sound trailer for the first episode, to be broadcast on BBC Radio. This was as follows:

   My name is William Hartnell and, as Doctor Who, I make my debut on Saturday 23 November at 5.15.

   The Doctor is an extraordinary old man from another world who owns a time and space machine.

   He and his grand-daughter, Susan (played by Carole Ann Ford), have landed in England and are enjoying their stay, until Susan arouses the curiosity of two of her school-teachers (played by William Russell and Jacqueline Hill). They follow Susan and get inside the ship, and Doctor Who decides to leave Earth, starting a series of adventures which I know will thrill and excite you every week.

- The first letter ever to be received by the *Doctor Who* production office from members of the public was written by two correspondents, Miss Johnson and Mr Priddy of Wimbledon Park, London SW19, immediately after transmission of *The Cave of Skulls* on 30 November 1964. They criticised the episode on the grounds that it: depicted a tribe without fire in an era when fire had already been discovered; assumed that the tribe would have a patriarchal society, although archaeological evidence for this was slender; and showed an articulated skeleton when this was anatomically impossible as there would have been nothing to hold the bones together. Story editor David Whitaker replied on 10 December 1963, refuting some of these points and justifying others on the grounds of dramatic licence.

- Margot Maxine, one of the walk-ons hired to play non-speaking members of the Stone Age tribe, refused to have her teeth blackened for the recording of *The Cave of Skulls* on 25 October 1963 and walked out of the studio at 3.00 p.m.
- The interior TARDIS set was constructed by Shawcraft Models (Uxbridge) Ltd., the freelance effects contractors who would be responsible for meeting the great majority of *Doctor Who*'s special props and effects requirements during the first Doctor's era.
- *An Unearthly Child* was repeated on 30 November 1963, immediately before *The Cave of Skulls*, as many viewers had been deprived of the opportunity to see the original transmission due to a widespread power failure. This repeat was not shown in Northern Ireland.

QUOTE, UNQUOTE

- **Barbara Wright:** 'But you are one of us! You look like us, you sound like us ...' **Susan Foreman:** 'I was born in another time, another world ...'
- **Ian Chesterton:** 'I know that free movement in time and space is a scientific dream I don't expect to find solved in a junkyard!' **The Doctor:** 'Your arrogance is almost as great as your ignorance!'
- **The Doctor:** 'Have you ever thought what it's like to be wanderers in the fourth dimension? Have you? To be exiles ...?'
- **Za:** 'My father made fire.' **Old Mother:** 'They killed him for it. It is better that we live as we have always done.' **Za:** 'Without meat we go hungry. Without fire we die!'
- **Barbara Wright:** 'You're trying to help me.' **The Doctor:** 'Fear makes companions of all of us, Miss Wright.'

ANALYSIS

100,000 BC can be subdivided into two distinct sections with very different settings and qualities: the first episode and the remaining three.

Contemporary reaction from the general viewing public to the first episode, *An Unearthly Child*, seems to have consisted mainly of bemusement, and in some cases even hilarity. While acknowledging that it was 'all good, clean fun,' a retired Naval officer quoted in the BBC's internal Audience Research Report on the episode said: 'Tonight's new serial seemed to be a cross between Wells' *The Time Machine* and a space-age *Old Curiosity Shop*, with a touch of Mack Sennett comedy. It was in the grand style of the old pre-talkie films to see a dear old police box being hurtled through space and landing on Mars or somewhere. I almost expected to see a batch of Keystone Cops emerge on the Martian landscape.' These sentiments were echoed by the *Daily Mail*'s TV reviewer Michael Gowers, who wrote in a piece published on 25 November 1963: 'William Hartnell gazing from under locks of flowing white, and the appealing Carole Ann Ford, represent the Unknown Them, William Russell and Jacqueline Hill the ignorant, sceptical Us, and their craft is cunningly disguised as a police callbox. The penultimate shot of this, after a three-point touchdown, in a Neolithic landscape, must have delighted the hearts of the *Telegoons* who followed.'

More recent reaction to the story's opening episode has been almost uniformly positive, and it is now generally regarded as a *bona fide* TV classic. John Peel, writing in 1980 in the fan reference work *Doctor Who – An Adventure in Space and Time*, was positively rapturous: 'Mysterious origins, flights across forever, and the chance meeting in a junk yard of two teachers and that which is utterly beyond their comprehension. *An Unearthly Child* was a work of loving craftsmanship, worked out to perfection by all concerned.'

Certainly the episode is very effective in establishing the premise of the series and in introducing its principal characters and concepts. The dialogue between the four regulars in their earliest scenes together is superbly written and well conveys the sense of wonder and incredulity of the two ordinary schoolteachers coming up against the complete unknown. William Russell and Jacqueline Hill strike just the right note as Ian and Barbara, making them instantly recognisable characters to the thousands of youngsters in the viewing audience. Carole Ann Ford is also suitably quirky and mysterious as Susan Foreman, complete with her specially created Vidal Sassoon hairstyle. The real acting honours, though, go to William Hartnell as the intriguing and irascible Doctor. His performance is quite simply superb. The only thing that matches it for impact in *An Unearthly Child* is the revelation of the TARDIS interior. Even today this scene is breathtaking, but just imagine how it would have struck the viewer of 1963, when nothing like it had ever been seen before and the idea of a ship bigger inside than out was truly novel. Designer Peter Brachacki's short involvement with the series was, by all accounts, not a happy experience, but in creating the TARDIS interior he was responsible for one of the most outstanding, innovative and memorable sets in TV history.

The impact of this set is arguably all the greater for the stark contrast it presents to the ship's mundane police box exterior. The shockingly incongruous sight of the latter standing on a barren, rocky landscape at the end of *An Unearthly Child* provides the series with an excellent first cliff-hanger and neatly sets the scene for the remainder of the opening story.

Reaction to these following episodes set in the Stone Age has been relatively lukewarm. It has been noted that they were completely untypical of the kinds of settings and situations that would normally be seen in *Doctor Who* – arguably not a good idea for the opening story of a series, which really ought to give viewers a fair idea of what they can expect. It has also been said that the Stone Age setting was inadvisable, as it resulted in the story having a narrow scope and lacking in visual interest. Even its producer Verity Lambert later opined that to open with a story in which the guest cast wore costumes akin to fur rugs and could communicate in little more than grunts was a mistake. These criticisms are somewhat unfair, however. While they may admittedly lack the impact of the phenomenal opening episode, these three instalments are nevertheless intense, highly dramatic and, as Peel noted, pervaded by 'an atmosphere of violence, squalor and a grotesque horror … Dismembered skeletons, burning skulls, rotting animal carcasses. A succession of macabre images masterfully create a realistic picture of life at the dawn of time.'

There are some interesting contrasts here between the different attitudes, expectations and abilities of the three groups of characters – the alien time travellers, the human schoolteachers and the primitive cave dwellers. As Peel put it, 'In theme, we see in *An Unearthly Child* Ian and Barbara as two modern-day intelligent humans. Yet to the Doctor they are as primitive savages. Ian and Barbara are unable to understand this until, ironically, the roles are reversed. In the prehistoric past it is Ian and Barbara who are the intelligent "aliens", and the cavemen the primitive savages.' The environment into which

Ian and Barbara (and, by identification with them, the viewing audience) are thrust is certainly just as strange and threatening as that of any far-distant planet.

All in all, *100,000 BC* gave the new series a positive start – particularly in its opening episode – and provided a solid foundation upon which it could build as the season progressed.

THE MUTANTS

Note: Also known as *The Daleks*.

Writer: Terry Nation. **Director:** Christopher Barry[1,2,4,5], Richard Martin[3,6,7]. **Designer:** Raymond P Cusick[1-5,7], Jeremy Davies[6]. **Costumes:** Daphne Dare. **Make-Up:** Elizabeth Blattner. **Incidental Music:** Tristram Cary. **Film Cameraman:** Stewart Farnell. **Film Editor:** Ted Walter. **Studio Lighting:** John Treays, Geoff Shaw. **Studio Sound:** Jack Clayton, Jack Brummitt. **Production Assistant:** Norman Stewart. **Assistant Floor Manager:** Michael Ferguson, Jeremy Hare.

	First UK TX	Scheduled TX	Actual TX	Duration	Viewers	Chart Pos.
The Dead Planet	21/12/63	17.15	17.16	24'22"	6.9	67
The Survivors	28/12/63	17.15	17.16	24'27"	6.4	78
The Escape	04/01/64	17.15	17.15	25'10"	8.9	45
The Ambush	11/01/64	17.15	17.15	24'37"	9.9	29
The Expedition	18/01/64	17.15	17.15	24'31"	9.9	27
The Ordeal	25/01/64	17.15	17.15	26'14"	10.4	29
The Rescue	01/02/64	17.15	17.18	22'24"	10.4	25

Plot: The TARDIS has brought the travellers to the planet Skaro where they meet two indigenous races – the Daleks, malicious mutant creatures encased in armoured travel machines, and the Thals, beautiful humanoids with pacifist principles. They convince the Thals of the need to fight for their own survival. Joining forces with them and braving Skaro's many dangers, they launch a two-pronged attack on the Dalek city. The Daleks are all killed when, during the course of the fighting, their power supply is cut off.

Episode endings:
1. Exploring their apparently deserted city, Barbara encounters one of the Daleks and is menaced by its telescopic sucker arm.
2. Having fetched some Thal anti-radiation drugs for herself and her companions, Susan reluctantly prepares to leave the safety of the TARDIS and head back to the Dalek city through Skaro's terrifying petrified forest.
3. The Doctor and Ian have removed one of the Dalek creatures from its travel machine and left it wrapped in a Thal cloak on the metallic floor of the cell in which they and their two companions have been held prisoner. Unseen by them, a Dalek claw pushes its way out from beneath the cloak.
4. The travellers have escaped from the Daleks but Ian realises that the TARDIS's fluid link, a vital component without which the ship cannot leave Skaro, is still in their possession.

5. Ian and Barbara are accompanying a party of Thals through a treacherous swamp of mutations to try to infiltrate the Dalek city from the rear. One of the Thals, Elyon, goes to fetch water. He screams and the others rush to his aid.

6. Ian, Barbara and their Thal allies are making their way through a dangerous cave system leading to the Dalek city. One of the Thals, Antodus, falls into a crevasse and hangs from a rope as Ian struggles to maintain his grip on the other end and is himself pulled toward the edge.

7. The TARDIS leaves Skaro but, as the Doctor busies himself with the controls, the ship lurches violently and the travellers are all thrown to the floor.

IT WAS MADE WHERE...?

Ealing filming: 28.10.63-01.11.63 on Stage 3, 26.11.63 on Stage 2, 02.12.63 (Stage unknown).
Studio recording: 15.11.63 (not transmitted), 22.11.63, 29.11.63, 06.12.63 (remount), 13.12.63, 20.12.63, 03.01.64, 10.01.64, all in Lime Grove D.

ADDITIONAL CREDITED CAST

Dalek Voices (Peter Hawkins[2-7], David Graham[2-7]), Daleks (Robert Jewell[2-7], Kevin Manser[2-7], Michael Summerton[2-4], Gerald Taylor[2-7], Peter Murphy[5-7]), Temmosus (Alan Wheatley[3,4]), Alydon (John Lee[3-7]), Dyoni (Virginia Wetherell[3-7]), Ganatus (Philip Bond[3-7]), Antodus (Marcus Hammond[4-7]), Kristas (Jonathan Crane[4-7]), Elyon (Gerald Curtis[4-5]), Thals (Chris Browning[7*], Katie Cashfield[7*], Vez Delahunt[7*], Kevin Glenny[7*], Ruth Harrison[7*], Lesley Hill[7*], Steve Pokol[7*], Jeanette Rossini[7*], Eric Smith[7*]).

* Also in *The Escape*, *The Ambush*, *The Expedition* and *The Ordeal*, but uncredited.

POPULAR MYTHS

- Terry Nation named the Daleks after seeing the letters DAL-LEK on a set of encyclopaedias. (Nation simply made up the name, but needed something a little more romantic to tell the press at the time.)
- There was a transmission fault at the start of the first episode resulting in the opening moments being in negative. (The story was made this way all along to give the impression of intense heat on the surface of Skaro.)
- The story was intended to feature a glass Dalek. (It never was. The glass Dalek was invented by David Whitaker for his 1964 novelisation of the story.)
- The first episode of the story was remade between the third and the fourth as there was electronic interference on the tape of the original recording. (The episode was indeed remade, but the real reason was that talkback – i.e. the sound of instructions relayed to the studio floor from the control gallery – was picked up and clearly audible on the soundtrack of the original recording.)
- Raymond Cusick based the shape of a Dalek on that of a pepper pot. (He based it on the shape of a man seated on a chair; the only time he used a pepper pot was to demonstrate to somebody in conversation how he envisaged the Daleks moving.)

THINGS TO WATCH OUT FOR

- The series' first monster is the dead Magneton in the petrified forest.
- There is a wonderfully tense scene leading up to the death of Antodus.
- The Doctor is apparently willing to give the Daleks the secrets of the TARDIS and of time travel if they abandon their plan to release deadly radiation onto the planet's surface – or is he just bluffing?

THINGS YOU MIGHT NOT HAVE KNOWN

- Working titles: *The Survivors*, *Beyond the Sun*. The story is now more commonly referred to as *The Daleks* to avoid confusion with the 1972 *Doctor Who* story also entitled *The Mutants*. The working title of the sixth individual episode was *The Caves of Terror*, and that of the seventh was *The Execution*.
- It was director Richard Martin rather than writer Terry Nation who suggested that the Thal anti-radiation drugs should be lethal to the Daleks.
- William Hartnell at one point cut himself on one of the metal bands around a Dalek's shoulder section. For all subsequent scenes these bands had sticky tape affixed along their edges as a safety measure.
- In writer Terry Nation's original storyline, entitled *The Survivors*, the conclusion was completely different from the one eventually transmitted. It involved the Daleks joining forces with the Thals in order to repel an anticipated attack by a force of alien invaders whose rockets had been detected approaching Skaro; when the aliens landed, however, the Doctor realised that they were in truth peaceful beings:

  > These people come from the planet that two thousand years before fired neutron bombs on Skaro. Since that time, their own civilisation has progressed and they have realised the enormity of the crime committed by their forefathers. They have waited until the radiation level has fallen, and now they come to make reparations and assist in rebuilding the planet. With Skaro's safe future assured, Dr. Who and the others leave for new times and distance.

- It was Terry Nation's idea that the Daleks should draw their power from the floor of their city, but associate producer Mervyn Pinfield's suggestion that the power source should be static electricity.
- The names of the Thal characters were all changed shortly before the story went into the studio. The original names (with the final names in brackets) were: Stohl (Temmosus), Vahn (Alydon), Kurt (Ganatus), Jahl (Kristas), Ven (Antodus), Daren (in the earliest draft scripts a male character, changed to the female Dyoni) and Zhor (Elyon).
- Kurt was originally to have been played by Dinsdale Landen and Stohl by David Markham.
- The draft script for episode seven, *The Rescue*, contained scenes where the Daleks loaded a neutron bomb onto a small, self-propelled truck which took it out of their city and came to rest in a clearing near the Doctor's ship. The Doctor then defused it with split-second timing.
- In considering how to realise the Daleks' voices, Christopher Barry first approached J N Shearme of the Post Office's Joint Speech Research Unit, who sent him on 18 October 1963 a tape of examples of two types of 'synthetic speech,' the first

produced using a vocoder and the second by computer generation. Shearme indicated that as much material as required could be processed by the first method, but a maximum of thirty seconds by the second owing to the amount of staff effort involved. Barry replied on 25 October, saying that the vocoder material was of particular interest but that it had been decided that something similar would have to be produced in the BBC's own studios as part of the speech would have to be done live rather than processed from tapes at a later date.

QUOTE, UNQUOTE

- **Alydon:** [Speaking of the Daleks.] 'If they call *us* mutations … what must *they* be like.'
- **Temmosus:** 'I wonder what they'll be like. How they'll be disposed towards us?' **Ganatus:** 'They are Daleks.' **Temmosus:** 'Yes, but we've changed over the centuries. Why shouldn't they? The once famous warrior race of Thals are now farmers.' **Dyoni:** 'But the Daleks were teachers weren't they, Temmosus.' **Temmosus:** 'Yes they were, and philosophers.' **Ganatus:** 'Perhaps they are the warriors now.'
- **Dalek:** 'The only interest we have in the Thals is their total extermination!'
- **The Doctor:** [Speaking to Alydon.] 'You wanted advice, you said. I never give it. Never. But I might just say this for you. Always search for truth. My truth is in the stars, and yours … is here.'

ANALYSIS

From the opening moments of *The Mutants* it appears that the TARDIS has arrived in a forest not too dissimilar from the one that it has just left. It soon becomes very apparent, however, that this is no normal forest. Indeed, *The Mutants* is no normal story. Its importance in *Doctor Who*'s history cannot be overstated, and there is one simple reason for this: it introduced the Daleks.

The Daleks are undoubtedly the highlight of the story. Nothing even remotely like them had ever been seen before, either on television or in the cinema, and they dominate every scene in which they appear. Their sedate, gliding movements and harsh, electronic voices make for an unforgettable combination. The fact that they are constantly in motion, their three stick-like 'limbs' twitching with alien life even when they are otherwise stationary, creates a very creepy effect. Their weaponry seems devastating, blistering a wall in moments – although when turned on the Thals it simply causes them to go negative, fall over and die (or, in one case, get up again to continue fighting). The Daleks, as Ian realises, are xenophobes – they hate other races simply because they are different from themselves. They are also intelligent, cunning and ruthless, all of which adds to their appeal – particularly in comparison with the rather wishy-washy pacifist Thals.

It has often been claimed that villains are far more interesting than heroes, and nowhere is this more evident than in *The Mutants*. The main problem with the Thals is that their charismatic leader Temmosus, played by Alan Wheatley, is unceremoniously killed off in the fourth episode and the remainder, with the possible exception of Alydon, are essentially rather faceless stereotypes – the coward, the ladies' man and so on – to be used by Nation according to the dictates of the plot. Certainly they have little regard for fashion – the men wear leather trousers with holes cut up the sides, while the women wander about in leotards and plastic tabards!

This rather less-than-inspiring costume design is perhaps the only weak point in what is otherwise a very impressive production. Among its many strong points are the sets. Belying the tiny budget that he was allocated, designer Raymond P Cusick managed to create settings which emphasise just how different Skaro is from the Palaeolithic era that the travellers have just left behind. These include the eerie petrified forest; the stark and gleaming Dalek city, the doors of which are too small for the humans to walk through without ducking; an impressive swamp filled with horrific mutations; and a network of tunnels and caverns.

On the technical side, good use is made of electronic inlay in the sequence where the travellers first see the Dalek city in the distance, and then later in the one where a massive whirlpool caused by a swamp mutation appears alongside the terrified Elyon. Other clever sequences include a number of Dalek-eye-views of the action, and one where Susan runs through the forest back to the TARDIS – although in this latter case it is perhaps a little too apparent that Carole Ann Ford is simply running on the spot while studio hands whip her with branches.

One of the potential problems with *The Mutants* is its length. Nation had a job to sustain the action over the full seven episodes, and the travellers seem to spend their time moving between the Dalek city and the Thal encampment. The master-stroke was to ensure that the only way of approaching the city for a final covert attack was to do so via a lake of mutations, a pipeline going up a sheer cliff-face and a dangerous cave system, helping to ensure that the story remains watchable and interesting throughout. These sequences are not merely padding, though; rather, they pay homage to the Jules Verne school of science-fiction storytelling, as exemplified in books such as *Journey to the Centre of the Earth* and *Around the World in Eighty Days*, in which an arduous trek through a series of strange and hazardous environments is typically not just an interlude in the story but *is* the story.

It is however the work of another well-known science-fiction author that provides one of the most apparent sources for Nation's story, as Trevor Wayne noted in *Gallifrey* Issue Thirteen dated winter 1980/81:

'The basic story is taken directly from H G Wells' *The Time Machine* ... In the famous book, the time traveller is transported to a strange, dream-like future landscape with sad ruined buildings set in a huge park. Mankind has been reduced to two types of creature: the childlike Eloi who live in an apparently halcyon existence on the surface, and the brutal troglodyte Morlocks who tend huge machines that provide food and other necessities for the Eloi, who are in turn themselves the food of the carnivorous Morlocks. *The Time Machine* is ... a political and scientific allegory owing much to Darwin and Huxley and to the Socialist philosophy in the latter years of the 19th Century. Society has been reduced to one food cycle.

'Taking the basic ingredients of the book, Terry Nation penned an allegory of his time, the 1960s. The setting is removed from Earth to Skaro ... The landscape is that of a post-atomic nightmare; ashen and petrified. And there are two types of creature. The first is monstrous [and] lives in an underground city (fall-out shelter?) ... The [other is] the image of human perfection (... in fact uncomfortably like the Nazis' stated ideal; tall, blond and – presumably – blue eyed) [and] of a gentle disposition.'

Another apparent source for the story is the first Dan Dare serial from the *Eagle* comic. In this, the Pilot of the Future, having braved perils such as a swamp full of monsters and a treacherous cave system, gets captured by a race of evil technocrats and then encounters a group of blond-haired pacifists whom he shames into fighting them.

The arrival of the Daleks has often been cited, with some justification, as the development that sealed *Doctor Who*'s popular success. Certainly the creatures' appeal was immediately noted by journalists, as is apparent from the following review by Peter Quince that appeared in the *Huddersfield Daily Examiner* dated 11 January 1964: 'As for spine chillery ... well, I take back what I said a few weeks ago about *Doctor Who* having got off to such a bad start it could never recover. It has recovered, and, though it still has its daft moments, it also produces some first class sensations – as, for example, last Saturday, when, after the Dalek "intelligence" had been lifted unseen from its robot and placed in a blanket on the floor, the episode closed with something very horrible indeed just beginning to crawl from under the blanket. So horrible was it, that I very much doubt whether I shall have the courage this evening to switch on to see what it was. Lovely stuff!'

The Mutants was a turning point for *Doctor Who*. And one that would continue to resonate in viewers' minds long after it was over.

THE CREATION OF THE DALEKS

The Daleks are one of those science fiction ideas that, in retrospect, seem so ridiculously simple that it is hard to understand why no-one had done anything similar before. There had been many different robotic monsters previously created for films and television shows, but these had always turned out looking like a man in a suit. Terry Nation must have realised this and, in his scripted description of the Daleks, specified that the creatures should have no visible legs and should glide along on a base (an idea inspired when he saw some Russian dancers whose feet were concealed beneath large skirts so that they appeared to glide across the stage). BBC designer Raymond P Cusick took this concept and decided to base the shape of the Dalek on that of a man seated on a chair. He initially considered fixing a small tricycle within each of the fibreglass shells to provide the smooth motion desired, but as none of the right size could be found he eventually resorted to mounting the prop on castors so that the actor inside could push it along with his feet. The resultant prop was both unsettling and unique. The simple 'pepperpot' shape with its three emerging appendages – eye-stalk, sucker-stick and gun-arm – was memorable, as was the strange gliding motion. The illusion of an alien creature was completed by the harsh electronic voice that grated instructions and barked out orders.

To viewers, the Daleks seemed truly alien beings – indeed, fooled by their relatively small stature, many initially believed that they were operated by remote control rather than by actors inside them. This was the intended effect, and the Daleks were a huge success. The impact that this had on *Doctor Who* itself was enormous. Virtually overnight, this gentle, partly educational family series for Saturday teatimes was transformed into the show that, for many people, just had to be watched at all costs. Playgrounds across the UK were alive with discussion about the creatures, and the demands for their return started to grow. The BBC, meanwhile, had been caught off guard by the incredible interest that the Daleks had provoked both from the press and in terms of letters and calls to the *Doctor Who* production office. They had to do something to try to satisfy

the many demands for the Daleks, and so turned to Australian entrepreneur Walter Tuckwell, who was already handling merchandise licensing for several other BBC shows, to see if he would handle the Daleks and *Doctor Who*. Tuckwell was delighted, and the stage was set for one of the most phenomenal marketing successes of the sixties.

INSIDE THE SPACESHIP

Note: Also known as *The Edge of Destruction* and *Beyond the Sun*.

Writer: David Whitaker. **Director:** Richard Martin[1], Frank Cox[2]. **Designer:** Raymond P Cusick. **Costumes:** Daphne Dare. **Make-Up:** Ann Ferriggi. **Incidental Music:** stock. **Studio Lighting:** Dennis Channon. **Studio Sound:** Jack Brummitt. **Production Assistant:** Tony Lightley. **Assistant Floor Manager:** Jeremy Hare.

	First UK TX	Scheduled TX	Actual TX	Duration	Viewers	Chart Pos.
The Edge of Destruction	08/02/64	17.15	17.15	25'04"	10.4	21
The Brink of Disaster	15/02/64	17.15	17.17	22'11"	9.9	31

Plot: As they slowly recover from the shock of being thrown to the TARDIS floor, the Doctor, Susan, Ian and Barbara all seem to be acting strangely. A number of unexplained events occur and suspicions are raised that some alien force may have entered the ship. The Doctor at one point even accuses Ian and Barbara of sabotage. It gradually dawns on the travellers that what they have been experiencing is an attempt by the TARDIS itself to warn them of something. The Doctor ultimately realises that the 'fast return' switch he used when leaving Skaro has stuck, and the ship has been plunging back to the beginning of time and its own destruction. Once the problem – a faulty spring – is corrected, the TARDIS returns to normal and the Doctor is forced to make some apologies.

Episode endings:
1. Having drugged his companions' drinks with a sleeping draught, the Doctor returns to the TARDIS control room. There he inspects the controls and is about to try operating them when he is interrupted by someone apparently intent on strangling him.
2. The TARDIS arrives in a new location where the weather is very cold. Leaving the ship to explore, Susan and Barbara find what appears to be a giant's footprint in the snow.

IT WAS MADE WHERE...?
Studio recording: 17.01.64, 24.01.64 both in Lime Grove D.

ADDITIONAL CREDITED CAST
None.

POPULAR MYTHS
• This story had the working title *Beyond the Sun*. (This was a working title for the previous story, *The Mutants*.)

- The story was written as a late addition to the schedule because the sets for *Marco Polo* were not ready in time. (It was a late addition, but the real reason was that Donald Baverstock, the Chief of Programmes for BBC1, had yet to give his approval for any more than thirteen episodes to be made. Thus, with *100,000 BC* at four episodes and *The Mutants* at seven, an additional two part story was required in case the series should then be cancelled.)

THINGS TO WATCH OUT FOR

- 'Fast Return' is written in felt tip pen on the console.
- The Doctor is initially astonished at the suggestion that the TARDIS might actually be alive.
- This is the only story in *Doctor Who*'s history to feature no other characters apart from the Doctor and his companions.
- This is the only story to be set almost entirely within the TARDIS.

QUOTE, UNQUOTE

- **Barbara Wright:** [To the Doctor.] 'Accuse us! You ought to go down on your knees and thank us! Gratitude's the last thing you'll ever have ... or any sort of common sense either!'
- **Barbara Wright:** 'We had time taken away from us and now it's being given back to us ... because it's running out!'
- **The Doctor:** 'As we learn about each other so we learn about ourselves.'

ANALYSIS

Considering its origins as a hasty 'filler' written to bring the initial episode count up to thirteen, *Inside the Spaceship* works remarkably well. As Deanne Holding put it in *TARDIS* Volume 6 Number 3/4 dated October 1981: '[*Inside the Spaceship*] is unique in that it features no alien menace, no strange planets to be explored, no supporting cast and no sets other than the TARDIS interior. It is a suspense story, in the Hitchcock tradition, and, as such, it is quite stunning.'

Even at this early stage, though, the impact of the Daleks was being felt. 'The first week of *Doctor Who* without Daleks was flat,' wrote Peter Quince in the *Huddersfield Daily Examiner* dated 15 February 1964. 'Admittedly, Susan went mad with a pair of scissors, clocks were smashed [sic] most mysteriously and Barbara thought the ship had been invaded by an unseen presence, but none of these excitements could make up for the loss of those ravishing robots. They have been the hit of the winter on all channels, though I doubt whether the BBC's plans to market them in do-it-yourself form will be all that successful. The craze will have died away by the time the Daleks reach the shops – unless of course the designer can include a real live death-ray in each packet – but I doubt whether the post-master general would like that.'

The restriction imposed on the production of having to take place largely within stock sets resulted in two episodes set entirely within the confines of the TARDIS. This allowed David Whitaker to devise a story in which the still fragile relationships between the leading characters initially fall apart, and then crystallise into far stronger friendships than existed before. The first episode is full of misdirection as the characters try to come to terms with what might have happened to them. This involves some strangely stilted acting from Carole Ann Ford and William Russell, who speak their lines as though they are simply reciting them from a page, and one really starts to get the feeling that – as the Doctor suspects – the ship may have been invaded by some outside force that is now masquerading as one of the travellers. The analogy with a theatrical play is not too off beam, as the limited number of sets and the relatively static camera angles give the viewer the impression of watching as the action unfolds, act by act, on a stage.

It is unfortunate that this approach does not appear to suit Ford, who seems ill at ease with the strange and dislocated Susan that she is called upon to play. Russell settles down after initial problems, while Jacqueline Hill and William Hartnell seem unaffected by the demands of the claustrophobic scripts. This 'staginess' could be seen as a failing of the production, but this would perhaps be unfair. 'The technical limitations of the production are obvious to the modern viewer,' commented Trevor Wayne in *Gallifrey* Issue Twelve dated autumn 1980, 'but this is largely due to the fact that [it was] almost experimental in [its] own day. Not only that, the producers stretched television technology to its limits to achieve a sense of wonder in the programme that to today's viewer, used to slick bland productions, will just seem shabby. But let us not forget that such programmes cannot be taken out of time and context; they reflect the abilities of the time in which they were produced. The world was a vastly different place in the early sixties to the one we live in today.'

By the end of the first episode, all the options have been exhausted and the Doctor drugs his companions so that he might investigate the problems without further interference. But the drugs don't work, and Ian attempts, for no apparent reason (other than to provide an episode ending), to strangle the Doctor.

After an uncertain first episode, the second is far better. Richard Martin, the director for the former, was relatively new and inexperienced at the job (which is why Christopher Barry was brought in to assist on the previous story), and Frank Cox, handling the latter, does much better. The action is tighter and the whole thing gathers momentum as the travellers realise that the danger may be of their own making. There are revelations and a conclusion that is elegant in its simplicity. The undoubted high point of the adventure comes when the Doctor is forced to confront a furious Barbara, who is understandably upset at the accusations he earlier directed at her and Ian, and has to do the one thing that it appears he is most uncomfortable with: apologise and admit he was wrong. Nick Davison, writing in *Star Begotten* Volume 2 Number 1 dated winter 1988, put it well: 'The complete success of the character development is apparent when you realise the drama – the *real* drama – comes from the desire to see the characters reconcile their differences.'

Although the majority of fans regard this most simple of adventures with considerable fondness, there are others who take a different view. 'The greatest pity ... is that it had real potential,' wrote Vanessa Bishop in *Skaro* Volume V No. II dated October/November 1990. 'It is perhaps the [series'] only venture into the realms of a disaster movie ... The "stuck-in-a-lift" – albeit a big one – scenario could've equalled the two previous tales. The TARDIS is [a brilliant invention] and yet, in this tale, becoming the fifth protagonist, it is immediately sent up – with its vast technology, it throws its crew into oblivion because of a jammed spring! Ironic, quaint, or just plain ridiculous? But the crowning (clowning) glory has to go to the dear old Doc himself – having discovered the problem, he then proceeds to explain the ins and outs of a gammy old spring to, of all people, Susan, who is supposed to be an alien. Susan is therefore either completely thick or raving mad. Who said *Doctor Who* never talked down to its audience? The TARDIS, of course, cannot warn them of the danger (why?) but only gives them clues through such crass and kitchy inventions as the food machine. It's a cracker! Decked out in its fifties design, it reminds me of something you draw at school when you're five and then rip up because you've thought of something better to do. The TARDIS continues to be helpful by electrocuting them through the console!'

Whatever one's feelings about the plot, there is no denying that at the conclusion all the characters are on good terms again, and their relationships have been strengthened in a way that simply having them experience adventures together arguably could not have achieved. *Inside the Spaceship* provides a respite from the monsters and allows the characters to grow. This makes them all the more real for the viewer, who, in turn, cares more what happens to them next.

MARCO POLO

Writer: John Lucarotti. **Director:** Waris Hussein[1-3,5-7], John Crockett[4]. **Designer:** Barry Newbery. **Costumes:** Daphne Dare. **Make-Up:** Ann Ferriggi. **Incidental Music:** Tristram Cary. **Sword Fight Arranged By:** Derek Ware. **Film Cameraman:** unknown. **Film Editor:** John House, Elmer Davies, Richard Barclay. **Studio Lighting:** John Treays, Howard King. **Studio Sound:** Jack Brummitt, Hugh Barker, Derek Martin-Timmins[4]. **Production Assistant:** Douglas Camfield, Penny Joy. **Assistant Floor Manager:** Catherine Childs.

	First UK TX	Scheduled TX	Actual TX	Duration	Viewers	Chart Pos.
The Roof of the World	22/02/64	17.15	17.15	24'12"	9.4	33
The Singing Sands	29/02/64	17.15	17.15	26'34"	9.4	33
Five Hundred Eyes	07/03/64	17.15	17.16	22'20"	9.4	34
The Wall of Lies	14/03/64	17.15	17.15	24'48"	9.9	31
Rider from Shang-tu	21/03/64	17.15	17.16	23'26"	9.4	37
Mighty Kublai Khan	28/03/64	17.30	17.30	25'36"	8.4	49
Assassin at Peking	04/04/64	17.30	17.30	24'48"	10.4	22

Plot: Arriving in Central Asia in 1289, the Doctor and his companions join the caravan of the famous Venetian explorer Marco Polo as it makes its way from the snowy heights of the Pamir Plateau, across the treacherous Gobi Desert and through the heart of imperial Cathay. Having witnessed many incredible sights and survived a variety of dangers, they eventually arrive at the mighty Kublai Khan's Summer Palace in Shang-tu, where the Doctor strikes up an extraordinary friendship with the now-aged ruler. They move on at last to the even more sumptuous Imperial Palace in Peking, where the travellers manage to save the Khan from an assassination attempt by the Mongol warlord Tegana – supposedly on a peace mission – before departing once more in the TARDIS.

Episode endings:

1. Tegana acquires from a Mongol subordinate a phial of poison with which he aims to poison Marco Polo's water gourds as his caravan crosses the Gobi desert. He confides that when everyone is dead he intends to return to the caravan and collect the TARDIS – 'the thing of magic that will bring the mighty Kublai Khan to his knees!'
2. Tegana arrives at a desert oasis and gleefully pours water onto the sand: 'Here's water, Marco Polo. Come for it!'
3. The Doctor, Susan and Ping-Cho (a young girl travelling with Marco Polo) enter the Cave of Five Hundred Eyes searching for Barbara. Suddenly Susan screams, pointing at one of the faces carved on the wall. Its eyes moved!
4. Having cut his way through the tent in which he and his fellow travellers have been held prisoner, Ian emerges into the clearing in the bamboo forest. The guard offers less resistance than expected – as Ian touches him, he keels over, a knife protruding from his torso.
5. Susan crosses from the Cheng-Ting way station to the stables, where her friends are waiting for her in the TARDIS, ready to make good their escape. As she rushes toward the ship, Tegana appears from the shadows and seizes her about the neck.
6. Ian holds the bandit Kuiju at knife-point, allowing Ping-Cho to retrieve her money. Kuiju reluctantly admits that it was Tegana who paid him to steal it. Suddenly Tegana arrives. He beckons to Ian, cutting the air with his sword.
7. As Marco Polo wonders where the time travellers are now, an image of the TARDIS console is seen superimposed against a starscape.

IT WAS MADE WHERE...?

Ealing filming: 13.01.64-17.01.64 on Stage 3B.
Studio recording: 31.01.64, 07.02.64, 14.02.64, 21.02.64, 28.02.64, 06.03.64, 13.03.64, all in Lime Grove D.

ADDITIONAL CREDITED CAST

Marco Polo (Mark Eden), Tegana (Derren Nesbitt), Ping-Cho (Zienia Merton), Man at Lop (Leslie Bates[1]), Chenchu (Jimmy Gardner[3,4]), Malik (Charles Wade[3]), Acomat (Philip Voss[3-5]), Mongol bandit (Michael Guest[5]), Ling-Tau (Paul Carson[5,7]), Wang-lo (Gabor Baraker[5,6]), Kuiju (Tutte Lemkow[5-7]), Vizier (Peter Lawrence[6,7]), Kublai Khan (Martin Miller[6,7]), Office Foreman (Basil Tang[6*]), Empress (Claire Davenport[7]).

* Also in *Assassin at Peking*, but uncredited

THINGS TO WATCH OUT FOR

• The horses of the Mongol bearers were the first live animals to be used in the making of *Doctor Who*.
• An animated map is used to illustrate the progress of the journey, accompanied by voice-over diary entries by Marco Polo.

THINGS YOU MIGHT NOT HAVE KNOWN

• Kuiju, the mercenary bandit with the pet monkey, is never referred to by name in the story's dialogue; his name is given only in the closing credits.

- Although not on holiday as such, William Hartnell had only one line of dialogue in *The Singing Sands*.
- The Doctor acquires from Kublai Khan a wooden walking stick which he is then seen to use in several subsequent stories. Its distinctive design includes a spiral section on the stem, with a small carved figure of a monkey climbing up it.
- Working title: *A Journey to Cathay*. The working title of the third individual episode was *The Cave of Five Hundred Eyes*, and this was actually given as the title in the 'Next Episode:' caption at the end of the previous episode.
- Zienia Merton, who played Ping-Cho, was required to deliver a lengthy recital in *Five Hundred Eyes*, telling of Ala-Eddin and his band of Hashashins. Zohra Segal, who played her attendant in the story, was booked to coach her for this as she was highly experienced in dance and mime.
- Books used by designer Barry Newbery in researching his sets for this story included: *Chinese Houses and Gardens* by Henry Inn and S.C. Lee, *Chinese and Indian Architecture* by Nelson I. Wu, *Ruins of Old Cathay* Volumes I and II by Sir Aural Stein and *Imperial Peking* (author unknown).

QUOTE, UNQUOTE

- **Tegana:** 'Hear me, Mongols. In these parts live evil spirits who take our likeness to deceive us and then lead us to our deaths. Let us therefore destroy these evil spirits before they destroy us!'
- **Susan Foreman:** 'One day, we'll know all the secrets of the skies, and we'll stop our wanderings.'
- **The Doctor:** [Mimicking Wang-lo's comment about the TARDIS.] '"I couldn't place it in the hanging-garden, now could I" What does he think it is? A potting shed, or something?'
- **Marco Polo:** 'On my travels to Cathay, Ian, I have come to believe many things I'd previously doubted. For instance, when I was a boy in Venice they told me that in Cathay there was a stone that burned. I did not believe, but there *is* such a stone – I have seen it … And if stone burns, why not a caravan that flies? Birds fly; I have even seen *fish* that fly. You are asking me to believe that your caravan can defy the passage of the sun? Move not merely from one place to another, but from today into tomorrow, today to yesterday? No Ian, that I cannot believe.'
- **Kublai Khan:** [To Ping-Cho.] 'Your beloved husband-to-be, so anxious to be worthy of your love, drank a potion of quicksilver and sulphur, the elixir of life and eternal youth … and expired.'
- **Marco Polo:** 'But what is the truth? I wonder where they are now – the past or the future?'

ANALYSIS

Marco Polo is an amazing *tour de force*; a superbly-executed epic that well illustrates the full and very considerable potential of *Doctor Who*'s early historical story type. From the Pamir Plateau in the Himalayas, across the Gobi Desert (with its terrifying 'singing sands'), via the Cave of Five Hundred Eyes to Kublai Khan's Summer Palace in Shang-tu and finally to the grand Imperial Palace in Peking, the action moves from one fascinating and convincingly-realised location to another as the time travellers join

Marco Polo's caravan for a hazardous journey through 13th Century Cathay.

John Lucarotti's excellent scripts, full of wonderful dialogue and finely drawn characters, are well matched by Waris Hussein's polished direction; and the highly detailed and often lavish sets and costumes, designed by Barry Newbery and Daphne Dare respectively, make the whole thing a sumptuous visual treat. Performances from the principal cast – including Mark Eden's distinguished Marco Polo, Derren Nesbitt's devious Tegana, Zienia Merton's innocent Ping-Cho, Martin Miller's frail yet commanding Kublai Khan and of course the four regulars – are uniformly strong. Tristram Cary's charming incidental score, as different as can be imagined from his weird (but nonetheless effective) electronic compositions for *The Mutants* earlier in the season, adds to the overall impression of a near-flawless production.

It is in the historical stories rather than the science-based ones that the semi-educational aspect of the series' original format arguably comes most to the fore, and here we learn about all manner of things ranging from altitude sickness to the derivation of the word 'assassin'. In fact, if there is one criticism that could be validly levelled at the story it is that this eagerness to educate as well as to entertain is occasionally rather too obvious. Nevertheless, these little tutorials certainly served their purpose, as is obvious from the following reminiscences by John Peel in *Oracle* Volume 2 Number 2 dated November 1978:

'A large number of people, it appears, are engaged in debate over whether television influences young minds ... I'd come down very strongly of the opinion that it does. For one thing, it influenced mine ... *Doctor Who* made me broaden my entire outlook, and one show in particular opened a new world to me. That was ... *Marco Polo*.

'Until this time, I had always thought of history as one of those horrible, boring lessons that school-kids were forced ... to learn, and [in which they got] rotten marks for forgetting the date of the Spanish Armada or bonfire night or some equally obscure number. Now, watching the Doctor and his companions meet a traveller on the way to the court of Kublai Khan, I began to realise that history could be fun! I was enthralled; was this really the same sort of thing as that tedious subject I hated at school? It did not seem like it ... Battle, intrigue, humour; they were real-life things, not the stuff from which text books were made ...

'I went back to school filled with a strong desire to learn more about history – and an equally strong opinion that text books were the worst place to learn such facts!'

There are, it must be admitted, some viewers who simply dismiss the historical stories as dull and uninspiring by comparison with the science-based ones. If there is any story that gives the lie to that assessment, it is *Marco Polo*. As Peel put it, writing this time in *Doctor Who – An Adventure in Space and Time* in 1980: 'Gorgeous, fast, tense, funny and filled with character and feel for the period – *Marco Polo* is one of the true classics of television.'

THE KEYS OF MARINUS

Writer: Terry Nation. **Director:** John Gorrie. **Designer:** Raymond P Cusick. **Costumes:** Daphne Dare. **Make-Up:** Jill Summers. **Incidental Music:** Norman Kay.

Studio Lighting: Peter Murray. **Studio Sound:** Jack Brummitt, Tony Milton. **Production Assistant:** David Conroy, Penny Joy. **Assistant Floor Manager:** Timothy Combe.

	First UK TX	Scheduled TX	Actual TX	Duration	Viewers	Chart Pos.
The Sea of Death	11/04/64	17.30	17.32	23'20"	9.9	22
The Velvet Web	18/04/64	17.30	17.31	25'37"	9.4	25
The Screaming Jungle	25/04/64	17.30	17.30	23'45"	9.9	22
The Snows of Terror	02/05/64	17.30	17.30	24'54"	10.4	20
Sentence of Death	09/05/64	17.15	17.15	25'03"	7.9	29
The Keys of Marinus	16/05/64	17.15	17.18	25'11"	6.9	43

Plot: The TARDIS arrives on the planet Marinus on an island of glass surrounded by a sea of acid. The travellers are forced by the elderly Arbitan to retrieve four of the five operating keys to a machine called the Conscience of Marinus, of which he is the keeper. These have been hidden in different locations around the planet to prevent them falling into the hands of the evil Yartek and his Voord warriors, who plan to seize the machine and use its originally benevolent mind-influencing power for their own sinister purposes. Now the machine has been modified to overcome the Voords and can be reactivated, so the keys must be recovered. In their quest, the travellers – transported from place to place by Arbitan's wristwatch-like travel dials – have adventures in the city of Morphoton; in a building besieged by ambulatory plants; with a lecherous and murderous trapper; and in the city of Millennius where Ian is falsely accused of murder and discovers that the legal rule is 'guilty until proven innocent'. The keys are eventually retrieved and the travellers return to the island. Arbitan has been killed by Yartek, who apparently tricks Ian into handing over the final key. Ian, however, passes a fake key instead and when Yartek tries to use it the machine explodes, killing him and the Voords.

Episode endings:
1. The Doctor, Susan and Ian arrive at the location of the first key shortly after Barbara, but find that she is nowhere to be seen. Ian sees her travel dial on the floor – there is blood on it.
2. Susan moves on to the second location before the others and finds herself in a jungle. She covers her ears in pain as an unearthly screaming sound echoes round.
3. Ian and Barbara turn their travel dials and arrive in a freezing cold environment. Barbara is paralysed by the cold and Ian tells her that they must move or they won't stand a chance.
4. Arriving in the city of Millennius, Ian finds a body on the floor of a museum-like room. He sees the final key in one of the cases but is knocked unconscious before he can get it. His unknown assailant places Ian's hand on a ceremonial mace before taking the key from the cabinet himself, which causes alarm bells to ring.
5. While investigating all the possibilities to try and clear Ian of the murder of Eprin, Barbara receives a telephone call. It is Susan, who explains that she has been kidnapped and will be killed if the Doctor reveals the location of the final key.
6. Having said their farewells to their friends Altos and Sabetha, the Doctor, Susan, Ian and Barbara leave in the TARDIS.

IT WAS MADE WHERE...?

Ealing filming: March 1964 (exact dates unknown).

Studio recording: 20.03.64, 27.03.64, 03.04.64, 10.04.64, 17.04.64, 24.04.64, all in Lime Grove D.

ADDITIONAL CREDITED CAST

Arbitan (George Colouris[1]), Voords (Martin Cort[1,6], Peter Stenson[1,6], Gordon Wales[1]), Altos (Robin Phillips[2-6]), Sabetha (Katharine Schofield[2-6]), Voice of Morpho (Heron Carvic[2]), Warrior (Martin Cort[3]), Darrius (Edmund Warwick[3]), Vasor (Francis de Wolff[4]), Ice Soldiers (Michael Allaby[4], Alan James[4], Peter Stenson[4], Anthony Verner[4]), Tarron (Henley Thomas[5,6]), Larn (Michael Allaby[5,6]), Senior Judge (Raf de la Torre[5]), First Judge (Alan James[5]), Second Judge (Peter Stenson[5]), Kala (Fiona Walker[5,6]), Aydan (Martin Cort[5]), Eyesen (Donald Pickering[5,6]), Guard (Alan James[6]), Yartek (Stephen Dartnell[6]).

POPULAR MYTHS

- Yartek's people are called the Voord. (Although 'Voord' is used as the plural of their name on a couple of occasions, 'Voords' is used more often and is the spelling that appears on the closing credits of the relevant episodes.)

THINGS TO WATCH OUT FOR

- The Voords wear clichéd but surprisingly effective wet-suit costumes, the cleverly-designed rubber masks of which bear – except in Yartek's case – antennae of various different shapes.
- The surprisingly adult scene in which the burly trapper Vasor tries to rape Barbara.
- The Doctor does not appear in either the third or the fourth episode as William Hartnell was on holiday in the weeks when they were recorded.
- The TARDIS arrives and leaves without the engine sound being heard outside the ship.

THINGS YOU MIGHT NOT HAVE KNOWN

- Darrius, the friend of Arbitan's whom the travellers meet in *The Screaming Jungle*, is never referred to by name in the story's dialogue; his name is given only in the closing credits.
- Scripts for this story were delivered behind deadline by Terry Nation as it was a late replacement for a historical story entitled *The Red Fort* which he had been due to write.
- Three heads and three pairs of webbed gloves were made for the Voords by Jack Lovell and his son John; freelance contractors who did much of *Doctor Who*'s specialist costume work during the first Doctor's era. The price quoted was less than £70.
- The Conscience Machine prop was accidentally damaged after the recording of the first episode but repaired again in time for its next appearance in the concluding one. The BBC's Scenic Servicing department footed the bill.

QUOTE, UNQUOTE

- **Arbitan:** 'For the sake of all my people, I hope you succeed.'
- **The Doctor:** 'I don't believe that man was made to be controlled by machines.'

First Doctor

The premise of the tale is simple: the Doctor and his friends must find and collect four hidden keys, using 'travel dials' to move instantaneously between their predetermined locations around the planet. One wonders, in fact, why Arbitan did not travel to collect the keys himself. (The Conscience machine is useless without them, and he could have returned with reinforcements should the Voords have invaded in his absence.) Be that as it may, the immediate difficulty presented by a plot such as this in production terms is that new settings and often new creatures need to be designed and created for virtually every episode, rather than just once per story. It is a tribute to the talents of designer Raymond P Cusick that he manages to bring this off effectively here on an extremely tight budget.

The opening episode features the island of glass and, more particularly, Arbitan's pyramid housing the Conscience. Aside from some fairly blatant painted cloths to represent the sides of the pyramid extending into the distance, this building, with its hidden doors and winding corridors, provides a convincingly mysterious location for the scene-setting action.

The travellers next find themselves in the city of Morphoton, ruled by a collective of bodiless brains in jars. Despite having arrived only minutes ahead of the others, Barbara has apparently found time to have a dress made, get changed, have the concepts of the city explained to her and embark on a sumptuous meal, but this glaring plot inconsistency is conveniently glossed over. Fortunately things improve in the later scenes where, having alone escaped full hypnotic conditioning, she sees through the illusory beauty of the city and realises its true squalor; this is very nicely handled by the director, so that things are seen from Barbara's point of view when appropriate and from the standard 'viewer's eye' perspective when the illusion is perceived by the Doctor, Ian and Susan.

The brain creatures are eventually destroyed when Barbara hits their glass cases with a piece of equipment, and the travellers move on accompanied by Arbitan's daughter Sabetha and her friend Altos, whom they have rescued from Morphoton. Their next arrival point is a jungle where the 'tempo of destruction' – entropy, roughly speaking – has been increased and the plants are running amok. The sequences outside the heavily overgrown walls of the house of Arbitan's scientist friend Darrius are somewhat painful to watch as first Susan calls out and Barbara fails to respond, although she is in no danger at the time, and then Barbara calls out and Ian takes an age to answer. This may help to increase the tension, but it also makes the characters appear slightly deaf. Matters are not improved by the fact that Ford is unfortunately rather less than convincing when trying to appear terrified, although Russell and Hill are again on top form.

As the episodes pass, so Nation continues to rely on the technique, already becoming well worn by this stage, of splitting the travellers up and subjecting them to different dangers. First the Doctor decides to travel on alone to the location of the final key (allowing Hartnell a couple of weeks' holiday), then Susan, Altos and Sabetha move on to the next location ahead of Ian and Barbara.

The Snows of Terror's ice cave sequences stretch credulity. One wonders how Arbitan ever thought that the travellers would find the key when it turns out to be hidden inside a block of ice inside a cave inside an ice mountain that is riddled with tunnels. The 'Ice Soldiers' are also something of a mystery. They are frozen solid and yet come alive when the key is defrosted. One of them screams when he falls down a crevasse, so they must be something approaching human and feel fear. Their origins and exact nature are never explained, however.

As the story draws to a close, Ian finds himself facing some rough justice in the city of Millennius, where one is assumed guilty of a crime until proven innocent. This taxes the Doctor, but his obvious delight at working out all the twists and turns in the plot is a joy to watch. Entertaining though this part of the story is, though, it would perhaps have been even better if the script had clearly indicated why the culprit wanted to steal the key in the first place.

Fortunately the story comes to a satisfying conclusion in the final episode when the fake key obtained in the third is put to good use by Ian.

The Keys of Marinus was not universally liked by those who saw it on its original transmission. 'The overall plot seemed very complicated at the time and I struggled to follow the subplots such as the frame-up of Ian in the human colony,' wrote Stephen Poole in *Oracle* Volume 2 Number 10 dated July 1979. 'It was all very overwhelming, especially since new monsters were constantly being introduced to us – a trend of *Doctor Who* in those days. New creatures would suddenly appear for one episode, more often than not, never to be seen again. The Voords ... for example only appeared in parts one and six – a great waste of potential.' It would however be fair to say that, despite its rather disjointed nature, this story is one that ultimately rewards the viewer. In each episode Nation presents an obstacle – sometimes mental, sometimes physical – and the Doctor and his friends have to figure out how to escape so that they can continue with their quest. In these early days, viewers of *Doctor Who* were really kept on their toes, not even knowing for sure where one story ended and the next began as they were generally linked by cliffhangers in exactly the same way as were episodes within stories. This element of unpredictability was one of strongest features of *Doctor Who*'s original format, and was to continue to stand the series in good stead throughout its long run.

THE AZTECS

Writer: John Lucarotti. **Director:** John Crockett. **Designer:** Barry Newbery. **Costumes:** Daphne Dare, Tony Pearce[3]. **Make-Up:** Jill Summers. **Incidental Music:** Richard Rodney Bennett, conducted by Marcus Dods. **Fight Arranger:** David Anderson, Derek Ware. **Studio Lighting:** Howard King. **Studio Sound:** Jack Brummitt, John Staple. **Production Assistant:** Ron Craddock. **Assistant Floor Manager:** Ken Howard.

	First UK TX	Scheduled TX	Actual TX	Duration	Viewers	Chart Pos.
The Temple of Evil	23/05/64	17.15	17.16	23'56"	7.4	25
The Warriors of Death	30/05/64	17.15	17.16	24'11"	7.4	34
The Bride of Sacrifice	06/06/64	17.15	17.15	25'27"	7.9	19
The Day of Darkness	13/06/64	17.15	17.15	25'30"	7.4	34

Plot: The TARDIS arrives in 15th Century Mexico inside the tomb of one-time Aztec High Priest Yetaxa. The travellers become cut off from the ship when they explore the temple outside and the tomb door closes behind them. Barbara is proclaimed by the High Priest of Knowledge, Autloc, as Yetaxa's divine reincarnation. However, she incurs the enmity of the High Priest of Sacrifice, Tlotoxl, when – against the Doctor's advice – she attempts to use her new-found authority to put an end to the Aztec practice of human sacrifice. Events reach a climax on the Day of Darkness – the time of a solar eclipse. Ian's unwilling conflict with the Aztecs' 'chosen warrior', Ixta, ends in a fight in which the latter falls to his death from the temple roof. The Doctor manages to reopen the tomb door using a wheel-and-pulley that he has carved (the Aztecs not having mastered the use of the wheel) and the travellers make good their escape.

Episode endings:
1. Tlotoxl proclaims that Barbara is a false goddess and that he will destroy her.
2. Tlotoxl cries out for Ixta to kill the overpowered Ian. Barbara suddenly arrives and orders that the fight be stopped. Tlotoxl challenges her – if she is indeed Yetaxa, then let her save her servant …
3. Ian is trapped inside a dark tunnel leading to Yetaxa's tomb as it rapidly fills with water.
4. Leaning over the TARDIS console, the Doctor tells his companions that they have a problem: one set of readings shows that the TARDIS has stopped, but another insists that they are still in motion.

IT WAS MADE WHERE...?
Ealing filming: 13.04.64 (Stage unknown).
Studio recording: 01.05.64 in Lime Grove D, 08.05.64 in TC3, 15.05.64 in TC3, 22.05.64 in Lime Grove D.

ADDITIONAL CREDITED CAST
Autloc (Keith Pyott), Tlotoxl (John Ringham), Ixta (Ian Cullen), Cameca (Margot van der Burgh), First Victim (Tom Booth[1]), Aztec Captain (David Anderson), Tonila (Walter Randall[2-4]), Perfect Victim (André Boulay[2-4]).

POPULAR MYTHS
- For reasons of decency, the costumes for the Aztec characters covered more of their bodies than would have been the case in reality. (The costumes were thoroughly researched and accurate.)

THINGS TO WATCH OUT FOR
- Carole Ann Ford appears only in pre-filmed inserts in the second and third episodes as she was on holiday during the weeks when those episodes were recorded.

THINGS YOU MIGHT NOT HAVE KNOWN
- The closing credits for *The Bride of Sacrifice* had to be reshot during the studio day for *The Day of Darkness* as the original roller caption was considered too erratically printed to be suitable for transmission.

QUOTE, UNQUOTE
- **Barbara Wright:** 'Oh, don't you see? If I could start the destruction of everything that's evil here, then everything that's good will survive when Cortes lands.' **The**

Doctor: 'But you can't rewrite history! Not one line! Barbara, one last appeal: what you are trying to do is utterly impossible. I know! Believe me, I know!'

- **Tlotoxl:** 'I will ask you – how shall a man know his gods?' **Barbara Wright:** 'By the signs of their divinity.' **Tlotoxl:** 'And what if thieves walk among the gods?' **Barbara Wright:** 'Then indeed, how *shall* a man know?' **Tlotoxl:** 'By the secrets of the gods' minds.' **Barbara Wright:** 'That is true; their knowledge will reveal them.'
- **Susan Foreman:** 'You're monsters! All of you, monsters ...'
- **Ian Chesterton:** [Speaking of the brooch carried by the Doctor.] 'Where did you get hold of this?' **The Doctor:** 'My fiancee.' **Ian Chesterton:** 'I see ... *Your what?*' **The Doctor:** 'Yes, I made some cocoa and got engaged ...'

ANALYSIS

The Aztecs, John Lucarotti's second contribution to the series, is another superb historical adventure. While it lacks the epic quality of his debut story, *Marco Polo*, it makes up for this with its fascinating and compelling depiction of the Aztec civilisation, which combined great beauty with great savagery – the latter being exemplified in particular by its practice of human sacrifice. As Brian J Robb noted in *Cameca's Summer Special*, dated July 1986, these two seemingly contradictory aspects of the Aztec culture are personified in the characters of the two High Priests: 'Tlotoxl and Autloc are not so much characters as signifiers. Tlotoxl represents the savagery of the Aztec way of life – he has a guarantee of power through the fear generated by sacrifice. In the classic mould, the signifier of savagery is imperfect. Tlotoxl has a limp ... Autloc, the signifier of civilisation, has no ... prominent deformities ... [He] realises within himself that [human] sacrifice is not necessary but is simply a tool to rule.'

This issue of human sacrifice provides the basis of the story and, as Robb observed, it is foregrounded right from the opening scene: 'The tomb into which the TARDIS crew emerge contains a human skeleton surrounded by various implements of torture ... The Doctor and his companions, through the visual juxtapositions, are set the task (no matter what they say) of ending [human sacrifice]. The meta-discourse in the visual text positions the characters as the medium through which the practice ... will die.'

It is Barbara, temporarily elevated to the position of a divine reincarnation, who takes the initiative in trying to bring human sacrifice to an end. In fact, of the regulars, Barbara is very much to the fore in this story, although the other three are also well catered for: Ian engages in a feud with the 'chosen warrior' Ixta; Susan finds herself consigned to a seminary, where her refusal to accept an arranged marriage to the Perfect Victim creates further trouble for the travellers; and the Doctor has a charming romance with the elderly Aztec lady Cameca.

Lucarotti's excellent characterisation is one of the story's greatest merits and, as Tim Munro commented in Issue One of *Star Begotten* dated winter 1986, the nature of its historical setting makes it easy for the viewer to identify with the travellers' plight: 'The problem facing our heroes is purely the question of their own personal survival, and [this] is far more credible and frightening than [some] grand apocalyptic galactic catastrophe. This is a major advantage that the historical stories have ... For instance, the collapse of the fabric of time is impossible for an audience to visualise, since [it] is outside their experience. Knives are not. It is therefore not difficult for the audience to imagine what, given half a chance, a knife-wielding Aztec priest will do to our heroes. Because the threat is localised and easy to visualise, the viewer's sense of involvement is increased.'

The Doctor tries to dissuade Barbara from the course upon which she has embarked. With his broader alien perspective, he knows that her attempts to transform the Aztec civilisation are futile, and that it is doomed to destruction at the hands of Cortes's Spanish forces. The story can indeed be seen as an exploration of the reasons underlying the ultimate downfall of this strange, almost paradoxical culture, as Rob Byrne argued in *Perigosto Stick* Issue One dated February 1991: 'Through the Doctor's words and Barbara's experiences, John Lucarotti is telling us that the Aztecs were doomed through the very nature of their society. The paradigm to which they subscribe is a dead end alley, and they have cut off all hope of turning back, through their own institutionalised violence and the startling gaps in their knowledge – metal rather than wooden swords would have given them a far greater chance against the Spaniards.'

This sense of doom is well captured by the story's closing scenes, as Robb described: 'Susan is to have her eyes gouged out, Barbara is to have her heart cut out, and Ian is to be thrown from the parapet ... The TARDIS crew escape [but] the violent, savage death of the Perfect Victim goes ahead, and Tlotoxl's power is renewed for a little longer. Autloc is the hope for the future of the Aztec nation. History, though, as both Ian and the viewer know it, [reveals] that the TARDIS crew failed ... This results in a revision to the opening meta-discourse. The crew return to the tomb, now to be read as the signifier of the death of the Aztec nation through savagery.'

The BBC's Audience Research Report on *The Bride of Sacrifice* episode recorded some (with hindsight surprising) comment from viewers who apparently thought that the series was already becoming somewhat tired: 'A local government officer wrote, fairly typically here, that he was "afraid that this series has gone on far too long; the danger and escape therefrom fall into a never varied pattern length and repetition – result, ennui".'

However, the report went on to note:

'A large minority made it plain that they continue to be well satisfied with the entertainment offered by the *Doctor Who* scripts, about situations contrived with sufficient ingenuity to engross adult attention and exciting enough for all the family to enjoy. Some viewers speaking for their children said that the Aztec instalments had been voted "smashing" (several children of school age writing down their own impressions called it "super" or "fab"), though a few youngsters, apparently, did not find the Mexican background as appealing as some of the earlier space-time encounters of Doctor Who and his young scientists [sic] ...

'The production ... was the subject of a good deal of comment, much of this directed (very favourably) at the settings and the exotic-looking costumes and ornaments worn by the Aztec characters, which a housewife, for one, thought not only sumptuous but "presumably historically correct". There was hardly any concerted criticism on points of presentation, but one or two viewers noted that the stone at the entrance of the tunnel was moved without much semblance of weight.'

This high standard of production remains apparent today, and is one of the many reasons for the story's enduring appeal. As Munro put it:

'*The Aztecs* is a beautiful piece of work and all involved can feel justly proud of the end result. [It has] adventurous production, clarity of plot, tension, viewer involvement and high acting standards ...

'From Barbara's first exploration of Yetaxa's tomb to the Doctor's final snatching up of Cameca's [brooch], *The Aztecs* is entrancing television – full of magical moments. The first sacrifice, Tlotoxl's testing of Barbara with poison, Ian's journey through the tunnels, the splendid fights between Ian (or "Eeyan" as the Aztecs pronounce it!) and Ixta … these scenes are all full of that oft-quoted and much-abused phrase "the *Doctor Who* magic".'

THE SENSORITES

Writer: Peter R Newman. **Director:** Mervyn Pinfield[1-4], Frank Cox[5,6]. **Designer:** Raymond P Cusick. **Costumes:** Daphne Dare. **Make-Up:** Jill Summers, Sonia Markham[6]. **Incidental Music:** Norman Kay. **Studio Lighting:** Peter Murray. **Studio Sound:** Les Wilkins, Jack Brummitt. **Production Assistant:** David Conroy. **Assistant Floor Manager:** Val McCrimmon, Dawn Robertson.

	First UK TX	Scheduled TX	Actual TX	Duration	Viewers	Chart Pos.
Strangers in Space	20/06/64	17.15	17.15	24'46"	7.9	17
The Unwilling Warriors	27/06/64	17.15*	17.40	24'44"	6.9	39
Hidden Danger	11/07/64	17.15	17.15	24'53"	7.4	22
A Race Against Death	18/07/64	17.15	17.15	24'49"	5.5	58
Kidnap	25/07/64	17.15	17.15	25'47"	6.9	29
A Desperate Venture	01/08/64	17.15	17.15	24'29"	6.9	39

* This episode was transmitted approximately twenty-five minutes late as the preceding programme, *Summer Grandstand*, had been extended to give additional coverage to the Wimbledon tennis tournament.

Note: There was a one week break between *The Unwilling Warriors* and *Hidden Danger* due to *Summer Grandstand* being extended on that occasion to give additional coverage to the Wimbledon tennis tournament and a cricket test match. This was the only time in the series' history that such a break occurred mid story.

Plot: The TARDIS arrives on board a spaceship in orbit around a planet called the Sense-Sphere. The alien Sensorites have trapped the ship's human crew, Captain Maitland, Carol and John, in a state of semi-permanent paralysis. When the Doctor investigates, the aliens steal the lock mechanism from the TARDIS, thus trapping him and his companions. The Sensorites allow all but Maitland and Barbara down to the planet, where Ian falls ill from a sickness that has been wiping out the Sensorites. The Doctor finds a cure. His investigations into the cause of the sickness are hampered by the subversive activities of the City Administrator, but eventually he uncovers three deranged human survivors from a past expedition who have been adding deadly nightshade to the water supply.

Episode endings:
1. The whistling sound of the approaching Sensorite ships stops and Carol can sense the creatures all around. As the travellers wait apprehensively, it is Ian who first sees the shape

of a Sensorite pressed against the ship's viewing port.

2. The Sensorites telepathically contact Susan and she accedes to their request. Telling the Doctor and the others to stay where they are, she opens the control room hatch and reveals two of the alien creatures waiting for her beyond. She explains that she has agreed to go with them down to their planet. She leaves with them and they close the hatch behind them.

3. Having drunk some of the aqueduct water provided by the Sensorite leader, Ian quickly falls sick and starts choking. He collapses to the floor and the First Elder sadly confirms that there is no hope; Ian is dying.

4. The Doctor goes to the aqueduct in the hope of finding the cause of the poisoning and finds some deadly nightshade. He looks up as a low animal growl sounds in the darkness.

5. Carol is on her way to see what is keeping the Doctor and Ian. Suddenly a hand is clamped over her mouth and she is dragged away.

6. Watching the image of Maitland's ship heading back to Earth on the TARDIS scanner, Ian comments that at least he and his crew know where they are going. The Doctor takes offence at this comment and determines to eject Ian from the TARDIS at their very next port of call.

IT WAS MADE WHERE...?

Ealing filming: May 1964 (exact dates unknown, Stage unknown)
Studio recording: 29.05.64 in TC3, 05.06.64 in TC3, 12.06.64 in Lime Grove D, 19.06.64 in TC4, 26.06.64 in Lime Grove D, 03.07.64 in Lime Grove D.

ADDITIONAL CREDITED CAST

John (Stephen Dartnell), Carol (Ilona Rodgers), Maitland (Lorne Cossette[1-3]), 1st Sensorite (Ken Tyllsen[2]), 2nd Sensorite (Joe Greig[2]), Commander (John Bailey[6]), First Human (Martyn Huntley[6]), Second Human (Giles Phibbs[6]), SENSORITES: First (Ken Tyllsen[3]), Second (Joe Greig[3]), Third (Peter Glaze[3-6]), Fourth (Arthur Newall[3-6]), First Elder (Eric Francis[3-6]), Second Elder (Bartlett Mullins[3-5]), First Scientist (Ken Tyllsen[4,5]), Second Scientist (Joe Greig[4]), Warrior (Joe Greig[5,6]) and Anthony Rogers[3-6]* Gerry Martin[3-5].

* Also in *Strangers in Space*, but uncredited.

POPULAR MYTHS

• The bearded and dishevelled human astronauts responsible for poisoning the Sensorites' water supply are members of an organisation known as INEER. (The initials 'INEER' seen by the Doctor and Ian on a piece of material torn from one of the astronauts' uniforms are intended to be the end of the word 'ENGINEER' – although undue confusion is caused by the fact that Hartnell fluffs his line and reads them as 'INNER'.)

THINGS TO WATCH OUT FOR

• When the Doctor and his friends leave the TARDIS in the first episode, the camera follows them, and then, in the same take, pans back to see Susan locking the doors. This simple sequence is effective in helping to establish the reality of the TARDIS's seemingly impossible interior dimensions.

- Barbara does not appear in *A Race Against Death* or *Kidnap* as Jacqueline Hill was on holiday in the weeks when they were recorded.
- Comic actor Peter Glaze (best known for his appearances on the BBC children's variety show *Crackerjack*) played the scheming City Administrator.

THINGS YOU MIGHT NOT HAVE KNOWN

- Writer Peter R Newman committed suicide in the late sixties.

QUOTE, UNQUOTE

- **The Doctor:** 'It all started out as a mild curiosity in the junkyard and now it's turned out to be quite a great spirit of adventure.'
- **John:** 'The Sensorites, they want me to forget. All the voices, begging me and imploring me to forget ... I don't like the voices. I want to have silence in my head.'
- **City Administrator:** 'These Earth creatures are working to destroy the Sensorite nation. Their pleasant smiles conceal sharp teeth, their soft words hide deadly threats.' **Second Elder:** 'Please ... don't listen.' **City Administrator:** 'And who opposes them? Weak and timid creatures like this Second Elder here whose sash I wear.' **Second Elder:** 'Thief!' **City Administrator:** 'Weakling! Betrayer of our people! Coward! I should imprison you in some room wherein no light can shine and fill that room with noise!'

ANALYSIS

One of the things that sets *The Sensorites* apart from many other *Doctor Who* adventures is its convincing and sympathetic presentation of an alien race and its culture. Just as the travellers' adventure with the Aztecs showed that human beings can sometimes be 'monsters' (to use Susan's description) so their encounter with the Sensorites, whose susceptibility to bright light and loud noise is rather charming and childlike, demonstrates that just because an alien race has a strange and possibly startling appearance, this does not necessarily mean that it is evil – even if, as in this case, it may be somewhat misguided. 'Although the alien Sensorites were strange, they were essentially good beings, whereas the evil-doers were deranged spacemen,' commented Stephen Poole in *Oracle* Volume 2 Number 5 dated February 1979. 'This angle of good versus evil was quite an original concept in 1964.'

The set-up is very nicely handled. The first two episodes, which take place on Maitland's spaceship, are full of the menace of the often spoken about but not yet seen Sensorites. We do not know who or what they are, only that they seem to have great powers and a strange ulterior motive for trapping the humans on the ship. This sense of threat is heightened by the mystery of the locked portions of the ship and the activities of John, banished from the control room as his mind has been broken by the aliens. In a classic piece of sixties sexism, Susan and Barbara are given the task of preparing a meal, and it is their quest for water that brings them into contact with the sad and deranged John. This is a bravura performance from Stephen Dartnell, who manages to convey threat and hopelessness through his speech and actions. Maitland and Carol are also well defined, if a little wet around the gills. Although there would seem to be a way around the Sensorites' control, neither of them has tried to escape – instead they sit in petrified silence as the creatures board their ship. What is odd is that Carol is able to sense the

Sensorites' arrival in the second episode, and yet they must already have been on the ship at the start of the first episode (one of them took the lock from the TARDIS). The Sensorites' own ships were not heard at that point in the first episode, so the theory that they returned to their planet and then came back again seems a little weak. These quibbles aside, when the creatures are eventually revealed, they fully live up to expectations. Short actors were hired to play them, and their almost balletic movements and whispering voices, combined with their strange faces and domed heads, bring over a sense of the truly alien.

The main theme underlying the story is that of trust and mistrust. The Sensorites implicitly trust all other members of their race (although, in the light of this, it has to be asked why they have a Warrior class and possess a fearful disintegrator weapon with which enemies can be eradicated from a remote location), and this is shown to be misguided as it gives the ruthless City Administrator the key to pursuing his objectives. Humans and Sensorites, on the other hand, do not trust each other at all. The astronauts from Earth want to obtain quantities of the rare metal molybdenum, which can be found in great abundance on the Sense-Sphere, and the Sensorites know this. Rather than set up some sort of trade agreement, however, the Sensorites drive the humans mad (albeit somewhat inadvertently) and the deranged humans in turn determine to wipe out the Sensorites by poisoning their water supply. In the meantime, the City Administrator, feeling that the First Elder is a fool to trust the Doctor and his friends, takes matters into his own hands and through deception tries to discredit them. All this mistrust between races is ultimately shown to be equally wrong.

This leads to perhaps the most unlikely aspect of the plot. That the Sensorites are all alike in appearance is well established. They even wear badges and sashes to denote their role in the society – the First Elder has two crossing sashes, the Second Elder wears one sash, the Scientist has a decal on his chest, the Warriors have black bands on their arms and the Administrator has a black collar – and yet, amazingly, it takes Carol to point out to the Administrator that without these symbols it would be difficult to tell them apart. He then makes this the basis of his whole plan – if he wears the Second Elder's sash, he reasons, how will others know he is *not* the Second Elder?

The multiple strands of the plot unfortunately tend to make the story drag, and the resolution of the mystery of what may or may not be lurking in the aqueduct ('monsters' say the Sensorites, but not one of them realises that these creatures appeared at the same time as the original human visitors disappeared!) has to wait until the Doctor has found a cure for the sickness that afflicts Ian. This slowness of pace has alienated some viewers. Gareth Wigmore, for example, hated the story, as he explained in *Matrix* Issue 52 dated spring 1996: 'On several occasions, something happens, some spark of dialogue that makes you think Peter R Newman was trying to write serious, intelligent science-fiction here, but David Whitaker wouldn't let him – or maybe that Peter R Newman wrote dire, childish rubbish which David Whitaker tried to spice up with the odd good line here and there.'

Despite the shortcomings of the plot, *The Sensorites* has much to commend it in production terms. The final shot of Maitland's ship heading off into space is a marvellous piece of effects work (and is also the earliest instance of *Doctor Who* presenting a ship flying in space), and the Sensorite city, cleverly designed by Raymond Cusick to contain no angles, only curves, is both alien in appearance and effective. The Sensorites too are blessed with good make-up and simple but effective costumes.

As the first attempt by *Doctor Who* to present a truly alien culture, and one based unusually on peace and trust, *The Sensorites* achieves a great deal. Nevertheless, we will let the final comment go to Wigmore: 'Everything in the story is boring beyond comprehension, give or take a bit of humour based around how stupid the Doctor is. Anything good in the script is killed by the production ... The ending is weak, we never see the growling monster, the men with the beards appear and are terrible, and suddenly, without having reached any kind of climax, the whole thing is over.'

THE REIGN OF TERROR

Writer: Dennis Spooner. **Director:** Henric Hirsch[1,2,4-6], John Gorrie[3*]. **Designer:** Roderick Laing. **Costumes:** Daphne Dare. **Make-Up:** Jill Summers[1,2], Sonia Markham[2-6]. **Incidental Music:** Stanley Myers. **Film Cameraman:** Peter Hamilton. **Film Editor:** Caroline Shields. **Studio Lighting:** Howard King. **Studio Sound:** Ray Angel, Chick Anthony. **Production Assistant:** Timothy Combe. **Assistant Floor Manager:** Michael Cager.

* Uncredited

	First UK TX	Scheduled TX	Actual TX	Duration	Viewers	Chart Pos.
A Land of Fear	08/08/64	17.15	17.15	24'24"	6.9	37
Guests of Madame Guillotine	15/08/64	17.15	17.15	24'04"	6.9	35
A Change of Identity	22/08/64	17.30	17.30	25'23"	6.9	34
The Tyrant of France	29/08/64	17.15	17.15	24'46"	6.4	36
A Bargain of Necessity	05/09/64	17.30	17.31	23'51"	6.9	39
Prisoners of Conciergerie	12/09/64	17.30	17.30	25'04"	6.4	38

Plot: The TARDIS materialises not far from Paris in 1794 – one of the bloodiest years following the French Revolution. The travellers become involved with an escape chain rescuing prisoners from the guillotine and get caught up in the machinations of an English undercover spy, James Stirling – alias Lemaitre, governor of the Conciergerie Prison. Twice, the Doctor – posing as a Regional Officer of the Provinces – is brought before the great tyrant, Robespierre himself, and has to talk himself out of trouble. Ian and Barbara, meanwhile, have a close encounter with a future ruler of France, Napoleon Bonaparte. As events reach their climax, Robespierre is overthrown – shot in the jaw and dragged off to the prison – and the Doctor and his friends slip quietly away.

Episode endings:
1. The Doctor lies unconscious in a locked room in a deserted house as fire spreads rapidly through the building.
2. In the Conciergerie Prison, Ian watches helplessly through a grille in his cell wall as Barbara and Susan are led away to be taken to the guillotine.

3. The shopkeeper from whom the Doctor obtained his disguise as a Regional Officer of the Provinces tells the prison jailer that he has evidence of a traitor – and holds out the Doctor's ring.
4. Ian meets Léon Colbert in the crypt of a disused church. Revolutionary soldiers suddenly appear, but when Ian turns to warn Léon he finds that the man is aiming a pistol at him. The traitorous Léon announces that Ian has walked into his trap.
5. The Doctor arrives at Jules Renan's house – but he has brought Lemaitre with him. Jules exclaims that the Doctor has betrayed them.
6. As the viewer sees an image of a spectacular starscape, the Doctor tells Ian that they must search for their destiny in the stars.

IT WAS MADE WHERE...?

Location filming: 15.06.64.
Locations: Isle of Wight Farm, over the Misbourne Road, Gerrards Cross, Bucks; White Plains, Tilehouse Lane, Denham Green, Bucks.
Ealing filming: 16.06.64-18.06.64 on Stage 3A (and 3B for 18.06.64)
Studio recording: 10.07.64, 17.07.64, 24.07.64, 31.07.64, all in Lime Grove G, 07.08.64, 14.08.64, both in TC4.

ADDITIONAL CREDITED CAST

Small boy (Peter Walker[1,2]), Rouvray (Laidlaw Dalling[1]), D'Argenson (Neville Smith[1]), Sergeant (Robert Hunter[1]), Lieutenant (Ken Lawrence[1]), Soldier (James Hall[1]), Judge (Howard Charlton[2]), Jailer (Jack Cunningham[2-6]), Webster (Jeffry Wickham[2]), Road works overseer (Dallas Cavell[2]), Peasant (Denis Cleary[2]), Lemaitre (James Cairncross[2-6]), Jean (Roy Herrick[3,4]), Jules Renan (Donald Morely[3-6]), Shopkeeper (John Barrard[3,4]), Danielle (Caroline Hunt[3,4]), Léon Colbert (Edward Brayshaw[3-5]), Robespierre (Keith Anderson[4-6]), Physician (Ronald Pickup[4]), Soldier (Terry Bale[5]), Paul Barrass (John Law[6]), Napoleon (Tony Wall[6]), Soldier (Patrick Marley[6]).

POPULAR MYTHS

- An elaborate model of Paris was constructed for the production but ultimately unused. It was later given to Carole Ann Ford as a present. (There was no such model. What Ford was given was a design model made by Roderick Laing to help him in his work.)

THINGS TO WATCH OUT FOR

- William Russell appears only in pre-filmed inserts in the second and third episodes as he was on holiday during the weeks when they were recorded.
- The second episode features *Doctor Who*'s first ever location filming: some shots of the Doctor walking through the countryside supposedly toward Paris, with Brian Proudfoot doubling for William Hartnell.

THINGS YOU MIGHT NOT HAVE KNOWN

- This story was a replacement for a postponed and ultimately abandoned David Whitaker six-parter about 16th Century Spain after the Armada, which was to have been directed by Gerald Blake.

- As producer and story editor respectively of the 'Saturday afternoon serial', it was originally intended that Verity Lambert and David Whitaker should provide a replacement programme to run in *Doctor Who*'s slot while it was off air for its between-seasons break. They were eventually spared this requirement and the slot was filled instead by repeats of a comedy series called *The Valiant Varneys* starring Reg Varney.
- This story's director, Henric Hirsch, was a member of the same bridge club as its writer, Dennis Spooner.
- Hirsch was dissatisfied with the scenic painting of the sets for the early episodes of the story and on 27 July 1964 sent the following memo to relevant members of the design and scenic servicing teams and to producer Verity Lambert:

    I would like to make a strong protest regarding the standard of artist painting on the sets for my series of *Dr. Who*. We have had large areas of stone walls painted by scenic artists and the results have been dreadful. The stone-work has just been hurriedly brushed in and looks just like wallpaper. The whole realism of the production has been ruined by such disappointing artist painting.

    I have been informed by my designer that we were charged nearly 300 man-hours to have this dungeon set artist painted and, in fact, it was rushed during the last day by two men in less than six hours.

    I hope that it will be possible to have better results on my final three productions.

- Leon Colbert's surname was originally to have been Corneille.

QUOTE, UNQUOTE

- **Road works overseer:** 'I suppose you think you're very clever.' **The Doctor:** 'Well, without any undue modesty, yes!'
- **Robespierre:** 'Death, always death! Do you think I want this carnage?'
- **The Doctor:** 'What do you find so amusing, hm?' **Barbara Wright:** 'Oh, I don't know … Yes I do. It's this feverish activity to try and stop something that we know is going to happen. Robespierre will be guillotined, whatever we do.' **The Doctor:** 'I've told you of our position so often.' **Barbara Wright:** 'Yes, I know. You can't influence or change history. I learned that lesson with the Aztecs.' **The Doctor:** 'The events will happen, just as they are written. I'm afraid so, and we can't stem the tide. But at least we can stop being carried away with the flood!'
- **The Doctor:** 'Our lives are important, at least to us. And as we see, so we learn.' **Ian Chesterton:** 'And what are we going to see and learn next, Doctor?' **The Doctor:** 'Well, unlike the old adage, my boy, our destiny is in the stars, so let's go and search for it …'

ANALYSIS

The Reign of Terror is the first of the series' historical stories to feature some truly historic events: specifically the downfall of Robespierre in 1794 and the first steps on the road to power of the young Napoleon Bonaparte.

Perhaps conscious that the violent, bloody nature of the French Revolution might otherwise make for unduly grim subject matter for *Doctor Who*, Dennis Spooner has leavened his scripts with occasional moments of whimsical humour – something of a departure for the series – perhaps most notably through the essentially comic character of the jailer of the Conciergerie Prison. He has also avoided focusing on the executions themselves – the guillotine is seen only in a stock film shot. Instead, drawing inspiration from *The Scarlet Pimpernel*, he has woven his story around a covert organisation rescuing people from the guillotine and helping them to escape to safety in England.

The time travellers stumble upon this escape route shortly after the TARDIS arrives in France, when they come upon a secluded house that turns out to be the meeting point where fleeing aristocrats are given disguises and documentation to help them on their way. There they meet two such escapees, Rouvray and d'Argenson, who are subsequently killed when Revolutionary soldiers descend upon the house. 'There is excellent attention to detail in this scene,' noted Andrew Thomas, writing in the Premiere Issue of *Dreamwatch* dated October 1994. 'The [soldiers' costumes] are authentic and demonstrate the kind of patched together helmets, "night cap" forage caps and uniforms typical of this period, which saw the clothing and armament industries of France overwhelmed by the sheer numbers of untrained conscripts forced into service in the Revolutionary armies. The "citizen's army" is also well brought to life, with one soldier sneering roundly at an officer, who has ordered him to cover the back of the house, "Cover it yourself – Citizen". He is persuaded to do his duty by reminding himself ... "It's a long time since I had a Royalist to myself." That one line chillingly symbolises the class hatreds which erupted in France as the Revolution unfolded.'

Subsequently the action moves to Paris, where the viewer is introduced to some of the leading figures in the escape committee – Jules Renan, his friend Jean and their associate Léon Colbert. The portrayal of these characters, however, was rather less to Thomas's liking: 'The presentation of the Royalists as pipe-smoking, jolly good chaps – "Not all Frenchmen can allow innocent people to be led to the guillotine, Barbara" – and the Revolutionaries as foul-mouthed and stupid clearly [reflects] ... Dennis Spooner's schoolbook vision of the events of the Revolution. Nowhere are there references to the bloody Royalist uprisings then going on in Brittany and the Vendee and the continuing threat from the none-too libertarian monarchs of Europe, just waiting to have another go at the Revolution after receiving a bloody nose in the days of its birth.' Although there is some validity in this observation, it should in fairness be pointed out that Jules in one scene specifically states that he is not an aristocrat, and that when Colbert is revealed to be a traitor to the escape committee, Spooner has Barbara challenging Ian over just such naïve assumptions about the respective merits of the two factions: 'The Revolution isn't all bad, and neither are the people who support it ... You check your history books, Ian, before you decide what people deserve.' The fact that Barbara has had a brief romantic association with Léon in no way diminishes the force of the point that she makes.

Characterisation is, in fact, one of Spooner's fortés, and of particular note in this regard are his depictions of Lemaitre (ultimately revealed to be the English spy James Stirling), Robespierre and Napoleon. Also well served are the four regulars; Tim Munro, writing in *Star Begotten* Volume 3 No. 3 dated Summer 1989, was particularly admiring of the treatment of the Doctor: 'Spooner covers every aspect of the first Doctor, allowing Hartnell to give one of his finest performances. We see his developing affection for the teachers … But we also see his pig-headedness; threatening to put them off the ship out of wounded pride. There is also his delightful rapport with children; patting Jean-Pierre on the head and treating him like a grandson after the boy saves him from the burning farm – Hartnell's farewell salute is wonderful! There's his encounter with a chain-gang and their sadistic overseer …, who puts him to work at gunpoint! Clobbering the overseer with his spade, Hartnell reveals a gift for mime worthy of a silent comic, prolonging his lead-in to the blow so that the audience anticipate it …

'We see his unquestionable authority when he acquires the uniform of a Regional Officer of the Provinces from John Barrard's shopkeeper, whose ghoulish Revolutionary zeal is unsettling (with reason!), by persuading him to do a swap for his own "fancy dress outfit" and ring. The Doctor's abilities include forging his own papers, and so thoroughly intimidating Jack Cunningham's jailer that the man scarcely glances at them anyway.'

Production values, while not perhaps reaching the dizzy heights of the previous historicals, are generally good. Director Henric Hirsch found the production a stressful one (he reportedly collapsed in the studio before recording of the third episode, resulting in John Gorrie having to stand in for him), but this is not at all apparent from the finished product, which is very polished. There are good performances from virtually all the cast (a rare exception being James Cairncross, whose delivery of his lines as Lemaitre tends to be rather wooden); and Keith Anderson as Robespierre and Tony Wall as Napoleon are both deserving of special praise.

One of the less successful aspects of the production is Stanley Myers' incidental music, which tends to be rather trite and irritating, but even this has its admirers, including Munro: 'Stanley Myers' richly-textured and detailed music uses an unusually large range of instruments. His constant echoing of the "Marseillese" is effective, and there is a wonderful "Doctor theme", which blends oboe, flute and harpsichord.'

All things considered, *The Reign of Terror* rounded off the series' first season in fine style.

By the end of its first season *Doctor Who* had proved itself a big success – due in no small part to the phenomenal impact made by the Daleks. Opposition to the series within the BBC had been largely silenced – for the time being, at least – and the last two stories made as part of the first production block had been held back to launch a second season on air.

Despite adjustments made in the wake of the Daleks' unexpected popularity, the stories of the first season had adhered quite faithfully to the format originally laid down for the series. There had been a few developments – perhaps most notably, the character of the Doctor had mellowed considerably so that, by the end of the run, there was little doubt that he was a champion for good – but stability had been ensured by the fact that the regular team, both in front of and behind the cameras, had remained unchanged throughout. With the coming of the second season, however, a number of important changes lay in store …

DOCTOR WHO SEASON TWO [1964-1965]

Regular Cast:

Dr. Who (William Hartnell)
Ian Chesterton (William Russell) until *The Chase: The Planet of Decision*
Barbara Wright (Jacqueline Hill) until *The Chase: The Planet of Decision*
Susan Foreman (Carole Ann Ford) until *The Dalek Invasion of Earth: Flashpoint*
Vicki (Maureen O'Brien) from *The Rescue: The Powerful Enemy* onwards
Steven Taylor (Peter Purves) from *The Chase: The Planet of Decision* onwards

Regular Crew:

Producer: Verity Lambert.
Associate Producer: Mervyn Pinfield until *The Romans: Inferno*.
Story Editor: David Whitaker until *The Dalek Invasion of Earth: Flashpoint*. Dennis Spooner from *The Rescue: The Powerful Enemy* until *The Chase: The Planet of Decision*. Donald Tosh from *The Time Meddler: The Watcher* onwards.
Title Music: Ron Grainer and the BBC Radiophonic Workshop, arranged by Delia Derbyshire.
Special Sounds: Brian Hodgson.

The second season of *Doctor Who* saw the first changes taking place in the series' regular cast and production team.

Contemporary documentation relating to the negotiations that took place when the contracts of the four leads came up for renewal shows that the production team were keen to retain the services of William Hartnell and William Russell but regarded Jacqueline Hill's continued involvement as less important and were disinclined to keep Carole Ann Ford in the series – in large part because the actress herself wanted to leave. In the end, Hill's agents did not push for the large pay increase that would have priced their client off the show (although she and Russell did both receive a small increase of around £16 per episode), so Ian and Barbara remained with the Doctor – at least for the time being. Susan, however, was written out, and another young girl introduced in her place.

The most important change in the production team was the exit of the original story editor, David Whitaker, and the entrance of his successor, Dennis Spooner. Spooner's tenure was to be relatively short, and by the end of the season he himself had left and passed on the reigns to Donald Tosh. A further notable development was the departure of associate producer Mervyn Pinfield (who made his last contribution in this role around the time that *The Dalek Invasion of Earth* went into studio, although he continued to be credited up until the end of *The Romans*). No new associate producer was appointed as it was considered that Verity Lambert had by this time fully justified Sydney Newman's faith in her and no longer needed such assistance.

PLANET OF GIANTS

Writer: Louis Marks. **Director:** Mervyn Pinfield[1-3], Douglas Camfield[4]. **Designer:** Raymond P Cusick. **Costumes:** Daphne Dare. **Make-Up:** Jill Summers[1], Sonia Markham[2-4]. **Incidental Music:** Dudley Simpson. **Studio Lighting:** Howard King. **Studio Sound:** Alan Fogg. **Production Assistant:** Norman Stewart. **Assistant Floor Manager:** Valerie McCrimmon, Dawn Robertson.

Note: This story was written and made in four episodes, but just two weeks before transmission the original third and fourth episodes – entitled *Crisis* and *The Urge to Live* respectively – were edited together to form a single episode, with sufficient material removed to bring the running time down to fit the standard slot. This was done at the instigation of Head of Serials Donald Wilson who felt that the action needed tightening up, particularly in view of the fact that the story had been held back to launch the second season on air.

	First UK TX	Scheduled TX	Actual TX	Duration	Viewers	Chart Pos.
Planet of Giants	31/10/64	17.15	17.16	23'15"	8.4	37
Dangerous Journey	07/11/64	17.15	17.15	23'40"	8.4	45
Crisis	14/11/64	17.15	17.15	26'35"	8.9	33

Plot: The main doors of the TARDIS open of their own accord just before it materialises, causing it to run out of control. On emerging, the travellers discover that the ship has been reduced in size and they are now only about an inch tall. In this miniaturised state, they stumble across a plot by a ruthless businessman, Forester, and his misguided scientist colleague, Smithers, to launch a new insecticide named DN6 – a product so destructive that it would kill not only those insects harmful to agriculture but also those vital to it. Forester is even willing to commit murder to ensure the success of his business, as civil servant Arnold Farrow discovers to his cost. The criminals are eventually brought to justice when the Doctor and his friends – hampered by the fact that Barbara has herself been made ill by the insecticide – tamper with the telephone in Smithers' laboratory, thus fuelling the suspicions of the local exchange operator, Hilda Rowse, who sends her police constable husband Bert to investigate.

Episode endings:
1. Farrow has been shot by Forester and the miniaturised time travellers investigate the body. Suddenly Susan realises that they are being intently watched by a giant black cat.
2. After cleaning Farrow's blood from the patio stones outside, Smithers goes into the laboratory to wash his hands, unaware that the Doctor and Susan are hiding in the water outlet from the sink. As a helpless Ian and Barbara watch, he fills the sink with water, washes, and then pulls out the plug.
3. With everything returned to normal, the Doctor checks the newly repaired scanner screen for their next destination. It shows only interference. The ship starts to materialise and the Doctor hopes to discover its latest arrival point.

FIRST DOCTOR

IT WAS MADE WHERE...?

Ealing filming: 30.07.64, 13.08.64 (Stage unknown).
Studio recording: 21.08.64, 28.08.64, 04.09.64, 11.09.64, all in TC4.

ADDITIONAL CREDITED CAST

Forester (Alan Tilvern), Farrow (Frank Crawshaw[1,2]), Smithers (Reginald Barratt[2,3]), Hilda Rowse (Rosemary Johnson[3]), Bert Rowse (Fred Ferris[3]).

THINGS TO WATCH OUT FOR

- The is no noise heard either inside or outside the TARDIS as it arrives at the start of the story and leaves at the end.
- This is the first instance of Dudley Simpson providing incidental music for the series. Simpson would continue to work on *Doctor Who* periodically until the end of the seventeenth season in 1979.

THINGS YOU MIGHT NOT HAVE KNOWN

- Working title: *The Miniscules*. The working title of the second individual episode was *Death in the Afternoon*.
- Fred Ferris, who played policeman Bert Rowse, was a popular Liverpudlian comedian.
- Hilda Rowse's first name was originally to have been Emma.
- Actor John Dawson was originally considered to play policeman Bert Rowse.
- The third and fourth episodes of the story as recorded were edited together into a single, standard length episode prior to transmission. Roughly half the material from each was discarded. The fourth episode was to have been entitled *The Urge to Live*. Terrance Dicks incorporated some of the cut material in his later novelisation of the story for the Target range.

QUOTE, UNQUOTE

- **Ian Chesterton:** 'You can get us back to normal size, can't you?' **The Doctor:** 'Oh yes, of course I can, dear boy. Yes ... of course I can ... I hope!'
- **Forester:** 'Do you know why I'm a success, Mr Farrow? Because I've never allowed the word "can't" to exist.'

ANALYSIS

It is rather puzzling now to note the apparent determination of *Doctor Who*'s creators to feature a story in which the time travellers find themselves in a miniaturised state. It had at first been intended that the series should actually be launched with an adventure of this type, C E Webber's *The Giants*. When that had fallen through, the idea had been passed on to freelance writer Robert Gould. Then, when that too had come to nothing, the project had finally been assigned to another freelancer, Louis Marks. While stories involving giants and people being reduced in size have long been a staple ingredient of popular fiction – incidents in *Gulliver's Travels* and fifties sci-fi films like *The Incredible Shrinking Man* come immediately to mind in this context – it is difficult to understand exactly why the *Doctor Who* team considered it so essential that the series should explore this territory. Nevertheless, this much-desired adventure eventually turned up at the start of the second season, with only a six week gap following the conclusion of *The Reign of Terror*.

The element that Marks brought to the mix was the idea of an indiscriminately destructive insecticide, for which he drew inspiration from environmentalist Rachel Carson's seminal book *Silent Spring*. This was the first time that *Doctor Who* had dealt with an ecological theme, but would be by no means the last.

The most immediately striking aspect of the story is its sets. Considering the limited budget with which he had to work – as always – Raymond P Cusick's incredible scaled-up versions of a laboratory bench and a sink are astonishingly convincing, as are his 'patio cracks' complete with ants' eggs and dead earthworm. The 'live' giant fly that causes Barbara to faint in shock is also worthy of special mention. This is an incredible construction and looks totally realistic, rubbing its mandibles together and swivelling its head. 'A masterpiece of visual effects,' commented Paul Mount in *Doctor Who – An Adventure in Space and Time* in 1981.

The limited studio space available to accommodate the deliberately outsized sets must have presented considerable problems for principal director Mervyn Pinfield. Some of these he was unable to solve – for example, Susan apparently fails to see the bulk of the ants eggs, even though they are within touching distance, until she has stood up and stepped over to them – but for the most part one can only admire the way in which this technically demanding story is realised on screen. Indeed, Mount went so far as to suggest that 'visually *Planet of Giants* is faultless, with all director Mervyn Pinfield's considerable camera expertise coming into play admirably'. The BBC's Audience Research Report on the first episode was similarly full of praise for 'the special effects and "props" which, according to most ... "really made it look as if [the travellers] were only inches high".'

Jacqueline Hill gets another chance to shine in this story as Barbara becomes infected with the insecticide. The urgency of getting her back to the TARDIS is heightened by her insistence to her friends that she is okay – the viewer knows that she is not, and this adds to the drama. William Hartnell and William Russell are also superb in this story, although Carole Ann Ford's performance as Susan is rather less impressive.

The other characters, unfortunately, are a pretty grim lot. Farrow and Forester are two dimensional and wooden, and Smithers seems totally out of place. Bert and Hilda Rowse give the impression of having wandered in by mistake from the set of *Dixon of Dock Green*.

The plot itself is also one of the weakest featured in the series up to this point. Smithers seems genuinely surprised when he realises that DN6 is lethal to all life, and yet every impression is given that he developed and helped to test it. Forester kills Farrow to ensure that he can profit from the chemical (and would clearly be quite happy to kill Smithers as well), and yet seems unconcerned as to who will make and distribute the stuff. There is very little substance to the drama here; and, as the TARDIS crew never interact with the other characters (the Doctor points out that the 'giants' will be unable to hear them as their voices will be on a different wavelength – although paradoxically he later suggests using the telephone to try to call for help), it all makes for fairly dull viewing.

One can only wonder just how much more the action would have dragged had the story not been edited down from four episodes to three, as much of the deleted material – including some additional sequences with Hilda and Bert in the post office in which further 'clues' were heavy-handedly brought to light, and scenes showing the travellers escaping down the drain-pipe after engineering the explosion of a can of insecticide at the story's climax – was unnecessary and frankly rather tedious.

Given the story's shortcomings it is perhaps surprising to note that the BBC's Audience Research Report indicated a generally positive response to the series' return from viewers at the time: 'There can be no doubt that the sample at large welcomed the re-appearance of the *Doctor Who* series and were well satisfied ... Of course the whole thing was all great nonsense, viewers would insist, but at the same time they had to admit that they quite enjoyed the adventures of Doctor Who and his companions of the TARDIS, preposterous though they might be. And certainly the situation on this occasion, with the Doctor, Susan, Ian and Barbara reduced to Lilliputian proportions, offered ample opportunities for intriguing events, and thrills and excitements to come. True, just one or two declared they "had no time" for this "far fetched" nonsense, but though some were inclined to react with a somewhat amused condescension, most were firm *Doctor Who* addicts and very pleased to embark on yet another of what promised to be a very exciting science-fiction adventure.'

Paul Mount's summation is arguably rather nearer the mark: '*Planet of Giants* is something of a curate's egg in that the aspects of it which worked did so quite brilliantly, but other facets which did not work quite plainly failed ... [It] is probably the first major chink in the otherwise unflawed armour of *Doctor Who* at the time.'

THE DALEK INVASION OF EARTH

Writer: Terry Nation. **Director:** Richard Martin. **Designer:** Spencer Chapman. **Costumes:** Daphne Dare[1,2,5,6], Tony Pearce[3,4]. **Make-Up:** Sonia Markham[1-3,5,6], Elizabeth Blattner[4]. **Incidental Music:** Francis Chagrin. **Fight Arranger:** Peter Diamond. **Film Cameraman:** Peter Hamilton. **Film Editor:** John Griffiths. **Studio Lighting:** Howard King. **Studio Sound:** Jack Brummitt. **Production Assistant:** Jane Shirley. **Assistant Floor Manager:** Christina Lawton.

	First UK TX	Scheduled TX	Actual TX	Duration	Viewers	Chart Pos.
World's End	21/11/64	17.40	17.41	23'42"	11.4	12
The Daleks	28/11/64	17.40	17.41	24'19"	12.4	10
Day of Reckoning	05/12/64	17.40	17.40	26'50"	11.9	10
The End of Tomorrow	12/12/64	17.40	17.40	23'23"	11.9	11
The Waking Ally	19/12/64	17.40	17.41	24'29"	11.4	18
Flashpoint	26/12/64	17.55	17.59	25'41"	12.4	12

Plot: The TARDIS materialises in London sometime after the year 2164. Dalek invaders are now ruling the Earth with the aid of humans converted into zombie-like Robomen, but they are opposed by a group of resistance fighters led by the wheelchair-using Dortmun. The travellers discover that the Daleks have established a huge mine in Bedfordshire, their aim being to remove the Earth's core using a huge bomb and replace it with a powerful drive system so that they can pilot the planet around the galaxy. Ian manages to create a barrier in the shaft in order to intercept the bomb. The resulting explosion destroys the Daleks and their mine and creates a huge volcanic eruption. Susan has fallen in love with the resistance fighter David Campbell, and the Doctor decides to leave her on Earth to find a new life with him, while he continues on his travels with Ian and Barbara.

Episode endings:

1. The Doctor and Ian, menaced by a group of Robomen, prepare to escape by diving into the Thames. As they turn, they see rising slowly from the water the familiar shape of a Dalek.
2. The Doctor lies helpless on a bench beneath a robotising machine in the Dalek saucer as the Dalek commander gives orders for the operation to commence.
3. The Doctor, Susan and David decide to wait for a few minutes before departing for Bedfordshire as there are Daleks nearby. Unseen by them, two Robomen have deposited a large oblong casing on the walkway above. The casing begins to tick ominously, and an indicator on a dial starts to move round ...
4. Ian and his friend Larry are trapped on the lip of a sheer drop as the ferocious Slyther bears straight down on them.
5. Ian is trapped inside the Daleks' bomb as the countdown begins and it moves toward the shaft where it is to be released ...
6. The TARDIS dematerialises and, comforted by David, Susan moves away. Her TARDIS key lies discarded on the ground, with an image of a starscape superimposed ...

IT WAS MADE WHERE...?

Location filming: 23.08.64, 25.08.64, 27.08.64, 28.08.64.
Locations: Hammersmith Bridge, Queen Caroline Street, Hammersmith, London, W6; Butler's Wharf, Southwark, London, SE1; 'A' Warehouse, St Katharine's Dock, London, E1; Irongate Wharf, St Katharine's Way, London, E1; White City Underground Station, Wood Lane, Shepherd's Bush, London, W12; Albert Embankment, London, SE11; Westminster Bridge, London, SW1; Whitehall, London, SW1; Trafalgar Square, London, SW1; Royal Albert Hall, Kensington Gore, Kensington, London, SW7; Albert Memorial, Kensington, London, SW7; Palace of Industry, Engineers Way, Wembley, Middx; John's Hole Quarry, Stone, Kent; Third Way, Wembley, Middx.
Studio recording: 18.09.64, 25.09.64, 02.10.64, 09.10.64, 16.10.64, 23.10.64, all in Riverside 1.

ADDITIONAL CREDITED CAST

Carl Tyler (Bernard Kay), David Campbell (Peter Fraser), Dortmun (Alan Judd[1-4]), Robomen (Martyn Huntley, Peter Badger), Dalek Operator[1]/Dalek Machines Operated By:[2-6] (Robert Jewell, Gerald Taylor[2-6], Nick Evans[2,3,5,6*], Kevin Manser[2-5], Peter Murphy[2-6]), Dalek Voices (Peter Hawkins[2-6], David Graham[2-6]), Jenny (Ann Davies[2-6]), Craddock (Michael Goldie[2,3]), Thomson (Michael Davis[2]), Baker (Richard McNeff[2,3]), Larry Madison (Graham Rigby[3-5]), Wells (Nicholas Smith[4-6]), Slyther operator (Nick Evans[4,5]), Ashton (Patrick O'Connell[4]), The Women in the Wood (Jean Conroy[5], Meriel Hobson[5]).

* Also in *The End of Tomorrow*, but uncredited

POPULAR MYTHS

- This story is set in the year 2164. (The Doctor and Ian find a calendar dated 2164, but it is lying in a disused warehouse and could have been there for years; it is most unlikely that anyone was still printing calendars after the Daleks invaded.)
- The Daleks are defeated due to their susceptibility to the Earth's magnetic forces.

FIRST DOCTOR

(They are defeated when they are caught in the explosion at their mine; the idea of their susceptibility to magnetic forces was exploited in the later cinema film adaptation of the story, *Daleks' Invasion Earth 2150 A.D.*)

THINGS TO WATCH OUT FOR

- The Daleks have enlarged fenders (accommodating small tricycles to enable the operators to move them over uneven ground on location) and energy collection discs (intended to explain the fact that they are no longer reliant on static electricity drawn from metal floors, as they were in their debut story).
- A Dalek attempts to interrogate a tailor's dummy – an early, isolated example of the creatures being treated as figures of fun, which would be seen more prominently in their next story, *The Chase*.
- This story features the first of many quarries to be used in the series' location filming – this one, John's Hole Quarry, actually representing a quarry rather than an alien landscape.
- The Black Dalek's 'pet', the Slyther, manages to change appearance somewhat between the end of the fourth episode and the beginning of the fifth. (This was due to dissatisfaction on the production team's part with the original version of the costume.)
- William Hartnell did not appear in the fourth episode (apart from in the film insert reprise from the third) as he was absent during the week in which it was recorded; this was due to him sustaining a bruised back in an on-set accident during camera rehearsal of the previous week's episode. Edmund Warwick briefly doubled for him.

THINGS YOU MIGHT NOT HAVE KNOWN

- Working titles: *The Daleks*, *The Return of the Daleks*.
- The title of the first episode is a pun, referring both to the devastation of the Earth by the Daleks and to the fact that the TARDIS arrives in an area of London near Battersea known as World's End.
- It was the production team's idea rather than writer Terry Nation's to write Susan out by way of a romance with the freedom fighter David (whose surname was originally to have been Somheim, then Archer). The story was also to have introduced a fifteen-year-old girl named Saida, played by Pamela Franklin, as a new companion by having her stow away aboard the TARDIS at the end of the last episode; this idea was subsequently dropped and Saida became just a one-off character, renamed Jenny and played by Ann Davies.
- Following transmission of this story's first episode, the production office received a letter dated 23 November 1964 from a viewer, Mrs Patricia Stern of Uxbridge in Middlesex, who complained that it had been too horrific and had scared her children. Verity Lambert replied on 2 December 1964, defending the episode in question and making some more general points about the series' content:

  1) *Doctor Who* is an adventure serial. There are bound to be some unpleasant incidents to sustain suspense and to show the ultimate triumph of good over evil.

  2) There were two bodies in last week's episode of *Doctor Who*, but we do not feel that too much attention was paid to 'gruesome detail.' For

example, there were no pools of blood or other unpleasant details. After all, death is a part of life. I do not feel that *Doctor Who* goes any further in portraying this than the average Western.

3) In Grimm's fairytales and in some classics, which are acceptable to children, there is just as much, if not more, 'horror and violence' as there is in *Doctor Who*.

It is our aim to entertain children and not frighten them out of their wits, and a great many children watch and enjoy *Doctor Who* with no ill effects.

- The Slyther was made by Shawcraft and consisted of a boiler suit with pieces of sponge and plastic added.
- The *Daily Mail* of 21 August 1964 reported that filming for this story was planned to take place in the Mall, with Buckingham Palace in the background, but could not go ahead due to the Changing of the Guard and other tourist attractions which, combined with Daleks, could have caused traffic jams.
- The *Daily Express* of 6 December 1964 claimed that the level of violence in *Doctor Who* was to be cut after scenes of 'William Hartnell being put on an operating table and threatened by whip-wielding Daleks' had brought complaints from some BBC executives.

QUOTE, UNQUOTE

- **Dalek:** 'We are the masters of Earth! We are the masters of Earth! We are the masters of Earth!'
- **Dalek:** 'Rebels of London, this is your last offer – our final warning. Leave your hiding places. Show yourselves in the open streets. You will be fed and watered. Work is needed from you … but the Daleks offer you life. Rebel against us and the Daleks will destroy London completely. You will all die. The males, the females, the descendants. Rebels of London, come out of your hiding places.' **Daleks:** 'The Daleks offer you life!'
- **The Doctor:** 'One day, I shall come back. Yes, I shall come back. Until then, there must be no regrets, no tears, no anxieties. Just go forward in all your beliefs, and prove to me that I am not mistaken in mine. Goodbye, my dear. Goodbye, Susan.'

ANALYSIS

While *Planet of Giants* must be deemed a partial failure, the same certainly cannot be said of *The Dalek Invasion of Earth*, which unquestionably ranks as one of the series' all-time greats.

Terry Nation's scripts are impressive, presenting an action-packed good-versus-evil struggle. The return of the Daleks was very much by popular demand and generated considerable excitement amongst viewers at the time, as is apparent from the following description in the BBC's Audience Research Report on the first episode:

'"My children introduced me to this series. I'm glad they did!", commented a representative from the majority of the sample who much enjoyed this episode … Viewers sometimes said that they realised these adventures were principally for juvenile consumption, but they too found them exciting and entertaining, and this was one of the best; others reported that their children sat with them enthralled – "This has great imagination again. Holds one's attention all the time. The children love it"; "My family has been talking about it all week." It was evident that the desire "to see what happened next" was pretty strong throughout the sample, and the suspense was said to have been well maintained.

'All the same, there were some protests from viewers who had been looking forward to the return of the Daleks that hardly anything had been seen of them – "Well, the Daleks are back! For about fifteen seconds we saw one Dalek. All I had was 'Where are the Daleks?' from my young sons. Rather a let down after all the publicity. Nevertheless, no doubt, under pressure we will see more next week." A small number of viewers in the sample seemed to regard the episode (and Doctor Who's travels generally) as rather beneath their notice although no doubt acceptable for children ("If you are catering for the eight to twelve age group, okay."). As against this, there were a few suggestions that part of today's adventure might prove rather alarming for the smaller fry – "It was rather gruesome for young children to watch, with drowned bodies and daggered bodies. Next week we hope for more Daleks and fewer bodies."'

Further evidence of children's reactions to this opening episode is provided by the following recollections from John Peel in *Oracle* Volume 2 Number 3 dated December 1978:

'I nearly fell out of my seat [as the end of the episode approached], excitement mounting as a familiar eye-stick rose from the dark waters and a Dalek slowly emerged, the end theme cutting in. I had honestly never expected to see these evil cyborgs back again, but what a place to see them – almost [in] my back yard ...

'They seemed far more evil in our world; deadly, pitiless – and totally exciting. No-one missed more of this story than they had to; it was the talk of the school, all us crazy kids "exterminating" wholesale lots of fellow pupils and secretly-addicted teachers! ...

'Dalekmania had begun; that strange fever that gripped the young (and not so young) with the desire to stick out their arms and grate "Exterminate!" to all and sundry ...'

On the other hand, the episode did have, as Bevan Thomas observed in *TSV* 22 dated April 1991, 'embarrassments such as the model flying saucer and the slow-moving, slow-talking, slow-thinking and utterly stupid-looking Robomen. It climaxed well with the ... Dalek rising from the river. [This] poses an interesting question, though. What the hell was it doing in the river in the first place?'

Richard Martin's studio direction of the story is perhaps a little clumsy in places, but this is more than made up for by his excellent location work – the first major use of location filming in *Doctor Who* – which is very effective in helping to convey the impression of a Britain under the rule of the alien forces. The images of the shattered London are stark and chilling, while those of the huge mining area the invaders have established in Bedfordshire are no less impressive.

'The idea of invaders from space encased in metal machines is not a new one,' observed Trevor Wayne in *Gallifrey* Issue Thirteen dated winter 1980/81. 'H G Wells' ... *The War of the Worlds* provided a splendid source of inspiration ...; although very little of the structure or plot of the novel actually find their way into the script. Desolate, devastated riverside buildings and a Roboman committing suicide [provide] a harrowing urban analogue for the petrified forest of the first Dalek story.'

The story can also be seen as a 'what if ...?' depiction of how things might have turned out had the country been occupied during World War II (which would still have been very fresh in the minds of many viewers when the story was first transmitted, having ended less than twenty years earlier), and it is all the more evocative for that, as Wayne elaborated: 'The resistance groups ... are clearly modelled on the brave bands of patriots who resisted the superbly armed and equipped Wehrmacht in occupied Europe during the last war. All the characters [wear] contemporary dress, with only a few remarks about moon bases to indicate that they [are] citizens of a future Britain. All they [have with which] to resist the Daleks [are] conventional 20th Century firearms.'

Nation's scripts essentially equate the Daleks with Adolph Hitler's Nazis. The Black Dalek is referred to as the 'commandant' of the mining camp; the creatures describe the extermination of all humans as their 'final solution'; and, as if to ensure that nobody misses the point, there is even a scene in the second episode in which a group of Daleks raise their sucker sticks in a Nazi salute. This is appropriate, given the creatures' xenophobic natures as originally established in their debut story and re-emphasised in this one. In some respects, however, the Daleks of *The Dalek Invasion of Earth* are rather different from their forerunners – and, as Wayne explained, these differences extend beyond the minor design changes to their casings: 'The Daleks of this story are far removed from the basically pitiful creatures on Skaro ... The [scene of the] Dalek emerging from the river speaks volumes; the invaders are [now] mobile in any element they choose ... The Doctor's explanation [to Ian] as to how the Daleks could be [on Earth] when they had witnessed their total destruction on Skaro [i.e. that this is an earlier point in the Daleks' history] is nonsense ... But we are not left to dwell on this logical inconsistency.'

The Daleks' scheme – to extract the Earth's core and replace it with a propulsion unit – is pure B-movie material, but the quality of writing and production transcends such limitations. Characterisation is another of the story's strong points, the human resistance workers being an interesting and believable group; and the climax of the action, as the Daleks and their mine are consumed in a huge explosion, leading to the extraordinary phenomenon of a volcanic eruption in England, is suitably awe-inspiring.

The closing moments of the story stand as an important landmark in *Doctor Who*'s history as they feature the first departure of a companion – namely the Doctor's grand-daughter Susan who, following the logical character development begun in *The Sensorites*, has grown from a child into a young woman and fallen in love with the resistance fighter David Campbell. This final scene is a poignant and moving one, beautifully written by story editor David Whitaker, which must have left many viewers wondering if the series would ever be quite the same again. The following week, however, would see the Doctor, Ian and Barbara embarking on another adventure, in which they would encounter a new regular character to take Susan's place.

THE RESCUE

Writer: David Whitaker. **Director:** Christopher Barry. **Designer:** Raymond P Cusick. **Costumes:** Daphne Dare. **Make-Up:** Sonia Markham. **Incidental Music:** Tristram Cary (from stock). **Film Cameraman:** Dick Bush. **Film Editor:** Jim Latham. **Studio Lighting:** Howard King. **Studio Sound:** Richard Chubb. **Production Assistant:** David Maloney. **Assistant Floor Manager:** Valerie Wilkins.

	First UK TX	Scheduled TX	Actual TX	Duration	Viewers	Chart Pos.
The Powerful Enemy	02/01/65	17.40	17.40	26'15"	12.0	11
Desperate Measures	09/01/65	17.40	17.41	24'36"	13.0	8

1 FIRST DOCTOR

Plot: Arriving on the planet Dido in the late 25th Century, the time travellers come upon a crashed spaceship from Earth. Its two occupants – a paralysed man named Bennett and a young girl, Vicki – are living in fear of a creature called Koquillion, a native whose people have apparently killed the other members of the human expedition. However, the Doctor quickly deduces that Koquillion is in fact Bennett in disguise; it was he who killed the others in order to conceal an earlier murder he had committed on the ship. Confronted by two of the humanoid Dido natives – whom he thought he had completely wiped out – Bennett falls from a high rock ledge to his death. As Vicki's father was amongst the murdered crewmen and she is now an orphan, the Doctor offers her a place aboard the TARDIS.

Episode endings:
1. Making their way along a narrow ledge to escape from the cave in which Koquillion has trapped them, the Doctor and Ian find some metal wall rings, apparently intended as hand-holds. One of them comes loose as Ian pulls on it, activating a mechanism that traps him between two sets of sharp spears. More spears emerge from the wall behind him and start to push him toward the edge while, below, a horrific monster awaits.
2. The travellers leave the planet Dido taking Vicki with them. The Doctor hopes that they might get some rest at their next port of call. The TARDIS materialises on the edge of a cliff, however, and slowly topples off …

IT WAS MADE WHERE...?
Ealing filming (models): 16.11.64-17.11.64 on Stage 2
Studio recording: 04.12.64, 11.12.64, both in Riverside 1.

ADDITIONAL CREDITED CAST
Bennett (Ray Barrett), Space Captain (Tom Sheridan), Koquillion (Sydney Wilson[1]*, Ray Barrett[2]).

* 'Sydney Wilson' was a name invented for the first episode to hide Koquillion's true identity. The name was taken from *Sydney* Newman and Donald *Wilson*, the BBC's Head of Drama and Head of Serials respectively.

POPULAR MYTHS
• The inhabitants of Dido are called Didonians. (They are never referred to as such in the televised story).

THINGS TO WATCH OUT FOR
• The TARDIS makes the familiar 'wheezing and groaning' noise both inside and outside the ship as it materialises in this story.

THINGS YOU MIGHT NOT HAVE KNOWN
• Working title: *Doctor Who and Tanni*.

- Jacqueline Hill sustained shock and a sore face when the wooden effects gun used in the scene where she shot the Sand Monster detonated with greater ferocity than expected.
- Tom Sheridan, who played the Space Captain heard but not seen in this story, was also inside the Sand Monster costume. He was also originally due to play one of the inhabitants of Dido.
- Earlier names considered for Vicki included Tanni, Millie, Valerie and Lukki (pronounced Lucky).
- Bernard Archard was at one point considered to play the role of Bennett but turned it down, apparently due to other commitments.
- Director Christopher Barry decided to use for the death of the Sand Monster the same sound effect as had been used for the death of a Dalek in *The Mutants*. He sent a tape of this to Brian Hodgson at the Radiophonic Workshop and asked him to ensure that the Monster's other sounds matched it.

QUOTE, UNQUOTE

- **Barbara Wright:** 'Oh, but Doctor, the trembling's stopped!' **The Doctor:** 'Oh my dear ... I'm so glad you're feeling better ... hm?' **Barbara Wright:** 'No! Not me! The ship!'
- **Vicki:** 'What are you looking like that for?' **Barbara Wright:** 'Like what?' **Vicki:** 'You're sorry for me aren't you? I'm perfectly all right, you know. I don't care if nobody ever comes. I'm fine. I'm perfectly all right!'
- **The Doctor:** 'We can travel anywhere and everywhere in that old box as you call it. Regardless of space and time ... and if you like adventure, my dear, I can promise you an abundance of it.'

ANALYSIS

The Rescue, as a relatively unambitious two-parter nestling between the epic *The Dalek Invasion of Earth* and the amusing historical *The Romans*, is a story that sometimes seems to get overlooked. This is a pity, as it is actually one of the best examples of character-driven drama from this period of the series' history.

With Susan out of the way, attention focuses initially on the Doctor, Ian and Barbara, and the story opens with a lovely scene illustrating just how far these people have come since we first met them. Primarily, however, the story is a vehicle to introduce the new companion, Vicki, and this is done with the minimum of fuss. The newcomer's character is sketched in nicely, and Maureen O'Brien plays the part with great skill and conviction – even Vicki's distress at the death of 'Sandy', a hideous but tame monster that she has adopted as a pet, is made completely believable. Vicki actually steals the show here, having some nicely written and acted exchanges with Barbara and the Doctor. Her decision to come on board the TARDIS at the end is also nicely handled and bodes well for the future. As Trevor Wayne wrote in *Gallifrey* Issue Twelve dated autumn 1980, 'Vicki was a very sympathetic character throughout, and portrayed a variety of emotions. She was certainly very brave, despite her predicament. She could be amusing, as she was when she reckoned Ian and Barbara were over 550 if they came from 1963! It was also very sad to see her break down when she thought about her dead parents and friends. Perhaps this was what ultimately attracted her to the Doctor. He saw that she needed protection, and she would of course suit his own inner desire for someone to alleviate the loss of his Susan.'

The plot itself is rather lightweight – perhaps not surprisingly, given the story's relative brevity. That Bennett has managed to keep his masquerade as Koquillion going well enough to fool Vicki is just about believable, although the Doctor sees through it immediately and it is really a little difficult to accept that a masked man carrying a jewelled spanner could strike terror anywhere. To his credit, though, Ray Barrett plays the 'dual role' very well and manages to bring a certain intensity to the supposed creature's demeanour, making it a memorable creation.

The climax of the story is visually impressive but a little strange, as John Peel described in *TARDIS* Volume 6 Number 3/4 dated October 1981: 'The ... sequence, where the Doctor is seated in the Didonian Hall of Judgment, long, dark and gloomy, has to be one of the most marvellous climaxes to a story I have ever seen. Hartnell sits with his back to the door, by the sacrificial altar, lit dimly by candles, and Koquillion enters silently behind him, moving quietly towards his unprotected back ... It sent a shiver down my spine! But the Doctor has heard him, and faces him down, forcing a confession of guilt from the mentally sick Bennett, only to suddenly realise that he is in terrible danger from this homicidal maniac! He is saved only by the intervention of two silent Didonians – a very weak plot device, and I still find it dreadfully hard to believe that the sight of these two unarmed aliens (totally human looking) should scare Bennett so much that he should fall off a cliff after backing away from them.'

The appearance of these two Dido natives, dressed in white jogging suits, is totally unexplained. One can only assume that Bennett did not, after all, kill all the natives in his engineered explosion; but if that is the case, where have they been all the time? And their wrecking of the crashed ship's radio transmitter at the end of the story (presumably intended to signify that they wanted nothing more to do with alien outsiders) is rather odd; surely the approaching rescue ship would not turn back simply because of this?

These unexplained plot threads are, however, only a minor irritation and scarcely detract from the viewer's overall appreciation of the story, which stands as an enjoyable interlude effectively allowing for a new regular to be introduced and for the other travellers to recover from their recent adventure against the Daleks.

THE ROMANS

Writer: Dennis Spooner. **Director:** Christopher Barry. **Designer:** Raymond P Cusick. **Costumes:** Daphne Dare. **Make-Up:** Sonia Markham. **Incidental Music:** Raymond Jones. **Fight Arranger:** Peter Diamond. **Film Cameraman:** Dick Bush. **Film Editor:** Jim Latham. **Studio Lighting:** Howard King[2-4]*. **Studio Sound:** Richard Chubb. **Production Assistant:** David Maloney. **Assistant Floor Manager:** Valerie Wilkins.

* It is unknown who handled the lighting for *The Slave Traders*. Howard King was due to do so (as for the rest of the story) but was on sick leave with flu.

	First UK TX	Scheduled TX	Actual TX	Duration	Viewers	Chart Pos.
The Slave Traders	16/01/65	17.40	17.40	24'14"	13.0	7
All Roads Lead to Rome	23/01/65	17.40	17.40	23'14"	11.5	15
Conspiracy	30/01/65	17.40	17.40	26'18"	10.0	28
Inferno	06/02/65	17.40	17.40	23'09"	12.0	13

Plot: The four time travellers are enjoying a rare holiday, staying at a villa not far from Rome in the year 64 AD. The Doctor soon becomes restless and sets off to visit the city, taking Vicki with him. In their absence, Ian and Barbara are kidnapped by slave traders. Having been mistaken for the famous lyre player Maximus Pettulian and asked to perform at the Emperor Nero's Court, the Doctor has to devise ever more elaborate schemes to avoid revealing that he cannot actually play the instrument. Ian meanwhile becomes a galley slave, while Barbara is sold to Nero's slave buyer Tavius at an auction in Rome. Ian and a fellow slave named Delos escape from the galley when it is wrecked in a storm and make their way to Rome to try to find and rescue Barbara. There they are recaptured and forced to fight as gladiators in the arena. Events reach their climax when, by accidentally setting light to the Emperor's plans for the rebuilding of Rome, the Doctor gives him the idea of having the city razed to the ground. Nero plays the lyre while Rome burns, and the Doctor and Vicki and a reunited Ian and Barbara make their separate ways back to the villa.

Episode endings:
1. Resting overnight at a house in Assissium, the Doctor attempts to play the lyre but manages only a few discordant notes. He chuckles to himself, unaware that the mute assassin Ascaris, who earlier murdered Maximus Pettulian, is entering the room through a curtained entrance, a sword in his hand.
2. Ian and Delos are imprisoned and faced with the prospect of being trained to fight as gladiators in the arena – but against what? Suddenly they hear a ferocious roar, and when Ian looks out through the cell bars he sees a pride of hungry lions roaming about a compound. Horrified, he turns away.
3. Ian and Delos are reluctantly fighting each other in the arena. Ian suddenly loses his balance, giving Delos the upper hand. As the Greek holds his sword to Ian's neck, Nero gives the command to cut off his head.
4. The Doctor tells a confused Ian that the TARDIS has materialised for a split second and become imprisoned by a force from which it cannot break free. Something, somewhere, is slowly dragging them down. Ian asks: 'Dragged down? To where?'. But the Doctor can only return his companion's stare.

IT WAS MADE WHERE...?

Ealing filming: 17.11.64-18.11.64 on Stage 2
Studio recording: 18.12.64, 01.01.64, 08.01.65, 15.01.65, all in Riverside 1.

ADDITIONAL CREDITED CAST

Sevcheria (Derek Sydney), Didius (Nicholas Evans[1]), Centurian (Dennis Edwards[1]), Stall holder (Margot Thomas[1]), Slave buyer (Edward Kelsey[1]), Maximus Pettulian (Bart Allison[1]), Ascaris (Barry Jackson[1,2]), Delos (Peter Diamond[2-4]), Tavius (Michael

Peake[2-4]), Woman Slave (Dorothy-Rose Gribble[2,3]), Galley Master (Gertan Klauber[2]), 1st Man in Market (Ernest Jennings[2]), 2nd Man in Market (John Caesar[2]), Court Messenger (Tony Lambden[2]), Nero (Derek Francis[2-4]), Tigilinus[2]/Tigilinus (Cup Bearer) [3] (Brian Proudfoot[2, 3], Poppaea (Kay Patrick[3, 4]), Locusta (Ann Tirard[3]).

POPULAR MYTHS

- It was new story editor Dennis Spooner who wanted to make *The Romans* an overtly humorous story. (It was producer Verity Lambert's idea to do a story in this vein to try to extend the series' dramatic range – although Spooner was certainly no stranger to comedy and so ideally suited to write it.)

THINGS TO WATCH OUT FOR

- There is a slapstick fight scene between the Doctor, aided by Vicki, and the mute assassin Ascaris, which ends with the latter falling from a first floor window not to be seen again ...
- The Doctor convinces Nero and his courtiers that he is a skilled lyre player, without ever playing a note – a scene that pays homage to Hans Christian Andersen's 1837 story *The Emperor's New Clothes*.

THINGS YOU MIGHT NOT HAVE KNOWN

- Derek Francis, a well-known comic actor, was initially reluctant to take the part of Nero but was persuaded to do so by Jacqueline Hill, whose husband Alvin Rakoff was a close friend of his.
- The scripts for this story underwent some late rewriting. One change was the introduction of the minor character of Nero's servant, Tigilinus. Actor Brian Proudfoot, who played this character, was thus a late addition to the cast.
- The part of Tigilinus was further expanded to incorporate that of another minor slave character. Similarly the slave trader Sevcheria was 'promoted' after the first episode to become the captain of Nero's guards, originally envisaged by Spooner as a separate individual.
- During the making of the story, director Christopher Barry queried the rule that, for copyright reasons, specially composed incidental music could be played back only in the studio and not during rehearsals. He pointed out that this was likely to deprive musicians of work as it encouraged directors to use stock music instead. However, he was informed that the rule could not be changed.

QUOTE, UNQUOTE

- **Nero:** 'I have a little surprise for you. Guess what it is.' **The Doctor:** 'Now, let me think. You want me to play in the arena?' **Nero:** 'You guessed.' **The Doctor:** 'It's no problem at all. After all, you want to do your very best for your fellow artists: why not the arena?' **Nero:** 'Yes, yes, of course. That is exactly right.' **The Doctor:** 'Well, I promise you, I will try to make it *a roaring success.*' **Nero:** 'You'll have to play something special, you know.' **The Doctor:** 'Of course, of course. Something serious, yes. Something they can *really get their teeth into.*' **Nero:** [muttering] 'You can't know, you can't. I've told no-one.' **The Doctor:** 'Caesar Nero. I've always wanted to put on a good show; to give a great performance. After all, who knows, if I *go down well*, I might even make it my *farewell performance*. You see, I've always wanted to be considered as an artist of *some taste*, generally considered as *palatable*, hm?'

- **Nero:** 'They wouldn't let me build my new Rome. But if the old one is burnt … If it goes up in flames they'll have no choice. Rome will be rebuilt to my design! Brilliant! Brilliant!'

ANALYSIS

The Romans, although likewise directed by Christopher Barry, is a very different style of production from *The Rescue*, relying far more heavily than any previous *Doctor Who* story on the use of humour to complement the drama. The four-parter that Dennis Spooner came up with is an amusing romp through Emperor Nero's Rome, drawing heavily on the traditions of farce but still having its serious moments, such as the scene where the slave-master Tavius is revealed as secretly being a Christian.

It has indeed been argued by some reviewers that *The Romans'* reputation as a 'comedy story' is not entirely justified, and that the humour is largely confined to its third episode, *Conspiracy*. David Auger, writing in *The Frame* No. 16 dated November 1990, drew attention to the harrowing nature of many of the events depicted, and particularly those involving Ian and Barbara:

'The first episode features a lurking assassin who carries out a brutal murder and a group of unscrupulous slave traders who kidnap Ian and Barbara. The two school teachers are faced with the daunting prospect that … the Doctor might be forced to depart [in the TARDIS] without them. Soon they no longer have even each other for comfort … as … Ian is purchased by a passing slave-buyer, leaving Barbara alone and distraught. It doesn't read like the plot of a comedy so far, does it?'

'The situation for the two companions becomes even more dire in the second episode.'

John Peel, writing in *Gallifrey* Issue 13 dated winter 1980/81, shared Auger's view that the more overt humour in the story was to be found mainly in its third episode: 'Nero chases Barbara around his palace and attempts to seduce her. In the dodging in and out of doors, the Doctor and Vicki (both guests in the palace) narrowly miss seeing her … The [sequence] has [a] strong comic flavour to it (let's face it, with Derek Francis playing Nero, it can't be meant very seriously!), but that is by no means true of the entire story. It provides light relief against the more horrific sequences – such as Ian chained in a galley, or threatened with being fed to the lions.'

'Such humour as there is [in the final episode],' noted Auger, 'is generally of a very dark nature; and the scene in which the Doctor teases Nero about the "roaring" fate the Emperor has waiting for him … is funnier than the events in the third episode because the comic element is kept under a tighter rein once again. The humour is complementing the drama, rather than the other way around.'

Ian K McLachlan, writing in *DWB* No. 130 dated September 1994, also argued that *The Romans* featured some unusually violent scenes: 'Nero, while comic, is not above killing. He causes one of his slaves to die by forcing him to drink from [a] poisoned chalice, and in a particularly nasty moment sticks his sword through the heart of one of his guards … [the director] having first convinced the viewer that it is Barbara he is about to kill. The scenes with Locusta are unnerving, and an interesting moral point is made when the supplier of poison maintains that she has nothing to do with the deaths of the victims. After all, she is only providing a service. Perhaps the same sort of argument that a hangman would have used in 1964.'

Although these points are largely valid, there is no denying that at the time of its original transmission *The Romans* seemed quite a radical departure from what had gone before, as is clear from the BBC's Audience Research Report on the final episode: '"This programme gets more and more bizarre; in fact it's so ridiculous it's a bore!", declared one of a number of viewers reporting who apparently agreed that *Doctor Who* was "suitable only for morons". Indeed, the conclusion of the adventure in ancient Rome, though not always provoking quite such stringent condemnation, found the majority of the sample audience in a carping mood. It was evident that the sequence had often been a disappointment – some viewers alleged that, after a promising start, the story had steadily declined to a farcical and pathetic anticlimax, while others were "not keen on *Doctor Who* going historical" ... On the other hand, there were complaints (though fewer) that there had been too much violence in this sequence, and that it was unsuitable for children. A fairly common criticism, however, was its lack of realism – everything, it was said, was "transparently phony".'

Revisionist analysis notwithstanding, *The Romans* remains one of the more humorous of the series' early stories. The depiction of Nero as a vain, comical oaf is in marked contrast to the serious, realistic portrayal of such historical figures as Marco Polo and Robespierre in the previous season; and it is somewhat difficult to come to terms with the Doctor engaging in near-slapstick fight sequences and reeling off a succession of excruciating puns.

William Hartnell, though, seems to enjoy having lighter material to work with for once. 'Hartnell [is] at his best in *The Romans*,' commented Tim Archer on an internet newsgroup in 1997. 'He really takes on the foolish nature of the Doctor and comes across as being quite funny in that story. Great relationship with Nero.' Another particular delight, as Auger observed, is the story's sympathetic depiction of the new companion, Vicki: 'Vicki's exuberant character fits more easily into Spooner's new format for the series than the more conventional Susan would have done. She acts as a good sparring partner for the Doctor, highlighting how much he has mellowed ... The repartee between them is entertaining, especially near the end of the story when Vicki suggests that the history books are inaccurate as they don't mention the Doctor's involvement in the fire that destroyed Rome! It is a shame that in some later stories the writers would neglect Vicki.'

The issue of the story's historical accuracy is one on which a number of reviewers have commented. Martin J Wiggins, writing in *Oracle* Volume 3 Number 5 dated February/March 1980, found the story to be greatly lacking in this respect:

'[Nero's] love of art, and Greek art in particular, was what led to his law of 59 AD (five years before the story was set) outlawing the unhellenistic practice of killing defeated gladiators. Indeed, as Emperor, Nero could have whatever measure he pleased passed by the Senate, which had no authority to resist. And when the fire of Rome started, despite slanderous rumours of his responsibility, he was in Antium, more than thirty miles away; on his return, it was he who was ... directing fire fighting. Hardly the sort of behaviour one might expect from a man who wanted to burn down Rome to force through his own architectural ideas by way of replacement.

'The reason for [these] errors is simply that Dennis Spooner failed to research his script adequately, preferring to rely on hearsay and the most biased ancient "authority" who ever wrote, Suetonius. This story is a prime example of the dangers of lack of research. Put in any fact that can be checked up on without checking up on it yourself, and you'll have certain members of the audience rolling in the aisles.'

This view has however been challenged by some other commentators, including Peel:

'In a recent book [*Suetonius' Nero*] by B H Warmington, Reader in Ancient History at the University of Bristol, ... I read: "The close similarity between Suetonius, Tacitus and Dio, all of whom wrote independently of each other, is all the more striking in view of the different forms ... There are few stories to the discredit of Nero which are not to be found in Tacitus as well as Suetonius, who is more likely to accept as truth what Tacitus has doubts about; an obvious case of this is the story that Nero set fire to Rome ... Since we have no external control for judging the veracity of the stories, though some are so outrageous that Suetonius' inclusion of them can hardly be condoned, ... similar condemnation must fall on Tacitus, who is only superficially more fastidious." In other words, Suetonius does record some stories which are probably just scandal, but this is by no means the majority of what he wrote ...

'On the subject of the fire [and] attempts to whitewash Nero (something that Warmington points out is futile and only works by discounting the facts), the book adds: "Only Tacitus suggests the possibility that Nero was not responsible ... Nero's responsibility was accepted by the Elder Pliny ... Tacitus appears to combine two versions, one of which stressed Nero's activities in organising the relief work."'

In the final analysis, regardless of the story's degree of success in educating the viewer about the realities of life in ancient Rome, it is for its innovative use of humour that *The Romans* will always be best remembered, and in this respect it represents a worthwhile attempt at finding new dramatic ground for the series to cover.

THE WEB PLANET

Writer: Bill Strutton. **Director:** Richard Martin. **Designer:** John Wood. **Costumes:** Daphne Dare. **Make-Up:** Sonia Markham. **Incidental Music:** stock. **Insect Movement By:** Roslyn de Winter. **Film Cameraman:** Peter Hamilton. **Film Editor:** Gitta Zadek. **Studio Lighting:** Ralph Walton. **Studio Sound:** Ray Angel. **Production Assistant:** Norman Stewart. **Assistant Floor Manager:** Gillian Chardet, Elizabeth Dunbar.

	First UK TX	Scheduled TX	Actual TX	Duration	Viewers	Chart Pos.
The Web Planet	13/02/65	17.40	17.40	23'57"	13.5	7
The Zarbi	20/02/65	17.40	17.42	23'20"	12.5	12
Escape to Danger	27/02/65	17.40	17.42	22'52"	12.5	11
Crater of Needles	06/03/65	17.40	17.40	25'50"	13.0	9
Invasion	13/03/65	17.40	17.40	26'04"	12.0	12
The Centre	20/03/65	17.55	17.55	24'32"	11.5	14

Plot: A strange power drain forces the TARDIS to materialise on the planet Vortis. There, the Doctor, Ian, Barbara and Vicki become involved in the plans of the butterfly-like Menoptra to reclaim their planet from the parasitic Animus that is slowly enveloping it with its web-like domain, the Carsenome. Joining forces with an advance party of Menoptra and the underground-dwelling Optera, the travellers manage to destroy the Animus, freeing the ant-like Zarbi and death-spitting larvae guns from its control and releasing the TARDIS from its influence.

Episode endings:

1. Left alone in the TARDIS, Vicki panics as the ship lurches violently. She operates the controls and the dematerialisation sequence starts. Returning to the ship to fetch help for the web-ensnared Ian, the Doctor is horrified to find that it is no longer there.

2. The Doctor, Ian and Vicki have been captured by the Zarbi and taken into a control centre. Their attempts to communicate with the creatures fail. A hood-like device descends from the ceiling and the Doctor is positioned under it. A voice asks the Doctor why he has come to this planet now.

3. Ian and the Menoptra Vrestin try to escape from some pursuing Zarbi by squeezing into a fissure in a rock-face. The ground gives way beneath them and they fall. The Zarbi and larvae guns swarm around the fissure.

4. The Menoptra forming the spearhead invasion force arrive and battle with the Zarbi. Barbara and Prapillus are caught in the middle of the fighting and find themselves surrounded.

5. Returning to the Carsenome with the Menoptra's isop-tope device, the Doctor and Vicki are herded into a chamber where they are enveloped in a web-like substance sprayed from wall-mounted nozzles.

6. The TARDIS dematerialises from the surface of Vortis. Prapillus vows that the Earth people will never be forgotten and warns that the Animus must never again be allowed to take root on the planet. The main Menoptra force is contacted and summoned back to Vortis.

IT WAS MADE WHERE...?

Ealing filming: 04.01.65-08.01.65, 11.01.65 on Stage 2
Studio recording: 22.01.65, 29.01.65, 05.02.65, 12.02.65, 19.02.65, 26.02.65, all in Riverside 1.

ADDITIONAL CREDITED CAST

Zarbi Operators[1]/THE ZARBI:[2-6] (Robert Jewell, Jack Pitt, Gerald Taylor, Hugh Lund[2-6], Kevin Manser[2-6], John Scott Martin[2-6]), Animus Voice (Catherine Fleming[2-4,6]), THE MENOPTRA: Vrestin (Roslyn de Winter[2-6]), Hrostar (Arne Gordon[2,4-6]), Hrhoonda (Arthur Blake[2]), Prapillus (Jolyon Booth[4-6]), Hlynia (Jocelyn Birdsall[4-6]), Hilio (Martin Jarvis[4-6]), THE OPTERA: Hetra (Ian Thompson[4-6]), Nemini (Barbara Joss[4, 5]).

POPULAR MYTHS

- The strange misty effect seen on the surface of the planet Vortis was created by smearing Vaseline on the camera lenses. (The effect was created by means of special filters fitted to the camera lenses.)
- The butterfly-like creatures seen in this story are called Menoptera. (The correct spelling is 'Menoptra'.)

THINGS TO WATCH OUT FOR

- The Menoptra captain Hilio is played by well-known actor Martin Jarvis in an early television role.
- Barbara does not appear in *Escape to Danger* and Jacqueline Hill is not credited in the closing credits of that episode.

THINGS YOU MIGHT NOT HAVE KNOWN

- The working title of the final episode was *Centre of Terror*.
- The Menoptra were designed by costume supervisor Daphne Dare and made by the Costume Department. There were eight in all, and four of these each had a flying harness and a pair of wings added by freelance contractors Shawcraft Models (Uxbridge) Ltd. The costumes, which were black with stripes of pale yellow fur, were slightly redesigned between the pre-filming at Ealing 2 and the studio recordings at Riverside 1.
- Shawcraft also provided four Zarbi costumes and two Venom Guns, built to scenic designer John Wood's drawings, as well as a number of special props and a model set of the Carsenome.
- The scenes of the Menoptra flying through the air were supervised by Kirby's Flying Ballet.
- Jacqueline Hill was concerned to see that her name was omitted from the closing credits of *Escape to Danger* as she was on holiday when it was recorded. She was under the impression that the regular cast were to be credited even if they did not appear, and she subsequently asked for her name to be reinstated in case the episode was sold abroad. No action was taken on this, however.
- While director Richard Martin was out of the country on holiday, having completed his work on this story, producer Verity Lambert edited out from episode six a shot of the Carsenome web dissolving. On 10 March 1965 she sent him a memo in which she explained: 'I did not like taking this decision, but honestly I thought nobody would know what on earth was happening. It simply did not work.'
- Two special filters were made to be fitted onto the camera lenses for scenes set on the planet's surface, giving them their misty, alien quality. At one point during recording both filters broke and had to be hastily replaced.

QUOTE, UNQUOTE

- **The Doctor:** 'Apart from rubbing our legs together like some sort of grasshopper, I doubt if we can get on speaking terms with them.'
- **Prapillus:** 'The Menoptra have no wisdom for war. Before the Animus came, the flower forest covered the planet in a cocoon of peace.'
- **Animus:** 'What Vortis is, I am. What you are, I will become.'

ANALYSIS

Bill Strutton's *The Web Planet* is one of the most ambitious stories ever attempted in *Doctor Who*, and this may be seen as its great strength or its great weakness, depending on the spirit in which it is approached.

The story is unique in that all the characters featured, aside from the Doctor and his friends, are non-humanoid. The viewer is instead presented with an incredible array of giant insects and other life-forms: the ant-like Zarbi; butterfly people called Menoptra; the Optera, worm-like jumping creatures; the larvae guns, a kind of venom-spitting giant woodlice; and finally the Animus, a pulsating tentacled creature akin to a spider, lurking at the heart of its web. All these are seen against the backdrop of the planet Vortis, a bleak and echoing world, replete with rocky crags and pools of deadly acid. The sky is always dark and the many moons and stars are visible at all times.

It would be a challenge for any blockbuster film to realise all these requirements convincingly and yet, with their comparatively tiny budgets, *Doctor Who*'s designers managed not only to create all the wonders required by the scripts but also to make them look quite decent – at least for the time of the story's production.

The Zarbi are introduced first, running about the planet on their two hind legs and trilling away to each other. In a way they are the most laughable of the creations as, despite the best efforts of the designers and actors involved, it is quite obvious that they are just men with ant costumes strapped to their backs. That said, they do work well as long as the viewer is prepared to become involved in the action and suspend disbelief. Brigid Cherry discussed this aspect of the story in *DWB* No. 81 dated September 1990: 'The oversized insect is a form of monster more usually to be found in a strain of films that began with *Them!* [in the mid-fifties] and continued in a line of (often bad, sometimes abysmal) B-movies of the likes of *Tarantula*, *The Black Scorpion* and *The Deadly Mantis*. The special effects which allowed the creation of ants in *Them!* were a high point of fifties science-fiction. In contrast with … *The Web Planet*, which has actors running around in fancy dress as ants, moths and woodlice, there were only two principal ants provided for the filming of *Them!*, and these were animated models … *Doctor Who*'s … men in black tights with [fibreglass] ants on their heads may look ridiculous, but are at least comparatively active. They have to be, as these are substantial "speaking" roles …'

Rather less effective are the Menoptra. Again the actors involved clearly expend a great deal of effort in trying to make them appear alien and strange; and their balletic movements, devised and co-ordinated by Roslyn de Winter (who played Vrestin), are largely effective in achieving this. The costumes created for them are also good; particularly the impressive translucent wings. In this case it is unfortunately the scripting of the characters that rather lets the side down. They come across as a fairly disorganised bunch of pacifists, and it is hard for the viewer to accept that they hope to defeat the Animus armed only with some sharp pieces of rock and an egg-like 'isop-tope' weapon. Indeed, given that no Menoptra has ever actually seen the Animus and lived to tell the tale (as illustrated by the fact that, contrary to their expectations, it has no 'dark side'), it is difficult to understand how they could have developed an effective weapon against it in the first place

The underground Optera, by contrast, are marvellously characterised and presented, with grunting voices, strange speech patterns and a curious leaping gait. The only negative point here is the costume's inclusion of what are supposed to be four vestigial arms, which just look daft. These creatures decide to help Ian and Vrestin to reach the Animus and, along the way, one of their number, the female Nemini, dies in a most horrific manner: in order to save the others, she uses her own body to plug a hole in the rock wall through which a stream of deadly acid is flowing. This is perhaps the most unsettling part of the whole story and, to his credit, William Russell as Ian manages to reflect the audience's feelings without saying a word.

A special mention must also go to designer John Wood for his amazing sets, which are at times quite breathtaking.

Leaving aside the incredible and fantastic characters and landscapes that the story presents, the plot itself is actually very simple and straightforward. At times, in fact, it seems that the writer and director have thrown in odd incidents of unexplained weirdness just to spice things up a bit. Examples include the TARDIS doors opening of their own accord and the control console spinning round for no apparent reason; Ian managing to put his foot – literally – in a Menoptra chrysalis when it is clearly visible on the ground with nothing else around it; and the Animus's strange influence over anything made of gold, including Barbara's bracelet, Ian's pen (although in the scene where this flies out of his hand, the wire by means of which the effect is achieved is unfortunately clearly visible) and the strange necklets used to subdue prisoners.

The story was certainly the weirdest the series had featured up to this point, and judging from the BBC's Audience Research Report on *The Centre* it was all a bit much for most contemporary viewers to take: '"Thank goodness this particular story is finished," commented a quantity surveyor from the substantial number of the sample for whom this episode had scant appeal. It also appeared that many viewers had found this last set of adventures centring round *The Web Planet* something of a disappointment, less arresting and entertaining than other *Doctor Who* stories they had seen, ridiculous to the point of being ludicrous, "silly instead of gripping", it was sometimes maintained – "*Doctor Who* is one of my favourite programmes, but just recently and especially the last episode, it seemed to become too stupid and I just couldn't get interested." The whole series based on the Zarbi was "like a third-rate kiddies' pantomime," according to a library assistant. Quite a few of the sample in criticising this particular episode gave it as their opinion that *Doctor Who* as a series had deteriorated, lost its entertainment value and should be rested or "scrapped". Plainly, ideas were running out.'

The criticism of a shortage of ideas seems particularly inapt when applied to *The Web Planet*, however, and indeed there were some in the Audience Research Report's sample who took a different view: 'A few … seemed quite intrigued – "The Menoptra, Zarbi etc were most appealing. I adore science-fiction, so anything pleases me in this line"; "We always start off by saying how stupid this is and how far-fetched, but we always watch it and end up by sitting on the edges of our seats and thoroughly enjoying it, especially this one."'

Conceptually, *The Web Planet* is magnificent, a classic story of good versus evil played out with the fate of a planet hanging in the balance. There are good performances from all the leads and, despite occasional lapses, the direction is fine. The success or failure of the story ultimately depends almost entirely on one factor: whether the viewer is prepared to appreciate the on-screen realisation of Strutton's bold concepts as the *tour de force* that it undoubtedly was for the time of its making, or whether the admittedly now very dated look of the production presents too much of an obstacle and it is seen simply as six episodes of tedium in which a bunch of actors run around in silly insect costumes.

THE CRUSADE

Writer: David Whitaker. **Director:** Douglas Camfield. **Designer:** Barry Newbery.

Costumes: Daphne Dare. **Make-Up:** Sonia Markham. **Incidental Music:** Dudley Simpson. **Fight Arranger:** Derek Ware. **Film Cameraman:** Peter Hamilton. **Film Editor:** Pam Bosworth. **Studio Lighting:** Ralph Walton. **Studio Sound:** Brian Hiles. **Production Assistant:** Viktors Ritelis. **Assistant Floor Manager:** Michael Briant.

	First UK TX	Scheduled TX	Actual TX	Duration	Viewers	Chart Pos.
The Lion	27/03/65	17.40	17.42	24'56"	10.5	16
The Knight of Jaffa	03/04/65	17.40	17.43	23'28"	8.5	29
The Wheel of Fortune	10/04/65	17.40	17.41	24'51"	9.0	32
The Warlords	17/04/65	17.40	17.40	23'40"	9.5	27

Plot: The TARDIS arrives in 12th Century Palestine where a holy war is in progress between the forces of King Richard the Lionheart and the Saracen ruler Saladin. Barbara is abducted in a Saracen ambush and the Doctor, Ian and Vicki make their way to King Richard's palace in the city of Jaffa. Ian is granted permission to ride in search of Barbara – the King knighting him Sir Ian of Jaffa to fit him for the role – while the Doctor and Vicki stay behind and try to avoid getting involved in court politics. King Richard secretly plans to marry his sister Joanna to Saladin's brother Saphadin in order to bring the war to an end, but Joanna finds out about this and refuses. The Doctor and his young ward are forced to flee after making an enemy of the King's adviser, the Earl of Leicester. Ian has meanwhile rescued Barbara from the clutches of the vicious Saracen emir El Akir. All four meet up in the wood where the TARDIS materialised and narrowly manage to escape the Earl of Leicester's men.

Episode endings:
1. King Richard refuses to help the travellers to rescue Barbara, telling them that she can rot in a Saracen prison before he will trade with Saladin.
2. Barbara is fleeing from El Akir's men down a dark alleyway when suddenly a hand appears from behind her and clamps across her mouth.
3. Barbara is brought before El Akir, who tells her that the only pleasure left for her is death – and that is very far away.
4. The TARDIS control room suddenly falls dark and silent. Only the console itself remains illuminated as the central column continues its steady rise and fall, the light reflecting on the faces of the now-motionless time travellers.

IT WAS MADE WHERE...?
Ealing filming: 16.02.65-18.02.65 (Stage unknown).
Studio recording: 05.03.65, 12.03.65, 19.03.65, 26.03.65, all in Riverside 1.

ADDITIONAL CREDITED CAST
William des Preaux (John Flint[1,2]), El Akir (Walter Randall), Richard the Lionheart (Julian Glover), Reynier de Marun (David Anderson[1]), William de Tornebu (Bruce Wightman[1,2]), Ben Daheer (Reg Pritchard[1-3]), Thatcher (Tony Caunter[1,2]), Saphadin (Roger Avon[1-3]), Saladin (Bernard Kay[1-3]), Saracen Warriors (Derek Ware[1], Valentino Musetti[1], Chris Konyils[2,3], Raymond Novak[2-4], Anthony Colby[3,4]), Joanna (Jean Marsh[2,3]), Chamberlain (Robert Lankesheer[2,3]), Sheyrah (Zohra Segal[2]), Luigi Ferrigo (Gabor Baraker[2]), Haroun (George Little[3,4]), Safiya (Petra Markham[3]), Earl of

77

Leicester (John Bay[3,4]), Turkish Bandit (David Brewster[3]), Maimuna (Sandra Hampton[4]), Fatima (Viviane Sorrél[4]), Hafsa (Diana McKenzie[4]), Ibrahim (Tutte Lemkow[4]), Man-at-arms (Billy Cornelius[4]).

POPULAR MYTHS

- This story was never sold overseas as it was felt that the content might be considered offensive in some countries. (It was sold widely overseas – although not to countries in the Middle East.)
- Ian climbs up a tree and over a balcony to rescue Barbara from El Akir's harem. (The harem was on the ground floor; the tree and balcony were introduced by David Whitaker in his later novelisation of the story).
- The Doctor and Vicki are forced to flee from the King's court because he thinks they revealed his secret marriage plan to Joanna. (They make their peace with the King, who realises that they were not the ones who gave away his secret but nevertheless advises them to leave as they have made an enemy of the powerful Earl of Leicester; the myth again derives from Whitaker's novelisation.)

THINGS TO WATCH OUT FOR

- This story marks the debut *Doctor Who* appearances by Jean Marsh (first wife of later Doctor Jon Pertwee) and Julian Glover – one of the most distinguished actors to have taken a guest role in the series up to that point – both of whom would go on to play further parts later in the series' history.
- Bandits stake Ian out in the sand and smear honey on his arm to attract hungry ants in an attempt to force him to reveal the whereabouts of his money – a scene in which production assistant Viktors Ritelis's arm doubled for William Russell's.
- William Russell's only appearance in the third episode is in a brief pre-filmed fight sequence as he was on holiday during the week when it was recorded.

THINGS YOU MIGHT NOT HAVE KNOWN

- Working title: *The Saracen Hordes*. The working title of the second individual episode was *Damsel in Distress*, that of the third was *Changing Fortunes* and that of the fourth was *The Knight of Jaffa*.
- David Whitaker's original scripts for this story contained hints of an incestuous relationship between King Richard and his sister Joanna, but these were removed before recording, apparently at the insistence of William Hartnell.

QUOTE, UNQUOTE

- **Joanna:** [To the Doctor.] 'There is something new in you, yet something older than the sky itself. I sense that I can trust you.'
- **Earl of Leicester:** 'I urge you, sire, abandon this pretence of peace!' **The Doctor:** 'Pretence, sir? Here is an opportunity to save the lives of many men … and you do nought but turn it down …' **Earl of Leicester:** 'Why are we here in this foreign land if not to fight? The Devil's Horde, Saracen and Turk, possess Jerusalem and we will not wrest it from them with honeyed words.' **The Doctor:** 'With swords, I suppose?' **Earl of Leicester:** 'Aye, with swords and lances, or the axe!' **The Doctor:** 'You stupid butcher! Can you think of nothing else but killing, hm?'

- **Richard the Lionheart:** 'Joanna, I beg of you to accept.' **Joanna:** 'No!' **Richard the Lionheart:** 'I entreat you, Joanna.' **Joanna:** '*No!*' **Richard the Lionheart:** 'Very well. I am the King. *We command it!*' **Joanna:** 'You cannot command *this* of me.' **Richard the Lionheart:** '*Cannot?*' **Joanna:** 'No. There is a higher authority than yours to which I answer!' **Richard the Lionheart:** 'I am the King. Where is there any man who has greater power over his subjects?' **Joanna:** 'In Rome! His Holiness the Pope will not allow this marriage of mine to that *infidel*!'

- **Vicki:** 'Are we going back to the ship?' **The Doctor:** 'As fast as our legs can carry us, my dear.' **Vicki:** 'Doctor? Will he really see Jerusalem?' **The Doctor:** 'Only from afar. He won't be able to capture it. Even now his armies are marching on a campaign that he can never win.' **Vicki:** 'That's terrible. Can't we tell him?' **The Doctor:** 'I'm afraid not, my dear. No. History must take its course.' [The Doctor and Vicki depart. Richard's hands are on his crucifix, folded in prayer.] **Richard the Lionheart:** 'Help me, Holy Sepulchre. Help me!'

ANALYSIS

David Whitaker's *The Crusade* – his second contribution to the season, but his first as a fully freelance writer – is a magnificent story, well up to the standard of the season one historicals. Eschewing the lighter approach of *The Romans*, Whitaker gives a gripping account of King Richard the Lionheart's attempts to win peace during the Third Crusade by having his sister Joanna married to Saphadin, brother of the Saracen ruler Saladin, and of our heroes' efforts to avoid getting caught up in a web of intrigue.

'No other story has [attained] such a high level of literary achievement,' enthused Tim Munro in *Star Begotten* Volume 3 Number 1/2 dated winter/spring 1989. 'Whitaker's beautiful poetic dialogue had a rhythm and a style all too often absent from *Doctor Who*. Here the words come close to the level of Shakespeare; breathtaking they are in their power ... Whitaker's wordy lines flow like a gentle stream, unjarring, finely crafted – used by a craftsman to enhance the illusion the viewers see. The smallest phrases convey vivid pictures, and few stories contain such rich three-dimensional characters.'

The comparison with Shakespeare might perhaps be a little overstated, but in bringing the story to the screen Douglas Camfield clearly treated it with the seriousness it merited, and it is easy to see why he is now generally regarded as one of the finest directors ever to have worked on *Doctor Who*.

'The plot romped along compulsively,' commented Paul Mount in *Doctor Who – Adventure in Space and Time* in 1981, 'with escapes, captures and recaptures becoming the norm, and the political intrigue and wrangling of the royal families adding just that little extra. The individual adventures of the travellers were equally enthralling ... Ian [battled] to get to Lydda, despite the intervention of the eye-patched bandit Ibrahim ... Barbara, too, had a thoroughly unpleasant time of it; struggling against the scarred El Akir, who harboured a hatred of all women; falling in with the friendly but [vengeful] Haroun, whose wife and son had been slaughtered by the emir some time earlier; and [eventually being recaptured] by El Akir, ready for the denouement in the harem. The climax itself was well worthy of the swashbuckling nature of what had gone before, with Ian bursting into the harem to rescue ... Barbara from the evil villain, whose life was eventually taken by the gentle Haroun.'

The third episode is perhaps the best of the entire story, featuring some highly dramatic and brilliantly acted confrontations between the various characters at the King's court in Jaffa. It is here, too, that William Hartnell gives one of his best and most intense performances as the Doctor, as if he has just realised the seriousness with which everyone else is taking the story – in the first two episodes he delivers his lines in the same rather jokey manner that he adopted in *The Romans* (although, to be fair, the material he is given in the scripts is itself more humorous in the early part of the story).

A particular strength of many of the early historical stories is Barry Newbery's exquisite scenic design work. *The Crusade* proves no exception to the rule, boasting some fine sets that go a long way towards capturing the atmosphere of 12th Century Palestine. Also of a high quality are other aspects of the production such as the incidental music, the costumes and the make-up (including the 'blacking up' of the actors playing the Saracen characters – a practice which would generally be considered unacceptable today but which was quite standard and unremarkable at the time).

Given the excellence of historical adventures such as *The Crusade*, it is all the more surprising – and, for those who appreciate this type of story, disappointing – to think that within less than two years they would be unceremoniously dropped from the series.

THE SPACE MUSEUM

Writer: Glyn Jones. **Director:** Mervyn Pinfield. **Designer:** Spencer Chapman. **Costumes:** Daphne Dare, Tony Pearce[3]. **Make-Up:** Sonia Markham. **Incidental Music:** stock. **Fight Arranger:** Peter Diamond[3,4]. **Studio Lighting:** Howard King. **Studio Sound:** George Prince, Ray Angel. **Production Assistant:** Snowy White. **Assistant Floor Manager:** John Tait, Caroline Walmesley.

	First UK TX	Scheduled TX	Actual TX	Duration	Viewers	Chart Pos.
The Space Museum	24/04/65	17.40	17.41	23'38"	10.5	16
The Dimensions of Time	01/05/65	17.50	17.55	22'00"	9.2	23
The Search	08/05/65	18.00	18.00	23'33"	8.5	22
The Final Phase	15/05/65	17.40	17.43	22'15"	8.5	27

Plot: The TARDIS jumps a time track and the travellers arrive on the planet Xeros. There they discover their own future selves displayed as exhibits in a museum established as a monument to the galactic conquests of the warlike Morok invaders who now rule the planet. When time shifts back to normal, they realise that they must do everything they can to try to avert this potential future. Vicki helps the native Xerons to obtain arms and thereby to revolt against the Moroks. The revolution succeeds and the travellers go on their way, confident that the future has been changed.

Episode endings:
1. The Doctor and his friends have found themselves displayed in the Morok museum. As they watch, time shifts back onto the correct track. The exhibits vanish; the Moroks find the TARDIS and the travellers' footprints in the sand; and the Doctor portentously announces that he and his companions have arrived.

2. Having failed to obtain any useful information from interrogating the Doctor, the Morok governor Lobos has him taken away to the preparation room to be converted into a museum exhibit.
3. Ian uses a stolen gun to force a guard to take him to Lobos, who tells him that the Doctor is in the second stage of preparation and nothing now can help him. Ian insists on being taken to the Doctor and, when Lobos complies, Ian is astounded by what he sees.
4. On an apparently barren planet, somewhere in space, a Dalek reports that the TARDIS has left Xeros. A Dalek voice emanating from a communications panel states that the Daleks' own time machine will shortly be in pursuit and that the Doctor will soon be exterminated.

IT WAS MADE WHERE...?

Ealing filming: 11.03.65 (Stage unknown).
Studio recording: 02.04.65, 09.04.65, 16.04.65, 23.04.65, all in TC4.

ADDITIONAL CREDITED CAST

Sita (Peter Sanders), Dako (Peter Craze), Third Xeron (Bill Starkey[1]), Morok Guards (Lawrence Dean, Ken Norris, Salvin Stewart[3,4], Peter Diamond[3,4], Billy Cornelius[3,4]), Lobos (Richard Shaw[2-4]), Tor (Jeremy Bulloch[2-4]), Morok Messenger (Salvin Stewart[2]), Morok Technician (Peter Diamond[2]), Morok Commander (Ivor Salter[3,4]), Xerons (Michael Gordon[3,4], Edward Granville[3,4], David Wolliscroft[3,4], Bill Starkey[3,4]), Dalek Voice (Peter Hawkins[4]), Dalek Machine Operated by (Murphy Grumbar[4]).

POPULAR MYTHS

- *The Space Museum* was a low-budget story – hence the rather drab look of some of the sets. (The story had a budget similar to, and cost much the same to make as, other four-parters at this point in the series' history.)

THINGS TO WATCH OUT FOR

- In a nice piece of continuity, William Russell starts gently banging his fists together as he leaves the TARDIS interior set and carries this through to the next scene, following a recording break, as he emerges from the police box onto the Xeros surface set; this gives the effect of a continuous piece of action, and helps maintain the illusion that the TARDIS interior really is inside the police box shell.
- Some of the tables from the Sensorite city (in *The Sensorites*) turn up in the Moroks' museum.
- Jeremy Bulloch, now better known for his role as Boba Fett in the *Star Wars* films *The Empire Strikes Back* and *The Return of the Jedi*, plays Tor. He would later appear in the season eleven story *The Time Warrior*.
- The Doctor's only appearance in the third episode is in the opening reprise from the second, as William Hartnell was on holiday during the week in which it was recorded.
- There is an amusing scene in which the Doctor hides inside a Dalek casing – an exhibit in the Moroks' museum.
- In the sequence in which Lobos tries to interrogate the Doctor using a machine that displays his prisoner's thoughts on a screen; the Doctor feeds the machine a series of amusing false images, including a photograph of himself wearing a Victorian bathing costume.

THINGS YOU MIGHT NOT HAVE KNOWN

- The working title of this story's opening episode was *The Four Dimensions of Time* and that of the fourth was *Zone Seven*.
- Writer Glyn Jones later had an acting role in the season twelve story *The Sontaran Experiment*.

QUOTE, UNQUOTE

- **Vicki:** 'We must have changed the future … we must have done!' **Barbara Wright:** 'Must we, Vicki? Or were all the things that happened planned out for us?'

ANALYSIS

The Space Museum starts strongly, as reflected in the comments recorded in the BBC's Audience Research Report on its fine first episode: '[It] made a promising start … according to many in the sample, who found the idea of time as the fourth dimension and the "jumping of a time track" most intriguing, and one which apparently stimulated much discussion in several households. This was a novel theory that had obviously been cleverly thought out, it was often remarked, and there was plenty of excitement and mystery here, they said, to whet the appetite for future instalments. A docker voiced the opinion of a substantial proportion of those reporting in his comment that "We are now getting back to the real appeal of *Doctor Who* – the unknown and out of the ordinary" … '

Paul Mount, writing in *Doctor Who – An Adventure in Space and Time* in 1982, was similarly enthusiastic about this early part of the story: 'The magic of the serial lay in its excellent first two episodes, where time itself played some rather unusual tricks on the Doctor and his friends.'

Unfortunately, after this promising beginning, the whole thing falls as flat as a pancake. The problem rests mainly with the guest cast. Richard Shaw as Lobos gives one of the worst performances yet seen in the series. His delivery of the dialogue is stilted and unreal, and he is altogether wooden. The other Morok actors are almost as bad, making them a very weak and ineffective bunch of conquerors. The Xerons, with their strange double eyebrows, fare hardly any better. They are given little to do in the scripts and come over as a pretty wet and nondescript bunch.

It is only the four regulars who manage to give a good account of themselves, their natural and experienced performances so overshadowing all the others' that this just serves to highlight the inadequacies of the latter. Of particular note is Maureen O'Brien as Vicki, who manages to shine in a story that allows her far more scope than of late.

All this is a great shame as the central question posed by the story – that of whether the future is predestined or can be changed – is a very interesting one. This issue dominates the travellers' thoughts as they realise that everything they do, every decision they make, may be either leading them closer to becoming exhibits or taking them further away from that fate. The problem is that they don't know, and are even forced to consider the possibility that to do nothing might be the best option – or is *that* the path to their unpleasant demise?

The failure of the story to deliver on its initial promise was noted in the BBC's Audience Research Report on *The Final Phase*: '"A very poor ending to what promised at first to be a better story" was a comment that represented the view of a large proportion of the sample, several of whom remarked that this was not the first time that the plot had "crumpled" in the final episode, as if, they suggested, the writer had suddenly lost interest and was in a hurry to get the TARDIS and its occupants away to another adventure. Too many loose ends were tied up too hastily, they protested, and ideas were not fully developed ... A substantial minority considered it "a load of drivel": this "crazy fantasy" was evidently too silly and ridiculous to have any entertainment value for them, and several expressed the opinion that the whole series was becoming stale.'

In some respects the scripting of the story is a bit sloppy. Vicki obtains a glass of water from the TARDIS's food machine at the start of the first episode only because the script requires her to drop and break the glass, and disregarding the fact that in *Inside the Spaceship* the food machine dispensed water in plastic bags. The Moroks' museum is flooded with a supposedly paralysing gas and yet Barbara and Dako manage to make their way to the exit and stop coughing and wheezing the moment they get outside. Some of the Morok guns appear simply to stun while others apparently cause pain and even kill. Vicki manages to reprogram the computer guarding the armoury to accept incorrect but truthful answers to a series of predetermined questions, and yet only two of the questions are asked. Finally, with the Moroks defeated, the Xerons dismantle their museum in what appears to be a matter of hours, making a nonsense of the travellers' earlier comments to the effect that it was the biggest museum they had been in, not to mention the fact that they had managed to get lost in its multitude of corridors.

Once these flaws are considered alongside the story's good points (the first episode in particular), the viewer's overall reaction to *The Space Museum* has to be one of disappointment. Things do look up right at the very end, however, as Paul Mount explained: 'The real killer to end this enjoyable, albeit unexceptional, serial occurred in the final sequence. The TARDIS was on its way, and on the far-distant world of Skaro, an all-too-familiar shape glided over to a wall console ... The return of the Daleks was just one week away.'

THE CHASE

Writer: Terry Nation. **Director:** Richard Martin. **Designer:** Raymond P Cusick, John Wood. **Costumes:** Daphne Dare. **Make-Up:** Sonia Markham. **Incidental Music:** Dudley Simpson. **Fight Arranger:** Peter Diamond. **Film Cameraman:** Charles Parnell. **Film Editor:** Norman Matthews. **Studio Lighting:** Howard King. **Studio Sound:** Ray Angel, Brian Hiles. **Production Assistant:** Alan Miller, Colin Leslie. **Assistant Floor Manager:** Ian Strachan.

	First UK TX	Scheduled TX	Actual TX	Duration	Viewers	Chart Pos.
The Executioners	22/05/65	17.40	17.41	25'25"	10.0	14
The Death of Time	29/05/65	17.40	17.41	23'32"	9.5	12
Flight Through Eternity	05/06/65	17.45	17.47	25'23"	9.0	12
Journey Into Terror	12/06/65	17.40	17.41	23'49"	9.5	8
The Death of Doctor Who	19/06/65	17.40	17.41	23'27"	9.0	11
The Planet of Decision	26/06/65	17.40	17.40	26'29"	9.5	7

Plot: The travellers are forced to flee in the TARDIS when they learn from the Time/Space Visualiser taken from the Moroks' museum that a group of Daleks equipped with their own time machine are on their trail with orders to exterminate them. The chase begins on the desert planet Aridius and takes in a number of stopping-off points including the observation gallery of New York's Empire State Building, the 19th Century sailing ship Mary Celeste (the Daleks' appearance causing all the crew and passengers to jump overboard) and a spooky haunted house which, although the Doctor and his friends do not realise it, is actually a futuristic fun-fair attraction. Eventually both time machines arrive on the jungle planet Mechanus, where the Daleks try to infiltrate and kill the Doctor's party using a robot double of him. The travellers are taken prisoner by the Mechanoids* – a group of robots sent some fifty years earlier to prepare landing sites for human colonists who, in the event, never arrived – and meet Steven Taylor, a stranded astronaut who has been the Mechanoids' captive for the past two years. The Daleks and the Mechanoids engage in a fierce battle which ultimately results in their mutual destruction, and the Doctor's party seize this opportunity to escape. The Doctor reluctantly helps Ian and Barbara to use the Daleks' time machine to return home.

* The robots encountered by the time travellers in the last two episodes are called 'Mechonoids' throughout the scripts and in the closing credits of *The Planet of Decision*. The name was however spelt 'Mechanoid' in the closing credits of *The Death of Doctor Who* and we have adopted that spelling in this book as it is the one first seen on screen.

Episode endings:
1. The Doctor and Barbara watch as, making rough choking sounds, a Dalek emerges from the sands of Aridius.
2. The TARDIS dematerialises as the Daleks fire at it in vain. Chorusing 'Eradicate!', 'Obliterate!', 'Exterminate!' the Daleks determine to set off after it at once: the Dalek Supreme has ordered that the travellers be pursued through all eternity and exterminated!
3. The travellers have escaped from the *Mary Celeste* and the TARDIS hurtles through the space/time vortex, pursued by the Dalek ship.
4. The leader of the Dalek executioners asks the robot double of the Doctor if it understands its orders. It replies in the affirmative: it is to infiltrate and kill.
5. A door in the wall of the cave where the travellers are hiding slides down with a crash to reveal a small compartment containing a spheroidal robot. The robot, in a strange electronic voice, says: 'Eight hundred – Thirty – Mechanoid – English – Input – Enter'. The Daleks can be heard approaching outside, so at Ian's suggestion the four travellers move to join the robot in the compartment …
6. Having assured himself and Vicki that Ian and Barbara have arrived safely home, the Doctor operates the TARDIS controls. The ship dematerialises and flies through the space/time vortex en route for a new destination.

IT WAS MADE WHERE...?

Location filming: 09.04.65, 10.05.65.
Locations: Camber Sands, Camber, East Sussex; garage behind Studio 3A/B, Ealing Film Studios, Ealing, London, W5.
Ealing filming: 12.04.65-15.04.65, 10.05.65 on Stage 3A/B

Studio recording: 30.04.65, 07.05.65, 14.05.65, 21.05.65, 28.05.65, 04.06.65, all in Riverside 1.

ADDITIONAL CREDITED CAST

Abraham Lincoln (Robert Marsden[1]), Francis Bacon (Roger Hammond[1]), Queen Elizabeth I (Vivienne Bennett[1]), William Shakespeare (Hugh Walters[1]), Television Announcer (Richard Coe[1]), Dalek Voices (Peter Hawkins, David Graham), Daleks (Robert Jewell, Kevin Manser, John Scott Martin[1-4], Gerald Taylor), Mire Beast (Jack Pitt[1,2]), Malsan (Ian Thompson[2]), Rynian (Hywel Bennett[2]), Prondyn (Al Raymond[2]), Guide (Arne Gordon[3]), Morton Dill (Peter Purves[3]), Albert C Richardson (Dennis Chinnery[3]), Capt Benjamin Briggs (David Blake Kelly[3]), Bosun (Patrick Carter[3]), Willoughby (Douglas Ditta[3]), Cabin Steward (Jack Pitt[3]), Frankenstein (John Maxim[4]), Count Dracula (Malcolm Rogers[4]), Grey Lady (Roslyn de Winter[4]), Robot Dr. Who (Edmund Warwick[5]), Mechanoid Voice[5]/Mechonoid Voice[6] (David Graham[5,6]), Mechanoid[5]/Mechonoids[6] (Murphy Grumbar[5,6], Jack Pitt[6], John Scott Martin[6]), with Jack Pitt[5], John Scott Martin[5], Ken Tyllson[5,6].

Note: Derek Ware played a bus conductor at the end of *The Planet of Decision* and was credited in the *Radio Times* but not on screen.

POPULAR MYTHS

- The scene of Ian and Barbara taking a bus ride following their return to Earth was shot on location. (It was shot in the BBC's Television Film Studios at Ealing, with back projection used behind the window of the bus to give the impression of movement.)

THINGS TO WATCH OUT FOR

- The Daleks sport a slightly modified design, complete with 'solar panel' slats around their shoulder sections.
- Stock film from *Top of the Pops* of the famous pop group The Beatles singing 'Ticket to Ride' was used in the Time/Space Visualiser scene in the first episode.
- Distinguished thespian Hywel Bennett appears in an early role as Aridian Rynian.
- There are a number of instances of the Daleks being sent up – most notably in the depiction of a 'thick' Dalek barely able to complete a sum.
- Some adapted cinema film Daleks – and, inadvertently, a studio camera – lurk in the foliage of Mechanus.

THINGS YOU MIGHT NOT HAVE KNOWN

- Working title: *The Pursuers*.
- *The Chase* was hastily commissioned from Terry Nation when another of his stories, apparently a revival of his abandoned season one historical *The Red Fort*, fell through.
- The film inserts of Ian and Barbara celebrating their return to Earth were made as part of the film shoot for the following story, *The Time Meddler*, and so were the responsibility of that story's director Douglas Camfield and designer Barry Newbery.
- The director initially considered for this story was Christopher Barry.
- The Mechanoids were called Mechons in Terry Nation's first draft scripts, and their

planet Mechanus was called Mechon.

- Three Mechanoid props were built by Shawcraft from Raymond Cusick's designs, at a total cost of £812.
- The Mire Beast was designed by costume supervisor Daphne Dare and constructed by Jack Lovell Ltd. It was orange in colour.
- The young astronaut introduced in the final episode of *The Chase* underwent a last-minute change of name from Michael to Steven. Earlier, in the first draft scripts, he was called Bruck.
- Director Richard Martin arranged to borrow from Aaru Productions eight of the Daleks used in their cinema film *Dr. Who and the Daleks*. He intended to have six of these modified to resemble more closely the BBC's own Daleks so that they could be featured in *The Chase*. This proved impracticable, however, so in the end only two of them were used, standing in the background of a couple of shots. Four of the BBC's own Daleks were refurbished, at a total cost of £118. £100 was paid towards this by the Publicity Department, who had been making extensive use of the props for promotional purposes.
- It was originally intended that the scenes of Abraham Lincoln delivering the Gettysburg address would be achieved using stock footage. Nothing suitable was available, however, so they were mounted in the studio with actor Robert Marsden playing Lincoln.
- An early idea was that The Beatles might actually appear in the first episode of this story, made up to look like old men and supposedly playing a concert in the 21st Century. Although the group themselves were apparently keen on the idea, it was vetoed by their manager Brian Epstein. The production team then explored the possibility of using a clip of the group from a *Top of the Pops* appearance, but the only one that had not been wiped was a recording of 'I Feel Fine', which had already been used the maximum number of times permitted under the contract. Fortunately, however, The Beatles were due to perform their new single 'Ticket to Ride' at Riverside Studios on 10 April 1965, and production assistant Alan Miller was able to arrange for a copy of that tape to be made available.
- Richard Martin's first choice of incidental music composer for this story was Max Harris, but the job eventually went to Dudley Simpson.
- David Newman and Barbara Joss doubled for William Russell and Maureen O'Brien for certain shots in the first and second episodes.
- It was originally intended that Peter Hawkins should provide all the Dalek voices for this story, but on 12 April 1965 it was decided that David Graham should also be used, as for the previous Dalek stories.
- The scenic design work on this story was split between Raymond Cusick and John Wood. Wood designed the sets for the Empire State Building and the Mary Celeste, the latter of which featured a thirty-three foot long ship's boom hired from Pinewood, while Cusick was responsible for the Dalek time machine, Frankenstein's House of Horrors and the Mechanoid city.

QUOTE, UNQUOTE

- **Dalek:** 'Final termination is inevitable!'
- **Robot Doctor:** 'Understand? Of course I understand, my dear fellow! Don't fuss so.

I am to infiltrate and kill. Infiltrate and kill …'
- **Mechanoid:** 'Enter – Enter – Zero – Stop.'
- **Daleks:** 'Advance and attack! Attack and destroy! Destroy and rejoice!'
- **Vicki:** 'I'm not very good on heights …'

ANALYSIS

The Chase is nowhere near as strong as for the Daleks' first two stories. It revolves, as the title implies, around the simple premise of a chase – the Daleks pursuing the TARDIS through time and space in their own ship (referred to in the scripts – though mercifully not on screen – as a 'DARDIS'!), with the aim of catching and killing the four travellers. 'The first episode is … possibly the worst of … the six …' noted Christopher Williams in *Zodin* No. 3 dated 1986. '[It] begins with a scene in the Daleks' time machine which basically has the Daleks talking to each other, obviously to fill the viewers in with the plot. The TARDIS is then seen flying through space. This has to be the worst and most annoying effect in the whole story, as it is … just a two dimensional photograph of the TARDIS being moved across a starry background.'

This effect is repeated on numerous occasions during the course of the story, both for the TARDIS and for the Daleks' time machine, as the action moves from place to place. Each episode has a different setting from the previous one (or in some cases more than one setting), and in this sense *The Chase* is similar to Nation's season one story *The Keys of Marinus*. Where it falls down in comparison with that earlier 'epic', though, is in the nature of its settings, which are for the most part rather too jokey and unbelievable. The apparent tendency of the scripts to want to send the Daleks up is also irritating, although in fairness to Nation it should be noted that this aspect was almost certainly introduced by story editor Dennis Spooner – in fact, *The Chase* is far more deserving of the 'comedy story' tag than is Spooner's own *The Romans* from earlier in the season.

There are, it must be acknowledged, some commentators for whom this approach worked. Gareth Roberts, writing in *DWB* No. 117 dated September 1993, positively welcomed Spooner's input: 'The Daleks' blundering silliness in this story is crucial to the credibility of the narrative, because they have become too powerful for the series' infant format to withstand. They have a time-space machine that actually works and a tracking device to follow the TARDIS. Given these abilities it should not be too difficult for them to execute a doddery old fellow, two suburban teachers and a teenage girl who keeps tripping over. Having written himself into this corner, the writer keeps trying to get himself out of it rather than abandon the whole thing as the bad idea it obviously is.'

The mixed reaction to the story from fan reviewers mirrors that of viewers at the time of its original transmission, if the following comments in the BBC's Audience Research Report on the *Journey into Terror* episode are anything to go by: 'Although the viewer who described this as a "delightful piece of spine-chilling fun" was, perhaps, rather more enthusiastic than most, a substantial proportion of those reporting evidently felt that this episode … [was] very entertaining and, several added, refreshingly different from the usual run of *Doctor Who* stories. This particular blend of horror and science-fiction was, it seemed, very much to their liking and displayed considerable ingenuity and imagination on the part of the scriptwriter. "This episode appealed to me more than many because of the introduction of the 'house of mystery' and all that happened in it." Some, however, found the programme rather a jumble – Frankenstein, Dracula, the

Daleks – everything seemed to be thrown in but the kitchen sink, they declared, and the result was too much of a hotch-potch to be particularly entertaining – "All we need now is Yogi Bear and we've had the lot!". Others said that, while they themselves had enjoyed it well enough, the episode might have given nightmares to children. For a sizeable minority, however, the episode was stupid and far-fetched in the extreme and there was evidence that viewers were becoming rather tired of Doctor Who and his exploits and that even the Daleks were losing their appeal. The stories were increasingly ludicrous, it was often said, and followed the same pattern with monotonous regularity – "Why does Doctor Who make such unholy blunders all the time? It is irritating to watch people make the same mistakes over and over again. The party *always* gets split up, someone *always* gets lost and Doctor Who *always* falls into an obvious trap". Nevertheless, even those who disliked the programme frequently added that their children "revelled in it", and there was, obviously, a regular and enthusiastic young audience for whom *Doctor Who* has become something of an institution, whatever their elders might think.'

Generally regarded as the story's saving grace is its excellent final episode, and more specifically the spectacular battle it features between the Daleks and their new rivals, the robotic Mechanoids (another excellent Raymond Cusick design). This drew a much more favourable report from the BBC's Audience Research Department: 'According to the majority of the sample here was evidently an exciting episode to end a varied and ingenious story in the *Doctor Who* saga. There was plenty of event and action in it, it was said, what with the escape from imprisonment of Doctor Who and his companions, the lively and "dramatic" battle between the Mechanoids and the Daleks and the final wholesale destruction of the Mechanoids' city ... "Full of adventure" was how one viewer (a telephone engineer) summed up the episode approvingly, and a commercial artist called it "an exciting, lively and quite convincing episode which kept my daughter glued to the set – and Dad too". Clever sets and effects added a great deal to the interest as well, apparently.'

'The Mechanoids ...' noted Christopher Williams, 'are almost as good a creation as the Daleks themselves, and certainly deserved a comeback. The weapons they used looked very effective if not dangerous on screen, and the only real major fault they have is [the electronic effect used for] their voices. I couldn't understand a word they said ...

'The ... much-acclaimed fight ... between the Daleks and the Mechanoids ... is extremely well-executed, with some impressive model work for the time, mixed in with some lovely camera angles. The Daleks and the Mechanoids all explode convincingly and I'm even prepared to overlook the *Batman*-style [explosion captions] that appear now and then. The action is thick and fast and [this] must go down as a classic *Doctor Who* moment.'

These battle scenes are undoubtedly the most impressive aspect of *The Chase*. The story is, however, noteworthy for one other reason: like the previous Dalek adventure, it ends with a change in the regular line-up of characters. This time, it is Ian and Barbara who depart, to be replaced by Steven Taylor (although, as Steven simply disappears at the end of the last episode, it is not until the following story that the viewer finds out that he has 'stowed away' aboard the TARDIS).

'What I like about Ian and Barbara,' reflected Gareth Roberts, 'is that they represent an England that has ceased to exist, if it ever existed. They are what you imagine your well adjusted friend's parents to have been like in the early sixties, all cardigan and slacks and politeness and halves of lager and leather key straps ...

'Their return to London 1965, accomplished in a blaze of still photographs, is amusing and tear-jerking. One imagines them today as grey haired and still marvellously in love, delivering Liberal Democrat leaflets through letterboxes in North London.'

It is probably fair to say that William Russell and Jacqueline Hill chose just about the right time to leave the series. By this stage, it was becoming clear that they had really done all that they could with their respective roles; had they stayed any longer, they might well have become stale. In deciding to bring in just one new companion to replace the two teachers, rather than trying to come up with direct substitutes as had happened, in a sense, when Carole Ann Ford left, the production team broke the 'four regulars' mould and established a new 'one girl, one boy' set-up that would become the norm until the end of the sixties.

Peter Purves, cast as Steven after appearing earlier in the story as the hillbilly character Morton Dill, gives a creditable and promising first performance as the young astronaut. 'Mr Purves's acting is very good,' observed Williams, 'as [Steven] meets the first humans he has seen in two years. His relief is very convincing indeed. Our first impression of the character ... is of a brave bloke, if not a little stupid as he returns to the burning Mechanoid city to retrieve his teddy bear which has kept him company for his two year imprisonment.'

Despite sillinesses such as this, and all its other undoubted faults, it is still somehow strangely difficult not to like *The Chase*. At the end of the day, perhaps the best way to view it is as being very much a story of its time. This, it must be remembered, was an era when 'Doctor Who' was featuring in his own weekly *TV Comic* strip, while the Daleks were appearing as 'guests' on programmes such as *Crackerjack* and *Late Night Line-up* and being mimicked on novelty pop records with titles like 'I'm Gonna Spend My Christmas With a Dalek'. Steve Lyons, writing in *Cosmic Relief* in 1994, summed up perfectly the story's curious appeal:

'*The Chase* has it all, from Vicki missing her cue to the puppet Mire Beasts – and Barbara's little dash to the falling "wall" in time to get captured – to the pathetic Dalek in the time machine ("Um, ah ... ten minutes"). It uses an unconvincing double for the Doctor in scenes where there's no reason to, and you couldn't dub Hartnell's voice worse if you tried. It contains one of the most ludicrous concepts in the history of science-fiction, as the Time/Space Visualiser sifts through an infinity of places and events to tune into some silly pieces of costume drama and eventually (by an insanely unlikely coincidence) happens to chance upon a gaggle of scheming Daleks. The Empire State Building scenes are painfully protracted, the haunted house could have come out of a *TV Comic* strip, and the slapstick aboard the *Mary Celeste* is downright embarrassing ...

'Without a doubt, *The Chase* is one of the most appallingly scripted, the most shoddily produced and the most apathetically performed pieces of TV trash that has ever ... given me such immense pleasure. And I guess that's something I love about *Doctor Who*: that indefinable magic that can make such a load of rubbish so thoroughly enjoyable to watch.'

DALEKMANIA

The return of the Daleks in *The Dalek Invasion of Earth* had generated even greater interest in them than there had been before. The ploy of bringing them to Earth had worked; now that children had seen them patrolling the streets of London, they all wanted their very own Dalek.

Walter Tuckwell, having been given by the BBC the job of handling the licensing of the Daleks, decided that rather than wait for potential clients to contact him, he would go out and actively sell the product. Thus if a toy manufacturer had an existing range of guns, for example, he would go to them and suggest a couple of Dalek-related additions to their range. Indeed, the Anti-Dalek Fluid Neutraliser was actually a water-pistol created for Dan Dare but, repackaged, it could be a weapon to be used against the machine-creatures from Skaro.

At the end of 1964, there had been only a handful of *Doctor Who* and Dalek toys in the shops: two plastic Dalek badges, a Dalek birthday card, an annual and a novel, a comic strip in *TV Comic* and a couple of records. What everyone wanted was a toy Dalek, and although one manufacturer had picked up the license to produce a dressing-up costume, a fire in their factory in April 1964 meant that all the components were destroyed and the product was never widely available. By the time *The Chase* was transmitted in the middle of 1965, however, Tuckwell was able to run an eighteen page advertisement feature in *Games and Toys* magazine featuring all the different Dalek products that were in production and would be available by the end of the year. In total there were over eighty different products released during the year, and by Christmas the Daleks were the hot seller in all the shops, far outstripping the competition. Due to Tuckwell's efforts, every child that wanted a Dalek for Christmas could now have one.

By this time, however, interest in Dalek products, and in *Doctor Who* products more generally, had already started to wane. The following year would see far fewer new items released, and by 1967 the craze would be almost over. This would also be reflected in *Doctor Who*'s viewing figures, which during the second season reached a peak that would not be equalled until some ten years later.

1964/1965 was the boom time for *Doctor Who*, both in terms of the numbers of people watching the show and in terms of the amount of interest from the press, the public and the shops. Dalekmania was aptly named.

THE TIME MEDDLER

Writer: Dennis Spooner. **Director:** Douglas Camfield. **Designer:** Barry Newbery. **Costumes:** Daphne Dare. **Make-Up:** Sonia Markham[1,2,4], Monica Ludkin[3]. **Percussion:** Charles Botterill[2-4]. **Fight Arranger:** David Anderson. **Film Cameraman:** unknown. **Film Editor:** unknown. **Studio Lighting:** Ralph Walton. **Studio Sound:** Ray Angel, Brian Hiles. **Production Assistant:** David Maloney. **Assistant Floor Manager:** Gillian Chardet.

	First UK TX	Scheduled TX	Actual TX	Duration	Viewers	Chart Pos.
The Watcher	03/07/65	18.55	18.55	24'05"	8.9	15
The Meddling Monk	10/07/65	17.40	17.39	25'17"	8.8	19
A Battle of Wits	17/07/65	17.40	17.41	24'10"	7.7	28
Checkmate	24/07/65	17.40	17.41	24'00"	8.3	24

Plot: The TARDIS arrives on an English coastline in the year 1066. Exploring, the Doctor discovers that one of his own people, the Monk, is conspiring to wipe out the Viking fleet and thus allow King Harold to face the forces of William of Normandy with a fresh army at the Battle of Hastings. The Doctor succeeds in thwarting the Monk's plans and leaves him trapped in England.

Episode endings:
1. The Doctor explores the ruined monastery he has seen, and finds that the sound of monks chanting is coming from a record player hidden in an alcove. As he stops the player, metal bars descend from the ceiling to trap him in the alcove. The Monk appears outside, laughing at the Doctor's plight.
2. Vicki and Steven explore the monastery looking for the Doctor and also discover the record player. Eventually they find the cell in which the Doctor has been placed, but when they enter he is not there: beneath his cloak there is just a pile of furs.
3. Stephen and Vicki return to the monastery, still in search of the Doctor. Vicki finds a cable leading to an ancient altar and then a door leading into the altar. They pass through and find themselves standing inside a TARDIS.
4. The TARDIS dematerialises and leaves England.

IT WAS MADE WHERE...?

Ealing filming: 10.05.65 on Stage 3A/B
Studio recording: 11.06.65 in TC4, 18.06.65 in TC3, 25.06.65 in TC4, 02.07.65 in TC4.

ADDITIONAL CREDITED CAST

Monk (Peter Butterworth), Edith (Alethea Charlton), Eldred (Peter Russell), Wulnoth (Michael Miller), Saxon Hunter (Michael Guest[1]), Ulf (Norman Hartley[2-4]), Viking Leader (Geoffrey Cheshire[2]), Sven (David Anderson[2-4]), Gunnar the Giant (Ronald Rich[2]).

POPULAR MYTHS

- Peter Butterworth was chosen for the part of the Monk on the strength of his appearances in the *Carry On* films. (He had yet to appear in any of the films at the time *The Time Meddler* was made in May 1965. Butterworth's first *Carry On* film was *Carry on Cowboy*, filming for which started in August of that year.)
- The Doctor's race are identified in this story as Gallifreyans. (They aren't.)

THINGS TO WATCH OUT FOR

- When asked what 'TARDIS' stands for, Vicki says that it is 'Time And Relative Dimensions In Space'. This is the first instance of the acronym being explained since the series' debut episode, and the first of the 'D' being said to stand for 'Dimensions' (as would then become the norm) rather than 'Dimension'.
- The interior of the Monk's TARDIS utilises the same set as the Doctor's except that the central control console is stood on a dais.
- The closing credits of the final episode are played over images of Steven, Vicki and the Doctor superimposed against a starscape and, for the first time in the series' history, there is no 'Next Episode ...' caption giving the title of the

following instalment.

- The Doctor's appearance in *The Meddling Monk* is limited to the filmed reprise from the end of *The Watcher* and a pre-recorded voice-over as William Hartnell was on holiday during the week when it was recorded.

THINGS YOU MIGHT NOT HAVE KNOWN

- Working title: *The Monk*. The working title of the first individual episode was *The Paradox*.
- This story was originally to have been recorded in studio Riverside 1, but was eventually done at Television Centre.
- The story included stock film of 'Viking ships' taken from BBC archives.

QUOTE, UNQUOTE

- **Steven Taylor:** 'I've seen some spaceships in my time, admittedly nothing like this, but ... what does this do?' **The Doctor:** 'That is the dematerialisation control, and that over yonder is the horizontal hold. Up there is the scanner, those are the doors, that is a chair with a panda on it ... Sheer poetry, dear boy! Now please stop bothering me!'

ANALYSIS

'*The Time Meddler* [contains] a number of "firsts" for *Doctor Who*,' pointed out Graham Howard in *TSV* 33 dated April 1993. 'It is the first "pseudo-historical", i.e. a historical that contains science-fiction elements (aside from the Doctor and his companions ...). It is the first time that the viewer is introduced to another person who is a member of the Doctor's own race (although ...the name of that race is not revealed ...). [It] is also the first full story in which Steven Taylor appears, having secretly entered the TARDIS at the end of *The Chase*. Indeed one of the more interesting parts of this story is Steven's bafflement and the Doctor's and Vicki's bemusement as Steven attempts to grapple with the capabilities of the TARDIS and the concept of time travel.'

The 'pseudo-historical' aspect of the story was one that drew considerable comment, and most of it very favourable, from viewers whose reactions were recorded in the BBC's Audience Research Report on *The Watcher*. 'It was apparently the intriguing discovery of a wrist watch, a gramophone and electric light amongst the Saxons of Northumbria in 1066 that made this episode particularly fascinating for many of the sample who looked forward to learning the explanation of this mystery next week; it had certainly given an interesting twist to the "time travel theme" and, they said, promised exciting new developments to come; a housewife's comment, for example, indicates the speculation that went on amongst a sizeable group: "We can hardly wait for the next episode to find out if there are more time travellers around, and if the Monk is one of them, and if the Battle of Stamford Bridge will be seen". Several remarked that it was rather a relief to get back into history in order to have a change from monsters and Daleks and they also welcomed the addition of Steven, the new passenger in the TARDIS ("a fresh face adds interest to the series").'

Steven does indeed show a lot of promise. He is teamed with Vicki for much of *The Time Meddler*, and their verbal sparring is lively and interesting. Previously, exchanges of this sort tended to be between the Doctor and Ian or Barbara (or sometimes both), but now there is a new dynamic for the writers to play with. The success of this character interplay is fortunate, as it manages to keep the viewer entertained during what is fundamentally quite a dull story. The BBC's Audience Research Report on the second episode, *The Meddling Monk*, recorded a much more mixed reaction than that on the first:

'"I still can't understand this new *Doctor Who* story. I was completely baffled after last week's episode and am even more so after this, with its mixture of Saxons and Vikings, electric toasters and electric frying pans. The sooner he gets back to the future the better – these historical stories are a bit of a bore."

'This comment reflects the majority, somewhat dissatisfied reaction to this particular *Doctor Who* adventure, and it is quite clear that most reporting viewers are finding this excursion into the past a rather uninteresting and uneventful affair so far. Certainly there was much speculation as to how various electrical gadgets and other 20th Century refinements came to be in use in [11th] Century Britain, but this seemed to irritate rather than intrigue many viewers ("Vikings and electrical toasters! What rubbish." – "Can't understand what a gramophone etc has to do with early Britons. It seems just silly.") who in addition complained that the story lacked incident and excitement and seemed to them "very tame and slow"...

'However, there were plenty like a dental surgeon who considered this "A most intriguing and interesting story, with plenty of action and very mysterious incident to keep you guessing – particularly the puzzle of electrical gadgets turning up in early Britain. All *very* odd.", while others, no less enthusiastic, remarked that the introduction of science-fiction into this particular historical adventure certainly seemed to supply the element they had felt was missing in previous historical episodes. Be that as it may, they were certainly finding this story very interesting and exciting."

Despite these positive comments from some of those surveyed by the BBC, it has to be acknowledged that nothing very much happens in the story. Steven and Vicki spend practically the whole four episodes running around trying to find the Doctor, while the Doctor, in turn, gets captured, escapes and then gets recaptured. The resolution is absurdly simple: the Doctor just removes the dimensional control from the Monk's TARDIS so that he can't use it. There is no apparent concern as to what havoc the Monk might wreak left stranded in 1066.

Peter Butterworth's Monk is, however, an excellent addition to *Doctor Who* mythology. The actor gives a deft, understated performance and imbues the character with a wicked sense of humour. His scenes with the Doctor are a particular joy to watch (especially the one in which the Doctor uses a stick to convince him that he has a gun poking in his back). 'The meddling Monk himself, wonderfully played by Peter Butterworth with just the right amount of humour, is actually a rather likeable character,' noted Graham Howard, 'in that he seems more mischievous than evil – although the enormity of what he was attempting to accomplish by changing history ... could probably [justify his actions being] called evil. One of the story's appeals is the verbal double act between the Doctor and the Monk which indicates that the Doctor does not view the Monk as a serious threat – more like an irritating child.'

The Vikings and Saxons, on the other hand, are sketched in merely as caricatures, and the scripts give them next to nothing to do except fight each other. Even the implied rape of Edith is glossed over, and when the Doctor arrives at her home she serves him a drink as though nothing has happened. This simply does not ring true – although it is perhaps understandable, given the series' family audience.

Douglas Camfield's direction is very polished and features some nice touches, such as the back-projection shots of the sky with moving clouds which are, for the mid-sixties, very innovative. The use of stock footage also adds to the impression of times past, convincing the viewer that the action really does take place by the sea, that seagulls do fly overhead and that a Viking fleet is approaching the coastline.

There are in fact some reviewers who rate this story very highly indeed. '*The Time Meddler* is a classic *Doctor Who* and a brilliant, entertaining piece of television,' asserted John Pettigrew in *DWB* No. 100 dated April 1992. This was an opinion shared by Paul Mount, who wrote in *Doctor Who – An Adventure in Space and Time* in 1982:

'It was another of those drastically under-rated and often-forgotten stories which tends nowadays to be overshadowed by some of the more spectacular and lavish space serials which surrounded it. Despite its shortage of alien worlds and extraterrestrial cultures, for me at least, *The Time Meddler* was far more enjoyable than the aimless *The Chase* and the colourless *The Space Museum* ...

'In the end, though, it was the Monk's story – a serial which lived and breathed through Peter Butterworth's shining performance. With William Hartnell absent from episode two all eyes were upon the bizarre Monk.

'With a perfect blend of subtle humour and strong, tightly-directed drama, *The Time Meddler* is certainly in the running as the best serial of its type, and served as a very satisfying end to the second season of *Doctor Who*.'

Doctor Who's second season had seen it consolidating and building upon the success of the first and becoming one of the UK's most popular series. Producer Verity Lambert and new story editor Dennis Spooner had been determined to keep it fresh and to stretch its dramatic boundaries, and this had resulted in it venturing into previously unexplored territory such as with the overt humour of *The Romans* and *The Chase*, the pseudo-historical content of *The Time Meddler* and the downright weirdness of *The Web Planet*. By the season's end, only William Hartnell still remained of the four original leads, while in the production office only Verity Lambert still survived from the team responsible for launching the series. Season three would see further behind-the-scenes changes taking place, and an even greater variety in the content of the stories.

DOCTOR WHO SEASON THREE [1965-1966]

Regular Cast:
Dr. Who (William Hartnell)
Vicki (Maureen O'Brien) until *The Myth Makers: Horse of Destruction*
Steven (Peter Purves) until *The Savages* Episode 4
Katarina (Adrienne Hill) from *The Myth Makers: Horse of Destruction* to *The Daleks' Master Plan: The Traitors*
Dodo (Jackie Lane) from *The Massacre of St Bartholomew's Eve: Bell of Doom* until *The War Machines* Episode 2
Polly (Anneke Wills) from *The War Machines* Episode 1 onwards
Ben Jackson (Michael Craze) from *The War Machines* Episode 1 onwards

Regular Crew:
Producer: Verity Lambert until *Mission to the Unknown: Mission to the Unknown*. John Wiles from *The Myth Makers: Temple of Secrets* to *The Ark: The Bomb*. Innes Lloyd from *The Celestial Toymaker: The Celestial Toyroom* onwards.
Story Editor: Donald Tosh until *The Massacre of St Bartholomew's Eve: Priest of Death*. Gerry Davis from *The Massacre of St Bartholomew's Eve: Bell of Doom* onwards.
Title Music: Ron Grainer and the BBC Radiophonic Workshop, arranged by Delia Derbyshire.
Special Sounds: Brian Hodgson.

Verity Lambert, although credited as producer on the first two stories of the new season, was in the process of handing over to her successor John Wiles during the making of *Galaxy 4* and had almost completely relinquished her responsibility for the series by the time that *Mission to the Unknown* went into studio.

Wiles quickly developed a good working relationship with story editor Donald Tosh, himself a relative newcomer to the production team. The two men found that they had very similar ideas about the direction in which the series ought to be steered: both wanted to see it becoming more adult and sophisticated. The fruits of this approach can perhaps be best appreciated in *The Myth Makers* and *The Massacre of St Bartholomew's Eve*, although the epic *The Daleks' Master Plan* – a carry-over from Lambert's time – was also unusually grim and horrific in content, making a marked contrast to the Daleks' previous major outing in *The Chase*.

William Hartnell – who had always regarded *Doctor Who* as primarily a children's series and, as the only one left of the original team, saw himself in some ways as the guardian of its true spirit – greatly disliked this new approach. This resulted in a number of clashes between actor and producer. Indeed, Wiles seriously considered having Hartnell written out and replaced after scenes in *The Celestial Toymaker* in which the Doctor becomes invisible for a time. In the end however Gerald Savory, Donald Wilson's successor as Head of Serials, renewed Hartnell's contract against Wiles's wishes. Wiles resigned shortly afterwards; and, in what Wiles would later describe as an unnecessary act of loyalty, Tosh decided to go as well.

Tosh was in fact the first to leave, handing over to his successor Gerry Davis part-way through the making of *The Massacre of St Bartholomew's Eve*. Wiles then gave way to new producer Innes Lloyd, who accepted the job only reluctantly as he had no prior interest in science-fiction.

Lloyd and Davis were never on the best of terms but nevertheless formed a very effective team on the series. After working through a number of stories essentially inherited from Wiles and Tosh – which, possibly because of the change of team, ended up being rather lacklustre – they started to introduce some new ideas of their own, giving *Doctor Who* a fresh impetus and paving the may for more major changes to come …

GALAXY 4

Writer: William Emms. **Director:** Derek Martinus*. **Designer:** Richard Hunt. **Costumes:** Daphne Dare. **Make-Up:** Sonia Markham. **Incidental Music:** stock. **Film Cameraman:** unknown. **Film Editor:** unknown. **Studio Lighting:** Derek Hobday, Ralph Walton. **Studio Sound:** George Prince. **Production Assistant:** Angela Gordon. **Assistant Floor Manager:** Marjorie Yorke, Sue Willis.

* The director originally assigned to this story was Mervyn Pinfield; he selected the cast and carried out some initial work on the shooting of film inserts at Ealing. Failing health meant that he was unable to continue, so he was replaced and received no credit on the finished production.

	First UK TX	Scheduled TX	Actual TX	Duration	Viewers	Chart Pos.
Four Hundred Dawns	11/09/65	17.40	17.41	22'21"	9.0	23
Trap of Steel	18/09/65	17.50	17.50	24'51"	9.5	22
Air Lock	25/09/65	17.50	17.52	24'19"	11.3	13
The Exploding Planet	02/10/65	17.50	17.50	24'47"	9.9	20

Plot: The Doctor, Vicki and Steven arrive on an arid planet where they meet the occupants of two crashed spaceships: the beautiful Drahvins and the hideous Rills. The latter prove to be friendly, compassionate explorers while the former are a group of mindless cloned soldiers terrorised by a warlike matriarch, Maaga. Both ships were damaged when the Drahvins precipitated a confrontation in space, but whereas the Rills' is almost ready to take off again (having been repaired by their robot drones, which Vicki nicknames 'Chumblies'), the Drahvins' is irreparable. When the planet is discovered to be on the point of disintegration, Maaga tries to force the time travellers to help her steal the Rills' ship. Instead, the Doctor allows the Rills to draw power from the TARDIS in order to refuel and escape, leaving the Drahvins to their fate.

Episode endings:
1. Inside the TARDIS control room, the Doctor consults his instruments while Steven waits impatiently. The Doctor announces that the Rills were correct; but the planet has even less time left than they thought. They must leave immediately, for tomorrow is the last day this

planet will ever see!

2. The Doctor and Vicki make their way through the Rill Centre, pursued at a distance by a Chumbley. They enter a chamber where they discover a deactivated Chumbley. Suddenly Vicki screams; from behind a cloudy glass partition a pair of eyes is looking out at them.

3. Steven, trapped in the air-lock of the Drahvins' ship as Maaga has the air drawn out, collapses slowly to the floor.

4. The travellers relax in the TARDIS following their ordeal. They see a planet on the scanner screen and Vicki wonders what is happening on it ... On a planet, a man named Garvey is lying on his back on the ground in a jungle. There is a terrifying animal screech and he wakes with a start, muttering: 'I remember, now. I must ... I must kill ... I must kill ... I must kill.'

IT WAS MADE WHERE...?

Ealing filming: 22.06.65-25.06.65 on Stage 3
Studio recording: 09.07.65, 16.07.65, 23.07.65, all in TC4, 30.07.65 in TC3, 06.08.65 in TC4

ADDITIONAL CREDITED CAST

Maaga (Stephanie Bidmead), Drahvin One (Marina Martin), Drahvin Two (Susanna Carroll), Drahvin Three (Lyn Ashley), Chumblies (Jimmy Kaye[1], William Shearer, Angelo Muscat, Pepi Poupée[3, 4], Tommy Reynolds[4]), Rill Voice (Robert Cartland[3,4]), Garvey (Barry Jackson[4]).

POPULAR MYTHS

- The Rill voices were originally to have been provided by Anthony Paul, and the change of casting was so late that he was still credited in the *Radio Times* listing for the third episode. (Robert Cartland, the voice artist who replaced Paul, was correctly listed in *Radio Times*.)
- William Emms, who scripted this story, was a schoolteacher who wrote only in his spare time. (Emms had once been an English teacher but had been a full-time freelance writer for some four years by the time he submitted his unsolicited idea for *Galaxy 4* to the *Doctor Who* production team.)

THINGS TO WATCH OUT FOR

- The Chumblies were cleverly realised by scenic designer Richard Hunt. Four of the robots were made. Each was around a metre tall – just large enough to accommodate one of the midget actors who operated them – and consisted of a fibreglass shell mounted on castors. A light was positioned at the top to indicate when the Chumbley was communicating with its Rill masters, and several rod-like arm attachments were fixed between the dome sections to represent ray-guns and other instruments. A number of pendulum-like objects were suspended around the base to represent the robot's motive units. Whenever a Chumbley was attacked or deactivated, its dome sections collapsed on top of each other; a dummy version was used for these shots.

THINGS YOU MIGHT NOT HAVE KNOWN

- Working title: *The Chumblies*.

- The Drahvins' uniforms were predominantly green, with white leather accessories.
- The trailer for this story, broadcast the day before the first episode's transmission, was narrated by Shaw Taylor, better known for his work on *Police 5*.
- The Drahvins were originally written as male characters, the leader of whom was called Gar.
- Contemporary documentation indicates that the Drahvins were created jointly by William Emms and Verity Lambert – presumably due to the latter deciding that they should be female rather than male, as they had been in Emms's draft scripts – and that the BBC is therefore part-owner of the rights to them.
- The Rills vaguely resembled wart-hogs and were seen lurking in their spaceship behind glass screens and swathed in 'ammonia gas' – in reality carbon dioxide dry ice. Four costumes were made, out of fibreglass and rubber. They were grey-green in colour and each large enough to house an actor who could operate the creature's arm-like appendages and thereby bring some movement to its otherwise static form.
- Actor Anthony Paul was originally due to provide the Rills' voices but in the event was unable to do so and was replaced by Robert Cartland. Paul was still credited for episode three on the recording script as it was too late for the entry to be amended. David Brewster was a late replacement for Bill McAllister playing one of the Rills.

QUOTE, UNQUOTE

- **Steven:** 'You ... you don't belong here?' **Maaga:** 'No. Nor do the Rills. There is no life on this planet. We come from Drahva. Some four hundred dawns ago we were investigating this section of the galaxy. We were looking for a planet such as this, capable of supporting life, so that we might colonise it. There are too many of us on Drahva.' **Steven:** 'All women?' **Maaga:** 'Women?' **Steven:** 'Women ...' **The Doctor:** 'Yes, women, female.' **Maaga:** 'Oh, we have a small number of men, as many as we need. The rest we kill. They consume valuable food and fulfil no particular function. [Referring to the other Drahvins.] And these are not what you would call ... human. They are cultivated, in test tubes. We have very good scientists. I am a living being. They are ... products. And inferior products. Grown for a purpose, and capable of nothing more.' **Steven:** 'Grown for what purpose?' **Maaga:** 'To fight. To kill.'
- **Rill Voice:** 'It is easy to help others when they are so willing to help you. Though we are beings of separate planets, you from the solar system and we from another space, our ways of thought, at times, do not seem all that different. It has been an honour to know you and serve you.' **Vicki:** 'Good luck!' **Rill Voice:** 'Thank you. We shall give you time to get clear before we take off. Now we are going. Goodbye. We wish you well.'

ANALYSIS

At the heart of *Galaxy 4* is a relatively simple and straightforward moral message: never judge by appearances. The Rills are hideously ugly reptilian creatures (although their full forms are generally obscured as they lurk in smoky compartments within their ship), but they are eventually revealed to be civilised, peaceful and highly advanced travellers. Even the Doctor, before he learns their true nature, makes the false assumption that they are aggressive and almost brings about their deaths by sabotaging the machine that converts the planet's air into the ammonia that they need to survive. To be fair, though, he has not properly met them at this stage and is having to rely on information supplied by the Drahvins, which misleadingly suggests that their intentions match their appearance; and he may well believe that his sabotage will only inconvenience rather than kill them.

The treacherous Drahvins provide the contrast to the Rills, and Verity Lambert's decision to make them beautiful women was an astute one – not only because it has the effect of demonstrating that beauty may be only skin deep, and thereby reinforcing the basic moral of the story, but also because it guaranteed a considerable amount of advance publicity in the popular press for the start of the series' third season. The only downside to this was that the press reports also highlighted the Drahvins' villainous tendencies – the *Daily Mail* of 25 June 1965, for example, ran a story headlined 'Enter Dr Who's new foes: The ray-gun blondes', claiming that their 'one aim in life [is] to kill with their ray guns' – tipping readers off to what would otherwise have been a surprising plot twist.

The Drahvins in fact constitute one of the most interesting and well thought-out of the series' early attempts at representing an alien culture. We learn that on their planet Drahva in Galaxy 4 women are the dominant sex; that Maaga, the leader of the group encountered by the Doctor and his friends, is a 'true' Drahvin who has been sent on a mission to 'conquer space', but her crew are just unintelligent soldier drones 'cultivated' in test tubes; and that Maaga has a 'special' type of food and ray-gun, while the others have to eat what look like leaves and twigs and carry ineffective weapons. The Doctor immediately observes that the Drahvins' technology is relatively primitive; he is able to scratch the outer hull of their ship with ease.

'The serial was rather daring for its day,' noted John Peel in *Fantasy Empire* Issue 4 in 1982, 'treating subjects such as cloning, which was new to TV then, and the possibility of a world [with] men [subservient to women].' These factors have indeed led some reviewers to draw parallels between *Galaxy 4* and Aldous Huxley's *Brave New World*. (Another frequently expressed view that the depiction of the Drahvins represents a reactionary comment on feminism – or 'women's lib' as it was commonly referred to in the mid-sixties – is arguably misconceived, given that they were originally to have been male characters and that only minor amendments were made to the scripts to reflect the late change of plan.) In dramatic terms, however, the fact that the Drahvins are less advanced than the Rills, with only Maaga capable of intelligent thought, means that their potential as adversaries for the Doctor is somewhat diminished, as Trevor Wayne observed in *Doctor Who – An Adventure in Space and Time* in 1981:

'Everything is weighted against the Drahvins, and that ultimately must tell against them as villains; as they are in an inferior position, they are not the great threat to the Doctor's continued existence that his enemies usually are.

'Besides the Doctor … and his … companions, the only real 'character' *per se* in the production is the belligerent Drahvin leader, Maaga. She is simply the bellicose product of a military society; indeed, the hints we are given about Drahva indicate that life there is not too different [from] that in a huge army barracks, where the strong lord it over the weak.'

Even the rather appealing Chumbley robots, which initially seem quite menacing, turn out to pose no threat at all to the travellers once they are revealed to be servants of the peaceful Rills.

The story is nevertheless an unfailingly entertaining one boasting some fresh ideas – including the effective concept of an unstable planet on the point of disintegration – and high production values. Wayne summed it up well: 'Despite all the little problems that, on reflection, seem to beset this story, it remains both memorable and extremely enjoyable. Its simple plot, coupled with inspired direction and lavish work on the models, props and costumes, all added up to a very impressive start to the third season.'

MISSION TO THE UNKNOWN

Note: Also known as *Dalek Cutaway*.

Writer: Terry Nation. **Director:** Derek Martinus. **Designer:** Richard Hunt, Raymond P Cusick. **Costumes:** Daphne Dare. **Make-Up:** Sonia Markham. **Incidental Music:** stock. **Film Cameraman:** unknown. **Film Editor:** unknown. **Studio Lighting:** Ralph Walton. **Studio Sound:** George Prince. **Production Assistant:** Angela Gordon. **Assistant Floor Manager:** Marjorie Yorke.

	First UK TX	Scheduled TX	Actual TX	Duration	Viewers	Chart Pos.
Mission to the Unknown	09/10/65	17.50	17.50	24'42"	8.3	37

Plot: On the planet Kembel, Space Security Service agent Marc Cory is investigating a recent sighting of a Dalek spaceship. His suspicion that the creatures may have established a base here proves well-founded. His two companions, Jeff Garvey and Gordon Lowery, both fall victim to the poisonous thorns of Varga plants – ambulatory flora indigenous to the Daleks' home world, Skaro – and he has no choice but to shoot them before they are themselves transformed into Vargas. Having overheard the Daleks plotting with representatives of the six outer galaxies to overthrow the solar system, Cory records a warning message and prepares to send it into orbit with a rocket launcher. Before he can do so, however, he is discovered and exterminated.

Episode endings:
1. Malpha vows to turn the galaxies to ashes and their people to dust. The first planet to be conquered will be Earth.

IT WAS MADE WHERE...?
Ealing filming: 25.06.65 on Stage 3
Studio: 06.08.65 in TC4.

ADDITIONAL CREDITED CAST
Jeff Garvey (Barry Jackson), Marc Cory (Edward de Souza), Gordon Lowery (Jeremy Young), Malpha (Robert Cartland), Dalek Voices (David Graham, Peter Hawkins), Dalek Operators (Robert Jewell, Kevin Manser, John Scott Martin, Gerald Taylor).

POPULAR MYTHS
• The members of the alliance were named Malpha, Desmir, Stifka, Hjbuj, Pteron,

Dbremen and Leemon. (These names, apart from Malpha, were made up for an Australian fan-published novelisation of the story in 1980. In the transmitted story only Malpha and the planet Gearon are named. The names used by John Peel in his 1989 Target novelisation derive from the later story, *The Daleks' Master Plan*.)

THINGS TO WATCH OUT FOR

- The regular cast do not appear in this episode, although William Hartnell was still credited on screen.
- Terry Nation made rather cavalier use of the term 'solar system', which he appears to have equated to the Milky Way as a whole. This perhaps suggests that by the era in which the story takes place – identified in *The Daleks' Master Plan* as being circa 4000 AD – humanity's empire extends throughout the galaxy, with the solar system at its hub. Skaro is also implied to be in this galaxy; hence the Daleks' alliance with representatives of 'the outer galaxies' against the forces of the solar system. The alternative interpretation that Skaro is actually within the solar system itself appears untenable.

THINGS YOU MIGHT NOT HAVE KNOWN

- This episode was made for all intents and purposes as if it was a fifth episode of *Galaxy 4* – e.g. the production crew were all the same, all the film inserts for both stories were shot together etc.

QUOTE, UNQUOTE

- **Marc Cory:** 'I'll tell you this: there's something very big going on here, and if the Daleks are involved, you can bet your life our whole galaxy is in danger.'
- **Malpha:** 'This is indeed an historic moment in the history of the universe. We six from the outer galaxies joining with the power from the solar system, the Daleks. The seven of us represent the greatest war force ever assembled. Conquest is assured!'

ANALYSIS

This single episode story was devised as a trailer for a longer (as it turned out, much longer) Dalek story later in the season. None of the regulars appears – this was always planned, as the episode was additional to the projected recording pattern and the artistes were not contracted for it – but it must be said that their presence is hardly missed as an excellent Terry Nation script and some fine direction combine to offer the viewer a gripping and highly entertaining adventure.

The atmosphere is tense and claustrophobic throughout. Following on from the previous week's cliffhanger, the episode opens with one of the astronauts running through a forest on the planet Kembel. He has been pricked by a Varga thorn, and the sight of his body being slowly covered with Varga fur and spines is terrifying. Later the plants are seen advancing slowly but surely on the astronauts' camp, making for some very gripping scenes. Robert Franks, writing in *Queen Bat* Issue 2 in 1985, observed: 'The Varga ... are another typical Nation device – "normally harmless" aspects of nature given a more malignant streak by the author in his efforts to provide locations which are both exotic and threatening. The Varga have their forerunners in both [John Wyndham's] Triffids and Nation's own Fungoids in *The Chase* ... [They] are the principal factor in the episode's claustrophobic quality – dragging themselves along by their roots, they are gradually closing … in around the two survivors.'

Nation also introduces his alliance of outer galaxies, although only a creature called Malpha is given any significant lines in this story. These creatures come in a variety of weird and wonderful designs and provide a sinister group of aliens allied with the Daleks against the planets of the solar system. 'I was deeply impressed at the time at the array of creatures portrayed,' recalled Ian Levine in *A Voyage Through 25 Years of Doctor Who* dated December 1988, 'especially Malpha who had a sort of cracked and ugly face looking something like a grotesque parody of someone with eczema. The Varga plants were particularly menacing; a combination of cotton wool and thorns which frightened me by the fact that somebody who became infected by them could actually become taken over and turn into vegetable matter … The Daleks were interesting and well-portrayed as usual, and the scenario was beautifully set for the epic to follow.'

Also worthy of mention are the superb jungle sets designed by Richard Hunt, which provide an effective contrast to the stark and simple lines of the Dalek control centre, equally well realised by Raymond P Cusick.

Although just a single episode, *Mission to the Unknown* is a thrilling and entertaining interlude that leaves the viewer eagerly anticipating the forthcoming Dalek epic. First, however, there is a trip back in time to consider …

THE MYTH MAKERS

Writer: Donald Cotton. **Director:** Michael Leeston-Smith. **Designer:** John Wood. **Costumes:** Daphne Dare[1,3,4], Tony Pearce[2]. **Make-Up:** Elizabeth Blattner[1,2], Sonia Markham[3,4]. **Incidental Music:** Humphrey Searle. **Fight Arranger:** Derek Ware. **Film Cameraman:** Peter Hamilton. **Film Editor:** Caroline Shields. **Studio Lighting:** Ralph Walton. **Studio Sound:** Dave Kitchen, Bryan Forgham. **Production Assistant:** David Maloney, Richard Brooks. **Assistant Floor Manager:** Dawn Robertson.

	First UK TX	Scheduled TX	Actual TX	Duration	Viewers	Chart Pos.
Temple of Secrets	16/10/65	17.50	17.51	24'45"	8.3	34
Small Prophet, Quick Return	23/10/65	17.50	17.49	24'43"	8.1	40
Death of a Spy	30/10/65	17.50	17.50	25'39"	8.7	33
Horse of Destruction	06/11/65	17.50	17.50	24'25"	8.3	38

Plot: When the TARDIS arrives on the plains of Asia Minor, not far from the besieged city of Troy, the Doctor is hailed by Achilles as the mighty god Zeus and taken to the Greek camp, where he meets Agamemnon and Odysseus. Forced to admit that he is a mere mortal – albeit a traveller in space and time – he is given just two days to devise a scheme to capture Troy. Steven and Vicki, meanwhile, have been taken prisoner by the Trojans, and Vicki – believed to possess supernatural powers – is given two days to banish the Greeks and thus prove that she is not a spy. Having initially dismissed the famous wooden horse as a fiction of Homer's, the Doctor is eventually driven to 'invent' it himself, thereby giving the Greeks the means to defeat the Trojans. In the climactic battle Steven is wounded by a sword-thrust to his shoulder and

Katarina, handmaiden to the Trojan prophetess Cassandra, helps the Doctor to get him back to the TARDIS. Vicki meanwhile, having adopted the guise of Cressida, elects to remain behind on Earth with the Trojan prince Troilus, with whom she has fallen in love.

Episode endings:
1. The Doctor has only two days in which to devise a scheme to enable the Greeks to capture Troy. Night has fallen on the sandy plains outside the city, but still visible is a Trojan plaque bearing the symbol of a horse's head …
2. Cassandra denounces Vicki as a spy and orders that both she and Steven be killed. Vicki runs to Steven's arms as the guards draw their swords.
3. Paris dismisses Cassandra's cries of woe by telling her that it is 'too late to say woe to the horse' and that he has given instructions to have it brought into Troy.
4. As Katarina tends to the wounded Steven in the TARDIS control room, the Doctor laments Vicki's departure and hopes that the ship will land somewhere where he can get proper drugs to treat the young astronaut.

IT WAS MADE WHERE...?
Location filming: 27.08.65, 30.08.85-02.09.65.
Locations: Frensham Little Pond, Frensham, Surrey; Ham Polo Club, Petersham Road, Ham, Middx.
Ealing filming: c. 03.09.65 (exact date unknown).
Studio recording: 17.09.65, 24.09.65, 01.10.65, 08.10.65, all in Riverside 1.

ADDITIONAL CREDITED CAST
Achilles (Cavan Kendall[1,4]), Hector (Alan Haywood[1]), Odysseus (Ivor Salter), Agamemnon (Francis de Wolff[1-3]), Menelaus (Jack Melford[1,3]), Cyclops (Tutte Lemkow[1-3]), King Priam (Max Adrian[2-4]), Paris (Barrie Ingham[2-4]), Cassandra (Frances White[2-4]), Messenger (Jon Luxton[2]), Troilus (James Lynn[3,4]).

POPULAR MYTHS
- William Hartnell refused to appear in scenes with Max Adrian as the latter actor was both Jewish and gay. (He didn't. It was coincidental that the scripts contained no scenes in which the two actors appeared together.)
- Actress Frances White, who played Cassandra, was uncredited. (She was credited at the end of each episode in which she appeared, although at her own request her name was not included in any publicity for the story, including the entries in *Radio Times*.)

THINGS TO WATCH OUT FOR
- Designer John Wood created an excellent wooden horse model and fine sets.
- There is a poignant and well written departure scene for the always underrated Vicki.

THINGS YOU MIGHT NOT HAVE KNOWN
- During recording of the first episode, William Hartnell was struck on the back by a camera and sustained a bruised left shoulder.
- A comment by Vicki in this story implies that she is sixteen years old.

- Working titles: *The Mythmakers*, *The Trojans* and *The Trojan War*. The working title of the first individual episode was *Deus ex Machina*; that of the third individual episode was recalled by Donald Cotton to have been *Is There a Doctor in the Horse?*
- Derek Martinus was at one point considered as the director for this story, but in the end Michael Leeston-Smith was allocated to it.

- **Paris:** 'Achilles, Achilles! Come out and fight, you jackal! Paris, Prince of Troy, brother of Hector, seeks revenge. You must dare to face me!' **Steven:** 'I dare to face you, Paris. Come out and draw your sword!' **Paris:** 'Ah. [He laughs.] No, you're not Achilles, are you?' **Steven:** 'I'm Diomede, friend of Odysseus.' **Paris:** 'Ah, Diomede. I do not want your blood. It's Achilles I seek.' **Steven:** 'And must my lord Achilles be roused to undertake your death, adulterer?' **Paris:** 'I ... er ... well, I'm prepared to overlook that, for the moment. I assure you I have no quarrel with you.' **Steven:** 'I'm Greek, you're Trojan. Is that not quarrel enough?' **Paris:** 'Yes, well, personally I think this whole business has been carried just a little bit too far. That Helen thing was just a misunderstanding.'
- **The Doctor:** 'How you can sit there so peacefully defeats me. Have you no feelings, hm? No emotions?' **Odysseus:** 'I was thinking, Doctor ... With luck, either Agamemnon or Achilles will not come through.' **The Doctor:** 'Do you think they'll desert us, hm?' **Odysseus:** 'No – die! That hope ... A greater share in the booty for me ...' **The Doctor:** 'That is a most immoral way of looking at life!'
- **Katarina:** 'The princess Cressida tells me all will be well. [She looks around the TARDIS control room.] And I knew it was to come.' **The Doctor:** 'What was to come?' **Katarina:** 'That I was to die.' **The Doctor:** 'My dear child, you're not dead! That's nonsense!' **Katarina:** 'But this is not Troy; this is not even the world; this is the journey through the beyond.' **The Doctor:** 'No ... Yes, yes, yes – as you wish, child. Now, I want you to keep an eye on that young man, will you?'

The Myth Makers, like *The Romans*, is a historical story with a distinctly humorous slant. As in the case of that earlier story, however, the importance of this factor has sometimes been over-stated, as Mark Wyman argued in *Flight Through Eternity* No. 2 in 1986: 'I'm not denying that there were many funny lines in the script, and not all the characters were played wholly straight ..., but there was also a genuine atmosphere of doom, danger and chaos, especially in the last episode. No room for laughter there.' A further consideration is that the style of humour in evidence in *The Myth Makers* is rather different from that seen in *The Romans*, as Wyman went on to explain: 'The BBC press release described Cotton's scripts as "the most sophisticated used in the series", and to a large extent that [was] true. Many of the Hartnell stories had wonderful ideas, and were brilliant achievements ... But *The Myth Makers* was one of the very first to feature the blend of sparkling dialogue and intellectual (as opposed to simply educational) references that came to be such an integral part of *Doctor Who* in later years.'

In a further parallel with *The Romans*, one of the most frequently discussed issues in reviews of *The Myth Makers* has been that of its faithfulness to historical sources.

'The stories by Homer and Virgil make up ... the original legend of the Trojan war,' noted Felicity Scoones in *TSV* 29 dated July 1992. 'The romance of Troilus and Cressida was not part of these original poems. Its first known source is the 12th Century French poet Benoit de St Maure, but the Chaucer/Shakespeare versions are the most familiar.

'Based on these sources the accuracy of *The Myth Makers'* account of the fall of Troy is mixed ... Achilles did kill Hector and Paris did abduct Menelaus's wife Helen. Traditionally the abduction was the cause of the war, but Donald Cotton embellishes on this, saying that what the Greeks really wanted was to gain some control of the trade routes and that this was just a convenient excuse ...

'In a post Homeric poem Paris [kills] Achilles ... However in Cotton's version Troilus kills Achilles ... This is an ironic change ... because in *Troilus and Cressida*, Troilus himself is killed by Achilles. It is difficult to see why Cotton made this reversal. Except in that it allows Troilus to live and thus keeps Vicki happy, it does not enhance the story.'

'The story of Troy was familiar to everyone who had studied Greek at school,' pointed out Trevor Wayne in *Doctor Who – An Adventure in Space and Time* in 1982. 'However, by the 1960s Greek and even Latin were being taught at very few schools; so the idea to make a joke from the subject matter ... was a rather dated one ...

'At first the Doctor dismisses the wooden horse as a fiction of Homer's, but he is finally compelled by circumstances to "invent" it himself. This provides us with the impression that the whole [story is] little more than an extended version of the jokey idea of how the intervention of time travellers ... caused the mysterious abandonment of the *Mary Celeste* in *The Chase*.'

Donald Cotton's characterisation of the Greeks and Trojans, and the way in which they were brought to life by the actors, drew favourable comment from Wyman: 'The performance of Barrie Ingham as Paris – which lies somewhere between Bertie Wooster and Black Adder, if you can imagine such a thing – tends to turn the whole Trojan court into a theatre of comedy. Cassandra is thus a spiteful high priestess of wonderfully ludicrous fury, Priam the cynical warlord and so on. But Odysseus is a real threat in his tempestuous changes of moods, capable of a hearty belly-laugh, sure, but also a piratical adventurer with more than a hint of barbarism.' Wayne, on the other hand, was less generous: 'Despite an impressive cast the characterisation is generally weak and superficial. At times it is little more than shallow caricature of one element of each of the Homeric heroes. Although Barrie Ingham's camp Paris is rather engaging ... most of the time the players exude the air of a tired music hall act. The strongest character is Ivor Salter's Odysseus, a cynical pirate, who is given the lion's share of the lines. For the Trojans, Priam has probably the best part; but his air of impatience with his children – the cowardly Paris and the wailing, pessimistic Cassandra – serves only to remind the viewer of his own boredom and impatience to return to the Daleks.'

The failure of *The Myth Makers* to deliver on *Mission to the Unknown*'s promise of an exciting Dalek story was a source of some irritation to viewers at the time, as evidenced by the BBC's Audience Research Report on the *Temple of Secrets* episode: 'This episode had scant appeal for a substantial number of the sample. Some reporting viewers, having seen the previous week's *Doctor Who* in which the Daleks turned up again, were apparently unprepared for the switching of the scene back in time to the Trojan war ... (several, in fact, wondered if a mistake had been made, and the wrong programme put out) and were perplexed and rather resentful – ... "I had been looking forward to the sequel of the previous week's excellent episode. The result – acute disappointment." ...

In fact *Doctor Who* in this setting struck some of the sample as quite ridiculous – "A travesty. A doddering old man trying to be smart in the presence of Greek heroes. Or is it an attempt to debunk?" A few reporting viewers, in criticising this particular story, gave it as their opinion that *Doctor Who* as a series had outstayed its welcome – "This programme has run too long and appears to have run out of ideas, episodes lately very poor and do not even tie up with the previous weeks."'

Fortunately, there were others who took a different view, as the Audience Research Report went on to note: '"One has to take this programme for what it is and not be too critical," commented an architect, and a good proportion of the sample liked *Temple of Secrets* moderately well (and several who were not themselves much taken with the episode admitted that children watching with them took a more favourable view), and about a quarter seemed very intrigued. According to various comments, Doctor Who's spaceship had landed in a fascinating period, it made a change to go back in time, also to have "all humans" in the episode and to be spared "weirdies from outer-space", and the story had originality and a welcome touch of humour.'

Also in the story's favour is its polished production – including, as Wyman observed, a fine incidental music score: 'The music by Humphrey Searle … was, again, an element taken to almost unprecedented levels of sophistication in *The Myth Makers*. Strident and militaristic in the opening scenes, subdued and soothing as a backdrop to the courtship of Vicki (sorry, Cressida) and Troilus. I don't suppose an orchestral score in a vaguely modernist style is in keeping with everyone's taste (I'm not sure that I *really* liked it myself!) but it was a bold innovation … and for that it must be applauded.'

Perhaps, in the final analysis, this is the most fitting verdict that can be returned on the story as a whole.

THE DALEKS' MASTER PLAN

Writer: Terry Nation[1-5,7], Dennis Spooner[6,8-12] from an idea by Terry Nation[6,8-12]. **Director:** Douglas Camfield. **Designer:** Raymond P Cusick[1,2,5-7,11,12], Barry Newbery[3,4,8-10]. **Costumes:** Daphne Dare[1-6,8-12], Tony Pearce[7]. **Make-Up:** Sonia Markham. **Incidental Music:** Tristram Cary. **Fight Arrangers:** Derek Ware, David Anderson. **Special Photographic Transparencies:** George Pollock. **Film Cameraman:** Peter Hamilton. **Film Editor:** Keith Raven. **Production Assistant:** Viktors Ritelis, Michael Briant. **Assistant Floor Manager:** Catherine Childs, Caroline Walmesley.

	First UK TX	Scheduled TX	Actual TX	Duration	Viewers	Chart Pos.
The Nightmare Begins	13/11/65	17.50	17.51	22'55"	9.1	35
Day of Armageddon	20/11/65	17.50	17.50	24'25"	9.8	31
Devil's Planet	27/11/65	17.50	17.51	24'30"	10.3	29
The Traitors	04/12/65	17.50	17.50	24'42"	9.5	34
Counter Plot	11/12/65	17.50	17.52	24'03"	9.9	26
Coronas of the Sun	18/12/65	17.50	17.50	24'45"	9.1	40
The Feast of Steven	25/12/65	18.35	18.36	24'36"	7.9	71
Volcano	01/01/66	17.50	17.51	24'42"	9.6	31

Golden Death	08/01/66	17.50	17.51	24'38"	9.2	43
Escape Switch	15/01/66	17.50	17.51	23'37"	9.5	37
The Abandoned Planet	22/01/66	17.50	17.51	24'34"	9.8	35
Destruction of Time	29/01/66	17.50	17.51	23'31"	8.6	39

Plot: The TARDIS materialises on Kembel. There the Doctor and his friends meet Space Security Service agent Bret Vyon, who has been sent in search of Marc Cory. Learning of the Daleks' scheme, which hinges on the use of a weapon called the time destructor, they determine to warn the authorities on Earth. This proves problematic as the human leader Mavic Chen, Guardian of the Solar System, is a traitor in league with the Daleks. Fortunately the Doctor has managed to make off with the taranium core of the time destructor, disrupting the Daleks' plans. In one of a number of attempts to regain the taranium, Chen dispatches Space Security Service agent Sara Kingdom to track down the Doctor's party. Sara, unaware of Chen's treachery, kills Bret – her own brother – before the time travellers can convince her of the truth. She then joins forces with them and, after an encounter with their old adversary the Monk, they all arrive back on Kembel. There, the Doctor contrives to steal the time destructor and turn it against the Daleks, annihilating them. Sara has ignored his instruction to return to the TARDIS, however, and she too is killed.

Episode endings:
1. The Doctor, having learned that there are Daleks on Kembel and discovered Marc Cory's skeleton and recorded warning message, hurries back to the TARDIS. He is stopped in his tracks when he sees that there are three Daleks standing guard on the ship. Horrified, he whispers 'Steven ... Katarina ...'.
2. Having snatched the taranium core from the Daleks, the Doctor heads back to the Spar spaceship. On board, however, Bret Vyon decides that he can wait no longer. Ignoring protests from Steven and Katarina, he starts the take-off procedure.
3. Having escaped from the prison planet Desperus in the Spar just as the Daleks arrive, the Doctor asks Katarina to check that the airlock door is secure. As she does so, the convict Kirksen emerges holding a knife. Katarina screams.
4. The Doctor and his friends are confronted by Sara Kingdom, who appears to be in league with Mavic Chen. The Doctor and Steven make a run for it, but Bret tries to appeal to her. She casually shoots him dead. Summoning Borkar, she tells him that two fugitives are still at loose and must be shot on sight – 'But aim for the head.'
5. The Doctor, Steven and Sara have been transported to the planet Mira, where they hide in a cave from the invisible Visians and invading Daleks. As the Daleks surround them, the Doctor concedes that the creatures have won.
6. The travellers have escaped once more from the Daleks. The TARDIS arrives at their next destination and, checking the controls, the Doctor discovers that the atmosphere outside is completely poisonous.
7. The travellers journey on in the TARDIS. Realising that they never got a chance to celebrate Christmas during their recent visit to Earth, the Doctor produces a bottle of champagne and some glasses. He toasts Steven and Sara and then turns and wishes everyone at home a happy Christmas as well.
8. Escaping from New Year revellers at Trafalgar Square in London, the TARDIS moves on again. The Daleks despatch a ship in pursuit. They are confident that they will conquer the

universe.

9. The TARDIS has arrived in ancient Egypt and materialised in a tomb. Steven and Sara return to the ship to find the lid of a nearby sarcophagus moving. From inside, a bandaged hand emerges.

10. The Doctor fits within the TARDIS control console a directional circuit stolen from the Monk's ship. He warns Steven and Sara that its operation will be very dangerous. Nevertheless, he comes to a decision and activates the controls. Suddenly a bright light explodes from the console.

11. Back on Kembel, Steven and Sara are captured by Mavic Chen and marched at gun-point into the Dalek base.

12. With the Daleks destroyed and Sara dead, the Doctor and Steven return to the TARDIS and leave the planet Kembel.

IT WAS MADE WHERE...?

Ealing filming: 27.09.65-01.10.65 on Stage 3A/B, 04.10.65-08.10.65 on Stage 3A/B, 18.10.65 (remount of model filming) on Stage 2, 21.10.65 (remount of model filming) on Stage 2, 15.11.65 (remount of model filming) on Stage 3B, 23.12.65 on Stage 2. Studio recording: 22.10.65, 29.10.65, 05.11.65, 12.11.65, 19.11.65, 26.11.65, 03.12.65, 10.12.65, 17.12.65, 31.12.65, 07.01.66, 14.01.66, all in TC3 except 19.11.65 in TC4.

ADDITIONAL CREDITED CAST

Kert Gantry (Brian Cant[1]), Bret Vyon (Nicholas Courtney[1-4]), Lizan (Pamela Greer[1, 4]), Roald (Philip Anthony[1]), Mavic Chen (Kevin Stoney[1-6,8-12]), Interviewer (Michael Guest[1]), Dalek Voices (Peter Hawkins[1-6,8-12], David Graham[1-6,8-12]), Daleks (Kevin Manser[1-6,8-12], Robert Jewell[1-6,8-12], Gerald Taylor[1-6,8-12], John Scott Martin[1-6,8-12]), Zephon (Julian Sherrier[2,3]), Trantis (Roy Evans[2,4,8]), Kirksen (Douglas Sheldon[3,4]), Bors (Dallas Cavell[3]), Garge (Geoff Cheshire[3]), Karlton (Maurice Browning[4,5]), Sara Kingdom[4-6]/Sara[7-12] (Jean Marsh[4-12]), Daxtar (Roger Avon[4]), Borkar (James Hall[4,5]), Froyn (Bill Meilen[5]), Rhymnal (John Herrington[5]), Station Sergeant (Clifford Earl[7]), First Policeman (Norman Mitchell[7]), Second Policeman (Malcolm Rogers[7]), Detective-Inspector (Keneth Thornett[7]), Man in Macintosh (Reg Pritchard[7]), Blossom Lefavre (Sheila Dunn[7]), Darcy Tranton (Leonard Grahame[7]), Steinberger P Green (Royston Tickner[7]), Ingmar Knopf (Mark Ross[7]), Assistant Director (Conrad Monk[7]), Arab Sheikh (David James[7]), Vamp (Paula Topham[7]), Clown (Robert G Jewell[7]), Professor Webster (Albert Barrington[7]), Prop Man (Buddy Windrush[7*]), Cameraman (Steve Machin[7]), Celation (Terence Woodfield[8,11]), The Meddling Monk (Peter Butterworth[8-10]), Trevor (Roger Brierley[8]), Scott (Bruce Wightman[8]), Khepren (Jeffrey Isaac[9,10]), Tuthmos (Derek Ware[9,10]), Hyksos (Walter Randall[9,10]), Malpha (Bryan Mosley[11]).

* This was the real name of Bryan Mosley, an alias he adopted for his stunt work and by which he was credited as Malpha in the penultimate episode.

POPULAR MYTHS

• Sara Kingdom was going to be a replacement companion for Katarina. (Not quite true. When it was realised that the character of Katarina would not work as a regular, Nation was asked to write her out as soon as he could. A replacement 'companion' character was then requested for the remainder of this story. There was never any intention for Sara to continue past the end of *The Daleks' Master Plan*.)

- The incident at the end of the seventh episode when the Doctor looks directly into camera and proposes a toast to everyone at home was an unscripted ad lib on William Hartnell's part and outraged the production team. (This action was scripted and rehearsed. It was in fact a tradition in the sixties for scenes of this kind to be included in special Christmas editions of popular series. Besides which, if the production team had really disliked it they could simply have edited it out.)

THINGS TO WATCH OUT FOR

- Brian Cant plays the hapless Kert Gantry in the first episode. Cant later went on to become a popular children's presenter, appearing in shows like *Playaway* and *Play School*.
- The green uniformed Technix all have bald heads – and the actors involved all had to agree to their heads being shaved for this purpose.
- Nicholas Courtney makes his first appearance in *Doctor Who*. Courtney's next role was in *The Web of Fear* as Colonel Lethbridge-Stewart, a character who was subsequently to appear with all but the sixth and eighth Doctors in the series (although he did appear with the sixth Doctor in the charity skit *Dimensions in Time*, and with the eighth in an audio adventure, *Minuet in Hell*, produced by Big Finish), and who was one of the series' regulars during the early seventies.
- The Doctor appears unaware of what cricket is when the TARDIS materialises at the Oval during a Test Match between England and Australia.
- The date of the Dalek invasion of Earth is given as 2157 AD.
- The starfish like Dalek creatures seen after the time destructor has done its work in the final episode are implied to be the form from which the Daleks evolved over a period of millions of years.

THINGS YOU MIGHT NOT HAVE KNOWN

- The working title of the fifth episode was *There's Something Just Behind You*, that of the sixth was *Counter-Plot*, that of the ninth was *Land of the Pharoahs*, that of the tenth was *Return to Varga* (the planet Kembel being called Varga in Terry Nation's draft scripts) and those of the twelfth were *The Mutation of Time* and *A Switch in Time*.
- The death scene of Katarina, shot as a film insert at Ealing during the week beginning 27 September 1965, was the first work that Adrienne Hill had done in the role.
- The story was originally to have been set in 1,000,000 A.D., but this was amended to 4,000 A.D. for the transmitted version.
- Original character names (with final names in brackets) were: Brett Walton (Bret Vyon), Mavick Chen (Mavic Chen, whose designation was also changed from Galactic President to Guardian of the Solar System), Kert Gantry (Kurt Gantry), Reinman (Lizan), Gilson (Roald, after the intermediate Ronald had been suggested) and Carlton (Karlton).
- An early draft of the script for *The Feast of Steven* suggested that some original footage of the Keystone Cops should be incorporated. This idea was later dropped.

- Head of Drama Sydney Newman sent director Douglas Camfield a memo on 11 January 1966 in which he told him: 'I think you have done a splendid job on the current DALEKS serial. Maybe it's a bit short on humour, but it's exciting, well shot and well acted. Very good.'
- Barry Newbery was due to design the final episode of this story, but around 20 December 1965 it was agreed that Raymond Cusick should take charge of it instead. This was because Newbery was by that stage tied up on preparatory work for *The Ark*.
- Trampoline instructor Rob Walker donned a wig and beard to double for actor Doug Sheldon in two high trampoline shots for the film insert scene where Sheldon's character, Kirksen, was ejected into space.
- The Technix were originally to have been called Technocrats.
- In *Golden Death*, the Doctor tampers with the chameleon circuit of the Monk's TARDIS so that it changes appearance from a block of stone to: a motor cycle, a state coach, a Western wagon, a tank and finally a police box.

QUOTE, UNQUOTE

- **Mavic Chen:** '... you must admit, the Daleks have a genius for war!'
- **The Doctor:** [On the death of Katarina.] 'She didn't understand ... She couldn't understand. She wanted to save our lives. And perhaps the lives of all the other beings of the solar system. I hope she's found her perfection. We shall always remember her as one of the daughters of the gods. Yes, as one of the daughters of the gods.'
- **The Doctor:** 'I am a citizen of the universe, and a gentleman to boot.'
- **The Doctor:** 'Here's a toast, a happy Christmas to all of us.' **Steven:** 'The same to you, Doctor, Sara.' **The Doctor:** 'And incidentally, a happy Christmas to all of you at home!'
- **Steven:** 'Let's go, Doctor, I've seen enough of this place.' **The Doctor:** 'Well, my boy, at last we've rid this planet of Daleks.' **Steven:** 'Bret ... Katarina ... Sara ...' **The Doctor:** 'What a waste ... What a terrible waste.'

ANALYSIS

'An all-round masterpiece,' was Ian Levine's assessment of *The Daleks' Master Plan* in *A Voyage Through 25 Years of Doctor Who* dated December 1988. 'The direction of Douglas Camfield combined with the scripting of Terry Nation and Dennis Spooner gelled in ... a way that defied description ... Rich characters, such as Kevin Stoney's Mavic Chen, and tense moments, such as the pathetic Katarina's self-sacrifice – the first time we discovered that a companion could actually die – abounded.'

The story, telling over twelve episodes of the Daleks' attempt to conquer the empire of the solar system, is indeed a remarkable one with a genuinely epic quality quite unmatched by anything else in this era, and perhaps in the entire history of *Doctor Who*. The events depicted span a wide variety of different times and places as the Doctor and his friends try to foil the master plan, and a whole host of intriguing and well-conceived characters are introduced, most of them ultimately to perish during the course of the action. The story's success is all the more impressive considering that it was written by two people working on different episodes, and that its unprecedented episode count was a result of the production team being instructed by one of their BBC superiors (reportedly because his mother was a fan of the Daleks) to make it double the length originally intended.

In many ways the central character is the evil Mavic Chen, who engages in a battle of wits both with the Doctor and with the Daleks and – aside from the regulars – is given the most screen time. Kevin Stoney's inspired portrayal of a man driven by greed and ambition makes him one of the greatest *Doctor Who* villains ever. Chen is already 'Guardian of the Solar System' and yet wants more. He has forged an allegiance with the Daleks to supply them with the taranium they need to power their fearsome time destructor weapon. All along, however, he plays his cards close to his chest, never trusting the Daleks completely and always allowing himself an escape route, as he works toward his ultimate goal of taking charge of the alliance. Of course the Daleks are doing exactly the same thing and, in this story more than most, they come over as a scheming and devious race, prepared to sacrifice almost anything in order to achieve their objectives.

The imagination and quality of the scripting is well matched by Douglas Camfield's excellent direction, and the succession of fantastic settings – from the jungles of Kembel to the Dalek headquarters, from spacecraft interiors to the prison planet Desperus, from Earth control to the steaming tropics of Mira, from a police station in Liverpool to a pyramid in Egypt – are all realised with consummate skill by two of the show's most prolific and talented scenic designers, sharing the massive workload between them.

If the story has a failing, it is that – perhaps inevitably, given its length – the plot tends to meander at times; and matters are not helped in this respect by the inclusion of what can almost be seen as a two episode interlude in the form of *The Feast of Steven* and *Volcano*.

The Feast of Steven, transmitted on Christmas Day, is intentionally distinct from the rest of the story. It features, amongst other things, the TARDIS arriving on a film set and the travellers becoming involved in a madcap, silent film-style encounter with the likes of Charlie Chaplin and the Keystone Kops. Ian K McLachlan, writing in *Gallifrey* Issue 9 dated winter 1979, recalled his feelings on watching this episode: 'I did not enjoy *The Feast of Steven*. Up to then I had believed in *Doctor Who*. Not in the sense that it really was happening, but rather that it *could* happen. And I wanted more than anything else for it to happen. I wanted to be transported away from my rather boring life into fantastic adventures and places! This episode, which was rather far-out and artificial, temporarily shattered the illusion.'

Contemporary reaction recorded in the BBC's Audience Research Report on the episode was similarly unfavourable: '"One of the worst programmes I have seen and definitely not Christmas material," commented a laboratory assistant, one of a large number of viewers (in fact, close on half the sample audience) who had no good word for this Christmas Day edition of *Doctor Who*. These viewers would certainly have taken issue as to the entertainment value of *The Feast of Steven* with anyone from the minority group (about one out of every five supplying evidence) who really enjoyed watching what happened when the crew of TARDIS deserted space travel for some Earthly adventures. These involved them with a "brush" with the police ("I thought Doctor Who and co had joined *Z-Cars* at the beginning of the story") and much further tribulation when TARDIS "materialised" (circa 1919, apparently) in a Hollywood film studio with a Keystone Kops feature at "shooting" point.'

The following episode, *Volcano*, continues in the same light hearted vein, with the TARDIS arriving first at a cricket match and later during New Year festivities in Trafalgar Square. It is only after these diversions that the focus returns to the main plot. Worth mentioning here, though, is the reappearance of the Doctor's old acquaintance the

Monk from *The Time Meddler* – the first instance in the series' history of a (non-regular) character from one story returning in a later one. The contemporary verdict on *Volcano*, as evidenced in a further Audience Research Report, was certainly more favourable than that on the previous week's instalment: 'This episode in which Doctor Who met up again with his enemy the Monk and the Daleks [was] increasingly menacing [and] appealed a good deal to a large minority, about of the quarter of the sample evidently finding it thoroughly gripping and entertaining – "A very good episode, particularly the well thought out difficulties and the solving of them by Doctor Who". More often reporting viewers were only moderately attracted by the episode which had apparently only just about held their interest, although several whose enjoyment was not particularly keen were bound to admit that children watching with them were of a different turn of mind – "Unable to fully appreciate, being in my fifties, but junior members of family delighted." Although various viewers found fault with this particular episode as padded out, lacking in suspense, somewhat confusing ("The storyline gets more and more complicated. Only *Who* addicts would follow this episode.") or too absurd, criticisms were often directed against the series as a whole as having "gone off"; it had got into a rut, was repetitive, becoming too fantastic, and the Daleks were getting played out, according to comment from viewers whose interest was on the wane – "I'm fed up with *Doctor Who* and the Daleks and such impossible situations."'

The Audience Research Report on *Escape Switch* suggests that the length of the story was proving increasingly irksome to viewers as the weeks went by: 'There was a sizeable amount of feeling, apparently, that this particular story is running out of good, solid ideas, that it is becoming confusingly meandering in plot. "Gets more involved every week and I continue to find difficulty in understanding it"; "Now needs something new. We have just Daleks, Daleks, Daleks. For a programme with a wealth of possibilities it has become very dull." Evidently these [viewers] are tiring a bit of Doctor Who's adventures with the taranium core, finding them now rather protracted and predictable, and they seem to have found this episode just "the mixture as before", and lacking in excitement or novelty. The others, however, apparently continue to find Doctor Who either quite exciting, admirably ingenious or just amusing as "picturesque nonsense".'

One particularly notable aspect of the story is the large number of characters who come to a nasty end. The Trojan handmaiden Katarina is killed after four episodes when she ejects herself into space through an airlock, as is Bret Vyon when he is shot by his own sister Sara Kingdom. Sara, who fulfils the 'female companion' role for the remainder of the adventure, is also killed at the end, aged to death by the time destructor. The Daleks exterminate most of their allies, and then are killed themselves when the Doctor turns the time destructor against them. All things considered, it is a very bleak tale indeed – a point that attracted comment in the generally favourable Audience Research Report on the climactic final episode: 'This episode, in which Doctor Who finally succeeded in engineering the destruction of the Daleks, appealed a good deal to roughly two thirds of the sample audience, many of whom remarked that, in their opinion, this had been the most thrilling and exciting episode for a very long time. Packed with action and momentous events, not the least of which was the "horrifyingly" rapid ageing and final disintegration of Sara caused by the activating of the "time destructor", this episode had brought Doctor Who's adventure on the planet Kembel to a spectacular close, they thought. A good many other viewers, however, considered this episode "much as usual":

the *Doctor Who* series was not of much interest to them and many, in fact, said they only tolerated it for the sake of their children, who were "absolutely crazy about *Doctor Who*". The disintegration of Sara caused them some unease – this was a "bit too nasty" even for such a juvenile space-fiction adventure as *Doctor Who*, in their opinion – but again the whole serial was so naïve it was impossible to take even this "horrible" event seriously. Nevertheless, it may be said that if adult viewers start by "tolerating" this serial for the sake of their children, it seems clear that they often find that it has its attractions and on this occasion there were, in fact, plenty who considered *Doctor Who* excellent entertainment by any standards.'

Like most of the longer *Doctor Who* stories, *The Daleks' Master Plan* is perhaps best appreciated at the rate of an episode per week, as was originally intended; it is simply too much to take in all in one go. As Gary Russell commented in *Ark in Space* No. 7 dated May 1983: 'It had its lame bits, [including] the nonsensical Monk character; and its strong bits, such as Katarina's unexpected demise; it had seriousness, [as in] the Doctor's final thought; and humour, notably the marvellous cricket match scene.'

For a single story to encompass as much as this one did was indeed quite an achievement.

THE MASSACRE OF ST BARTHOLOMEW'S EVE

Note: Also known as *The Massacre*.

Writer: John Lucarotti, Donald Tosh[4]. **Director:** Paddy Russell. **Designer:** Michael Young. **Costumes:** Daphne Dare. **Make-Up:** Sonia Markham. **Incidental Music:** stock. **Film Cameraman:** Tony Leggo. **Film Editor:** Bob Rymer. **Studio Lighting:** Dennis Channon. **Studio Sound:** Gordon Mackie. **Production Assistant:** Gerry Mill. **Assistant Floor Manager:** Fiona Cumming, Richard Valentine.

	First UK TX	Scheduled TX	Actual TX	Duration	Viewers	Chart Pos.
War of God	05/02/66	17.15	17.15	24'51"	8.0	45
The Sea Beggar	12/02/66	17.15	17.15	24'43"	6.0	96
Priest of Death	19/02/66	17.15	17.15	24'33"	5.9	92
Bell of Doom	26/02/66	17.15	17.15	25'06"	5.8	94

Plot: The TARDIS materialises in Paris in the year 1572 and the Doctor decides to visit the famous apothecary Charles Preslin. Steven, meanwhile, is befriended by a group of Huguenots from the household of the Protestant Admiral de Coligny. Having rescued a young serving girl, Anne Chaplet, from some pursuing guards, the Huguenots gain their first inkling of a plan by the Catholic Queen Mother, Catherine de Medici, to have all French Protestants massacred. A further shock is in store for Steven, as it appears that the hated Catholic dignitary the Abbot of Amboise is actually the Doctor in disguise. Held responsible for the failure of a plot to assassinate de Coligny, the Abbot is executed by the Catholic authorities and his body left lying in the gutter. To Steven's relief, it transpires that the Abbot was not the Doctor after all, but merely his physical double. The two time travellers meet up again at Preslin's shop, where Steven has gone in search of the TARDIS key, and regain the safety of the ship just as the massacre begins. The TARDIS then lands on Wimbledon Common in 1966 and the Doctor and Steven gain a new companion, Dorothea 'Dodo' Chaplet, who may be a descendent of Anne's.

Episode endings:

1. Simon Duvall brings the Abbot of Amboise news that Anne Chaplet has taken refuge at Admiral de Coligny's house. As the Abbot speaks, demanding that the girl be brought to him the next day, the viewer sees him for the first time: he is apparently the Doctor in disguise.

2. Admiral de Coligny tells his assistant Nicholas Muss that he has seen the King and almost persuaded him to ally with the Netherlands against the Spanish. The King told him that he would go down in history as the 'Sea Beggar'. De Coligny, unaware that Marshal Tavannes has given orders that the 'Sea Beggar' be assassinated the next day, reflects that it is a title he would be proud of ...

3. The Abbot of Amboise lies dead in the gutter, a crowd of angry Catholics gathering around his body. When Steven protests that the Huguenots were not responsible, Roger Colbert incites the crowd against him. Steven flees for his life through the Paris streets ...

4. A young girl enters the TARDIS, believing it to be a real police box. Steven, having previously stormed out in a rage at the Doctor's failure to rescue Anne Chaplet, returns and warns him that two policemen are approaching. The old man closes the doors and dematerialises the ship. Steven is shocked by his actions, but the young girl herself is unconcerned. She introduces herself as Dorothea Chaplet, or Dodo for short. Steven expresses astonishment at her surname – could she be Anne's descendant? The TARDIS journeys on with a new crew member.

IT WAS MADE WHERE...?

Ealing filming: 03.01.66-06.01.66 on Stage 3A/B
Location filming: 07.01.66.
Location: Windmill Road, Wimbledon Common, Wimbledon, London, SW19.
Studio recording: 21.01.66, 28.01.66, 04.02.66, 11.02.66, all in Riverside 1.

ADDITIONAL CREDITED CAST

Gaston (Eric Thompson[1,2,4]), Nicholas (David Weston), Simon (John Tillinger[1,2,4]), Landlord (Edwin Finn[1,2]), Roger (Christopher Tranchell[1-3]), Preslin (Erik Chitty[1]), Anne (Annette Robertson), Captain of the Guard (Clive Cazes[1,3]), Servant (Reginald Jessup[1-3]), Abbot of Amboise (William Hartnell[2,3])*, Marshal Tavannes (André Morell[2-4]), Admiral de Coligny (Leonard Sachs[2-4]), Old Lady[2]/Old Woman[3] (Cynthia Etherington[2,3]), Catherine de Medici (Joan Young[3,4]), Charles IX (Barry Justice[3]), Teligny (Michael Bilton[3,4]), Priest (Norman Claridge[3]), 1st Man (Will Stampe[3]), 2nd Man (Ernest Smith[3]), Officer (John Slavid[4]), 1st Guard (Jack Tarran[4]), 2nd Guard (Leslie Bates[4]).

* William Hartnell also appeared as the Abbot in *War of God*, but was credited only as the Doctor. He was credited only as the Abbot for *The Sea Beggar* and *Priest of Death*.

POPULAR MYTHS

• Donald Tosh was credited as co-writer on *Bell of Doom* because he supplied the final scene introducing Dodo. (Tosh wrote the final draft scripts of all four episodes, amending John Lucarotti's originals extensively. He was credited only on *Bell of Doom* because during production of the first three episodes he was still on BBC staff as *Doctor Who*'s story editor.)

- Anne's surname was Chaplette. (It was Chaplet – the same as Dodo's – according to the scripts.)
- 1st Man was played by Roy Denton. (He was played by Will Stampe – Denton, who was originally due to take the role, dropped out the day before recording and was credited in the *Radio Times* as it was too late for this to be changed.)
- The tolling of the tocsin bell is heard at the beginning and end of each episode. (It isn't.)

THINGS TO WATCH OUT FOR

- Admiral de Coligny is well portrayed by Leonard Sachs – who was better known as presenter of *The Good Old Days* music hall show and would appear again in *Doctor Who* in the season twenty story *Arc of Infinity*.
- Michael Young's design work, including a large split-level set for the Ealing film sequences of the Paris streets, is excellent.
- William Hartnell appears only in pre-filmed inserts in the second episode as he was on holiday during the week when it was recorded.

THINGS YOU MIGHT NOT HAVE KNOWN

- Working title: *The Massacre*.
- G. Evans was at one point considered as the scenic designer for this story, but the job eventually went to Michael Young.
- Gerry Davis received his first *Doctor Who* story editor credit on the *Bell of Doom* episode, while his predecessor Donald Tosh received a co-writer credit with John Lucarotti.
- The massacre itself was represented by way of some prints obtained from the British Museum. One definitely known to have been used was entitled *La Maison appartenant de Bretonuilliers a Paris*, credited to Martin Engelbrecht.

QUOTE, UNQUOTE

- **Marshal Tavannes:** 'At dawn tomorrow this city will weep tears of blood.'
- **The Doctor:** 'My dear Steven, history sometimes gives us a terrible shock, and that is because we don't quite fully understand. Why should we? After all, we're too small to realise its final pattern. Therefore don't try and judge it from where you stand. I was right to do as I did. Yes, that I firmly believe. [Steven leaves the TARDIS.] Steven … Even after all this time, he cannot understand. I dare not change the course of history. Well, at least I taught him to take some precautions; he did remember to look at the scanner before he opened the doors. And now, they're all gone. All gone. None of them could understand. Not even my little Susan. Or Vicki. And as for Barbara and Chatterton – Chesterton – they were all too impatient to get back to their own time. And now, Steven. Perhaps I should go home. Back to my own planet. But I can't … I can't …'

ANALYSIS

The Massacre of St Bartholomew's Eve is the last of the three historical stories contributed to the series by arguably the genre's finest exponent, John Lucarotti. In this case though the final version of the scripts was written by departing story editor Donald Tosh (whose idea it had been in the first place to base a story around the St Bartholomew's Eve massacre of Huguenots by Protestants in Paris 1572) and did not entirely meet with Lucarotti's approval.

Perhaps the story's most well-remembered aspect is the dual role it affords William Hartnell as both the Doctor and the Abbot of Amboise. The actor's icily intense performance as the cruel Abbot is excellent, and such a contrast to his familiar portrayal of the Doctor that it serves to remind the viewer just how great that is, as well as giving the lie to the oft-made assumption that the time traveller's doddery and eccentric manner is merely a reflection of Hartnell's own.

The Abbot and the Doctor never actually meet during the course of the story, and in some respects it is misleading to describe this as a dual role at all: the Doctor disappears part-way through the first episode and does not turn up again until part-way through the fourth; in the meantime it is only the Abbot that is seen. The Doctor's absence from much of the action allows Steven to take centre stage for once – in fact, this can be seen as the first time in the series' history that a companion is accorded the lead role in a story. Peter Purves rises to the occasion and, as always, gives an excellent performance, emphasising just what a good companion he makes.

John Lucarotti later recalled that in his original scripts he had given the Doctor a much more prominent role in the action, and that it was this aspect of Donald Tosh's subsequent rewriting to which he had particularly objected. If this was indeed the case, one can only conclude that – in this instance at least – Tosh had the better judgment. Quite apart from the fact that the limited nature of the editing facilities available to the series at the time would have made it very difficult if not impossible to achieve the frequent switches between the Doctor and the Abbot that Lucarotti had apparently envisaged, one of the most appealing aspects of the story as transmitted is that the viewer, like Steven, is kept guessing until virtually the last minute as to the Abbot's true identity – is he the Doctor in disguise, as it at first appears, or simply his physical double? To have had the Doctor popping up at regular intervals during the course of the action would have made it impossible for this element of mystery to have been sustained – at least for the viewer, if not for Steven.

Another aspect that arguably works in the story's favour – and another that Lucarotti disliked – is that the historical events depicted are relatively little known, as Robert Tweed observed in *DWB* No. 117 dated September 1993: 'While the average sixties schoolchild or Mum or Dad might be expected to know at least something about the travels of Marco Polo or the warlords of the Third Crusade, the horrific slaying of 3,000 Protestants in 16th Century France is hardly in common cultural currency. The Doctor himself, absent from most of the story, doesn't realise what is about to happen until midway through the final episode. Crucially, however, it is Steven's ignorance of the significance of his surroundings that propels the narrative to its heart-rending conclusion.'

Whatever differences there may have been between Lucarotti and Tosh, their creative conflict gave birth to a story that is full of incident, atmosphere and fascinating period detail, with some rich and finely-drawn characters afforded some wonderful lines of dialogue. Paddy Russell's accomplished direction complements the scripts very well, and there are some fine performances from a high-powered cast.

'The atmosphere is perhaps more grim than that of any other story,' noted Tweed. 'Each episode shows the events of one day ... The stock incidental music, crashing drums and cymbals, goes a long way towards heightening the tension. The performances are all excellent, with particular credit to Leonard Sachs and former Quatermass André Morell. Annette Robertson as the doomed Anne, following on from the doomed Katarina and [the] doomed Sara, is a much more interesting and better acted character than her descendent and successor and might perhaps have made a worthier addition to the TARDIS crew, although that would have invalidated the point of the story.'

The production team did in fact give some consideration to the possibility of making Anne a new regular. In the end however they decided against this, both because of the problems inherent in having a companion from the past – as they had realised with Katarina, the Doctor would have had to explain to her many things of which the viewer would already have been aware – and because her rescue from the massacre could have been seen as undue interference with history on the Doctor's part. Consequently they decided instead to introduce a possible descendent of Anne's, namely Dodo Chaplet. This did however present a slight conundrum: 'What I've never been able to work out,' mused John Peel in *Fantasy Empire* Issue 4 in 1982, 'is how Dodo is descended from Anne, unless Anne married someone with the same surname as herself.'

THE ARK

Writer: Paul Erickson, Lesley Scott*. **Director:** Michael Imison. **Designer:** Barry Newbery. **Costume Designer:** Daphne Dare. **Make-Up:** Sonia Markham. **Incidental Music:** Tristram Cary (stock). **Film Cameraman:** Tony Leggo. **Film Editor:** Noel Chanan. **Studio Lighting:** Howard King. **Studio Sound:** Ray Angel. **Production Assistant:** David Maloney. **Assistant Floor Manager:** Chris D'Oyly John.

*Although credited, Lesley Scott – Paul Erickson's wife at the time of the story's production – apparently made no contribution to the scripts.

	First UK TX	Scheduled TX	Actual TX	Duration	Viewers	Chart Pos.
The Steel Sky	05/03/66	17.15	17.15	24'00"	5.5	102
The Plague	12/03/66	17.15	17.15	25'00"	6.9	70
The Return	19/03/66	17.15	17.15	24'19"	6.2	85
The Bomb	26/03/66	17.15	17.15	24'37"	7.3	71

Plot: The TARDIS arrives some ten million years in the future on a giant spaceship carrying all the Earth's surviving plant, animal and human life (much of it miniaturised and in suspended animation) on a 700 year voyage to a new home on the planet Refusis II. Dodo is suffering from a cold – an unknown affliction in this era – and as the human Guardians of the ship and their servant race the Monoids have no resistance, a plague breaks out. The Guardians place the travellers on trial and Steven is forced to defend them against allegations that they spread the disease deliberately. Fortunately, the Doctor finds a cure. The TARDIS leaves the spaceship, which Dodo has nicknamed the Ark, only to arrive back there as it is approaching the end of its voyage. Partly as a result of the earlier plague, the Monoids have now grown strong and enslaved the humans. They plan to make Refusis II their own but, with the help of the invisible Refusians, the Doctor is able to persuade the two races to live together in peace.

Episode endings:
1. With the Commander suffering from the same fever that has killed a Monoid, Zentos demands that the strangers be made to suffer for the crime that they have committed. If the Guardians die now, it will have been pointless them leaving the Earth in the first place. On the Ark's scanner screen, the Earth is seen moving toward its final destruction …
2. Having arrived back on the Ark, the travellers head for the control room. On the way, Dodo notices that the statue that they earlier saw under construction has now been completed – but it has the head not of a human but of a Monoid.
3. Dodo is horrified that the Ark's launcher has exploded, stranding her and the Doctor on Refusis II. The Doctor states that the two of them will have to wait until another party arrives; and if no one comes, they will just have to stay on the planet.
4. The TARDIS is arriving at a new destination. Suddenly the Doctor vanishes from sight. Dodo suggests that this might have something to do with the Refusians, but the invisible Doctor tells his companions that it is some form of attack!

It Was Made Where…?

Ealing filming: 31.01.66-04.02.66 (Stage unknown).
Studio recording: 18.02.66, 25.02.66, 04.03.66, 11.03.66, all in Riverside 1.

Additional Credited Cast

Commander (Eric Elliott[1,2]), Zentos (Inigo Jackson[1,2]), Manyak (Roy Spencer[1,2]), Mellium (Kate Newman[1,2]), 1st Monoid (Edmund Coulter[1,2]), 2nd Monoid (Frank George[1,2]), Rhos (Michael Sheard[2]), Baccu (Ian Frost[2]), 1st Guardian (Stephanie Heesom[2]), 2nd Guardian (Paul Greenhalgh[2]), Maharis (Terence Woodfield[3,4]), Monoid Two (Ralph Carrigan[3]), Yendom (Terence Bayler[3]), Monoid One (Edmund Coulter[3,4]), Dassuk (Brian Wright[3,4]), Venussa (Eileen Helsby[3,4]), Monoid Three (Frank George[3,4]), Monoid Voices (Roy Skelton[3,4], John Halstead[3,4]), Refusian Voice (Richard Beale[3,4]), Monoid Four (John Caesar[4]).

Things To Watch Out For

- The Monoids, who have no visible mouths, apparently eat through holes in their necks.
- Jackie Lane, in her debut appearance as Dodo, delivers her lines with a somewhat variable accent. She had originally rehearsed the role with a Cockney accent but, before recording got under way, the production team were instructed by their superiors that it was unacceptable for a regular character in *Doctor Who* to speak in anything other than 'BBC English'.
- There is a wonderfully dramatic moment at the end of *The Plague*, when the completed statue with the Monoid head is revealed for the first time.
- In the sequences set in the Ark's kitchen in the third and fourth episodes, small pills are seen to be transformed into recognisable food items – such as vegetables and fruit – when dropped into bowls of water.

QUOTE, UNQUOTE

- **Baccu:** [Acting as prosecutor in the Guardians' trial of the time travellers.] 'My contention is that it was no accident that this disaster has happened. I say that you intentionally came here to spread the disease.' **Steven:** 'Look, that's utter nonsense.' **Baccu:** 'I maintain that you are agents of the planet towards which this spaceship is proceeding; that you came here to destroy us!' **Steven:** 'Why? We're human beings like you are. Why should we?' **Zentos:** 'And there's the crux of the matter. Do you expect us to believe that nonsense? That you managed in that ridiculous machine called the TARDIS to travel through time? Guardians, Monoids, these beings, or whatever they are, they place a heavy strain on our credulity.' **Steven:** 'Well that's not difficult. If your medical records are anything to go by, this segment of time, far from being one of the most advanced in knowledge, is one of the worst.' **Zentos:** 'We can cope with all things known to the fifty-seventh segment of time, but not with strange diseases brought by you as agents of the intelligences that inhabit Refusis.' **Steven:** 'You're still on about that? I told you before, we know nothing of that planet.' **Zentos:** 'My instinct, every fibre of my being, tells me differently.' **Steven:** 'That, unfortunately, tells me only one thing.' **Zentos:** 'What is that?' **Steven:** 'That the nature of man, even in this day and age, hasn't altered at all. You still fear the unknown like everyone else before you.'

ANALYSIS

The idea of a giant spaceship taking the last survivors of Earth on a generation-spanning voyage to a new planet provides a strong basis for this story, and was a far-sighted and innovative one for the time of its production – another example of the increased sophistication brought to *Doctor Who* by John Wiles and Donald Tosh. Also of considerable interest is the depiction of the apparently long established relationship between the human Guardians and their Monoid servants (or should that be slaves?), which the former seem to think is quite cosy and amicable but – at least judging from the events of the second segment of the story, after the TARDIS returns to the Ark – the latter clearly (and perhaps understandably) consider somewhat less satisfactory. The Monoids' ultimate overthrowing of their masters makes for an interesting reversal of fortunes – and it is, in a way, a pity that the script attributes this partly to the lingering effects of the cold virus unwittingly introduced by Dodo, as this rather dilutes the moral questions that the story implicitly poses about the humans' treatment of the Monoids in the first two episodes.

This subdivision of the story into two distinct segments was novel and interesting in itself. '[An] important thing to remember about *The Ark*,' noted Ian K McLachlan in *Matrix* Issue 6 dated May 1980, '[is] that it was really two two-part adventures stitched together. This is what makes it stand out in my mind and really made use of the Doctor's ability to travel in both space and time … In those days, the viewers had no idea at all how long an adventure was going to last. Each episode ran into the next one and the whole series was joined together … I loved the strange ending of episode two – which could not work to the same extent today with [viewers] knowing the length of a story [in advance].'

There is however a negative aspect to this story structure, which is that there is little time in either segment for detailed plotting or extensive characterisation. This results in both being rather too simple for their own good, and the humans and Monoids being somewhat one-dimensional and faceless. One is actually tempted to wonder how the human race survived long enough to build the Ark in the first place, as those seen here are a very feeble bunch. The Monoids are quite effectively realised as alien races go – the inspired idea of having the actor hold the 'eye' of the costume in his mouth and move it with his tongue works very well indeed, and it is surprising that this simple effect has not been used more widely – but the scripts' failure to develop them and provide a convincing background to their relationship with the humans ultimately tells against them. They are perhaps at their least successful in the second segment of the story when, despite writer Paul Erickson's attempts to liven things up by having them quarrel amongst themselves, they become basically just clichéd monsters and the whole thing degenerates into a simplistic 'good versus evil' conflict.

On the plus side, the production has a very polished and surprisingly expensive look. The effects – including a giant statue, Earth burning up as it approaches the Sun and an exploding space shuttle – are quite ambitious and uniformly good. Even the sequences of the invisible Refusians causing objects to move seemingly by themselves, which could have been a great let-down, are very well achieved. Other points of note include the jungle set – another piece of excellent design work by Barry Newbery – which has the added bonus of being populated with live animals, including a snake, a toucan and even a baby elephant!

Overall though, despite its many good points, *The Ark* must be deemed only a qualified success.

THE CELESTIAL TOYMAKER

Writer: Brian Hayles, scripts by Donald Tosh. **Director:** Bill Sellars. **Designer:** John Wood. **Costumes:** Daphne Dare. **Make-Up:** Sonia Markham. **Incidental Music:** Dudley Simpson. **Choreography:** Tutte Lemkow. **Studio Lighting:** Frank Cresswell. **Studio Sound:** Alan Fogg. **Production Assistant:** Snowy White. **Assistant Floor Manager:** Elizabeth Dunbar.

	First UK TX	Scheduled TX	Actual TX	Duration	Viewers	Chart Pos.
The Celestial Toyroom	02/04/66	17.50	17.50	24'40"	8.0	44
The Hall of Dolls	09/04/66	17.50	17.50	24'45"	8.0	49
The Dancing Floor	16/04/66	17.50	17.50	24'10"	9.4	32
The Final Test	23/04/66	17.50	17.51	23'57"	7.8	36

Plot: The travellers arrive in a strange domain presided over by the Celestial Toymaker – an enigmatic, immortal entity who forces them to play a series of games, failure at which will render them his playthings. The Doctor has to solve the complex Trilogic game while Steven and Dodo are faced with defeating a succession of apparently child-like but potentially lethal animated toys in contests such as 'blind man's buff', musical chairs and 'hunt the key'. The Doctor finally overcomes the Toymaker by imitating his voice in order to complete the Trilogic game from within the TARDIS, which then dematerialises as his foe's universe is destroyed.

Episode endings:

1. The Doctor has passed move 350 in the Trilogic game. Meanwhile Dodo and Steven have discovered a riddle set by the Toymaker: 'Four legs, no feet; Of arms no lack; It carries no burden on its back; Six deadly sisters, seven for choice; Call the servants without voice.'*

2. The Doctor has passed move 700 in the Trilogic game. Steven and Dodo, being pursued by three life-sized ballerina dolls, have another riddle to solve: 'Hunt the key, to fit the door; That leads out on the dancing floor. Then escape the rhythmic beat; Or you'll forever tap your feet.'*

3. The Doctor has reached move 902. Cyril meanwhile leads Steven and Dodo to their next game, and warns them that they will not find it so easy this time – because they will be playing against him. The Doctor continues the Trilogic game: 'Lady luck will show the way; Win the game, or here you'll stay.'*

4. With the TARDIS in flight once more, the Doctor takes from Dodo the sweets that Cyril gave to her and pops one of them in his mouth. Suddenly he cries out and doubles up in pain, dropping the bag of sweets to the floor ...

* These riddles appeared as caption slides at the ends of the episodes.

IT WAS MADE WHERE...?

Ealing filming: 03.03.66 (Stage unknown).
Studio recording: 18.03.66, 25.03.66, 01.04.66, 08.04.66, all in Riverside 1.

ADDITIONAL CREDITED CAST

Toymaker (Michael Gough), Joey (Campbell Singer[1]), Clara (Carmen Silvera[1]), King of Hearts (Campbell Singer[2]), Queen of Hearts (Carmen Silvera[2]), Knave of Hearts (Peter Stephens[2]), Joker (Reg Lever[2]), Dancers (Beryl Braham[3], Ann Harrison[3], Delia Lindon[3]), Sergeant Rugg (Campbell Singer[3]), Mrs Wiggs (Carmen Silvera[3]), Kitchen Boy[3]/Cyril[3,4] (Peter Stephens[3,4]).

THINGS TO WATCH OUT FOR

- Peter Stephens' portrayal of Cyril, very much in the style of the popular Billy Bunter character created by Frank Richards. This reportedly brought a complaint from Richards' representatives, and the BBC transmitted a voice-over announcement following the story's last episode disclaiming any intentional similarity between characters in the story and existing fictional characters.

THINGS YOU MIGHT NOT HAVE KNOWN

- Working titles: *The Toymaker, The Trilogic Game*.
- Brian Hayles' scripts for this story were completely rewritten, first by story editor Donald Tosh with additional input from producer John Wiles and then by Tosh's successor Gerry Davis.

QUOTE, UNQUOTE

- **Toymaker:** 'The last time you were here I hoped you'd stay long enough for a game, but you hardly had time to turn around.' **The Doctor:** 'And very wise I was, too.'
- **Toymaker:** 'I'm bored. I love to play games but there's no-one to play against. The

beings who call here have no minds, and so they become my toys. But you will become my perpetual opponent. We shall play endless games together, your brain against mine.'

- **Toymaker:** 'Play the game according to the rules I set, or give up now.' **Steven:** 'The rules *you* set? Your own players break them. They cheat!' **Dodo:** 'How can we believe anything you say? Everything's so strange!' **Steven:** 'We can't even be certain that was the Doctor's voice we heard before. It could have been you leading us into another trap.' **Toymaker:** 'I am glad to see you are at last treating me with respect.'

- **Toymaker:** 'Make your last move, Doctor. Make your move.' **The Doctor:** 'But if I do, this place vanishes, hm?' **Toymaker:** 'And then you have won completely.' **The Doctor:** 'And if this place vanishes, then the TARDIS and the rest of us will vanish also?' **Toymaker:** 'Correct. That is the price of success. Make your last move, Doctor. Make your *last* move.'

ANALYSIS

Much of *Doctor Who* could arguably be more appropriately classified as science-fantasy than as science-fiction, but every so often there would come along a story that ventured an unusually long way in that direction. *The Celestial Toymaker* was the first of these forays into the realms of pure fantasy – and, as would be borne out by reactions to later stories in a similar vein, it seems that fans of the series were much better disposed to this departure from the norm than were members of the general viewing public. The opinions of the latter were recorded in the BBC's Audience Research Report on the closing episode, *The Final Test*:

'The final instalment of the story of *The Celestial Toymaker* had little appeal for a large proportion of the sample, over a third of whom actually disliked it: they found nothing very exciting in the closing moves of the game between Doctor Who and the Toymaker (a handful remarking that they knew all along that Doctor Who would get out of this "impossible" situation "with absurdly impossible ease"), or in the game that Steven and Dodo played with the doll, Cyril. There was not enough action, according to a sizeable group who obviously soon got tired of watching their leaps from triangle to triangle, and of Cyril's "very predictable" attempts to cheat; some, too, protested that the acting was either "ham" or under-rehearsed. A considerable number, however, took a very different view, declaring that the cast's performance (especially that of Michael Gough as the Toymaker) was the redeeming feature of the episode, and many of them also praised the imaginative production...

'The sample was asked to comment on *The Celestial Toymaker* adventure as a whole, and from their replies it was clear that many of them did not care for this adventure into the realm of "fantasy gone mad"; it was too far removed from the original conception of Doctor Who's travels through space and time, they claimed, and there was widespread support for the viewer who declared, "We can accept adventure into space, yes; back into history and even pre-history, yes; but this dabbling in pure whimsy, no". The games were very difficult for children to understand, it was sometimes said, especially as the rules were not clearly explained at the outset and the dolls' persistent cheating made them all the more confusing: there was nothing mysterious or thrilling about this "drawn-out series of glorified Snakes and Ladders", it seems, and a substantial minority dismissed it as "ridiculous rubbish"; in their view it was a complete waste of time and talent, and it was suggested (not infrequently) that it was time the series was rested as "ideas are evidently running out". Nevertheless, although some reporting viewers disliked it themselves, they were often at pains to point out that their children had enjoyed it, and there were also some who found it a welcome change from "the more usual horrors like Daleks and monsters": the battle of wits had been well maintained throughout the four episodes, it was claimed, but few went so far as to agree that "this adventure seemed fresher and more credible than previous ones".'

Fan reviews of *The Celestial Toymaker* present such a marked contrast to this more general reaction that it is sometimes difficult to believe that they are considering the same production. 'This was one of the weirdest, cleverest and most successful *Doctor Who* stories ever,' enthused John Peel in *Fantasy Empire* Issue 4 in 1982. 'Its ingenious blend of childishness and death-traps, the stunning villain and the wonderful plot gave us a rare treat, a blend of magical qualities.' Similarly, while acknowledging that there were some flaws, John Binns, writing in *Matrix* Issue 45 dated spring 1993, asserted: 'In some ways the story is a masterpiece. Particularly in the first episode, there is an excellent sinister feel to it which is heightened considerably by Michael Gough's superb performance. A clever contrast is created between the brutality of the Toymaker's games, the deceptive friendliness of the clowns, and the other characters ... The clowns in part one, Joey and Clara, are especially sinister ...'

A fair assessment arguably lies somewhere between these two extremes of opinion. The story's underlying concept – that of a deceptively welcoming domain presided over by a god-like being who engages visitors in a series of potentially lethal games in order to relieve the boredom of his immortal existence – is undoubtedly an intriguing one; and for the most part, as Trevor Wayne noted in *Doctor Who – An Adventure in Space and Time* in 1982, the production succeeds in achieving an effective blend of the childlike and the macabre: 'The curiously surreal, yet obviously studio, sets work extremely well, coupled with a rapid direction that give one little impression of the size or shape of the Toymaker's dimension ... *Doctor Who* often shows evidence that its budget cannot stretch as far as the writer's imagination. Here, though, we have a splendidly "televisual" analogue of the over-full nursery of a spoiled brat; what appears to be the set for *Play School* or some such programme made for very young children. But in the realm of the Toymaker simple games like "blind man's buff" and hopscotch, usually played sheepishly by adult presenters to teach their young audience, take on a completely different and deadly twist for Steven and Dodo, because their props are potentially deadly chairs and electrified floors.'

There are, however, parts of the story during which the action unquestionably flags; and, as suggested by the opinions recorded in the Audience Research Report, the games that Steven and Dodo are forced to play are rather less than thrilling in themselves and tend to be unduly protracted, testing the viewer's patience. Nevertheless, the differing reactions of the two companions to the toy opponents that they come up against constitute one of the story's most interesting elements. 'Steven sees all his opponents as extensions of the Toymaker himself,' noted Wayne. 'They are all the same to him, and this impression is reinforced by the way a small cast is used, with the actors "leapfrogging" to play the opponents in every other game. Dodo realises that the toys, too, are victims, but her generous nature almost blinds her to the fact that these people have been with the Toymaker a long time and are shot through with his personality which has overwhelmed their own.' 'Throughout the story,' observed Binns, 'Steven and Dodo are tricked and betrayed again and again, and slowly (Dodo more slowly than Steven) they learn that nothing can be trusted: their eyes, their ears, the "rules" of the games, and especially the characters they play against. At the heart of this paranoia is the knowledge that the omnipotent Toymaker has them completely at his mercy, and is taking a perverse enjoyment in the proceedings.'

One aspect of the story that has always attracted almost universal praise – even in the Audience Research Report – is Michael Gough's wonderful performance as the Toymaker. 'It is [this] that sustains the atmosphere of threat through the latter three episodes,' asserted Binns, 'and particularly part three where the Doctor has been made invisible, intangible and mute … Indeed, it's a pity that he isn't used more in the story … Gough really comes across as a powerful being, limited by nothing but his own whim and equal, if not superior, to the Doctor.' This excellent character is, arguably, *The Celestial Toymaker*'s greatest legacy to the *Doctor Who* universe.

THE GUNFIGHTERS

Writer: Donald Cotton. **Director:** Rex Tucker*. **Designer:** Barry Newbery. **Costumes:** Daphne Dare. **Make-Up:** Sonia Markham. **Ballad Music:** composed by Tristram Cary, lyrics by Donald Cotton and Rex Tucker, played by Tom McCall **, sung by Lynda Baron. **Film Cameraman:** Ken Westbury. **Film Editor:** Les Newman. **Studio Lighting:** George Summers. **Studio Sound:** Colin Dixon. **Production Assistant:** Tristan de Vere Cole, Angela Gordon. **Assistant Floor Manager:** Tom O'Sullivan.

* Rex Tucker received no director credit on *The OK Corral* as he had asked to have his name removed from it following a disagreement with producer Innes Lloyd over editing of the episode.
** In *Don't Shoot the Pianist* only, Winifred Taylor rather than Tom McCall played the piano accompaniment for the studio scenes in which the Ballad was played in the Last Chance Saloon.

	First UK TX	Scheduled TX	Actual TX	Duration	Viewers	Chart Pos.
A Holiday for the Doctor	30/04/66	17.50	17.51	23'48"	6.5	50
Don't Shoot the Pianist	07/05/66	17.50	17.50	23'47"	6.6	45
Johnny Ringo	14/05/66	17.55	17.56	23'52"	6.2	51
The OK Corral	21/05/66	17.50	17.52	23'53"	5.7	60

Plot: The TARDIS arrives in the town of Tombstone in the Wild West and the Doctor, having hurt a tooth on one of Cyril's sweets, decides he must visit a dentist. The local dentist is Doc Holliday, currently engaged in a feud with the Clanton family. Lawmen Wyatt Earp and Bat Masterson are meanwhile doing their best to keep the peace. The Doctor, Steven and Dodo narrowly survive a lynch mob, the attentions of Holliday and Earp and various other dangers; they finally return to the TARDIS after witnessing the famous gunfight at the OK Corral, in which the young Clanton brothers and their gunman ally Johnny Ringo are all killed by Holliday, Earp and Earp's brother Virgil.

Episode endings:
1. Having been set up by Doc Holliday, the Doctor makes his way back to the Last Chance Saloon, wherein the Clanton Brothers are making Steven and Dodo sing and play the piano while they wait to kill Holliday as he comes through the doors.
2. The Clantons decide to lynch Steven in order to try to get the Doctor (whom they still believe to be Doc Holliday) to face them. They give Earp an ultimatum: either the Doctor comes out of the jail house or Steven will be hanged.
3. The other Clantons come to rescue their brother Phineas from jail. Warren Earp, one of Wyatt's brothers, is shot, and all the Clantons escape.
4. In the TARDIS control room, the Doctor announces to Steven and Dodo that he believes he knows exactly where they are: in the future, at a time of peace and prosperity. As the travellers leave the ship, the scanner shows the image of a savage-looking man approaching.

IT WAS MADE WHERE...?

Ealing filming: 28.03.66-31.03.66 on Stage 3A/B
Location filming: 01.05.66.
Location: Callow Hill Sandpit, Callow Hill, Viginia Water, Surrey.
Studio recording: 15.04.66 in TC4, 22.04.66, 29.04.66, 06.05.66 in Riverside 1.

ADDITIONAL CREDITED CAST

Ike Clanton (William Hurndall), Phineas Clanton (Maurice Good), Billy Clanton (David Cole), Kate (Sheena Marshe), Seth Harper (Shane Rimmer[1,2]), Charlie (David Graham[1-3]), Wyatt Earp (John Alderson), Doc. Holliday (Anthony Jacobs), Bat Masterson (Richard Beale), Pa Clanton (Reed de Rouen[3,4]), Johnny Ringo (Laurence Payne[3,4]), Warren Earp (Martyn Huntley[3,4]), Virgil Earp (Victor Carin[4]).

POPULAR MYTHS

- *The Gunfighters* was the lowest rated *Doctor Who* story ever. (There were a number of stories with lower ratings, including *The Savages, The War Machines* and *The Smugglers*.)
- Sheena Marshe, who played Kate Fisher, was director Rex Tucker's daughter. (She was unrelated to him; his daughter Jane Tucker, later to find fame as one third of the Rod, Jane and Freddy group of children's entertainers, did however appear as a walk-on in the story.)

THINGS TO WATCH OUT FOR

- *Thunderbirds* voice artistes David 'Brains' Graham and Shane 'Scott Tracey' Rimmer appear as Charlie the barman and Seth Harper respectively. Graham had also provided Dalek voices for a number of earlier *Doctor Who* stories.
- The caption at the end of the final episode reads: 'Next Episode: Dr. Who and the Savages'. *The Gunfighters* was the last story to have individual episode titles.

THINGS YOU MIGHT NOT HAVE KNOWN

- Working title: *The Gunslingers*.

- Patrick Troughton was one of the actors considered for the role of Johnny Ringo.
- An unusual feature of this story was *The Ballad of the Last Chance Saloon*, passages from which were heard throughout all four episodes. The main lyrics were written by Donald Cotton, the score by incidental music composer Tristram Cary and additional lyrics by director Rex Tucker. It was largely pre-recorded, the singer being Lynda Baron and the pianist Tom McCall.
- For the scenes in which Steven was forced to sing the ballad to Dodo's accompaniment, the singer was Peter Purves himself while Jackie Lane mimed playing the piano. As originally scripted, Dodo was to have sung to Steven's accompaniment, but the roles were reversed at the insistence of Jackie Lane, who considered her singing voice too poor. Tom McCall played the piano in the studio (out of vision) for episode one, and Winifred Taylor for episode two.
- It was originally intended that Sheena Marshe, as Kate, should also be heard singing *The Ballad of the Last Chance Saloon*, and she was present at the initial sound recording session on 5 April 1966, but Tucker decided her voice was not suited to the song. She therefore mimed to Lynda Baron's pre-recorded voice in the transmitted episodes.
- It was actor Maurice Good's idea to give his character Phineas Clanton a stutter.
- Head of Drama Sydney Newman was less than impressed with this story, sending Head of Serials Gerald Savory the following memo of comment on 23 May 1966:

   We have talked a lot about this particular serial in the *Dr. Who* series but I thought it might be useful if I got some of it down on paper.

   In my view it was a very sad serial despite the fact it was quite well acted and certainly well shot. The trouble was that the entire attack was misconceived. Somehow or other *Dr. Who* audiences, as proven from many past successes, always want to believe in the particular life-and-death situation that Dr. Who and his companions find themselves in. The mickey-taking aspects of this particular one I think alienated all except the most sophisticated – and I'm not even sure about the latter.

   The use of the song was a drag. It seemed to me that every time the story began to gallop, it was slowed down to a desperate crawl by the use of the song. I also didn't like the way Lynda Baron sang. Somehow or other she could not sustain this type of ballad.

- An unusual requirement for *The O.K. Corral*, recorded on 6 May 1966, was conveyed in a memo of 4 May 1966 from props assistant June Gillespie to the catering manageress of Riverside Studios:

   Please make fully practical:

   Sixteen lamb chops and baked beans – *eight of these* to be delivered to studio Riverside 1 at 5.15 p.m. with equal amount of beans on four separate plates and the rest of the chops to be delivered at 8.15 p.m. also on four separate plates with beans. i.e. two chops and spoonful of beans for each of the four Clantons for the actual take.

   Two glasses of ice cold milk for Doctor Who to be delivered to studio Riverside 1 at 8.15 p.m.

QUOTE, UNQUOTE

- **The Doctor:** 'You can't walk into the middle of a Western town and say you've come from outer space! Good gracious me. You would be arrested on a vagrancy charge!'

ANALYSIS

The Gunfighters is a curious mixture; some aspects of it work quite well, but others leave a great deal to be desired.

The basic concept of the story – that of the Doctor and his friends arriving in Tombstone in time for the famous gunfight at the OK Corral – must have looked good on paper, but sadly the realisation falls flat. One of the main reasons for this is the obvious difficulty of trying to realise a Western on *Doctor Who*'s relatively small budget and without the benefit of any location work – although it must be said that designer Barry Newbery's faithful recreation of a Western town by way of studio sets is simply superb, and the use of live horses also adds to the illusion. Another problem is the rather jokey tone of Donald Cotton's scripts – the story is, in essence, a comedy. As John Peel, writing in *Fantasy Empire* Issue 4 in 1982, put it: 'Despite the sorry lessons of *The Romans* and *The Myth Makers* that comedy as such wouldn't work in *Doctor Who*, this was yet another [story in that vein]. Full of embarrassing lines … intended to spoof the popular Western craze of the day, it simply turned into a sorry mess. *Thunderbirds* voices Shane Rimmer and David Graham turned up in person, adding a little extra humour, but even they couldn't save such a story.' Ian Levine, commenting in *A Voyage Through 25 Years of Doctor Who* dated December 1988, went even further: 'This story, in short, should never have been made, and will forever remain a true embarrassment to *Doctor Who*.'

A particular irritation is the dreadful 'Ballad of the Last Chance Saloon'. Sung off-camera by Lynda Baron, this comments on and summarises the plot at the start and end of each episode and at critical points in between. As if that wasn't enough, Steven also gets to sing it during the course of the action, as does bar girl Kate. It seems that there is no escape from it. Ian K McLachlan, writing in *Matrix* Issue 8 dated May 1981, expressed the feelings of many: 'I thought that the [Ballad] was a bad thing. It gave the whole [story] the air of unreality which I have always hated in *Doctor Who*. I like it to appear "possible" – something like a ballad singer wailing in the background spoils the illusion!'

Some of the incidental characters are nicely written and acted – Doc Holliday and Wyatt Earp being probably the best – but there are also some weak links – Kate is rather dreadful, as is Billy. The whole thing starts to get somewhat confused when Earp's brothers begin arriving, along with Pa Clanton and the sub-Clint Eastwood Johnny Ringo, whose only good deed is to get Charlie the bar tender 'early retirement'. The Doctor and his friends unfortunately seem totally out of place on this occasion. The portrayal of the Doctor, in particular, makes him appear far too naive and trusting. It seems to take him forever to realise that Doc Holliday has set him up, and his invention of impromptu cover names for himself (Doctor Caligari), Dodo (Dodo Dupont, pianist) and Steven (Steven Regret, tenor) just adds to their problems. Straining credibility to breaking point, both Steven and Dodo are seen to be able to play the piano to a professional standard – convenient for the plot, maybe, but completely out of character.

Further plot problems occur later on. In one sequence, for example, Kate manages to arrive at the saloon well before the Doctor, despite having left some minutes after him and without him seeing her on the way. To cap it all, in the much vaunted gunfight, the Clantons all turn out to be dreadful shots, repeatedly missing the Earps even though they are simply walking down the middle of the street.

Contemporary reaction to the story was certainly very negative, as is apparent from the BBC's Audience Research Report on the final episode: 'The OK Corral story in general and this final episode in particular came under [a] critical barrage from the viewers in the sample. A majority evidently neither liked the idea of "Doctor Who and his team" being placed in a Wild West setting nor did they consider the story good as Westerns go. Doctor Who, it was said, fits much better into the "space-age sort of story". "The series", one viewer went so far as to say, "has deteriorated from pure science-fiction into third-rate story telling". Perhaps if the OK Corral story had not seemed to them so much of a tenth rate Western, some of the reporting viewers might have been better pleased. As it was, it all "fell absolutely flat", many obviously thought, being ridiculous in its story and in the way Doctor Who was involved, and corny in its script. The final episode was apparently widely considered even more idiotic than the preceding ones, with a good deal of gratuitous violence thrown in ("All that shooting for such ridiculously trifling misdemeanours."): "The story was hackneyed, ridiculous and dull"; "A weak and puerile plot"; "The script, even for a children's programme, was absolute rubbish"; "Appeared crude even beside the worst that reaches us from America". A small minority of the sample did seem to quite like the OK Corral story, because they like Westerns anyway and thought this one fairly exciting in the "old style Western" manner, and because it made a change from the "monsters" of previous *Doctor Who* stories. However, the reporting viewers on the whole seemed pretty disgusted with a story that was not in the science-fiction genre they associate with *Doctor Who*, and which was not in itself, in their opinion, convincing or exciting.'

In more recent years a number of reviewers have attempted to salvage *The Gunfighters'* reputation. Simon Black, for example, made the following points in *Spectrox* Issue 7 in 1988: 'The plot is theoretically historical, though if you read the actual details you'll find this story none too accurate, but who cares? ... For a Hartnell story it doesn't lose pace or the viewer's attention too often over ninety minutes, and raises many a deliberate laugh along the way. Despite the criticisms levelled at Donald Cotton, the story works reasonably well; the situations may be clichés, especially by today's standards, but they're fun to watch ... Okay, so it's hardly the most phenomenally gripping of stories, but does it have to be?'

This rather half-hearted defence is less than convincing, and at the end of the day the story must be adjudged one of the least effective of the Hartnell era.

THE SAVAGES

Writer: Ian Stuart Black. **Director:** Christopher Barry. **Designer:** Stuart Walker. **Costumes:** Daphne Dare. **Make-Up:** Sonia Markham. **Incidental Music:** Raymond Jones. **Film Cameraman:** unknown. **Film Editor:** unknown. **Studio Lighting:** Gordon Sothcott. **Studio Sound:** Norman Greaves. **Production Assistant:** Norman Stewart. **Assistant Floor Manager:** Gareth Gwenlan.

	First UK TX	Scheduled TX	Actual TX	Duration	Viewers	Chart Pos.
Episode 1	28/05/66	17.35	17.36	23'41"	4.8	62
Episode 2	04/06/66	17.35	17.35	23'57"	5.6	50
Episode 3	11/06/66	17.35	17.35	24'59"	5.0	66
Episode 4	18/06/66	17.35	17.35	24'41"	4.5	93

Plot: The TARDIS has arrived on a far-distant and seemingly idyllic world, but the Doctor, Steven and Dodo discover that it hides a terrible secret: the apparently civilised Elders maintain their advanced society by draining off and transferring to themselves the life-force of a group of defenceless Savages. Outraged at this exploitation, the Doctor is seemingly helpless to prevent it when some of his own life-force is tapped by the Elders' leader, Jano. In the process, however, Jano also acquires some of the Doctor's attitudes and conscience. Turning against his own people, he enlists the help of the Savages to destroy the Elders' transference laboratory – a task with which the time travellers gladly assist. Steven agrees to remain behind on the planet to become leader of the newly united Elders and Savages.

Episode endings:
1. Seeing the dishevelled figure of one of the Savages, Wylda, approaching her down the corridor, Dodo screams.
2. On Jano's orders, Senta prepares to subject the Doctor to the transference process. As power builds up around the Doctor's prostrate body, Senta comments that this will be the Elders' greatest achievement yet …
3. Dodo and Steven struggle to get the semi-conscious Doctor clear of the corridor as gas pours in. They begin to cough and choke as the gas engulfs them …
4. The TARDIS dematerialises from the surface of the planet.

IT WAS MADE WHERE…?

Location filming: 27.04.66, 29.04.66, 01.05.66.
Location: Callow Hill Sandpit, Callow Hill, Viginia Water, Surrey; Shire Lane Quarry, Chalfont St Peter, Bucks.
Ealing filming: 27.04.66-28.04.66 (Stage unknown).
Studio recording: 13.05.66, 20.05.66, 27.05.66, 03.06.66, all in Riverside 1.

ADDITIONAL CREDITED CAST

Chal (Ewen Solon), Tor (Patrick Godfrey), Captain Edal (Peter Thomas), Exorse (Geoffrey Frederick[1,3,4]), Jano (Frederick Jaeger), Avon (Robert Sidaway[1,2]), Flower (Kay Patrick[1,2]), Nanina (Clare Jenkins), Senta (Norman Henry), Wylda (Edward Caddick[1-3]), First Assistant[2]/Assistant[3] (Andrew Lodge[2,3]), Second Assistant (Christopher Denham[2]), Third Assistant (Tony Holland[2]), Savage (John Dillon[3]), Guard (Tim Goodman[3]).

POPULAR MYTHS

• The Elders' 'light guns' were realised on screen simply by means of a powerful light positioned at the end of the prop. (Although they did incorporate a light, the guns also emitted 'dry ice' smoke.)

THINGS TO WATCH OUT FOR

- A warm welcome is given by the Elders to the TARDIS crew, whose arrival has unusually been anticipated as they have been tracking the ship's journeys for 'many light years' and have accorded the Doctor the title of 'The Traveller from Beyond Time'.
- Frederick Jaeger mimics Hartnell excellently in the scenes after some of the Doctor's life-force is transferred to Jano – a performance in which he was extensively coached by Hartnell himself.

THINGS YOU MIGHT NOT HAVE KNOWN

- Working title: *The White Savages.*

QUOTE, UNQUOTE

- **Jano:** 'Doctor, do you realise that with our knowledge we can make the brave man braver, the wise man wiser, the strong man stronger. We can make the beautiful girl more beautiful still. You see the advantages of that in the perfection of our race.'
- **Jano:** [Speaking to Captain Edal about the Doctor.] 'He is a very sophisticated man, Captain. It is impossible to know what he thinks.'
- **Jano:** 'We do not understand you, Doctor. You have accepted our honours gladly. How can you condemn this great artistic and scientific civilisation because of a few wretched barbarians?' **The Doctor:** 'So, the rewards are only for the people that agree with you?' **Jano:** 'No. No, of course not. But if you are going to oppose us ...' **The Doctor:** 'Oppose you! Indeed I am going to oppose you – just as in the same way that I oppose the Daleks, or any other menace to common humanity!' **Jano:** 'I'm sorry you take this attitude, Doctor. It is most unscientific. You are standing in the way of human progress.' **The Doctor:** 'Human progress, sir! How dare you call your treatment of these people progress!' **Jano:** 'They are hardly people, Doctor. They are hardly like us.' **The Doctor:** 'I fail to see the difference.' **Jano:** Do you not realise that all progress is based on exploitation?' **The Doctor:** 'Exploitation indeed! This, sir, is protracted murder!'

ANALYSIS

The Savages, like many stories of this era of the series' history, boasts a very interesting central premise; specifically that of a seemingly civilised and admirable society owing its advancement to the parasitic leeching of life-force from a group of apparent savages – another variation on the 'never judge by appearances' theme explored in *Galaxy 4* and, to a certain extent, *The Celestial Toymaker*. This was, nevertheless, the third story in a row to receive a distinctly less than enthusiastic response from viewers whose opinions were reflected in the BBC's Audience Research Report on its final episode:

'"At least this particular adventure wasn't one of those boring historical ones and it was miles better than that awful Wild West affair but even so I couldn't work up much interest. The plain truth of the matter is I've got tired of the series which I think is overdue for a long rest."

'This comment was typical of the majority, rather unenthusiastic response to this [story], and to the series as a whole. Even if this was the sort of adventure they preferred in that the action had taken place in the future rather than the past, and even if, considered dispassionately, the story compared favourably with most of Doctor Who's previous expeditions into the future, many viewers in the sample admitted that they had lost their appetite for a series which, in their opinion, had gone on far too long. At the same time not a few of these viewers remarked that their children were certainly not losing interest – "The kids liked this adventure and said it was 'super smashing' but then they still think the series is marvellous, unlike me, who tired of it long since". And there were plenty of adult viewers who evidently still have a taste for this "imaginative" and "exciting" serial. According to this group, this particular expedition had been "one of Doctor Who's most eventful, thrilling and exciting to date". More generally, however, viewers were somewhat indifferent. No matter how ingenious the plot and how eventful the development – and no matter how inventive the "inhabitants" of the planet the TARDIS happened to arrive on – for them Doctor Who had now outstayed his welcome.

'Whatever their opinion of the series as such, viewers clearly considered the standard of acting on this occasion most satisfactory. There was praise in plenty, for instance, for Ewen Solon (Chal) and also to a lesser extent for Frederick Jaeger (Jano) and Peter Thomas (Captain Edal). There was little specific praise for the regulars but it was sometimes said that they had, as usual, given of their best.'

While the Audience Research Reports in general often seem unduly critical of the series – perhaps not surprisingly, given that they recorded the reactions of members of the viewing public at large rather than of those with a particular affection for *Doctor Who* or for science-fiction as a genre – it is difficult not to agree with the sentiments expressed on this occasion. Interesting though the central premise of the story is, the way in which it is developed and realised on screen leaves something to be desired. 'Though there are nice ideas in this story,' commented John Peel in *Fantasy Empire* Issue 4 in 1982, 'it is slow and dry, and Ian Stuart Black seemed never to really understand the show. I could never understand how the TARDIS could be tracked through its journeys, as it wandered randomly, but that was only one of the minor points of this dull story.' A similar assessment was delivered by Trevor Wayne in *Doctor Who – An Adventure in Space and Time* in 1983: 'For all its sincerity, high production values – such as the skilful use of the quarry location for the Savages' domain – *The Savages* remains "forgettable". There is no visual hook for the viewer's imagination, and the story contains nothing new. It is ultimately a rather tired reworking of a clichéd *Doctor Who* formula, which in itself is clearly derived from much earlier sources.'

Another source of sadness in this story is the departure of Steven, one of the best of the sixties companions, excellently portrayed throughout by Peter Purves. Fortunately he is given a good exit, presented with the formidable task of leading the now reconciled Elders and Savages – a challenge befitting his abilities.

The overall impression left by *The Savages* is of a series in need of a fresh approach. Fortunately, such a change was just around the corner.

THE WAR MACHINES

Writer: Ian Stuart Black, based on an idea by Kit Pedler. **Director:** Michael Ferguson. **Designer:** Raymond London. **Costumes:** Daphne Dare[1,2,4], Barbara Lane[3]. **Make-Up:** Sonia Markham. **Incidental Music:** stock. **Film Cameraman:** Alan Jonas. **Film**

Editor: Eric Mival. **Studio Lighting:** George Summers. **Studio Sound:** David Hughes.
Production Assistant: Snowy White. **Assistant Floor Manager:** Lovett Bickford,
Margot Hayhoe.

	First UK TX	Scheduled TX	Actual TX	Duration	Viewers	Chart Pos.
Episode 1	25/06/66	17.35	17.35	24'01"	5.4	71
Episode 2	02/07/66	18.55	18.56	24'00"	4.7	76
Episode 3	09/07/66	17.35	17.35	23'58"	5.3	62
Episode 4	16/07/66	17.15	17.17	23'11"	5.5	67

Plot: The TARDIS arrives in London in 1966 and the Doctor and Dodo visit the Post Office
Tower. There they meet Professor Brett, whose revolutionary new computer WOTAN (Will
Operating Thought ANalogue) can actually think for itself and is shortly to be linked up to other
major computers around the world – a project overseen by civil servant Sir Charles Summer. It
transpires however that WOTAN considers that humans are inferior to machines and should
therefore be ruled by them. Exerting a hypnotic influence, it arranges the construction of War
Machines – heavily-armed, self-contained mobile computers – with which to take over the
world. These prove more than a match for troops, but by establishing a magnetic force field the
Doctor is able to capture one of them, which he then reprograms to destroy WOTAN. Dodo,
now back in her own time, decides to remain on Earth. The Doctor enters the TARDIS alone,
but Brett's secretary Polly and her merchant seaman friend Ben Jackson follow him inside just
before it dematerialises.

Episode endings:
1. Dodo is hypnotised by WOTAN over the telephone and instructed to go to the control room
   in the Post Office Tower. There, she is given her instructions. She is to bring Doctor Who
   to WOTAN.
2. Having been asked by the Doctor to investigate around the Covent Garden area, Ben finds
   a warehouse in which a War Machine is being tested. The Machine suddenly homes in on
   him and approaches relentlessly.
3. The army attack the Covent Garden warehouse but cannot stop the War Machine. It
   chases the soldiers from the area and they retreat. Outside, however, the Doctor steps
   forward and stands his ground as the Machine approaches.
4. The Doctor is waiting by the TARDIS for Dodo when Ben and Polly arrive with a message
   from her: she wishes to stay in London. The Doctor enters the TARDIS, leaving Polly
   puzzled as to what he is doing inside a police box. Ben remembers that they still have
   Dodo's key, so the two friends follow the Doctor into the TARDIS just before it
   dematerialises.

IT WAS MADE WHERE...?

Location filming: 22.05.66, 25.05.66, 26.05.66.
Locations: Bedford Square, Bloomsbury, London, WC1; Conway Street, Fitzrovia,
London, W1; Covent Garden, Strand, London, WC2; Royal Opera House, Bow Street,
Strand, WC2; Ealing Film Studios Backlot, Ealing Green, Ealing, London, W5;
Charlotte Street, Fitzrovia, London W1; Gresse Street, Fitzrovia, London, W1;
Cornwall Gardens/Cornwall Gardens Walk, South Kensington, London, SW7; Berners

Mews, Fitzrovia, London, W1; Maple Street, Fitzrovia, London, W1.
Ealing filming: 23.05.66-25.05.66 on Stage 3A/B
Studio recording: 10.06.66, 17.06.66, 24.06.66, 01.07.66, all in Riverside 1.

ADDITIONAL CREDITED CAST

Major Green (Alan Curtis), Professor Brett (John Harvey), Kitty (Sandra Bryant[1,2]), Flash (Ewan Proctor[1]), Sir Charles Summer (William Mervyn), Professor Krimpton (John Cater), American Journalist (Ric Felgate[1]), Interviewer (John Doye[1]), Worker (Desmond Cullum-Jones[2]), Tramp (Roy Godfrey[2]), Taxi-driver (Michael Rathbone[2]), Machine Operator (Gerald Taylor[2-4]), Worker (Eddie Davis[3]), Captain (John Rolfe[3,4]), Sergeant (John Boyd-Brent[3,4]), Corporal (Frank Jarvis[3]), Soldier (Robin Dawson[3]), Television Newsreader (Kenneth Kendall[4]), The Minister (George Cross[4]), Garage Mechanic (Edward Colliver[4]), Man in telephone box (John Slavid[4]), Radio Announcer (Dwight Whylie[4]), US Correspondent (Carl Conway[4]), The voice of WOTAN (Gerald Taylor[4]) and WOTAN[1-3].

POPULAR MYTHS

- Pat Dunlop contributed to the writing of this story. (Dunlop was the writer originally commissioned to turn Kit Pedler's story idea into script form but had to pull out due to a clash of commitments with another BBC series, *United!*. Ian Stuart Black used none of Dunlop's work when he took over.)

THINGS TO WATCH OUT FOR

- Comedian and actor Mike Reid, perhaps best known for his role in *EastEnders*, makes an early television appearance as an army soldier, waiting beside the electrical trap for the War Machine in Episode 4.
- Special 'computer lettering' is used in the opening title graphics for each episode.
- WOTAN is given its own credit in the closing titles for the first three episodes. This is the only time in the series' history that a fictional creation receives a cast credit.
- Newsreader Kenneth Kendall and radio announcer Dwight Whylie appear as themselves.
- WOTAN refers to the Doctor throughout as 'Doctor Who', the only time that the character is ever given this name in the series' dialogue (although he is credited as such on almost every episode up to and including those of the eighteenth season, adopts the alias 'Doctor von Wer' – a rough German approximation of 'Doctor Who' – in *The Highlanders* and signs himself 'Dr. W' in *The Underwater Menace*).
- Episode 3 has a wonderful cliffhanger: the Doctor stands his ground, haughty and unafraid, as the War Machine advances upon him.

THINGS YOU MIGHT NOT HAVE KNOWN

- Working title: *The Computers*.
- Michael Craze provided the voice of a policeman heard in Episode 4.
- Sir Charles was originally to have been called Sir Robert.
- The taxi in which the Doctor is seen arriving at the Royal Scientific Club in Bedford Square was a genuine London cab hailed by the production crew on location. Its driver, Mr. W. Busell, was paid £2 and signed a form giving the BBC all rights to his contribution.

- John Boddimeade, the driver of a fork lift truck seen in the second episode, and Bill Taylor, the driver of a lorry seen in the third, were BBC scene men who each received a staff contribution fee in payment.
- Comedian and impressionist Mike Yarwood was to have appeared as a walk-on in Episode 3 but left the studio at 1.00 p.m. to go to hospital for an X-ray and did not return.

QUOTE, UNQUOTE

- **The Doctor:** 'You know there's something alien about that tower, I can sense it!' **Dodo:** 'Smells okay to me. Good old London smoke!' **The Doctor:** 'I can feel it … it's got something … sort of powerful … it's … Look at my skin! Look at that! I've got that prickling sensation. The … sensation again … the same … just as I had when I fought the Daleks … those Daleks were near!'
- **WOTAN:** 'Doctor Who is required … bring him here.'

ANALYSIS

The War Machines is in a sense ahead of its time, as its approach and subject matter are very similar to those that would become a regular format for the Earth-based UNIT adventures of the third Doctor's era. As in those later stories, the Doctor is depicted here almost as an establishment figure. Early in the first episode he simply walks into the Post Office Tower and is accepted by everyone. A little later he attends the press launch for WOTAN and, again, no one questions his credentials. He is apparently known to Sir Charles Summer, and seems to have a knack for being in the right place at the right time. This seems hard to reconcile with everything that the viewer has learnt about the Doctor over the previous three years.

The very fact that this is the first *bona fide* 'contemporary England' adventure does, though, make it refreshingly novel. To see the Doctor doing such mundane, down-to-earth things as engaing in phone conversations, as he does in the second episode, is strangely unsettling; and, whether by accident or design (one hopes the latter), the way in which Hartnell plays this action – holding and using the phone in a cuiously awkward manner, as if it is some unfamiliar alien communications device – is quite extraordinary.

The ideas around which the story is based are, once more, very interesting. There are however a few problems with Ian Stuart Black's plotting, such as the unbelievable coincidence of the warehouse where the first War Machine is built being right next door to the Inferno night club that Dodo visits with Polly. Then there is the question of the time period over which the story takes place. During the first day the Doctor arrives, views WOTAN, attends the press conference and visits Sir Charles at his home. Brett has meanwhile been taken over by WOTAN and is apparently the first of its human slaves. That evening Polly and Dodo go to the night club, where Dodo is hypnotised and heads off to receive instructions. She later returns to meet up with the Doctor, and they see a tramp who is shortly afterwards killed. Given that the night club has closed, these events must take place around one or two in the morning. At breakfast time the same day, the Doctor sees the tramp's death reported in a newspaper (very unlikely as most morning papers were printed by ten the previous evening – and in any case, would the death of such an unimportant person really be reported in this way, complete with a photograph?) and Ben heads off to the warehouse where there are numerous boxes of components for the construction of War Machines, as well as a completed Machine and a team of controlled workers. Now that is fast work! There is no way that WOTAN could have arranged for the manufacture, packing and shipping of War Machine components (all in boxes emblazoned with a 'W' logo), as well as the complete construction of a whole Machine in the space of about twelve hours! The only positive point in all this is that, as WOTAN's deadline for world domination is midday, the viewer has no time to dwell on the problem.

WOTAN itself is terribly anachronistic. On the one hand it is voice activated and can speak, but on the other it gives answers to questions on a teleprinter. Obviously no-one had considered television monitors as a means of passing information between human and computer and vice versa. The War Machines, however, are quite impressive, although they seem to prefer knocking over piles of boxes to actually doing anything useful like taking over the world. At the end of the story, when the Doctor reprograms one of the Machines to attack WOTAN, it somehow manages to get up to the top of the Post Office Tower. That building obviously has very large lifts!

When Dodo's conditioning is uncovered, the Doctor swiftly packs her off to the countryside to recover, and this is the last we see of her – surely one of the most ignoble departures of any companion. Jackie Lane's exit is in fact somewhat welcome, as she never managed to make much of an impact as Dodo, although she does at least give a good performance in her final story, particularly in the scenes where she falls under WOTAN's influence. It has to be said that Ben, played by Michael Craze, and Polly, played by Anneke Wills (then the wife of Michael Gough, who had been cast as the Celestial Toymaker earlier in the season), show right from the outset much more promise as companion characters.

Contemporary reaction to the story recorded in the BBC's Audience Research Report on the last episode was distinctly mixed: 'The last episode … held little or no appeal for about half the sample: the whole idea of a computer able to think for itself, and with power over human beings as well as machines, was "preposterous", according to a large number of reporting viewers who evidently considered the denouement of the battle between WOTAN and a reformed War Machine was altogether too absurdly fantastic to accept ("I like science-fiction but this was ridiculous"). Some were particularly disappointed with this adventure as it had made quite a promising start, they said: after the "careful build-up" in previous weeks the ending seemed to them an anticlimax and so rushed that all sense of suspense was lost. A sizeable number compared the War Machines unfavourably with the Daleks ("very poor relations"), and claimed that it was all too clear that new ideas were running out; it was time the programme was rested, they declared, and the only complaint of one small group was that the autumn was too early for its return.'

In fairness, though, the story is not all that bad, and remains quite watchable. Graham Howard, writing in *TSV* 28 dated April 1992, had this to say: 'I believe this story to be vastly underrated. I wouldn't call it a classic – a misused term if ever there was one – and viewed by today's standards it would probably appear rather dated. Nevertheless, in terms of what makes a good *Doctor Who* story, I would claim that *The War Machines* is superior to many other Hartnell stories.'

Due in large part to the transition of producers from Verity Lambert to John Wiles to Innes Lloyd, and the accompanying change of story editors from Donald Tosh to Gerry

Davis, the stories of *Doctor Who*'s third season were amongst the most varied in terms of subject, setting and style of any in the series' history. Unfortunately, particularly toward the end of the season, they also tended to be somewhat varied in terms of quality and degree of appeal to the viewing audience. *The War Machines*, however, saw Lloyd and Davis really starting to make their own mark on the series.

Lloyd had been keen from the outset to update the style of *Doctor Who* – which in his opinion had previously been rather old-fashioned and whimsical – and to make the Doctor's adventures more action-orientated and 'gutsy'. To this end, he and Davis recruited an unofficial scientific adviser to the series in the person of Dr Kit Pedler, whose first real contribution was to provide the basic story idea for *The War Machines*. Lloyd also took this opportunity to change the image of the Doctor's companions. The original intention had been that Dodo should continue as a regular, with a new character called Richard, or Rich for short, brought in to replace Steven, following his departure in *The Savages*. Eventually, however, Lloyd decided that Dodo should also be written out, paving the way for the introduction of a completely new male and female companion team: seaman Ben Jackson and secretary Polly Wright (whose surname was never given on screen) – two up-to-date, 'swinging sixties' characters very much in line with the aim of bringing a greater degree of realism to the series.

The following season would see the production team continuing to mould the series to their preferences – a process that would involve undoubtedly the most momentous change so far …

DOCTOR WHO SEASON FOUR [1966-1967]

Regular Cast:

Dr. Who (William Hartnell) until *The Tenth Planet* Episode 4
Dr. Who (Patrick Troughton) from *The Power of the Daleks* Episode One onwards
Polly (Anneke Wills) until *The Faceless Ones* Episode 6
Ben (Michael Craze) until *The Faceless Ones* Episode 6
Jamie (Frazer Hines) from *The Highlanders* Episode 1 onwards
Victoria (Deborah Watling) from *The Evil of the Daleks* Episode 2 onwards

Regular Crew:

Producer: Innes Lloyd.
Associate Producer: Peter Bryant on *The Faceless Ones* and *The Evil of the Daleks.**
Story Editor: Gerry Davis until *The Evil of the Daleks* Episode 3. Peter Bryant from *The Evil of the Daleks* Episode 4 onwards.
Title Music: Ron Grainer and the BBC Radiophonic Workshop, arranged by Delia Derbyshire.
Special Sounds: Brian Hodgson.

* Peter Bryant was credited as associate producer on only the first three episodes of *The Faceless Ones*; otherwise, his work in that capacity was uncredited.

By the end of 1966, *Doctor Who* was well on its way to becoming a much-loved national institution, although its popularity had declined somewhat since the peak of the second season. The process of change initiated by new producer Innes Lloyd and his story editor Gerry Davis during the latter part of the third season would continue during the fourth, facilitated by a general relaxation of the restrictions placed on the series by their BBC superiors. Thus they encountered no apparent objection to their introduction, in the person of Ben, of a companion with a Cockney accent – a move that only a few months earlier had been vetoed in the case of Dodo – and were able to drop the historical story type, which had originally been seen as an integral part of the series' format. And whereas the then Head of Serials Gerald Savory had overruled John Wiles when he had thought to write out William Hartnell and introduce a new Doctor, his successor Shaun Sutton proved much more willing to go along with this idea …

When the fourth season got under way, however, viewers could scarcely have suspected that in just a few weeks' time *Doctor Who* would have a new lead actor. At this point, the series appeared much the same as ever as Hartnell's Doctor embarked on another adventure in history with his new companions Polly and Ben.

THE SMUGGLERS

Writer: Brian Hayles. **Director:** Julia Smith. **Designer:** Richard Hunt. **Costumes:** Daphne Dare. **Make-Up:** Sonia Markham. **Incidental Music:** none. **Fight Arranger:** Derek Ware. **Film Cameraman:** Jimmy Court. **Film Editor:** Colin Eggleston. **Studio Lighting:** Cyril Wilkins. **Studio Sound:** Leo Sturgess. **Production Assistant:** John Hobbs. **Assistant Floor Manager:** John Hansen, Tony Gilbert, Maggie Saunders.

	First UK TX	Scheduled TX	Actual TX	Duration	Viewers	Chart Pos.
Episode 1	10/09/66	17.50	17.50	24'36"	4.3	96
Episode 2	17/09/66	17.55	17.55	24'27"	4.9	77
Episode 3	24/09/66	17.50	17.50	23'55"	4.2	96
Episode 4	01/10/66	17.50	17.52	23'37"	4.5	109

Plot: The TARDIS arrives on the coast of 17th Century Cornwall – much to the astonishment of Polly and Ben. Pirates led by Captain Samuel Pike and his henchman Cherub are searching for a hidden treasure, while a smuggling ring masterminded by the local Squire is trying to off-load contraband. The Doctor is kidnapped by Pike's men after inadvertently learning, from churchwarden Joseph Longfoot (who is subsequently murdered), a cryptic rhyme that holds the key to the treasure's whereabouts. Although he manages to escape, the Doctor is eventually forced to tell Pike the rhyme's meaning – it refers to names on tombstones in the church crypt – and the treasure is uncovered. At this point, however, the militia arrive, having been summoned by Revenue officer Josiah Blake. A fight ensues in which Pike and many of his men are killed and the rest taken prisoner. The Doctor and his companions meanwhile slip back to the TARDIS.

Episode endings:
1. On board the pirates' ship, the *Black Albatross*, Cherub explains to Captain Pike that the captive Doctor has learned of the treasure's whereabouts but refuses to talk. The Captain turns to the Doctor and, exclaiming 'Well, by thunder you'll talk to me, or my name's not Samuel Pike!', crashes his left arm down on the table top; it ends not in a hand but in a metal spike.
2. Ben leaves Blake struggling to free himself in the crypt and heads for the stairs, determined to find his fellow travellers so that they can escape through the secret passage to the TARDIS. He finds his way blocked by the Squire, accompanied by Cherub and a bound and gagged Polly. The Squire advances on him, pistol raised …
3. In the crypt, inn-keeper Jacob Kewper warns that the Squire will join him on the gallows if he is to be hanged. From the stairs, Cherub throws a knife at Kewper. It strikes him in the middle of the back and he falls to the ground. Polly screams.
4. The Doctor tells Polly and Ben that the TARDIS has now brought them to the coldest place on Earth.

IT WAS MADE WHERE…?

Location filming: 19.06.66-23.06.66.
Locations: Nanjizal Bay, Nanjizal, Cornwall; St Grada Church, Grade, Cornwall; Church

Cove, Cornwall; Farmland between Helston and Wendron, Cornwall; Trethewey Farm, Trethewey, Cornwall; Bonny Mary, Newlyn Harbour, Newlyn, Cornwall; Bosistow Cliffs, Nanjizal, Cornwall.
Studio: 08.07.66, 15.07.66, 22.07.66, 29.07.66, all in Riverside 1.

ADDITIONAL CREDITED CAST

Churchwarden (Terence de Marney[1]), Cherub (George A Cooper), Jacob Kewper (David Blake Kelly[1-3]), Tom (Mike Lucas[1-3]), Squire (Paul Whitsun-Jones), Spaniard (Derek Ware[1,4]), Captain Pike (Michael Godfrey), Jamaica (Elroy Josephs[2,3]), Blake (John Ringham[2-4]), Gaptooth (Jack Bligh[4]).

POPULAR MYTHS

- Pike has a metal hook in place of his right hand. (He has a metal spike in place of his left hand.)
- For the fight between smugglers and Revenue men in episode four, so few stuntmen were used that they had to play multiple roles achieved by means of frantic behind-the-scenes costume changes. (Although Terry Walsh, one of those involved, recalled the scene being shot in this way, in fact the ten stuntmen under the direction of fight arranger Derek Ware, of whose HAVOC organisation they were members, played only one role each.)

THINGS TO WATCH OUT FOR

- The title sequence film is used to represent the space/time vortex as seen on the TARDIS scanner screen in Episode 1, with the story title, writer's credit and episode number captions overlaid in black on the swirling patterns.
- The story makes extensive use of film inserts shot on location in Cornwall. This was the first *Doctor Who* story on which the crew stayed away from London for a time on a location shoot.
- The wording of the rhyme revealing the treasure's location changes from episode to episode – depending on how well the relevant cast members remembered their lines.

THINGS YOU MIGHT NOT HAVE KNOWN

- Michael Craze fell through a trapdoor during the making of this story and sustained a minor injury to his arm.
- Writer Brian Hayles was asked by story editor Gerry Davis to come up with an idea for a historical adventure and decided that the 17th Century would make a good setting. Davis agreed that smuggling would be a suitable theme to explore as this was in line with his desire for the series' historical stories to be based on identifiable, romantic areas of fiction – in this case, Russell Thorndike's Doctor Syn books.

QUOTE, UNQUOTE

- **The Doctor:** [To Ben and Polly.] 'How dare you follow me into the TARDIS! The distractions … I really thought I was going to be alone again.'
- **The Doctor:** 'You are now travelling through time and space.' **Ben:** 'Yes, well, make sure I get back by tea-time!'
- **The Doctor:** [To Polly.] 'You may know where you are, my dear, but not when! I

can foresee oodles of trouble!'

- **Cherub:** [Speaking of the Doctor.] 'He's like a snake, Captain!' **Captain Pike:** 'One more word out of you and I'll slit your gizzard! [To the Doctor.] Now, let us talk together like gentlemen ...'
- **The Doctor:** [To Polly.] 'Superstition is a strange thing, my dear. Sometimes it tells the truth.'

ANALYSIS

It would, of course, be absurd to suggest that because, say, *The Space Museum* was rather dull or *The Chase* was unduly jokey and unbelievable, futuristic stories should have been dropped altogether from *Doctor Who* in favour of the more successful historicals. Yet this is exactly the sort of approach that reviewers often take when discussing the historicals themselves; they point to the perceived inadequacies of, say, *The Romans* and *The Gunfighters* and use this as a basis for arguing that the stories set in Earth's past never worked and were surplus to requirements. This is largely because these reviewers tend to consider the matter very much out of context. Nowadays, *Doctor Who* is generally regarded as being first and foremost a science-fiction series (however dubious that classification might be), and this can make the historicals seem like something of an aberration; an early experiment that proved unsuccessful and was wisely discontinued. In truth, however, they were just as integral and as important a part of the series' original format as were the futuristic stories, and just as successful. To write them all off simply on the basis that one or two were below par would be to make the same mistake that Innes Lloyd did when, in the light of critical comments such as those contained in the Audience Research Report on *The Gunfighters*, he assumed – rather conveniently, given that he himself disliked this type of story – that the historicals were generally unpopular. This overlooks the fact that a number of the futuristic stories – perhaps most notably *The Web Planet* – attracted equally unfavorable feedback, and that while it is undoubtedly true that many viewers expressed a preference for the futuristic stories, many others expressed a preference for the historical ones.

The Smugglers, the last of the Hartnell era historicals, may not be in quite the same league as earlier gems such as *Marco Polo*, *The Crusade* and *The Massacre of St Bartholomew's Eve*, but it is a lively and highly entertaining yarn that gets *Doctor Who*'s fourth season off to a strong start. It also provides the first illustration of Gerry Davis's preferred approach to the historical story type, which was to draw on the settings and subject matter of popular, easily identifiable areas of 'romantic' fiction. In this case, Russell Thondike's Dr Syn novels were apparently the main source of inspiration although, as Tim Robins noted in *Doctor Who – An Adventure in Space and Time* in 1983, a number of other influences were readily discernible: 'Brian Hayles cobbles together *Jim Davis*, *Treasure Island*, *Kidnapped* and *Peter Pan*'s Captain Hook to create a blood and thunder yarn of 17th Century smuggling. Having at one time been a schoolteacher he would have been [well] aware of such literary sources, and indeed *The Smugglers* seems more derived from these and the traditions of Hollywood than historical fact or research. The [guest] cast shamble their way through the adventure with an excess of "oohs" and "ahhs"; but, although stereotyped, their portrayals add a great deal of atmosphere which passes as authenticity. Moreover, *The Smugglers* never becomes a farce or a pantomime, despite such portrayals and despite a great deal of humorous dialogue. Much of the story involves a lot of running around through caves and secret tunnels, with most of the characters being captured and escaping, only to be captured again at various points in the plot. The result [is] harmless fun, and more than just a little diverting.'

One of the story's greatest joys is its wonderful array of colourful characters. Perhaps most notable of these are the misguided smuggler Squire Edwards who, although corrupt, still sees himself as a gentleman and balks at the idea of his pirate allies resorting to murder; the menacing Captain Pike, who also likes to see himself as a gentleman but has no such qualms; and the dashing and determined Revenue man Blake – a strong performance by John Ringham. Much of the interest for the viewer lies in the interaction between these larger-than-life figures and in working out where their true loyalties lie; and, as Robins noted, this is a story in which appearances can often be deceptive: 'The Doctor is mistaken for a real physician; Ben and Polly for murderers; the Revenue man for a smuggler; the Squire, the churchwarden and the inn-keeper are all revealed as smugglers; and Pike mistakes himself for a powerful man able even to defy the curse of Avery's treasure. Cherub is the ultimate deception. His angelic name belies the fact that he is the most bloodthirsty villain of all.'

Another notable aspect of *The Smugglers* is its unusually extensive use of location filming – the result of several days' shooting in Cornwall (the time for which could be found only by virtue of the fact that this was the last story of the series' third production block). This adds considerably to the atmosphere and, along with the very effective sets, costumes and make-up, helps to give the production a relatively high-budget look.

Anneke Wills and Michael Craze continue to impress as new companions Polly and Ben, and are given plenty of good material to work with in Hayles's scripts. William Hartnell is also on top form as the Doctor, effortlessly taking centre stage with his customary dignity, authority and mischievous twinkle in the eye. Certainly he shows little or no signs of the ill health to which many would later attribute his imminent departure from the series – mention of which leads nicely on to …

THE TENTH PLANET

Writer: Kit Pedler, Gerry Davis[3,4]. **Director:** Derek Martinus. **Designer:** Peter Kindred. **Costumes:** Sandra Reid. **Make-Up:** Gillian James. **Incidental Music:** stock. **Film Cameraman:** unknown. **Film Editor:** unknown. **Studio Lighting:** Howard King. **Studio Sound:** Adrian Bishop-Laggett. **Production Assistant:** Edwina Verner. **Assistant Floor Manager:** Jenny McArthur.

	First UK TX	Scheduled TX	Actual TX	Duration	Viewers	Chart Pos.
Episode 1	08/10/66	17.50	17.52	23'08"	5.5	77
Episode 2	15/10/66	17.50	17.50	23'15"	6.4	57
Episode 3	22/10/66	17.50	17.54	23'31"	7.6	46
Episode 4	29/10/66	17.50	17.51	24'02"	7.5	48

Plot: The TARDIS arrives in December 1986 at a South Pole Space Tracking station where the personnel, under the command of General Cutler, are engaged in trying to talk down a manned space capsule that has got into difficulty. The Doctor realises that the problem stems from the gravitational pull of another planet that has entered the solar system and is now heading for Earth. His words are borne out when the base is invaded by a force of alien Cybermen. The Cybermen's world, Mondas, is draining energy from Earth – once its 'twin planet' – and the situation will soon become critical. The Cybermen propose to take the humans back to Mondas for conversion into further members of their race. The humans fight back – although sabotage by Ben prevents Cutler from taking the highly dangerous step of launching a powerful Z-bomb – and Mondas eventually disintegrates due to absorbing too much energy. All the remaining Cybermen collapse and die, having been totally dependent on their planet. The Doctor has become weak during the ordeal, and hurries back to the TARDIS ...

Episode endings:
1. The Snowcap base Sergeant and one of his men, Tito, examine the TARDIS and decide to use cutting equipment to try to get inside. Tito returns to the base to fetch this. The Sergeant is meanwhile confronted by strange figures that approach across the snow. Impervious to bullets, they club him to the ground. When Tito and Joe return with the equipment, they too are attacked by the alien beings and knocked down. One of the aliens turns Tito's body over to check that he is dead.
2. Cutler is engrossed in trying to rescue a second space capsule, this one piloted by his son, which has been sent up to try to help the first. Suddenly the radar operator reports that there are hundreds of Cyberman spaceships approaching in formation.
3. The countdown to the launch of the Z-bomb proceeds. Ben, who was caught trying to sabotage it by Cutler and knocked unconscious, is unable to remember whether or not he succeeded. The countdown reaches zero and the missile's rockets fire.
4. The Doctor returns to the TARDIS, closely followed by Ben and Polly. The ship's controls move of their own accord and the Doctor collapses to the floor. His companions enter and, before their astonished eyes, the Doctor's face transforms into that of a younger man.

IT WAS MADE WHERE...?

Ealing filming: 30.08.66-02.09.66 on Stage 3A/B
Studio recording: 17.09.66, 24.09.66, 01.10.66, 08.10.66, all in Riverside 1.

ADDITIONAL CREDITED CAST

General Cutler (Robert Beatty), Dyson (Dudley Jones), Barclay (David Dodimead), Schultz (Alan White[1,2]), Williams (Earl Cameron[1,2]), Tito (Shane Shelton[1]), American Sergeant (John Brandon[1]), Wigner (Steve Plytas), Radar Technician (Christopher Matthews), Krail (Reg Whitehead[2]), Talon (Harry Brooks[2]), Shav (Gregg Palmer[2]), Geneva Technician (Ellen Cullen[2-4]), T.V. Announcer (Glenn Beck[2]), Cyberman Voices (Roy Skelton[2,4], Peter Hawkins[4]), R/T Technician (Christopher Dunham[3,4]), Terry Cutler (Callen Angelo[3,4]), Krang (Harry Brooks[4]), Jarl (Reg Whitehead[4]), Gern (Gregg Palmer[4]).

Note: Although uncredited, the new Doctor, played by Patrick Troughton, is seen at the conclusion of Episode 4.

POPULAR MYTHS

- Pat Dunlop contributed to the writing of this story. (He had no involvement with it whatsoever.)
- Mondas's draining of Earth's energy is an attack by the Cybermen. (It is a natural process; the Cybermen aim to end it by destroying the Earth, realising that if it is allowed to continue unchecked it will eventually lead to the disintegration of Mondas – as is borne out at the story's conclusion.)
- An attempt was once made to colourise parts of this story. (This was an April Fool's joke in *Doctor Who Magazine*.)
- The master copy of the fourth episode of this story was lost in 1973 after being lent out to the BBC's children's magazine programme *Blue Peter* for use in a feature that they were compiling about the series. (It is unknown how this episode came to be lost; the episode that was lost after being lent out to *Blue Peter* was actually *The Daleks' Master Plan: The Traitors*.)

THINGS TO WATCH OUT FOR

- The first episode's writer's credit is to 'Kitt Pedler', and the third episode's to Pedler and 'Gerry Davies'.
- The Cybermen's helmets are held together with clear sticky tape in Episode 2.
- The Doctor does not appear in Episode 3 as William Hartnell was unwell during the week when it was recorded.
- Special 'computer tape'-style opening and closing title graphics were created for this story by graphic designer Bernard Lodge.

THINGS YOU MIGHT NOT HAVE KNOWN

- Michael Craze met his future wife, production assistant Edwina Verner, on this story; she threw some of the polystyrene 'snow' into his face as a practical joke, inadvertently aggravating an injury he had recently sustained to his nose.
- The master videotape of Episode 4 was lent to the production office of *Junior Points of View* after transmission as they wished to use extracts from it on their programme on 4 November 1966.
- Bernard Hepton was at one point considered for a role in this story.
- Seven Cyberman costumes were made for this story. The guns, chest units and head gear were supplied by Shawcraft to costume supervisor Sandra Reid's specifications.

QUOTE, UNQUOTE

- **Krail:** 'You must come and live with us.' **Polly:** 'But we cannot live with you! You're different. You've got no feelings.' **Krail:** 'Feelings? I do not understand that word.' **The Doctor:** 'Emotions. Love. Pride. Hate. Fear. Have you no emotions, sir?' **Krail:** 'Come to Mondas and you will have no need of emotions. You will become like us.'
- **Polly:** 'What's happened to you Doctor?' **The Doctor:** 'Oh, I'm not sure my dear. Comes from an outside influence. Unless this old body of mine is wearing a bit thin.'
- **The Doctor:** 'What did you say, my boy? It's all over? That's what you said … but it isn't at all. It's far from being all over …'

The Tenth Planet marks the end of an era. It features William Hartnell's final regular appearance as the Doctor and provides an early indication of the type of story that would come to typify Patrick Troughton's time in the series. 'This is what makes *The Tenth Planet* important – it's a nebulous picture of things to come,' wrote Mark Clapham in *Matrix* Issue 53 dated autumn 1996. 'It's a prototype Troughton monster tale, one restrained by the nature of the series at the time. Trapped between two eras, it shows neither the innocence of an early Hartnell, nor the full-blooded good versus evil conflict of the best Troughton stories.'

The format can be summarised as follows: take an isolated community (in this case the Snowcap base) under the command of a misguided authority figure (Cutler), add a monstrous menace (the Cybermen), kill off some of the community and allow the Doctor to find a solution before the end. This relatively simple approach would lead during the Troughton era to some of the best and most memorable *Doctor Who* stories ever, and *The Tenth Planet* was the first of its kind.

The story opens with – unusually for the series' early years, although it would become the norm later on – a scene not featuring the Doctor and his companions but establishing the situation into which they are to arrive. This is the Snowcap base with its multinational team of men led by the redoubtable General Cutler – a fine performance by Robert Beatty, bringing the character to life as a man who can galvanise all the others on the base. 'Kit Pedler gives us a hopeful view of the future ... (despite the story being set in 1986),' noted Joe Bishop in *Capitol Spires* Issue 2 dated July 1993. 'The diversity of [races and creeds amongst the human characters] highlights the sense of international cooperation, where the world is a better place if we all work together ... The variation in clothes, roles (military and civilians working together) and accents contrasts totally with the homogeneity of the Cybermen, [who] all look alike and sound alike and are probably capable of the same tasks and would [probably] do them in exactly the same way – regimentation gone mad.'

We have to wait until the end of the first episode before the Cybermen are revealed – as usual where a story's 'monster' is concerned – and they present a terrifying image for the cliffhanger. The pale, expressionless and noseless face of one of the creatures hanging over the prone form of a dead soldier must have given many a young viewer nightmares for the week ahead. Once they have been established, the Cybermen dominate the story, despite the fact that they make a significant appearance in only two of the four episodes, and even then, not for long. The combination of their massive frames, towering over the rest of the cast, and their strange, harmonic, sing-song voices emerging from mouths that are simply held open, is extremely unnerving. They seem powerful and unstoppable.

The Cybermen's reliance on logic is key to their characters, as Bishop explained: 'They are tragic creatures because they have lost their humanity ... There is no evil intent in their actions; they are just trying to ensure the survival of their race in the only logical way open to them. They do not consider trying to cooperate with mankind to their mutual advantage. The energy drain from Earth will eventually destroy Mondas, therefore Earth must be destroyed before that can happen. [However] there is no logic in letting [mankind] be destroyed along with [its] planet; the Cybermen [see it] as a resource to be utilised. The humans will be taken to Mondas to be made into Cybermen ...'

The contrast between humans and Cybermen effectively enables writer Kit Pedler to raise questions about the nature of humanity, as Clapham observed: 'Although it is doubtful that Cutler could have reached the rank of general while being the sort of man who gives priority to rescuing his son over minor concerns such as saving the Earth, there is a point being made. While the other characters act against their own interest by fighting the Cybermen, Cutler adopts his enemies' mode of thinking. Cutler's primary interest is the survival of his son, at the expense of all else. Like the Cybermen, who admit to being "only interested in survival", Cutler wishes above all else to preserve his line, for the Cutlers to survive even if he does not. This theme of self-interest being the root of dehumanisation is far more subtle primarily because a desire to protect one's own children is usually seen as admirable. When Cutler puts the life of his son before the interest of the rest of humanity, he shows us a harsh truth – when we help those close to us, those who enrich our lives, we may in fact not be acting out of kindness but from a veiled selfish instinct.'

Cutler aside, the Snowcap personnel are a rather sorry bunch of one-dimensional characters. Most of the work of repelling the Cybermen is thus left to the General and to the Doctor's party. An exception to this comes in the very good scene where the invaders are picked off outside the base with a battery of their dead comrades' weapons fired by some of Cutler's men hidden in the snow. A superb idea. It does, though, raise the question of how the second wave of Cybermen manage to get into the base in the fourth episode. It would appear that this defensive strategy has for some reason been abandoned; or perhaps the Cybermen have simply overwhelmed Cutler's men with the speed of their attack, as – rather implausibly – they are seen to storm the base less than a minute after their spaceships land.

Fortunately the viewer has no opportunity to linger on unexplained plot points such as these as the action comes thick and fast, alternating between Cutler trying to ensure that his son is safe up in space and the Cybermen trying to attack the base. The final episode all but hurtles toward a climax, with the Doctor and Polly facing an unknown fate on board a Cyberman ship, Ben and the Snowcap scientist Barclay trying to figure out how to use radiation against the invaders, and Mondas posing a constant threat to the Earth. To cap everything, at the end of the story, the Doctor starts behaving very strangely indeed. Is he sick? Have the Cybermen done something to him? No clear answers are forthcoming as he rushes back to the TARDIS. The final shock in this highly dramatic and enjoyable story comes when, after he falls to the TARDIS floor, his features shimmer and change …

Doctor Who would never be quite the same again.

THE CREATION OF THE CYBERMEN

The Cybermen were devised by *Doctor Who*'s unofficial scientific adviser Kit Pedler in collaboration with story editor Gerry Davis as a potential replacement for the Daleks. Pedler's initial idea had been for a group of Star Monks inhabiting a world that appears to be Earth's 'twin', but this had been modified in discussions with Davis to incorporate, in place of the Star Monks, a new threat personifying one of Pedler's own phobias – that of dehumanising medicine. Pedler foresaw a time when spare part surgery – the replacement of limbs and organs – would become as commonplace as changing a shirt, and that eventually people might have so many prosthetic parts that they would become uncertain whether they were human or machine. He was also interested with the differences and similarities between the human brain and advanced computers, and with the science of cybernetics – a term coined by mathematician Norbert Weiner in 1948 for the study of self-regulating systems (and not, as is commonly believed, for the development of animal-machine hybrids). Pedler and Davis reasoned that people whose brains had been cybernetically enhanced would lose the capacity for emotion and act totally logically, like robots. Thus was born the concept of the Cybermen.

In the scripts for *The Tenth Planet*, the Cybermen were described as 'tall, slim, with one-piece, close-fitting silver mesh uniforms,' with normal faces and heads but 'a shining metal plate stretching from centre hair-line to occiput' under their hair. On the front of their trunks they were to have 'a mechanical computer-like unit consisting of switches, two rows of lights and a short, moveable proboscis'. The were to carry 'exotic side arms' and at their shoulders they were to have 'small, ram-like cylinders acting over the joints'. Instead of flesh was to be 'a transparent, "arm-shaped" forearm covering containing shining rods and lights, but [with] a normal hand at the end of it.' Costume designer Sandra Reid, following discussions with Pedler and with scenic designer Peter Kindred and director Derek Martinus, created costumes based on her interpretation of the writers' ideas. Certain aspects – such as the moveable proboscis – were dropped for cost reasons. It was also decided that the best way to realise the Cybermen's faces was to have them wearing grey jersey masks. Holes were cut in the material for the eyes and mouth, and silver make-up applied to disguise the actor's own features underneath. The hands were, however, left bare, as suggested in the original description.

The Cybermen proved an instant hit with viewers, and would go on to become second only to the Daleks in popularity amongst *Doctor Who*'s many monster races.

The Second Doctor (Patrick Troughton) 1966-1969

PATRICK TROUGHTON IS THE SECOND DOCTOR

'I loved playing the part!' exclaimed Patrick Troughton in a 1984 interview about his time as the second Doctor. 'Playing one part for three years – I'd never done that in my life, you see. I'd gone from one character part to another, playing wildly different things … and just to come to one part for three years which was happy, and people liked, was an absolute joy. It was wonderful!'

Born in 1920, Troughton had spent his early life in North London. In his teens he had trained at the Embassy School of Acting in Swiss Cottage, from where he had won a scholarship to the John Drew Memorial Theatre on Long Island in New York, USA. Returning to Britain on the outbreak of the Second World War, he had acted in the Tonbridge Repertory Company for a year. Then he had joined the Royal Navy, rising through the ranks to become captain of a motor gun boat on duty in the North Sea. After demob in 1945 he had resumed his theatrical career, working with the Amersham Repertory Company, the Bristol Old Vic Company and the Pilgrim Players at the Mercury Theatre in Nottingham. He had first broken into television – always to remain his favourite medium – in 1947, and into films a year later. Specialising in character parts, often submerged beneath elaborate costume and make-up, he had found himself in great demand from directors throughout the fifties and early sixties.

It was while he was on location in Ireland for a Hammer Films production entitled *The Viking Queen* that he was approached by the BBC and invited to take over the starring role in *Doctor Who*. He eventually accepted, overcoming some initial reluctance, mainly because he realised that the regular income would help to pay for his sons' education.

Troughton's Doctor, instantly recognisable in his disreputable old frock coat and baggy checked trousers, was impish and mischievous. He was like Merlin, the Pied Piper and Charlie Chaplin all rolled into one, and yet something quite unique too. The viewer felt reassured in his presence, yet thrilled and excited at the same time. Throughout his three years in the role, the actor gave a consistently superb performance, endearing himself to adults and children alike. He had demonstrated that the series could survive a change of lead actor – by no means a foregone conclusion, given how popular and well-established William Hartnell had been – and would prove a hard act for his successors to follow.

THE POWER OF THE DALEKS

Writer: David Whitaker*. **Director:** Christopher Barry. **Designer:** Derek Dodd. **Costumes:** Sandra Reid. **Make-up:** Gillian James. **Incidental Music:** Tristram Cary (from stock). **Film Cameraman:** Peter Sargent. **Film Editor:** Jim Latham. **Studio Lighting:** Graham Sothcott. **Studio Sound:** Buster Cole. **Production Assistant:** Michael Briant. **Assistant Floor Manager:** Marjorie Yorke. **Daleks Created By:** Terry Nation**.

*The final version of the scripts was written by Dennis Spooner, who received no credit.
** Terry Nation received this credit as joint owner with the BBC of the rights to the Daleks.

	First UK TX	Scheduled TX	Actual TX	Duration	Viewers	Chart Pos.
Episode One	05/11/66	17.50	17.50	25'43"	7.9	44
Episode Two	12/11/66	17.50	17.49	24'29"	7.8	50
Episode Three	19/11/66	17.50	17.52	23'31"	7.5	52
Episode Four	26/11/66	17.50	17.50	24'23"	7.8	50
Episode Five	03/12/66	17.50	17.52	23'38"	8.0	48
Episode Six	10/12/66	17.50	17.52	23'46"	7.8	37

Plot: The TARDIS brings the new Doctor, Polly and Ben to the Earth colony planet Vulcan. The Doctor witnesses a murder and, investigating the body, discovers a pass badge allowing him unrestricted access to the colony. The dead man was an Earth Examiner who had been secretly summoned by Deputy Governor Quinn to investigate the activities of a group of rebels – a problem regarded as insignificant by Governor Hensell. A scientist, Lesterson, has meanwhile discovered a crashed space capsule containing inert Daleks, which he is now in the process of reactivating. The Doctor's warnings are ignored when the Daleks claim to be the colonists' servants. As the rebels grow in strength, their operations covertly led by Head of Security Bragen, the Daleks take advantage of the colonists' naive trust to establish a reproduction plant – on a conveyor belt system – with which to increase their numbers. The Doctor eventually destroys the Daleks by turning the colony's power source against them. The defeat of the Daleks, to whom Bragen and the rebels had allied themselves, gives Quinn an opportunity to re-establish control, Hensell having previously been killed. The Doctor and his friends slip back to the TARDIS.

Episode endings:
1. The Doctor, Ben and Polly have found two seemingly dormant Daleks inside the crashed capsule. Examining the floor, the Doctor realises that there was once a third. He fails to notice as a tentacled creature begins to emerge from a hole at the base of the wall behind him …
2. To the astonishment of the Doctor and the colonists, the reactivated Dalek grates 'I am your servant!'. The Doctor tries to warn that the Daleks destroy human beings without mercy or conscience, but his voice is almost drowned out by the Dalek loudly repeating its phrase.
3. The three reactivated Daleks chant 'We will get our power!' as Lesterson looks on with growing concern …
4. As a horrified Lesterson looks on, a line of newly created Daleks roll off the conveyor belt on their ship …
5. The Daleks stream out of their capsule chanting 'Daleks conquer and destroy! Daleks conquer and destroy!'
6. The TARDIS dematerialises from Vulcan. The lingering notes of a tune on the Doctor's recorder are heard as the eye-stalk of one of the apparently destroyed Daleks slowly rises up as if to watch the ship depart.

IT WAS MADE WHERE…?

Ealing Filming: 26.09.66-30.09.66 on Stage 2
Studio Recording: 22.10.66, 29.10.66, 05.11.66, 12.11.66, 19.11.66, 26.11.66, all in Riverside 1

ADDITIONAL CREDITED CAST

The Examiner (Martin King[1]), Quinn (Nicholas Hawtrey), Bragen (Bernard Archard), Lesterson (Robert James), Janley (Pamela Ann Davy), Hensell (Peter Bathurst[1-5]), Resno (Edward Kelsey[2]), Valmar (Richard Kane[3-6]), Daleks (Gerald Taylor[3-6], Kevin Manser[3-5], Robert Jewell[3-6], John Scott Martin[4-6])*, Dalek Voices (Peter Hawkins[3-6])*, Guards (Peter Forbes-Robertson[4-6], Robert Russell[5,6], Robert Luckham[5]), Kebble (Steven Scott[4-6]).

* The Dalek in Episode Two was played by Gerald Taylor and voiced by Peter Hawkins, but neither was credited.

POPULAR MYTHS

- *Doctor Who*'s planet Vulcan predated *Star Trek*'s. (*Star Trek* made its on-air debut in the US on 8 September 1966, predating transmission of *The Power of the Daleks* by almost two months; and although Spock's home planet was referred to initially as 'Vulcanis' it became 'Vulcan' just a few episodes later.)
- David Whitaker's scripts included a lengthy scene involving the TARDIS food machine, which Dennis Spooner removed when he rewrote them. (Although Dennis Spooner made this claim in a number of later interviews, there was in fact no such scene in Whitaker's scripts; Spooner appears to have been misremembering a lengthy scene involving a diagnostic machine in the colony's medical centre, which he did indeed remove in rewriting.)
- The Tristram Cary incidental music used in this story was taken entirely from the first Dalek story, *The Mutants*. (Some of it was taken from season three's *The Daleks' Master Plan*.)

THINGS TO WATCH OUT FOR

- The Doctor's clothes transform along with his appearance.
- This story affords the first clear sight in the series' history of fully-evolved Dalek creatures; tentacled blobs placed into the casings of the new Daleks created in their capsule. (Those seen in *The Daleks' Master Plan* were implied to have been regressed to a primordial form by the time destructor.)
- Polly is absent from Episode Four and Ben from Episode Five as Anneke Wills and Michael Craze were on holiday during the respective weeks in which they were recorded.

THINGS YOU MIGHT NOT HAVE KNOWN

- Working title: *The Destiny of Doctor Who*. The rehearsal scripts for Episodes 3 and 4 bear sub-titles of *Servants of Masters* and *The Destiny of Doctor Who*.
- Patrick Troughton made an appearance in Verity Lambert's *Adam Adamant Lives!* in the guest role of General Mongerson immediately before beginning work on *The Power of the Daleks*.
- A still photograph of William Hartnell was used in a scene when the newly regenerated Doctor sees his 'old' face in a hand mirror.
- No date was given for the story in the scripts, but contemporary BBC documents specify it as 2020 AD.

QUOTE, UNQUOTE

- **Ben:** [Picking up the old Doctor's ring.] 'The Doctor always wore this. If you are him it should fit. [He tries the ring on the Doctor's finger, but it is too big.] That settles it.' **The Doctor:** 'I'd like to see a butterfly fit into a chrysalis case after it spreads its wings.' **Polly:** 'Then you *did* change.' **The Doctor:** 'Life depends on change, and renewal.' **Ben:** 'Oh, *that's* it, you've been renewed, have you?' **The Doctor:** 'Renewed? Have I? That's it, I've been renewed. It's part of the TARDIS. Without it I couldn't survive.'

- **The Doctor:** [Rummaging through a trunk.] 'The Doctor was a great collector, wasn't he?' **Polly:** 'But *you're* the Doctor!' **The Doctor:** 'Oh, I don't look like him.' **Ben:** 'Who are *we*?' **The Doctor:** 'Don't you know?'

- **The Doctor:** [Speaking of the reactivated Dalek.] 'It knew who I am, Ben.' **Ben:** 'Well, if a Dalek takes you for the proper Doctor, then I suppose I can.' **Lesterson:** [To the other colonists present.] 'This creation is called, I understand, a Dalek. Look at it. I have simply given it electrical power, and do you know what? It is capable of storing it! Furthermore, it responds to orders. [To the Dalek.] Turn around. Move that chair. Stop. [The Dalek obeys each command.] You see! Imagine what it is going to do to our mining programme; to our processing; our packaging. Dozens of labour jobs, Governor. It may even be the answer to this colony's problems.' **The Doctor:** 'Yes, it will end the colony's problems – because it will end the colony!'

ANALYSIS

The transition from William Hartnell to Patrick Troughton received remarkably little coverage in the popular press (certainly by comparison with that accorded to the later changes of Doctor). The only significant report appeared in the *Daily Sketch* on the day that the first episode of the *The Power of the Daleks* was transmitted:

'If you believe the programme overlords, most viewers have a compelling urge ... to be frightened out of their wits. And that explains the strange affair of The Changing Face of Doctor Who.

'The time travelling Doctor is back as usual on BBC1 this afternoon – and advance reports say that his return will be an explosive event to woo the kids away from Guy Fawkes bonfires.

'But something is very much out of the ordinary – instead of being played by William Hartnell, the Doctor is spooky character actor Patrick Troughton.

'When veteran Bill Hartnell decided to drop out it could have meant the end for Doctor Who.

'Scriptwriters have been turning mental somersaults to explain why a new hero is appearing, without warning, to young fans. Full details of his debut are being kept a secret, until today ...'

As it turned out, viewers' opinions of the new Doctor were sharply divided, as is apparent from two letters that appeared in the 24 November edition of *Radio Times*. The first, from G Howard of Leeds, read:

'I would like to send my heartiest congratulations to the production team of BBC1's *Doctor Who*.

'Patrick Troughton and the superb character he has created have dragged the programme out of the unfortunate mess it had degenerated into. Given sensible scripts the programme could possibly emerge as one of the real successes of television science-fiction.

'I look forward to the time when *Doctor Who* is performed for adults only.'

Mrs Estelle Hawken of Wadebridge in Cornwall, on the other hand, was distinctly unimpressed:

'What have you done to BBC1's *Doctor Who*? Of all the stupid nonsense! Why turn a wonderful series into what looked like Coco the Clown?

'I think you will find thousands of children will not now be watching *Doctor Who*, which up to now has been the tops.'

This unenthusiastic reaction was largely echoed in viewers' comments recorded in the BBC's Audience Research Report on the third episode of the story. 'Once a brilliant but eccentric scientist, he now comes over as a half-witted clown,' complained a teacher. 'The family have really "gone off" *Doctor Who* since the change,' noted another viewer. 'They do not understand the new one at all, and his character is peculiar in an unappealing way.' The report contained much criticism, too, of Troughton's performance – although one person conceded that he 'seemed to be struggling manfully with the idiotic new character that Doctor Who has taken on since his change'. Typical opinions were that he was overacting, 'playing for laughs' and making the Doctor into 'something of a pantomime character'. 'I'm not sure that I really like his portrayal,' was one verdict. 'I feel the part is over-exaggerated – whimsical even – I keep expecting him to take a great watch out of his pocket and mutter about being late like Alice's White Rabbit'. A number frankly stated that they had preferred William Hartnell in the role. There was however a recognition from a minority that Troughton had yet to settle down and that there was still time for him to become 'fully acceptable'. Perhaps the most positive comment came from a student, who said that 'Patrick Troughton, a brilliant actor, had improved the programme greatly'.

In retrospect it can be seen that Troughton makes quite a good debut as the Doctor. His less than rapturous reception at the time is probably accounted for mainly by the fact that his somewhat outlandish initial characterisation takes a bit of getting used to after William Hartnell's more serious interpretation. This difference in approach was elaborated on by Anthony Clark in *DWB* No. 117 dated September 1993: 'What is most remarkable about this story is just how little Patrick Troughton does. Okay, so he's on screen for quite a lot of the time, but right up until the end he does little more than half allude to his suspicions whilst getting in the way. In fact, this early manifestation of the hands-off approach established itself as one of the new Doctor's main characteristics, at least up until the departure of the Davis/Lloyd axis.'

If the Audience Research Report is anything to go by, it seems that doubts about the new Doctor may have coloured contemporary viewers' opinons of the story as a whole. 'Viewers in the sample who were enthusiastic about this episode …' noted the Report's compiler, 'were confined to a minority, less than a quarter … finding it appealing to an appreciable degree'. Amongst this enthusiastic minority, it seemed that the Daleks were the main attraction. 'This is supposed to be for the "kids",' commented a 'senior clerk', 'but I must confess that I found the programme quite gripping. As an ardent sci-fiction fan I think the Daleks are the most sinister "aliens" I've come across'. More often, though, 'viewers in the sample reported a very moderate degree of enjoyment, and a number were scarcely interested at all'. For some, even the Daleks had lost their appeal. 'They have made their impact, served their usefulness,' commented one malcontent, 'now they just seem hackneyed and more unreal than usual'.

With the benefit of hindsight these comments can again be seen as being far too harsh. The enclosed, claustrophobic nature of the story's setting and the relatively small scale of the threat posed by the Daleks – the destruction of a single human colony – present a marked and very effective contrast to the epic nature of the previous Dalek story, *The Daleks' Master Plan*, which ended its on-air run earlier the same year. The plotting and dialogue are excellent and the guest characters all very believable and compelling. Of particular note in this regard are the crazed Lesterson, brilliantly portrayed by Robert James, and the Daleks themselves, who as scripted by David Whitaker seem far more cunning and evil than in many of their previous appearances as scripted by their creator Terry Nation. There are also some highly memorable set-pieces including, as Clark recalled, the famous 'Dalek production line' sequence: 'Partly because it was a real spectacle, and partly because we the viewers got to see just how much trouble was in store for the colonists and Doctor, this vision of "breeding" Daleks is probably the fulcrum of *The Power of the Daleks*. To be able to breed an army to order is chilling enough, but to have that reproduction taking place in the midst of a human colony with the aid of its power, really heightens the catastrophic ambience that permeates the whole story. Quite simply, this single sequence represents just how threatening the Daleks can be when handled properly.'

All things considered, *The Power of the Daleks* gets the second Doctor's era off to a great start.

THE HIGHLANDERS

Writer: Elwyn Jones*, Gerry Davis. **Director:** Hugh David. **Designer:** Geoffrey Kirkland. **Costumes:** Sandra Reid. **Make-Up:** Gillian James. **Incidental Music:** stock. **Fight Arranger:** Peter Diamond. **Film Cameraman:** unknown. **Film Editor:** unknown. **Studio Lighting:** Gordon Summers, Ken McGregor. **Studio Sound:** Larry Goodson. **Production Assistant:** Fiona Cumming. **Assistant Floor Manager:** Nicholas John.

*Although commissioned to write this story, Elwyn Jones in fact carried out no work on it. The scripts were written by story editor Gerry Davis, by virtue of which he was given a co-writer's credit on the transmitted episodes.

	First UK TX	Scheduled TX	Actual TX	Duration	Viewers	Chart Pos.
Episode 1	17/12/66	17.50	17.49	24'38"	6.7	67
Episode 2	24/12/66	17.50	17.50	23'41"	6.8	89
Episode 3	31/12/66	17.50	17.52	22'54"	7.4	68
Episode 4	07/01/67	17.50	17.50	24'19"	7.3	66

Plot: The time travellers arrive in Scotland in the aftermath of the battle of Culloden. The Doctor gains the trust of a small band of fleeing Highlanders by offering to tend their wounded Laird, Colin McLaren; but while Polly and the Laird's daughter, Kirsty, are away fetching water, he and the others are all captured by Redcoat troops under the command of Lieutenant Algernon ffinch. Grey, a crooked solicitor who sells prisoners for transportation to slavery in the West Indies, then secures the group into his custody. Polly and Kirsty blackmail ffinch into helping, and the Doctor eventually wins the day by smuggling arms to the Highlanders, who are being held on board a stolen ship, the *Annabelle*. Grey and the ship's unscrupulous captain, Trask, are overpowered and the vessel returned to its rightful owner, MacKay, who agrees to take the Scots to safety in France. The Doctor, Polly and Ben return to the TARDIS, where they are joined on their travels by the young piper Jamie McCrimmon.

Episode endings:
1. Leaving Kirsty hiding in a cave, Polly heads off to try to rescue her friends. Unable to see in the dark, she falls into a covered pit. She tries to climb out, but a hand clutching a knife reaches down to her. Polly screams.
2. Jamie, Ben and the Highlander prisoners are being taken out to the *Annabelle* in a rowing boat by Trask. Trask warns them that the only way off the ship is straight down to the bottom of the sea – a point graphically illustrated as a prisoner is pushed over the side and bubbles are seen rising from the depths.
3. Ben has been captured and tied up for daring to cross Grey. Sentenced to be dropped from the yard arm, he is lifted from the deck and swung out over the side of the *Annabelle*. He is dropped into the sea, hauled out, and then dropped again. Trask smiles as bubbles rise to the surface ...
4. The Doctor, Ben and Polly enter the TARDIS, accompanied by Jamie. The TARDIS dematerialises.

IT WAS MADE WHERE...?

Location Filming: 14.11.66-15.11.66, 21.11.66
Location: Frensham Ponds, Surrey.
Ealing Filming: 16.11.66 on Stage 3A/B
Studio Recording: 03.12.66, 10.12.66, 17.12.66, 24.12.66, all in Riverside 1

ADDITIONAL CREDITED CAST

Alexander (William Dysart[1]), The Laird (Donald Bisset), Kirsty (Hannah Gordon), Lt. Algernon ffinch (Michael Elwyn), Sergeant (Peter Welch), Solicitor Grey (David Garth), Perkins (Sydney Arnold), Sentry (Tom Bowman[2]), Trask (Dallas Cavell[2-4]), Mollie (Barbara Bruce[2]), Willie Mackay (Andrew Downie[3,4]), Sailor (Peter Diamond[4]), Colonel Attwood (Guy Middleton[4]).

POPULAR MYTHS

- It was decided to keep Jamie on as a companion due to positive audience reaction. (Gerry Davis and Innes Lloyd were initially uncertain how Jamie would work as an ongoing character and so Frazer Hines' initial contract for the part allowed provision for three further options to be taken up on a further three four-part stories. Hines' contract was signed on 2 November 1966 and location filming for *The Highlanders* took place from 14 November. On 21 November an extra piece of location filming was scheduled, believed to be a revised final scene in which Jamie enters the TARDIS – Hines' performance during the location filming having convinced Lloyd and Davis that the character had the potential to become a regular. Location filming for *The*

Underwater Menace, which also featured Jamie, took place on 13 December, three days before the first episode of *The Highlanders* was transmitted.)

THINGS TO WATCH OUT FOR

- Well known actors Hannah Gordon and Donald Bisset play Kirsty and the Laird respectively.
- The Doctor uses an array of disguises: German doctor, aged washer woman and Redcoat.

THINGS YOU MIGHT NOT HAVE KNOWN

- Working title: *Culloden*.
- This story was commissioned from Elwyn Jones, a distinguished writer who had recently returned to a freelance career after a spell as the BBC's Head of Series. He had been introduced to story editor Gerry Davis by Head of Serials Shaun Sutton, and on learning that Jones had no particular ideas for a story, Davis (in accordance with his preference for the series' historicals to draw on popular areas of fiction, in this case stories in the style of Robert Louis Stevenson's *Kidnapped*) had suggested that something about Culloden might be suitable. When he later checked to see how the scripts were progressing, though, he discovered that Jones had been too busy even to start them. He consequently had to write the story himself. As this was an emergency, he was allowed an on-screen credit for his work, although Jones was also credited as co-writer.
- *The Highlanders* was originally scheduled to be made and transmitted after *The Underwater Menace* but the two stories were switched in the running order after director Hugh David protested that the budget available for the latter was insufficient to meet the demands of its scripts.

QUOTE, UNQUOTE

- **The Doctor:** 'Down with King George!' **Jamie:** 'So you are for the Prince after all.' **The Doctor:** 'No, I just like hearing the echo!'

ANALYSIS

Like the previous season's *The Gunfighters*, *The Highlanders* is a curious mixture of the dramatic and the comedic. It is also the second – and last – of the historical stories conforming to Gerry Davis's idea of drawing inspiration from popular areas of 'romantic' fiction, the main source on this occasion being Robert Louis Stevenson's *Kidnapped* (although John Prebble's *Culloden* may also have been influential).

It is arguably Polly and Ben who are the focal characters of the story, as the Doctor plays little part in the main action. Polly strikes out on her own, joins forces with Kirsty and manages to embarrass Lieutenant ffinch into helping them to achieve their objectives. Ben is similarly active, finding himself kidnapped and taken on board a slave ship, escaping by the use of one of Harry Houdini's tricks and managing to swim ashore. While all this is going on, the Doctor is simply messing about, confusing everyone he meets with an array of accents and disguises. This makes for some highly amusing scenes; in particular the one where he so befuddles Solicitor Grey's servant, Perkins, that the man ends up having a nap on the table while Grey himself is trussed up and bundled into a cupboard behind him!

This new image of the Doctor as a clown has its fullest expression here. Almost every scene featuring the Doctor has him either speaking in a false accent or pretending to be someone else. This is taken to ridiculous extremes when Ben, having escaped from the *Annabelle*, hauls himself up onto the quayside only to be confronted by a patrolling Redcoat. 'Oh no!' thinks the viewer – but it is only the Doctor in yet another disguise. This new characterisation does have its merits, however. Here is a Doctor who can bemuse and confuse with words; who can use sleight of hand to procure items that he may need; and who, if all else fails, can turn on the charm and have people eating out of his hand. 'Troughton masterfully balances his role as a broody, bustling, bumbling, often absent-minded old "granny" with that of a knife-sharp, energetic, brilliant schemer,' enthused Tim Robins in *Doctor Who – An Adventure in Space and Time* in 1983.

The story also boasts a fine collection of guest characters. Dallas Cavell's Captain Trask is an archetypal sea-dog in the mould of the classic Long John Silver – all he needs are the wooden leg and the parrot for the image to be complete. Cavell's delivery of his dialogue, with suitable 'ah harrrr's and 'me hearties', is totally over the top and provides a balance to David Garth's polite, gentlemanly Solicitor Grey – a performance seemingly modelled on Grytpype-Thynne from BBC radio's comedy classic *The Goon Show*. Grey of course has his own foil, the perpetually put-upon Perkins, who takes the brunt of his master's ire and wit.

As in the case of the some of the earlier historicals, the accuracy of the events depicted in *The Highlanders* has been called into question. The following letter from T S Cunningham of London E17 appeared in the 12 January 1967 edition of *Radio Times*:

'In the recent adventure of *Doctor Who* the Jacobite Rebellion of 1745 was once again represented as an Anglo-Scottish conflict.

'The '45 was in fact an attempt to restore the Stuart dynasty to the throne of the United Kingdom of Great Britain, and although the supporters of Prince Charles Edward were mainly from Scotland that country as a whole did not favour the Jacobite cause.

'At Culloden something like a quarter of the Duke of Cumberland's army consisted of Scottish regiments.'

The Highlanders was never intended to be a documentary, however, and by this stage of its history the series was not even expected to be fulfilling the partly educational aspect of its initial remit. Thus it was that Innes Lloyd was able to phase out the historical stories altogether. 'It's hard to believe that *The Highlanders* sounded the death-knell for the purely historical adventure,' wrote Robins. 'Troughton seems equally comfortable in science-fiction and historical stories (whereas Hartnell always seemed distinctly ill at ease [in] the former). Both *The Smugglers* and *The Highlanders* are excellent examples of their genre, although *The Highlanders* possesses an air of gritty realism that is decidedly absent [from] the offerings which followed.'

At ease though Troughton may appear, *The Highlanders* nevertheless seems curiously out of place in the new, more dynamic style of series initiated by Lloyd and Davis. In fact, in some ways, it does not really seem like a *Doctor Who* story at all, being devoid of many of what would come to be accepted as the series' standard ingredients.

Aside from its status as the last of the true historicals (at least until *Black Orchid* in the nineteenth season), *The Highlanders* will always be remembered for one other thing: the introduction of Frazer Hines as Jamie, who would go on to become one of the most popular and enduring of the Doctor's companions – a testament to the production team's shrewdness in quickly recognising the potential of the character and deciding to keep him on.

THE UNDERWATER MENACE

Writer: Geoffrey Orme. **Director:** Julia Smith. **Designer:** Jack Robinson. **Costumes:** Sandra Reid[1,2], Juanita Waterson[3,4]. **Make-up:** Gillian James. **Incidental Music:** Dudley Simpson. **Fight Arranger:** Derek Ware. **Film Cameraman:** Alan Jonas. **Film Editor:** Eddie Wallstab. **Studio Lighting:** George Summers. **Studio Sound:** Bryan Forgham. **Production Assistant:** Norman Stewart. **Assistant Floor Manager:** Gareth Gwenlan.

	First UK TX	Scheduled TX	Actual TX	Duration	Viewers	Chart Pos.
Episode 1	14/01/67	17.50	17.50	24'18"	8.3	43
Episode 2	21/01/67	17.50	17.51	25'00"	7.5	64
Episode 3	28/01/67	17.50	17.51	24'09"	7.1	59
Episode 4	04/02/67	17.50	17.51	23'20"	7.0	65

Plot: The TARDIS arrives on an extinct volcanic island. Before long, the travellers are captured and taken into the depths of the Earth, where they find a hidden civilisation – the lost city of Atlantis. The Atlanteans worship a goddess named Amdo and use Fish People – men and women operated upon so that they can breathe under the sea – to farm the plankton-based food on which they survive. A deranged scientist, Professor Zaroff, has convinced them that he can raise their city from the sea, but actually he plans to drain the ocean into the Earth's molten core, so that the resultant superheated steam will cause the planet to explode. The travellers meet up with two shipwreck survivors, Sean and Jacko, who manage to persuade the Fish People to rebel and stop work. The Doctor eventually manages to foil Zaroff's plan, but only by breaking down the sea walls and flooding the city. Zaroff drowns, but everyone else escapes.

Episode endings:
1. The struggling Polly is held down on an operating table as the Atlantean scientist Damon tells her that after she is injected she will know nothing more until her conversion into a Fish Person is complete. He advances on her with a syringe …
2. King Thous tells the Doctor and the priest Ramo that he has given much thought to their words and come to a decision. His attendants open the doors and Zaroff enters with a group of guards. Thous tells Zaroff that he can do what he likes with the two men.
3. Zaroff shoots Thous and has his guards do likewise to the King's attendants. Triumphant, he announces 'Nothing in the world can stop me now!'
4. As the Doctor attempts to materialise on Mars, the TARDIS suddenly goes out of control.

IT WAS MADE WHERE…?

Location Filming: 12.12.66-13.12.66
Location: Winspit Quarry, Worth Matravers, Dorset.

Ealing Filming: 14.12.66-16.12.66 on Stage 2
Studio Recording: 07.01.67, 14.01.67, 21.01.67, 28.01.67, all in Riverside 1

ADDITIONAL CREDITED CAST

Ara (Catherine Howe), Ramo (Tom Watson[1-3]), Lolem (Peter Stephens[1,3]), Damon (Colin Jeavons), Zaroff (Joseph Furst), Damon's assistant (Gerald Taylor[2]), Overseer (Graham Ashley[2,4]), Zaroff's guard (Tony Handy[2-4]), Jacko (Paul Anil[2-4]), Sean (P. G. Stephens[2-4]), Thous (Noel Johnson[2-4]), Nola (Roma Woodnutt[3]).

POPULAR MYTHS

- Joseph Furst adopted an outrageous East European accent in his portrayal of Zaroff. (Furst spoke in his own normal accent.)

THINGS TO WATCH OUT FOR

- In the opening TARDIS scene, Polly, Ben and the Doctor are each heard 'thinking' about where they would like to land next. (Polly hopes for Chelsea in 1966, Ben wants *not* to meet the Daleks and the Doctor relishes the idea of encountering prehistoric monsters.) This was achieved by prerecording the actors' voices and playing them back during the making of the episode.
- Noel Johnson, appearing here as King Thous, was better known as the voice of Dick Barton in the famous radio serial *Dick Barton: Special Agent*. He would later play Grover in the season eleven story *Invasion of the Dinosaurs*.
- Zaroff has a pet octopus.
- The effect of the fish people swimming in the sea was achieved by 'flying' the artistes playing the creatures on Kirby wires supplied by Kirby's Flying Ballet.

THINGS YOU MIGHT NOT HAVE KNOWN

- Working titles: *Doctor Who Under the Sea*, *The Fish People*.
- Zaroff is described as 'the greatest living scientist since Leonardo'.
- In Orme's original draft scripts, Zaroff's motivation was explained as being a sort of warped revenge for the deaths of his wife and children in a car crash. This was edited out before recording.
- The production history of *The Underwater Menace* was somewhat chequered. It had been in development for some time and had almost been cancelled in October 1966 when a William Emms story called *The Imps* (to be directed by Julia Smith and designed by Raymond London, with costumes and make-up by Sandra Reid and Gillian James respectively) had been scheduled to be made in its place. By 9 November, though, Emms had fallen seriously ill and the production team knew that requested re-writes to his story were not going to be completed in time. Then, less than a week later, *The Imps* had been moved back in the running order (subsequently to be cancelled altogether) and *The Fish People* – Orme's story – had been resurrected to replace it. The scripts and rewrites were hastily delivered by Orme in a flurry of correspondence between 16 and 29 November. Due to the late start of production, *The Underwater Menace* went into recording one week later than originally scheduled.
- A short, five foot clip of a shark was obtained from stock for inclusion in Episode 1.
- Incidental music composer Dudley Simpson made use of the Cliff Adam Singers to

provide the chanting and other background singing for scenes set in the temple of Amdo.

- Following transmission of the first episode, a member of the public, Mrs N Safford, wrote to the production office with concerns about the content of the show – and in particular, a sequence at the end showing Polly being prepared for an operation to turn her into a fish person. A response was drafted by the production office as follows:

> Thank you for your letter about last week's episode of 'Dr. Who' – obviously the last thing any programme such as ours wishes to do is to cause fear which can be carried into ordinary life, especially where children are concerned. 'Dr. Who', though, is, I believe, accepted by children as a fantasy, which bears little relation to their everyday existence and the 'goggle-eyed creature with plastic gills' is and was to our minds an unreal creature which they have become very used to in this serial. One hopes that very young children, if they are frightened of such creatures, are only frightened when they are watching them perform on the television screen. The very fact that, in this particular episode, there were so many fantastic situations, such as pulling the plug out of the Atlantic or the feeding of the heroes to the sharks, one believed would dissipate any reality which they felt about the operation scene at the end, and that they would accept it also with a 'pinch of salt'.
>
> We are, naturally, most concerned if the effect does frighten children, who are faced with an operation, and certainly in future scripts we will pay particular attention to the points you have raised. Unhappily, the programme is recorded some weeks before transmission, so there is nothing we are able to do about the second episode. However, the operating room atmosphere will not reappear again throughout this serial thereafter.

- The sequences of Zaroff drowning in the final episode were shot in the tank at Ealing on 14 December 1966. Actor Joseph Furst later gave the following account of this in an interview with Rod Scott for the Australian fanzine *Sonic Screwdriver*: 'They had a small swimming pool inside the studio and I spent half an hour to an hour in it, as the sequences had to be shot in reverse. We started with a full pool, because it took longer to fill than to let the water out. When I came out I was wet, and for a cut in between it had to be reversed the other way around. I had four costumes that I could change into, a hot shower and a hairdresser standing by to get my hair in order again. It *seemed* like I spent hours and hours on end in the water, and so finally when the death scene came, it was a very painful experience.'

- **Zaroff:** 'So you're just a little man after all, Doctor, like all the rest. You disappoint me.' **The Doctor:** 'You disappoint *me*, Professor. I didn't think that a man of science needed the backing of thugs!' **Zaroff:** 'Have a care, Doctor, your life is in the balance!'
- **The Doctor:** 'Let's not say goodbye Professor. We'll be seeing each other again.' **Zaroff:** 'Not in *this* world, Doctor!'
- **Thous:** 'To think that after so long the great day is at hand. We shall surprise the whole of mankind.' **Zaroff:** 'Yes, a very great surprise … Perhaps the greatest ever!'
- **The Doctor:** 'Zaroff, I think you ought to know the sea has broken through and is

about to overwhelm us here.' **Zaroff:** [To his assistants.] 'Don't listen to him! The man lies!' **The Doctor:** 'Then perhaps the distant roaring that we can hear is just the goddess Amdo with indigestion.'

The Underwater Menace has a number of points in its favour. Geoffrey Orme gives his characters some reasonable and often amusing, if generally rather hackneyed, dialogue; there are a few charming and well-executed location scenes; Dudley Simpson's incidental music is quite nice; and Jack Robinson's studio sets are also effective, in some cases appearing surprisingly large-scale. In addition, the effects work by way of which the final destruction of Atlantis is realised is splendid. Otherwise, however, it is very difficult to find anything good to say about this story, which is undoubtedly the weakest of the second Doctor's era, if not of the sixties as a whole.

The plot is tedious and clichéd in the extreme; the guest characters are all one-dimensional; the companions get a very raw deal (particularly poor Polly, who seems to spend most of her time crying, whimpering and screaming); and the overall production is simply not up to the series' usual standard, the scripts' demands clearly far exceeding the resources available to meet them. The costumes and make-up are particularly unimpressive, looking like something thrown together for a dodgy amateur dramatics production. While this may perhaps be partly excused by the fact that the story, having originally been dropped during scripting, was resurrected as an emergency measure when another one had to be abandoned after the writer fell ill, it has to be said that it makes for less than satisfying viewing.

The Fish People are perhaps the most poorly realised 'monsters' in the series' entire history, and their presence is made all the more painful by the thought that they need not have been included at all. 'Surprisingly, as guest "monsters" for the serial, the Fish People are a little superfluous,' noted Tim Robins in *Doctor Who – An Adventure in Space and Time* in 1983. 'The most violent action on their part is throwing shells at the taunts of the Irishman Sean. Episode 3 contains an underwater "ballet" which seems largely unnecessary – despite being the only long scene featuring them. In fact, they even look a little boring, as at least half their number are only partially made-up, wearing rather obvious wet-suits and goggles … On the whole they are rather drippy as "monsters", and their revolt is due more to outside manipulation than any revolutionary fervour.'

To be fair, it should be noted that the Fish People's 'ballet', if somewhat pointless, is at least well staged. It could also be speculated that the wet-suits and goggles sported by some of the creatures are intended to suggest that the process of conversion is a gradual one; although, against this, it has to be admitted that in the scene where Polly is menaced by Damon, the implication seems to be that just a single operation is involved.

The standard of acting on display from the guest cast leaves a lot to be desired. Most disappointing in this regard is Joseph Furst's Zaroff. 'Furst has to be one of the most monumentally awful actors ever to grace *Doctor Who*,' asserted Nick Cooper in *Star Begotten* Vol. 4 No. 1 dated May 1990. 'Indeed, he wouldn't have looked out of place as the stock loony in a late Roger Moore James Bond as he takes manic glee in ranting every line.' Furst is actually a distinguished and accomplished actor whose performances in other productions are generally admirable; on this occasion however he is certainly very much over the top.

All in all, *The Underwater Menace* is reminiscent of nothing so much as a poorly-scripted, uninspired and low-budget B-movie.

THE MOONBASE

Writer: Kit Pedler. **Director:** Morris Barry. **Designer:** Colin Shaw. **Costumes:** Sandra Reid, Mary Woods[1,2], Daphne Dare[3,4]. **Make-Up:** Gillian James[1-3], Jeanne Richmond[4]. **Incidental Music:** stock. **Film Camerman:** Peter Hamilton. **Film Editor:** Ted Walter. **Studio Lighting:** Dave Sydenham. **Studio Sound:** Gordon Mackie. **Production Assistant:** Desmond McCarthy. **Assistant Floor Manager:** Lovett Bickford.

	First UK TX	Scheduled TX	Actual TX	Duration	Viewers	Chart Pos.
Episode 1	11/02/67	17.50	17.52	24'12"	8.1	56
Episode 2	18/02/67	17.50	17.51	24'42"	8.9	36
Episode 3	25/02/67	17.50	17.51	26'11"	8.2	49
Episode 4	04/03/67	17.50	17.51	23'28"	8.1	44

Plot: The TARDIS arrives in 2070 AD on the Moon, where a weather control station under the command of a man named Hobson is in the grip of a plague epidemic – in reality the result of an alien poison planted by the Cybermen. Polly realises that as the Cybermen's chest units are made of plastic they must be vulnerable to attack by solvents. She and her friends manage to destroy all the Cybermen on the base with a 'cocktail' of such chemicals shot at them through fire extinguishers. A second wave of Cybermen advances across the lunar surface but, prompted by the Doctor, Hobson uses the base's gravity-generating weather control device, the Gravitron, to send them flying off into space.

Episode endings:
1. Polly is looking after the injured Jamie in the base's medical section. He asks for some water and she leaves to get it. When she has gone, a Cyberman enters the medical unit from the store-room and heads for Jamie – who, in his delirium, thinks that it is 'the Phantom Piper' come to claim him …
2. The Doctor and Hobson try to work out how the Cybermen got into the base and where they have been hiding. They start to make a search of the medical unit and notice a pair of Cyberman shoes protruding from under a sheet on one of the beds. The Cyberman suddenly throws back the sheet and draws its weapon, advancing on the humans.
3. The Cybermen advance in force across the lunar surface toward the moonbase.
4. The travellers return quietly to the TARDIS, where the Doctor decides to consult the time scanner – a device capable of giving them a glimpse of their future. It shows a picture of a huge crustacean claw.

IT WAS MADE WHERE...?

Ealing Filming: 17.01.67-20.01.67 on Stage 3 A/B
Studio Recording: 04.02.67, 11.02.67, 18.02.67 in Riverside 1, 25.02.67 in Lime Grove D

ADDITIONAL CREDITED CAST

Hobson (Patrick Barr), Benoit (Andre Maranne), Nils (Michael Wolf), Sam (John Rolfe), Voice from Space Control (Alan Rowe[1-3]), Ralph[1]/Scientist[3] (Mark Heath[1, 3]), Dr. Evans (Alan Rowe[1,3,4]), Scientists (Barry Ashton, Derek Calder, Arnold Chazen[1-3], Leon Maybank[1-3], Victor Pemberton, Edward Phillips[1-3], Ron Pinnell[1-3], Robin Scott, Alan Wells), Voice of Controller Rinberg (Denis McCarthy[2]), Cybermen (John Wills, Sonnie Willis[1,3,4], Peter Greene[2-4], Keith Goodman[3,4], Reg Whitehead[3,4]), Cybermen Voices (Peter Hawkins[3,4]).

THINGS TO WATCH OUT FOR

- There is an unusual sequence in Episode 3 where the Doctor debates with himself what the Cybermen might be afraid of; this was achieved by pre-recording his whispered 'thoughts' and playing them back in the studio with Patrick Troughton muttering the responses in between (see 'Quote, unquote').
- Talkback from the headphones of the crew on the studio floor is clearly audible at times during Episode 4 (the same problem as had earlier caused the opening episode of the first Dalek story to have to be remounted) – for example, a voice can be clearly heard saying 'cue' at the start of the scene where the controlled scientists are first activated by the Cybermen.
- John Levene, later to play the more prominent role of Benton, appears as a Cyberman extra in the third and fourth episodes.
- An early example of an optical effect is seen as the Cybermen fire their cannon at the dome of the lunar base.

THINGS YOU MIGHT NOT HAVE KNOWN

- Working title: *The Return of the Cybermen*.
- John Wills, who plays one of the Cybermen in this story, earlier appeared as 'Frankenstein' in *The Chase* under the name John Maxim.
- Innes Lloyd was keen to feature a story set on the Moon to tap in to all the news coverage of NASA's Apollo Moon missions. With the transmission of *The Moonbase*, the Doctor beat NASA to the Moon by two years.
- Kit Pedler was asked to produce the scripts for *The Moonbase* with the stipulation that the action had to take place on the Moon and should involve no more than one large set and two smaller ones.
- As Jamie was a last minute addition to the story, Davis chose to have him be unconscious for most of the time. What lines Jamie did have were taken from Ben and the Moonbase crew.
- To make space for the other sets, the TARDIS control room was cut down from its normal size and some of its walls were represented simply by photographic blow-ups, a technique that had been used previously in the series.
- For a brief shot of microbes under a microscope slide in Episode 2, a fifteen foot piece of stock footage was taken from an episode called *Science and Life* in a series called *Men and Microbes*.
- The relocating of the final episode's recording to Studio D of Lime Grove resulted in the loss of a 'fast re-wind telecine' facility. This was noted in a memo dated 15 February 1967 from producer Innes Lloyd to the BBC's Head of Serials. 'The

problem is acute on 25th February,' wrote Lloyd, 'for the last episode of "Moonbase". I can anticipate that in future serials it will be a serious debilitating factor to the programme. The only answer I can think of ... is to transfer all our film onto videotape and sue for a third machine to play into the recording. As I am sure you will agree it would be most unfortunate for this particularly good programme "The Moonbase" to be so inhibited because of lack of facilities.'

- Following the recording of the final episode, a problem was encountered with audible talk-back (the instructions of the director and PA to the cast and crew) on the soundtrack. Morris Barry, the director, was forced during editing to remove it wherever possible. Barry alerted technical managers Brian Clemett and Dave Sydenham to the problem and pointed out that as all *Doctor Who*s were planned to be recorded in Lime Grove for the foreseeable future, it should be addressed with some urgency.

- In an attempt to gain additional promotion for the story, Lloyd on 27 January 1967 sent a memo to Robin Scott of the BBC's promotion unit:

> I am exceedingly keen to get the maximum screen promotion for this programme as our audience figures begin to show a marked upward trend, which, obviously, we want to maintain.
>
> The serial is set on the moon and in it there are some excellent film sequences, shot at Ealing, showing Doctor Who and his companions, in futuristic space suits, encountering the effects of weightlessness. It has the appeal of being fairly topical, as far as lunar exploration is concerned, and I am sure it could provide an exhilarating and interesting trail for the serial.

Possibly as a result of this, a twenty-five second trailer for the story was broadcast at 18:14 on 4 February 1967, with live narration by John Benson.

- The name tags commissioned from the Graphics Department on 16 January 1967 for the various crew members of the Moonbase crew were listed as follows:

Hobson T.	U.K.
Benoit J.	FRANCE
Jensen N.	DENMARK
Evans G.	U.K.
Elliot J.	AUSTRALIAN
Becket S.	N. ZEALAND
Anders R.	AUSTRALIAN
Wise C.	U.K.
Benson J.	U.K.
Faure J.	FRANCE
Baker P.	CANADIAN
Braun E.	CANADIAN
Schultz F.	GERMAN
Adebayo R.	NIGERIAN
Stacey N.	N. ZEALAND

- The shot of a claw seen on the TARDIS scanner screen at the end of the final episode was filmed on Stage 3A/B at Ealing on 17 February 1967 during the making of *The Macra Terror*.
- Consideration was at one point given to delaying the start of transmission of *The Moonbase* by one week, to re-establish a two week gap between the recording and transmission of episodes. This idea was taken no further though.

QUOTE, UNQUOTE

- **The Doctor:** 'There are some corners of the universe which have bred the most terrible things. Things that act against everything we believe in. They must be fought.'
- **Polly:** 'Are you a medical doctor?' **The Doctor:** 'Yes I think I was once, Polly, I think I took a degree in Glasgow … 1888, I think … Lister.'
- **The Doctor:** [*Thinking* and talking to himself.] *Funny* … 'Funny' … *Go to all that trouble to make the men do the work … why?* … 'Do it themselves, easy' … *They're using the men as tools … why?* … 'Don't know' … *Yes I do, though* … 'There must be something in here they don't like' … *Pressure?* … 'No' … *Electricity?* … 'No' … *Radiation?* … 'Maybe' … *Grav … Gravity … now, there's a thought … Gravity!* … 'Oh yes … Gravity.'
- **The Doctor:** 'Everything's got a weak point. It's just a question of waiting until it shows up, that's all.'

ANALYSIS

The Moonbase is all but a remake of the first Cyberman adventure, *The Tenth Planet*. In this remix, the Antarctic is replaced with the Moon, Cutler with Hobson, and the sub-plot involving the space capsule in danger with one about a mysterious illness. However, this is by no means to suggest that *The Moonbase* is a poor relation. On the contrary, it is far superior in many ways, not least of which being the depiction of the Cybermen themselves.

In *The Tenth Planet*, the creatures were impressive both in their physical size and in their alien nature, but their effectiveness was diminished slightly by the somewhat chunky nature of their costumes and by the strange sing-song effect used for their voices. The new look that the designers have given them for *The Moonbase* – cloth face swapped for an impassive metal helmet, chunky chest unit and gun for a smaller affair incorporating a hand-held weapon, plastic suit for a loose fitting one-piece silver garment – is far sleeker and more polished, making them more impressive still. Similarly their radically rethought voices – sing-song lilt replaced with a totally electronic drawl created by Peter Hawkins using a vibrating palate originally developed as a medical aid for people with throat and vocal cord problems – are simply chilling, and still sufficiently different from the Daleks' to preserve the Cybermen's distinctiveness.

The Cybermen do not in fact make much of an appearance in the first two episodes, but in the last two they dominate the proceedings. This story, far more than their debut, can be seen as the one that truly established them as popular recurring monsters in the series. '*The Moonbase* was a superior story all round [to the one that preceded it],' agreed Bruce Campbell in *A Voyage Through 25 Years of Doctor Who* dated December 1988. 'The newly [redesigned] Cybermen had a more menacing feel to them, and arguably these "mark two" versions are the most effectively realised Cybermen to date. The storyline, although slightly implausible at times, kept the action flowing with some fine moments of suspense throughout ..., aided by some effective stock music.'

Another point in the story's favour is that it features some great performances from the regular team. Patrick Troughton has now clearly settled into his role as the new Doctor and is well served by the scripts, in which the comedic excesses of *The Highlanders* and *The Underwater Menace* have given way to a more subtle and effective use of humour. The crew of the Moonbase, on the other hand, are unfortunately something of a washout. The best character is Hobson, and he is still nowhere near as strong as Cutler, his equivalent in *The Tenth Planet*.

On the production side, the stock music used for this story is – as Campbell observed – very effective, providing themes for the Cybermen as well as action stings and general background atmosphere. The sets, however, seem somewhat spartan, particularly after the relatively lavish look of *The Underwater Menace*, and the Gravitron is far too wobbly to be convincing as a machine supposedly capable of projecting some form of gravity beam with great precision onto the Earth. Worse still is the modelwork, which is dreadful. The effects shots of the Cybermen's ships landing, and later being thrown off the Moon by gravitational forces, are amongst the worst ever seen in *Doctor Who*, and nowhere near as good as similar shots in *The Tenth Planet* and in other earlier stories.

Morris Barry's studio direction, too, is rather lacklustre in places. An example of this is the unconvincing lumbering about of the men possessed by the Cybermen. It would be interesting to know, too, how the possessed Sam Beckett manages to get into the Gravitron control room without anyone seeing him, given that he has black neutrotropic viral lines all over his face and a Cyberman control device on his head! Fortunately the film work done at Ealing is very much better, suggesting that this was Barry's main strength. The scenes set on the lunar surface are excellent (and it is no surprise that Innes Lloyd made a special request of his BBC colleagues that they be used to promote the show). Particularly effective is the one in Episode 3 – probably the strongest episode of the story altogether – where a Cyberman attacks Benoit and Ben hurls a cannister of 'Polly Cocktail' at it by hand, as the fire extinguishers won't work in the vacuum.

In the final analysis, the negative points of the story are far outweighed by the positive – a view shared by those whose opinions were recorded in the BBC's Audience Research Report on the final episode. 'This particular ... adventure ... seems on the whole to have kept many in the sample fairly happily entertained,' it was noted. 'They often took it with a large grain of salt, but, even so, enjoyed a situation that, as a fitter pointed out, reflects "the dream of many to reach the Moon".' In what could be considered a vindication of Lloyd's efforts to introduce more 'hard science' into the series, the Report continued: 'The idea of being able to control the Earth's weather from a Moon station was original too, as other viewers maintained, and the story won approval from another group because it was real science-fiction, at least in reference to the electronic technicalities with which Hobson, Doctor Who and the rest of the team were concerned.' There remained 'a large minority' whose comments reflected 'some asperity', mainly directed towards *Doctor Who* in general. There was also a 'not inconsiderable degree of fairly lacklustre feeling' about the climax to this particular story, a typical comment being that it 'lacked credibility; not good enough to win through by accident'. Overall, though, the tone was upbeat: 'A large minority were ... much intrigued by the events of this final episode and found them very exciting. There was plenty of imaginatively-devised incident, it was said, before the last of the Cyber attacks was foiled, and all with an out-of-this-world touch, that, as various viewers observed, makes the science-fiction sequences in the *Doctor Who* series generally more thrilling than when the TARDIS travels backwards rather than forwards in time. The rout of the Cybermen was ingeniously managed, further comment went on, and the episode had its agreeably gruesome moments ("but this is what we love – makes us shiver", said a customs officer), was lively too, and not unbelievably far-fetched.'

Their popularity now assured, the Cybermen were well on the way to becoming the archetypal monsters of the second Doctor's era.

THE MACRA TERROR

Writer: Ian Stuart Black. **Director:** John Davies. **Designer:** Kenneth Sharp. **Costumes:** Daphne Dare, Vanessa Clark[1]. **Make-Up:** Gillian James, Jean Richmond[1]. **Music:** Dudley Simpson. **Film Cameraman:** Peter Hamilton. **Film Editor:** Eddie Wallstab. **Studio Lighting:** Frank Cresswell. **Studio Sound:** Hugh Barker, Gordon Mackie. **Production Assistant:** Chris D'Oyly John. **Assistant Floor Manager:** Ann Faggetter.

	First UK TX	Scheduled TX	Actual TX	Duration	Viewers	Chart Pos.
Episode 1	11/03/67	17.50	17.51	22'58"	8.0	37
Episode 2	18/03/67	17.50	17.51	23'21"	7.9	42
Episode 3	25/03/67	17.50	17.51	23'24"	8.5	45
Episode 4	01/04/67	17.50	17.51	24'41"	8.4	39

Plot: The time travellers visit a human colony that appears to be a happy place run along the lines of an enormous holiday camp but has in fact been infiltrated and taken over by a race of giant crab-like creatures – the Macra. The brainwashed inhabitants are forced to mine a gas toxic to themselves but vital for their oppressors' survival. Ben at one point comes under the Macra's malign influence and turns against his friends. He eventually regains his senses, however, and under the Doctor's guidance destroys the gas pumping equipment, thus killing the Macra and restoring the colony's freedom.

Episode endings:
1. The rebellious colonist Medok looks on in disgust and the Doctor in amazement as a Macra appears in the moonlight in the ruined building ...
2. Polly realises with horror that the Macra are in Control. The colony's Pilot summons security chief Ola and a guard and angrily orders that the prisoners be taken away. Polly cries out again that, 'The Macra are in Control!'
3. Jamie is trapped in a mine tunnel as two Macra approach ...
4. The Doctor is horrified on learning from Ben that the colonists want to make him their next Pilot. Determined to avoid this fate, he leads his companions away in a dance through the celebrating colonists.

IT WAS MADE WHERE...?

Location Filming: 15.02.67

Location: Associated Portland Cement Quarry, Dunstable, Bedfordshire.
Ealing Filming: 17.02.67 on Stage 3 A/B
Studio Recording: 04.03.67, 11.03.67, 18.03.67, 25.03.67, all in Lime Grove D

ADDITIONAL CREDITED CAST

Pilot (Peter Jeffrey), Barney (Graham Armitage[1]), Questa (Ian Fairbairn[1]), Sunnaa (Jane Enshawe[1,3,4]), Chicki (Sandra Bryant[1], Karol Keyes[4]), Drum Majorette (Maureen Lane[1,4]), Medok (Terence Lodge[1-3]), Ola (Gertan Klauber), Controller (Graham Leaman), Alvis (Anthony Gardner[1]), Control Voice (Denis Goacher), Broadcast Voice[1,3]/Broadcast and Propaganda Voice[2] (Richard Beale), Macra Operator (Robert Jewell), Officia (John Harvey[3,4]), Guards (John Caesar[4], Steve Emerson[4], Danny Rae[4]*), Cheerleaders (Roger Jerome[4], Terry Wright[4], Ralph Carrigan[4]).

*John Caesar and Steve Emerson also appear uncredited in Episodes 1 to 3 and Danny Rae in Episodes 1 and 2.

POPULAR MYTHS

- The image of the Controller seen on the screen in the Pilot's office was a photograph of story editor Gerry Davis. (It was a photograph of Graham Leaman, who played the Controller.)

THINGS TO WATCH OUT FOR

- The opening episode of this story saw the debut of the first new opening title sequence since *Doctor Who* began. Although early experiments with the 'howl-around' technique back in 1963 had included the distorting and blending of faces, the series' original producer Verity Lambert had found this effect too disturbing and vetoed its use. When called upon to update the titles in 1966, graphic designer Bernard Lodge recalled the effect and decided to include a photograph of Patrick Troughton in the sequence. This was combined with a new title graphic in a different typeface from that used in the original sequence, and a new set of 'howl-around' patterns generated around these images. This version of the title sequence was shot by Lodge and engineering expert Ben Palmer on 9 December 1966 in Studio TC2. The costs were charged to *The Power of the Daleks*' production budget, and the original intention was that the sequence should first be used for *The Underwater Menace*. Following its eventual debut, it was to be used for the remainder of the second Doctor's episodes.
- Ken Sharp's sets are without exception excellent.
- The Macra seen to be in charge in the last episode is white rather than black (for which the Macra prop had to be repainted).
- The character Chicki was played by two different actresses. Sandra Bryant, who took the role for Episode 1, asked to be released from her contract so that she could accept another, more attractive offer of work. This was agreed, and so for Episode 4 (the only other episode in which Chicki appears) the part was recast, going instead to Karol Keyes.

THINGS YOU MIGHT NOT HAVE KNOWN

- Working titles: *The Spidermen*, *The Insect-Men*, *The Macras*.
- Transmission of the final episode of this story was followed by a fifty-four second

trailer for the following one, *The Faceless Ones*, featuring a montage of shots taken at Gatwick Airport.

- Only one Macra prop was built. Clever camera angles and trick photography were used by director John Davies to create the illusion that there were many more of the creatures. To enable the Macra to move. the prop was placed on the back of a van with its claws and antennae operated by Robert Jewell.

QUOTE, UNQUOTE

- **The Doctor:** 'I think you've been listening to some very bad advice.' **Polly:** 'But I've been asleep.' **The Doctor:** 'Yes, I know you have. Fast asleep. Very fast asleep. Polly, do you smell anything; a sort of sweet perfume?' **Polly:** 'No.' **The Doctor:** 'Never mind. Now, Polly, I want you to forget everything you've been dreaming.' **Polly:** 'Why do you say that?' **The Doctor:** 'It's just possible that you've been given a series of orders while you've been asleep. You know, "Do this", "Do that", "Do the other thing". My advice to you is: don't do anything of the sort. Don't just be obedient. Always make up your own mind.'
- **The Doctor:** [Interrupting an argument between Ola and the Pilot.] 'Oh, come now, we can't have bad temper and differences of opinion in this happy-type colony! Say you're sorry, Ola. Say you're sorry, Pilot.'
- **Control Voice:** 'This is an emergency! Control must be believed and obeyed! No-one in the colony believes in Macra! There is no such thing as Macra! Macra do not exist! There are no Macra!'

ANALYSIS

The Macra Terror is on the surface a relatively straightforward tale about alien invasion and control of an apparently idyllic human colony. On consideration, though, it can be seen to have far deeper levels. Writer Ian Stuart Black later said that he had wanted to explore the idea of a substance being poisonous to one life form but vital to the survival of another. This is certainly apparent in the transmitted episodes. Perhaps even more readily discernible, however, are themes of indoctrination, propaganda and unquestioning obedience to authority. This has caused some commentators to draw not unreasonable parallels with weighty literary sources such as Kafka and Orwell – the televised addresses of the Controller being likened to those of Big Brother in the latter's *Nineteen Eighty-Four*, for example. Others, however, have taken the view that this attempt at social comment falls rather flat, and that the story comes across as being simply pretentious.

'What doesn't work is the holiday camp backdrop,' wrote Tim Robins in *Doctor Who – An Adventure in Space and Time* in 1983. '"We regulate our day by music," the companions are informed; and, sure enough, cheery jingles are interspersed throughout the proceedings, exhorting the colonists to work hard and have fun. Muzak assaults the ear at every opportunity, and a friendly Controller pops up every now and then to reassure the colonists that everything is … well … under control! The colony hierarchy spout the usual platitudes … whilst every activity is given some grandiose name, such as "The Danger Gang" or "The Refreshing Department" …

'Of course, all this is supposed to jar. The idea is to provide a chilling contrast between the superficially relaxed, happy life of the colony and the sinister schemes of the Macra.

At the same time a rather crude message is being put across about brainwashing and the dangers of obeying commands without question; but as serious or satirical political comment it just doesn't wash. The contrast is lost because so much of the story is focused upon the action, chaos and danger ...'

This assessment is probably unduly harsh, but nevertheless it is undoubtedly true that the story's more serious aspects are somewhat undermined by the presence of the Macra themselves, which tends to take it into traditional monster mayhem territory. Having said this, the Macra, although neither the most interestingly characterised nor the most convincingly realised of monsters, are undoubtedly a very creepy concept, making for a number of extremely suspenseful scenes – particularly in the earlier parts of the story when the viewer catches only the occasional, mist-swathed glimpse of them.

The story's production values are generally fine, and another plus point is that the guest cast (in keeping with the regulars) are all excellent, bringing to life some interesting and well-drawn characters. On the minus side, the denouement is perhaps rather less dramatic than it might be. That, though, is a relatively minor quibble.

All things considered, the story must certainly be adjudged a success – albeit, as Robins suggested, perhaps only a partial one: 'Doctor Who is a versatile programme. Doubtless the bizarre, the symbolic, the satirical can all be encompassed in its timeless theme. However, what The Macra Terror does show is that if you want to attempt a subtle story, it's best not to include large, alien crabs roving around a holiday camp ...'

THE FACELESS ONES

Writer: David Ellis, Malcolm Hulke. **Director:** Gerry Mill. **Designer:** Geoffrey Kirkland. **Costumes:** Daphne Dare, Sandra Reid. **Make-up:** Gillian James. **Incidental Music:** stock. **Film Cameraman:** Tony Imi. **Film Editor:** Chris Hayden. **Studio Lighting:** Howard King. **Studio Sound:** Gordon Mackie. **Production Assistant:** Richard Brooks. **Assistant Floor Manager:** Sue Marlborough.

	First UK TX	Scheduled TX	Actual TX	Duration	Viewers	Chart Pos.
Episode 1	08/04/67	17.50	17.50	23'47"	8.0	47
Episode 2	15/04/67	17.50	17.51	25'22"	6.4	70
Episode 3	22/04/67	17.50	17.50	23'10"	7.9	43
Episode 4	29/04/67	17.50	17.50	24'28"	6.9	62
Episode 5	06/05/67	17.50	17.52	23'34"	7.1	39
Episode 6	13/05/67	17.50	17.50	23'38"	8.0	33

Plot: The TARDIS arrives on Earth in 1966 – on a runway at Gatwick airport. Polly witnesses a murder in a nearby hangar and is then kidnapped by the perpetrator, Spencer of Chameleon Tours. Subsequently Ben also vanishes. The Doctor and Jamie are left to try to convince the sceptical airport Commandant that there has been foul play. It transpires that a great many other young people have also vanished, all of them while on Chameleon Tours holidays. With the help of Samantha Briggs, the sister of one of the missing youths, the Doctor and Jamie uncover a plot by the alien Chameleons to kidnap human youngsters in order to take their identities – for the Chameleons have lost their own in an accident on their home planet. The Doctor offers to help the Chameleons find another solution to their problem and the kidnapped humans are released.

Episode endings:
1. Spencer and Chameleon Tours' Captain Blade help a figure swathed in heavy clothing through the airport terminal buildings to the medical centre. There they sit the figure on a table and remove its hat and coat. Although seen only from behind, the features thus revealed appear distinctly alien.
2. Investigating the Chameleon Tours hangar, the Doctor becomes trapped in a secret room that starts rapidly to fill with freezing gas.
3. Detective Inspector Crossland, investigating the disappearances of Sam Briggs' brother Brian and of his own colleague Gascoigne (the man seen murdered by Polly), is kidnapped by Blade on a Chameleon Tours plane and taken to the flight deck, which is bedecked with alien equipment. He is horrified to see on a screen that all the passengers on board have apparently vanished.
4. The wings of the Chameleon Tours plane fold back and the craft becomes a rocket which shoots into space and docks with a large space station.
5. Having arrived on the Chameleon space station, the Doctor and Nurse Pinto are captured by Blade and a group of Chameleons.
6. The Doctor and Jamie say their farewells to Ben and Polly who have decided to stay on Earth as they have learned that this is the same day on which they first left to travel with the Doctor. When they have gone, the Doctor tells Jamie that the TARDIS is not where they left it.

IT WAS MADE WHERE...?

Location Filming: 10.03.67, 13.03.67-14.03.67, 17.03.67
Location: Gatwick Airport, Gatwick, Surrey.
Ealing Filming: 15.03.67-16.03.67 on Stage 3 A/B, 11.04.67 on Stage 3A
Studio Recording: 01.04.67, 08.04.67, 15.04.67, 22.04.67, 29.04.67, 06.05.67, all in Lime Grove D

ADDITIONAL CREDITED CAST

Policeman (James Appleby[1]), Commandant (Colin Gordon), Meadows (George Selway[1-3,5,6]), Jean Rock (Wanda Ventham), Spencer (Victor Winding), Inspector Gascoigne (Peter Whitaker[1]), Blade (Donald Pickering), Jenkins (Christopher Tranchell[1,2,4-6]), Nurse Pinto (Madalena Nicol[2,4-6]), Crossland (Bernard Kay[2-6]), Samantha Briggs (Pauline Collins[2-6]), Ann Davidson (Gilly Fraser[2-6]), Announcer (Brigit Paul[2,4]), Heslington (Barry Wilsher[3-6]), R.A.F. Pilot (Michael Ladkin[4]), Supt. Reynolds (Leonard Trolley[6]).

POPULAR MYTHS

- The only surviving copy of Episode 1 is a print edited by the censors in Australia. (The copy of this episode in the BBC's archives is complete and unedited.)
- *The Faceless Ones* was, by a strange coincidence, the first story to feature the Doctor's face in the opening title sequence. (It wasn't. The first story to feature the new title sequence was *The Macra Terror*.)

THINGS TO WATCH OUT FOR

- Episode 2 of this story saw the debut of a slightly rearranged version of the series' opening theme music, supplied by Delia Derbyshire of the BBC's Radiophonic Workshop.
- Ben and Polly do not appear in Episodes 3 to 5, and appear only in a pre-filmed insert in Episode 6.
- Frazer Hines speaks without his normal Scots burr in Episodes 5 and 6 as the Chameleon copy of Jamie.
- Popular actress Pauline Collins appears in an early role as Sam Briggs.

THINGS YOU MIGHT NOT HAVE KNOWN

- Working title: *The Chameleons.*
- The original plan was to film the exterior sequences for this story at London Airport (better known today as Heathrow Airport) between 8 and 17 March 1967, and permission was sought from the relevant authorities to proceed around the start of February. However, in a letter of 21 February to the Public Relations Office there, production assistant Richard Brooks explained that due to expensive script-re-writes which put the overall costs of the story higher, their fees could no longer be afforded. On the same day, Brooks confirmed with the Public Relations Officer at Gatwick Airport that the production team would be using this as the location. Shooting would take place in the passenger concourse and the car park, and permission was also gained from a company called Air Couriers Ltd to film on the concrete apron alongside their premises at the airport.
- This story was developed out of an original proposal by Malcolm Hulke and David Ellis for a four part adventure called *The Big Store.* Set in a large department store, this concerned a small group of alien colonists who wanted to take over the Earth by releasing a virulent strain of bubonic plague. If this plan failed, then the aliens sent to carry out the mission would simply leave. The aliens consisted of two types: a highly intelligent master race and a race of faceless and mindless servants able to take on the external characteristics of humans. The storyline for the first episode was dated 15 November 1966 and read as follows:

PART ONE

TARDIS arrives in the central area of a big department store in the middle of the night. Doctor Who and his friends emerge and discover that they are on Earth, in England, 1973. Doctor Who is delighted they have landed in this place, because in the big store's electrical department he hopes to be able to find equipment to remedy an electrical fault which has developed in TARDIS. As Ben and Polly look at the partly familiar, partly strange, merchandise on display, we cut to the roof of the store.

Roof of Store (Film)

On the heliport, a flying saucer has just landed. Standing by it, waiting for the hatch to open, are three men dressed in 1973 lounge suits. They are:

SECOND DOCTOR 2

No. 1   The tough, strong, ruthless commanding officer of the group. An intelligent man of action.

No. 739   Scientist; weak dilatory man.

No. 50   A heavy. Not too bright.

The hatch opens, and No. 800 emerges, dressed in black, flying suit.

No.800   Scientist; intelligent, ruthless.

No. 1 greets 800, and it is later established that he has been sent to 'assist' 739 because the latter is behind time in his work. It is clear that 739 resents the presence of 800 but must accept the situation. 800 asks if the laboratory has been set up yet; 739 says yes, but there are problems. 800 smiles, and says that all problems can be solved.

No.1 takes 800 to the edge of the roof, so that 800 can see his first Earth city. No.1 says; "With your help, 800, it will soon be ours."

Central Store Area

Ben and Polly are in the food section, sampling everything in sight. It is a change from the TARDIS-type diet. They hear some other people and quickly hide. Into their view come a smartly dressed man and woman. To the surprise of Polly and Ben, the smartly dressed couple begin to help themselves to food. However, they don't eat it; having filled a couple of electrically-operated baskets-on-wheels, the couple move off to the lifts. As Ben and Polly watch, the couple get into a lift; the doors close, and the indicator shows the lift has gone into the sub-basement.

Neither Polly nor Ben can understand this. But it reminds Polly of that fact that in the morning people will be coming into the store, and will find the police box. They set off towards Doctor Who to warn him of this possibility.

However, when they arrive back at the TARDIS they discover that Doctor Who has foreseen this eventuality. There is now a little white rope around the police box, which has become the focal point of a POLICE RECRUITMENT WEEK display.

In the men's wear section, No. 1 and his colleagues arrive at a rack of men's clothes. 800 looks around, asking if this is the way to the laboratory. No. 1 explains that he has brought No. 800 here to be suitably dressed for his mission. 800 is amused, but agrees to put on these strange Earth clothes.

At TARDIS, Ben has told Doctor Who about the two smartly-dressed thieves. Doctor Who gives this little attention, and goes off in search of spare parts for the TARDIS. Ben and Polly further discuss the mystery of the two thieves.

In the TV-set section (cinemascope television screens), Doctor Who is fiddling with the back of one of the sets. As Doctor Who works, No. 1 and his colleagues come walking by, in step like soldiers. One of them, 800, has over his arm a black flying suit. Doctor Who keeps out of sight. But as the four men have passed him by, he is about to resume work when he sees them go into the lift. The lift doors open and from the indicator he can see that it goes down to the sub-basement.

Sub-basement

No. 1 introduces 800 to the smartly dressed food thieves, who had been getting the regular nightly food supplies for their group. No. 1 refers to the two thieves as Z and L, whom of course 800 has met before on their own planet. 800 is amazed at the transformation of Z and L. Z and L report on the presence of two Earth people whom they believe were watching them take the food. 800 says he presumes No. 1 will have these two Peeping Toms hunted down and killed immediately.

Central Store Area

Looking around, Polly finds teenage clothes of 1973, some of which are on models. Intrigued, she tries on one or two jackets. As she admires herself in a mirror, one of the dummies begins to walk, hands reaching for Polly's throat.

- Samantha Briggs was at one point considered as a new female companion for the Doctor. However actress Pauline Collins declined to continue with the role.
- At one point during the scripting process Samantha was to have been called Cleo Briggs, and before that Mary Dawson. Similarly Nurse Pinto was to have been called Nurse O'Brien, and Chameleon Tours were to have been known as Pied Piper Tours.
- Both Michael Craze, playing Ben, and Anneke Wills, playing Polly, were originally contracted to appear up until the second episode of the following story, *The Evil of the Daleks*, but were written out at the end of *The Faceless Ones* (although the BBC paid them in full for all their contracted episodes). This decision appears to have been taken by Head of Serials Shaun Sutton on or around 8 February 1967.

QUOTE, UNQUOTE

- **Jamie:** [About an aeroplane.] 'It's a flying beastie!'
- **Blade:** 'We could eliminate a whole squadron of their toy planes, and they'd never get on to us. Their minds can't cope with an operation like this. Remember the teaching of our Director – the intelligence of Earth people is comparable only to that of animals on our planet.'
- **The Doctor:** 'Why are you abducting all these young people?' **Meadows:** 'We had a catastrophe on our planet. A gigantic explosion. As you've seen, we've lost our identities. My people are dying out.'

The Faceless Ones sees *Doctor Who* approaching the end of a period of transition. It still has something of the feel of a first Doctor story about it and yet shows the series casting off just about the last of its direct links to that era with the departure of Polly and Ben. The way in which the two companions are written out is actually rather abrupt and offhand, as was noted by Chris Marton in *Wheel in Space* No. 9 dated May 1980: 'It was sad that the retiring companions' appearances were so sparse, and one suspects that contractual hassles were the main reason; a pity, as this would have been an excellent story to remember them by. Their love/hate interplay, with the Doctor as amiable mediator, set the style of the soon-to-be-developed platonic (?) friendships Jamie enjoyed with Victoria and Zoe.'

The fact that *The Faceless Ones* takes place on (and above) contemporary Earth now seems unremarkable, given the numerous uses of that setting in subsequent years. It should be borne in mind however that this was actually only the second story of its type to be seen in the series (the first having been *The War Machines*). As Marton commented: 'Fans have been so inundated with 20th Century invasions of Earth set in England that the original novelty value of it being [Patrick Troughton's] premier appearance in this setting has long worn off.'

The Faceless Ones also provides a welcome contrast to the monster-filled tales of the earlier part of the season, making use of the convenient plot device of having the aliens take on the appearance of humans for much of the story. Not only does this save the production team the expense of creating elaborate monster costumes, it also means that the story has to rely for its excitement more on effective dialogue and action than on the shock appearance of an alien being. The Chameleon creatures, when they do eventually appear, are nevertheless suitably gruesome: 'The first appearance of the face of a Chameleon is a behind-the-sofa *Doctor Who* gem,' enthused Marton. 'The hideously veined face with its similarities to delegate Malpha in *The Daleks' Master Plan* was a make-up classic.'

'It was a pity that the Chameleons themselves were a bit unbelievable,' wrote Robert Shearman in *Cloister Bell* 6/7 in 1983. 'They lacked any chill that the Macra may have had and, while not being a stupid race, they weren't as clever as they imagined themselves to be. The clichéd idea of a race being able to assume human features (overtly plagiarised from *Invasion of the Body-Snatchers*) was touched on again after *The Faceless Ones* ... but was dealt with in this story far better than [in] any other ... [As they were] forced to remain in the identity they [had] stolen, or they [would] die, you could feel their fear as the Doctor threatened to remove the armbands which held their identity together.'

The Chameleons aside, the story's special effects tend to be rather lacklustre. More significantly, the scripts by David Ellis and Malcolm Hulke contain far too much talk and not enough action to maintain the viewer's interest over the full six episodes, making this a rather unmemorable adventure. It does, however, have its good points. 'The plot was full of mystery and excitement, such as ... at the end of Episode 3 when we find that somehow the passengers on the Chameleon flight have [apparently] vanished in mid flight,' wrote Gordon Roxburgh in *Matrix* Issue 4 dated November 1979. 'There was also the suspense [factor] that you didn't know who was a Chameleon. Jamie ... fell head first into this and divulged all to the Chameleon leader (the Director) thinking him to be the real Crossland. [An example of] Frazer Hines' technique of getting the audience involved, shouting at home, "No! He's not real, he's the alien!".'

'The plot is not going to win an award,' commented Tim Munro in *Star Begotten* Volume

3 Number 4 dated autumn 1989. 'The Chameleon kidnappings raise the question of why nobody (other than Samantha Briggs) notices that their holidaying relatives never seem to come back. Generally, though, *The Faceless Ones* is carried off with such skill that one ignores the holes in it … The scripts cannot really be faulted … The characters are sympathetic, often hilariously funny, but *nobody* is reduced to mere comic relief. They're realistic people with many facets. Above all, there is excellent handling of Patrick Troughton's Doctor, capturing perfectly the schizoid blend of childlike playfulness and unquestionable authority.'

Overall, the positive aspects of the story probably just about outweigh the negative. 'Somewhat out of place in a season still deeply-rooted in the Hartnell era,' concluded Tim Robins in *Doctor Who – An Adventure in Space and Time* in 1983, '[it is a] bizarre, often camp action-adventure; a trendy, yet successful attempt to drag *Doctor Who* into the second half of the '60s [and] a blueprint for the future.'

THE EVIL OF THE DALEKS

Writer: David Whitaker. **Director:** Derek Martinus, Timothy Combe[7]*. **Designer:** Chris Thompson. **Costumes:** Sandra Reid. **Make-up:** Gillian James. **Incidental Music:** Dudley Simpson. **Visual Effects:** Michealjohn Harris, Peter Day. **Fight Arranger:** Peter Diamond. **Film Cameraman:** John Baker. **Film Editor:** Ted Walters. **Studio Lighting:** Wally Whitmore. **Studio Sound:** Bryan Forgham. **Production Assistant:** Timothy Combe. **Assistant Floor Manager:** David Tilley, Margaret Rushton. **Dalek Stories Created By:** Terry Nation**.

* Dalek fight film sequence only.
** As on *The Power of the Daleks*, Terry Nation received this credit on Episodes 3 to 7, with a voice-over credit on Episode 2, as joint owner with the BBC of the rights to the Daleks.

	First UK TX	Scheduled TX	Actual TX	Duration	Viewers	Chart Pos.
Episode 1	20/05/67	18.00	18.00	24'07"	8.1	37
Episode 2	27/05/67	17.50	17.51	25'13"	7.5	37
Episode 3	03/06/67	17.45	17.45	24'27"	6.1	61
Episode 4	10/06/67	17.45	17.45	24'43"	5.3	51
Episode 5	17/06/67	17.45	17.45	25'23"	5.1	62
Episode 6	24/06/67	17.45	17.45	24'48"	6.8	38
Episode 7	01/07/67	18.25	18.25	24'33"	6.1	50

Plot: The TARDIS has been stolen by antiques dealer Edward Waterfield, who lures the Doctor and Jamie into a trap. They are transported back to Waterfield's own time, 1867, where his daughter Victoria is being held hostage by the Daleks to ensure his cooperation. The Daleks force the Doctor to monitor Jamie's performance of a test – the rescue of Victoria – with the supposed intention of identifying the human factor: the special quality possessed by humans that enables them always to defeat the Daleks. The Doctor, having succeeded in this task, implants the human factor into three test Daleks – with the result that they become friendly and playful! Everyone is transported back to Skaro where the Doctor discovers that the Daleks' true aim has been to isolate the Dalek factor – the impulse to destroy – and implant it into humans. The Emperor Dalek informs him that his TARDIS will be used to spread the Dalek factor throughout all time. By a ruse, however, the Doctor is able to infuse many more Daleks with the human factor. A civil war breaks out between the two Dalek factions and they are apparently all destroyed. As Waterfield has been killed during the course of the action, the Doctor offers Victoria a place aboard the TARDIS.

Episode endings:

1. Waterfield's henchman Kennedy, absorbed in rifling his boss's secret safe, fails to notice as a Dalek materialises behind him. He turns and stares in horror as the Dalek grates 'Who are you?' and demands that he answer.
2. Two Daleks wait for the test on Jamie to begin. One intones that the humans have been warned that any delay will result in their death. Unaware that Jamie is currently missing, the other replies: 'There will be no delay!'
3. Jamie makes his way cautiously through the booby-trapped corridors of the house. Suddenly a figure looms out of the darkness ahead of him. He calls out, asking who is there. The burly Turk Kemel prepares to attack him …
4. Jamie and Kemel reach Victoria's room. Jamie bangs on her door to bring her out. Suddenly a door opens behind them, and a Dalek emerges …
5. Jamie looks on in bemusement as the humanised Daleks play a game of 'trains' with the Doctor, who rides around on the back of one of them …
6. An alcove is illuminated, revealing the captured TARDIS. The Emperor Dalek announces that the Doctor will 'take the Dalek factor and spread it through the entire history of Earth'.
7. The Doctor looks down at the Dalek city and mutters 'The final end'. The city is in ruins, with exterminated Daleks all around. One Dalek, however, is still alive …

IT WAS MADE WHERE…?

Location Filming: 20.04.67-21.04.67, 24.04.67-25.04.67
Locations: BBC Outside Broadcasts and Transport Base, Kendal Avenue, Ealing, London, W3; Warehouse Lane, Hammersmith, London, W1; Grimsdyke Rehabilitation Centre, Old Redding Road, Harrow Weald, Harrow.
Ealing Filming: 26.04.67-28.04.67 on Stage 2, 16.05.67-17.05.67 on Stage 3 A/B
Studio Recording: 13.05.67, 20.05.67, 27.05.67, 03.06.67, 10.06.67, 17.06.67, 24.06.67, all in Lime Grove D

ADDITIONAL CREDITED CAST

Bob Hall (Alec Ross[1]), Kennedy (Griffith Davies[1,2]), Edward Waterfield (John Bailey), Perry (Geoffrey Colville[1,2]), Daleks (Robert Jewell, Gerald Taylor[3-7], John Scott Martin[5-7], Murphy Grumbar[6,7], Ken Tyllsen[7]), Dalek Voices (Roy Skelton[1,6,7*], Peter Hawkins[2-7]), Mollie Dawson (Jo Rowbottom[2-5]), Theodore Maxtible (Marius Goring[2-7]), Ruth Maxtible (Brigit Forsyth[2-5]), Toby (Windsor Davies[2-4]), Arthur Terrall (Gary Watson[3-5]), Kemel (Sonny Caldinez[3-7]).

* Roy Skelton provided Dalek voices for Episode 5 as well, but this was a late change of plan and he received no credit on the episode (although he did in *Radio Times*).

THINGS TO WATCH OUT FOR

- The Beatles' 'Paperback Writer' and the Seekers' 'Nobody Knows the Trouble I've Seen' were used as background music on the juke box in the coffee bar scenes in the first episode.
- The theme given to the Daleks by Dudley Simpson in his incidental music was based on the series' own signature tune.
- Patrick Troughton and Deborah Watling appear only in film inserts in the fourth episode as they were on holiday during the week when it was recorded.
- Sound effects from *The Mutants* and *The Daleks' Master Plan* were re-used for the Dalek city.
- Some Louis Marx 'tricky action' toy Daleks were used in modelwork for the scenes of the destruction of the Dalek city.
- This story features the first individual visual effects designer credits ever given on the series, to Michealjohn Harris and Peter Day. Previously visual effects had been handled by the series' scenic designers rather than by the BBC's Visual Effects Department, although the Department as a whole did receive a credit on the first story, *100,000 BC*.

THINGS YOU MIGHT NOT HAVE KNOWN

- Michealjohn Harris is the person whose name is most often misspelt on *Doctor Who*'s closing credits.
- Individual episode titles were included on all scripts, bar that for Episode 6. These were as follows: 1: *To Set a Trap...*; 2: *The Net Tightens*; 3: *A Trial of Strength*; 4: *A Test of Skill*; 5: *The Human Factor*; 7: *The End of the Daleks*.
- David Whitaker's original story breakdown for *The Evil of the Daleks* was headed simply *Daleks* and dated 4 January 1967. It read as follows (with 'C.H.' standing for cliffhanger):

> Ep.1: Tardis stolen. Waterfield reports to Daleks success of mission – asks for Victoria to be returned to him. We learn the Dalek 3 phase plan: Steal Tardis: Trap Doctor and take him back to 1880: Use Tardis to investigate human factor in man's evolution.
> C.H.: Dr. finds Waterfield's shop, etc.
>
> Ep.2: Waterfield lures Dr. to his two-man time machine with Jamie. Ben and Polly return to London life. Dr. etc. whisked back to 1880.
> C.H.: They are confronted by the Daleks.
>
> Ep.3: We meet Anne Waterfield, Etc. Waterfield uses pressure on Dr. to show him how Tardis operates and take him back to 20,000 B.C.
> C.H.: They return to Savage Cave in 20,000 B.C.
>
> Ep.4: Sequence in Cave. Og is captured. Tardis scene. He is brought back to 1880. Studied by Waterfield.
> C.H.: Og escapes.

Ep.5: Og recaptured. Anne and Og. Jamie taken to Skaro. He meets Victoria.
C.H.: Daleks take over investigation of Og.

Ep.6: Daleks learn what it is that makes mankind tick. They plan to return
to B.C. to destroy this quality.
C.H.: They return to B.C. with Dr. and Og as prisoners.

Ep.7: B.C.: Battle with Daleks. Skaro, Jamie etc. escape. Final scene in
Victorian London.

- Deborah Watling was not the first choice of actress to play the new companion, Victoria Waterfield. After auditions that took place around the end of March/beginning of April 1967, and a camera test on the afternoon of 11 April, Denise Buckley appears to have been chosen for the part. On 13 April, however, Innes Lloyd dropped Buckley from the cast of *The Evil of the Daleks* and confirmed that Deborah Watling (who was not listed for audition) was to play the part instead. Lloyd asked for an option on her services for *The Tomb of the Cybermen*, the next story to be recorded, and also on *The Abominable Snowmen*, which was the first story due to be made after the summer break.
- The Daleks' creator Terry Nation was paid £15 per episode for their use in this story.
- The decision to remove Ben and Polly from the first two episodes of *The Evil of the Daleks* resulted in David Whitaker having to re-work his scripts for those episodes, which he had already delivered.
- The designer for this story was originally to have been Colin Shaw. It was eventually Chris Thompson.
- Actor Barry Ashton's hands doubled for Patrick Troughton's in close up during filming at Ealing on 28 April 1967 for the first episode of this story.
- An experimental session to try out an inlay effect was carried out in Lime Grove Studio D between seven and eight in the evening of 18 May 1967. No recording was done.

QUOTE, UNQUOTE

- **Dalek:** 'The human discovered our communications system.' **Edward Waterfield:** 'And you murdered him!' **Dalek:** 'He would have betrayed us.' **Edward Waterfield:** 'You don't have to kill!' **Dalek:** 'Silence!' **Edward Waterfield:** 'I won't be silent! What are you dragging me into? You've destroyed a human life, don't you understand that?' **Dalek:** 'That is of no consequence.' **Edward Waterfield:** 'No *consequence*!' **Dalek:** 'There is only one form of life that matters – Dalek life!'
- **Jamie:** [To the Doctor] 'Anyone would think that it's a little game, and it's not. People have died. The Daleks are all over, fit to murder the lot of us, and all you can say is that you've had a good night's work. Well, I'm telling you this, we're finished. You're just too callous for me. Anything goes by the board, anything at all. You don't give that much for a living soul except yourself. Just whose side are you on?'
- **Dalek Emperor:** 'So you are the Doctor.' **The Doctor:** 'We meet at last. I wondered if we ever would.' **Dalek Emperor:** 'The experiment is over?' **The Doctor:** 'Yes. I have implanted the human factor in the three Daleks that you gave me. [To Waterfield and Jamie.] When I say "run", run.' **Dalek Emperor:** 'Speak louder!'

The Doctor: 'I was merely telling my friend that the day of the Daleks is coming to an end.' **Dalek Emperor:** 'Explain.' **The Doctor:** 'It's very simple. Somewhere in the Dalek race there are three Daleks with the human factor. Gradually they will come to question. They will persuade other Daleks to question. You will have a rebellion on your planet.' **Dalek Emperor:** 'No!' **The Doctor:** 'I say yes! I've beaten you, and I don't care what you do to me now.'

ANALYSIS

'The final end,' whispers the Doctor as the seventh and last episode of *The Evil of the Daleks* draws to a close. The momentous event to which he is referring is the ultimate destruction (or so he thinks) of his old enemies the Daleks in a devastating civil war that has reduced their gleaming metal city to a smouldering ruin. Coming at the conclusion of the fourth season – a season that has seen *Doctor Who* successfully negotiating its crucial first change of lead actor – it can also be said to mark the end of the first major chapter in the series' long history.

This sense of closure is engendered not only by the apparent destruction of the Daleks (something in no way invalidated by the fact that they were, in the event, later resurrected) but also by the fact that the story harks back to the series' roots and showcases many of the main elements that have contributed towards its early success. In taking the unusual course of splitting the action between three very different settings – Earth in the present, Earth in the past and an alien planet in the future – it provides an excellent illustration of the flexibility afforded by the concept of space and time travel and encompasses all the principal story types established within the basic *Doctor Who* format. It even sees the Doctor revisiting the Daleks' home planet, Skaro, the scene of his original encounter with them in the second transmitted story. Such return visits may now seem unremarkable, but in 1967 this was thrilling stuff.

Also reminiscent of the series' roots is the fact that the Doctor appears during certain parts of the story to be acting in a decidedly furtive and suspect manner. More so than at any other time since the early part of the first season, he seems an enigmatic and potentially dangerous figure with a distinctly dark side to his nature. Jamie is even moved at one point to denounce him as being 'too callous' and threaten to part company with him as soon as they reach their next destination – an echo of feelings expressed by the Doctor's original human companions, Ian and Barbara, in the early days of their travels in the TARDIS. The Doctor's dispassionate manipulation of individuals and events in order to bring about the Daleks' destruction provides an effective reminder of his alien qualities. 'I am not a student of human nature,' he comments at one point, 'I am a professor of a far wider academy of which human nature is merely a part'.

David Whitaker was an ideal person to script this virtual homage to the series' own ethos. As one of the small group of individuals responsible for developing the format in the first place, he understood perhaps better than any other writer what it was that made it so successful and gave it its unique appeal. His scripts for the story are superbly crafted, recounting a suspenseful and epic tale with a wealth of striking images and memorable dialogue. Particularly outstanding are his compelling and finely-drawn characters, including the naïvely misguided scientist Edward Waterfield and his innocent young daughter Victoria; the ruthless entrepreneur Theodore Maxtible, obsessed with the alchemist's dream of transforming base metal into gold; Maxtible's prim, deluded daughter Ruth; her hapless suitor Arthur Terrall, driven half insane by the Daleks' malign influence; the mute Turkish wrestler Kemel; and, of course, the Daleks themselves, positively radiating evil in one of their strongest ever vehicles.

The story's production values are also high. The scenes set in Victorian England, evoking impressions of sources as diverse as H G Wells and Lewis Carroll, are especially well-realised, consistent with the BBC's reputation for excellence in the production of period drama. Those set on Skaro, while perhaps lacking the distinctive look of earlier Dalek stories, are nonetheless effective. The imposing Dalek Emperor is a truly awe-inspiring innovation, and now one of the series' great icons.

The Evil of the Daleks is, in short, one of those rare stories truly deserving of that much over-used label 'classic'. *Doctor Who* had featured many excellent stories before, but rarely had it been as enthralling, as gripping or as exciting as this. 'It is *Doctor Who* at its very, very best,' commented Jeremy Bentham in *DWB* No. 50 dated December 1987, 'not only obeying all the rules of good drama production but rising to the challenge of making credible science-fiction melodrama while neatly avoiding all the temptations either to send it up or, worse, camp it up.'

Many scenes stay fresh in the viewer's memory long after they are witnessed: the TARDIS being stolen and driven away on a lorry; the Daleks gliding through the wood-panelled corridors of Maxtible's home; the Doctor playing 'trains' with three humanised Daleks; Jamie growing distrustful of the Doctor as he seems to fall under the Daleks' influence; the possessed Maxtible walking around with his arms outstretched like a Dalek, mirroring the 'make believe' actions of many thousands of schoolchildren over the previous four years; and the climactic civil war on Skaro, with the Emperor's increasingly desperate cries of 'You must not fight in here!' and copious quantities of gunge spewing from the tops of exterminated Daleks.

It is unsurprising to find that the BBC's Audience Research Report on the story's final episode, while indicating that there were as usual a minority who simply disliked the series and 'hoped that, as this episode suggested, this was indeed the last of the Daleks – and, for that matter, Doctor Who, the TARDIS and "the whole stupid, childish, silly boiling lot",' indicated an overwhelmingly positive response from contemporary viewers. The most commonly expressed opinion was that the story had been 'as amusing and exciting as ever' and that 'the entire *Doctor Who* series, if undoubtedly "pure escapism", was nevertheless "good fun" and certainly utterly harmless'. Children, it was found, 'still adored the Daleks, and were devastated by the suggestion that these amusing and fantastic creatures had been finally and irrevocably wiped out'. Adult fans, too, insisted that 'the *Doctor Who* series (and particularly those adventures involving the Daleks) were hard to beat … and they would be sorry indeed if there were to be no more'.

Gerry Davis's departure from the post of story editor around the end of April 1967 brought to a close a period of relative stability for *Doctor Who*'s production team. It also marked the end of Kit Pedler's regular involvement as the series' unofficial scientific adviser (although he would continue to provide storylines for Cyberman adventures throughout the remainder of the second Doctor's era). Innes Lloyd was also keen to move on by this stage, feeling that he had contributed all he could to the series, but remained as producer for the time being as no suitable successor was available; Davis had in fact been invited to take over from him, but had declined.

The new story editor appointed to the series was former actor and radio writer, director and producer Peter Bryant, who had been trailing Davis as an assistant since around mid-January 1967. Bryant was also seen as a potential replacement for Lloyd; indeed it had initially been thought that he would take the role of associate producer on the series, hence his credit as such on *The Faceless Ones*. Around the time that he took over from Davis, Bryant also brought in a new assistant of his own, namely writer and sometime actor Victor Pemberton (who had actually appeared in *The Moonbase* as one of the base personnel).

The fourth season had been, all things considered, a successful one for *Doctor Who*. A critical change of lead actor had been well accomplished; a period of experimentation had led to the development of an effective new format; and, with the arrival of Jamie in *The Highlanders* and Victoria in *The Evil of the Daleks*, two promising new companion characters had been introduced in place of Polly and Ben. The changes overseen by Lloyd and Davis had, in short, revitalised the series. The task facing Lloyd and Bryant for the fifth season was to consolidate and build upon that success.

DOCTOR WHO SEASON FIVE (1967-1968)

Regular Cast:
Dr. Who (Patrick Troughton)
Jamie (Frazer Hines)
Victoria (Deborah Watling) until *Fury from the Deep* Episode 6
Zoe (Wendy Padbury) from *The Wheel in Space* Episode 2

Regular Crew:
Producer: Peter Bryant on *The Tomb of the Cybermen*. Innes Lloyd from *The Abominable Snowmen* Episode One to *The Enemy of the World* Episode 6. Peter Bryant from *The Web of Fear* Episode 1 onwards.
Story Editor: Victor Pemberton on *The Tomb of the Cybermen*. Peter Bryant from *The Abominable Snowmen* Episode One to *The Enemy of the World* Episode 6. Derrick Sherwin from *The Web of Fear* Episode 1 onwards.
Title Music: Ron Grainer and the BBC Radiophonic Workshop, arranged by Delia Derbyshire.
Special Sounds: Brian Hodgson.

Viewers tuning in for the start of *Doctor Who*'s fifth season could have been forgiven for thinking that there was a new production team in charge. In fact the crediting of Peter Bryant as producer and Victor Pemberton as story editor on *The Tomb of the Cybermen* was merely a one-off trial run for what Innes Lloyd hoped would eventually become a permanent arrangement. Thus on the following story, *The Abominable Snowmen*, Lloyd regained his usual producer credit while Bryant reverted to story editor and Pemberton to his uncredited assistant. It was not until later in the season that Lloyd was finally granted his wish to move on to pastures new and Bryant was allowed to take over from him. Bryant's eventual successor as story editor – Pemberton having by this point become aware that he was not cut out for the job – was a young freelance writer named Derrick Sherwin, who brought in his own uncredited assistant in the person of another young freelancer, Terrance Dicks.

Unlike previous changes of production team, these behind-the-scenes developments had little discernible impact on the style and content of the Doctor's adventures. Bryant very much approved of the way in which Lloyd had handled the series and the direction in which he had steered it and saw no need for any major shake-up. The transition was thus a smooth one; a factor that no doubt contributed greatly to the remarkable consistency of quality attained by the season – a season that many now consider a strong contender for the title of best in the series' history.

THE TOMB OF THE CYBERMEN

Writer: Kit Pedler, Gerry Davis. **Director:** Morris Barry. **Designer:** Martin Johnson. **Costumes:** Sandra Reid[1,2], Dorothea Wallace[3,4]. **Make-Up:** Gillian James. **Incidental Music:** stock. **Visual Effects:** Michealjohn Harris, Peter Day. **Film Cameraman:** Peter Hamilton. **Film Editor:** Alan Martin. **Studio Lighting:** Graham Sothcott. **Studio Sound:** Brian Hiles. **Production Assistant:** Snowy Lidiard-White. **Assistant Floor Manager:** Sue Willis, Catherine Sykes.

	First UK TX	Scheduled TX	Actual TX	Duration	Viewers	Chart Pos.
Episode 1	02/09/67	17.50	17.50	23'58"	6.0	57
Episode 2	09/09/67	17.50	17.50	24'44"	6.4	57
Episode 3	16/09/67	17.50	17.50	24'14"	7.2	38
Episode 4	23/09/67	17.50	17.50	23'22"	7.4	34

Plot: The TARDIS arrives on the planet Telos where an Earth archaeological expedition, led by Professor Parry, is attempting to uncover the lost tombs of the Cybermen. With a lot of help from the Doctor the archaeologists enter the tombs. There, one of the party, Klieg, reveals himself and his business partner, Kaftan, to be planning to revive the Cybermen. He wants to use their strength, allied with the intelligence of his own Brotherhood of Logicians, to create an invincible force for conquest. It transpires however that the tomb is actually a giant trap designed to lure humans suitable for conversion into further Cybermen – a fate that almost befalls Kaftan's assistant Toberman. After fending off an attack by Cybermats – small but dangerous cybernetic creatures – the Doctor eventually defeats the revived Cybermen, led by their Controller, and reseals the tombs. The Controller is apparently destroyed in the process.

Episode endings:

1. In a room within the excavated complex, Jamie and the archaeologist Haydon have found a machine that creates patterns on a wall. They experiment with it, and when Jamie activates a previously unused switch the figure of a Cyberman appears. Moments later Haydon falls dead to the ground – he has been shot.

2. The Cybermen have released their Controller from his tomb. Klieg appeals to the creature, explaining that he represents the Brotherhood of Logicians and needs their help. The creature grabs his arm and flatly intones: 'You belong to us. You will be like us.'

3. The Cybermen send Cybermats to attack the archaeologists. The Doctor renders them harmless and then goes to check on Kaftan and Klieg, who have been locked in the weapons testing room. Kaftan and Klieg suddenly appear, having escaped with the aid of an X-ray laser found in the room. Klieg fires the laser, apparently aiming at the Doctor.

4. The Doctor, Jamie and Victoria depart from Telos, leaving behind a live Cybermat and the dead body of the partially cybernised Toberman.

Location Filming: 12.06.67
Location: Gerrards Cross Sand and Gravel Quarry, Wapsey's Wood , Gerrard's Cross, Bucks.

Ealing Filming: 13.06.67-16.03.67 on Stage 2
Model Filming: 19.06.67 in Puppet Theatre
Studio Recording: 01.07.67, 08.07.67, 15.07.67, 22.07.67, all in Lime Grove D

ADDITIONAL CREDITED CAST

Toberman (Roy Stewart), Professor Parry (Aubrey Richards), John Viner (Cyril Shaps[1,2]), Jim Callum (Clive Merrison[1,3,4]), Kaftan (Shirley Cooklin), Captain Hopper (George Roubicek), Eric Klieg (George Pastell), Ted Rogers (Alan Johns[1]), Peter Haydon (Bernard Holley[1,2]), Crewman (Ray Grover[1]), Cyberman Controller (Michael Kilgarriff[2-4]), Cybermen (Hans de Vries[2-4], Tony Harwood[2-4], John Hogan[2-4], Richard Kerley[2-4], Ronald Lee[2-4], Charles Pemberton[2-4], Kenneth Seeger[2-4], Reg Whitehead[2-4]), Cybermen Voices (Peter Hawkins[2-4]).

POPULAR MYTHS

- The only surviving copy of this story is slightly edited. (The prints in the BBC's archives are complete and unedited.)

THINGS TO WATCH OUT FOR

- Martin Johnson's set designs are excellent, and include some striking bas-relief Cyberman images on the walls of the tomb complex.
- Producer Peter Bryant's then wife Shirley Cooklin appears in the role of Kaftan, which was written specially for her.
- Klieg's mention in the first episode of 'Whitehead logic' was probably a nod to the actor Reg Whitehead, who had played a Cyberman in all their stories to date.
- There is a wonderfully moving scene in which the Doctor comforts a frightened Victoria and tries to help her to come to terms with the death of her father by telling her that he can recall his own family, but only when he chooses to.

THINGS YOU MIGHT NOT HAVE KNOWN

- Working titles: *The Cybermen Planet*, *The Ice Tombs of Telos*.
- Toberman was described in the original scripts as wearing a hearing aid (tying in with the fact that he was virtually mute and perhaps with the story's theme of cybernisation), but this idea was dropped at the request of director Morris Barry.
- Klieg was originally to have been played by Vladek Sheybal and the Cyber Controller by John Wills (who had appeared as a Cyberman in *The Moonbase*).
- Orange squash was specially provided in the studio for the actors playing the Cybermen, who got very hot inside their heavy costumes.

QUOTE, UNQUOTE

- **Eric Klieg:** 'How did you know in the first place?' **The Doctor:** 'Oh, I used my own, special technique.' **Eric Klieg:** 'Oh, really, Doctor … and may we know what that is?' **The Doctor:** 'Keeping my eyes open and my mouth shut!'
- **The Doctor:** 'Well, if we count in Earth terms I suppose I must be about 400 … yes, about 450 years old! Yes. Well. Quite …'
- **The Doctor:** 'Our lives are different to anybody else's. That's the exciting thing. Nobody in the universe can do what we're doing.'

ANALYSIS

'*The Tomb of the Cybermen* is, quite simply, the best [Cyberman] story,' enthused Martin Day in *Cloister Bell* 10/11 dated March 1985. 'Accompanied by superb acting from Pat Troughton and many others, scenes such the Doctor's recollections of his family become steeped in emotion and the mysteries of the time traveller, guaranteed to bring a lump to the throat and to stick in the mind for a long time after.'

The production team had apparently learned from the mistakes of the previous two Cyberman adventures and, although *The Tomb of the Cybermen* follows the same basic pattern (isolated group of humans picked off by the Cybermen), it manages to develop the idea to greater advantage and, as a result, achieves a considerable success.

Perhaps in recognition that this is the start of a new season, and also that the TARDIS has a newcomer in the person of Victoria Waterfield, the story starts with a brief recap of what the TARDIS does and of the Doctor's role in the proceedings. This piece of background out of the way, the action cuts to some very impressive location filming as our isolated group of humans – archaeologists in this case – uncover the doors leading to the lost tombs of the Cybermen. The story really picks up when the Doctor arrives; in fact, although this is not dwelt on, it is the Doctor who allows the men access to the tomb complex and, ultimately, to the frozen Cybermen lying dormant below. This aspect of the plot was highlighted by Graham Howard in *TSV* 29 dated July 1992: 'In this story the Doctor always seems two steps ahead of the others in the expedition and basically appears to be the only one capable of solving the Cybermen's puzzles ... This used to bother me in that it seemed if it hadn't been for the Doctor no-one would have been able to get down into the tombs. I now consider he probably thought that once the tombs had been discovered it was only a matter of time before someone would be successful in entering [them], and so it was better to bring out and destroy the evil now rather than let it have a chance to develop ... This superiority makes him instrumental to the advancement of a good deal of the plot and at times made him appear more like a "cosmic Columbo" than a "cosmic hobo".'

It seems to be a minor failing of all Kit Pedler's stories that, while the nominal leader of the human team (be it Cutler, Hobson or Parry) is a fairly strong character (although in Parry's case this in itself is questionable), the others are faceless and weak. The exception to the rule provided by *The Tomb of the Cybermen* is the inspired addition of a rogue factor in the form of the mysterious, but oddly named, Kaftan, her servant Toberman and Klieg, the expedition's financier, all of whom have ulterior motives for being there. These characters work well and provide much entertainment – especially effective are Klieg's verbal sparring with the Doctor, and his insane determination to achieve his aims come what may.

The Cybermen, when they eventually appear, are again impressive, and the addition of the Cyberman Controller is interesting, if only because it reduces the rest of the creatures to mostly non-speaking stooges – a problem that would similarly beset the Daleks when Davros was introduced in 1975. The voices used for the Cybermen here are the same as those in *The Moonbase* and just as chilling, the emotionless electronic drone serving to emphasis the horror of the prospect of being physically transformed into one of these creatures.

'The [Cybermen] were at their best in *The Moonbase* and *The Tomb of the Cybermen*,' opined Jeremy Bentham in *DWB* No. 101 dated May 1992. 'There is something about those smooth, featureless masks, with their dark, hollow eyes and that "grinning skull" expression, that is truly chilling. Add into the recipe their flat [electronic] voices and the illusion of inhuman technology made flesh is virtually complete.

'[The] visualisation, or even just the threat, of "body horror" has always been an effective tool in [*Doctor Who*'s] workshop. [The idea of having] your humanity wrenched away and replaced with the mind or the artefacts of an alien invader has sent children scurrying behind sofas from *The Dalek Invasion of Earth* [onwards]. It's done with classic, blood-curdling style in *The Tomb of the Cybermen* as Toberman's cloak falls open to reveal a shining metal and plastic arm where once [were] flesh and blood.'

The story is by no means perfect, however. As in *The Moonbase*, the Cybermen make a strange electronic quacking noise when they are attacked, which just sounds silly. While Morris Barry's direction is generally good, he also allows through two inexcusably poor action shots. The first occurs in a scene where a Cyberman lifts Toberman to throw him across the room; the problem is that the Kirby wire supporting actor Roy Stewart is all too clearly visible. The second comes where, similarly, Toberman lifts the Controller to throw him against some instrument panels; in this case, it is unfortunately very obvious that Stewart is actually holding nothing more than a lightweight empty suit. The scene in which Victoria falls asleep after being drugged by Kaftan is rather poorly acted by Deborah Watling; and the viewer's credulity is further strained by the subsequent scene where, on recovering, she manages to hit an attacking Cybermat with the very first shot that she fires from Kaftan's gun. Other flaws have more to do with the plotting than with the on-screen realisation. How, for example, does Kaftan know which switch to use in the scene where she closes the doors of the revitalising chamber in order to trap Victoria? A lucky guess, perhaps? And on the subject of the revitalising chamber, one wonders why the Cybermen didn't spot the flaw of placing it on the upper level of the tomb complex rather than by the tombs themselves, given that the Controller needs to be revitalised in order to survive ... Finally, although the attack by the Cybermats on the sleeping humans is well staged, these creatures are never actually seen to hurt anyone and it is very unclear exactly what threat they pose. Thus it seems rather strange when everyone backs away at the sight of a lone Cybermat; wouldn't they just assume that they could simply jump (or step) over it?

Fortunately, none of these little script and production niggles detracts too much from the overall impact of the story. It is well-paced, gripping and, in places, genuinely frightening. As Jeff Stone commented in *TSV 29* dated July 1992: 'From the lead in prologue following *The Evil of the Daleks* to the genuinely moving end, *The Tomb of the Cybermen* was one hundred minutes of sheer magic.'

THE ABOMINABLE SNOWMEN

Writer: Mervyn Haisman, Henry Lincoln. **Director:** Gerald Blake. **Designer:** Malcolm Middleton. **Costumes:** Martin Baugh. **Make-Up:** Sylvia James. **Incidental Music:** none. **Visual Effects:** Ron Oates, Ulrich Grösser. **Film Cameraman:** Peter Bartlett, Ken Westbury. **Film Editor:** Philip Barnikel. **Studio Lighting:** Howard King. **Studio Sound:** Norman Bennett, Alan Edmonds. **Production Assistant:** Marjorie Yorke. **Assistant Floor Manager:** Roselyn Parker.

	First UK TX	Scheduled TX	Actual TX	Duration	Viewers	Chart Pos.
Episode One	30/09/67	17.25	17.26	24'15"	6.3	57
Episode Two	07/10/67	17.25	17.26	23'15"	6.0	71
Episode Three	14/10/67	17.25	17.25	23'55"	7.1	51
Episode Four	21/10/67	17.25	17.25	24'11"	7.1	60
Episode Five	28/10/67	17.25	17.25	23'51"	7.2	61
Episode Six	04/11/67	17.25	17.26	23'31"	7.4	56

2 Second Doctor

Plot: The TARDIS arrives in Tibet in 1935 and the Doctor visits the remote Detsen monastery in order to return a sacred bell, the ghanta, given to him for safe keeping on a previous visit. There he meets an Englishman, Travers, on an expedition to track down the legendary Abominable Snowmen or Yeti. It transpires that the Yeti roaming the area are actually disguised robots, which scare away or kill anyone who approaches. The High Lama Padmasambhava, whom the Doctor met hundreds of years earlier on his previous visit, has been taken over by a nebulous alien being, the Great Intelligence, which has artificially prolonged his life and is now using him to control the Yeti by way of models on a chessboard-like map. The Intelligence's aim is to create a material form for itself and take over the Earth. The Doctor banishes it back to the astral plane, allowing Padmasambhava finally to die in peace.

Episode endings:
1. Jamie and Victoria are trapped inside a mountain cave as a Yeti attacks. Jamie attempts to hold it off with a sword, but the creature breaks this in two and lumbers after him. Victoria screams in terror.
2. The Doctor discovers a sphere-shaped cavity in the chest of a captured Yeti. Outside the monastery, a shiny metal sphere that was earlier dislodged from the Yeti and that began to move of its own accord now emits a high-pitched bleeping noise and gathers speed. Inside, at the feet of a statue of the Buddha, a similar sphere brought back by Jamie from the mountain cave follows suit.
3. The metal control sphere floats into the captured Yeti's chest cavity, which opens and closes automatically in order to accept it. Victoria, having just returned to the main hall where the Yeti has lain immobile beneath a spirit trap erected by the monks, lets out a horrified scream as the creature snaps its restraining chains and rears up to confront her …
4. Victoria, bidden by a strange disembodied voice, enters the monastery's inner sanctum. Inside, a curtain draws aside to reveal the wizened form of Padmasambhava. 'Come in,' the voice continues. 'You have no alternative.'
5. On the mountainside, a foam-like substance – the corporeal form of the Great Intelligence – starts to spew from the mouth of the cave.
6. As Travers hurries away, determined to catch the real Yeti that they have spotted further up the mountain, the time travellers head back to the TARDIS. Jamie hopes that next time the Doctor can land them somewhere warmer …

IT WAS MADE WHERE...?

Ealing Filming: 23.08.67-25.08.67 (Stage unknown)
Location Filming: 04.09.67-09.09.67
Location: Nant Ffrancon Pass, Gwynedd, North Wales.

Studio Recording: 15.09.67, 16.09.67, 23.09.67, 30.09.67, 07.10.67, 14.10.67, all in Lime Grove D

ADDITIONAL CREDITED CAST

Travers (Jack Watling), Khrisong (Norman Jones), Thonmi (David Spenser), Rinchen (David Grey[1-5]), Sapan (Raymond Llewellyn), Yeti (Reg Whitehead, Tony Harwood[2-6], Richard Kerley[2-6], John Hogan[3-6]), Songsten (Charles Morgan[2-6]), Padmasambhava (Wolfe Morris[2-6*]), Ralpachan (David Baron[2-6]).

* Wolfe Morris also supplied the harsh, sibilant voice of the Great Intelligence, but was uncredited for this.

THINGS TO WATCH OUT FOR

- Jack Watling, who played Professor Travers, was the real-life father of Deborah Watling, who played Victoria.
- The make-up effect created for Padmasambhava by Sylvia James is highly impressive.

THINGS YOU MIGHT NOT HAVE KNOWN

- The names of a number of the Tibetan characters were appropriated by Mervyn Haisman and Henry Lincoln from real historical figures. The real Padmasambhava, for instance, lived in the 8th Century and founded the Tibetan branch of Buddhism. When Terrance Dicks novelised the story in 1974 he made slight changes to the names of these characters – Padmasambhava became Padmasambvha, Songsten became Songtsen, Thonmi became Thomni and so on – apparently on the advice of *Doctor Who*'s then producer Barry Letts who, as a follower of Buddhism, considered that what Haisman and Lincoln had done was unnecessary and risked causing offence.
- The start of location filming was delayed by two days due to high winds at Llyn Ogwen.
- Twelve model Yeti were constructed for use on the relief map of the monastery and surrounding mountain. These were designed so that they could be made to blow up in Episode Six.
- The final episode of *The Abominable Snowmen* was followed on transmission by a trailer for *The Ice Warriors*. This ran as follows:

  Clent is at a desk in the main Ioniser Control room: 'My name is Clent. I'm a scientist in charge of stopping the second Ice Age from destroying the European Zone. A complex task at the best of times, a challenge, great and hard. One of the most brilliant scientists on my staff has rebelled against the way I run the base. And now he lives the life of a scavenger, a useless, non-productive waste of talent.'

  Cut to a straggly bearded man sitting in a hut: 'He's talking about me, I'm the scientist who rebelled. The name's Elric Penley. There's no point in arguing with a man like Clent, he's a machine. I chose this existence because, well, because I demand the right to be an individual. Clent may be able to control the glacier, but there's a far greater menace that he hasn't reckoned with. I mean the creature from the ice.'

Cut to the Warrior in a block of ice. It starts to come alive.

Announcer: 'The Doctor and his companions find themselves embroiled in this life or death struggle in *Doctor Who and the Ice Warriors*, next Saturday at 5:25.'

QUOTE, UNQUOTE

- **Travers:** [Describing the Yeti] 'They're shy, elusive creatures. Why do you think it's taken me so long to track them down?'
- **Jamie:** [Faced with the problem of a Yeti standing guard outside the TARDIS.] 'Have you thought of a clever plan, Doctor?' **The Doctor:** 'Yes, Jamie, I believe I have.' **Jamie:** 'What are you going to do?' **The Doctor:** 'Bung a rock at it!'
- **The Great Intelligence:** 'Why are you here? Why did you not heed my warning?' **The Doctor:** 'Who are you?' **The Great Intelligence:** 'You know well. It is I, the master Padmasabhava, who speaks.' **The Doctor:** 'Oh no, it isn't. I know Padmasambhava. He's my friend. Where have you come from? Why are you using his body in this fashion?' **The Great Intelligence:** 'Such a brain as yours is too small to grasp my purpose.' **The Doctor:** 'Too small!'

ANALYSIS

The Abominable Snowmen is a highly atmospheric and suspenseful tale. Its setting is unusual for the series and well-realised throughout, both in the mountainside location work – of which there is a pleasingly generous amount – and in the Detsen monastary studio scenes. 'A monastery should be a place of safety, a haven,' wrote Justin Richards in *Shada* 15 dated May/June 1983, 'yet here there is a sense of evil almost everywhere, emanating from the inner sanctum, the holy of holies. The only place that feels at all safe is the interior of the TARDIS, and that is guarded by a Yeti ... Having discovered that Padmasambhava is not the benevolent sage he is held to be, we are faced with the horror of the greatest evil being actually inside the monastery, with our heroes (and heroine). This, more than the Yeti roaming the slopes outside, from whom we can escape by closing the monastery doors, is what provokes the aura of impending doom.'

The monastery is perhaps at its most eerie when the Doctor first arrives there to find it apparently deserted. Brian Hodgson of the Radiophonic Workshop deserves particular credit for his goosebump-inducing sound effects of the wind whistling icily around the walls of the building; indeed, this story's sound effects as a whole are particularly good – as, arguably, they have to be, given the complete absence of any incidental music. Another fine example is the memorable – and, as schoolchildren throughout the country quickly discovered, easily imitable! – bleeping noise emitted by the Yeti control spheres.

The scripts for the story, by newcomers Mervyn Haisman and Henry Lincoln, are very well written. To have the Doctor revisiting the scene of a previous adventure, unseen by viewers and unrelated to the present one, is a good and novel idea (the only possible precedent being the mention in season three's *The Celestial Toymaker* of a previous visit by the Doctor to the Toymaker's domain). The central premise, of the Great Intelligence attempting to escape from the astral plane and achieve corporeal existence on Earth, is both intriguing and horrific, and makes for some very frightening scenes – particularly those involving the 'possessed' Padmasambhava. 'The storyline continues well throughout,' observed Kenny Smith in *The Paisley Pattern Dr Who Annual* in 1993, 'leaving several questions unanswered till virtually the climax ... Padmasambhava comes over as a pathetic man, only held together by the will of the Great Intelligence. The changes in his voice, from the cool, calm [tones of the] abbot into the malevolent, hoarse whisper of the Intelligence [constitute] one of the most effective uses of vocals in the whole of the show's history. Padmasambhava is brilliantly [portrayed] by Wolfe Morris.'

The Yeti are impressive, if somewhat cuddly, monsters with suitably mysterious origins, and their appeal is further enhanced by all the associated imagery – including their metal control spheres and the little model figures by means of which their movements are directed. 'For me,' wrote Nick Page in *Cloister Bell* 10/11 dated March 1985, 'the best monster of the sixties must be the Yeti. When they first emerged from the shadows in *The Abominable Snowmen* they did tend to spend a lot of the time standing motionless on what were supposed to be the slopes of the Himalayan mountains, but what made [them] so terrifying ... was that you never knew exactly when one was going to grab you – the Great Intelligence ... was obviously a conservationist and always turned off the robots' power whenever it was not required. This meant that as a character approached a seemingly dead Yeti, we the viewers never knew when it would burst into savage life ...'

The story features some great supporting characters as well – most notably the English explorer Travers, wonderfully portrayed by Deborah Watling's father Jack.

'As a piece of television drama the finished story is hard to fault,' summed up Justin Richards, 'boasting as it does an extremely high standard of story, script, design and production. There are few *Doctor Who* stories which achieve the [reputation] of [a] classic almost universally ... but *The Abominable Snowmen* is one.'

It is a reputation that is well deserved.

THE ICE WARRIORS

Writer: Brian Hayles. **Director:** Derek Martinus. **Designer:** Jeremy Davies. **Costumes:** Martin Baugh. **Make-Up:** Sylvia James. **Incidental Music:** Dudley Simpson. **Visual Effects:** Bernard Wilkie, Ron Oates. **Film Cameraman:** Brian Langley. **Film Editor:** Michael Lockey. **Studio Lighting:** Sam Neeter. **Studio Sound:** Bryan Forgham. **Production Assistant:** Snowy Lidiard-White. **Assistant Floor Manager:** Quenton Annis.

	First UK TX	Scheduled TX	Actual TX	Duration	Viewers	Chart Pos.
ONE	11/11/67	17.10	17.10	24'21"	6.7	68
TWO	18/11/67	17.25	17.25	24'10"	7.1	71
THREE	25/11/67	17.25	17.25	23'58"	7.4	64
FOUR	02/12/67	17.25	17.26	24'23"	7.3	63
FIVE	09/12/67	17.25	17.24	24'25"	8.0	44
SIX	16/12/67	17.25	17.25	23'58"	7.5	59

Plot: The TARDIS arrives on Earth at the time of a new ice age and the travellers make their way into a base where scientists commanded by Leader Clent are using an ioniser device to combat the advance of a glacier. A giant humanoid creature, termed an Ice Warrior by one of the scientists, has been found buried in the glacier nearby. When thawed, it revives and is revealed to be Varga, captain of a Martian spacecraft that landed on Earth centuries ago and is still in the glacier. Varga sets about freeing his comrades and formulating a plan to conquer the Earth – Mars itself now being dead. The scientists meanwhile realise that continued use of the ioniser could cause the alien ship's engines to explode. Their trusted computer is unable to advise them without further information, and it seems that disaster is imminent. The disaffected scientist Penley, supported by the Doctor, eventually decides to risk activating the ioniser. There is only a minor explosion, which destroys the Martians and, at the same time, checks the ice flow.

Episode endings:

1. The frozen creature has been brought to the ioniser base and is left to thaw out while the scientists hold a meeting. Jamie and Victoria debate the merits of the clothes worn by the female scientists, oblivious to the fact that behind them the massive creature is starting to move ...

2. Varga has escaped from the base, taking with him a hostage in the person of Victoria and some portable power packs to thaw out his still frozen crew. Having blasted away the ice wall, Varga attaches the power packs to his comrades and stands back as they begin rapidly to thaw out.

3. Victoria escapes from the Martians' ship and uses one of the scientists' communicators to contact the Doctor at the base. She tells him that the aliens are ruthless killers and will stop at nothing. Inside the ship, the Martians' sonic cannon is trained on Victoria and the operator, Zondal, awaits the order to fire.

4. The Doctor goes to the Martians' ship, where Varga allows him to enter the airlock. Sealing the outer door, Varga threatens to reduce the atmospheric pressure in the airlock to zero unless the Doctor answers his questions.

5. Zondal has been left in charge of the Martians' sonic cannon while Varga and the others try to gain entry to the base. The Doctor and Victoria, held prisoner in the ship, use a vial of hydrogen sulphide to incapacitate Zondal. The collapsing Warrior makes a desperate attempt to activate the cannon, while the Doctor struggles to hold back his arm.

6. The Martians' ship is destroyed and Clent is happy to have Penley back working with him once more. The Doctor, Jamie and Victoria have meanwhile slipped quietly back to the TARDIS, which dematerialises from the snowy landscape.

IT WAS MADE WHERE...?

Ealing Filming: 25.09.67-29.09.67, 02.10.67 on Stage 3 A/B
Studio Recording: 21.10.67, 28.10.67, 04.11.67, 11.11.67, 18.11.67, 25.11.67, all in Lime Grove D

ADDITIONAL CREDITED CAST

Miss Garrett (Wendy Gifford), Clent (Peter Barkworth), Arden (George Waring[1-3]), Walters (Malcolm Taylor[1,5,6]), Davis (Peter Diamond[1]), Storr (Angus Lennie[1-4]), Penley (Peter Sallis), Varga, the Ice Warrior (Bernard Bresslaw[1,2]), Voice of Computer (Roy Skelton[1,2,5]), ICE WARRIORS: Varga, the Leader (Bernard Bresslaw[3-6]), Zondal (Roger Jones[3-6]), Turoc (Sonny Caldinez[3,4]), Rintan (Tony Harwood[3-6]), Isbur (Michael Attwell[3-6]).

Note: The way in which Bernard Bresslaw was credited on the first two episodes differed from the way in which he was credited on the remaining four. This is reflected in the above listing.

POPULAR MYTHS

- The base computer is called ECCO. (This name was invented by writer Brian Hayles for his later novelisation of the story.)

THINGS TO WATCH OUT FOR

- There is an unusual fading in and out of the opening story title, episode number and writer credits, with the episode number being presented in the format indicated in the transmission date listing above.
- Gentle giant Bernard Bresslaw, best known today for his many appearances in the *Carry On …* films, plays the impressive Martian leader, Varga.
- Peter Sallis, now well known as one of the stars of *Last of the Summer Wine*, appears as the scientist-turned-scavenger Penley.
- A real live bear was used in specially shot film inserts (as opposed to stock footage). It was hired from a company called Zoo-Rama Ltd, for a fee of £70, and used at Ealing on 29 September.
- Miss Garrett's entire costume unexpectedly changes between the fifth and sixth episodes.
- The TARDIS materialises on its side at the beginning of the first episode, and yet it is upright when it dematerialises at the end of the sixth.

THINGS YOU MIGHT NOT HAVE KNOWN

- The year in which this story was set was stated in publicity material as circa 3000 AD, but no date was given in the transmitted episodes themselves.
- During the recording of *The Ice Warriors*, two of the special effects models were destroyed due to 'careless handling' after their use in the second episode, while being retained for the fourth and fifth. These had to be re-built. In addition, a set was inadvertently destroyed between recording days and had to be reconstructed.
- Singer Joanne Brown was used by composer Dudley Simpson to provide the wordless vocals for his music for this story.

QUOTE, UNQUOTE

- **Victoria:** 'You won't succeed! You can't be so inhuman!'
- **Varga:** 'We only fight to win.'

ANALYSIS

One of the most immediately striking aspects of *The Ice Warriors* is the costumes; not only the Ice Warriors' impressive reptilian forms – now justly famous – which designer Martin Baugh based around the idea of a crocodile with an armoured shell, but also the human scientists' distinctive outfits. The latter consist of figure-hugging unitards for the women and tight suits for the men, all adorned with strange psychedelic patterns based on printed circuits, which Baugh derived from the notion that at this point in the Earth's future there might be machines that could automatically spray clothes onto a person.

Director Derek Martinus's casting of large actors to play the Martians was a good move, as the creatures tower over the rest of the characters and look very imposing. Their hissing voices and terrifying presence are what really give this story the edge. His choice of Bernard Bresslaw to play Varga was a particularly inspired piece of casting, and Bresslaw makes the part totally his own. Martinus's decision to have the Warriors' voices recorded separately was also astute, as it meant that the lips of the masks could be attached directly to those of the actors, allowing their mouths a full range of movement and reinforcing the impression of a race of truly alien creatures.

The rest of the guest cast playing the base personnel – who have to overcome not only the Martians but also the glacier and even their own internal conflicts – are uniformly excellent. Peter Barkworth deserves a special mention for his superb portrayal of Clent; and praise is also due to whoever came up with the simple but highly effective idea that he should play the part with a pronounced limp and walk aided by a stick. It is in the characterisation of Clent – and perhaps even more so in that of his assistant Miss Garrett, also well portrayed by Wendy Gifford – that writer Brian Hayles makes what is arguably the story's main point, specifically that it is dangerous for human beings to become too reliant on computers. This theme of man's relationship to machine is established early in the first episode, when the scientists at the base are seen to be so dependent on their computer to tell them what to do that they do not even realise that it is about to blow up until the Doctor arrives and manages to prevent the disaster. It is then explored throughout the rest of the story, principally through the symbolic conflict between Clent and Garrett on the one hand and Penley and his scavenger friend Storr on the other.

'Hayles was not trying to convince us that anti-technology was the right path,' argued Robert Shearman in *Cloister Bell* 10/11 dated March 1985. 'Penley was the most sympathetic character because, while he hated the effects that computerisation had on characters such as Clent and Garrett (and presumably most of the world), "We're not all like Clent. He's the kind that uses scientists' skulls as stepping stones to top jobs ..." He does respect science and the great good it is capable of doing for mankind – "Discovery is as exciting and purposeful to me as hunting game is to you" [he tells Storr]. The reason ... the Ioniser was used [by Hayles] to solve the problem [at the end of the story] was ... to emphasise that technology is good if under control. It is the humans who decide to use the Ioniser, whatever the dangers which cause the computer to run down.'

'Brian Hayles comes out firmly in favour of Penley,' agreed Martin J Wiggins in *Oracle* Volume 3 Number 4 dated January 1980. 'It is shown that only the individual can take initiative or risks, so that individualism is the key to an unpredictable, changing society, while regimentation yields only staticism. However, the case against individual freedom is well put by Clent, who asserts that people may misuse this freedom by trying to escape their own responsibility to others ... The story suggests that there are two clear choices – one can either have dictatorship entailing repression of individual rights, but also service to others, or else individual freedom with no such repression, but a possible lack of such service.'

A possible error in Brian Hayles' scripts was pointed out by a Miss J Kirkcaldy of Grays in a letter printed in the 14 December 1967 edition of *Radio Times*. 'I would like to point out to Doctor Who that there have already been four great ice advances and retreats, three of which, to give them their German names, are Guntz, Wurm and Mindel. This is what my geography mistress states and what I am learning for my O Level. Therefore if Doctor Who has to be in the grip of the Second Ice Age he will have to go back in time – not forward to AD 3000.' Hayles himself provided an answer to this, albeit not an entirely convincing one, in the same edition: 'The glacial advances known as Guntz, Mindel, Riss and Wurm were all "surges" within the overall Ice Age period, also known as Pleistocene or Quaternary.'

Another, perhaps more serious problem with Hayles's story is that it fails to give the viewer any real sense of where all the various settings are in relation to one other. The glacier face could be just a few hundred yards from the base, as could the shack where Storr and Penley hide out, but they could just as easily be miles away. Sometimes it takes people ages to travel from one place to another, yet on other occasions they do so quite quickly. The avalanche at the glacier face in the first episode does not appear to affect the base, and yet the glacier is supposed to be almost upon it. This, though, is no more than a minor irritation. Otherwise, there is very little to fault in *The Ice Warriors*, making it another in a succession of superb stories.

An important element in the success of this era of *Doctor Who* is the excellence of the three regulars, and again they are in fine form here. Patrick Troughton manages to make the most of certain scenes that allow for touches of humour, such as when the travellers emerge from the TARDIS at the start (the Doctor freezes in apparent terror, staring off into the distance ... because Jamie has knelt on his hand!), when the Doctor asks about a machine used for creating chemicals (he needs to use it urgently ... because he's thirsty!) and when he prepares to attack Zondal with ammonium sulphide (he cannot get the stopper off the test tube!). He is equally good, however, in scenes where the Doctor is forced to accept the gravity of the situation, such as when he approaches the Martian ship and when he speaks with Varga in the base. Frazer Hines and Deborah Watling also give a good account of themselves in their respective roles.

'The relationships of the trio from the TARDIS were at a zenith at this time, with each playing off and complementing the others,' wrote Marc Platt in *Shada* 14 dated March/April 1983. 'Although Jamie is confined mainly to buckling his swash, Victoria remains the enchanting innocent, even when she spends most of her time close to hysteria. Her vulnerable sense of wonder is undampened by her adventures and is an essential element of the magic that thrived throughout the fifth season. Troughton's Doctor is a constant surprise and it is that quality that makes him so admirable. The only obvious aspect is that he will be totally unpredictable. He marches into the base, is marked out by his scruffiness as a Scavenger, patches up the ioniser on the spot and takes over Penley's job. He uses an automatic chemical dispenser as a drinks supply, and when Miss Garrett proudly announces the base to be fully computerised, he says "Well, never mind" ... He then sets off into the blizzard to rescue Victoria from the Martians, whom he hopes will treat him as a guest! Troughton's magnificent gift is that the more outlandishly he behaves, the further ahead of us we know his quicksilver mind to be.'

The following story, however, would see the three time travellers playing strangely unaccustomed roles in the action ...

THE ENEMY OF THE WORLD

Writer: David Whitaker. **Director:** Barry Letts. **Designer:** Christopher Pemsel. **Costumes:** Martin Baugh. **Make-up:** Sylvia James. **Incidental Music:** stock. **Film Cameraman:** Fred Hamilton. **Film Editor:** Philip Barnikel. **Studio Lighting:** Howard King. **Studio Sound:** Tony Millier. **Production Assistant:** Martin Lisemore. **Assistant Floor Manager:** Edwina Verner.

	First UK TX	Scheduled TX	Actual TX	Duration	Viewers	Chart Pos.
Episode 1	23/12/67	17.25	17.25	23'45"	6.8	89
Episode 2	30/12/67	17.25	17.26	23'48"	7.6	75
Episode 3	06/01/68	17.25	17.26	23'05"	7.1	79
Episode 4	13/01/68	17.25	17.26	23'46"	7.8	66
Episode 5	20/01/68	17.25	17.25	24'22"	6.9	73
Episode 6	27/01/68	17.25	17.26	21'41"	8.3	55

Plot: The time travellers arrive in Australia in the near future and learn from a man named Giles Kent that the Doctor is the physical double of Salamander, a scientist and politician who has discovered a means of storing and distributing solar energy and thus ending starvation in a world ravaged by earthquakes, floods and the like. Most people see Salamander as a hero, but Kent and others believe him to be establishing himself as a dictator. The Doctor uncovers the truth by impersonating Salamander and gaining access to his research station. Salamander and Kent were originally working together. Almost five years ago, they convinced a group of people undergoing an endurance test in a bunker beneath the station that a war had broken out on the surface. It is these people, led by a man named Swann, who – deceived into thinking that they are striking back against an evil enemy – have been engineering the so-called natural disasters. Kent, now exposed as a traitor, blows up the station. Salamander meanwhile tries to escape in the TARDIS by impersonating the Doctor. He neglects to close the doors before dematerialisation, however, and is sucked out into the vortex.

Episode endings:
1. Salamander's security chief Bruce enters Kent's office with an armed guard. He directs the guard to open the door to an inner room. Salamander – or could it possibly be the Doctor impersonating him? – emerges and asks Bruce what he is doing there.
2. Salamander orders that Denes, the Controller of the European Zone, be arrested for traitorous incompetence. Denes appeals to his deputy, Fedorin, for support. Salamander, however, reveals that Fedorin is to be the chief witness at Denes's trial. Wracked by guilt, Fedorin turns away ...
3. Bruce tells Salamander that he saw him in Kent's office. Salamander retorts that he hasn't seen Kent in months. 'It was you,' insists Bruce. 'Or ... someone like you.'
4. The Doctor is with Kent and his assistant Astrid in the caravan overlooking Salamander's research station. Suddenly Bruce enters with an armed guard and confronts the Doctor.
5. A badly injured Swann tells Astrid that it was Salamander who attacked him, and that the attack took place below ground.
6. Salamander is sucked out through the open TARDIS doors and into the vortex as the Doctor and his companions struggle to save themselves from the same fate.

IT WAS MADE WHERE...?
Location Filming: 05.11.67-09.11.67
Locations: Clymping Beach, Climping, West Sussex; BBC Villiers House fire escape, Ealing Broadway, Ealing, London; Walpole Park, Ealing, London.
Ealing Filming: 10.11.67-11.11.67, 13.11.67 (Stage unknown)
Studio Recording: 02.12.67, 09.12.67, 16.12.67, 23.12.67, 30.12.67, 06.01.68, all in Lime Grove D

ADDITIONAL CREDITED CAST

Anton (Henry Stamper[1]), Rod (Rhys McConnochie[1]), Curly (Simon Cain[1]), Astrid (Mary Peach), Giles Kent (Bill Kerr), Donald Bruce (Colin Douglas), Salamander (Patrick Troughton[2-6])*, Benik (Milton Johns[2-6]), Denes (George Pravda[2,3]), Fedorin (David Nettheim[2,3]), Fariah (Carmen Munroe[2-4]), Guard Captains (Gordon Faith[2,3], Elliott Cairnes[4-6]), Guard on Denes (Bill Lyons[3]), Griffin, the Chef (Reg Lye[3]), Sergeant to Benik (Andrew Staines[4]), Fighting Guard (Bob Anderson[4]), Guard in Corridor (William McGuirk[4-6]), Swann (Christopher Burgess[4-6]), Colin (Adam Verney[4-6]), Mary (Margaret Hickey[4-6]), Guard in Caravan (Dibbs Mather[5]).

*Patrick Troughton was credited on Episodes 2 to 6 as playing 'Dr. Who Salamander'. He also appeared as Salamander in episode 1, but was credited only as 'Dr. Who.'

THINGS TO WATCH OUT FOR

- Episode 3 features no reprise from Episode 2.
- Neither Deborah Watling nor Frazer Hines appears in Episode 4, as they were on holiday during the week when it was recorded.
- There are some dramatic scenes at the end of Episode 6 in which, courtesy of trick photography, the Doctor and Salamander are seen on screen together.

THINGS YOU MIGHT NOT HAVE KNOWN

- Two Episode 1 characters, Rod and Curly, were originally called 'Tibor' and 'Otto' in the scripts.
- The novelisation of this story was first proposed to the publishers, W H Allen, by the original scriptwriter David Whitaker, but he had got no further than starting to draft out a rough plan of the book when he died on 4 February 1980. None of Whitaker's work was included in the final novelisation.
- Playing one of the guard extras in Episodes Five and Six was Patrick Troughton's son, David Troughton. This was his first *Doctor Who* role. He went on to appear again in *The War Games* and once more, as King Peladon, in the third Doctor story *The Curse of Peladon*.
- Playing a Central European guard in Episodes 2 and 3 was Frazer Hines's brother, Ian Hines. He also appeared in the season six story *The Mind Robber* as one of the Clockwork Soldiers.
- Following the end of the final episode, a specially recorded trailer for the following story, *The Web of Fear*, was transmitted. The script for this one minute forty second sequence read as follows:

INT. TUNNEL/PLATFORM	
LS Tunnel.	(FROM OUT OF THE TUNNEL WE SEE THE DOCTOR RUNNING INTO SHOT. HE LOOKS BACK OVER HIS SHOULDER AS HE RUNS.
DR. appears.	
As he comes to cam. he starts.	HE COMES INTO FOREGROUND, GIVES ONE LAST LOOK BEHIND

HIM, THEN TURNS INTO CAMERA
AGAIN.

Pan him L. to sitting pos.
on platform

HE STARTS WITH SURPRISE AS HE
SEES THE CAMERA.)

Doctor: Oh! (HE SMILES WITH
RELIEF) Oh dear, I thought for a minute
it was ...
(HE LOOKS QUICKLY BEHIND
HIM AGAIN.)

Doctor: You see they weren't far behind
me and ... oh, I must sit down – excuse me.
(HE SITS ON PLATFORM)

Doctor: That's better. I'm glad I bumped
into you actually because there's something
I wanted to talk to you about. Now, when
Jamie and Victoria and I go off into our
next adventure we meet some old friends ...
(HE SMILES, AND THEN THE SMILE
FADES.) ... and some old enemies.

(HE CASTS A WORRIED AND
HASTY LOOK OFF.)

Doctor: Yes, some old enemies. The Yeti
actually – only this time they're a little more
frightening. But I thought I'd just warn you
so that if your Mummy and Daddy are
frightened watching, you can tell them to
hold your hand.

Grams.
Distant shooting
Let him rise
& exit L

(HE WINKS AND SMILES INTO CAM.)

Oh dear, time to go! See you next week ...
(SHOOTING GETS NEARER)

I hope! (HE TURNS & GOES)

This pre-recorded sequence was followed by a clip of film from *The Web of Fear*. A voice-over was provided at the end by BBC announcer John Revel and a forty second clip from the Martin Slavin, Norman Ramin stock record 'Space Adventure' was also used.

- **Victoria:** 'Perhaps we've landed in a world of madmen?' **The Doctor:** 'They're human beings, if that's what you mean.'
- **The Doctor:** 'People spend all their time making nice things, and then other people come along and break them.'
- **Griffin, the Chef:** 'Dinner tonight's going to be a national disaster! First course interrupted by bomb explosion. Second course affected by earthquakes. Third course ruined by interference in the kitchen. I'm going out for a walk. It'll probably rain …'
- **Astrid:** 'I suggested that we meet under a disused jetty by the river.' **The Doctor:** 'Disused Yeti?'

ANALYSIS

The Enemy of the World is *Doctor Who*'s first serious venture into James Bond territory, and as such it is only partially successful, owing for one thing to the fact that – inevitably – the production is relatively cheap and conspicuously lacks the sort of grand spectacle for which the Bond films are renowned.

'*Doctor Who* meets James Bond?' mused David Gibbs in *Star Begotten* Vol. 4 No.1 dated May 1990. 'Hardly. Not on a BBC budget. And yet one has the suspicion that David Whitaker had this in mind all along. Salamander is definitely a graduate of the Blofeld school of villainy, with perhaps just a touch of Scaramanga about him. Many of the plot devices are pure 007 [and] the whole format seems to be leaning that way. Jamie is presented as a Bond substitute (incredible, but true!), with his two lovely female sidekicks, Victoria (the Moneypenny type) and Astrid (the leggy beauty with the lethal kick). The intrigue and plot complexity, not to mention the humour and the general feel, closely resemble numerous Fleming tales, or perhaps more specifically the films.

'Sadly, while the idea of Bond-inspired *Doctor Who* is fine in concept, it falls down in realisation. "My name's McCrimmon, James McCrimmon" just isn't the same, is it? And where does the Doctor fit into the 007 format? Answer: in his Troughton persona, he doesn't, which is why *The Enemy of the World* isn't totally successful. It's either *Doctor Who* or a spy tale, but it isn't both at the same time.'

'The first thing to be admitted is that this story has very little to do with *Doctor Who* in the mid-sixties …' agreed Thomas Patrickson in *Cloister Bell* 10/11 dated March 1985. 'But is there really anything so dreadful in having such a serial? In a season so full of monsters, it was surely a good idea to pause for breath and replace a new monster with an ingenious new idea – that of Salamander. It also has to be admitted that it is asking the audience a lot to accept that the TARDIS should just *happen* to land in the same place as the Doctor's double. That granted, though, we are presented with a tale written by a master of his craft [with] interesting Nazi style characters ranging from the jackbooted Benik to the conscientious objector Bruce and the pitiful food taster Fariah, with a skeleton in her cupboard. We are given a range of locations unparalleled in Earth *Doctor Who* stories … All right, so we know that Australia was actually Littlehampton … and that Hungary was firmly based in Shepherds Bush, but the pure strength and excitement of the scripts more than compensate for that.'

The scripts are indeed quite good, given the limitations within which they have to work, and feature some typically sparkling David Whitaker dialogue. Jamie and Victoria are admittedly seen to act somewhat out of character – giving the impression that, for the sake of the plot, they have been shoe-horned into roles for which they are not really suited – but there is some good material for the Doctor and, as Patrickson noted, Troughton's dual role is very well handled: 'The dual role was a real field day for Troughton … Playing the lovable clown must have palled somewhat [by this point], and it is obvious from his acting that it was nice to play the smooth deceptive villain for a change."

Particularly memorable is the scene at the end of the story in which Salamander is sucked into the time vortex through the open TARDIS doors. 'The whole story builds up to an explosive climax with some chilling laughter from Pat [Troughton] as the murderous villain, and all ending with a battle of wits aboard the TARDIS,' enthused Chris Marton in *Wheel in Space* No. 10 dated August 1980.

'In *The Enemy of the World*,' concluded Patrickson, 'we have a gripping story executed on screen with a considerable amount of panache … It is unique in [having] a present day/slightly future setting and yet containing no real science-fiction. However good the story itself was, it will almost inevitably be the fascinating Salamander who will be best remembered.'

In the final analysis, despite attracting some favourable comments, *The Enemy of the World* must still be considered the weakest story of the fifth season, and one so markedly different in style from the others – most obviously in its lack of alien monsters (although Salamander could perhaps be seen as a human monster!) – that it really sticks out like a sore thumb.

THE WEB OF FEAR

Writer: Mervyn Haisman, Henry Lincoln. **Director:** Douglas Camfield. **Designer:** David Myerscough-Jones. **Costumes:** Martin Baugh. **Make-up:** Sylvia James. **Incidental Music:** stock. **Fight Arranger:** Derek Ware. **Visual Effects:** Ron Oates. **Film Cameraman:** Alan Jonas, Jimmy Court. **Film Editor:** Philip Barnikel, Colin Hobson. **Studio Lighting:** Clive Leighton*. **Studio Sound:** Ray Angel. **Production Assistant:** Gareth Gwenlan. **Assistant Floor Manager:** Roselyn Parker.

* Geoff Shaw was incorrectly credited for lighting in the on-screen credits at the end of Episode 6. Shaw was in fact the story's TM2, i.e. technical co-ordinator.

	First UK TX	Scheduled TX	Actual TX	Duration	Viewers	Chart Pos.
Episode 1	03/02/68	17.25	17.25	24'53"	7.2	82
Episode 2	10/02/68	17.15	17.15	24'38"	6.8	80
Episode 3	17/02/68	17.25	17.25	24'34"	7.0	71
Episode 4	24/02/68	17.25	17.25	24'50"	8.4	52
Episode 5	02/03/68	17.25	17.25	24'19"	8.0	48
Episode 6	09/03/68	17.25	17.25	24'41"	8.3	36

Plot: The TARDIS narrowly avoids becoming engulfed in a web-like substance in space. It then arrives in the London Underground railway system, the tunnels of which are being overrun by the web and by the Great Intelligence's robot Yeti. The time travellers learn that this crisis was precipitated when Professor Travers, whom they first met in the Himalayas some forty years earlier, accidentally caused one of the Yeti to be reactivated, opening the way for the Intelligence to make another invasion attempt. The travellers work alongside army forces – led initially by Captain Knight and then by Colonel Lethbridge-Stewart – as they battle against the alien menace, hampered by the fact that one of their number has fallen under the Intelligence's influence and is a traitor in their midst. The Intelligence's ultimate aim is to drain the Doctor's mind. The Doctor manages to sabotage the device with which it intends to achieve this, so that he can drain the Intelligence's mind instead, but he is 'rescued' by his friends before he can bring his plan to fruition. The Intelligence is repelled into space, and the Doctor and his friends leave the army to clear up the mess.

Episode endings:
1. In one of the Underground tunnels, the Doctor watches from hiding as two Yeti cover some crates with web fired from guns held in their claws. The crates contain explosives and, back at the army base, Captain Knight gives the order for detonation. The explosives are set off and the web-covered crates glow with light.
2. Making their way through the tunnels in search of the Doctor, Jamie and Private Evans see a wall of web surging towards them.
3. In a room within the army base, Professor Travers finds one of the model Yeti control devices beside the body of Craftsman Weams. He is suddenly confronted by a Yeti that has entered the room behind him.
4. Professor Travers reappears in the army base. He is flanked by Yeti and under the control of the Intelligence. 'I am the Intelligence,' he whispers ...
5. Evans finishes dressing Sergeant Arnold's wounds and returns to the base laboratory, the walls of which are beginning to bulge under the pressure of the web outside. Suddenly one of the walls gives way, releasing a flood of glowing web.
6. The Doctor, Jamie and Victoria return to the TARDIS at Covent Garden station. They hurry through the tunnels as the Doctor realises that although the Yeti have gone, the trains might soon start running again.

IT WAS MADE WHERE...?

Ealing Filming: 15.12.67, 18.12.67-20.12.67 on Stage 3 A/B, 03.01.68 (Stage unknown)
Location Filming: 17.12.67, 14.01.68, 20.12.67
Locations: Yard of T J Poupart Ltd, Shelton Street, rear of Long Acre, Covent Garden, London WC2; Ealing Film Studios backlot, Ealing Green, Ealing, London, W5.
Model Filming: 08.01.68 in Puppet Theatre
Studio Recording: 13.01.68, 20.01.68, 27.01.68, 03.02.68, 10.02.68, 17.02.68, all in Lime Grove D

ADDITIONAL CREDITED CAST

Professor Travers (Jack Watling), Anne Travers (Tina Packer), Julius Silverstein (Frederick Schrecker[1]), Corporal Lane (Rod Beacham[1-4]), Corporal Blake (Richardson Morgan[1-4]), Captain Knight (Ralph Watson[1-4]), Harold Chorley (Jon Rollason[1-3,6]), Staff Sgt. Arnold (Jack Woolgar), Craftsman Weams (Stephen Whittaker[1-3]), Soldier (Bernard G High[1]), Yeti (John Levene[1,2,4-6], John Lord[2,4,6], Gordon Stothard[1,2,4-6], Colin Warman[1,4*], Jeremy King[2,3**], Roger Jacombs[6]), Soldier (Joseph O'Connell[2]), Driver Evans (Derek Pollitt[2-6]), Col. Lethbridge-Stewart (Nicholas Courtney[3-6]).

* Also in Episode 2, but uncredited.
** Also in Episode 4, but uncredited.

THINGS TO WATCH OUT FOR

- John Levene makes his second *Doctor Who* appearance, as one of the Yeti. Levene later went on to play Benton, one of the regular UNIT 'team' during the seventies.
- Jack Watling returns as Professor Travers.
- Nicholas Courtney (who had previously played Bret Vyon in *The Daleks' Master Plan*) makes his debut in Episode 3 as Colonel Lethbridge-Stewart, promoted to Brigadier in a later adventure (*The Invasion*). The Colonel's debut is actually in Episode 2, when only his boots are seen walking through the tunnels. For this sequence, the part was played by an uncredited Maurice Brooks.
- The closing credits for each episode apart from Episode 6 are rolled against an image of the pulsing web.
- The stock incidental music accompanying the Yeti attack at Covent Garden in Episode 4 is the same as that previously used as a theme for the Cybermen.
- A number of props – a small pyramid, the model Yeti and the silver control spheres – were reused from *The Abominable Snowmen*.

THINGS YOU MIGHT NOT HAVE KNOWN

- On 7 November 1967, Gareth Gwenlan, PA to director Douglas Camfield, wrote to the Chief Press Officer of London Transport requesting permission to film on a platform and, if possible, in the Underground tunnels at Aldwych station, and also at the exterior of the booking hall and gate of Covent Garden station. A suitable deal could not be reached, however, and so all the sequences set in the Underground tunnels and on station platforms were recorded in studio instead.
- It was at one point intended that the opening sequence of the story should be set in the Natural History Museum in London, and Gwenlan wrote to the Museum on 8 November to try to secure permission for location filming to take place there on 21 December. This was refused, so the scenes were set instead in Julius Silverstein's private museum, staged at Ealing on 3 January 1968. Actor Desmond Cullum-Jones, who was to have appeared as a commissionaire in the location filming, was paid an *ex gratia* fee.
- It was confirmed on 28 November 1967 that neither David Langton nor Nicholas Selby was interested in playing 'Colonel Lethbridge'. Nicholas Courtney, who had been cast as Captain Knight, was therefore given the role, and the part of Knight recast.
- Gwenlan ordered a number of still photographs, on each of which was to be superimposed an image of a Yeti. These were for use in the sequence in the story where the creatures are shown to be marauding through a deserted London, and Gwenlan requested any six of the following images: Steps of St. Pauls, Lions at Trafalgar Square, Buckingham Palace, Tower Bridge, Westminster Abbey, Tower of London, Admiralty Arch, Courtyard of the Houses of Parliament, Downing Street.

QUOTE, UNQUOTE

- **Harold Chorley:** [Proffering a microphone and tape recorder.] 'Tell me, Professor. Will you be in charge of the scientific section, or will your daughter?' **Professor Travers:** 'Mind your own business!' **Harold Chorley:** '... and how long do you think it's going to take for you to come up with the answer, eh? One week? Three perhaps?' **Professor Travers:** 'Well how the hell should I know. 'Ere, that thing working?' **Harold Chorley:** 'Of course.' **Professor Travers:** [Into microphone.] 'Erm. It's more than likely that we won't be able to defeat this menace. And that London, in fact the whole of England, might be completely wiped out. [To Chorley.] There. Did you get that?'

- **Col. Lethbridge-Stewart:** 'This Intelligence. Exactly what is it?' **The Doctor:** 'Well I wish I could give you a precise answer. Perhaps the best way to describe it is a sort of formless, shapeless thing, floating about in space like a cloud of mist only with a mind and will.' **Col. Lethbridge-Stewart:** 'What's it after? What's it want?' **The Doctor:** 'I wish I knew. The only thing I know for sure is that it brought me here.'

- **The Great Intelligence:** 'Revenge is a petty human emotion. My purpose for you is far more interesting.' **The Doctor:** 'And what's that?' **The Great Intelligence:** 'Through time and space I have observed you, Doctor. Your mind surpasses that of all other creatures.' **The Doctor:** 'What do you want?' **The Great Intelligence:** 'You! Your mind will be invaluable to me, therefore I have invented a machine that will drain all past knowledge and experience from your mind.'

ANALYSIS

Dark and gloomy underground tunnels … cobwebs … engulfing mist … the feeling of being hunted by a relentless foe that will kill you when it catches you. All the stuff of nightmares, and all found in *The Web of Fear*.

Doctor Who has, at its best, a quality that makes the viewer accept what he or she is seeing without questioning it. The combination of Yeti and web in this story really makes no sense at all. Why should the Yeti have web-guns? 'Why not?' is the viewer's resounding reply, and the fact is simply accepted.

As a sequel to *The Abominable Snowmen*, *The Web of Fear* works very well indeed. By transporting the Yeti from the open spaces of the Himalayas to the familiar yet incongruous environment of the London Underground, writers Mervyn Haisman and Henry Lincoln increase their menace a hundredfold and plug into the hidden fears of millions of commuters and train users who have secretly wondered what might be lurking in those dark places.

The suspenseful and exciting scripts are perfectly complemented by the superb dramatic and atmospheric direction of Douglas Camfield, including some nice touches such as the use of a very effective passage of stock music by composer Bela Bartok for the scene in Episode 1 in which the Yeti is reactivated. A combination that chilled the spines of all who saw the story.

The sets too are superb. Denied the use of a real London Underground station and tunnels, designer David Myerscough-Jones created his own highly convincing replica. Indeed a letter of complaint was apparently later received from London Underground alleging that filming had taken place on their property without permission – a true testament to the merits of Myerscough-Jones's work.

If the story has a drawback, it is that the action seems somewhat padded out over the six episodes. There is a lot of to-ing and fro-ing as people wander off into the tunnels only to reappear at some later point. This may well have been intentional, though, as it certainly adds to the sense of unease – knowing that there is at least one traitor in the army camp, eyes and fingers point to whoever appears to be acting the most suspiciously.

'Basically *The Web of Fear* was a whodunit, with the viewers at home being enticed into guessing the identity of the Intelligence's pawn,' wrote Michael B Holder in *Entropy* Issue One in 1981. 'All of the way through the obvious suspect was [television reporter] Harold Chorley, especially when, armed with Victoria's information and directions, he made off to escape in the TARDIS. Certainly I never thought of Staff [Sergeant] Arnold as being a possibility – he was a straightforward [and] unremarkable man.'

Nick Page, writing in *Cloister Bell* 10/11 dated March 1985, felt that the idea of the Great Intelligence using a human host was not as well realised as in its debut story. 'The only disappointment was the voice used by the Intelligence ... In *The Abominable Snowmen* the Intelligence spoke in an icy whisper with a distinct hissing quality which blended in brilliantly with the baritones of the controlled Padmasambhava. This was especially apparent in the scenes where Padmasambhava was communicating with the Intelligence: you could almost feel the hatred of the Intelligence for mankind. Unfortunately the voice adopted in *The Web of Fear* was somewhat pathetic in comparison. This time [it] used much more human tones when it used the loudspeaker system on the Underground to speak to Travers and Victoria. Even at the end when it revealed that Staff Sergeant Arnold was the human working for [it], the alien parasite used Arnold's own voice to communicate with the humans. A disappointing end to an otherwise perfect production.'

The Web of Fear is a rare beast. A *Doctor Who* story that manages to terrify on a basic level, while still managing to tell a good and exciting story. It is no wonder that the production team looked to this type of contemporary Earth-based adventure when they came to consider how the series might best be developed for the future ...

FURY FROM THE DEEP

Writer: Victor Pemberton. **Director:** Hugh David. **Designer:** Peter Kindred. **Costumes:** Martin Baugh. **Make-up:** Sylvia James. **Incidental Music:** Dudley Simpson. **Visual Effects:** Peter Day, Len Hutton. **Film Cameraman:** Ken Westbury. **Film Editor:** Colin Hobson. **Studio Lighting:** Sam Neeter. **Studio Sound:** David Hughes. **Production Assistant:** Michael Briant. **Assistant Floor Manager:** Margot Hayhoe.

	First UK TX	Scheduled TX	Actual TX	Duration	Viewers	Chart Pos.
Episode 1	16/03/68	17.15	17.15	24'54"	8.2	46
Episode 2	23/03/68	17.15	17.16	23'08"	7.9	40
Episode 3	30/03/68	17.15	17.16	20'29"	7.7	47
Episode 4	06/04/68	17.15	17.15	24'17"	6.6	62
Episode 5	13/04/68	17.15	17.16	23'40"	5.9	73
Episode 6	20/04/68	17.15	17.15	24'24"	6.9	42

Plot: The TARDIS lands on the surface of the sea, just off the East coast of England. The time travellers use a rubber dinghy to get to shore, where they are shot with tranquiliser darts and taken prisoner by security guards as they have arrived in the restricted area of a gas refinery. At the refinery base, run by a man named Robson, the Doctor learns that there have been a number of unexplained problems with the pressure in the feed pipes from the offshore drilling rigs. It is later revealed that one of the rigs has sucked up a parasitic form of seaweed, which is capable of releasing poisonous gas or a strange kind of foam that allows it to take control of the minds of those it touches. The weed spreads rapidly and seems set on establishing a huge colony centred around the rigs. The Doctor makes the chance discovery that it is very susceptible to high pitched noise; consequently he is able to use the amplified sound of Victoria's screams to destroy it. Victoria elects to stay with the family of one of the refinery workers, Harris. The Doctor, although sharing Jamie's sadness at her departure, understands her decision to settle down to a quieter life.

Episode endings:
1. Victoria, trapped in a store room at the base, screams as foam pours in through an open grille and advances toward her. Within the foam are fronds of animated weed ...
2. Supported by the base's Chief Engineer, the Dutch consultant van Lutyens makes a renewed attempt to persuade Robson that the heartbeat-like sound that they can hear emanating from the pipeline is made by something alive. 'It's down there. In the darkness. In the pipeline. Waiting ...'
3. Maggie Harris and Robson, both infected by the weed creature, meet on the beach. The former tells the latter that he will obey his instructions. Then she turns and walks straight out into the sea, eventually becoming completely submerged beneath the waves ...
4. 'The advance guard,' mutters the Doctor as a mass of weed creature is seen writhing inside an observation pipe. Motioning his companions and the base personnel to remain where they are, he advances toward the pipe ...
5. The Doctor and Jamie enter the central area of the control rig to find themselves confronted by the terrifying sight of Robson standing in the middle of a mass of weed and foam. 'Come in Doctor,' he whispers. 'We've been waiting for you.'
6. As the image of Victoria waving goodbye recedes on the TARDIS scanner screen, the Doctor admits to the forlorn Jamie, 'I was fond of her too, you know, Jamie.'

IT WAS MADE WHERE...?

Location Filming: 04.02.68-06.02.68, 12.02.68
Locations: Red Sands Sea Fort, Thames Estuary; Botany Bay, Margate, Kent; fields nr. Denham Aerodrome, Bucks.
Ealing Filming: 07.02.68-09.02.68 on Stage 3 A/B, 05.03.68-06.03.68 (Stage unknown)
Studio Recording: 24.02.68, 02.03.68, 09.03.68, 16.03.68, 23.03.68 in Lime Grove D, 29.03.68 in TC1

ADDITIONAL CREDITED CAST

Robson (Victor Maddern), Harris (Roy Spencer), Price (Graham Leaman), Guard (Peter Ducrow[1]), Maggie Harris (June Murphy[1-4,6]), Carney (John Garvin[1]), Chief Engineer (Hubert Rees), Van Lutyens (John Abineri[1-4]), Chief Baxter (Richard Mayes[1, 4]), Quill (Bill Burridge[1-5]), Oak (John Gill[2-5]), Megan Jones (Margaret John[4-6]), Perkins (Brian Cullingford[4-6]).

THINGS TO WATCH OUT FOR

• This story boasts some truly cracking cliffhangers.

- The Doctor's sonic screwdriver makes its debut appearance when it is used to unseal a pipeline inspection hatch in Episode 1.
- The scene where the weed-infected technicians Quill and Oak attack Maggie Harris is particularly terrifying.

THINGS YOU MIGHT NOT HAVE KNOWN

- Working title: *The Colony of Devils*.
- Victor Pemberton had previously written a seven-part radio serial called *The Slide* in which an intelligent form of mud threatened to engulf a new town called Redlow. *Fury from the Deep* was heavily influenced by this.
- Pemberton recalls that after *Fury from the Deep* had been made he was asked by producer Peter Bryant to develop another story. The idea that he came up with was entitled *The Eye in Space* and concerned a giant octopoid eye in space that could see everything and attract objects – including the TARDIS – toward it. Nothing further came of this.

QUOTE, UNQUOTE

- **Van Lutyens:** 'Whatever it is that's in the pipeline, that's jamming the impeller, that's taken over the rigs, is a menace and a threat to us all.'
- **Megan Jones:** 'What's happening?' **The Doctor:** 'The first part of the invasion.' **Victoria:** 'Doctor, don't go near.' **The Doctor:** 'It's begun. The battle of the giants!'
- **Victoria:** [To Jamie] 'Why can't we go somewhere pleasant? Where there's no fighting, just peace and happiness?'

ANALYSIS

Few threats can be more potent than that of mental and physical possession by an alien entity. *Fury from the Deep* plays on this fear to great effect in its depiction of the menace posed by the latest monster to be introduced to *Doctor Who* – a monster that, as Mathew Prince noted in *Cloister Bell* 10/11 dated March 1985, neatly sidesteps all the clichés of adventure stories featuring undersea creatures: 'What saved *Fury from the Deep* from the depths of banality was the total failure of gigantic (model) squids, lobsters, octopi or reptiles to surface with seemingly random stealth and/or shock-horror ferocity. Here the aggressor was seaweed. Whether this was true inventiveness on the part of Victor Pemberton or budget considerations on the part of Peter Bryant, the resulting idea, with the help of the then omnipresent foam machine, proved far more frightening than hulks of angry scale and muscle. Fronds of seaweed. Silent, unobtrusive and above all disturbingly commonplace. And it was not even a species of seaweed mutated by the incessant pollution of the sea (a concept already reaching cliché status in 1968); just a previously unencountered deep sea variety brought to the surface by the laying of gas pipes on the sea bed. There was ... the unfortunate adoption of world domination/destruction as the weed's motive for attack [but] at least there weren't hordes of extras in plastic weed suits – the threat proved to be more psychological and therefore more frightening than that.'

Director Hugh David pulls no punches, either, in his treatment of Victor Pemberton's story, creating some truly terrifying and horrific scenes. Amongst the most memorable of these are Victoria trapped in the store room as the weed creature breaks in behind her;

Maggie Harris being attacked by the mysterious Oak and Quill and subsequently walking impassively into the sea as if to commit suicide; van Lutyens coming to grief in the impeller shaft and the Doctor and Jamie going in after him; and the final gripping confrontation on the control rig. This must be, all in all, one of the most frightening stories ever to be presented by *Doctor Who*. As Gary Hopkins put it in *Doctor Who – An Adventure in Space and Time* in 1984: 'If viewing figures were judged by the number of people who watched from between parted fingers or behind the settee – *Doctor Who* is never better than when it causes sleepless nights – then *Fury from the Deep* would surely have found its way into the *Guinness Book of Records*!'

Chief Robson and his colleagues are excellently characterised and well portrayed throughout by a fine cast. Particularly memorable is Robson himself, of whom Hopkins wrote: 'Victor Maddern plays the stubborn, hard-boiled Chief Robson who, like most stereotyped work obsessed commanders, cracks under the strain in the second reel. To his credit, though, Maddern rises above the stereotype by giving Robson a human side during his lapses into gibbering hysteria. His close friendship with Megan Jones, the reasonable director of the Euro-Sea board, also hints at a humanity he otherwise conceals beneath a tough exterior.'

Prince considered that 'large, isolated complexes with impractically long corridors were becoming a shade too predictable [by] this stage … along with the tough, no-nonsense Northerners like Hobson – sorry, I mean Robson – who run them until events prove too much for them and their cool 'n collected seconds-in-command have to take over.' Paul Clifton, however, writing in *DWB* No. 119 dated November 1993, considered this aspect of the story a particular asset: 'It may be set in a technological complex, but this is a simple industrial facility, piping natural gas from offshore rigs to the rest of Britain, not some top-secret scientific base. The people running this facility are ordinary men and women, concerned with office protocol and keeping their jobs. The whole thing seems based in the real world in a way that few other stories are … There are no great "boy's own" expeditions across mountains or glaciers – instead, people venture into darkened rooms and chambers, and as contact is lost with the rigs the control staff wait helplessly, because the officials with enough authority to order up a helicopter have all gone away. It's all very parochial.' And therein lies the key to much of its very considerable impact.

The story ends with a nice change of pace, too, as the poignant closing scenes of Victoria bidding farewell bring a distinct lump to the throat. The Doctor and Jamie travel on alone again – but only for the time being …

THE WHEEL IN SPACE

Writer: David Whitaker, from a story by Kit Pedler. **Director:** Tristan de Vere Cole. **Designer:** Derek Dodd. **Costumes:** Martin Baugh. **Make-up:** Sylvia James. **Incidental Music:** Brian Hodgson/BBC Radiophonic Workshop. **Visual Effects:** Bill King/Trading Post. **Film Cameraman:** Jimmy Court. **Film Editor:** Ron Fry. **Studio Lighting:** Michael Jefferies. **Studio Sound:** John Holmes. **Production Assistant:** Ian Strachan. **Assistant Floor Manager:** Marcia Wheeler.

	First UK TX	Scheduled TX	Actual TX	Duration	Viewers	Chart Pos.
Episode 1	27/04/68	17.15	17.15	23'47"	7.2	40
Episode 2	04/05/68	17.15	17.17	22'50"	6.9	59
Episode 3	11/05/68	17.15	17.15	24'25"	7.5	40
Episode 4	18/05/68	17.25*	18.00	24'14"	8.6	28
Episode 5	25/05/68	17.15	17.17	21'55"	6.8	44
Episode 6	01/06/68	18.00**	18.06	23'10"	6.5	51

* This episode was actually transmitted approximately thirty-five minutes late as the preceding programme, *Grandstand*, overran due to coverage of the FA Cup Final football match.

** This episode was actually transmitted approximately six minutes late as *Grandstand* overran due to coverage of an England -v- West Germany football match.

Plot: The TARDIS materialises on board a spaceship, the *Silver Carrier*, where the Doctor and Jamie are attacked by a Servo Robot. Jamie manages to contact a nearby space station known as the Wheel and they are rescued. Meanwhile, the *Silver Carrier* discharges some Cybermats, which also travel to and enter the station. These pave the way for the penetration of the station by Cybermen, who intend to use its direct radio link with Earth as a beacon for their invasion fleet. The Doctor sends Jamie and a young woman named Zoe Heriot over to the *Silver Carrier* to fetch the TARDIS's vector generator rod. Meanwhile he manages to free the Wheel's crew from the Cybermen's hypnotic control and to destroy the two Cybermen on the station. When Jamie and Zoe return, he installs the rod in the station's X-ray laser, making it powerful enough to destroy the Cyber-fleet. An approaching force of space-walking Cybermen is also vanquished.

Episode endings:
1. Convinced that the *Silver Carrier* poses a threat to the Wheel, Controller Jarvis Bennett decides to turn the X-ray laser on it and destroy it completely.
2. On the *Silver Carrier* two large egg-like objects start rocking backwards and forwards. One of them becomes translucent and the shape of a Cyberman can be seen within. It punches its fist through the shell of the egg.
3. Laleham and Vallance, two of the Wheel's crew, space-walk over to the *Silver Carrier* to fetch fresh supplies of bernalium. There they encounter and are hypnotised by two Cybermen. They are ordered to take the Cybermen to the Wheel and assist them there.
4. The Doctor and Jamie are investigating the crates of bernalium in a storage area on the Wheel when suddenly a Cyberman appears on the stairs behind them.
5. Jamie and Zoe are space-walking across to the *Silver Carrier* to fetch the TARDIS's vector generator rod. Zoe suddenly sees that the approaching meteorite storm is heading straight for them.
6. The Doctor finds Zoe hiding on board the TARDIS. She wants to join him and Jamie on their travels. He decides to give her a taste of what this might be like by using a thought scanner to 'show' her one of his past adventures. She sees a man – Kennedy – being exterminated by a Dalek*.

* This was a clip from the end of the first episode of *The Evil of the Daleks*.

IT WAS MADE WHERE...?

Ealing Filming: 18.03.68-22.03.68 (Stage unknown)
Studio Recording: 05.04.68 in Lime Grove D, 12.04.68 in TC3, 19.04.68 in TC1, 26.04.68 in TC3, 03.05.68, 10.05.68 in Riverside 1

ADDITIONAL CREDITED CAST

Victoria (Deborah Watling[1])*, Servo Robot (Freddie Foote[1]), Leo Ryan (Eric Flynn), Dr. Gemma Corwyn (Anne Ridler[1-5]), Tanya Lernov (Clare Jenkins), Jarvis Bennett (Michael Turner), Enrico Casali (Donald Sumpter), Bill Duggan (Kenneth Watson[2-4]), Elton Laleham (Michael Goldie[2-5]), Armand Vallance (Derrick Gilbert[2-6]), Kemel Rudkin (Kevork Malikyan[2,3]), Chang (Peter Laird[2-4]), Sean Flannigan (James Mellor[2-6]), Cybermen (Jerry Holmes[2-6], Gordon Stothard[3-6]), Voices (Peter Hawkins[3-6], Roy Skelton[3-6]).

* Deborah Watling received an on-screen credit on Episode 1 for her appearance as Victoria in the reprise from the end of *Fury from the Deep*.
Note: Griffith Davis and Robert Jewell received no credit on Episode 6 for their respective appearances as Kennedy and a Dalek in the clip from *The Evil of the Daleks*.

POPULAR MYTHS

- This story went considerably over budget. (It was one of the few stories of the second Doctor's era to come in under budget.)
- Zoe's surname is spelt 'Herriot'. (In David Whitaker's script it is spelt 'Heriot'.)
- There is a suspenseful scene in which the two Cybermen menace Zoe in the Wheel's library. (There is no such scene. The photographs that exist of this were specially posed for publicity purposes only.)
- Only two Cyberman costumes were used in the making of this story. (A third was put together from stock for the sequence in Episode 6 where a force of Cybermen space-walk toward the Wheel.)

THINGS TO WATCH OUT FOR

- The Doctor's face creases in pain in Episode 1 as he rummages in his pocket. Following Jamie's apparent concern, the Doctor pulls out a bag of lemon sherbets and offers one to the boy.
- Patrick Troughton makes no appearance in Episode 2 as he was on holiday during the week when it was recorded. The Doctor is seen only as an unconscious figure, with Chris Jeffries doubling for Troughton.
- Jamie gives the Doctor the alias 'John Smith' – a name he sees printed on the side of a piece of medical equipment on the Wheel.
- This story is the first to have an incidental music score as well as sound effects provided by the BBC's Radiophonic Workshop.

THINGS YOU MIGHT NOT HAVE KNOWN

- Working title: *The Space Wheel*.
- Eric Flynn, who plays Leo Ryan in this story, was the son of Hollywood film star Errol Flynn.

- Production of this story was affected by a scene-shifters strike at the BBC, which necessitated several last minute changes of studio.
- Kit Pedler provided the basic idea for this story, from which David Whitaker was commissioned on 18 December 1967 to write the scripts. These were to include the Cybermen and the Cybermats. The delivery deadline was 31 January 1968, on which date incoming producer Peter Bryant wrote to Whitaker confirming a telephone conversation the previous night in which Whitaker had agreed to deliver episodes three and four on time and the final two episodes not later than Friday 2 February. It is apparent from the tone of Bryant's note that he had inadvertently upset Whitaker in asking for the scripts to be delivered by the agreed date. He explained that the lack of scripts made life difficult for him at a time when he, as a very new producer, needed the show to run smoothly.
- The story ended with a sequence in which Zoe Heriot joined the TARDIS as the Doctor's new companion, and dialogue was specifically written to tie in with the repeat of *The Evil of the Daleks,* which would bridge the seven week gap between seasons. For viewers, it would be as though *Doctor Who* had not been off the air at all.

QUOTE, UNQUOTE

- **Jamie:** 'Just you watch your lip or I'll put you across my knee and larrap you.' **Zoe:** 'Oh, this is going to be fun. I shall learn a lot from you.'
- **Zoe:** 'You can't disprove the facts. It's pure logic.' **The Doctor:** 'Logic, my dear Zoe, merely enables one to be wrong with authority.'
- **Dr. Gemma Corwyn:** 'Do you ever feel anything emotional, Zoe?' **Zoe:** 'Emotional? Do you know that's the second time I've been asked that in the last few hours. Leo Ryan said I was all brain and no heart.' **Dr. Gemma Corwyn:** 'Yes, it's your training. I shouldn't worry about it.' **Zoe:** 'Oh, but I do. I don't want to be thought of as a freak. Leo said I was like a robot, a machine. Well I think he's right. My head's been pumped full of facts and figures which I reel out automatically when needed. But, well, I want to feel things as well.'
- **Cyberman:** 'You know our ways.'

ANALYSIS

The Wheel In Space is fundamentally a very straightforward story about Cybermen attacking a space station. Some commentators have indeed suggested that it lacked the substance to sustain six episodes. 'The four episode length that suited *The Tomb of the Cybermen* so well should also have been [used for] *The Wheel in Space*,' asserted Martin Day in *Cloister Bell* 10/11 dated March 1985. '[Having] six episodes led to all being padded, especially the tedious second episode.' This opinion is not universally shared, however, and overall the story seems quite nicely paced. The interest level is increased by the fact that, unusually, the viewer is almost always ahead of the Doctor in realising what is going on: the viewer is the first to know that the Cybermen are involved (having seen the Cybermats); that a Servo Robot lurks inside the locked control room on the *Silver Carrier;* and that the TARDIS is potentially in danger (first from the Wheel's X-ray laser and later from rogue meteorites). The viewer is even the first to learn what the Cybermen's plan is, step by step. This is highly effective in helping to build up tension and anticipation.

'Although Pedler's basic plot [was] fine,' observed Martin Day, '[it repeated an idea] used previously in *The Tenth Planet* and *The Moonbase* … – that of [a] vital [base] being captured from which to launch [an attack] on Earth.' This is certainly true, but equally there is no denying that the claustrophobic space station setting is very well used, as Martin J Wiggins noted in the appropriately titled *Wheel in Space* No. 10 dated August 1980: '*The Wheel in Space* is perhaps the ideal story to disprove Jon Pertwee's [theory] that it is always less frightening to see a Yeti in Tibet than sitting on the loo in Tooting Bec. This is in fact a crutch for lazy writers to lean on, and in *The Wheel in Space* there were many apparently safe places created by skilful writing, made safe because people were doing what they would normally do in them … As with many classic stories, the safe places were slowly cut down until the humans were besieged in their own control room.'

Things do indeed get very tense when the Cybermen start killing off the crew of the Wheel. The death of Gemma is quite nasty and effective, and Leo Ryan's one-man-stand against a Cyberman is also somewhat affecting in its pointlessness. The impact of these scenes, and of the story as a whole, is greatly enhanced by the acting of the guest cast, which is generally extremely good.

The story is not without its faults, however. As Martin Day pointed out, 'The Cybermats … look so sweet scuttling around chomping the bernalium rods, it's difficult to take the damn things seriously.' And '[The sets are] boring in the extreme, but then making an original-looking hi-tech setting is rather difficult …' Day also found the design of the Servo Robot bizarre.

The voice of the Cyber Planner (apparently a sort of super-evolved Cyberman, but represented here only as a kind of flashing computer bank) is the same as that of the Cybermen in *The Moonbase* and *The Tomb of the Cybermen*, and remains very effective, but the one used on this occasion for the Cybermen themselves is awful – squeaky and very human-sounding – and also changes slightly between film and studio sessions (apparently because the appropriate equipment was unavailable for the former).

The biggest flaw, though, is that the Cybermen's plan, despite being logical and well worked out, is so convoluted that it seriously strains the viewer's credulity. It goes something like this. The Cybermen first attack and take over the *Silver Carrier*, refuelling it and setting it on course for the Wheel with a cargo of numerous small egg-like objects. The latter drift over to the Wheel and hatch Cybermats, which proceed to consume supplies of the metal bernalium. The Cybermen then ionise a star and thereby create a shower of meteorites on a collision course for the Wheel. They have predicted – correctly, as it turns out – that the Wheel's crew, powerless to destroy the meteorites without the bernalium vital to the functioning of their X-ray laser, will discover that there is a further supply of the metal on the *Silver Carrier* and send people over to get it. Two larger egg-like objects on the *Silver Carrier* have meanwhile hatched Cybermen, who proceed to hypnotise the men from the Wheel and hitch a lift over to the station hidden in the crates of bernalium. Once on board, they intend to cut off the air supply and kill the humans so that the Wheel can be used as a beacon for their fleet to home in on. One has to wonder why they go to all this trouble just to get on board the Wheel when simply invading it by force would presumably be very much easier. After all, the Cybermats manage to get on board with little trouble, so an attack by a Cyber-fleet should surely be a walkover. And in any case, the question remains: if the Cybermen want a beacon, why don't they just set up one of their own?

Perhaps it is best not to dwell on these plot problems, as in other respects the story is a very enjoyable one. Wiggins preferred to focus on the atmosphere and tension created by writer David Whitaker and director Tristan de Vere Cole: 'What was interesting about the use of the Cybermen in *The Wheel in Space* ... was their apparent ubiquity, and the way in which this was used to increase the tension – anywhere you went, there was danger of finding one; for example, at the end of Episode 4, the Doctor and Jamie went down to the hold to examine the crates, and then a Cyberman began to come down.'

The story also makes a promising debut for new companion Zoe Heriot, brought to life with infectious enthusiasm by Wendy Padbury. Her initial lack of emotion and reliance on logic show how people can easily fall into the trap of acting like Cybermen without the need for physical conversion – the difference in Zoe's case being that as a result of her contact with the Doctor and Jamie she comes to question and change her outlook on life.

Certainly viewers at the time were well disposed toward the story, if the BBC's Audience Research Report on the final episode gives a good indication: 'The overall response to *The Wheel in Space* was favourable. There were, certainly, those who thought the whole thing ridiculous in the extreme and who could not imagine either children or adults finding much in it to appeal to them. Another group enjoyed it fairly well but felt that invention was, perhaps, beginning to flag. The stories were becoming repetitive; the series needed new ideas and new antagonists for Doctor Who rather than Daleks, Cybermen and the like. This was a rather tame adventure, it was said, and there was too much use of pseudo-technical jargon that would be over the heads of most younger viewers. Whether they took it seriously or not, however, the bulk of the sample enjoyed Doctor Who's encounter with his old enemies, two or three going on to say that they preferred his science fiction adventures to the historical ones. It was pleasant to escape now and then to the world of fantasy, viewers remarked ("the 'impossible' always appeals to me and this was no exception") and this particular story had proved both interesting and exciting, even those who watched with tolerant amusement rather than absorbed interest often saying that their children "lapped it up".'

Sandwiched between the horror classic *Fury from the Deep* and a repeat of one of the best Dalek stories, *The Evil of the Daleks*, *The Wheel in Space* is sometimes unfairly overlooked. While perhaps not quite deserving Wiggins' summation – 'well written, well performed: a classic' – it provides a satisfying end to an excellent season.

On 1 July 1967, viewers of *Doctor Who* had seen the Dalek race apparently destroyed in the seventh and final instalment of *The Evil of the Daleks*. Less than a year later, however, the machine-creatures from Skaro were back on the nation's screens in a repeat transmission of the very story in which they had been so soundly defeated. This was the first instance of any *Doctor Who* story being given a second airing in the UK, the only previous repeat having been a reshowing of the series' opening episode, *An Unearthly Child*, just one week after its original transmission. The repeat of *The Evil of the Daleks* was also unique in that it was actually incorporated into the ongoing narrative of the series itself, being presented as an attempt by the Doctor to give newcomer Zoe Heriot, played by Wendy Padbury, a taste of what she could be letting herself in for by joining him and Jamie on their travels. Although the production team did not go so far as to edit a reprise of *The Wheel in Space* into the first episode of the repeat, they nevertheless ensured that viewers were reminded of the link between the two stories by having a short conversation between the Doctor and Zoe dubbed onto the beginning of the episode, immediately after the opening titles and music. This went as follows:

> **The Doctor:** 'Now as I remember, Zoe, it all started when Jamie and I discovered somebody making off with the TARDIS.' **Zoe:** 'But what about those Daleks you showed me?' **The Doctor:** 'We're coming to that, Zoe. Just let me show you the story from the beginning ...'

Although the last episode of *The Wheel in Space* and the first episode of the repeat were transmitted in consecutive weeks, the repeat itself did not have an uninterrupted run; there were two Saturdays without *Doctor Who* (originally scheduled to be only one) following the third episode, to make way for the BBC's coverage of the Wimbledon tennis tournament. The story resumed with the fourth episode on 13 July 1968, and the seventh and final episode went out three weeks later on 3 August. The sixth season began the following Saturday, 10 August, with the opening episode of *The Dominators* (which included dialogue referring back to the repeat), so from the viewer's perspective it was almost as if there had been no between-seasons break at all.

DOCTOR WHO SEASON SIX (1968-1969)

Regular Cast:
Dr. Who (Patrick Troughton)
Jamie (Frazer Hines)
Zoe (Wendy Padbury)

Regular Crew:
Producer: Peter Bryant until *The Space Pirates* Episode Six. Derrick Sherwin on *The War Games*.
Script Editor: Derrick Sherwin until *The Mind Robber* Episode 5. Terrance Dicks from *The Invasion* Episode One until *The Seeds of Death* Episode Six. Derrick Sherwin on *The Space Pirates*. Terrance Dicks on *The War Games*.
Title Music: Ron Grainer and the BBC Radiophonic Workshop, arranged by Delia Derbyshire.
Special Sounds: Brian Hodgson.

The sixth season, as the last to be made in monochrome and the last to feature Patrick Troughton as the Doctor, marked the end of an era for *Doctor Who*. It was also made during a rather unsettled period for the series behind the scenes and, perhaps as a result of this, lacked the consistency of the previous season. It did however contain a number of stories that would later come to be regarded as particularly fine examples of sixties *Doctor Who*, and three of these – *The Seeds of Death*, *The Invasion* and *The War Games* – contained elements that, with hindsight, can be seen to have foreshadowed the revamping of the series that would take place for the first season of the seventies.

THE DOMINATORS

Writer: Norman Ashby*. **Director:** Morris Barry. **Designer:** Barry Newbery. **Costumes:** Martin Baugh. **Make-Up:** Sylvia James. **Incidental Music:** none. **Visual Effects:** Ron Oates. **Film Cameraman:** Peter Hamilton. **Film Editor:** Chris Hayden. **Studio Lighting:** Sam Neeter. **Studio Sound:** Richard Chubb. **Production Assistant:** John Bruce. **Assistant Floor Manager:** Barbara Stuart.

* This was a pseudonym for Mervyn Haisman and Henry Lincoln. Derrick Sherwin also made a significant input to the writing of Episode 5.

	First UK TX	Scheduled TX	Actual TX	Duration	Viewers	Chart Pos.
Episode 1	10/08/68	17.15	17.15	24'25"	6.1	54
Episode 2	17/08/68	17.15	17.15	24'07"	5.9	61
Episode 3	24/08/68	17.15	17.15	24'06"	5.4	65

Episode 4	31/08/68	17.15	17.15	23'54"	7.5	33
Episode 5	07/09/68	17.15	17.15	24'19"	5.9	64

Plot: The TARDIS materialises on the planet Dulkis, currently under threat from two alien Dominators, Rago and his subordinate Toba, who have landed in a spaceship. Aided by their robotic servants, the Quarks, and slave workers drawn from the native Dulcian population, the Dominators set about drilling bore holes, through which they plan to fire rockets into the planet's molten core. Their intention is then to drop an atomic seed capsule into the resulting eruption, turning Dulkis into a radioactive mass – fuel for the Dominators' space fleet. The Dulcian Councillors, being pacifists, refuse to retaliate, although Cully, the rebellious son of their leader Senex, has already joined forces with the time travellers. The Doctor eventually defeats the Dominators by intercepting the seed capsule as it is dropped and placing it on board their ship, which is then destroyed shortly after take off. Dulkis suffers only a minor volcanic eruption, as a result of the rockets fired into its magma.

Episode endings:
1. The Doctor and Jamie have discovered the Dominators' spaceship. Jamie points out that they are being observed by two Quarks from a nearby hilltop. Toba joins the Quarks and they ask him if they should destroy.
2. Zoe and Cully are trapped in the Dulcian survey unit as it is fired upon by the Quarks. Explosions rock the building and rubble crashes down around them.
3. Toba orders the Quarks to destroy totally the Dulcian museum in which Jamie and Cully are taking cover. The Quarks fire and the building collapses around the two friends. A smiling Toba is informed by a Quark that the task has been completed.
4. Toba tells his prisoners that they will die one by one unless they reveal where Jamie is. They refuse to answer, and the Dulcian Educator Balan is the first to be gunned down by a Quark. The Doctor is next in line, and the Quarks get ready to fire again.
5. The Doctor tells Jamie that Dulkis is safe; there will be just a minor eruption confined to one island. Jamie points out that they themselves are on the island and the Doctor reacts in horror as lava flows towards them.

IT WAS MADE WHERE...?
Location Filming: 25.04.68, 28.04.68-29.04.68, 02.05.68-03.05.68
Locations: Olley (Wrotham) Ltd sand pit, Trottiscliffe, Nr. Maidstone, Kent; Gerrards Cross Sand and Gravel Quarry, Wapsey's Wood, Gerrard's Cross, Bucks.
Model Filming: 26.04.68 in Puppet Theatre
Ealing Filming: 30.04.68-01.05.68 on Stage 2
Studio Recording: 17.05.68, 24.05.68 in TC4, 31.05.68, 07.06.68, 14.06.68 in TC3

ADDITIONAL CREDITED CAST
Rago (Ronald Allen), Toba (Kenneth Ives), Cully (Arthur Cox), Wahed (Philip Voss[1]), Etnin (Malcolm Terris[1]), Tolata (Nicolette Pendrell[1]), Kando (Felicity Gibson), Teel (Giles Block), Balan (Johnson Bayly[1-4]), Quarks (John Hicks, Gary Smith, Freddie Wilson[2-5]), Quark voices (Sheila Grant), Senex (Walter Fitzgerald[2-4]), Council Members (John Cross[2-4], Ronald Mansell[2-4]), Bovem (Alan Gerrard[2-4]), Tensa (Brian Cant[3,4]).

POPULAR MYTHS

- The third episode of this story had no on-screen episode number caption. (The episode's 35mm transmission print - which still survives in the archives - bore no such caption, but the production team, having noticed this omission, arranged for one to be superimposed live during the transmission itself - as evidenced by the 16mm telerecording made of the transmission, which also survives.)
- The location scenes of this story were shot on colour film as a test exercise. (They weren't. Despite persistent rumours to the contrary, the BBC did no colour filming or recording on any of the sixties Doctor Who stories.)

THINGS TO WATCH OUT FOR

- Some impressive explosions were filmed on location, perhaps most notably that of Cully's ship in the first episode.
- A surprisingly gruesome disintegration effect was used for the Quarks' killing of the Dulcians Etnin and Tolata in the first episode. (A simpler, but still quite horrific, smoke effect was substituted for the later deaths.)
- Chris Jeffries doubled for Patrick Troughton in all location-shot scenes featuring the Doctor.
- Ronald Allen, then better known for his starring role in the soap opera *Compact* and now for that in the soap opera *Crossroads*, played Rago, and Kenneth Ives, once a HAVOC stuntman and subsequently a distinguished director, played Toba.
- Brian Cant, better known as a presenter of children's programmes including *Play School*, played the minor Dulcian character Tensa.
- The Quarks' distinctive voices were created by recording actress Sheila Grant laughing, and then playing a synthesised version of the sound back as words.

THINGS YOU MIGHT NOT HAVE KNOWN

- Working title: *The Beautiful People*.
- *The Dominators* was originally commissioned as a six-part story from writers Mervyn Haisman and Henry Lincoln. The writers were late delivering their scripts, however, and script editor Derrick Sherwin decided that a major re-vamp was required, including cutting the story down from six episodes to five. As a result of this, Haisman and Lincoln requested that their names be removed from it. This was done, and the on-screen credit was given to Norman Ashby, a pseudonym created from the forenames of the writers' respective fathers-in-law.
- During the making of the previous story, *The Wheel in Space*, chief drama designer Lawrence Broadhurst had been asked by the Head of Serials to undertake an investigation into the cost of supplying scenic services to *Doctor Who*. It is unclear what lay behind this request – but as an intermediate statement by Broadhurst quoted an estimated overspend figure of £1300 for that story, this may well have been what prompted it. *The Dominators* came under scrutiny because designer Barry Newbery's initial estimate showed an overall £400 overspend. When the visual effects budget for the story (approximately £800) was added in, Newbery was able to predict that he could bring each episode in at an acceptable sum of around £406, but only because of 'an immense reduction in effects panels and controls, and also because of thorough planning to reduce the original script content, and physical effort in the studio.'
- The Quarks were played by school children as they were the only artistes who would

fit into the small casings. By law, they had to be accompanied by a chaperone on location and in studio.

- Costume designer Martin Baugh's original idea for the Quarks was that their heads should spin around as they orientated on their victims. This idea was abandoned when Baugh discovered that he could not obtain the required type of ball bearings needed to make it happen.
- Extras Eve Martin, Valerie Stanton, Jean Callaghan and Valerie Wood were booked to play 'statues' in the Dulcian city, but subsequently this idea was dropped and they were not used.
- Recording for this story was originally scheduled to be carried out in Studio D at Lime Grove.

QUOTE, UNQUOTE

- **Cully:** [Speaking of Zoe.] 'She can't be a Dulcian – she has an enquiring mind.'
- **Rago:** [To Senex.] 'You will provide me with certain statistics …' **Tensa:** 'Really, sir, I must protest.' **Rago:** 'Protest? You defy a Dominator?' **Tensa:** 'Senex is our leader, and as such demands respect.' **Rago:** 'I warn you. A Dominator must be obeyed. Your leader means nothing to me. I respect only one thing – superior force.'

ANALYSIS

The Dominators makes a disappointingly lacklustre start to the sixth season. 'We are faced with nothing more terrifying than a couple of intergalactic bully boys with very large chips on their shoulders,' complained David Miller in *DWB* No. 82 dated October 1990. 'The plot (for want of a better word) … goes something like this. Some nasty men in strange costumes land their flying saucer on the planet Dulkis. They get out, stamp about, shout a bit and generally duff up the indigenous population. The Dulcians, who wear even stranger clothes, are such a monumentally dull lot that, by the end, you don't care if they *do* get stomped on by the Dominators. After five mind shattering episodes, in which we discover nothing whatsoever about the invaders and precious little about the Dulcians, the nasty Dominators are defeated by a bit of fancy footwork on the part of the Doctor.'

In fairness, the two Dominators, although hardly amongst the best of the series' alien creations, are at least quite well realised on screen; and, as Chris Marton and Mark Woodward observed in *Cerebration Mentor* Number 2 in 1982, the running disagreements between them provide much of the story's interest: 'The aliens are portrayed as a quirky, dispassionate duo with distinct bloodlust traits, and there is a great deal of interplay between the two. Navigator Rago, the senior …, is the more responsible …, being more aware of [their] critically low energy levels and accordingly careful, and is determined to make a success of his mission. Toba is the sadist, and it is he who causes the [greatest] tribulations to the Dulcians. He casually wastes the sparse energy of the Quarks in the self-gratification of his sadistic tendencies. There are inevitable clashes between the two Dominators as Toba depletes the energy reserves Rago is so desperately trying to save, and in one big argument Rago tells Toba that he [risks being left] on Dulkis to perish with the Dulcians. Ronald Allen is mangificent as the superior Rago … [He] keeps his eyes and face locked in an unsettling demeanour of emotionless fanaticism (if such a thing is possible) and can be equally as ruthless as Toba when the need arises. The towering height of them over the Dulcians and the TARDIS crew alike gives them an extra measure of menace.'

'The Quarks were also well done,' asserted Martin Wiggins in *Wheel in Space* Issue Two in 1977, 'with very good retractable arms and rather odd feet, which [were effective] because, [rather than] gliding along or shuffling, [they] *walked*. It was also good to have the Quarks talking with squeaky female voices rather than the usual boring monotone.' In essence however the Quarks are really no more than robot drones with guns and spiky heads, and David Miller had rather more mixed feelings about them: 'Their appearance at the end of Episode 1 is at once compelling and ridiculous. The initial reaction is to laugh, but considering that we have already seen a demonstration of their colossal fire power, there is something genuinely macabre in their childlike [question] "Shall we destroy?" ... Although they look small and unimposing next to their Dominator masters, they are actually quite large ... Their clumsiness of shape and movement is at the same time unnerving and endearing, rather like malicious children ... But, for all their advantages, seeing the Quarks toddling about on screen with their fluting, high-pitched voices, is nothing short of hilarious. All hope of menace is lost as they have the living daylights kicked out of them by Jamie and Cully (the only Dulcian who actually *does* anything!). The Quarks are ludicrously easy to destroy, and just about the best thing they do on location is explode!'

The Dulcians, it must be admitted, are a singularly dull bunch, and, as Miller noted, it is difficult for the viewer to get overly worked up about their plight: 'There is a problem with the ... central idea itself – the Dulcians are pacifists. The story hinges on the conflict between aggression and pacifism. This is hardly a new concept for *Doctor Who* (it was the basis of the very first Dalek story). Unfortunately it is not a very televisual [one] – the aggressors arrive, pacifists give in, end of drama. Most aggravating of all, *The Dominators* offers no solution to the problem. In a ridiculous conclusion, the planet is ... saved from destruction by the Doctor. "Hooray!" you cry, but it does lead one to ponder what might have happened had he not been around ...' Director Morris Barry's casting of some of the Dulcian parts can also be criticised. 'No disrespect to Arthur Cox,' commented Chris Marton and Mark Woodward, 'but most rebel figures in the [series] are younger, more athletic and very handsome. The middle aged Cully, who has a [distinct] pot belly, is not quite in this class.'

Contemporary viewers whose reaction was recorded in the BBC's Audience Research Report on the opening episode were similarly unenthusiastic:

'In the opinion of dissatisfied viewers, this particular episode ... was typical of the recent trend in the series, by which the idea of going backwards in time to various historical events (which several much preferred) had been largely discarded in favour of concentrating on the science-fiction stories. Consequently, in order to maintain interest, the non-human characters had become more and more fantastic and improbable, it was said, and at least three in ten of those reporting dismissed this latest story as absolute rubbish. The series had long since lost all element of surprise, they declared, as, apart from minor details, each adventure followed the same pattern ("they arrive, separate, someone gets captured and the rest of the story is taken up with their rescue"); the new Quarks were nothing but "square Daleks", and the development of the plot was much too slow: "this sort of thing needs to get off to an exciting start".

'According to just over a third, however, *Doctor Who*, which they had long enjoyed as an entertaining "escapist" serial, continued to maintain a good level of inventiveness. The writers always seemed able to come up with something new, it was said, and *The Dominators*, with its interesting collection of characters, including a race of robots even more terrible than the Daleks, would seem to possess the ingredients of another first class

Second Doctor

space adventure. At the same time, it was clear that a further number (while less critical than the majority) were beginning to lose interest: "although I am a *Doctor Who* fan of many years standing, my enjoyment is steadily decreasing every week," commented one typically, and some doubts were expressed as to its ability to appeal even to children.'

Fortunately, better was to come as the season progressed.

THE MIND ROBBER

Writer: Derrick Sherwin[1]*, Peter Ling[2-5]. **Director:** David Maloney. **Designer:** Evan Hercules. **Costumes:** Martin Baugh[1-4], Susan Wheal[5]. **Make-Up:** Sylvia James. **Incidental Music:** stock. **Fight Arranger:** B H Barry, John Greenwood. **Visual Effects:** Jack Kine, Bernard Wilkie. **Film Cameraman:** Jimmy Court. **Film Editor:** Martyn Day. **Studio Lighting:** Howard King. **Studio Sound:** John Holmes. **Production Assistant:** John Lopes. **Assistant Floor Manager:** Edwina Verner.

* Derrick Sherwin, as *Doctor Who*'s script editor, received no credit for writing this episode, which thus became the only episode in the series' history to feature no writer's credit on screen.

	First UK TX	Scheduled TX	Actual TX	Duration	Viewers	Chart Pos.
Episode 1	14/09/68	17.20	17.17	21'27"	6.6	55
Episode 2	21/09/68	17.20	17.18	21'39"	6.5	54
Episode 3	28/09/68	17.20	17.20	19'29"	7.2	45
Episode 4	05/10/68	17.20	17.20	19'14"	7.3	44
Episode 5	12/10/68	17.20	17.21	18'00"	6.7	84

Plot: To escape from the volcanic eruption on Dulkis, the Doctor uses an emergency unit which moves the TARDIS out of normal time and space. The travellers find themselves in an endless void, where they are menaced by White Robots. Having regained the safety of the TARDIS, they believe they have escaped – until the ship suddenly explodes apart. They then find themselves in a land of fiction, where they are hunted by life-size clockwork soldiers and encounter characters like Rapunzel and Swift's Lemuel Gulliver. This domain is presided over by a man known only as the Master – a prolific English writer from 1926 – who in turn is controlled by a Master Brain computer. Now the Master is desperate to escape and wants the Doctor to take his place, while the Master Brain plans to take over the Earth. The Doctor engages the Master in a battle of wills using a variety of fictional characters. Zoe and Jamie meanwhile succeed in overloading the Master Brain and, in the confusion, the White Robots destroy the computer, finally freeing the Master.

Episode endings:
1. The TARDIS is in flight, the travellers having apparently escaped from the void. A low, throbbing hum is heard which grows in intensity until it is unbearable. Suddenly the TARDIS explodes. The Doctor spins away through space while Jamie and Zoe are left clinging to the console as it is engulfed in swirling mist.
2. Escorted to the edge of a forest of words by the clockwork soldiers, the Doctor, Jamie and Zoe find themselves in a black void. Suddenly they see a white unicorn charging straight at them.

3. Exploring a labyrinth, the Doctor and Zoe find themselves facing a statue of the Medusa, which starts to come to life. The Doctor tells Zoe to deny its existence or it will turn them both to stone. Zoe is unable to do so. As the Medusa approaches, the Doctor desperately tells Zoe not to look into its eyes.
4. The travellers are taken to see the Master. Jamie and Zoe attempt to escape through a library but are caught by the White Robots and forced between the pages of a giant book, which starts to close on them.
5. The travellers and the Master all escape as the White Robots destroy the Master Brain computer. A mist envelops them and the TARDIS reforms in space.

IT WAS MADE WHERE...?

Location Filming: 09.06.68
Locations: Harrison's Rocks, nr Groombridge, Sussex; Kenley Aerodrome, Croydon.
Model Filming: 10.06.68-11.06.68 in Puppet Theatre
Ealing Filming: 12.06.68-14.06.68 on Stage 2
Studio Recording: 21.06.68, 28.06.68 in TC3, 05.07.68, 12.07.68 in Lime Grove D, 19.07.68 in TC3

ADDITIONAL CREDITED CAST

The Master (Emrys Jones), Robots (John Atterbury[1,4,5], Ralph Carrigan[1,4,5], Bill Wiesener[1,4,5], Terry Wright[1,4,5]), Jamie (Hamish Wilson[2,3]), A Stranger[2]/Gulliver[3-5] (Bernard Horsfall[2-5]), Children (Barbara Loft[2,5], Sylvestra Le Tozel[2,5], Timothy Horton[2,5], Chistopher Reynolds[2,5*], David Reynolds[2,5*], Martin Langley[2,5]), Soldiers (Paul Alexander[2,3,5], Ian Hines[2,3,5], Richard Ireson[2,3,5]), Redcoat (Philip Ryan[2,3]), Princess Rapunzel (Christine Pirie[3,5**]), The Medusa (Sue Pulford[3,4]), Karkus (Christopher Robbie[4,5]), D'Artagnan and Sir Lancelot (John Greenwood[5]), Cyrano (David Cannon[5]), Blackbeard (Gerry Wain[5]).

* The surname of these child actors was spelt 'Reynolds' on the closing credits of Episode 2 and 'Reynalds' on the closing credits of Episode 5.
** Christine Pirie also contributed, uncredited, a voice-over reading of an extract from *Little Women* in Episode 3. Similarly, Richard Ireson also played, uncredited, the Minotaur.

POPULAR MYTHS

- Hamish Wilson, who played Jamie in Episodes 2 and 3, is Frazer Hines's cousin. (He isn't, but Ian Hines, who played one of the Clockwork Soldiers in this story, is Hines's brother.)

THINGS TO WATCH OUT FOR

- The character Gulliver speaks only lines written for him by Jonathan Swift in *Gulliver's Travels*.
- Distinguished actress Sylvestra Le Touzel, then acting as Sylvestra Le Tozel, plays one of the children.

THINGS YOU MIGHT NOT HAVE KNOWN

- Working title: *Man Power, The Fact of Fiction*.
- Although the Master is never named, it is strongly implied that he is a real historical

SECOND DOCTOR 2

writer: Bracebridge Hemyng (1829-1904). The Master states at one point that he wrote the adventures of Captain Jack Harkaway in the *Ensign* comic; in reality, it was Hemyng who created Harkaway and wrote his adventures. (Peter Ling himself had also written for boys' comics.)

- The costumes used for the White Robots had originally been seen in the *Out of the Unknown* play *The Prophet*, when they had been black and borne identification numbers on their chests. They were repainted for *The Mind Robber* but were not in fact white; rather, three were yellow and one was grey. The reason for this was that pure white tended to be too bright for the monochrome cameras in use at the time, causing picture flaring. (For the same reason, the TARDIS control console was painted pale green rather than white.)

- **Zoe:** 'They don't want us to find a way out ... only a way in.'
- **The Master:** [Speaking of the Doctor.] 'You cannot escape ... but we will play your game a little longer.'
- **The Doctor:** 'Sausages! Man will become like a string of sausages – all the same!'

ANALYSIS

Doctor Who, with its highly flexible format, was able from time to time to present a story that could be considered 'experimental'. *The Mind Robber* is a good example of this. It is often compared to the third season story *The Celestial Toymaker* (and also to the eighteenth season story *Warriors' Gate*, although in that case the main similarity seems to be that the action takes place partly in a white void). Both adventures pit the Doctor and his friends against some initially unseen and intangible force; both involve them being forced to solve puzzles; and both present the possibility of the Doctor having to stay in his adversary's domain as the ultimate threat. Both also fall more clearly into the category of science-fantasy than of science-fiction, although they do have a firm science-fiction basis.

Writing in *Ark in Space* No.7 dated May 1983, David Owen felt that *The Mind Robber* worked better than *The Celestial Toymaker*, 'since the Doctor and co are left to deduce exactly where they are, and what the rules of the game are. This draws more on the Doctor's mental resources and hence makes for a far more interesting story, as he solves riddles and puzzles, such as replacing Jamie's face. Quite a stroke of luck that Frazer Hines should be unavailable during *this* story, since the necessary rewrite is indistinguishable from its surroundings ...'

On the downside, *The Mind Robber* is a bit of a jumble. Principal writer Peter Ling has thrown into the mix a large number of disparate elements from all manner of works of fiction: nursery rhymes, Gulliver, clockwork soldiers, Rapunzel, a superhero called the Karkus, a unicorn, pirates and so on. And yet the whole thing works despite this. The reason may be that the fictional characters play no real part in the plot; they are, cleverly, just characters that appear, interact with the time travellers (or just say their lines) and then vanish when their usefulness is over. It is puzzling, however, that some of these supposedly fictional characters actually existed (Blackbeard and Cyrano de Bergerac for example); and it is never explained where the White Robots come from, although to give the production team the benefit of the doubt this could perhaps be a supreme piece of cleverness as they (or at least their costumes) were originally created for one of the BBC's *Out of the Unknown* plays and so could be considered fictional as well. (A later *Out of the Unknown*, *Get Off My Cloud*, featured both the TARDIS and the Daleks ... the blurring of fact and fiction continued.)

The opening episode is generally considered the most memorable, and rightly so. It works incredibly well – especially considering that it was a last-minute addition (necessitated by scripting problems that had seen *The Dominators* reduced from six episodes to five) and that it was constrained by the fact that no guest cast or additional sets could be afforded. The 'white featureless void' is very well realised, and the use of subtle mixes between shots adds to the impression of a place devoid of landmarks. The camerawork is, indeed, some of the best ever seen in the series. John Peel, writing in *Oracle* Volume 2 Number 7 dated April 1979, remembered the impact of this episode:

'The first episode had me unsettled, with most of the action centred in the TARDIS and weird images filling the minds of the two companions ... whilst the Doctor strove to repair the [ship] before it was destroyed. Then ... the TARDIS exploded, whirling fragments carrying off the Doctor and his companions ...

'I was hooked. I didn't miss a single moment of this story, and it easily ranks as the veritable classic ... of the Troughton age in my mind ... It was a story where literally anything could happen, where nothing was what it seemed and there was no way of guessing what would happen next ...'

After this wonderful opening, things do go downhill slightly. Amongst the problems are that the ground-level sets for the 'forest of words' in which the travellers find themselves, although quite effective as such, simply do not tie up with the overhead view (a shame, as this was a nice idea); that the route Zoe suggests taking to the centre of the labyrinth does not match the route as seen on a map of the tunnels; and that the Karkus can be regarded only as a complete joke or perhaps, to be more generous, as another good idea that just didn't work out. Perhaps more fundamentally, despite the fact that the episodes are somewhat shorter than normal (in fact, some of the shortest in the series' history – the last one is only about eighteen minutes long), the story contains quite a bit of material that comes across like padding. The ending is also somewhat rushed and confused: the White Robots, having been told to destroy, destroy their controller; the Doctor and friends are then engulfed in mist; and the TARDIS re-forms. End of story, and not terribly satisfying.

The BBC's Audience Research Report on the final episode suggests that, in common with most other fantasy-orientated stories, *The Mind Robber* was less than well received by contemporary viewers:

'It seemed that this episode only served to confirm the growing feeling that the element of fantasy in *Doctor Who* was getting out of hand. This was one of the most far-fetched they had yet seen, most of the sample said, and, with the exception of a few who considered the ending a "bit of a let down" to a promising adventure, the remarks of those reporting also applied to the story as a whole.

'For many, *Doctor Who* was clearly something watched "for the children's sake" rather than from personal inclination. Never one of their favourite programmes, it had now deteriorated into ridiculous rubbish which could no longer be dignified with the term science-fiction, they declared. This latest adventure, with its weak storyline, was too silly for words and, in their opinion, Doctor Who had had his day.'

'Just under a third' of the sample were reported to have considered the story 'an enjoyable fantasy,' commenting favourably on the idea of a 'master mind' being able to turn people into fictional characters. 'On the other hand, several who welcomed the theme as a refreshing departure from "the more usual punch-up" between the Doctor's party and their current enemies thought the action terribly disjointed and difficult to follow and, although they personally found the story one of the best for a long time, ended by condemning it as far too complicated for younger viewers – who were, after all, its main audience'.

It must be said however that, despite its arguable shortcomings, *The Mind Robber* remains a hugely enjoyable story, and one that stands up to repeated viewing. It contains at its heart a sound idea, and the writing is highly inventive. The introduction of a 'different' Jamie – again necessitated by circumstances; in this case the fact that Frazer Hines had succumbed to chicken pox and could not appear – is truly innovative, and Hamish Wilson does a pretty good job of playing the Scot for two episodes. Peel summed up the feelings of many when he suggested that the story stands as a milestone in *Doctor Who*'s history: 'It had been years since *Doctor Who* had aroused this kind of interest in me, and this story ranks among the best of my ... memories [of the series]; weird sets, superb humour (when the Doctor meets Rapunzel, he asks to use her hair to climb down; she says "You may as well, everyone else does ..."); strange twists and a brilliant writer.'

THE INVASION

Writer: Derrick Sherwin, from a story by Kit Pedler. **Director:** Douglas Camfield. **Designer:** Richard Hunt. **Costumes:** Bobi Bartlett. **Make-Up:** Sylvia James. **Incidental Music:** Don Harper. **Visual Effects:** Bill King/Trading Post. **Film Cameraman:** Alan Jonas. **Film Editor:** Martyn Day. **Studio Lighting:** Robbie Robinson. **Studio Sound:** Alan Edmonds, Bryan Forgham. **Production Assistant:** Chris D'Oyly John. **Assistant Floor Manager:** Sue Willis.

Note: Episode Eight bore an additional credit reading 'The BBC wish to acknowledge the help given to them by the Ministry of Defence in the making of this programme.'

	First UK TX	Scheduled TX	Actual TX	Duration	Viewers	Chart Pos.
Episode One	02/11/68	17.15	17.15	24'32"	7.3	55
Episode Two	09/11/68	17.15	17.15	24'26"	7.1	55
Episode Three	16/11/68	17.15	17.15	23'44"	7.1	66
Episode Four	23/11/68	17.15	17.15	24'18"	6.4	73
Episode Five	30/11/68	17.15	17.15	23'25"	6.7	67
Episode Six	07/12/68	17.15	17.15	23'20"	6.5	72
Episode Seven	14/12/68	17.15	17.15	24'46"	7.2	51
Episode Eight	21/12/68	17.15	17.15	25'03"	7.0	80

Plot: The TARDIS materialises in England in the 1970s and the time travellers meet a girl named Isobel whose uncle, computer scientist Professor Watkins, has recently gone missing. The Doctor offers to help track him down, starting at the place where he last worked – the London HQ of International Electromatics, the world's major supplier of electronic equipment. His initial suspicions about IE's managing director, Tobias Vaughn, are confirmed after he becomes reacquainted with Lethbridge-Stewart, now promoted to Brigadier and in charge of the British branch of the United Nations Intelligence Taskforce (UNIT), and learns that there have been other disappearances at IE premises. He discovers that Vaughn is in league with the Cybermen in a plan to invade Earth, but is also plotting against them with the aim of seizing power for himself. Watkins is being forced by Vaughn to develop the cerebration mentor, a machine designed to generate emotional impulses as a weapon against the Cybermen. The Cybermen immobilise most of Earth's population – sending a hypnotic signal through special circuits incorporated in all IE equipment – and launch their invasion. The Doctor has managed to protect himself and his friends from the signal and – with help from an embittered Vaughn, who is killed during the fighting – the invasion is eventually defeated.

Episode endings:

1. Tobias Vaughn crosses to the wall of his office and activates a switch on a control panel. The wall pivots upwards to reveal a strange, alien-looking device within a hidden compartment.

2. The Doctor and Jamie see guards placing an unconscious Zoe and Isobel into crates ready for transportation to the IE factory. Jamie attacks Vaughn's sadistic security chief, Packer, but the guards are alerted by the sounds of their struggle. The Doctor tells his companion to run, but they are both caught and brought before Packer at gunpoint.

3. To avoid capture by guards, the Doctor and Jamie each hide inside a crate loaded aboard the IE train. Jamie finds himself lying next to some sort of cocoon. To his horror, something inside the cocoon starts to move …

4. The Doctor and Jamie watch from hiding as technicians attach cables to one of the cocoons and activate the device to which they are connected. The cocoon is split open from inside and a Cyberman emerges.

5. Jamie, Zoe and Isobel are trapped in a London sewer as Cybermen converge on them from both directions. Suddenly a rogue Cyberman that Vaughn earlier sent mad using the cerebration mentor appears and lurches toward them …

6. The Cybermen emerge from the sewers and march through the streets of London as the invasion begins.

7. The Cyber Director tells Vaughn that the Cybermen no longer need him; they intend to deliver a Cyber megatron bomb that will destroy all life on Earth. The Doctor asks Vaughn if this is what he wanted – to be the ruler of a dead world.

8. The Doctor, Jamie and Zoe enter the TARDIS, watched with bemusement by Isobel and UNIT's Captain Turner. The ship dematerialises.

IT WAS MADE WHERE…?

Model Filming: 31.08.68 (Stage unknown)
Location Filming: 03.09.68-13.09.68
Locations: Williamstrip Farm, Coln St Aldwyns, Cirencester; Associated British Maltsters building, Wallingford; Hatherop Road, nr aerodrome, Fairford; Kingston Minerals, Kempford Road, Fairford; St Peter's Hill, off Queen Victoria Street, London; Queen Victoria Street, London; TCC Condensers, Wales Farm Road, London; Princedale Road; Heathfield Street; Walmer Road; St James' Gardens, all Notting Hill Gate, London; Guinness Factory, Park Royal, London; Knightrider Street; Moor Lane; Distaff Lane; St Nicholas Cole Abbey; Queen Victoria Street; Fore Street; St Paul's Churchyard all City, London; Millbank Tower, Millbank, London; Maida Hill Tunnel, Regent's Canal, Lisson Grove, London; Cumberland Terrance, Regent's Park, London; Australia

House, Strand, London; Denham Aerodrome, Tilehouse Lane, Denham Green, Bucks.
Ealing Filming: 13.09.68 (Stage unknown)
Studio Recording: 20.09.68, 27.09.68, 04.10.68, 11.10.68, 18.10.68, 25.10.68, 01.11.68, 08.11.68 all in Lime Grove D

ADDITIONAL CREDITED CAST

Lorry Driver (Murray Evans[1]), Patrolman (Walter Randall[1]), Isobel (Sally Faulkner[1,2,4-8]), Benton (John Levene[1-3,6,8*]), Tracy (Geoffrey Cheshire[1,2]), Tobias Vaughn (Kevin Stoney), Packer (Peter Halliday**), Gregory (Ian Fairbairn[2,5,6]), Brigadier Lethbridge-Stewart (Nicholas Courtney[2-8]), Sergeant Walters (James Thornhill[2-7]), Captain Turner (Robert Sidaway[2-8]), Professor Watkins (Edward Burnham[3,4,6,7]), Phone Operator (Sheila Dunn[4,5]), Major-General Rutlidge (Edward Dentith[4,5]), Workman (Peter Thompson[5]), Policeman (Dominic Allan[5]), Private Perkins (Stacy Davies[6]), Cybermen (Pat Gorman[6-8], Ralph Carrigan[6-8***] Charles Finch[6-8], John Spradbury[6-8], Derek Chafer[6], Terence Denville[6], Peter Thornton[7,8], Richard King[7,8]), Major Branwell (Clifford Earl[7,8]), Sergeant Peters (Norman Hartley[7,8]).

* Also appeared in film sequences in Episode Five, but uncredited.
** Peter Halliday also provided, uncredited, the voices of the Cybermen and of the Cyber Director hidden in a concealed compartment in Vaughn's office.
*** On the closing credits of Episode Five Ralph Carrigan's surname was misspelt 'Carrigon'.

THINGS TO WATCH OUT FOR

- The TARDIS becomes (temporarily) invisible after materialising.
- There is a cameo appearance by director Douglas Camfield playing a car driver in the first episode.
- This story marks the debut appearance by John Levene (who had previously played monsters in the series) as future regular Benton. In Episode Eight he replaced James Thornhill, who was originally planned to have appeared as Sergeant Walters.
- Douglas Camfield's wife Sheila Dunn provided voice-overs as a phone operator.
- Zoe makes no appearance in Episode Four of the story as Wendy Padbury was on holiday during the week when it was recorded. Similarly Jamie appears only in a pre-filmed insert in Episode Eight as Frazer Hines was due for a break.
- The story features some excellent and highly distinctive incidental music (albeit only about four minutes in total) by jazz musician Don Harper.
- Extensive use was made of stock footage of radar dishes, missiles etc.
- An appearance was made by the 2nd Battalion of Coldstream Guards as UNIT troops in the battle scenes in Episode Eight.

THINGS YOU MIGHT NOT HAVE KNOWN

- Working title: *Return of the Cybermen*.
- Like the previous Cyberman stories, *The Invasion* was based on an idea by Kit Pedler, who was paid a fee of £280 for the original idea, the basic storyline and general background advice. He was also paid a copyright payment of £120 for the use of the Cybermen and the Cybermats – although the latter ultimately did not appear in the story.
- The production team originally intended that both Professor Travers and Colonel

Lethbridge-Stewart from *The Web of Fear* should appear in this story. Despite the recent disagreement over *The Dominators*, the characters' creators Mervyn Haisman and Henry Lincoln agreed to this on 6 May 1968. The idea was that both characters would be seen in seven of the eight episodes. Subsequently however producer Peter Bryant expressed concern in a memo to assistant head of copyright John Henderson that during the scripting process the involvement of Travers had been reduced to the point where the part was too small to offer to an actor of Jack Watling's standing. A decision was therefore made that this character, although he would be referred to, would not appear. There was also concern that Nicholas Courtney might not be available on the required dates to play the Colonel. The suggestion was that if this turned out to be the case, then a similar character could be substituted, and no payment would be due to Haisman and Lincoln. Henderson however replied that 'a change of name (in which there is no copyright anyway) and performer will not alter the fact that your new character "Joe Soap" will really be Lethbridge-Stewart in disguise, who belongs to Haisman and Lincoln; and I think we ought to pay for him whatever he is called and whoever plays him!' The two writers were ultimately paid £5 per episode for the use of Lethbridge-Stewart.

- Edward Burnham (Professor Watkins) was contracted to appear in the last episode but ultimately was not used.

QUOTE, UNQUOTE

- **Brigadier Lethbridge-Stewart:** 'You still making a nonsense of it, Doctor, in your … what's it called? TARDIS?' **The Doctor:** 'Yes, we're still travelling, yes.' **Brigadier Lethbridge-Stewart:** 'Yes, Miss Travers told me all about it. It's … um … well, it's to say the least an unbelievable machine.' **The Doctor:** 'Any more unbelievable than the Yetis, hm?' **Brigadier Lethbridge-Stewart:** 'No, true. I'm not quite so much a sceptic as I was before *that* little escapade!'
- **Tobias Vaughn:** 'My body may be cybernetic but my mind stays human!'
- **Professor Watkins:** 'You're an evil man, Vaughn. You're sadistic. You're a megalomaniac. You're insane. I pity you. But if I get half a chance, I'll kill you.'
- **Tobias Vaughn:** 'The world is weak, vulnerable, a mess of uncoordinated and impossible ideals. It needs a strong, single mind, a leader.'

ANALYSIS

The Invasion, originally conceived as a sequel of sorts to *The Web of Fear* (although in the end Professor Travers and his daughter Anne effectively became Professor Watkins and his niece Isobel), is one of the very best stories to feature the Cybermen. That this should be the case is actually quite ironic, given that the silver giants are kept firmly in the background throughout and don't really constitute characters in their own right – indeed, they don't even appear until Episode Four and have only a couple of brief lines of dialogue in the entire story. They are instead represented by the Cyber Director (presumably, like the Cyber Planner in *The Wheel in Space*, a kind of super-evolved Cyberman) and more particularly by the part-converted human entrepreneur Tobias Vaughn – a great character, wonderfully portrayed by Kevin Stoney (who had already endeared himself to the series' fans with his fine performance as Mavic Chen in the third season story *The Daleks' Master Plan*).

'It is [Vaughn's] battle with the Doctor that gives substance and form to the plot,' wrote Anthony Clark in *DWB* No. 114 dated June 1993. 'In the end, this conflict plays out so well that the Cybermen are almost an irrelevance at times … *Doctor Who* has never had a better written and acted villain, and all his scenes are a *tour de force* of character portrayal … By the end of the story you really feel that you have come to know Vaughn's motives so well that he becomes almost sympathetic, if not likeable.

'Thematically *The Invasion* makes great play out of spreading its net wider than most *Doctor Who* stories. This is partly facilitated by its length, although Derrick Sherwin's script is so neatly precise that each episode is stocked with meat and little else. Therefore, there is ample opportunity to explore that plot's potential as both an exciting roller-coaster yarn and as a commentary on faceless transnational corporations and their amorphous, and therefore ill-defined, role in the world's establishment. In this scheme of things, the Cybermen provide the thrills and spills while Vaughn and … IE … [tease] out the bigger questions. To my mind this is one of the great strengths of the story – monsters for the kids and some serious "adult" content.'

This may not be a 'standard' Cyberman story, but the idea of the Earth being attacked through its electronic equipment is perfectly in tune with the concepts underlying the creatures, and the influence of their creator Kit Pedler can be discerned here. The Cybermen also look very good on screen, due partly to the superb new costumes designed for them by Bobi Bartlett but perhaps more particularly to Douglas Camfield's excellent direction. 'Although the new Cybermen are more in line with conventionally styled robots,' commented Philip Packer in *Star Begotten* Vol. 3 No. 1/2 dated June 1989, 'they can look stunning in some of Camfield's shots, notably those in the sewers, where they gleam menacingly, and especially in one of the most perfectly executed and celebrated invasion sequences ever made for *Doctor Who*, or any other telefantasy series: … the moment at the end of Episode [Six] when the Cybermen climb out of the sewers and march down the steps of St Paul's … In fact, [this scene] is even more similar than I first thought to the famous 'Odessa Steps' sequence of *Battleship Potemkin* … I don't think Camfield went out of his way to ape Eisenstein simply for the sake of it. It seems more likely that the locations offered this possibility of exploiting the effectiveness of the sequence and adapting it to suit the situation … Consider also the similarity with certain sections of Akira Kurosawa's *Shichi-nin no Samurai* [aka *Seven Samurai*] too.'

Sherwin's creation (as an addition to Pedler's original storyline) of the UNIT organisation – headed by Lethbridge-Stewart from *The Web of Fear* – is inspired; and in retrospect the story can be considered even more significant than it seemed at the time of its original transmission, given that it was in effect a 'dummy run' for the early part of the third Doctor's era.

'*The Invasion* was careful to portray a vision of the future,' noted Mark Jones in *Matrix* Issue 49 dated spring 1994. 'Treated by the production team and publicity alike as being set in 1975, [it] presented a frightening but believable view of the world of [that time] … The Earth is closer towards unity, with UNIT operating as an effective multinational force: the Brigadier in Episode Seven is able to pick up a file containing the scheduled launch times of Russian rockets and is equally able to launch those [rockets] at the incoming invasion fleet …The emphasis of the story is on International Electromatics, a company which, as its name suggests, is a huge … conglomerate operating across the globe. Watkins is firmly convinced that Vaughn is using specific circuits to corner the world electronics market, and this is not totally unbelievable … [This makes IE] a suitable cipher for the Cybermen's plans.

'This future world draws on the technophobic roots of such stories as *The War*

Machines, which is also associated with Kit Pedler. There are such devices as videophones and computer doormen. The Doctor frequently says that he hates computers ..., and Zoe destroys one, much to Vaughn's amusement ... Vaughn has at his disposal a group of armed security men, referred to by the Brigadier as "Vaughn's private army", whose effectiveness and brutality [are] not left to the imagination.'

'*The Invasion* is a totally successful blend of good characterisation (with suitably convincing performances from Nicholas Courtney as Lethbridge-Stewart and Kevin Stoney as the evil Tobias Vaughn) and taut plotting,' enthused Trevor Wayne in *Doctor Who – An Adventure in Space and Time* in 1984. 'Despite [its] prodigious length ... there are no dull patches and little let-up in the pace and excitement; for once the defeat of the invasion and the downfall of the aliens are not reserved for the last ten minutes of the final episode. Excellent use of film and locations and the proliferation of soldiers, guns, missiles, helicopters and other military hardware once again prove that Douglas Camfield's forté was the strong action-packed adventure.'

The Invasion is, in short, one of the highlights of the sixth season, and a veritable classic.

THE KROTONS

Writer: Robert Holmes. **Director:** David Maloney. **Designer:** Raymond London. **Costumes:** Bobi Bartlett. **Make-Up:** Sylvia James. **Incidental Music:** none. **Visual Effects:** Bill King/Trading Post. **Film Cameraman:** Alan Jonas. **Film Editor:** Martyn Day. **Studio Lighting:** Howard King. **Studio Sound:** John Holmes. **Production Assistant:** Edwina Verner. **Assistant Floor Manager:** David Tilley.

	First UK TX	Scheduled TX	Actual TX	Duration	Viewers	Chart Pos.
Episode One	28/12/68	17.15	17.16	23'00"	9.0	55
Episode Two	04/01/69	17.15	17.16	23'03"	8.4	54
Episode Three	11/01/69	17.15	17.17	21'47"	7.5	61
Episode Four	18/01/69	17.15	17.17	22'39"	7.1	68

Plot: The TARDIS arrives on the unnamed planet of the Gonds, who are ruled and taught in a form of self-perpetuating slavery by the alien Krotons – crystalline beings whose ship, the Dynatrope, crash-landed there thousands of years ago after being damaged in a space battle. The Krotons are at present in suspended animation, in a crystalline slurry form, awaiting a time when they can be reconstituted by absorbtion of mental energy. Periodically, the two most brilliant Gond students are received into the Dynatrope, apparently to become 'companions of the Krotons' but in truth to have their mental energy drained, after which they are killed. When the Doctor and Zoe take the students' test, their mental power is sufficient to reanimate the Krotons. The Doctor discovers that their life system is based on tellurium and, with help from the Gond scientist Beta, he is then able to destroy them and their ship using an impure form of sulphuric acid.

Episode endings:
1. Gond students start smashing up the teaching machines. When Selris, the Gond leader, arrives with the Doctor, a snake-like probe emerges from the Dynatrope. It homes in on the

Doctor and extends toward him.

2. The Doctor and Zoe, after reanimating the Krotons, have escaped through the back of the Dynatrope. Jamie however is still trying to enter through the main door. The Krotons allow him through in the belief that he can supply more mental energy. They subject him to the intelligence draining device and discover that he is not as intelligent as the Doctor and Zoe. One Kroton remarks that, in that case, the power will kill him.

3. The Gonds attack the Krotons' ship by attempting to undermine its foundations. The Doctor arrives too late to stop them and the ceiling starts to cave in. The Doctor is buried under a pile of rubble.

4. With the Dynatrope destroyed, the Gonds must find their own solutions from now on. The TARDIS leaves the planet.

IT WAS MADE WHERE...?

Location Filming: 10.11.68-11.11.68
Locations: West of England Quarry and Tank Quarry, Malvern, Worcestershire.
Ealing Filming: 12.11.68-13.11.68 (Stage unknown)
Studio Recording: 22.11.68, 29.11.68, 06.12.68, 13.12.68 all in Lime Grove D

ADDITIONAL CREDITED CAST

Selris (James Copeland), Abu (Terence Brown[1]), Vana (Madeleine Mills), Thara (Gilbert Wynne), Eelek (Philip Madoc[1,3,4]), Axus (Richard Ireson[1,3,4]), Beta (James Cairncross[1,3,4]), Student (Bronson Shaw[1]), Custodian (Maurice Selwyn[1]), Kroton Voices (Roy Skelton, Patrick Tull[2-4]), Krotons (Robert La'Bassiere[2-4]* Miles Northover[2-4])

* Robert La'Bassiere was the name under which actor Robert Grant asked to be credited.

POPULAR MYTHS

- This story was based on an idea by Robert Holmes for a science-fiction play that was passed on to the *Doctor Who* office after being rejected by Roger Parkes, the script editor of the BBC's *Out of the Unknown* anthology series. (It was based on a storyline that Holmes had originally submitted to the *Doctor Who* office some three years earlier – although apparently, at an even earlier stage, when Irene Shubik rather than Roger Parkes was script editor, it had indeed started life as an unsuccessful submission to *Out of the Unknown*.)
- The Krotons were the winning entry in a *Blue Peter* 'design a monster' competition. (They weren't. Confusion may have arisen as one of the winning entries in a *Blue Peter* 'design a monster to beat the Daleks' competition, the 'Aqua-Man', resembled a cardboard box with legs and arms – not too dissimilar from the Krotons' appearance.)

THINGS TO WATCH OUT FOR

- Popular Welsh actor Philip Madoc makes an early television appearance as Eelek.

THINGS YOU MIGHT NOT HAVE KNOWN

- Working titles: *The Trap*, *The Space Trap*.
- Frazer Hines had originally intended to leave the series at this point but decided to stay on to the end of the season after he learned that Patrick Troughton would also

be bowing out then. This was the main reason why a comedy-flavoured story entitled *The Prison in Space* by Dick Sharples, in which Jamie was to have been written out and a new companion character called Nik introduced, was dropped at the last minute, even though costume and set design work had already begun and some members of cast (including Barrie Gosney) had already been contracted. *The Krotons* was brought forward from later in the season to fill the slot.

- Script writer Robert Holmes had originally submitted an outline of *The Space Trap* to the *Doctor Who* production office on 25 April 1965, when it had been rejected by story editor Donald Tosh. It was while clearing out some files that he came across his original letter and outline and sent it in again, with a note to the effect that the production team could throw it away if they felt it was of no use. Assistant script editor Terrance Dicks liked the idea and developed it with Holmes over a relatively long period as a 'fall back'. Consequently it was ready and available for use when Dick Sharples' *The Prison in Space* fell through.

QUOTE, UNQUOTE

- **Zoe:** 'The Doctor's almost as clever as I am.'
- **Beta:** [To the Doctor.] 'We've been slaves for one thousand years. Do you think you can free us in one day?'
- **Kroton:** 'Where are the high brains?'

ANALYSIS

The very first shot in this story is of a small hatch sticking as it opens to allow Selris to receive instructions from within, and this production glitch unfortunately sets the tone for the remainder of the adventure.

In design terms, *The Krotons* is very basic. There is little to be seen here that excites or even shows promise. The interior of the Kroton ship, or the Dynatrope as they call it, consists of bland metal walls and hanging ribbed plastic tubing (perhaps the Krotons use the same supply house as the Cybermen?) rather than something truly alien-looking. The model shots used to depict the exteriors of the Gond dwellings and the Dyantrope, which appears to be a massive golf ball-like structure, are unconvincing and inconsistent with the studio sets – a problem that is most painfully obvious in a scene where some of the characters notice that the Dynatrope is damaged, and the next shot is of a view that they could not possibly be seeing from their vantage point. This is simply shoddy work, and director David Maloney wisely keeps such effects to a minimum.

The scripts, the first from future *Doctor Who* stalwart Robert Holmes, can be most generously described as workmanlike. *The Krotons* is a simple tale of a group of humanoids enslaved by an initially unseen power. It could be viewed as some sort of political allegory, but it is doubtful that this was the impetus behind it. Holmes had yet to master *Doctor Who*'s particular requirements and, perhaps as a result, many of the characters come across as being bland and faceless. One notable exception is Eelek, played with relish by Philip Madoc, who all but steals every scene in which he appears. Another strong character is Beta, a scientist to whom certain areas of learning have been denied. His obvious joy at being 'allowed' to mix up sulphuric acid is pleasing to see, and yet this does raise the question of how he happens to be aware of acids at all, given that the Gonds supposedly know only what the Krotons have taught them and that this does not include chemistry.

Where this story does succeed is in the quality of its soundtrack. In the absence of any incidental music, special sounds supervisor Brian Hodgson fills the air with the most wonderful pulsing and throbbing noises as the Krotons are reanimated and move about their ship. The Krotons' voices too are superb: harsh, grating and totally authoritative. In some ways this is a story that is better listened to than watched, as the mind can conjure up a far more impressive series of images than its makers were able to achieve on screen.

Some commentators, though, take a much more positive view of the story. 'The Krotons was entertainment,' argued David Gibbs, writing in *DWB* No. 87 dated March 1991. 'It stood up ... as a tight, crisp one hundred minutes of enjoyable television. Its sets were small, sometimes cheap; the acting tended towards the wooden on occasions; the Krotons themselves could quite conceivably have been drawn from a *Blue Peter* "design a monster" competition, as legend for so many years insisted. It was devoid of music, special effects on any real scale, even action, in the contemporary sense of the word. And yet it worked, so well. It needs no apologies, just your appreciation.'

Contemporary viewers, too, seem to have derived a fair amount of pleasure from the story, judging from the BBC's Audience Research Report on the first episode: 'The start of a new adventure in space and time in this popular family series was thoroughly enjoyed by a number of viewers in the sample audience. It was said to be an "intriguing" and "compelling" episode that promised another excellent science-fiction story, with sufficient suspense at the end to make viewers look forward to the next instalment. Children were particularly fascinated, apparently, but adults also judged it exciting and innovative.'

As usual, such positive reaction was not universal, although much of the negative comment recorded seemed to relate more to the current state of the series as a whole than to this particular story: 'Those who were less satisfied had various complaints. The adventures of Doctor Who had become too familiar and repetitive, it was said, and thus were becoming "stale" and "boring". New ideas and themes were required, it was occasionally suggested: "Why must all other space-beings be baddies or monsters – cannot Doctor Who meet a friendly alien?"; "Why in the future? Can't we have something in the past for once?". The happenings were "too horrific" and "too far-fetched", even for a children's serial, it was sometimes remarked. The start of this story was too slow and unexciting, in the opinion of a few, though lack of action while the scene was set in the first episode was only to be expected, some thought. For a small minority it was all "the usual predictable rubbish", it seemed, some saying they only watched because their children enjoyed it, while others felt the series had been going on too long.'

'I remember [*The Krotons*] for the appalling acting of James Copeland and for the terrible Kroton legs,' wrote Ian K McLachlan in *TARDIS* Volume 6 Number 5 dated January 1982. 'It was probably one of the poorest [Troughton] stories. And yet there were still some good parts in it. The lovely voices of the Krotons. The enchanting scenes when the Krotons actually come to life. The great dialogue between the Doctor and Zoe when they are taking the tests. One sequence which did surprise me was the almost slapstick [one] between Frazer Hines and James Cairncross when they were mixing the acid.'

This is probably the fairest assessment of the story – it was disappointing, but by no means a total disaster. As Gibbs commented: 'No irrelevant sub-plots, few scenes that deviate from the main thrust of the story – *The Krotons* just gets on with telling the story, and telling it well.'

THE SEEDS OF DEATH

Writer: Brian Hayles, Terrance Dicks[3-6]*. **Director:** Michael Ferguson. **Designer:** Paul Allen. **Costumes:** Bobi Bartlett. **Make-Up:** Sylvia James. **Incidental Music:** Dudley Simpson. **Visual Effects:** Bill King/Trading Post. **Film Cameraman:** Peter Hall. **Film Editor:** Martyn Day. **Studio Lighting:** Howard King**. **Studio Sound:** Bryan Forgham. **Production Assistant:** Fiona Cumming. **Assistant Floor Manager:** Trina Cornwell.

* Terrance Dicks wrote the final version of the scripts for these episodes but was uncredited for this on screen.
** Fred Wright was incorrectly credited for lighting in the on-screen credits at the end of Episode Six. Wright was in fact the story's TM2, i.e. technical co-ordinator.

	First UK TX	Scheduled TX	Actual TX	Duration	Viewers	Chart Pos.
Episode One	25/01/69	17.15	17.16	23'11"	6.6	68
Episode Two	01/02/69	17.15	17.15	24'26"	6.8	72
Episode Three	08/02/69	17.15	17.15	24'10"	7.5	65
Episode Four	15/02/69	17.15	17.15	24'57"	7.1	74
Episode Five	22/02/69	17.15	17.14	24'56"	7.6	65
Episode Six	01/03/69	17.15	17.15	24'31"	7.7	59

Plot: The TARDIS brings the time travellers to Earth in the 21st Century, where they learn that human society is now reliant on T-Mat – a matter transmitting device that beams people and freight instantly to destinations all around the globe. The system, overseen by a Commander Radnor and his assistant Gia Kelly, is currently malfunctioning and the travellers agree to pilot an obsolete rocket, designed by an old-timer, Professor Daniel Eldred, to the Moon relay station to investigate. They find the place overrun by Ice Warriors, who are preparing for an invasion attempt. To weaken Earth's resistance the Warriors are using the T-Mat to send Martian seed pods to selected points on the planet's surface. These emit a fungus that draws oxygen from the surrounding atmosphere, making it lethal to humans but ideal for the Martians themselves. The travellers manage to use the T-Mat to get back to Earth, where the Doctor discovers that the only thing effective in destroying the pods is water. At the local weather control bureau, having disposed of a Warrior left on guard there, he adjusts the instruments so as to cause a downpour, thus ending the threat of the pods. He then returns to the Moon where, by a ruse, he is able to misdirect the Martian invasion fleet into orbit around the Sun, where it will be destroyed. The remaining Warriors are all killed.

Episode endings:
1. A technician, Locke, reports to Radnor from the Moon station, telling him that his colleague Osgood has been killed. He is able to say no more as the alien Slaar appears and destroys the video link device. Slaar summons his guard – an Ice Warrior – and orders him to kill Locke. The Ice Warrior fires and Locke dies.
2. The Doctor, Jamie and Zoe are approaching the Moon in Eldred's rocket when the homing beacon is deactivated. The Doctor tries frantically to reactivate it, while Jamie worriedly contemplates the fact that if he fails they will either crash or drift on endlessly through space.

3. A Martian seed pod arrives in the T-Mat cubicle on Earth and a technician, Brent, draws it to the attention of Radnor and Eldred. They go to examine the pod and, when Brent touches it, it starts to expand like a balloon being inflated ...

4. With the help of a technician named Phipps, Zoe manages to slip unseen into the Moon station control room and turn up the heating thermostat to 'full on'. She is making her escape when an Ice Warrior turns and sees her. Phipps shouts a warning and is killed by the Ice Warrior, which then advances on Zoe ...

5. The Doctor tries in vain to gain entry to the weather control bureau as the foam-like Martian fungus threatens to engulf the building. One of the seed pods starts to expand right in front of him and he desperately shields his face from its potentially lethal effects ...

6. The Doctor, Jamie and Zoe enter the TARDIS and it dematerialises.

IT WAS MADE WHERE...?

Ealing Filming: 13.12.68, 16.12.68-18.12.68, 20.12.68, 23.12.68 on Stage 2
Location Filming: 19.12.68
Location: Hampstead Heath Extension, West Heath Road, opposite Templewood Avenue, Hampstead, London.
Studio Recording: 03.01.69, 10.01.69, 17.01.69, 24.01.69, 31.01.69, 07.02.69, all in Lime Grove D

ADDITIONAL CREDITED CAST

Gia Kelly (Louise Pajo), Computer Voice (John Witty), Brent (Ric Felgate[1-4]), Osgood (Harry Towb[1]), Radnor (Ronald Leigh-Hunt), Fewsham (Terry Scully[1-5]), Phipps (Christopher Coll[1-4]), Locke (Martin Cort[1,2]), Eldred (Philip Ray), Slaar (Alan Bennion), Ice Warriors* (Steve Peters, Tony Harwood[2-6], Sonny Caldinez[4-6]), Security Guard (Derrick Slater[4]), Sir James Gregson (Hugh Morton[5]), Grand Marshall (Graham Leaman[5,6]).

* Steve Peters was billed as 'Alien' in the *Radio Times* listing for Episode One so as not to spoil the surprise of the Ice Warriors being in the story.

POPULAR MYTHS

• Slaar is an Ice Lord. (He is never referred to as an 'Ice Lord' or even as a 'Lord', but is presented simply as the commander of the Martian forces. His superior is however identified as a Grand Marshal (misspelt 'Grand Marshall' on the closing credits).)

THINGS TO WATCH OUT FOR

• Model sequences of the Earth and the Moon form a backdrop to the story title, writer and episode number captions at the start of each episode.
• Patrick Troughton's side-burns appear and disappear depending on whether he is seen in a pre-filmed sequence or in a studio scene.
• A prop previously seen as the TARDIS astral map, as introduced in season two's *The Web Planet*, appears as one of the exhibits in Eldred's museum of space flight.
• Patrick Troughton made no appearance in Episode Four as he was on holiday during the week when it was recorded. Tommy Laird doubled for him in shots where the Doctor's unconscious form is seen.

THINGS YOU MIGHT NOT HAVE KNOWN

- Working title: *The Lords of the Red Planet.*
- Zoe's leather outfit was primrose yellow in colour. Actress Wendy Padbury was allowed to keep it as an addition to her own wardrobe after recording of the story was completed.
- Brian Hayles' original outline for *The Seeds of Death* (which was the title given at its head) was followed quite faithfully in the transmitted story up until the point at which the Doctor and his friends arrive on the Moon in one of Eldred's rockets; then it took a somewhat different course. The outline for the remainder of the story was as follows:

The journey itself is eventful, but when they arrive on the Moon, it is to find that it has been taken over by the Ice Warriors, under the supervision of two Martian Warlords – a more intelligent and humanoid version of the Warriors. The Martian plan is elaborate. By taking over the despatch centres of T-MAT, they have immediate access to the major population centres of Earth – and similarly, if they require, all the subsidiary planets in the system. They intend to send one Warrior to each of these cities – not to attack or destroy, but to plant the spore-bearing algae that normally grows on Mars. This plant is adaptable, but basically anaerobic – doesn't need oxygen. Its spores contain an hereditary virus which breaks down the chlorophyll molecule. With chlorophyll destroyed, the process of photosynthesis in plants is impossible – thus, no oxygen is produced to replenish Earth's natural supply, the carbon dioxide level of the atmosphere increases, and the "free" nitrogen content of the air becomes unbearable. This in addition to the toxic gas produced by the spores at close range, will soon make Earth uninhabitable to humans – but perfect for the coming of the Martians. The main body of these are waiting in deep space, for the peaceful invasion that will take place when Earth is "prepared" for them. The spores "burst" and spread inside four weeks – and once the secondary coverage is achieved, there is no hope for human life.

Having discovered the essential purpose of the "suicide Warriors", the Doctor's plan is twofold – first to destroy the spores before they burst, and then to somehow beat back the Warriors – who, if they cannot conquer by their more subtle method, will invariably use force, even though this will mean having to repair the destruction.

The spores are eventually destroyed by being sprayed by oxygen – possibly liquid, for visual effect – while the Warriors are allowed to enter the despatch chambers, but diverted into open space, whilst still in their dematerialised state. The Professor is left happily in charge of an emergency transport system.

This outline was later further developed by Hayles into a fourteen page scene breakdown in which the two Martian Warlords were named as Slaar and Visek, the part of 'Kelly' was male and a separate character called Mary was included as the T-Mat expert.

- In November 1968, it became apparent that Hayles' scripts were not what the production office wanted. Therefore agreement was reached with Hayles that assistant script editor Terrance Dicks could rework the final four episodes, for which he would share the writer's credit (although not on screen or in publicity material). Dicks was paid an additional fee of £125 per episode for this work.

- **The Doctor:** 'You can't kill me … I'm a genius!'
- **Slaar:** 'Have you lost my signal?' **Grand Marshal:** 'Your signal is being received clearly, but we are off course.' **Slaar:** 'Are you sure your calculations are correct?' **Grand Marshal:** 'Our calculations have been checked. You have sent us into an orbit close to the Sun!' **Slaar:** 'Use your retroactive rockets to change course!' **Grand Marshal:** 'It is too late. We have insufficient fuel for manoeuvre. You have failed us, Slaar. We shall all die. We are being pulled into the orbit of the Sun …' **Slaar:** 'This is impossible …' **Ice Warrior:** 'The signal – there is no power.' **Slaar:** [To the Doctor.] 'You did this.' **The Doctor:** 'Yes. That signal has been going no further than this control room.' **Slaar:** 'But they were receiving my signal.' **The Doctor:** 'Not yours – ours.'

In some respects *The Seeds of Death* can be considered a relatively straightforward sequel to *The Ice Warriors*, with the T-Mat system providing the same sort of technological backdrop as did the ioniser equipment – and its controlling computer – in that earlier story. The main supporting characters are also similar – for Clent, Penley and Miss Garrett in *The Ice Warriors* read Radnor, Eldred and Miss Kelly in *The Seeds of Death*. There are admittedly a number of additional elements this time, but even these tend to bring a sense of *deja vu* – the base on the Moon and the weather control station on Earth, for example, both evoke memories of the fourth season story *The Moonbase*. 'The Seeds of Death* is the sort of story that leaves you with very little new after you have finished watching it,' observed Philip Packer in *Star Begotten* Vol. 4 No. 2 dated October 1990. 'It is basically an adventure romp with a happy ending. Enjoyable, certainly, but nothing really lasting comes out of it except … the concept of the [different "classes" amongst the Martians]. The regulars are wonderful, but they always were! It is probably the only story in season six – apart from *The Space Pirates* – that doesn't attempt to make some sort of point designed to endure beyond the story. The fact that man shouldn't put all his transport eggs in one basket is purely a plot device, since it is irrelevant to the contemporary audience who couldn't foresee a time when a system such as T-Mat could exist without some sort of back-up.'

'The real beauty of *The Seeds of Death*,' wrote John Connors in *Shada* 14 dated March/April 1983, 'was its plot and pace. Brian Hayles knew how to write material that was fast, but well thought through … Where [it] was drawn out, it was important that it was, like in [Episode One] where Radnor is trying to convince Eldred to give permission for the former to use the latter's rocket to sort out the problems with the T-Mat on the Moon. It was rather a circular conversation, but that's what it takes to convince someone as stubborn as Eldred. It's far better than the usual "no, I won't let you use it; oh, okay then, you can" business where people are talked out of a lifetime's convictions in thirty seconds. Where the script did go awry was the idea of man having no alternative transport other than T-Mat. It seems to be stretching the imagination to its elastic limit to propose that we'd drop everything for something which, despite being called "ultimate", looked more likely to go wrong than the average TV set.'

While this criticism is certainly valid, the concept of T-Mat is at least quite thoughtfully presented, as Tim Westmacott observed in *Star Begotten* Issue One dated winter 1986:

'The world's total commitment to the system is cleverly demonstrated by the fact that for T-Mat staff to distinguish one transmission from another, the monitoring computer has to report each one in a different vocal pitch, there being no time for a pause in between.

'Famine has been eliminated, but so evidently has the concept of storage, since even minor delays lead to serious food shortages between countries of differing ideology. Thus ... the system – which ideally seems a marvellous innovation – is shown to cause far greater problems by ceasing to work than it cured when introduced. The fact that things are not always as they first appear is a theme which recurs throughout the story.'

Michael Ferguson's direction is excellent, and contributes much to the brisk pace of the action. 'The Moon sequences really worked best,' thought John Connors, 'and the narrow corridors were a perfect setting for the Ice Warriors to stalk in. These aliens looked magnificent here ... I'd like them to have moved a little faster, though ... Anyway, they managed to capture the Doctor, which led to the only really bad sequence [with] the totally unconvincing rescue of his [unconscious] body via a convenient grille at the back of the T-Mat kiosk ... All a little too contrived for my liking. It was also unfortunate that the spread of fungus on crops was portrayed by the same foam used earlier in *Fury from the Deep*, though seeing the Ice Warrior trampling around the countryside was a nice juxtaposition.'

The BBC's Audience Research Report on the story's concluding instalment indicated that two in five of the contemporary viewers in the sample considered the episode 'an exciting end' to the story, while the rest were 'rather less enthusiastic'. The Ice Warriors attracted particular comment, some likening their appeal to that of the Daleks. 'I loved the wheezy Warriors!' enthused 'a student', who had found the story 'way-out but fascinating and comic'. Several amongst the sample had apparently considered the creatures unsuitable for children – 'When I saw crusty skin showing below the helmet,' said one, 'it quite made my flesh creep' – while others 'had feared initially that the young ones might be scared by the monster but apart from a toddler here and there, this was apparently not the case – "my kids thrived on the horror"'.

'Whilst it would be incorrect to say that [*The Seeds of Death*] is a multi-layered story,' concluded Philip Packer, 'its one layer is a very whole and rewarding one ... The acting and music are at all times spellbinding, and [Michael] Ferguson's direction imbues even the most banal of scenes with a wonderfully slick and purposeful flavour.

'Brian Hayles' scripts need little padding, and like all six (and above) parters of the period, I find [this] preferable to many shorter stories which lose so much through a lack of characterisation.'

Perhaps the most serious criticism that can be made of the story is that, Slaar notwithstanding, the Ice Warriors themselves are rather less well characterised and presented here than in their debut outing. *The Seeds of Death* nevertheless helps to confirm their status as one of the 'big four' monsters of the second Doctor's era – the others being, of course, the Daleks, the Cybermen and the Yeti – and paves the way for further return appearances in later years.

THE SPACE PIRATES

Writer: Robert Holmes. **Director:** Michael Hart. **Designer:** Ian Watson. **Costumes:** Nicholas Bullen. **Make-Up:** Sylvia James[1-5], Sallie Evans[6]. **Visual Effects:** John Wood. **Incidental Music:** Dudley Simpson. **Film Cameraman:** Peter Hall. **Film Editor:**

Martyn Day. **Studio Lighting:** Peter Winn. **Studio Sound:** David Hughes. **Production Assistant:** Snowy Lidiard-White. **Assistant Floor Manager:** Liam Foster.

	First UK TX	Scheduled TX	Actual TX	Duration	Viewers	Chart Pos.
Episode One	08/03/69	17.15	17.16	24'11"	5.8	96
Episode Two	15/03/69	17.15	17.15	25'02"	6.8	74
Episode Three	22/03/69	17.15	17.15	23'50"	6.4	75
Episode Four	29/03/69	17.15	17.17	22'25"	5.8	83
Episode Five	05/04/69	17.15	17.15	24'44"	5.5	70
Episode Six	12/04/69	17.15	17.15	24'26"	5.3	98

Plot: The TARDIS materialises in Earth's future on a space beacon just before it is attacked by pirates. The travellers find themselves trapped in a sealed section of the beacon as it is blown apart and flown to where the pirates will plunder it of the precious mineral argonite. They then witness a conflict between the pirates and the Interstella Space Corps, led by General Hermack and Major Warne. The ISC are convinced that the pirates' mastermind is an innocent yet eccentric space mining pioneer named Milo Clancey, while their true leader is a man named Caven. Caven has a secret base on the planet Ta and is assisted by Madeleine Issigri, daughter of his ex-partner Dom, who – unknown to her – is now his captive. When Madeleine discovers Caven's full treachery she helps to bring him to justice. The time travellers are given a lift back to the TARDIS by Clancey in his rickety old ship, the LIZ 79.

Episode endings:
1. Beacon Alpha 4 is exploded into sections and the Doctor, Jamie and Zoe are thrown to the floor.
2. Milo Clancey boards the segment of the beacon in which the time travellers are trapped and shoots Jamie with a gun. Zoe screams that he is a murderer.
3. Chased through tunnels on Ta, the Doctor and his friends fall into a black pit.
4. Milo leads ISC Lieutenant Sorba and the time travellers to Madeleine's office on Ta. Suddenly Caven and his men burst in. Sorba reaches for a gun and is shot dead. The pirates' weapons are then trained on the Doctor and his friends as Caven comments: 'You must have walked in here with your eyes open, Clancey ... How very naïve of you ...'
5. The Doctor is searching for Jamie and Zoe beneath the LIZ 79 when Caven decides to launch the ship by remote control. The Doctor is caught in the blast as the ship lifts off into space.
6. With Madeleine under arrest and the pirates vanquished, the time travellers face the daunting prospect of a trip in the LIZ 79 to find the TARDIS.

IT WAS MADE WHERE...?

Ealing Filming: 07.02.69, 10.02.69-14.02.69, 19.02.69 on Stage 2
Studio Recording: 21.02.69, 28.02.69, 07.03.69, 14.03.69, 21.03.69, 28.03.69, all in Lime Grove D

ADDITIONAL CREDITED CAST

Dervish (Brian Peck[1,3-6]), Caven (Dudley Foster[1,3-6]), General Hermack (Jack May), Major Ian Warne (Donald Gee), Technician Penn (George Layton), Lt. Sorba (Nik Zaran[1,4,5]), Space Guard (Anthony Donovan[1]), Milo Clancey (Gordon Gostelow[2-6]), Madeleine Issigri (Lisa Daniely[2-6]), Pirate Guard (Steve Peters[4-6]), Dom Issigri (Esmond Knight[5,6]).

THINGS TO WATCH OUT FOR

- The story boasts some superb model effects courtesy of designer John Wood. Wood was at this point a freelancer but had previously worked for the BBC, where his assignments had included designing the sets for *The Web Planet*, *The Chase* (with Raymond P Cusick), *The Myth Makers* and *The Celestial Toymaker*. The models were made by Ted Dove of Magna Models, and Wood then supervised the shooting of them at Bray Studios by Nick Allder and Ian Scoones of the Bowie Group, who had previously worked on a number of Gerry Anderson's puppet series.

- The story title, episode number and writer's caption credits for each episode are shown in black against a white background following (except in Episode One's case) the reprise from the previous episode.

- Patrick Troughton, Frazer Hines and Wendy Padbury appeared only in pre-filmed inserts in Episode Six as they were all away on location for *The War Games*. This thus became the only sixties episode apart from *Mission to the Unknown* to have none of the regulars present for a studio recording.

THINGS YOU MIGHT NOT HAVE KNOWN

- *The Space Pirates* was a replacement for another story dropped from this season at a relatively late stage; this time *The Dream Spinner* by Paul Wheeler. Impressed by his work on *The Krotons*, Terrance Dicks asked Robert Holmes to write it at short notice. The storyline was commissioned on 28 November 1968, the serial having been confirmed seven days earlier.

- The vocalist heard in the incidental music was Mary Thomas who, together with instrumentalists Terrance MacDonagh and Eric Allen, was hired by composer Dudley Simpson to realise his score.

- *The Space Pirates* holds a record in that (with the exception of *Mission to the Unknown*, which does not feature the regular characters at all) the time elapsed before the first appearance of the Doctor and his companions is longer than in any other story in *Doctor Who*'s history.

QUOTE, UNQUOTE

- **The Doctor:** 'Mr Clancey ... would it be going out of your way to drop us off ... at ... at the space station?' **Milo Clancey:** 'I can't do that. It's blown to bits, isn't it.' **The Doctor:** 'Oh dear ... Oh my word ... uh ... Well, do you know where we are?' **Milo Clancey:** 'No ... Well, no ... Only the argonite pirates know that. They're taking them off for salvage.' **The Doctor:** 'Oh dear. That will be difficult won't it.'

- **Zoe:** 'Milo, there's one thing I don't understand.' **Milo Clancey:** 'Well you're very lucky, girl. There's about a hundred thousand things I don't understand but I don't stand around asking fool questions about them, I do something useful. Why don't you do something useful? Why don't you ... um ... make us all a pot of tea or something?'

- **The Doctor:** 'Oh ... the TARDIS ... well that's no problem. It's orbiting Lobos, Milo's home planet, in one of the beacon sections.' **Zoe:** 'Well, no problem, eh? Well how are we going to get to it?' **The Doctor:** 'Well, Milo's very kindly offered to give us a lift in the *LIZ*.' **Jamie:** 'Oh no ... not the *LIZ* again. Frankly I'd rather walk.' **The Doctor:** 'You never know ... you might have to!'

ANALYSIS

The Space Pirates sees *Doctor Who* striking out into new territory. Constrained by the lack of any budgetary provision for new monsters, writer Robert Holmes turned instead to the idea of space exploration and came up with the first 'space opera' that the series had ever attempted. In this he was no doubt inspired to a certain degree by Stanley Kubrick's film of Arthur C Clarke's *2001: A Space Odyssey*, which had been released in 1968, and perhaps more particularly by NASA's then current Apollo programme of missions to the Moon. This gave the story a fresh, up-to-date feel, aided considerably by some excellent model spaceship effects – arguably the best yet seen in the series – shot in a style very similar to that of the numerous Apollo simulations being presented in news and current affairs programmes of the time. Leaving aside the hi-tech trappings, however, it can be seen that what Holmes has actually done is cleverly to take some of the traditional and well-worn motifs of the Western genre and give them a fresh spin by transferring them to an outer-space setting – a variation on the '*Wagon Train* to the stars' idea that formed the basis of the contemporary American series *Star Trek*. With pirates, old-time prospectors, government lawmen, miners and a beautiful young woman involved, and some good old fashioned conspiracy afoot, the stage is set for a potentially exciting adventure.

'Was [it] really a *Doctor Who* story though?' mused Chris Dunk in *Oracle* Volume 3 Number 7 in 1980. 'Quite honestly, in parts the Doctor and his companions might not have bothered to turn up. Their first appearance was not until well past the half-way stage of the first episode, and even then they merely succeeded [in becoming] trapped – helpless aboard one of the argonite sections jettisoned into space by Caven and Dervish.

'By fleshing out the roles of Warne and Hermack, the TARDIS crew could easily have been eliminated, especially with the extremely sensitive portrayal of Madeleine Issigri around whom much of the subplot was based. Was she a dirty double-crosser (espionage rears its head), was her father really dead, or was she really the innocent girl caught up in events over which she had little control?'

The reworking of Western conventions in a science-fiction vein is perhaps most successfully achieved in Milo Clancey – a classic old-time prospector type – who is the story's best and most engaging guest character, stealing every scene in which he appears. His clapped-out old ship, the *LIZ 79*, seems to get by on a wing and a prayer, but it has a wonderful and extremely memorable design and far more character than the large and impersonal V-ship and the smaller Minnows that the ISC forces use. 'Clancey was a superb creation,' agreed Dunk, 'and his disrespect for the authorities (evident particularly in the earlier episodes) was a joy to watch. Everything about him smacked of individualism – the sort of person you would like to be with. Totally unreliable, mind you!'

Another highlight of the story is the characterisation of the Doctor, which is exceptionally good. The idea of him keeping a collection of pins and a bag of marbles in his pockets is very apt. Highly amusing, too, is his embarrassment – and Jamie's gleeful reaction – when Madeleine kisses him toward the end of the story.

It has indeed been suggested by some commentators that *The Space Pirates* largely lived up to its considerable promise. Dunk, for instance, argued that the viewer 'could become involved on any level of the story' and that it was 'one of the unsung successes of the era'. This is very much a minority view, however, and it has to be admitted that story as a whole is extremely disappointing. The least successful element of all is probably General Hermack and his crew – tedious, one-dimensional characters portrayed in a uniformly wooden manner with terrible mid-Atlantic accents. More fundamentally, the basic structure of the story is frankly a complete mess. This is chiefly due to poor pacing arising from the fact that the various space journeys involved are generally shown to take a considerable length of time – which may well be accurate in scientific terms but, at least in this case, makes for rather poor drama. General Hermack and his crew seem to spend virtually the entire story arriving at places just too late to catch the pirates.

In short, *The Space Pirates* drags interminably. Gavin French, writing in *A Voyage Through 25 Years of Doctor Who* dated December 1988, was not impressed. 'I'm afraid that *The Space Pirates* was another fairly disappointing story [from Robert Holmes]. In typical Holmesian style there [were] some interesting characters and some interesting dialogue, but overall it was a rather slow and uninspiring piece of fiction for which, try as I might, I can gather no real enthusiasm.'

With the pirates captured, Madeleine's treachery uncovered and the Doctor and co heading back to the TARDIS, things are on course for the season finale. But if the general view was that six episodes was quite long enough for *The Space Pirates*, what would be made of the ten episode epic that was to follow …?

THE WAR GAMES

Writer: Terrance Dicks, Malcolm Hulke. **Director:** David Maloney. **Designer:** Roger Cheveley. **Costumes:** Nick Bullen. **Make-Up:** Sylvia James. **Incidental Music:** Dudley Simpson. **Fight Arrangers:** Peter Diamond, Arthur Howell. **Visual Effects:** Michealjohn Harris. **Film Cameraman:** Alan Jonas. **Film Editor:** Chris Hayden. **Studio Lighting:** Howard King. **Studio Sound:** John Staple. **Production Assistant:** Edwina Verner. **Assistant Floor Manager:** Marion McDougall, Caroline Walmesley.

	First UK TX	Scheduled TX	Actual TX	Duration	Viewers	Chart Pos.
Episode One	19/04/69	17.15	17.15	25'00"	5.5	88
Episode Two	26/04/69	17.15	17.15	25'00"	6.3	68
Episode Three	03/05/69	17.15	17.15	24'30"	5.1	81
Episode Four	10/05/69	17.15	17.16	23'40"	5.7	63
Episode Five	17/05/69	17.15	17.15	24'30"	5.1	87
Episode Six	24/05/69	17.15	17.15	22'53"	4.2	91
Episode Seven	31/05/69	17.15	17.16	22'28"	4.9	83
Episode Eight	07/06/69	17.15	17.15	24'37"	3.5	96
Episode Nine	14/06/69	17.15	17.15	24'34"	4.1	91
Episode Ten	21/06/69	17.15	17.15	24'23"	5.0	66

Plot: The TARDIS arrives on a planet where a race known only as the Aliens have gathered soldiers from a number of different wars in Earth's history, brainwashed them and put them to battle. Their aim is to form an invincible army from the survivors and use this to take over the galaxy. The War Lord is assisted by a Security Chief and a War Chief, the latter of whom the Doctor quickly recognises as a member of his own race, the Time Lords. The War Chief has provided the Aliens with the time vessels, SIDRATs, that are essential to their scheme; but he secretly plans to double-cross them and seize power for himself. When the War Lord learns of the War Chief's duplicity he has him shot down by guards. By this time, however, the Doctor, aided by a band of human resistance fighters who have shaken off the Aliens' control, has already managed to put a stop to the war games. Unfortunately he has no way of returning all the human soldiers to their proper times and places and so has to call on the Time Lords for help. Having thus revealed his position to them, he is taken prisoner, placed on trial for the crime of interfering in the affairs of other races and subsequently sentenced to a period of exile on Earth. Jamie and Zoe, meanwhile, are sent back to their own respective points of origin. Before being dispatched to begin his exile, the Doctor is told that he must again take on a new appearance ...

Episode endings:
1. In the First World War zone the Doctor has been found guilty of spying against the English forces and is tied up before a firing squad. Captain Ransom brings his men to order, tells them to present arms and opens his mouth to give the order to fire. A shot rings out and the Doctor grimaces.
2. The Doctor, Jamie and Zoe, together with their new friends Lieutenant Carstairs and Lady Jennifer Buckingham, have left the First World War zone in the latter's military ambulance. They encounter fresh danger, however, as soldiers from ancient Rome charge down a hill towards them. The others clamber back into the ambulance as Carstairs tries desperately to restart the engine using a crank handle. The Roman soldiers are almost upon them ...
3. The time travellers and Lady Jennifer see one of the Aliens' time machines arrive in a barn in the American Civil War zone and a number of Confederate soldiers emerge. When the soldiers have left, the Doctor enters the machine to investigate. Suddenly shooting is heard from outside the barn. Zoe goes to fetch the Doctor but when she too is inside the machine the door closes and it dematerialises – much to Jamie's consternation.
4. Zoe encounters Carstairs in the Aliens' landing bay. Her initial relief quickly fades when he pulls his revolver on her and, unmoved by her attempts to remind him who he is, insists that she is a German spy and that it is his duty to shoot her. His finger tightens on the trigger ...
5. The Doctor, Zoe and Carstairs watch from hiding as one of the Aliens' time machines returns to the landing bay. Jamie and three of the human resistance fighters, including their leader Russell, emerge. Zoe realises that they have walked into an ambush. Alien guards open fire on the newcomers, who writhe in agony and fall to the floor, apparently dead.
6. The Doctor, Jamie and Carstairs are trapped inside one of the Aliens' time machines as the internal dimensions are gradually reduced. The War Chief informs them that they have thirty seconds to decide whether to surrender or be crushed to death ...
7. The Aliens mount a successful raid on the First World War chateau that the resistance fighters have adopted as their base. They capture the Doctor and reclaim the mental processing machine that he earlier stole from them. Jamie, Zoe, Russell and Carstairs are powerless to stop them as they leave in their time machine.
8. The Doctor has delivered the leaders of all the different groups of human resistance fighters into the clutches of the Security Chief and the War Chief. Jamie and Zoe react in horror to this apparent act of treachery.
9. The Doctor, Jamie and Zoe try desperately to regain the safety of the TARDIS as the Time Lords cause them to move as if in slow motion. They slump down beside the ship's police box exterior and the Doctor strains to turn the key in the lock ...

10. A still protesting Doctor spins away through a dark void to begin his sentence of exile on Earth with a new appearance. His face is shrouded in shadow ...

IT WAS MADE WHERE...?

Location Filming: 23.03.69-01.04.69
Locations: Sheepcote Tip, Wilson Avenue, Brighton; Seven Sisters Country Park, Exceat, Seaford, Sussex; Bridle Path, Nr Coombe Down Pumping Station, off Underhill Lane, Clayton, Sussex; Eastbourne Waterboard Road, West Dean, Sussex; Westdean and 'Church only' road, West Dean, Sussex; High Park Farm, Ditchling Road, Brighton; Birling Farm, East Dean, Sussex.
Ealing Filming: 03.04.69 on Stage 2
Studio Recording: 11.04.69, 18.04.69, 25.04.69, 02.05.69 in TC4, 08.05.69, 15.05.69 in TC8, 22.05.69 in TC1, 29.05.69 in TC8, 05.06.69 in TC6, 12.06.69 in TC8

ADDITIONAL CREDITED CAST

Lady Jennifer Buckingham[1]/Lady Jennifer[2-4]/Jennifer[5] (Jane Sherwin[1-5]), German soldiers (John Livesey[1], Bernard Davies[3]), Lieutenant Carstairs[1]/Lieut. Carstairs[2,3]/Carstairs[4-9] (David Savile[1-9]), Major Barrington (Terence Bayler[1]), Sergeant Willis (Brian Forster[1]), General Smythe (Noel Coleman[1-3,7]), Captain Ransom (Hubert Rees[1-3]), Sgt. Major Burns (Esmond Webb[1,7]), Redcoat (Tony McEwan[2]), Commandant Gorton (Richard Steele[2]), Military Chauffeur (Peter Stanton[2]), Military Policeman (Pat Gorman[2]), Lieut. Crane (David Valla[3]), Lieut. Lucke (Gregg Palmer[3]), von Weich (David Garfield[3-6]), War Chief (Edward Brayshaw[3-9]), Sgt. Thompson (Bill Hutchinson[4]), Corporal Riley (Terry Adams[4]), Leroy (Leslie Schofield[4]), Scientist (Vernon Dobtcheff[4-6]), Harper (Rudolph Walker[4, 5]), Alien Guard (John Atterbury[4]), Spencer (Michael Lynch[5]), Russell (Graham Weston[5-9]), Security Chief (James Bree[5-9]), Alien Technician (Charles Pemberton[5]), Moor (David Troughton[6]), War Lord (Philip Madoc[7-10]), Du Pont (Peter Craze[7]), Arturo Villar (Michael Napier-Brown[8,9]), Petrov (Stephen Hubay[8]), First Time Lord (Bernard Horsfall[10]), Second Time Lord (Trevor Martin[10]), Third Time Lord (Clyde Pollitt[10]), Tanya (Clare Jenkins[10]).

Note: Also credited for Episode Ten in the *Radio Times*, but not on screen, were: Quark (Freddie Wilson), Yeti (John Levene), Ice Warrior (Tony Harwood), Cyberman (Roy Pearce) and Dalek (Robert Jewell). These monsters were seen on a screen as evidence presented by the Doctor in his trial by the Time Lords.

POPULAR MYTHS

- Derrick Sherwin was credited as producer on this story because Peter Bryant had been assigned to troubleshoot an ailing BBC detective series called *Paul Temple*. (Sherwin was deputising as producer because Bryant was ill.)
- *Doctor Who* was under serious threat of being cancelled at the end of this season. (Although this is Terrance Dicks's recollection, it has been denied by both Peter Bryant and Derrick Sherwin and is not borne out by contemporary documentary evidence. The series would however face the threat of cancellation at the end of the *following* season.)

- The story title, episode number and writers' credits for each episode are shown over a stock footage montage of explosions and gunfire.
- Producer Derrick Sherwin's then wife Jane appears in the role of Lady Jennifer Buckingham.
- A real First World War ambulance was used in the location scenes.
- Patrick Troughton's son David (who had previously been an extra in *The Enemy of the World*) appears in the minor speaking role of Private Moor.
- This story marks the first mention by name, and ultimately the first appearance, of the Doctor's own race, the Time Lords.
- Episode Ten features short clips from the opening episodes of *The Web of Fear*, *Fury from the Deep* and *The Wheel in Space*.
- There is a tear-jerking departure scene for popular companions Jamie and Zoe.

THINGS YOU MIGHT NOT HAVE KNOWN

- Like *The Krotons* and *The Space Pirates*, *The War Games* was taken up as a late replacement after other stories fell through. In this case the stories in question are presumed to have been a six-parter by Malcolm Hulke entitled *The Impersonators*, rejected by Derrick Sherwin on 30 December 1968, and a four-parter by Sherwin himself.
- A Kroton was originally to have been seen amongst the monsters presented by the Doctor on the Time Lords' screen in episode ten, and a copyright payment was made to Robert Holmes for this purpose. However, the idea was subsequently dropped.

QUOTE, UNQUOTE

- **Arturo Villar:** [To Zoe] 'For such a little woman, your mouth is too big.'
- **The Doctor:** 'It is a fact, Jamie, that I do tend to get involved with things.'
- **The Doctor:** [To the Time Lords.] 'Give me a thought channel and I'll show you some of the evils I have been fighting against.' [A screen appears behind the Doctor and displays images as he speaks.] 'The Quarks. Deadly robot servants of the cruel Dominators. They tried to enslave a peace-loving race. Then there were the Yeti. More robot killers, instruments of an alien Intelligence trying to take over the planet Earth.' **Second Time Lord:** 'All this is entirely irrelevant.' **The Doctor:** 'You asked me to justify my actions. I am doing so. Let me show you the Ice Warriors. Cruel Martian invaders. They tried to conquer the Earth too. So did the Cybermen, half creature, half machine. But worst of all were the Daleks, a pitiless race of conquerors, exterminating all who came up against them. All these evils I have fought, while you have done nothing but observe! True, I am guilty of interference. Just as you are guilty of failing to use your great powers to help those in need!' **First Time Lord:** 'Is that all you have to say?' **The Doctor:** 'Well isn't it enough!' **First Time Lord:** 'Your defence has been heard, and will be considered. But you have raised ... difficult issues. We require time to think about them. You will be recalled when we have made our decision.'
- **Zoe:** 'Will we ever meet again?' **The Doctor:** 'Now, Zoe, you and I know that time is relative, isn't it?'

ANALYSIS

'Just as *The Power of the Daleks* proved to be an excellent introduction, so *The War*

Games makes the finest exit any Doctor could hope for.' So wrote Chris Marton in *Wheel in Space* No. 9 dated May 1980, and it would be difficult to disagree with his assessment. The story certainly gets off to a cracking start as the TARDIS materialises in what appears to be No Man's Land during the First World War. The viewer is initially led to think that this may mark a return to the purely historical story format of years gone by – an impression reinforced by some highly effective location-filmed scenes of the war-scarred landscape. Then however the eerie General Smythe, brilliantly portrayed by Noel Coleman, dons a pair of thick-lensed reading glasses with which to hypnotise his Captain and uncovers a wall-mounted video screen concealed behind a picture in his room. The overt science-fiction elements suggest that the story is actually going to be another of the pseudo-historical type pioneered in *The Time Meddler*. Only later does it become apparent that the TARDIS has in fact arrived on an alien planet split into various different war zones.

A commonly expressed view is that, after this strong beginning, the story becomes dull and repetitive, picking up again only in the closing stages when the Time Lords are introduced. Richard Walter, for example, wrote in *Matrix* Issue 5 dated February 1980 that 'sadly it turned sour … and ended up being a runabout' until 'the one thing that saved the story: the introduction of the Time Lords.' This assessement has however been challenged by other commentators. Chris Marton for one felt that, while it did admittedly contain some padding, including an encounter between the young 19th Century soldier Private Moor and the Alien von Weich in the American Civil War zone, 'it is the middle part [of the story] that is the most exciting, entertaining and deftly constructed'. Nick Pegg made a similar point, albeit rather more bluntly, in *Perigosto Stick* Issue Two dated August 1991: 'People who go on about how boring episodes one to nine of this story are are clearly talking out of their bottoms because, even disregarding the always exciting and strongly motivated "Earth" sequences, the tension surrounding the Doctor's growing apprehension about who he might be about to bump into is incredible, so that when he suddenly comes face to face with the War Chief and we see clear recognition in *both* their faces, the moment is doubly electrifying.' In fairness, even those who are critical of the story often find things that they like in the middle section. Richard Walter, for example, wrote: 'The idea of kidnapping soldiers from Earth to fight their own wars until only the strongest were left to form the Aliens' army was very good, and the story did have some strong features – the time zones and the mist between them; people breaking the hypnotic hold over them and forming resistance groups; the use of SIDRATS; and the War Chief recognising the Doctor.'

Another point in the story's favour is the excellence of the design work by way of which the various war zones are depicted, again recalling the glory of the series' early historical stories. These sets also provide a very stark contrast to the Aliens' clinical base. The realisation of the latter is itself highly effective, boasting a number of nice touches such as unusual hi-tech wall units, strange controls in the form of magnetic shapes to be moved about on vertical panels, and weird spiral patterns adorning some of the surfaces.

What really makes *The War Games*, though, is the wonderful dialogue given to the characters by Malcolm Hulke and Terrance Dicks. It must be every actor's dream to play parts as well written as these; and, as Chris Marton pointed out, both the guest cast and the regulars rise to the occasion, delivering uniformly excellent performances:

'Edward Brayshaw is particularly impressive as the ruthless War Chief, remaining a formidable adversary, though not as wholly evil as Philip Madoc's marvellously silky War Lord.

'Jamie had one of his best outings as Troughton's muscle, a role that seemed to have fallen off in his last season, and Zoe remained constantly engaging. Troughton showed that he can be slyly subtle and play full-blooded melodrama with equal aplomb, especially in [a] fateful conversation with the War Chief, in which we learned more about the Doctor in one scene than we had in the whole of the previous six years.'

The story's amazing conclusion, with its momentous revelations about the Doctor's origins and the cliffhanger ending to the final episode, provides the icing on the cake. 'During the last couple of episodes it becomes steadily apparent that the Doctor is genuinely terrified of the Time Lords,' observed Nick Pegg, 'and this, together with their imaging as godlike, floating creatures with an impressive line in crashing organ music … ensures that we're aware that this is the Big One – but for a change the fear is explicitly not one of universal domination. The Doctor's in danger of being absorbed, forced to conform, to drop back into a mechanism which he alone has been viewing from without. For our hero it is this, not a close shave with a bunch of Daleks, that is the ultimate terror. It is entirely fitting that the second Doctor, who more than any of his counterparts was pitted against the meaning of monstrousness, should be brought to his knees not by an army of Ice Warriors or Cybermen but by the evil that men do. His downfall is the reality of the essential difference which originally separated him from his own people. His forfeit is to live among humanity. The death of Troughton's Doctor seems also to be his ultimate triumph.'

The final episode of *The War Games* attracted the most uniformly positive Audience Research Report for some time. Notwithstanding the story's epic length, the reaction of those contemporary viewers – roughly two thirds of the sample – who had seen all or most of the ten episodes was said to be 'decidedly favourable'. Some were admittedly 'inclined to damn with faint praise', but the only really negative comment recorded was that children seemed disappointed by the lack of monsters – and even this was balanced by the observation that 'not a few adult viewers' considered the story 'all the better for the absence of "inhuman creatures"'.

'Although there was little evidence of any great enthusiasm for this final episode of *The War Games*,' it was noted, 'nevertheless it is clear that the majority of the sample audience were very well satisfied. Certainly there were those, but in minority numbers only, who dismissed it as "the usual rubbishy nonsense", while others apparently found it disappointingly inconclusive. According to most, however, this exciting and action-packed episode had not only brought this adventure on the planet of the Time Lords to a most satisfactory ending, but also cleared up the mystery surrounding Doctor Who's origin besides (most ingeniously) setting the scene for the "new" Doctor Who …

'There was much praise for Patrick Troughton's "superb" interpretation of Doctor Who, and indeed it was often said that the talents of this fine actor had been rather wasted here. In addition, many viewers remarked that they were extremely sorry he had relinquished this role and that they could only hope that when the new series started … the new Doctor Who would prove as effective as he had been.'

The production of season six proved generally problematic. Of particular significance was the fact that during this period both Peter Bryant and Derrick Sherwin became involved with other projects – notably the military drama *S P Air*, a two-part pilot for which was actually made and transmitted – and so were unable to give *Doctor Who* their undivided attention.

The Dominators went out under the pseudonym Norman Ashby after writers Mervyn Haisman and Henry Lincoln objected to Sherwin's rewriting of it, including its reduction from six episodes to five. *The Mind Robber*, which had at one point been planned as a six episode story itself, was ultimately lengthened from four episodes to five in order to fill the extra slot. Perhaps even more significantly, three of the seven transmitted stories – *The Krotons*, *The Space Pirates* and *The War Games* – were late additions to the season after a number of other stories, including Dick Sharples' *The Prison in Space*, Paul Wheeler's *The Dream Spinner*, Malcolm Hulke's *The Impersonators* (which may have evolved into *The War Games*) and one by Derrick Sherwin of unknown title, had for one reason or another been abandoned.

The season was nevertheless more varied than the previous one not only in terms of quality but also in terms of settings and plots, eschewing its heavy reliance on Earth-based stories and the 'isolated group of humans infiltrated and attacked by alien monsters' formula. This time there were only three stories – *The Invasion*, *The Krotons* and *The Seeds of Death* – that could really be considered traditional monster tales. This however was more a matter of economic necessity than an artistic decision. The production team continued to amortize the series' costs as far as possible by commissioning relatively long stories, but found that the budget would simply no longer stretch to the creation of large numbers of convincing alien costumes and environments (or even of much incidental music – hence the dearth of this, particularly in the first few stories). They had in any event concluded at an early stage of the season's production that *Doctor Who* was no longer working in its current format and ought to be revamped. Inspired by Nigel Kneale's highly successful Quatermass serials of the fifties, in which Professor Quatermass and his scientific and military colleagues had been seen to battle a succession of alien menaces in near-contemporary England, they felt – based in part on the perceived success of *The Web of Fear*, a story that had itself been somewhat influenced by the Quatermass serials – that the Doctor's adventures would be far more effective if they became less fantastical and took place on Earth in familiar, everyday settings with recognisable characters.

To facilitate the remoulding of *Doctor Who* in this image, Sherwin created UNIT – the United Nations Intelligence Taskforce. This was to be an international military intelligence unit, established to investigate UFOs and other strange phenomena, with which the Doctor could work while on Earth. Having liked the character Colonel Lethbridge-Stewart in *The Web of Fear* the production team decided, subject to actor Nicholas Courtney's agreement, to bring him back as the commander of the British branch of UNIT. UNIT's debut in *The Invasion*, with Lethbridge-Stewart promoted to Brigadier, was thus always intended to be simply the first step in a process of moving towards a more permanent Earth-bound setting – something that would have happened even if Patrick Troughton had not made clear his intention to leave at the end of the season.

By the time of the making of *The Invasion*, Sherwin was effectively deputising for Bryant as producer of *Doctor Who*, leaving Dicks to take over as script editor (as the story editor post had now been renamed). A young writer named Trevor Ray was meanwhile brought in to replace Dicks as assistant script editor. Bryant himself was becoming less and less actively involved with the series due to health problems. His last credit as producer was on *The Space Pirates*, for which Sherwin temporarily returned to script editing duties while Dicks was busy rewriting episodes of *The Seeds of Death*. The producer's credit on *The War Games* then went solely to Sherwin.

The conclusion of *The War Games*, with the Doctor being captured by his own people and sentenced to a period of exile on Earth, was specifically designed to usher in the new format that Sherwin and Bryant had devised for *Doctor Who*. The next season – following an unprecedented six-month break during which the series' slot would be occupied by a debut package of episodes from the American import *Star Trek* – would see that new format finally coming to fruition.

THE TIME LORDS

It was established in the very first episode of the series' introductory story, *100,000 BC*, that the Doctor and his grand-daughter Susan were aliens from another world and time. Subsequent references to their origins, however, were confined to occasional tantalising hints, such as in *Marco Polo* when Susan, asked how far away her home is, replied 'as far as a night star', and in *The Sensorites* when she said: 'Grandfather and I don't come from Earth. It's ages since we've seen our planet. It's quite like Earth, but at night the sky is a burnt orange, and the leaves on the trees are bright silver.' The Doctor's reasons for leaving his home planet were kept similarly vague. In *100,000 BC* he admitted that he and Susan were 'wanderers' and 'exiles'; in *The Sensorites* he contemplated the possibility that they might one day return home; but in *The Massacre of St Bartholomew's Eve*, when he considered this possibility again, he concluded 'I can't … I can't.' Only one other native of the Doctor's and Susan's home planet was featured during the series' early years – namely the Monk in *The Time Meddler* and *The Daleks' Master Plan* – and just about the only significant thing to be revealed about him was that he had a TARDIS of his own. The Doctor's origins were, in short, left very much a mystery throughout this period – a fact that arguably contributed much to the character's appeal.

All this changed in *The War Games*, when the Doctor's people were named for the first time as the Time Lords; his reason for leaving them was said to be boredom arising from their practice of merely observing rather than exploring other worlds; and the majority of the final episode was actually set on their home planet. The Time Lords themselves were presented as aloof and mysterious beings dressed in long, flowing robes. Little more was actually revealed about them at this point other than that they were awesomely powerful – their capabilities included placing a whole planet in a force field and 'dematerialising' people (in this case, the War Lord) so that it was as though they had never existed. Now that they had been established, however, it was arguably inevitable that they would become an increasingly important part in the series' mythology as writers succumbed to the temptation to revisit and base further stories around them; and early signs of this were indeed to be seen during the era of the third Doctor.

The Third Doctor
(Jon Pertwee)
1970-1974

JON PERTWEE IS THE THIRD DOCTOR

'I went to see Shaun Sutton, who was Head of Drama at the BBC and a very old friend – we'd started in the business together. I said, "How do you want this played?" and Shaun replied, "Well – as you." I said, "What is me? I don't know what I am!" You see, I had always "hidden under a green umbrella" – meaning one has always played character parts. I had never played "me". He told me, "We know what you are, that's why you've been cast, and if you play it as you, it will come out all right." So Doctor Who was me!'

Thus did Jon Pertwee often describe his initiation into *Doctor Who*. Born in 1919 in the Chelsea area of London, into a family with a long tradition of involvement in the performing arts, he had gained his first taste of the stage in a number of school productions. In 1936 he had joined, and subsequently been expelled from, the Royal Academy of Dramatic Arts. Undaunted, he had then gone on to work in repertory theatre and in 1938 progressed to London's West End. He had also made his debut in feature films (initially as an extra and then from 1939 onwards in speaking roles) and in radio, a medium with which he was to become particularly associated in the years to come.

His theatrical career was temporarily put on hold when the Second World War broke out and he joined the Navy, although he often appeared in shows for his fellow servicemen. Eventually he was appointed to the Naval Broadcasting Section where he became involved in producing and recording programmes for the 'pleasure and edification' of the services. In 1946 he joined the cast of *HMS Waterlogged*, the Naval edition of the forces radio show *Mediterranean Merry-Go-Round*, after being sent by his senior officers to investigate the production for 'irregularities' such as jokes about members of the government. It was in this that he first indulged a flair for accents for which he was later to became renowned. The fictional *HMS Waterlogged* subsequently became the subject of a highly successful spin-off show, *The Waterlogged Spa*. In the late forties, following his departure from the Navy, Pertwee amongst other things joined a vaudeville troupe, appeared in music hall and made many further radio shows and films, being contracted to the Associated British Pictures Corporation (ABPC) to appear in their productions. In 1959 he was invited to front a new BBC radio series and asked if he could come up with a suitable idea. The result was *The Navy Lark*, based very much upon Pertwee's wartime experiences, which became a great success and ran for almost twenty years.

During the sixties, Pertwee concentrated on stage work and film acting and appeared in several productions of note, including three of the popular *Carry On* ... series. The seventies, however, saw him becoming best known for his work in television, a medium in which he had debuted some twenty years earlier. And, although his later success as Worzel Gummidge undoubtedly runs it a close second, his most popular role of all was arguably that of the Doctor.

'I got away with murder on *Doctor Who*,' joked the actor. 'I was just playing me for the first time really, and I made him a dashing bloke dressed in pretty clothes. This was in the seventies when people were very clothes conscious and wore frilly shirts and colours. All that hooked at the right time. I put in the martial arts and my love of gadgetry, motorcycles, cars, Bessie, helicopters – these were things that I liked anyway, so I just adapted them into *Doctor Who*. Apart from being hard work, it was a piece of cake!'

DOCTOR WHO SEASON SEVEN (1970)

Regular Cast:
Doctor Who (Jon Pertwee)
Liz Shaw (Caroline John)
Brigadier Lethbridge-Stewart (Nicholas Courtney)

Regular Crew:
Producer: Derrick Sherwin on *Spearhead from Space*. Barry Letts from *Doctor Who and the Silurians* Episode 1 onwards.
Script Editor: Terrance Dicks.
Title Music: Ron Grainer and the BBC Radiophonic Workshop, arranged by Delia Derbyshire.
Special Sounds: Brian Hodgson.

3 THIRD DOCTOR

It had originally been intended that Peter Bryant, after recovering from a period of ill health, would return to *Doctor Who* to produce the whole of the seventh season. In the event however he, Derrick Sherwin and Trevor Ray were all assigned around the beginning of October 1969 to revamp the problematic *Paul Temple* series. Bryant was consequently involved with the production of only the first two stories of the season, eventually transmitted under the titles *Spearhead from Space* and *Doctor Who and the Silurians*, and received a credit on neither: the producer's credit on the former went to Sherwin, and that on the latter to Bryant's eventual successor, Barry Letts, whose only previous work on the series had been directing *The Enemy of the World* for the fifth season. Letts had been invited to take on the job, after a number of others including Douglas Camfield had turned it down, and agreed on condition that he would also be allowed to direct at least one story per season. Terrance Dicks remained as the series' script editor and quickly struck up an excellent working relationship with Letts. Trevor Ray meanwhile was briefly replaced by Robin Squire – a young former pop singer who had written a novel about the music business and gained an attachment to the production team – until he too moved on and the assistant script editor post was dropped.

Although Bryant and Sherwin formally oversaw only the first part of the season (which, consisting of only twenty-five episodes, was by far the shortest to date), their influence was strongly felt throughout. For one thing, it was Bryant who had cast Jon Pertwee and set the parameters for his characterisation of the Doctor (although in the event the actor gave a far less whimsical performance than Bryant had envisaged). For another, it was Bryant and Sherwin who had chosen to overhaul the series' format by having the Doctor exiled to Earth and allied with UNIT in a succession of relatively adult-orientated adventures. It was they, too, who had decided to introduce a sophisticated Cambridge University scientist as the Doctor's new assistant rather than another of the naïve youngsters who had tended to be his companions in the recent past.

The following production block would see Letts bringing much more of his own influence to bear on the series, leaving season seven as a tantalising glimpse of how *Doctor Who* might have continued had Bryant and Sherwin remained in charge.

SPEARHEAD FROM SPACE

Writer: Robert Holmes. **Director:** Derek Martinus. **Designer:** Paul Allen. **Costumes:** Christine Rawlins. **Make-Up:** Cynthia Goodwin. **Incidental Music:** Dudley Simpson. **Visual Effects:** John Horton. **Film Cameraman:** Stan Speel, Robert McDonnell. **Film Editor:** William Symon, Adam Dawson. **Production Assistant:** Peter Grimwade. **Assistant Floor Manager:** Liam Foster.

	First UK TX	Scheduled TX	Actual TX	Duration	Viewers	Chart Pos.
Episode 1	03/01/70	17.15	17.16	23'38"	8.4	54
Episode 2	10/01/70	17.15	17.16	24'21"	8.1	57
Episode 3	17/01/70	17.15	17.15	24'16"	8.3	49
Episode 4	24/01/70	17.15	17.15	24'47"	8.1	51

Plot: The TARDIS arrives on Earth in the middle of a meteorite shower and the Doctor is found by UNIT troops and taken to a nearby hospital. The Brigadier is faced with having to cope not only with the mysterious meteorites but also with Ransome, an ex-employee of a local plastics factory who claims he has seen a walking mannequin. The meteorites turn out to be hollow globes containing the Nestene consciousness, a disembodied alien intelligence with an affinity for plastic. A Nestene agent, Channing, has infiltrated the plastics factory and is using energy from the globes to animate Autons – mannequin-like figures and realistic replicas of senior establishment figures – with the aim of colonising the Earth. Aided by newly-recruited UNIT scientist Dr Elizabeth Shaw, the Doctor thwarts this scheme by repelling the Nestene consciousness into space and thereby neutralising the Autons and the monstrous tentacled form that it has been creating for itself in a tank within the factory. Channing, revealed to be no more than a sophisticated Auton, is likewise deactivated.

Episode endings:
1. The Doctor has been kidnapped from the hospital by two strange men under the instruction of Channing. He manages to escape in a wheelchair, but then abandons it and tries to return to the TARDIS on foot. A UNIT soldier guarding the police box shoots the Doctor as he crashes through the trees.
2. Ransome returns to the plastics factory and breaks into his old workshop to find it full of new equipment. As he inspects a strange computer-like device, a plastic shop dummy steps down from a plinth behind him and advances.
3. The Brigadier telephones his regular army contact General Scobie to ask for support in investigating Auto Plastics. Scobie agrees to meet the Brigadier but hangs up as there is a knock at his front door. Scobie opens the door to reveal an exact duplicate of himself, who advances on him.
4. The Doctor agrees to continue helping the Brigadier in exchange for facilities to repair the TARDIS and a vintage car similar to one that he appropriated from the hospital. The

Brigadier goes to prepare the paperwork and asks the Doctor what his name is. 'Smith,' replies the Doctor. 'Doctor John Smith.'

IT WAS MADE WHERE...?

Location Filming (ext): 13.09.69-19.09.69

Locations: Favourite Doll Factory, Georges Road, Holloway, London, N7; Junction of Euston Road and Midland Road, London, NW1; National Car Parks, Rear of St Pancras Station, Midland Road, London, NW1; John Sanders Ltd, The Broadway, Ealing, London, W5; Lancaster Road, Ealing, London, W5; High Street, Ealing, London W5; Royal Horticultural Society, Wisley, Surrey; Hatchford Park School, Ockham Lane, Hatchford, Surrey; TCC Condensors, Wales Farm Road, Ealing, London, W3; Wood Norton Estate, Evesham, Hereford and Worcestershire; Mansion House Hotel, Coopers Lane, Evesham, Worcs; Wheelbarrow Castle Cottage, Radford, Worcs; Madame Tussauds, Marylebone Road, London, NW1.

Location Filming (int): 08.10.69-18.10.69, 20.10.69-24.10.69, 30.10.69-31.10.69, 03.11.69-07.11.69, 22.11.69 all BBC Training Centre, Wood Norton, Hereford and Worcestershire

ADDITIONAL CREDITED CAST

Channing (Hugh Burden), Seeley (Neil Wilson[1-3]), Mullins (Talfryn Thomas[1]), Captain Munro (John Breslin), Dr. Henderson (Antony Webb[1,2]), Nurse (Helen Dorward[1]), Corporal Forbes (George Lee[1,2]), UNIT Officer (Tessa Shaw[1]), Technician (Ellis Jones[1]), Wagstaffe (Allan Mitchell[1]), 2nd Reporter (Prentis Hancock[1]), Major General Scobie (Hamilton Dyce[2-4]), Dr. Beavis (Henry McCarthy[2]), Hibbert (John Woodnutt[2-4]), Ransome (Derek Smee[2,3]), Meg (Betty Bowden[2,3]), Sergeant (Clifford Cox[3]), Attendant (Edmund Bailey[4]).

THINGS TO WATCH OUT FOR

- This story introduced a new opening title sequence – designed, like the previous ones, by Bernard Lodge – accompanied by a slightly rearranged version of the familiar theme music; and, for the first time in the series' history, a matching closing title sequence (whereas previously the closing credits had generally been shown against a black background). Lodge used the same techniques as had been used for the Troughton sequence, but added colour to the electronic feedback patterns using tinted filters. Lodge experimented with several different feedback patterns and tried incorporating an image of the Doctor with his hands raised up by his shoulders as well as the head and shoulders photograph that appears in the final title sequence. Extracts from this footage were to be seen on the 1992 BBC Video release *The Pertwee Years*; and a complete early edit of the opening title sequence, featuring some of the ultimately unused material, was included as a hidden "Easter egg" feature on the 2000 BBC DVD of *Spearhead from Space*

- The title sequences for *Spearhead from Space* have two unique features: first, the camera zooms in on the story title caption in the opening credits so that it appears to rush toward the viewer; secondly, the music accompanying the closing credits fades down part way through (at a different point in each of the four episodes) and simultaneously fades up at a different point, the net result being a rather disjointed-sounding edit.

- The Doctor is credited for the first time as 'Doctor Who' in the closing credits as opposed to 'Dr. Who'.
- *Spearhead from Space* was the first of only two *Doctor Who* stories to be originated entirely on film as opposed to videotape (the other was the 1996 TV movie); this was an emergency measure necessitated by the unavailability of studios due to industrial action at the BBC.
- The establishing shots of the plastics factory in operation are accompanied by an extract from Fleetwood Mac's popular contemporary single 'Oh Well – Part 1'.
- The Autons' wrist guns have a highy memorable design, being concealed within their hands behind a hinged finger section.
- Scenes featuring real waxworks were shot at Madame Tussaud's in London.

THINGS YOU MIGHT NOT HAVE KNOWN

- Working title: *Facsimile*.
- Production of this story was hit by a strike which meant that all the material due to be recorded in studio had to be hastily rescheduled to be filmed on location instead.
- Outgoing producer Derrick Sherwin made a cameo appearance in Episode 2 as the UNIT commissionaire guarding the underground entrance to UNIT HQ.
- Holmes's script echoed many great alien invasion themes of the past, but it most closely resembled a 1966 screenplay, written by Roger Marshal from a story by Holmes, for a Merton Park film called *Invasion*, which starts with two humanoid aliens crash-landing on Earth outside a country hospital. They are taken in and the doctors realise that they are not quite human …

QUOTE, UNQUOTE

- **Technician:** 'I suppose they must have been meteorites … mustn't they?'
- **Brigadier Lethbridge-Stewart:** 'We deal with the odd … the unexplained. Anything on Earth … or beyond.'
- **Brigadier Lethbridge-Stewart:** 'In the last decade, we've been sending probes deeper and deeper into space. We've drawn attention to ourselves, Miss Shaw.'

ANALYSIS

It is apparent from the first few seconds of the opening episode of *Spearhead from Space* that *Doctor Who* has changed. Gone are the moody black and white swirls and in come new and vibrantly coloured patterns of glowing lines. The Doctor's face appears and then vanishes, and the patterns twist and spin in time with the hypnotic music. Then … something is approaching the Earth, something alien … and inevitably the Doctor has to be involved somehow.

Spearhead from Space boasts a number of 'firsts'. It is the first story to have been made in colour; the first to star Jon Pertwee as the time travelling hero; the first to feature UNIT as a regular part of the series' format; and arguably the first to really go for the viewer's jugular with a potent combination of horror and science-fiction.

The opening episode sets the scene. Some mysterious meteorites have fallen (shades of Nigel Kneale's 1955 serial *Quatermass II*) and, when uncovered, they glow with a strange internal light and emit an eerie trilling sound. The mystery of what they are will have to wait, however, as it is the new Doctor who attracts the most interest. The viewer's eagerness to find out what he is going to be like is cleverly maintained as for much of the first two episodes he is either unconscious or at best semiconscious in hospital, recovering initially from his change of appearance and then from a wound sustained when he is shot by a jumpy UNIT soldier. After his eventual recuperation he is at first presented as someone who does not take things too seriously. In fact certain scenes, like one in which he takes a shower to escape the attentions of the hospital staff, are positively comedic – something that at the time seemed not entirely surprising, given that Jon Pertwee's background was as a light entertainment and comedy performer. The viewer is however reminded of the Doctor's alien nature by way of a number of revelations, such as that he has two hearts and can put himself into a recuperative coma.

The pace of the story is slow and measured in this initial section but really starts to pick up after the Doctor discharges himself from hospital and steals a car with which to drive to UNIT HQ, where he quickly establishes his credentials and sets about helping Liz Shaw to analyse some meteorite fragments. The focus of the story now shifts to the main plot – the invasion attempt by the Nestene consciousness and its Auton dummies. Writer Robert Holmes's concept of an alien intelligence that can inhabit and animate plastic is inspired if, as Simon M Lydiard pointed out in *Skaro* Volume Three Number One dated October/November 1982, not wholly original: 'The idea of a planet-hopping intelligence using robot slaves to take over the planet Earth was not, even at this time, a particularly new one and had been featured in *Doctor Who* in both *The Abominable Snowmen* and *The Web of Fear* … Despite the unoriginality of the story, which could have easily degenerated into something not entirely unlike a 1950s B-movie, it came across as remarkably fresh, due to Robert Holmes's entertaining script, Derek Martinus's stylish direction and Jon Pertwee's refreshing characterisation.'

It is the terrifying and well-realised concept of killer shop dummies that makes *Spearhead from Space* one of the most horrific *Doctor Who* stories ever. The first time that one of the plastic mannequins is seen to move, stepping down from a plinth behind Ransome at the end of Episode 2, the viewer gasps. They are spooky, effective and oh so very real. The scene in Episode 4 in which they 'come to life' *en masse* is wonderful, and one of the all-time great *Doctor Who* moments. The dummies kill indiscriminately, and yet they themselves are unstoppable for they are simply plastic objects. 'The Autons proved to be … terrifying, especially their "drop away" wrist guns and their sheer power,' wrote Chris Dunk in *Oracle* Volume 2 Number 8 dated May 1979. 'The fact that they resembled human beings yet were so starkly divorced from mankind enhanced their evil, and when they chose to strike, the moment was right. Streams of killer mannequins smashing effortlessly free from shop windows is horrifying. It is something that I could really shudder at.'

Particularly notable is the uncompromising, adult quality of the story's realisation, which sets it apart from much of sixties *Doctor Who* and contributes greatly to its success. When a jeep driven by one of the Brigadier's men crashes, blood is seen on the cracked windscreen; people are clearly terrified by the emotionless, blank-faced Autons; and the fact that all this takes place on a familiar, recognisable Earth only adds to its effectiveness. Derek Martinus's direction is characteristically dynamic and inventive, and his casting is also very good. Hugh Burden's icy Channing deserves particular mention, as does John Woodnutt's tormented plastics factory manager Hibbert. The UNIT set-up is also well defined and re-established, with Nicholas Courtney effortlessly reprising his engaging

THIRD DOCTOR

portrayal of Lethbridge-Stewart and newcomer Caroline John making a promising debut as the sceptical Liz Shaw.

Surprisingly, given the quality of the story and the significant change of format that it represented for the series, the BBC's Audience Research Report on the opening episode noted that the reaction of contemporary viewers could 'hardly be described as enthusiastic,' although 'the majority ... were clearly quite satisfied with it ... It was perhaps early days to judge, most would say, but at least this introductory episode seemed up to standard and if the story so far merely "set the scene" and, rather neatly and quite convincingly, introduced the "new" Doctor Who, there was every indication that, once under way, the story would develop into the usual quite diverting "science-fictionish escapist" tale they had come to expect of the series. A few (but very few) admitted that they never had any time for this "childish rubbish", while a considerable number remarked that although a new *Doctor Who* series was not unwelcome and this first episode had appeal, compared to the series it replaced, *Star Trek*, it seemed naïve, and, to them, less satisfying. "Hardly an adequate substitute for *Star Trek*, and by comparison rather childish. But time will tell, and it's good enough in its own way." Altogether the consensus of opinion seemed to be that this new series gave every indication of becoming a *Doctor Who* adventure in the expected tradition – and certainly (many added) it appealed very much to children.'

Contemporary press reaction suggests that some journalists were rather more on the ball. 'This *Doctor Who* adventure wins my vote as the best in the lifetime of the series so far,' commented Matthew Coady in the *Daily Mirror*. 'What it did was to suggest an authentic sense of the uncanny.' Gerard Garrett of the *Daily Sketch* was similarly enthusiastic, asserting that the series had returned, in colour, with 'a production so slick that it made many adult series look like lumbering oxen'.

Contributing significantly toward this slickness of production is the fact that, making a virtue of necessity, this story was shot entirely on film. The first example of the new style *Doctor Who* of the seventies, *Spearhead from Space* fairly grips the viewer from start to finish and sets the scene for even greater things to come. As Simon M Lydiard concluded, 'For sheer production quality, *Spearhead from Space* remains a towering landmark in *Doctor Who* history.'

DOCTOR WHO AND THE SILURIANS

Writer: Malcolm Hulke. **Director:** Timothy Combe. **Designer:** Barry Newbery. **Costumes:** Christine Rawlins. **Make-Up:** Marion Richards[1-4], Teresa Wright[5-7]. **Incidental Music:** Carey Blyton. **Visual Effects:** James Ward. **Film Cameraman:** Fred Hamilton. **Film Editor:** Bill Huthert. **Studio Lighting:** Ralph Walton. **Studio Sound:** John Staple. **Production Assistant:** Chris D'Oyly-John. **Assistant Floor Manager:** Sue Hedden.

	First UK TX	Scheduled TX	Actual TX	Duration	Viewers	Chart Pos.
Episode 1	31/01/70	17.15	17.16	24'15"	8.8	41
Episode 2	07/02/70	17.15	17.16	23'08"	7.3	68

Episode 3	14/02/70	17.15	17.16	23'16"	7.5	59
Episode 4	21/02/70	17.15	17.15	25'00"	8.2	46
Episode 5	28/02/70	17.15	17.17	23'58"	7.5	52
Episode 6	07/03/70	17.15	17.15	24'15"	7.2	63
Episode 7	14/03/70	17.15	17.15	22'55"	7.5	54

Plot: Summoned by the Brigadier to an underground research centre at Wenley Moor, the Doctor and Liz Shaw learn from its director, Dr Lawrence, that work on a new type of nuclear reactor is being hampered by inexplicable power losses and by an unusually high incidence of stress-related illness amongst staff. Investigating a nearby cave system, the Doctor discovers it is the base of a group of intelligent reptiles, termed Silurians, who went into hibernation millions of years ago but have now been revived by power from the research centre. The Doctor strives for peace between reptiles and humans and manages to gain the trust of the old Silurian leader, but then a rebellious young Silurian seizes power and releases a deadly virus that threatens to wipe out humanity. The Doctor finds an antidote, but the Silurians retaliate by taking over the research centre and preparing to destroy the Van Allen Belt, a natural barrier shielding the Earth from solar radiation harmful to humans but beneficial to reptiles. The creatures are tricked into returning to their caves when the Doctor overloads the reactor, threatening to cause a nuclear explosion. The Brigadier, to the Time Lord's disgust, then has the Silurian base blown up.

Episode endings:
1. The Doctor is exploring the cave system when he hears a roaring noise. He continues, and encounters the terrifying form of a supposedly extinct dinosaur.
2. Liz is examining the barn where an injured Silurian earlier attacked a farmer, Squire, and terrorised his wife. She turns and screams as the Silurian comes up behind her and knocks her to the ground.
3. The Doctor visits the cottage of research centre scientist Dr Quinn, whom he correctly suspects has made contact with the Silurians, and finds him dead. In the man's hand he discovers a device that, when activated, emits a bleeping signal. Suddenly the injured Silurian enters the room.
4. In the Silurians' base, the young Silurian returns to the cage in which the Doctor is being held prisoner. It tells him that it has destroyed the soldiers in the cave system and will now destroy him too. The creature's third eye glows and the Doctor's face contorts in agony.
5. The Doctor and the Brigadier arrive at the local hospital and find the research centre's security officer, Major Baker, lying dead outside – the first victim of the Silurian virus.
6. The Doctor is in the laboratory at the research centre, desperately trying to isolate an antidote to the Silurian virus. Suddenly the wall behind him scorches and melts and two Silurians break through. One of the creatures turns its third eye on the Doctor, causing him to collapse.
7. The Doctor and Liz are leaving Wenley Moor in the Doctor's vintage car, Bessie. The car breaks down, but the Doctor manages to get it started again. Suddenly they see a huge explosion in the distance. The Doctor realises with horror that the Brigadier has had the cave system blown up and thereby destroyed an entire race of intelligent beings. He rejoins Liz in the car and drives away.

IT WAS MADE WHERE...?

Location Filming: 12.11.69-14.11.69, 17.11.69-20.11.69, 24.11.69
Locations: Milford Chest Hospital, Milford, Surrey; transmitter station, Hog's Back, Surrey; Marylebone Station, Melcombe Place, London, NW1; Hankley Common MOD base, Godalming, Surrey; Godalming High Street, Godalming, Surrey; Sheephatch Farm, Tilford, Surrey; Melcombe Place, Marylebone, London NW1; Dorset Square/Balcombe Street, Marylebone, London, NW1; Walkway by Swanscombe House, Edward Woods Estate, corner Queensdale Crescent and St Ann's Road, Shepherd's Bush, London, NW11.
Studio Recording: 08.12.69 in TC3, 15.12.69, 21.12.69-22.12.69, 05.01.70, 12.01.70 all in TC1, 19.01.70, 26.01.70 both in TC8

ADDITIONAL CREDITED CAST

Dr. Quinn (Fulton Mackay[1-3]*), Major Baker (Norman Jones[1-5]), Dr. Lawrence (Peter Miles[1-6]), Miss Dawson (Thomasine Heiner[1-5]), Dr. Meredith (Ian Cunningham[1]), Roberts (Roy Branigan[1]), Spencer (John Newman[1]), Davis (Bill Matthews[1]), Captain Hawkins (Paul Darrow[2-7]), Doris Squire (Nancie Jackson[2]), Squire (Gordon Richardson[2]), Silurians (Pat Gorman[2-4], Paul Barton[4,5,7], Simon Cain[4-7], John Churchill[4,5,7], Dave Carter[7]), Silurian Voices (Peter Halliday[2,4-7]), Masters (Geoffrey Palmer[4-6]), Sergeant Hart (Richard Steele[4,6]), Travis (Ian Talbot[4]), Old Silurian (Dave Carter[4,5]), Young Silurian (Nigel Johns[4-7]), Private Robins (Harry Swift[5]), Silurian Scientist (Pat Gorman[5-7]), Corporal Nutting (Alan Mason[6,7]), Private Wright (Derek Pollitt[6]), Hospital Doctor (Brendan Barry[6]).

* Also in Episode 4, as a corpse in the reprise from Episode 3, but uncredited.

POPULAR MYTHS

- The Silurians have a 'pet' tyrannosaurus rex. (The dinosaur featured in the story is unidentified but appears to be an allosaurus.)

THINGS TO WATCH OUT FOR

- This is the only instance in the series' history of an on-air story title beginning '*Doctor Who and* …' (although *The Savages*, *The Highlanders*, *The Underwater Menace*, *The Moonbase* and *The Macra Terror* were all referred to as *Dr. Who and the*… in the 'next episode' caption at the end of the preceding story's closing episode, and there would later be a BBC radio serial entitled, at the beginning of each episode, *Doctor Who and the Ghosts of N Space*).
- The Doctor's yellow-liveried vintage car, nicknamed Bessie, makes its first appearance.
- This story marks the debut use in *Doctor Who* of Colour Separation Overlay – an effects technique, often known as Chromakey outside the BBC, whereby all areas of a camera image that are in a particular key colour (usually blue or, a little later, yellow) are electronically replaced with the equivalent areas of another camera image, giving a composite of the two. Examples in *Doctor Who and the Silurians* include the creation of a cave background and the presentation of an image of Major Baker on a screen in the Silurians' base.
- Paul Darrow, now better known for his role as Avon in the BBC science-fiction series

Blake's 7, plays UNIT's Captain Hawkins. He would later appear as Tekker in the season twenty-two story *Timelash*.

- Fulton Mackay, now better known for his role as Mr Mackay in the classic BBC sitcom *Porridge*, plays Dr Quinn. He was later considered for the role of the fourth Doctor when Jon Pertwee left the series.
- Well known comedy actor Geoffrey Palmer appears as Masters. He would later take a further role in the series, as the Administrator in the season nine story *The Mutants*.
- Non-speaking cameo appearances are made by members of the production team, including Barry Letts, Terrance Dicks and, most prominently, Trevor Ray (who plays a ticket collector struck down by the Silurian virus), in the location scenes shot at Marylebone Station in London. Ray has since claimed that a number of renowned actors, including Diana Rigg (famous for her role as Emma Peel in *The Avengers*), also appeared incognito as dying commuters in these scenes, although there is no documentary evidence to support this.
- This story has very distinctive incidental music, which was composed and conducted by Carey Blyton and played by Paul Harvey (Eb, Bb and A clarinets, bass clarinet, contra-bass clarinet), Michael Oxenham (Bb and A clarinets, sopranino and descant recorders, medieval, wide-bore variet and soprano, alto, tenor and bass krumhorns), Neill Sanders (Horn), Vivian Joseph (Cello), Gordon Kember (Piano-prepared and unprepared) and Stephen Whittaker (percussion).

THINGS YOU MIGHT NOT HAVE KNOWN

- Working title: *The Monsters*.
- Sheila Grant, who had performed the Quark voices for the season six story *The Dominators*, was hired for an experimental session to record voices for this story. Her contribution was ultimately not used.
- Three Alsation dogs were hired at a cost of 40 guineas (£42) from Animal Kingdom in Denham for filming in the Farnham area on 17 November.
- This was the first story made on colour videotape.

QUOTE, UNQUOTE

- **Dr. Quinn:** 'The knowledge I shall gain is worth any risk!'
- **Dr. Lawrence:** 'This is the Permanent Under Secretary.' **The Doctor:** 'Yes, well, I've got no time to talk to under secretaries – permanent or otherwise.' **Masters:** 'May I ask who you are?' **The Doctor:** 'You may ask!'
- **The Doctor:** 'I'm beginning to lose confidence for the first time in my life – and that covers several thousand years.'

ANALYSIS

'*Spearhead from Space* provided a more than adequate foundation for this new era [of] *Doctor Who*,' observed Chris Dunk in *Oracle* Volume 2 Number 9 dated June 1979, 'but *Doctor Who and the Silurians* was just as important in its own way. The new format had to be built upon, enlarged and firmly established. Time also had to be allowed for the Doctor to [cement] his forced alliance with UNIT and to modify his character to suit his new existence. For the first time in many, many moons he [finds] himself to be not quite the top dog. Even he, albeit grudgingly, has to accept being bossed around to an extent – as by the Brigadier right at the start of this ambitious seven-part serial.'

There was, in short, a great deal riding on the success of *Doctor Who and the Silurians*. Fortunately all concerned rose to the occasion and came up with a great story that fully exploits the considerable potential of the 'Earth exile' format. 'The plot was not one I would associate with either of the ... two [previous] Doctors, somehow,' continued Dunk. 'It seemed different right from the word go (*Spearhead from Space* was very Troughtonesque in parts) and this ... [showed] that the [series was] on the move, exploring new ground, as indeed it should ... The basic premise was a good one as well, and one long overdue for examination in *Doctor Who*. I have always been fascinated by the birth of mankind [and] ancient history ...'

The story keeps the viewer glued to the screen throughout, giving the lie to the oft-made assertion that any that are longer than four episodes are bound to sag. It is expertly structured and highly intelligent too, raising some real moral issues, and writer Malcolm Hulke has been almost universally praised for his scripts, including by Gordon Roxburgh in *Matrix* Issue 6 dated May 1980:

'"In science-fiction there are only two stories. They come to us, or we go to them." [So] said the late Malcolm Hulke. However, for the Silurians story [he] wrote what must be one of the most novel ideas ever in the [series]. A "they come to us" story with a difference ... they've always been here! ...

'Perhaps the most striking feature ... was the plausibility of it all. It was just possible that a power plant could trigger off an underground shelter of millions of years ago. The history of the then approaching Moon also added to the reasons why the Silurians were there at all ... The Silurian race was believable. There were those capable of seeing reason, seeing both sides of the issue – as in the old Silurian – or the complete opposite as shown by the younger Silurians. One could find some sympathy for the creatures; they were given a credible background with their civilisation and attitudes to the human race [who] now ruled what was their world.'

'Tim Combe was an excellent choice [of] director,' wrote Michael Kenwood in *Skaro* Volume Three Number One dated October/November 1982. 'He [cast] and brought out the best in several excellent actors while still remaining adept technically, this [being] obvious from several superb pieces of photography. Among my favourite [parts] were the shots of the sun after the wounded Silurian emerged from the darkness of the caves, and the horrific scenes of Londoners dying off in their droves ... Also fascinating was the "Silurian's eye view" before it was revealed fully. The horror present in this story came nowhere near [to that in] *Spearhead from Space* ... but there were still some very frightening scenes, especially those in the gloomy caves.'

Dunk, although being in the minority in feeling that the story failed to hold up over its full seven episode length, also thought that it contained many highly effective sequences: 'The very first scene has to be classified as brilliant, with the sudden and brutal death of the pot-holer in the caves. In fact it was the element of death that I found to be very well done throughout this story. (Aren't I morbid!) The spreading of the virus first through England then all across Europe was also extremely worrying and entertaining while it lasted.'

The representation of the effects of the virus is much aided by some excellent and disturbing make-up by Teresa Wright, particularly in the case of Dr. Lawrence. A scene in which Lawrence, very well portrayed by Peter Miles, lunges across his desk to attack the Brigadier is particularly shocking, and unusually violent even for this period in the series' history.

Just as the final battle between UNIT and the Autons in *Spearhead from Space* paralleled that between UNIT and the Cybermen in *The Invasion* (even down to being shot in a similar way at the same location), so the scenes of people dying of the plague in *Doctor Who and the Silurians* recall those of people succumbing to the Cybermen's hypnotic signal in that sixth season serial, so serving to confirm its status as a template for the early part of the third Doctor's era. If anything, however, the effect is even more dramatic this time around.

The Silurians themselves, although perhaps not amongst the top flight of the series' monster races, are nevertheless competently realised and memorable. 'The Silurians were reasonable,' agreed Michael Kenwood. 'While simply men in rubber suits, and with slightly loose masks at that, they looked very effective in the darkness of the caves … The voices, however, were not the best that have been heard in the [series] … The third eye effect could have been better with rays, but it was okay with lights. The heads looked convincingly alien and reptilian too.' Even the Siluarians' voices are popular with many. Ken Tod, for instance, wrote in *TSV* 25 dated October 1991: 'The actors playing the Silurians do a very good job and the voices by Peter Halliday are excellent.'

Jon Pertwee has clearly settled into his role as the Doctor by this point, and gives an assured performance. The BBC's Audience Research Report on the story's closing episode recorded that amongst contemporary viewers the actor 'was again warmly praised, several adding that they preferred his playing of Doctor Who to that of his predecessors: "Not bumbling like the others, much more modern and sensible", one of them wrote.' Caroline John as Liz Shaw meanwhile proves to be a very good foil, far removed from the naïve young companions of the past. The Brigadier and UNIT are also at their peak here; and it is on the morality of their actions in destroying the Silurian base that attention is focused as the story builds to its excellent climax. 'There was a sense of urgency in the last few episodes,' noted Roxburgh. 'Eventually the Silurians had to be tricked into returning to their underground shelter but the Doctor alone, as we would expect, still thought that man and Silurian could live in peace. We could feel the sadness he felt as the caves were blown up, the anger boiling inside him at losing the chance to find out.'

The overall impression given by the BBC's Audience Research Report is of a rather mixed response. Over two-fifths of the sample of viewers responded 'warmly', and considered that 'a well contrived "surprise" ending had made "a fitting climax to a thrilling serial"'. Some of those who reacted 'less whole-heartedly', however, thought it 'a rushed and "rather tame and routine" finish to an otherwise "exciting and at times frightening tale"'. One commented that the Silurians 'gave in too easily', while others complained that the episode was 'slow and lacking in action'. As usual, a small minority clearly found little to enjoy in *Doctor Who*, holding it to be 'far-fetched rubbish'. The fact that the series had undergone a change of format now seemed to be registering, but opinions on this development were again divided. 'I preferred this serial to many of the earlier ones,' noted one viewer, 'because one is more interested in a possible threat to this world one lives in, than some unknown planet as so often featured in *Doctor Who*.' Others, however, 'did not think the present story as effective as previous series, some obviously regarding an Earthbound Doctor Who as less exciting than the space traveller. They also said that the story had seemed slow in places and overlong, several judging it "ridiculous" and the "monsters" far too unrealistic or, alternatively, it had become "too adult now". Although some said that they did not regard *Doctor Who* as entertainment for adults, more commented that it made suitable viewing for all age groups.'

'This has got to be one of the best Pertwee stories,' judged Stephen Haywood in *Capitol Spires* Issue 2 dated July 1993. 'It has everything: monsters in the form of fairly well-executed dinosaurs; strong, diverse characters all acting in believable and consistent ways; a threat to mankind which, without the Doctor, probably could not be diverted; and, of course, the Silurians, a truly inspired creation on the part of Malcolm Hulke.'

THE AMBASSADORS OF DEATH

Writer: David Whitaker, Trevor Ray[1]*, Malcolm Hulke[2-7]*. **Director:** Michael Ferguson. **Designer:** David Myerscough-Jones. **Costumes:** Christine Rawlins. **Make-Up:** Marion Richards, Teresa Wright. **Incidental Music:** Dudley Simpson. **Action:** HAVOC. **Visual Effects:** Peter Day, Ian Scoones. **Film Cameraman:** A A Englander, Tony Leggo. **Film Editor:** Don Godden, Chris Wimble. **Studio Lighting:** Ralph Walton, Geoff Shaw, Dave Sydenham. **Studio Sound:** Gordon Mackie, Brian Hiles. **Production Assistant:** Nick John. **Assistant Floor Manager:** Margot Heyhoe.

* Trevor Ray wrote the final version of Episode 1 and Malcolm Hulke that of Episodes 2-7. They were uncredited for this work. David Whitaker himself never wrote anything beyond Episode 3 in script form.

	First UK TX	Scheduled TX	Actual TX	Duration	Viewers	Chart Pos.
Episode 1	21/03/70	17.15	17.16	24'33"	7.1	60
Episode 2	28/03/70	17.15	17.15	24'39"	7.6	59
Episode 3	04/04/70	17.20	17.21	24'38"	8.0	60
Episode 4	11/04/70	17.15*	17.44	24'37"	9.3	46
Episode 5	18/04/70	17.15	17.14	24'17"	7.1	57
Episode 6	25/04/70	17.15	17.16	24'31"	6.9	70
Episode 7	02/05/70	17.15	17.15	24'32"	5.4	80

* This episode was transmitted approximately thirty minutes late due to an overrun of the preceding programme, *Cup Final Grandstand*.

Plot: The Doctor joins UNIT's investigation into the mystery surrounding Mars Probe 7. Space Control, headed by Professor Ralph Cornish, has had no contact with the three astronauts on board since it started back from Mars seven months ago, and now the Recovery 7 rescue mission has run into similar difficulties. This second ship does get back to Earth, but the astronauts are kidnapped after landing and Liz Shaw notices that the Geiger counter is at maximum. It transpires that the ship's occupants were not the human astronauts after all but a trio of radiation-dependent alien ambassadors who had swapped places with them. The Doctor makes a solo flight in Recovery 7 and docks with Mars Probe 7, still orbiting in space. He is then intercepted by a huge alien spaceship and taken on board, where he finds the real astronauts unharmed. The aliens' Captain threatens to destroy the Earth unless their three ambassadors are released. The Doctor is allowed to go and, after returning to Space Control, discovers that the kidnapping of the ambassadors is part of a scheme devised by xenophobic ex-astronaut General Carrington to discredit the aliens and convince the world's authorities to wage war against them. The Doctor and UNIT are able to thwart his plans and arrange the safe exchange of ambassadors for astronauts.

Episode endings:

1. The Doctor and Liz go to see Bruno Taltalian, a scientist on Cornish's team, to request the use of his computer to analyse the alien messages that have been received. When they enter the computer room he pulls a gun on them.

2. The sealed Recovery 7 capsule has been taken to Space Control after its return to Earth. Astronaut Charles Van Lyden's voice can be heard over a radio link, but Cornish cannot get a reply when he tries to talk to the man. The Doctor asks some additional questions which are also ignored. He instructs a workman, standing by with a blowtorch, to cut the capsule open.

3. Liz Shaw receives a note, apparently from the Brigadier, asking her to meet him in Hertfordshire. She sets off but discovers that this is a trap. She is chased by two thugs and tries to escape across a bridge over a weir. Mid-way across she is caught. She manages to knock one of the men into the water, but is then herself flipped over the edge by the other.

4. One of the alien astronauts is taken by their kidnapper, Reegan, to kill Sir James Quinlan, the man in charge of the space programme. This done, the creature then destroys the contents of a safe. The Doctor arrives to see Quinlan and hurries to the dead man's side. Behind him, the astronaut approaches, hand outstretched to kill him too.

5. The Doctor makes a solo flight in Recovery 7 and docks with Mars Probe 7 to try to find out where the human astronauts might have gone to. Ground radar suddenly reports a massive alien craft heading straight for the Doctor.

6. The Doctor has been captured by Reegan and taken to his secret base. Reegan wants the Time Lord to build him a translation device so that he can communicate with the aliens. Suddenly, Carrington enters the room. He has been behind all the kidnappings and now wants the Doctor dead. He produces a gun with which to kill him, explaining that he sees it as his 'moral duty' to do so.

7. Carrington has been exposed and prevented from engineering a conflict with the aliens. The Doctor leaves to continue his attempts to repair the TARDIS while Liz remains to assist Cornish with the ambassadors.

IT WAS MADE WHERE...?

Location Filming: 23.01.70, 26.01.70-27.01.70, 29.01.70-31.01.70, 02.02.70-04.02.70

Locations: Southall Gas Works, White Street, off Gas Works Ford, North London; White Street, Southall, Middx; TCC Factory (BBC), Wales Farm Road, Acton; Claycart Bottom, off Rushmoor Road, Aldershot, Hampshire; Puckeridge Hill Road Bridge, Basingstoke Canal, Aldershot, Hampshire; Royal Engineers Driving Circuit, Aldershot; Wycombe Air Park, Clay Lane, High Wycombe, Bucks; Folley's Gravel Pit, Spade Oak, Little Marlow, Bucks; Gossmore Lane, Marlow, Bucks; Marlow Weir (Lock Side), Mill Road, Marlow; Beacon Hill, Beacon Hill Road, nr Ewshot, Hants; Wycombe RDC Sewage Purification Works, Little Marlow, Bucks; Blue Circle Cement Works, Northfleet, Kent.

Studio Recording: 13.02.70, 20.02.70, 27.02.70, 06.03.70, 13.03.70 all in TC3, 20.03.70 in TC4, 27.03.70 in TC1

ADDITIONAL CREDITED CAST

Ralph Cornish (Ronald Allen), Taltalian (Robert Cawdron[1,2,4]), Carrington[1-3]/General Carrington[4-7] (John Abineri), Van Lyden (Ric Felgate[1-3,6]), John Wakefield (Michael Wisher[1,2,7]), Miss Rutherford (Cheryl Molineaux[1,2]), Grey (Ray Armstrong[1,2]), Collinson (Robert Robertson[1,2]), Quinlan (Dallas Cavell[2-5]), Control Room Assistants (Bernard Martin[2], Joanna Ross[5-7], Carl Conway[5,6]), Dobson (Juan Moreno[2]), Corporal Champion (James Haswell[2]), Unit Sergeant (Derek Ware[2]), Reegan (William Dysart[3-7]), Lennox (Cyril Shaps[3-5]), Heldorf (Gordon Sterne[3]), Astronauts (Steve Peters[3-5,7]*, Neville Simons[3-5,7]*, Ric Felgate[4,5,7]*), Unit Soldier (Max Faulkner[4]), Masters (John Lord[4]), Flynn (Tony Harwood[5]), Sergeant Benton (John Levene[5,7]), Private Parker (James Clayton[5]), Technician (Roy Scammell[5]), Alien Space Captain (Peter Noel Cook[6,7]), Aliens' Voices (Peter Halliday[6,7]), Lefee (Steve Peters[6]), Michaels (Neville Simons[6]), Private Johnson (Geoffrey Beevers[7]).

* Steve Peters, Neville Simons and Ric Felgate were credited as the alien astronauts on the episodes in which they appeared as such only if their equivalent human characters did not also appear in the same episodes.

THINGS TO WATCH OUT FOR

- The opening title sequences of this story are unique for two reasons. First, they break off part-way through to make way for a short 'teaser' of the action before resuming to display the story title, writer and episode number captions. Secondly, the story title actually appears in two stages – 'The Ambassadors' first and then 'of Death' below it a few moments later – the latter punctuated by a gunshot noise added to the theme music.
- Actor Michael Wisher appears in the role of John Wakefield, a television reporter. Wisher later became best known for playing Davros in the season twelve story *Genesis of the Daleks* and made numerous other appearances in the series.
- There are some excellent model sequences of Mars Probe 7, Recovery 7 and the alien spaceship, accompanied by some unusual and highly effective incidental music courtesy of Dudley Simpson.

THINGS YOU MIGHT NOT HAVE KNOWN

- Working titles: *The Invaders from Mars*, *The Carriers of Death*
- This was the first story on which Derek Ware's stunt organisation, HAVOC, received an on-screen credit. They had been involved with the series since the season four story *The Smugglers*.
- Episode 5 saw the first appearance of Sergeant Benton in a regular role within the UNIT organisation.
- The rocket capsule set was the same one as used in an episode of *Doomwatch* called *Re-Entry Forbidden*. The two productions shared the cost for the set, which was designed by Ian Watson.
- A special trailer was made for *The Ambassadors of Death*. It opened with a big close

up of the Doctor saying: 'There's been no radio contact for seven months. Something's gone badly wrong with Mars Probe 7.' There then followed a shot of the capsule in space and and one of Van Lyden screaming with the aliens' signal noise over. Then the Doctor says: 'We've got to find out who's sending that signal.' There followed an excerpt from the fight sequence in Episode 1, and the Doctor continues: 'Someone is determined to steal the recovery capsule!' There were then excerpts from the ambush sequence in Episode 2, before the Doctor says: 'The people behind this are trying to kidnap Liz Shaw!' The kidnap was illustrated by excerpts from that sequence. Finally the Doctor says: 'I don't know what we brought back in Mars Probe 7, but it certainly wasn't human!' The last shot was of an astronaut approaching a UNIT sentry. The entire trailer was concluded by an announcer's voice-over: 'Mars Probe 7 returns – carrying a terrifying cargo that endangers the whole world. Next week, the Doctor battles alien enemies and their human allies in *The Ambassadors of Death*!' This trailer was included on the BBC video release of *The Ambassadors of Death* in 2002.

QUOTE, UNQUOTE

- **Ralph Cornish:** '*Something* took off from Mars!'
- **The Doctor:** 'I don't know what came down in Recovery 7, but it certainly wasn't human!'

ANALYSIS

The Ambassadors of Death, like David Whitaker's previous story *The Enemy of the World*, is a curious mixture of James Bond-style action and hardware and science-fiction concepts. Its main point is often said to be to illustrate the lengths to which some people are capable of going in their irrational hatred of other races. Strangely, however, this emerges only in General Carrington's xenophobic attitude toward the apparently friendly aliens that he first encountered on Mars. Normally one might expect some additional sub-plots exploring the same theme, but these are absent here. This tends to suggest that Whitaker might actually have had a different message in mind, but if that is so then it is hard to discern what it might have been. Nick Cooper, writing in *Star Begotten* Issue Two dated summer 1987, tried to rationalise this:

'The unnamed alien race are, without doubt, the "monsters", yet they are certainly not the villains. Reegan is a villain in the literal sense, but he is not to blame for the situation, only for taking advantage of it once it had arrived. And Carrington? All I can say is that of all the *Doctor Who* "bad guys", none prompted my *sympathy* more so than he … He *is* insane and so he cannot really be blamed for his actions – no-one warrants that blame. How's that for a difference? A story in which *no* one person or group is to blame for all the "evilness"?

'If anything is to blame for the near destruction of Earth, it is the baser and primitive urges within all people: xenophobia and hatred from Carrington, greed from Reegan (for money) and Wakefield and Quinlan (for fame), a desire for petty revenge from Lennox and so on. And in the face of these? The courage, compassion and humanity of the Doctor, Liz and Cornish and the Brigadier's basic sense of right and wrong and faith in the Doctor.

'*The Ambassadors of Death* holds a deep message for all of us – we should not fear or hate those who are different from ourselves, because the threat is more likely to come from ourselves …'

There are a number of inconsistencies and plot problems apparent in the story, no doubt due in large part to its difficult development and the involvement of several different writers in its scripting. Such a combination of different styles and ideas generally does a story no good at all, and this is very apparent here. The eclectic nature of the story was highlighted by Lance Parkin in *Matrix* Issue 52 dated spring 1996: 'The *Ambassadors of Death* is a peculiar mix of archetypal action-by-HAVOC two-fisted UNIT romp and leisurely [ramble in the style of the] sixth [season] stories that almost appear to be made up as they go along. Most of Episode 5 is taken up with Reegan's attempt to sabotage the Doctor's rocket, an attempt eventually foiled by the Doctor in thirty seconds. That said, the action sequences are lavish and the cliffhangers are among the best in the show's history.'

There is nothing wrong as such with either the direction or the acting, but the aforementioned plot problems result in the story dragging somewhat over its seven episodes. The aliens are deliberately sidelined and, on the single occasion that the viewer does get to see one of their true faces, it is on screen for less than a second. Even the alien Captain is seen only through a louvre blind, making any detail impossible to discern. Quite why this was done is unclear. Perhaps the alien make-up was deemed unsatisfactory, or perhaps, as the story isn't really about the aliens at all, it was felt that there was simply no need to showcase them. Parkin put forward another theory: 'Keeping the aliens at a distance really makes them, well, *alien*. Glimpsed behind slats, or in a moment after Liz removes one of their helmets, [they remain largely a mystery]. Their voices are strange, disembodied, their vast spacecraft mixes the mundane (a recreated quarantine area to keep the astronauts in) [with] a surreal CSO landscape. We hear that they have "invaded our galaxy" and that "they were on Mars before us," but only from Carrington, and we don't know whether they are really Martians or not. We know they need radiation … to live, but not why (or how). Although some fans have expressed dissatisfaction with this obscurity, it's a deliberate device that only adds to the mystery, suspense and paranoia – it's a trick that *The X-Files* uses on a weekly basis nowadays, over twenty years later.'

The comparison with *The X-Files* is an interesting one, as in some ways the format of that highly successful series mirrored that of season seven-style *Doctor Who*, with Mulder and Scully fulfilling dramatic functions similar to those of the Doctor and Liz, and their boss Skinner and his FBI colleagues being in a position akin to that of the Brigadier and his UNIT team. And the incorporation of a shadowy recurring "villain" in the person of the Cigarette Smoking Man could perhaps be seen as paralleling a development that would occur in *Doctor Who* in the following season …

The Ambassadors of Death arguably shows what the remainder of the third Doctor's era could have held in store, if events had follwed a slightly different course. Impressive military hardware, soldiers running about with guns, and barely glimpsed or present aliens to provide the science-fiction backdrop. It is perhaps just as well that this did not, in the event, become the norm. Some, however, have celebrated *The Ambassadors of Death* for its relatively adult content and realisation. 'From scene one we were plunged into a tale far deeper and more complex than perhaps any that had preceded it,' wrote Simon M Lydiard in *Skaro* Volume Three Number Three dated February/March 1983. '*Doctor Who* had at last reached full maturity, a quality which, along with Jon Pertwee's surprising acting talents, would take the series' ratings, popularity and reputation to new heights.'

INFERNO

Writer: Don Houghton. **Director:** Douglas Camfield, Barry Letts*. **Designer:** Jeremy Davies. **Costumes:** Christine Rawlins. **Make-Up:** Marion Richards. **Incidental Music:** stock. **Action:** HAVOC. **Visual Effects:** Len Hutton. **Film Cameraman:** Fred Hamilton. **Film Editor:** Martyn Day. **Studio Lighting:** John Green. **Studio Sound:** John Staple. **Production Assistant:** Chris D'Oyly-John. **Assistant Floor Manager:** Sue Hedden.

* Barry Letts directed, uncredited, the studio recordings for Episodes 3 to 7 as Douglas Camfield had been taken ill, suffering an adverse reaction to drugs that he had been prescribed for a heart condition.

	First UK TX	Scheduled TX	Actual TX	Duration	Viewers	Chart Pos.
Episode 1	09/05/70	17.15	17.15	23'21"	5.7	72
Episode 2	16/05/70	17.15	17.16	22'04"	5.9	66
Episode 3	23/05/70	17.15	17.16	24'34"	4.8	85
Episode 4	30/05/70	17.15	17.16	24'57"	6.0	54
Episode 5	06/06/70	17.15	17.16	23'42"	5.4	54
Episode 6	13/06/70	17.25	17.26	23'32"	5.7	73
Episode 7	20/06/70	17.15	17.15	24'33"	5.5	79

Plot: The Doctor is an observer and UNIT are providing security cover at an experimental drilling project designed to penetrate the Earth's crust and release a previously-untapped source of energy, named Stahlman's Gas after its discoverer. Professor Stahlman dismisses the concerns of the project's Executive Director Sir Keith Gold and exceeds all safety margins in order to expedite the work. Soon however the drill head starts to leak an oily green liquid that transforms those who touch it into vicious primeval creatures with a craving for heat. The Doctor is accidentally transported by the partially-repaired TARDIS control console into a parallel universe where England is ruled by a military dictatorship. The drilling project is at a more advanced stage here and, thwarted by his friends' ruthless *alter egos*, he is unable to prevent the penetration of the Earth's crust, which ultimately causes the planet's destruction. Escaping back to his own universe, where the drilling is still in progress, the Doctor tries to warn of impending disaster. At first he is disbelieved, but his words are borne out when the power-crazed Stahlman is himself transformed into one of the hideous primordial creatures. The Doctor, aided by consultant Greg Sutton, kills Stahlman with ice-cold blasts from fire extinguishers. He is finally able to shut down the drilling with only moments to spare.

Episode endings:
1. The Doctor and the Brigadier discover missing maintenance worker Harry Slocum in the switch room of the project's nuclear reactor. He has mutated into a vicious sub-human creature.
2. The Brigadier and Liz rush into the hut in which the Doctor has been attempting to repair the TARDIS control console. They are just in time to see the Doctor, the console and Bessie all vanish.

3. In the parallel universe, the project workers are trying to cope with an emergency caused by a leak in one of the drill head output pipes. The Doctor tries surreptitiously to repair their broken-down computer but is confronted by Platoon Under Leader Benton, who tells him that he can either go with him to face a firing squad or be shot where he stands.

4. The Doctor tries desperately to persuade the project workers in the parallel universe to stop the drilling, warning that if they penetrate the Earth's crust they will release forces that they never dreamed existed. Stahlman tells Brigade Leader Lethbridge Stewart to shoot the Doctor and then, as a distant rumbling and screeching noise is heard, he raises a gun to do so himself. The countdown to penetration reaches zero ...

5. The Doctor, sheltering in an office with the Brigade Leader, Section Leader Elizabeth Shaw, Greg Sutton and the project's Assistant Director Dr. Petra Williams, tries to persuade them to help him to return to his own universe. He tells them that he has a plan. Suddenly the arm of one of the primordial creatures smashes through the window in the office door.

6. The Section Leader shoots the Brigade Leader in order to give the Doctor a chance of escaping. The Doctor tries desperately to activate the TARDIS console as a wall of lava rolls toward the hut ...

7. The Doctor bids farewell to Liz and the Brigadier, telling the latter that he is a 'pompous, self-opinionated idiot,' and then dematerialises with the TARDIS console. He walks back into the hut moments later, sheepishly admitting that he got no further than the nearby rubbish tip. Making light of his earlier remarks, he tries to persuade the Brigadier to have his troops help in retrieving the console. Liz laughs as the two men leave the hut together.

IT WAS MADE WHERE...?

Location Filming: 31.03.70-03.04.70
Location: Berry Wiggins of Rochester, Kingsnorth-on-the-Medway, Kent.
Ealing Filming: 06.04.70-08.04.70 on Stage 2
Studio Recording: 23.04.70-24.04.70, 06.05.70-08.05.70 all in TC3, 21.05.70-22.05.70 in TC6, 29.05.70 in TC3. NB: Although all these dates were scheduled for studio recording, the way that Camfield elected to work was to do all camera rehearsals on the first day of each block, leaving all the recording to the subsequent days.

ADDITIONAL CREDITED CAST

Professor Stahlman[1-4,6,7]/Director Stahlman[5] (Olaf Pooley), Sir Keith Gold (Christopher Benjamin[1-5,7]), Greg Sutton (Derek Newark), Petra Williams[1-4,7]/Dr. Petra Williams[5,6] (Sheila Dunn), Sergeant Benton[1,2,6,7]/Platoon Under Leader Benton[3-5] (John Levene), Private Latimer (David Simeon[1,3]), Private Wyatt (Derek Ware[1-3]), Harry Slocum (Walter Randall[1,2]), Bromley (Ian Fairbairn[1-5,7]), RSF Sentry (Roy Scammell[4]), Patterson (Keith James[5]), Primords (Dave Carter[5,6], Pat Gorman[5,6], Philip Ryan[5,6], Peter Thompson[5,6], Walter Henry[6]).

Note: Nicholas Courtney was credited as playing Brigade Leader Lethbridge Stewart and Caroline John as playing Section Leader Elizabeth Shaw for Episode 5. In general, actors were credited under the names and ranks of their parallel universe characters only if – as in the cases of Courtney and John in this episode – their normal universe characters did not also appear in the same episode.

POPULAR MYTHS

- The 'parallel universe' aspect of the story was added to the scripts at the production team's suggestion to ensure that there was sufficient material to fill seven episodes. (This aspect of the story was present in writer Don Houghton's original outline; the aspect added to the scripts at the production team's suggestion was that of the Primord creatures.)
- This was Caroline John's last story as Liz as she was pregnant and could not return for the following season. (Although it is true that the actress was pregnant, Barry Letts was unaware of this when he decided against renewing her contract.)

THINGS TO WATCH OUT FOR

- The story title, writer's credit and episode number captions for each episode are faded up and focused over a special stock footage montage of volcanic eruptions following the opening title sequence.
- This story marks the last appearance in the series of the original TARDIS control console prop.
- The primordial mutant creatures are named 'Primords' in the closing credits of the episodes in which they appear and in publicity material but are unnamed in the story's dialogue.
- Professor Stahlman's *alter ego* in the parallel universe at one point wears a radiation suit bearing a label on which his surname is prominently spelt 'Stahlmann' – although it is unclear whether this was an intentional indication of a further difference between the two universes or simply an error. He is named as 'Director Stahlman' in the closing credits to Episode 5, but this could itself be an error.

THINGS YOU MIGHT NOT HAVE KNOWN

- Working titles: *Operation: Mole-Bore*; *The Mo-Hole Project*, *Project Inferno*
- The face of the 'Leader' seen on a poster in the Doctor's hut in the parallel universe was in fact that of visual effects designer Jack Kine.
- The make-up for this story went over budget as three full Primords more than planned were created: nine instead of six.
- There is an additional scene in the BBC video release of this story, of the Doctor listening to a radio report of the end of the world in the parallel universe. The voice on the radio was provided by Pertwee doing an impression of Lord Haw Haw (a propogandist for the Nazis in the Second World War). The scene was cut for the original transmission as it was felt that viewers would recognise Pertwee's voice.

QUOTE, UNQUOTE

- **The Doctor:** 'I keep telling you, Brigade Leader, I don't exist here!' **Brigade Leader Lethbridge Stewart:** 'Then you won't feel the bullets when we shoot you.'
- **The Doctor:** 'Listen to that! It's the sound of the planet screaming out its rage!'
- **Greg Sutton:** 'Marvellous, isn't it? The world's going up in flames and they're still playing at toy soldiers.'
- **Brigadier Lethbridge-Stewart:** '"Pompous, self-opinionated idiot," I think you said, Doctor.' **The Doctor:** 'Yes, well, we don't want to bear a grudge for a few hasty words, do we? No, not after all the years that we've worked together. Now, come along, my dear fellow. Put on a smile …'

'*Doctor Who* ... had "come of age" with the horror of *Spearhead from Space*, ... the conservationist attitudes of *Doctor Who and the Silurians* and the anti-racist tones of *The Ambassadors of Death*. Would *Inferno*, the final story of that monumental seventh season, live up to the quality of its predecessors? The answer is, it did, and in such a way that, to me, it became an all-time *Doctor Who* classic.' This assessment by Darren Giddings in *Skaro* Volume Three Number Three, dated February/March 1983, hit the nail right on the head. *Inferno* provides a superb ending to the series' seventh season, its style – often described by reviewers as 'gritty realism' – strongly recalling that of the seminal Quatermass serials, which had been so inspirational in the formulation of the new 'Earth exile' format. The scenes set on the parallel Earth as it nears its destruction are wonderfully realised, and almost unbearably tense. Nicholas Courtney and Caroline John really rise to the occasion and give superb performances as the 'alternative' Republican Security Forces (RSF) versions of their regular characters, and Jon Pertwee is also at his best here. These parallel Earth scenes are, indeed, the most memorable aspect of the story, and the one that has attracted the most comment from reviewers. Mike Ashcroft, for instance, wrote in *Oracle* Volume 2 Number 11 dated August 1979: '[The story] could almost have run as a four-parter, totally cutting out the trip to the alternative universe which was virtually inconsequential to the plot. After all, the Doctor could surely have deduced the fate of the world from other sources nearer at hand – it would have been just as plausible.

'This sojourn into alternative reality was though, funnily enough, just about the most interesting part of the proceedings ... It gave the production team and the writer, Don Houghton, an almost unique chance to parody the UNIT set-up and, indeed, as much of the world as they wanted to, and the changes they made were very much appreciated by this reviewer ... The costume changes and the slight realignment of ranks were well thought out to give a feeling of familiarity, yet with unease mingled in too. For instance, ... the Brigadier [was] transformed effortlessly into the aggressive and tough Brigade Leader while donning an [eye-patch] and a totally new uniform to complement this reformed image. He soon became an object of fear rather than a comforting friend.'

Don Houghton's scripts are extremely well written, and the direction is fantastic throughout – remarkably so, given the difficulties that must have been caused when Douglas Camfield fell ill part-way through production. There are some wonderful touches, such as in the first episode where the infected Harry Slocum raises a wrench to brain someone and the next shot is of a hammer knocking a nail into a wall, neatly conveying a sense of extreme violence without actually showing it. The location work, shot in an oil refinery, is very stark and effective – particularly in the scenes where the Doctor is on the run, being chased by RSF forces and menaced by Primords, after his arrival on the parallel Earth.

'Unlike many of the early Pertwee stories,' wrote Giddings, 'this is one which revolves entirely around the Doctor – he is the man alone, not backed up by UNIT, in fact hunted by them in the guise of the RSF; he is the only one who knows the effects of the drilling and, by Episode 7, the only one remotely concerned with stopping it. He does stop it, of course, but not until the very last moment.

'There are many scenes in the production which create a very tense atmosphere, especially those where the Doctor is being hunted on the high metal walkways. We all know a mutating human is going to spring out, but when will it happen? It is scenes such as this which have given *Doctor Who* its reputation of "behind the sofa" viewing.'

The arrogant and acerbic Stahlman (both versions) is well portrayed by Olaf Pooley and probably the best of the guest characters, although Greg Sutton, played by Derek Newark (who had been caveman Za in *Doctor Who*'s debut story *100,000 BC*), and the slightly underused Sir Keith Gold, played by Christopher Benjamin, are also very good. Petra Williams is rather less impressive, owing mainly to a slightly lacklustre performance by Sheila Dunn (Camfield's wife), but still fulfils her function in the narrative quite adequately.

The only really negative point to be made about the story is that the make-up of some of the Primords is unintentionally rather comical, and that the creatures in general seem rather surplus to requirements – perhaps a reflection of the fact that they had not been part of Houghton's original storyline. 'For better or worse, a staple ingredient of most *Doctor Who* stories is a monster,' noted Geraint Jones in *Doctor Who – An Adventure in Space and Time* in 1985. 'In the case of *Inferno*, I did feel that it was for the worse. The miraculous metamorphosing of humans into hairy, screeching beasts seemed to me to be quite superfluous to the main story, and the problem was compounded by the fact that the make-up used was not as effective it might have been (the only flaw in an otherwise superb production which would have done many a feature film proud).'

These however are mere quibbles; overall, *Inferno* stands as one of the finest stories of the third Doctor's era.

It seemed at one point that *Doctor Who*'s seventh season might be its last. Barry Letts was informed during the course of its production that his BBC superiors were seriously considering cancelling the series and wanted him to come up with a suggestion for a possible replacement. He devised an idea entitled *Snowy Black* concerning the exploits of an innocent Australian cowboy trying to come to terms with city life in London – a forerunner of sorts to the *Crocodile Dundee* films – and even got to the point of lining up an actor, Mark Edwards, to take the title role. Before the first scripts were commissioned, however, *Doctor Who* was finally confirmed for a further season and *Snowy Black* was no longer needed.

Although pleased that the style of *Doctor Who* had shifted away from science-fantasy toward science-fiction, Letts disliked the idea of the series' stories being set almost exclusively on near-contemporary Earth and determined to have the Doctor journeying once more into space and time. Terrance Dicks strongly supported this move, finding himself much more in tune with Letts's ideas than he had been with Peter Bryant's and Derrick Sherwin's. Another element of the seventh season with which both Letts and Dicks had been dissatisfied was Liz Shaw. This was on the basis that the independent, self-confident scientist had little need to rely on the Doctor for explanations and so, in their eyes, failed to fulfil the basic dramatic functions of aiding plot exposition and acting as a point of audience identification. Letts therefore decided against renewing actress Caroline John's contract for a further season and the two men set about devising a new companion for the Doctor. Other changes also lay in store as the series underwent what was, in effect, a further revision of its format for the eighth season.

DOCTOR WHO SEASON EIGHT (1971)

Regular Cast:
Doctor Who (Jon Pertwee)
The Master (Roger Delgado)
Jo Grant (Katy Manning)
Brigadier Lethbridge-Stewart (Nicholas Courtney)

Regular Crew:
Producer: Barry Letts.
Script Editor: Terrance Dicks.
Title Music: Ron Grainer and the BBC Radiophonic Workshop, arranged by Delia Derbyshire.
Special Sounds: Brian Hodgson.

The eighth season was to see *Doctor Who* coming in for renewed criticism from certain quarters – particularly the media, although questions were also asked in the House of Lords – over the level of horror and violence contained in its stories. This was somewhat ironic, given that the previous season had actually been rather more adult in tone and had attracted no such odium. New producer Barry Letts, working closely with script editor Terrance Dicks, was keen to steer the series back more toward its family viewing roots, feeling that under the new format introduced by his predecessors it had become too focused on hard-edged science-fiction and military action at the expense of the lighter, fantasy-based entertainment and warm, identifiable characters that it had featured in the past.

It was with this in mind that the two men introduced in place of Liz Shaw a new companion character – Jo Grant, an impetuous teenager assigned to UNIT (originally planned to be a UNIT lieutenant) as a result of some string pulling by an influential relative – who was much more akin to the old-style companions. They also decided to give the Brigadier a new second-in-command more suited to his status than the relatively lowly Sergeant Benton (who would nevertheless continue as a regular). This was Captain Yates, who was envisaged also as a possible love interest for Jo – although, in the event, little came of this in the transmitted stories. Thus was formed the basis of what would eventually come to be referred to by fans as the 'UNIT family'.

Another, arguably even more significant innovation at this point was the introduction of a new regular villain in the person of the Master – a renegade Time Lord dedicated to evil – whose relationship to the Doctor would be similar to that of Moriarty to Sherlock Holmes. Indeed, so taken were Letts and Dicks with this character that they decided to have him appearing as the Doctor's adversary in all five of the eighth season's stories – an occurrence that was to remain unparalleled in the series' history.

TERROR OF THE AUTONS

Writer: Robert Holmes. **Director:** Barry Letts*. **Designer:** Ian Watson. **Costumes:** Ken Trew. **Make-Up:** Jan Harrison. **Incidental Music:** Dudley Simpson. **Action:** HAVOC. **Visual Effects:** Michealjohn Harris. **Film Cameraman:** John Baker. **Film Editor:** Geoffrey Botterill. **Studio Lighting:** Eric Monk. **Studio Sound:** Colin Dixon. **Production Assistant:** Nicholas John. **Assistant Floor Manager:** Bruce Best. **Circus Sequences by Courtesy of:** Robert Brothers.

* There was no director credit on screen in view of the fact that Barry Letts was the series' producer.

	First UK TX	Scheduled TX	Actual TX	Duration	Viewers	Chart Pos.
Episode One	02/01/71	17.15	17.15	24'56"	7.3	78
Episode Two	09/01/71	17.15	17.15	24'48"	8.0	71
Episode Three	16/01/71	17.15	17.15	23'28"	8.1	58
Episode Four	23/01/71	17.15	17.16	22'10"	8.4	59

Plot: The Master arrives on Earth at a circus run by a man named Rossini and steals a dormant Nestene energy unit from a museum. He reactivates it using a radio telescope and uses his hypnotic abilities to take control of a small plastics firm run by the Farrel family, where he organises the production of deadly Auton dolls, chairs and daffodils. Humanoid Auton dummies distribute the daffodils – designed to spray a suffocating plastic film over their victim's mouth and nose – by giving them away free to members of the public in a fake promotional campaign. The Master plans to activate the flowers with a signal from the radio telescope, which he will then use to bring the main Nestene Consciousness to Earth. The Doctor manages to persuade the Master that the Nestenes will have no further use for him once they arrive. The two Time Lords then work together to send the Consciousness back into space.

Episode endings:
1. Jo Grant, having been hypnotised by the Master, tries to open a metal box that has been brought into the lab at UNIT HQ. The Doctor shouts for someone to stop her – the box is a bomb!
2. The Doctor and Jo are investigating Rossini's circus when they are surrounded by an angry mob of carnival folk. A police car comes to their rescue and they jump in. As they are driven away, a suspicious Doctor attracts the attention of one of the policeman and reaches forward to rip away a plastic face mask, revealing an Auton beneath.
3. The Master, disguised as an engineer, installs in the UNIT lab a new telephone with a lengthy cord. Later, he calls the Doctor from a phone box. When the Doctor answers, the Master uses a signalling device to cause the plastic cord to come alive and start to strangle him.
4. The Doctor reveals that the Master is now trapped on Earth like himself and confesses that he is quite looking forward to him turning up again.

IT WAS MADE WHERE...?

Location Filming: 17.09.70-18.09.70, 21.09.70-23.09.70
Locations: St Peter's Court, Chalfont St Peter, Bucks; car park, Church Lane, Chalfont St Peter, Bucks; Hodgemoor Wood, Nr Chalfont St Giles, Bucks; Queen's Wharf, Queen Caroline Street, Hammersmith, London, W6; Robert Brothers Circus, Lea Bridge Road Playing Fields, Leyton, London, E10; Totternhoe Lime and Stone Quarry, Tottenhoe, Beds; GPO Relay Station, Zouches Farm, nr Caddington, Beds; Thermo Plastics Ltd, Luton Road, Dunstable, Beds.
Studio Recording: 09.10.70-10.10.70 in TC8, 23.10.70-24.10.70 in TC6

ADDITIONAL CREDITED CAST

Captain Mike Yates (Richard Franklin), Sergeant Benton (John Levene[1,2,4]), Rex Farrel (Michael Wisher), McDermott (Harry Towb[1,2]), Time Lord (David Garth[1]), Radio Telescope Director (Frank Mills[1]), Professor Philips (Christopher Burgess[1,2]), Goodge (Andrew Staines[1]), Rossini (John Baskcomb[1,2]), Museum Attendant (Dave Carter[1]), Farrel Senior (Stephen Jack[2]), Mrs. Farrel (Barbara Leake[2,3]), Strong Man (Roy Stewart[2]), Brownrose (Dermot Tuohy[3]), Telephone Mechanic (Norman Stanley[3]), Policeman (Bill McGuirk[3])*, Auton Policeman (Terry Walsh[3])**, Auton Leader (Pat Gorman[3,4]), Auton Voice (Haydn Jones[3,4])

* Although credited on screen, Bill McGuirk did not appear; the material featuring him as the policeman character was cut at the video editing stage.
** Also in Episode Two, but uncredited.
Note: Jon Pertwee was credited as 'Dr. Who' on Episodes Three and Four.

POPULAR MYTHS

- The production team had initially envisioned the new regular villain for the series as a female character, possibly called the Controller, to be played by Susan Jameson. (The role was always envisioned as a male character called the Master, and Roger Delgado was the only actor considered for it.)

THINGS TO WATCH OUT FOR

- The Master's TARDIS is disguised as a horse box.
- The Nestene energy unit in this story is blue, whereas in *Spearhead from Space* they were red.

THINGS YOU MIGHT NOT HAVE KNOWN

- Working title: *The Spray of Death*
- Haydn Jones was originally contracted both to provide the Auton voices and to play the telephone engineer who turns out to be the Master in disguise, but the latter part was recast when Jones was given the more substantial one of Vosper in *The Mind of Evil*.
- In this story, the Doctor reveals that his TARDIS takes a Mark I dematerialisation circuit, whereas the Master's takes a Mark II.
- Bobby Roberts, owner of the Roberts Brothers circus used as the location, makes a cameo appearance leading a line of elephants from the ring. Agreement was reached to use the circus as a location as long as it received an on-screen credit.

- The last line of the story was changed on the suggestion of BBC Head of Serials Ronnie Marsh from 'Until I destroy him, or until he destroys me!' to 'As a matter of fact, Jo, I'm quite looking forward to it.' Marsh felt the original line to be too stark and explicit.
- In Robert Holmes's original outline, both daffodils and troll dolls were distributed to the public and were to be activated by rain. In an undated note to Holmes, the production team noted that they 'just can't swallow the Master's plan depending on notoriously unreliable English weather. Why not go to Morocco?' The note went on to outline, as an alternative, the scenario that is seen in the transmitted story.

QUOTE, UNQUOTE

- **The Master:** 'The human body has a basic weakness. One which I shall exploit to assist in the destruction of humanity.'
- **The Doctor:** 'I sometimes think that military intelligence is a contradiction in terms.'
- **The Master:** 'I have so few worthy opponents. When they're gone I always miss them.'
- **The Master:** 'Death is always more frightening when it strikes invisibly.'
- **Jo Grant:** [Responding to the Doctor's prediction that the Master is bound to turn up again.] 'You don't seem very worried about it, Doctor.' **The Doctor:** 'I'm not, Jo. As a matter of fact, I'm rather looking forward to it.'

ANALYSIS

The eighth season of *Doctor Who* gets off to a strong start with an adventure that sees the return of the Nestenes and their animated plastic mannequins, the Autons, which had been so successful in *Spearhead from Space*. Simon Lydiard, writing in *A Voyage Through 25 Years of Doctor Who* dated December 1988, spotted the only problem with this: 'In almost every respect *Terror of the Autons* was a success, bar one – originality … It is … blindingly obvious that [it] is a thinly disguised rewrite of … *Spearhead from Space*. Nevertheless, it is still terrific entertainment.'

Terror of the Autons is, in fact, not quite as effective as *Spearhead from Space* in depicting the threat of the Autons. They are very much reduced to the role of 'heavies' here, their function being simply to kill, and there are no detailed facsimiles like Channing and Scobie in the earlier story – indeed, at one point the Master actually states that the Nestenes will be sending forces to invade Earth, whereas in *Spearhead from Space* they created them in Hibbert's plastics factory. The Autons in this story also move about silently, whereas in their debut they emitted an eerie buzzing noise that added greatly to their menace. There are however some memorable scenes featuring the Autons, the best being the one at the start of Episode Three in which two Auton policemen attempt to kill the Doctor and Jo in a quarry and one gets knocked down a steep incline by a car driven by Mike Yates; after a very long fall – an excellent piece of stunt work – it simply gets back to its feet and starts climbing up again. This is a powerful statement of how invulnerable these creatures are, and yet the idea is not developed further. Instead, the story concentrates more on introducing the new 'team' that will see *Doctor Who* through the next year of adventures.

Amongst the newcomers the greatest impact is made by the Master. As Roger Delgado was the only actor ever considered for this part, one might say that it was written specifically for him. Whatever the circumstances, he makes it very much his own, giving a performance of great charisma and bringing to life the Doctor's evil nemesis with a degree of success that no-one could have predicted. The Master is charming, sophisticated, silver-tongued, witty and intelligent, yet at the same time cruel, callous and implacably evil. Arguably he is the most interesting character to have been introduced to the series since the Doctor himself. Stephen Haywood's reaction, described in *Capitol Spires* Issue 1 dated spring 1993, was typical: 'The surprise of seeing a horse box materialise *a la* TARDIS is one of my lasting recollections, as is the dark mysterious stranger who turns out to be the Master. For me, this is *the* Master story; Roger Delgado's portrayal is excellent. The Master of *Terror of the Autons* is just that bit more suave, self-confident and, more importantly, restrained [than in] later stories. One really gets the feeling of great evil when watching Delgado ...'

The only less than successful aspect of the way the Master is presented in this story is that, although he has gone to great lengths to plan and bring to fruition the Nestenes' invasion of Earth, it takes barely a single comment from the Doctor to persuade him to change his mind and help to repel them back into space. The suggestion may be that his arrogance sometimes leads him to bite off more than he can chew; or possibly that he has a devil-may-care attitude and will switch allegiance to whichever side seems to be having the most fun. Perhaps, on the other hand, writer Robert Holmes could simply think of no other way in which to resolve the story.

Barry Letts's direction is excellent, although on the technical side a problem looms with the over-enthusiastic use of CSO. The scenes employing this effect look false and strained here, the objects moving about on the blue-screen background having a tell-tale line around them (a problem that would not be eliminated until technical advances were made later in the decade). Paul Cornell, writing in *DWB* No. 112 dated April 1993, disliked this and many other aspects of the story: 'In a show where there's obviously the ability to film exterior shots and cars, we get a CSO car interior. And a CSO wall. And a CSO kitchen. Indeed, the show becomes a comic strip visually at the same time as it does in dramatic terms ... Often, we don't see who's speaking, and the incredible prissiness of not letting us see the Doctor dissect solid plastic ... The mind fails to boggle.'

Aside from the Auton policemen, the most memorable images in the story are those of the carnival-masked Autons that distribute the plastic daffodils, the daffodils themselves and the black plastic chair that engulfs the hapless plastics factory manager McDermott and suffocates him to death. It was these instances of everyday people and objects turning out to be instruments of death that provoked the uproar – perhaps the greatest yet to beset *Doctor Who* – over the series' level of violence. Although simply a continuation of the theme established in *Spearhead from Space* of shop dummies turning out to be killers, this was far nearer to home. Children were supposed to be able to trust a policeman, not be frightened that he might turn out to be a killer Auton in disguise. 'What level of horror is acceptable in a teatime programme?' queried Sylvia Clayton in the *Daily Telegraph* of 18 January 1971. 'The present *Doctor Who* adventure makes this question pertinent by the very effectiveness of its attack on the nerves. These plastic monsters come from within the range of a child's domestic scene. There is a murderous mannequin doll with deadly fangs, a chair which inflates to suffocate the victim, a telephone flex which strangles the caller. Policemen with apparently normal faces whip off their masks [sic] to show a hideous non-face underneath. Small children of my acquaintance have found these devices terrifying in a way fantasy figures such as the

Daleks and the Cybermen were not ... *Doctor Who* is placed at a time when the smallest children will be watching, and adult frissions will be best left to *Doomwatch*.'

'*Terror of the Autons* is perhaps best remembered for precisely that – terror,' wrote Simon Lydiard. 'It contained some of the most frightening moments in the [series'] history up to that point, and possibly beyond. Who can forget McDermott being "swallowed" by the inflatable armchair in Episode Two, or the unmasking of the Auton policeman at the conclusion of that episode? ... In Episode Three, the Doctor opens a safe in Farrel's office to be confronted by an Auton which fires off a shot, just narrowly missing the Brigadier. Most terrifying of all is the concept of the plastic daffodils which spray out a clear plastic film that covers the nose and mouth, thus suffocating the victim.' Chris Dunk, writing in *Oracle* Volume 2 Number 9 dated June 1979, went even further: 'I still think today that this is the most frightening *Doctor Who* story that I have ever seen, and it proved to me beyond a shadow of doubt that danger from "familiar" objects is much more real that something with which one can't associate. Especially to a child.'

Cameron Pritchard summed things up well in *TSV* 28 dated April 1992: 'I think this has to be undoubtedly one of the best stories of the Pertwee era. It is, after all, a very special story, introducing the Master and Jo Grant as well as bringing back the Autons and getting season eight off to a great start.'

I AM THE MASTER . . .

Barry Letts and Terrance Dicks generally cite Sherlock Holmes's great adversary Moriarty as their chief inspiration for the creation of the Master. The fictional concept of the arch-enemy goes back a long way, however, and was well established in many of the genres and sources upon which *Doctor Who* drew in its seventh and eighth seasons. Thus the Master can also be seen as being akin to James Bond's deranged yet brilliant super-criminal adversaries, intent on taking over or destroying the world, and to the various supervillains, each with his or her own special abilities and trademarks, opposed by superheroes such as Batman and Superman. The Master's name is itself evocative of those of similar characters in other series, such as Batman's adversaries (the Joker, the Riddler, the Penguin and so on) and Adam Adamant's recurring foe the Face in *Adam Adamant Lives!*; and it had been used once before in *Doctor Who*, for the controller of the Land of Fiction in season six's *The Mind Robber*. As Letts and Dicks recall, however, their main reason for choosing this name was that, in common with the Doctor's, it corresponded to an academic qualification.

The closest *Doctor Who* antecedent to the Master in terms of character traits can be found in season ten's *The War Games* in the person of the War Chief, an evil renegade Time Lord cynically exploiting his alien 'allies' as part of a scheme to gain power for himself – something that the Master would also attempt in a number of stories. The curious rapport that the Doctor had with the War Chief would also be mirrored in his relationship with the Master; he would actually seem to relish each new encounter with his arch-enemy, admitting at the end of *Terror of the Autons* that he was 'almost looking forward to it'. The closest antecedent in terms of appearance, on the other hand, was the same story's War Lord, with his bearded, saturnine countenance and his plain black suit, complete with Nehru-style high-collared jacket. The hypnotic powers displayed by the War Lord's race, the Aliens, similarly foreshadowed those of the Master.

It was Letts who chose Roger Delgado for the role, having worked with him on a number of occasions during his own earlier career as an actor. 'He was always precisely right,' the producer later reflected, 'always finding that nice balance between smoothness and villainy, which was the hallmark of the Master.'

'I love playing the Master,' Delgado once said. 'He is the man the fans love to hate.'

THE MIND OF EVIL

Writer: Don Houghton. **Director:** Timothy Combe. **Designer:** Ray London. **Costumes:** Bobi Bartlett. **Make-Up:** Jan Harrison. **Incidental Music:** Dudley Simpson. **Action:** HAVOC. **Visual Effects:** Jim Ward. **Film Cameraman:** Fred Hamilton, Max Samett. **Film Editor:** Howard Billingham. **Studio Lighting:** Eric Monk. **Studio Sound:** Chick Anthony. **Production Assistant:** John Griffiths. **Assistant Floor Manager:** Sue Hedden.

	First UK TX	Scheduled TX	Actual TX	Duration	Viewers	Chart Pos.
Episode One	30/01/71	17.15	17.15	24'39"	6.7	61
Episode Two	06/02/71	17.15	17.14	24'31"	8.8	54
Episode Three	13/02/71	17.15	17.15	24'32"	7.5	70
Episode Four	20/02/71	17.15	17.15	24'40"	7.4	63
Episode Five	27/02/71	17.15	17.16	23'34"	7.6	58
Episode Six	06/03/71	17.15	17.15	24'38"	7.3	65

Plot: The Doctor and Jo visit Stangmoor Prison for a demonstration of the Keller Machine – a device claimed to be capable of extracting negative emotions from hardened criminals. The Doctor's scepticism seems valid when a prisoner called Barnham collapses whilst undergoing the treatment. The Brigadier is meanwhile in charge of security at a World Peace Conference, where documents go missing and the Chinese delegate dies in mysterious circumstances. Captain Yates is away on another mission, transporting a banned Thunderbolt missile across country to be destroyed. The Doctor joins the Brigadier at the conference and they foil an attempt by the Chinese delegate's aide, Captain Chin Lee, to kill the American delegate. Lee is under the hypnotic control of the Master – otherwise known as Professor Emil Keller. The Master uses the evil impulses stored within the Keller Machine – actually the container for an alien mind parasite – to cause unrest at Stangmoor. He then enlists the convicts' aid to hijack the Thunderbolt missile, planning to use it to blow up the peace conference and start World War Three. Shielded by Barnham, now immune to the effects of the parasite, the Doctor transports the Keller Machine to a nearby airfield where the missile is being held. Using the Machine to keep the Master occupied, he reconnects the missile's auto-destruct circuit and gets clear just before the Brigadier triggers it. The parasite is presumed destroyed in the resulting explosion, but the Master escapes in a van, running Barnham down in the process.

Episode endings:

1. The Doctor is alone in the process chamber at the prison when the Keller Machine activates. He tries in vain to stop it and reacts in terror as he is engulfed in images of a raging inferno.
2. The American delegate Senator Alcott calls on the Chinese delegate Fu Peng at the latter's apparent request but finds his suite empty. Chin Lee enters the room behind him and instructs him to sit down. He does so, but jumps to his feet again when she turns out the light and a strange pulsing glow illuminates the room. The Senator is horrified as a shimmering image of a dragon appears to menace him.
3. In the process chamber, the Master has Mailer handcuff the Doctor to a chair beside the Keller Machine and then follows him out. The Machine activates and the Doctor reacts in terror as he hears the voice of a Dalek and sees images of many of his old foes.
4. The Keller Machine materialises in the process chamber before the Doctor and Jo. Mailer shoots at it ineffectually and then runs out, leaving the Doctor and Jo to its mercy.
5. UNIT troops are battling the convicts for control of the prison and Mailer releases the Doctor and Jo from the cell in which they have been held, intending to use them as hostages. As they descend a flight of steps, Jo throws herself back against Mailer in order to give the Doctor a chance to escape. This plan backfires, however, and Mailer aims his gun at the Doctor. A shot rings out.
6. The Doctor complains to Jo that while the Master now has a fully operational TARDIS he himself is still stuck on Earth – with the Brigadier.

It Was Made Where...?

Location Filming: 26.10.70-31.10.70, 02.11.70-04.11.70

Locations: Dover Castle, Dover, Kent; Archers Court Road, Whitfield, Kent; Hangar, Alland Garage RAF Manston, Manston, Kent; RAF Swingate, Dover, Kent; Pineham Road, Pineham, Kent; Commonwealth Institute, Kensington High Street, London, W8; Cornwall Gardens, London, SW7.

Studio Recording: 12.10.70 (R/T voices for film), 20.11.70-21.11.70 in TC3, 04.12.70-05.12.70 in TC6, 18.12.70-19.12.70 in TC3

Additional Credited Cast

Captain Mike Yates (Richard Franklin), Captain Chin Lee (Pik-Sen Lim[1-3]), Prison Governor (Raymond Westwell[1-3]), Dr. Summers (Michael Sheard[1-4,6]), Professor Kettering (Simon Lack[1]), Barnham (Neil McCarthy[1-3,5,6]), Corporal Bell (Fernanda Marlowe[1-4]), Linwood (Clive Scott[1]), Chief Prison Officer Powers (Roy Purcell[1-3]), Senior Prison Officer Green (Eric Mason[1-3]), Prison Officers (Bill Matthews[1-4,6], Barry Wade[1-4,6], Dave Carter[1-4,6], Martin Gordon[1-4,6]), Sergeant Benton (John Levene[2-6]), Mailer (William Marlowe[2-5*]), Vosper (Haydn Jones[2-4]), Fu Peng (Kristopher Kum[2,3]), Senator Alcott (Tommy Duggan[2**]), Charlie (David Calderisi[4]), Major Cosworth (Patrick Godfrey[5,6]), Fuller (Johnny Barrs[5]), Main Gate Prisoner (Matthew Walters[5***]).

* Also in Episode Six, in the reprise from Episode Five, but uncredited.
** Also in Episode Three, in the reprise from Episode Two, but uncredited.
*** Also in Episodes Three and Four, but without dialogue and uncredited.

3 THIRD DOCTOR

Note: Jon Pertwee was credited as 'Dr. Who' on this story. Roger Delgado did not appear in, and was not credited on, Episode One.

POPULAR MYTHS

- The Doctor makes a comment in Episode One that suggests he supports capital punishment. (His comment is ironic and suggests precisely the opposite.)

THINGS TO WATCH OUT FOR

- The Master smokes a fat cigar.
- There is an excellent performance as Captain Chin Lee by Pik-Sen Lim, who was the wife of writer Don Houghton.
- This story features the first use of on-screen subtitles in *Doctor Who* (not counting the silent film style caption cards displayed in *The Daleks' Master Plan: The Feast of Steven*) as the Doctor converses with the Chinese delegate Fu Peng in Hokkien.
- The dragon that attacks Senator Alcott was referred to as 'Puff the Magic Dragon' by the unimpressed production crew during the making of the story.
- BBC publicity photographs were used to represent the Doctor's mental impressions of past 'adversaries' in the cliffhanger to Episode Three. Shown passing rapidly over an image of flames (perhaps intended to recall the fiery destruction of the parallel Earth in the season seven story *Inferno*), these depicted, respectively: a Silurian, a Zarbi, Slaar, a War Machine and a Cyberman. The voice of a Dalek is also heard in this sequence.

THINGS YOU MIGHT NOT HAVE KNOWN

- Working titles: *The Pandora Machine*, *Man Hours*, *The Pandora Box*.
- Short-lived UNIT regular Corporal Bell was named Corporal Bates in early drafts of the scripts of this story.
- William Marlowe, who played Mailer in this story, was at the time married to Fernanda Marlowe, who played Corporal Bell. He later married as his second wife Roger Delgado's widow Kismet.
- The mind parasite was made from cooked spaghetti and macaroni liberally covered with green washing up liquid.
- The character of Vosper was named after Marjory Vosper Ltd, Don Houghton's agent.
- After the location filming was complete, the negatives were found to be damaged and so a further location session had to be arranged at a cost of £436.10. Because none of the original actors was available, Tim Coombe and his crew took the parts of the battling UNIT soldiers and prisoners themselves.
- Andy Ho was originally contracted for the part of Fu Peng but was not used. Kristopher Kum was cast as a replacement.

QUOTE, UNQUOTE

- **Professor Kettering:** [Speaking of the Keller Machine.] 'Science has abolished the hangman's noose and substituted this infallible method.' **The Doctor:** 'People who talk about infallibility are usually on very shaky ground.'
- **The Doctor:** 'We believe what our minds tell us to, Jo.'
- **The Doctor:** [To the Brigadier.] 'Do you think for once in your life you could manage to arrive *before* the nick of time!'

The Mind of Evil suffers from the same problem as *The Wheel in Space* in season five: the scheme cooked up by the Doctor's adversary is so convoluted that it seriously lacks credibility. The Master has apparently been posing as Emil Keller for some six months (which – given that his TARDIS is out of action, and assuming that he didn't anticipate the failure of the Nestene Consciousness's invasion attempt – means that at least that amount of time must have elapsed since *Terror of the Autons* ended). In the end, though, the success of his carefully laid plans relies on the very unlikely coincidence of him being able to get his hands on the Thunderbolt missile at exactly the same time that the World Peace Conference is taking place. What would have happened if the transportation of the missile had been delayed by a couple of weeks? Surely not out of the question, given the apparent tactlessness of it being trundled about the country while the Conference is in progress. Perhaps the Master's original intention was to do nothing more than cause havoc with the Keller Machine, and his adoption of the aim of precipitating a Third World War by using the missile to destroy the Conference was simply a piece of opportunism on his part. The story suggests otherwise, however, and he does not even seem to be fully aware of the dangers posed by the creature within the Machine.

The creature's origins are never adequately explained, either, and it gives the impression of having been added to the story merely to provide a token 'monster'. If the Master really had to be seen to recruit a group of convicts as a sort of private army, it would have been just as easy in plot terms to have had him infiltrating the prison and using his hypnotic powers to gain control. His apparent inability to hypnotise the convicts' leader, Mailer, smacks of near desperation on writer Don Houghton's part to explain the need for the Machine's inclusion. 'The alien parasite appeared as a rather inauspicious little thing (something of a cross between Cyclops and the Blob ...),' wrote Philip Ince in *Oracle* Volume 3 Number 1 dated October 1979, 'but, as with the Nestenes, one got the impression that the Master had bitten off more than he could readily chew. I would have preferred a more expanded explanation as to what the parasite actually did rather than the continual "It feeds on the evil of the mind". As far as I could make out, it could lock onto people's thoughts [and] pluck out their greatest fears, which it then turned against them [so that it could] subsequently [feed] on the fear that was generated in the brain.'

What makes all these plot problems seem almost excusable, and in a sense almost irrelevant, is that the action is brought to the screen with such style and panache that the viewer hardly notices them. Director Timothy Combe must therefore take much of the credit for the story's undoubted success. The prison scenes are very well realised, the quite extensive location work is impressive and the cast – regular and guest alike – give excellent performances throughout. In the one instance where the design work falls significantly below par, specifically in the realisation of the illusory dragon that attacks the American delegate, Combe manages largely to disguise the inadequacies of the awful costume through clever camerawork and editing. He is even able to make the Keller Machine an effective menace, despite its uninspiring appearance.

The concept underlying the alien parasite is undeniably a frightening one, and the fact that it develops the ability to teleport, so that no-one knows exactly when or where it is going to appear next, adds greatly to the tension. Also significant factors are the excellent theme and sound effects created for the Machine by, respectively, incidental music

THIRD DOCTOR

composer Dudley Simpson and special sounds maestro Brian Hodgson. These considerably enhance the sense of horrific relentlessness about the Machine's attacks, even though the cliffhanger episode endings tend to be rather samey – repetition being another failing of Houghton's scripts.

Philip Ince considered that all the incidental music and the special sound effects featured in the story were 'outstanding' and attributed this in part to the realisation of Simpson's score on the Radiophonic Workshop's new Delaware synthesiser: 'Dudley Simpson ... by skilful use of a synthesiser ... formed a classic piece that [was] very evidently [amongst] the first of its kind – on television at least. It matched perfectly the effects from the Radiophonic Workshop which enhanced the evil of the Keller Machine by increasing the tempo and volume of its deep, throbbing operational sound. Perhaps the effectiveness of these pieces can also be attributed to their being constantly repeated and linked with horrible death, so that, when [they were] heard, the adrenaline [started] to flow in expectation.'

Ince also had some positive comments to make about the Doctor's new companion: 'Jo Grant's character [had] greatly advanced [by this story], more than Liz's ever did as she had exhausted the possibilities of her portrayal in the first couple of stories and showed no more than a professional interest for the Doctor's welfare. In *Terror of the Autons*, Jo was shown as a rather weak and naïve companion but suddenly she became a warm, caring *person*. [She] adopted the attitude of a loving daughter and, as was seen at the climax of Episodes One and Two where the Doctor [was] attacked by the parasite, it was she who attempted to calm her "master" as a mother might comfort a small child in the grip of a nightmare.'

There are indeed a lot of good elements in this story, but the viewer is left with the nagging suspicion that, with the extraneous plot elements and repetition removed, it might have worked even better in only four episodes.

THE CLAWS OF AXOS

Writer: Bob Baker, Dave Martin. **Director:** Michael Ferguson. **Designer:** Kenneth Sharp. **Costumes:** Barbara Lane. **Make-Up:** Jan Harrison, Rhian Davies. **Incidental Music:** Dudley Simpson. **Action:** HAVOC. **Visual Effects:** John Horton. **Film Cameraman:** A A Englander. **Film Editor:** Bob Rymer. **Studio Lighting:** Ralph Walton. **Studio Sound:** Dave Kitchen. **Production Assistant:** Marion McDougall. **Assistant Floor Manager:** Roselyn Parker.

	First UK TX	Scheduled TX	Actual TX	Duration	Viewers	Chart Pos.
Episode One	13/03/71	17.15	17.16	23'51"	7.3	57
Episode Two	20/03/71	17.15	17.16	24'00"	8.0	43
Episode Three	27/03/71	17.15	17.16	24'05"	6.4	70
Episode Four	03/04/71	17.15	17.16	25'19"	7.8	49

Plot: An approaching alien spaceship is detected on monitoring equipment at UNIT HQ, where the Brigadier is entertaining two visitors – Chinn, a civil servant making a security inspection, and Bill Filer, an American agent sent to discuss the threat of the Master. The ship lands in England and the UNIT team, joined by Hardiman and Winser from the nearby Nuton power station, meet its occupants: beautiful golden-skinned humanoids called Axons. The Axons claim that their ship, Axos, is damaged and that they need time in which to repair it. In return, they offer Axonite, a substance that can cause animals to grow to enormous sizes and thus end food shortages. The Doctor is suspicious, and rightly so: Axos, Axonite and the Axons – whose true appearance is hideous – are all part of a single parasitic entity brought to Earth by the Master to feed on the planet's energy. The Doctor manages to materialise his TARDIS, with the Master on board, at the centre of Axos. He offers to link the two ships together to make one giant time machine, on condition that Axos in return helps him to take revenge on the Time Lords for exiling him to Earth. This is merely a trick, however, and Axos is locked in a time loop from which it can never escape. The Doctor returns to Earth in the TARDIS, where he reluctantly admits to the Brigadier that the Master may also have escaped.

Episode endings:

1. The Doctor, the Brigadier, Chinn, Hardiman and Winser are all being 'entertained' by the Axons. Jo is meanwhile searching elsewhere in Axos for Bill Filer, whose voice she has heard. She screams as from the wall behind her emerges a horrific monster.
2. In the lab at the Nuton complex, the Doctor tells Jo and Filer that Axos, the Axons and Axonite are all part of the same creature. Suddenly tentacled Axon monsters arrive and advance on the Doctor and his friends.
3. The Master, in return for his freedom, is helping UNIT to deal with a potentially catastrophic build up in power being channeled from Nuton's nuclear reactor to Axos. He plans first to store the power in the Doctor's TARDIS and then to boost it into Axos all in one go. The Brigadier is concerned that this could cause the deaths of the Doctor and Jo, who are held prisoner in Axos. The Master however presents a stark choice: either they destroy Axos, or Axos destroys the world. The Brigadier gives the go-ahead and the Master puts his plan into action. In Axos, the Doctor and Jo are buffeted about as they try to escape.
4. The Doctor realises that the Time Lords have programmed the TARDIS so that it will always return to Earth. It seems that he is some kind of galactic yo-yo.

IT WAS MADE WHERE...?

Location Filming: 04.01.71-08.01.71
Locations: Dengemarsh Road, Lydd, Kent; St Martin's Plain Camp, Cheriton High Street, Shorncliffe, Kent; Beach by Dungeness Road, Dungeness, Kent; Dungeness 'A' Nuclear Power Station, Dungeness, Kent.
Studio Recording: 22.01.71-23.01.71 in TC3, 05.02.71-06.02.71 in TC4

ADDITIONAL CREDITED CAST

Captain Mike Yates (Richard Franklin), Sergeant Benton (John Levene), Chinn (Peter Bathurst), Filer (Paul Grist), Hardiman (Donald Hewlett), Winser (David Savile[1,2]), Pigbin Josh (Derek Ware[1]), Axon Man (Bernard Holley), 1st Radar Operator (Michael Walker[1,2]), 2nd Radar Operator (David G. March[1,2]), Corporal Bell (Fernanda Marlowe[1]), Axon Woman (Patricia Gordino[1,2]), Axon Boy (John Hicks[1]), Axon Girl (Debbie Lee London[1]), Captain Harker (Tim Piggot-Smith[2,3]), The Minister (Kenneth Benda[3*]), Technician (Royston Farrell[4]).

* Also in a voice-over telephone conversation in Episode Two, but uncredited.

THINGS TO WATCH OUT FOR

- The interior of the TARDIS is seen for the first time since *The War Games*.
- Distinguished actor Tim Piggot-Smith makes an early television appearance as Captain Harker. He would later appear as Marco, friend to Duke Giuliano, in the season fourteen story *The Masque of Mandragora*.
- *Z Cars* actor Bernard Holley plays the golden lycra-clad Axon Man and the uncredited voice of Axos.

THINGS YOU MIGHT NOT HAVE KNOWN

- Working titles: *The Gift*, *The Friendly Invasion*, *The Axons*, *The Vampire From Space*
- The title of this story was changed at a very late stage to *The Claws of Axos*. The first studio session was recorded using *The Vampire From Space* on the opening title sequences.
- The Axon monsters were made by a freelance contractor named Jules Baker.
- To play the various forms of the Axon creatures, numerous cast and stuntmen were hired. The following artistes were used in the capacities indicated: Globby Axon: Clinton Morris, Douglas Roe; Axon Glob: Douglas Roe, Clive Rogers; Rolling Axon Glob: Eden Fox, Stuart Myers; Axon Men: Roger Minnis, Geoff Righty, Steve King, David Aldridge; Axon Monsters: Marc Boyle, Jack Cooper, Peter Holmes, Clinton Morris, Steve Smart; Double For Axon Man: Nick Hobbs; Stunt Double For Axon Woman: Sue Crosland; Stunt Axons: Steve Emerson, Stuart Fell, Reg Harding, Derek Martin.

QUOTE, UNQUOTE

- **Axos:** 'Axos calling Earth. Fuel systems exhausted. Request immediate assistance ...'
- **Axos:** 'Data confirms space/time travel possible using additional power from complex. You see, Doctor, we can call upon the additional power of the complex whenever we need it.' **The Doctor:** 'How? You can't just walk in there and take it!' **Axos:** 'On the contrary, Doctor. We can.'

ANALYSIS

The Claws of Axos is a story that manages to combine an effective alien menace with some excellent location work to present a seamless tale of invasion by stealth. The scripts by Bob Baker and Dave Martin are original and ambitious and the production manages, for the most part, to achieve their vision.

'It still amazes me that *The Claws of Axos* was Bob Baker and Dave Martin's first televised script,' wrote Simon Lydiard in *A Voyage Through 25 Years of Doctor Who* dated December 1988. 'It was so good. Perhaps the fact that it took a year to write, and numerous rewrites, accounts for it being so well-polished and intelligent. The concept of an organic culture, in which even spaceships are grown, is most interesting, particularly when it turns out that that culture is parasitical.

'*The Claws of Axos* is [also] remarkably well produced, boasting some excellent special effects (and a few awful ones). The dichotomy between the beautiful, golden-skinned Axons and the malevolent orange, tentacled monsters they become is most effective. The slow-motion shots of the tentacled Axons running are almost nightmarish, and when first transmitted seemed quite frightening to me ...

'Despite the obvious merits of this story, there is still one rather irritating flaw. If the Axons held the Master captive originally, why did they need to torture the Doctor to gain the secret of time travel?'

The story opens in much the same way as *Spearhead from Space* and, as spotted by Martin J Wiggins in *Oracle* Volume 3 Number 2 dated November 1979, there are other elements that seem less than original: 'The details of [the Master's] appearance were repetitive. As in *Terror of the Autons*, he brings [a] hungry horde of horrors down to Earth, becomes their slave (an irony, considering what he calls himself), his plan backfires on [him] and he ends up a temporary ally of the Doctor in cleaning up the mess.' On the whole, though, the story is highly imaginative and inventive; indeed, it is fairly brimming over with interesting ideas. One particularly notable aspect is the impression given that nothing is quite what it seems. Axos, apparently a benevolent alien, is really a hostile parasite; the Axons, although initially peaceful and beautiful, turn out to be hideous monsters; the Master, someone we know to be evil, ends up helping UNIT and the Doctor; Chinn, an obnoxious civil servant who tries to keep Axonite for Britain's use alone, turns out to have done exactly the right thing by preventing the parasite from spreading across the world; and finally the Doctor himself, well established as the series' hero, seems to abandon his friends to Axos by escaping in the TARDIS with the Master. All it needed was for Bill Filer to turn out to be a double agent working for the Soviet Union and the picture would have been complete.

The Axons are incredibly powerful creatures. Their abilities include draining energy from just about anything, as the tramp Pigbin Josh discovers to his cost, and transmuting matter to their own ends, as in the scene where they accelerate Jo's ageing process to force the Doctor to cooperate with them. Axos is, in effect, a gestalt being, each part of it able to communicate instantaneously with every other, and is a master of deception. Even the Master cannot get the better of it. There are few other alien races presented by *Doctor Who* that are as well thought-out, adaptable and interesting. Technically, the Axon monsters and Axos itself are very well realised, as indeed is the entire story. Clever use of CSO and the frequent cross-mixing and fading of images give the scenes set in the interior of Axos an almost hallucinogenic quality. The model shots of it in space are superb and, along with the excellent location scenes of it buried in shingle, help to create the impression of a highly credible alien menace. The impact is added to by Dudley Simpson's incidental music and Brian Hodgson's special sound effects, which combine to provide a fitting aural accompaniment to the visual treats.

It should perhaps be acknowledged at this point that there are some fans, albeit in a minority, who greatly dislike the direction in which Barry Letts and Terrance Dicks steered *Doctor Who* in the early seventies. Anthony Brown, for example, had some strong words to offer on this subject when he reviewed *The Claws of Axos* in *DWB* No. 100 dated April 1992: '*The Claws of Axos* epitomises everything Barry Letts ever did wrong when he got control of *Doctor Who*. Though it's customary to refer to the Letts, UNIT and Pertwee eras as if they were one and the same, they weren't. Throughout the seventh season, even after Barry Letts took over responsibility for the mechanics of production on *Doctor Who* (at which he excelled), the creative impetus behind the series remained that of Derrick Sherwin and Douglas Camfield [sic]. It wasn't until *Terror of*

THIRD DOCTOR

3

the Autons that Barry Letts put his stamp on the series, introducing a number of elements which turned the superb, adult science-fiction drama of the previous year back into a shallow 'family' adventure. The fascinating barbed relationship between the Doctor and the Brigadier was converted into the sort of "I insult him, but I love him really" relationship which makes cliché cop shows so nauseating. UNIT, until now a vaguely menacing international taskforce, became a boys' drinking club and, in a prime example of Letts' parochialism, was brought back into the fold of the British Army.'

Brown went on to criticise Pertwee's 'lovable uncle persona' and the dropping of Liz Shaw – 'perhaps the most promising companion since Barbara' – in favour of the 'incompetent' Jo Grant: 'As a character, she was made bearable only by the cuteness of Katy Manning.' Brown's summation of *The Claws of Axos* was damning: 'The problem is simply that *The Claws of Axos* is the last of the transitional serials. In basic content and setting, it belongs to the seventh season, and that means that – when it's produced in the Letts style – it shows all the inadequacies of that style.'

This, though, is a rather cynical view. In fact, particularly when viewed in context as a product of early seventies pop culture, *The Claws of Axos* stands up very well indeed. Such failings as it does exhibit are relatively inconsequential production and plotting glitches. The omission of a CSO background as Benton drives a land rover through rampaging Axon monsters, for example, makes the scene in question look very false, and the Doctor's casual appropriation of a nuclear reactor with which to run tests on Axonite seems somewhat unbelievable – especially as it has been said that the reactor supplies electricity to most of Southern England.

Whatever view one takes of it, *The Claws of Axos* encompasses all the Pertwee era's best-remembered elements – scary monsters, a near-contemporary Earth setting, UNIT, the Master, Jo and of course the third Doctor himself – and fairly typifies Barry Letts' time as producer.

COLONY IN SPACE

Writer: Malcolm Hulke. **Director:** Michael Briant. **Designer:** Tim Gleeson. **Costumes:** Michael Burdle. **Make-Up:** Jan Harrison. **Incidental Music:** Dudley Simpson. **Visual Effects:** Bernard Wilkie. **Film Cameraman:** Peter Hall. **Film Editor:** William Symon. **Studio Lighting:** Ralph Walton. **Studio Sound:** David Hughes, Tony Millier. **Production Assistant:** Nicholas John. **Assistant Floor Manager:** Graeme Harper.

	First UK TX	Scheduled TX	Actual TX	Duration	Viewers	Chart Pos.
Episode One	10/04/71	18.10	18.12	24'19"	7.6	41
Episode Two	17/04/71	18.10	18.13	22'43"	8.5	28
Episode Three	24/04/71	18.10	18.14	23'47"	9.5	26
Episode Four	01/05/71	18.10	18.12	24'20"	8.1	28
Episode Five	08/05/71	18.10	18.13	25'22"	8.8	23
Episode Six	15/05/71	18.10	18.12	25'22"	8.7	23

Plot: The Time Lords discover that the Master has stolen their secret file on the Doomsday Weapon and decide to send the Doctor to retrieve it for them. The TARDIS takes the Doctor and Jo to the desolate planet Uxarieus in the year 2472. There they become involved in a dispute between some beleaguered colonists and the crew of an Interplanetary Mining Corporation (IMC) spaceship over the ownership rights to the planet. The Doctor learns that the indigenous Primitives and their High Priests worship a large machine tended by a creature called the Guardian. The Master meanwhile arrives in the guise of an Adjudicator sent from Earth to decide the fate of the planet. He forces the Doctor to take him to the Primitives' underground city, where they learn that the machine is in fact the Doomsday Weapon, capable of destroying entire planets. Its radiation emissions have brought about the decline of the Guardian's race and are also responsible for the crop failures that the colonists have been experiencing. The Doctor persuades the Guardian to destroy the Weapon rather than let it fall into the Master's hands. The two Time Lords get clear just in time as the machine explodes, and the Master then escapes in his TARDIS. The colonists, meanwhile, attack the IMC men and force them to surrender.

Episode endings:
1. The Doctor, investigating the colonist Leeson's dome, is menaced by a robot.
2. The Doctor, investigating the colonist Leeson's dome, is again menaced by the IMC's mining robot, which is now directed by the security chief Morgan and wields a pair of vicious claws at the ends of its arms.
3. The Primitives drag Jo into their city through a door that swings open in a rock face.
4. A gun battle breaks out between the colonists and the IMC men. The Master tells the Doctor and Jo that they are both about to become the victims of 'stray bullets' and aims a gun at them ...
5. The Master sees on a hand-held scanner device that Morgan and the IMC scientist Caldwell are about to rescue Jo from his TARDIS, where she is held prisoner in a sealed transparent tube. He prepares to press the button on the front of the device that will cause the tube to be flooded with poison gas ...
6. The TARDIS materialises back in the UNIT lab, where the Doctor and Jo find the Brigadier waiting for them. The Doctor tells Jo that they have arrived back only seconds after they left. The Brigadier is confused, but the Doctor cautions Jo not to try to explain – he would never understand.

IT WAS MADE WHERE...?
Location Filming: 10.02.71-12.02.71, 15.02.71, 16.02.71
Location: The Old Baal Clay Pit, Carclaze, St Austell, Cornwall.
Studio Recording: 05.03.71-06.03.71 in TC4, 19.03.71-20.03.71, 02.04.71-03.04.71 all in TC3

ADDITIONAL CREDITED CAST
Winton (Nicholas Pennell), Ashe (John Ringham), Leeson (David Webb[1]), Jane Leeson (Sheila Grant[1]), Norton (Roy Skelton[1-4]), Mary Ashe (Helen Worth), Martin (John Line[1]), Mrs. Martin (Mitzi Webster[1]), Primitive and Voice[1,2]/Primitive[4,6] (Pat Gorman[1,2,4,6]), Robot (John Scott Martin[1-3]), Time Lords (Peter Forbes-Robertson[1], John Baker[1], Graham Leaman[1]), Caldwell (Bernard Kay[2-6]), Dent

(Morris Perry[2-6]), Morgan (Tony Caunter[2-6]), Holden (John Herrington[2]), Allen (Stanley McGeagh[3]), Long (Pat Gorman[3]), Alec Leeson (John Tordoff[4]), Guardian (Norman Atkyns[4,6]), Alien Priest (Roy Heymann[4,6]), Colonist (Pat Gorman[5]).

Note: Although Pat Gorman was credited as providing a 'Voice' for Episodes One and Two – specifically, that heard accompanying a propaganda film watched by the Doctor on the IMC spaceship – it was apparently director Michael Briant who actually spoke this commentary. Roger Delgado did not appear in, and is not credited on, the first three episodes of this story. For the remainder he was credited as 'Master' rather than 'The Master'. Nicholas Courtney did not appear in, and is not credited on, Episodes Two to Five inclusive.

POPULAR MYTHS

- The main action of this story takes place on the planet Exarius. (The name given to the planet in Malcolm Hulke's script for Episode One is Uxarieus.)

THINGS TO WATCH OUT FOR

- The TARDIS materialises and dematerialises instantaneously, rather than fading in and out as usual.
- Mary Ashe is played by Helen Worth, now best known for her long-standing role in *Coronation Street.*
- The Master's TARDIS is now disguised as the Adjudicator's spaceship and its interior is seen for the first time (barring a tight shot of one wall seen on a screen in *Terror of the Autons*).

THINGS YOU MIGHT NOT HAVE KNOWN

- Working title: *Colony*
- The colonists had left Earth in the year 2471 and the date of the Doctor's arrival is 2 March 2472.
- Director Michael Briant had originally cast Susan Jameson as the vicious and sadistic Morgan, but this decision was overrruled by Ronnie Marsh, the BBC's Head of Serials, as he felt that casting a woman in that role would not be suitable for a family audience.
- The buggies used for transport by IMC were Haflinger Cross Country vehicles supplied by Steyr-Daimler-Pach (Gt Britain) Ltd and were returned in a damaged state costing the BBC £74.40 in repairs.
- The mining robot was built by an outside contractor, Magna Models, for £450. It was damaged by being left out in the rain overnight and cost £60.70 to repair. It was found that the paint was lifting and that the plywood broke on handling. This was not considered to be 'fair wear and tear' by Peter Wigzell, the BBC's Studio Operations Manager. Jack Kine, the head of Visual Effects, backed up his request for the money to come from other than the Effects Department budget.

QUOTE, UNQUOTE

- **The Doctor:** 'I am every kind of scientist.'
- **Captain Dent:** 'All colonists are eccentric. That's why they're colonists.'
- **The Master:** 'One must rule or serve. That is the basic law of life. Why do you

hesitate? Surely it's not loyalty to the Time Lords, who exiled you to one insignificant planet?' **The Doctor:** 'You'll never understand. I want to see the universe, not to rule it.'

Like season six's *The Space Pirates*, *Colony in Space* can be seen as a reworking of certain elements of the Western genre in an outer space setting. This is most apparent in the conflict between the simple but good-hearted settlers (or colonists), eking out a poor living from a hostile landscape, and the unprincipled mining company (IMC) trying to cheat them out of their rightful land allocation. The spear-wielding Primitives are the science-fiction equivalent of Red Indians, while the Master takes on the role of the local lawman who has to adjudicate between the competing interests.

'This classic *Doctor Who* story is well remembered for being the third Doctor's first adventure away from Earth,' noted Gordon Roxburgh in *Matrix* Issue 8 dated May 1981, 'and unfortunately that's its only redeeming factor in the eyes of many people. *Colony in Space* is undoubtedly one of the best written stories of the Pertwee era. I cannot think of any other serial which flows so smoothly along without boring the viewer. Malcolm Hulke was indeed a master at writing the longer stories, but like *Doctor Who and the Silurians* [this one] tends to be underrated when compared with other stories in the same season ([particularly] *The Dæmons*).'

Roxburgh is not the only commentator to have expressed such a positive view of the story. Chris Dunk, for example, writing in *Oracle* Volume 3 Number 3 dated December 1979, described it as 'an epic saga with so very much to commend it to the *Doctor Who* fan at various different levels'. The problem with this assessment is that, although the story is indeed refreshing in its setting and contains some interesting ideas and well-drawn characters, it is distinctly short on visual interest and dramatic incident and consequently comes across as being rather dull and lifeless. Attempting to defend it against such criticisms, Dunk argued that it 'was nowhere near as dull as the landscape' and indeed 'pulsated with excitement', and went on to suggest that 'one of the most interesting things about it was the great number of differing factions involved, leading to confrontations galore, cloak and dagger espionage and general thrills 'n spills.' This, however, overstates the story's appeal. Such action as there is tends to be of the 'cowboys and Indians' variety – the colonists use rifles, as in a Western, and there is an (admittedly superb) fist fight in the final episode between the colonist Winton and the IMC security man Rogers (played by stuntman Terry Walsh) that involves them both getting covered in slurry in a watery area of the clay pit location used for the story. The most exciting moment in the entire six episodes is probably the revelation of the Master in the guise of the Adjudicator from Earth, but even this has less impact than it might have done, owing to the predictability of his arrival (this having been telegraphed in the very first scene of the opening episode).

Another flaw in the story is that the history of Uxarieus's indigenous civilisation, although interesting in itself and well presented, is revealed almost entirely through the Doctor's own deductions. The Primitives and their High Priests could hardly be described as characters in their own right – unlike, say, the Silurians in Malcolm Hulke's previous credited contribution to the series – and even the Guardian, incidentally the most poorly realised of all the aliens on show here, makes only brief appearances to

THIRD DOCTOR 3

deliver pronouncements from on high.

All in all, *Colony in Space* was a rather unfortunate choice of story for the third Doctor's initial foray away from Earth. 'Although [it] is by no means a bad story,' agreed Paul Mount in *Doctor Who – An Adventure in Space and Time* in 1985, 'it somehow seems a shame that something a little more unusual and out-of-the-ordinary couldn't have been created for such an auspicious event.'

We will leave the last word, though, to the enthusiastic Gordon Roxburgh: 'So many scenes stand out in this story: for example, Jo and Winton imprisoned in the Primitives' shelter chained to a bomb; the fight in the colonists' dome; the Doctor and Jo listening in to the conversation [between the colonists' leader] Ashe and the Master (with tumblers and all); and scenes in the Master's TARDIS ... As usual in Malcolm Hulke's stories there is [an] underlying moral message. In *Colony is Space* it is pretty well disguised; but hints of pollution on Earth, and this being the entire [reason] why the colonists left Earth in the first place, are well brought over ... The story is a masterpiece [and] still one of my [favourites] ... The whole thing was neatly tied up – even to the end with the TARDIS arriving just a few seconds after it [had] left Earth, with the Brigadier totally unaware of the incredible adventure that the Doctor and Jo had [gone] through.'

THE DÆMONS

Writer: Guy Leopold*. **Director:** Christopher Barry. **Designer:** Roger Ford. **Costumes:** Barbara Lane. **Make-Up:** Jan Harrison. **Incidental Music:** Dudley Simpson. **Fight Arranger:** Peter Diamond. **Visual Effects:** Peter Day. **Film Cameraman:** Fred Hamilton. **Film Editor:** Chris Wimble. **Studio Lighting:** Tony Millier. **Studio Sound:** Ralph Walton. **Production Assistant:** Peter Grimwade. **Assistant Floor Manager:** Sue Hedden.

* This was a pseudonym for Robert Sloman and Barry Letts.

	First UK TX	Scheduled TX	Actual TX	Duration	Viewers	Chart Pos.
Episode One	22/05/71	18.15	18.17	25'05"	9.2	26
Episode Two	29/05/71	18.10	18.11	24'20"	8.0	23
Episode Three	05/06/71	18.10	18.11	24'27"	8.1	34
Episode Four	12/06/71	18.10	18.11	24'25"	8.1	24
Episode Five	19/06/71	18.10	18.11	24'04"	8.3	17

Plot: The Doctor becomes alarmed on seeing a television report of an archaeological dig by a Professor Horner into an ancient barrow near the village of Devil's End. He hurries to the scene with Jo. The Master is posing as the local vicar, Mr Magister, and using black magic rituals to summon Azal, the last of a race known as the Dæmons, whose miniaturised spaceship is buried within the barrow. Benton and Yates arrive in a UNIT helicopter but, before the Brigadier and his troops can join them, a heat barrier appears and cuts the village off from the outside world. Azal will appear three times and on the last of these occasions will decide whether to transfer his awesome powers to another or to destroy the planet as a failed experiment. The

Master hopes to be the recipient of the powers, but in the event Azal offers them to the Doctor instead. The Doctor declines, arguing that the human race should be allowed to develop at its own pace. Azal decides to kill him, but Jo then offers to take his place and, unable to comprehend this act of self-sacrifice, the Dæmon self destructs. The Master is finally captured by UNIT and taken away to await trial for his crimes against humanity.

Episode endings:
1. The Doctor and Jo arrive at the site of the dig at the stroke of midnight, just as Professor Horner breaks through a stone wall that he has uncovered. A freezing wind blasts through the hole, apparently killing both Horner and the Doctor.
2. The Doctor and Jo enter the barrow to investigate further. They find what looks like a model spaceship but the Doctor explains that it is a real ship that has been miniaturised. Suddenly, a gargoyle-like creature sent by the Master attacks them.
3. In a cavern beneath the village church, the Master summons Azal the Dæmon. There is what appears to be a minor earthquake and the Master falls back, urging the Dæmon to obey him.
4. The Master summons Azal once more, this time in a black magic ceremony involving his full coven of acolytes. Jo, who has been watching from hiding, sees him preparing to sacrifice a chicken and rushes out to try to stop him. It is too late as Azal materialises and grows to giant size before her eyes.
5. Azal's death results in a huge explosion that destroys the church. The Master is then captured by UNIT troops and driven away. As Devil's End starts to return to normal, the Doctor, Jo and Benton join the local white witch Miss Hawthorne in a dance around the maypole while the Brigadier and Yates retire to the pub for a drink.

IT WAS MADE WHERE...?

Location Filming: 19.04.71-24.04.71, 26.04.71-30.04.71
Locations: Aldbourne, Wiltshire; 'The Four Barrows', nr. Aldbourne, Wilts; Cambell Aircraft Company, Membury Airfield, Membury, Wilts; crossroads adjacent to Airfield; lane by Oaken Coppice, Knighton, Wilts; Old Airfield by Darrells Farm, Nr. Ramsbury, Wilts. Studio Recording: 11.05.71, 19.05.71 in TC4, 26.05.71 in TC3

ADDITIONAL CREDITED CAST

Captain Mike Yates (Richard Franklin), Sergeant Benton (John Levene), Miss Hawthorne (Damaris Hayman), Bert the Landlord (Don McKillop), Winstanley (Rollo Gamble[1-3]), Prof. Horner (Robin Wentworth[1]), Alastair Fergus (David Simeon[1]), Harry (James Snell[1,2]), Garvin (John Joyce[1,2]), Dr. Reeves (Eric Hillyard[1-3]), Tom Girton (Jon Croft[1-3]), PC Groom (Christopher Wray[1,2]), Baker's Man (Gerald Taylor[2]), Bok (Stanley Mason[2,3,5]), Sgt. Osgood (Alec Linstead[3-5]), Thorpe (John Owens[3-5]), Azal (Stephen Thorne[4,5]), Morris Dancers (The Headington Quarry Men[4]), Jones (Matthew Corbett[5]).

POPULAR MYTHS

- There was originally a sixth episode. (This was an April Fool's joke in the fanzine *DWB*.)
- A helicopter was destroyed during the making of this story. (Although a helicopter is seen to explode as it hits the heat barrier, this was actually a piece of footage taken from the James Bond film *From Russia With Love*.)

- The original intention was that Michael Kilgarriff, seen previously in the series as the Cyberman Controller in *The Tomb of the Cybermen*, would play Azal on screen and that Stephen Thorne would provide only his voice. (The original intention was that Thorne would play Azal on screen and vocal artist Anthony Jackson would provide his voice. In the end, Thorne both played and voiced the character.)
- Jo Grant's own clothes are left behind in the cavern when she escapes dressed in a sacrificial tabard just before the church explodes, and yet she is seen wearing them again at the end of the story. (Jo is clearly seen carrying her clothes under her arm when she escapes from the church.)

THINGS TO WATCH OUT FOR

- Part of the Master's incantation to summon Azal is based on the nursery rhyme 'Mary Had A Little Lamb' spoken backwards.
- The area under the church is always referred to as 'the cavern' and never 'the crypt'. This was a BBC requirement to avoid the risk of causing offence to viewers with religious sensibilities. Similarly, much to director Christopher Barry's amazement, no mention of God was permitted to be made in the story's dialogue, although references to the Devil were acceptable.
- Azal at one point implies that his race were responsible for the destruction of Atlantis (apparently at odds with events seen in *The Underwater Menace*).
- Matthew Corbett, whose father Harry created and operated the popular children's puppet character Sooty and eventually sold the rights to him, appears as one of the Master's devil-worshipping acolytes in Episode Five. He was a late addition to the cast, replacing Bill Wiesener.

THINGS YOU MIGHT NOT HAVE KNOWN

- Working title: *The Demons*
- The script for *The Dæmons* was inspired by an audition piece written by Barry Letts when casting the role of Jo Grant.
- The barrow was originally to have been called the Devil's Dyke.
- A genuine troupe of Morris Dancers, the Headington Quarry Men, was hired for the location filming.
- The helicopter used on location was hired from Gregory Air Services at Denham Aerodrome.

QUOTE, UNQUOTE

- **Miss Hawthorne:** [To the Master in the guise of Mr. Magister.] 'A rationalist, existentialist priest indeed!'
- **Captain Mike Yates:** 'I see. So all we've got to deal with is something which is either too small to see or thirty feet tall, can incinerate you or freeze you to death, turn stone images into homicidal monsters and looks like the devil.' **The Doctor:** 'Exactly.'
- **Brigadier Lethbridge-Stewart:** 'Jenkins … chap with wings, there. Five rounds rapid.'
- **Azal:** [To the Master.] 'Take care, creature. With your few pitiful grains of knowledge, you have summoned me here. But I am not your slave, and you are not immortal!'

ANALYSIS

The Dæmons is often cited, by those who worked on it and reviewers alike, as the best of the third Doctor's stories, and it is easy to see how this view has arisen. Like *The Claws of Axos*, it encapsulates all the era's most well-remembered aspects – such as the UNIT 'family' and the Master – in a story with an interesting background, including in this case black magic rituals and an archaeological dig, and some scary 'monsters'. The production too is excellent, boasting some extensive and impressive location filming in the Wiltshire village of Aldbourne, and Christopher Barry's direction is well up to scratch. As J Jeremy Bentham wrote in *Oracle* Volume 3 Number 4 dated January 1980, 'Every so often … a story comes along with the capacity to stun the viewer with the sheer excellence of its presentation, and for me *The Dæmons* was such a story.'

Admittedly the plot is not the most groundbreaking to have been presented in the series. The 'clandestine witchcraft in an English village' story is, indeed, almost a staple ingredient of television action-adventure series, and there are echoes of Nigel Kneale's 1958/59 serial *Quatermass and the Pit*. The idea of a village cut off by an impenetrable dome-shaped barrier had previously been used in John Wyndham's *The Midwich Cuckoos* and, although it is at least handled with a degree of originality here, the rationale for its inclusion is less than clear. It would suggest that Azal feels the need to protect himself, but why? He is, after all, immensely powerful, can kill at a glance, and intends either to pass on his power or to destroy the Earth. Hardly the sort of creature that needs to hide himself away.

On the subject of Azal, it must be acknowledged that his on-screen realisation is one of the weaker aspects of the production, being achieved via the wonders of CSO. As Bentham pointed out: 'This serial perfectly emphasised the value of keeping the principal creature hidden from the viewing public until the last possible moment. That way millions of minds were at work trying to visualise Azal long before his emergence at the end of Episode [Four].'

The story's underlying theme, that of science versus magic, is established early in the first episode in a nice scene where the Doctor demonstrates to Jo and Captain Yates that something should never be assumed to be 'magic' just because the explanation for it is not immediately apparent. It is then explored throughout the remainder of the five episodes (an unusual but effective story length), in which the viewer learns that many of the magical traditions and images are in fact a product of the Dæmons' secret 'psionic science'. The fact that this scientific basis for magic was never developed further in later stories is surprising – one can certainly imagine the Master finding many uses for it. It is a fascinating idea and allows for the presentation of many elements (or should that be elementals?) that would otherwise be beyond the bounds of credibility. A nice example is the stone gargoyle Bok that comes to life (although whether as a result of the Master's rituals or simply as a side effect of Azal's appearance is never made clear) and even flies. Another is the Dæmon's ability to shrink or grow at will – and the fact that such changes are accompanied by a rush of energy shows that the writers have, commendably, given some consideration to the physics involved. The point is perhaps stretched a little too far, however, in the suggestion that the Dæmons are able also to miniaturise their own spaceships, as this immediately raises the question why they do not simply build small spaceships in the first place, achieving considerable savings in energy and raw materials, and then adjust their own size to fit.

The story's guest characters are all well written and acted. The short-lived Professor

Horner is a joy to watch as he puts down the pushy television reporter Alastair Fergus. Miss Hawthorne is very memorable as well, and Damaris Hayman is perfectly cast in the role, her engaging performance adding much to the story. The regulars too are generally very well served. It is nice to see Yates and Benton in 'civvies' for once; the Brigadier gets some good action and dialogue; and the Master is the epitome of evil charm, looking wonderful both when posing as Mr. Magister in his vicar's garb – complete with dog collar – and later when leading the coven in his scarlet ceremonial robes. 'The Master, alias Mr. Magister, was used remarkably well,' agreed Alan Early, writing in *Ark in Space* No.7 dated May 1983, 'and this was no mean feat considering that it was the fifth consecutive story the character had appeared in. Delgado was in top form, and it was at about this time that the … Master threatened [to rival] the popularity of the [Doctor]. I can think of no other villain in *Doctor Who* who merited a cliffhanger ending when his life was threatened.'

Given that *The Dæmons* is so archetypal of Barry Letts' period as producer, it is no surprise that the minority of fans who greatly dislike the approach that he brought to the series have, contrary to the general reaction, been vociferously critical of it. Perhaps the most scathing review of all was by Chris Newbold in *Perigosto Stick* Issue Two dated August 1991: 'It is my considered opinion, as someone who has seen almost all the *Doctor Who* stories it is possible to see, that *The Dæmons* is without doubt one of the worst. I say that in full possession of the knowledge that it is thought of as an example of the very best of *Doctor Who*, an "all-time classic". Naturally I find it hard to see how this view can possibly have come about, unless it is part of a more general belief that the Pertwee years represent *Doctor Who* at its best. I do not subscribe to such a view.'

Newbold's criticisms were wide ranging. He disliked the story's opening, disapproved of the use of pseudo-science to overcome the heat barrier and took issue with the general handling of the science-versus-magic theme. His major problem, however, was with the Doctor himself: 'The story … succeeds in emphasising all that is bad about the third Doctor's character. In the "with horns" scene in Episode Three he behaves like the archetypal bad parent – intolerant, patriarchal, inconsistent in attitude and impossible to please. He is a patronising know-it-all who deliberately gives either ambiguous or oversimplified explanations, expects everyone to know what he is talking about and snaps at them if they don't. Obviously these "nuances" to his character are intended to convey his irritation at being exiled on a planet of "primitives", but their result is to render him utterly unlikeable. Jo is the principal target of his annoyance and, by the end of the aforementioned scene, it is hard to discern quite why she should hold so much affection for the man. His irritation at her difficulty in understanding his explanation of recent changes in the mass of the Dæmon spaceship (this is hardly surprising when all she has to work on is explanations such as "$e=mc?!$") is made all the more unreasonable by the fact that she, like some rejected daughter, is trying so hard to please him. Later in the scene she even mimics his usual attitude toward the Brigadier in an effort to gain his acceptance. This fails and [he] simply retorts: "Jo, the Brigadier is doing his best to cope with an almost impossible situation, and since he is your superior officer, you might at least show him a little respect". The bastard.'

It is difficult to disagree with many of Newbold's observations, and it has to be admitted that – surprisingly, given that Letts was one of the writers – the characterisation of the third Doctor in this story is rather odd. Perhaps the most cringe-inducing moment comes in the fifth episode, with his monumentally inappropriate description of Hitler as a 'bounder'. To focus exclusively on these aspects of his character, however, while ignoring his undeniable charm and charisma, and the compassion and kindness he often shows to the weak and oppressed, is to present only half the picture.

The Dæmons may not be perfect, but it has earned its place as one of the most widely admired and acclaimed adventures of the Pertwee era.

Season eight can be seen as having provided a template for the remainder of the third Doctor's era. Barry Letts and Terrance Dicks had succeeded in their aim of taking *Doctor Who* back into family viewing territory, and the gritty realism of the previous year's stories had consequently given way to a lighter, more fantasy-based style. UNIT continued to constitute an important element in the format, but characterisation and humour now took precedence over military hardware and action set-pieces. There had also been established a group of reassuringly familiar regular characters – the Doctor, the Master, the Brigadier, Jo, Yates and Benton – and the actors who portrayed them had bonded together into a highly effective team, their affection and respect for each other clearly evident from the transmitted episodes. All these developments would be carried forward and built upon in the seasons that followed.

THIRD DOCTOR

DOCTOR WHO SEASON NINE (1972)

Regular Cast:
Doctor Who (Jon Pertwee)
Jo Grant (Katy Manning)

Regular Crew:
Producer: Barry Letts.
Script Editor: Terrance Dicks.
Title Music: Ron Grainer and the BBC Radiophonic Workshop, arranged by Delia Derbyshire.
Special Sounds: Brian Hodgson except on *The Mutants* and *The Time Monster*. Dick Mills on *The Mutants* and *The Time Monster*.

Season nine saw no changes taking place amongst either the production team or the regular cast of *Doctor Who* – the first time this had happened since season one. It was also very similar to the previous season in terms of style and content (although it did have an extra episode overall, which allowed for it to be subdivided into two four-part stories and three six-part stories – a pattern that would be repeated for the remainder of Jon Pertwee's time as the Doctor). The most significant change was that the Master was featured in only two of the stories, rather than in all of them as had been the case the year before. This left the way clear for the Doctor to be faced with a wider variety of adversaries – including a number making return appearances from earlier periods of the series' history. The first story, indeed, would see him coming up against the most popular monster creations of all …

DAY OF THE DALEKS

Writer: Louis Marks. **Director:** Paul Bernard. **Designer:** David Myerscough-Jones. **Costumes:** Mary Husband. **Make-Up:** Heather Stewart. **Incidental Music:** Dudley Simpson. **Fight Arranger:** Rick Lester. **Visual Effects:** Jim Ward. **Film Cameraman:** Fred Hamilton. **Film Editor:** Dan Rae. **Studio Lighting:** Alan Horne. **Studio Sound:** Tony Millier. **Production Assistant:** Norman Stewart. **Assistant Floor Manager:** Sue Hedden. **Daleks Originated By:** Terry Nation*.

* Terry Nation received this credit as joint owner with the BBC of the rights to the Daleks.

	First UK TX	Scheduled TX	Actual TX	Duration	Viewers	Chart Pos.
Episode One	01/01/72	17.50	17.53	23'36"	9.8	38
Episode Two	08/01/72	17.50	17.53	23'52"	10.4	29
Episode Three	15/01/72	17.50	17.52	24'18"	9.1	38
Episode Four	22/01/72	17.50	17.52	24'17"	9.1	40

Plot: Sir Reginald Styles, organiser of a world peace conference, narrowly survives an assassination attempt by a combat-uniformed guerrilla who vanishes like a ghost. Later the guerrilla is attacked by huge, ape-like creatures called Ogrons and found unconscious by UNIT troops in the grounds of the house. The Doctor deduces that he comes from about two hundred years in the future and that a device found with him is a time machine. While Styles is away, the Doctor and Jo keep watch. The guerrillas attack again, but the Time Lord convinces them that he is not Styles. One of their party, Shura, is later injured by an Ogron. Jo meanwhile accidentally activates one of the guerrillas' time machines and is transported to the 22nd Century. When the guerrillas return there, the Doctor goes with them. He learns that the Earth of this period is ruled by the Daleks with the help of the Ogrons and human collaborators, whose leader is known as the Controller. Jo and the Doctor are both taken prisoner at the Dalek base. The guerrillas rescue them and explain that they are attempting to kill Styles because he caused an explosion at the peace conference, starting a series of wars that left humanity vulnerable to Dalek conquest – a history that they wish to change. The Doctor realises that the explosion was actually caused by Shura in a misguided attempt to fulfil his mission. Returning to the 20th Century with Jo, he has Styles' house evacuated. Daleks and Ogrons arrive in pursuit, but are destroyed when Shura detonates his bomb.

Episode endings:
1. The Controller reports to his Dalek masters that a time transmitter has been detected operating in the 20th Century and that the coordinates are being fixed. He is told that whoever is operating it is an enemy of the Daleks and must be destroyed. The three Daleks take up a chant of 'Exterminate them!'
2. The Doctor follows the guerrillas into a disused railway tunnel that acts as their arrival point in the 20th Century. The menacing form of a Dalek materialises nearby.
3. The Doctor is lying strapped to a table attached to a mind analysis device as the Daleks attempt to confirm his identity. Images of his two previous incarnations appear on a screen and the Daleks triumphantly shriek that he is the Doctor and an enemy of the Daleks who will be exterminated.
4. The Doctor urges Sir Reginald Styles to make sure that his peace conference is a success. Sir Reginald tells him not to worry as everyone knows what will happen if it fails. The Doctor confirms that he and Jo know too: they have seen it.

IT WAS MADE WHERE...?

Location Filming: 13.09.71-16.09.71
Locations: Dropmore Park, Burnham, Bucks; Harvey House, Green Dragon Lane, Brentford, Middx; Bull's Bridge, Hayes, Middx.
Studio Recording: 04.10.71-05.10.71 in TC4, 18.10.71-19.10.71 in TC8

ADDITIONAL CREDITED CAST

Brigadier Lethbridge-Stewart (Nicholas Courtney[1,2,4*]), Controller (Aubrey Woods), Captain Yates (Richard Franklin[1,2,4]), Sergeant Benton (John Levene[1,2,4]), Anat (Anna Barry), Shura (Jimmy Winston[1,2,4]) , Boaz (Scott Fredericks), Sir Reginald Styles (Wilfrid Carter[1,4]), Miss Paget (Jean McFarlane[1,4]), Girl Technician (Deborah Brayshaw[1,3]), U.N.I.T. Radio Operator (Gypsie Kemp[1,2]), Guerilla (Tim Condren[1]), Ogrons (Rick Lester, Maurice Bush, David Joyce[2-4], Frank Menzies[2-4], Bruce Wells[2-

[4], Geoffrey Todd[2-4]), Daleks (John Scott Martin, Ricky Newby, Murphy Grumbar), Dalek Voices (Oliver Gilbert, Peter Messaline), Monia (Valentine Palmer[3,4]), Manager (Peter Hill[3]), Senior Guard (Andrew Carr[3,4]), Guard at Work Centre (George Raistrick[3]), Television Reporter (Alex MacIntosh[4]).

* Also in Episode Three, in the reprise from the end of Episode Two, but uncredited.

POPULAR MYTHS

- Terry Nation was not consulted in advance about the use of the Daleks in this story and, when he found out about it, this led to a row between him and the BBC. (Although Terrance Dicks recalls such a dispute, Barry Letts does not, and it is clear from contemporary BBC documentation that it is the latter who is correct. Nation was consulted in advance, and his agents ALS Management confirmed in a letter dated 22 April 1971 that he had no objection to the Daleks being used in a story for the 1972 season, subject to the usual negotiations. The story the production team had in mind at that point was one called *The Daleks in London* by Robert Sloman. This was then abandoned, however, and in June 1971 they decided instead to have the Daleks incorporated into Louis Marks's story, which had not originally featured them. Nation was sent Marks's amended scripts to read, and told Terrance Dicks in a letter dated 20 July 1971 that they seemed 'a very good and exciting batch of episodes'. Nation was ultimately paid a fee of £25 per episode for the use of his creations, and agreement was reached that he would write their next story.)

THINGS TO WATCH OUT FOR

- The story's on-screen title is *Day of the Daleks*, although it was incorrectly referred to in the *Radio Times* listings (and on the later BBC video release) as *The Day of the Daleks*.
- In Episodes Two and Three, the initial 'sting' of the closing title music is retained at the end of the reprise from the previous episode.
- A section of the closing title sequence appears in the background on the screen of the Daleks' mind analysis machine at the end of Episode Three. Images of the Doctor's two previous selves (publicity photographs of William Hartnell and Patrick Troughton) are also shown on screen, thus convincing the Daleks that they have their old enemy. The first of the episode's closing credits is superimposed over this scene just before the foreground images are removed, leaving just the title sequence. The rest of the credits then follow.
- BBC television news reporter Alex MacIntosh appears as himself in Episode Four.

THINGS YOU MIGHT NOT HAVE KNOWN

- Working titles: *The Ghost Hunters*, *Years of Doom*
- Episode Four was originally to have featured a confrontation between the Doctor and the Daleks in which the Daleks explain how they destroyed those of their number who were impregnated with the human factor in the events seen in *The Evil of the Daleks* and then turned their attention to conquering Earth by means of time travel. This scene was actually recorded but had to be cut at the editing stage for timing reasons.
- This was the first of a number of stories in which the key colour used for the CSO effects was yellow rather than blue.

- The Ogrons were neither named nor described in Louis Marks's scripts.

- **The Doctor:** 'There are many sorts of ghosts, Jo. Ghosts from the past, and ghosts from the future.'
- **Controller:** [To the Doctor and Jo.] 'You don't understand. No-one who didn't live through those terrible years can understand. Towards the end of the 20th Century, a series of wars broke out. There were hundreds of years of nothing but destruction and killing. Nearly seven eighths of the world's population wiped out. The rest living in holes in the ground, starving, almost reduced to the level of animals.' **The Doctor:** 'So Earth is now a giant factory, all the wealth, the minerals, located and taken to Skaro?' **Controller:** 'Exactly. The men who are strong enough are sent to the mines. The others work in factories.' **Jo Grant:** 'Why? Why are they doing all this?' **Controller:** 'They need a constant flow of raw materials. Their empire's expanding.'
- **Controller:** [To the Daleks.] 'Who knows? I may have helped to exterminate *you*.'

The long-awaited return of the Daleks is very welcome indeed; and the fact that *Day of the Daleks* happens to be something of a minor classic is an added bonus. 'From the start to the end,' wrote Mike Ashcroft in *Oracle* Volume 3 Number 5, dated February/March 1980, 'the story was utter entertainment to me.'

For a series in which time travel plays such a crucial role, *Doctor Who* had previously dwelt surprisingly little on the possible implications and ramifications of moving through the 'fourth dimension'. With a few exceptions, the stories of the first eight seasons had tended to use the TARDIS simply as a device to get the Doctor and his companions into whatever situation the writer wanted to develop – whether that situation happened to be in the past, present or future, on Earth or on some unfamiliar alien world. In *Day of the Daleks*, however, the concept of time travel is dealt with rather more thoughtfully than this, and is arguably more important and central to the plot than in any previous story. The idea of the creation of a time paradox whereby the guerrillas are themselves responsible for the history of the world into which they are born is really quite mind boggling, and writer Louis Marks deserves full credit for the intelligence and sophistication of his scripts.

The scenes set in the 22nd Century are particularly effective, conveying a chilling impression of what life might be like under Dalek rule, and Aubrey Woods gives a superb performance as the conscience-stricken Controller who acts as the invaders' quisling. *Day of the Daleks* is in fact one of only two *Doctor Who* stories ever to have presented a scenario in which an alien race has actually *succeeded* in taking over the Earth, the other being – curiously enough – *The Dalek Invasion of Earth*, which depicts another Dalek invasion of exactly the same time period. The likely explanation for this coincidence is that Marks simply drew some of his inspiration for *Day of the Daleks* from that earlier story (which he would almost certainly have seen in production while working on his one previous *Doctor Who* commission, *Planet of Giants*). By a happy coincidence, however, it actually ties in rather well with the time paradox theme, the apparent implication being that just because one Dalek invasion of the 22nd Century has been defeated, that is not to say that they cannot use their time travel capability to make a second attempt – indeed, a Dalek actually states at one point that they have invaded Earth 'again'.

It would however be wrong to suggest that this is purely or even primarily a story of ideas. *Doctor Who* is often at its best when it works on more than one level, and that is certainly the case here. *Day of the Daleks* boasts not only some fascinating underlying concepts but also plenty of action and some good, old-fashioned monsters to keep the viewer on the edge of the seat, or even behind the sofa.

'The Ogrons made a nice addition to the *Doctor Who* mythos,' commented Ashcroft. 'It made a change to see the Daleks using someone else rather than humanity as their puppets. It also helped to make them believable as the supremely terrifying creatures they should be …

The only pity is that the Daleks themselves are somewhat underused in this story; in the scenes set in the 22nd Century they are kept rather too much in the background, and in those where they finally emerge from their base and travel back to the 20th Century, their appearance could hardly be described as spectacular. This is due in large part to the fact that director Paul Bernard – who otherwise does a fine job – is sadly unsuccessful in his valiant attempts to conceal the fact that he has only three Dalek props at his disposal.

The BBC's Audience Research Report on the story's penultimate episode indicates that contemporary viewers gave it a rather cautious welcome: 'The majority … evidently enjoyed this episode at least moderately, some tolerating it for the sake of their children ("not my cup of tea but they adore it"), others admitting to being "a sucker" for this ingenious "rubbish", and quite a number finding it altogether enthralling ("I have become a big fan of *Doctor Who*; this was a gripping episode; I can't wait till next week"). There was noticeable feeling, however, that it was rather slow-moving, lacking in tension and action, and some viewers complained that the series seemed not as good as its predecessors; it was less "imaginative" and exciting, they said, or was becoming stale and predictable. ("Seems to have lost its impact; I no longer feel for the Doctor or share his adventures"; "Maybe children viewing for the first time would find this good, but to me it's just repetition; I wish the Daleks would get Doctor Who for good this time", are comments echoed by several, one or two noting that "the Daleks have had their day".)'

The Audience Research Report on the story's closing episode reveals that viewer reaction was again 'moderate rather than enthusiastic': 'Some of those reporting, certainly, were great fans of *Doctor Who*: science-fiction was all too rare on television, and this was good, imaginative stuff, they said, and well thought out. More often, however, viewers in the sample tended to regard it as a "bit of a giggle" – entertaining enough in its way (and undoubtedly a great hit with children) but hardly to be taken seriously – and others confessed that they watched only because other members of their family wanted to do so. More specifically, there were complaints that, after three episodes in which nothing much seemed to happen, this last one appeared very rushed and the Daleks vanquished all too easily – "as though they couldn't get rid of them quickly enough". In any case, some added, they were "sick of the Daleks" and hoped that they had now seen the last of them.'

As is often the case, these comments – drawn from a sample of the general viewing audience rather than of those with a particular interest in or affinity for *Doctor Who* or science-fiction as a genre – give an unduly negative impression. *Day of the Daleks* is a story with much to commend it, and it gets the series' ninth season off to a flying start.

THE CURSE OF PELADON

Writer: Brian Hayles. **Director:** Lennie Mayne. **Designer:** Gloria Clayton. **Costumes:** Barbara Lane. **Make-Up:** Sylvia James. **Incidental Music:** Dudley Simpson. **Fight Arranger:** Terry Walsh/PROFILE. **Visual Effects:** Bernard Wilkie, Ian Scoones. **Film Cameraman:** Fred Hamilton, Peter Sargent. **Film Editor:** Michael Sha-Dyan. **Studio Lighting:** Howard King. **Studio Sound:** Tony Millier. **Production Assistant:** Chris D'Oyly-John. **Assistant Floor Manager:** Ros Anderson.

	First UK TX	Scheduled TX	Actual TX	Duration	Viewers	Chart Pos.
Episode One	29/01/72	17.50	17.52	24'32"	10.3	36
Episode Two	05/02/72	17.50	17.52	24'33"	11.0	20
Episode Three	12/02/72	17.50	17.53	24'21"	7.8	49
Episode Four	19/02/72	17.50	17.50	24'16"	8.4	27

Plot: The Doctor and Jo make a test flight in the TARDIS and arrive on the planet Peladon. Seeking shelter, they enter the citadel of the soon to be crowned King Peladon, where the Doctor is mistaken for a human dignitary summoned to act as Chairman of a committee assessing an application by the planet to join the Galactic Federation. The other committee members – Alpha Centauri, Arcturus and the Martian Lord Izlyr and his Warrior subordinate Ssorg – have already arrived, but are disconcerted by the death of one of the King's advisors, Chancellor Torbis. High Priest Hepesh, who opposes the union with the Federation, attributes Torbis's death to the Curse of Aggedor, the sacred beast of Peladon. Other incidents occur and the Doctor concludes that a saboteur is at work. At first he suspects the Ice Warriors, but the guilty parties are eventually revealed to be Hepesh and Arcturus. Arcturus has convinced Hepesh that the Federation would only exploit Peladon for its mineral riches, whereas this is in fact his own race's intention. Arcturus is destroyed with a blast from Ssorg's sonic gun, but Hepesh escapes into a network of tunnels beneath the citadel, where he foments rebellion amongst the guards. The rebels storm the citadel and take the King prisoner. Hepesh then orders Aggedor – a real beast he has been using for his own ends – to kill the Doctor. The Doctor, however, has tamed Aggedor, and it is Hepesh who dies.

Episode endings:
1. As the Doctor and the committee delegates leave Peladon's throne room, a large stone statue of Aggedor overlooking the passage outside the door topples from its ledge and starts to fall towards them …
2. Hepesh accuses the Doctor of desecrating the planet's holy of holies – the inner sanctum of the Temple of Aggedor. Peladon reluctantly proclaims that to this charge there can be no defence and only one sentence – death.
3. The Doctor and the King's Champion Grun have been fighting each other in a trial of strength in a deep pit. The Doctor is victorious but spares Grun's life. Peladon raises his hand to declare the trial over. Then, in a rapid succession of events, Arcturus extends his energy weapon, Jo screams and Ssorg fires his sonic gun …
4. The real Earth delegate arrives and looks on in open-mouthed astonishment as the TARDIS dematerialises.

IT WAS MADE WHERE...?

Ealing Filming: 16.12.71-17.12.71 on Stage 2
Studio Recording: 17.01.72-18.01.72 in TC4, 31.01.72-01.02.72 in TC3

ADDITIONAL CREDITED CAST

Peladon (David Troughton), Hepesh (Geoffrey Toone), Torbis (Henry Gilbert[1]), Izlyr (Alan Bennion), Ssorg (Sonny Caldinez), Alpha Centauri (Stuart Fell), Voice of Alpha Centauri (Ysanne Churchman), Arcturus (Murphy Grumbar[1-3]), Voice of Arcturus (Terry Bale[1-3]), Grun (Gordon St. Clair), Aggedor (Nick Hobbs), Guard Captain (George Giles[3,4]), Amazonia (Wendy Danvers[4]).

POPULAR MYTHS

- The natives of the planet Peladon are called Pels. (They are not called by this name here.)
- Izlyr is an Ice Lord. (Although he is referred to as a Lord, the term 'Ice Lord' is never used.)

THINGS TO WATCH OUT FOR

- This story is an allegory of the UK's accession to the Common Market – a highly topical issue at the time of its original transmission.
- This story accords the only on-screen credit to Terry Walsh's short-lived stunt group PROFILE. Walsh had by this point superseded Derek Ware as the series' regular stunt co-ordinator, but would be subsequently credited simply under his own name.

THINGS YOU MIGHT NOT HAVE KNOWN

- Working title: *The Curse* (unconfirmed).
- David Troughton, who played King Peladon, was the son of the actor who played the second Doctor, Patrick Troughton. He had previously appeared in *Doctor Who* twice, in the second Doctor stories *The Enemy of the World* and *The War Games*. At the time of making this story, he shared a flat with future Doctor Colin Baker.
- Sonny Caldinez replaced David Purcell at a late stage as Ssorg. Producer Barry Letts, rather than Caldinez, spoke all Ssorg's lines, but was uncredited.
- Amazonia, the real delegate from Earth, is never referred to by name in the story's dialogue; her name is given only in the closing credits.
- Prior to being commissioned to write *The Curse of Peladon*, Brian Hayles submitted two other storylines, called *The Brain Dead* and *Shape of Terror* respectively, which contain similar elements to some of those within *The Curse of Peladon*.

QUOTE, UNQUOTE

- **Jo Grant:** [To Peladon]: 'I don't understand you! One minute you're condemning the Doctor to death and the next you're proposing to me!'
- **Izlyr:** 'We reject all violence ... except in self defence.'
- **Hepesh:** 'I wanted to save our world ... to preserve the old ways. Perhaps I was wrong, Peladon. I hope so. Your future, which you set so much store by, is yours now.'

ANALYSIS

One of *Doctor Who*'s most celebrated and popular features is the wide variety of weird and wonderful alien races that it presents. Every so often there comes along a story in which the Doctor encounters not just one or two different types of creature but a veritable menagerie. A good example of this is season two's *The Web Planet*, the only story (with the obvious exception of *Inside the Spaceship*) to involve no humanoid characters at all, apart from the Doctor and his companions. Another is *The Curse of Peladon*, featuring the cowardly hermaphrodite hexapod from Alpha Centauri; the delegate from Arcturus encased in his elaborate life support machine; Izlyr and his Warrior companion Ssorg from Mars; and Peladon's legendary sacred beast Aggedor. These creatures are fascinating, not only because of their striking appearances – although the designers certainly deserve considerable credit for the excellence of their on-screen realisation – but also because they each have their own particular 'characteristics'; in effect, their own personality. Much of this is down to Brian Hayles's fine scripting, but much too is conveyed by the different and distinctive ways in which the creatures move and speak. In the case of Alpha Centauri, for example, it is not only the physical appearance that is striking but also the timid, shuffling gait and nervous movements effected by actor Stuart Fell within the costume, and the shrill, high-pitched voice created by vocal artist Ysanne Churchman (who was apparently instructed by director Lennie Mayne to make the creature sound like a gay civil servant!). Similarly, in the case of the Martians, it is their slow, lumbering movements and rasping, whispered speech that stick in the memory.

The presentation of the Ice Warriors as 'reformed characters' (a suggestion made by the production team) is inspired, and the Doctor's initial misguided distrust of them a nice twist. 'The handling of the Ice Warriors was the best I [had] seen aliens dealt with for a long time,' concurred Martin J Wiggins in *Oracle* Volume 3 Number 6 dated May 1980. 'While there [had] been instances of aliens being apparently good and turning out evil, this was a rare occurrence of the opposite happening. Brian Hayles was able to play on [the viewer's] old prejudices against the Martians … and then to turn the situation on its head. This had two advantages: it obscured the true villains and made the story more of a mystery, and it made the Warriors more real. It is all very well to have them as slavering conquerors all the time, but this story showed that they were motivated not by dedication to evil but by self-interest.'

Izlyr is perhaps the only one of the alien delegates to come across as a three dimensional character in his own right – it is a perennial problem in *Doctor Who* that where creatures lack any recognisable features there is little that can be achieved in the way of in-depth characterisation – but this is more than made up for by the excellent portrayal of the Peladon natives. The complex relationship between Peladon and Hepesh is a particular highlight of the story, as is the nascent romance between Peladon and Jo. Indeed, the planet Peladon and its civilisation as a whole are wonderfully conceived and realised.

'Peladon was a compelling setting from the first,' noted Wiggins. 'A barbaric, medieval castle was juxtaposed with the sophisticated technology of the Federation delegates. This clash between barbarism and civilisation went down to the very roots of the story, with the political leaders' desire for progress checked by opposition from [a] religious leader.

'As the story progressed, it was shown that Hepesh was willing to do anything to prevent the planet being jerked into civilisation, even to commit sacrilege by cruelty to the royal beast, or be false to his own beliefs by conspiring with one of the aliens he professed to hate. As it was, he omitted to give thought to Arcturus's reasons for giving help … Hepesh is thus a very interesting character: a fanatic, a patriot, but above all, a man doomed to failure.'

'Brian Hayles' script is a masterpiece,' enthused Anthony Brown in *DWB* No. 116 dated August 1993, 'superbly structured and filled with exquisite characters, whose depth makes it possible for them to behave in utterly unexpected ways without acting atypically. Plot twists come out of nowhere, the point behind Hepesh's machinations always unclear until the moment when the trap closes around his victim. Every cliffhanger is integral to the plot, twisting it in a new direction which provokes reactions from the characters, in turn driving the plot.'

The Curse of Peladon is a hugely enjoyable story, and one of the real gems of the third Doctor's era.

THE SEA DEVILS

Writer: Malcolm Hulke. **Director:** Michael Briant. **Designer:** Tony Snoaden. **Costumes:** Maggie Fletcher. **Make-Up:** Sylvia James. **Incidental Music:** Malcolm Clarke. **Action:** HAVOC. **Fight Arranger:** Derek Ware. **Visual Effects:** Peter Day. **Film Cameraman:** Peter Sargent. **Film Editor:** Martyn Day. **Studio Lighting:** Mike Jefferies. **Studio Sound:** Tony Millier, Colin Dixon. **Production Assistant:** Colin Dudley. **Assistant Floor Manager:** John Bradburn.

Note: All episodes bore an additional credit reading: 'The BBC wish to acknowledge the help given to them by the Royal Navy in the making of this programme.'

	First UK TX	Scheduled TX	Actual TX	Duration	Viewers	Chart Pos.
Episode One	26/02/72	17.50	17.51	24'40"	6.4	76
Episode Two	04/03/72	17.50	17.52	24'30"	9.7	26
Episode Three	11/03/72	17.50	17.50	24'05"	8.3	45
Episode Four	18/03/72	17.50	17.51	24'21"	7.8	40
Episode Five	25/03/72	17.45	17.46	24'53"	8.3	39
Episode Six	01/04/72	17.50	17.51	24'24"	8.5	47

Plot: The Doctor and Jo visit the Master in his high-security prison on an island off the south coast of England and hear from the governor, Colonel Trenchard, that ships have been mysteriously disappearing at sea. Investigating, the Doctor learns from Captain Hart, commander of a nearby Naval base, that the sinkings have centred around an abandoned sea fort. He and Jo then visit the fort and are attacked by what one of the men there terms a Sea Devil – an amphibious breed of the prehistoric creatures encountered by the Doctor shortly after his exile to Earth. The Master, aided by a misguided Trenchard, is stealing equipment from the Naval base in order to build a machine to revive the Sea Devils from hibernation. The Doctor takes a diving bell down to the Sea Devils' underwater base to try to encourage peace. His efforts are frustrated by a depth charge attack ordered by a pompous politician, Walker, but in the confusion he manages to free a captured submarine and escape back to the surface. The Sea Devils then capture the Naval base, and the Master has the Doctor taken back to their control centre, where he forces him to help finish the machine. The Doctor sabotages the machine and the two Time Lords escape together just as the base is destroyed in an explosion.

Episode endings:

1. The Doctor and Jo head for the sea fort to investigate further. Once there, their boat is destroyed, trapping them inside. They hear the shuffling gait and rasping breath of something approaching them down a corridor.
2. The Doctor returns to the prison to see the Master and walks into his trap. The two Time Lords fight with swords. The Doctor seems to gain the upper hand but, when he turns his back, the Master pulls a knife and throws it straight at him.
3. With Jo's help, the Doctor escapes from the Master's prison. The two head for the beach, where they find themselves caught between a squad of castle guards, a minefield and a Sea Devil that the Master has summoned from the sea.
4. The Doctor determines to descend in a diving bell to try to make contact with the reptiles. Jo watches anxiously as the bell is lowered. After a short time contact is lost and it is hauled back up again. Jo looks inside and sees to her horror that the Doctor has gone.
5. The Master leads an attack by the Sea Devils on the Naval base. The Doctor and Jo, on their way with Captain Hart to try to make contact with the reptiles once more, find themselves facing the creatures on the base.
6. With the Sea Devil base destroyed, the Master contrives to escape in a hovercraft.

IT WAS MADE WHERE...?

Location Filming: 21.10.71-22.10.71, 25.10.71-30.10.71
Locations: Fraser Gunnery Range, *HMS St George*, Eastney, Portsmouth, Hants; *HMS Reclaim*, Portsmouth Harbour, Hants; Whitecliff Bay, Nr. Bembridge, Isle of Wight; Bembridge Sailing Club, Bembridge, Isle of Wight; on small boats outside Bembridge Harbour; Norris Castle, East Cowes, Isle of Wight; No-Man's Land Fort, the Solent; Red Cliff, Sandown, Isle of Wight; Priory Bay, Seaview, Isle of Wight.
Studio Recording: 15.11.71-16.11.71, 29.11.71-30.11.71, 13.12.71-14.12.71 all in TC8

ADDITIONAL CREDITED CAST

Master (Roger Delgado), Captain Hart (Edwin Richfield), Trenchard (Clive Morton[1-4]), Robbins (Royston Tickner[1]), Radio Operator (Neil Seiler[1]), Clark (Declan Mulholland[1, 2]), Hickman (Hugh Futcher[1]), 3rd Officer Jane Blythe (June Murphy), Ldg. Telegraphist Bowman (Alec Wallis[1,4-6]), Castle Guard Wilson (Brian Justice[1]), Castle Guard Barclay (Terry Walsh[1,3*]), Sea Devil (Pat Gorman[1,2,4-6]), C.P.O. Smedley (Eric Mason[2]), Commander Ridgeway (Donald Sumpter[3-5]), Lt. Commander Mitchell (David Griffin[3-5]), Ldg. Seaman Lovell (Christopher Wray[3,5]), Castle Guard Drew (Stanley McGeagh[3,4]), C.P.O. Summers (Colin Bell[4,5]), Lt. Commander Watts (Brian Vaughan[4]), A/B Girton (Rex Rowland[5]), Walker (Martin Boddey[5,6]), Rear Admiral (Norman Atkyns[5]), Chief Sea Devil (Peter Forbes-Robertson[5,6]), C.P.O. Myers (John Caesar[6])

* Also in Episodes Two and Four, but uncredited.

- The Master watches *The Rock Collector* episode of *Clangers* on a television in his prison cell and fails to realise that it is a children's puppet show until this is pointed out to him by Colonel Trenchard. (The Master fully realises the nature of what he is watching. His comment to Trenchard that the Clangers seem to be 'a rather interesting extraterrestrial life-form' is intended to be a joke, and his expression clearly shows his frustration at Trenchard's lack of a sense of humour when he takes it literally.)
- Roger Delgado was afraid of the water and it took great courage for him to film the scene in which the Master and the Doctor are rescued from the sea by the Navy. (This was frequently recalled by Jon Pertwee in later interviews but, according to Delgado's widow Kismet, it is untrue. Delgado was actually worried about getting his costume wet, as there was no spare available.)

- Stuntman Stuart Fell doubles, rather unconvincingly, for Katy Manning in the scene in Episode One where Jo climbs up a ladder to the sea fort.
- The Doctor claims that the earlier description of the Earth's one-time reptilian rulers as 'Silurians' was incorrect, and that they should really have been referred to as 'Eocenes'. This piece of dialogue was included by writer Malcolm Hulke in response to claims by one or more viewers that it was impossible in evolutionary terms for the Silurian era to have spawned man-sized reptiles; ironically, however, it is equally unlikely that the Eocene era could have been the origin of such creatures.
- This was the last instance of Derek Ware's stunt organisation HAVOC being contracted to perform a story's stunt work.

- Working title: *The Sea Silurians*.
- The Navy waived all royalty fees on the use of stock film clips showing ships in action, as they considered that the publicity they derived from the programme was sufficient recompense.
- The No-Man's Land sea fort used as a location for this story was sold by the Ministry of Defence in 1988 for £30,000 to a Sussex businessman named Roger Penfold. Penfold renovated the entire structure, converting it into two luxury homes, adding a helicopter landing pad, a garden, a gazebo, a swimming pool, tennis court, clay pigeon shoot, numerous fitted bedrooms, a den, study, lounge, a dining room big enough to seat 25 people and a self contained flat in the lighthouse. In 1990 he was asking £5,750,000 for the renovated property.
- A programme called *Television Club* looked at the making of *The Sea Devils* in an edition on 7 Feb 1972.
- John Baker was originally assigned to compose the music for this story but he was replaced by Malcolm Clarke.

- **The Doctor:** [Speaking of the Master.] 'He used to be a friend of mine once … a very good friend. In fact, you might almost say we were at school together.'
- **The Doctor:** 'If Horatio Nelson had been in charge of this operation, I hardly think

that he would have waited for official instructions.' **Captain Hart:** 'Yes … a pretty impulsive fellow. If one can believe the history books.' **The Doctor:** 'History books? Captain Hart, Horatio Nelson was a personal friend of mine.'

- **The Doctor:** 'Why begin a long and bloody war where thousands will be killed on both sides?' **Chief Sea Devil:** 'We shall destroy man and reclaim the planet.' **The Doctor:** 'Is there nothing I can say to make you reconsider?' **Chief Sea Devil:** 'Nothing.' **The Doctor:** 'I'm sorry.'

ANALYSIS

We open on a ship. Screams and shouts can be heard over the clamour of alarms, and a panicked sailor calls for help into the radio. Suddenly an alien hand reaches out and grasps the microphone as the sailor screams in terror …

From this dramatic beginning *The Sea Devils* unfolds as a colourful adventure yarn in much the same vein as *The Claws of Axos* and *The Dæmons*. '*The Sea Devils* was intended to be fun, and that's exactly what it succeeds in being,' wrote Alistair Hughes in *TSV* 48 dated August 1996. 'From the Doctor's famous "Horatio Nelson" quote in Episode One to the Master's cavalier wave as he makes his escape in Episode Six, we are treated to an enjoyable ride filled with memorable moments and fine portrayals.'

Despite the story's near-contemporary Earth setting, UNIT is for once totally absent, leaving the Royal Navy to deal with this latest threat to the planet's security. The implication may perhaps be that UNIT is a purely land-based force with no jurisdiction over incidents occurring at sea, but this is left as a matter for speculation as no explanation is provided in the story itself. Fulfilling the Brigadier's usual narrative function as an incredulous military figurehead is Captain Hart, ably played by Edwin Richfield, who also has a trusty number two in the person of 3rd Officer Jane Blythe. The most interesting guest character of all, however, is Colonel Trenchard, brilliantly portrayed by Hugh Morton – although it must be seen as a damning indictment of the British authorities that they are content to entrust the security of the Master, supposedly their number one prisoner, to this bumbling ex-colonial official. It would indeed be difficult to imagine any less suitable person than Trenchard to be placed in charge of the Master, who manages to win him over without even using his hypnotic abilities, purely by the power of persuasion!

The monsters on this occasion are the eponymous Sea Devils (although the only character to refer to them as such is Clark, one of the hapless caretakers of the sea fort, who babbles incoherently about 'sea devils' when he is found by the Doctor and Jo). 'The finned, turtle-like Sea Devil heads are especially striking and stand lingering close-ups on many memorable occasions,' wrote Hughes. 'The head masks were worn as "top hats" by the actors to increase the neck length and break up the human shape, and the [result] brings to mind large aquatic creatures like whales and dolphins, which have very large heads with long tapering bodies. As has always been a strength in *Doctor Who*, the Sea Devils behave intelligently, not as lumbering "man-in-suit" monsters. Generally, they are used well, and it's refreshing to see them move quickly and agilely when they have to, pursuing the Doctor through the sea fort and capturing the Naval base as efficiently as any commando team (or should that be SEALs?).'

The creatures have a statuesque quality and, in the case of the Chief Sea Devil (the only one that speaks), a strange nobility imparted largely by Peter Forbes-Robertson's sensitive portrayal. They work very well in the action scenes, too, as they attack, get shot at and die in a variety of imaginative stunt falls – and even, on one occasion, a back-flip. Their weapons – silver, saucer-like discs that can blast or burn as required – are well designed and memorable, as Dallas Jones appreciated in *A Voyage Through 25 Years of Doctor Who* dated December 1988: 'The gun itself I consider to be one of the most ingenious props in the series' history – simply because it doesn't *look* like a gun! It is so simple in appearance and [this] makes it seem all the more real.'

Another notable aspect of the story is that it showcases a wide variety of different forms of transport, including a motor boat, a scooter, a hovercraft, some one-man speedboats, a submarine, a diving vessel, a diving bell and a number of customised Citröens. This contributes greatly to its action-packed flavour. The same can be said also of the liberal use of stock footage of depth charges being laid and ships moving into attack; and so well integrated are these sequences with the location footage specially shot for the story that it is hard to see where one stops and the other starts. Apparently the Navy agreed to contribute to the production on condition that the story presented them in a good light, but given its underlying moral message – that blowing your perceived enemies to pieces might not always be the best solution – it is debatable whether or not they actually got their wish.

This moral dimension is a characteristic feature of Malcolm Hulke's stories. Here the viewer is presented with the plight of the reptiles, caught between the Master, the Doctor and the humans – who should they trust? Ultimately they are betrayed by all three, although it is the humans whose actions are shown to be the most irrational as the (admittedly somewhat clichéd) faceless civil servant Walker orders an attack on their base, thereby throwing away any chance of a peaceful solution to the conflict. The reptiles are left convinced that humanity is prepared to listen only to the language of violence.

Michael Briant's direction of the story is splendid, and the production values are high. The performances by all the leads are, as usual, excellent and believable, and the location work lends an air of reality to the proceedings. Perhaps the only area of contention is the incidental music, which is quite radically different from the norm for this period of *Doctor Who*'s history – or indeed for any period. Radiophonic Workshop composer Malcolm Clarke, making his first contribution to the series, came up a score that can best be described as experimental. It is in effect a collection of atonal sounds that punctuate the action, in some parts melodic but in others simply a background noise (for example a low bubbling for the sequences set in the submarine). Opinions differ greatly as to the merits of this approach, but one thing that is certain is that no-one who watches *The Sea Devils* can possibly fail to miss what is arguably its most striking aspect.

THE MUTANTS

Writer: Bob Baker, Dave Martin. **Director:** Christopher Barry. **Designer:** Jeremy Bear. **Costumes:** James Acheson. **Make-Up:** Joan Barrett. **Incidental Music:** Tristram Cary. **Fight Arranger:** Terry Walsh. **Visual Effects:** John Horton. **Film Cameraman:** Fred Hamilton. **Film Editor:** Dave King. **Studio Lighting:** Frank Cresswell. **Studio Sound:** Tony Millier. **Production Assistant:** Fiona Cumming, Chris D'Oyly-John. **Assistant Floor Manager:** Sue Hedden.

	First UK TX	Scheduled TX	Actual TX	Duration	Viewers	Chart Pos.
Episode One	08/04/72	17.50	17.51	24'25"	9.1	29
Episode Two	15/04/72	17.50	17.51	24'24"	7.8	38
Episode Three	22/04/72	17.50	17.50	24'32"	7.9	36
Episode Four	29/04/72	17.50*	17.50	24'00"	7.5	44
Episode Five	06/05/72	17.50	17.51	24'37"	7.9	44
Episode Six	13/05/72	17.50	17.52	23'43"	6.5	67

* In Wales the scheduled TX time was 17.10.

Plot: The Time Lords send the Doctor and Jo on a mission to deliver a sealed message pod to an unknown party aboard a Skybase orbiting the planet Solos in the 30th Century. Solos is due to gain independence from Earth's empire but its Marshal is determined to prevent this. He arranges the murder of the Earth Administrator and, with his chief scientist Jaeger, plans to transform Solos's atmosphere into one more suited to humans. Ky, a young Solonian leader, is falsely accused of the murder and flees to the planet, taking Jo with him. The Doctor follows and joins them in an old thaesium mine. Ky turns out to be the intended recipient of the message pod, which opens automatically for him. Inside are stone tablets carved with ancient inscriptions. The Doctor's party then meet Sondergaard, a human scientist leading a hermit-like existence in the mine while searching for a cure for the mutating disease that afflicts the Solonians. The Doctor and Sondergaard decipher the inscriptions, deducing that the mutations are part of a natural life-cycle in which thaesium radiation plays a vital role. The Doctor retrieves a crystal from a cave where the radiation is concentrated and returns to the Skybase to analyze it. He is recaptured by the Marshal and, with his friends held hostage, is forced to perfect the machine with which Jaeger plans to transform Solos. Sondergaard meanwhile gives Ky the crystal, which turns him first into a mutant and then into an ethereal super-being – the ultimate stage of the Solonians' life-cycle. Jaeger is killed when the Doctor sabotages his machine, and the Marshal is vaporised by Ky.

Episode endings:
1. Ky and his people, trying to escape from the Skybase, enter a transmat cubicle with Jo as their hostage. The Marshal orders his guards to open fire and the cubicle explodes.
2. The Doctor is on his way to the Skybase transmat cubicle when he is seized by the Solonian warrior chief Varan, who mutters 'Die, Overlord!'
3. The Doctor has found Ky and Jo in the mine caves but the Marshal is close behind. Stubbs and Cotton, two of the Skybase guards, go to search for the Doctor, but the Marshal orders the cave exits sealed and poisonous gas pumped in.
4. Varan and his warriors, together with Stubbs, Cotton, Jo and Ky, attack the Skybase. The Marshal is ready for them however and, in the ensuing skirmish, Varan is sucked through the exterior wall into space. As Jaeger launches the atmosphere reconditioning missiles at Solos, Jo and the others struggle to avoid being sucked into space themselves.
5. To ensure the Doctor's cooperation in convincing an Investigator from Earth that all is well, the Marshal places Jo, Ky and Cotton in the refuelling lock under threat of death. The Investigator's ship docks, and Cotton realises with horror that when it refuels the chamber will flood with thaesium, killing them all.
6. The Doctor and Jo return to the TARDIS, avoiding awkward explanations to the Investigator.

IT WAS MADE WHERE...?

Location Filming: 07.02.72-12.02.72

Locations: Chislehurst Caves, Chislehurst, Kent; Frindsbury Caves, Stone House Farm, Lower Rochester Road, Frindsbury, Kent; Associated Portland Cement Manufacturers Quarry, Bean Road, Northfleet, Kent.

Studio Recording: 22.02.72 (tannoy voices), 28.02.72-29.02.72 in TC4, 13.03.72-14.03.72 in TC8, 27.03.72-28.03.72 in TC3

ADDITIONAL CREDITED CAST

Marshal (Paul Whitsun-Jones), Varan (James Mellor[1-4]), Ky (Garrick Hagon), Administrator (Geoffrey Palmer[1]), Stubbs (Christopher Coll[1-5]), Cotton (Rick James), Varan's Son (Jonathan Sherwood[1,2]), Jaeger (George Pravda[2-6]), Sondergaard (John Hollis[3-6]), Old Man (Sidney Johnson[3]), Solos Guard (Roy Pearce[4]*, Damon Sanders[5]), Warrior Guard (David Arlen[4]), Skybase Guard (Martin Taylor[5]), Mutt (John Scott Martin[5]**), Investigator (Peter Howell[6]).

* Also in Episodes Three and Five, but uncredited.

** Also in all the other episodes of the story, but uncredited.

Note: Jon Pertwee was credited as 'Dr. Who' on the first four episodes of this story.

POPULAR MYTHS

- The incidental music for the story's final episode was composed not by Tristram Cary but by Dudley Simpson. (Tristram Cary composed the incidental music for all six episodes.)

THINGS TO WATCH OUT FOR

- Well known comedy actor Geoffrey Palmer appears as the quickly assassinated Administrator in Episode One.

THINGS YOU MIGHT NOT HAVE KNOWN

- Working titles: *Independence*, *The Emergents*.
- Christopher Barry felt that he had become 'typecast' as a *Doctor Who* director and, in order to avoid being assigned to the series again, let it be known within the BBC that he had had a serious disagreement with Jon Pertwee during the making of *The Mutants* – a claim that was in fact untrue. He eventually returned to the series to direct Tom Baker's first story.
- Episode Six of this story is the first in the series' history to bear an on-screen copyright date.
- Author Salman Rushdie refers to *The Mutants* in his controversial book *The Satanic Verses* and implies that its characterisation of mutations as evil just because they look different from human beings encourages racist attitudes. He thereby completely misses the point of the story, which in fact has an anti-racist message.
- The tannoy voices heard on board Skybase were provided by Garrick Hagon. The voice from the *Hyperion* was that of John Hollis.
- An experimental effects session was arranged for 20 March for director Christopher Barry to try out some CSO effects for the story.

- There were a great many problems with the sets for this story. The Marshal's office was over the studio fire line and had to be re-set; a section of corridor was missing; the transfer cubicles were not ready in time and the casters were put in the wrong position, preventing the revolving doors from working; a part of the radiation cave set was not constructed even though it was on the designer's drawing; and props were missing from Varan's village hut.

QUOTE, UNQUOTE

- **The Doctor:** [Speaking of Earth in the 30th Century.] 'Grey cities linked by grey highways across a grey desert. Slag, ash and clinker – the fruits of technology.'
- **Jaeger:** 'This planet as it stands is no longer of any use unless we make the atmosphere breathable.' **The Doctor:** 'Even if it means wiping out every Solonian in the process?' **Jaeger:** 'Earth is fighting for its survival – the side effects are of no importance.' **The Doctor:** 'Genocide as a side effect! You ought to write a paper on that, Professor.'
- **The Doctor:** 'Marshal, you are quite mad.' **Marshal:** 'Only if I lose.'

ANALYSIS

This story is in essence very similar to the previous season's *Colony in Space*. Both feature two sides battling over an inhospitable planet apparently inhabited by a mysterious race of monsters whose origins are unknown. The difference in *The Mutants* is that the action is viewed mostly from the point of view of the oppressing humans rather than from that of the oppressed natives; but, as in *Colony in Space*, it takes the Doctor to figure out what is really going on.

The idea of the Doctor being stranded on Earth is, by this point, really starting to wear thin. The Time Lords have already been responsible (or so it is implied) for his trips to Uxarieus in *Colony in Space* and Peladon in *The Curse of Peladon*, but now we have them giving him a far more blatant mission: to deliver a message pod. One wonders, in passing, why they could not simply have materialised the pod in front of its intended recipient – but then of course there would have been no story. As it is, the Doctor and Jo dash off to Solos, there to lock horns with the obsessive Marshal as he dedicates himself to 'cleansing' the planet. The Doctor's distaste for this imperialistic attitude is well brought across; and one of the nice things about the story is the way he manages to stay one step ahead of the Marshal and his scientist Jaeger all the way through, even when supposedly working in a forced alliance with them.

Some fine scripts by Bob Baker and Dave Martin are well served by Christopher Barry's characteristically polished direction. The mutants themselves are both well conceived and nicely designed; most people have a fear of insects, and the thought of the hapless Solonians transforming involuntarily and seemingly at random into giant ant-like creatures is quite terrifying – especially as they seem to be the 'good guys'. The scenes set on the planet's surface and in the caves are particularly well shot and directed, making Solos one of the most effectively realised alien worlds ever presented in *Doctor Who*. 'There is a surprising amount of film in this story,' noted David Gibbs in *Star Begotten* Volume 3 Number 1/2 dated winter/spring 1989. 'All scenes set in the underground mines were filmed on location, as were the bulk of the planet exteriors (and even those in the studio – Varan's village – were melded in almost imperceptibly). For once a *Doctor Who*

3 THIRD DOCTOR

planet really does [look] like an alien world, helped in no small part by the copious amounts of the swirling mist that pervades every inch of the "Solonian" surface. In one scene, Jon Pertwee runs from the mist, cape billowing, and fells a guard before disappearing back into the talons of the dense atmosphere. Somehow, one really feels that this *is* a planet on the edge of the 30th Century Earth empire, rather than a quarry somewhere.'

One of the less praiseworthy aspects of the production on this occasion is the acting of the guest cast, none of whom is particularly impressive. Probably the best is Paul Whitsun-Jones as the single-minded Marshal, a worthy opponent for the Doctor who manages to make the act of threatening into an art form. Undoubtedly the worst is Rick James as Cotton, who puts in a strong bid for the title of worst performance ever seen in *Doctor Who*. His woodenness and apparent inability to deliver his lines with any degree of conviction unfortunately tend to undermine every scene in which he appears, while Christopher Coll as his partner Stubbs struggles gamely to make the script work. Even the weakest elements in a story can have their admirers, however, and Dallas Jones took a rather different view in *A Voyage Through 25 Years of Doctor Who* dated December 1988: 'The story had two characters I thoroughly enjoyed watching, namely Stubbs and Cotton … It was nice to see Cotton played by a black actor, especially as the story could be seen as commenting on the South African apartheid problem.'

Another aspect of the *The Mutants* that has attracted both condemnation and praise is the incidental music by Tristram Cary, with whom Christopher Barry had previously worked on the Daleks' debut story – also called, by a strange coincidence, *The Mutants*. Like Malcolm Clarke on *The Sea Devils*, Cary adopted an atonal *musique concrète* approach, creating an electronic landscape of beeps and whistles that, while admittedly quite in keeping with the story's themes and settings, is highly distracting.

Overall, though, *The Mutants* is a good story – and one that, with its strong anti-apartheid and anti-colonial messages, gives a good illustration of the increasingly moralistic tone that producer Barry Letts was bringing to the series at this time.

THE TIME MONSTER

Writer: Robert Sloman, Barry Letts*. **Director:** Paul Bernard. **Designer:** Tim Gleeson. **Costumes:** Barbara Lane. **Make-Up:** Joan Barrett. **Incidental Music:** Dudley Simpson. **Visual Effects:** Michealjohn Harris, Peter Pegrum. **Film Cameraman:** Peter Hamilton. **Film Editor:** Martyn Day. **Studio Lighting:** Derek Hobday. **Studio Sound:** Tony Millier. **Production Assistant:** Marion McDougall. **Assistant Floor Manager:** Rosemary Hester.

* Barry Letts received no credit on screen in view of the fact that he was producer of the series.

	First UK TX	Scheduled TX	Actual TX	Duration	Viewers	Chart Pos.
Episode One	20/05/72	17.50*	17.51	25'04"	7.6	37
Episode Two	27/05/72	17.50	17.52	25'05"	7.4	60
Episode Three	03/06/72	17.50	17.52	23'59"	8.1	36
Episode Four	10/06/72	17.50	17.51	23'55"	7.6	28

Episode Five	17/06/72	17.45	17.46	24'29"	6.0	67
Episode Six	24/06/72	17.45	17.47	24'55"	7.6	39

* In Wales the scheduled TX time was 17.05.

Plot: The Master, in the guise of Professor Thascales, has constructed at the Newton Institute in Wootton a device known as TOMTIT – Transmission Of Matter Through Interstitial Time – with which to gain control over Kronos, a creature from outside time. The creature is summoned but the effect proves uncontrollable, so the Master flees. The Doctor shuts TOMTIT down but the Master later reactivates it, using it first to ensnare Krasis, High Priest of the lost city of Atlantis, and then to attack UNIT forces by way of a series of timeslips. The Master takes Krasis back to Atlantis in his TARDIS in the hope of stealing the sacred Crystal of Kronos, with which he aims finally to dominate the creature. The Doctor follows with Jo but is unable to prevent his enemy from seducing Queen Galleia and staging a coup. Galleia turns against the Master when she learns that he has caused the death of her husband, King Dalios. The Master then unleashes Kronos, destroying Atlantis. The two Time Lords escape in their respective TARDISes and confront each other in the time vortex. The Doctor threatens to trigger a 'time ram' – a devastating collision – but cannot bring himself to do it. Jo, held hostage by the Master, has no such qualms, and operates the controls herself. The two TARDISes reappear in a strange void presided over by Kronos – who now appears as a beautiful female face. The time ram has released Kronos, who agrees to return the Doctor and Jo to Earth. The creature plans to subject the Master to eternal torment, but the Doctor pleads on his behalf and he too goes free.

Episode endings:
1. A radiation-suited Master is demonstrating TOMTIT to Newton Institute director Dr Percival and a group of observers, including Brigadier Lethbridge-Stewart. The device succeeds in instantaneously transporting a cup and saucer from the main area of the lab to a smaller inner area. From the inner area, lab assistant Stuart Hyde calls for the power to be switched off. Instead however the Master boosts it and shouts to Kronos to come to him.
2. The Master activates TOMTIT again and, as an astonished Dr Percival and a stunned Sergeant Benton look on, Krasis materialises in the inner area of the lab.
3. The Master directs a V1 flying bomb from the Second World War to fall on a UNIT convoy led by Captain Yates. The Doctor, Jo and the Brigadier witness the explosion from a distance. The Brigadier tries desperately to raise Yates on his walkie-talkie, but in vain.
4. The Master laughs as he sends the Doctor's TARDIS spinning into the time vortex with Jo left alone aboard it.
5. Jo is seized by Krasis and thrown into the Atlantean vault wherein lurks the Minotaur. She hears the creature roar and looks round in alarm.
6. Benton, having previously been regressed to a baby by TOMTIT, reverts to his normal age. He stands naked in the laboratory and demands to know what has been happening as the Doctor, Jo, the Brigadier, Stuart Hyde and Newton Institute scientist Dr Ruth Ingram look on in amusement.

IT WAS MADE WHERE...?

Ealing Filming: 29.03.72-31.03.72, 03.04.72 on Stage 2
Location Filming: 04.04.72-07.04.72

Locations: Swallowfield Park, Swallowfield, Berks; Stratfield Saye Park, Stratfield Saye, Hants; Roads near Strathfield Saye, Hants; Mortimer Lane, Mortimer, Berks; Heckfield Heath, School Lane, Heckfield Heath, Berks; Road near Old Church Farm, Old Church Lane, Hartley Wintney, Hants.

Studio Recording: 25.04.72-26.04.72 in TC3, 09.05.72-10.05.72 in TC4, 23.05.72-24.05.72 in TC3

ADDITIONAL CREDITED CAST

Master (Roger Delgado), Brigadier Lethbridge-Stewart (Nicholas Courtney), Captain Mike Yates (Richard Franklin[1-4]), Sergeant Benton (John Levene[1-4,6]), Dr. Ruth Ingram (Wanda Moore[1-4,6]), Stuart Hyde (Ian Collier[1-4,6]), Dr. Percival (John Wyse[1-3]), Dr. Cook (Neville Barber[1,2]), Proctor (Barry Ashton[1,2]), Window Cleaner (Terry Walsh[1]), Krasis (Donald Eccles[2-6]), Hippias (Aidan Murphy[2,3,5,6]), Neophite (Keith Dalton[2]), Unit Sergeant (Simon Legree[3,4]), Kronos (Marc Boyle[3,4,6]), Dalios (George Cormack[3,5,6]), Knight (Gregory Powell[3]), Roundhead Officer (Dave Carter[3]), Farmworker (George Lee[4]), Galleia (Ingrid Pitt[5,6]), Crito (Derek Murcott[5,6]), Lakis (Susan Penhaligon[5,6]), Miseus (Michael Walker[5,6]), Guard (Melville Jones[5,6]), Minotaur (Dave Prowse[6]), Face of Kronos (Ingrid Bower[6]).

Note: Jon Pertwee was credited as 'Dr. Who' for this story.

POPULAR MYTHS

- Well-known actress Susan Penhaligon, making an early television appearance as Galleia's handmaiden Lakis, was originally to have been credited as Virginia Mull. (Virginia Mull was a different actress who had a small uncredited walk-on role as a serving girl in the Atlantis scenes of this story. Susan Penhaligon was always to have been credited under her own name.)

THINGS TO WATCH OUT FOR

- This story boasts a new TARDIS interior set, designed by Tim Gleeson.
- The costumes for the Atlantean characters are highly detailed and elaborate.
- Popular horror film star Ingrid Pitt appears as Queen Galleia.
- Dave Prowse, later to play (but not voice) the masked Darth Vader in the *Star Wars* films, appears in an equally incognito role as the Minotaur.

THINGS YOU MIGHT NOT HAVE KNOWN

- An experimental session was undertaken on Monday 27 March 1972 in studio 4A to test out several effects. The morning was given over to Christopher Barry to carry out a further test of CSO effects for *The Mutants* on a telecine loop, while the afternoon was for Paul Bernard to test effects for *The Time Monster*. These latter effects were described in contemporary documentation as: small true crystal of Kronos, light box fx, Minotaur head, emitted light from crystal, effervescent fizz, motif for crystal, limb of fire, water dazzle, Kronos' 'suit of lights' (with Marc Boyle) and Stuart Hyde's ageing make-up (with Ian Collier).
- Susan Penhaligan replaced Ann Michelle at a late stage after the latter actress was let go by Paul Bernard for unpunctuality after a week's rehearsal.

- **The Master:** 'Ah, the tribal taboos of army etiquette. I find it difficult to identify with such primitive absurdities.'
- **The Doctor:** 'When I was a little boy, we used to live in a house that was perched halfway up the top of a mountain. Behind our house, there sat under a tree an old man. A hermit, a monk. He'd lived under this tree for half his lifetime, so they said, and had learned the secret of life. So, when my black day came, I went and asked him to help me.' **Jo Grant:** 'And he told you the secret? Well, what was it?' **The Doctor:** 'I'm coming to that, Jo, in my own time. I'll never forget what it was like up there. All bleak and cold, it was, a few bare rocks with some weeds sprouting from them and some pathetic little patches of sludgy snow. It was just grey. Grey, grey, grey. The tree the old man sat under was ancient and twisted, the old man himself – he was as brittle and as dry as a leaf in autumn.' **Jo Grant:** 'But what did he say?' **The Doctor:** 'Nothing. Not a word. He just sat there, silently, expressionless, and he listened while I poured out my troubles. I was too unhappy even for tears, I remember. When I'd finished, he lifted a skeletal hand and he pointed. Do you know what he pointed at?' **Jo Grant:** 'No.' **The Doctor:** 'A flower. One of those little weeds. Just like a daisy it was. I looked at it for a moment and suddenly I saw it through his eyes. It was simply glowing with life like a perfectly cut jewel, and the colours were deeper and richer than you could possibly imagine. It was the daisiest daisy I'd ever seen.' **Jo Grant:** 'And that was the secret of life? A daisy? Honestly, Doctor!' **The Doctor:** 'Yes, I laughed too when I first heard it. Later, I got up and ran down the mountain and I found that the rocks weren't grey at all. They were red and brown, purple and gold. And those pathetic little patches of sludgy snow were shining white in the sunlight!'
- **Galleia:** [Speaking of the Master.] 'Handsome? Aye, he looked well enough. But his face, Lakis. It was a face of power. Such a man would risk the world to win his desires …'

The Time Monster is one of a number of stories in relation to which the weight of fan opinion has shifted significantly over the years. The views expressed by J Jeremy Bentham in *Oracle* Volume 3 Number 9, dated May 1981, are representative of those that saw print in the late seventies and early eighties:

'From start to finish the serial is just loaded with unexpected bonuses. The TARDIS is used widely …; there are some excellent sets; and the action never flags throughout the whole 150 minutes. Best of all is the stunning interplay between the Doctor and his principal adversary. Robert Sloman has carefully drawn out the personality of each Time Lord, giving them strengths and weaknesses that are not only delightful to observe but totally fitting …

'*The Time Monster* is a true example of *Doctor Who* at its best – an adventure in space and time in the classical sense, combining science-fiction with adventure with historical drama.'

In marked contrast is the following assessment by Jonathan Burt in *Five Hundred Eyes* Issue 5 dated summer 1990, which typifies the far more negative response that the story has received in later years: 'Although the ideas behind the story were solid, they were strained by the six episode format. Padding is obvious throughout … and especially during the Wootton section. The pace is terribly slow – the action could have fitted into half the time. Indeed, Episode Two and the first part of Episode Three further the plot not at all between the Master's first and second call of "Come, Kronos, come!" When Kronos does make one of its irregular appearances, its "white dove" costume looks rather silly ... The climax of Episode Six when Kronos is depicted as a huge yet distant god-like face, proving its asexuality, power and a beauty of its own type, is more effective in realising the potential of the "most fearsome" Chronivore.'

This distinctly lukewarm reaction corresponds more closely to that of contemporary viewers, as evidenced by the BBC's Audience Research Report on the story's closing episode: 'There was evidently some feeling among reporting viewers that *Doctor Who* was "ready for a rest" ... Some, certainly, enjoyed this imaginative and enjoyable fantasy about the possible fate of the fabled city of Atlantis, which had some tense moments, but, on the whole, it was felt to reflect the general "tiredness" of the series, several dismissing it as "absolute rubbish" which was too obvious and stereotyped to hold their attention. "I see the Master has escaped again, so no doubt we are in for a further series of confrontations", remarked one viewer drily.'

Some fan commentators have been even more damning in their criticism. 'It is a story which covers some four thousand years of history – and even goes beyond the calculable boundaries of time,' noted David Auger in *Doctor Who – An Adventure in Space and Time* in 1986. 'A simple artifact provides the common denominator ...: a piece of quartz in the configuration of a trident; the very crystal which was once used by the priests of Atlantis to draw Kronos from beyond those temporal boundaries and into time itself. However, despite there being such an imaginative concept to link them, these diverse elements fail to meld successfully as a *Doctor Who* serial. It is almost as if someone has grasped the crystal and let it slip through their fingers to shatter on the floor. While still retaining some individual splendour, the resulting fragments lack coherence and can never match the magnificence of the original crystal.'

This is a persuasive analogy; and indeed, with hindsight, it is difficult to see how *The Time Monster* acquired its initial high reputation in the first place. It is easily the weakest story of the ninth season. Quite apart from its lack of dramatic focus and poorly worked out plot, it also features some of the silliest ideas ever to be presented in *Doctor Who* – most notably Bessie's 'minimum inertia superdrive' and the Doctor's use of a wine bottle and assorted kitchen implements to construct a device to jam TOMTIT. Some of the characters – particularly Ruth and Stuart, with their terribly clichéd 'battle of the sexes' sniping, and Hippias, who is far too camp to be taken seriously as the lover of the voluptuous Galleia – are frankly cringe-inducing. The realisation of Kronos is also less than impressive, as even Bentham was forced to admit: '[When it was] framed against the crystal, wings beating in slow motion like a malevolent dragonfly, a very powerful image was conjured up, which was totally lost on the few occasions we saw it in full view – swinging about the set on its flying harness like an apoplectic budgerigar.' Even worse is the depiction of the story's other 'monster', the Minotaur. 'Paul Bernard's direction really slips here,' wrote Jonathan Burt. 'The Minotaur, looking ... ridiculous, is fully lit by a white floodlight, so the viewer can appreciate all its inadequacies! The Doctor plays the toreador, and, inexplicably, the beast runs on and fatally crashes into the wall, conveniently exposing the crystal. Words cannot hope to sum up the ineptness of this sequence: it has to be experienced.'

The fragments of 'individual splendour' to which Auger referred are to be found mainly in the section of the story set in Atlantis, which boasts excellent performances from Ingrid Pitt as Galleia and George Cormack as Dalios and an unusual but highly effective subplot of the Master seducing the Queen. The characterisation of the regulars is also one of the story's best features – the sequence in which Captain Yates and his UNIT men are confronted by a knight on horseback and Roundhead troops, although admittedly superfluous to the plot, is wonderful – and reviewers have often singled out the Master for particular praise. 'The Master is the best aspect of the story,' asserted Jonathan Burt, 'brilliantly portrayed by Roger Delgado. There are several subtle touches …, one of the best being in Episode One when [he] pretends to be a "life-long pacifist" to avoid eating lunch opposite the Brigadier. Although he hypnotises Percival with ease ("Just like the old days"), this is a story when his tricks do not always come off. Benton is not fooled [by his impersonation of the Brigadier over the telephone], because the Master calls him "dear fellow" … Furthermore the Master fails to hypnotise Dalios, and, although he controls his ire externally, we can see he is seething inside. Despite these setbacks, [he] is given opportunities to display his magnetism and power as a character … [He] is able to exert a non-hypnotic influence over Krasis and Galleia … The Master's "infernal courtesy" is on display throughout … His exchanges with the Doctor in the TARDISes verge on friendly banter, but both Delgado and Pertwee inject [them] with an underlying seriousness. Despite his evil, Delgado's Master is a likeable character, and this is at the root of his success.' It must be said however that even the universally admired Delgado has an uncharacteristic lapse when he overacts woefully in the scene where he pleads with Kronos to spare him.

One senses that the production team's aim in *The Time Monster* was to try to repeat the perceived success of the previous season's closing story, *The Dæmons*, also written by Robert Sloman and Barry Letts. There are, indeed, a number of similarities between the two, as David Auger observed: 'The structure of the first episode in each case is very similar; The *Time Monster* has Jo Grant informing the Doctor about some of the latest theories on Atlantis, where *The Dæmons* saw her telling him about witchcraft and the occult; both episodes feature the two lead characters racing along in Bessie to get to the location around which the action is centred; and both climax with the Master calling upon a powerful being to come forth and do his bidding. Similarities extend beyond these first episodes, though. For example, the crystal of Kronos cannot be moved, just as the miniaturised spacecraft of the Dæmon could not be moved. And to cap it all, Kronos and Azal come from two different alien races, both of which were apparently responsible for the destruction of Atlantis!' Despite all these similarities, the two stories are sadly far apart in quality, and *Doctor Who*'s ninth season ends on a disappointing note.

Season nine had been another successful one for *Doctor Who*, it ratings and audience appreciation figures both showing a marked overall improvement for the third year in succession. Producer Barry Letts and script editor Terrance Dicks had both contemplated moving on to other projects at the end of the ninth production block – which continued beyond *The Time Monster* to include one of the following season's stories, *Carnival of Monsters* – but, delighted with what they had achieved on the series, their BBC superiors persuaded them to stay on and take it into its tenth year of production.

DOCTOR WHO SEASON TEN (1972-1973)

Regular Cast:
Doctor Who (Jon Pertwee)
Jo Grant (Katy Manning)

Regular Crew:
Producer: Barry Letts.
Script Editor: Terrance Dicks.
Title Music: Ron Grainer and the BBC Radiophonic Workshop, arranged by Delia Derbyshire.
Special Sounds: Dick Mills except on *Carnival of Monsters*. Brian Hodgson on *Carnival of Monsters*.

Season ten saw the continuation of a period of unprecedented behind-the-scenes stability on *Doctor Who*. It was the fourth successive season on which Barry Letts had worked as producer – a stint unequalled by any of his predecessors – and the sixth for Terrance Dicks as a member of the production team. The series' regular and semi-regular cast also remained unchanged for the third year in a row. One change that Letts wanted to make was to introduce a new version of the series' theme music, arranged by Brian Hodgson and realised on the Radiophonic Workshop's Delaware synthesiser. This proved unpopular with others at the BBC, however, and so at a late stage the familiar Delia Derbyshire arrangement was reinstated.

A policy that the production team liked to pursue was to launch each season with a 'gimmick' that would attract publicity and entice viewers to tune in for the start of the new run of episodes. For season eight it had been the introduction of the Master, and for season nine the return of the Daleks. This time, it was a special story to celebrate a significant landmark – the series' tenth anniversary.

THE THREE DOCTORS

Writer: Bob Baker, Dave Martin. **Director:** Lennie Mayne. **Designer:** Roger Liminton. **Costumes:** James Acheson. **Make-Up:** Ann Rayment. **Incidental Music:** Dudley Simpson. **Visual Effects:** Michealjohn Harris, Len Hutton. **Film Cameraman:** John Baker. **Film Editor:** Jim Walker. **Studio Lighting:** Clive Thomas. **Studio Sound:** Derek Miller-Timmins. **Production Assistant:** David Tilley. **Assistant Floor Manager:** Trina Cornwell.

	First UK TX	Scheduled TX	Actual TX	Duration	Viewers	Chart Pos.
Episode One	30/12/72	17.50	17.51	24'39"	9.6	41
Episode Two	06/01/73	17.50	17.50	24'18"	10.8	22

Episode Three	13/01/73	17.50	17.51	24'22"	8.8	44
Episode Four	20/01/73	17.50	17.51	25'07"	11.9	17

Plot: A gel-like plasma creature arrives on Earth and hunts down the Doctor, who calls on the Time Lords for help. The Time Lords themselves are in crisis as their energy is being drawn off into a black hole. They send the Doctor's earlier selves to join him. The first Doctor, caught in a time eddy and able only to advise, deduces that the creature is a time bridge. The third Doctor and Jo then give themselves up to it and are transported to a world of antimatter beyond the black hole. On Earth, the second Doctor is forced to take refuge in the TARDIS along with the Brigadier and Sergeant Benton. On the advice of the first Doctor he switches off the ship's force field, and the whole UNIT building is transported through the black hole. Behind these events is Omega, a figure from Time Lord history whose solar engineering provided the power for time travel. He has been trapped in the black hole ever since and now wants the Doctor to swap places with him, but it transpires that the corrosive properties of his domain have already destroyed his physical form, leaving only his will. He threatens to destroy the universe but is tricked into touching the second Doctor's recorder – the only thing not converted to antimatter when the TARDIS passed through the black hole – and is consumed in the resulting supernova. Everyone else is returned home.

Episode endings:
1. The third Doctor switches off the TARDIS force field and goes outside. Jo follows him and both are engulfed in a blinding flash from the plasma creature.
2. The second Doctor switches off the TARDIS force field and the whole of UNIT HQ is transported through the black hole.
3. The second and third Doctors find the point of singularity within the black hole: the source of Omega's power. Omega catches them there and exacts retribution: the third Doctor is consigned to a black void where he is forced to fight a troll-like creature – the dark side of Omega's mind – that eventually gets him in a stranglehold.
4. Having bid farewell to his predecessors, who fade away to their rightful times and places, the third Doctor discovers that the Time Lords have rewarded him by sending him a new dematerialisation circuit for the TARDIS and returning to him his knowledge of time travel lore and dematerialisation codes. Explanations are hard for Mr Ollis, however, and he skirts the issue by asking his wife if supper is ready.

IT WAS MADE WHERE...?

Ealing Filming: 06.11.72 on Stage 3A
Location Filming: 07.11.72-10.11.72
Locations: Harefield Lime Works, Springwell Lock, Springwell Lane, Rickmansworth; YMCA/MOD Hostel, Hayling House, Hayling Lane, Higher Denham; Springwell Reservoir, Springwell Lane, Rickmansworth; Summerfield Bungalow, Springwell Lane, Rickmansworth.
Studio Recording: 27.11.72-28.11.72 in TC1, 11.12.72-12.12.72 in TC8

ADDITIONAL CREDITED CAST

Dr. Who (Patrick Troughton), Dr. Who (William Hartnell), Brigadier Lethbridge-Stewart (Nicholas Courtney), Sergeant Benton (John Levene), Dr. Tyler (Rex

Robinson), President of the Council (Roy Purcell), Mr. Ollis (Laurie Webb), Chancellor (Clyde Pollitt[1,2]), Time Lord (Graham Leaman), Mrs. Ollis (Patricia Prior[1,4]), Corporal Palmer (Denys Palmer[1,2]), Omega (Stephen Thorne[2-4]).

POPULAR MYTHS

- The production team decided to make a story involving all three Doctors after William Hartnell visited the *Doctor Who* office looking for work. (The idea for such a story had often been suggested to the production team, including in many viewers' letters, and they decided to go ahead with it as they thought it would be a fitting way to launch the tenth anniversary season. Hartnell had effectively retired by this point and was not looking for work.)
- The initial sequence of the second Doctor seen on the Time Lords' scanner was a clip from *The Macra Terror*. (It was specially shot for this story at Harefield Lime Works.)
- The scenes of the first Doctor stuck in the time eddy were filmed in William Hartnell's garage. (They were shot at the BBC's Television Film Studios in Ealing on 6 November.)

THINGS TO WATCH OUT FOR

- This story is the second in succession to introduce a new TARDIS interior set.. On this occasion it was designed by Roger Liminton and based closely on the original. The one that had been used for *The Time Monster* had been disliked by the production team and had in any case been damaged in storage so that it was no longer useable.
- This story features the final performance by William Hartnell in *Doctor Who*. He was suffering badly from arteriosclerosis and had to read all his lines from cue cards while seated in a chair. The scripts were hastily rewritten to circumvent this problem, and he was seen only in pre-filmed inserts displayed on screens. This was to be his last work as an actor and he died some three years later, on 24 April 1975.

THINGS YOU MIGHT NOT HAVE KNOWN

- Working title: *The Black Hole*

QUOTE, UNQUOTE

- **Brigadier Lethbridge-Stewart:** 'As long as he does the job, he can wear what face he likes.'
- **Third Doctor:** 'Well Sergeant, aren't you going to say that it's bigger on the inside than it is on the outside – everybody else does.' **Sergeant Benton:** 'That's pretty obvious isn't it?'
- **First Doctor:** 'So you're my replacements – a dandy and a clown. Have you done anything?' **Second Doctor:** 'Well, er, we've assessed the situation ...' **First Doctor:** 'Just as I thought. Nothing.' **Third Doctor:** 'Well it's not easy, you know.' **Second Doctor:** 'It's not as if we knew what that stuff is.' **Third Doctor:** 'No.' **First Doctor:** 'Then I'll tell you. It's a time bridge.' **Second Doctor:** 'It's a what?' **Third Doctor:** 'I see.' **First Doctor:** 'Now what's a bridge for, eh?' **Second Doctor:** 'Well ... um ...' **Third Doctor:** 'Crossing?' **First Doctor:** 'Right. So stop dilly dallying, and cross it!'
- **Omega:** 'I was to be the one to find and create the power source that would give us mastery over time itself.' **Third Doctor:** 'Well you succeeded. And are revered for

it.' **Omega:** 'Revered? Here? I was abandoned.' **Third Doctor:** 'Histories say that you were lost in the supernova.' **Omega:** 'I was sacrificed to that supernova. I generated those forces, and for what? To be blown out of existence into this black hole of antimatter. My brothers became Time Lords ... but I was abandoned and forgotten.' **Third Doctor:** 'No, not forgotten. All my life I've known of you and honoured you as our greatest hero.' **Omega:** 'A hero? I should have been a god!'

ANALYSIS

As a story designed to celebrate the series' tenth anniversary, *The Three Doctors* serves its purpose very well. The views expressed by Keith Miller in *DWFC Monthly* Number 13, dated February 1973, are not far wide of the mark: 'A brilliant start to what I'm sure is going to be one of the best series in the history of the programme. The story, acting, sets [and] music were all fantastic, the best I've seen and heard for a long time. It showed how much the Doctor has changed in the ten years he has been in our homes.'

With William Hartnell effectively sidelined due to ill health, the limelight is shared between just the current lead Jon Pertwee and his immediate predecessor Patrick Troughton, and they are afforded sufficient scope to carry the plot along in their own inimitable ways – an opportunity of which they take full advantage.

Omega provides a suitably awe-inspiring threat for such an auspicious occasion and constitutes a superb addition to the ranks of megalomaniacal crazies that have appeared over the years. Stephen Thorne gives a bravura performance in the role, and almost steals the show. This is all the more impressive considering that his head is totally encased in a mask and he has to convey everything through just his voice and body movement. An obstacle rather less within his ability to overcome, however, is that – as in all areas of the production – the story's limited budget is sadly inadequate to do full justice to the grandeur of the scripted concepts. 'The Doctor's opponent ... deserves better than he gets,' wrote Marc Platt in *Shada: A Special* dated December 1983. 'As controller of singularity, Omega has a one-track mind, but surely the world he has created from his own intellect should be more imaginative than yet another quarry? He boasts that for him everything is possible, and to prove it he produces ... a chair! Omega may be having a hard time keeping up appearances (particularly his own!) but his accommodation and lifestyle betray a lack of funds and a frugality of imagination on the director's behalf. (Tilting the camera angles does not make a fantasy world.)'

The story starts well enough, and soon the Doctor and Jo are being threatened by a pulsating lump of crackling goo that emerges from a drain. The use of video effects to create this menacing blob was a good move, as in the later scenes when it transforms into a horde of rampaging Gel Guards things do become a little silly. The costumes for the Gel Guards look like nothing more than mobile blobs of coloured cellophane; and the inclusion of a large illuminated claw that can fire blasts of energy, although a nice idea in principle, is distinctly unthreatening in practice. 'The Gel Guards I thought were rather comical, although of course they weren't meant to be,' commented Keith Miller. 'Nevertheless, they did look funny hobbling around making that burping sound.' To be fair, the creatures do seem rather more menacing in the scenes set inside Omega's castle, where the walls are of a matching design and the doorways are just the right size to accommodate them, but attacking *en masse* outside UNIT HQ they look somewhat pathetic.

One must always remember, though, that this is primarily a celebratory reunion tale, and on that basis it works. As Julian Knott commented in *A Voyage Through 25 Years of Doctor Who* dated December 1988: 'It is in the finest tradition of the Christmas pantomime – and *The Wizard of Oz* – that the story progresses, with a villain in the mould of the Wizard himself – Omega.'

The Three Doctors stands as a milestone in *Doctor Who*'s history, both because it marked the end of the Doctor's period of exile on Earth and thereby started a process that would eventually lead to the phasing out of UNIT as a regular presence, and also because it was the first story actively to celebrate the series' own past – an approach that, in later years, would arguably be taken to extremes.

CARNIVAL OF MONSTERS

Writer: Robert Holmes. **Director:** Barry Letts. **Designer:** Roger Liminton. **Costumes:** James Acheson. **Make-Up:** Angela Seyfang. **Incidental Music:** Dudley Simpson. **Visual Effects:** John Horton. **Film Cameraman:** Peter Hamilton. **Film Editor:** Peter Evans. **Studio Lighting:** Clive Thomas. **Studio Sound:** Gordon Mackie. **Production Assistant:** Chris D'Oyly-John. **Assistant Floor Manager:** Karilyn Collier.

	First UK TX	Scheduled TX	Actual TX	Duration	Viewers	Chart Pos.
Episode One	27/01/73	17.50	17.50	24'46"	9.5	29
Episode Two	03/02/73	17.50	17.50	25'00"	9.0	36
Episode Three	10/02/73	17.50	17.51	24'49"	9.0	44
Episode Four	17/02/73	17.50	17.51	24'10"	9.2	38

Plot: The Doctor and Jo take the TARDIS on a test flight. They arrive on a cargo ship, the *SS Bernice*, that appears to be crossing the Indian Ocean in 1926 but is in fact trapped inside a Miniscope – a banned peepshow of miniaturised life-forms – on the planet Inter Minor. They enter another section of the scope but find themselves confronted by ferocious Drashigs. The Doctor eventually breaks out of the scope and returns to full size. The device is owned by a pair of Lurman entertainers, Vorg and Shirna, who hope to make a quick profit from Inter Minor's hitherto reclusive natives. They have run into trouble, however, as the bureaucratic Minorians are dissatisfied with their credentials. The Doctor's efforts to rescue Jo from the scope, which is on the point of breaking down, are hampered by the schemes of two Minorians, Kalik and Orum, who plan to dupe their superior, Pletrac, and overthrow the planet's president, Zarb, by allowing the Drashigs to escape. Vorg destroys the Drashigs with an eradicator weapon and the Doctor, by linking the scope to the TARDIS, manages to return all the exhibits to their points of origin. Jo materialises beside the wrecked device, and she and the Doctor then depart in the TARDIS.

Episode endings:
1. The Doctor and Jo manage to get back to the TARDIS but look on in horror as a huge hand descends from above to pick the police box up.
2. The Doctor and Jo, making their way through the internal workings of the scope, find a hatch. They go through it and emerge into a cave leading to what appears to be an area

of swampland. Suddenly a Drashig rears up out of the swamp before them.

3. The Doctor emerges, still miniaturised, from the base of the scope and collapses to the ground.
4. The Doctor and Jo leave Inter Minor as Vorg, with a variation of the old 'three card trick' using three magum pods and a yarrow seed, sets about trying to earn enough credit bars for a trip off the planet.

IT WAS MADE WHERE...?

Location Filming: 30.05.72-02.06.72
Locations: Howe Farm, Tillingham Marshes, Tillingham, Essex; Cawoods Quarry, Asheldham, Essex; *RFA Robert Dundas*, Naval Dockyard, Chatham, Kent.
Studio Recording: 19.06.72-20.06.72 in TC4, 03.07.72-04.07.72 in TC6

ADDITIONAL CREDITED CAST

Major Daly (Tenniel Evans), John Andrews (Ian Marter), Claire Daly (Jenny McCraken), Vorg (Leslie Dwyer), Shirna (Cheryl Hall), Pletrac (Peter Halliday), Kalik (Michael Wisher), Orum (Terence Lodge), Captain (Andrew Staines[3]).

POPULAR MYTHS

- The second episode as seen on the BBC video release of this story, which is about four minutes longer than the one originally transmitted and features the abandoned Delaware synthesiser arrangement of the theme music, is a specially extended version. (It is a rough cut that was prepared during the original editing of the story and never intended for public consumption. It still exists only because BBC Enterprises inadvertently included it a package of episodes supplied to the Australian Broadcasting Company. It features Paddy Kingsland's different arrangement of the title music and includes some material that was cut before transmission from the UK version.)

THINGS TO WATCH OUT FOR

- A brief appearance is made by a Cyberman as one of the specimens seen on the screen of Vorg's Miniscope.
- Vorg is played by Leslie Dwyer, who later appeared as the miserable child-hating Punch and Judy man Mr Partridge in the BBC comedy series *Hi-de-Hi!*.
- Tenniel Evans, appearing here as Major Daly, was one of Jon Pertwee's co-stars in *The Navy Lark* and, back in 1969, had prompted him to put his name forward to the *Doctor Who* office as a possible successor to Patrick Troughton; unknown to either of them, Pertwee's name had already been on the production team's short list.
- Ian Marter plays John Andrews. Marter had earlier auditioned for the role of Captain Mike Yates and would later play the Doctor's companion Harry Sullivan.

THINGS YOU MIGHT NOT HAVE KNOWN

- Working title: *Peepshow*
- A programme called *Looking In* did a feature on the location filming for *Carnival of Monsters*.
- The cliffhanger for Episode Three was originally to have been completely different from that transmitted. In this version, as the Doctor secures the rope to descend the shaft, he hears a roar and sees a Drashig advancing on him. Catching his foot in the

rope, he overbalances and falls down the shaft. At the start of the following episode, the Drashig falls after him, revealing that the Doctor is hanging from the rope. After the Drashig has fallen, the Doctor climbs down after it. This sequence, along with several others over the course of the story, was cut due to the episodes over-running their allotted time.

- *Carnival of Monsters* was the final story on which Brian Hodgson was to handle the series' special sounds. Thereafter they would be supplied by Dick Mills.
- A BBC2 screening of Episode Four as part of the 'Five Faces of Doctor Who' repeat season in 1981 was edited at the request of Barry Letts to remove some material in the closing scenes in which he considered Pletrac's 'bald wig' make-up to be less than satisfactory. It was this repeat version of the episode that was included on the original BBC video release of *Carnival of Monsters*. It was also included as an 'extra' on the subsequent DVD release.

QUOTE, UNQUOTE

- **Orum:** [Speaking of the Minorian class known as Functionaries.] 'They've no sense of responsibility. Give them a hygiene chamber and they store fossil fuel in it.'
- **Pletrac:** 'The function of this tribunal is to keep this planet clean. This Tellurian creature comes from outside our solar system and is a possible carrier of contagion. Furthermore the creature may be hostile.' **The Doctor:** 'Would you kindly stop referring to me as "the creature", sir. Or I may well become exceedingly hostile!'

ANALYSIS

Carnival of Monsters opens with the Doctor exercising his newly-reinstated freedom by attempting to take Jo on a trip to the 'famous blue planet' Metebelis 3. The failure of the TARDIS to reach its intended destination is no surprise, but the way in which the viewer is kept guessing as to where it has actually arrived – there is at first no apparent connection between the scenes set on the *SS Bernice* and those set on Inter Minor – helps to make this a very enjoyable adventure.

The guest characters in the story are fewer than usual, but writer Robert Holmes manages to make the most of them. The first signs of his penchant for creating memorable 'double acts' (something for which he would later become renowned amongst the series' fans) can be found here in the two Lurmans – the verbose Vorg and his cynical assistant Shirna – and the two principal Minorians – the duplicitous Kalik and his fawning supporter Orum. The interaction between these two sets of characters serves to crystallise the·planet's political situation and drive forward the plot. The roles are all well acted, too, although special mention must go to Michael Wisher, who makes full use of his voice and expressions to bring Kalik to life. On the downside, it has to be said that Vorg and Shirna have a whimsical, larger than life quality – a point that could in fact be made of the story as a whole – and this has tended to alienate some reviewers. As Ian K McLachlan commented in *TARDIS* Volume 6 Number 5 dated January 1982: '*Carnival of Monsters* … could have been much improved with Vorg and Shirna very much toned down. Perhaps it was their costumes which were most at fault. They reminded me so much of a bad *Lost in Space* story.' Gary Russell, on the other hand, wrote in *Oracle* Volume 3 Number 11/1, dated Christmas 1981, that 'the costumes were rich and elegant, especially the two Lurmans'.' Of the Minorians, Paul Scoones gave the following rather unenthusiastic assessment in *TSV* 44 dated June 1995:

'Kalik's plan to overthrow his brother, the unseen but much mentioned President Zarb, fails to engender any interest. This subplot seems to serve no other purpose ... than to facilitate the escape of the Drashigs, and ultimately provide Vorg with an opportunity to earn the respect and acceptance of the Minorian government.

'The Minorian tribunal is petty, procrastinating and officious, but we only realise just how much so when the Doctor arrives on the scene to tell them off. The Pertwee era is loaded with scenes of the Doctor displaying his contempt for petty bureaucracy and although this story is no exception, for once his words are not directed against the Brigadier, scientists or British politicians.'

The only really disappointing characters, however, are the Functionaries – Minorian workers who apparently have little to do except stand around and grunt. Their make-up suggests that they are not of the same race as Kalik, Orum and Pletrac, but there is no evidence of any other Minorians about – perhaps they are all confined to their homes. Given that the Functionaries are evidently oppressed, it is strange to note that the Doctor fails to take up their cause. 'At the outset it would appear that the moral wrong-doing that will be put right by the Doctor's intervention is the treatment of the Functionaries ...,' observed Paul Scoones, 'but this is not in fact the case. References are made to the Functionaries' unrest and refusal to work. At the beginning [one of them] dares to ascend to a higher level – perhaps metaphorically as well as literally – apparently protesting at his working conditions, but he is gunned down by Kalik without hesitation ... It is odd that this aspect of the plot has no resolution, and that the Doctor does not even appear to be aware of the Functionaries' plight.'

The characters on board the *SS Bernice* are all well written and played. The repetition of lines and actions resulting from the fact that they are supposedly caught in a time loop does eventually become rather wearing but nevertheless allows for some nice pieces of plotting as the Doctor and Jo escape, get captured and escape once more while their captors are left none the wiser. Julian Knott, writing in *A Voyage Through 25 Years of Doctor Who* dated December 1988, thought these sequences impressive, liking the juxtaposition of the hi-tech scope with the pseudo-historical setting of the ship: 'Soon ... viewers are taken through the initial SF wrappings of the story and enter the 1926 Holmes version of a Wodehouse BBC classic series adaptation. The script is excellent, the plot thickens, and interest is recaptured.'

The Drashigs are excellently realised monsters, and fulfil their admittedly limited role in the narrative very nicely. The plesiosaur that terrorises the *SS Bernice* is, on the other hand, rather less successful, owing both to the unconvincing nature of the model used and to the dodgy CSO by way of which it is inserted into the picture.

Carnival of Monsters is perhaps best viewed as a pleasant and light-hearted interlude between the self-congratulatory *The Three Doctors* and the more serious *Frontier in Space*.

FRONTIER IN SPACE

Writer: Malcolm Hulke. **Director:** Paul Bernard, David Maloney6*. **Designer:** Cynthia Kljuco. **Costumes:** Barbara Kidd. **Make-Up:** Sandra Shepherd. **Incidental Music:** Dudley

Simpson. **Visual Effects:** Bernard Wilkie, Rhys Jones. **Film Cameraman:** John Tiley. **Film Editor:** John Bush. **Studio Lighting:** Ralph Walton. **Studio Sound:** Brian Hiles. **Production Assistant:** Nicholas John. **Assistant Floor Manager:** John Bradburn.

* David Maloney directed, uncredited, the final moments of the story.

	First UK TX	Scheduled TX	Actual TX	Duration	Viewers	Chart Pos.
Episode One	24/02/73	17.50	17.51	23'17"	9.1	32
Episode Two	03/03/73	17.50	17.53	24'10"	7.8	53
Episode Three	10/03/73	17.50	17.52	24'00"	7.5	57
Episode Four	17/03/73	17.50	17.51	23'35"	7.1	55
Episode Five	24/03/73	17.50	17.52	23'57"	7.7	57
Episode Six	31/03/73	17.50	17.53	24'44"	8.9	40

Plot: The TARDIS arrives in the year 2540 on board an Earth spaceship, which then comes under attack. The crew perceive the Doctor, Jo and the attackers as Draconians, whose empire currently rivals Earth's for control of the galaxy. The Doctor and Jo, however, see that the attackers are really Ogrons. The Ogrons stun everyone on board and steal the ship's cargo – including the TARDIS. Accused by the Earth authorities of spying for the Draconians, the Doctor is sent to a penal colony on the Moon while Jo is placed in the custody of a Commissioner from Sirius 4 – actually the Master. The Master rescues the Doctor and locks him and Jo up aboard a stolen police spaceship. Once in flight, the ship is intercepted by the Draconians. Taken to Draconia, the Doctor is able to convince the Emperor of the Master's scheme to provoke a war using the Ogrons and a hypnotic device that makes those affected see whatever they most fear. Jo is recaptured by the Master and taken to the Ogrons' home planet, where he also has the Doctor's TARDIS. The Doctor follows with General Williams – an emissary from the President of Earth – and a Draconian Prince. Behind the Master's plot are the Daleks, who want a war to break out so that they can invade in the aftermath. The Doctor and his party are placed in the Master's custody as the Daleks leave to prepare their forces, but they manage to escape. Williams and the Draconian Prince depart to warn their respective peoples of the Daleks' intentions. The Doctor, though, is injured in the confusion. Jo helps him into the TARDIS, where he sends a telepathic message to the Time Lords ...

Episode endings:
1. When questioned by their rescuers, the crew of the cargo ship denounce the Doctor and Jo as stowaways and traitors in league with the Draconians.
2. Ogrons attack the prison and break into the cell where the Doctor and Jo are being held by the Earth authorities. One of the creatures, brandishing its gun, instructs the two travellers: 'You – come!'
3. In the penal colony, the Doctor is accompanying the elderly peace campaigner Professor Dale in an escape attempt. They enter an airlock where spacesuits and breathing apparatus have been left for them by an apparent ally, the trustee prisoner Cross, so that they can go outside. In fact they have walked into a trap: the breathing apparatus is empty, and Cross seals them in and starts to pump out the air ...
4. The Doctor, Jo and the Master are held in a cell aboard the police spaceship as the Draconians direct it toward their home planet. Unseen by his fellow prisoners, the Master

activates a signalling device on which a light begins to flash. Elsewhere, the signal registers on a screen before which is seated an Ogron.

5. The Master threatens a horrified Jo with his hypnotic fear-inducing device, telling her 'It works directly on the fear centres deep in your mind!'

6. Jo helps the injured Doctor into the TARDIS, where he activates the controls and sends a telepathic message to the Time Lords. The police box rushes away through the void ...

IT WAS MADE WHERE...?

Model Filming: 21.08.72 (studio unknown)
Location Filming: 10.09.72-13.09.72
Locations: Riverside Walk and around Hayward Gallery, Royal Festival Hall, South Bank, Waterloo, London; Fuller's Earth Works (Beachfields Quarry), Cormongers Lane, Redhill, Surrey; 8a Fitzroy Park, Highgate, London.
Ealing Filming: 14.09.72 (studio unknown)
Studio Recording: 02.10.72-03.10.72, 16,10.72-17,10,72 all in TC4, 31.10.72-01.11.72 in TC3

ADDITIONAL CREDITED CAST

President of Earth (Vera Fusek[1-3,5,6]), General Williams (Michael Hawkins[1-3,5,6]), Draconian Prince (Peter Birrel[1,2,5,6]), Gardiner (Ray Lonnen[1,2]), Kemp (Barry Ashton[1,2]), Hardy (John Rees[1,2]), Stewart (James Culliford[1,2]), Newscaster (Louis Mahoney[1,2]), Draconian Space Pilot (Roy Pattison[1,2]), Secretary (Karol Hagar[1-3]), The Master (Roger Delgado[3-6]), Professor Dale (Harold Goldblatt[3,4]), Patel (Madhav Sharma[3]), Prison Governor (Dennis Bowen[3,4]), Cross (Richard Shaw[3,4]), Sheila (Luan Peters[3]), Technician (Caroline Hunt[3]), Lunar Guard (Lawrence Harrington[3]), Draconian Captain (Bill Wilde[4,5]), Draconian Emperor (John Woodnutt[5]), Draconian Messenger (Ian Frost[5]), Earth Cruiser Captain (Clifford Elkin[5]), First Ogron (Stephen Thorne[5,6]), Second Ogron (Michael Kilgarriff[5,6]), Third Ogron (Rick Lester[5,6]), Congressman Brook (Ramsay Williams[6]), Newscaster (Bill Mitchell[6]), Pilot of Space Ship (Stanley Price[6]), Daleks (John Scott Martin[6], Cy Town[6], Murphy Grumbar[6]), Dalek Voice (Michael Wisher[6]).

Note: The above listing reflects an error made at the time of production, whereby one of the on-screen cast credit slides for Episode One was inadvertently substituted for one of those for Episode Two. This meant that two cast members – Roy Pattison as Draconian Space Pilot and Louis Mahoney as Newscaster – received a credit on Episode Two even though they did not appear, while two others – Lawrence Davidson as Draconian First Secretary and Timothy Craven as Cell Guard – received no credit even though they did appear.

POPULAR MYTHS

- The fifth episode as seen on the BBC video release of this story, which is about a minute longer than the one originally transmitted and features the abandoned Delaware synthesiser arrangement of the theme music, is a special 'extended version'. (It is a rough cut that was prepared during the original editing of the story and never intended for public consumption.)

- This story features Roger Delgado's last appearance in *Doctor Who*. On 18 June 1973 he was killed in a car crash in Turkey while on the way to the location for a film called *Bell of Tibet*.
- The Master is seen reading a copy of H G Wells's *The War of the Worlds*.
- There are brief shots of a Sea Devil, a Solonian mutant and a Drashig in the scene in Episode Six where the Master subjects Jo to the effects of his fear-inducing device.

- The masks for the Draconian 'extras' were modelled from a bust of the face of comedian Dave Allen.
- The 'Ogron eater' monster did not turn out as successfully as had been hoped, and Letts insisted that the director, Paul Bernard, re-edit the final episode to minimise the time that the creature was seen on screen. The monster was played by AFM John Bradburn.

- **General Williams:** 'I prefer to put my faith in the mind probe.'
- **The Master:** 'In a reminiscent mood are you, Doctor? Poor Miss Grant, you have my deepest sympathies.'
- **The Master:** [To the Draconian Emperor.] 'No-one is more concerned about the cause of peace than I.'
- **Draconian Emperor:** 'An emperor who does not rule deposes himself.'

Frontier in Space is a surprisingly rare foray by *Doctor Who* into the realms of 'space opera' – stories of interplanetary conflict in which model shots of spaceships flying about the galaxy are a predominant feature. One of the few other examples is *The Space Pirates* in season six. Unlike that rather lacklustre earlier story, however, this one works brilliantly, being both very well scripted by Malcolm Hulke and superbly brought to the screen by director Paul Bernard and his team. '*Frontier in Space* is very good TV drama,' wrote Charles Daniels on an internet newsgroup in 1997. 'The very basic nature of the conflict works extremely well – both sides are convincingly characterised, and Malcolm Hulke … manages to avoid making the Draconians into bad guys. (Indeed, sympathetic monsters is one of the best overall features of the Pertwee era.) The idea of altering people's perceptions so that they see false images is great. The Master is at his best as an amoral agitator and expert con-man … The representations of Earth hint at a broad and convincing human empire … and seem utterly realistic. (Even the stereotypical mad American evangelist warmonger type isn't too [over the top]) … The costumes and sets are lavish and well designed, and the [location] filming at the South Bank … is very entertaining.'

The model filming for the space scenes is excellent, and the frequent changes of planetary location put the whole thing on a suitably grand scale. The Draconians are well conceived and realised creatures, with their superb 'half masks' created by visual effects sculptor John Friedlander, and it is easy to see how they became Jon Pertwee's own personal favourite of all the alien creations that appeared during his time as the Doctor. The Master is as charmingly evil as ever, and it is just a pity that he does not get a proper farewell scene given that (although obviously no-one could have known it at the time) this was Roger Delgado's last appearance in the series. It is good to have the Ogrons back again, and the surprise arrival of the Daleks for the final episode is very welcome and effective, its impact all the greater for the fact this is the first time that the series has featured a twist ending of this kind. On the downside, the Master's fear inducing device repeats an idea used to rather better effect with the Keller Machine in *The Mind of Evil*, and the story's lack of a clear resolution is undeniably disappointing, although this may have been unavoidable given that it was always intended to serve as a lead in to the Doctor's next adventure.

Contemporary viewers certainly gave *Frontier in Space* an overwhelmingly positive reception, according to the BBC's Audience Research Report on the closing episode:

'Despite some criticism that the story ... was dull, predictable and came to an unsatisfactory conclusion, this last episode was evidently enjoyed by the majority of those reporting. This had been an exciting and entertaining tale, they said, and the reappearance of the Daleks certainly "got things humming", while the somewhat open-ended conclusion had its advantages in leaving scope for a new but "related" adventure ...

'[With] scattered exceptions, those reporting had the warmest praise for the way in which the whole cast made the very most of the script. Jon Pertwee was, as always, excellent as the Doctor, it was said, and both Katy Manning (Jo Grant) and Roger Delgado (the Master) were warmly commended. A few felt the production lacked pace or offered nothing new in the way of "effects", but most were quite satisfied with this aspect of the serial, settings, costumes and make-up (especially for the various "alien" species) being considered very good indeed.

'As always, there was a hard core of opinion that the *Doctor Who* series had long outlived its entertainment value ... Nevertheless, it was clear from viewers' comments that it was still widely regarded as excellent family entertainment, from those who said that their children would never miss it to the rather older viewer who wrote: "I sometimes feel, at 64, that I shouldn't be watching this!", and a considerable number evidently agreed with the member of the sample who said: "I feel this enjoyable piece of fantasy could go on for ever – each new generation is potentially a new race of *Doctor Who* fans".'

These pleasingly positive sentiments are testament to the fact that *Frontier in Space* is, overall, one of the strongest stories of the tenth season.

PLANET OF THE DALEKS

Writer: Terry Nation. **Director:** David Maloney. **Designer:** John Hurst. **Costumes:** Hazel Pethig. **Make-Up:** Jean McMillan. **Incidental Music:** Dudley Simpson. **Visual Effects:** Clifford Culley. **Film Cameraman:** Elmer Cossey. **Film Editor:** Dave Thomas. **Studio Lighting:** Derek Slee. **Studio Sound:** Tony Millier. **Production Assistant:** George Gallaccio. **Assistant Floor Manager:** Sue Hedden, Graeme Harper, John Cook.

	First UK TX	Scheduled TX	Actual TX	Duration	Viewers	Chart Pos.
Episode One	07/04/73	18.10	18.11	24'51"	11.0	09
Episode Two	14/04/73	17.50	17.54	24'08"	10.7	18
Episode Three	21/04/73	17.50	17.54	22'34"	10.1	26

Episode Four	28/04/73	17.50	17.51	23'36"	8.3	29
Episode Five	05/05/73	17.50	17.52	22'31"	9.7	21
Episode Six	12/05/73	17.50	17.51	23'06"	8.5	24

Plot: The TARDIS materialises in a hostile jungle on the planet Spiridon. Jo sets out alone to find help for the Doctor, who has fallen into a coma. She meets a party of Thals and is left in hiding aboard their crashed spaceship while they go to the Doctor's aid. The Time Lord, now recovered, learns of their mission to destroy a party of Daleks sent here to discover the native Spiridons' secret of invisibility. Another Thal spaceship crash-lands in the jungle, and the survivors bring news that somewhere on Spiridon there is an army of ten thousand Daleks. Jo meanwhile meets a friendly Spiridon named Wester, who cures a deadly fungus disease that she has contracted. It transpires that the Daleks' army is frozen in suspended animation in a cavern below their base. The Doctor, with the help of the Thals, explodes a bomb in the cavern wall and thereby causes one of the planet's natural ice volcanoes to erupt, entombing the army in a torrent of liquid ice. The newly-arrived Dalek Supreme and his aides are left stranded on Spiridon as the Thals steal their ship and the Doctor and Jo depart in the TARDIS.

Episode endings:
1. The Thal leader Taron tells the Doctor that if he joins them in spraying liquid paint over the incapacitated invisible creature that they have come across he will see what they are up against. He does so, and before them is revealed the familiar shape of a Dalek.
2. A Thal spaceship crash-lands on Spiridon. Rebec, one of three survivors, gives Taron the astounding news that somewhere on the planet there are ten thousand Daleks.
3. The Doctor and his Thal allies have sealed themselves in a refrigeration plant deep within the Dalek base as the Daleks attempt to cut through the door. At the Doctor's suggestion, they rig up a large plastic sheet as a makeshift balloon in the hope that they can use this to float to safety on the hot exhaust gases rising up a large chimney. The balloon seems unable to lift their combined weight however and, although the Doctor urges the Thals to give it time, Rebec cries out that it is not going to work.
4. The rebellious Thal Vaber is captured by a group of Spiridons, one of whom orders that he be taken to the Daleks.
5. The Doctor and the Thals have infiltrated the Daleks' base. Rebec is inside a captured Dalek casing, while the others are disguised in Spiridon furs. A Dalek sees a Thal boot protruding from under one of the furs and raises the alarm, declaring an emergency.
6. Jo asks the Doctor to take her home to Earth. He agrees to do so and adjusts the TARDIS controls.

IT WAS MADE WHERE...?

Location Filming: 02.01.73, 03.01.73
Location: Beachfields Quarry, La Porte Industries Ltd, Cormonger Lane, Redhill, Surrey.
Ealing Filming: 04.01.73, 05.01.73, 08.01.73, 09.01.73 on stage 3B
Studio Recording: 22.01.73-23.01.73 in TC4, 05.02.73-06.02.73 in TC6, 19.02.73-20.02.73 in TC1

ADDITIONAL CREDITED CAST

Taron (Bernard Horsfall), Vaber (Prentis Hancock[1-5]), Codal (Tim Preece), Rebec (Jane How[2-6]), Wester (Roy Skelton[2,3,5]*), Dalek Voices (Michael Wisher[2-6], Roy Skelton[2-6]), Dalek Operators (John Scott Martin[2-6], Murphy Grumbar[2-6], Cy Town[2-6]), Marat (Hilary Minster[3]), Latep (Alan Tucker[3-6]).

* Roy Skelton also provided, uncredited, other Spiridon voices.

POPULAR MYTHS

- The Dalek Supreme was operated in this story by Tony Starr. (Starr could not have operated the Dalek Supreme in the scenes set in the Spiridon jungle, as he was not present when they were recorded. He did operate a Dalek in other scenes in Episode Six, and was credited for this in *Radio Times*, but there is no evidence that it was the Dalek Supreme and, particularly given that he was uncredited on screen, this seems unlikely. It is probable that John Scott Martin, who was credited as Chief Dalek in *Radio Times*, played the Dalek Supreme in all instances.)

THINGS TO WATCH OUT FOR

- There is an addition to the TARDIS set in the form of a cupboard unit containing a slide-out bed.
- Wester becomes visible – and thereby reveals the Spiridons' true appearance – after he dies due to exposure to a virus with which the Daleks plan to wipe out all other life on the planet.

THINGS YOU MIGHT NOT HAVE KNOWN

- Working title: *Destination: Daleks*
- Rebec was named after Terry Nation's daughter, Rebecca.

QUOTE, UNQUOTE

- **Taron:** 'In our legends there is a being, a figure from another planet who came to Skaro when the Thals were in their greatest peril. In something called a TARDIS. He had three companions.' **The Doctor:** 'Yes, Barbara, Ian and Susan.' **Vaber:** 'And their leader was called?' **The Doctor:** 'The Doctor.' **Taron:** 'Are you trying to tell us that you are the Doctor?' **The Doctor:** 'That's right.'
- **The Doctor:** [After destroying a Dalek.] 'You know, for a man who abhors violence, I took great satisfaction in doing that.'
- **The Doctor:** 'Courage isn't just a matter of not being frightened, you know. It's being afraid and doing what you have to do anyway.'

ANALYSIS

The observation most often made by reviewers about *Planet of the Daleks* is that it is virtually a rewrite of the first Dalek story from 1963/64. There is certainly a good deal of truth in this. Once again the Doctor is seen to aid a group of Thals in an attack on a gleaming Dalek base. In place of a petrified forest, a lake of mutations and a treacherous cave system they are faced with a hostile jungle, a lake of 'liquid ice' and, as before, a treacherous cave system. Again the Doctor's companion becomes ill and is cured by the

3 THIRD DOCTOR

indigenous people's drugs, and again someone uses a Dalek casing as a disguise. The Daleks intend to unleash a lethal virus on the planet's surface, just as in the earlier story they planned to release deadly radiation. The inclusion of the Dalek Supreme meanwhile reminds the viewer of other sixties Dalek stories, and even the invisible Spiridons recall the invisible Visians from *The Daleks' Master Plan*. All these similarities are by no means to the story's detriment, however. Rather, they serve to give it a pleasantly nostalgic quality perfectly appropriate to the tenth anniversary season. Episode One's explicit dialogue references to the Doctor's initial visit to Skaro with Barbara, Ian and Susan are a particularly nice touch.

'Parallels and reworkings aside, *Planet of the Daleks* actually compares quite favourably with its 1963/64 progenitor,' wrote Tim Robins in *Doctor Who – An Adventure in Space and Time* in 1986. 'Although it lacks the sense of wonder, it tries to evoke a similar epic atmosphere and aspires to the spectacle delivered by the Daleks' appearances in [the comics] *TV Century 21* and *TV Action*. "Somewhere on this planet there are ten thousand Daleks!" exclaims a Thal – although unfortunately most of them prove to be of the [Louis Marx] variety.'

The use of painted Dalek toys to depict the Dalek army is admittedly rather obvious but nevertheless does not detract too much from the viewer's enjoyment of these scenes; and it must be said that the idea of a ten thousand strong force of the creatures just waiting to be revived and sent into action is really quite awe-inspiring. The new-look Dalek Supreme – adapted from a sixties cinema film Dalek, which writer Terry Nation still had in his possession – is also very impressive, with its black and gold livery and its customised eye-stalk and dome-lights; and indeed the Daleks as a whole are far more effective here than in their previous story, *Day of the Daleks*.

Other aspects of the story's on-screen realisation are rather hit and miss, as Robins observed: 'Dalek head lights continually flash out of synchronisation – as does the curious torch-like eye-stalk of the Dalek Supreme – and this problem is exacerbated by the fact that ... [unusually] ... one Dalek [sounds] exactly like another. Even the camera angles fail to indicate which Dalek is speaking. The studio is the right place to create truly alien environments, but unfortunately the Spiridon jungle is uninteresting and its denizens faintly ludicrous – particularly as a crowd of glowing eyes in the dark. The Spiridons' bright furs make one wonder what poor large, furry and very hot animals they originally belonged to. The Dalek flying saucer – which appears to be a couple of lampshades stuck together – is particularly lamentable. However, ... [a] plus is the effective and convincing use made of CSO to convey the Spiridons' invisibility, which otherwise serves very little dramatic purpose.'

Another criticism that could be made of the story is that the Thals – who have now clearly abandoned their earlier pacifist ways in favour of waging all-out war against the Daleks – are rather clichéd and two-dimensional characters and, with the exception of Bernard Horsfall's Taron, not all that well acted. Such considerations are not too important, though, as this story clearly has no real pretensions toward being serious drama. Robins was perhaps not far wrong when he wrote: 'This serial represents what *Doctor Who*, for better or worse, has almost always been about – pulp sci-fi adventure for kids and like-minded adults. A universe where prose is purple and death comes in various shades of green.' All in all, *Planet of the Daleks* is a very enjoyable tale that provides a satisfying conclusion to the epic storyline begun in *Frontier in Space*.

THE GREEN DEATH

Writer: Robert Sloman, Barry Letts*. **Director:** Michael Briant. **Designer:** John Burrowes. **Costumes:** Barbara Kidd. **Make-Up:** Ann Rayment. **Incidental Music:** Dudley Simpson. **Fight Arranger:** Terry Walsh. **Visual Effects:** Ron Oates, Colin Mapson, Richard Conway. **Film Cameraman:** Bill Matthews, Ken Lowe. **Film Editor:** Alastair Mackay. **Studio Lighting:** Mike Jefferies. **Studio Sound:** Richard Chubb. **Production Assistant:** John Harris, Michael McDermott. **Assistant Floor Manager:** Karilyn Collier.

* Barry Letts received no credit on screen in view of the fact that he was producer of the series.

	First UK TX	Scheduled TX	Actual TX	Duration	Viewers	Chart Pos.
Episode One	19/05/73	17.50	17.51	25'55"	9.2	18
Episode Two	26/05/73	17.50	17.51	25'55"	7.2	38
Episode Three	02/06/73	17.50	17.51	25'12"	7.8	29
Episode Four	09/06/73	17.50	17.50	25'47"	6.8	32
Episode Five	16/06/73	17.50	17.50	25'20"	8.3	15
Episode Six	23/06/73	17.50	17.51	26'06"	7.0	30

Plot: UNIT is called in after a miner from the Welsh village of Llanfairfach is found dead, his skin glowing bright green. Jo joins forces with a local environmental group, led by Professor Clifford Jones, while the Doctor investigates the nearby plant of a company called Global Chemicals. They discover that the mine workings are full of giant maggots and green slime – both lethal to touch – that have been produced by chemical waste pumped from the Global plant. Stevens, the director of Global, has been taken over by the BOSS – Bimorphic Organisational Systems Supervisor – a computer with a will of its own. The BOSS plans to seize power by linking itself to every other major computer in the world, but the Doctor uses a blue crystal – a souvenir from a brief visit to the planet Metebelis 3 – to break its hold over Stevens, who then programs it to self-destruct. The maggots, on the point of pupating into giant insects, are destroyed with a type of fungus. Jo falls in love with Professor Jones and decides to leave UNIT in order to accompany him on an expedition up the Amazon – and to marry him. The Doctor gives her the blue crystal as an early wedding present.

Episode endings:
1. Jo and a miner named Bert descend into the mine to help another miner who has got into difficulties. The Doctor and the Brigadier arrive at the surface and ask Dave, a third miner, to stop the cage's descent. Dave discovers that the brake won't work – the cage is out of control!
2. The Doctor meets up with Jo in the mine workings and she shows him a vast lake of green slime and giant maggots that lies ahead. They try to turn back but the tunnel collapses. From the rubble emerge several giant maggots, which advance on them.
3. Jo has decided to stay up late to read in the environmentalists' cottage. She is unaware that a giant maggot, hatched from an egg that the Doctor brought back from the mine, is

making its way across the floor towards her.

4. The Doctor, having infiltrated Global Chemicals to investigate further, makes his way to a computer room. There the computer – the BOSS – introduces itself.

5. The Doctor has used the crystal from Metebelis 3 to free Captain Yates from the BOSS's hypnotic influence. Yates returns to the Global Chemicals factory and likewise uses the crystal to clear the mind of an employee named Mr James, who reveals that the BOSS intends to take over at four o'clock that afternoon. Suddenly James suffers an acute pain and falls dead to the ground. Stevens, who has entered the room unseen by Yates, coldly observes that no-one can be depended upon.

6. A party is thrown to celebrate Jo's engagement to Professor Jones. The Doctor downs a glass of wine and leaves quietly, seen only by Jo. Outside it is growing dark and, with the sound of the party fading into the distance, the Doctor gets into Bessie and drives off.

IT WAS MADE WHERE...?

Location Filming: 12.03.73-16.03.73, 19.03.73-20.03.73
Locations: Ogilvie Colliery, Deri, Nr Bargoed, Glamorgan; Colliery Quarry, Deri, Nr Bargoed, Glamorgan; farm above Colliery, Troed-y-rhiw Jestyn, Deri; RCA Factory, Brynmawr, Breconshire.
Studio Recording: 02.04.73-03.04.73, 16.04.73-17.04.73, 29.04.73-30.04.73 all in TC3

ADDITIONAL CREDITED CAST

Brigadier Lethbridge-Stewart (Nicholas Courtney), Stevens (Jerome Willis), Clifford Jones (Stewart Bevan), Elgin (Tony Adams[1-4]), Hinks (Ben Howard[1-4]), Dai Evans (Mostyn Evans[1,2]), Dave (Talfryn Thomas[1-3]), Bert (Roy Evans[1,2]), Nancy (Mitzi McKenzie[1,3-6]*), Milkman (Ray Handy[1,4]), Hughes (John Scott Martin[1]), Fell (John Rolfe[2,3]), Boss's Voice (John Dearth[2-6]), Minister of Ecology (Richard Beale[3]), Captain Yates (Richard Franklin[4-6]), Sergeant Benton (John Levene[4-6]), Cleaner (Jean Burgess[4]), Yate's Guard** (Brian Justice[4]), Guard (Terry Walsh[4]***), James (Roy Skelton[5]).

* Mitzi McKenzie was credited on but did not appear in Episode One.
** Although grammatically incorrect, this is how the credit appeared on screen.
*** Also in Episodes One, Two and Six but uncredited on screen.

THINGS TO WATCH OUT FOR

- The Doctor finally gets to visit Metebelis 3, which he first indicated an intention to do in *Carnival of Monsters*. The scenes set on Metebelis 3 were filmed at the Ogilvie Colliery.
- The Doctor disguises himself as a Welsh milkman and a cleaning woman.
- Tony Adams, better known for his role as Adam Chance in *Crossroads*, plays Elgin. Adams was taken ill during the recording, so Roy Skelton was brought in to play a replacement character called Mr James, who was given the lines written for Elgin.
- The Brigadier takes a phone call from the Prime Minister, who is named as 'Jeremy' – a joke by the production team intended to suggest that the Liberal Party, then led by Jeremy Thorpe, could win the next General Election.
- Some of the giant maggots were created from inflated condoms.
- For Episodes Two, Five and Six, the title sequence film over which the closing credits

were superimposed was played backwards and upside-down (a result of the film being played backwards through the projector in order to save time during recording).

THINGS YOU MIGHT NOT HAVE KNOWN

- Katy Manning was romantically involved with actor Stewart Bevan at the time he was cast to play Professor Jones in this story.
- Sets from the Gerry Anderson series *UFO* were used to create BOSS.

QUOTE, UNQUOTE

- **The Doctor:** 'Metebelis 3, Jo? Or where else would you like to go? You choose for yourself.' **Jo Grant:** 'But I've only got ten minutes.' **The Doctor:** 'Jo, you've got all the time in the world … and all the space. I'm offering them to you.' **Jo Grant:** 'But Doctor, don't you understand? I've got to go. This Professor Jones, he's fighting for everything that's important. Well, everything that you've fought for. In a funny way, he reminds me of a sort of … younger you.' **The Doctor:** 'I don't know whether to feel flattered or insulted. It's all right, Jo. I understand.' **Jo Grant:** 'Thanks Doctor. Thank you.' **The Doctor:** 'Jo? Tell the Brigadier that I'll follow him down.' **Jo Grant:** 'Right.' **The Doctor:** 'Later.' **Jo Grant:** 'Right … Bye.' **The Doctor:** 'Goodbye …' [Jo exits.] 'So … the fledgling flies the coop …'
- **Boss's Voice:** 'You disappoint me, Doctor. I should have thought you'd have guessed. I am the BOSS. I'm all around you. Exactly. I am the computer.'
- **The Doctor:** 'Stevens, listen to me. You've seen where this efficiency of yours leads. Wholesale pollution of the countryside. Devilish creatures spawned by the filthy by-products of your technology. Men … men walking around like brainless vegetables. Death. Disease. Destruction.'
- **Jo Grant:** 'You don't mind, do you?' **The Doctor:** 'Mind? He might even be able to turn you into a scientist.' **Jo Grant:** 'Don't go too far away, will you. And if you do, come back and see us sometimes.'

ANALYSIS

Doctor Who goes green. *The Green Death* is a prime example of producer Barry Letts's favoured approach of presenting stories that not only entertain but also enlighten with a strong moral message. The underlying theme here is concern for the ecology; an issue that remains as topical today as when the story was originally transmitted.

But first, the Doctor finally manages to get to Metebelis 3, and what he finds there is not what Keith Miller expected, as he explained in *DWFC Monthly* Number 17 dated August/September 1973: 'At last the Doctor landed on Metebelis 3, and what a place! I thought it would be a blue heaven but it seemed to be the exact opposite. It was quite terrifying to see that tentacle lash around the Doctor's body and hear that unearthly scream pierce the silence.'

The main part of the action, however, takes places in Wales, and the conflict between Global Chemicals and Professor Jones's Wholeweal community – referred to locally as the Nuthutch – is nicely set up. It must be said, on the other hand, that writers Barry Letts and Robert Sloman do have a tendency to resort to stereotypes in their characterisation. This was evident with Dr Ruth Ingram and Stuart Hyde in their previous story, *The Time Monster*, but is even more so here with the clichéd hippies at the Nuthutch and the frankly rather patronising 'boyo' type Welshmen. The revelation that the menace behind Global Chemicals is a megalomaniacal computer is not exactly original, either, a similar idea having been presented in *The War Machines* back in season three. On the whole, though, the scripts are well written and dramatic, providing some good material for the regulars – it is particularly pleasing to see Mike Yates working in an undercover capacity – and plenty of action and excitement.

On the production side, *The Green Death* suffers from an over-reliance on CSO – particularly in the scenes where it is used to substitute patently false photographic backgrounds for location shots that there was no time to film. It works best in the more traditional effects sequence of the Doctor and Jo pushing a coal truck through an underground lake of slime and maggots, although even here a tell-tale fringing problem is all too apparent. Fortunately the story's other effects, including the front-axial projection used to create the pulsing green markings on those infected by the slime and the giant fly into which one of the maggots transforms, are very much better.

On the acting front, things are not so good. Aside from Professor Jones and Nancy, none of the Wholeweal community makes much of an impression. Stevens is a suitably icy villain, but everyone else at Global Chemicals wanders around as though in a trance – which in plot terms of course many of them are. The chopping and changing of characters does not help: Elgin and Hinks one episode, then Fell, then finally James (who should have been Elgin but was substituted due to illness on actor Tony Adams's part).

The Green Death is still primarily recalled as 'the one with the maggots', and there are certainly some excellent and highly memorable scenes featuring these well-realised creatures. Perhaps the best, as cited by Keith Topping in *DWB* No. 123 dated February 1994, occurred at 'the climax to Episode Three as Jo Grant sits alone in the Nuthutch, with her back to the maggot closing in on her. It's disturbing …, it's chillingly phallic … and it also reinforces the central concepts of *Doctor Who*'s space-monster fixations. A woman in peril, ecologically engineered menace (mankind's greed for profit and technological advancement juxtaposed with a threat to innocence) and the horror of unseen danger. Classic episode ending devices when used separately but, when combined, having the serendipity of being almost the definitive *Doctor Who* moment.'

The other particularly notable aspect of this story is that it was the last to feature Katy Manning as Jo Grant. Jo had by this point become very much an integral part of the third Doctor's era, and her presence had certainly livened things up. There is a genuine sense of sadness in her final scenes with the Doctor, and a feeling of melancholy rarely matched in the series. This was well summed up by Keith Miller: 'Climbing aboard Bessie, the Doctor takes one last look back, alone with his thoughts of times gone by. Starting the engine, he slowly drives off into the distance, once more … alone. And so the end of another companionship for the Doctor, and a very sad ending (which I liked) to a truly fantastic series. That final shot … [conveyed] the feeling of loneliness which the Doctor had experienced so many times before. Now, if you'll excuse me, I think I've got something in my eye …'

The lifting of the Doctor's exile by the Time Lords was a logical culmination of the policy pursued by Barry Letts and Terrance Dicks over the previous two years of gradually loosening his ties with Earth and allowing him once more to travel through space and time (albeit initially only on predetermined missions). It meant that the original rationale for his joining forces with UNIT was no longer valid, and the viewer was left to assume that he now maintained his association with the organisation through choice rather than necessity, perhaps because of the friendships he had formed with the Brigadier, Jo and the others. At the same time, behind the scenes, the death of Roger Delgado and the departure of Katy Manning marked the beginning of the end of the period of stability that the series had enjoyed since *Terror of the Autons*; and further, more significant changes were looming on the horizon.

DOCTOR WHO SEASON ELEVEN (1973-1974)

Regular Cast:
Doctor Who (Jon Pertwee)
Sarah Jane Smith (Elisabeth Sladen)

Regular Crew:
Producer: Barry Letts.
Script Editor: Terrance Dicks*.
Production Unit Manager: George Gallaccio from *The Monster of Peladon* Part One onwards**.
Title Music: Ron Grainer and the BBC Radiophonic Workshop, arranged by Delia Derbyshire.
Special Sounds: Dick Mills.

* Robert Holmes contributed to the script editing of *Invasion of the Dinosaurs* and *Death to the Daleks* but was uncredited on screen.
** Production unit manager was a new post created at this time. The functions of this post – basically financial planning – had previously been carried out by the producer.

Season eleven was planned during a period when producer Barry Letts and script editor Terrance Dicks were dividing their time between *Doctor Who* and *Moonbase 3*, a new six part space adventure series that they had created and been asked to make for the BBC. *Moonbase 3*'s studio recordings were scheduled to be carried out in the break between *Doctor Who*'s tenth and eleventh production blocks so that there would be no direct clash of commitments, but the two men nevertheless had their work cut out to ensure that neither series suffered through lack of attention. Adding further to their workload was the need to devise and cast a new companion for the Doctor following the departure of Katy Manning's Jo Grant at the end of *The Green Death*. The character they eventually came up with, after a false start involving an unknown character played by an unknown actress, was journalist Sarah Jane Smith, and the actress Letts chose, with Jon Pertwee's approval, was Elisabeth Sladen. Sladen made her debut in the season's opening story, *The Time Warrior* – which, like *Carnival of Monsters* the previous year, was made not at the beginning of the new production block but at the end of the old one.

THE TIME WARRIOR

Writer: Robert Holmes. **Director:** Alan Bromly. **Designer:** Keith Cheetham. **Costumes:** James Acheson. **Make-Up:** Sandra Exelby. **Incidental Music:** Dudley Simpson. **Fight Arranger:** Marc Boyle, Terry Walsh. **Visual Effects:** Jim Ward, Peter Pegrum. **Film Cameraman:** Max Samett. **Film Editor:** William Symon. **Studio Lighting:** Mike Jefferies. **Studio Sound:** Tony Millier. **Production Assistant:** Marcia Wheeler. **Assistant Floor Manager:** Rosemary Webb.

	First UK TX	Scheduled TX	Actual TX	Duration	Viewers	Chart Pos.
Part One	15/12/73	17.10	17.10	24'15"	8.7	34
Part Two	22/12/73	17.45	17.46	24'10"	7.0	75
Part Three	29/12/73	17.10	17.11	23'30"	6.6	89
Part Four	05/01/74	17.30	17.30	24'57"	10.6	22

Transmission of Part Three was scheduled for 19.15 on BBC Cymru
Transmission of Part Four was scheduled for 19.10 on BBC Cymru

Plot: Journalist Sarah Jane Smith is impersonating her aunt, virologist Lavinia Smith, in order to gain access to a research centre where top scientists are being held in protective custody while UNIT investigates the disappearance of a number of their colleagues. The missing scientists have been kidnapped by a Sontaran, Linx, and taken back to medieval England, where they are working under hypnosis to repair his crashed spaceship. The Doctor follows in the TARDIS, and Sarah stows away. In return for shelter, Linx has provided a robber baron called Irongron with anachronistically advanced weapons to use in attacks on neighbouring castles. The Doctor helps Sir Edward of Wessex to repel one such attack, then he and Sarah conspire to drug the food in Irongron's kitchens so that the weapons can be removed while the men are unconscious. Aided by one of the kidnapped scientists, Rubeish, he then sends the others back to the 20th Century using Linx's primitive time travel equipment. Linx shoots Irongron down and gets ready to leave in his repaired ship. Hal, one of Sir Edward's archers, fires an arrow into the vulnerable probic vent at the back of his neck, killing him. The Doctor, Sarah and Hal escape just before the ship explodes, destroying the castle.

Episode endings:
1. As the Doctor watches from hiding, Linx removes his helmet and reveals the monstrous features beneath.
2. The Doctor fights off Irongron and his men in the castle courtyard. He falls to the ground and Irongron, declaring 'He who strikes Irongron dies!', raises an axe to kill him.
3. The Doctor attempts to bargain with Linx, offering to help repair his spaceship in return for being allowed to dehypnotise the scientists and send them back to the 20th Century. Linx gives his answer: he raises his weapon and fires it at the Doctor.
4. The TARDIS dematerialises before the astonished gaze of Hal.

Location Filming: 07.05.73-10.05.73
Location: Peckforton Castle, Peckforton, Nr Tarporly, Cheshire.
Studio Recording: 28.05.73-29.05.73 in TC6, 11.06.73-12.06.73 in TC1

ADDITIONAL CREDITED CAST

Brigadier Lethbridge-Stewart (Nicholas Courtney[1]), Linx (Kevin Lindsay), Professor Rubeish (Donald Pelmear), Irongron (David Daker), Bloodaxe (John J. Carney), Eleanor (June Brown), Edward of Wessex (Alan Rowe), Hal (Jeremy Bulloch), Meg (Sheila Fay[1,3,4]), Eric (Gordon Pitt[1]), Sentry (Steve Brunswick[3]*).

* Also in Parts One, Two and Four, but uncredited.

POPULAR MYTHS

• There was another actress cast as Sarah before Elisabeth Sladen. (There was another companion, played by a different actress, originally intended to appear in this story. Sarah was a completely fresh character, and Sladen the first choice to play her, after the production team had second thoughts.)

THINGS TO WATCH OUT FOR

• *The Time Warrior* marks the debut of a new opening and closing title sequence designed by Bernard Lodge and realised using a process known as 'slit scan'. The opening title sequence features for the first time the distinctive diamond-shaped logo for the series.
• June Brown, now better known as Dot Cotton in *EastEnders*, appears as Sir Edward's wife Eleanor.
• The Doctor's home planet is named for the first time as Gallifrey.

THINGS YOU MIGHT NOT HAVE KNOWN

• Working titles: *The Time Fugitive*, *The Time Survivor*
• A romantic subplot between Hal and a serving wench named Mary (played by Jacqueline Stanbury) at Sir Edward's castle was edited from the final transmission.
• Robert Holmes's storyline for *The Time Warrior* took the form of a communication between a Sontaran named Terran Cedicks and his base.

QUOTE, UNQUOTE

• **Brigadier Lethbridge-Stewart:** [Speaking of the assembled scientists.] 'Most of their work's so secret, they don't know what they're doing themselves.'
• **The Doctor:** 'A straight line may be the shortest distance between two points, but it is by no means the most interesting.
• **Irongron:** 'Is this "Doctor" a long-shanked rascal with a mighty nose?'
• **Sarah Jane Smith:** 'You're talking as if you weren't human.' **The Doctor:** 'Yes, well, the definition of the word "humanity" is always a rather complex question, isn't it?'
• **Sarah Jane Smith:** 'You're serious, aren't you?' **The Doctor:** 'About what I do, yes. Not necessarily about the way I do it.'

The Time Warrior, like the similarly titled *The Time Monster* from season nine, is another of the relatively small number of stories falling into the pseudo-historical category – in other words, mixing a period setting with overt science-fiction elements. Writer Robert Holmes apparently took some persuading to adopt this approach, having disliked the series' early historical stories, and this may perhaps explain why the scripts, although entertaining, are not amongst his very best for the series. A particular problem is that the curiously-named Rubeish and his (non-speaking) scientist colleagues are a rather clichéd and unbelievable bunch, making it very difficult for the viewer to become involved in their plight.

The medieval setting in which much of the action takes place is welcome in principle but doesn't work too well in practice, owing mainly to a lack of convincing period atmosphere – although this is a failing for which director Alan Bromly, with his rather uninspired handling of the proceedings, can arguably be held as much responsible as Holmes. Where this section of the story does win out however is in its wonderful dialogue – one sometimes suspects that Holmes couldn't have written a bad line of dialogue if he had tried – and, as Steven Grace observed in *Star Begotten* Vol. 3 No. 1/2 dated June 1989, in its superior characterisation:

'Even the most minor characters, such as Meg the maid, benefit from having a life of their own and [having been] created with a credible background in mind, [and] I should like to … claim that Linx and Irongron are the finest of [the writer's] legendary double acts …

'During the whole story some fine parallels are drawn between Irongron and Linx; from the moment that each is introduced we are presented with the perfect match of the two boastful warriors equal in their great arrogance. In the very first scene …, as Linx's ship comes crashing down on the wood outside the castle, Irongron immediately claims the apparent "falling star" for himself – "Irongron's star". His men are cowering in terror and horrified at the idea of riding into the wood at night, but Irongron does not share their fears. Similarly, Linx claims Earth [for the Sontaran empire] with no fear of the band (or should that read "rabble") of "knights" surrounding him.'

Irongron and his loyal but simple henchman Bloodaxe, well portrayed by David Daker and John J Carney respectively, also work well together. The story's best feature however is undoubtedly Linx the Sontaran, an inspired and memorable creation with a very striking design, complete with 'potato head' mask, excellently brought to life by actor Kevin Lindsay.

The other particularly notable aspect of *The Time Warrior* is that it introduces Elisabeth Sladen as Sarah Jane Smith, now widely considered the best of all the Doctor's travelling companions. Her potential as a character is apparent right from the outset, as Keith Miller observed in *DWFC Monthly* Number 19 dated January 1974: 'I found Sarah Jane Smith very promising as the Doctor's new assistant. Her acting was very good, showing she has a mind of her own … [Her] reluctance to admit she had been transported back in time was well handled.' These sentiments were echoed by John Peel when he reviewed the story in *Doctor Who – An Adventure in Space and Time* in 1987:

'Given the brief that she was into women's lib, Holmes made the most of the humour in the situation. In a medieval cloakroom, [Sarah] complains about a serving woman's attitudes. "You're living in the middle ages!" she yells, before realising what a stupid comment this is. Holmes gently poked fun at the libbers' concepts, whilst endorsing them at the same time. Sarah is given plenty to do, and demonstrates her bravery and versatility throughout the tale. "There's always something you can do," she tells Sir

Edward, "it is just a matter of working out what."

'Elisabeth Sladen was absolutely wonderful in her first serial. She made Sarah aggressive ("Get lost!"), wistful ("I could just murder a cup of tea …") and cute as well. She had an infectious smile and an air of conviction about what she did … She was courageous and charming, clever and annoying – all at once.'

The story as a whole was well received by contemporary viewers, judging from the BBC's Audience Research Report on Part Four: 'The majority … evidently found this episode up to the accepted standard of *Doctor Who* adventures, making good entertainment at least for their children and very often for themselves as well. ("Can be really enjoyed whatever age you are.") It was a very good ending, they often said, to a story which "worked up to a good climax" with "lots of excitement". There was some minority feeling, however, that this was "not one of the best *Doctor Who* episodes" and that it was too far-fetched ("the miraculous escapes of Doctor Who from impossible situations strain credulity to the limit"), "corny" and "cliché ridden"; or "slapstick rather than the science-fiction we have come to expect".'

Keith Miller was another admirer of the story's climax: 'The last fifteen minutes were great, where Linx was shot [in] the back of his neck, the Doctor … [escaped] by that fantastic swing from the balcony to the door, and lastly … Irongron's castle [exploded].'

It is perhaps a pity that *The Time Warrior* was not a mid-season story as, although it makes for enjoyable viewing, it lacks the sort of impact ideally needed to launch a new run of adventures. John Peel summed things up well when he wrote: 'In the end, *The Time Warrior* will really be best recalled as Sarah's first story and the first appearance of a Sontaran. As far as that goes, it achieves its aims. It is by no means a bad story – simply a simple one. The action is there to join the quips together, and to prevent the children from falling asleep. The Doctor is there because it's his show, after all. As for the rest – well, it's lightweight fun, and never pretends to be anything else.'

INVASION OF THE DINOSAURS

Note: The on-screen title of the first episode of this story is simply *Invasion* – an abbreviation intended to preserve the surprise that the story features dinosaurs.

Writer: Malcolm Hulke. **Director:** Paddy Russell. **Designer:** Richard Morris. **Costumes:** Barbara Kidd. **Make-Up:** Jean McMillan. **Incidental Music:** Dudley Simpson. **Visual Effects:** Clifford Culley. **Film Cameraman:** Keith Hopper. **Film Editor:** Robert Rymer. **Studio Lighting:** Alan Horne. **Studio Sound:** Trevor Webster. **Production Assistant:** George Gallaccio. **Assistant Floor Manager:** John Wilcox.

	First UK TX	Scheduled TX	Actual TX	Duration	Viewers	Chart Pos.
Part One	12/01/74	17.30	17.30	25'29"	11.0	24
Part Two	19/01/74	17.30	17.31	24'43"	10.1	26
Part Three	26/01/74	17.30	17.30	23'26"	11.0	27
Part Four	02/02/74	17.30	17.34	23'33"	9.0	34
Part Five	09/02/74	17.30	17.30	24'38"	9.0	23
Part Six	16/02/74	17.30	17.30	25'34"	7.5	54

Plot: The Doctor and Sarah return to 20th Century London to find it deserted. Initially arrested as looters, they are soon back with UNIT. The Brigadier explains that central London has been evacuated due to the unexplained and random appearance of prehistoric monsters. The Doctor and Sarah discover that the monsters are being brought through time by two scientists, Whitaker and his henchman Butler, as part of a conspiracy to clear London of people. The Doctor's investigations are deliberately hindered first by Captain Yates and then by the Army's General Finch, both of whom are involved in the conspiracy. Sarah visits Sir Charles Grover, the Government Minister in charge during the emergency, but discovers that he too is involved. Captured and hypnotised, she revives to find herself apparently on board a spaceship en route to colonise another world. She soon realises that the ship is just a mock-up and those on board, led by a number of elders, have been duped. The conspirators in fact intend to use a time machine to return London to a 'Golden Age' before the Earth became polluted, so that they and the would-be colonists can start civilisation afresh. The Doctor and the Brigadier mount a raid on their underground headquarters. Grover makes a last-ditch attempt to operate the time machine, but the Doctor has changed the settings and he succeeds only in sending himself and Whitaker back to the era of the dinosaurs. The Brigadier arranges for the misguided Yates to be given a chance to resign quietly from UNIT.

Episode endings:

1. The Doctor and Sarah are being taken to a detention centre in a Land Rover. The vehicle suddenly screeches to a halt and the Doctor looks out of the back to see a tyrannosaurus rex looming over them.

2. The Doctor goes to capture a brontosaurus using a gun he has built for the purpose. Yates, under instruction from Whitaker, has disabled the gun and it does not work. The brontosaurus vanishes and, as the Doctor turns, a tyrannosaurus rex appears. UNIT troops start firing at it.

3. Sarah goes to see Sir Charles Grover in the hope that he may help her to discover the location of Whitaker's base. Grover takes her captive and she is placed in a room where she is sent to sleep with flashing lights. When she wakes she is told that she is on board a spaceship heading for 'New Earth'.

4. Whitaker telephones the Doctor and asks the Time Lord to meet him. When the Doctor arrives at the rendezvous, there is no sign of Whitaker, but suddenly a stegosaurus appears. General Finch bursts in with the Brigadier and accuses the Doctor of being responsible for the dinosaur invasion.

5. Trying to make his way back to Whitaker's London base, the Doctor finds himself facing a final wave of dinosaurs. He is suddenly confronted by a tyrannosaurus rex.

6. The Doctor tries to persuade Sarah to take another trip in the TARDIS, this time to the planet Florana.

Location Filming: 02.09.73, 23.09.73-29.09.73

Locations: Albert Embankment, London; Westminster Bridge, London; Whitehall, London; Trafalgar Square, London; Margaret Street, London; Haymarket, London; Billingsgate Market, Lower Thames Street, London; Covent Garden, London; Outer Circle (by Cambridge Gate), Regent's Park, London; Clayponds Avenue, Brentford, Middx; Wilmer Close, Kingston Upon Thames, Surrey; Canbury Gardens, Lower Ham Road, Kingston Upon Thames, Surrey; Lower Ham Road, Kingston Upon Thames, Surrey;

THIRD DOCTOR

Southall Gas Works, White Street, Southall, Middx; Phillips Jewellers, Arcade, Moorfields, London, EC2; Moorgate Underground Station, Moorfields, London, EC2; New Union Street, London, EC2; Northfield's School, Balfour Road, London, W13; GPO Sorting Office, Orchard Road, Kingston Upon Thames, Surrey; Palmer Crescent, Kingston Upon Thames, Surrey; Pickford's Depositories, Brownlow Road, Ealing, London, W13; Kingston Meat Market, The Bittoms, Kingston Upon Thames, Surrey; South Lane, Kingston-Upon-Thames, Surrey; The Straight, Southall, Middx; Chamberlain Road, Ealing, London, W13; Central Electricity Generating Board Sub Station, Elderberry Road, Ealing, London, W5; White Street, Southall, Middx; Parkfields Road, Kingston-Upon-Thames, Surrey; Long Lane, Smithfield, London, EC1; Wimbledon Common, Wimbledon, London, SW19; Lindsay Street, Smithfield, London, EC1; Riverside Drive, Ham, Middx.
Studio Recording: 15.10.73-16.10.73 in TC6, 29.10.73-30.10.73 in TC8, 12.11.73-13.11.73 in TC3

ADDITIONAL CREDITED CAST

Brigadier Lethbridge-Stewart (Nicholas Courtney), General Finch (John Bennett), Captain Yates (Richard Franklin), Sergeant Benton (John Levene), Lieutenant Shears (Ben Aris[1]), Sergeant Duffy (Dave Carter[1]), Corporal Norton (Martin Taylor[1]), Private Ogden (George Bryson[1,2]), R/T Soldier (John Caesar[1]), Phillips (Gordon Reid[1]), Lodge (Trevor Lawrence[1]), Warehouse Looter (Terry Walsh[1]), Charles Grover M.P. (Noel Johnson[2-6]), Professor Whitaker (Peter Miles[2-6]), Butler (Martin Jarvis[2-6]), Peasant (James Marcus[2]), UNIT Corporal (Pat Gorman[2]), Mark (Terence Wilton[3-6]), Ruth (Carmen Silvera[4,6]), Adam (Brian Badcoe[4-6]), Private Bryson (Colin Bell[5,6]), Robinson (Timothy Craven[6]).

POPULAR MYTHS

- Robert Holmes, who on this story made his uncredited debut as a script editor, accepted the post only reluctantly and after some persuasion. (He actually telephoned the production office to put himself forward as a candidate for the post, and was delighted to find that he was already under consideration for it.)
- The master tape of the first episode of this story was mistakenly wiped when it was confused with season six's *The Invasion*. (There is no evidence to suggest that this is why the tape was wiped; all the tapes for *The Invasion* were wiped in 1972, more than two years before *Invasion of the Dinosaurs* was transmitted.)

THINGS TO WATCH OUT FOR

- Well-known actor Martin Jarvis plays Butler. Jarvis had previously portrayed Hilio in the season two story *The Web Planet*, and went on to make one further *Doctor Who* appearance, as the Governor in the season twenty-two story *Vengeance on Varos*.
- This story marks the first appearance of the Doctor's futuristic new car, named the Alien by its makers but referred to generally (although never on screen) as the Whomobile. It had still to be fully completed by the time the filming for this story took place, so it is seen with no roof and only a makeshift windscreen.

THINGS YOU MIGHT NOT HAVE KNOWN

- Working titles: *Bridgehead from Space*, *Timescoop*.
- The effects for this story were contracted out to Clifford Culley of Westbury Design

and Optical Ltd, working out of Pinewood studios, and the making of the dinosaur models (which were too big for Culley to handle) subcontracted to a designer named Robert Fuller.

- *Bridgehead from Space* was the title of the original story outline submitted by Malcolm Hulke on 18 December 1972. In it, the TARDIS materialises in a deserted London and the Doctor learns from a few remaining humans that aliens have landed and taken over the city. To ensure that London remains clear, the aliens have released monsters onto the streets, hatched from eggs. The aliens start to demand more and more parts of England for themselves. This is intended as a parallel to the tactics of Hitler – divide and rule. The Doctor's goal is to find the aliens' master plan and to prove to the world's population that unless they work together, they are doomed.

- Hulke was unhappy at the change in title from *Timescoop* to *Invasion of the Dinosaurs* and more unhappy still that the first episode was billed simply as *Invasion*, which prompted him to write a letter of complaint to the production office. He felt that many millions of viewers would have been lost because the title was so uninteresting. He felt that this reflected on him as a writer – as people would assume that the title was his idea – and with lowered ratings as a result, his professional reputation might suffer. Terrance Dicks replied to Hulke's letter on 17 January 1974, recalling that *Timescoop* as a title originated in the *Doctor Who* office, as did the title as finally used. Dicks commented that the *Radio Times'* use of drawings of the Doctor being attacked by a pterodactyl and a caption referring to 'pre-historic monsters' made a nonsense of their decision to change the title for the first episode, but noted that *Radio Times* 'are a law unto themselves'. Dicks concluded by stating that he agreed that the decision to change the title was a dubious one and that he now regretted making it.

- The police box shell was completely referbished for this story. The interior was painted black, the doors re-hung, the base re-clad with hardboard and the entire box repainted, blown down and aged to match the original colour – Prussian blue. Finally, all the graphics were repainted.

QUOTE, UNQUOTE

- **The Doctor:** 'Look, I understand your ideals. In many ways I sympathise with them. But this is not the way to go about it, you know. You've got no right to take away the existence of generations of people.' **Captain Yates:** 'There's no alternative.' **The Doctor:** 'Yes there is. Take the world that you've got and try and make something of it. It's not too late.'

- **Brigadier Lethbridge-Stewart:** 'We've got company.' **The Doctor:** [In the process of planting a bomb in the lift leading to the conspirators' base.] 'Good grief, it's a triceratops! Look Brigadier, try and keep it occupied while I'm finishing this off, will you?'

- **The Doctor:** 'It's not the oil and the filth and the poisonous chemicals that are the real cause of pollution, Brigadier. It's simply greed.'

ANALYSIS

Given that the production team decided to commission a story about dinosaurs only because they had been approached by a freelance effects designer who assured them that he could produce highly realistic models of such creatures, it is rather ironic that the one major respect in which *Invasion of the Dinosaurs* fails in its on-screen realisation is … the dinosaurs!

The opening episode starts very promisingly but ends terribly, as Keith Miller described in *DWFC Monthly* Number 19 – Special Review Edition in the spring of 1974: 'The deserted London streets created a brilliant atmosphere, and set the scene for what I thought was going to be the Malcolm Hulke version of *The Dalek Invasion of Earth* but with dinosaurs. The scenes that followed were very good, what with the public telephone being out of order and the streets being devoid of any bus service. The looter in the jewellery shop was brought to a quick and mysterious end when his car crashed some distance down the road. Very good, I thought, the mystery deepens. Then came the pterodactyl, which was quite well done, [although] its wings didn't flap enough. The Doctor and Sarah being arrested was a novel twist ... After escaping they came up against the first dinosaur and, oh dear, shades of Basil Brush! A glove puppet nervously skiing about London streets didn't exactly fill me with fright ...'

The model dinosaurs were not in fact glove puppets, but there is undeniably a resemblance to the popular children's character Basil Brush in the way that they move, and not for one moment do they look convincing. What's more, it is painfully obvious that only a small number were created for the story; the Doctor seems to encounter a tyrannosaurus rex every time he turns a corner. The CSO by way of which the creatures are combined with the live action is not wonderful, either, and the scenes in question actually look much better if viewed in black and white. The effects team have obviously tried hard to make the miniature sets in which the dinosaurs appear match their live action counterparts, but ultimately the creatures – in whatever setting – are laughable rather than frightening.

The great pity is that the awfulness of the dinosaur scenes tends to overshadow the excellence of Paddy Russell's direction of the rest of the story and the high quality of the performances by the assembled cast – particularly Noel Johnson as Grover and John Bennett as Finch, although Martin Jarvis is rather wasted as the one-dimensional Butler. Craig Hinton recognised this dichotomy in a review in *A Voyage Through 25 Years of Doctor Who* dated December 1988: 'Marred by terrible special effects, enriched by superb acting and character development by all concerned, the story seemed ... to exist [solely] to fill up six episodes.'

It is perhaps fortunate that Malcolm Hulke's scripts use the dinosaurs really only as window dressing to what is, in essence, another moralistic tale about the problems of pollution and the lengths to which mankind might go to try to solve them. In a neat about-turn from *The Green Death*, where the ecologists were the good guys and the 'establishment' most definitely at fault, here the ecologists are unreasonable fanatics and the 'establishment', as represented by the Doctor and the Brigadier, are the saviours of humanity. John Peel, writing in *Fantasy Empire* Issue 11 dated May 1984, highlighted the story's strong plot and characterisation: 'Once again, we were treated to another of Malcolm Hulke's complex and believable plots. The villains genuinely believed that what they were doing was for the ultimate good of the human race, and tried to justify their beliefs. None of them [was a] sadistic [killer], and all were sorry for the deaths incurred in the project, but they felt that it was worth it to achieve a Golden Age. The revelation of Mike Yates as a traitor was quite a shock to the viewers, as for the previous [three] seasons he had been one of the staunchest of allies for the UNIT crew. It was an unexpected and clever plot move, and seemed to mark the end of Yates in the show.'

This is not to suggest that Hulke's scripts are perfect, however. On the downside, the story is poorly paced and contains a tremendous amount of padding, most particularly in Part Five which seems to be almost entirely taken up with the Doctor driving about Wimbledon Common being chased by helicopters and Land Rovers. The subplot concerning the people supposedly *en route* to 'New Earth', although one of the story's most effective elements, is also superfluous and could easily have been cut, perhaps leaving this as a rather tighter four-part adventure. There is, moreover, a big credibility problem in the idea that Sir Charles Grover and his chums were able to construct a spaceship mock-up in the basement of a Government building and then recruit notable (and newsworthy) sportsmen and writers supposedly to fly off to another planet, all without anyone else noticing. It is impossible to imagine something of this magnitude happening without the newspapers getting wind of it, and yet it comes as a complete surprise to Sarah. Still, at least Sarah has a chance to use her journalistic skills in this story – an aspect of her character that would later be somewhat neglected – and is given lots to do while the Doctor faffs about trying to capture a dinosaur.

Keith Miller summed things up well: 'After the battle of the bendy toys with Basil and Bronty, the Doctor guides UNIT down to the Underground station where he combines forces with the elders and brings about the ironic ending of all the baddies being transported back to the time they wanted to bring forwards. The story, on the whole, was well written, but the effects let it down badly, I'm sorry to say.'

Unfortunately, *Invasion of the Dinosaurs* is destined to be remembered as 'the one with the awful dinosaurs'.

DEATH TO THE DALEKS

Writer: Terry Nation. **Director:** Michael Briant. **Designer:** Colin Green. **Costumes:** L Rowland Warne. **Make-Up:** Magdalen Gaffney, Cynthia Goodwin. **Incidental Music:** Carey Blyton, performed by the London Saxophone Quartet. **Fight Arranger:** Terry Walsh. **Visual Effects:** Jim Ward. **Masks:** John Friedlander. **Film Cameraman:** Bill Matthews. **Film Editor:** Bob Rymer. **Studio Lighting:** Derek Slee. **Studio Sound:** Richard Chubb. **Production Assistant:** Chris D'Oyly-John. **Assistant Floor Manager:** Richard Leyland.

	First UK TX	Scheduled TX	Actual TX	Duration	Viewers	Chart Pos.
Part One	23/02/74	17.30	17.30	24'32"	8.1	49
Part Two	02/03/74	17.30	17.30	24'25"	9.5	30
Part Three	09/03/74	17.30	17.30	24'24"	10.5	20
Part Four	16/03/74	17.30	17.35	24'35"	9.5	21

Plot: The TARDIS arrives on the planet Exxilon, where all electrical energy is drained off by an unknown force. The Doctor meets a Marine Space Corps expedition from Earth who tell him that a plague is sweeping the galaxy and that the antidote, parrinium, can be found only on Exxilon. Their ship has been disabled by the energy drain, so they are unable to leave with the mineral. Sarah meanwhile has seen a magnificent white edifice with a flashing beacon on top. She is captured by a group of savage Exxilons and taken to their cave to be sacrificed for defiling their city. The Doctor and the humans enter into an uneasy alliance with a group of Daleks who also land on the planet and whose weapons are rendered inactive by the energy drain. They too are taken prisoner by the Exxilons. The Doctor interrupts Sarah's execution but is then sentenced to death himself. The two travellers escape into some tunnels as the cave is attacked by a second force of Daleks armed with mechanical guns. There they meet Bellal, an enlightened Exxilon, who tells them that the city was created by his own race but then brought about their downfall. The Doctor, realising that the city's beacon is causing the energy drain, resolves to put it out of action. He and Bellal enter the city and, by passing a series of potentially deadly tests, reach its centre. There the Time Lord uses his sonic screwdriver to give the controlling computer a brainstorm. The Daleks plan to take all the parrinium but their ship is destroyed with a bomb triggered by one of the humans who has stowed away on board. Sarah then reveals that she and another of the humans had already smuggled off all the parrinium and transferred it to the Earth ship.

Episode endings:

1. A spaceship lands on the planet and the Doctor goes with the MSC group to greet it. A door opens and Daleks glide out. The Daleks fire their weapons.
2. Making his way through the tunnels beneath the Exxilon city, the Doctor is confronted by a metallic root that rears up before him.
3. The Doctor and Bellal, progressing through the corridors of the Exxilon city, come to an area where the floor is marked in a red and white pattern. Suddenly the Doctor says 'Stop – don't move!'
4. As the Exxilon city collapses, the Doctor sadly muses that the universe now has only 799 wonders.

IT WAS MADE WHERE...?

Location Filming: 13.11.73-16.11.73, 19.11.73
Location: sand and gravel pit, Amey Roadstone Corp Ltd, Puddletown Road, Gallows Hill, Dorset.
Studio Recording: 03.12.73-04.12.73, 18.12.73-19.12.73 in TC3

ADDITIONAL CREDITED CAST

Dan Galloway (Duncan Lamont), Richard Railton (John Abineri[1,2]), Commander Stewart (Neil Seiler[1, 2]), Peter Hamilton (Julian Fox), Jill Tarrant (Joy Harrison), High Priest (Mostyn Evans[1,2]), Dalek voices (Michael Wisher), Dalek Operators (John Scott Martin, Murphy Grunbar*, Cy Town), Bellal (Arnold Yarrow[2-4]), Gotal (Roy Heymann[3]).

* Murphy Grumbar's surname was mis-spelt on all episodes.

THINGS TO WATCH OUT FOR

- When testing their new weapons system, the Daleks use a small model police box for target practice.

THINGS YOU MIGHT NOT HAVE KNOWN

- Working title: *The Exxilons*
- The Exxilon masks were designed by the costume designer L. Rowland Warne but made by John Friedlander.

- **The Doctor:** [Speaking of the Daleks] 'Inside each of those shells is living, bubbling lump of hate.'
- **Bellal:** 'Exxilon had grown old before life began on other planets.'

ANALYSIS

The knowledge that a story is to feature the Daleks always induces a feeling of excitement and anticipation. Expectations are higher than they would normally be, and if the story proves to be anything less than spectacular this can sometimes lead to it being judged unduly harshly. This may perhaps help to account for the fact that *Death to the Daleks* has, over the years, come in for far more than its fair share of criticism. An example of this is to be found in Trevor Wayne's evaluation in *Doctor Who – An Adventure in Space and Time* in 1987: 'The arrival of the Daleks in the closing minutes [of the first episode] sets the scene for a nightmare … Unfortunately it is a recurring nightmare; *deja vu* rather than death seems to be stalking the Daleks. If *Planet of the Daleks* … was a rewrite of the seminal Dalek story, then *Death to the Daleks* contains a wealth of SF clichés, many of which have turned up before in Dalek stories and in *Doctor Who* more generally: mysterious cities degenerating; ancient civilisations; the inevitable tunnels and corridors; the quest/race through the elaborate IQ test; and clichéd and monotonous dialogue. Although there is little wrong with the basic storyline, ultimately I always have to remember it as "the story in which the Daleks were painted silver" or "the one with Sarah in" in order to separate it in my mind's eye from other serials.'

Admittedly the action is somewhat low key and played out on a relatively small scale (although references to the space plague sweeping the galaxy give a tantalising glimpse of the bigger picture), but the scripts are still well-written and entertaining, with a good premise and some interesting concepts. The Daleks are at their scheming best here and also look very impressive, their casings having been refurbished for the production. Even before they arrive on the scene, there is much to enjoy in a first episode that begins very effectively with the violent slaying of an astronaut (played by stuntman Terry Walsh) and the apparent 'death' of the TARDIS as all its power is drained away, and then continues in a suitably creepy and atmospheric vein as the Doctor and Sarah venture out to explore the mist-swathed surface of the planet Exxilon.

The subplot involving the Exxilons and their city is one of the story's most intriguing aspects, although again Trevor Wayne felt that it was both unoriginal and inadequately developed: 'Central to [the plot] is one of Terry Nation's obsessions …: that science and invention may become too complex or clever for the scientist or inventor. This is, of course, a legitimate concern, which Kit Pedler and Gerry Davis had spread beyond *Doctor Who* to their own series, *Doomwatch*. But whereas such ideas can be fully developed in a [series] like *Doomwatch*, they all too often get buried under the weight of plotting needed to sustain a *Doctor Who* story over four or six episodes. In the case of *Death to the Daleks*, the message trying to claw its way to the surface is apparent when Bellal tells the Doctor the sorry tale of how the wise and noble Exxilons constructed the perfect city controlled by the perfect computer which, seeing that its creators were not perfect, evicted them.'

Keith Miller, writing in *DWFC Monthly* Number 19 – Special Review Edition in the spring of 1974, liked the modelwork by way of which the Exxilon city was realised, and indeed the depiction of the Exxilons as a whole: 'The [exterior of] the citadel was a magnificent piece of alien architecture. Really terrific. After Sarah had been captured, the Exxilon singing was great and frightening.' On the downside, however, the closing model shots of the city disintegrating are very unconvincing. And while the Exxilons are good characters, being both well written and effectively presented with some great masks courtesy of visual effects sculptor John Friedlander, the members of the human expedition are all rather one-dimensional, and in a couple of cases not very well acted. Carey Blyton's incidental music is another aspect of the story's production that is less than wholly successful, tending to grate on the nerves after a while – and quite a short while at that – although some commentators have praised it, and it does undeniably blend in well with the superb atmospheric sounds created for the planet by the Radiophonic Workshop's Dick Mills.

Above all else, though, this is a story of excellent set pieces and impressive images. Notable examples not already mentioned include Sarah fending off an Exxilon attacker in the TARDIS in the first episode; the Daleks using a model police box for target practice with their new weapons; and one of the city's defensive roots emerging from a lake in the mining area, where it spectacularly destroys a Dalek. The various challenges that the Doctor and Bellal face as they make their way through the Exxilon city are also memorable – although the cliffhanger ending to Part Three is rather strange. (In fairness, it was not originally supposed to be a cliffhanger at all, and became one only because the episode had to be edited for timing reasons.) The Doctor's subsequent use of 'Venusian hopscotch' to overcome the problem of the booby trapped pattern on the floor is also stretching things a bit. 'Venus must rate pretty highly in the [Doctor's] book,' observed Keith Miller, 'what with Venusian measurements, karate, lullabies and now hopscotch! The lightning bolts as the Dalek skimmed over the floor were well done, as was the floor repairing itself.'

Death to the Daleks is overall a highly enjoyable story, and probably the best of the series' eleventh season.

THE MONSTER OF PELADON

Writer: Brian Hayles. **Director:** Lennie Mayne. **Designer:** Gloria Clayton. **Costumes:** Barbara Kidd. **Make-Up:** Elizabeth Moss. **Incidental Music:** Dudley Simpson. **Visual Effects:** Peter Day. **Film Cameraman:** Keith Hopper. **Film Editor:** William Symon. **Studio Lighting:** Ralph Walton. **Studio Sound:** Tony Millier. **Production Assistant:** Marcia Wheeler. **Assistant Floor Manager:** Roselyn Parker.

	First UK TX	Scheduled TX	Actual TX	Duration	Viewers	Chart Pos.
Part One	23/03/74	17.30	17.30	24'59"	9.2	23
Part Two	30/03/74	17.30	17.30	23'26"	6.8	55
Part Three	06/04/74	17.30	17.30	24'47"	7.4	42
Part Four	13/04/74	17.30	17.30	24'50"	7.2	37
Part Five	20/04/74	17.30	17.31	23'56"	7.5	42
Part Six	27/04/74	17.30	17.31	23'48"	8.1	30

Plot: The TARDIS returns to Peladon some fifty years after the Doctor's last visit. The planet is now ruled by Queen Thalira – daughter of the late King Peladon – with advice from Chancellor

Ortron. The Doctor and Sarah are arrested by Ortron for trespassing on sacred ground but their names are cleared by Alpha Centauri, now Galactic Federation ambassador to Peladon. A ghost-like image of Aggedor has been responsible for some deaths in the planet's trisilicate mines, heightening unrest amongst the miners. The Doctor discovers that the apparitions are really the result of the use of a matter projector and a directional heat ray by a human engineer, Eckersley. Eckersley is in league with a group of renegade Martian warriors, led by Commander Azaxyr, in a plot to seize the trisilicate deposits for Galaxy 5, a power bloc at war with the Federation. Azaxyr mounts an attack on the throne room and kills Ortron. The Doctor however turns the heat ray on some of the Martians, while others are dispatched by the miners. Eckersley flees, taking the Queen hostage, but the Doctor uses the real Aggedor to track him down. Eckersley is killed, but Aggedor also dies in the skirmish. Its plans thwarted, Galaxy 5 surrenders to the Federation. The Doctor is invited by Thalira to take over as Chancellor but he declines, suggesting the miners' leader Gebek would make a better candidate.

Episode endings:
1. Queen Thalira agrees to let the Doctor investigate the cave where the Federation mining engineer Vega Nexos was killed by the spirit of Aggedor. As the Doctor and Blor, the Queen's Champion, enter the cave, a disaffected miner named Ettis, intending to sacrifice them to Aggedor, detonates some explosives. The resulting rock fall traps the Doctor and Blor in the cave. Suddenly a roaring image of Aggedor appears, killing Blor.
2. The Doctor and Sarah are thrown into a pit beneath the temple to face the judgment of Aggedor. A low growl alerts them to the fact they're not alone. The Doctor pulls out a small flashlight and they see the beast Aggedor looming out of the shadows towards them.
3. The Doctor suspects that the image of Aggedor may be controlled from the supposedly shut refinery in the mine workings. He and the leading miner, Gebek, go there to investigate. The Doctor disarms the automatic protection system and the refinery door opens to reveal a Martian warrior.
4. The Doctor struggles with Ettis to prevent him from destoying the citadel with a sonic lance aimed at it from a neighbouring peak. They are unaware that Azaxyr has set the lance to self destruct and that if it is operated anyone in the vicinity will be killed. Ettis overpowers the Doctor and operates the lance, which explodes.
5. The Doctor, Gebek and Sarah enter the refinery in order to use the Aggedor statue – which is linked to a matter transmitter and a heat ray – against the Martians. Azaxyr's deputy Sskel and some other Warriors start to burn their way through the refinery door.
6. The Doctor and Sarah make their way back to the TARDIS and leave Peladon.

IT WAS MADE WHERE...?

Ealing Filming: 14.01.74-18.01.74 on Stage 3A
Studio Recording: 28.01.74-29.01.74 in TC8, 11.02.74-12.02.74, 26.02.74-27.02.74 all in TC6

ADDITIONAL CREDITED CAST

Eckersley (Donald Gee), Thalira (Nina Thomas), Ortron (Frank Gatliff[1-5]), Gebek (Rex Robinson), Ettis (Ralph Watson[1-4]), Voice of Alpha Centauri (Ysanne Churchman), Body of Alpha Centauri (Stuart Fell), Vega Nexos (Gerald Taylor[1]), Preba (Graeme Eton[1,2,4]), Blor (Michael Crane[1]), Guard Captain (Terry Walsh[1-4]), Aggedor (Nick

Hobbs[2,3,6]), Miner (Roy Evans[3,4]), Azaxyr (Alan Bennion[4-6]), Sskel (Sonny Caldinez[4-6*]), Miner (Max Faulkner[6]).

* Also at the end of Part Three, but uncredited.

POPULAR MYTHS

- Azaxyr is an Ice Lord. (Although he is referred to as a Lord, the term 'Ice Lord' is never used.)

THINGS TO WATCH OUT FOR

- In an attempt to recapture the feel of *The Curse of Peladon*, the same director and designer were assigned to this story and many of the props that still existed (including the Alpha Centauri, Aggedor and Ice Warrior costumes) were reused.
- There is a careless shot in the fight scene at the end of Part Four, where the viewer can clearly see that stuntman Terry Walsh is doubling for Jon Pertwee.

THINGS YOU MIGHT NOT HAVE KNOWN

- In Brian Hayles's original outline for this story, which is undated and does not have a title, the old King Peladon is still ruling the planet. Ortron is conspiring to sell mineral rights for money and weapons which he will use to make himself King. To do this he is in league with Eckersley, a mining contractor who has promised Ortron this deal. Megeshra is a character in all this, as is Thalira, but it is unclear from the outline what their roles are. Thalira appears to be the spurned 'girlfriend' of King Peladon whom he dropped when he went 'all moony' over Jo. The Ice Warriors are also included, but their alliegance is unclear from the outline. There is a suggestion that Sarah be driven into the arms of Eckersley so that she could discover that nasty-looking aliens can be good, while good looking humans can be bad.
- The story's scene breakdown (also undated and untitled) does not feature the sonic lance. It is the Federation who sends troops to the planet, not Alpha Centauri who summons them. The scene breakdown also features the Doctor causing a critical overload in the main reactor and ends with him tricking Axazyr into revealing his plans while a radio-link to the Federation is open, thus thwarting him.
- Producer Barry Letts, rather than actor Sonny Caldinez, spoke all of Sskel's lines, but was uncredited.

QUOTE, UNQUOTE

- **Sarah Jane Smith:** 'There's nothing "only" about being a girl.'
- **Sarah Jane Smith:** [Speaking of the Doctor, who has apparently been killed.] 'I still can't believe it. I can't believe that he's dead. You see, he was the most alive person I ever met.'

ANALYSIS

A sequel is something that should be attempted only if a) the original was successful enough to warrant it and b) the writer has something fresh to say on the subject. In the case of *The Monster of Peladon* the first of these criteria is met but unfortunately the second is not, as was immediately spotted by Keith Miller writing in *DWFC Monthly* Number 19 – Special Review Edition in the spring of 1974: 'Ortron [had] taken the place of Hepesh, the ruler [had] changed sex, but the story was almost the same [as *The Curse of Peladon*], with Ortron trying to show the Queen how wrong she [was and] trying to get rid of the Doctor and anyone else who dared to defy [him]. Then Grun, the King's Champion, was reincarnated as the [Queen's] Champion … It seemed as if it was just going to be *The Curse of Peladon* drawn out into six episodes. How disappointing!'

That *The Monster of Peladon* should suffer from this obvious shortcoming is all the more regrettable given the rarity of direct sequels in *Doctor Who*. The repetition of so many elements from *The Curse of Peladon* is not only unoriginal but also creates problems in terms of believability. It seems very unlikely that Alpha Centauri would still be on Peladon some fifty years after the events seen in the earlier story (unless the creature has a high boredom threshold!) or that Aggedor, the last surviving beast of its kind, would still be alive – especially if it has been kept in a pit all this time – and more unlikely still that the Ice Warriors would again be involved. Although perhaps less significant in plot terms, the biggest coincidence of all is that the mineral trisilicate, said by the Doctor in *The Curse of Peladon* to be exclusive to Mars and Martian technology, is now to be found in abundance on Peladon and is being used by Galaxy 5 as the basis for their technology!

Quite apart from its unsatisfactory nature as a sequel, *The Monster of Peladon* drags awfully. The plot fairly groans under the weight of Peladon's political intrigue and unrest amongst the miners. Like *The Curse of Peladon*'s allegory about entry into the Common Market, these were topical issues at the time of the story's original transmission, when miners' strikes seemed to be part and parcel of life in the UK, but unfortunately they are simply not very interesting. The characterisation is also rather weak on this occasion. The miners, with their daft badger hairstyles, are a stereotypical bunch of revolutionary hotheads. Their taking up of arms against the authorities would seem to suggest that they are very aggrieved indeed, but their motivation just does not come across. Nina Thomas's Queen Thalira, meanwhile, is such a drip that it is hard to believe that she could hold on to power for any time at all. Eckersley is also poorly defined. He seems to have constructed the trisilicate refinery, which is now disused (although why this should be the case is unclear), and also to have provided the communications room and the special security doors for the armoury. A further puzzle is that the refinery has a hi-tech sonic defence system but the armoury – which would seem more in need of it – does not. Why not have such a system in both places?

The one bright point in all this is that the Martians are well characterised and – at least in this small breakaway group – back to their old warlike ways. Alan Bennion, who played Slaar in *The Seeds of Death* and Izlyr in *The Curse of Peladon*, turns in another excellent performance as Azaxyr, and skilfully manages to make him seem subtly different from both those earlier characters. Unfortunately, with one exception, the other Warriors are let down by poor costumes with mismatched heads and bodies cobbled together from what was left in the BBC's stores after *The Seeds of Death*. The exception is Sskel played by Sonny Caldinez, who also appeared as Ssorg, the sole regular Warrior in *The Curse of Peladon*, and so was presumably able to reuse the same, better assembled costume. Craig Hinton, writing in *A Voyage Through 25 Years of Doctor Who* dated December 1988, thought that the creatures nevertheless had a considerable impact, although he was rather less well disposed toward the story as a whole: 'Looking unfortunately very tatty in seven year old costumes designed for other actors, the Ice Warriors still managed to maintain that air of menace that had made them so popular in the sixties – when they appeared, that was. *The Monster of*

Peladon seemed to drag over six episodes, introducing – then ignoring – plot developments, and leaving the "cruel Martian invaders" until the last moment. It was … creaking under weak special effects and mediocre direction from Lennie Mayne.'

The Monster of Peladon is tedious and uninspiring. Only Sarah's grief when the Doctor apparently gets killed during the course of the action seems real, foreshadowing what is to come in the very next adventure …

PLANET OF THE SPIDERS

Writer: Robert Sloman, Barry Letts*. **Director:** Barry Letts. **Designer:** Rochelle Selwyn. **Costumes:** L Rowland Warne. **Make-Up:** Deanne Turner. **Incidental Music:** Dudley Simpson. **Visual Effects:** Bernard Wilkie. **Film Cameraman:** Fred Hamilton. **Film Editor:** Bob Rymer. **Studio Lighting:** Ralph Walton. **Studio Sound:** John Holmes. **Production Assistant:** Marion McDougall. **Assistant Floor Manager:** Graeme Harper.

* Barry Letts received no credit on screen in view of the fact that he was producer of the series.

	First UK TX	Scheduled TX	Actual TX	Duration	Viewers	Chart Pos.
Part One	04/05/74	17.45	17.47	24'40"	10.1	17
Part Two	11/05/74	17.40	17.40	25'02"	8.9	26
Part Three	18/05/74	17.40	17.40	24'58"	8.8	22
Part Four	25/05/74	17.30	17.31	23'53"	8.2	24
Part Five	01/06/74	17.35	17.36	24'01"	9.2	19
Part Six	08/06/74	17.35	17.38	24'43"	8.9	25

Plot: Sarah is invited by Mike Yates to visit him at a Buddhist meditation centre where he has been staying. A group of people there, led by a man named Lupton, are misusing the meditation rituals in order to make contact with powerful alien forces, which manifest themselves as a giant spider. The spider is an emissary from the ruling council on the planet Metebelis 3, sent to recover the blue crystal that the Doctor previously found there and that has now been returned to him by Jo. The Doctor and Sarah journey to Metebelis 3 and aid its human colonists in an attempt to overthrow the 'eight legs'. They then return to Earth in the TARDIS. The Doctor recognises the meditation centre abbot K'anpo as his former Time Lord guru and, at his prompting, returns to Metebelis 3, where the humans' revolt has ultimately failed. He demands an audience with the Great One – a huge mutated spider revered by the others – and offers her the crystal. The Great One uses it to complete a crystal lattice, which she believes will increase her mental powers to infinity. Instead, the rising power kills her. The other spiders also die as their mountain explodes. K'anpo has meanwhile been killed while protecting Yates from an attack by the spider-controlled residents of the meditation centre, only to be reborn in the form of his assistant Cho-je – his own future self. Some weeks later, the Doctor is brought back to UNIT HQ by the TARDIS, having been fatally affected by the radiation in the Great One's cave. K'anpo appears and, with his help, the Doctor regenerates.

Episode endings:
1. Mike Yates and Sarah watch from hiding as the meditation centre residents, seated around

a mandala, chant the Tibetan 'jewel of the lotus' mantra. Suddenly a giant spider appears on the mandala.

2. Lupton flees in a speedboat and the Doctor gives chase in a one-man hovercraft. The hovercraft finally draws level and the Doctor jumps across into the speedboat. When he looks round, however, Lupton has vanished.

3. On Metebelis 3, the Doctor gets into a fight with the Queen spider's guards. The Guard Captain fires a blast of energy from his fingertips and the Doctor collapses to the ground just outside the TARDIS.

4. Sarah is lying cocooned in the spiders' larder. The Doctor appears in the doorway, but Sarah's initial relief turns quickly to disappointment when she sees guards behind him and realises that he too is a prisoner.

5. The Doctor and Sarah talk with K'anpo while, outside the room, the meditation centre handyman Tommy tries to prevent the spider-controlled residents Barnes, Keaver, Land and Moss from entering. They blast him with energy from their fingertips.

6. As Sarah and the Brigadier look on, the Doctor regenerates.

IT WAS MADE WHERE...?

Location Filming: 11.03.74-15.03.74
Locations: Tidmarsh Manor, Tidmarsh, Berkshire; Mortimer Station, Stratfield Mortimer, Nr. Reading; roads around station; Membury Airfield, Membury, Wiltshire; La Marchant Barracks, Devizes, Wilts; river's edge at Strand, Nr. Westbury on Severn, Gloucs.
Studio Recording: 02.04.74-03.04.74 in TC1, 16.04.74-17.04.74 in TC8, 30.04.74-01.05.74 in TC6.

ADDITIONAL CREDITED CAST

Brigadier Lethbridge-Stewart (Nicholas Courtney[1,2,6]), Mike Yates (Richard Franklin), Sergeant Benton (John Levene[1,2]), Professor Clegg (Cyril Shaps[1]), Lupton (John Dearth), Barnes (Christopher Burgess), Moss (Terence Lodge), Land (Carl Forgione[1, 2,4-6]), Keaver (Andrew Staines[1,2,4-6]), Cho-je (Kevin Lindsay[1-3,5,6]), Tommy (John Kane), Policeman (Chubby Oates[2]), Soldier (Pat Gorman[2]), Man with boat (Terry Walsh[2]), Hopkins (Michael Pinder[2]), Tramp (Stuart Fell[2]), Spider Voices (Ysanne Churchman[2-6]), Kismet Delgado[3-6], Maureen Morris[3-6]), Arak (Gareth Hunt[3-6]), Sabor (Geoffrey Morris[3-5]), Neska (Jenny Laird[3-5]), Rega (Joanna Monro[3-5]), Tuar (Ralph Arliss[3-6]), Guard Captains (Walter Randall[3-5], Max Faulkner[5*]), K'anpo (George Cormack[6**]).

* Also in Part Four, but uncredited.
** Also in Part Five, but uncredited.
Note: Ysanne Churchman provided the voice of Lupton's spider, Kismet Delgado – Roger Delgado's widow – that of the spider Queen, and Maureen Morris that of the Great One. Although uncredited, the new Doctor, played by Tom Baker, is seen at the conclusion of Part Six.

POPULAR MYTHS

• Roger Delgado's Master was originally to have been written out in *Planet of the Spiders*, and after the actor's death the story was revised to incorporate Lupton in

THIRD DOCTOR

place of the Master. (If Delgado had not died it is likely that he would have been written out in the final story of season eleven – the production team had it in mind that the Master would sacrifice his life in order to save the Doctor's and thus achieve a kind of redemption – but this idea, provisionally entitled *The Final Game* and also intended to be written by Robert Sloman and an uncredited Barry Letts, was never developed further and *Planet of the Spiders* was a completely different story.)

THINGS TO WATCH OUT FOR

- The spiders' method of taking over humans is by leaping on their backs and remaining there, invisibly, while they exert telepathic control.
- The second and final appearance of the Whomobile occurs in this story.
- Gareth Hunt, later to become one of the stars of *The New Avengers* and of a popular series of coffee commercials, plays Arak.
- The cliffhanger for Part Five was artifically created by editing on a scene from some way into Part Six. This explains why there are several additional scenes at the start of Part Six before Part Five's cliffhanger is reached.
- This story marks the first use of the term 'regeneration' to describe the process by way of which Time Lords take on a new body when their old one wears out.

THINGS YOU MIGHT NOT HAVE KNOWN

- John Kane, who played Tommy in this story, also worked as a television writer, including on the sitcom *Terry and June*.
- In the scene where Clegg holds and gains mental impressions from the Doctor's sonic screwdriver, the original intention was to show a clip from *The Green Death* as well as one from *Carnival of Monsters*. This idea was dropped and only the clip from *Carnival of Monsters* was used.
- The gyroplane used on location for this story was hired from Campbell Aircraft Ltd of Membury Airfield and flown by A. M. W. Curzon-Herrick.
- The Skima hovercraft used in the filming was hired from Michael Pinder of Teddington, who also played 'Hopkins', the man from whom the Doctor takes the vehicle when chasing Lupton.
- The tractor seen by Yates and Sarah was driven by J. R. Balsdon from Barn Elms Farm near Reading.
- To help the production crew's understanding of the story, Barry Letts prepared a glossary of terms extracted from a book called *The Message of the Tibetans*.
- Future companion Harry Sullivan effectively makes his debut here, but off-screen: the Brigadier rings up the medical section of UNIT and speaks to "Sullivan" on the phone.

QUOTE, UNQUOTE

- **Sarah Jane Smith:** 'You're just like everybody else.' **Tommy:** 'I sincerely hope not.'
- **K'anpo:** 'We are all apt to submit ourselves to domination … Not all spiders sit on the back.'
- **Cho-je:** 'The old man must die, and the new man will discover to his inexpressible joy that he has never existed.'
- **The Great One:** 'You see this web of crystal above my head? It reproduces the pattern of my brain. One perfect crystal and it will be complete. That is the perfect crystal I need!'

Doctor Who's writers over the years seem to have been somewhat fixated on the idea of presenting giant-sized creepy-crawlies. *Planet of the Spiders* takes this to the ultimate extreme with its artificially enlarged talking spiders with delusions of grandeur, and the viewer is called upon to do even more than usual in the way of suspension of disbelief. The realisation of the spiders is admittedly sound – their voices are particularly memorable – and the story caused something of a stir at the time of its original transmission, with accusations being made in the press that it was too horrific. Even so, it is hard to imagine that anyone but the most arachnaphobic could be truly scared of these 'eight legs' (as they like to be known); and certainly as far as the Great One is concerned it is a pity that the rather more realistic model originally prepared by the Visual Effects Department was vetoed by producer Barry Letts.

Perhaps the best aspect of *Planet of the Spiders* is its characterisation of Mike Yates, having retreated to a Buddhist meditation centre to re-evaluate his life following his rather ignominious parting from UNIT at the end of *Invasion of the Dinosaurs*. It is rare indeed for a genre series like *Doctor Who* to afford one of its regulars this sort of significant character development, and all concerned deserve to be congratulated on such a thoughtful and well worked out departure from the norm.

Another point in the story's favour is that it not only draws on the overt trappings of Buddhism – such as the meditation rituals and the 'jewel of the lotus' mantra (*om mane padme hum*) – to enhance its atmosphere but also takes that philosophy as the whole basis of its plot, making it in effect a Buddhist parable. This is both appropriate and subtly done, being obvious to those with a knowledge of Buddhism but unobtrusive to those with no such interest. 'The Doctor's ego is … out of control,' observed Paul Cornell in *DWB* No. 88 dated April 1991, 'ignoring Sarah, getting Professor Clegg killed in his dilettante psychic experiments ("my greed for knowledge"), and basically displaying all the paternalistic traits that so annoy modern viewers. That he is to be criticised for this, and killed for it, is surely a huge testament to Letts' helmsmanship of the show. The Doctor's disquiet before K'anpo is a revealing moment that shows that even he has a monkey (or a spider) on his back. Even the Doctor must submit to his own principles.'

These virtues apart, it is difficult to find much to praise in *Planet of the Spiders*, and one can only assume that it was a case of initial over-enthusiasm when Keith Miller wrote in *DWFC Magazine* Number 20 dated June/July 1974: 'This story was fantastic! It brimmed over with emotion, sadness and adventure.' Geraint Jones was rather nearer the mark in his assessment in *Doctor Who – An Adventure in Space and Time* in 1987: 'There was far too much padding and repetitive to-ing and fro-ing to make the script and production a tight one; had the story been told in four episodes, it would undoubtedly have ensured a far more satisfactory swansong for Pertwee's Doctor. Good indications of the quality of drama in an episodic serial are surely the episode cliffhangers. Apart from the regeneration scene which closed the story … not one of the others in *Planet of the Spiders* was particularly exciting or audience-grabbing. Rather than thundering towards a climax, every episode gave the impression that it was slowly but surely running out of steam.'

Given that it was included solely in order to afford Jon Pertwee a final opportunity to indulge his passion for different forms of transport, it is hardly surprising that the lengthy chase scene in Part Two seems self-indulgent and pointless (although still not as bad as the totally gratuitous one in *Invasion of the Dinosaurs* Part Five). More regrettable still is that the characterisation of the Brigadier reaches its absolute nadir in this story – the culmination of a slow but steady decline over the previous three years. The shrewd, no-nonsense professional soldier of season seven has by this point been reduced almost to the level of a buffoon. His casual manner, near shoulder-length hair, failure to comprehend even the simplest of scientific concepts and almost total reliance on the Doctor to tell him what to do make it impossible to believe in him as a realistic character; and the writers' continual poking of fun at him, such as in the scene where he suggests that a belly-dancer's movements could be adapted as exercises for his men and the one where he becomes embarrassed at the revelation of a 'dirty weekend' spent in Brighton, serves only to make him seem a pompous idiot.

The best of the story's guest characters is Tommy, who is initially mentally retarded but subsequently cured by the Doctor's blue crystal – a transformation sensitively portrayed by actor John Kane. John Dearth's Lupton, Kevin Lindsay's Cho-je and George Cormack's K'anpo are also worthy of special mention. Lupton's human cronies are rather nondescript, however, and the humanoid inhabitants of Metebelis 3 are a singularly dull bunch. Jenny Laird's performance as Neska is particularly noteworthy, being one of the most cringe-inducingly awful ever seen in the series.

The BBC's Audience Research Report on the story's concluding instalment suggests that contemporary viewers were none too impressed: 'The conclusion of *Planet of the Spiders* ... met with a tolerant rather than enthusiastic response from most of the adult viewers who constituted the sample audience. However, a minority of about one in three found it very enjoyable. The "death" of Doctor Who in the shape of Jon Pertwee – the most likeable and subtle Doctor so far, according to a few long-term viewers – was greeted with some regret; nevertheless, several said they liked the flexibility of the Time Lord concept ... and felt that the "translation" was neatly effected in this episode. The acting and production were generally commended, although some viewers thought the minor roles were sometimes stiffly or hammily performed, or the giant spiders in this story (perhaps mercifully) less life-like than some monsters the series had created.' Children in the BBC's sample were, as always, far more positive, their views being neatly exemplified by the one who said: 'Exciting, frightening, a must every Saturday. When will it come back, Mum?' Nevertheless, there is no escaping the conclusion that *Planet of the Spiders* makes for a disappointing end to the third Doctor's era.

The eleventh season, while certainly having some high points, is arguably the weakest of Jon Pertwee's time as the Doctor. The impression given is that, with the notable exception of newcomer Elisabeth Sladen, the series' regulars – both in front of and behind the cameras – were running short of energy, ideas and enthusiasm. Regeneration was in store however not only for the Doctor – the departure of Pertwee, following on from the death of Roger Delgado and the bowing out of Katy Manning and Richard Franklin, marking the end of an era in more ways than one – but also for the production team. *Planet of the Spiders* was Terrance Dicks's last story as script editor and Barry Letts's penultimate one as producer; although Letts would stay on to oversee the early part of season twelve, it would be his successor Philip Hinchcliffe, along with new script editor Robert Holmes, who would be responsible for steering *Doctor Who* into the next phase of its history.

The Fourth Doctor
[Tom Baker]
1974-1981

TOM BAKER IS THE FOURTH DOCTOR

Tom Baker was born in 1934 and brought up in a devout Roman Catholic family in the poverty-stricken Scotland Road area of Liverpool. After leaving school he went to Jersey to join a monastic order called the Brothers of Ploermel, later moving to Shropshire in England as a novitiate. He followed the monastic life for some six years before deciding at the age of twenty-one that it was not for him. After a period of National Service in the Army's medical corps he obtained a scholarship and enrolled at the Rose Bruford Drama School in London. His first professional job was reading poetry in a Soho coffee bar called the Partisan. Toward the end of the fifties he began to work with repertory companies around Britain, taking roles in numerous productions. Then in the late sixties he got his first big break when he was spotted by a National Theatre talent scout while appearing in a revue called *Late Night Lowther* – Lowther being the name of the pub in York where it was staged – and subsequently offered a job with the company.

In 1968 Baker made his television debut in an episode of *Dixon of Dock Green*. This was followed by roles in series including *Market in Honey Lane*, *George and the Dragon* and *Softly, Softly: Task Force*. He had already made his big-screen debut in a production of Shakespeare's *A Winter's Tale*, which although shot in 1966 was not released until 1968, but his most famous film role came in 1970 when he played Rasputin in *Nicholas and Alexandra*. Other film work in the early seventies included roles in Pasolini's *The Canterbury Tales*, the horror anthology *Vault of Horror* and the fantasy adventure *The Golden Voyage of Sinbad*. In the theatre, meanwhile, he followed his two and a half year stint at the National Theatre with leading parts at the Bristol Old Vic, the Hampstead Theatre Club and the Shaw Theatre.

Despite a number of recent roles, Baker was down on his luck at the point when, partly on the strength of his performance in *The Golden Voyage of Sinbad*, he was chosen by Barry Letts to succeed Jon Pertwee in *Doctor Who*. Three films in which he had landed major parts had all been cancelled within a short space of time due to budgetary problems, and for the past month or so he had been working on a building site as a hod-carrier and tea-maker. His role as the fourth Doctor transformed his life. Over the next seven years he became a hugely popular and instantly recognisable figure to television audiences in Britain and around the world, with his imposing stature, dark curly hair, broad toothy grin, rich booming voice and outlandish attire – including a trademark wide-brimmed hat and long, multicoloured scarf.

'I didn't know how I was going to do *Doctor Who*,' admitted the actor in a 1992 interview. 'I had no idea at all – not until the very first rehearsal, and even then I didn't know … I just did it. I just played the script and something evolved and the audience liked the way I did it, obviously, so we kept it like that. But sometimes it was funny and sometimes not so funny and sometimes it was thrilling. It was just an accident really.'

For many viewers, Tom Baker's characterisation of the Doctor remains the most memorable, eclipsing those of his predecessors and successors and making him arguably the most popular Time Lord of them all.

DOCTOR WHO SEASON TWELVE [1974-1975]

Regular Cast:
Doctor Who (Tom Baker)
Sarah Jane Smith (Elisabeth Sladen)
Harry Sullivan (Ian Marter)

Regular Crew:
Producer: Barry Letts until *Robot* Part Four. Philip Hinchcliffe from *The Ark in Space* Part One onwards.
Script Editor: Robert Holmes.
Production Unit Manager: George Gallaccio.
Title Music: Ron Grainer and the BBC Radiophonic Workshop, arranged by Delia Derbyshire.
Special Sounds: Dick Mills.

Aside from the new Doctor, there was little to distinguish season twelve's first story, *Robot*, from the type of *Doctor Who* to which viewers had become accustomed over the previous few years. It was set – like the majority of the Jon Pertwee stories – in near-contemporary England and featured not only the Doctor's established companion Sarah Jane Smith but also Brigadier Lethbridge-Stewart, Sergeant (now Warrant Officer) Benton and the familiar UNIT organisation. The idea behind this was to reassure viewers that, although the Doctor might have changed, the series itself was still the same. Similarly, although the remainder of the season followed the trend of the later Pertwee stories in moving away from the tried-and-trusted UNIT set-up and into more unfamiliar territory, continued viewer reassurance was provided by the inclusion of a succession of returning monsters.

Robot was the last story of the series' eleventh production block and saw Barry Letts bowing out as producer. His successor Philip Hinchcliffe had already been trailing him for some weeks by this point. Letts would however remain on hand to offer comment and advice during the making of the next two stories, *The Sontaran Experiment* and *The Ark in Space* (the season's stories again being made out of transmission order), and his influence would be felt throughout the twelfth season as all the scripts had already been commissioned during his time as producer. A large part of the responsibility for shaping the new season, however, fell to new script editor Robert Holmes, who had some strong ideas of his own about the type of stories that the series ought to be featuring.

ROBOT

Writer: Terrance Dicks. **Director:** Christopher Barry. **Designer:** Ian Rawnsley. **Costumes:** James Acheson. **Make-Up:** Judy Clay. **Incidental Music:** Dudley Simpson. **Visual Effects:** Clifford Culley. **OB Cameraman:** unknown. **Studio Lighting:** Nigel Wright. **Studio Sound:** John Holmes, Trevor Webster. **Production Assistant:** Peter Grimwade. **Assistant Floor Manager:** David Tilley.

	First UK TX	Scheduled TX	Actual TX	Duration	Viewers	Chart Pos.
Part One	28/12/74	17.35	17.35	24'11"	10.8	25
Part Two	04/01/75	17.30	17.33	25'00"	10.7	17
Part Three	11/01/75	17.30	17.30	24'29"	10.1	22
Part Four	18/01/75	17.30	17.32	24'29"	9.0	30

Plot: A newly regenerated Doctor joins UNIT in an investigation into the theft of top secret plans and equipment from supposedly secure premises. Sarah discovers that the raids have been carried out by a robot invented by scientist Professor Kettlewell while he was working for Think Tank, a body involved in developing emerging technologies. The robot has been reprogrammed on the orders of Miss Winters, the director of Think Tank, and used to obtain the means for constructing a disintegrator gun with which the Scientific Reform Society – of which she is a leading member – can steal the computer codes controlling the nuclear weapons of the world's leading powers. In this way, the SRS hope to hold the world to ransom unless their demands for a purer way of life are met. Kettlewell is killed by the robot after he balks at Miss Winters' ruthlessness. The robot then suffers an electronic mental breakdown and tries to activate the nuclear weapons. The Brigadier attempts to destroy it with the disintegrator gun, but this merely causes it to grow to gigantic proportions, following which it goes on the rampage. The Doctor, assisted by UNIT medical officer Harry Sullivan, destroys it with a metal virus described in Kettlewell's notes.

Episode endings:

1. Sarah, suspicious of a patch of oil she found on the floor of Kettlewell's deserted lab at the Think Tank, sneaks back there to investigate further. Suddenly, with a loud grating noise, a hidden door opens and a huge silver robot strides forward demanding to know who she is and why she is there. Sarah backs away in panic as the robot advances.
2. The Doctor is contacted by Professor Kettlewell, who asks the Time Lord to meet him at his lab. When he gets there, he is confronted by the robot who has instructions to kill him. The robot knocks the Doctor to the ground and advances.
3. The Doctor manages to open the doors to the SRS's underground bunker, but the robot emerges armed with the disintegrator gun. It vaporises a soldier and a tank before giving its ultimatum: the Doctor and UNIT are to go now or it will destroy them all.
4. Sarah is upset at the destruction of the robot and the Doctor suggests a trip to cheer her up. Harry arrives and believes that the idea of the Doctor travelling around in a police box is absurd. The Doctor invites him to take a look inside, just to prove how absurd it is, and Harry agrees. The Doctor and Sarah follow him inside and the TARDIS departs. The Brigadier

arrives to ask the Doctor about 'dinner at the Palace'. Seeing the TARDIS dematerialising, he muses to himself that he will have to explain that the Doctor will be a little late.

IT WAS MADE WHERE...?

OB: 28.04.74-02.05.74, 05.05.74-06.05.74
Location: BBC Engineering Training Centre, Wood Norton Hall, Wood Norton, Evesham, Worcs.
Studio: 21.05.74, 02.06.74, 06.06.74-07.06.74 all in TC3

ADDITIONAL CREDITED CAST

Brigadier Lethbridge-Stewart (Nicholas Courtney), Sergeant Benton (John Levene), Miss Winters (Patricia Maynard), Robot (Michael Kilgarriff), Professor Kettlewell (Edward Burnham), Jellicoe (Alec Linstead), Short (Timothy Craven2).

THINGS TO WATCH OUT FOR

- This story sees the debut of another new opening and closing title sequence, again designed by Bernard Lodge and realised using the 'slit scan' process, but in this instance featuring Tom Baker rather than Jon Pertwee and, for the first time, the TARDIS's police box exterior.
- This was the first *Doctor Who* story to have all its location scenes recorded on outside broadcast (OB) video rather than shot on film (although its interior scenes were still recorded in studio in the normal way).
- Benton reveals in Part Two that he has been promoted to Warrant Officer, but this is not reflected in the closing credits, which continue to give his rank as Sergeant.
- The shots of the Doctor's regeneration at the beginning of the first episode were taken from the *Planet of the Spiders* recording but those of Sarah Jane Smith and the Brigadier in the same scene were re-recorded for this story.
- Surgeon-Lieutenant Harry Sullivan, played by Ian Marter, makes his first appearance in this story. Marter had previously been in *Doctor Who* in the Jon Pertwee story *Carnival of Monsters*, playing Lt John Andrews, and before that had auditioned for the part of Pertwee-era regular Mike Yates. Marter later successfully novelised several *Doctor Who* stories, and wrote the spin-off novel *Harry Sullivan's War*. He died in 1986.

THINGS YOU MIGHT NOT HAVE KNOWN

- *Robot* was inspired in part by the 1933 film *King Kong*.
- Director Christopher Barry considered, amongst other people, Colin Baker, better known as the actor who played the sixth Doctor, to play the part of Miss Winters' number two, Arnold Jellicoe. The part eventually went to Alec Linstead.

QUOTE, UNQUOTE

- **The Doctor:** 'Never cared much for the word "impregnable". Sounds a bit too much like "unsinkable".' **Harry Sullivan:** 'What's wrong with "unsinkable"?' **The Doctor:** 'Nothing. As the iceberg said to the Titanic.' **Harry Sullivan:** 'What?' **The Doctor:** 'Gloop, gloop, gloop, gloop, gloop, gloop, gloop.'
- **Brigadier Lethbridge-Stewart:** 'You know, just once I'd like to meet an alien menace that wasn't immune to bullets.'

4 FOURTH DOCTOR

- **The Doctor:** 'There's no point in being grown up if you can't be childish sometimes.'

Robot was not a good choice of story to launch a new Doctor. It lacks both the popular returning monster of the second Doctor's debut adventure, *The Power of the Daleks*, and the freshness and originality of the third Doctor's, *Spearhead from Space*. Despite this, it does have some redeeming features.

First and foremost is the Doctor himself. Admittedly Tom Baker's shambling, bohemian eccentric is initially a little hard to take after Jon Pertwee's dashing and debonair 'dandy'. In fact, the high humour content of the early part of *Robot* – well exemplified by the scene in which the Doctor tries on the costumes of a Viking warrior, a playing card jack and a pierrot clown before settling on his standard outfit – echoes that of *The Power of the Daleks* and *Spearhead from Space*, almost as though the production teams responsible always felt it necessary to resort to this approach as a way of smoothing the transition between Doctors. As in those earlier cases, however, the latter part of the story sees the new Doctor really getting to grips with the problem at hand and starting to make his mark on the series. Jonathan Way, writing in *A Voyage Through 25 Years of Doctor Who* dated December 1988, liked the way the Doctor was presented: 'The fourth Doctor's character is highlighted and thrown into sharp relief against the familiar background of characters and situations that we'd seen for years. A lot of the fun of *Robot* is to see how the new Doctor will deal with a situation that we all knew the third Doctor could have dealt with admirably.' Robert Cope also appreciated Tom Baker's performance, as he explained in *DWB* No. 96 dated December 1991: 'Tom Baker's debut performance is formidable, his charismatic qualities outshining all those sharing the screen. The rapport between Sladen and Baker is instant; even the almost intrusive presence of Ian Marter's Harry Sullivan cannot disguise the fact that Baker's [over the top] madcap approach contrasts marvellously with Sladen's no-nonsense nosy but vulnerable Sarah … This Doctor is a bohemian to the core, the weirdly alien qualities that comprise the fourth Doctor's persona evident from the outset.'

It is really the regulars, both old and new, who carry this story. Nicholas Courtney gives his usual dependable performance as the Brigadier, despite again being handed some rather poor material to work with; it is good to see John Levene's stalwart Benton at last getting a promotion; Elisabeth Sladen shines as Sarah; and Ian Marter makes a promising debut as Harry Sullivan, marking the welcome return of the male companion figure after over five years without one.

None of the other characters in this tale of Nazi-like scientists at work makes much of an impression – none, that is, except the eponymous robot, otherwise known as K1. Designed by James Acheson and constructed by Allister Bowtell, this is a masterpiece of costuming, being both visually impressive and functionally practical – even to the extent of being able to walk up and down steps. The concept of a machine that thinks for itself and develops emotional responses is not exactly original, but is nevertheless well handled in Terrance Dicks's scripts. The fact that it ends up taking a liking to Sarah is somewhat strange, but this does lead to the final episode's pleasing pastiche of the 1933 RKO film *King Kong* as, courtesy of CSO, it is enlarged to giant size by the disintegrator gun and carries Sarah off to safety before being cut down by the Doctor's timely application of a metal-eating virus. Ultimately the viewer is made to feel sorry for the robot, which is a tribute to Michael Kilgarriff's sterling performance, both physical and vocal.

The story's climax is less impressive than it should be, however, owing to some poor visual effects. 'B-movie freaks will revel in the final episode sequence when K1 is fired on by the Brigadier and starts a growth acceleration of tacky CSO proportions,' suggested Robert Cope. 'As the military back-up moves in on the attack, [a] model [tank gets destroyed], K1 throws some Action Man [toys] around and generally things adopt a *Blue Peter* sticky-backed plastic feel.'

The BBC's Audience Research Report on Part One indicates that contemporary viewers had rather mixed feelings about it: 'A minority of about three in ten felt it was definitely enjoyable (some were long-term followers of the series) while a smaller group were distinctly unimpressed. It was suggested, here and there, that this episode had been slow – the story had not got very far by the end.' Naturally enough, the major subject for comment was the new Doctor himself. 'At this early stage,' it was reported, 'many did not know whether they were going to like him or not; viewers often said he would "take some getting used to". First impressions among those who volunteered an opinion were seldom entirely favourable. Some considered the new personality too clownish and eccentric (occasionally, "too stupid for words") or too unlike the previous Doctor. Also, Jon Pertwee had been a favourite with some viewers, and they missed him. On the other hand, a small group seem to have been instantly attracted, or won over by the end of the episode. The new Doctor had "more life and humour", it was said, and seemed likely to "buck the series up".' The report highlighted in particular the reactions of younger viewers amongst the sample. Specific comments included: 'The new Doctor is not quite as good as Jon Pertwee, but the programme is still just as exciting' (boy aged eleven); 'It was nice and creepy but I like the other Doctor Who best' (boy aged twelve); 'My little boy didn't like the new Doctor, he thought he was too silly. Loved the robot' (parent); 'I would like him calmed down a bit, because he's crazy' (boy aged eight); and 'It was ever so good. I liked that tin thing with the clippy hands' (girl aged eight).

Robot is perhaps best seen as being a showcase for the talents of Tom Baker – after all, no-one knew whether or not the series could survive yet another change of lead actor – and in that at least it does succeed.

THE ARK IN SPACE

Writer: Robert Holmes*. **Director:** Rodney Bennett. **Designer:** Roger Murray-Leach. **Costumes:** Barbara Kidd. **Make-Up:** Sylvia James. **Incidental Music:** Dudley Simpson. **Visual Effects:** John Friedlander, Tony Oxley. **Studio Lighting:** Nigel Wright. **Studio Sound:** John Lloyd. **Production Assistant:** Marion McDougall. **Assistant Floor Manager:** Russ Karel.

* Robert Holmes wrote this story from an idea by John Lucarotti, who received no on-screen credit.

	First UK TX	Scheduled TX	Actual TX	Duration	Viewers	Chart Pos.
Part One	25/01/75	17.35	17.36	24'58"	9.4	27
Part Two	01/02/75	17.30	17.31	24'49"	13.6	5
Part Three	08/02/75	17.30	17.32	24'05"	11.2	17
Part Four	15/02/75	17.30	17.32	24'37"	10.2	24

Plot: The TARDIS arrives on an apparently deserted and deactivated space station Nerva, otherwise known as the Ark, orbiting Earth in the far future. There the Doctor, Sarah and Harry discover the last survivors of the human race held in suspended animation, Earth having been evacuated thousands of years earlier when solar flares threatened to destroy all life. The station has been visited by a Wirrn, an insect life form, which has laid its eggs in the solar stacks and absorbed the body and mind of one of the sleeping humans. The Doctor's reactivation of the station's systems causes the humans to start to revive. Their leader, nicknamed Noah, becomes infected by one of the emerging larvae and is slowly taken over. The Doctor and his friends meanwhile gain the trust of the other humans, now led by a med-tech named Vira. Together they manage to lure the hatched Wirrn insects into a shuttle craft and then eject it into space. In a final act of humanity, Noah – by this time fully transformed into a Wirrn – deliberately neglects to set the shuttle's stabilisers, causing it to explode.

Episode endings:
1. Sarah has inadvertently been placed in suspended animation with the other sleeping humans. Harry searches in some cupboards for a resuscitation unit with which to revive her. The first is empty, but when he opens the second, a huge green insect lurches towards him.
2. A revived human named Libri goes after Noah, who is acting strangely. Noah persuades Libri to hand over his gun and then shoots him. Turning, Noah pulls his left hand from his pocket and stares at it in horror. It is engulfed in a green, larva-like skin.
3. The Wirrn turn off the Ark's main power and the Doctor heads for the solar stacks to try to reconnect it. There he finds numerous Wirrn hanging in chrysalises. He is about to turn on the power when he is confronted by a fully grown Wirrn creature with Noah's features still just visible. As he watches, Noah's face vanishes to be replaced by that of the Wirrn adult.
4. The Doctor decides to pop down to Earth using the Ark's transmat system to ensure that the diode receptors are in good working order to receive the returning sleepers. Sarah and Harry go with him.

IT WAS MADE WHERE...?
Studio: 28.10.74-29.10.74 in TC3, 11.11.74-12.11.74 in TC1

ADDITIONAL CREDITED CAST
Voices (Gladys Spencer[1], Peter Tuddenham[1]), Vira (Wendy Williams[2-4]), Noah (Kenton Moore[2-4]), Libri (Christopher Masters[2]), Rogin (Richardson Morgan[3,4]), Lycett (John Gregg[3]), High Minister's Voice (Gladys Spencer[3]), Wirrn Operators (Stuart Fell[3,4], Nick Hobbs[4]).

THINGS TO WATCH OUT FOR
- No-one but the regulars takes part in the action of the first episode – the only instance of this occurring after season one's *Inside the Spaceship*.

- The Doctor uses his yo-yo to take a gravity reading and a cricket ball to try to hit the switch controlling the Ark's defence systems.
- *The Ark in Space* shares a number of ideas with the season three story *The Ark*.

THINGS YOU MIGHT NOT HAVE KNOWN

- *The Ark in Space* started life as a story by John Lucarotti which turned out to be unsuited to the series's current style. As there was no time for Lucarotti to work on it further, this task fell to script editor Robert Holmes. As Holmes had to change so much, the story was transmitted under his name.
- The Wirrn grubs were constructed by designer John Friedlander out of plastic bubble-wrap packaging, painted with latex and sprayed green.
- Sets from this story were reused in *Revenge of the Cybermen*, mainly as a cost-saving exercise.
- The music played to Sarah in Part One is Handel's *Largo*.

QUOTE, UNQUOTE

- **The Doctor:** 'Homo Sapiens. What an inventive, invincible species. It's only a few million years since they crawled up out of the mud and learned to walk. Puny, defenceless bipeds. They've survived flood, famine and plague, they've survived cosmic wars and holocausts and now, here they are, out among the stars ready to begin a new life, ready to outsit eternity. They're indomitable ... indomitable.'
- **Vira:** 'You claim to be med-techs?' **The Doctor:** 'Well, my doctorate is purely honorary, and Harry here is only qualified to work on sailors.'
- **The Doctor:** 'It may be irrational of me, but humans are quite my favourite species.'

ANALYSIS

After the lightweight action-adventure of *Robot*, *Doctor Who* returns to its forté with a scary monster story to chill the viewer's blood. *The Ark in Space* in fact contains some of the most horrific material to have been featured in the series up to this point.

'*The Ark in Space* could hardly have been more different [from] *Robot*,' wrote Jonathan Way in *A Voyage Through 25 Years of Doctor Who* dated December 1988. 'Gone were the large casts, omnipresent location [recording] and arrays of stunts and explosions; instead replaced by a sense of claustrophobia ... The fact that [the first] episode ... stands alone, carried by the three regular cast and two special voice-overs, is testimony enough to the skill of Robert Holmes's writing.'

Each new discovery by the time travellers leads to new questions. What has caused the strange trails of green slime on the floor? Why has the power been cut off? What has happened to Sarah? The effectiveness of these scenes is enhanced considerably by Roger Murray-Leach's superb sets, which convincingly convey the impression of being in a cold, clinical space station. Even the surprisingly large scale and impressive chambers in which Nerva's human occupants are found in suspended animation have an enclosed, claustrophobia-inducing quality to them. '[All] four episodes were crammed full of tension and horror,' wrote Richard Walter in the appropriately titled *Ark in Space* No. 7 dated May 1983, 'and the feeling that there was very little chance of our heroes escaping from the eerie metallic corridors of the Ark.'

The terror mounts with the discovery that the Wirrn larvae are able to infect humans

FOURTH DOCTOR

and physically convert them, taking over their minds and memories in the process. Kenton Moore almost steals the show with his depiction of a man being slowly transformed, cell by cell, into an alien creature that wants to kill everyone else – including his intended partner. The sight of the tormented Noah wrestling with his alien hand in Part Three is an enduring image, as is that of the pitiful and mutating creature later seen scuttling through the corridors.

'*The Ark in Space* is all about possession ...,' wrote Tim Robins in *In-Vision* Issue Two dated January 1988. 'On one level [it] again pays homage to ... Quatermass ... The possession of Noah closely mirrors the fate of ... astronaut Carroon [in *The Quatermass Experiment*]. Carroon is slowly absorbed by an alien entity which has already absorbed his two ship mates ... In the climax of this story ... Quatermass appeals to the last vestiges of the three astronauts' humanity to help destroy the creature ...

'Also fascinating is the serial's focus on what is now termed "body horror" ... Examining the contents of films including *Alien* (1979), *The Thing* (1982) and *Mutant II* (1985), Pete Boss notes (in *Screen*, volume 27 number 1), "What is common is the sense of disaster being visited at the level of the body itself – an intimate apocalypse. The enduring image is of the body irreversibly self-destructing ..."

'In this "apocalyptic" battle, health and sickness, order and chaos, compete in the body. In *The Ark in Space*, the Doctor makes the point that to revive Sarah, the medication Vira has administered has "turned her body into a battlefield". More starkly, the Wirrn's invasion of the Ark is also played out within Noah ... His psychic battle for the control of his consciousness, his self-identity, is mirrored by a physical battle with his own mutating cells.'

The Wirrn grubs and the alien flesh of Noah's hand were constructed principally from bubble-wrap packaging material sprayed green, but never has such an innocuous material been made to seem so terrifying. The adult Wirrn creatures are also well designed and effective, despite the fact that they seem to be able to scuttle about with remarkable ease – full marks to the director here for avoiding showing their lower half, as the sight of a pair of feet protruding from the costume would have spoiled the illusion somewhat!

The regulars are all in fine form in this story, and the guest cast are very good too, as John Harding pointed out, also in *In-Vision* Issue Two: 'Among the station crew, Richardson Morgan's Rogin stands out – excellently played, with the kind of cynical delivery that brings a wry smile to the face. His character, noticeably out of step with his acceptingly obedient fellows, appeals from the first complaint ("Didn't I tell you, Lycett, I said five thousand years ago, 'There'll be a snitch up!'") to the last noble act of sacrifice. Wendy Williams also turned in a creditable performance as Vira. She was somehow unearthly, cold and calculating, but allowed flashes of humanity to show; this was [most] apparent when coming to terms with Noah's destruction ...'

The Ark in Space is a wonderful story that restores the viewer's confidence in *Doctor Who* after the lacklustre *Robot* and launches it on a new, more adult and horrific course.

THE SONTARAN EXPERIMENT

Writer: Bob Baker, Dave Martin. **Director:** Rodney Bennett. **Designer:** Roger Murray-Leach. **Costumes:** Barbara Kidd. **Make-Up:** Sylvia James. **Incidental Music:** Dudley

Simpson. **Fight Arranger:** Terry Walsh. **Visual Effects:** John Friedlander, Tony Oxley. **OB Cameraman:** unknown. **Production Assistant:** Marion McDougall. **Assistant Floor Manager:** Russ Karel.

	First UK TX	Scheduled TX	Actual TX	Duration	Viewers	Chart Pos.
Part One	22/02/75	17.30	17.30	24'27"	11.0	18
Part Two	01/03/75	17.30	17.30	25'00"	10.5	17

Plot: The Doctor, Sarah and Harry arrive on a desolate and apparently deserted Earth to discover that a group of shipwrecked astronauts from a human colony, GalSec, have been lured there by a fake distress call. One of their number, Roth, tells Sarah of an alien conducting gruesome experiments on him and his crewmates. The alien turns out to be a Sontaran, Field-Major Styre, who is compiling a report on human physical and mental capabilities as a prelude to an invasion of Earth. The Doctor challenges Styre to unarmed combat. The Sontaran agrees but is quickly weakened in Earth's unfamiliar gravity. Harry meanwhile enters Styre's ship and uses the Doctor's sonic screwdriver to remove the vital terullian diode bypass transformer, so that when the alien returns there to revitalise himself he is drained of all his energy and destroyed. The Doctor sends a message to the Sontaran fleet, warning them that without Styre's report they cannot invade.

Episode endings:
1. The alien emerges from its ship and removes its helmet. It is a Sontaran.
2. The Doctor, Sarah and Harry leave Earth via the transmat with the intention of returning to Nerva.

IT WAS MADE WHERE...?
OB: 26.09.74-02.10.74
Locations: Hound Tor, nr Manaton, Dartmoor, Devon; Headland Warren, nr Postbridge, Devon.

ADDITIONAL CREDITED CAST
Vural (Donald Douglas), Krans (Glyn Jones), Erak (Peter Walshe), Styre[1]/Styre and The Marshal[2] (Kevin Lindsay), Roth (Peter Rutherford), Zake (Terry Walsh[1]), Prisoner (Brian Ellis[2]).

THINGS TO WATCH OUT FOR
- This was the first story to be recorded with no interior scenes.
- Kevin Lindsay makes his last *Doctor Who* appearances, playing Styre and the Sontaran Marshal. As the actor suffered from a heart condition (which had resulted in him collapsing at one point during the recording of *The Time Warrior*) Styre's latex mask and helmet were redesigned to be less bulky and to give better ventilation for breathing. Lindsay's heart condition led to his death not long after the making of this story.
- The GalSec astronaut Krans is played by Glyn Jones, the writer of the season two story *The Space Museum*.
- Tom Baker broke his collar bone during the making of this story on Sunday 29 October 1976, and he is consequently doubled by Terry Walsh in many of the scenes where the Doctor is required to move or engage in physical action.

FOURTH DOCTOR

- Field-Major Styre had five fingers on each hand, rather than three as sported by Linx in *The Time Warrior*.

THINGS YOU MIGHT NOT HAVE KNOWN

- Working title: *The Destructors*.

QUOTE, UNQUOTE

- **Harry:** 'Doctor! I thought you were dead.' **The Doctor:** 'Not me …' [He holds up a piece of metal.] 'Piece of the synestic locking mechanism from Nerva's rocket – popped it in my pocket.' **Harry:** 'Fortuitous.' **The Doctor:** 'Foresight. You never know when these bits and pieces will come in handy. Never throw anything away, Harry.' [He throws it away.] 'Now, where's my five hundred year diary? I remember jotting some notes on the Sontarans … It's a mistake to clutter one's pockets, Harry.'

ANALYSIS

'*The Sontaran Experiment* is an experiment for the show as well as for Field-Major Styre,' reckoned Nick Pegg in *DWB* No. 93 dated September 1991. 'The first two-parter for over ten years and the first story shot entirely on OB videotape, it comes across in dramatic terms as a series of heavily stylised statements about where the show is headed under the new line-up. Conventions and expectations which had formed the bedrock of the Pertwee years are yanked from beneath the viewer's feet; the emphasis on such standard lines as "characterisation" and "morality" gives way to what looks like an experiment in pure atmosphere. Untrammelled by the need for complex exposition (because the actual plot is so delightfully nonexistent and silly), the story concentrates on generating a series of effects.'

The idea that a Sontaran battle fleet would hold back from invading a totally uninhabited Earth while a lone Field-Major conducts a lengthy assessment of the ability of humans to withstand an attack is indeed a rather silly one. The revelation that groups of human colonists have 'built an empire' since leaving their planet of origin also sits rather uneasily with the scenario presented in *The Ark in Space*, in which it was suggested that the sleepers aboard Nerva were the only ones to have survived the solar flares that had supposedly devastated the Earth. These awkwardnesses are neatly glossed over, however, and writers Bob Baker and Dave Martin present a highly entertaining story with just the right amount of plot to fill its unusual two episode length.

It is in terms of atmosphere and imagery that *The Sontaran Experiment* really triumphs. The tension builds nicely during the first episode with the GalSec crew's hints of an alien menace lurking in the rocks and the ominous sound and eventually sight of an imposing robot patrolling the area, all leading up to the cliffhanger introduction of Styre – initially mistaken by Sarah for *The Time Warrior*'s Linx (although the Sontaran actually looks slightly different on this occasion, with his redesigned mask and five fingers instead of only three). Then in the second episode the story takes on a really horrific quality as the sadistic nature of Styre's tests on his human victims becomes fully apparent. The scene in which Harry finds one of the astronauts left chained up to die of thirst is truly shocking, and the subjection of Sarah to a series of terrifying hallucinations is also, as Pegg put it, 'genuinely sinister' – although perhaps the most gruesome test of all, involving an assessement of human resistance to 'immersion in fluid', is thankfully only heard about rather than seen. The climactic fight scene between the Doctor and Styre is also well done, and the simple but quite effective shot of the Sontaran 'deflating' as the energy drains out of him is another enduring image.

Rodney Bennett makes an excellent debut as a *Doctor Who* director (*The Ark in Space*, although the first of his stories to be screened, was actually the second to be made) and the astutely chosen and well used Dartmoor location adds much to the story's atmosphere and effectiveness. It is indeed refreshing to have, for once, a story recorded entirely in the open air.

The Sontaran Experiment is a pleasing interlude between the two more substantial stories either side of it, and is memorable in its own right as an exciting and well crafted adventure.

GENESIS OF THE DALEKS

Writer: Terry Nation. **Director:** David Maloney. **Designer:** David Spode. **Costumes:** Barbara Kidd. **Make-Up:** Sylvia James. **Incidental Music:** Dudley Simpson. **Visual Effects:** Peter Day. **Davros Mask:** John Friedlander. **Film Cameraman:** Elmer Cossey. **Film Editor:** Larry Toft. **Studio Lighting:** Duncan Brown. **Studio Sound:** Tony Millier. **Production Assistant:** Rosemary Crowson. **Assistant Floor Manager:** Karilyn Collier.

	First UK TX	Scheduled TX	Actual TX	Duration	Viewers	Chart Pos.
Part One	08/03/75	17.30	17.30	24'30"	10.7	23
Part Two	15/03/75	17.30	17.30	24'51"	10.5	15
Part Three	22/03/75	17.30	17.30	22'38"	8.5	42
Part Four	29/03/75	17.30	17.31	23'38"	8.8	36
Part Five	05/04/75	17.30	17.30	23'27"	9.8	30
Part Six	12/04/75	17.30	17.32	23'30"	9.1	26

Plot: The Time Lords intercept the transmat beam taking the Doctor, Sarah and Harry back to Nerva and deposit them instead on the planet Skaro at an early point in its history. There a Time Lord gives the Doctor both a mission to prevent or alter the Daleks' development so that they become less of a threat to the universe and a time ring that will enable him and his companions to return to the TARDIS once this is done. Skaro is currently in the grip of a long war of attrition between its two humanoid powers, the Kaleds and the Thals. The Kaleds' chief scientist, Davros, has been experimenting to discover the final form into which his race will mutate – the weapons used in the war have already produced genetically scarred 'mutos', who have been consigned to the wastelands – and has devised a protective casing in which they can continue to survive. This is instantly recognised by the Doctor and Sarah as a Dalek. Escaping from the bunker where Davros and his Elite, led by the sadistic Nyder, are based, the Doctor and Harry persuade the Kaled leaders to put the Dalek experiments on hold. Davros retaliates by conspiring with the Thals to destroy the Kaled city with a rocket. He then activates the Daleks and orders them to wipe out the Thals. Some members of the Elite revolt, protesting at the genetic alterations that Davros has made to the Daleks, and they too are exterminated. The Daleks then seize control, killing the remainder of the Elite and ultimately Davros himself. Thal survivors detonate explosives at the entrance to the bunker, sealing the Daleks inside. Having earlier passed up an opportunity to destroy the Dalek mutants at birth, the Doctor estimates that his intervention will have delayed their development by about a thousand years.

Episode endings:

1. Sarah stumbles across a half ruined building in the wastelands. Through a hole in the wall she sees two humanoids, one of them in a mobile chair, and a Dalek. On the electronic-voiced command of the chair-bound figure, Davros, the Dalek destroys a number of targets with its gun. Davros contentedly concludes that the weaponry is perfect: 'Now we can begin.'

2. Sarah organises her fellow prisoners in the Thal rocket silo to stage a breakout. They start to clamber up the gantry, intending to make their way out onto the surface of the dome above. Thal soldiers shoot up at them but they keep climbing. Sarah gets into difficulties and the muto Sevrin urges her on. Suddenly she loses her grip and falls ...

3. Sarah and Harry head for the Kaled dome to warn of the impending attack while the Doctor remains behind in the Thal base to try to sabotage the rocket. A Thal guard activates a defence system and the Doctor convulses in pain as an electrified fence sends waves of current through him.

4. The Doctor is captured by Davros, who threatens to torture Sarah and Harry unless he reveals details of future Dalek defeats so that these can be averted. The Doctor hesitates and Davros's demands grow ever louder.

5. The Doctor decides to blow up the Dalek incubator room and enters to place explosive charges. Sarah and Harry, waiting outside, start to become anxious as the minutes pass. Suddenly the door opens and the Doctor staggers out, struggling with an embryonic Dalek mutant that has wrapped itself in a stranglehold around his throat.

6. Their task completed, the Doctor, Sarah and Harry take hold of the time ring. They spin away through space and time on their way to rendezvous with the TARDIS.

IT WAS MADE WHERE...?

Filming: 06.01.75-09.01.75
Location: Betchworth Quarry, Pebblehill Road, Betchworth, Surrey.
Ealing filming: 13.01.75-14.01.75 on Stage 2
Studio: 27.01.75-28.01.75 in TC1, 10.02.75-11.02.75 in TC8, 24.02.75-25.02.75 in TC6

ADDITIONAL CREDITED CAST

Davros (Michael Wisher), Nyder (Peter Miles), Gharman (Dennis Chinnery[1,2,4-6]), Ravon (Guy Siner[1,3]), Time Lord (John Franklyn-Robbins[1]), Kaled Leader (Richard Reeves[1-3]), Dalek Operators (John Scott Martin, Cy Town[3-6], Keith Ashley[3-6]), Sevrin (Stephen Yardley[2-6]), Ronson (James Garbutt[2-4]), Tane (Drew Wood[2]), Gerrill (Jeremy Chandler[2]), Thal Soldier (Pat Gorman[2]), Kavell (Tom Georgeson[3-5]), Mogran (Ivor Roberts[3]), Thal Politician (Michael Lynch[3,4]), Thal Soldier (Hilary Minster[3]), Thal Guard (Max Faulkner[3]), Dalek Voice (Roy Skelton[3-6])*, Bettan (Harriet Philpin[4-6]), Kaled Guard (Peter Mantle[5]), Kravos (Andrew Johns[6]), Thal Soldier (John Gleeson[6]).

* An additional Dalek Voice was provided by Michael Wisher in Part Two, but without on-screen credit.

THINGS TO WATCH OUT FOR

- There is a freeze-frame cliffhanger at the end of Part Two – the series' first use of this technique.
- Guy Siner and Hilary Minster, two of the actors playing Kaled soldiers, later appeared in the BBC sitcom *'Allo, 'Allo*.
- Some of the Thal guns were previously used by the Drahvins in the season three story *Galaxy 4*.
- Part of an Ice Warrior costume is seen in one shot, representing one of the mutant creatures produced by Davros in his experiments.

THINGS YOU MIGHT NOT HAVE KNOWN

- Working title: *Genesis of Terror*.
- Michael Wisher rehearsed for his role as Davros with a paper bag over his head.
- *Genesis of the Daleks* marked the first occasion that viewers gained an insight into the origins of the Daleks on screen. Previously Terry Nation had told a completely different version in the *TV Century 21* Dalek comic strip of the sixties; and the *Radio Times* had also presented an alternative account of their origins in a text story *We are the Daleks!*, again by Nation, in its special publication marking *Doctor Who*'s tenth anniversary.

QUOTE, UNQUOTE

- **Sevrin:** 'Why must we always destroy beauty? Why kill another creature because it is not in our image?'
- **Davros:** 'Today, the Kaled race is ended, consumed in a fire of war. But, from its ashes will rise a new race. The supreme creature. The ultimate conqueror of the universe. The Dalek!'
- **The Doctor:** 'Davros, if you had created a virus in your laboratory. Something contagious and infectious that killed on contact. A virus that would destroy all other forms of life … would you allow its use?' **Davros:** 'It is an interesting conjecture.' **The Doctor:** 'Would you do it?' **Davros:** 'The only living thing …the microscopic organism … reigning supreme … A fascinating idea.' **The Doctor:** 'But would you do it?' **Davros:** 'Yes. Yes. To hold in my hand, a capsule that contained such power. To know that life and death on such a scale was my choice. To know that the tiny pressure of my thumb, enough to break the glass, would end everything. Yes. I would do it. That power would set me up above the gods. And through the Daleks I shall have that power!'
- **The Doctor:** 'Just touch these two strands together and the Daleks are finished. Have I that right?' **Sarah Jane Smith:** 'To destroy the Daleks, you can't doubt it.' **The Doctor:** 'But I do. You see some things could be better with the Daleks. Many future worlds will become allies just because of their fear of the Daleks.' **Sarah Jane Smith:** 'It isn't like that!' **The Doctor:** 'But the final responsibility is mine and mine alone. Listen. If someone who knew the future, pointed out a child to you and told you that that child would grow up totally evil, to be a ruthless dictator who would destroy millions of lives … could you then kill that child?' **Sarah Jane Smith:** 'We're talking about the Daleks. The most evil creatures ever invented. You must destroy them. You must complete your mission for the Time Lords!' **The Doctor:** 'Do I have the right? Simply touch one wire against the other and that's it. The Daleks

cease to exist. Hundreds of millions of people, thousands of generations can live without fear … in peace, and never even know the word "Dalek".' **Sarah Jane Smith:** 'Then why wait? If it was a disease or some sort of bacteria you were destroying, you wouldn't hesitate.' **The Doctor:** 'But if I kill. Wipe out a whole intelligent life form, then I become like them. I'd be no better than the Daleks.' **Sarah Jane Smith:** 'Think of all the suffering there'll be if you don't do it.'

- **Dalek:** 'We are entombed, but we live on. This is only the beginning. We will prepare. We will grow stronger. When the time is right we will emerge and take our rightful place as the supreme power of the universe!'
- **The Doctor:** 'I know that although the Daleks will create havoc and destruction for millions of years, I know also, that out of their evil, must come something good.'

ANALYSIS

Terry Nation's previous two Dalek stories, *Planet of the Daleks* and *Death to the Daleks*, had been somewhat clichéd and unoriginal and it had seemed that the Doctor's greatest adversaries were destined for an ignoble end playing out ever more hackneyed and repetitive material. *Genesis of the Daleks* changed all that. Indeed, as Nathan Roberts commented in *Star Begotten* Volume 3 Number 1/2 dated winter/spring 1989: 'The problem with reviewing a story like *Genesis of the Daleks* is that it is easy to run out of superlatives … Like a lot of Hinchcliffe's and Holmes's work, it is dramatic, gritty and uncompromising, pushing the show to its creative boundaries in almost every sphere of production.'

Not only are Terry Nation's scripts well written and full of new ideas, while still remaining true to the Daleks' roots by effectively equating them with the Nazis of the Second World War (perhaps the most obvious example of this after season two's *The Dalek Invasion of Earth*), but the story's production values are also extremely high. Director David Maloney is able to make an otherwise standard *Doctor Who* quarry really look like a mist-shrouded alien planet, and his slow motion opening sequence of a group of soldiers being massacred in a hail of bullets sets the scene for an unusually grim and horrific six-parter. This is a story about survival at any cost, and neither its writer nor those responsible for bringing it to the screen shirk from conveying the harrowing implications.

The story really kicks into gear with the introduction of Davros. It has by this point become virtually standard procedure in *Doctor Who* for a dominant central character to be brought in to act as the leader of a race of popular monsters, who are then reduced to the status of mere 'heavies' standing around in the background, handling the violent action and – if they are lucky – uttering the occasional line of dialogue. The Cybermen have been made subservient to their Controller (*The Tomb of the Cybermen*), their Planner (*The Wheel in Space*) and their Director (*The Invasion*), and similarly the Ice Warriors have been given their commanding officers in the form of Slaar (*The Seeds of Death*), Izlyr (*The Curse of Peladon*) and Azaxyr (*The Monster of Peladon*). Now it is the turn of the Daleks to play second fiddle; and although the conclusion to Part Six encouragingly suggests that they are going to buck the trend by killing their creator and reasserting their own dominance, later stories would prove this not to be the case.

Davros is, however, a masterful creation. Almost every line that he is given to speak is quotable, and Michael Wisher, who could have been born to play the part, turns in a truly electrifying performance that overshadows all other aspects of the story. This near-perfect combination of scripting and acting brings Davros to life as an utterly compelling character, whose deranged genius is portrayed with such conviction that the audience holds its collective breath whenever he is on the screen. 'Michael Wisher's [performance] as Davros must rate as one of the most powerful ever ... in *Doctor Who*,' enthused Richard Walter in *Baker's Best* in 1981. 'Undoubtedly the superb make-up helped, but having an actor who had previously been a Dalek "voice" was a great idea. At times Davros could have been a Dalek, the tone of his voice changing dramatically depending on his mood and often demonstrating just how ruthless he was.' Roberts was similarly impressed. 'The real stars of the story ... are undoubtedly Peter Miles as Nyder and Michael Wisher as Davros, and both give remarkable performances; the latter especially so considering that the only way for him to project the character was through his voice – the normal range of facial and bodily expression (with the exception of a slightly moving right arm) were unavailable to him. This alone makes Wisher's performance all the more breathtaking.' It could be argued that, despite its title, this story is not really about the creation of the Daleks at all; it is first and foremost Davros's story, and it is for him that it is chiefly remembered.

The story's faults are few and far between. There is a rather daft scene in which Harry clumsily puts his foot into the mouth of a giant clam that promptly tries to eat him; and many of the scientist characters serve no other purpose than to act as Dalek-fodder. In addition, although the cliffhanger ending to the first episode is great, being perfect in its timing and sense of anticipation of things to come, some of the others are a bit duff. Sarah falling from a gantry (only to land safely on a previously unseen beam at the start of the following episode) and the Doctor somehow becoming attached to an electrified fence are not exactly the stuff of nightmares.

These few minor failings are quickly forgotten, however, amongst all the wonderful things that this story has to offer. Scenes such as the one in which the Doctor debates with Davros the morality of the creation of the Daleks, likening them to a deadly virus with the potential to wipe out all life in the universe, and the one in which he agonises over whether or not he has the right to commit genocide by blowing up the Daleks' incubation chamber and destroying them at birth, are amongst the most dramatic and intelligent that the series ever produced. The BBC's Audience Research Report on the story's concluding instalment suggests that many contemporary viewers realised that it was something a bit special: 'A little more complex than some *Doctor Who* adventures, perhaps, and with underlying questions of conscience, the serial had been "different" it was occasionally felt and, although dismissed in some quarters as far-fetched, long drawn-out, confused and/or predictable, had provided acceptable escapist entertainment for the majority.'

Genesis of the Daleks is a gem of a story, with little padding as six-parters go and fine performances from all the cast. 'So Frankenstein is once more destroyed by his monster,' wrote Keith Miller in *DWFC Mag* Number 24 dated May/June 1975. 'The Doctor, Sarah and Harry say a very rushed goodbye to the Thals, grab hold of the time ring and whiz into outer space. The ending left me very puzzled. The Thals wandered away as if the Daleks had been destroyed. The Doctor and co faded away. What about the Daleks? It would only take them a matter of minutes to get through the blocked-up corridor.'

It seemed that the Daleks were destined to cross the Doctor's path again. More immediately, though, the very next story promised the long-awaited return of another of the series' most famous monster races ...

REVENGE OF THE CYBERMEN

Writer: Gerry Davis. **Director:** Michael E Briant. **Designer:** Roger Murray-Leach. **Costumes:** Prue Handley. **Make-Up:** Cecile Hay-Arthur. **Incidental Music:** Carey Blyton, Peter Howell*. **Visual Effects:** James Ward. **Film Cameraman:** Elmer Cossey. **Film Editor:** Sheila S Tomlinson. **Studio Lighting:** Derek Slee. **Studio Sound:** Norman Bennett. **Production Assistant:** John Bradburn. **Assistant Floor Manager:** Rosemary Hester, Russ Karel.
* Uncredited.

	First UK TX	Scheduled TX	Actual TX	Duration	Viewers	Chart Pos.
Part One	19/04/75	17.35	17.36	24'19"	9.5	24
Part Two	26/04/75	17.30	17.31	24'24"	8.3	28
Part Three	03/05/75	17.50	17.51	24'32"	8.9	25
Part Four	10/05/75	17.35	17.31	23'21"	9.4	22

Plot: The time ring takes the Doctor, Sarah and Harry back to Nerva, but to a period many thousands of years earlier than their previous visit. The station is currently acting as a beacon warning space traffic of the existence of a new asteroid orbiting Jupiter. This is Voga, also known as the planet of gold as that metal can be found in abundance there. The three friends learn that a space plague has killed all but a handful of Nerva's crew. A visiting civilian scientist named Kellman is in fact a traitor working with a group of Cybermen who want to destroy Voga as gold dust can coat their breathing apparatus and suffocate them. The 'plague' is the result of poison injected into its victims by Cybermats. The Cybermen invade the beacon and force the Doctor and two of the remaining humans to carry some cobalt bombs down into the heart of Voga. Kellman however is really a double agent, secretly working with one faction of the Vogan race on the planet below. Their plan has been to lure the Cybermen onto the beacon and destroy it with a rocket, known as the Skystriker. The Doctor rids himself of the bomb he has been forced to carry and returns to the beacon, which the Cybermen evacuate on learning of the Vogans' intentions. The missile is launched, but the Doctor gives instructions for it to be redirected away from the beacon and onto a collision course with the Cybermen's ship, which is thus destroyed.

Episode endings:
1. Sarah screams as a Cybermat leaps from the floor and attacks her neck.
2. The Doctor tries to get away as the Cybermen board the beacon, but the Cyberleader fires its head-mounted weapon at him and he collapses to the ground. The Cyberleader announces to the other Cybermen that all resistance is overcome and the beacon is theirs.
3. Harry examines the unconscious Doctor and concludes that there is nothing seriously wrong with him. He starts to unbuckle the straps by means of which the Cybermen's bomb is attached to the Doctor's back, unaware that this will cause it to detonate …
4. The TARDIS arrives on the beacon, having been gradually drifting back to this point in time, and the Doctor, Sarah and Harry leave for a rendezvous with the Brigadier, who has sent an urgent message requesting assistance with a problem on Earth.

IT WAS MADE WHERE...?

Location filming: 18.11.74-21.11.74
Location: Wookey Hole Caves, Wookey Hole, Wells, Somerset.
Studio: 02.12.74-03.12.74 in TC1, 16.12.74-17.12.74 in TC3

ADDITIONAL CREDITED CAST

Kellman (Jeremy Wilkin[1-3]*), Commander Stevenson (Ronald Leigh-Hunt), Lester (William Marlowe), Warner (Alec Wallis[1]), Vorus (David Collings), Magrik (Michael Wisher), Cyberleader (Christopher Robbie), Tyrum (Kevin Stoney[2-4]), Sheprah (Brian Grellis[2-4]), First Cyberman (Melville Jones[2-4]).

* Also in Part Four, in the reprise from Part Three, but uncredited.

POPULAR MYTHS

• The Cybermen's desire for revenge in this story, as reflected in the title, is out of keeping with their unemotional characters. (The Cybermen are not seeking revenge in their attack on Voga but trying to destroy a potential threat; it is the Vogans who incorrectly assume that their motive is revenge.)

THINGS TO WATCH OUT FOR

• A number of sets in this story were reused from *The Ark in Space*, which was recorded immediately before it.
• *Revenge of the Cybermen* saw the Cybermen return to the screen in their own story for the first time since *The Invasion* (1968). They had appeared fleetingly in *The War Games* (1969), *The Mind of Evil* (1971) and *Carnival of Monsters* (1973).
• The Cybermen's voices were provided for the first time by the actors inside the costumes.
• Five of this story's guest cast had played notable roles earlier in *Doctor Who*'s history: Kevin Stoney as Mavic Chen in *The Daleks' Master Plan* and as Tobias Vaughn in the previous Cyberman story, *The Invasion*; Christopher Robbie as the Karkus in *The Mind Robber*; Ronald Leigh-Hunt as Commander Radnor in *The Seeds of Death*; and William Marlowe as Mailer in *The Mind of Evil*. Michael Wisher would go on to play Davros in *Genesis of the Daleks*, which came after *Revenge of the Cybermen* in production order.
• The launching of the Skystriker is represented by (rather obvious) NASA stock footage of a Saturn V rocket taking off.

THINGS YOU MIGHT NOT HAVE KNOWN

• The Radiophonic Workshop's Peter Howell, later to become one of the series' regular incidental music composers, made his uncredited debut on this story when he was asked by producer Philip Hinchcliffe to add to and enhance the score provided by Carey Blyton.
• Gerry Davis wrote the script *Return of the Cybermen*, which Holmes then re-wrote extensively, adding the Vogans and the new sub-plot involving them, as *Revenge of the Cybermen*.

QUOTE, UNQUOTE

• **The Doctor:** [To the Cyberleader] 'You're nothing but a pathetic bunch of tin soldiers skulking about the galaxy in an ancient spaceship.'

- **Cyberleader:** 'Cybermen can survive more efficiently than animal organisms. That is why we will rule the galaxy.'

Revenge of the Cybermen holds the dubious distinction of having received what may well be the only one-word review in *Doctor Who*'s critical history when Keith Miller, assessing it in *DWFC Mag* Number 24 dated May/June 1975, wrote simply: 'Yeauch.' John Connors, on the other hand, suggested in *Aggedor* Issue 4 in 1983 that it was 'a gem' almost unsurpassed 'as an example of the rich quality of the mid seventies stories'. A fair appraisal lies somewhere between these two extremes. Connors himself went on to identify, and then rather half-heartedly to try to excuse, the story's major failing: 'Possibly the only weak point was the script, but bearing in mind that no Cyberstory has ever been innovative ... then *Revenge of the Cybermen* comes out well. Perhaps Cybermen fail to inspire good plots.'

A story with a weak script and a poor plot is always going to have a struggle to impress the viewer, and *Revenge of the Cybermen* is no exception. It does however contain some good characters, and David Owen, writing in *In-Vision* Issue Five dated June 1988, was impressed by its use of symbolism:

'The story's boundaries are clearly defined. At no point does Commander Stevenson radio Earth to ask them to come and nuke the Cybership. Earth and its society are not represented literally in this story, but represented by the symbol of the beacon and its occupants. Stevenson and Lester stand for human good and the value of cooperation. Kellman is human greed and corruption. At stake is the survival of the sympathetic characters and their world of the beacon, with Voga a secondary concern ...

'[The] Vogans ... constitute a fairly typical *Doctor Who* alien race in suffering leaders who talk a lot, looking indistinguishable and having troops who die easily. Contrast with the Cybermen has to be shown by civil unrest in the opposed camps of Vorus's Guardians and Tyrum's City Militia. The pre-story policy of safety through seclusion compares with the Cybermen's idea of safety through domination. Even the two Vogan camps do not show much unity – it is one of Vorus's own people [that] the Guardians slay for trying to warn Nerva of his intentions.'

The return of the Cybermen themselves, after an absence of more than six years (barring the odd cameo appearance), is undoubtedly the story's main talking-point. Their costumes have once more undergone a slight redesign and, although disliked by some commentators, this new look is actually quite effective. 'The Cybermen seemed to disappoint many,' noted John Connors, 'but I found them wholly acceptable (apart from their flared trousers!) and ... loved their head guns – they were much more practical than hand-held weapons, because to disarm them you'd have to blow their heads off.' Again it is the scripting that lets things down, as the Cybermen appear uncharacteristically emotional and have some terrible dialogue to deliver. The idea of them being susceptible to attack with gold dust is also less than inspired; previous stories have shown them to be vulnerable to such diverse things as radiation, solvents, gravity, low temperatures, electric currents, force fields, emotional impulses and grenades, and the revelation of this latest weakness only serves to reduce their potency still further.

As far as the story's on-screen realisation is concerned, the direction by the ever-dependable Michael E Briant is fortunately very good – although shots of the Cyberleader strutting around with his hands on his hips are an unfortunate lapse – and, as John Connors observed, the production values are uniformly high:

'The visual scope of *Revenge of the Cybermen* was marvellous. The Vogan surface looked so mystical and genuine, it's put all subsequent attempts to recreate that feel in a studio to shame. Cardboard caves just don't work. *Revenge of the Cybermen* had real ones, and a nice large number of extras clambering about them to make it look totally convincing ...

'*Revenge of the Cybermen* was made when the big rock bands of the seventies still held sway, and, although [doubtless] unintentional ..., [its incidental music] reflected the bombastic gestures of that period, as well as showing the militaristic overtones with the superbly chilling Cybertheme used at the end of [Part Two] and the start of [Part Three].'

Revenge of the Cybermen is not a particularly bad story, but it is not a particularly good one either, and coming after three real crackers it can only be considered a disappointing way to end the season.

At only twenty episodes, the twelfth season had been by far the shortest of *Doctor Who*'s history up to this point. The original intention had been that *Revenge of the Cybermen* would be followed by a further six-part story, but the BBC's programme planners had decided to cut short this run of transmissions and bring forward the next so that *Doctor Who*'s seasons would in future span from autumn to spring, rather than from spring to summer. The twelfth season had done well in the ratings and it was felt that the move to an autumn start would give the BBC an added edge against the rival ITV network in the competition for viewers, particularly as many ITV regions were about to start screening a major new Gerry Anderson series called *Space: 1999*. This change of scheduling meant that production of the next batch of twenty-six episodes had to be advanced by some three months to ensure that it would be ready in time for transmission. The division between the twelfth and thirteenth production blocks was consequently more notional than real, as work continued effectively without a break.

The stories of the twelfth season, despite containing some reassuringly traditional elements, had given a clear indication that *Doctor Who* was undergoing a significant change of style under the new production team of Philip Hinchcliffe and Robert Holmes. *Robot*, for all its military hardware, gun battles and explosions, had been essentially larger than life, fantasy-based family drama, very much akin to most of the Pertwee-era UNIT tales, but the other stories – particularly *The Ark in Space*, *The Sontaran Experiment* and *Genesis of the Daleks* – had possessed a much more realistic and horrific quality. *Genesis of the Daleks*, with its themes of warfare, racial hatred and genetic experimentation, had even provoked complaints from some viewers and from the self-appointed moral watchdogs of the National Viewers and Listeners Association, headed by Mary Whitehouse. This was a trend that would be continued in season thirteen.

DOCTOR WHO SEASON THIRTEEN [1975-1976]

Regular Cast:
Doctor Who (Tom Baker)
Sarah Jane Smith (Elisabeth Sladen)
Harry Sullivan (Ian Marter) until *Terror of the Zygons* Part Four

Regular Crew:
Producer: Philip Hinchcliffe.
Script Editor: Robert Holmes.
Production Unit Manager: George Gallaccio on *Terror of the Zygons*, *Pyramids of Mars* and *The Seeds of Doom*, Janet Radenkovic on all stories except *Terror of the Zygons*.
Title Music: Ron Grainer and the BBC Radiophonic Workshop, arranged by Delia Derbyshire.
Special Sounds: Dick Mills except on *Planet of Evil*. Peter Howell on *Planet of Evil*.

Season thirteen consisted of five four-parters and one six-parter, establishing a pattern that would be repeated for the next four years (although season seventeen would lose its six-parter due to industrial action at the BBC). This season was wholly the responsibility of Philip Hinchcliffe and Robert Holmes, who were thus able to ensure that it fully reflected their shared vision of the series. The horror content of the stories was even higher than before, and the gradual phasing out of UNIT that had been begun in the third Doctor's era was finally completed. Harry Sullivan – a character originally conceived as someone who could take care of the action scenes if the fourth Doctor happened to be played by an older actor – was also now considered surplus to requirements and written out. The resultant season was not only one of significant change, however, but also one considered by many to be amongst the very best in the series' history.

TERROR OF THE ZYGONS

Writer: Robert Banks Stewart. **Director:** Douglas Camfield. **Designer:** Nigel Curzon. **Costumes:** James Acheson. **Make-Up:** Sylvia James. **Incidental Music:** Geoffrey Burgon. **Visual Effects:** John Horton, John Friedlander. **Film Cameraman:** Peter Hall. **Film Editor:** Ian McKendrick. **Studio Lighting:** John Dixon. **Studio Sound:** Michael McCarthy. **Production Assistant:** Edwina Craze. **Assistant Floor Manager:** Rosemary Webb.

	First UK TX	Scheduled TX	Actual TX	Duration	Viewers	Chart Pos.
Part One	30/08/75	17.45	17.46	21'41"	8.4	29
Part Two	06/09/75	17.45	17.45	25'08"	6.1	61
Part Three	13/09/75	17.45	17.47	24'09"	8.2	32
Part Four	20/09/75	17.20	17.22	25'22"	7.2	45

Plot: The Doctor, Sarah and Harry return to Earth in response to the Brigadier's summons. UNIT are investigating a series of attacks on North Sea oil rigs and have set up a temporary HQ in the Scottish village of Tullock. The attacks are the work of a huge cyborg, the Skarasen, controlled by a group of aliens called Zygons whose spaceship lies at the bottom of Loch Ness. The Zygons plan to take over the Earth as a substitute for their own planet, which has been devastated by solar flares. They are using their shape-shifting abilities to take on the identities of locals whose inert bodies are held aboard their ship. The Doctor releases the Zygons' prisoners and causes their ship, which has now emerged from the Loch, to self-destruct. Only their leader, Broton, survives. He has assumed the identity of the Duke of Forgill and travelled to London. There he plans to give a show of strength by destroying a World Energy Conference with the Skarasen, which is now approaching up the Thames. Broton is shot by UNIT troops and the Doctor throws the Skarasen its homing device, which it devours. Without a controlling influence, the creature makes its way back to Loch Ness.

Episode endings:
1. Sarah telephones the Doctor from the infirmary where Harry has been taken to recover from a head wound sustained when he was shot by the Duke of Forgill's retainer, the Caber. Their conversation is interrupted as Sarah is attacked by a Zygon and lets out a terrified scream.
2. The Doctor races across the moors to try to escape from the pursuing Skarasen but eventually trips and falls to the ground. Broton, watching on a screen in the Zygon ship, gives the order to kill, and the Skarasen bears down on its victim.
3. As the UNIT team look on, the Zygon spaceship rises from Loch Ness and takes to the air.
4. The TARDIS dematerialises and the Duke of Forgill expresses astonishment that the Brigadier, a Scot, did not think to ask the Doctor and Sarah for their return rail tickets to get a refund on them.

IT WAS MADE WHERE...?

Location filming: 17.03.75-21.03.75, 24.03.75–25.03.75 (extension due to bad weather)
Locations: Climping Beach, Climping, West Sussex; Ambersham Common, South Ambersham, West Sussex; Hall Aggregates Quarry, Storrington, West Sussex; Charlton, West Sussex; Furnace Pond, Mill Lane, Crabtree, West Sussex; Millbank Tower, Millbank, London SW1.
Studio: 07.04.75-08.04.75 in TC3, 22.04.75-23.04.75 in TC4

ADDITIONAL CREDITED CAST

Duke of Forgill (John Woodnutt*), Brigadier Lethbridge-Stewart (Nicholas Courtney), RSM Benton (John Levene), Sister Lamont (Lillias Walker), The Caber (Robert Russell), Angus (Angus Lennie[1,3]), Huckle (Tony Sibbald[1,2]), Munro (Hugh Martin[1]), Radio Operator (Bruce Wightman[1]), Zygons (Keith Ashley, Ronald Gough[2-4]), Corporal (Bernard G High[2]), Soldier (Peter Symonds[3]).

* John Woodnutt also played Broton in all four episodes, but was uncredited for this on screen.

FOURTH DOCTOR

POPULAR MYTHS

- The village in which much of the action takes place is called Tulloch. (It is called Tullock, according to a sign board seen on screen.)

THINGS TO WATCH OUT FOR

- There are some excellent model shots of the Zygon spaceship.
- Superb performances are given by John Woodnutt – previously seen in the series as Hibbert in season seven's *Spearhead from Space* and as the Draconian Emperor in season ten's *Frontier in Space* – as both the local laird, the Duke of Forgill, and Broton.
- Angus Lennie, who had previously appeared as Storr in season five's *The Ice Warriors* but was better known for his role as Shughie McFee in the soap opera *Crossroads*, plays landlord Angus McRanald.
- This was the last story to feature the full UNIT team of the Brigadier, RSM Benton and Harry Sullivan.
- The effects featuring the Skarasen were achieved using two puppets. The first was three feet long and designed for stop-motion work of the creature moving about on land. The other was a large version of the head and neck section, used mainly for scenes of the monster emerging from the River Thames at the end of Part Four.

THINGS YOU MIGHT NOT HAVE KNOWN

- Working titles: *The Loch Ness Monster*, *The Loch Ness Terror* and *The Zygons*.
- This story was originally planned as a six-parter to end season twelve, but was cut down to four parts at the scripting stage when it was held back to launch season thirteen.
- The design of the Zygons was based partly on a human embryo.
- The Zygons were designed to glow internally by the provision of a series of lights inside the rib cage and the head, all powered from a concealed battery pack. This idea was not used much during recording.
- A scene of the TARDIS arriving invisibly at the start of Part One was dropped after filming because of technical difficulties discovered during editing.

QUOTE, UNQUOTE

- **The Doctor:** 'You brought me back 270 million miles just to sort out a little trouble at sea?' **Brigadier Lethbridge-Stewart:** 'Three serious disasters ...' **The Doctor:** 'When I left that psionic beam with you, Brigadier, I said that it was only to be used in an emergency!' **Brigadier Lethbridge-Stewart:** 'This *is* an emergency!' **The Doctor:** 'Oil? An emergency? Ha! It's about time the people who run this planet of yours realised that to be dependent on a mineral slime just doesn't make sense.'
- **The Doctor:** [To Broton] 'You can't rule the world in hiding. You've got to come out on to the balcony sometimes and wave a tentacle.'

ANALYSIS

After the Yeti in *The Abominable Snowmen*, giant sea monsters in *Fury from the Deep* and the Minotaur in *The Time Monster*, *Doctor Who* presents its own version of yet another creature of popular legend (or should that be myth?), namely the Loch Ness Monster. 'I always wondered just how long it would take the writers to get round to Nessie as subject matter ...' wrote Keith Miller in *DWFC Mag* Number 25 dated March/April

1976. 'Anyway, this story of Broton and co was written with quite a lot of originality, but also with a generous helping of tried and trusted ... scenes [from *The Sea Devils*]. Take for instance the opening scenes with [Munro] on the oil rig ... The shots where the rig collapsed at night were quite well done, [though].'

Another third Doctor story to which *Terror of the Zygons* bears a certain similarity is *The Green Death*, in that it relies for much of its atmosphere on a somewhat stereotypical depiction of the people and culture of the country in which it is set – in this case Scotland rather than Wales. 'Television shorthand is employed from the opening moments,' noted Tim Robins in *In-Vision* Issue 7 dated August 1988, 'when an oil rig worker is heard to request: "Can ye no send over a few haggis? The chef we have here disnae ken the first thing aboot ...". At this point, the Skarasen thankfully puts an end to this walking cliché.' *Terror of the Zygons* differs from *The Green Death* however in that its stereotypes, such as Angus the bagpipe-playing landlord with 'second sight', seem less patronising – perhaps a consequence of the fact that writer Robert Banks Stewart was himself a Scot – and that it contains no equivalent to the earlier story's allusions to contemporary issues like pollution and loss of employment in the mining industry. '[It] represents a tourist-eyes view of Scotland,' concluded Robins. 'Rituals (bagpipes playing), the social status of the laird, dress (the kilt), language (accent and references to Gaelic), artefacts (the stag's head [on the wall of the pub]) and food (haggis) exoticise the Scottish culture – taking on a mythic quality as well as providing local colour.'

The featuring of UNIT serves to highlight just how much *Doctor Who* has changed since Barry Letts and Terrance Dicks were in charge. Under Philip Hinchcliffe and Robert Holmes the series has become far less cosy and taken on what has often been described as a gothic horror quality. There are many scenes in this story that it is impossible to imagine having been included a few seasons earlier. A good example is the one in which a Zygon, having taken on the appearance of Harry, attacks Sarah. As Keith Miller put it: 'Harry turned very nasty in his guise of a Zygon (or vice versa) and the sequence with Sarah in the barn was very well done – the slow climbing of the ladder and the shot of Harry, hidden in shadow except for a single eye, glaring at her. Chilling ... Then Harry picks up a pitchfork and lunges at the young journalist, misses and plummets to his death ... below, with a lot of synthesised groaning. Ooh, nasty ...'

The Brigadier and his UNIT team are themselves depicted much more realistically on this occasion than in their last few appearances, regaining some of their dignity and believability. This is no doubt attributable in part to the influence of Douglas Camfield, renowned for his interest in all things military, who – returning for the first time since season seven's *Inferno* – again proves himself to be one of the series' very best directors. His earlier *Doctor Who* work had shown him to have a predeliction for presenting scary material, and his characteristically dynamic and stylish approach is perfectly in tune with the more horrific quality brought to the series by Hinchcliffe and Holmes.

The Zygons are not particularly original in their conception. As far back as season four's *The Faceless Ones* the series had presented creatures capable of appropriating people's appearances, which is in fact a stock idea in science-fiction, and their organic technology recalls that of the Axons in *The Claws of Axos*, who also had to quit their home planet due to solar flare activity. Where they really succeed however is in their wonderful on-screen realisation. Their costumes, the responsibility of James Acheson and John Friedlander, are a masterpiece of monster design and, coupled with the highly effective way in which they are directed by Camfield, make them a chilling and memorable foe for the Doctor.

For a time it seems that *Terror of the Zygons* is to be an almost faultless production. But then the Skarasen appears. The realisation of this creature is undoubtedly the major weakness of the story. The two models used for the purpose are less than convincing in themselves, and the stop-motion filming by way of which they are animated is truly terrible. Even the dramatic final scenes are let down by the Skarasen, as Keith Miller noted: 'The fight in the cellar between Broton and the Doctor, Sarah and the Brigadier was quite good, with Broton coming to [a] predictably nasty end. Then, to wrap things up, [the Skarasen] rises very unconvincingly from the Thames to the humorous squeaky screams of the passers-by.'

In the *Lively Arts* documentary *Whose Doctor Who* in 1977, Philip Hinchcliffe made the observation that just a single unsuccessful effect can result in the failure of an entire production. It would be surprising if the Skarasen from *Terror of the Zygons* was not one of the effects that he had in mind. Even with this impediment, however, the story remains a strong one.

PLANET OF EVIL

Writer: Louis Marks. **Director:** David Maloney. **Designer:** Roger Murray-Leach. **Costumes:** Andrew Rose. **Make-Up:** Jenny Shircore. **Incidental Music:** Dudley Simpson. **Visual Effects:** Dave Havard. **Film Cameraman:** Stan Speel, Kenneth McMillan. **Film Editor:** M A C Adams. **Studio Lighting:** Brian Clemett. **Studio Sound:** Tony Millier, Brendan Shaw. **Production Assistant:** Malachy Shaw Jones. **Assistant Floor Manager:** Karilyn Collier.

	First UK TX	Scheduled TX	Actual TX	Duration	Viewers	Chart Pos.
Part One	27/09/75	17.45	17.45	24'02"	10.4	19
Part Two	04/10/75	17.45	17.46	22'30"	9.9	24
Part Three	11/10/75	18.05	18.07	23'50"	9.1	29
Part Four	18/10/75	17.45	17.46	23'43"	10.1	26

Plot: The TARDIS picks up a distress call and the Doctor and Sarah arrive on the planet Zeta Minor. There they discover that a Morestran geological expedition has fallen prey to an unseen killer and only the leader, Professor Sorenson, remains alive. A military mission from Morestra has also arrived to investigate. The culprit is revealed to be a creature from a universe of antimatter, retaliating for the removal by Sorenson of some antimatter samples from around the pit that acts as an interface between the two universes. The Morestrans take off in their ship, but it is slowly dragged back towards the planet due to the antimatter on board. Sorenson himself becomes infected by antimatter and gradually transforms into antiman, a monster capable of draining the life from others. The Morestran commander, the increasingly unhinged Salamar, attacks Sorenson with a radiation source but this only causes him to multiply, and soon the ship is overrun by deadly creatures. The Doctor finds the original Sorenson, takes him back to the planet in the TARDIS and throws both him and his samples into the pit, fulfilling a bargain he earlier made with the antimatter creature. Sorenson reappears unharmed and the Doctor returns him to the Morestran ship, which is now freed of the planet's influence.

Episode endings:
1. The shimmering red outline of a huge creature looms over the Doctor and Sarah. Sarah tries to get away but falls to the ground, and the creature advances toward them.
2. The Doctor arrives at the black pit leading to the universe of antimatter. As Sarah watches from the bridge of the Morestran ship, the events being relayed there via an oculoid tracking device, the antimatter creature emerges from the pit and the Doctor is dragged forward and topples over the edge.
3. The Doctor and Sarah are restrained in pallets in the Morestran ship to be ejected into space. The outer hatch opens and Salamar orders his deputy, Vishinsky, to activate the ejection switch. Vishinsky refuses, and a struggle ensues in which Salamar pushes the older man's arm down onto the switch. The pallets slide forward and through an inner hatch.
4. The Doctor and Sarah leave to keep an appointment with the Brigadier, and the TARDIS spins away through space and time.

IT WAS MADE WHERE...?
Ealing filming: 11.06.75-13.06.75 on Stage 2
Studio: 30.06.75-01.07.75 in TC6, 14.07.75-15.07.75 in TC3

ADDITIONAL CREDITED CAST
Sorenson (Frederick Jaeger), Vishinsky (Ewen Solon), Salamar (Prentis Hancock), De Haan (Graham Weston[1-3]), Ponti (Louis Mahoney[1,2]), Morelli (Michael Wisher[1-3]), Braun (Terence Brook[1]), Baldwin (Tony McEwan[1]), O'Hara (Haydn Wood[1,2]), Reig (Melvyn Bedford[3,4]).

THINGS TO WATCH OUT FOR
- The TARDIS control room makes its first appearance since season eleven's *Death to the Daleks*. This slightly redesigned set was first used for *Pyramids of Mars*, which preceded *Planet of Evil* in production order.
- Frederick Jaeger and Ewen Solon, appearing in this story as Sorenson and Vishinsky, had previously played Jano and Chal in season three's *The Savages*.
- Salamar was played by Prentis Hancock, fresh from making the first season of *Space: 1999*, in which he played Paul Morrow.
- There is a dramatic freeze-frame cliffhanger at the end of Part Two.

QUOTE, UNQUOTE
- **The Doctor:** 'Here on Zeta Minor is the boundary between existence as you know it and the other universe which you just don't understand. From the beginning of time it has existed side by side with the known universe. Each is the antithesis of the other. You call it "nothing", a word to cover ignorance. And centuries ago scientists invented another word for it. "Antimatter", they called it. And you, by coming here, have crossed the boundary into that other universe to plunder it. Dangerous ...'
- **The Doctor:** [To Sorenson] 'You and I are scientists, Professor. We buy our privilege to experiment at the cost of total responsibility.'

FOURTH DOCTOR

'With the Zygons now bygones,' quipped Keith Miller in *DWFC Mag* Number 25 dated March/April 1976, 'the Doctor persuades Sarah, but not Harry (aw!) to journey once more in the TARDIS and whisks her off to the "edge of the universe", to quote the *Radio Times*, to the rather shrivelled remains of a survey team. [The first] episode ... didn't wait around! Bodies disappeared and half baked skeletons took their place. Quite nasty.'

Planet of Evil is another wonderfully creepy story; and although a number of its central elements are clearly plundered from old cinema films – a practice that would become a defining characteristic of the Hinchcliffe and Holmes approach to the series – it is all done with such style and panache that the viewer, far from complaining about a lack of originality, delights in spotting all the familiar sources to which the writer and the production team are paying homage. Professor Sorenson's transformation into antiman is only one of a number of references to Robert Louis Stevenson's 1886 novel *The Strange Case of Doctor Jekyll and Mr Hyde*, as adapted in numerous horror films over the years; and the antimatter creature – very well realised as a shimmering red outline superimposed by way of electronic effects – is, in all but name, the Id monster from the 1956 MGM feature film *Forbidden Planet*.

The planet Zeta Minor becomes almost a character in its own right as, in keeping with the Jekyll and Hyde theme, it transforms from a relatively safe place during the day to a very dangerous one at night. The opposition between the known world of matter and the unknown one of antimatter, although deeply unscientific, also works well in dramatic terms. The scenes in which the Morestran ship is dragged back toward the planet due to the antimatter on board are very memorable, and the whole thing has the quality of an epic struggle about it.

One of *Forbidden Planet*'s most celebrated features is its excellent design work, and the same could be also said of *Planet of Evil*. Particularly noteworthy is the superb watery jungle set created by Roger Murray-Leach for the film insert sequences shot at Ealing. 'The main asset of the story was ... the scenery,' judged Keith Miller. 'I thought the sets were fantastic, with the flooded ground and dangling creepers. It created a great atmosphere of a totally alien planet. Best I've seen in a long time.' 'The Zeta Minor jungle looks suitably alien,' agreed Kenny Smith in *The Paisley Pattern Dr Who Annual* in 1993, 'but only during the filmed sequences. With no bright studio lights reflecting off plastic leaves, you're looking at one of the best alien jungles to be seen in the whole of the [series'] history ... Just try to ignore the terrible videotaped bits, though.' In fact the video recorded jungle scenes are by no means as bad as Smith suggested; but the criticisms he made of some other aspects of the production were arguably more valid: 'Character-wise, only Professor Sorenson is of note – the rest are just a bunch of boring old spacemen. Sorenson is a nutter, totally obsessed with his work ... He is totally deranged, and not at all helped by the antimatter infection. A pity about the brown spacesuit, though ... As with every other story made in the seventies, the attempts at space clothes are laughable. The groovy flares and open-necked, *Star Trek*-style shirts, complete with shoulder pads, look dated.'

Of the story's guest cast, Frederick Jaeger gives the stand-out performance as the tortured Professor Sorenson. Ewen Solon is also very acceptable as Vishinsky, and most of those playing the more minor Morestran roles give a good account of themselves. On the downside, Prentis Hancock unfortunately follows up a rather wooden portrayal of

Vaber in season ten's *Planet of the Daleks* with an equally poor attempt at Salamar here. Regulars Tom Baker and Elisabeth Sladen, meanwhile, have really got to grips with their respective roles by this point, and both give flawless and highly engaging performances.

The story's closing episode received 'a mainly moderately favourable response' from contemporary viewers, according to the BBC's Audience Research Report: 'It did not have such an exciting plot as some, viewers commented, some also having found it difficult to follow the gist, especially if the preceding episodes had been missed. One minority group regarded it as "ludicrous rubbish" – the monsters too unbelievable even for science fiction – "only fit for children", usually observing that they had watched as their family enjoyed it, but sometimes admitting that they had found it quite diverting, all the same. Another regarded it as not only ridiculous but rather horrible, with "some frightening moments": altogether unsuitable viewing for young children.' Over a third of those in the sample commented more favourably, however, indicating that '"all the family" had enjoyed this episode and the whole story, commending the series as one geared for the young but also acceptable to adults; a few especially welcomed the ingredient of "idealism" as well as adventure, with good triumphing over evil, promises kept, and experience prevailing. Several sci-fi enthusiasts had found it suitably terrifying and thrilling. Children too, from three to thirteen ... had relished the monsters: though decidedly frightening for some of the youngest, they refused to have the set switched off and sat spellbound, sometimes open-mouthed; older children thought the episode interesting and exciting, being also absorbed.'

The welcome reappearance of the TARDIS interior reinforces the impression that the Doctor is finally breaking free of his ties to Earth and resuming his space and time travels in earnest; and although Part Four ends with him and Sarah leaving to rendezvous with the Brigadier, as promised at the end of *Terror of the Zygons*, the opening scenes of the following story would confirm his increasing reluctance to continue his long-standing association with UNIT.

PYRAMIDS OF MARS

Writer: Stephen Harris*. **Director:** Paddy Russell. **Designer:** Christine Ruscoe. **Costumes:** Barbara Kidd. **Make-Up:** Jean Steward. **Incidental Music:** Dudley Simpson. **Visual Effects:** Ian Scoones. **Film Cameraman:** John McGlashan. **Film Editor:** M A C Adams. **Studio Lighting:** Ron Koplick. **Studio Sound:** Brian Hiles. **Production Assistant:** Peter Grimwade. **Assistant Floor Manager:** Paul Braithwaite.

* This was a pseudonym for Robert Holmes and Lewis Greifer.

	First UK TX	Scheduled TX	Actual TX	Duration	Viewers	Chart Pos.
Part One	25/10/75	17.45	17.47	25'22"	10.5	28
Part Two	01/11/75	17.45	17.48	23'53"	11.3	15
Part Three	08/11/75	17.45	17.46	24'32"	9.4	37
Part Four	15/11/75	17.45	17.45	24'52"	11.7	22

Plot: The TARDIS materialises on Earth in the year 1911 inside an old priory owned by Egyptologist Marcus Scarman. Scarman has been possessed by Sutekh, last survivor of the god-like Osirans, who is held prisoner inside a pyramid in Egypt by a signal transmitted from one on Mars. Sutekh desires his freedom and instructs Scarman to construct servicer robots – which look like Egyptian mummies – to build a missile with which to destroy the Martian pyramid. The Doctor foils this plan by blowing up the missile. He then falls under Sutekh's control himself and is made to transport Scarman to Mars in the TARDIS. Scarman cuts off the signal but the Doctor, now freed of Sutekh's influence, realises that there will be a short delay before it ceases to have effect, owing to the time taken for it to reach Earth. He rushes back and uses the time control from the TARDIS to move into the far future the end of the space-time tunnel that links the priory to the Egyptian pyramid. Sutekh, travelling down the tunnel, is unable to reach the end in his lifetime, and dies.

Episode endings:

1. Marcus Scarman's servant Namin plays the priory's organ as three robot mummies line up in front of a sarcophagus mounted on a raised dais. The front of the sarcophagus becomes a vortex and Namin comes to kneel before it as a black-robed figure steps through. The figure grasps Namin's shoulders. Smoke pours from the Egyptian's body and he falls dead to the ground.

2. The Doctor, Sarah and Marcus Scarman's brother Laurence return to the latter's house, where they discover the body of Scarman's friend Dr Warlock. The Doctor plans to block Sutekh's control of Marcus Scarman and thus cause him to collapse. Outside, a poacher named Clements is crushed to death between two mummies. Laurence shoots at them but they advance into the cottage, where one of them grabs Sarah by the throat.

3. The Doctor, disguised as a mummy, places a box of dynamite in the missile being prepared for launching. Sarah then fires a rifle at it. The box ignites but there is no explosion as Sutekh is mentally containing the blast. The Doctor travels to Sutekh's pyramid in Egypt using the sarcophagus space-time tunnel. Once there he breaks the Osiran's concentration and the missile is destroyed. Sutekh blasts the Doctor with light from his eyes.

4. With Sutekh dead from old age, the space-time tunnel explodes as the thermal balance equalises. A fire begins to rage in the priory and the Doctor and Sarah make a hasty departure so as not to be blamed for starting it – as the Doctor comments, he had enough of that in 1666.

IT WAS MADE WHERE...?

Location filming: 29.04.75-02.05.75
Location: Stargrove Manor, East End, Hants.
Studio: 19.05.75-20.05.75 in TC3, 02.06.75-03.06.75 in TC6, 10.6.75 (gallery only) in TC1

ADDITIONAL CREDITED CAST

Marcus Scarman (Bernard Archard), Laurence Scarman (Michael Sheard[1-3]), Dr. Warlock (Peter Copley[1,2]), Namin (Peter Mayock[1,2]), Collins (Michael Bilton[1]), Ahmed (Vik Tablian[1]), Mummies (Nick Burnell, Melvyn Bedford, Kevin Selway), Ernie Clements (George Tovey[2]), Sutekh (Gabriel Woolf[3,4*]).

* Gabriel Woolf also provided Sutekh's voice in Part Two and Horus's voice in Part Four, both uncredited.

POPULAR MYTHS

- Sutekh is an Osirian. (The name of his race is pronounced 'Osiran' throughout. The story's scripts and other paperwork also spell it as 'Osiran' in numerous places, although as 'Osirian' in others.)

THINGS TO WATCH OUT FOR

- This story features the last appearance of a traditional-look TARDIS control room set until *The Invisible Enemy* eleven stories later.
- There is a chilling sequence in which the Doctor takes Sarah to an alternative 1980 to show her the destruction that Sutekh would wreak on the Earth if allowed to escape.
- The Doctor's age is given as 750 years.

THINGS YOU MIGHT NOT HAVE KNOWN

- Although the script states that Sarah Jane is wearing an old dress of Victoria Waterfield's, it is not a costume that had previously been used in the series.
- *Pyramids of Mars* was voted best story of the season by the *Doctor Who* Appreciation Society in their first ever season poll.
- The story was originally commissioned from writer Lewis Greifer, but Robert Holmes completely re-wrote the scripts, resulting in the pseudonym Stephen Harris being used on transmission. Greifer's original story involved alien seeds hidden in the British Museum and mummies chasing around the exhibits.

QUOTE, UNQUOTE

- **The Doctor:** 'The Earth isn't my home, Sarah. I'm a Time Lord.' **Sarah:** 'Oh, I know you're a Time Lord.' **The Doctor:** 'You don't understand the implications. I'm not a human being. I walk in eternity.'
- **Servant of Sutekh (Marcus Scarman):** [Killing Namin.] 'I am the servant of Sutekh. He needs no other ... Die ... I bring Sutekh's gift of death to all humanity.'
- **The Doctor:** 'Deactivating a generator loop without the correct key is like repairing a watch with a hammer and chisel. One false move and you'll never know the time again.'

ANALYSIS

In *Pyramids of Mars*, the gothic horror style brought to *Doctor Who* by Philip Hinchcliffe and Robert Holmes is given its fullest expression yet. Here we have an ancient evil entombed in a pyramid, a possessed human and walking mummies: all the elements of classic 'Egyptian mummy' horror movies. Given the *Doctor Who* twist, however, the ancient evil is revealed to be an alien worshipped by the Egyptians, while the mummies turn out to be robots.

Robert Franks, writing in *Aggedor* Issue 4 in 1983, thought the story an excellent one: 'The plot ... stands out as one of the freshest and most stimulating in *Doctor Who*'s twenty years. The concept of a race of universally powerful beings, capable of destroying whole planets with the slightest thought (even though ... Sutekh the Destroyer was the only one to do such with such evil intent), may not have been entirely original, either in *Doctor Who* terms or otherwise, but for once there was a genuine feeling of panic and

4 FOURTH DOCTOR

desperation associated with the pace of the story.'

'The beginning, one of the most important bases for a story, was just great,' enthused Steve Ocock in the *Doctor Who Appreciation Society Yearbook 1976*. 'The idea of a certain Professor Scarman opening up a tomb is captivating enough, but when he begins to scream we find ourselves in the TARDIS control room. A very clever move this; you've just got to watch the programme now to find out what happened to the Professor!'

The first episode is indeed an excellent scene-setter, and ends on a superb cliffhanger as a terrifying black-robed figure emerges from the vortex within the sarcophagus in Scarman's house and walks down a short flight of steps, smoke billowing from its feet as treads on the carpet, to grip Namin by the shoulders and end his life in grisly fashion. This is just one of many memorable moments throughout the story. Chris Dunk and Rosemary Fowler, writing in *Baker's Best* in 1981, pointed out some other noteworthy aspects: 'The old priory being the site of UNIT HQ (only years before), [and burning] down due to the Doctor's own actions ... was a nice link. Sarah's appropriation of Victoria's old dress was also a nice touch ... The notion that the TARDIS controls are isomorphic must be controversial [though]. Other people have been able to gain access to the TARDIS [in the past] so presumably one must suppose that the Doctor was lying to Sutekh [when he told him that] ... Visually, the story worked superbly. The sets and costumes were magnificent from the first to the last. The BBC has ... always specialised in these period pieces and they came up trumps once more. The lodge and the country house (actually owned by Mick Jagger) were so true to the feel of the story that it would certainly not have worked so well otherwise. The grounds gave a chance for some nice, fresh location work too, enhanced by nice direction on the part of Paddy Russell ... The mummies were effective in their simplicity, powerful-looking yet basic and menial servants ... Sutekh himself [had] a macabre appearance ...'

Other highlights include Marcus Scarman being shot by Clements, the poacher, only for time to go into reverse and the bullet to fly back out of his body; Clements running into the deflection barrier placed around the priory by Sutekh, and later meeting a gruesome end as he is crushed to death between two mummies; Dr Warlock being killed by the possessed Marcus Scarman; Laurence Scarman having a similarly fatal meeting with his brother; and the Doctor, in a tellingly alien moment, pointing out to Sarah that grief is a luxury they cannot afford as the deaths they have seen will just be the first of many if Sutekh is not stopped – 'Know thine enemy,' as he puts it.

The story also has very high production values, including some fine incidental music by Dudley Simpson, and uniformly excellent performances from the small guest cast. Gabriel Woolf's icily understated Sutekh – another in a long line of masked villains – is particularly effective, and a good match for Tom Baker's Doctor. 'The initial blast from Sutekh's eyes was a chilling intro to the fascinating confrontation between Time Lord and god,' wrote Keith Miller in *DWFC Mag* Number 25 dated March/April 1976. 'The cool, calm yet malicious voice of Sutekh was superb, as was [Tom Baker's] acting ... when the evil alien extracted information from the Doctor's brain. Especially notable was the Doctor's humiliation when Sutekh forced [him] to his knees.'

It is not hard to see why this near-flawless story is so well remembered. As Stephen Cole put it in *DWB* No. 126 dated May 1994: 'This is one of those much-loved classics of *Doctor Who*, packaging a solid plot, chilling adversaries, fine acting performances and smooth direction with the lead actor effortlessly moving towards his disarming, charmingly alien peak of performance. And really, after all this time "up there" as one of the golden reasons we're all fans in the first place, is there much more to be said?'

THE ANDROID INVASION

Writer: Terry Nation. **Director:** Barry Letts. **Designer:** Philip Lindley. **Costumes:** Barbara Lane. **Make-Up:** Sylvia Thornton. **Incidental Music:** Dudley Simpson. **Fight Arranger:** Terry Walsh. **Visual Effects:** Len Hutton. **Film Cameraman:** Ken Newson. **Film Editor:** Mike Stoffer. **Studio Lighting:** Duncan Brown. **Studio Sound:** Alan Machin. **Production Assistant:** Marion McDougall. **Assistant Floor Manager:** Felicity Trew.

	First UK TX	Scheduled TX	Actual TX	Duration	Viewers	Chart Pos.
Part One	22/11/75	17.45	17.47	24'21"	11.9	17
Part Two	29/11/75	17.45	17.46	24'30"	11.3	24
Part Three	06/12/75	17.45	17.47	24'50"	12.1	14
Part Four	13/12/75	17.55	17.56	24'30"	11.4	15

Plot: The TARDIS arrives on the planet Oseidon where the alien Kraals have created an exact replica of the English village of Devesham and its nearby Space Defence Station and populated it with androids in order to rehearse for an invasion attempt. A human astronaut, Guy Crayford, has been duped into collaborating with them. The TARDIS travels on to Earth alone, and the Doctor and Sarah follow in Crayford's rocket, which is being used to carry the spearhead of the invasion force. The Kraals' chief scientist, Styggron, intends to release a deadly virus in order to weaken resistance to the forthcoming invasion. On reaching Earth, the Doctor and Sarah try to convince UNIT troops at the Space Defence Station of the danger. The Brigadier is away in Geneva, however, and Crayford is being hailed as a hero. The Doctor uses the Station's transmitters to jam the control signals of the now active androids – including duplicates of himself, Harry Sullivan and RSM Benton – and prevents Styggron from releasing his virus. Styggron accidentally infects himself during a fight with the android Doctor and is killed.

Episode endings:

1. The Doctor is captured trying to escape from the replica Space Defence Station but Sarah sees him being taken to a cell and creeps up to release him once the android guards have gone. Unseen by Sarah or the Doctor, a communicator on the wall swings back to reveal an alien face peering out at them.

2. The Doctor and Sarah return to where the TARDIS landed, but it has gone. The Doctor now knows that this is not the real Earth – and that his companion is not the real Sarah. He grabs her and, as she struggles to free herself, she falls over. The front of her face falls off to reveal that she is an android.

3. The Kraals are preparing Crayford's rocket to leave for Earth. The Doctor and Sarah hurriedly make their way on board, where they find pods containing androids. They start to move the androids out so that they can get into the pods themselves – otherwise, they will

be crushed by the g-force on take-off. Sarah manages to get into one of the pods, but the rocket takes off and the force starts to crush her.

4. The Doctor and Sarah locate the TARDIS on Earth and depart.

IT WAS MADE WHERE...?

Location filming: 21.07.75-25.07.75
Locations: National Radiological Protection Board, Harwell, Oxon; Worsham Quarry, Witney, Oxon; Tubney Wood, Tubney, Oxon; East Hagbourne, Oxon.
Studio: 11.08.75-12.08.75 in TC3, 25.08.75-26.08.75 in TC8

ADDITIONAL CREDITED CAST

Guy Crayford (Milton Johns), Morgan (Peter Welch[1-3]), Corporal Adams (Max Faulkner), Styggron (Martin Friend), Grierson (Dave Carter[1,4*]), Harry Sullivan (Ian Marter[2-4]), Chedaki (Roy Skelton[2,3]), RSM Benton (John Levene[2-4]), Kraal (Stuart Fell[3]), Colonel Faraday (Patrick Newell[4]), Matthews (Hugh Lund[4]), Tessa (Heather Emmanuel[4]).

* Although credited on Part One, Dave Carter did not appear.

POPULAR MYTHS

• This story was originally written to feature the Daleks rather than the Kraals. (It wasn't.)

THINGS TO WATCH OUT FOR

• A major source of inspiration for this story was the 1956 Allied Artists/Walter Wanger film *Invasion of the Body Snatchers*.
• Tom Baker had a bad throat while the location filming was being done, and his voice is much huskier than usual during these scenes.
• Marshal Chedaki sounds very similar to Zippy from the children's television series *Rainbow*. Actor Roy Skelton provided the voices for both parts.
• Like the Skystriker in the previous season's *Revenge of the Cybermen*, Crayford's rocket is represented by NASA stock footage of a Saturn V.
• Ian Marter and John Levene make their final appearances in *Doctor Who* as, respectively, Harry Sullivan and RSM Benton (and their android doubles).
• Patrick Newell, appearing here as Colonel Faraday, was better known as Mother in the espionage thriller series *The Avengers*.

THINGS YOU MIGHT NOT HAVE KNOWN

• Working title: *The Kraals*.
• Nicholas Courtney was not available to play the part of the Brigadier, and his lines were instead given to Colonel Faraday, played by Patrick Newell.
• This was the first non-Dalek story written for *Doctor Who* by Terry Nation since *The Keys of Marinus* (1964).

QUOTE, UNQUOTE

• **The Doctor:** [To one of the android drones with a finger-mounted gun.] 'Is that finger loaded?'
• **Styggron:** 'The androids will disseminate a virus. It will cause a contagion so lethal,

the Earth will be rid of its human population within three weeks, then it will burn itself out and the world will be ours.'

- **The Doctor:** 'Once upon a time there were three sisters, and they lived in the bottom of a treacle well. Their names were Olga, Marsha and Irena ... Are you listening, Tillie? ... I feel disorientated.' **Sarah:** 'This is the disorientation centre!' **The Doctor:** 'That makes sense.'

ANALYSIS

The Android Invasion is the weak link in an otherwise outstanding season and has received decidedly mixed reviews over the years. Keith Miller, giving an early reaction in *Doctor Who Digest* Number 1 dated July 1976, was unimpressed: 'I must be fair and say that the story was average, and I suppose some [people] thought it was good, but it left me cold. It created very little atmosphere and wasn't worthy of [Terry Nation's] talents.' Graham Howard, commenting almost twenty years laer in *TSV* 44 dated June 1995, was only a little better disposed toward the story: 'Taking everything into account I would describe *The Android Invasion* as good but not great. A qualified success.'

Terry Nation had taken a conscious decision to write a story featuring a new race of monsters rather than his famous creations the Daleks, and the Kraals – a sort of cross between a human and a rhinoceros – are a somewhat unoriginal but otherwise reasonable addition to the ranks of the Doctor's adversaries. Their on-screen realisation by visual effects sculptor John Friedlander is not too bad either, although Miller thought otherwise: 'The [Kraals'] masks were terribly false, I'm afraid to say; even funny.'

Actor Martin Friend makes the most of his role as the hunchbacked and conniving Styggron and brings over well the single-mindedness of the character. Indeed, all the guest cast in this story give good performances. Milton Johns as Crayford cuts a tragic figure as he comes to terms with the Kraals' duplicity and with their intention of using his rocket as a proverbial Trojan horse in their invasion of Earth; it's good to see Ian Marter and John Levene again; and Patrick Newell is perfectly adequate as Colonel Faraday, although the viewer suspects – quite correctly – that he is simply a stand-in for the unavailable Nicholas Courtney. Even those actors required to play the standard androids do so with an eerie stillness that seems to work.

The direction by Barry Letts – returning to *Doctor Who* for the first time since he relinquished the post of producer – is fine, indeed perhaps his best for the series. The location filming is good, and there are some very memorable moments, including a disconcertingly twitching UNIT soldier apparently committing suicide by throwing himself off the edge of a cliff at the beginning of Part One (in fact it is an android malfunctioning); some creepy scenes in the replica village, particularly those in the pub; and the classic ending to Part Two where the front of the android Sarah's face falls off to reveal the electronic circuitry beneath.

It is in its plotting that the story really falls down. The Kraals are clearly intelligent creatures and have some formidable technology at their disposal: they can create convincing android duplicates, drain the minds of others and place their knowledge in a computer, develop a killer virus and, perhaps most impressive of all, construct a near-perfect replica of an English village, including all the flora and fauna, buildings, smells, sky, clouds and everything needed to convince the Doctor that he is actually on Earth. And yet they are unable to come up with a solution to the rising levels of radiation on their home planet and instead devise a highly convoluted plan to take over the Earth.

Graham Howard pointed out some other problems: 'The "make Crayford believe he lost an eye by giving him an eye-patch" [scenario] is probably the most infamous plot weakness, but it is not the only one. The inability of people to shoot straight takes on almost farcical proportions. The soldiers cannot hit their target – even with a machine gun; the "robot mechanics" cannot shoot straight with their fingers; and even the android version of the Doctor has a woefully inaccurate aim! But this is a relatively minor … point … Less easy to dismiss as dramatic licence are some of the other plot deficiencies.

'For a start, why was it necessary for the Kraals to go to such extraordinary lengths to copy Devesham and the Space Defence Centre in such meticulous detail if they were ultimately going to destroy the replica anyway? Especially if the only purpose behind the infiltration of these areas was to facilitate the dissemination of the virus. Surely a rough approximation … would have been sufficient? … If the androids are "indestructible" why did the face of the android version of Sarah fall off so easily? Why did the calendar in the pub have only one date? Why is it that when Styggron is killed, the threat of invasion seems to disappear, when surely the Kraal invasion fleet is still out there?'

While not all these criticisms are entirely fair – it is clearly indicated in the story that the reason why the pub calendar has only one date is that the Kraals' replica of Devesham is imperfect – the general thrust of them is valid. There are some bold ideas and concepts here but they are inadequately thought through, and things happen for no good reason other than to progress the plot. It is quite obvious, to take the most blatant example, that Terry Nation has invented the previously unheard of TARDIS pause control, which bizarrely causes the ship to move from Oseidon to Earth when the key is inserted in the lock, simply because he is unable to think of any other way to get it from one planet to the other if the Doctor and Sarah travel in Crayford's rocket.

In a lesser season *The Android Invasion* might perhaps have held its own, but in season thirteen, with shining *Doctor Who* gems all around, it can manage only to glimmer dully.

THE BRAIN OF MORBIUS

Writer: Robin Bland*. **Director:** Christopher Barry. **Designer:** Barry Newbery. **Costumes:** L Rowland Warne. **Make-Up:** Jean McMillan. **Incidental Music:** Dudley Simpson. **Movement by:** Geraldine Stephenson. **Visual Effects:** John Horton. **Studio Lighting:** Peter Catlett. **Studio Sound:** Tony Millier. **Production Assistant:** Carol Wiseman. **Assistant Floor Manager:** Felicity Trew.

* This was a pseudonym for Terrance Dicks and Robert Holmes.

	First UK TX	Scheduled TX	Actual TX	Duration	Viewers	Chart Pos.
Part One	03/01/76	17.55	17.56	25'25"	9.5	30
Part Two	10/01/76	17.45	17.47	24'46"	9.3	32
Part Three	17/01/76	17.45	17.46	25'07"	10.1	23
Part Four	24/01/76	17.55	17.55	24'18"	10.2	28

Plot: The planet Karn is home both to a mystic Sisterhood, whose sacred flame produces an elixir of life, and to Mehendri Solon, a fanatical scientist who is using the remnants of spaceship crash victims to put together a new body for the still-living brain of the executed Time Lord criminal Morbius. When the Doctor and Sarah arrive on the planet, Solon decides that the Doctor's head is just what he needs to complete his work. The Sisterhood meanwhile fear that the Doctor has been sent by the Time Lords to steal the last drops of elixir produced by the dying flame. They kidnap him and plan to burn him at the stake but he is rescued by Sarah, who is temporarily blinded in the process. The Doctor is tricked by Solon into believing that his companion's condition is permanent. He asks the Sisterhood for help and restores their sacred flame to its former glory using a firework to clear its blocked chimney. Returning to Solon's citadel, the Doctor and Sarah become trapped in the cellar. The Doctor releases cyanide fumes into the ventilation system and Solon is killed, but not before he has used an artificial brain case to complete Morbius's new body. The now-mobile Morbius accepts the Doctor's challenge to a mind-bending contest, which takes a heavy toll on both of them. The Sisters force the crazed Morbius over a cliff and he falls to his death. They then use the elixir to heal the Doctor.

Episode endings:

1. Sarah sneaks into Solon's laboratory, left in darkness by a power failure, to investigate. She pulls aside some curtains and sees a humanoid figure lying on a raised platform. She initially believes that this is the Doctor, but suddenly the power comes back on and she sees that it is in fact a hideous monster with no head and a huge claw in place of its right hand. The monster lunges towards her.

2. Sarah, still unable to see, makes her way down into Solon's cellar, trying to locate the source of a guttural electronic voice that she can hear. On a bench in front of her stands a cylindrical tank in which Morbius's brain is suspended in bubbling green fluid. Morbius thinks that Sarah is one of the Sisterhood and rants that she has been sent by Maren to destroy him before his vengeance can begin …

3. Sarah, left by Solon in his laboratory after the completion of the operation to install Morbius's brain in an artificial brain case, realises that her sight is returning. The Morbius monster, having risen from the operating table, lurches towards her from behind, raising its claw to her neck …

4. The Doctor and Sarah enter the TARDIS and it vanishes in a flash and a puff of smoke.

IT WAS MADE WHERE…?

Studio: 06.10.75-07.10.75 in TC1, 20.10.75-21.10.75 in TC3, 24.10.75 (studio unknown)

ADDITIONAL CREDITED CAST

Solon (Philip Madoc), Maren (Cynthia Grenville), Ohica (Gilly Brown), Sisters (Sue Bishop, Janie Kells, Gabrielle Mowbray, Veronica Ridge), Condo (Colin Fay), Kriz (John Scott Martin[1]), Voice of Morbius (Michael Spice[2-4]), Monster (Stuart Fell[3,4])*.

* In Parts One and Two the headless monster was played uncredited by Alan Crisp.

POPULAR MYTHS

• Barry Newbery's sets for this story were inspired by the work of the Spanish architect

Antoni Gaudí. (They weren't, although at director Christopher Barry's request Newbery did look at some of Gaudí's work during the course of his research.)

- The Doctor mentions a race called the Hoothi who travel in silent gas dirigibles – a reference later picked up by author Paul Cornell when he featured the creatures in his original *Doctor Who* novel *Love and War*. (They are called the Muthi, according to Terrance Dicks's script.)

THINGS TO WATCH OUT FOR

- This story reused a number of elements from Terrance Dicks's 1974 stage play *Doctor Who and the Daleks in Seven Keys to Doomsday*.
- Kriz, a creature killed by Solon's servant Condo in Part One after its spaceship crash-lands on Karn, is a Solonian mutant from the season nine story *The Mutants*.
- Images of the Doctor's previous three incarnations appear on the screen of the mind-bending machine during the battle between the Doctor and Morbius. A number of other images, apparently intended to represent even earlier incarnations, also appear. These were photographs of behind-the-scenes personnel – directors Christopher Barry and Douglas Camfield, script editor Robert Holmes, production unit manager George Gallaccio, producer Philip Hinchcliffe, writer Robert Banks Stewart and production assistants Chris Baker and Graeme Harper – wearing stock costumes.
- At the end of Part Four the TARDIS dematerialises instantaneously, with a flash and a puff of smoke, rather than fading away gradually, and the dematerialisation sound is played at a higher speed than usual.

THINGS YOU MIGHT NOT HAVE KNOWN

- Colin Fay, who played Condo, was an opera singer.

QUOTE, UNQUOTE

- **The Doctor:** 'I thought I recognised the stars.' **Sarah Jane Smith:** 'You've been here before?' **The Doctor:** 'I was born in these parts.' **Sarah Jane Smith:** 'Near here?' **The Doctor:** 'Well, within a couple of billion miles, yes.'
- **Voice of Morbius:** 'I am still here. I can see nothing, feel nothing. You have locked me into hell for eternity. If this is all there is, I would rather die now … Trapped like this, like a sponge beneath the sea. Yet even a sponge has more life than I. Can you understand a thousandth of my agony? I, Morbius, who once led the High Council of the Time Lords, reduced to this – to the condition where I envy a vegetable.'
- **The Doctor:** [Speaking of the elixir of life.] 'The impossible dream of a thousand alchemists, dripping like tea from an urn.'

ANALYSIS

'A lightning-streaked sky, a barren landscape, an eerie castle and a clap of thunder. Nope, this isn't the latest Hammer Horror picture, it was the opening sequence of *The Brain of Morbius*.' So wrote Keith Miller in *Doctor Who Digest* Number 2 dated September 1976, and this story does indeed owe a great deal of its style and substance to the horror film genre. The principal sources this time are the numerous cinematic adaptations of Mary Shelley's 1818 novel *Frankenstein, or The Modern Prometheus* (the idea of a mad scientist putting together bits of corpses in order to create and animate a composite body, later encountered by a blind person who fails to realise its monstrous aspect) and H Rider Haggard's 1886 novel *She: A History of Adventure* (a woman jealously tending a rejuvenating sacred flame). 'You couldn't exactly call the story original,' continued Miller, 'but I thought it was an excellent adaptation of the Frankenstein legend, with the exception of the Sisterhood. It had very strong atmosphere, and carefully planned mood changes. Tom Baker's light acting in contrast to Philip Madoc's excellent characterisation of Solon made a thoroughly delightful combination.'

Jeanette Napier writing in *TARDIS* Volume 1 Number 6 dated May 1976 also considered the Sisterhood to be the story's weakest element: 'While there are dark doings at the castle, we have also been introduced to the Sisterhood – [a] women's lib version of the Time Lords. I really wasn't all that impressed with them. All those flashing eyes and waving arms and chanting spells were just too much for me! I loved the idea of a group of women on equal terms with the Time Lords, but surely they could have been made more elegant, as well as being sinister. Why couldn't they have been portrayed as mysterious females in long, dark robes who flitted around in near silence, thus making it more sinister when they used their strange powers? They reminded me of freaked out go-go dancers!' Napier did however share Miller's enthusiasm for Solon: 'I must admit I was really sorry to see Solon get killed. I thought he was a marvellous baddie and had visions of him taking over from the Master as the Doctor's arch enemy.'

Solon is indeed an excellent character, and much of the credit for his considerable impact must go to actor Philip Madoc. 'Philip Madoc excels as Solon,' wrote Nick Cooper in *DWB* No. 79 dated July 1990, 'undoubtedly a brilliant man, yet one driven beyond all reasonable bounds by a personal desire for revenge and the reflected glory the resurrected Morbius will bring him. He retains from his former life the ability to exude charm as he invites the Doctor and Sarah into his home, but he can then almost casually order Condo to kill Sarah simply because he has no use for her. Condo himself draws not only on Igor, but on Quasimodo as well, with Sarah as his rather unwilling Esmerelda.' Cynthia Grenville is also good as Maren, the head of the Sisterhood, and Michael Spice does a great job providing Morbius's suitably malevolent-sounding voice. The regulars too are wonderfully assured in their respective roles, and Elisabeth Sladen deserves special praise on this occasion for her affecting portrayal of Sarah's temporary blindness.

Also worthy of note are the story's sets – particularly as, for once, there is no location work or Ealing filming. Barry Newbery, the series' longest serving designer, again comes up trumps with a wonderfully alien-seeming planetary landscape, complete with some strange hexagonal pillars that appear to be huge basalt structures, and a suitably gothic-looking interior for Solon's citadel.

One of the story's main talking points is the climactic mind bending contest, chiefly because it seems to contradict all other *Doctor Who* lore in indicating that the Doctor had eight previously unseen incarnations before the William Hartnell one. This certainly appears to have been what the production team intended to suggest at the time, although an equally valid alternative interpretation is that the images in question are actually those of Morbius's earlier selves – it is, after all, Morbius who loses the contest, the aim of which is apparently to force one's opponent back mentally to the point of their birth; and if he does seem to be gloating in triumph when the images appear this can presumably be attributed to his unsound state of mind. At the end of the day, maybe all that matters is that the scene provides a dramatic and intriguing resolution to the action.

Perhaps the most extraordinary aspect of the story is the adult nature of some of its content. The shot of Morbius's brain falling to the floor of Solon's laboratory in a pool of green slime is often recalled as a particularly gruesome image, but the following incident in which Solon pulls a gun and shoots Condo repeatedly in the chest (his tunic is later seen to be soaked in blood) is surely one of the most realistically violent moments in the series' entire history. This, predictably enough, did not go down well with Mary Whitehouse, who was quoted in the press as saying that *The Brain of Morbius* 'contained some of the sickest and most horrific material seen on children's television'. The series' fans, on the other hand, lapped it all up. 'I thought it was wonderful! ...' wrote Jeanette Napier. 'We could do with a few more stories like this – give the Doctor some really nasty human-like adversaries with an evil intelligence and less bloodthirsty creatures who want to conquer planets just for the fun of it, and I'm sure the number of *Doctor Who* fans would increase tenfold!' The following story was another that would fit this description almost to a tee.

THE SEEDS OF DOOM

Writer: Robert Banks Stewart. **Director:** Douglas Camfield. **Designer:** Jeremy Bear[1, 2], Roger Murray-Leach. **Costumes:** Barbara Lane. **Make-Up:** Ann Briggs. **Incidental Music:** Geoffrey Burgon. **Fight Arranger:** Terry Walsh. **Visual Effects:** Richard Conway. **Film Cameraman:** Keith Hopper. **Film Editor:** M A C Adams. **OB Cameraman:** unknown. **Studio Lighting:** John Dixon. **Studio Sound:** John Holmes. **Production Assistant:** Graeme Harper. **Assistant Floor Manager:** Sue Shearman.

	First UK TX	Scheduled TX	Actual TX	Duration	Viewers	Chart Pos.
Part One	31/01/76	18.00	18.01	24'10"	11.4	16
Part Two	07/02/76	17.30	17.31	24'09"	11.4	30
Part Three	14/02/76	17.55	17.57	24'51"	10.3	32
Part Four	21/02/76	17.45	17.47	24'26"	11.1	23
Part Five	28/02/76	17.45	17.48	25'06"	9.9	26
Part Six	06/03/76	17.45	17.47	21'51"	11.5	15

Plot: Two alien seed pods are found buried in the Antarctic permafrost and the Doctor realises that they are from a Krynoid, a form of plant life that infects and transforms all animal life on planets upon which it becomes established. One of the pods infects a scientist at an Antarctic base but the developing Krynoid is destroyed by a bomb set by two men, Scorby and Keeler, who have made off with the other pod for their boss, eccentric plant collector Harrison Chase. At his mansion in England, Chase arranges for the pod to be opened under controlled conditions while a human host – Sarah – is held nearby. The Doctor rescues Sarah, but Keeler is infected. Keeler's transformation into a Krynoid is accelerated by Chase, who has him fed with raw meat. The creature escapes and goes on the rampage, rapidly growing to giant proportions. Chase decides to turn the Doctor into compost by feeding him into a pulverising machine. The Time Lord escapes, but Chase falls into the machine and is killed. UNIT have meanwhile been called in, and they arrange for the Krynoid to be bombed before it can spread its pods across the Earth.

Episode endings:

1. In the Antarctic base the scientist Winlett is rapidly changing into a plant. The Doctor suggests amputating his arm, as that is the source of the Krynoid infection. Of the others at the base only Moberley is qualified to perform the operation. He gets the necessary equipment together, but then encounters the sick man in a corridor. Winlett, all but unrecognisable, attacks Moberley.

2. The Doctor rescues Sarah from the power plant of the Antarctic base with only moments to spare before the bomb planted there by Scorby and Keeler is set to explode. The Krynoid enters behind them but they manage to escape, locking it in. The bomb explodes.

3. Chase decides to use Sarah as a part of his experiment. He holds her bare arm to a table beside the Krynoid pod, which starts to open.

4. Richard Dunbar of the World Ecology Bureau, having failed to make Chase see sense, flees through the grounds of the mansion chased by Scorby. He suddenly comes across the Krynoid, now about ten feet tall and totally inhuman. He is killed, but his scream alerts the Doctor and Sarah, who run to help. Sarah screams as the creature surges towards them.

5. The Doctor and Sergeant Henderson from UNIT arrive with defoliant sprays and rescue Sarah and Scorby from the Krynoid-controlled plants in Chase's mansion. The Doctor decides to move all the plants outside and they start to do so. Chase, however, locks the door behind them and they find themselves trapped outside as the giant Krynoid approaches. Chase smiles faintly.

6. The danger over, the Doctor and Sarah leave for a holiday on Cassiopeia – but are taken back to the Antarctic by the ever-unpredictable TARDIS.

IT WAS MADE WHERE...?

OB: 30.10.75-03.11.75, 07.12.75-08.12.75
Locations: Buckland Sand and Silica Co Ltd, Reigate Road, Buckland, Surrey; Athelhampton House, Athelhampton, Dorset; BBC Television Centre, Wood Lane, Shepherd's Bush, London, W12.
Studio: 17.11.75-18.11.75, 01.12.75-02.12.75 all in TC4, 15.12.75-16.12.75 in TC8, 19.12.75 in TC4.

ADDITIONAL CREDITED CAST

Harrison Chase (Tony Beckley), Scorby (John Challis), Arnold Keeler (Mark Jones[1-4]), John Stevenson (Hubert Rees[1,2]), Charles Winlett (John Gleeson[1,2]), Derek Moberley (Michael McStay[1,2]), Richard Dunbar (Kenneth Gilbert[1-4]), Sir Colin Thackeray (Michael Barrington[1,3-6]), Hargreaves (Seymour Green[1,3-5]), Amelia Ducat (Sylvia Coleridge[3-5]), Guard Leader (David Masterman[3,4]), Doctor Chester (Ian Fairbairn[3]), Chauffeur (Alan Chuntz[3]), Guard (Harry Fielder[4*]), Major Beresford (John Acheson[5,6]), Sergeant Henderson (Ray Barron[5,6]), The Krynoid's voice (Mark Jones[5]).

* Also in Part Three, but uncredited.
Note: The uncredited actors inside the second stage Krynoid costume were Ronald Gough and Keith Ashley.

POPULAR MYTHS

• This story was originally written as a four-parter and the opening two episodes were added by script editor Robert Holmes and/or director Douglas Camfield. (It was commissioned and written as a six-parter by Robert Banks Stewart from the outset.)

- The location scenes for this story were shot at a house owned by rock star Mick Jagger. (Jagger's house, Stargrove Manor near Newbury in Hampshire, was used as a location for *Pyramids of Mars*; the house seen in *The Seeds of Doom* is Athelhampton House in Athelhampton, Dorset.)

THINGS TO WATCH OUT FOR

- The costume for the humanoid stage of the Krynoid was created by taking one of the surviving Axon costumes from *The Claws of Axos* and spraying it green.
- The Doctor gives his age as 749.
- This was the last story to feature the UNIT organisation until *Battlefield* (1989).

THINGS YOU MIGHT NOT HAVE KNOWN

- A scene of Keeler strapped to a bed, struggling to resist eating a plate of raw meat as the Krynoid within him slowly takes control, was cut by producer Philip Hinchcliffe as being too terrifying.
- The first two episodes bore plot similarities to the 1951 Christian Nyby film *The Thing From Another World*. The story was also reminiscent of numerous hostile-plants-attack-mankind tales like John Wyndham's *The Day of the Triffids* and, on TV, *The Quatermass Experiment* (1953) and the *Out of the Unknown* episode *Come Buttercup, Come Daisy, Come ..?* (1965).
- This was the final serial directed by Douglas Camfield before his death in 1984.
- Production of the serial was plagued with problems including a flu epidemic hitting the cast, an actor being injured in a car crash and replaced, and Part One's edited tape going temporarily missing shortly before transmission.

QUOTE, UNQUOTE

- **The Doctor:** 'I suppose you could call it a galactic weed, though it's deadlier than any weed you know. On most planets the animals eat the vegetation. On planets where the Krynoid gets established, the vegetation eats the animals.'
- **The Doctor:** [To the World Ecology Bureau's Sir Colin Thackeray.] 'If we don't find that pod before it germinates, it'll be the end of everything. Everything, you understand? Even your pension!'
- **Harrison Chase:** 'What do you do for an encore, Doctor?' **The Doctor:** 'I win.'
- **Harrison Chase:** 'The plants must win. It will be a new world. Silent and beautiful.'

ANALYSIS

The Seeds of Doom is an odd story as it is one in which the Doctor, aside from finding the second of the two Krynoid pods in the ice and thereby arguably precipitating the major crisis, plays no significant part in the unfolding of events or in their resolution. The plot would still hold up if he and Sarah were not in it at all. Tim Munro, however, suggested in *DWB* No. 129, dated August 1994, that the story was in many respects typical of its era: 'It's an intriguing hybrid of the new and the old; a fascinating indicator of how much the show had improved. Its basic elements – its Earthbound setting, action set-pieces, establishment troubleshooter Doctor, rampaging monster, [Quatermass] plot and big bang finale – could all fit comfortably into a Pertwee story. What's striking is how much better is the presentation. For all its regressionist aspects, the story's rich characterisations, inventive dialogue, dark atmosphere, memorable villain and intense portrayal of violence and emotion make it quintessentially Hinchcliffe/Holmes. In this era, more than any other, everything came right; a production team was formed with a clear vision of what the show should be, the talent to achieve it and the freedom to do so. *The Seeds of Doom* may not ascend to the heights of season fourteen, but it is a superb example of the qualities which make this era the most highly regarded in the show's history.'

Alistair Pegg, writing in *The Black Scrolls of Rassilon* Issue 4 dated winter 1995, shared these sentiments: 'The question that springs to my mind when watching a story that is as entertaining and enjoyable as this is – just how do they do it? It's a query that can be levelled at much of the Hinchcliffe era. Just how did they make the programme so consistently superb? Why do other periods of the show's history never match up to the excellence nearly always evident in the serials from 1974 to 1977? After all, other producers had many of the factors that made up *The Seeds of Doom* at their disposal: Tom Baker giving his all; strong companion(s); a good cast; well-constructed plot; and scary monsters etc. *The Seeds of Doom* is good because it possesses all these elements. But it has more, and in my opinion it is the following that really lift this adventure from routinely good into the realms of greatness. It is a) money, b) a fertile writer and c) Douglas Camfield.'

Writer Robert Banks Stewart consciously structured the story as a two-part segment set in the Antarctic followed by a four-part segment set in England, and this works extremely well. The initial segment draws inspiration from the 1951 RKO/Winchester horror film *The Thing from Another World*, in which an alien is found buried in the Arctic ice and subsequently goes on the rampage, and is equally gripping – even if the snow looks terribly fake in the closer shots of the Doctor uncovering the pod. The characters are all well written and played, but it is really the make-up that is the star here as the hapless Winlett undergoes a horrific transformation into a Krynoid.

The segment set in England is no less effective. Tony Beckley is simply excellent as Chase, with an icy calm and level of control worthy of the Master (whose habit of wearing black leather gloves he also shares). As Jeanette Napier commented in *TARDIS* Volume 1 Number 8 dated July 1976: 'I found it a nice change to have a baddie whose chief love wasn't money or power, but plants.' Chase's 'number one heavy', Scorby, is also well acted by John Challis, who neatly conveys the character's sense of increasing desperation when faced with the growing Krynoid. The Krynoid itself, after it has been unwisely fed by Chase, turns first into a large green sack with tentacles and suckers and then into some vast thrashing creature that towers above his mansion. The modelwork by way of which the latter scenes are achieved is very nice, and overall the Krynoid is a good addition to the ranks of *Doctor Who*'s monstrous foes – although the revelation that it is able to talk places an unnecessary strain on the viewer's credulity, and the idea of it being able somehow to influence other plants and cause them to lash out at people is, frankly, rubbish.

The only really disappointing aspect of *The Seeds of Doom* though is its portrayal of UNIT. With none of the old regulars present, they come across as a faceless and characterless bunch whose sole function in the story is to resolve the situation by arranging for the Krynoid (and, in the process, Chase's mansion) to be blown to pieces. This is all the more regrettable with hindsight, given that UNIT would subsequently be absent from the series for a lengthy period. 'The story's biggest flaw,' wrote Guy Blythman in *TSV* 43 dated March 1995, 'particularly when everything that comes before it is so good, is the ending, with the Krynoid bombed to bits by the RAF. It isn't so much the use of stock footage that annoys me here as the feebleness of resorting to conventional means to remove the threat to civilisation. The Doctor should employ original and interesting methods to defeat his enemies. His loss of touch here is rather alarming. I feel the imagination of the [writer] deserted [him] at this point.' This is perhaps a little hard on Robert Banks Stewart, but the story does certainly close on a rather odd note as the TARDIS takes the Doctor and Sarah back to Antarctica. 'The part that made me puzzle,' wrote Keith Miller in *Doctor Who Digest* Number 2 dated September 1976, 'was when Sarah said at the South Pole, "You forgot to reprogram the coordinates!" Considering they [originally] landed at the Pole in a helicopter, that was rather unlikely, wasn't it?'

The departure of Harry as a regular at the end of *Terror of the Zygons* left the Doctor with only one companion, as had been the case during the Jon Pertwee era. The difference this time was that UNIT were also written out during the course of the season. This meant that for season fourteen there would be no other regulars or semi-regulars to divert attention from the central Doctor-companion relationship, which would thus became arguably more important than ever before, initially with Sarah and then with newcomer Leela. Season fourteen would also see a continuation of the gothic horror approach instituted by Philip Hinchcliffe and Robert Holmes, and some of the highest production values that the series had ever boasted.

DOCTOR WHO SEASON FOURTEEN (1976-1977)

Regular Cast:
Doctor Who (Tom Baker)
Sarah Jane Smith (Elisabeth Sladen) until *The Hand of Fear* Part Four
Leela (Louise Jameson) from *The Face of Evil* Part One onwards

Regular Crew:
Producer: Philip Hinchcliffe.
Script Editor: Robert Holmes.
Production Unit Manager: Chris D'Oyly-John on all stories, John Nathan-Turner uncredited on *The Talons of Weng-Chiang*.
Title Music: Ron Grainer and the BBC Radiophonic Workshop, arranged by Delia Derbyshire.
Special Sounds: Dick Mills.

Season fourteen was the third and final season on which Philip Hinchcliffe worked as producer of *Doctor Who*. In many ways it built on the success of the previous one, but on the other hand it also brought further controversy about the levels of horror and violence in the series, which culminated in BBC executives giving an unprecedented written apology to Mary Whitehouse over a scene at the end of Part Three of *The Deadly Assassin* in which the Doctor is apparently on the point of being drowned. The repercussions of this incident were to be felt in subsequent seasons, when much tighter controls would be imposed on the production team and the series would arguably never be quite the same again. Another significant development during the course of season fourteen was the departure of the well established and popular Sarah Jane Smith and the introduction of a new, very different type of companion in the person of Leela, played by Louise Jameson. Tom Baker, meanwhile, was well into his stride as the Doctor, and still going strong.

FOURTH DOCTOR

THE MASQUE OF MANDRAGORA

Writer: Louis Marks. **Director:** Rodney Bennett. **Designer:** Barry Newbery. **Costumes:** James Acheson. **Make-Up:** Jan Harrison. **Incidental Music:** Dudley Simpson. **Visual Effects:** Ian Scoones. **Film Cameraman:** John Baker. **Film Editor:** Clare Douglas. **Studio Lighting:** Dennis Channon. **Studio Sound:** Colin Dixon. **Production Assistant:** Thea Murray. **Assistant Floor Manager:** Linda Graeme.

	First UK TX	Scheduled TX	Actual TX	Duration	Viewers	Chart Pos.
Part One	04/09/76	18.10	18.12	24'31"	8.3	40
Part Two	11/09/76	18.05	18.07	24'44"	9.8	22
Part Three	18/09/76	18.10	18.12	24'34"	9.2	29
Part Four	25/09/76	18.10	18.13	24'45"	10.6	23

Plot: The TARDIS is temporarily captured by the Mandragora Helix, a spiral of energy with a controlling influence, at the centre of which the ship is infiltrated by a sparkling ball of energy. The travellers then move on to the Dukedom of San Martino in Renaissance Italy, where the Doctor quickly realises that the Mandragora energy is loose. The energy enters an underground temple and reveals itself to the outlawed Brotherhood of Demnos, whose leader, the court astrologer Hieronymous, is instructed to make ready for Mandragora's full appearance. Hieronymous is a pawn in Count Federico's schemes to usurp his young nephew Giuliano, whose accession to the Dukedom is being marked with a celebratory masque. At the height of the ball, the Brethren attack the court and kill many guests. Hieronymous, now completely absorbed by Mandragora, confronts the Doctor in the underground temple and attempts to blast him down. The Doctor however has earthed both himself and the altar so that the energy simply drains away, leaving the planet safe – at least until the constellations are again in the correct configuration for the Helix to make contact.

Episode endings:
1. The Doctor is brought before a leather-masked executioner as Count Federico watches from an overlooking balcony. At a signal from Federico, the executioner raises his heavy sword and prepares to swing it down to cut off the Doctor's head.
2. Giuliano and Sarah are waiting outside while the Doctor investigates the tunnels leading to the Brotherhood's underground temple. Suddenly Federico arrives with a group of men and, leaving Giuliano to fend them off, Sarah races to alert the Doctor. In the tunnels she is recaptured by the Brotherhood, who were earlier thwarted in an attempt to sacrifice her. The High Priest tells her: 'Demnos will not be cheated of his pleasure, little one.'
3. Federico and the Doctor arrive in the underground temple, where the masked Hieronymous has been leading the Brotherhood in a ceremony to receive the Helix energy. Federico strides up to Hieronymous and, branding him a traitor, snatches away his mask. Beneath is nothing but a halo of light. Hieronymous fells Federico with a blast of energy from his hand.
4. The Doctor tells Sarah that Mandragora's constellation will be in a position for it to make a further attack on the Earth in about five hundred years' time – at the end of the 20th Century. They enter the TARDIS and, as Giuliano watches from a distance, it dematerialises.

IT WAS MADE WHERE...?

Location filming: 03.05.76-06.05.76
Location: Portmeirion, Penrhyndeudraeth, North Wales.
Studio: 24.05.76-25.05.76, 06.06.76-08.06.76 all in TC3

ADDITIONAL CREDITED CAST

Count Federico (John Laurimore[1-3]), Captain Rossini (Antony Carrick), Giuliano (Gareth Armstrong), Marco (Tim Piggott-Smith), Hieronymous (Norman Jones), High Priest (Robert James), Brother (Brian Ellis[1]), Soldier (Pat Gorman[1]), Guards (James Appleby[2]**, John Clamp[2]**), Pikemen (Peter Walshe[2], Jay Neill[2]), Titan Voice (Peter Tuddenham[2]**), Dancers (Peggy Dixon[4], Jack Edwards[4], Alistair Fullarton[4], Michael Reid[4], Kathy Wolff[4]), Entertainer (Stuart Fell[4]).

*Also in Part Four, in the reprise from Part Three, but uncredited.
** Also in Part One, but uncredited.

POPULAR MYTHS

• Many of the period costumes seen in this story were first used in Franco Zeffirelli's 1968 feature film production of *Romeo and Juliet*. (They were first used in Renato Castellani's 1954 feature film production of *Romeo and Juliet*.)

THINGS TO WATCH OUT FOR

• This story marks the first use of a new style of lettering, in a serif font, for the series' on-screen titles.
• The TARDIS's wood-panelled secondary control room is introduced in this story
• A new police box prop was created for the TARDIS exterior, the old one having by this point worn out.
• The Doctor explains for the first time that he and his companions are able to understand unfamiliar languages by virtue of a 'Time Lord gift'.

THINGS YOU MIGHT NOT HAVE KNOWN

• Working titles: *The Catacombs of Death* and *The Curse of Mandragora*.

QUOTE, UNQUOTE

• **The Doctor:** 'Humans have got such limited little minds. I don't know why I like you so much.' **Sarah Jane Smith:** 'Because you have such good taste.' **The Doctor:** 'That's true. That's very true.'
• **Sarah Jane Smith:** [To the Doctor.] 'The worse the situation, the worse your jokes get.'
• **Hieronymous:** 'Had it not been you, there would have been other travellers drawn into Mandragora's Helix. Earth had to be possessed and checked. Man's curiosity might lead him away from this planet until, ultimately, the galaxy itself might not contain him. We of Mandragora will not allow a rival power within our domain.'

ANALYSIS

The new season starts in a relatively low-key fashion with the Doctor and Sarah exploring some unfamiliar areas of the TARDIS and eventually coming upon a 'second control

FOURTH DOCTOR

room' that will henceforth be used instead of the traditional one (albeit, as it turns out, only for this season). 'After visiting the rather large and superimposed boot cupboard,' observed Keith Miller in *Doctor Who Digest* Number 3 dated October 1976, 'we catch our first glimpse of the new control room. My first impression of it was "Oh ... " but now that I've seen it a couple of times since, I *really* like it and am beginning to prefer it to the old one! I love the idea of the wood panelling effect throughout the room. Nice touches were the [third Doctor's] frilly shirt and [the second Doctor's recorder], but how on earth were they supposed to have gotten there? One thing that adds a touch of class to the final setting is the flight of steps leading up to the exit. I think it's super! ... I noticed too that the exterior of the TARDIS had changed. It's a slightly lighter blue, smoother and generally "newer" looking.'

The short sequence at the centre of the Mandragora Helix works quite well, with some good visual effects in evidence, although it seems rather odd that the gravity and atmosphere are normal here and that the Doctor and Sarah are able to walk about as if they are on a floor – which, of course, the actors are! The action moves quickly on to the story's main setting of 15th Century Italy, and here the viewer is treated to some superb location work done in and around the Welsh village of Portmeirion – a folly created by architect Sir Clough Williams-Ellis with the Italian harbour town of Portofino as its inspiration.

'It is a little hard to define the exact nature of *The Masque of Mandragora*,' wrote Jeremy Bentham in the *Doctor Who Appreciation Society Yearbook 1977/78*. '[Do] its roots lie with the supernatural or with historical drama? ... At the beginning it was pure *Hamlet* as the dastardly Count Federico forged intricate plots and intrigues to win for himself the coveted crown of San Martino held by the rightful heir, Duke Giuliano – whose father he had already disposed of. Schemes were hatched, clandestine agreements made and cunning arrangements forged, all to secure the power of the evil Count. Almost in the background at first was the "old fraud" Heironymous ...

'With the arrival of the Mandragora sparkler the accent of the story changed, ever so gradually and subtly, into that of a true sword and sorcery tale; in fact the change was so gradual that an audience might easily be forgiven for missing [it]. By [Part Four], Federico was dead and the possessed Brethren of Demnos ... were ready to begin their mystical attack on the palace. Rodney Bennett, the director, ... handled well the blending of history and black magic. The two rarely met head on as the intercutting of Federico's ambitions with Heironymous's powers showed. Often the only bridging of the two was the Doctor.'

The scripts by Louis Marks are very well written and highly intelligent, using the Mandragora energy to symbolise the forces of superstition that would ultimately be overthrown by those of science – 'the dawn of a new reason', to use the Doctor's description – at the time of the Renaissance. As John Ainsworth put it in *DWB* No. 92 dated August 1991: 'The Mandragora Helix is a personification of the story's basic premise – that astrology is not just a nonsense, that there is a power in the stars. Louis Marks arrived at this concept by applying what he described as "*Doctor Who* thinking", and indeed one can see immediately how appropriate [it] is to the series. Renaissance Italy provided the perfect setting for the serial, being something of an historical turning point, as well as being visually stimulating.'

Early reaction to the story, however, was only lukewarm. Gordon Blows wrote in *TARDIS* Volume 1 Number 11 dated October/November 1976: 'Despite all I've got to say for the quality of the production and story of *The Masque of Mandragora*, it did come over just a little flat. Perhaps historical style stories so thickly flavoured with period scenes need about fifty minutes an episode so that the usual amount of Doctor and companion reaction to "goings on" can be maintained. In other words, I think the period setting interfered with the story. Perhaps it *should*, but *not* to the point where it makes the story seem slow ... I think on reflection though that when looking back on *The Masque of Mandragora* it will be thought of as a good story. It certainly wasn't a bad one.'

The BBC's Audience Research Report on the final episode suggests that viewers in general had similarly mixed feelings: 'At the extreme, critical viewers dismissed the programme as utterly silly and "corny", quite often adding that the acting was hammy – although it was suggested that this was hardly surprising in view of the script. The more lukewarm tended to remark that the plot had "dragged" rather and that the series as a whole was running out of ideas. Occasionally, too, members of the sample compared Tom Baker's flippant Doctor Who unfavourably with his predecessors. However, the bulk of the reporting audience reacted with at least moderate approval of the storyline which involved the right amount of colourful action and suspense as the Doctor fittingly defeated the powers of evil once again and, on the whole, seemed disposed to praise both acting and a production in which historical settings and special effects contributed to the programme's general appeal, and in some views, even, were the best part of it.' Children's views were as usual noted as being particularly positive. Specific comments on this occasion included: 'I was frightened a bit but enjoyed it'; 'It was very good. I liked the power coming from their fingers'; 'Very funny'; 'My seven-year-old wouldn't miss it for anything; he explains the plot to me'; and 'My three-year-old always wants to watch – from the safety of Daddy's knee. She finds it confusing at times and can't always pick out the baddies'.

A fair assessment would rate *The Masque of Mandragora* much more highly than these contemporary comments would suggest. It has excellent scripts and a polished production – including some lavish and exquisitely detailed sets designed by Barry Newbery – and some first-rate performances from a strong cast.

THE HAND OF FEAR

Writer: Bob Baker, Dave Martin. **Director:** Lennie Mayne. **Designer:** Christine Ruscoe. **Costumes:** Barbara Lane. **Make-Up:** Judy Neame. **Incidental Music:** Dudley Simpson. **Fight Arranger:** Max Faulkner. **Visual Effects:** Colin Mapson. **Film Cameraman:** Max Samett. **Film Editor:** Christopher Rowlands. **Studio Lighting:** Derek Slee. **Studio Sound:** Brian Hiles. **Production Assistant:** Marion McDougall. **Assistant Floor Manager:** Terry Winders.

	First UK TX	Scheduled TX	Actual TX	Duration	Viewers	Chart Pos.
Part One	02/10/76	18.10	18.11	24'50"	10.5	24
Part Two	09/10/76	17.50	17.51	24'48"	10.2	29
Part Three	16/10/76	18.05	18.07	24'22"	11.1	20
Part Four	23/10/76	18.00	18.03	25'00"	12.0	19

Plot: The TARDIS arrives on contemporary Earth, where Sarah comes into contact with what appears to be a fossilised human hand. This is in fact the last surviving fragment of a Kastrian called Eldrad, who was blown up in space as a punishment for attempting to wipe out his own people. Eldrad's essence lives on in a blue-stoned ring, which the possessed Sarah removes from the hand and places on her own. She then takes the hand to the nearby Nunton nuclear research and development complex where it soaks up the radiation from the reactor core and regenerates into a complete being. Eldrad – who, having patterned his new body on Sarah's, appears to all intents and purposes female – persuades the Doctor to take him back to Kastria where he might reclaim his heritage. There he discovers only a dead planet: the Kastrians are extinct and their race banks were destroyed by their last King, Rokon, in case Eldrad should ever return. Furious, Eldrad, whose body has now been reconfigured into its proper form, tries to get the Doctor to return him to Earth so that he might rule there instead. The two time travellers use the Doctor's scarf to trip him into a deep crevasse. Back in the TARDIS, the Doctor receives a summons to return to Gallifrey and, as he cannot take Sarah there, endeavours to drop her off at her home.

Episode endings:
1. Sarah places a box containing the fossilised hand on the floor of a lead-lined room in the Nunton complex. She watches as it first regenerates a missing finger and then starts to move.
2. A technician named Driscoll takes the hand to the reactor core. The complex is evacuated as he pulls open the door and enters. In the control room, Nunton's director Professor Watson is thrown to the floor as the computers start exploding.
3. The Doctor and Sarah take Eldrad back to Kastria. Eldrad uses his ring to summon a lift to take them to the thermal chambers on the lower levels, but when the lift doors open a spear-like syringe thuds into his chest.
4. The Doctor receives a summons from Gallifrey and, realising that he cannot take Sarah there, redirects the TARDIS to Hillview Road, South Croydon, so as to return her home. Sarah reluctantly disembarks with the assertion that travel does broaden the mind. After the TARDIS has gone, she realises that she is not in Hillview Road and may not even be in South Croydon. Whistling a tune, she picks up her things and walks off, pausing only to glance up at the sky.

IT WAS MADE WHERE...?

Location filming: 14.06.76-18.06.76
Locations: Cromhall Quarry, Cromhall, Wootton-under-Edge, Gloucs; Oldbury Power Station, Oldbury Naite, Thornbury, Gloucs; Stokefield Close, Thornbury, Gloucs.
Studio: 05.07.76-07.07.76, 19.07.76-20.07.76 all in TC8

ADDITIONAL CREDITED CAST

Dr. Carter (Rex Robinson[1,2]), Intern (Renu Setna[1]), Abbott (David Purcell[1]), Zazzka (Roy Pattison[1]), King Rokon (Roy Skelton[1,4]), Guard (Robin Hargrave[1]), Professor Watson (Glyn Houston[2,3]), Driscoll (Roy Boyd[2*]), Miss Jackson (Frances Pidgeon[2*]), Elgin (John Cannon[2]), Eldrad (Judith Paris[3,4]), Kastrian Eldrad (Stephen Thorne[4]).

* Also in Part Three in the reprise from Part Two, but uncredited.

THINGS TO WATCH OUT FOR

- For once, the TARDIS arrives in a quarry that is exactly what it appears to be: a quarry.
- There is a highly effective freeze frame ending to the final episode as Sarah glances up into the sky. *The Hand of Fear* marked Elisabeth Sladen's last regular appearance in the role. The character returned in the twentieth anniversary special *The Five Doctors*, in the fifty minute special *K-9 and Company* and in a number of later radio and audio plays.
- The design of the Kastrian obliteration module was based on that of the Martian war machines in George Pal's 1952 film *The War of the Worlds*.

THINGS YOU MIGHT NOT HAVE KNOWN

- Working title: *The Hand of Time*.
- During the explosion in the quarry, one of the cameras recording material from ground level was destroyed. Luckily the film in the camera was salvaged and footage was used in the completed programme.

QUOTE, UNQUOTE

- **Eldrad:** 'Can this be the form of the creatures who have found me and who now seek to destroy me? No matter. They shall fail as the obliteration has failed. Strange form or not ... Eldrad lives and shall again rule Kastria!'
- **King Rokon:** 'So now you are king, as was your wish. I salute you from the dead. Hail Eldrad. King ... of nothing.'
- **Sarah Jane Smith:** 'I must be mad. I'm sick of being cold and wet and hypnotised left, right and centre. I'm sick of being shot at, savaged by bug eyed monsters, never knowing if I'm coming or going ... or been ... I want a bath, I want my hair washed, I just want to feel human again ... and, boy, am I sick of that sonic screwdriver. I'm going to pack my goodies and I'm going home ... I said, I'm going to pack my goodies and I am going home!'
- **Sarah Jane Smith:** 'Don't forget me.' **The Doctor:** 'Oh, Sarah, don't you forget me.'

ANALYSIS

Once again Bob Baker and Dave Martin come up trumps with a story that combines all the best features of *Doctor Who* in this era. '*The Hand of Fear* made a refreshing and welcome comeback for two of the [series'] veteran writers,' enthused Steven Evans in the *Doctor Who Appreciation Society Yearbook 1977/78*, 'continuing their grand tradition of original plots, excellent dialogue and believable aliens. It also marked, [for the first time in] six years, [a] contemporary Earth story not to feature UNIT.'

The first episode revolves around the titular hand. What is it? Whose is it? And why is Sarah acting so strangely? The scenes of the possessed Sarah escaping from the hospital and making her way to the Nunton complex are all the more effective for the use of a fish-eye lens to distort the picture and make her seem uncharacteristically threatening. Elisabeth Sladen does a superb job here, causing the viewer to regret all the more that this is to be her final story as a regular. The brash and aggressive Sarah of season eleven has by this point given way to a far more trusting and likeable character. Her relationship with the Doctor has become wonderfully relaxed – mellow, even – and the interplay between them ever more naturalistic. In this story, her quips as she tries to persuade him to let her accompany him into the complex are particularly nice, as is her playful baiting of him by proclaiming 'Eldrad must live' *after* he has freed her of the Kastrian's influence.

If the depiction of Sarah is one of the high points of *The Hand of Fear*, then that of the female Eldrad is the other. Certainly many older boys and men in the viewing audience must have perked up when she made her impressive entrance in Part Three. From her husky voice to her tight fitting costume, she presents the classic dilemma of a physically attractive woman who is also deadly and ruthless. As Keith Williams wrote in *TARDIS* Volume 1 Number 12 dated December 1976: 'The female Eldrad's first appearance was impressive enough – a magnificent creature, all crystalline; purple skin; glowing eyes darting sideways suspiciously.' Judith Paris is excellent in the role, and it is a considerable let-down when Stephen Thorne takes over after Eldrad's transformation in the final episode. Although Thorne makes good use of his voice – the costume allows him little scope to convey things by way of facial expression – he unfortunately sounds and acts almost exactly like Omega, the villain he portrayed in the same writers' season ten story *The Three Doctors*. Even some of the lines he is given are practically the same. This negative development is a shame, as Eldrad is essentially an interesting and in many ways tragic character. Misguided and egocentric, yes, but also quite sympathetic. As Sarah says: 'I quite liked her, but I couldn't stand him.'

Tim Dollin, also writing in *TARDIS* Volume 1 Number 12, found the story's resolution disappointing as a whole: 'I thought we were in for a story where Eldrad would try and save her people beneath the surface. Instead we go downstairs in a particularly false lift and try and drag Eldrad across those terrible sets. They looked like something out of pantomime. Then all is forgotten about Eldrad's plight and she becomes a he. This I thought was stupid! Now all that happens is that the Doctor trips Eldrad up and he falls down a hole. I thought the story should have been extended to a six-parter, with the last three episodes describing Eldrad's fight to defeat "her enemies". The only thing to save the episode was the last five minutes.'

It is the last five minutes that really distinguish *The Hand of Fear*. As Keith Miller put it in *Doctor Who Digest* Number 4 dated January 1977: 'The farewell scene between the Doctor and Sarah was well acted out, and although not a tear was shed, it was to me ... far sadder ... than the famous death sequence in *Love Story*. Sarah's sudden flare up at the Doctor, deciding to leave [and] then saying that the "Time Lord story" was just a ruse to get her to stay [were] perfectly executed by Lis Sladen and ... a fitting tribute to one of the most popular of *Doctor Who*'s assistants.' Martin Wiggins must have echoed the thoughts of many when he wrote, again in *TARDIS* Volume 1 Number 12: 'I felt a little lost when Sarah left. She was the only person I could really identify with in *Doctor Who*, and now she's gone.'

THE DEADLY ASSASSIN

Writer: Robert Holmes. **Director:** David Maloney. **Designer:** Roger Murray-Leach. **Costumes:** James Acheson, Joan Ellacott. **Make-Up:** Jean Williams. **Incidental Music:** Dudley Simpson. **Fight Arranger:** Terry Walsh. **Visual Effects:** Len Hutton, Peter Day. **Film Cameraman:** Fred Hamilton. **Film Editor:** Ian McKendrick. **Studio Lighting:**

Brian Clemett. **Studio Sound:** Clive Gifford. **Production Assistant:** Nicholas John. **Assistant Floor Manager:** Linda Graeme.

	First UK TX	Scheduled TX	Actual TX	Duration	Viewers	Chart Pos.
Part One	30/10/76	18.05	18.09	21'13"	11.8	15
Part Two	06/11/76	18.05	18.05	24'44"	12.1	11
Part Three	13/11/76	18.05	18.07	24'20"	13.0	12
Part Four	20/11/76	18.05	18.07	24'30"	11.8	12

Plot: The Doctor arrives on Gallifrey, where he is accused of the assassination of the Time Lord President. Investigating with the aid of Co-ordinator Engin and Castellan Spandrell, he discovers that this is part of a plot hatched by his old adversary the Master. Having used up all twelve of his regenerations, the Master is now a wizened husk. He is seeking to control the presidency in order to obtain the official regalia, the Sash and Rod of Rassilon, which are really keys to the Eye of Harmony, the source of all the Time Lords' power. The Doctor links his mind to the Amplified Panatropic Computer Net, containing the accumulated wisdom of the Time Lords, in the hope of tracking the Master down. In the virtual reality of the Matrix, he finds himself in a life-or-death struggle with a hooded opponent. The Doctor proves the stronger and his opponent is revealed as Chancellor Goth, the leading presidential candidate, whom the Master has been using as a puppet. Following his defeat, Goth dies. The Master meanwhile seizes the Sash and Rod of Rassilon and starts to access the Eye of Harmony, located beneath the floor of the Panopticon meeting hall, in the hope of drawing off enough energy to enable himself to regenerate. The Doctor manages to stop him before Gallifrey is destroyed, and the Master falls down one of the fissures that have opened up in the floor. The Doctor then departs in the TARDIS, unaware that the Master has survived his fall and escaped to fight another day.

Episode endings:
1. The Doctor finds a weapon on the deserted balcony overlooking the Panopticon, where the Time Lord President is about to make his resignation speech. He fires a shot into the crowd below, and the President is hit and falls toward the floor.
2. In the unreal environment of the Matrix, the Doctor's foot is caught in some railway tracks as the points change. He struggles desperately to free himself as a train rushes towards him.
3. Goth gains the upper hand in his battle with the Doctor within the Matrix. He holds the Doctor's head underwater, intent on drowning him.
4. The Master leaves Gallifrey in his TARDIS, which is disguised as a grandfather clock, moments after the Doctor. Spandrell speculates to Engin that the universe is not a big enough place for the two of them.

IT WAS MADE WHERE...?

Location filming: 26.07.76-30.07.76
Locations: Betchworth Quarry, Pebblehill Road, Betchworth, Surrey; Royal Alexandra and Albert School, Rocky Lane, Merstham, Surrey; Wycombe Air Park, Clay Lane, High Wycombe, Bucks.
Studio: 15.08.76-17.08.76 in TC3, 01.09.76-02.09.76 in TC8

ADDITIONAL CREDITED CAST

The President (Llewellyn Rees[1,2]), Chancellor Goth (Bernard Horsfall), Castellan Spandrell (George Pravda), Cardinal Borusa (Angus Mackay[1,2,4]), The Master (Peter Pratt), Commentator Runcible (Hugh Walters[1,2]), Co-ordinator Engin (Erik Chitty), Commander Hilred (Derek Seaton[1,2,4]), Gold Usher (Maurice Quick[1]), Time Lords (John Dawson[1,2], Michael Bilton[1]), Solis (Peter Mayock[3]), Voice (Helen Blatch[4]*).

* Also in Part One, but uncredited.

THINGS TO WATCH OUT FOR

- There is an excellent performance as Chancellor Goth by Bernard Horsfall, who had previously played a Time Lord in season six's *The War Games* as well as Gulliver in the same season's *The Mind Robber* and the Thal Taron in season ten's *Planet of the Daleks* – all three directed, like *The Deadly Assassin*, by David Maloney.
- The Prydonian seal seen in this story (referred to later in the series' history as the seal of Rassilon) had previously appeared as the Vogans' emblem in season twelve's *Revenge of the Cybermen* – a consequence of both stories having the same designer, Roger Murray-Leach.
- This story was the first to feature the Master since the death of Roger Delgado, the first actor to play the role, in 1973.
- The Doctor appears without a companion character for the only time in the series' history.

THINGS YOU MIGHT NOT HAVE KNOWN

- Working title: *The Dangerous Assassin*.
- When the story was repeated, the freeze-frame cliff-hanger ending to Part Three was edited out of the original master-tape following earlier complaints, from self-appointed television 'watchdogs' , about the graphic depiction of the near-drowning of the Doctor. Part Four was also slightly edited.

QUOTE, UNQUOTE

- **The Doctor:** [In a voice-over accompanying a roller-caption text presented at the beginning of Part One.] 'Through the millennia, the Time Lords of Gallifrey led a life of ordered calm, protected against all threats from lesser civilisations by their great power. But this was to change. Suddenly, and terribly, the Time Lords faced the most dangerous crisis in their long history ...'
- **The Doctor:** 'Vapourisation without representation is against the constitution!'
- **Borusa:** 'As I believe I told you long ago, Doctor, you will never amount to anything in the galaxy while you retain your propensity for vulgar facetiousness.'

ANALYSIS

The Deadly Assassin is a landmark *Doctor Who* story. 'There are many parts of *Doctor Who* lore ... now taken for granted that saw their introduction in [this story],' wrote David Saunders in *Shada* 18 dated July 1984. 'It had been hinted at in *The Brain of Morbius* that regeneration might have its limits, but it is *The Deadly Assassin* which establishes the figure at twelve. The ranks and chapters of the Time Lords are outlined here for the first time, as are their ceremonial costumes and those of the Chancellery guards. The revered Rassilon ... and his bequeathed symbols of presidential office ... have their first mentions in this Gallifreyan tale, as does the location and function of the Panopticon ... This is the first serial to give actual names to individual Time Lords and we must not overlook the establishment of the Doctor as a member of the Prydonian chapter [who] was expelled from the Academy [or the fact] that the TARDIS is listed for the first time as a Type 40 capsule.'

At the time of the story's original transmission, however, many fans took the view that it contradicted the minimal details that had previously been revealed about the Doctor's race, and were absolutely infuriated by this. 'What must have happened is that at the end of *The Hand of Fear* the Doctor was knocked out when the TARDIS took off and had a crazy mixed up nightmare about Gallifrey,' suggested Jan Vincent-Rudzki in *TARDIS* Volume 2 Number 1 in 1977. 'As a *Doctor Who* story, *The Deadly Assassin* is just not worth considering. I've spoken to many people ... and they all said how this story shattered their illusions of the Time Lords and lowered them to ordinary people. Once, Time Lords were all-powerful, awe-inspiring beings, capable of imprisoning planets forever in force fields, defenders of truth and good (when called in). Now, they are petty, squabbling, feeble-minded, doddering old fools. WHAT HAS HAPPENED TO THE MAGIC OF *DOCTOR WHO*?' These outspoken criticisms from someone who was, at the time, President of the *Doctor Who* Appreciation Society had a very influential effect and were echoed and expanded upon by numerous other reviewers, including David Fychan in *Oracle* Number 12 dated September 1978:

'Here was a whole four episodes about the Time Lords; a chance to gaze deep into a society of immeasurable age; a chance to see what the Doctor left behind; an insight into the Doctor's mentality (why does he prefer the human race?) – and as such, it was incredibly, unbelievably wasted. It failed badly as anything but a thriller-SF story about an Earthly society. Time Lords were really only humans – for every emotion they showed, for every motive they possessed, there are clear parallels simply on Earth ...

'What we "learnt" in *The Deadly Assassin* was quite revealing: no Time Ladies; a stiff caste system; a fact-adjusting society; torture; a constitution; a police force; Shabogan hooligans – all these go to make up the Gallifrey that we found. Perhaps more important: no time scanners; Goth's unnatural alliance with the Master; and only twelve regenerations?

'So, the most important question about the adventure is not "How does it fit in?" but "Is it worth trying to fit in?". *The Deadly Assassin* is an incongruity in *Doctor Who*.'

With the passage of time, the story has been re-evaluated, as was recognised by John C Harding in *Frontier Worlds* 9 dated June 1981: 'All civilisations rise and fall, and the idea of showing the Time Lords at the nadir of their civilisation was, in theory, a good one. At the time ... I – like most fans – was incensed at this treatment of these previously god-like beings. It [was], however, a logical progression.' 'The degeneration of the Time Lord race is portrayed reasonably and realistically,' agreed David Saunders, 'if one assumes that those seen in *The War Games* with the almost omniscient powers in fact belonged to the Celestial Intervention Agency [as referred to in this story] ... This would seem to have been the reason for casting Erik Chitty and the (ever fascinating) George Pravda – I just love his intonation – as well as the two Prydonians from whom the Doctor "borrowed" his ceremonial robes. That our mysterious, pacifistic observers have now, in the main, become a bunch of old dodderers ... would seem to explain the necessity of the Chancellery Guard.'

Harding also liked the way in which the principal Time Lords in this story were portrayed: 'By far my favourite character was Spandrell. Although at times the dry accent of George Pravda brought [it] close to going over the top, for the most [part] he maintained a sardonic and superbly cynical character ... Cardinal Borusa (Angus MacKay) was perhaps the strongest character – a Gallifreyan Disraeli. He had the rare ability to bridge the gap between appearances and reality, although he was too ready to tip the balance in favour of appearances. He was played with disdainfully reserved authority, which is the only way to treat such a character without demeaning him: it is impossible to work behind the scenes and be seen as powerful at the same time.

'These two characters, more than anything, served to accentuate the nature of Gallifrey according to *The Deadly Assassin*. There was an inner rot within the powerful facade, which was quickly ignored and swept away – eradicate the symptoms ... and no-one will mind the illness. A dangerous practice ...'

With the depiction of the Time Lords put in its proper perspective, the other aspects of the story can be judged on their own merits – which are very considerable. The scripts by Robert Holmes are well up to his usual high standard, and again draw much of their inspiration from a classic cinema film. '*The Manchurian Candidate* (1962, directed by John Frankenheimer, from the novel by Richard Condon) ... is the obvious source ...,' pointed out Tat Wood in *Perigosto Stick* Issue Two dated August 1991. 'The blindingly obvious connection, leaving aside the wholesale theft of the plot for a moment, is Commentator Runcible. The whole film is about the role of television in American politics, news management, rewriting history to create heroes, making people "remember" things that never happened, hypnosis, manipulation and paranoia in general ... The climax [comes when] an assassin, disguised as a priest to allow him uninhibited access to the Republican Party convention at Madison Square Garden (including documentary footage ...), goes into a lighting gallery, puts together a two-piece rifle and sets his sights on the presidential candidate (copied shot-for-shot by David Maloney). His friend Marco, who has been given the job of investigating the murders after he and a colleague have identical nightmares, is unable to get to him because everyone has to stand up and salute when some old cow screeches "The Star-Spangled Banner". But then the assassin overcomes his conditioning and shoots his controller.'

One unique feature of *The Deadly Assassin* is the absence of any companion character to share the adventure with the Doctor. This is particularly noticeable in the extraordinary Matrix sequences in the second and third episodes which, as noted by Harding, take *Doctor Who* into previously unexplored dramatic territory: 'Here was the Doctor in dashing white shirt ... fighting physically in a tropical, oppressive atmosphere – the pioneer New Romantic? There was an eerie surrealism in the landscape: a surgeon in a desert with a large hypodermic; a horse wearing a gas-mask – powerfully horrific imagery ... Later, the Doctor shouting "I deny this reality" and the dreamscape fading was a great *Doctor Who* moment. There is something very evocative in that phrase, and the fact that it worked for a moment or two heightened its effect. The imbalance between the two opponents worked well for the show: a well-prepared, well-kitted-out hunter with a high-powered rifle versus an unprepared, weaponless and wounded man ... Obviously [this segment] was different in atmosphere from the rest of the story, but David Maloney didn't try to ignore this; he heightened its effect by making it deliberately surreal. This was a master stroke of direction which delighted me.'

The reintroduction of the Master after some three and a half years' absence from the screen works very well, and the idea of showing him in an emaciated transitional state is a good one. Peter Pratt turns in a fine performance under difficult circumstances – it can never be a very comfortable experience for an actor to have to step into the shoes of a much-admired predecessor who has met a tragic death – and this is all the more admirable given that the restrictive nature of his mask and costume leaves him to rely almost entirely on his voice.

The Deadly Assassin is, all things considered, a truly remarkable story, as Jon Blum argued on an internet newsgroup in 1997: 'There's a tremendous sense of pacing to the first episode – it actually takes place on quite a small canvas, just a few sets, but everything about the writing and direction is calculated to make the story barrel along, while at the same time giving a sense of scale. Event follows event at breakneck speed, characters like Spandrell, Engin and Hilred are introduced on the run, and a huge number of background details are slotted in unobtrusively … What's interesting is that the plot takes a sharp turn [at the end] … Strangely enough, the story could work just fine without the entire Eye of Harmony subplot, introduced part way through Part Four … I wonder what the consequences for future *Doctor Who* would have been if they'd never brought in Rassilon, the Eye of Harmony and all that?'

THE FACE OF EVIL

Writer: Chris Boucher. **Director:** Pennant Roberts. **Designer:** Austin Ruddy. **Costumes:** John Bloomfield. **Make-Up:** Ann Ailes. **Incidental Music:** Dudley Simpson. **Fight Arranger:** Terry Walsh. **Visual Effects:** Mat Irvine. **Film Cameraman:** John McGlashan. **Film Editor:** Pam Bosworth, Tariq Anwar. **Studio Lighting:** Derek Slee. **Studio Sound:** Colin Dixon. **Production Assistant:** Marion McDougall. **Assistant Floor Manager:** Linda Graeme.

	First UK TX	Scheduled TX	Actual TX	Duration	Viewers	Chart Pos.
Part One	01/01/77	18.20	18.22	24'58"	10.7	23
Part Two	08/01/77	18.30	18.30	24'58"	11.1	19
Part Three	15/01/77	18.20	18.22	24'40"	11.3	20
Part Four	22/01/77	18.25	18.27	24'46"	11.7	19

Plot: The TARDIS arrives on a planet where a savage tribe called the Sevateem worship a god called Xoanon. The Doctor discovers that Xoanon is in fact a spaceship computer that he tried to repair at some point in his past and inadvertently drove mad by giving it a multiple personality. It is tended to by another tribe of humanoids, the ascetic Tesh. These are the descendants of the ship's original technicians, while the Sevateem are the descendants of the original survey team. The Doctor, with the help of a Sevateem girl called Leela, manages to gain access to the ship and wipe the additional personalities from the computer, leaving it sane and in proper control once more. Leela, deciding that she no longer wants to stay on her own planet, pushes her way on board the TARDIS. The Doctor has gained another companion.

Episode endings:

1. Leela takes the Doctor to see the image of the Sevateem's 'Evil One' carved into the side of a cliff. It is the Doctor's own face. The Doctor muses that he must have made quite an impression.
2. The Doctor and Leela climb into the carving of the Doctor's face through the mouth and see the shadow of a figure moving in the tunnel ahead of them. Xoanon meanwhile psychically attacks the Sevateem with invisible creatures. A young man named Tomas attempts to hold the creatures off with a gun, and the energy it discharges reveals them to have the likeness of the Doctor's face. The tribe's leader Andor is killed and Tomas fires repeatedly in the creatures' direction in a desperate attempt to defend himself.
3. The Doctor tries to convince Xoanon of his identity but the computer determines not to listen and bombards him with images of his own face shouting out denials. Finally the image of the Doctor shouts in a child's voice: 'Who am I?'
4. The Doctor returns to the TARDIS, where Leela is waiting for him. She asks him to take her with him but he declines. She darts into the TARDIS ahead of him and refuses to come out. As the Doctor follows her in, she operates the controls and the TARDIS dematerialises.

It Was Made Where...?

Ealing filming: 20.09.76-24.09.76 on Stage 2
Studio: 11.10.76-12.10.76, 25.10.76-26.10.76 all in TC3

Additional Credited Cast

Neeva (David Garfield), Andor (Victor Lucas[1,2]), Tomas (Brendan Price), Calib (Leslie Schofield), Sole (Colin Thomas[1]), Lugo (Lloyd McGuire[1]), Guards (Tom Kelly[1], Brett Forrest[2]), Xoanon (Rob Edwards[2,3], Pamela Salem[3], Anthony Frieze[3], Roy Herrick[4]), Jabel (Leon Eagles[3,4]), Gentek (Mike Ellis[3,4]), Acolyte (Peter Baldock[4]).

Note: Tom Baker also supplied uncredited one of the voices of Xoanon.

Things To Watch Out For

- Pamela Salem and Rob Edwards supply two of the voices of Xoanon. Both actors were at the time rehearsing for the following story, *The Robots of Death*.
- Anthony Frieze, credited as one of the voices of Xoanon, was the young winner of a competition to visit the *Doctor Who* studios. Philip Hinchcliffe arranged for a recording of his voice to be made shouting 'Who am I?' for the climax to Part Three.

Things You Might Not Have Known

- Working title: *The Day God Went Mad*.
- This story was promoted in *Radio Times* as the first in a new season of *Doctor Who*. This was due to the fact that, unusually, the season had broken for five Saturdays at the end of 1976.
- The timing of the Doctor's first encounter with Xoanon was said in Terrance Dicks's novelisation of this story to have been immediately after his regeneration in *Robot*. This was not derived from any information given in the televised version.
- The mad computer was inspired by Harry Harrison's *Captive Universe*.
- Leela was based on a cross between Mrs Emma Peel from *The Avengers* and the terrorist Leila Khalid.

- **Leela:** 'The Evil One!' **The Doctor:** 'Well, nobody's perfect, but that's overstating it a little.'
- **The Doctor:** 'Now drop your weapons or I'll kill him with this deadly jelly baby.'
- **Neeva:** 'We start getting proof and we stop believing.' **Tomas:** 'With this proof, we don't have to believe.'
- **The Doctor:** 'You know the very powerful and the very stupid have one thing in common. They don't alter their views to fit the facts. They alter the facts to fit the views. Which can be uncomfortable if you happen to be one of the facts that needs altering.'
- **The Doctor:** 'You can't expect perfection, even from me!'

ANALYSIS

This story was at one point to have been called *The Day God Went Mad*, which is not a bad title for what is in essence an 'all-powerful machine runs riot' tale. Xoanon's multiple personality is excellently depicted. The computer itself is never seen, but the walls of its chamber consist of a series of large screens that display images and feed information from the surrounding environment – something that is used to very good effect, particularly at the end of Part Three in what must rate as one of the strangest and most unsettling of the series' cliffhangers. The only 'face' ever associated with Xoanon is the Doctor's own face, and the sequence in which the Sevateem battle huge roaring images of it is quite disturbing. The scripts by new writer Chris Boucher also make clever play of the theme of schizophrenia, as David Richardson discussed in *Skaro* Volume Four Numbers Three/Four dated February 1984:

'The battle between the two aspects of Xoanon's nature is reflected in the macrocosmic world by the conflict between the Tesh and the Sevateem; intelligence against strength. Xoanon wishes to combine these to obtain the optimum blend of the two qualities, but he can only conceive of doing this by separating them out and making them clash, like the two aspects of himself. Xoanon believes "we must become one" and requires that strength and intelligence become one through "racial" conflict.

'The fight between the Tesh and [the] Sevateem is basically about prejudice. The former see the latter as "mindless savages", whilst Leela is repulsed by the Tesh: "It had two heads – one inside the other!" Just as if they were separate races, the Tesh and [the] Sevateem show dislike of each other for mindless superficial reasons. However, the irony is that they are the same race – another example of separation from one.'

The first two episodes concentrate on the savage Sevateem and their battle to breach the 'wall' separating them from their god Xoanon so that they might rescue him from the clutches of the evil Tesh. The casting here is very good, with Brendan Price as Tomas and Leslie Schofield as Calib coming over particularly well. Less impressive is David Garfield as Neeva – partly because his slight Welsh accent is readily discernible in certain scenes, notably those where the tribe are required to 'speak the litany', and seems distinctly out of place.

By far the most memorable of the Sevateem is, naturally enough, Leela, a primitive but resourceful young woman with a heart of gold who, for no apparent reason, decides to go off with the Doctor at the story's conclusion. The convenient coincidence of someone wanting to join the Doctor on his travels just after his last companion has parted from him has by this point become a familiar and somewhat overused device, but

Leela herself seems to have been universally welcomed to the series. André Willey gave her the following enthusiastic reception in *TARDIS* Volume 2 Number 2 dated 27 February 1977: 'The introduction of Leela was good – I like the idea of a primitive girl who seems to be quite brave – it makes a nice change.' Keith Miller, writing in *Doctor Who Digest* Number 5 dated May 1977, commented a little more wryly: 'The first thing I noticed was her sparsity of clothing, which I found out afterwards was noticed by quite a few million other people too.' The new companion was also a hit with an unknown writer in *New Musical Express* dated 29 January 1977:

'About the most successful and apparently liberated lady in the current crop of telly heroines has to be Doctor Who's new sidekick Louise Jameson who plays the savage amazon Leela.

'Where all previous *Doctor Who* female interest seemed to have a taste for appalling Carnaby Street clothes, an inability to avoid being captured by the bad guys and a terrible tendency to cry "eek" every time danger threatens, Leela is a very different matter.

'Supposedly born into a primitive tribe of degenerate galactic colonists, she has so far proved a deft hand at throwing around hunky male opponents, wields a mean crossbow and has yet to utter a single "eek".

'She provides a much more cynically suitable back-up to Tom Baker's whimsical, almost Harpo Marx portrayal of the Doctor.

'*Doctor Who*, in fact, seems to get better and better.'

In the last two episodes, the impressively-realised jungle gives way to the sterile corridors of the Tesh's spaceship. The Tesh are intentionally bland and emotionless characters, but unfortunately as a result make little impression. The prospect of these ascetic individuals being reconciled with the aggressive Sevateem after the story's conclusion seems somewhat unlikely, and one wonders if the Doctor realises what a mess he might have left behind on the planet even with Xoanon restored to normal.

At the end of the day, though, *The Face of Evil* is an impressive tale that manages to intrigue and delight, mainly due to some great performances from the cast. Like many other stories of this era it recalls some familiar science fiction sources – including *2001: A Space Odyssey* with its deranged spaceship computer Hal – but as our unknown *New Musical Express* correspondent noted: '*Doctor Who* may not be the most original show ever to come down the tube, but the way things are today, the very act of ripping off the best qualifies the *Doctor Who* writers and production team for a merit badge.'

THE ROBOTS OF DEATH

Writer: Chris Boucher. **Director:** Michael E Briant. **Designer:** Kenneth Sharp. **Costumes:** Elizabeth Waller. **Make-Up:** Ann Briggs. **Incidental Music:** Dudley Simpson. **Visual Effects:** Richard Conway. **Film Cameraman:** Peter Chapman. **Film Editor:** unknown. **Studio Lighting:** Duncan Brown. **Studio Sound:** Tony Millier. **Production Assistant:** Peter Grimwade. **Assistant Floor Manager:** David Tilley.

	First UK TX	Scheduled TX	Actual TX	Duration	Viewers	Chart Pos.
Part One	29/01/77	18.20	18.20	24'06"	12.8	14
Part Two	05/02/77	18.20	18.22	24'15"	12.4	17
Part Three	12/02/77	18.20	18.23	23'51"	13.1	15
Part Four	19/02/77	18.20	18.26	23'42"	12.6	18

Plot: The TARDIS materialises on board a massive sandminer vehicle combing an alien world for precious minerals. The miner is run by a small human crew with the aid of numerous robots split into three classes: Dums, Vocs and a single controlling Super Voc. The crew are currently being picked off one by one by an unseen killer. The Doctor and Leela immediately come under suspicion but are able to convince two undercover government agents – Poul and his robot associate D84, a Super Voc posing as a Dum – that they are innocent. The real culprit is one of the human crew, Dask, who is in truth the scientist Taren Capel. Raised by robots, Capel regards them as superior to humans and has been reprogramming those on board with orders to kill the other members of the crew. He is tricked by the Doctor into outlining his plans for conquest while a helium canister discharges itself into the room, and is consequently killed by one of the robots as it can no longer recognise his voice.

Episode endings:
1. The Doctor is trapped in a storage unit within the sandminer as it rapidly fills with sand.
2. The sandminer's engines run out of control, threatening it with destruction. The Doctor opens an inspection hatch, intending to fight sabotage with sabotage, but is restrained by Dask. As the power builds to a near critical eighty-five percent, Toos desperately shouts: 'She's going!'
3. A robot with orders to kill the Doctor seizes him about the neck with its hands.
4. The Doctor and Leela return to the TARDIS, which dematerialises from the sandminer.

IT WAS MADE WHERE...?
Visual Effects filming: 02.11.76-05.11.76 at Visual Effects Stage, 250 Western Avenue, Ealing, London
Studio: 22.11.76-23.11.76, 05.12.76-07.12.76 (studio unknown)

ADDITIONAL CREDITED CAST
Uvanov (Russell Hunter), Toos (Pamela Salem), Dask (David Bailie), Poul (David Collings), Borg (Brian Croucher[1,2]), Zilda (Tania Rogers[1,2]), Cass (Tariq Yunis[1,2]), Chub (Rob Edwards[1]), D.84 (Gregory de Polnay), S.V.7 (Miles Fothergill), Robots (Mark Blackwell Baker, John Bleasdale, Mark Cooper, Peter Langtry, Jeremy Ranchev, Richard Seager).

THINGS TO WATCH OUT FOR
- Russell Hunter, well known for his role as Lonely in the counterespionage series *Callan*, plays Commander Uvanov.
- Brian Croucher, now renowned for his portrayal of Travis in *Blake's 7*, plays Borg.
- Robophobia, an irrational fear of robots, is at one point referred to as 'Grimwade's syndrome'. This was an in-joke reference to production assistant Peter Grimwade (later to become a director and writer on the series) who had bemoaned the fact that the stories on which he was assigned to work almost always involved robots.
- The designer, Ken Sharp, based his concept for the look of the sandminer and the

FOURTH DOCTOR 4

robots on an *art deco* style. This idea was carried forward into the make-up and the costumes for the human crew.

- The TARDIS's secondary control room, introduced in *The Masque of Mandragora*, makes its final appearance in this story.

- Peter Grimwade directed, uncredited, all the film insert sequences for this story.
- The music tracks played to the crew in Part One are 'None but the Weary' by Tchaikovsky and 'Girl with the Flaxen Hair' by Debussy.
- The sandminer was inspired by a similar ship in Frank Herbert's *Dune*.

- **Chub:** 'There was a Voc therapist in Kaldor City once. Specially programmed, equipped with vibro-digits, subcutaneous stimulators, the lot. You know what happened, Borg? Its first client wanted treatment for a stiff elbow. The Voc therapist felt carefully all round the joint, and then suddenly just twisted his arm off at the shoulder. *Shoompf.* All over in two seconds.'
- **D.84:** [Speaking of a tool used on board the sandminer.] 'It is a Laserson probe. It can punch a fist-sized hole through six-inch armour plate, or take the crystals from a snowflake one by one.'

The Robots of Death is another in a succession of high quality stories, and one of the very best to be produced by Philip Hinchcliffe. Excellent writing, superb direction, great performances and wonderful design work combine to make it a true classic.

'Chris Boucher's script was magnificent,' wrote Chris Dunk in *Oracle* Volume 2 Number 8 dated May 1979, 'containing something basic with which virtually everyone can identify – namely a petrifying fear of violent death. This phobia was personified in the sleek and lethal robots ... The [thought] of a Voc clamping its vice-like digits around [someone's] throat ... never ceases to terrify me. There is no surer way of death, and the pulsing theme invented for this act of murder by Dudley Simpson instantly recalls the emotionless machine lowering a cadaver gently to the floor. Their finesse totally belied their true intentions.

'Throughout many years as a *Doctor Who* fan, I can remember nothing more vividly than this. It scared me.'

The sandminer clearly owes a debt of inspiration to Frank Herbert's *Dune*, and another source cited for the story is Agatha Christie's *Murder on the Orient Express*, although *Ten Little Niggers* is closer to the idea of a group of people being killed off one by one by an unknown murderer. However, as Gordon Blows pointed out in the *Doctor Who Appreciation Society Yearbook 1977/78*, there is much more to *The Robots of Death* than this:

'Most *Doctor Who* stories these days seem to be based upon a well-known film. But to compare *The Robots of Death* [to] *Murder on the Orient Express* is only a joke, this [story's] sophistication lying very obviously with the contemporary science-fiction novel.

'Although the more science-fiction-style adventures tend to be the most popular *Doctor Who* stories, the first and foremost factor of all successful series has to be a strong cast of interesting and believable characters. *The Robots of Death* won hands down on this. Commander Uvanov and his restless crew, more at war with each other than the adversaries that became of their servants, were each interested only in their own ideals ...

'The Doctor's defeat of Capel was simple but ingenious, and very well contrived on the part of ... Chris Boucher ... Writing two stories on the trot, he was able to characterise Leela, and she has remained as close to the Sevateem and her savage instincts as the day she left the jungle of her home world.'

The robots themselves recall the stories of Isaac Asimov – no doubt one of the novelists whose work Blows had in mind – and make for a very effective threat when reprogrammed to ignore his famous First Law of Robotics: 'A robot may not injure a human being or, through inaction, allow a human being to come to harm'. D.84 is particularly well portrayed by Gregory de Polnay, successfully coming across as a character in his own right, and the calm, well-mannered voices used for all the speaking robots only serve to increase their effectiveness still further. 'I must say that the format for *The Robots of Death* was very imaginative,' observed Owen Tudor in *TARDIS* Volume 2 Number 3 in 1977. 'The restrictions placed on the script by the setting were used well, and the idea of a robot revolt was good. However, I did not like the way in which it was shown that it was all the fault of the baddie that the robots were being nasty. I think it would have been better if the robots revolted because they wanted to be regarded as equals with the humans, because of the way humans maltreated them. Still, that might have been a little difficult – the robots would have had to be *very* advanced.'

The adoption of an *art deco* look for the story's sets and costumes is a real master stroke, giving the whole thing a sumptuous and highly distinctive look and further emphasising the contrast between the outward refinement of the robots and the violent actions they are called upon to perform. 'The production was excellent,' agreed Gordon Blows, 'and for once the special effects and exterior designs corresponded perfectly with the interior sets, even to the point of superimposing the control deck across the window of the [model] sandminer, so that one had the impression of looking into the ship.'

The Robots of Death is a fine example of a story on which everyone involved was clearly committed to achieving the best they possibly could. The results speak for themselves.

THE TALONS OF WENG-CHIANG

Writer: Robert Holmes*. **Director:** David Maloney. **Designer:** Roger Murray-Leach. **Costumes:** John Bloomfield. **Make-Up:** Heather Stewart. **Incidental Music:** Dudley Simpson. **Fight Arranger:** Stuart Fell. **Visual Effects:** Michealjohn Harris. **Film Cameraman:** Fred Hamilton. **Film Editor:** David Lee. **OB Cameraman:** unknown. **Studio Lighting:** Mike Jefferies. **Studio Sound:** Clive Gifford. **Production Assistant:** Ros Anderson. **Assistant Floor Manager:** Linda Graeme.

* Robert Holmes wrote this story from an idea entitled *The Foe from the Future* by Robert Banks Stewart, who received no on-screen credit.

	First UK TX	Scheduled TX	Actual TX	Duration	Viewers	Chart Pos.
Part One	26/02/77	18.30	18.32	24'44"	11.3	16
Part Two	05/03/77	18.35	18.37	24'26"	9.8	28

Part Three	12/03/77	18.30	18.32	21'56"	10.2	22
Part Four	19/03/77	18.30	18.32	24'30"	11.4	21
Part Five	26/03/77	18.30	18.31	24'49"	10.1	18
Part Six	02/04/77	18.30	18.31	23'26"	9.3	32

Plot: Arriving in London at the end of the 19th Century, the Doctor and Leela make friends with a police pathologist, Professor Litefoot, and learn that hairs taken from the clothing of a dead body found floating in the Thames seem to have originated from a very large rat. The Doctor's investigations take him first to the sewers, where there are indeed giant rats on the loose, and then to the Palace Theatre, where a stage magician, Li H'sen Chang, is procuring young girls for his master, the ancient Chinese god Weng-Chiang. Weng-Chiang is in fact Magnus Greel, a war criminal from the 51st Century. The journey back through time has disrupted his molecular structure and he now needs to feed on the life force of others – hence his use for the young girls. He has come to London to retrieve his lost time cabinet, which is in the possession of Litefoot. Infiltrating Litefoot's home with Chang's ventriloquist doll Mr Sin – a computerised homonculus with the brain of a pig – he retrieves the cabinet and prepares to travel back to his own time. The Doctor, aided by Leela, Litefoot and Henry Gordon Jago, the proprietor of the Theatre, tracks him down to his lair and traps him before he can escape. Greel falls into his life force extraction machine and disintegrates. The Doctor is then attacked by Mr Sin but manages to disconnect its circuitry, rendering it inanimate.

Episode endings:
1. The Doctor and Leela descend into the sewers, where they are confronted by a giant rat. The Doctor ushers Leela in the opposite direction as the rat scurries towards them.
2. Leela has been dining with Litefoot at his house. The Professor goes outside to investigate after spotting a prowler in the grounds, and on his return is struck down by an unseen assailant. Leela is suddenly confronted by the squat figure of Mr Sin advancing on her with a knife.
3. Leela flees from Weng-Chiang's lair through the sewers, chased by a giant rat. The Doctor, who is also in the sewers with a gun borrowed from Litefoot, hears her coming and prepares to fire. She turns the corner and falls, and the rat bears down on her.
4. Professor Litefoot is left unconscious in his house as Weng-Chiang, laughing maniacally, speeds away in a horse-drawn carriage with the time cabinet strapped to the back.
5. Weng-Chiang returns to Litefoot's house to fetch a missing bag containing the key to the time cabinet. He ambushes Leela and presses a chemical-soaked pad over her mouth. She struggles with him and pulls the mask from his face, revealing a bent and twisted visage beneath.
6. Leela and the Doctor enter the TARDIS and it dematerialises. Litefoot is amazed, but Jago takes it all in his stride: it is a good trick, and one that Li H'sen Chang himself would have appreciated.

IT WAS MADE WHERE...?

Location filming: 13.12.76-17.12.76, 20.12.76-24.12.76
Locations: Ealing Film Studios; Wapping Pier Head, Wapping High Street, London, E1; Clink Street, Southwark, London SE1; Ivory House, St Katharine's Dock, East Smithfield, London, E1; St Mary Overy's Wharf, Cathedral Street, Southwark, London, E1; Bridewell Place, Wapping, E1; Bankside, Southwark, SE1; Broad Oak, 24

Cambridge Park, Twickenham, Middx; East Dock/Centre Basin, St Katharine's Dock, East Smithfield, London, E1;
OB: 07.01.77, 09.01.77-13.01.77
Locations: Northampton Repertory Theatre, Swan Street, Northampton; St Crispin's Hospital, Duston, Northampton; Empty Rates Office, Fish Street, Northampton.
Studio: 11.01.77 (studio unknown), 24.01.77-25.01.77 in TC1, 08.02.77-10.02.77 in TC8

ADDITIONAL CREDITED CAST

Li H'sen Chang (John Bennett[1-5]), Jago (Christopher Benjamin), Casey (Chris Gannon[1-4]), Professor Litefoot (Trevor Baxter), Mr. Sin (Deep Roy), Sergeant Kyle (David McKail[1,2]), P.C. Quick (Conrad Asquith[1,2]), Buller (Alan Butler[1]), Ghoul (Patsy Smart[1]), Lee (Tony Then[1,4,5]), Coolie (John Wu[1]), Weng-Chiang (Michael Spice[2-6]), Teresa (Judith Lloyd[3]), Cleaner (Vaune Craig-Raymond[3]), Singer (Penny Lister[4]), Ho (Vincent Wong[5,6*]).

* Also in Part One, but uncredited.

THINGS TO WATCH OUT FOR

- There is a cameo appearance by the series' incidental music composer Dudley Simpson as the conductor of the orchestra at the Palace Theatre.
- A pile of straw seen in the road as Weng-Chiang searches for the time cabinet was placed there to hide a modern car which had, despite requests to the contrary, been parked in the road prior to filming.

THINGS YOU MIGHT NOT HAVE KNOWN

- Working title: *The Talons of Greel*.
- Writer Robert Holmes said that the story was influenced by *The Phantom of the Opera* and by the numerous *Fu Manchu* films and books.
- Because the script called for Li H'sen Chang to perform some magic tricks on stage during Parts One and Four, two advisers were brought in to assist. These were Larry Barnes and Ali Bongo.
- The making of *The Talons of Weng-Chiang* was examined in detail in *The Lively Arts* documentary *Whose Doctor Who* in 1977.

QUOTE, UNQUOTE

- **Leela:** 'Doctor, you make me wear strange clothes, you tell me nothing, you are trying to annoy me.'
- **Li H'sen Chang:** 'He came like a god. He appeared in a blazing cabinet of fire. I saw him and helped him. He was tired from his journey. He was ill for many months, I was but a humble peasant but I gave him sanctuary while the soldiers searched. I nursed him ...'
- **The Doctor:** '"Eureka" is Greek for "this bath is too hot".'
- **Jago:** 'That's my trouble, Litefoot.' **Professor Litefoot:** 'What?' **Jago:** 'Well I'm not awfully ... Well, I'm not so bally brave when it comes to it. I try to be but I'm not.' **Professor Litefoot:** 'Well when it comes to it, I don't suppose anybody is.'

Every so often, *Doctor Who* would produce a story that almost defies the reviewer to find something wrong with it. *The Talons of Weng-Chiang* is such a story. As Jan Vincent-Rudzki wrote in *TARDIS* Volume 2 Number 4 in 1977: 'Dark, fog-laden streets, oriental mystery, alien technology, a walking sinister doll and amateur sleuths all added up to a very atmospheric and enjoyable story.' The BBC is justly renowned for its excellence in producing period costume drama. This is combined here with a cracking set of scripts from Robert Holmes, showcasing all the best aspects of his writing, and superb direction by series veteran David Maloney, whose casting and use of locations is as usual immaculate, to create what is arguably one of the best *Doctor Who* adventures ever.

'For the first time Leela appears fully dressed,' observed Keith Miller in *Doctor Who Digest* Number 6 dated August 1977, 'looking suspiciously like Tinker to complement the Doctor's mixture of Sexton Blake and Sherlock Holmes. The BBC is rather expert at recreating Victorian London – after all, they've had enough practice with *The Forsyte Saga*, *The Pallisers*, *The Duchess of Duke Street*, *The Onedin Line* etc – and it was a joy to watch the Doctor and Leela strolling through the cobbled streets before being attacked by a horde of Chinamen and then arrested for creating a disturbance.'

Arthur Conan Doyle's Sherlock Holmes canon has often been cited as one of the story's major influences, but this was disputed by Andy Lane in *In-Vision* Issue Twenty-One dated December 1989: '[It] picks up not on the truth of Sherlock Holmes, but on what people think the truth is. In fact, the vast majority of Holmes's cases do not take place in London, do not involve fog and hansom cabs, and revolve around villains smaller, rather than larger, than life ... The Doctor's costume of deerstalker and cloak is suitably Holmesian, except that Holmes never wore a deerstalker – that was the invention of one of the original artists ... Sherlock Holmes's reputation rests upon his powers of observation, memory and deduction ... In comparison, the Doctor puts up a bad showing. Fair enough, his memory is as good – he immediately recognises scorpion venom, the Tong of the Black Scorpion, the rat hairs on the murdered cab driver and the effects of opium. But his ratiocinations are few and far between ... In fact ... one [is put] more in mind of Sir Denis Nayland Smith, arch-enemy of ... Doctor Fu-Manchu. The connections here are more obvious: the fog, the alleys, the crowds of orientals skulking through the streets spoiling for a fight, the base on the river, the villain who expands his lifespan through strange scientific means, the hero and his sidekick who blunder into trouble but escape more by luck than judgment, the melodrama, the plot device that could affect the world. It's almost too good to be true.'

It is the characters that really make *The Talons of Weng-Chiang* shine. John Bennett is faultless as the inscrutable Li H'sen Chang, and his performance and make-up are so convincing that it is difficult to believe that he is not actually Chinese. Christopher Benjamin gives his all as the ebullient theatre manager Henry Gordon Jago, and Chris Gannon also comes across well as his weasly side-kick Casey; the two characters make a marvellous duo, their relationship contrasting nicely with that of Chang and Weng-Chiang, alias Magnus Greel. Following in the footsteps of other notable villains like Azal, Omega, Davros and Sutekh, Greel as ably portrayed by Michael Spice is a chilling depiction of evil and insanity. Although he is to some extent a tragic figure, it is hard to feel any sympathy for him as he casually murders young girls in order to extract their life essence for himself. Last but not least, Trevor Baxter is brilliant as the gentlemanly Professor Litefoot. The teaming of Jago and Litefoot during the course of the action works extremely well, and it is easy to see why there was at one point some consideration given to according them their own spin-off series. This knack of writing memorable 'double acts' is Robert Holmes's great forté, and here we have several fine examples: the Doctor and Leela, Jago and Casey, Litefoot and Leela, Jago and Litefoot and Chang and Weng-Chiang.

The story does have one fault, however, and that is the poor realisation of the giant rats used by Greel to keep people away from his lair beneath the Palace Theatre. The shots in which they are shown by way of real rats in a miniature sewer work relatively well, but sadly the same cannot be said of those involving stuntman Stuart Fell in a furry costume. The worst moment of all comes when a rat attempts to eat some raw meat that Greel has hung over the bars of a grille leading to the sewers. It is quite apparent here that the rat's teeth are made of foam rubber, and it is about as frightening as a Beatrix Potter character. The scene in which it chases after Leela in the sewers is a little better though, mainly because rather less is seen of it. 'If only it was as Robert Holmes said in [his recent interview in the *Daily Express*],' reflected Vincent-Rudzki, 'that it would be seen only in the shadows, or just its tail. Instead we saw that terrible cuddly-looking thing that I just couldn't help laughing at, even when Leela joined the so-called trait of typical companions when she was screaming as it caught her leg.' Keith Miller agreed: 'It's not very long before the Doctor and Leela are splashing about in the sewers, the set of which looked very realistic, which is more than I can say about the giant rat which, even in long shot as seen at the end of [Part One], looked, to quote Margaret Forwood in the *Sun*: "… as chilling as a pantomime horse and as lifelike. It looked, not to mince words, as if it had been stuffed." … [Later on,] the rats attack and for the first time in the series, [Leela] screams. A lot of you wrote to me saying, "But she's a warrior. It's spoilt the effect!", but wouldn't *you* scream if you had a giant rodent gnawing at *your* limb? The jaws are chomping away at the end of [Part Three] and when the Doctor manages to save her with the aid of Litefoot's Chinese rifle, Leela is seen to have only a bruised ankle! Hmmmmm …'

The giant rats aside, this story still contains its fair share of gruesome and disturbing material – not to mention, when Chang retreats to an opium den, the first scene in the series' history of someone taking illicit drugs. The horrific nature of *Doctor Who* at this time, and of *The Talons of Weng-Chiang* in particular, was discussed by Richard Landen in the *Doctor Who Appreciation Society Yearbook 1977/78*: '[A] rather surprising aspect of this [story] was the amount of violence shown, especially after the outcry against *The Deadly Assassin*. It seems, though, that an axe in the back, multiple stabbings, being eaten by rats and even self-poisoning are all less gruesome than someone holding their breath underwater! Personally I feel that the [series'] violent scenes should be more prominent, but then *News at Nine* might feel a slight challenge to its undisputed reign in this category.'

The Talons of Weng-Chiang was Philip Hinchcliffe's *Doctor Who* swansong, his BBC superiors having decided to reassign him to a new police series called *Target* devised by a man named Graham Williams – who, by a strange coincidence, was to be his successor on *Doctor Who*. Established script editor Robert Holmes remained on the production team for the time being but was keen to move on and so would also be bowing out before long. Season fifteen would thus be one of behind-the-scenes changes for the series – not to mention considerable difficulties, as a number of problems combined to make it a baptism of fire for the incoming team.

FOURTH DOCTOR

DOCTOR WHO SEASON FIFTEEN (1977-1978)

Regular Cast:
Doctor Who (Tom Baker)
Leela (Louise Jameson)
Voice of K9 (John Leeson) on *The Invisible Enemy* and from *The Sun Makers* Part One onwards

Regular Crew:
Producer: Graham Williams.
Script Editor: Robert Holmes until *The Sun Makers* Part Four. Anthony Read from *Underworld* Part One onwards*.
Production Unit Manager: John Nathan-Turner.
Title Music: Ron Grainer and the BBC Radiophonic Workshop, arranged by Delia Derbyshire.
Special Sounds: Dick Mills except on *The Sun Makers*. Paddy Kingsland on *The Sun Makers*.

* Anthony Read also contributed to the script editing of *Image of the Fendahl* and *The Sun Makers* but was uncredited on screen.

Graham Williams encountered problems almost as soon as he arrived as *Doctor Who*'s producer. The intention had been that season fifteen would open with a Terrance Dicks vampire story entitled *The Witch Lords* (also referred to as *The Vampire Mutation*), but this was vetoed at a late stage by Head of Serials Graeme McDonald on the grounds that it could be interpreted as a send-up of a lavish BBC production of Bram Stoker's *Dracula* that was then in preparation. Consequently the production team – on which Robert Holmes was shortly to be succeeded as script editor by a highly experienced writer/producer named Anthony Read – had to find a hasty replacement and rearrange the season's production order so as to allow time for it to be written and recorded. The first story to be made was consequently the second to be transmitted. This was *The Invisible Enemy*, which saw the introduction of a rather unusual new companion to join the Doctor and Leela on their travels. The robot dog K9 had been envisaged by writers Bob Baker and Dave Martin as simply a one-off character for their story, but Williams decided that it was too good a creation to waste on just a single appearance. He saw it as a potential ratings winner, particularly amongst children, and hoped that it would help to boost the level of humour in the series – something he was keen to do as he was under considerable pressure from BBC management to tone down the horror content that had caused such controversy during his predecessor's tenure. Tom Baker, by contrast, was less than happy about the dog's introduction, believing that the Doctor really had no need of any companions at all. Fortunately though he did get on well with John Leeson, the actor chosen to provide its voice. The replacement first story, meanwhile, was another Terrance Dicks contribution that would see the Doctor and Leela battling for their lives in a uniquely isolated historical setting …

HORROR OF FANG ROCK

Writer: Terrance Dicks. **Director:** Paddy Russell. **Designer:** Paul Allen. **Costumes:** Joyce Hawkins. **Make-Up:** Jackie Hodgson. **Incidental Music:** Dudley Simpson. **Visual Effects:** Peter Pegrum. **Film Cameraman:** John Walker. **Film Editor:** unknown. **Studio Lighting:** Bob Gell. **Studio Sound:** David Hughes. **Production Assistant:** Peter Grimwade. **Assistant Floor Manager:** Bill Hartley.

	First UK TX	Scheduled TX	Actual TX	Duration	Viewers	Chart Pos.
Part One	03/09/77	18.15	18.18	24'10"	6.8	52
Part Two	10/09/77	18.15	18.15	24'10"	7.1	51
Part Three	17/09/77	18.15	18.18	23'12"	9.8	23
Part Four	24/09/77	18.15	18.16	23'49"	9.9	23

Plot: The TARDIS arrives on Fang Rock, a small island off the English coast, around the start of the 20th Century. The Doctor and Leela seek shelter at a lighthouse where the island's only inhabitants – Ben, Vince and Reuben – operate the recently-installed electric lamp to warn ships off the treacherous rocks. Vince has just seen a bright object fall from the sky into the sea. Ben then disappears and his body is later discovered hidden behind the generator – he has been electrocuted. A passing ship crashes on the rocks as a freak fog bank descends, and the survivors – Colonel Skinsale, Lord Palmerdale, Adelaide Lesage and Harker – stumble into the lighthouse. There they find themselves prey to a Rutan – one of the race engaged in a perennial war with the Sontarans – whose spaceship has crashed in the sea. The Rutan can change its form at will and has been masquerading as Reuben, having killed the old keeper and hidden his body. Vince and the wreck survivors are also killed but the Doctor fights back by blasting the Rutan, now reverted to its natural form of an amorphous jelly, with a makeshift mortar bomb. The Doctor then rigs up the lighthouse lamp with a diamond taken from a cache held by the now dead Skinsale, thereby creating a powerful laser beam to destroy the approaching Rutan mothership.

Episode endings:
1. With the lighthouse lamp out of action, a ship approaches the rocks in the thick fog. The Doctor sends up a flare and the fog-horn is sounded, but to no avail. The ship crashes onto Fang Rock.
2. Reuben is tending the lighthouse generator and goes into the coal store to fetch more fuel. Upstairs, Palmerdale is in the middle of explaining to Adelaide that nothing is happening when an horrific scream from Reuben echoes through the lighthouse.
3. The Doctor finds Reuben's body in the coal store and realises that the man they have seen walking about the lighthouse is in fact the Rutan. The Doctor has locked the enemy in with them.
4. The Doctor and Leela return to the TARDIS. As it leaves, the Doctor recites lines from Wilfred Gibson's poem 'The Ballad óf Flannen Isle'.

IT WAS MADE WHERE...?

Ealing filming: 04.05.77-06.05.77 (studio unknown).
Studio: 25.05.77-26.05.77, 07.06.77-09.06.77 all at Pebble Mill.

FOURTH DOCTOR

Vince (John Abbott), Reuben (Colin Douglas), Ben (Ralph Watson[1]), Lord Palmerdale (Sean Caffrey[2-4]), Skinsale (Alan Rowe[2-4]), Adelaide (Annette Woollett[2-4]), Harker (Rio Fanning[2,3]).

Note: Colin Douglas also provided the voice of the Rutan in Part Four.

POPULAR MYTHS

- Designer Paul Allen researched the lighthouse sets from a book called *Lighthouses, Lightships and Buoys* by E G Jerrome. (He didn't – although that book was used for research purposes by others involved in the production. Allen visited two lighthouses, took lots of photographs of them, and based his designs on those.)

THINGS TO WATCH OUT FOR

- This was the only *Doctor Who* story to have studio scenes recorded at the BBC's Pebble Mill studios in Birmingham, rather than in London.
- This story marks the one and only appearance in the series of a Rutan – seen in its natural state as an amorphous green blob with trailing tentacles. The Rutans had been mentioned in two previous stories, *The Time Warrior* and *The Sontaran Experiment*, as being engaged in a long war with the Sontarans.
- Louise Jameson stopped wearing brown contact lenses at the end of this story. The reason given for Leela's consequent change of eye colour was that the flash from the explosion of the Rutan ship caused pigment dispersion in her eyes, changing them from brown to blue.
- At the end of the serial, the Doctor recites *The Ballad of Flannen Isle* by Wilfred Gibson.

THINGS YOU MIGHT NOT HAVE KNOWN

- Working titles: *The Monster of Fang Rock, The Beast of Fang Rock*.
- *Horror of Fang Rock* was seen by Philip Segal, executive producer of the 1996 television movie, as a 'model' *Doctor Who* story, and was used by him in trying to sell the idea to Fox in 1995.

QUOTE, UNQUOTE

- **The Doctor:** '... The localised condition of planetary atmospheric condensation caused a malfunction in the visual orientation circuits. Or to put it another way, we got lost in the fog.'
- **Lord Palmerdale:** 'Are you in charge here?' **The Doctor:** 'No, but I'm full of ideas.'
- **The Doctor:** 'The chameleon factor ... sometimes called lycanthropy. Leela, I've made a terrible mistake. I thought I'd locked the enemy out. Instead I've locked it in ... with us!'

ANALYSIS

Horror of Fang Rock maintains the high standard established by *The Talons of Weng-Chiang* at the end of the previous season. Terrance Dicks's well written scripts take full advantage of the isolated nature of the story's setting and are very effective in building up tension. The scenes that take place outside the lighthouse on the rocks are eerie and atmospheric, the clever use of smoke and lighting effects helping to make this a convincing locale despite the fact that it was created entirely in studio. In fact, all the sets for this story are superb. The lighthouse itself is totally realistic – even down to the curved doors leading onto the main spiral staircase – and engenders a palpable feeling of claustrophobia as the action unfolds.

Some reviewers, however, have been less than enthusiastic about the story. Keith Miller, writing in *Doctor Who Digest* Number 8 dated April 1978, found the whole thing tedious: 'The main characters of Vince and Reuben were so melodramatic and stagy that I couldn't believe in them at all. The modelwork, which at first looked quite promising, quickly deteriorated when the ship ran aground. The limited space … of the lighthouse could have been exploited far better than it was, the story being reduced to an uninteresting runabout up and down stairs from the unseen enemy. The fact that … the monster [was kept] unseen until the last episode was, I think, the only thing that held the audience's attention throughout the tedious plot. And then to find out the alien was only a balloon with spaghetti attached to its rear was a vast disappointment.' Howard D Langford, commenting on the story in *TARDIS* Volume 3 Number 3 dated May/June 1978, had similar misgivings: 'I thought there was rather too much rushing about the lighthouse. Also the Doctor's speeches were too abrupt – he appeared to be constantly in a bad mood, and this is a feature of the series in general: there was little genuine humour. I wish *everyone* hadn't been killed. Nevertheless, on the whole I liked this story.'

The small guest cast are generally very good, although Annette Woollett's Adelaide is a little annoying (there's a nice moment where Leela slaps her round the face to stop her screaming). Top marks to Colin Douglas and John Abbott, who are excellent in their respective roles as Reuben and Vince and whose scenes together in the opening episode are important in helping to create a sense of impending doom. Vince's eventual death is particularly poignant, especially as it seems to come at the hands of Reuben, his one-time friend and mentor – although it is actually, of course, the work of the Rutan masquerading as Reuben. This is indeed a rather depressing story in many respects, as it is one, as Langford noted, in which everyone aside from the Doctor and Leela is ultimately killed. Skinsale's death is particularly pointless, caused purely by his greed for a handful of diamonds casually discarded by the Doctor.

Horror of Fang Rock is a tightly constructed drama that succeeds because of, rather than in spite of, its confined setting and limited cast. If any story proves that *Doctor Who* has no need of a huge budget and eye-popping visual effects in order to succeed, it is this one.

THE INVISIBLE ENEMY

Writer: Bob Baker, Dave Martin. **Director:** Derrick Goodwin. **Designer:** Barry Newbery. **Costumes:** Raymond Hughes. **Make-Up:** Maureen Winslade. **Incidental Music:** Dudley Simpson. **Visual Effects:** Tony Harding, Ian Scoones. **Film Cameraman:** Nick Allder. **Film Editor:** Glenn Hyde. **Studio Lighting:** Brian Clemett. **Studio Sound:** Michael McCarthy. **Production Assistant:** Norman Stewart. **Assistant Floor Manager:** Tony Garrick, Christabel Albery.

	First UK TX	Scheduled TX	Actual TX	Duration	Viewers	Chart Pos.
Part One	01/10/77	18.15	18.20	23'09"	8.6	40
Part Two	08/10/77	18.05	18.04	25'13"	7.3	55
Part Three	15/10/77	18.10	18.13	23'28"	7.5	65
Part Four	22/10/77	18.10	18.13	21'22"	8.3	50

Plot: The TARDIS is infiltrated by the Swarm – a space-borne intelligence that wishes to spread itself across the universe – and the Doctor is infected by its nucleus. The ship then materialises on Titan, one of the moons of Saturn, where the human occupants of a refuelling station have also been taken over. The Doctor eventually collapses as a result of his infection, but first manages to relay to Leela the coordinates of a local hospital asteroid. At the Bi-Al Foundation, based on the asteroid, Professor Marius clones the two time travellers, miniaturises the clones using the relative dimensional stabiliser from the TARDIS and then injects them into the Doctor's body in the hope that they can find and destroy the nucleus. The plan backfires as the nucleus escapes from the Doctor in place of the clones and is enlarged to human size. The creature arranges for itself to be taken back to Titan, where breeding tanks have been prepared for it. The Doctor, now cured of its influence, enlists the help of K9, Professor Marius's dog-shaped robot computer, and sets a booby-trap that results in the breeding tanks being blown up, killing the nucleus. Marius gives K9 to the Doctor as a parting gift.

Episode endings:
1. The Doctor, infected by the Swarm, aims a gun at Leela's back and prepares to fire.
2. Marius injects the miniaturised clones of the Doctor and Leela into the Doctor's neck, and they spiral down into his bloodstream.
3. Marius collects from the Doctor's tear duct what he believes to be the miniaturised clones of the Doctor and Leela and places them into the cloning booth. He operates the controls of the relative dimensional stabiliser to return them to normal size, but instead it is the prawn-like nucleus that appears in the booth.
4. Marius suggests to the Doctor that he take K9 with him in the TARDIS. The Doctor is reluctant, but Leela is delighted. In the end, K9 decides for himself by trundling in through the open police box doors. The Doctor and Leela follow and, as the ship dematerialises, Marius reflects: 'I only hope he's TARDIS trained.'

IT WAS MADE WHERE...?
Bray filming: April 1977
Studio: 10.04.77-12.04.77, 24.04.77-26.04.77 all in TC6

ADDITIONAL CREDITED CAST
Lowe (Michael Sheard), Safran (Brian Grellis[1,2,4]), Meeker (Edmund Pegge[1]), Silvey (Jay Neill[1]), Crewman (Anthony Rowlands[1]), Nucleus Voice* (John Leeson), Professor Marius (Frederick Jaeger[2-4]), Parsons (Roy Herrick[2,3]), Marius' Nurse (Elizabeth Norman[2,3]), Reception Nurse (Nell Curran[2]), Opthalmologist (Jim McManus[2-4]), Cruikshank (Roderick Smith[2,3]), Hedges (Kenneth Waller[2]), A Medic (Pat Gorman[3,4**]), Nucleus (John Scott-Martin[3,4]).

* On Parts Two to Four John Leeson was credited as 'Nucleus and K9 Voice'.
** Also at the end of Part Two, but uncredited.

- *The Invisible Enemy* sees the return of the traditional TARDIS control room set, albeit slightly redesigned by Barry Newbery.
- K9 makes its first appearance here. It was realised as a radio controlled electronic robot dog designed by Tony Harding and built by the BBC Visual Effects Department. One earlier idea had been to use a huge robotic Doberman costume with an actor inside.

THINGS YOU MIGHT NOT HAVE KNOWN

- Working titles: *The Enemy Within, The Invader Within, The Invisible Invader.*
- The decision to keep K9 on as a regular companion was made fairly late in the day with the consequence that a means had to be contrived in some of the following stories to incapacitate the dog, as he had not been included in the plot.

QUOTE, UNQUOTE

- **Lowe (and other characters infected by the Swarm):** 'Contact has been made!'
- **The Doctor:** '5000 AD! We're still in the time of your ancestors.' **Leela:** 'Ancestors?' **The Doctor:** 'Yes. That was the year of the great breakout.' **Leela:** 'The great what?' **The Doctor:** 'Mmm. When your forefathers went leapfrogging across the solar system on their way to the stars. Yes. Asteroid belt's probably teeming with them now. New frontiersmen ... pioneers ... waiting to spread across the galaxy like a tidal wave ... or a disease.' **Leela:** 'Why "disease"? I thought you liked humanity.' **The Doctor:** 'Oh I do, I do. Some of my best friends are humans. When they get together in great numbers other lifeforms sometimes suffer.'
- **Nucleus:** 'It is the right of every creature across the universe to survive, multiply and perpetuate its species. How else does the predator exist? We are all predators, Doctor. We kill ... we devour ... to live. Survival is all ... You agree?' **The Doctor:** 'Oh yes, I do, I do. And on your argument, I have a perfect right to dispose of you.'

ANALYSIS

After the promising start made in *Horror of Fang Rock*, many viewers would no doubt have entertained hopes that the quality of the fifteenth season would match that of the fourteenth. Such hopes would have been soundly dashed by *The Invisible Enemy*, which is one of the weakest stories of the fourth Doctor's era. Reviewers over the years have struggled to find a good word to say about it. 'The basic idea behind this story of an enemy invading from within the human nervous system was an interesting and novel one,' conceded Howard D Langford in *TARDIS* Volume 3 Number 3 dated May/June 1978. 'However, having said this, the story was handled badly. The action seemed to be at too fast a rate – I preferred the slower tempo of *Horror of Fang Rock*. The introduction of K9 was a disaster which led to inevitable tedious fighting. If we want lasers blasting we can watch *Star Wars*, not *Doctor Who* ... Finally, the blowing up of the nucleus was the sort of action that the Doctor deplored in *Doctor Who and the Silurians*, yet here we find him resorting to destruction *a la* Leela. He was supposed to be educating her, not vice versa!'

A particularly notable aspect of this story is its heavy reliance on visual effects. The model shots are the most extensive and ambitious to be featured in the series thus far, and are undoubtedly one of the highlights of the production. Even they have come in for criticism, however. 'It was the visual effects that spoiled the show,' argued Kevin Davies in *Quark* 1 dated November 1977. 'The spaceship models were excellent ... but were reduced to "things on strings" once on screen. The Titan base was straight from *Space: 1999*, and its eventual destruction was awful. Blaster rays issued from anywhere but the gun nozzles, CSO screens looked unconvincing, as usual, and K9 fired at a *precracked* wall in order to make a barrier small enough for a puppy K9 to jump over.'

In fairness to designer Barry Newbery, whose characteristically excellent work is the other highlight of the production, it should be pointed out that the pre-cracking of the wall fired at by K9 was successfully disguised when the scene in question was first recorded; unfortunately director Derrick Goodwin called for retakes and the broken section of the wall had to be replaced with insufficient time available for the join to be repaired.

The scenes in which the clones (or rather pseudo-clones, complete with clothes, produced by something referred to as the 'Kilbracken technique') make their way through the Doctor's body are highly reminiscent of the 1966 Twentieth Century Fox production *Fantastic Voyage*. They work nowhere near as well, however. One reason for this is that, whereas in the film the voyagers had a ship with its own atmosphere, here the clones are moving about as if they are in the open air. Another is that, on *Doctor Who*'s relatively small budget, the effects that could be achieved were visibly inferior. These scenes are nevertheless some of the more successful ones in the story – although the appearance of the human-sized version of the nucleus of the Swarm at the end of Part Three is very much a let-down, as Keith Miller pointed out in *Doctor Who Digest* Number 8 dated April 1978:

'I really liked the scene when the Doctor "short circuited" his liver to save Leela from the balloon-type antibodies. The chasm between the brain and the mind left a lot to be desired, but who knows, perhaps such a thing does exist. Anyway, Leela leads the Doctor to the nucleus, that particularly nasty blob with one arm. Very effective. The meeting between it and the Doctor was very good, expertly written and acted. However, it isn't long before the nucleus escapes through the Doctor's tear duct and enlarges into one of the funniest *Doctor Who* monsters I've seen in a long time ...

'The remaining struggle to get back to the hive and its inevitable destruction [were] quite well done, but all believability was gone because of the farcical monster. Pity. I had enjoyed the other three episodes.'

Writers Bob Baker and Dave Martin seem to have developed a liking for giving their characters 'catchphrases'. In *The Hand of Fear* it was 'Eldrad must live!', this time it is 'Contact has been made!' (and later in the season in *Underworld* it is 'The quest is the quest!'). Unfortunately this is one of the few memorable aspects of the scripts, which generally consist of clichéd and undemanding action-adventure material. We will leave the final word to the particularly unimpressed John Peel, who wrote in *TARDIS* Volume 2 Number 8 in 1977: 'The production team seem convinced that *Doctor Who* is really a kid's show, and have proved it so admirably with the latest serial. Despite superficial glitter, good miniatures and Frederick Jaeger's superb acting [as Professor Marius] (didn't seem a bit like Sorenson [in *Planet of Evil*], did he?), *The Invisible Enemy* failed miserably as entertainment ... The Doctor now has a mechanical pet to go with his savage. With stories like this one and *Horror of Fang Rock*, why not a new time slot as well? Straight after *Watch with Mother*. (The [series] is going to the dogs!)'

IMAGE OF THE FENDAHL

Writer: Chris Boucher. **Director:** George Spenton-Foster. **Designer:** Anna Ridley. **Costumes:** Amy Roberts. **Make-Up:** Pauline Cox. **Incidental Music:** Dudley Simpson. **Visual Effects:** Colin Mapson. **Film Cameraman:** Elmer Cossey. **Film Editor:** unknown. **Studio Lighting:** Jim Purdie. **Studio Sound:** Alan Fogg. **Production Assistant:** Prue Saenger. **Assistant Floor Manager:** Karilyn Collier.

	First UK TX	Scheduled TX	Actual TX	Duration	Viewers	Chart Pos.
Part One	29/10/77	18.10	18.12	24'38"	6.7	70
Part Two	05/11/77	18.10	18.10	24'44"	7.5	64
Part Three	12/11/77	18.05	18.07	24'22"	7.9	63
Part Four	19/11/77	18.10	18.14	20'32"	9.1	46

4 · FOURTH DOCTOR

Plot: An anachronistic twelve million year old human skull has been discovered by archaeologists and is now being used by Professor Fendelman in his time scanner experiments at Fetch Priory in contemporary England. The skull is actually an artifact of the Fendahl, an ancient creature that feeds on the life force of others. Drawn by the operation of the scanner, the Doctor and Leela arrive as the experiments reach a peak. The skull is exerting an influence over the mind of Thea Ransome, one of the scientists in Fendelman's team, and glowing with power each time the scanner is activated. Thea is eventually transformed into the Fendahl core, and a group of acolytes assembled by Maximillian Stael – another of Fendelman's team, who is trying to harness the creature's power for his own ends – are converted into snake-like Fendahleen. The Doctor shows the remaining scientist, Adam Colby, and two locals, Martha Tyler and her son Jack, how to defend themselves against the Fendahleen using rock salt. By activating the scanner once more, he triggers an implosion that destroys both the Priory and the Fendahl core.

Episode endings:
1. Thea falls into a trance-like state as the scanner is activated. Outside, a large unseen creature approaches the Doctor through the woods, and he seems unable to move.
2. The Doctor escapes from the store room where he has been imprisoned and finds the skull, which starts to hum and glow with power. He is compelled to place his hand on it, at which point the power greatly intensifies. The Doctor writhes in pain.
3. As Thea begins her transformation into the Fendahl core in the Priory cellar, the Doctor, Leela, Jack and Martha meet in the corridors above. Suddenly they find that they are unable to move. Around the corner and towards them slides a huge Fendahleen.
4. Back in the TARDIS, the Doctor prepares to dump the skull in the vicinity of a star that is about to go supernova. He also plans to repair K9. Leela chides the Doctor for calling K9 'him' rather than 'it', something that he had earlier pulled her up on. The Doctor claims that he is allowed to do this as K9 is his dog. K9 nods in agreement.

IT WAS MADE WHERE...?

Location filming: 01.08.77-04.08.77
Location: Stargrove Manor, East End, Hampshire.
Studio: 20.08.77-21.08.77, 04.09.77-05.09.77 all in TC6

ADDITIONAL CREDITED CAST

Thea Ransome (Wanda Ventham), Martha Tyler (Daphne Heard), Dr. Fendelman (Denis Lill[1-3]), Ted Moss (Edward Evans), Maximillian Stael (Scott Fredericks), Adam Colby (Edward Arthur), David Mitchell (Derek Martin[1,2]), Hiker (Graham Simpson[1]), Jack Tyler (Geoffrey Hinsliff[2-4]).

POPULAR MYTHS

- This story had a working title of *The Island of Fandor*. (It didn't. This myth originated when Gordon Blows, then editor of the *Doctor Who* Appreciation Society magazine *TARDIS*, misheard the title of the story over the phone and reported it incorrectly.)

THINGS TO WATCH OUT FOR

- K9 appears only briefly, in the opening and closing TARDIS scenes. *Image of the Fendahl* had been written before it was known that K9 would be joining the series on a regular basis.
- Leela wears a new costume for this adventure.
- Two sizes of Fendahleen were created for the show. Several small hand-operated versions were made for the sequence in which the Fendahl core converts her followers into the creatures, and one full sized monster was also built.

THINGS YOU MIGHT NOT HAVE KNOWN

- This was the first story in which *Radio Times* credited the lead character as 'The Doctor' rather than 'Doctor Who'. This did not happen again until *The Power of Kroll*. With *Castrovalva* (1982), the fifth Doctor's debut story, the credit became 'The Doctor' permanently.

QUOTE, UNQUOTE

- **Leela:** 'He came armed and silent.' **The Doctor:** 'You must have been sent by providence.' **Ted Moss:** 'No, I was sent by the council to cut the verges.' **Leela:** 'Your council should choose its warriors more carefully.'
- **The Doctor:** 'There are four thousand million people here on your planet, and if I'm right, within a year, there will just be one left alive. Just one.' **Adam Colby:** 'What are you exactly, some sort of wandering Armageddon pedler?'
- **Adam Colby:** 'Are you saying that about twelve million years ago, on a nameless planet which no longer exists, evolution went up a blind alley? Natural selection turned back on itself, and a creature evolved which prospered by absorbing the energy wavelengths of life itself? It ate life, all life, including that of its own kind?' **The Doctor:** 'Yes. In other words, the Fendahl. Then the Time Lords decided to destroy the entire planet, and hid the fact from posterity. They're not supposed to do that sort of thing, you know.'

Image of the Fendahl ends the run of gothic horror stories initiated by Philip Hinchcliffe and Robert Holmes back in the thirteenth season. The theme this time is that of mankind being manipulated by an ancient alien power to enable that power to manifest itself at some later point – another *Doctor Who* reworking of ideas contained in Nigel Kneale's *Quatermass and the Pit*.

'It would be easy to dismiss *Image of the Fendahl* as just a revamped *The Dæmons*,' wrote Jeremy Bentham in the *Doctor Who Appreciation Society Yearbook 1977/78*, 'were it not for the presence of the double-level plotline ... Looked at from the superficial point of view, [the story's] roots lie not with *The Dæmons* ... but with a mid-sixties film penned by the team of Haisman and Lincoln – *Curse of the Crimson Altar* – which likewise took a premise of a "helpless girl steered by evil man into becoming a manifestation of destruction" ...

'Switching now to the second level, the plot required a little bit of thinking, on [the part] of the viewer, to appreciate the subtle twist in the story; that everything which happened, right up to the manifestation of the Fendahl core in Thea, was ordained millions of years ago by the Fendahl itself. Fendelman's genius with the time scanner, Stael's belief in power through magic and Thea's empathy with the skull ... All these seeds had been genetically sown within primeval apes who would one day produce the ideal circumstances for the Fendahl's reappearance. It was complex in principle, [and] the Doctor took fiendish relish in explaining [it] in as complicated a way as possible; fluent scientific jargon reeled off in a patter unrivalled since the soliloquies of Groucho Marx.'

In common with the other stories of this type, it is the characters that make it work. Here we have the driven Doctor Fendelman who, with his time scanner, is the man chosen to fulfil the destiny of the Fendahl. His assistants Maximillian Stael, Thea Ransome and Adam Colby represent, respectively, the misguided, the victim and the hero. All are nicely characterised, but Stael comes across a little less well than the others, perhaps because it is hard to understand precisely what he hoped to gain from summoning the Fendahl in the first place. The impression is given that he has been manipulating events behind the scenes from the start – a neat parallel with the idea of the Fendahl manipulating events since the dawn of mankind – and yet there is little evidence to substantiate this.

Chris Boucher's scripts have attracted many favourable comments from reviewers, including Amanda Murray writing in *DWB* No. 111 dated March 1993: 'All of Chris Boucher's contributions to *Doctor Who* have been of a very high calibre, and *Image of the Fendahl* is no exception. The dialogue is some of the best of the season, combining suspense and humour in appropriate and balanced doses, playing one off the other to great effect. It skirts round a mass of scientific and mystical jargon in a manner which always seems on the verge of cliché and technobabble, but which never quite tumbles over the edge.'

Of the guest characters, it is Martha Tyler, the old wise woman, who really stands out. The interplay between her and the security guard, David Mitchell, in the first episode is excellent, and her premonition of the Fendahl's coming is equally well handled. Daphne Heard plays the role to perfection and is largely responsible for conveying the sense of high tension and anticipation in the latter episodes.

The Fendahl itself is something of a disappointment. Given a big build-up as a

4 FOURTH DOCTOR

terrifying creature that feeds on death, it eventually manifests itself as nothing more than a rather attractive woman with eyes painted on the outside of her closed eyelids. She swishes her robes about a lot and turns acolytes into Fendahleen but does little else to justify the awe in which everyone seems to hold her. The Fendahleen, particularly in their large form, seem far more impressive, although Chris Dunk took a contrary view in *TARDIS* Volume 3 Number 1 dated January/February 1978:

'The one thing that possibly spoilt the adventure was the appearance of the Fendahleen at the end of [Part Three]. It looked rather ridiculous I thought (why have we had so many bug-eyed little monsters recently ...?) and when it was killed by salt it became even more so. Can a being that has teleported itself countless millions of miles across space really be killed by a handful of salt?

'But my faith in the BBC costumes and special effects people was restored when I saw the magnificent golden creature that Thea became. One couldn't help feeling awed at the magnificent spectacle that could hold you entranced just by the hypnotic effect of its eyes.'

The scripts are a little vague when it comes to certain details about the Fendahleen. It is never explained what causes the mark on the back of the neck of their victims, for example, nor what is their exact relationship with the core – they are a gestalt, we are told, and there must be twelve Fendahleen for it to operate, but otherwise it is all a bit of a mystery. However, these huge, slimy monsters creeping up to suck the life from their paralysed victims undoubtedly help to make *Image of the Fendahl* one of the last truly frightening *Doctor Who* stories. As Bentham wrote: 'Faults in the serial were hard to find, and where they did occur ... they were easily outweighed by all the many good points ... No matter if your taste is for costume, design, technical effects, photography, characterisation or storyline, *Image of the Fendahl* rated highly on them all.'

THE SUN MAKERS

Writer: Robert Holmes. **Director:** Pennant Roberts. **Designer:** Tony Snoaden. **Costumes:** Christine Rawlins. **Make-Up:** Janis Gould. **Incidental Music:** Dudley Simpson. **Visual Effects:** Peter Day, Peter Logan. **Film Cameraman:** John Tiley. **Film Editor:** Tariq Anwar. **Studio Lighting:** Derek Slee. **Studio Sound:** Michael McCarthy. **Production Assistant:** Leon Arnold. **Assistant Floor Manager:** Linda Graeme.

	First UK TX	Scheduled TX	Actual TX	Duration	Viewers	Chart Pos.
Part One	26/11/77	18.05	18.07	24'59"	8.5	48
Part Two	03/12/77	18.05	18.05	24'57"	9.5	36
Part Three	10/12/77	18.05	18.05	24'57"	8.9	35
Part Four	17/12/77	18.05	18.08	24'57"	8.4	42

Plot: The TARDIS arrives in the future on the planet Pluto where there are now six suns, a breathable atmosphere and a large industrial community. The Company that controls the planet exploits the workers, pays them a pittance and then taxes them on everything imaginable. The Doctor and Leela join forces with an underground band of rebels led by a man named Mandrel. They learn that the head of the Company's operations on Pluto, represented by the human official Gatherer Hade, is an Usurian known as the Collector. The Usurians enslave planets through economic means and then fleece the inhabitants with exorbitant taxes. The Company keeps the citizens in line by diffusing a calming gas, PCM, through the air conditioning system. The Doctor manages to stop this, and the workers then rise up against the Company and hurl Gatherer Hade to his death from the roof of a tall building. The Doctor meanwhile gains access to the Company computer and programs it to apply a two per cent growth tax. The Collector, unable to cope with the loss of his profits, reverts to his natural form – a type of poisonous fungus – and is rendered harmless.

Episode endings:

1. With Leela held hostage by the rebels, the Doctor is forced to attempt to withdraw some money – a thousand talmars – from a consumbank booth using a stolen and forged consumcard. Suddenly the door of the booth slams down and a strident alarm sounds. The booth fills with gas, and the Doctor is overcome.
2. Leela, K9 and two workers named Cordo and Bisham are trapped as a vehicle containing a group of armed guards rapidly approaches them down a corridor.
3. Leela is strapped to a trolley by the Collector's guards and rolled into a condensation chamber to face death by steaming. The Doctor tries to reach her through some vents, but time is running out as the temperature is building in the heat exchanger and the steam will very shortly have to be released into the system. Leela resolutely awaits her fate ...
4. Back in the TARDIS, K9 is waiting to finish the game of chess that he was on the point of winning against the Doctor when they arrived on Pluto. The Doctor makes an adjustment to the TARDIS controls that causes the ship to lurch violently, sending the chess pieces flying. He tells K9 that as soon as he has reset the coordinates, they can finish the game. K9 groans.

IT WAS MADE WHERE...?

Location filming: 13.06.77-17.06.77, 20.06.77
Locations: WD & HO Wills Tobacco Factory, Hartcliffe Way, Hartcliffe, Bristol, Avon; Camden Town Deep Tube Shelters, Stanmore Place, Camden Town, London, NW1.
Studio: 04.07.77-05.07.77 in TC3, 17.07.77-19.07.77 in TC6

ADDITIONAL CREDITED CAST

Hade (Richard Leech), Marn (Jonina Scott), Cordo (Roy Macready), Mandrel (William Simons), Goudry (Michael Keating), Veet (Adrienne Burgess), Nurse (Carole Hopkin[1]), Collector (Henry Woolf[2-4]), Bisham (David Rowlands[2-4]), Synge (Derek Crewe[3,4]), Commander (Colin McCormack[3,4]), Guard (Tom Kelly[4]).

THINGS TO WATCH OUT FOR

- The Gatherer uses many amusing forms of address for the Collector, including not only 'your Excellency' but also such gems as 'your Magnificence', 'your Sagacity' and 'your Enormity'.
- Michael Keating, now better known for his role as Vila in *Blake's 7*, plays the rebel Goudry.
- There are a number of Aztec influences in the story's costume and set designs – most notably in the Gatherer's crested hat, the badges worn by Company executives and the large 'sun god' symbol suspended at the back of the Gatherers' office. These

were a nod toward the original intention of set designer Tony Snoaden and costume designer Christine Rawlins to base their work on Mexican propogandist art; an idea that had been vetoed by director Pennant Roberts.

THINGS YOU MIGHT NOT HAVE KNOWN

• Robert Holmes wrote this story as a satire on the British tax system and there are numerous in-jokes within the script.

QUOTE, UNQUOTE

• **Cordo:** 'Praise the Company.' **Mandrel:** 'Stuff the Company!'
• **Hade:** 'Citizen Doc-tor. What an unusual name!' **The Doctor:** 'Yes, especially for an Ajacks.' **Hade:** 'Indeed. There are so many Wurgs and Keeks in Megropolis Three that I sometimes wonder how my colleague Gatherer Pyle manages to keep track of them all.'
• **The Collector:** [As Leela is about to be killed in the steamer, with microphones set up to broadcast her screams.] 'This is the moment when I get a real feeling of job satisfaction!'

ANALYSIS

Robert Holmes's time as script editor of *Doctor Who* is notable for the number of stories that he wrote (or heavily rewrote) himself, so it is fitting that it should have ended with another; and *The Sun Makers* provides a further excellent illustration of why many commentators regard him as one of the finest writers the series ever had. Indeed John McElroy, writing in the *Doctor Who Appreciation Society Yearbook 1977/78*, went so far as to suggest that it ranks 'as one of the best and most original *Doctor Who* stories ever':
'The story was so refreshing because it dealt with civil war – and although in the end the aliens were ultimately responsible, the story was delightfully free from "bug-eyed monsters".

'The story also worked because the humour level was judged to perfection – [for example] most of the corridors were named after [UK] tax forms (P45, P60 etc).'

It is the high level of sophisticated humour in the story that really sets it apart from those around it; in fact this is arguably the first story since season three's *The Myth Makers* to make humour its central focus, almost its *raison d'être*. Holmes uses a fairly straightforward, even clichéd science-fiction backdrop – that of a group of oppressed humans struggling to free themselves from the tyranny of their alien masters – to make what is in essence a wickedly barbed attack on bureaucracy and, in particular, the UK tax system as administered by the Inland Revenue.

'I thought this story an excellent political satire,' wrote Howard D Langford in *TARDIS* Volume 3 Number 3 dated May/June 1978, 'which well demonstrated the versatility of the *Doctor Who* format. The Gatherer was an amazing character, and his speeches especially to the Collector were very funny, run through with irony. The story was an example of how action and humour can be combined to make a point in an entertaining and thoughtful way. I liked the way the Gatherer was flung from the building, refusing to believe that rebellion was possible, demonstrating that he was just as much a pawn as the work units (very reminiscent of [Orwell's] *1984*) ...

'The Collector himself was a nice parody of certain attitudes to the economic system. The revelation that he was an alien being controlling the humans through economic means gave the story a new twist (and reminded me of the deception in *The Macra Terror*). The acting was very good indeed. I wouldn't say the story was a classic, but it wasn't far off.'

Andrew Pixley, reviewing the story in *In-Vision* Issue 27 dated October 1990, also thought that the humour worked extremely well:

'The emotionless nurse who tells Cordo that his father has died and then slams the screen shut as he offers her the Golden Death payment must remind many who have struggled with the officialdom of the Inland Revenue and got the "I'm sorry, you'll want our other department" brush off. The D-grade's discovery that the death tax has risen is also reminiscent of all those times when the everyday man finds that the rules set by officialdom have changed, and that ignorance of the law is no excuse.'

The BBC's Audience Research Report on the story's second episode suggests that it was greatly enjoyed by most contemporary viewers: 'In general, they warmly welcomed the more realistic, less "fantastic" nature of the theme (widely interpreted as an "exposé of super monopoly capitalism"), felt the story was well developed, intriguing and exciting, and liked the "more recognisable characters", considering them a nice change from monsters. In short, it was in their opinion, entertaining and even compelling viewing, which was "well up to the usual high standard of *Doctor Who* adventures". However, a substantial minority of the sample were less enthusiastic. They were in most instances unimpressed by this "departure from the outer galaxies and weird creatures", often feeling that a "new view of the future" was needed in order to retain the initial originality of this long-running series. Whilst they did criticise the story as "too far-fetched to be anything other than childish" and frequently condemned the characters as utterly stereotyped ("straight out of a third-rate *Mikado*"), most apparently thought it a fairly average "sci-fi" story (in which "goodies fight the baddies, as always") and rated it as such.'

The Report continued in a generally positive vein – indeed, this was to be perhaps the most positive of any produced on the fourth Doctor's episodes – and noted that the production values were highly acclaimed: 'The large majority thought the acting and the production "as good as ever" and rated both highly. Whilst several viewers liked what they saw as the "tongue in cheek" approach of the cast, most detected no change from the normal and thought the acting "of the usual high standard". Louise Jameson (Leela) was singled out for special praise for her performance in this episode, many feeling that she was more assured now than she had been previously ... There was particular praise for the imaginative and ingenious sets and costumes, which were in many viewers' opinions a welcome change from the disused quarries and dull army surroundings which have "featured so often of late", and some especially liked the introduction of K9.'

K9 drew a particularly enthusiastic response from children in the BBC's sample (who as usual had little but praise for the episode in general) and it does indeed fit in quite well in this story – despite its obvious technical limitations. It is however impossible to imagine K9 having worked in the context of one of the gothic horror stories produced by Philip Hinchcliffe, and its adoption as a regular in this season gives a good indication of the lighter, more fantastical quality that the series took on under Graham Williams.

'Several critics of *Doctor Who* have observed that the series' realism, or at least grittiness, declined during the late seventies,' noted David Owen, also in *In-Vision* Issue 27. 'While this can be attributed in part to intervention by powers above the production office calling for the show's shock content to be toned down, a considerable shift in [its] production style over and above this can be observed.

'Compare *The Sun Makers* with Robert Holmes's four-parter of the previous season –

The Deadly Assassin. Both stories parody aspects of contemporary human society. Yet by comparison the latter seems to hammer its point home with all the subtlety of a bolt from K9's nose. The content has little to do with this – it is the production style alone which makes this adventure more fitting for the label "family viewing" than its dozen or so predecessors. Which perhaps just goes to prove the old maxim that it's not *what* you say, it's the *way* that you say it.'

Pixley summed things up well: '*The Sun Makers* was a breath of fresh air. With its wacky dialogue and dose of Holmesian characters the story was a complete change from the dark intensities of Fetch Priory and Fang Rock, and even the fantastic voyage to the Bi-Al Foundation. Now it stands up as a clear indication of what was to come.'

UNDERWORLD

Writer: Bob Baker, Dave Martin. **Director:** Norman Stewart. **Designer:** Dick Coles. **Costumes:** Rupert Jarvis. **Make-Up:** Cecile Hay-Arthur. **Incidental Music:** Dudley Simpson. **Visual Effects:** Richard Conway. **Film Cameraman:** unknown. **Film Editor:** Richard Trevor. **Studio Lighting:** Mike Jefferies. **Studio Sound:** Richard Chubb. **Production Assistant:** Mike Cager. **Assistant Floor Manager:** Gary Downie.

	First UK TX	Scheduled TX	Actual TX	Duration	Viewers	Chart Pos.
Part One	07/01/78	18.25	18.25	22'36"	8.9	50
Part Two	14/01/78	18.25	18.27	21'27"	9.1	37
Part Three	21/01/78	18.25*	18.31	22'21"	8.9	37
Part Four	28/01/78	18.25	18.29	22'53"	11.7	27

* This episode was transmitted approximately six minutes late as the preceding programme, *Grandstand*, overran to give additional coverage to a Rugby Union international.

Plot: The TARDIS arrives on a Minyan space craft, the *R1C*, commanded by a man named Jackson. Jackson and his crew are on a long quest to recover the Minyan race banks from a ship called the *P7E* which left their planet centuries ago. The Doctor helps to free the *R1C* after it becomes buried in a meteorite storm, but it then crashes into another newly-formed planet. Inside the planet is a system of caves at the heart of which is the *P7E*. The *P7E*'s computer, the Oracle, was programmed to protect the race banks but subsequently went insane and – with the aid of its robotic servants, the Seers – imposed its rule upon the Minyan survivors and their descendants. It allows Jackson to take what appear to be the race banks, but they are actually imitations containing fission grenades. The Doctor realises the deception and obtains the genuine race banks. He then tricks the Oracle's guards into taking the grenades back to their leader. The resulting explosion destroys the planet and the *P7E* and boosts the *R1C* off on a voyage to Minyos II, carrying with it the Minyan survivors.

Episode endings:
1. Meteorites build up around the hull of the *R1C*, threatening to bury it at the heart of a new planet.

2. Fumigating gas floods into the caves around the Doctor as he struggles to gain access to the pumping controls and reverse the flow. The gas billows around him and he is on the point of being overcome.

3. The Doctor and Leela are attempting to gain access to the *P7E* by hiding in a dump truck used for transporting rocks to a crusher. The Minyan pushing the truck stumbles and loses his grip on it. The truck tips up, depositing the Doctor and Leela in the mouth of the crusher.

4. In the TARDIS control room, the Doctor tells Leela of Jason and the Argonauts and ponders that such myths might be not just stories of the past but also prophesies of the future. He asks K9 what he thinks and, to his annoyance, the robot dog disagrees. The Doctor storms out and Leela kisses K9 on the end of his nose.

IT WAS MADE WHERE...?

Studio: 03.10.77-04.10.77, 15.10.77-18.10.77 all in TC3, 21.10.77 (studio unknown)

ADDITIONAL CREDITED CAST

Jackson (James Maxwell), Herrick (Alan Lake), Orfe (Jonathan Newth), Tala (Imogen Bickford-Smith), Rask (James Marcus[2-4]), Tarn (Godfrey James[2-4]), Idmon (Jimmy Gardner[2-4]), Idas (Norman Tipton[2-4]), Guard Klimt (Jay Neill[2]), Ankh (Frank Jarvis[3,4]), Lakh (Richard Shaw[3,4]), Naia (Stacey Tendeter[3,4]), Voice of the Oracle (Christine Pollon[3,4]).

THINGS TO WATCH OUT FOR

- The Minyans have ingeniously designed shield guns – which, strangely, Leela knows how to operate apparently without having to be shown.
- The story was inspired by the myth of Jason and the Argonauts' quest for the Golden Fleece.

THINGS YOU MIGHT NOT HAVE KNOWN

- The sets of the Minyan spacecraft proved much more expensive than anticipated, leaving no scenery budget for the scenes set inside the new planet. To overcome this problem, Colour Separation Overlay was used in conjunction with models to give the impression of caves and tunnels.
- Alan Lake, who played Herrick, one of Jackson's crew, was the husband of Diana Dors.
- Imogen Bickford-Smith, who played Tala, another crew member, was optimistically promoted by her agent as being the next *Doctor Who* companion, as Louise Jameson had announced her intention to leave the series.

QUOTE, UNQUOTE

- **Jackson/Herrick/Orfe/Tala:** 'The quest is the quest!'
- **The Doctor:** 'Have you ever heard of the Flying Dutchman?' **Leela:** 'No.' **The Doctor:** 'Pity. I've often wondered who he was.'
- **Voice of the Oracle:** 'There are no gods but me! Have I not created myself?'

ANALYSIS

It has sometimes been suggested that *Doctor Who* is at its best when its roots are showing. Those who hold that view would no doubt find much to admire in

4 FOURTH DOCTOR

Underworld. 'Bob Baker and Dave Martin's second [story] for the fifteenth season ... is one of a long line ... with an uncredited extra author,' suggested Andrew Martin in *In-Vision* Issue 28 dated November 1990. 'In this case it is not the script editor or another trusted, experienced writer but the generations of Greek storytellers who created and refined the myth of Jason and the Argonauts. While stories such as *The Brain of Morbius* are reworkings of classic tales of literature under greater or lesser disguise, *Underworld* is an instance of a story owing so much to its roots that the authors feel obliged to acknowledge the fact in its closing moments: "I called Jackson 'Jason'? ... Jason was another captain on a long quest."'

It seems obvious that writers Baker and Martin intended the viewer to realise at an early stage that their story was based on Greek myth, and to take delight in spotting things like the similarities between names – Jackson/Jason, Herrick/Heracles, Tala/Atalanta, Orfe/Orpheus, Minyos/Minos, *R1C*/Argossey, *P7E*/Persephone, and so on – and the parallels between the Minyan race banks and the Golden Fleece sought by Jason and his crew. This actually works rather well, giving the story an extra level and lending the whole thing a mythic quality.

Underworld is however a story that has had a generally bad press over the years. The following comments by Howard D Langford in *TARDIS* Volume 3 Number 3 dated May/June 1978 are fairly typical: '*Underworld* I thought was a terrible story, with virtually nothing to recommend it. The first episode was very tedious, and the plot in general seemed very weak. The sets were bad, the acting was bad, the script was bad. There was far too much reliance on weapons. One of the most important characteristics of the Doctor has always been that he never carries a gun, but uses his wits to get out of tricky situations. The coming of K9 is a curse which has changed all this and has worked for ill on both the originality of the scripts and the fame of the Doctor as a moral agent who disapproves of violence except in extreme circumstances. As for the last episode – oh no! Not another megalomaniac computer.' Gordon Blows, reviewing the story in the *Doctor Who Appreciation Society Yearbook 1977/78*, also disliked the ending: 'Unfortunately, what started out to be an inventive and original story for *Doctor Who* disintegrated into a very over-used idea with the introduction of the Oracle. As the Doctor himself put it, "Simply ... another machine with megalomania!". The story became very close to ... *The Face of Evil*, with the slaves taking the place of Leela's Sevateem and the robots the place of the acolytes.'

Like the same writers' earlier story *The Invisible Enemy*, *Underworld* relies to an unusually great degree on visual effects. The modelwork on this occasion is arguably some of the finest ever seen in the series, the best shot of all being the one where the *R1C* crashes through the soft surface of the newly-formed planet around the *P7E*. The realisation of the robotic Seers, on the other hand, is less impressive. 'It's never really explained who or what the Seers are,' noted Keith Miller in *Doctor Who Digest* Number 8 dated April 1978, 'but toward the end of [Part Three] they reveal themselves as they [lift] off their [masks] and we see two of the most hilarious aliens ever seen on TV. Two jumping beans with eyes!' Undoubtedly the most contentious aspect of the production, however, is its very extensive use of CSO, by way of which all the scenes set in the caves of the planet were achieved. This has come in for some scathing criticism from reviewers, but is actually quite brilliantly done. Admittedly the viewer is never for one moment fooled into believing that the characters are walking through a real environment, but there is remarkably little of the peripheral fringing or image loss often associated with this effect (apparently it looks even better if watched in black and white), and in a strange sort of way it actually suits the slightly unreal quality of the Oracle's domain. In any event, given how difficult and time-consuming CSO effects can be to get right, one can only marvel at the technical prowess and commitment of all those involved in achieving these scenes.

There is far more to admire in *Underworld* than its reputation would suggest, and overall it stands up well as a good example of the *Doctor Who* of this period.

THE INVASION OF TIME

Writer: David Agnew*. **Director:** Gerald Blake. **Designer:** Barbara Gosnold. **Costumes:** Dee Kelly. **Make-Up:** Maureen Winslade. **Incidental Music:** Dudley Simpson. **Visual Effects:** Colin Mapson, Richard Conway. **Film Cameraman:** Ken Westbury. **Film Editor:** Chris Wimble. **OB Cameraman:** David Goutier, Alan Hayward. **Studio Lighting:** Mike Jefferies. **Studio Sound:** Anthony Philpott. **Production Assistant:** Colin Dudley. **Assistant Floor Manager:** Terry Winders, Romey Allison.

* This was a pseudonym for Graham Williams and Anthony Read.

	First UK TX	Scheduled TX	Actual TX	Duration	Viewers	Chart Pos.
Part One	04/02/78	18.25	18.25	25'00"	11.2	28
Part Two	11/02/78	18.25	18.24	25'00"	11.4	29
Part Three	18/02/78	18.25	18.24	25'00"	9.5	47
Part Four	25/02/78	18.25	18.25	23'31"	10.9	28
Part Five	04/03/78	18.25	18.27	25'00"	10.3	32
Part Six	11/03/78	18.25	18.25	25'44"	9.8	35

Plot: After a meeting in space with a group of unseen aliens the Doctor returns to Gallifrey and claims the presidency of the Time Lords. Leela meanwhile tries to work out why he is behaving out of character. At his induction, the Doctor is 'crowned' with a device giving him access to the Matrix. He then arranges for the transduction barriers around Gallifrey to be put out of action by K9. When this is done, his alien 'friends' materialise. They are telepathic invaders called Vardans. The Doctor links K9 to the Matrix in order to determine their point of origin. His plan is to place a time loop around their home planet, but he must avoid arousing their suspicions – hence his erratic behaviour. He banishes Leela to the wastelands of outer Gallifrey for fear that she might unintentionally jeopardise his plans. There she meets a group of Gallifreyan outsiders, and together they organise an attack on the Capitol to fight off the invaders. The Doctor finally springs his trap and the Vardans are banished. Then, however, Gallifrey is invaded by Sontarans who, unknown to the Doctor, were using the Vardans to enable them to conquer the Time Lords. The Doctor uses knowledge extracted from the Matrix by K9 to construct a forbidden de-mat gun, activated by the Great Key of Rassilon. He then uses this to kill the Sontarans, although his memory of recent events is wiped in the process. Leela announces that she wishes to stay behind with Andred, one of the Chancellery guards, with

FOURTH DOCTOR

whom she has fallen in love. K9 elects to remain with her.

Episode endings:
1. The presidential induction ceremony reaches its conclusion as the Matrix circlet is placed on the Doctor's head. Suddenly he writhes in pain and falls to the floor, clutching at the circlet.
2. K9 blasts the transduction barrier controls and the Vardan ship enters Gallifreyan space. The Doctor gathers the senior Time Lords in the Panopticon and introduces them to their new masters – the Vardans. Three shimmering shapes appear as the Doctor laughs in triumph.
3. The Doctor returns to the TARDIS, where K9 has been tracing the Vardans' point of origin. He places the matrix circlet on K9's head. Suddenly Andred enters the TARDIS with some guards. He sentences the Doctor to death as a traitor and raises his gun.
4. With the Vardan threat banished, the Doctor announces to Leela, Andred, Castellan Kelner and the others assembled in the Panopticon that the future of Gallifrey is assured. Realising that they are not looking at him, he turns to see four Sontarans standing on the steps behind him. The foremost Sontaran raises its gun and aims it at him.
5. As the Sontaran fleet approaches Gallifrey, Castellan Kelner, now cooperating with the Sontaran leader Stor, reverses the stabiliser banks and initiates a process that will throw the Doctor's TARDIS into a black star.
6. The Doctor leaves Leela to stay with Andred and K9 to look after her. As the TARDIS dematerialises, Leela wonders if the Doctor will be lonely. Inside, the Doctor produces a large box with 'K9 MII' printed on the side. He stands at the console, looks into the distance and smiles broadly.

IT WAS MADE WHERE...?

Bray filming: 01.11.77-02.11.77
Studio: 06.11.77-08.11.77 in TC8
Location filming: 14.11.77-15.11.77, 17.11.77-18.11.77, 13.12.77-16.12.77
Locations: Beachfields Quarry, Cormongers Lane, Redhill, Surrey; St Anne's Hospital, Redstone Hill, Redhill, Surrey; British Oxygen, Blacks Road, Hammersmith Broadway, London, W6.
OB: 16.11.77, 05.12.77-09.12.77, 12.12.77-16.12.77
Location: St Anne's Hospital, Redstone Hill, Redhill, Surrey.
Studio: 18.12.77 (gallery only) in TC8, 21.12.77, 04.01.78 (both gallery only) both in TC8, 05.02.78 (gallery only) in TC8

ADDITIONAL CREDITED CAST

Vardans (Stan McGowan[1-4], Tom Kelly[1,2,4]), Andred (Christopher Tranchell*), Kelner (Milton Johns), Borusa (John Arnatt[1-3,5,6]), Lord Gomer (Dennis Edwards[1-3]), Lord Savar (Reginald Jessup[1]), Gold Usher (Charles Morgan[1-3]), Guard (Christopher Christou[2**]), Rodan (Hilary Ryan[2-6]), Ablif (Ray Callaghan[3-5]), Jasko (Michael Mundell[3-5]), Bodyguard (Michael Harley[3***]), Nesbin (Max Faulkner[3-6]), Presta (Gai Smith[3-6]), Castellan Guard (Eric Danot[4****]), Stor (Derek Deadman[4-6]), Sontaran (Stuart Fell[5,6*****]).

* Christopher Tranchell was credited as 'Chris Tranchell' on Parts Three to Six inclusive.
** Also in Parts One and Three, but uncredited.

*** Also in Parts One, Two and Four, but uncredited.
**** Also in Parts One, Two and Three, but uncredited.
***** Also in Part Four, but uncredited.
Note: There is no voice credit for K9 on Part Five as he does not speak in this episode.

POPULAR MYTHS

- Robert Holmes and Terrance Dicks were involved in the writing of this story. (They weren't, although it was on Holmes's advice that Graham Williams and Anthony Read structured it as a four-part segment followed by an effectively separate two-part segment.)
- The story was originally to have ended with a scene in which the Sontarans deferred to the Doctor and knelt before him. (This myth arose when early publicity stills for the story showed the Sontarans apparently kneeling before the Doctor. These were in fact taken from a scene in Part Five in which Chancellor Borusa blasts the Sontarans with sound and they fall to their knees, clutching their helmets in pain.)
- Although three Sontarans are seen to enter the TARDIS, only two are killed, meaning that there is still a Sontaran lost in the TARDIS somewhere. (Only two Sontarans, Stor plus a trooper, are seen to enter. The trooper is killed with the de-mat gun, and Stor is also eventually killed with the same weapon, but outside the TARDIS.)
- The characters living outside the Time Lords' Citadel are the Shabogans, as mentioned in *The Deadly Assassin*. (There is nothing to link the two. In *The Deadly Assassin*, the Shabogans were mentioned by Spandrell as being responsible for vandalism around the Citadel. In this story, the outsiders are clearly described as Time Lords who have left the Citadel for varying reasons, and it seems unlikely that they would have returned to carry out acts of petty damage.)

THINGS TO WATCH OUT FOR

- A great deal of the TARDIS's interior is seen in this story. Among the rooms glimpsed are a swimming pool (described by the Doctor as a bathroom), a changing room, an art gallery and numerous corridors.
- Actor Derek Deadman's Cockney accent is unfortunately very noticeable in his performance as the Sontaran leader Stor.
- The Sontarans in this story have three fingers on each hand as in *The Time Warrior*, rather than five as in *The Sontaran Experiment*.

THINGS YOU MIGHT NOT HAVE KNOWN

- *The Invasion of Time* was a replacement for another story which fell through. This was *The Killer Cats of Geng Singh* (spelling uncertain) by David Weir. *The Invasion of Time* was hastily written by producer Graham Williams and script editor Anthony Read and transmitted under a BBC in-house pseudonym, David Agnew.

QUOTE, UNQUOTE

- **K9:** [To the TARDIS] 'You are a very stupid machine.'
- **Leela:** 'Discussion is for the wise or the helpless and I am neither.'
- **Andred:** 'You have access to the greatest source of knowledge in the universe.' **The Doctor:** 'Well, I do talk to myself sometimes.'

FOURTH DOCTOR

- **Stor:** [About the TARDIS] 'This machine is a load of obsolete rubbish.'
- **Stor:** 'If we cannot control the power of the Time Lords then we shall destroy it.'

ANALYSIS

After the previous season's acclaimed *The Talons of Weng-Chiang*, viewers could have been forgiven for expecting something rather special from the now-traditional closing six-parter. What they got with *The Invasion of Time* was something of a mess. To be fair, Graham Williams and Anthony Read had been obliged to write the scripts in record time as an emergency measure when the story originally planned to fill this slot fell through, and the production had been beset by problems – including near cancellation due to industrial action – throughout. It is just unfortunate that all these behind the scenes difficulties were reflected in the end product.

Keith Miller, writing in *Doctor Who Digest* Number 8 dated April 1978, hated the story with a vengeance: '*The Invasion of Time* was a complete and utter disaster … The whole six episodes was such a waste of time, actors and expense. The first four episodes were unbelievably *bad*, and the last two *worse*. The "special" effects were shabby ("Look, mummy, pieces of bacofoil with Glasgow accents have invaded Gallifrey!"), the script so confusing … and the acting … pathetic.

'The Sontaran episodes – I just couldn't believe my eyes. How *Doctor Who* could sink so *low*, I've no idea. The TARDIS scenes were abominable … Good grief, Graham Williams. What on earth do you think you're doing?'

Nick Pegg, on the other hand, argued in *Spectrox* VIII in 1990 that the story's detractors are rather missing the point: 'If people dismiss *The Invasion of Time* for devaluing or debunking the Time Lords, surely they're being rather selective in their appraisal of what is after all a clear, phased debunking of the Hinchcliffe [and] Holmes team's debunking of what had gone before. Gallifrey is certainly at its most complex and fascinating; its torpid evanescence, which Holmes and Maloney were content to image a season earlier as a series of (wonderfully evocative) gothic/haunted house signifiers, is reinvented for *The Invasion of Time* in accordance with Williams's equally rapacious but rather less one-track eclecticism, alongside a playful sense of art-house intellectualism – the atmosphere of seedy decline is still there, but the dusty shadows and cloistered galleries of *The Deadly Assassin* … give way to the sort of modern symptoms of cultural decline which are part of our immediate postmodern experience of life – the vaulted cobwebby cloisters are replaced by equally impractical diagonally-slashed corridors that probably seemed like a good idea to some piss-bored Time Lord architect; horrid one-coloured moulded plastic chairs appear with chunderous regularity; Coordinator Engin's intimidatingly mysterious bleepy HQ is supplanted by control rooms veering towards pukey late-seventies Bang & Olufsen kitsch – chairs and consoles are designer-moulded, there are desk-top executive toys and garish drinks sipped through daft loop-the-loop straws while communications and software storage depend on silly little coloured spheres …'

The changing depiction of the Time Lords was also of interest to David Fychan in *Oracle* Volume 2 Number 2 dated November 1978: 'This was a controversial [story]. It was clearly an attempt both to please *Doctor Who* fans and to cure the continuity errors made in *The Deadly Assassin*. To me it failed, and was therefore wasteful of an otherwise sound story ... Where [the writers] tried to correct *The Deadly Assassin* (such as over [the lack of] female Time Lords), they [only] complicated matters. Just as we were working out that female Time Lords did not exist, we were presented with one ... The Time Lords were made slightly more powerful, but still rather naïve – and we saw very few of them about. However, there were extremely interesting moments – and some great dialogue (viz: "His hearts are in the right places"). Especially interesting [were] the induction ceremony, ... the fact that the Castellan keeps files on political activists and the existence of a few Time Lords "outside".'

The plot – such as it is – involves the Doctor wanting, for reasons best known to himself, to trap the Vardans in a time loop, and failing to realise that his actions will leave Gallifrey open to invasion by the Sontarans. Like season thirteen's six-parter *The Seeds of Doom*, it can be subdivided into two distinct sections. The first, consisting of Parts One to Four, involves the Doctor acting strangely and appearing to help the Vardans invade Gallifrey, while the second, consisting of Parts Five and Six, features the Sontarans in what appears to be a tacked-on run-around. Howard D Langford, writing in *TARDIS* Volume 3 Number 3 dated May/June 1978, felt: 'The saving grace of the story [was] the appearance of the Sontarans *en masse* and the restatement of their own personal philosophy.' Deanne Holding, however, took the opposite view in *Baker's Best* in 1981: 'The first four episodes were intriguing, exciting and for the most part quite original in concept. Unfortunately, their promise was let down by [Parts Five and Six] as the drama lost its grip and the elements of surprise and tension evaporated.'

One of the story's main problems is a lack of good characters. Of the Time Lords, only John Arnatt's shrewd, dignified Chancellor Borusa and Milton Johns's conniving, obsequious Castellan Kelner hold the viewer's interest. The 'outsiders' are bland and vapid, and Rodan and Andred are hopeless. The Vardans meanwhile are one of the most pathetic alien races ever to be featured in the series. Initially they appear to be large pointy-headed creatures, but the viewer then realises that it is only the backs of their chairs that have been seen! When they finally show themselves on Gallifrey, they seem to consist of sheets of tinfoil that crinkle in the breeze – which raises the question why they need to sit in chairs in the first place; how does a formless creature 'sit' anywhere? Finally they transform themselves into rather boring humanoids with silly uniforms like something out of an old *Flash Gordon* serial. Very disappointing. They could perhaps have been improved had they been played by actors with authoritative voices, but this was not the case. Stan McGowan in particular sounds as though he is simply reading his lines, and there is no power therein. The Sontarans too fare badly, mainly due to Derek Deadman's variable performance as Commander Stor. Their motivation seems to be to obtain the secrets of the Time Lords, but all they do is run around a lot, get lost in the TARDIS, and finally attempt to blow the place to smithereens. Even Tom Baker is somewhat below par at times here as he – or director Gerald Blake – allows his usual madcap humour to descend into silliness in scenes such as the one where the Doctor plays hopscotch in the Citadel corridors, or where he continually trips as he passes a certain point within the TARDIS – although it must be acknowledged that his performance in some of the scenes where he is pretending to be the Vardans' ally is very intense and powerful. Perhaps the ultimate disappointment is the frankly unbelievable conclusion wherein Leela opts to stay with a man she hardly knows.

On a more positive note, the story does boast some very good special effects. The opening shot of the Vardan ship is reminiscent of the opening of *Star Wars* and imparts a similar sense of wonder, and the later shots of the Sontaran ship approaching Gallifrey are excellent. It is just a shame that the rest of the production is not up to this standard.

To add to all the many problems that Graham Williams had faced during his first year on *Doctor Who*, Leela had to be written out in *The Invasion of Time* after Louise Jameson decided against renewing her contract. Consequently a new companion character would have to be devised and cast in time for the next production block. *The Invasion of Time* had seen perhaps the greatest shift yet toward the more overtly humorous style that Williams was attempting to cultivate. There were indeed some within the BBC who considered that this had gone too far, and it was agreed that all the series' directors should in future receive a memo reminding them of the need to preserve the essentially serious nature of the stories. It was also agreed that Tom Baker's frequent and often comedic scripting suggestions and ad libs should be kept more closely in check during the course of the following season – a season that would adopt a format unprecedented in *Doctor Who*'s history.

THE SEARCH FOR THE KEY TO TIME

The unusual nature of season sixteen lies in the fact that its six individual stories are linked by a single over-arching plot. This idea had been conceived by Graham Williams when he was first appointed as producer and had originally been considered as the basis for season fifteen. The three page proposal put together by Williams for this purpose was accepted by Head of Serials Graeme McDonald, but the enforced abandonment of Terrance Dicks's vampire tale *The Witch Lords* and the shortage of time remaining for advance planning meant that it could not in the end be taken forward for that season. Williams therefore decided to hold it over and use it for season sixteen instead.

The basic premise of Williams's proposal was that there should be a higher power above the Time Lords, and that this should consist of two equal but opposing forces – the White Guardian, standing for 'good' and 'construction', and the Black Guardian, standing for 'evil' and 'destruction' – holding the cosmos in balance. The Doctor would be given by the White Guardian the task of retrieving the six scattered segments of the cube-shaped Key to Time – the source of the Guardians' power – and reassembling them in order to prevent the balance from being destroyed. Each of the six individual stories making up the twenty-six episode season would revolve around the search for one of the six segments but would be sufficiently self-contained to be enjoyed in its own right. What Williams did not have at the outset, however, was a clear idea of how the over-arching plot of the quest for the six segments should be resolved – that was something that would have to be worked out during the scripting of the season …

DOCTOR WHO SEASON SIXTEEN (1978-1979)

Regular Cast:
Doctor Who (Tom Baker)
Romana (Mary Tamm)
Voice of K9 (John Leeson)*

* Except on *The Power of Kroll*, in which K9 does not appear.

Regular Crew:
Producer: Graham Williams.
Script Editor: Anthony Read*.
Production Unit Manager: John Nathan-Turner.
Title Music: Ron Grainer and the BBC Radiophonic Workshop, arranged by Delia Derbyshire.
Special Sounds: Dick Mills except on *The Stones of Blood*. Liz Parker on *The Stones of Blood*.

* Douglas Adams also contributed to the script editing of *The Armageddon Factor* but was uncredited on screen.

The new character devised by Graham Williams as a replacement for Leela (after he had unsuccessfully attempted to persuade Elisabeth Sladen to return as Sarah Jane Smith) was a female Time Lord named Romanadvoratrelundar (or Romana for short) – the first companion of the Doctor's own race since his grand-daughter Susan in the series' first ten stories. He saw her as an 'ice maiden' in the mould of classic film star Grace Kelly, and envisaged that her academic prowess would be balanced by naïvety and a lack of practical experience. The actress chosen for the part, apparently out of some three thousand applicants, was Mary Tamm, previously best known for her role in the 1974 Columbia film production *The Odessa File*. K9 was also kept on as a companion – a relatively late decision – after Williams received assurances from the Visual Effects Department that the prop's internal workings could be redesigned to make it quieter and more controllable. This refit was carried out in collaboration with a firm called Slough Radio Control, who allowed employee Nigel Brackley to be seconded to *Doctor Who* on a semi-permanent basis to look after the mechanical dog. This season would also see Tom Baker matching his predecessor Jon Pertwee's five year stint on the series and well on his way to becoming the longest-serving of all the Doctors.

THE RIBOS OPERATION

Writer: Robert Holmes. **Director:** George Spenton-Foster. **Designer:** Ken Ledsham. **Costumes:** June Hudson. **Make-Up:** Christine Walmesley-Cotham. **Incidental Music:** Dudley Simpson. **Visual Effects:** Dave Havard. **Studio Lighting:** Jimmy Purdie. **Studio Sound:** Richard Chubb. **Production Assistant:** Jane Shirley. **Assistant Floor Manager:** Richard Cox.

	First UK TX	Scheduled TX	Actual TX	Duration	Viewers	Chart Pos.
Part One	02/09/78	17.45	17.44	25'02"	8.3	42
Part Two	09/09/78	18.20	18.21	24'46"	8.1	36
Part Three	16/09/78	18.30	18.32	24'42"	7.9	38
Part Four	23/09/78	18.20	18.21	24'50"	8.2	36

Plot: The White Guardian gives the Doctor a quest to find the six disguised segments of the Key to Time which, when assembled, will be used to restore the balance of the cosmos. To aid him he is given a new companion, a female Time Lord called Romana, and a tracer device. He tracks the first segment to the city of Shur on the planet Ribos. There con men Garron and Unstoffe are engaged in a scam to sell the entire planet to the Graff Vynda-K, deposed ruler of Levithia. The Graff has been tricked into believing that Ribos is a rich source of jethrik, a rare mineral vital for achieving space warp drive. His interest is further piqued when he sees a large lump of the mineral on display in a reliquary. The Doctor realises that this is actually the first segment but, before he can steal it, Unstoffe spirits it away. The Graff, having discovered the trick that has been played on him, hunts the con men down and captures them, along with the time travellers, in the catacombs beneath the city. He is on the point of having them executed when Riban guards blow up the entrance to the catacombs. The death of his loyal officer

Sholakh in the ensuing rock fall unhinges the Graff's mind. He storms into the dust and is killed by a thermite bomb with which he had intended to destroy the catacombs. The Doctor, Romana and K9 depart with the jethrik, leaving Garron and Unstoffe to make off with the Graff's ship of plundered loot.

Episode endings:

1. The Doctor and Romana are investigating the reliquary, the vicious Shrivenzale creature left on guard having been fed drugged meat by Unstoffe. The exit door suddenly starts to slide shut, threatening to trap them inside, and the Doctor quickly comes to Romana's aid in trying to halt its descent. Beyond the door, the Shrivenzale, its jaws soaked in blood, starts to stir ...
2. The Doctor, Romana and Garron are confronted by the Graff Vynda-K and his men. The Graff, asserting that no-one makes a fool of him and lives, orders that they be executed. Sholakh tells the guards to take aim and prepare to fire ...
3. The Doctor, Romana, Garron and K9 hide in the catacombs as the Graff and his men search for them. The Doctor inadvertently disturbs a skull with his foot, and it clatters to the ground, giving them away. The Graff is triumphant.
4. At the Doctor's invitation, Romana touches the tracer to the lump of jethrik, which is transformed into the first segment. 'Simple, wasn't it?' suggests the Doctor drily. 'Only five more to go.'

It Was Made Where...?

Studio: 09.04.78-11.04.78, 24.04.78-25.04.78 all in TC4, 03.05.78 (gallery only) in TC3.

Additional Credited Cast

The Guardian (Cyril Luckham[1]), Garron (Iain Cuthbertson), Unstoffe (Nigel Plaskitt), Graff Vynda-K (Paul Seed), Sholakh (Robert Keegan), Captain (Prentis Hancock), Shrieves (Oliver Maguire, John Hamill[1,2]), Binro (Timothy Bateson[3,4]), The Seeker (Ann Tirard[3,4]).

Note: K9 does not appear in and is not credited on Part Two.

Things To Watch Out For

- There are fine performances from this story's guest cast, including Timothy Bateson as Binro the Heretic and Iain Cuthbertson, particularly well known for his role as Charlie Endell in LWT's *Budgie* and its follow up series *Charles Endell Esquire*, as Garron. Nigel Plaskitt, seen here as Unstoffe, was better known for playing a young man named Malcolm in a series of television commercials for Vick's Sinex nasal spray.
- The Key to Time was a prop consisting of six clear resin segments that fitted together to form a cube. Several copies were constructed for use in the season's recording, and a complete Key was later sold at auction for £1300.

Things You Might Not Have Known

- Working titles: *Operation*, *The Ribos File*.

- **The Doctor:** 'Look, I'm sure there must be plenty of other Time Lords who'd be delighted ...' **The Guardian:** 'I have chosen you, Doctor.' **The Doctor:** 'I was afraid you might say that. Ah! You want me to volunteer, is that it? And if I don't?' **The Guardian:** 'Nothing.' **The Doctor:** 'You mean nothing'll happen to me?' **The Guardian:** 'Nothing. Ever.'
- **The Doctor:** 'I'll call you Romana.' **Romana:** 'I don't like Romana.' **The Doctor:** 'It's either Romana or Fred. **Romana:** All right, call me Fred.'
- **Binro:** 'Have you ever looked up at the sky at night and seen those little lights? They are *not* ice crystals! I believe they are suns just like our own sun, and perhaps each sun has other worlds of its own, just as Ribos is a world... I have made measurements of those little lights, and of our own sun, and I can prove that Ribos *moves*; it circles the sun, travelling far away and returning ...'

The sixteenth season – often referred to simply as the Key to Time season – gets off to an excellent start with a cracking set of scripts from Robert Holmes, brought to the screen with great style by director George Spenton-Foster. The opening scene, setting up the season's over-arching plot, was actually the work not of Holmes but of script editor Anthony Read. It is no less well written, however, and successfully establishes the White Guardian and his unseen Black counterpart as important new characters in the *Doctor Who* universe, representing a previously unknown power above the Time Lords themselves. 'It is somewhat ironic that after Robert Holmes successfully destroyed the image of Time Lords as superior beings,' observed Jan Vincent-Rudzki in *TARDIS* Volume 3 Number 6 dated December 1978, 'he finds in his most recent story the introduction of another super being, the White Guardian ... The Guardian himself is one of those marvellous ideas in the [series]. Instead of an awe-inspiring being we see someone calmly sitting in a chair chatting about the end of order in the universe, although I have no idea why the Guardian could not get each segment for himself.'

'It's traditional to talk a bit about Taoism [when discussing the Key to Time and the Guardians],' noted Tat Wood in *Perigosto Stick* Issue One dated February 1991, 'so I'll point out that the White Guardian uses the word "balance" four times in two minutes (five if you count "equilibrium"). One of the interesting features of Taoism is that it discourages any belief in privileged viewpoints – all aspects are equally valid. The underlying principle of this philosophy is the dynamic harmony and unity of opposing forces. Note the word "dynamic". The point is not the total exclusion of anything you don't want to accept, but embracing the necessity of both sides ...

'Now it's very tempting ... to go on and say that the Ice and Sun Gods [on Ribos] correspond to the Guardians, but this leads to [a] paradox ...: Binro's whole life is spent trying to get away from the parochial thinking that has Ribos at the centre of the universe and duelling gods over it. The shift in perspective from the astrological to the astronomical is at the core of the series ... If the local superstition is right all along, then Binro was only comic relief ..., and the Doctor's multitudinous speeches about superstition are pure humbug. The weight of past experience is on the side of Binro and the Doctor, so the Guardians have to be incorporated into the multiplex viewpoint. The Guardians are therefore not simply combatants but two sides of the same coin, as inseparable as a candle and the shadows it casts: it is the balance between them which is important.'

Binro is perhaps the most fascinating and well written of all the characters in the main part of the story set on Ribos – although Garron and Unstoffe are also highly memorable. In a sense the elderly heretic is irrelevant to the main plot, but at the same time he is the principal medium through which Holmes explores its underlying theme of superstition versus science.

'Holmes was a masterly creator of alien worlds,' wrote Tim Munro in *Star Begotten* Vol 4. No. 2 dated autumn 1990, 'who knew that all *Doctor Who*'s budgetary failings faded into insignificance if the sheer power of words could be harnessed to convince an audience that beyond the scenes on the screen there existed a whole real planetful of real people. To create this illusion of reality he deployed incredible detail. In the case of Ribos itself, we are fed scraps of its geography, its history, its economics, its class system and even its political and religious structures. Similarly we are given a jigsaw of information about the society which exists beyond it – the Cyrrhenic Alliance and its mighty galactic empire, a volatile mixture of expansionist military dictatorship and political dog-fight from which sprung the Graff Vynda-K.'

The Ribos Operation is notable for having very high production values – it certainly outshines most of the previous season's stories in this respect, looking altogether more sumptuous and polished. One gets the impression that rather more care and attention have been lavished on it than was generally the case the year before. A good illustration of this comes in the scenes set at the catacomb entrance, which is festooned with dozens of flickering candles and shot with a highly atmospheric soft focus effect.

'The most marks must be given to Dudley Simpson,' thought Jan Vincent-Rudzki. 'His music helped create the atmosphere so well, from organ music of the Guardians to that incredible music in the throne room.'

The other particularly notable aspect of *The Ribos Operation* is its introduction of Romana as a new companion to replace Leela. Leela had been an ambitious but never fully successful character. Partly this was due to the approach adopted by Louise Jameson, whose rather mannered performance and intentional avoidance of naturalism in the delivery of her dialogue – eschewing the use of contractions, for instance – meant that the viewer could never quite forget that this was not a real person but an actress playing a role. Partly however it was also due to the fact that the writers could not, in the end, keep her true to her 'noble savage' origins; the need to show her interacting with the Doctor and other relatively advanced characters led them to resort to what has sometimes been referred to as the 'Jamie syndrome' (although in his case it actually worked), having her reveal sudden and unexpected advances of knowledge and ability. With the creation of Romana the production team went to the opposite extreme of giving the Doctor a companion of supposedly equal, if not superior, intelligence to himself. This would bring its own problems, as the writers would have to contrive ways of explaining for the viewer's benefit things that the two Time Lords would really have no need to discuss between themselves, and Romana too would sometimes display a surprising knowledge of Earthly customs and expressions. Mary Tamm's initial performance is, in its own way, just as mannered as Louise Jameson's – in fact, she goes through the whole of *The Ribos Operation* giving the impression that she has got an unpleasant smell under her nose – but fortunately she would become rather more relaxed in later stories, and, as debuts go, it is not a bad one.

FOURTH DOCTOR

As for the Doctor, Munro was not far wrong when he wrote: 'Tom Baker is at his peak. The brooding alien of Hinchcliffe has blossomed into a vibrant overgrown schoolboy, gleefully revelling in his adventures. From the moment he hears Garron's Somerset accent his curiosity is piqued, and he follows wherever that curiosity leads. At this stage, his flippancy and clowning is still a defence mechanism, a cushion against the horrors around him, often used to get him out of trouble ... Baker's enjoyment of the role bubbles through, showing no sign of the boredom which [eventually] let his clowning out of control. Here it remains one facet of a complex man, and when death crowds in on him the clowning has to stop. "Aren't you frightened?" Romana asks, as their dawn execution [approaches]. "Yes," says the Doctor with utter sincerity. "Terrified."'

'A while ago I asked if there was any magic left in *Doctor Who*,' wrote Jan Vincent-Rudzki, referring back to an article written in the wake of his influential review of season fourteen's *The Deadly Assassin*. 'Well *The Ribos Operation* answered that with a resounding "Yes".'

THE PIRATE PLANET

Writer: Douglas Adams. **Director:** Pennant Roberts. **Designer:** Jon Pusey. **Costumes:** L Rowland Warne. **Make-Up:** Janis Gould. **Incidental Music:** Dudley Simpson. **Visual Effects:** Colin Mapson. **Film Cameraman:** Elmer Cossey. **Film Editor:** John Dunstan. **Studio Lighting:** Mike Jefferies. **Studio Sound:** Mike Jones. **Production Assistant:** Michael Owen Morris. **Assistant Floor Manager:** Ruth Mayorcas.

	First UK TX	Scheduled TX	Actual TX	Duration	Viewers	Chart Pos.
Part One	30/09/78	18.20	18.22	25'05"	9.1	30
Part Two	07/10/78	18.20	18.22	25'30"	7.4	52
Part Three	14/10/78	18.20	18.22	25'47"	8.2	44
Part Four	21/10/78	18.20	18.22	25'16"	8.4	46

Plot: The tracer detects the second segment on the planet Calufrax. The TARDIS makes a bumpy landing, and the Doctor and Romana soon discover that they are not on Calufrax at all. They are in fact on Zanak, a planet that has been hollowed out and fitted with engines so that it can transmat through space and materialise around others – such as Calufrax – to plunder their mineral wealth, leaving them as shrunken husks held by gravitational forces in a 'trophy room'. Ostensibly in charge is the Captain, whose body has been partially replaced with robotic parts following a near-fatal crash, but he is merely a puppet controlled by his nurse – a projection of Zanak's original ruler, the aged Queen Xanxia. Xanxia is using time dams, powered by the forces generated in the trophy room, to keep her body alive until this new, younger form has stabilised. The Captain prepares Zanak to 'jump' again – this time with Earth as its target. The Doctor attempts to thwart his plans, calling on the assistance of the Mentiads – a gestalt of telepaths amongst Zanak's indigenous population – to sabotage the engines. The Captain rebels against the nurse, but she kills him. The nurse herself is then destroyed by one of the Zanak natives whom the Doctor, Romana and K9 have befriended. The Doctor realises that the second segment comprises the whole of the planet Calufrax. He contrives to drop the compressed husks from the trophy room into a space-time vortex created by the TARDIS in the centre of Zanak, and is then able to pick up and convert the segment at his leisure.

Episode endings:

1. A group of Mentiads blast the Doctor with a bolt of mental energy. K9 blasts them back, but to no avail. The Mentiads turn again to the Doctor, who slumps to the floor under their attack.

2. The Doctor, Romana and the young native Kimus explore the mine workings under Zanak. The Doctor realises that the planet is hollow and that it has materialised around Calufrax. The three friends flee further into the mine as the Captain's guards arrive and give chase. Suddenly they are confronted by a group of Mentiads who state that they have come for the Doctor.

3. K9 destroys the Captain's robotic parrot, the polyphase avitron, and by way of retribution the Captain forces the Doctor to walk a plank suspended over a sheer drop. The Doctor reaches the end and pauses. The Captain fires a gun at his feet until, with a cry, he falls from the plank and disappears from view. The Captain laughs.

4. The Doctor helps to set up some explosives for the Mentiads, who then operate the detonator telepathically. Zanak's control centre, the Bridge, is totally destroyed in a spectacular explosion. The Doctor and Romana leave to return to the TARDIS.

IT WAS MADE WHERE...?

Location filming: 01.05.78-05.05.78
Locations: Disused Railway Tunnel, Daren-felen, Gwent, Wales; Big Pit, Blaenavon, Gwent, Wales; Coity Mountain, Gwent, Wales; Monmouthshire Golf Course, Llanfoist, Gwent, Wales; Bwlch y Garn, Ebbw Vale, Gwent, Wales; Cathedral Cave, Dan-yr-Ogof Showcaves, Dan-yr-Ogof, Powys, Wales; Berkley Power Station, Berkley, Gloucs.
Studio: 22.05.78-23.05.78, 03.06.78-05.06.78 all in TC6

ADDITIONAL CREDITED CAST

Captain (Bruce Purchase), Mr. Fibuli (Andrew Robertson), Balaton (Ralph Michael[1, 2]), Pralix (David Sibley[1,3,4]*), Kimus (David Warwick), Mula (Primi Townsend), Citizen (Clive Bennett[1]), Mentiad (Bernard Finch), Guard (Adam Kurakin[1-3]), Nurse (Rosalind Lloyd[2-4]).

* Also at the beginning of Part Two, but uncredited.

THINGS TO WATCH OUT FOR

- The Doctor has a visible cut on his top lip during this story as Tom Baker had been bitten by a dog whilst offering it a sausage. This is explained in plot terms by the Doctor banging his lip on the TARDIS console when it makes its bumpy landing on Zanak.

THINGS YOU MIGHT NOT HAVE KNOWN

- Douglas Adams's original draft of the story was extremely complex, involving a Time Lord trapped inside a giant aggression absorbing machine, and had to be considerably simplified at the script editing stage.
- Vi Delmar, who played (uncredited) old Queen Xanxia, asked for extra money to remove her false teeth in her scenes.

- **Guard:** [Taking a telescope from Romana] 'This is a forbidden object.' **Romana:** 'Why?' **Guard:** 'That is a forbidden question. You are a stranger?' **Romana:** 'Well, yes.' **Guard:** 'Strangers are forbidden.' **Romana:** 'I did come with the Doctor.' **Guard:** 'Who is the ...' **Romana:** 'Ah, now don't tell me. Doctors are forbidden as well.'

- **The Doctor:** [To the Captain.] 'What is it you're really up to, eh? What do you want? You don't want to take over the universe do you? No. You wouldn't know what to do with it beyond shout at it.'

- **Captain:** 'I'm gratified that you appreciate it.' **The Doctor:** 'Appreciate it ... *Appreciate it*! You commit mass destruction and murder on a scale that's almost inconceivable and you ask me to appreciate it! Just because you happen to have made a brilliantly conceived toy out of the mummified remains of planets!' **Captain:** 'Devilstorms, Doctor ... It is not a toy!' **The Doctor:** 'Then what's it for? Huh? What are you doing? What could possibly be worth all this?'

ANALYSIS

Douglas Adams's first story for *Doctor Who* was written at exactly the same time as his first radio serial of *The Hitch-Hiker's Guide to the Galaxy*, a concept that would eventually bring him fame and fortune. It is perhaps not surprising therefore to find that the two have much in common. The spectacular scientific gobbledegook that comes pouring from the mouths of the Doctor and Romana is a case in point, as is the incredible abundance of mind-blowing concepts vying for attention in the scripts. Here we are presented with engines capable of moving a planet across space via some sort of interstitial vortex; time dams; cybernetic control systems; living projections of matter; powerful telepaths; flying cars; and anti-inertia travel tubes. 'Whilst it would be inaccurate to say that *The Pirate Planet* is anything other than an engaging and diverting adventure serial,' suggested Philip Packer in *Star Begotten* Volume 4 Number 4 dated winter 1990/91, 'it is packed with some absolutely fascinating and (dare I say it) plausible concepts, although to be fair to Douglas Adams, most of his ideas seem workable, at least in the imagination. There is the idea of the hollow planet itself; the way in which the release of the crushed planets' energy – some of which is psychic – forces open the natural passages of any latent telepath on Zanak, thus causing another Mentiad to break out ...; the suspended inertia tunnel in which the occupants stand still whilst the tunnel whizzes past very effectively and which – after a minor adjustment by the Doctor – slams two of the Captain's guards straight into the wall of the anteroom at the end!; the concept of the time dams being able to hold back the flow of time; and so on.'

That there is room in all this for a plot is a wonder, and that the whole thing actually turns out to be quite enjoyable is an absolute marvel. 'I must admit that I had a lot of reservations about this story by new writer Douglas Adams,' noted Geraint Jones in *TARDIS* Volume 3 Number 6 dated December 1978. 'The idea of a hollow planet sucking worlds dry of their wealth, bionic parrots etc just did not seem right somehow for *Doctor Who*. As it turned out, I found it to be one of the most enjoyable adventures ever in the series.'

'Adams even makes a valiant attempt to provide an explanation for the Captain's plan to defeat Xanxia,' added Packer, 'which although steeped in neutron flowisms at least makes a vague sort of sense within the parameters of *Doctor Who* doublespeak. And then there are the overtly comic ideas such as the notion of the Doctor being able to walk the plank from the top of the mountain, which ties in with the pirate motif, as does ... the robotic parrot... Actually, the pirate theme is quite stylishly woven into the visual side of the story. Instead of the eye-patched and one-legged Long John Silver bombast, we have the hi-tech equivalent, whose torso and head are ... half mechanical.'

The story's success is due partly to Tom Baker and Mary Tamm who breeze through the madness as though they are in another show entirely, but partly also to marvellous performances from Bruce Purchase as the blustering Captain and Andrew Robertson as the Smee-like Mr Fibuli. The Captain is the sort of larger than life character that one could easily imagine an actor like Brian Blessed playing, and Purchase gives it his all. What makes it all work is the ending, where the Captain is revealed as being as much a pawn as those at whom he ranted; and his sorrow at the death of Mr Fibuli is nicely played. It is in fact just as well that the Captain and Mr Fibuli are so good, as the other incidental characters are simply awful. Rosalind Lloyd's nurse is one-dimensional and shallow, and the Zanak natives (just how they survive being thrust through a space vortex over and over again is never explained) are some of the most bland characters ever to be seen in *Doctor Who*. They look vaguely similar to the Dulcians from season six's *The Dominators*, and have the same annoying vacuuousness about them. The other main group, the Mentiads, seem to spend the entire story marching across fields to get to places, and one is reminded of numerous *Monty Python's Flying Circus* sketches in which characters do a similar thing to humorous effect.

Continuing a trend of increasing silliness in Tom Baker's portrayal of the Doctor, here we see him amongst other things talking directly to camera; tossing up a coin that then takes an inordinate length of time to fall; and ripping a sweet from a paper bag with his teeth, as though pulling the pin from a hand grenade. This more flippant approach to the character would flourish over the next couple of years, especially after Douglas Adams succeeded Anthony Read as script editor for season seventeen, but *The Pirate Planet* is arguably the story in which it really took root.

THE STONES OF BLOOD

Writer: David Fisher. **Director:** Darrol Blake. **Designer:** John Stout. **Costumes:** Rupert Jarvis. **Make-Up:** Ann Briggs. **Incidental Music:** Dudley Simpson. **Visual Effects:** Mat Irvine. **OB Cameraman:** Trevor Wimlett, Mike Windsor. **Studio Lighting:** Warwick Fielding. **Studio Sound:** Richard Chubb. **Production Assistant:** Carolyn Montagu. **Assistant Floor Manager:** Carol Scott, Nigel Taylor.

	First UK TX	Scheduled TX	Actual TX	Duration	Viewers	Chart Pos.
Part One	28/10/78	18.25	18.24	24'20"	8.6	38
Part Two	04/11/78	18.20	18.22	23'53"	6.6	75
Part Three	11/11/78	18.20	18.21	24'27"	9.3	38
Part Four	18/11/78	18.20	18.23	23'07"	7.6	66

FOURTH DOCTOR

Plot: The Doctor, Romana and K9 are led by the tracer to the Nine Travellers, a circle of standing stones on Boscombe Moor in present-day England, but the third segment is nowhere to be found. They meet elderly archaeologist Professor Emilia Rumford and her assistant Vivien Fay, who are surveying the site, and learn that the circle appears to have had a variable number of stones over the years. The Doctor encounters a group of Druids led by a man named de Vries and narrowly avoids becoming their latest sacrifice. De Vries is later killed by one of the stones from the circle – an Ogri, a life form that lives on blood. Miss Fay is the latest guise of the Cailleach, a being worshipped by the Druids, who has been on Earth for four thousand years. She transports Romana to a spaceship suspended in hyperspace at the same coordinates as the stone circle. The Doctor follows and accidentally releases two justice machines called Megara, which sentence him to death for breaking the seal on their compartment. When they attempt to carry out their sentence, however, he tricks them into knocking Miss Fay unconscious. Reading her mind, they learn that she is really Cessair of Diplos – the alien criminal they were originally sent to try. Having established her guilt, they transform her into an additional stone in the circle, but not before the Doctor has grabbed her necklace – the Seal of Diplos, alias the third segment of the Key to Time.

Episode endings:
1. Romana, led by the sound of the Doctor's voice calling her, arrives at the edge of a cliff. Backing away as an unseen presence, apparently the Doctor, advances menacingly toward her, she falls over the edge of the cliff.
2. Miss Fay shoves Romana roughly into the middle of the stone circle and aims a long staff at her. The staff emits pulses of energy and Romana vanishes.
3. Miss Fay, now with silver skin and wearing long, flowing robes, arrives on the spaceship accompanied by two Ogri. She triumphantly tells the Doctor and Romana that they are trapped in hyperspace forever. The spaceship hovers in the void of hyperspace.
4. As Romana looks on, the Doctor uses the tracer to convert Miss Fay's necklace into the third segment. He then attempts to fit the segments together, but finds to his embarrassment that he is unable to do so.

IT WAS MADE WHERE...?

OB: 12.06.78-15.06.78
Locations: The King's Men, Rollright Stones, Little Rollright, Oxfordshire; Reed Cottage, Little Compton, Warwickshire; Field belonging to Manor Farm, Oakham Road, Little Rollright, Oxfordshire; Little Rollright Quarry, Oakham Road, Little Rollright, Oxfordshire.
Studio: 03.07.78-04.07.78, 16.07.78-18.07.78 all in TC3, 21.07.78 (gallery only) in TC1

ADDITIONAL CREDITED CAST

Professor Rumford (Beatrix Lehmann), Vivien Fay (Susan Engel), De Vries (Nicholas McArdle[1,2]), Martha (Elaine Ives-Cameron[1,2]), Megara Voices (Gerald Cross[3,4], David McAlister[3,4]), Campers (James Murray[3], Shirin Taylor[3]).

Note: Gerald Cross provided the voice of the Guardian in Part One, but was uncredited on screen.

THINGS TO WATCH OUT FOR

- The cells of the spaceship in hyperspace contain both a dead Wirrn and what appears to be the 'skeleton' of a Kraal android. Shots of another creature, a Sea Devil, were lost at the editing stage
- Hints are given that Cessair of Diplos is an agent of the Black Guardian: aside from the evidence of a warning given by the White Guardian at the beginning of Part One, there is also the fact that Cessair knows what the segment of the Key is and tells the Doctor in the closing stages of Part Four that if he lets the Megara turn her into stone, he will never find what he is looking for.

THINGS YOU MIGHT NOT HAVE KNOWN

- Working title: *The Nine Maidens*.
- *The Stones of Blood* was *Doctor Who*'s 100th story and a scene involving the Doctor, Romana and K9 having a party in the TARDIS was scripted and rehearsed. It was dropped before recording, however, as producer Graham Williams felt it was too self-congratulatory.

QUOTE, UNQUOTE

- **Vivien Fay:** [Speaking of Professor Rumford's ownership of a police truncheon] 'Last year, when she was lecturing in New York, she took it with her in case she got mugged.' **Romana:** 'And did she get mugged?' **Vivien Fay:** 'No, she got arrested for carrying an offensive weapon.'
- **Professor Rumford:** 'But I still don't understand about hyperspace.' **The Doctor:** 'Well, who does?' **K9:** 'I do.' **The Doctor:** 'Shut up, K9!'
- **Professor Rumford:** 'Are you from outer space?' **The Doctor:** 'No. I'm more from what you'd call inner time.'

ANALYSIS

Doctor Who's one hundredth story is, fittingly, an extremely good one – and one that, in featuring a wide variety of different plot elements and two highly contrasting settings, manages to encapsulate much of what has made the series so successful over the years. 'The plot was great,' judged Chris Dunk in *Oracle* Volume 2 Number 5 dated February 1979, 'and although I was wary of an uninitiated author writing this centenary serial, my fears were quite unfounded ... David Fisher rose magnificently to the occasion and turned in a very creditable story ... This was very much a story of many facets, and from witchcraft and Druids we went on to the great contrast of gleaming metal sophistication in hyperspace. The greatly reduced cast [in the latter stages] allowed for [an] eerie "who's around the next corner?" feeling, but the stars of this sortie had to be the justice machines, the Megara ... The effects required to handle [them] were well executed too ... I suppose this was my favourite aspect of the show – the Doctor out on a limb, relying on his wits, and all the time gradually drawing nearer and nearer to death. Very witty too, of course.'

Geoffrey Saunders, writing in *Baker's Best* in 1981, liked the way the plot developed over the course of the four episodes: [Part One] was mainly an "atmosphere" episode, and the build up of mystery and tension was incredible. Those wheeling, squawking birds and mysterious heart-thumping, glowing stones, coupled with the nasty things which befell the Doctor and Romana, added a great deal of uneasiness to the nagging

4 FOURTH DOCTOR

suspicion that Vivien Fay was up to something ... The end ... with dear Romana walking barefoot over a cliff, was excellently handled and the mystery "pusher" was a good idea. (If we'd seen whoever it was pushing Romana, a great deal of the terror would have been lost.) ... The tension evoked so brilliantly in [Part One] mixed perfectly with [Part Two's] "run-around" feel ... as the Doctor and Professor Rumford found out about Vivien Fay being ... not of this world at the same time as Romana met up with her. The ending was superb, being more of the "What will happen next ...?" type than the "Is she dead?" kind ... The sudden change of focus from Earth to the hyperspace cruiser [in Part Three] was surprising, but did not spoil the feel of the story. The events leading up to [this] were archetypal *Doctor Who* with the Doctor escaping the monsters for a while ... in order to make one of his incredible lash-ups, all the while nattering away about the theory behind his invention ...The last episode was a real gem, with the Megara taking over as the Doctor's main worry. This switching of emphasis from one set of "baddies" to another was superbly achieved, as were the events leading up to the Doctor's "turning around" of the court case ...'

Ann Summerfield, writing in *In-Vision* Issue 34 dated October 1991, thought that the story could be classed as 'female gothic':

'Just read this list of gothic themes from a recent companion to literature: "the flow of blood, caves, spirits without body, guilt, imprisonment, physical terror, hunted virgins, stolen inheritance, and discrepancy between authority and the evidence of one's own senses". Doesn't that sound just like a description of *The Stones of Blood* (especially if we assume Romana's lack of experience is sexual as well as worldly!)? ...

'*The Stones of Blood* is a *feminine* adventure, and at times the Doctor himself seems ... alienated and overwhelmed ... It is only in the "theoretically absurd" territory of hyperspace that the Doctor's wit and ingenuity can come into play. Before venturing into hyperspace's futuristic and industrial environment it is the women who offer solutions or who solve problems.'

It is rather a pity that this proved to be the only *Doctor Who* story directed by Darrol Blake as he makes an excellent job of it, giving the scenes set on Earth a suitable degree of behind-the-sofa scariness and those set in hyperspace an appropriately claustrophobia-inducing hi-tech feel. Indeed, the whole production positively shines. There are several wonderful moments dotted throughout the story (although it is probably just as well that Graham Williams vetoed a scene of the Doctor celebrating his birthday, as this would have been too self-aware). Examples include the scene in which Romana exits from the TARDIS and turns to see a number of ravens perched on its roof; and, perhaps best of all, a surprisingly graphic incident in which two campers find an Ogri standing outside their tent and are reduced to skeletons when they touch it. What makes this latter scene even more noteworthy is that it is completely irrelevant to the plot (the campers play no other part in the proceedings) and is included purely for the purposes of heightening the atmosphere and reinforcing the threat posed by the Ogri – the kind of thing that many lesser writers and directors would not think to do.

Jan Vincent-Rudzki summed it up nicely in *TARDIS* Volume 4 Number 1 dated February 1979: 'This was deservedly the one hundredth story, and an indication of [the] high standards the [series] is reaching these days. Roll on the next one hundred!'

THE ANDROIDS OF TARA

Writer: David Fisher. **Director:** Michael Hayes. **Designer:** Valerie Warrender. **Costumes:** Doreen James. **Make-Up:** Jill Hagger. **Incidental Music:** Dudley Simpson. **Fight Arranger:** Terry Walsh. **Visual Effects:** Len Hutton. **Film Cameraman:** John Walker. **Film Editor:** David Yates. **Studio Lighting:** Brian Clemett. **Studio Sound:** Richard Chubb. **Production Assistant:** Teresa-Mary Winders. **Assistant Floor Manager:** Rosemary Webb.

	First UK TX	Scheduled TX	Actual TX	Duration	Viewers	Chart Pos.
Part One	25/11/78	18.20	18.22	24'53"	8.5	45
Part Two	02/12/78	18.20	18.21	24'27"	10.1	30
Part Three	09/12/78	18.20	18.21	23'52"	8.9	38
Part Four	16/12/78	18.20	18.20	24'49"	9.0	45

Plot: The tracer brings the TARDIS to the planet Tara. Romana finds the fourth segment disguised as part of a statue but is then taken prisoner by Count Grendel of Gracht. Grendel is plotting to seize the Taran throne from the rightful heir, Prince Reynart, and has mistaken Romana for an android duplicate of the Prince's betrothed, Princess Strella, to whom she bears a remarkable resemblance. The Doctor is meanwhile captured by Prince Reynart's men Zadek and Farrah and taken to his hunting lodge, where he is forced to repair an android double of the Prince to act as a decoy for potential assassins. Grendel then kidnaps the Prince, and the Doctor has to modify the android so that it can be crowned in his place. Grendel commissions an android duplicate of Romana equipped with a lethal ray and contrives for the Doctor to meet her. K9, recognising this as a trap, saves his master. Romana has meanwhile escaped from Castle Gracht, and she rescues the Doctor from Grendel's men. Grendel destroys the Reynart android and recaptures Romana. The Doctor gains access to the Castle by rowing across the moat and, having first found and pocketed the fourth segment, manages to thwart Grendel's plans to seize power. The Prince's men then attack the Castle in force. Romana saves Strella from being killed and the Doctor engages Grendel in a swordfight. Grendel, realising that he has been defeated, dives into the moat and escapes to fight another day.

Episode endings:
1. The Doctor, Reynart, Zadek and Farrah drink a toast to the King, but the wine has been drugged and they all start to fall unconscious. The Doctor manages to make his way to the door before collapsing. The door opens to reveal Grendel standing outside.
2. The presiding Archimandrite invests the android Reynart as the new King of Tara. The assembled courtiers rise and the android begins a speech of accession, slurring its words a little. Suddenly Princess Strella arrives, kneels before the android and offers her loyalty to the King. With a shout of 'No!', the Doctor crosses to Strella and strikes at her head with the King's staff. The courtiers gasp in horror.
3. Grendel throws a spear into the android Prince and escapes from Reynart's hunting lodge on horseback, recapturing Romana on the way.
4. K9 has been left stranded in a boat in the middle of the Castle moat, calling out plaintively to the Doctor. The Doctor looks down on him from the battlements and laughs.

IT WAS MADE WHERE...?

Location filming: 24.07.78-28.08.78
Location: Leeds Castle, Maidstone, Kent.
Studio: 14.08.78-15.08.78 in TC6, 28.08.78-29.08.78 in TC1

ADDITIONAL CREDITED CAST

Count Grendel (Peter Jeffrey), Zadek (Simon Lack), Prince Reynart (Neville Jason), Farrah (Paul Lavers), Lamia (Lois Baxter[1-3]), Till (Declan Mulholland[1,3,4]), Archimandrite (Cyril Shaps[2-4]), Kurster (Martin Matthews[2-4]).

THINGS TO WATCH OUT FOR

- Mary Tamm plays both Romana and Strella, as well as android doubles of each.
- For this story only, the opening title credits are in the order: title, part, writer (rather than the standard: title, writer, part).
- Some excellent location footage was shot at Leeds Castle in Kent – although the glass-painted additions to the Castle, intended to give it a more fairytale quality, never look anything other than false.

THINGS YOU MIGHT NOT HAVE KNOWN

- Working titles: *The Prisoner of Zend, The Androids of Zenda.*

QUOTE, UNQUOTE

- **The Doctor:** [Speaking to Swordsman Farrah.] 'Would you mind not standing on my chest, my hat's on fire.'
- **The Doctor:** 'I shall have to go alone of course. It's funny. They always want you to go alone when you're walking into a trap. Have you noticed that?'
- **The Doctor:** [Speaking of K9's efforts to cut through a wooden door with his nose laser] 'Do hurry up. A hamster with a blunt penknife could do it quicker.' **K9:** 'You ordered me to make no noise, Master.' **The Doctor:** 'Just get on with it.'

ANALYSIS

Following hot on the heels of *The Stones of Blood* comes a second story from David Fisher. *The Androids of Tara* is very obviously inspired by a specific literary source, namely Anthony Hope's *The Prisoner of Zenda* (in fact, its early working title was *The Androids of Zenda*), and its heavy reliance on that one particular romantic novel of 1894 may perhaps account for the fact that is rather less engaging than the other stories of the season, coming over more as a gentle run-around than as anything particularly significant. Owen Tudor, writing in *TARDIS* Volume 4 Number 1 dated February 1979, was less than enamoured: 'The script was too unspeakably plagiaristic for the work of the production team to shine through. From the peak of science-fiction cum fantasy in *The Stones of Blood*, David Fisher plumbed the depths of hack romantic swashbuckling in *The Androids of Tara* … Would it have made any difference [if] the crossbows had fired real bolts, if the swords had cut flesh rather than searing it? The androids, made so much of in the title, were little more than a way to create doubles. A certain Anthony Hope achieved the same effect with chance human doubles. The use of androids was perhaps the only difference between *The*

Androids of Tara and *The Prisoner of Zenda*.'

The basic idea that the planet Tara has a culture where the 'peasants' know about science and androids while the nobles spend their time developing electric swords and hunting wood beasts is a good one, but sadly gets lost somewhere along the way. What we are left with is a bit of swashbuckling, mostly involving a contingent of guards who cannot aim true to save their lives, and a lot of mucking about in woods and underground waterways (although this does allow the Doctor one of the best lines, involving hamsters and penknives). The quality of a story's cliffhangers often gives a good indication of how dramatic it is, and *The Androids of Tara*'s are all totally lacking in tension. It doesn't help matters, either, that virtually all the characters are bland and forgettable. The real Prince Reynart and Princess Strella are barely distinguishable from their emotionless android duplicates, so lacklustre are the performances by Neville Jason and Mary Tamm in these roles, and the proceedings are only marginally enlivened by the occasional appearances of Grendel's hunchbacked servant Till – a nice cameo from Declan Mulholland. The one saving grace in this area of the production is Peter Jeffrey as Count Grendel, as Mike Ashcroft pointed out in *Oracle* Volume 2 Number 6 dated March 1979: 'While *The Androids of Tara* did have a lot going for it, it seemed to have a ridiculously one-dimensional plot and relied much too heavily on the one forceful character to emerge – Count Grendel of Gracht, played in all his splendour by that notorious TV bad guy, Peter Jeffrey. Grendel was the pivot ... – if he failed to come across, then the story would fail. Luckily, he dredged some respect from the bottom of the barrel and we didn't quite have a disaster on our hands.'

Some fan commentators, it must be acknowledged, have taken a much more positive view of the story, a few even going so far as to try to characterise it as a sort of camp classic. Tim Munro, writing in *Star Begotten* Volume 5 Number 2 dated spring/summer 1992, argued that it worked despite its limitations: 'Nobody is ever going to claim that *The Androids of Tara* has hidden depths. It isn't multilayered or meaningful, and it isn't full of socio-political commentary. It has no message ... and couldn't support a ream of in-depth textual analyses as the series' classics do. But it is well-crafted television, and above all terrifyingly enjoyable entertainment. Being so different [from] the show's norm, it comes as an invigorating breath of fresh air. Instead of the usual crazed megalomaniac plotting galactic domination amidst rampaging monsters ... and white-tunicked humanoid cyphers, *The Androids of Tara* gives us a swashbuckling historical romance ... All the SF trappings – the androids, the static-charged swords, etc – are purely superficial, there to reassure regular viewers that they are still watching the same [series]. This is *Doctor Who* as fairytale, with all the genre's trademarks – handsome princes, beautiful princesses, black-hearted Counts, and malevolent hunchbacks – and this is picked up in all aspects of the production. Michael Hayes, star director of the Williams era, brings to the story an absolute understanding of its requirements, and this is reflected in Valerie Warrender's lavish sets and Doreen James's sumptuous costumes. On a purely visual level, *The Androids of Tara* is one of the [most] beautiful *Doctor Who* stories ever made.'

The Androids of Tara scarcely deserves such fulsome praise. It is not exactly a bad story, just a bland one, and at this stage of the sixteenth season bland is not what is needed. The search for the Key to Time is faltering, and something big is needed to rekindle the viewer's interest. Fortunately, the next story features something very big indeed ...

FOURTH DOCTOR

THE POWER OF KROLL

Writer: Robert Holmes. **Director:** Norman Stewart. **Designer:** Don Giles. **Costumes:** Colin Lavers. **Make-Up:** Kezia Dewinne. **Incidental Music:** Dudley Simpson. **Visual Effects:** Tony Harding. **Film Cameraman:** Martin Patmore. **Film Editor:** Michael Goldsmith. **Studio Lighting:** Warwick Fielding. **Studio Sound:** Richard Chubb. **Production Assistant:** Kate Nemet. **Assistant Floor Manager:** Chris Moss.

	First UK TX	Scheduled TX	Actual TX	Duration	Viewers	Chart Pos.
Part One	23/12/78	18.15	18.17	23'16"	6.5	85
Part Two	30/12/78	18.30	18.31	23'57"	12.4	26
Part Three	06/01/79	18.25	18.28	21'56"	8.9	51
Part Four	13/01/79	18.25	18.27	21'58"	9.9	31

Plot: The TARDIS arrives in the marshes of the third moon of the planet Delta Magna. While trying to get an accurate reading on the tracer, the Doctor is shot at by Thawn and Fenner, two men from a nearby methane refinery. Romana is meanwhile taken prisoner by the green-skinned natives, the Swampies, who decide to sacrifice her to their god Kroll as a prelude to an attack on the refinery. A man named Rohm-Dutt is running guns to the Swampies ostensibly on behalf of an anti-colonial organisation sympathetic to their cause. This however is part of a plot by Thawn to have the Swampies wiped out. The Doctor arrives at the Swampies' temple just in time to rescue his companion. The refinery crew notice that the lake bed is shifting, as if there is something moving beneath it. The Swampies, led by Ranquin, prepare their attack, but are stopped in their tracks when Kroll – an enormous squid-like creature – appears on the horizon. Kroll starts to assail them, while the Doctor, Romana and Rohm-Dutt are captured by the Swampies and sentenced to death. The Doctor and Romana manage to escape, but Rohm-Dutt is seized and killed by one of Kroll's tentacles. The two Time Lords reach the refinery, where they learn that Thawn is planning to destroy Kroll by blasting it with a rocket. The Doctor disables the rocket and Thawn is slain by the Swampies as they launch their attack. Kroll then returns but the Doctor, realising that it has ingested the fifth segment (disguised as a Swampie relic), uses the tracer to end its threat. The segment is converted, and in place of the giant Kroll there are countless smaller creatures left lying in the marshes.

Episode endings:
1. As the assembled Swampies chant their god's name, Ranquin calls on Kroll to arise from the depths. Romana, tied up inside a sacrificial compound, shrieks in horror as a creature appears and attacks her.
2. One of Kroll's tentacles breaks through a large metal pipe inside the refinery. It seizes a worker named Harg and, as his horrified colleagues look on, drags him into the pipe.
3. The Doctor and Romana flee from the Swampies in a canoe, but the huge form of Kroll rises up before them in the swamp.
4. The Doctor and Romana return to the TARDIS and it dematerialises.

IT WAS MADE WHERE...?

Location filming: 18.09.78-22.09.78, 25.09.78-29.09.78
Locations: The Maltings, Snape, Suffolk; Iken Cliff, Iken, nr Snape, Kent.
Studio: 09.10.78-11.10.78 in TC6, 26.10.78 (gallery only) in TC3, 08.11.78 (gallery only) in TC1
Bray filming: 19.10.78-20.10.78 in water tank

ADDITIONAL CREDITED CAST

Thawn (Neil McCarthy), Ranquin (John Abineri), Fenner (Philip Madoc), Rohm-Dutt (Glyn Owen[1-3]), Varlik (Carl Rigg), Skart (Frank Jarvis), Dugeen (John Leeson), Harg (Grahame Mallard[1,2]*), Mensch (Terry Walsh[1,2]).

* Also at the beginning of Part Three, but uncredited.

POPULAR MYTHS

- As reported by *Doctor Who Magazine*, this story was a replacement for one entitled *The Lords of Misrule* by distinguished screen writer Ted Willis. (Ted Willis never worked on *Doctor Who*. Thriller writer Ted *Lewis*, best known for the seminal *Get Carter*, did work on an ultimately unused Key to Time story, title unknown.)
- Philip Madoc accepted the role of Fenner due to a misunderstanding; he had thought that he was being invited to play the more substantial part of Thawn. (He agreed to take the role of Fenner after actor Alan Browning, who was to have done so, fell ill shortly before filming commenced. He had previously been invited to play Thawn, but this invitation had been withdrawn by the production team as Neil McCarthy had already accepted the role.)

THINGS TO WATCH OUT FOR

- John Leeson appears in person as Dugeen, rather than as the voice of K9. He replaced Martin Jarvis, who dropped out before recording commenced.
- This story presents *Doctor Who*'s largest ever monster.

THINGS YOU MIGHT NOT HAVE KNOWN

- Working title: *Horror of the Swamp*.
- Production unit manager John Nathan-Turner deputised for producer Graham Williams during this story's single studio session as Williams was absent due to illness.
- The green make-up used for the Swampies proved particularly difficult to remove, causing the cast to retire to a nearby air base to try and scrub it off, much to the amusement of the watching airmen.

QUOTE, UNQUOTE

- **The Doctor:** 'Well, you'd better introduce me.' **Romana:** 'As what?' **The Doctor:** 'Oh, I don't know, a wise and wonderful person who wants to help. Don't exaggerate.'
- **Thawn:** 'The authorities are far too soft. Once they start interfering, you can never get rid of them. We'll handle this one by ourselves, and in my way. Final. We get rid of the problem once and for all.'
- **Ranquin:** 'Kroll is all wise, all seeing ...' **The Doctor:** 'All baloney!'

FOURTH DOCTOR

ANALYSIS

'This story is not well remembered by many fans despite it being written by the late great Robert Holmes,' noted Paul Dunn in *Capitol Spires* Issue 2 dated July 1993. This is quite true; and Dunn's comment gives a clue as to the likely reason for its generally poor reputation: although it is by no means a bad story, it falls some way short of the very high standards of which Holmes is well known to have been capable. This was a point picked up by Chris Dunk in *Oracle* Volume 2 Number 6 dated March 1979:

'Robert Holmes is an incredibly talented author ... His scripts have always been laced with a fine blend of humour and originality, and sometimes satire ... So I've come to expect a lot of Mr Holmes, and it happened that this story proved to be, in my eyes, his downfall. Not that it was bad, I hasten to add; it just wasn't very good by his own excellent standards. In fact it was pretty average throughout, with even the superb Philip Madoc playing a subdued role [as Fenner] under the belligerent command of Thawn ...

'Flashes of inspiration were visible in places, but we really needed a spark to light the fire. Perhaps it was the lack of humour (much less prevalent than usual, and something that I thrive on) that did it, maybe the lack of sturdy subplots ... Parts of the script did show that *Doctor Who* is concerned with the real world though – encouraging and commendable. A few moral hints here and there are quite acceptable as long as the author doesn't tend to preach too much.'

This rather negative view of the story has not been universally shared, however. Owen Tudor, writing in *TARDIS* Volume 4 Number 2 dated 1 April 1979, suggested that the absence of Holmes's usual witticisms was more than made up for by 'the excellence of script, costumes, characterisations and acting,' and that '[the story] was an object lesson in television writing, as it used the possibilities and restrictions of the format presented with admirable skill and expertise.' Like Dunk, Tudor felt that the story contained a degree of social comment: 'Every day we face the technology-nature struggle. We are nature. The world we live in is predominantly technology. Nature is the unpredictable Kroll, technology is the scheduled rocket launches. *The Power of Kroll* tells us that both are dangerous, and that both can be defeated. The human colony is important to us because it represents the admirable human desire to expand, to explore, to seek and also the doubts we have had about what we will find, and, more importantly, how we will handle what we find. It is interesting to note that *The Power of Kroll* comes close [on] the heels of renewed interest in the mainly European-based problems of the African continent.'

This may well be true, but unfortunately any moral message that the viewer might have gleaned from the story is somewhat obscured by the fact that the depiction of the Swampies as green-skinned (obviously made-up) spear-wielding natives who are easily duped and betrayed by the gun runner Rhom-Dutt strongly recalls the patronising portrayal of black-skinned (and just as obviously made-up) African tribesmen in countless old 'jungle adventure' films of the *Tarzan* variety. Indeed the scene at the end of Part One in which Romana is tied up behind a stockade to be sacrificed to Kroll while the Swampies hop from foot to foot outside, shaking their spears and chanting their god's name, is very obviously copied from one in the 1933 RKO film *King Kong* in which a group of highly stereotyped African natives prepare to sacrifice Fay Wray to the giant ape of the title. This rather questionable aspect aside, the on-screen realisation of *The Power of Kroll* is generally good. Dunn drew attention to a number of notable points:

'The locations [for] the story are great, making a change from the overused gravel pit, with the Norfolk marshes being well used …

'The Kroll model itself was well executed, but was completely let down by the use of [a] split screen effect, resulting in a very hard line between the model and the live action footage.'

The unconvincing nature of the split screen effect used to integrate the model Kroll with the location shot landscape – apparently a consequence of film cameraman Martin Patmore having been given bad advice, without which it would have worked very much better – has certainly been the most frequently cited failing of the *The Power of Kroll*'s production. This is bound to be a problem in a story that makes such a big deal – both literally and metaphorically – of its principal monster. One can well understand Robert Holmes's reported unease at being asked to come up with a story featuring the biggest monster ever seen in *Doctor Who*, and it is perhaps unsurprising that in the circumstances he was unable to do his best work – indeed, it seems that he was always at his least inspired when working within constraints with which he was uncomfortable, such as the requirement to use a historical setting for season eleven's *The Time Warrior*. The last word on *The Power of Kroll*, however, goes to the appreciative Tudor: 'The segment [of the Key was] used more effectively in *The Power of Kroll* than anywhere else this season. It bound together all the layers [of the story]. It had created the great god Kroll. It had provided the methane resources that attracted the colonists to the swamp. It eventually threatened everybody, and its final disintegration into hundreds of little octopi provided an aftermath which fitted exactly the calm after the climax.'

THE ARMAGEDDON FACTOR

Writer: Bob Baker, Dave Martin. **Director:** Michael Hayes. **Designer:** Richard McManan-Smith. **Costumes:** Michael Burdle. **Make-Up:** Ann Briggs. **Incidental Music:** Dudley Simpson. **Visual Effects:** John Horton. **Studio Lighting:** Mike Jefferies. **Studio Sound:** Richard Chubb. **Production Assistant:** Ann Aronsohn. **Assistant Floor Manager:** Steve Goldie, Rosemary Padvaiskas.

	First UK TX	Scheduled TX	Actual TX	Duration	Viewers	Chart Pos.
Part One	20/01/79	18.25	18.25	24'39"	7.5	93
Part Two	27/01/79	18.25	18.27	23'56"	8.8	49
Part Three	03/02/79	18.25	18.28	25'03"	7.8	76
Part Four	10/02/79	18.25	18.28	25'09"	8.6	60
Part Five	17/02/79	18.20	18.26	24'42"	8.6	66
Part Six	24/02/79	18.25	18.30	25'09"	9.6	36

Plot: The final segment of the Key is traced to the planet Atrios, engaged in a long war with the neighbouring Zeos. The Marshal of Atrios intends a final strike to destroy the Zeons, but the Doctor and Romana discover that Zeos is deserted and the war is being co-ordinated by a computer called Mentalis, built by one of the Doctor's old Time Lord Academy friends, Drax. The computer is under the control of the Shadow, an agent of the Black Guardian. He and his servants, the Mutes, are inhabiting an unseen third planet positioned between Atrios and Zeos. The Doctor creates a temporary substitute for the final segment from a substance called

FOURTH DOCTOR

chronodyne and uses the Key to place a time loop around the ship from which the Marshal is about to launch his strike against Zeos. It transpires that Atrios's Princess Astra is the real sixth segment. The Shadow converts her into the segment, but the Doctor snatches it and escapes to the TARDIS, where he finally completes the Key. The White Guardian appears on the scanner screen and congratulates the Doctor. He asks that the Key be given over to him, but the Doctor decides that it is too powerful for any one being to control and orders it to re-disperse. Enraged, the Guardian reverts to his true colour – Black – and vows that the Doctor shall die for his defiance. In order to shake him off, the Doctor fits a randomiser to the TARDIS's controls. There is now no telling where or when his travels will take him.

Episode endings:

1. The Doctor and Romana escape from the Marshal by tricking his deputy, Major Shapp, into summoning K9, who blasts out the lights. Princess Astra has meanwhile been taken by a black-clad humanoid into a concealed booth from which they both vanish. The Doctor, Romana and K9 hurry back to where the TARDIS was left, only to find that it is no longer there.
2. The Marshal agrees that the Doctor can go to Zeos and directs him to a transmat point. The Doctor steps in to find himself flanked by two Mutes. Romana arrives, warning of a trap, but the door closes and the Doctor is transported away. Romana calls for him in vain outside the door.
3. Using K9 as an interpreter, the Doctor learns from Mentalis that the computer intends to destroy everything. In his ship heading towards Zeos, the Marshal prepares to attack the planet.
4. The Doctor, Romana and Astra arrive in the TARDIS on the Shadow's planet. The Shadow, sitting with K9, who calls him 'master', prepares to meet them, laughing that the Key to Time is his.
5. The Doctor is being escorted by a Mute to the TARDIS to fetch the first five segments of the Key to Time for the Shadow. Drax steps out and fires a special gun that he has constructed, hitting the Doctor and causing him to shrink.
6. The Black Guardian tries to trick the Doctor into handing over the Key to Time, but the Doctor orders it to disperse and breaks the tracer. Princess Astra appears back on Atrios with her lover, Merak. The Doctor tells Romana about the randomiser that he has fitted to the TARDIS, which means that in future neither the Black Guardian nor they themselves will know where or when they are going to land.

IT WAS MADE WHERE...?

Ealing filming: October 1978 (Stage unknown)
Studio: 05.11.78-07.11.78, 20.11.78-22.11.78, 03.12.78-05.12.78 in TC3, 29.12.78 (gallery only) in TC1

ADDITIONAL CREDITED CAST

Marshal (John Woodvine[1-4,6]), Princess Astra (Lalla Ward), Shapp (Davyd Harries[1-4,6]), Merak (Ian Saynor[1-4,6]), 'Hero' (Ian Liston[1]), 'Heroine' (Susan Skipper[1]), Guards (John Cannon[1], Harry Fielder[2]), The Shadow (William Squire[3-6]), Technician (Iain Armstrong[3]), Pilot (Pat Gorman[3,4]*), Drax (Barry Jackson[5,6]), The Guardian (Valentine Dyall[6]).

* Also in Part Six, but uncredited.

THINGS TO WATCH OUT FOR

- Lalla Ward plays Princess Astra. Ward was subsequently cast as the second incarnation of Romana as she had made a favourable impression on the production team.

THINGS YOU MIGHT NOT HAVE KNOWN

- Working title: *Armageddon*.
- Former *Doctor Who* director David Maloney deputised for producer Graham Williams during early preparations for this story as Williams was absent due to illness.
- Part One of *The Armageddon Factor* was the five-hundredth episode of *Doctor Who*.
- Part Five was interrupted by a break in transmission for several minutes. Music was played and a caption slide displayed until transmission resumed from a point just before the break occurred.

QUOTE, UNQUOTE

- **Marshal:** 'How can we have peace until we have the ultimate deterrent that will ensure a lasting peace?' **The Doctor:** 'Tell me Marshal, if you had this ultimate deterrent, what would you do?' **Marshal:** 'Use it of course, make sure it works.' **The Doctor:** 'Yes … You have a true military mind, Marshal.' **Marshal:** 'Thank you.'
- **The Shadow:** 'I have waited so long, even another thousand years would be nothing for me. But you. I have watched you and your jackdaw meanderings. I know you, and I know there is a want of patience in your nature.' **The Doctor:** 'That's right. Fools rush in …' **The Shadow:** 'Exactly. Leave him. He will make his own mistake. Then, Doctor, I shall be waiting.'
- **Drax:** 'Blimey, it's a dog! Who's a little tin dog, then?' **K9:** 'Your silliness is noted.'
- **The Doctor:** 'We have the power to do anything we like. Absolute power over every particle in the universe. Everything that has ever existed and ever will exist. As from this moment – are you listening to me Romana?' **Romana:** 'Yes of course I'm listening …' **The Doctor:** 'Because if you're not listening, I can make you listen. Because I can do anything. As from this moment there's no such thing as free will in the entire universe. There's only my will because I possess the Key to Time.' **Romana:** 'Doctor, are you all right?' **The Doctor:** 'Well of course I'm all right … But supposing I wasn't all right?'

ANALYSIS

A lot is asked of *The Armageddon Factor*. Not only does it have to tell a good story in its own right, but it also has to provide the resolution to the season-long hunt for the Key to Time – a largely successful experiment that has by this point created a high degree of expectation. Does it meet these twin requirements? Well, yes and no. It is entertaining enough in itself, with some good direction by Michael Hayes and generally fine production values, but ultimately fails to tie up all the loose ends and leaves the over-arching plot strangely unresolved.

As with other six-parters of this era, the story can be subdivided into a number of 'acts'. The first, consisting of Parts One and Two, focuses on the main protagonists on Atrios: the obsessed Marshal (a fine performance from John Woodvine); his deputy Shapp; the pacifist Princess Astra; her weedy lover Merak; plus an assortment of guards. Sadly, aside from the Marshal, all these characters are somewhat one-dimensional. Merak, in particular, is pathetic and seems to spend the entire story wandering around calling for Astra.

Parts Three and Four introduce the Shadow, agent of the Black Guardian, and things start to look up. The introductory scene itself is very effective, and the Shadow's presence permeates the remaining episodes. He is, indeed, by far the best thing about the whole story. Actor William Squire keeps the character totally believable and simply oozes evil. The only let-down is his use of small black Lego bricks to control others' minds. It is never explained how these work (and strangely they work on both Astra and K9 but not the Doctor) – although it is admittedly a rather more dramatic device than some possible alternatives such as swinging a watch in front of Astra's eyes or simply reprogramming K9. Geraint Jones liked the character, as he wrote in *TARDIS* Volume 4 Number 2 dated 1 April 1979: 'The Shadow proved an excellent villain. His evil was total as his little game on Atrios and Zeos showed. The face mask was very convincing, as were the scars on the jaw. The voice was one of the best we have ever heard: a low, hissing sound, but very clear as well as sinister.' Less impressed, however, was Mike Ashcroft writing in *Oracle* Volume 2 Number 8 dated May 1979: 'I didn't really like any of the characters, to tell the truth … The Shadow was too corny (as the name suggests – he was rather like a comic-strip fiend) for a commanding lead role, but given the situation the actor turned in a good performance.'

Also introduced in the middle section of the story is the computer Mentalis, a nice idea that works all the better for being presented in not too overblown a way – it is simply a computer in a room. It is also a nice touch that only K9 can communicate with Mentalis, giving him something to do in the story that is specifically tailored to his capabilities.

Parts Five and Six, set largely on the Shadow's 'planet' (obviously a spaceship of some description), bring the story and the search for the Key to Time to their conclusion. The biggest point of contention here is the character of Drax. 'I just didn't like him,' stated Ashcroft. '[Part Five] has to take first prize in the all-time "waste of time" category. It totally deflated my rising opinion of the intelligent, well-constructed storyline … After … the various parties roamed round endless corridors in "the valley of the Shadow" we were introduced to Drax, who encapsulates my distaste for this adventure. His instant recognition of the Doctor – "Theta Sigma" as he called him – made me fear for the worst; fears that were soon confirmed. The "Class of '92" must have had a remarkably poor success rate, as Drax was so phony it was beyond belief. He was completely out of character with the show (hopefully not a sign of Doug Adams's influence), and as a Time Lord did more to ruin the image of Gallifrey than Robert Holmes ever did. His [Cockney] accent was taking things a bit too far … and the intended humour just wasn't funny. I can't think of a single character who has aggravated me more since … since I can't remember when!'

The story ends reasonably well with Astra herself revealed as being the sixth segment – which may perhaps explain Lalla Ward's rather lifeless acting throughout the adventure – and the Doctor finally assembling the complete Key to Time. Now comes the problem: the resolution to the over-arching plot. Unfortunately it is something of a cop out. The Doctor simply decides that the Key is too powerful for anyone to possess and orders it to redisperse, thus thwarting the Guardian's plan. This all seems far too easy and makes a mockery of the preceding twenty-five and a bit episodes of adventure as the Doctor struggled to locate and assemble the six segments.

'My overall view on the last episode can only be [that it was an] anticlimax,' wrote Geraint Jones. 'It was very exciting, unpredictable and well produced. But as a successful conclusion to a twenty-six week lead up, it was a let-down.

'Everything was so rushed that explanations were far from being clear throughout. Was the universe stopped for a brief moment to restore the balance? Was this done by the White Guardian? How was Astra restored and the segment retained?

'It balanced the season nicely to meet the White Guardian at the opening and the Black at the end, but I think it would have worked far better with both in this last story …

'Surely it would have been better to have concluded the basic story of *The Armageddon Factor* in the first four episodes and [left] the last two to develop and conclude the running theme more successfully?'

Ashcroft had similar misgivings: 'The climax with the Black Guardian, at last, was … impressive but rather brief. The power of the Black Guardian was also a bit underplayed I felt. Since the White Guardian could trap and open the doors of the TARDIS in *The Ribos Operation*, then I was surprised that his counterpart couldn't act against the ship here – even if the defences *were* on. If the Key to Time had been instructed to act defensively, then it might have been a different kettle of fish, but no such order was given. Presumably this was an example of the forces of good being superior to those of evil. And where was the White Guardian during all the action?'

To be fair, the choice that the Doctor makes is the only one that allows Astra continued existence; and it is hard to see what other outcome could have been arrived at that would have allowed *Doctor Who* to continue without a major revision of its format. If the season had ended with the Black Guardian being given the Key, what would have happened? How could the Doctor have prevented him from running the universe exactly as he pleased? This dilemma could certainly have provided the basis for an interesting new strand of adventures – a revamping of the series akin to the Doctor's exile to Earth in the early seventies, perhaps – but clearly there was no call for such a grand scale development at this time. Then again, the season could have ended with the White Guardian being given the Key, in fulfillment of the Doctor's mission, but that would have been even more undramatic than what was actually transmitted – and, in any event, the closing scenes could be interpreted as suggesting that the two Guardians are really just two sides of the same individual, or else that the Doctor has been inadvertently working for the Black Guardian all along. So it is that the Doctor wins the day by denying anyone ultimate power and, fitting a randomiser to his TARDIS, heads off into the great unknown. *The Armageddon Factor* effectively marks the end of another of *Doctor Who*'s sub-eras and a return to the old days, where the Doctor was a wanderer in space and time, never knowing where or in what time period he would arrive next.

Anthony Read's first full season as *Doctor Who*'s script editor was also his last; he bowed out on *The Armageddon Factor* and handed over the reins to his successor, Douglas Adams. Production of season sixteen had been relatively trouble free by comparison with that of the previous one, but Graham Williams nevertheless considered that the use of a linking theme had imposed too many strictures to be repeated on a regular basis. Season seventeen would therefore see a return to the more familiar format of a succession of unconnected stories, the transmission order of which could if necessary be changed during the course of production. This was perhaps just as well, as production of *that* season would prove to be anything but trouble free …

DOCTOR WHO SEASON SEVENTEEN [1979-1980]

Regular Cast:
Doctor Who (Tom Baker)
Romana (Lalla Ward)
Voice of K9 (David Brierley)*

* Except *Destiny of the Daleks* and *City of Death*; in the former K9 does not speak and in the latter he does not appear.

Regular Crew:
Producer: Graham Williams.
Script Editor: Douglas Adams.
Production Unit Manager: John Nathan-Turner.
Title Music: Ron Grainer and the BBC Radiophonic Workshop, arranged by Delia Derbyshire.
Special Sounds: Dick Mills.

An early priority for Graham Williams and Douglas Adams in their preparations for *Doctor Who*'s seventeenth season was to decide how to replace Mary Tamm, who had resisted all attempts to persuade her to stay on for a further year as Romana. They concluded that the simplest plot explanation for Tamm's sudden disappearance would be to have Romana regenerate. Although they toyed with the idea of casting a different actress in the role for each story, they quickly realised that this would be impracticable. Eventually they offered the job to Lalla Ward, who had impressed them with her performance as Princess Astra in *The Armageddon Factor* and, importantly, had got on well with Tom Baker. John Leeson had also decided to move on at this point, and so someone new was required to voice K9. David Brierley was cast after two rounds of auditions by director Christopher Barry, who had been assigned to handle his debut story *The Creature from the Pit*. The season's first transmitted story, meanwhile, would see the robot dog out of action with 'laryngitis' as the Doctor faced once again his most notorious adversaries …

DESTINY OF THE DALEKS

Writer: Terry Nation. **Director:** Ken Grieve. **Designer:** Ken Ledsham. **Costumes:** June Hudson. **Make-Up:** Cecile Hay-Arthur. **Incidental Music:** Dudley Simpson. **Visual Effects:** Peter Logan. **Film Cameraman:** Philip Law, Kevin Rowley, Fred Hamilton. **Film Editor:** Dick Allen. **Studio Lighting:** John Dixon. **Studio Sound:** Clive Gifford. **Production Assistant:** Henry Foster. **Assistant Floor Manager:** David Tilley, Antony Root.

	First UK TX	Scheduled TX	Actual TX	Duration	Viewers	Chart Pos.
Episode One	01/09/79	18.10	18.14	24'03"	13.0	28
Episode Two	08/09/79	18.10	18.10	25'14"	12.7	39
Episode Three	15/09/79	18.10	18.08	24'32"	13.8	28
Episode Four	22/09/79	18.15	18.17	26'05"	14.4	27

Plot: The Doctor and a newly-regenerated Romana arrive on Skaro and discover that the Daleks are using explosive charges and a group of humanoid slave workers to mine the planet in search of their creator, Davros. A stalemate has arisen in an interplanetary war that the Daleks are waging against the robotic Movellans, and their hope is that Davros will be able to give them the edge. A force of Movellans has also arrived on Skaro, determined to thwart the Daleks' plan. Davros is found in the ruins of the old Kaled city and immediately revives, his life support systems having held him in suspended animation ever since his apparent death. He quickly deduces that the battle computers of the two warring races are locked in a logical stalemate and that he can break this by introducing an element of intuition. The Movellans, having reached the same conclusion, want the Doctor to do likewise for them. Davros attempts to destroy the Movellan ship using a suicide squad of Daleks loaded with bombs, but the Doctor returns to the Kaled city and tricks him into inadvertently detonating them before they reach their target. The Movellans are deactivated and Davros is cryogenically frozen on board their ship until the freed slave workers can take him to Earth and ensure that he is put on trial for his crimes.

Episode endings:
1. Romana, trapped in the ruins of the old Kaled city, backs uneasily away from a vibrating wall. Suddenly Daleks crash through the wall and advance towards her, repeatedly telling her not to move and asserting that she is their prisoner.
2. Davros flexes his fingers, and his artificial eye lights up as he revives.
3. The Movellans set a trap for the Doctor, placing an unconscious Romana in a transparent cylinder with a 'nova device' capable of causing the air inside to catch fire when the countdown reaches zero. The Doctor struggles desperately to find a way into the sealed cylinder as the countdown continues.
4. The TARDIS dematerialises from the surface of Skaro.

FOURTH DOCTOR

IT WAS MADE WHERE...?

Location filming: 11.06.79-15.06.79
Locations: Winspit Quarry, Worth Matravers, Dorset; Binnegar Heath Sand Pit, Puddletown Road, Wareham, Dorset.
Studio: 02.07.79-03.07.79 in TC3, 15.07.79-17.07.79 in TC1

ADDITIONAL CREDITED CAST

Tyssan (Tim Barlow), Commander Sharrel (Peter Straker), Agella (Suzanne Danielle), Lan (Tony Osoba), Dalek Operators (Cy Town, Mike Mungarvan), Dalek Voice (Roy Skelton)*, Davros (David Gooderson2-4), Jall (Penny Casdagli2,4), Veldan (David Yip2,4), Movellan Guard (Cassandra4**).

* David Gooderson also supplied some Dalek voices in this story, but uncredited.
** Although she is credited on Part Four, the appearance of the Movellan Guard played by Cassandra is actually in Part Three.
Note: Although K9 has no dialogue in this story he is heard to croak at the start of Episode One. The croak was provided by Roy Skelton.

Three 'alternative' physical forms of Romana seen in Episode One were played, uncredited, by Lee Richards, Maggy Armitage and Yvonne Gallagher.

THINGS TO WATCH OUT FOR

- The Skaro sound effects from the first Dalek story, *The Mutants*, are reused here.
- Romana wears a pink and white parody of the Doctor's costume.
- This story features the first use on the series of a steadycam – a rig used to obtain smooth, stable shots from a hand held camera – operated on this occasion by Fred Hamilton.
- David Yip, later to star in the BBC's *The Chinese Detective*, plays the Dalek prisoner Veldan.

THINGS YOU MIGHT NOT HAVE KNOWN

- Actor Tim Barlow, who played Tyssan, was deaf.
- Michael Wisher was not available to reprise his role of Davros from *Genesis of the Daleks* and so David Gooderson was cast. He was a voice artist and it was thought that he would be able to imitate Wisher's half-Dalek, half-human cadences.
- The influence of new script editor Douglas Adams is visible when the Doctor pulls from his pocket a book, *Origins of the Universe*, by Oolon Caluphid of *The Hitch-Hiker's Guide to the Galaxy* fame.
- During the opening credits, *Destiny of the Daleks*'s individual segments were called episodes, rather than parts as was the standard for all other fourth Doctor stories.

QUOTE, UNQUOTE

- **The Doctor:** [Reading a book called *Origins of the Universe* by Oolon Caluphid.] 'He got it wrong on the first line! Why didn't he ask someone who saw it happen?'
- **Daleks:** 'Seek – locate – exterminate!'

ANALYSIS

The opening scenes of *Destiny of the Daleks* get the new season off to a shaky start,

Romana's regeneration – in which she 'tries on' a number of unsuitable bodies before settling on the Lalla Ward version – being played very much for laughs. 'The [regeneration] scene was handled abysmally,' complained Chris Dunk in *Oracle* Volume 3 Number 3 dated December 1979. 'There was a total lack of convincing acting, although to be fair to the actresses involved, the script could hardly have allowed less for it. What really made me cross though was the lack of explanation. I am quite open to any new theories thrust at us and I will readily accept that Romana can change like this, but we were not told so. We were not even given the briefest mention of *why* she had to do it.' On a more positive note, Lalla Ward's debut performance as the new Romana is very promising, as Chris Marton suggested in *TARDIS* Volume 4 Number 6 in 1979: 'Lalla Ward's Romana seemed more natural and spontaneous than Mary Tamm's ..., and her mixture of ... Time Lord intellect and little girl innocence could prove a winning formula.'

Writer Terry Nation was not in fact responsible for the regeneration scene – it was added by script editor Douglas Adams – and, as Chris Marton noted, the story subsequently settles down into his well-established style: 'The usual Nation trademarks are well in evidence – the long exploration of a seemingly desolate, uninhabited terrain; the incapacitation of one of the TARDIS crew by a run-of-the-mill hazard, the other running off to locate help; return to the TARDIS barred; the encounter with a group of visitors to the planet; and the inevitable melodramatic appearance of the Daleks at Episode One's climax.'

Chris Dunk had mixed feelings about the story taking place on Skaro: 'It was courageous to return to Skaro, but with a randomiser fitted to the TARDIS helm I fail to see why and how that particular planet out of all the millions should have been arrived at. The odds must be heavily against it.' The scenes set on the planet's surface are very effective, however, as Richard Walter observed in *Matrix* Issue 4 dated November 1979: 'The location work gave [it] tremendous atmosphere and the effect of the Movellan ship landing was not at all bad. From their first appearance, the Movellans had a sense of mystery surrounding them. They looked human, and yet ...'

Nation had toyed before with the idea of the Daleks having a race of robot rivals – specifically the Mechanoids in season two's *The Chase* and, perhaps more particularly, in the *TV Century 21* comic strips of the mid-sixties – and the Movellans are a worthwhile addition to the series' mythology, even though their appearance leaves a little to be desired. Rather more surprising is the fact that in this story the Daleks themselves are on several occasions referred to as robots. This has been roundly condemned by most fan commentators, although William Gallagher made an interesting point in *Web Planet* Issue 2 dated July 1980: '"*He referred to the Daleks as robots!*" many of you have shrieked in your profound certainty that Mr Nation was wrong to do so. But was he? It was then many years since the Daleks had been created, so it was natural for them to have improved themselves in every way possible.' It does indeed seem that Nation – or could it have been Adams? – was quite consciously suggesting that the Daleks had evolved from organic creatures into robotic ones. The scene in which the Doctor finds a Kaled mutant lying on the ground and recalls that the Daleks were once organic themselves is particularly significant in this regard. If so, however, his motivation for introducing such a change remains a mystery. It is admittedly very difficult to believe that the Daleks could ever have become locked in a logical stalemate with the Movellans *unless* they had evolved into robots, given that they are normally highly emotional creatures, but Nation attempts to address this problem in a different way by suggesting that it is the races' respective *battle computers* that have led to this situation. In the end, the impression given is that Nation is simply struggling to come up with a plausible reason why the Daleks should need to go in search of their creator for assistance.

This brings us to the nub of the story's problems. Davros was a character positively crying out *not* to be resurrected after his unbeatable debut appearance in season twelve's *Genesis of the Daleks.* The plot device by way of which this is achieved in *Destiny of the Daleks* is frankly ludicrous, and the character in general is nowhere near as well-written or as subtle here as in the earlier story. It doesn't help matters, either, that Michael Wisher, whose wonderful performance in *Genesis of the Daleks* was such a crucial factor in Davros's success, proved to be unavailable on this occasion, necessitating a recasting of the part. David Gooderson's acting here is unfortunately not in the same league, and the net result is that this wonderful character is very much devalued. 'The biggest let down was in the handling of Davros,' wrote Chris Marton. 'David Gooderson tried, but [his version] seemed more crusty and bad tempered than Michael Wisher's ruthless fanatic. His somewhat humiliating fate reduced his evil stature greatly, though the possibility of his release by the Daleks is open ...' Even Davros's mask and chair, designed for an actor of a different build, are less effective this time around, as Ian Wishart pointed out in *Ark in Space* No. 1 in 1979: 'It was amusing to watch Davros – the evil genius, brilliant creator of the Daleks – bobbing up and down on his squeaky chair every time he moved about.'

Francis Danes, writing in *Fendahl* Number 6 dated August/September 1979, thought that the Daleks too were poorly presented in this story: 'The Dalek machines themselves were in appalling condition ... It is sad that the most famous monsters of science-fiction were so tatty ... The dummy Daleks were very obvious; they just looked completely unfinished. The one that stood behind Davros when the "real" Daleks had departed was particularly bad.' Richard Walter took a similar view in *Matrix* Issue 4 dated November 1979: 'Where in the universe can a Dalek get a respray and service? What did annoy me was that the four Daleks used were each slightly different, which meant that if one was blown up ... it was easy to spot the same one guarding a prisoner down the tunnel in another scene. It was made very obvious that the [BBC] only had the four machines.' Ian Wishart, however, argued that the Daleks came out quite well: '[They] appeared a little bashed up – but surely a race of space/time travellers in the middle of a gigantic space war would get a little knocked about now and then? At the end of Episode One, when [they] burst through the glass wall ... and captured Romana, I was really glad to see them portrayed as terrifying and callous, as they should be ... Some ... thought that the way the Daleks kept repeating what they were saying, and shouting things like "Seek, locate and destroy!" ... made them appear stupid and, to a certain degree, primitive. However, to me, this is exactly how they should be: thoroughly evil and really terrifying. It was interesting to note how less dominant the Daleks became after Davros came on the scene ...'

Destiny of the Daleks ultimately manages to rise above all its undoubted failings and provides a fair degree of entertainment. Contemporary viewers certainly thought so, if the BBC's Audience Research Report on the story gives any indication: 'Most viewers found the programmes enjoyable, feeling that the plot had been a good one. The teenage and adult audience did not find the story particularly exciting or at all frightening but they felt that children did. "The Daleks always create good opposition" was the general view, and respondents said that *Doctor Who* was "always reliable entertainment".' Opinions on Lalla Ward were mixed, but Tom Baker again 'was often praised for his portrayal of the central character, a few adding that his was "the best Doctor Who of all".'

As Chris Marton put it: 'After a couple of hit and miss seasons, the dreaded Daleks once more come to the aid of the Doctor in a most enjoyable, if not exactly vintage little story.'

CITY OF DEATH

Writer: David Agnew*. **Director:** Michael Hayes. **Designer:** Richard McManan-Smith. **Costumes:** Doreen James, Jan Wright. **Make-Up:** Jean Steward. **Incidental Music:** Dudley Simpson. **Visual Effects:** Ian Scoones. **Film Cameraman:** John Walker. **Film Editor:** John Gregory. **Studio Lighting:** Mike Jefferies. **Studio Sound:** Anthony Philpott. **Production Assistant:** Rosemary Crowson. **Assistant Floor Manager:** Carol Scott.

*This was a pseudonym adopted by Douglas Adams and Graham Williams, who put together the final scripts after initial drafts commissioned from writer David Fisher failed to meet with their approval.

	First UK TX	Scheduled TX	Actual TX	Duration	Viewers	Chart Pos.
Part One	29/09/79	18.05	18.07	24'25"	12.4	50
Part Two	06/10/79	18.15	18.17	24'33"	14.1	44
Part Three	13/10/79	18.00	18.04	25'25"	15.4	34
Part Four	20/10/79	18.15	18.16	25'08"	16.1	16

Plot: The Doctor and Romana are enjoying a holiday in Paris, 1979, when they become aware of a fracture in time. During a visit to the Louvre to see da Vinci's *Mona Lisa*, the Doctor purloins from a stranger, Countess Scarlioni, a bracelet that is actually an alien scanner device. He, Romana and a private detective named Duggan are then 'invited' to the chateau home of Count Scarlioni, where they find hidden in the cellar six additional *Mona Lisa*s – all of them originals! The Count is revealed as an alien called Scaroth, last of the Jagaroth race. He was splintered in time when his ship exploded above primeval Earth, and in his twelve different aspects has since been guiding mankind's development to a point where time travel is possible. His intention is to go back and prevent the destruction of his ship. To finance the final stages of this project, overseen by the misguided scientist Kerensky, he plans to steal the *Mona Lisa* from the Louvre and then secretly sell the multiple copies that one of his earlier splinters has forced da Vinci to paint. The Doctor realises that the Count must be prevented from carrying out his plan as the explosion of the Jagaroth ship provided the energy that initiated life on Earth. Following Scaroth's trail in the TARDIS, he travels back to primeval Earth. Duggan fells Scaroth with a punch, thereby ensuring that history stays on its proper course.

Episode endings:
1. Countess Scarlioni goes to Kerensky's laboratory to try to speak to her husband, but he has locked the door. Inside, the Count pulls off a mask to reveal beneath his human features the cyclopean alien face of Scaroth.
2. Investigating the mystery of the additional *Mona Lisa*s, the Doctor travels back in time to Leonardo's workshop to talk to the painter. There he is caught by a soldier and introduced

to Captain Tancredi – who looks identical to Count Scarlioni, and knows who the Doctor is.

3. The Count invites Kerensky to examine the field generator of the time travel equipment. When he does so, the Count operates the machine and Kerensky ages to a skeleton before the eyes of the startled Romana and Duggan.

4. The Doctor and Romana say farewell to Duggan at the top of the Eiffel Tower. A few moments later they wave up to him from the ground below, and run off into the distance.

IT WAS MADE WHERE...?

Location filming: 30.04.79-03.05.79

Locations: Eiffel Tower, Parc du Champ de Mars, Paris, France; Duplex Metro Platform (Line 6), Rue August Bartoldi, Paris, France; Trocadero Metro Platform (Line 6), Place du Trocadero, Paris, France; Avenue Kleber (Boissiere Metro and Entrance), Paris, France; Rue de Rivoli (Louvre Museum), Paris, France; Le Notre Dame Brasserie, Place du Petit Pont, Paris, France; Place de la Concorde, Paris, France; Denise Rene Gallery, Boulevard St Germain, Paris, France; Avenue des Champs Elysees, Paris, France; 47 Rue Vieille du Temple, Paris, France.

Bray filming: 08.05.79-10.05.79

Studio: 21.05.79-22.05.79 in TC3, 03.06.79-05.06.79 in TC6

ADDITIONAL CREDITED CAST

Count (Julian Glover), Countess (Catherine Schell), Duggan (Tom Chadbon), Kerensky (David Graham), Hermann (Kevin Flood), Louvre Guide (Pamela Stirling[1,3]), Soldier (Peter Halliday[2,3]), Art Gallery Visitors (Eleanor Bron[4], John Cleese[4]).

THINGS TO WATCH OUT FOR

- A source of inspiration for this story was the *Bulldog Drummond* tales of Herman McNeile.
- Kerensky's computer makes a sound very similar if not identical to that of WOTAN from the sesaon three story *The War Machines*.
- John Cleese and Eleanor Bron make a cameo appearance as eccentric art critics in Part Four.
- Popular film actor Julian Glover returned to *Doctor Who* to play Count Scarlioni. He had previously appeared as Richard the Lionheart with William Hartnell's Doctor in *The Crusade* (1965).
- Catherine Schell, who portrayed the Countess, had previously played the shape-changing character Maya during the second, 1976, season of Gerry Anderson's series *Space: 1999*.

THINGS YOU MIGHT NOT HAVE KNOWN

- Working title: *Curse of the Sephiroth*.
- *City of Death* was written by producer Graham Williams and script editor Douglas Adams when a script by David Fisher called *The Gamble with Time* had to be re-worked due to changing production requirements. As a result it was transmitted under the name David Agnew, a generic BBC pseudonym that, on *Doctor Who*, had previously been used for *The Invasion of Time*.

- **The Doctor:** 'I say, what a wonderful butler! He's so violent!'
- **Countess:** [Speaking of the Doctor.] 'My dear, I don't think he's as stupid as he seems.' **Count:** 'My dear, nobody could be as stupid as *he* seems!'
- **Duggan:** 'You can't make an omelette without breaking eggs'. **Romana:** 'If you made an omelette, I'd expect to find a pile of broken crockery, a cooker in flames and an unconscious chef!'
- **Count:** 'I am Scaroth. Me together in one. The Jagaroth shall live through me. Together we have pushed this puny race of Humans, shaped their paltry destiny to meet our ends. Soon we shall be. The centuries that divide me shall be undone.'
- **Romana:** 'Shall we take the lift or fly?' **The Doctor:** 'Let's not be ostentatious.' **Romana:** 'All right … let's fly, then.' **The Doctor:** 'That would look silly … we'll take the lift.'

Analysis

City of Death mixes time travel, spaghetti-headed aliens and hard-boiled detectives in a tale of an alien race's fight for survival; and the sublime Parisian ambience supplied by virtue of a brief location shoot in the French capital – made possible by judicious budget balancing on the part of Graham Williams and production unit manager John Nathan-Turner – is the icing on the cake.

From the opening shots of Scaroth in his ship the viewer gets the feeling that this story is going to be something really special. Visual effects designer Ian Scoones pulled out all the stops to present an alien landscape second to none, and the simple spider-like design of the Jagaroth ship is both elegant and effective. *Doctor Who* has often been derided for the questionable quality of its effects, and yet those showcased here still stand up to close scrutiny many years after they were created. As Chris Dunk wrote in *Oracle* Volume 3 Number 4 dated January 1980: 'The opening sequence could hardly have been more effective. The modelwork was great, and the backdrop, an empty, inert Earth, four million years past, was eerie and formidably exciting. Desolation and death were thus even suggested in the opening frames, but few could have had an inkling of how history would eventually turn full circle …'

City of Death succeeds in part simply because it is unlike any other *Doctor Who* story before or after. 'The way in which *City of Death* is played, scored, photographed and so on is not typical *Doctor Who*,' noted Tim Ryan in *Peladon* Issue Six dated May/June 1990. 'It has cinematic qualities. [Do] that famous shot-through-the-postcard-rack and the sequence that [follows] look like *Doctor Who* to you? [They seem] to me to have escaped from some weirdo French thriller! And what about Dudley Simpson's incidental music? … One can well believe that Dudley has flown over to Paris to sample the atmosphere – at least that's the way it sounds. His music for the story is positively epochal; it's ornately structured; cyclical yet free-falling; marvellously arranged – it's like a … well, a film score! And what about the special effects, the Jagaroth ship and all? … No painted washing-up liquid bottles here!'

Daniel O'Mahony praised the story to the skies in *Star Begotten* Volume 3 Number 1/2 dated winter/spring 1989: '*City of Death* has everything a classic needs – a cracking good storyline, mostly brilliant characterisations, the humour that should always be present in *Doctor Who* …, mucho-brilliant cliffhangers (all of them) and lots of gratuitous violence.' John Connors joined in the accolades in *DWB* No. 89 dated May 1991: 'In May 1979 the *Doctor Who* crew created a little slice of history ... by flying to Paris for ... film work – the first ever foreign location shoot the series had seen. But, in retrospect, it was more than that; from that moment on, they were on course to create the best blend of kitsch, surrealism, fantasy and comedy-drama seen in our favourite Time Lord's annals. Originally dismissed as too camp and silly to be of more than passing interest, *City of Death* has been reassessed and reconsidered to the point where it's now a strong contender for the crown of best story ever. It's not hard to see why.'

Early reaction to the story was, as Connors suggested, not always so positive. John Peel was particularly concerned about the level of humour on display, as he explained in *TARDIS* Volume 4 Number 6 in 1979: 'With Doug Adams joining, the format seems to have stabilised now – as pure farce. To my mind, the acting once more was appalling ... French gangsters in turned-up collars and hats! Good grief! And Duggan was so stupid as to be unbelievable. On the whole I simply couldn't believe that this was *Doctor Who*. Humour on the show is one thing; the continual buffoonery is getting completely on my nerves.' This point was also picked up by Chris Dunk: 'The only thing that I can find to fault the production team on ... is the apparent need for Tom Baker to "play for laughs" ... Whether these are ad libs or not, I believe that many of them are unnecessary, not contributing to the success that *Doctor Who* enjoys ... Stories should, and ultimately will, stand or fall by the calibre of the author's workmanship, ... not by cheap gags. Humour, yes, ... but not the farcical element.'

In retrospect these criticisms can be seen to have been misplaced. The humour in *City of Death* is actually quite delightful, and one of its main attractions. Tom Chadbon's performance as the ever-enthusiastic private eye Duggan is nicely light-hearted and David Graham's outrageously-accented portrayal of the ill-fated scientist Kerensky is excellent.

The story's major plus point in terms of casting, however, is Julian Glover as Count Scarlioni. Glover brings a certain dignity and authority to any production in which he appears, and here he is perfectly cast as the totally controlled and ruthless Scaroth. Catherine Schell is also admirable as his wife, although her attractiveness unfortunately serves to highlight the slight oddity that, presumably, they have never enjoyed conjugal rights – unless it is only Scaroth's head and hands that look alien! The mask used for the Jagaroth is actually the one aspect of the production that is less than wholly successful, in that it is clearly much larger than Julian Glover's own head and so could not logically be accommodated within the human disguise worn by Scaroth for most of the action. One can only assume that the creatures are able somehow to scrunch up their heads, which might also perhaps explain why Scaroth feels the need to relax by tearing off his human disguise at the end of Part One – an action that otherwise seems to serve no purpose but to provide the obligatory cliffhanger.

These are mere quibbles, though, and in no way detract from the fact that *City of Death* is in almost every way a triumph, totally belying the fact that its scripts were hurried last minute rewrites.

THE CREATURE FROM THE PIT

Writer: David Fisher. **Director:** Christopher Barry. **Designer:** Valerie Warrender. **Costumes:** June Hudson. **Make-Up:** Gillian Thomas. **Incidental Music:** Dudley Simpson. **Visual Effects:** Mat Irvine. **Film Cameraman:** David Feig. **Film Editor:** M A C Adams. **Studio Lighting:** Warwick Fielding. **Studio Sound:** Anthony Philpott. **Production Assistant:** Romey Allison. **Assistant Floor Manager:** David Tilley, Kate Osborne.

	First UK TX	Scheduled TX	Actual TX	Duration	Viewers	Chart Pos.
Part One	27/10/79	18.00	18.02	23'32"	9.3	43
Part Two	03/11/79	18.05	18.07	24'03"	10.8	23
Part Three	10/11/79	18.00	18.02	23'55"	10.2	36
Part Four	17/11/79	18.00	18.04	24'07"	9.6	36

Plot: The Doctor and Romana receive a distress signal and arrive on Chloris, a lush and verdant world that has only small quantities of metals, all of which are controlled by its ruler, Lady Adrasta. Adrasta keeps order with the aid of her Huntsman and his wolfweeds – mobile balls of vegetation – while a band of scruffy thieves, led by Torvin, organize raids on her palace to steal whatever metal they can. The Doctor identifies the distress signal's source as a large eggshell-like structure in the forest. He is taken prisoner by Adrasta's guards and, in order to escape, leaps into the Pit – the entrance to a cave system into which all those who incur Adrasta's wrath are consigned to be devoured by an immense green globular creature living within. The Doctor, with the aid of the elderly soothsayer Organon, discovers that the creature is not an unthinking killer but an ambassador from the planet Tythonus, which has a lack of chlorophyll but an abundance of metal. The Tythonians had hoped to trade with Chloris, but the first person their ambassador Erato encountered on arriving in his eggshell-like ship was Adrasta, who took his communicator device and trapped him in the Pit so as to preserve her monopoly on metal. Erato retrieves his communicator and kills Adrasta. He then warns the Doctor that the Tythonians have set a neutron star on a collision course with Chloris in retaliation for his imprisonment. With the Doctor's help he is freed from the Pit and, out in space, spins an aluminium shell around the star, allowing for it to be pulled off course by the TARDIS's gravitational tractor beam and thus saving Chloris.

Episode endings:
1. The Doctor, in order to escape from Adrasta and her guards, jumps into the Pit.
2. The huge alien creature presses up against an alarmed Doctor, threatening to crush him.
3. The hypnotised thieves, ignoring Adrasta's screams of protest, place against the creature's side the 'shield' earlier stolen from the wall of her throne room.
4. Organon tells the astonished Huntsman that the scroll he is holding is a draft contract for a trading agreement between Tythonus and Chloris. The Huntsman asks how he knows this and Organon, rather than admitting that he was told it by the Doctor, merely crosses his fingers and claims that it is 'written in the stars'.

IT WAS MADE WHERE...?

Ealing filming: 20.03.79-23.03.79, 26.03.79 on Stage 3B
Model reshoot: 17.04.79-18.04.79 on BBC Visual Effects Workshop model stage
Studio: 09.04.79-10.04.79, 22.04.79-24.04.79 all in TC6, 19.04.79 (voice-overs only)
(studio unknown), 27.04.79 (gallery only) in TC1

ADDITIONAL CREDITED CAST

Adrasta (Myra Frances), Karela (Eileen Way), Torvin (John Bryans), Edu (Edward
Kelsey), Ainu (Tim Munro), Huntsman (David Telfer[1,4]*), Tollund (Morris Barry[1]),
Doran (Terry Walsh[1]*), Organon (Geoffrey Bayldon[2-4]), Guardmaster (Tommy
Wright[2,3]), Guards (Philip Denyer[2,3], Dave Redgrave[3]).

* Also in Part Two, but uncredited.

THINGS TO WATCH OUT FOR

• Former *Doctor Who* director Morris Barry plays the small part of Adrasta's engineer
  Tollund in Part One.
• Eileen Way, who had appeared as Old Mother in the very first *Doctor Who* story,
  100,000 BC, features here as Lady Adrasta's assistant Karela.
• Geoffrey Bayldon, better known as Catweazle in the LWT series of the same name
  and as the Crowman in Southern's *Worzel Gummidge*, portrays Organon.
• David Brierley makes his debut replacing John Leeson as the voice of K9.

THINGS YOU MIGHT NOT HAVE KNOWN

• This was the last story to be directed by Christopher Barry, one of *Doctor Who*'s
  longest-serving contributors.

QUOTE, UNQUOTE

• **Organon:** [Introducing himself.] 'Astrologer extraordinary. Seer to princes and
  emperors. The future foretold, the present explained, the past – apologised for.'
• **Adrasta:** [Speaking of the Pit.] 'We call it "the Pit".'

ANALYSIS

It is a standard approach in science-fiction storytelling for the writer to posit a world
possessing one or two distinctive features and then, by logical extrapolation from those
features, develop a culture similar to and yet fascinatingly different from our own. David
Fisher starts out along the right lines in *The Creature from the Pit* by presenting a
scenario in which a planet rich in vegetable matter but short on metals receives trading
overtures from one with the converse problem. Unfortunately it seems that, having
come up with this ingenious idea, he then rested on his laurels and failed to move on to
the extrapolation stage. Aside from the presence of Torvin's band of thieves – and it
takes no great leap of the imagination to realise that if something is in short supply there
are bound to be thieves trying to steal it – there is nothing here to suggest what the
ramifications of the scarcity of metals might be for the wider community on Chloris.
Indeed there is nothing to suggest a wider community at all; the planet's entire
population seems to consist of about ten individuals.

In fact Fisher has set himself too difficult a task. Had he made Chloris short of one particular metal – copper, say – he might have had a reasonable chance of exploring the implications of this by researching all the things in which that metal is normally to be found and then speculating as to the effects of its absence in each case. A planet lacking in *all* metals would in reality be so different from our own as to be virtually impossible to represent on screen – at least within *Doctor Who*'s limited budgets. It is highly unlikely, scientifically speaking, that any animal or plant life existing here would even remotely resemble that of Earth; and it is questionable whether or not a planet could ever have formed in the first place without at least a certain quantity of metals having been present. A possible alternative approach for Fisher to have taken would have been to have made Chloris a planet on which metals were present in normal quantities but unobtainable due to the indigenous population's failure to discover mining skills – an idea with obvious potential for further development. It was not to be, however; and in fact one senses from the scripts that Fisher's grasp of scientific principles is none too sound. The most obvious illustration of this is the scene in which Erato launches itself into space and weaves an aluminium shell around a neutron star in order to minimise its gravitational pull (eh?) and allow the TARDIS to pull it off course with a tractor beam. Hmm …

The scripting of this story is actually pretty poor in almost every respect. The characters are all clichéd and one dimensional; the dialogue is generally atrocious; and the wolfweeds are just plain silly. The decision to make the thieves a bunch of stereotypical Jewish characters of the Fagin variety was apparently taken by script editor Douglas Adams rather than by Fisher, but the end result is that they seem to have wandered in off the set of a *Monty Python's Flying Circus* sketch. The three regulars are also poorly catered for here. It is all too obvious that Fisher has written Romana with Mary Tamm's characterisation rather than Lalla Ward's in mind (not his fault, as at that stage it had yet to be firmly established that Tamm was leaving); the Doctor seems to lose his senses altogether at the end of Part One as he leaps into the Pit of his own accord, knowing full well that to be consigned there is regarded as tantamount to a sentence of execution (another example of the 'anything for a cliffhanger' syndrome); and K9 is at his silliest and most irritating – although this is due not only to Fisher's writing but also to David Brierley's vocal performance, which is sadly not a patch on John Leeson's. Just about the only redeeming features as far as the story's characters are concerned are Geoffrey Bayldon's Organon and Myra Frances's Adrasta, both actors managing to work wonders with the material that they are given. 'The Lady Adrasta … was excellently evil,' opined Chris Dunk in *Oracle* Volume 3 Number 5 dated February/March 1980, 'and her confrontation with the creature was very dramatic although tended to be corny too. Never mind, the end of [Part Three] was quite the most exciting *Doctor Who* that I have seen for a long time. Marvellous stuff!'

'One word sums up this adventure,' suggested Richard Walter in *Matrix* Issue 5 dated February 1980. 'Disappointing. And it's a shame, because [it] boasted some fine sets, good actors and a rather interesting plot with some twists. For a start, the jungle set filmed at [Ealing] really did make a tremendous difference. It looked like the whole sequence had been filmed on location and gave the episode a heavy atmospheric quality which was never noticeable in the following episodes …

'The first part showed promise, and with the introduction of Geoffrey Bayldon in the second my hopes were high for an exciting romp. How wrong I was! The second and third

FOURTH DOCTOR

episodes were very tedious, with hardly anything of importance happening and with the Doctor and ... Organon wandering through tunnels in pursuit of a giant green blob (which incidentally was of a rather obscene design, I thought!) whilst Romana, now in the clutches of Adrasta, carted K9 around under her arm using him as a portable blaster!'

The blatantly phallic appendage that visual effects designer Mat Irvine saw fit to give Erato is indeed an unfortunate lapse in taste – the scene in which the Doctor raises it to his lips and blows into it, supposedly in an attempt to communicate, leaves the viewer similarly open-mouthed in astonishment – and the creature in general is very poorly realised. 'The "spherical mattress" was unconvincing enough,' wrote Dunk, 'although some children were apparently terrified by it, but the joking response to it offered by the Doctor destroyed all believability. Maybe he can defuse the scary bits, but there comes a limit; and why not let the kids be frightened anyway? TV can so often be condescending to the unrepresented minority.'

The use of humour in the story has come in for considerable criticism from reviewers. 'Isolated moments of humour ... are to me quite agreeable,' conceded Tim Westmacott in *TARDIS* Volume 5 Number 1 in 1980. '[It] is [the Doctor's] flippant remarks in a dangerous situation like "You're standing on my scarf!" as the creature looms over him that are not.' John Peel, writing in the same issue of *TARDIS*, was rather more forthright: 'After a shaky start to this season, the usual degeneration seems to have set in ... I can't help feeling that *The Creature from the Pit* didn't have humour to hold the plot together, but a bit of a plot to hold the humour together ... It's getting very embarrassing admitting to watching the [series] nowadays. Virtually all of my friends and family have given [it] up in disgust now.'

Even the usually dependable director Christopher Barry is somewhat off form on this story – his last for the series – although, in fairness, he had an uphill struggle to try to make it work. There is, all things considered, very little to recommend *The Creature from the Pit*.

NIGHTMARE OF EDEN

Writer: Bob Baker. **Director:** Alan Bromly, Graham Williams*. **Designer:** Roger Cann. **Costumes:** Rupert Jarvis. **Make-Up:** Joan Stribling. **Incidental Music:** Dudley Simpson. **Visual Effects:** Colin Mapson. **Studio Lighting:** Warwick Fielding. **Studio Sound:** Anthony Philpott. **Production Assistant:** Carolyn Montagu. **Assistant Floor Manager:** Val McCrimmon.

* Graham Williams decided to dispense with Alan Bromly's services toward the end of the story's second studio session and directed the remainder himself, without on-screen credit.

	First UK TX	Scheduled TX	Actual TX	Duration	Viewers	Chart Pos.
Part One	24/11/79	18.00	18.01	24'17"	8.7	41
Part Two	01/12/79	18.00	18.05	22'44"	9.6	31
Part Three	08/12/79	18.00	18.03	24'06"	9.6	32
Part Four	15/12/79	17.55	17.56	24'31"	9.4	32

Plot: The TARDIS arrives on the space liner *Empress* which has become locked together with a private ship, the *Hecate*, after colliding with it on emerging from hyperspace. The Doctor and Romana meet the scientist Tryst, who has with him a Continuous Event Transmuter (CET) machine containing crystals on which are stored supposed recordings of planets that he and his team have visited. Someone on board the liner is smuggling the dangerous addictive drug vraxoin, and to complicate matters the interface between the two ships allows some monstrous Mandrels from the mud-swamps of Eden to escape from the CET machine – which does not merely take recordings but actually displaces whole planetary areas into its crystals. The smugglers are revealed to be Tryst and the *Hecate*'s pilot, Dymond. Vraxoin is in fact the material into which the Mandrels decompose when they are killed. The Doctor thwarts this plan, separates the two ships and returns the Mandrels to Eden.

Episode endings:
1. Finding their progress through the *Empress* impeded by its interface with the *Hecate*, the Doctor instructs K9 to cut a hole in the wall to allow access. When he and the liner's Captain Rigg remove the cut metal panel, a huge monster rears out of the hole and, growling menacingly, starts waving its arms about.
2. The Doctor and Romana have sealed themselves in the lounge to escape the excise men Fisk and Costa. Romana calls up the image of Eden on the CET machine. The Doctor then tells Romana that he intends to test a theory, and the two of them leap into the projected image.
3. The Doctor plans to separate the two ships. Romana activates the drive of the *Empress* at the appropriate moment, but the Doctor is trapped in the interface and blurs and vanishes as the ships separate.
4. With Tryst and Dymond arrested, the Doctor takes charge of the CET crystals and intends to return all the projections to their correct planets of origin. Romana notes that she can think of one animal that would be at home in an electric zoo but, when asked, declines to name it.

IT WAS MADE WHERE...?

Studio: 12.08.79-14.08.79, 26.08.79-28.08.79 in TC6, 31.08.79 (gallery only) in TC5, 23.09.79 (gallery only) in TC6

ADDITIONAL CREDITED CAST

Tryst (Lewis Fiander), Dymond (Geoffrey Bateman), Rigg (David Daker[1-3]), Della (Jennifer Lonsdale[1,2,4]), Secker (Stephen Jenn[1]), Crewmen (Richard Barnes[1,3], Sebastian Stride[3,4], Eden Phillips[4]), Stott (Barry Andrews[2-4*]), Fisk (Geoffrey Hinsliff[2-4]), Costa (Peter Craze[2-4]), Passengers (Annette Peters[2], Lionel Sansby[2], Peter Roberts[2], Maggie Petersen[2, 3]).

* Also in Part One, but uncredited.

THINGS TO WATCH OUT FOR
• The idea of the CET machine and its stored life-forms recalls that of the Miniscope in season ten's *Carnival of Monsters*.

THINGS YOU MIGHT NOT HAVE KNOWN
• Working title: *Nightmare of Evil*.

- This story was the first solo *Doctor Who* project for writer Bob Baker, who had scripted many stories previously with his partner Dave Martin. Together they had created K9.

- **Romana:** 'I don't think we should interfere.' **The Doctor:** 'Interfere! Of course we should interfere. Always do what you're best at, that's what I say.'
- **Tryst:** 'I am helping to conserve endangered species.' **The Doctor:** 'By putting them in this machine?' **Tryst:** 'Oh yes.' **The Doctor:** 'Ah yes, of course. Just in the same way a jam maker conserves raspberries.'
- **Rigg:** 'First a collision, then a dead navigator and now a … monster roaming about my ship. Well it's totally inexplicable.' **The Doctor:** 'Nothing's inexplicable.' **Rigg:** 'Then explain it.' **The Doctor:** 'It's inexplicable!'
- **The Doctor:** 'Oh … my fingers … my arms … my legs … ah … my everything … aaargh!'

Nightmare of Eden is one of those stories that despite boasting an imaginative and well written set of scripts – with a good plot, some interesting ideas, crisp dialogue and a surprisingly adult drug-related theme – ultimately does not work due to the sheer quantity of production deficiencies stacked against it. Admittedly, like every other story, it has not been without its admirers. '*Nightmare of Eden* stands out as one of the best Baker stories of all time and certainly my favourite from last season,' wrote Richard Walter in *Matrix* Issue 5 dated February 1980. 'There were all the ingredients of a first class adventure – suspense, intrigue and lots of action. Also, perhaps surprisingly, the humour had been toned down and most was in fact relevant to the situation.' In general, however, even those who have praised the story have done so in full awareness of its flaws – Paul Trainer, for example, declared in *Ark in Space* No. 2 in 1980: 'Maybe it's the freak in me, but I found this an extremely enjoyable story' – and most commentators have been more in sympathy with the views expressed by John Peel in *TARDIS* Volume 5 Number 1 in 1980:

'A very discerning critic (in the *Daily Telegraph* …) summed it all up for me: "I have never met anyone who does not believe that this old series would not be better with a more conventional Doctor Who treating it with all the concentrated seriousness of William Hartnell." Too true, mate. "A very dud adventure." Well, I don't know anyone who would disagree with that.

'There seems to be a very strange idea that flits currently about the *Doctor Who* office that the show is for kids and can therefore be treated as casually as anyone pleases, since kids will watch any old rubbish. Who needs good actors, sensible plots or anything beyond a very obvious joke every two minutes or so to keep the brats happy?'

There are two major problem areas in the production: the Mandrels and Tryst. To take the Mandrels first, the original intention of writer Bob Baker – making his first solo contribution to the series – was that these should be mud monsters dripping with slime, but on screen they appear simply as hairy, growling beasties with overlong arms and glowing green headlamp eyes. It is hard for the viewer to feel any fear of them, as even when they attack people they do so with a kind of casual approach that renders the whole thing ludicrous. Even in the dark environment of Eden they fail to impress. 'The monsters, according to the *Sun*, were "terrifying",' noted John Peel. 'I can't think why. The build up in [Part One] so obviously had to have something stick [its] illuminated eyes through a wall that it was really quite boring. And all they did was growl a bit and hit people with their claws. They looked rather like … Yeti coming home from a poodle parlour …'

The problem with Tryst is his incredible Germanic accent, which sounds totally put-on and fake and renders the character – one of the main players in the drama – a figure of fun rather than, as he should be, a serious threat. Just as laughable, if not more so, are the rather less significant Fisk and Costa who, with their leather-boy outfits and cute caps, strut around being officious in a manner that is far too extreme to be realistic. The only effective guest characters in the story are Stott and Rigg, but the fine performances of Barry Andrews and David Daker in these roles are buried under the weight of tatty visuals and hammy acting elsewhere.

'*Nightmare of Eden* was ripe with faults,' complained Paul Trainer, 'which irritated … because they [occurred] in the most important places – viz the "Oooh my everything!" scene at what should have been the climax of the story … That most famed incident … was not only irritating but [also] out of character with other parts of the story, such as the Doctor's condemnation of the vraxoin smugglers. Indeed, after the somewhat camp tone of *The Creature from the Pit*, *Nightmare of Eden* was refreshing because of its tense, dramatic feel, which added to the excitement of it. It was the sort of *Flash Gordon* (or should that be updated to *Star Wars*?) excitement that I found prevalent throughout the whole season.'

Tom Baker's overplaying of certain scenes – in particular the infamous sequence, referred to by Trainer, in which the Doctor plays the Pied Piper and lures the Mandrels into the Eden projection only to be set upon by them before emerging unscathed but with his clothes ripped to shreds – tends seriously to undermine any dramatic impact that the story might otherwise have. The Mandrel sequence is a classic piece of pantomime shtick, something that *Doctor Who* had never needed to resort to in the past and that, in a way, eerily foreshadowed the approach that it would sometimes be accused of taking in the future.

THE HORNS OF NIMON

Writer: Anthony Read. **Director:** Kenny McBain. **Designer:** Graeme Story. **Costumes:** June Hudson. **Make-Up:** Christine Walmsley-Cotham. **Incidental Music:** Dudley Simpson. **Visual Effects:** Peter Pegrum. **Studio Lighting:** Nigel Wright. **Studio Sound:** John Hartshorn. **Production Assistant:** Henry Foster. **Assistant Floor Manager:** Rosemary Chapman.

	First UK TX	Scheduled TX	Actual TX	Duration	Viewers	Chart Pos.
Part One	22/12/79	18.10	18.11	25'41"	6.0	100
Part Two	29/12/79	17.50	17.54	25'00"	8.8	56
Part Three	05/01/80	18.20	18.22	23'26"	9.8	40
Part Four	12/01/80	18.05	18.06	26'45"	10.4	26

Plot: The inhabitants of the planet Skonnos have been promised by an alien Nimon that he will restore their empire to greatness if they in return provide young sacrifices and radioactive

FOURTH DOCTOR

hymetusite crystals, both of which they are obtaining from the nearby planet Aneth. With the TARDIS immobilised for repairs, the Doctor and Romana encounter the Skonnan spaceship transporting the latest sacrificial consignment from Aneth. Romana is captured and taken to Skonnos on board the ship, while the Doctor follows in the now semi-repaired TARDIS. Once there, they are consigned by the Skonnans' leader, Soldeed, into the Nimon's labyrinthine power complex. The two Time Lords discover that the Nimons are a race of parasites moving from planet to planet like a plague of locusts. The bull-headed creatures send a lone representative to an unsuspecting world, offering assistance in order to gain the trust of its inhabitants, then arrive in force to drain it of its resources. The power complex, fuelled by hymetusite, uses a black hole to create a space tunnel through which the Nimons cross from one planet to the next. The Doctor manages to destroy the complex on Skonnos, thereby trapping the Nimons on their last home, the dying planet Crinoth.

Episode endings:
1. The Doctor holds on to K9 in alarm as a planet-sized asteroid approaches the TARDIS on collision course.
2. The Nimon kills the Skonnan Co-Pilot and advances on Romana and the Anethan youngsters.
3. The Doctor reacts in horror as Soldeed fires bolts of energy from his staff and puts the controls of the Nimon's transmat capsule out of action, effectively trapping Romana on the planet Crinoth.
4. The Doctor sets about completing his repairs on the TARDIS control console.

IT WAS MADE WHERE...?
Studio: 24.09.79-26.09.79 in TC3, 07.10.79-09.10.79 in TC6, 15.10.79 (gallery only) in TC8

ADDITIONAL CREDITED CAST
Soldeed (Graham Crowden), Sorak (Michael Osborne), Co-Pilot (Malcolm Terris[1,2,3*]), Pilot (Bob Hornery[1]), Teka (Janet Ellis), Seth (Simon Gipps-Kent), Nimons (Robin Sherringham, Bob Appleby[4**], Trevor St. John Hacker[4**]), Voice of the Nimons (Clifford Norgate), Sezom (John Bailey[4]).

* Also in Part Four, as a dead body, but uncredited.
** Also in Part Three, but uncredited.

POPULAR MYTHS
• The creatures planning to invade Skonnos are called the Nimon. ('Nimons' is clearly given as the plural of the race's name both in the closing credits and in the story's dialogue.)

THINGS TO WATCH OUT FOR
• Janet Ellis, later to become a presenter of the popular children's magazine programme *Blue Peter* and mother of pop star Sophie Ellis-Bextor, appears here as the Anethan Teka.
• The famous 'Bloodnock's stomach' sound effect from the BBC radio classic *The Goon Show* is used in a scene in which the Doctor tries unsuccessfully to reactivate

the TARDIS control console.

- Graham Crowden, one of the actors considered for the role of the fourth Doctor and later well known for his role as Jock in *A Very Peculiar Practice*, plays Soldeed, the Nimons' high priest on Skonnos.
- The Nimon Power Complex was based around the idea of a giant printed circuit, the paths through which changed to trap any visitors and draw them to the Nimon at the centre.

QUOTE, UNQUOTE

- **The Doctor:** 'Come on old girl, quite a few millenia left in you yet.' **Romana:** 'Thank you, Doctor!' **The Doctor:** 'Not you – the TARDIS.'

ANALYSIS

It is fair to say that *The Horns of Nimon* has acquired something of a reputation amongst *Doctor Who* fans as an atrocious story with some of the sloppiest production ever seen in the series. The following assessment by Alan Jeffries in *Brave New World* Issue 1 in 1990 is not untypical:

'Tom Baker shows all the signs of a man long past his prime, and just appears to be going through the motions, sending the show up to alleviate his boredom – something a weak script can ill afford. [The actors portraying] Soldeed and the Co-Pilot also display more ham than a Danish abattoir, so that they stand out from an almost universally appalling cast by virtue of their sheer awfulness. The only person to emerge with any credit is Lalla Ward, who puts in a fiery performance ...

'[There is no excuse for] awful scenes such as the Doctor attempting to kick-start the TARDIS, or giving K9 the kiss of life. (Were these scenes recorded after a liquid lunch, one wonders?) Much of the "humour" is [cringe-makingly] embarrassing.'

Similar sentiments were expressed by John Peel in *TARDIS* Volume 5 Number 2 in 1980: 'I found this a rather silly, badly made story. I especially disliked those silly costumes for the Nimons themselves, and the very low level of acting. And who spotted Malcolm Terris's underpants peaking through a tear in his costume ...?' Joining in the chorus of disapproval, Richard Walter wrote in *Matrix* Issue 5 dated February 1980: 'How could anybody take a Nimon seriously? Skinny bodies, arms and legs with an enormous head – very obvious and it just looked like a mask – and boots with massive platform soles gave them [a] resemblance [to] the Frankenstein monster. Also, in common with many other *Doctor Who* monsters, they moved so slowly that they never stood a chance of capturing their victims let alone killing them. Perhaps had the Nimons looked a little more frightening and had the sets not looked as if they were constructed from overturned breadbaskets, the rather flawed plot wouldn't have [seemed] quite so bad. However, I have my doubts.'

Exactly why *The Horns of Nimon* should have attracted such vitriolic criticism is hard to fathom. It is admittedly a little more light hearted than usual, even for an era of the series that has often been said to have an 'undergraduate humour' quality, and some of the jokes do go too far – the worst being the use of a totally inappropriate comedy sound effect for the malfunctioning TARDIS control console. However, Tom Baker's Doctor

4 FOURTH DOCTOR

is actually rather more serious and intense here than in most other stories of a similar vintage, and it is clear that much of his flippancy – including his frequently criticised quip of 'Is this a private party or can anyone join in?' when he interrupts the Nimon as it is menacing Romana and the Anethans at the beginning of Part Three – is really just a ploy to put his adversary off guard; the sort of thing that he had done, without complaint by reviewers, many times in the past. The production values, too, are actually no worse than on many other stories of this era, and rather better than on some. Ian Wishart, writing in *Ark in Space* No. 2 in 1980, pointed out some highlights:

'I was glad to see CSO was not much used in this story. The shots of the spaceships in flight could have been improved if they had [been shot on] film instead of videotape. Two though I thought were marvellous: the first was of the extended TARDIS door leading to the Skonnos spaceship (Part One) and the second was ... of the Complex blowing up (Part Four), which *was* on film ...

'The sets were ... far, far the best of the season. Especially [those] inside the [Nimon's] Complex – they were really outstanding ...

'Probably the thing I liked [most] about this story ... was its fantastic aliens – the [Nimons] ... Their masks were very good, but what was most impressive about them was their magnificent voices. I think [they] are a race well worth bringing back!'

The Nimon costumes are indeed quite effective, although it is a pity that shortly before the story went into studio director Kenny McBain vetoed their freelancer constructor Roger Oldhamstead's original idea of giving the heads an intentionally artificial look so that they would actually appear to be masks concealing the Nimons' true, even more hideous nature. McBain's 'half way house' solution of keeping Oldhamstead's masks but having the transparent glass eyes painted red is the only less than satisfactory aspect of the costumes. Wishart was quite correct, however, in identifying the creatures' splendid voices as a real plus point.

Anthony Read's story, loosely based on the Greek tale of Theseus and the Minotaur, is ingenious and fun, and the idea of a race of creatures swarming locust-like from planet to planet, leaving each completely drained of its energy before moving on to the next, is actually quite chilling. Tim Westmacott, writing in *Oracle* Volume 3 Number 7 in 1980, had nothing but praise for the scripting:

'I think that writer Anthony Read came up with a brilliant idea for the method of invasion used by the Nimons. The situation [was] even more horrific than it first appeared because the Nimons obviously moved home fairly frequently, as [became apparent when], on Crinoth, Romana met Sezom.

'By far the [best] character in the story was the staff-carrying, power-hungry Soldeed. From his impressive entrance into the imposing Skonnos Control from the Nimon's Power Complex, through his apparent worshipping of "Lord Nimon" who blinded him to the truth with misleading promises of "conquest" and "Skonnos rising from its own ashes with wings of fire", to his eventual breakdown when he realised that the entity ... he had been playing "on a long string", far from being the last of its kind, was just the first of an invading race of parasitic nomads, his was the most interesting and memorable [part]. The overriding irony of this tale is that it was the Nimon ... that played upon Soldeed's greed and, instead of Skonnos regaining its imperial status, which it may well have done without the Nimon, it would have been finished. Hence the story's title.'

Perhaps what all this boils down to is that, in order to enjoy *The Horns of Nimon*, the viewer just has to approach it in the right spirit. David Saunders suggested as much in his observations in *TARDIS* Volume 5 Number 2 in 1980:

'The costumes and sets seemed to me to be straight out of a *Flash Gordon* adventure with Soldeed convinced that he must emulate Ming the Merciless! Even the cliffhanger endings to the episodes were a parallel with the 1950s serials – contrived menaces to the main characters which were instantly solved the following week because things were never as terrible as they had seemed, once viewed from a different angle.

'Admittedly *The Horns of Nimon* was not without its faults ... – but they were negligible because of the overall brilliance of the production ...

'The whole production was played mainly at the level of camp that made the sixties *Batman* show popular, but it worked because like that other series all the cast entered into the spirit of it and it meshed well because of this.'

Season seventeen proved to be a highly popular one with viewers, its ratings showing a marked reversal of a gradual downward trend seen during seasons fifteen and sixteen. Indeed *City of Death* received the highest ratings ever recorded for a *Doctor Who* story, the final episode reaching 16.1 million viewers – although this exceptional feat was admittedly due to the fact that a strike had blacked out the ITV network at the time, which meant that the series' only competition came in the form of minority interest programmes on BBC2. Behind the scenes, however, more changes were in store for the series. Douglas Adams had decided to relinquish the script editor's post after just one season, mainly because he was becoming increasingly busy with *The Hitch-Hiker's Guide to the Galaxy*. Even more significantly, Graham Williams had decided during production of *Nightmare of Eden* that he too would leave the series on completion of this season. His three year period as producer had arguably been the most problem-hit of any in the series' history, and he now felt in need of a break. He and Adams therefore left together, opening the way for a new production team to steer the series onto a different course for the eighties.

SHADA

The Horns of Nimon was originally intended to be followed on transmission by another story – a concluding six-parter entitled *Shada* – but a recurrence of an industrial dispute that had previously caused difficulties during production of *The Invasion of Time* and *The Armageddon Factor* eventually led to its cancellation, even though extensive location filming in the Cambridge area and the first of its three planned studio sessions had already been completed.

Written by Douglas Adams as his final contribution to *Doctor Who*, *Shada* was envisaged as a Time Lord story without a Gallifreyan setting. It sees the Doctor bringing Romana to present-day Earth to visit Professor Chronotis, an elderly Time Lord who absconded from Gallifrey and now lives a quiet academic life at St Cedd's College in Cambridge. Also seeking Chronotis is a scientist called Skagra who has a device, in the form of a floating sphere, with which he intends to steal the Professor's mind and thereby learn the location of a book entitled *The Worshipful and Ancient Law of Gallifrey*. Skagra eventually succeeds in obtaining the book, which had been borrowed from the Professor's study by a student named Chris Parsons. He then kidnaps Romana and hijacks the TARDIS. The book turns out to be the key to Shada, the ancient prison planet of the Time Lords. Skagra's objective is to use his sphere on one of the inmates, Salyavin, whose unique mental powers he can then exploit to project his own mind into every other creature in the universe. When the TARDIS reaches Shada, however, he discovers that Salyavin's cell is empty. After a number of close encounters with the Krargs – Skagra's monstrous crystalline servants – the Doctor, Chronotis and K9, along with Parsons and his friend Claire Keightley, arrive on Shada in Chronotis's TARDIS, which has been disguised as his study. Chronotis admits that he is in fact Salyavin; he escaped from Shada centuries ago and has been living on Earth ever since. The Doctor thwarts Skagra's plans by winning a mind battle against him.

Shada was formally dropped from the seventeenth season in December 1979, it having become apparent that due to the backlog of Christmas specials waiting to be recorded there was no prospect of studio time being found for its completion. A number of attempts were subsequently made to remount it but these ultimately came to nothing, and in June 1980 it was officially cancelled. A version of the story was eventually released on video in 1992 with Tom Baker providing a narration to cover the missing scenes. A completely new production of Douglas Adams's scripts was recorded, with Paul McGann as the eighth Doctor, as an audio-only drama for webcast on BBCi and CD release by Big Finish in 2003.

DOCTOR WHO SEASON EIGHTEEN (1980-1981)

Regular Cast:
Doctor Who (Tom Baker)
Romana (Lalla Ward) until *Warriors' Gate* Part Four
Adric (Matthew Waterhouse) from *Full Circle* Part One onwards
Nyssa (Sarah Sutton) from *The Keeper of Traken* Part One onwards*
Tegan (Janet Fielding) on *Logopolis*
Voice of K9 (John Leeson) until *Warriors' Gate* Part Four

* Nyssa was originally conceived as a one-off character for *The Keeper of Traken*. Even before rehearsals for that story began, however, actress Sarah Sutton was contracted for additional episodes. We have therefore chosen to regard her as a regular from *The Keeper of Traken* Part One onwards, although it is arguable that she might more properly be classed as one of the guest cast for that story and as a regular only from *Logopolis* Part Two onwards.

Regular Crew:
Executive Producer: Barry Letts.
Producer: John Nathan-Turner.
Script Editor: Christopher H Bidmead.
Production Unit Manager/Production Associate*: Angela Smith.
Title Music: Ron Grainer and the BBC Radiophonic Workshop, arranged by Peter Howell.
Special Sounds: Dick Mills.

* The title 'production unit manager' changes to 'production associate' from *Logopolis* onwards.

Season eighteen was the first to be produced by John Nathan-Turner, who would remain in charge of the series until 1989. He had spent the previous three years as its production unit manager, and Graham Williams had suggested on a number of occasions that he would be a good candidate to fill a new associate producer post, taking even more of the workload off his shoulders. These suggestions had not been taken up, however, and Williams had ultimately decided to move on.

Nathan-Turner was not the first choice of Head of Serials Graeme McDonald to take over from Williams, but when he was eventually offered the job he gratefully accepted, formally taking over the reins around the beginning of November 1979. McDonald himself was in the process of changing jobs during the latter part of 1979. The Serials Department had been merged with the Series Department in the first major reorganisation of the BBC's Drama Group to have taken place since 1963, and he had been appointed to head the new, larger Department thus created. Realising that his increased responsibilities left him less time than in the past to devote to individual series, and mindful also of Nathan-Turner's inexperience in his new post, he decided to appoint

4 FOURTH DOCTOR

former *Doctor Who* producer Barry Letts as executive producer. This in essence simply formalised and expanded an arrangement that had been operating informally since part-way through production of season sixteen, when – while first Nathan-Turner and then David Maloney deputised for Williams, who was absent from the office due to illness – Letts had been given a 'watching brief' over the series. Letts's executive producer role, which would not officially begin until around the second week of June 1980, basically entailed him offering comments on scripts, giving advice and approving major production decisions – in short, taking over the supervisory function normally performed by the head of department.

A new script editor was also required for the series to replace Douglas Adams. First choice was writer and poet Johnny Byrne, and also considered was writer Ted Rhodes. In the end however the post went to Christopher H Bidmead, who had been recommended to Nathan-Turner by former *Doctor Who* writer Robert Banks Stewart, who at this time was working as producer of the BBC detective series *Shoestring*. Although initially reluctant to join the production team, feeling that *Doctor Who* had abandoned its factual science roots and become 'very silly', Bidmead was won over on discovering that Nathan-Turner and Letts shared his concerns and wanted to return to the more serious style of earlier eras. Bidmead began work on the series in December 1979. With all members of the new production team in place, preparations began in earnest for the forthcoming season – which, as Nathan-Turner had managed to win an allocation of an extra two episodes above the usual twenty-six, would consist of seven four-part stories.

THE LEISURE HIVE

Writer: David Fisher. **Director:** Lovett Bickford. **Designer:** Tom Yardley-Jones. **Costumes:** June Hudson. **Make-Up:** Dorka Nieradzik. **Incidental Music:** Peter Howell. **Visual Effects:** Andrew Lazell. **Film Cameraman:** Keith Barton. **Film Editor:** Chris Wimble. **Studio Lighting:** Duncan Brown. **Studio Sound:** John Howell. **Production Assistant:** Romey Allison. **Assistant Floor Manager:** Val McCrimmon.

	First UK TX	Scheduled TX	Actual TX	Duration	Viewers	Chart Pos.
Part One	30/08/80	18.15	18.15	23'33"	5.9	77
Part Two	06/09/80	18.20	18.20	20'45"	5.0	103
Part Three	13/09/80	17.55	17.57	21'21"	5.0	111
Part Four	20/09/80	18.15	18.16	21'19"	4.5	111

Plot: The Doctor and Romana visit the Leisure Hive on the planet Argolis, the surface of which is uninhabitable following a twenty minute nuclear war between the Argolins and their enemies the Foamasi. The Argolins themselves are now sterile. Pangol, the youngest, was created by the Tachyon Recreation Generator, a machine that runs games in the Hive. He now secretly plans to use the Generator, modified by an Earth scientist named Hardin, to recreate himself many times over, forming an army of duplicates to destroy the Foamasi. Pangol's mother Mena, the controller of the Hive, is meanwhile coming under pressure from a supposedly human financier, Brock, to sell it to the Foamasi. Foamasi agents from their planet's government arrive and expose Brock and his assistant Klout as members of a renegade Foamasi group called the West Lodge. The Doctor then reconfigures the Generator equipment using components from the randomiser device previously linked to the TARDIS's navigation circuits, and Pangol's plan is foiled as he rejuvenates into a babe in arms.

Episode endings:

1. The Doctor enters the Recreation Generator to investigate but a Foamasi operates the controls, trapping him inside. As Romana tries to open the door, an image of the Doctor appears on a view screen and screams as its arms and lower torso are pulled off.
2. The Doctor agrees to help Romana and the Earth scientist Hardin test alterations made to the Recreation Generator. He enters the machine. Discovering on returning to Hardin's lab that the experiment is flawed, Romana hurries to stop it. She opens the door to the Generator to reveal the Doctor, who has aged immensely and now has a long white beard.
3. The Doctor, Romana, Hardin and two Foamasi enter the Argolin boardroom. One of the Foamasi advances on Brock and, despite his cries of terror, rips off his face and clothes to reveal another Foamasi.
4. The Doctor and Romana leave Argolis to sort out its problems, with Pangol rejuvenated to a baby and his mother Mena back in charge.

IT WAS MADE WHERE...?

Location filming: 20.03.80-21.03.80
Location: Brighton Beach, Fish Market Hard, Brighton, East Sussex.
Studio: 02.04.80-04.04.80 in TC1, 18.04.80-21.04.80 in TC3

ADDITIONAL CREDITED CAST

Mena (Adrienne Corri), Morix (Laurence Payne[1]), Brock (John Collin), Pangol (David Haig), Hardin (Nigel Lambert), Vargos (Martin Fisk), Guide (Roy Montague), Klout (Ian Talbot), Tannoy Voice (Harriet Reynolds[1,2,4]), Stimson (David Allister[2]), Generator Voice (Clifford Norgate[2,3]), Foamasi (Andrew Lane[3,4]).

Note: K9 appears only at the start of the first episode. Klout, unusually, is credited on screen even though he is a non-speaking character.

THINGS TO WATCH OUT FOR

- This story marks the debut of new opening and closing title sequences, complete with 'neon tube' logo, designed by the BBC's Sid Sutton, accompanied by a new Peter Howell-arranged version of Ron Grainer's theme music.
- Also seen for the first time in this story is a new TARDIS exterior prop, this time constructed of fibreglass rather than of wood and, with its stacked roof arrangement, somewhat truer to the design of a genuine police box than the previous version (first seen in *The Masque of Mandragora*).
- K9's original voice artiste, John Leeson, returns, having been persuaded by John Nathan-Turner to reprise the role for this season.
- The digital Quantel image processing system had its first use in *Doctor Who* on this

FOURTH DOCTOR 4

story. Amongst the effects created by way of this system was a moving shot of the TARDIS materialising on Argolis (whereas the 'roll back and mix' technique with which the materialisation was normally achieved necessitated a completely static shot).

- Working title: *The Argolins*.
- In the scene where the Doctor is apparently dismembered in the Tachyon Recreation Generator, the various parts of his body were played by David Rolfe, Roy Seeley and Derek Chafer as well as by Tom Baker.

QUOTE, UNQUOTE

- **Pangol:** [Speaking of the Recreation Generator.] 'How did you get out?' **The Doctor:** 'Through a hole in the back.' **Pangol:** 'But there isn't one.' **The Doctor:** 'There is now.'
- **Brock:** 'His scarf killed Stimson.' **The Doctor:** 'Arrest the scarf then!'
- **Pangol:** 'I am the child of the Generator.'

ANALYSIS

With the coming of the eighteenth season it is as though *Doctor Who* has undergone a complete transformation. So many changes have been introduced by new producer John Nathan-Turner that the series is almost unrecognisable from the one that ended its previous run with *The Horns of Nimon* earlier the same year. The familiar 'time tunnel' title sequence so associated with *Doctor Who* has been dispensed with in favour of a more conventional 'journey through space' effect, while the famous Delia Derbyshire arrangement of Ron Grainer's theme music has given way to a more modern but less exceptional synthesiser version courtesy of Peter Howell. Dudley Simpson, whose highly distinctive incidental music was for so many years a staple ingredient of the series, has been superseded by the BBC's own Radiophonic Workshop composers. The Doctor too has undergone a very noticeable change from the madcap wisecracker of recent years into a more sombre figure with a new, heavily stylised burgundy version of his traditional costume. Fan reaction to all these innovations has ranged from the ecstatic to the horrified, but one thing that no-one can deny is that Nathan-Turner made his mark on the series right from the word go.

The Leisure Hive itself exhibits all the glitz of state-of-the-art early eighties television, with imaginative direction and camera work, impressive visual effects, wall-to-wall incidental music and a plot involving intrigue, mystery – and a lot of scientific gobbledegook. In fact, watching the story, it is hard to believe that it was commissioned as something of an emergency measure when it was discovered that no other suitable scripts were held in reserve in the *Doctor Who* office. As John Peel wrote in *TARDIS* Volume 5 Number 6 in 1981: 'Direction was tight and gave a marvellous air of sophistication to the show, costumes (especially those of the Argolin) were faultless, effects were pleasing, for the most part ... In fact, only one thing marred this story for me, and that was the total lack of any rational explanations for anything.'

Director Lovett Bickford's decision to eschew the normal multiple camera recording technique of studio television and proceed instead by way of a succession of single camera set-ups, as on a film production, paid dividends in terms of the story's lavish and detailed visuals – as well as causing it to go over budget. His careful presentation of the Foamasi, relying on close-ups of their eyes, claws, feet and so on rather than showing them in their entirety, was wise as it helps to maintain the tension and avoids exposing too much the rather serious limitations of the costumes. The sequence at the beginning of Part Four in which the Foamasi impersonating Brock and his assistant Klout are stripped of their human disguises – a rather daft idea bearing in mind that, as with Scaroth in the previous season's *City of Death*, the creatures are clearly somewhat larger than humans – provides perhaps the best illustration of the success of this approach, as the rapid intercutting of a series of close-ups effectively conveys the impression of what is supposed to be happening without it ever actually being seen. Another aspect of the story's production that deserves particular praise is the make-up used for Tom Baker in the scenes after the Doctor has been unnaturally aged by the Recreation Generator. This is simply magnificent, perfectly complementing Baker's restrained and totally believable performance as an older version of his Doctor. In fact all the actors give a good account of themselves in this story. Adrienne Corri's performance as Mena is perhaps the best amongst the guest cast, being suitably dignified and stoical, although – strangely enough, given that he has no dialogue – Ian Talbot's creepy, unsettling portrayal of Klout is also particularly memorable.

Fan reviews of *The Leisure Hive* have tended to be rather mixed, reflecting the aforementioned differences of opinion as to the merits of the changes introduced by the new producer. Chris Dunk, writing in *Ark in Space* No. 5 dated Spring 1981, was highly enthusiastic: 'It gave what the [series] needed – a change in direction – and the credit for this must go almost totally to … John Nathan-Turner. To interfere with such an institution as *Doctor Who* is a tricky business, but he grabbed it firmly, and successfully, by the horns …' Tim Robins, on the other hand, tore the story apart in *The Doctor Who Review* Issue Seven in 1980: 'I'm truly sorry. I tried to like *The Leisure Hive*, but however hard I tried, the inconsistencies, the flaws, the plodding plot kept nagging at the back of my mind. Terrance Dicks is quoted as saying that [*Doctor Who*] is the only science-fiction series to successfully make the genre accessible to the general public at large. Alas, *The Leisure Hive* hardly did that.' One aspect of the story that Robins particularly disliked was the closing scene of Part Four, which he found to be unduly flippant and totally out of keeping with what had preceded it: 'It seemed to me as if everyone realised that *The Leisure Hive* had been too heavy-going and hoped to make up for it in the last few minutes, chucking characterisation out of the window in the process.'

The Leisure Hive was the last individual *Doctor Who* story to come under the scrutiny of the BBC's Audience Research Department. Most of those whose views were recorded were apparently pleased to see the series back, and their reactions were generally positive: 'The majority … derived a fair amount of enjoyment from the episodes of the story they had seen, the storyline being described as "intriguing", "compulsive", "exciting" and "tense" in various areas of the sample audience. There were viewers who thought that this story was below the usual standard for *Doctor Who*: some people found it hard to follow, while others considered it unexciting. Nevertheless, most of those reporting regarded the story as welcome escapism and found it very entertaining.' Tom Baker's performance was once more 'rated very highly' and Lalla Ward was also praised, although there was still 'some criticism of her acting ability'. Particular praise was also accorded to the overall standard of production: 'The production clearly impressed those reporting: the special effects were rated very highly and several people considered these the most important part of the programme. Praise was also accorded to the make-up, costumes and sets. Apart from some viewers who considered that few new ideas had been demonstrated in this production or described the series as a "mere special effects show", most people appreciated the series for its visual interest.'

From the general viewing public at least, then, a ringing endorsement of John Nathan-Turner's efforts to improve the look of *Doctor Who* and thereby, as he often put it, to 'bring it into the eighties'.

MEGLOS

Writer: John Flanagan, Andrew McCulloch. **Director:** Terence Dudley. **Designer:** Philip Lindley. **Costumes:** June Hudson. **Make-Up:** Cecile Hay-Arthur. **Incidental Music:** Paddy Kingsland[1], Peter Howell[2-4]*. **Visual Effects:** Steven Drewett. **Studio Lighting:** Bert Postlethwaite. **Studio Sound:** John Holmes. **Production Assistant:** Marilyn Gold. **Assistant Floor Manager:** Val McCrimmon, Karen Loxton.

* Peter Howell also composed the music for the cliffhanger ending to Part One but was uncredited on screen.

	First UK TX	Scheduled TX	Actual TX	Duration	Viewers	Chart Pos.
Part One	27/09/80	18.15	18.16	24'43"	5.0	105
Part Two	04/10/80	18.15	18.17	21'24"	4.2	139
Part Three	11/10/80	17.40	17.42	21'19"	4.7	129
Part Four	18/10/80	17.45	17.44	19'30"	4.7	127

Plot: The Doctor is invited to visit the planet Tigella by its leader, Zastor, who has become concerned about disputes between his people's two opposing factions, the religious Deons and the scientist Savants. The TARDIS is intercepted by the megalomaniacal xerophyte Meglos, last survivor of the planet Zolfa-Thura, and trapped in a chronic hysteresis – a time loop – but the Doctor and Romana manage to free it. Meglos, using the body of a kidnapped Earthling, transforms himself into a duplicate of the Doctor and steals the Tigellans' power source – a mysterious dodecahedron. He plans to use this to power an apocalyptic device with which he intends to destroy Tigella. The Doctor, although hindered by the activities of a group of Gaztak mercenaries hired by Meglos, ultimately brings about the xerophyte's destruction by tampering with the dodecahedron's controlling computers.

Episode endings:
1. Meglos traps the TARDIS in a chronic hysteresis and, with the aid of the Earthling's body, transforms himself into a perfect duplicate of the Doctor.
2. Romana is captured in the Tigellan forest by the Gaztaks' second in command, Brotadac, who states that she has seen too much. He orders his men to kill her.
3. The Deons' High Priest Lexa intends to sacrifice the Doctor to the god Ti in order to bring back the missing dodecahedron. The Time Lord is tied to the altar and flames placed under

ropes holding up a huge stone that will fall and crush him. The ropes are burned through one by one, and the Doctor looks on in horror as a Deon holds a flame under the final rope.

4. With Meglos and Zolfa-Thura destroyed, the Tigellans can get on with the task of rebuilding their lives – without the help of the dodecahedron. The Doctor tells the Earthling that he can get him home before he leaves. The Earthling is understandably puzzled.

It Was Made Where...?

Studio: 25.06.80-27.06.80 in TC8, 10.07.80-12.07.80 in TC3

Additional Credited Cast

General Grugger (Bill Fraser), Lieutenant Brotadac (Frederick Treves), Zastor (Edward Underdown), Lexa (Jacqueline Hill), Caris (Colette Gleeson), Deedrix (Crawford Logan), Earthling (Christopher Owen), Tigellan Guard (Simon Shaw).

Things To Watch Out For

- With the obvious exceptions of season one's *Inside the Spaceship* and single episode stories (season three's *Mission to the Unknown*, the twentieth anniversary special *The Five Doctors* and the 1996 television movie), this is the only story in the series' history in which all the credited cast members appear in all the episodes.
- Jacqueline Hill plays the leading Deon, Lexa. Hill had played the first Doctor's companion Barbara Wright in seasons one and two.
- The sound effect created for the approach of the Fendahl in season fifteen's *Image of the Fendahl* was re-used as background atmosphere for the Tigellan jungle.
- The scenes set on the surface of Zolfa-Thura were realised by way of a new effects technique referred to as scene-sync – a development of the established CSO process. This involved two cameras being electronically synchronised to follow identical movements so that they could be made to track in unison and maintain the composite image (created in the usual way), whereas previously CSO shots had almost invariably been static.

Things You Might Not Have Known

- Working titles: *The Golden Pentangle*, *The Last Zolfa-Thuran*.
- Some of the Gaztak costumes came from a BBC production of *Macbeth*.
- Bill Fraser agreed to play Grugger only if he could kick K9.

Quote, Unquote

- **Zastor:** 'Some fifty years ago I knew a man who solved the insoluble by the strangest means. He sees the threads that join the universe together and mends them when they break.' **Deedrix:** 'A Savant, or one of her madmen?' **Zastor:** 'A little of each and a great deal more of something else.'
- **Meglos:** 'I need you Earthling.' **Earthling:** 'Let go of me! You've no right.' **Meglos:** 'Quite right. But academic.'
- **Brotadac:** 'Do you think he'd let me have that?' **Grugger:** 'What, the coat? Not cold, are you?' **Brotadac:** 'It's rather a nice coat ... Now that he's finished playing the Doctor.'

FOURTH DOCTOR

Fan reviewers can be rough on *Doctor Who* when it fails to live up to their expectations. '*Meglos* was the sort of story that doesn't deserve a place *anywhere* in *any* season, let alone second in an allegedly new-look series which would revitalise the whole concept of *Doctor Who*,' asserted Paul Mount in *The Doctor Who Review* Issue 8 dated December 1980. 'To put it bluntly, *Meglos* was *The Horns of Nimon* revisited – but with good production values ... [It] was a disaster.' Although it certainly falls far short of the standards of production set by *The Leisure Hive*, *Meglos* is actually nowhere near as bad as these strong sentiments would suggest – especially if one makes allowances for the fact that it is about a talking cactus who wants to take over the universe.

'The story had very strong themes which were laid out carefully as it unfolded,' noted Martin Wiggins in *Fendahl* 13 dated November/December 1980. 'The division between Savants and Deons went beyond a simple sociological oddity, for it was a basic division between the two ways of looking at things – the Savants regard everything as explicable in terms of the physical universe; the Deons have to drag in metaphysics as well. As usual in *Doctor Who*, the Savant view was correct, the Deons' view of the arrival of the dodecahedron being merely a result of their "limited frame of reference" (Meglos's characteristic phrase dismissing the repeated references to impossibility). This religious theme was mingled with a heavy political beat to the story: each of the Tigellan characters represented one particular group on the planet – Lexa, the Deons; Deedrix, the Savants; Zastor, trying to maintain an uneasy balance between the two; and Caris, a splinter group of Savants advocating life on the surface.'

The problem with the Tigellans is that – with the exception of Jacqueline Hill, who manages a competent performance in a role not really worthy of her talents – the cast all give the impression of having been drafted in from an amateur dramatics group. Lines are spoken as though they are being read off cue-cards and there is a notable lack of conviction all round. The worst offender is Edward Underdown, playing Zastor, who drifts through the story without ever really seeming to have his heart in it. That Underdown, a quite distinguished actor, was seriously ill at the time may well account for this, but ultimately the viewer has to judge by what is seen on screen irrespective of any behind-the-scenes problems that might have prevented it from being better. It must be admitted, though, that the cast are not well served by the costumes and make-up that they are required to wear, which are ridiculous in the extreme. (Just why do all the Savants feel the need to have the same silly hairdos?)

Even more disappointing is the story's villain, as Paul Mount commented: '*Meglos* himself was the stereotype to end all stereotypes, despite some superb "spiky" makeup for both the Earthling ... and Tom Baker. Ignoring the glaring inconsistency of ... a race of cacti [surrounding] themselves with control rooms filled with dials and levers suitable only for human hands, Meglos ... had no depth, no character, no originality and no purpose.' Exactly why Meglos needs an unnamed Earthling to provide him with a body in the first place, when presumably one of the Gaztaks or even a Tigellan would do just as well, is never made clear; and indeed there is very little background information of any sort provided about the character.

The motley band of Gaztaks afford a little welcome light relief – although John Connors, writing in *Aggedor* Issue 5 in 1983, had rather mixed feelings about their depiction: 'Ironically, Brotodac, played by Frederick Treves, was one of the better [members of the guest cast], especially when he chose Meglos's coat rather than a world to be destroyed. I [use the word] "ironically" because "Brotodac" is an anagram of "bad actor" ... Bill Fraser managed a little more acting ability than the cactus (but not much) ... He bumbled about looking uncomfortable in that ridiculous false beard; such an important part could have been better allotted.'

Paul Trainer, writing in *Ark in Space* No. 5 dated Spring 1981, was generally happy with the story's production values: 'As far as most of the technical aspects went, the sets, effects and direction were almost faultless, although there was one painful moment when Tigella, [seen] in Zolfa-Thura's sky, was quite obviously held up by strings.' In fact the story's effects as a whole are nothing to write home about, although they are passable and – in the case of the scene-sync shots – innovative in technique, and there is little to distinguish the Tigellan jungle from many others seen previously in *Doctor Who*.

The best aspect of the entire story is the superlative contribution made by Tom Baker and Lalla Ward. Baker not only gives a good performance as the Doctor but also plays Meglos with aplomb and makes an excellent villain. Tim Dollin, writing in *TARDIS* Volume 5 Number 6 in 1981, was highly impressed: 'The star of the show was undoubtedly Tom Baker ... He really [gave] a brilliant performance as the doppelganger, and it was amazing to see the very real contrast between his Doctor and Meglos ... My favourite effect of the piece was when the Earthling and Meglos were superimposed over each other [as the former tried to free his body from the latter's control]. It was brilliantly done, far better than the wobbling model work that somehow let the show down at times. It is in Parts Two and Three that the story really works, due to Tom's amazing performance.' Lalla Ward likewise has Romana down to a tee in this story. She is witty and cunning and a perfect foil for the Doctor. The fact that K9 is also present almost passes the viewer by, and it is becoming apparent by this stage that the series' writers are really struggling to find something useful to give the robot dog to do.

Meglos is an entertaining tale with some good ideas and interesting themes, including the conflict between religion and science, the dilemma faced when a race realises that its essential power source is no longer reliable – or even present – and the lengths to which an individual will sometimes go in order to settle an old score. Unfortunately the production just doesn't quite gel and the whole thing ends up being something of a disappointment.

THE E-SPACE TRILOGY

The production team decided around the end of January 1980 to have three of this season's stories linked by a running theme. The theme that Bidmead came up with, setting it out in detail in a note dated 12 June 1980, concerned the dangers encountered by the Doctor and his companions after the TARDIS accidentally passes through a Charged Vacuum Emboitment (CVE) from their own universe, N-Space, into a completely different and rather smaller one, E-Space.

One function that the production team wanted the E-Space trilogy to fulfil was to provide a vehicle for the writing out of Romana and K9 and the introduction of a new companion to take their place. Lalla Ward was contracted for just the first twenty episodes of the season as she had agreed with Nathan-Turner that it would then be time

for her to move on, while K9's exit had been decreed by the producer as he disliked the character and felt that it provided too easy a solution to the problems that the Doctor encountered. The new companion devised by Nathan-Turner and Bidmead was Adric, a youthful 'Artful Dodger' type. The actor chosen by Nathan-Turner to take the role of Adric was Matthew Waterhouse, a young *Doctor Who* fan who had been working as a BBC clerk. He had been suggested to the production office by the BBC's internal Casting Advisory Service and been judged by Nathan-Turner, Barry Letts and director Peter Grimwade to be the best of all those who auditioned.

FULL CIRCLE

Writer: Andrew Smith. **Director:** Peter Grimwade. **Designer:** Janet Budden. **Costumes:** Amy Roberts. **Make-Up:** Frances Needham. **Incidental Music:** Paddy Kingsland. **Visual Effects:** John Brace. **Film Cameraman:** Max Samett. **Film Editor:** Mike Houghton. **Studio Lighting:** Mike Jefferies. **Studio Sound:** John Holmes. **Production Assistant:** Susan Box. **Assistant Floor Manager:** Alex Bridcut, Lynn Richards.

	First UK TX	Scheduled TX	Actual TX	Duration	Viewers	Chart Pos.
Part One	25/10/80	17.40	17.40	24'23"	5.9	106
Part Two	01/11/80	17.40	17.42	22'11"	3.7	170
Part Three	08/11/80	17.40	17.43	22'00"	5.9	115
Part Four	15/11/80	17.40	17.40	24'16"	5.5	127

Plot: The TARDIS falls through a CVE into E-Space and arrives on the planet Alzarius. There the inhabitants of a crashed Starliner and a group of young rebels called the Outlers, led by a boy named Varsh and including his brother Adric, are being terrorised by a race of Marshmen who emerge from the marshes at a time known as Mistfall. The Doctor discovers that the Starliner's inhabitants are not the descendants of its original crew, as has been claimed by their leaders the Deciders, but evolved Marshmen. With the Time Lord's help and encouragement, the Starliner is repaired and able to leave the planet.

Episode endings:
1. The Doctor and K9 look on as Marshmen emerge from the waters of the Alzarian marsh and start to move toward them.
2. As marsh spiders scuttle toward her, Romana picks up a river fruit with which to defend herself. Suddenly the fruit splits open and another marsh spider emerges, landing on her cheek. She fends it off but almost immediately falls to the ground, unconscious.
3. Romana, having been infected by the marsh spider, opens an emergency escape hatch on board the Starliner. Marshmen start to pour into the ship.
4. K9 confirms Romana's observation to the Doctor that unless they find another CVE, they are trapped. The TARDIS scanner screen displays the green-hued vista of E-Space.

IT WAS MADE WHERE...?

Location filming: 23.07.80-25.07.80

Location: Black Park, Fulmer, Bucks.
Studio: 07.08.80-08.08.80 in TC3, 21.08.80-23.08.80 in TC6, 27.08.80 (gallery only) in TC6

ADDITIONAL CREDITED CAST

Login (George Baker), Draith (Leonard Maguire[1]), Nefred (James Bree), Garif (Alan Rowe), Dexeter (Tony Calvin[1-3]), Varsh (Richard Willis), Tylos (Bernard Padden), Keara (June Page), Omril (Andrew Forbes[1-3]), Rysik (Adrian Gibbs[1]), Marshman (Barney Lawrence[2-4*]), Marshchild (Norman Bacon[2,3]).

* Also in Part One, but uncredited.
Note: There is no voice credit for K9 on Part Three as he does not speak in this episode, owing to his head having been knocked off by the Marshmen.

THINGS TO WATCH OUT FOR

* Alan Rowe makes his final *Doctor Who* appearance, as Garif. He had previously appeared as Doctor Evans and the voice of Space Control in season four's *The Moonbase*, as Edward of Wessex in season eleven's *The Time Warrior* and as Skinsale in season fifteen's *Horror of Fang Rock*.
* George Baker, who went on to star as Inspector Wexford in the TVS police drama series *The Ruth Rendell Mysteries*, plays Login.

THINGS YOU MIGHT NOT HAVE KNOWN

* Working title: *The Planet that Slept*.
* Adric's name was suggested by script editor Christopher H Bidmead as an anagram of that of eminent physicist P A M Dirac (who in 1930 was the first to predict the existence of antimatter).
* The writer, Andrew Smith, was a nineteen-year old fan of *Doctor Who* who finally got the opportunity to write for the show.

QUOTE, UNQUOTE

* **Romana:** 'The Time Lords want me back.' **The Doctor:** 'Yes, well, you only came to help with the Key to Time.' **Romana:** 'Doctor, I don't want to spend the rest of my life on Gallifrey – after all this!' **The Doctor:** 'Well, you can't fight Time Lords, Romana.' **Romana:** 'You did, once.' **The Doctor:** 'And lost.'
* **Nefred:** 'Seek out the Doctor. He can teach you to fly the Starliner. It is my wish that you all leave Alzarius.' **Login:** 'And return to Terradon?' **Nefred:** 'No, we cannot return to Terradon.' **Garif:** 'If the Doctor shows us how?' **Nefred:** 'We cannot return.' **Login:** 'Why?' **Nefred:** 'Because … we have never been there.'

ANALYSIS

After the major disappointment of *Meglos*, the eighteenth season gets back on track with *Full Circle*. As Peter Anghelides put it in *TARDIS* Volume 5 Number 6 in 1981: 'The new season promised much, and in *Full Circle* all the hopes of an excellent set of new stories have been realised. What makes it all the more impressive is that it is what might be defined as a "fan story", written by someone with a knowledge [of] *and* an obvious

4 FOURTH DOCTOR

regard for the show.' Andrew Smith was indeed the first fan of *Doctor Who* to have had a story accepted for the series – a notable achievement, notwithstanding the fact that he already had several other professional writing credits to his name by this point – and his affection for the series shines through in his work. This adds considerably to the story's effectiveness – although Martin Wiggins, writing in *Ark in Space* No. 5 dated spring 1981, felt that Smith sometimes allowed his enthusiasm to get the better of him:

'*Full Circle* ... is very much a story written by a fan for fans. Occasionally this got out of control – the first scene, for example, contained the Doctor's pointless prattle about *The Invasion of Time*, which was annoying because it was an ostentatious way of showing how continuity was being kept to and nothing more, when it could have been an interesting piece of discourse – Romana must have known of, or even known, Leela before she left Gallifrey, and one wonders how a confirmed wanderer, such as scene two showed her to be, would react to someone who voluntarily chose to spend the rest of her life on [that planet].

'This was, however, only an isolated lapse, and in general the dialogue was carefully used to expound the fairly complex plot with great economy.'

Wiggins also detected some religious inspiration in the story, as he went on to detail: 'The story presented a mish-mash of themes from the Book of Exodus (for example, the Procedure of Mistfall reflects the first Passover in Egypt) and this was heightened by the religious quality of [the incidental music] Paddy Kingsland used for the hall of books. It was no surprise to find Moses/Nefred dying before reaching Terradon, the final stages being supervised by his lieutenant Joshua/Login.'

Whether or not Smith consciously intended these parallels is open to question, but there is no denying that his scripts for the story are well written and thematically rich. Indeed they seem to have positively inspired director Peter Grimwade and everyone else involved in the production, as the on-screen realisation of the story is virtually faultless. 'A good plot needs to be exploited by fine acting,' pointed out Peter Anghelides, 'and everyone in the cast was convincing in the many and varied parts. The [walk-ons] showed refreshing enthusiasm, and the acting of the youngsters was particularly [good]. The main characters were rounded and believable, even though they were not necessarily on view at all times, and the secret of revelation of character *by what they say* seems to be one of Andrew Smith's strengths. Notice too how the deaths were well handled – the two Deciders' deaths were moving and believable, and the deaths of the two children, including Adric's brother, were effective and not overly dramatic. Tom Baker proved all his critics wrong this time, giving an excellent portrayal of the Time Lord ...'

Gary Hopkins, writing in *The Doctor Who Review* Issue 8 dated December 1980, was equally enthusiastic about Tom Baker's performance, and about Lalla Ward's too: 'The principals ... were as good as ever. The Doctor in Part Three facing up to [the scientist] Dexeter as he began his experiments on the Marshchild, and then roaring his accusations at the Deciders, was magnificent stuff ... Tom Baker at his spine-tingling best ... Romana too came over tremendously, especially in the first scenes in the TARDIS bedroom ... and also later on when under the influence of the spider bite. It's nice to see Lalla having a chance to do more than just her usual "goody-goody" act, which can get just a little bit wearing.'

The story's principal monsters, the Marshmen, look good, despite having rather conventional 'man-in-a-rubber-suit' type costumes, and are very well directed by

Grimwade. Hopkins was again enthusiastic: 'The beautiful final scene of [Part One], with a group of mud-encrusted Marshmen rising gracefully and, for one moment, in slow motion, from the marshes, must surely have brought a thrill of delight to even the most die-hardened fan … The design of the Marshmen – though not exactly original, with more than a shade of the Creature from the Black Lagoon and even the Silurians – was convincing, unlike recent creations such as the Mandrels, the Nimons and the Foamasi. Their rampage in Part Four (though woefully bloodless) brought to mind similar scenes in late sixties and early seventies classics too numerous to mention. The intriguing point about the Marshmen was that, despite their viciousness and their destructive nature, I couldn't really see them as *evil*. Only the most resilient cynic could have looked at the Marshchild's confusion as it was caught between two groups of humans in Part Two without some sympathy and sadness. Its death scene in the following episode was tinged with both relief and sorrow, as the creature died cut off from its own kind, alone, mistreated and abused, in the shattered remains of a clinical laboratory.'

One aspect of the production on which opinions differ is the depiction of the marsh spiders. Hopkins was impressed: 'The crab-spiders show just how much the BBC have improved in recent years with this sort of visual effect. Except for one or two dodgy scenes, [they] were totally convincing as they scuttled across the cave floor. A scene that will live for quite a while with me involved Romana picking up a river-fruit, ostensibly to defend herself from the encroaching spiders, when it splits open, depositing a rather large and nasty spider on to the side of her face. Classic stuff.' Frank Danes, on the other hand, was less than complimentary in *Fendahl* 13 dated November/December 1980: 'Where the special effects boys failed was in the creation of the spiders. Legs pedalling furiously, glowing eyes, long white fangs reminded one of a toy from Woolworth's rather than a *Doctor Who* monster.'

Danes was rather more generous in his comments on the Doctor's new companion, who actually shows little promise in this story: 'Adric was interesting. He was very well introduced, as a misfit in his brother's Outlers, and blended into the story rather well. Matthew Waterhouse isn't the best of young actors, but he's by no means the worst, and gave a fairly pleasing performance. The death of his brother showed Matthew at his best.' Be this as it may, one can only wish that it had been Richard Willis's superb Varsh who had survived to travel on with the Doctor.

The final word must go to Hopkins, whose overall assessment of the story was spot on: 'From its superb beginning in the TARDIS, with brilliant performances from Tom and Lalla as Romana realises that the Time Lords want her back on Gallifrey, right through to the final scene of Part Four, with the realisation that they are stuck in [E-Space], *Full Circle* was a joy to behold, a story that fans and casual viewers alike are sure to remember for some time.'

STATE OF DECAY

Writer: Terrance Dicks. **Director:** Peter Moffatt. **Designer:** Christine Ruscoe. **Costumes:** Amy Roberts. **Make-Up:** Norma Hill. **Incidental Music:** Paddy Kingsland. **Fight Arranger:** Stuart Fell. **Visual Effects:** Tony Harding. **Film Cameraman:** Fintan Sheehan.

FOURTH DOCTOR

Film Editor: John Lee. **Studio Lighting:** Bert Postlethwaite. **Studio Sound:** John Howell. **Production Assistant:** Rosalind Wolfes. **Assistant Floor Manager:** Lynn Richards.

	First UK TX	Scheduled TX	Actual TX	Duration	Viewers	Chart Pos.
Part One	22/11/80	17.40	17.42	22'24"	5.8	119
Part Two	29/11/80	17.40	17.41	23'16"	5.3	136
Part Three	06/12/80	17.40	17.40	24'13"	4.4	145
Part Four	13/12/80	17.40	17.40	24'54"	5.4	125

Plot: The Doctor, Romana, K9 and Adric – an Outler from Alzarius who has stowed away aboard the TARDIS – arrive on a planet where the native villagers live in fear of 'the Wasting' and of three Lords named Zargo, Camilla and Aukon who rule from an imposing Tower. The Lords are soon revealed to be vampire servants of the last of the Great Vampires, a race referred to in Time Lord mythology. The Great Vampire is about to be revived from its resting place beneath the Tower – in fact the spaceship in which the Lords, in their original human forms, came to E-Space – but the Doctor launches one of the ship's three shuttle craft and it pierces the heart of the creature, killing it. The Lords, deprived of their master, crumble to dust.

Episode endings:
1. The Doctor and Romana are making their way through the forest to the Tower when suddenly they are assailed by bats. Romana points out to the Doctor that the sky is full of the creatures.
2. The Doctor and Romana are exploring a cavern beneath the Tower when they encounter Aukon, who tells them that this is the 'resting place' and welcomes them to his domain.
3. Camilla and Zargo menace Romana and Adric, intending to drink their blood. Adric throws a knife at Zargo, and it hits him in the chest. Camilla then advances on the boy while Zargo, seizing the retreating Romana, pulls the still bloodless knife from his chest and drops it to the floor.
4. The time travellers depart in the TARDIS, the Doctor telling Adric that he must now be taken straight back home.

IT WAS MADE WHERE...?

Location filming: 30.04.80-01.05.80
Location: Burnham Beeches, Burnham, Bucks.
Ealing Filming: 02.05.80 in water tank
Visual Effects: 20.05.80-21.05.80 at 250 Western Avenue, Ealing, London
Studio: 15.05.80-16.05.80 in TC3, 29.05.80-31.05.80 in TC6

ADDITIONAL CREDITED CAST

Aukon (Emrys James), Camilla (Rachel Davies), Zargo (William Lindsay), Ivo (Clinton Greyn), Marta (Rhoda Lewis[1,2]), Tarak (Thane Bettany), Habris (Iain Rattray[1,2,4]), Kalmar (Arthur Hewlett), Veros (Stacy Davies), Karl (Dean Allen[1]), Roga (Stuart Fell[3]), Zoldaz (Stuart Blake[3]).

Note: There is no voice credit for K9 on Part Two as he does not speak in this episode.

POPULAR MYTHS

- This story's location scenes were shot at Black Park near Iver Heath in Buckinghamshire. (They were shot at Burnham Beeches near Amersham, also in Buckinghamshire – it was *Full Circle*'s location scenes that were shot at Black Park.)

THINGS TO WATCH OUT FOR

- *State of Decay* features the largest quantities of blood ever seen in a *Doctor Who* story – by a considerable margin!
- There is ingenious use of stock footage of bats in flight.

THINGS YOU MIGHT NOT HAVE KNOWN

- Working titles: *The Wasting, The Vampire Mutations*.
- For the only time during his era as the Doctor, Tom Baker had to have his hair permed before filming commenced. It had lost its natural curl due to the actor being in ill health.
- *State of Decay* started life in 1977, when a Terrance Dicks written vampire story, *The Witch Lords*, was put on hold due to a perceived clash with a BBC production of *Dracula*.

QUOTE, UNQUOTE

- **The Doctor:** 'Night must fall, Romana, even in E-Space.' **Romana:** 'It doesn't feel natural. There's that noise again.' **The Doctor:** 'Only bats. Quite harmless.' [A bat swoops down and bites him on the neck.] '*Argh*! Well, in theory. That one was a bit carnivorous.'
- **Romana:** 'You are incredible.' **The Doctor:** 'Well, yes, I suppose I am. I've never given it much thought.'
- **The Doctor:** '*Psst*, you are wonderful.' **Romana:** 'Suppose I am. I've never really thought about it.'

ANALYSIS

Following on from the excellent *Full Circle*, *State of Decay* is another story that – apart from a single unsuccessful model shot in Part Four – looks absolutely superb on screen, as Rosemary Fowler described in *Oracle* Volume 3 Number 9 dated May 1981:

'The whole production was given a definite atmosphere of gloom and foreboding by the darkly lit sets of the Tower, and the sumptuous, though sombre, dark grey and red costumes of the "Three Who Rule". I really liked their medieval-style robes and felt that they helped to underline the sense of separateness between them and the ragged peasants.

'Most of the visual effects were well executed, particularly the superimposing of the bat over Aukon's face near the end of [Part One]. Indeed, all the bat scenes were very well done; one area where most vampire films fall down to earth with a thud. Paradoxically, this production's pitfall was the one effect you would think the BBC knew how to do by now – yes folks, I do mean that awful rocket! ... If you cannot make a realistic shot of a rocket turning around in space, avoid it! A simple pair of shots of it going up and coming back down again would have been perfectly adequate and less of a strain on the viewers' [credulity]. I am merely grateful that they decided against showing a full-sized version of the Great Vampire. However, on a note of praise, the final sequence of the disintegration of the lesser vampires was as good if not better than the best efforts of Hammer Films.'

The story's suitably atmospheric location work is also a highlight, and director Peter Moffatt brings out some good performances from a fine guest cast. Fowler found Emrys James's Aukon particularly impressive: 'Emrys James gave a very creditable performance as Aukon, the real leader of the "Three". Where Camilla and Zargo were merely power mad, jealous freaks, who spent most of their time hissing at people and baring their fangs without ever once getting down to draining anyone's blood, Aukon was a subtle blend of the disciple of the Great One and the worldly, practical dictator. He was the one who was concerned to prepare all for the Time of Arising, he also the one whom the peasants were most in awe of. One can't help feeling that Camilla and Zargo were merely ornaments in the social structure of that claustrophobic community, the ones to distract the attention away from the more powerful Chancellor.'

Martin J Wiggins, writing in *Web Planet* Number 6 in 1981, considered the story reminiscent of the early part of the fourth Doctor's era: '*State of Decay* was an affectionate tip of the hat to Philip Hinchcliffe, who introduced gothic horror to *Doctor Who*. Indeed, this serial could have been more successful even than those he produced, for while he instigated take-offs of the horrific fictions of individual writers' minds ... the source for *State of Decay* was a horror more deeply ingrained, a genuine primitive fear rather than one created for the satisfaction of those seeking to be frightened. However, the potential of a vampire tale, ably fulfilled by the first two episodes, was sabotaged by the reproduction of two other characteristics of Hinchcliffe's reign – the "ancient enemy of the Time Lords" bit and the need to make every threat the biggest threat to the universe since sliced bread.'

Tim Robins found much to admire in Terrance Dicks's scripts, as he explained in *The Doctor Who Review* Issue 8 dated December 1980:

'I don't think I can remember a story that was as well plotted ... Terrance Dicks masterfully avoided the terrible plot clichés that were inherent in the story. The tower was a spaceship, the Lords vampires, commanders of the spaceship still alive after thousands of years. A lesser writer would have hinged the entire plot around these "surprises" which would, naturally, not have been revealed until an extremely rushed Part Four. But no. Terrance Dicks dispensed with these revelations in throwaway lines liberally scattered throughout the opening episodes and in doing so produced an enthralling plot – one of the few stories that has kept my interest through every single episode.

'The story ... succinctly encapsulated everything Tom Baker's Doctor should have been, the image the best Tom Baker stories have created... Tom's [Doctor] was ideally suited for that surprising blend of gothic horror, pseudo-science, Time Lord mythology and downright strangeness. It was a curious blend that few stories ever really achieved, but when they did they became instant classics ..: Dark stories with darker ideas that plunged the Doctor into the world of horror with one foot only tentatively in science-fiction ...'

Even so, Robins was in accord with Wiggins in feeling that the story was let down by its ending: 'The only place where I feel [it] slipped up, almost inevitably, was [Part Four]. Although it didn't sink into sheer awfulness like *The Leisure Hive* and that rather-to-be-forgotten *Meglos*, several scenes seemed out of focus with the quality of the previous three episodes. K9 made me squirm with embarrassment, particularly when the rebels' leader Ivo ... decided to apologise to it.' Geraint Jones, writing in *TARDIS*

Volume 5 Number 6 in 1981, likewise thought that while the story was 'one of the most enjoyable, and certainly best produced, … for a very long time' it was 'ultimately a disappointment' due to 'a wasted last episode' with a very predictable ending.

These criticisms seem somewhat churlish. After all, a vampire story would not be a vampire story without the obligatory dénouement involving stakes through the heart and the undead crumbling to dust before the heroes' eyes; anything less would be a disappointment. And at least here the whole thing is given a *Doctor Who* twist with the revelation that the Great Vampire and its kind were ancient enemies of the Time Lords. Atmosphere is the key thing in a story like this, and *State of Decay* has it in abundance. Scenes such as the one in which the Doctor runs up a hill to the TARDIS, and then accesses the antiquated Record of Rassilon to find out more about the vampires, are highly evocative. There are some great directorial touches here, including the stylised, almost choreographed movements of the three Lords and the aforementioned moment when a slow-motion shot of a bat in flight is superimposed over an image of Aukon. Wonderful stuff! Tim Robins, however, remained less than fully satisfied: '*State of Decay* was brilliant, but where was the moral? "Don't fall through E-Space or you'll get your neck bitten"? [It] was a great horror story but, when you think about it, it was rotten science-fiction. But then, *Doctor Who* has ceased being that. I did, however, enjoy it, and if any story this season deserves praise this one does. Just one question – what the heck *was* "the Wasting"?'

@@@

WARRIORS' GATE

Writer: Steve Gallagher. **Director:** Paul Joyce. **Designer:** Graeme Story. **Costumes:** June Hudson. **Make-Up:** Pauline Cox. **Incidental Music:** Peter Howell. **Visual Effects:** Mat Irvine. **Studio Lighting:** John Dixon. **Studio Sound:** Alan Fogg. **Production Assistant:** Graeme Harper. **Assistant Floor Manager:** Val McCrimmon.

	First UK TX	Scheduled TX	Actual TX	Duration	Viewers	Chart Pos.
Part One	03/01/81	17.20	17.21	22'54"	7.1	88
Part Two	10/01/81	17.10	17.10	23'47"	6.7	93
Part Three	17/01/81	17.10	17.11	22'15"	8.3	59
Part Four	24/01/81	17.10	17.10	24'53"	7.8	69

Plot: The TARDIS is hijacked in the vortex by a time sensitive Tharil named Biroc, and brought to a strange white void. Biroc wants to free the others of his race who are being transported in a slave ship, captained by Rorvik, which is also trapped in the void. The only other thing present in the void is an ancient gateway leading to a decrepit banqueting hall. This is the domain of the Tharils, who in a previous time were cruel masters to their human slaves but have now repented. The humans built the Gundan robots to kill the Tharils, and this led to the latter race's downfall. Rorvik tries to break through the gateway, and thereby gain access to N-Space, by blasting it with his engines. The blast is simply reflected back, however, destroying the ship and freeing its prisoners. Romana and K9 elect to remain in E-Space to help liberate the remainder of the Tharil race, while the TARDIS – now occupied only by the Doctor and Adric – is able to return to N-Space.

Episode endings:

1. The Doctor has followed Biroc to the gateway, wherein he finds a cobwebbed and deserted banqueting hall. He stoops beside a large mirror to examine Biroc's discarded chains. Behind him, one of the two armour-clad figures standing near the mirror comes to life. It strides towards the Doctor, raises an axe and sweeps it down at his back.

2. Aldo and Royce, two of Rorvik's crew, attempt to revive a Tharil prisoner but injure it instead. After they have gone, the Tharil rises from the table where it has been left and makes its way to the bridge. Romana, strapped immobile in the navigator's chair, strains at her bonds as the Tharil approaches. She screams as it reaches for her face.

3. The Doctor is led by a female Tharil to a feast taking place in the banqueting hall at the time of the Tharils' dominance. Romana, watching from a gallery, suddenly senses that the Doctor is in danger. As time contracts around them, Gundan robots invade the hall and smash an axe into the table. The Doctor and Romana suddenly find themselves back in the 'present', surrounded by Rorvik and his men. Rorvik comments that he is surprised to find them here.

4. Romana elects to stay with the Tharils in E-Space to help them free their people, and K9 stays with her. The Doctor and Adric leave in the TARDIS, heading back to N-Space.

IT WAS MADE WHERE...?

Location Photographs: 01.09.80
Location: Powys Castle, Welshpool, Powis, Wales
Studio: 24.09.80-26.09.80 in TC6, 02.10.80-04.10.80 in TC1, 07.10.80 (gallery only) in TC6

ADDITIONAL CREDITED CAST

Rorvik (Clifford Rose), Packard (Kenneth Cope), Lane (David Kincaid), Aldo (Freddie Earlle), Royce (Harry Waters), Biroc (David Weston[1,3,4]), Sagan (Vincent Pickering), Gundan (Robert Vowles[1,2]), Lazlo (Jeremy Gittins[2-4]).

THINGS TO WATCH OUT FOR

- Kenneth Cope plays Rorvik's second in command, Packard. He had previously starred as the ghostly detective Marty Hopkirk in the sixties series *Randall and Hopkirk (Deceased)*, amongst many other notable roles.
- Clifford Rose, who played Rorvik, was well-known as Kessler in *Secret Army*.
- Writer Stephen Gallagher has gone on to become one of Britain's most respected horror/thriller novelists and has adapted and directed several of his novels for television.

THINGS YOU MIGHT NOT HAVE KNOWN

- Working title: *Dream Time*.
- This story was promoted in *Radio Times* as the first in a new season of *Doctor Who*. This was due to the fact that, unusually, the season had broken for two Saturdays over the Christmas holiday period.
- Lazlo, the Tharil prisoner revived toward the end of Part Two, is never referred to by name in the story's dialogue; his name is given only in the closing credits.
- This was the last story to have visual effects designed by *Doctor Who*'s most well-known effects designer, Mat Irvine.

- **Biroc:** 'Others follow.' **The Doctor:** 'Others?' **Biroc:** 'Believe nothing they say. They're not Biroc's kind.' **Romana:** 'What are you?' **Biroc:** 'A shadow of my past and of your future.'
- **Rorvik:** 'Run Doctor! Scurry off back to your blue box. You're like all the rest. Lizards when there's a man's work to be done. I'm sick of your kind. Faint-hearted, do-nothing, lily-livered deadweights. This is the end for all of you. I'm finally getting something done!'
- **The Doctor:** 'One good solid hope's worth a cart-load of certainties.'
- **Adric:** 'Will Romana be all right?' **The Doctor:** 'All right? She'll be superb!'

ANALYSIS

'A mysterious white void; a crippled ship; an apathetic crew; the exit from E-Space? Thus began a superbly enigmatic *Doctor Who* story worthy of the excellent new production which has been the hallmark of the eighteenth season.' This positive assessment of *Warriors' Gate*, given by Peter Anghelides in *Oracle* Volume 3 Number 10 dated August 1981, has been echoed by many other reviewers. Often, however, the praise has been qualified by the observation that the scripts by debut writer Steve Gallagher (now better known as thriller writer Stephen Gallagher) expect rather too much of the viewer in terms of being able to work out what is going on from the limited clues provided. It is indeed doubtful that anyone could truly follow the story on just a single viewing. 'The confused plot resulted from a lack of clear explanations,' commented Robert Craker in *TARDIS* Volume 6 Number 1 dated April 1981. 'We had some glimmerings, but being told snippets a bit at a time is nearly as confusing as being told nothing at all.' The problem is that practically nothing is fully explained. The origins of the Tharils, the motivations of Rorvik and his crew, the functions of the gateway, the properties of the mirrors – all are left, to one degree or another, mysterious.

Visually, though, the story is undeniably stunning, boasting some superb utilitarian sets and an array of imaginative and well executed video effects, such as the one used to depict the Tharils moving through the void. There are some truly memorable moments scattered throughout the four episodes, including one in which time comes to a temporary standstill during the flipping of a coin in Part One, the harrowing electrocution of Lazlo in Part Two and the equally unsettling death of Sagan in Part Four.

The performances by the guest cast are also praiseworthy. David Weston's restrained and noble Biroc is one of the best, as is Clifford Rose's marvellously manic Rorvik. The light relief supplied by Freddie Earlle as Aldo and Harry Waters as Royce is also especially welcome in an otherwise bleak story. 'Rorvik and his crew are a mixed bunch,' wrote Karen Davies in *Celestial Toyroom* Issue 245 in 1997. 'Clifford Rose gives an excellent performance as a man whose sanity is hanging by the merest of threads. Exasperated by his crew's inefficiency, he is unable to grasp the seriousness of the situation. Kenneth Cope is the voice of reason, combined with the shrewd intelligence of a man who has realised exactly how little work he needs to do to keep his job.'

Another aspect of note is that the story's episode endings are all outstanding – always a good sign. In fact the cliffhanger conclusion to Part Three is one of the series' all-time classics: tense and full of drama, leaving the viewer on the edge of the seat and desperate to know what happens next. And then we come to the end of Part Four. The idea of

4 FOURTH DOCTOR

Romana, having effectively served her apprenticeship aboard the TARDIS, leaving to become a 'female Doctor' in E-Space, taking K9 with her for assistance, is quite wonderful, and arguably the most fitting departure ever given to one of the Doctor's companions. To have had her returning to Gallifrey and taking up some high office, which (particularly following the Time Lord summons in *Full Circle*) would perhaps have been a more obvious way for the production team to have written her out, would have been a betrayal of the character. As Peter J Finklestone wrote in *Web Planet* Number 7 in 1981: 'What price a *Romana and K9 in E-Space* offshoot series?'

THE KEEPER OF TRAKEN

Writer: Johnny Byrne. **Director:** John Black. **Designer:** Tony Burrough. **Costumes:** Amy Roberts. **Make-Up:** Norma Hill. **Incidental Music:** Roger Limb. **Visual Effects:** Peter Logan. **Studio Lighting:** Don Babbage. **Studio Sound:** John Holmes, Alan Fogg. **Production Assistant:** Alan Wareing. **Assistant Floor Manager:** Lynn Richards.

	First UK TX	Scheduled TX	Actual TX	Duration	Viewers	Chart Pos.
Part One	31/01/81	17.10	17.09	24'05"	7.6	72
Part Two	07/02/81	17.10	17.09	24'50"	6.1	106
Part Three	14/02/81	17.10	17.09	23'49"	5.2	112
Part Four	21/02/81	17.10	17.12	25'11"	6.1	103

Plot: The Doctor and Adric learn from the wizened Keeper of Traken that a great evil has come to his planet in the form of a Melkur – a calcified statue. The Keeper is nearing the end of his reign and seeks the Doctor's help in preventing the evil from taking control of the bioelectronic Source that is the keystone of the Traken Union's civilisation. The Melkur, via various deceptions, becomes the next Keeper. It is then however revealed to be the Master's TARDIS. Its owner, still blackened and emaciated as when last seen, hopes to use the Source's power to regenerate himself. The Doctor manages to expel him and install a new Keeper in his place, but in a last minute ploy the Master traps one of the Traken Consuls, Tremas, and merges with his body before fleeing the planet.

Episode endings:
1. Armed guards known as Fosters bring the Doctor and Adric as prisoners before the Keeper and his Consuls. The Doctor asks the Keeper to vouch for him. At that moment however, unseen by all but the Keeper, the Melkur appears in the doorway. The Keeper is affected by the Melkur's presence and is able to tell his Consuls only that they have been invaded by evil. He then vanishes and, as the Melkur moves out of sight, the Consuls and the Fosters close in on the Doctor and Adric.
2. The Doctor, Adric and Consul Tremas are taken prisoner by the Fosters. Consul Kassia, who has fallen under the Melkur's influence, tells it that her task is done. The Melkur replies that, on the contrary, it is only beginning.
3. The old Keeper dies and Kassia ascends to his chair to take his place. Consul Katura, despite attempts by the Doctor and Tremas to intervene, activates the controls that will give

the new Keeper access to the Source. Suddenly Kassia cries out and her body contorts in pain before vanishing altogether – to be replaced by the Melkur.

4. The Master takes Tremas's body as his own and then departs in his TARDIS. Tremas's daughter Nyssa comes looking for her father, but in vain.

IT WAS MADE WHERE...?

Studio: 05.11.80-07.11.80 in TC6, 21.11.80-22.11.80 in TC8, 26.11.80 (gallery only) (studio unknown), 17.12.80 in TC6

ADDITIONAL CREDITED CAST

Tremas (Anthony Ainley), Kassia (Sheila Ruskin),The Keeper (Denis Carey[1,2]), Seron (John Woodnutt[1,2]), Katura (Margot van der Burgh), Luvic (Robin Soans), Neman (Roland Oliver), Melkur (Geoffrey Beevers)*, Fosters (Liam Prendergast[3], Philip Bloomfield[4]).

* Geoffrey Beevers played the Master but was credited as the Melkur to conceal this plot twist. The walking Melkur statue was played by Graham Cole (now better known for his starring role in the ITV police series *The Bill*).

THINGS TO WATCH OUT FOR

- The Master has two TARDISes – one disguised as the Melkur and the other as a grandfather clock.
- Anthony Ainley was cast as Tremas (an anagram of Master) partly because of a perceived facial similarity to the late Roger Delgado.
- The emaciated Master was played by Geoffrey Beevers, the husband of actress Caroline John, who had played Liz Shaw in the seventh season.
- Although she did not join the TARDIS crew until the following story, *The Keeper of Traken* saw the introduction of Nyssa, played by Sarah Sutton.

QUOTE, UNQUOTE

- **The Keeper:** 'How vain one can still be. I thought the whole universe knew the history of our little empire.'
- **The Doctor:** [Speaking of the Traken Union.] 'They say the atmosphere there was so full of goodness that evil just shrivelled up and died.'
- **The Master:** 'A new body ... at last!'

ANALYSIS

John Peel, writing in *TARDIS* Volume 6 Number 1 dated April 1981, considered *The Keeper of Traken* to be the season's most impressive story yet: '[This] was the best Tom Baker story for many a long year, and one of the most pleasing stories I have ever seen in the series. Everything gelled to make this one of those rare creatures – a virtually flawless show.' If this is overstating the case, it is only by a little. Writer Johnny Byrne's debut contribution to the series has a welcome quality of freshness and originality about it, presenting some unusual and slightly quirky concepts including the Traken Union and the evil Melkurs that are calcified by the planet's goodness as soon as they arrive there. Director John Black, another newcomer to the series, makes a fine job of translating script to screen, showing a deft touch with the drama and a great visual flair. The only real failing in the story's on-screen presentation – and a minor one, at that – is that the grove in which the Melkur arrives never convinces the viewer as being in the open air; it always looks exactly like what it is, a studio set. Peter G Lovelady, writing in *Oracle* Volume 3 Number 10 dated August 1981, had some suitably positive comments to make about other aspects of the production: 'The lavish interior sets added to the atmosphere, and the rich, flowing costumes were a credit to Amy Roberts. The new radiophonic music has been another definite plus to the season. Roger Limb provided us with a number of themes … A particular favourite of mine was the party music for Tremas's wedding, … adding to the Renaissance feel. My only grumble [concerned] the visual effects – the reversion of nature to "destructive chaos" was very [poorly realised].' Robert Fairclough, writing in *Web Planet* Number 7 in 1981, was even more appreciative: 'Apart from one model shot of the TARDIS in [Part One], the production was flawless; the courts of Traken, the labyrinth beneath the grove, had a curious neo-classical quality, and Shakespearian undercurrents were also present in the vaguely Elizabethan costumes … The elements of tragedy-symbolism in the weeds and storm, undermining of the state and institution of a corrupt ruler … were also noticeably and effectively present, enhancing the fundamentally good SF yarn that *The Keeper of Traken* was.'

All Johnny Byrne's characters are well written and effectively brought to life by the guest cast. Soon-to-be companion Nyssa is given not an enormous amount to do in the story, but Sarah Sutton delivers a charming, nicely understated performance that shows considerable promise. Best of all, though, is Anthony Ainley's Tremas.

'Tremas was … solid flesh and blood,' agreed John Peel, 'the kind of person that you could believe in. It's very hard to create such a real-seeming person in a story, but Johnny Byrne gave us a superb one here. Tremas was kind, intellectual, curious (a fatal flaw!), well-mannered and witty. His lines were sparkling, the delivery faultless. Anthony Ainley was an excellent choice for the role, and played [it] to perfection … The other characters had all been believable and good, but Tremas was special in a story that was filled with such magic for me …

'The final scene, with good triumphant, evil defeated and Tremas about to go home was beautiful. But that fatal curiosity for the clock …! I revelled in the sequence … The Master creeping out, and clutching at the still form of Tremas, the merging of the two people, and then the regeneration of the old body into a virtual Delgado look-alike (he even regenerated the clothes …), and "A new body … at last!". I loved it!'

The resurrection of the Master in a new physical form is undoubtedly *The Keeper of Traken*'s most important and enduring contribution to the *Doctor Who* mythos. Lovelady felt that it was only moderately successful in this regard, but held out hope for the series' future: 'The build up to [the Master's] revelation was well handled, with nice little melodramatic bits … Alas, when the cowled figure finally turned round, I was disappointed. Although Norma Hill had done a creditable job with the make-up, Geoffrey Beevers actually looked *less* decayed than Peter Pratt [in *The Deadly Assassin*], and he was remarkably agile, considering he was near the end of this [thirteenth incarnation] … again! … Although Mr Beevers captured the Master's disregard for life, his reaction to the captured Doctor was … all wrong. Agreed, he would relish the moment, but he would not be drooling over the Doctor like a hungry bloodhound. He was also perhaps too volatile, especially when the Source was nearly destroyed. However, we now have Anthony Ainley, who, with more than a passing resemblance to Roger Delgado, looks very promising indeed.'

LOGOPOLIS

Writer: Christopher H Bidmead. **Director:** Peter Grimwade. **Designer:** Malcolm Thornton. **Costumes:** June Hudson. **Make-Up:** Dorka Nieradzik. **Incidental Music:** Paddy Kingsland. **Visual Effects:** John Horton. **Film Cameraman:** Peter Hall. **Film Editor:** Paul Humfress. **Studio Lighting:** Henry Barber. **Studio Sound:** John Holmes. **Production Manager:** Margot Heyhoe. **Assistant Floor Manager:** Val McCrimmon.

	First UK TX	Scheduled TX	Actual TX	Duration	Viewers	Chart Pos.
Part One	28/02/81	17.10	17.09	24'32"	7.1	84
Part Two	07/03/81	17.10	17.09	24'03"	7.7	57
Part Three	14/03/81	17.10	17.11	24'32"	5.8	102
Part Four	21/03/81	17.10	17.09	25'10"	6.1	97

Plot: The Doctor takes Adric and a young air hostess named Tegan Jovanka, who has come aboard the TARDIS by accident, to the planet Logopolis, home of a race of mathematicians whose help he hopes to enlist in reconfiguring the outer shell of the TARDIS. The mysterious, wraith-like Watcher brings Nyssa from Traken to join them and warns of impending danger – something that is borne out as the Master arrives and kills a number of the Logopolitans. The Logopolitans' leader, the Monitor, reveals that the universe passed its normal point of heat death long ago and has been preserved only by his people's calculations, which – by way of a signal beamed from a perfect copy of the Pharos Project radio telescope on Earth – have kept open numerous CVEs through which the excess entropy can drain. This process has now been halted by the Master's interference, and the Doctor is forced to join forces with his arch-enemy in order to save the universe. Their plan is to use the real Pharos Project to transmit a copy of the Logopolitan program and thus keep open the CVEs, but the Master seizes the opportunity to blackmail the peoples of the universe by threatening them with destruction unless they agree to his demands. In foiling this scheme the Doctor falls from the gantry of the radio telescope. As he lies injured on the ground the Watcher appears again and merges with the Doctor as he regenerates.

Episode endings:
1. The Doctor finds the police investigating Tegan's abandoned sports car. A Detective Inspector asks him to explain the presence in the car of two shrunken bodies: a policeman and Tegan's aunt Vanessa. The Doctor realises that the Master has escaped from Traken and must be somewhere near.
2. The Doctor attempts to reconfigure the TARDIS but it begins to shrink instead. As his friends watch from outside, the ship gets smaller and smaller.
3. The Doctor decides to collaborate with the Master to save the universe from entropy. He bundles Adric, Nyssa and Tegan into the TARDIS, then he and the Master shake hands on their agreement to work together. 'One last hope,' says the Doctor.

4. The Doctor goes out onto the gantry of the radio telescope and disconnects the power cable. The Master causes the gantry to move and the Doctor, unable to cling on to the cable, falls to the ground below. He is joined by Adric, Nyssa and Tegan who look on as the mysterious Watcher merges with him. The end result is a new incarnation of the Doctor, who sits up.

IT WAS MADE WHERE...?

Location filming: 16.12.80, 18.12.80, 22.12.80
Locations: 43 Ursula Street, Battersea, London, SW11; Albert Bridge, Kensington and Chelsea; London, SW3; Cadogan Pier, Chelsea Embankment, London, SW3; BBC Receiving Station, Crowsley Park, Blounts Court Road, Sonning Common, Berks; Lay-by, Amersham Road (A413), Denham, Bucks.
Studio: 08.01.81-09.01.81 in TC3, 22.01.81-24.01.81 in TC6, 28.01.81 (gallery only) in TC6

ADDITIONAL CREDITED CAST

Aunt Vanessa (Dolore Whiteman[1]), Detective Inspector (Tom Georgeson[1,2]), The Master (Anthony Ainley), The Monitor (John Fraser[2-4]), Doctor Who (Peter Davison[4]), Security Guard (Christopher Hurst[4]).

Note: Nyssa does not appear until Part Two and is not credited on Part One. The Master, although credited on Parts One and Two, is not seen until Part Three. Only his evil chuckle is heard in the earlier episodes. The Watcher – a wraith like intermediate stage between the Doctor's fourth and fifth incarnations – was played in all four episodes by Adrian Gibbs, but received no credit on screen or in the *Radio Times*.

THINGS TO WATCH OUT FOR

- This is Anthony Ainley's first full story as the Master.
- An electronic effect ws used on Part Four's closing title sequence to blur the usual image of Tom Baker's face.
- The lead up to the Doctor's regeneration at the conclusion of *Logopolis* included two compilations of clips featuring old enemies and friends of the Doctor. The enemies (and the episodes from which the clips were drawn) were: the Master (*The Deadly Assassin* Part One); a Dalek (*Destiny of the Daleks* Episode Four); the Pirate Captain (*The Pirate Planet* Part Four); a Cyberman (*Revenge of the Cybermen* Part Three); Davros (*Genesis of the Daleks* Part Five); a Sontaran (*The Invasion of Time* Part Five); a Zygon (*Terror of the Zygons* Part Three); and the Black Guardian (*The Armageddon Factor* Part Six). The companions were: Sarah (*Terror of the Zygons* Part Two), Harry (*The Sontaran Experiment* Part Two), the Brigadier (*Invasion of the Dinosaurs* Part Two), Leela (*The Robots of Death* Part One), K9 (*The Armageddon Factor* Part Two), Romana 1 (*The Stones of Blood* Part One) and Romana 2 (*Full Circle* Part One).
- The regeneration sequence at the end of this story was repeated with different music and overdubs as a pre-title sequence to the fifth Doctor's debut episode, *Castrovalva* Part One.

- It was decided only late in the day that Nyssa would be a continuing character, so the other new companion, Tegan, was actually cast first.

QUOTE, UNQUOTE

- **The Doctor:** 'Have you seen the state of the time column recently? Wheezing like a grampus.'
- **The Doctor:** [Speaking of the Master.] 'He must have known I was going to fix the chameleon circuit.' **Adric:** 'He read your mind?' **The Doctor:** 'He's a Time Lord! In many ways we have the same mind.'
- **The Doctor:** 'Never guess. Unless you have to. There's enough uncertainty in the universe as it is.'
- **The Doctor:** 'It's the end ... but the moment has been prepared for.'

ANALYSIS

Logopolis tries hard to be the epic tale that it really needs to be as the concluding story of Tom Baker's extraordinary seven year tenure as the Doctor, and for the most part it succeeds.

Script editor Christopher H Bidmead made it a top priority to introduce some harder science into *Doctor Who* and move away from what he saw as the unduly fantasy-based approach of the previous few years; in the self-written *Logopolis* he takes this reliance on scientific concepts to its furthest extreme, as Justin Richards pointed out in *Aggedor* Issue 5 in 1983: 'There can be little doubt that *Logopolis* boasted one of the best, and by that I mean deepest, yet still accessible as basic entertainment, scripts of the series; the philosophical and scientific theories and arguments are presented and questioned at a speed which the Logopolitan mathematicians themselves would find staggering – the argument for and against causality which runs through the story is made overt by passing references to Thomas Huxley and the causal nexus, while the computer nature of Logopolis itself is referred to in casual lines about subroutines and Algol. The brain-like structure of the model [of Logopolis] ... is not made as obvious as perhaps it could be.'

It has been argued, however, that the Logopolitans' power to create any event in space and time simply by reciting a string of mathematical expressions could be more properly described in another way. Jan Vincent-Rudzki, writing in *Baker's Best* in 1981, asserted: '[We] have in *Logopolis* a race of wizards practicing magic, something the Doctor has always pooh-poohed, yet nobody ... seemed to realise this or be particularly impressed. What should have been an amazing discovery for the Doctor was glossed over so quickly, when it should have been marvelled at. This was one of the main faults of the final [story]; people just did not react to situations in a normal manner. The exception to this was the brilliant first episode, which was probably the best bit of drama to have come from *Doctor Who* in quite a few years. In this episode people acted like normal people in everyday situations. But when thrust into an alien situation they became like cardboard cut-outs whose mouths opened to say the words. The best example of this was Tegan. In [Part One] she acted quite normally, chatting away to her aunt in a most delightful manner. Yet the moment she stepped into the TARDIS she changed.'

There are also, it must be pointed out, one or two staggeringly *un*scientific ideas in the story, such as the Doctor's proposal to open the TARDIS doors underwater and thereby 'flush out' the Master (conveniently overlooking the fact that both he and Adric would undoubtedly be killed in the process) and, in Part Four, the Master's attempt to broadcast to the 'peoples of the universe' using what looks like a transistor radio. In fact, seen here in his first full story, the new Master unfortunately comes across as merely a poor copy of the character portrayed by Roger Delgado in the seventies. 'After all the Master's evil laughter I half expected him to twirl his moustache,' commented Vincent-Rudzki, 'but thankfully the corn did not go that far, although he did press buttons in an incredibly over-dramatic way. Anthony Ainley seems a good choice for the Master in a Delgado mould, but I think it would have been better to give him a more definitive variation of the Master's character, as the Doctor has when he regenerates. Likewise, if this was the Delgado version reborn, then why did he wear that silly suit that made him look like a penguin? Yet despite these points it was good to see some hope for the return of the Master as a worthy opponent.'

These faults notwithstanding, *Logopolis* does undoubtedly fulfil its main function of providing a suitable lead-in to the Doctor's regeneration, as Peter Anghelides observed in *Oracle* Volume 3 Number 11/12 dated Christmas 1981: 'One way in which *Logopolis* continually entertained us was, strangely, by baffling us. However, this was not a blinding with science, but rather an increasing puzzlement as to the continuing plotline. Who is the distant stranger? How is the Master manipulating the Doctor's fortune? What is the "single great secret" of Logopolis which is the Master's goal? These are all admirably sustained throughout the story, until at the apposite moment they are devastatingly explained, and we are faced (as is the Doctor) with the prospect of the destruction of the universe. So skilfully is the problem introduced that I think we all felt, for once, that the Doctor faced real defeat, rather than believing that "he is on TV next week, so he can't get killed". To all intents and purposes, the Doctor *dies*! He is then born again, but we can reflect wryly that for once the Doctor has tasted true defeat, with the Master's continued (and renewed) existence only highlighting the Doctor's inadequacy (being forced to regenerate after the fall).'

Mark Woodward, writing in *Web Planet* Number 8 dated August 1981, summed up the thoughts of many: 'I had an overwhelming feeling of apprehension as the last seconds of this story ticked relentlessly away, the end of the Doctor's fourth incarnation drawing ever nearer, [his] past life flashing before his weary eyes as he clung desperately to the cable. Resolved to his destiny, Earth's gravity claimed his seemingly fragile form as he plunged to his doom ... And so it came to pass that Tom Baker should end his long reign as the Doctor, and he bowed out with dignity as he wished it. He did not scream as he fell. Then he uttered his final words: "It's the end, but the moment has been prepared for ..." I was overcome with waves of nostalgia by the shadows of his past uttering that single word, ["Doctor"], and I suddenly realised I was going to miss him.'

It is only with hindsight that one can see just how much Baker was missed. Certainly as far the series' popularity with the general viewing public was concerned, this story would prove to be a turning point.

⊛⊛⊛⊛⊛⊛⊛⊛⊛⊛⊛⊛⊛⊛⊛⊛⊛⊛⊛⊛⊛⊛⊛⊛⊛⊛⊛⊛⊛⊛⊛⊛⊛⊛⊛⊛⊛

During the early stages of production of season eighteen John Nathan-Turner had reached a mutual agreement with Tom Baker that the actor would bow out of the series upon the expiry of his current contract, bringing to an end his unprecedented seven year run as the Doctor. The producer had not been particularly happy with Baker's portrayal of the Doctor, considering that his increasingly assured and flippant interpretation made the character seem too dominant and invulnerable. He had also greatly disliked the general air of jokiness that Baker tended to inject into the proceedings. Baker, too, had come to feel that now was the right time for him to be moving on. So it was that on 24 October 1980, the day before transmission of the first episode of *Full Circle*, the BBC held a press conference to announce that the actor would be leaving at the end of the season.

This left Nathan-Turner not only with the task of finding a new leading man but also with the problem of trying to retain the loyalty of the series' regular audience. Baker had won an enormous following, and many were no doubt unaware that there had ever been other Doctors. To recast the lead role in a long-running and popular show is always a high-risk endeavour, and Nathan-Turner felt that Baker's successor would be bound to face an uphill struggle to win acceptance. One strategy that the producer developed with a view to alleviating this problem was to make the last two stories of season eighteen and the first of season nineteen a loosely-linked trilogy reintroducing the Master. Anthony Ainley was chosen as the new incarnation of the Doctor's arch-enemy largely on the strength of his portrayal of the villainous Reverend Emilius in *The Pallisers* – a 1974 BBC classic serial on which Nathan-Turner had worked as production manager.

Another idea that Nathan-Turner had considered with the aim of enticing viewers to stick with *Doctor Who* was to replace Romana with an already established companion character from the series' past. To this end he had approached both Elisabeth Sladen, who had played Sarah Jane Smith, and Louise Jameson, who had played Leela, to see if they would be interested in reprising their roles. Both had declined, so he had then decided instead that two completely new companions should be introduced toward the end of season eighteen – the theory being that these would quickly gain their own respective admirers who would want to see how they coped with the new Doctor. The first of the two to appear on screen was Nyssa. She had originally been created by writer Johnny Byrne as a one-off character for *The Keeper of Traken*, but Nathan-Turner had quickly decided to keep her on for at least a further three stories. The second new regular, Tegan Jovanka, made her debut in *Logopolis*. Created by Nathan-Turner and Bidmead before it was realised that Nyssa would also be a companion, she was originally to have had a three story 'trial run' but later became thought of as a more long-term regular. Her initial character description established her as a bossy, argumentative air hostess from Australia – a country of origin chosen by the producer partly in order to break the precedent of exclusively British human companions and partly, it has been suggested, with a view to obtaining co-production money from the series' Australian broadcasters, ABC. The actress chosen for the role was Janet Fielding, whose name had been put forward to Nathan-Turner by the Actors Alliance organisation, of which she was a member, on the basis that she was a genuine bossy Australian!

Tom Baker's era as the Doctor had been not only the longest but also arguably the most successful, overall, in *Doctor Who*'s history. When the series returned, it would have a new leading man in the person of twenty-nine year old Peter Davison.

K-9 AND COMPANY

The gap between seasons eighteen and nineteen was enlivened for *Doctor Who* viewers not only by *The Five Faces of Doctor Who*, a BBC2-transmitted run of repeats that for the first time ever featured stories from Doctors other than the current incumbent, but also by a one-off, fifty-minute special that John Nathan-Turner hoped would launch a whole new spin-off series.

Following the public outcry that had occurred when the news that K9 would be leaving *Doctor Who* filtered out in early June 1980, Nathan-Turner had put forward to his BBC superiors the suggestion that the robot dog be given its own show. This idea had been approved and a pilot production set in motion. The initial outline for the story was written by Nathan-Turner himself at the end of April 1981, under the working title *One Girl and Her Dog*. This sketched out a basic idea for a 'black magic yarn' set in an English country village, involving Sarah Jane Smith, her Aunt Lavinia's ward Brendan and K9 mark III – apparently a gift left for her by the Doctor, but in fact under the control of his arch-enemy the Master. In terms of style, the production was envisaged as being more in the mould of *The Avengers* than of *Doctor Who*.

At the beginning of May 1981, Nathan-Turner and new temporary *Doctor Who* script editor Antony Root produced a format document for the programme, now entitled *A Girl's Best Friend*, which contained character outlines of Sarah and K9 and a refined synopsis of the story, this time with no mention of K9 being under the Master's control. It was shortly after this, on 12 May, that Nathan-Turner first contacted Elisabeth Sladen to see if she would be willing to appear in the special. Fortunately she readily agreed – something she had previously resisted doing when invited first by Graham Williams and then by Nathan-Turner himself to return as a regular in *Doctor Who* itself. She would be joined by John Leeson, who agreed to reprise his role as K9's voice.

Terence Dudley was approached to script the special. After discussions and the preparation of a detailed scene breakdown he wrote a full draft script that stuck quite closely to the ideas developed by the production team but fleshed them out accordingly. Root's successor, Eric Saward, made a number of amendments to the script during September 1981 – by which time the special had acquired its final title of *K-9 and Company* (Nathan-Turner's superiors having requested that it refer explicitly to K9), with *A Girl's Best Friend* relegated to a subtitle.

Location shooting – including for the title sequence, which Nathan-Turner decided should be in the same style as those for the US series *Hart to Hart* and *Hawaii Five-0* – was carried out in November 1981 near Cirencester in the Gloucestershire countryside. A two-day studio session subsequently took place at the BBC's Pebble Mill studios in Birmingham.

K-9 and Company: A Girl's Best Friend, the first *bona fide* TV spin off from *Doctor Who*, was eventually seen by viewers on Monday 28 December 1981 as part of the Christmas season on BBC1. It won a quite respectable viewing figure of 8.4 million and would no doubt have done even better had it not been for the fact that the Winter Hill transmitter in the North West region suffered a power blackout at the time. The option of a full series was never pursued, however. The programme had a single repeat screening the following Christmas, on 24 December 1982 on BBC2, where it pulled an audience of 2.1 million.

Further details of this programme, including a full analysis, can be found in Appendix A to this book.

The Fifth Doctor
(Peter Davison)
1982-1984

PETER DAVISON IS THE FIFTH DOCTOR

Peter Moffett, now better known by his stage name Peter Davison, was born in 1951 in the Streatham area of London. Ten years later his family moved to Woking in Surrey, where he took parts in a number of school plays and eventually joined a local amateur dramatic society. On leaving school at the age of sixteen, with only modest academic qualifications, he had a variety of short-lived jobs ranging from hospital porter to clothes press operator. He was still keen to pursue an acting career, however, and managed to obtain a place at the Central School of Speech and Drama, where he trained for three years. His first professional acting work came shortly after this in 1972 when he secured a small role in a run of *Love's Labour's Lost* at the Nottingham Playhouse. This marked the start of a three year period in which he worked in a variety of different repertory companies around the UK, often in Shakespearian roles. He then made his television debut, appearing (alongside his future first wife, American-born actress Sandra Dickinson) as a blond-wigged space cowboy character in a story in the Thames TV children's science-fiction series *The Tomorrow People*. He spent the following eighteen months working as a filing clerk at Twickenham tax office and pursuing an interest in singing and songwriting, which led him to record several singles with Dickinson. He then secured prominent roles in two series. The first, LWT's 1977 period drama *Love for Lydia*, saw him playing the romantic lead, Tom Holland. It was in the second, however, that he was really to come to the attention of the general viewing public. This was the BBC's *All Creatures Great and Small*, a highly popular series based on the books of country vet James Herriot, which ran initially for three seasons between 1978 and 1980. Davison, co-starring with Robert Hardy and Christopher Timothy, played an impetuous young vet named Tristan Farnon.

Davison's success in *All Creatures Great and Small* brought him a lot more work, including the lead roles in two sitcoms – LWT's *Holding the Fort* and the BBC's *Sink or Swim* – which consolidated his status as a well-known and popular television actor. It was in September 1980 that John Nathan-Turner first suggested to Davison that he might take on the mantle of the fifth Doctor in *Doctor Who*. The actor's initial reaction was one of considerable scepticism, as he considered himself completely unsuitable for the role, but he was eventually won over, his acceptance being announced to the press at the beginning of November. '*Doctor Who* was a lot of fun to do,' he said in 1988. 'We had some terrific guest artists, and I wouldn't have missed it for anything. It was very demanding, and strikes delayed my last story so I was too tired to feel sad when it was all finally over, but, yes, one does suffer the odd pang.'

DOCTOR WHO SEASON NINETEEN (1982)

Regular Cast:
The Doctor (Peter Davison)
Adric (Matthew Waterhouse) until *Earthshock* Part Four
Nyssa (Sarah Sutton)
Tegan (Janet Fielding)

Regular Crew:
Producer: John Nathan-Turner.
Script Editor: Eric Saward on *Castrovalva*, *Kinda*, *Black Orchid* and *Time-Flight*, Antony Root on *Four to Doomsday*, *The Visitation* and *Earthshock**.
Production Associate: Angela Smith.
Title Music: Ron Grainer and the BBC Radiophonic Workshop, arranged by Peter Howell.
Special Sounds: Dick Mills.

* Although credited as script editor on *Earthshock*, Antony Root did little or no work on it. This was a ploy to avoid crediting Eric Saward as script editor on his own story.

A week after *K-9 and Company* was transmitted, *Doctor Who* itself was back on air for the start of the fifth Doctor's era – in an unfamiliar weekday evening slot, broadcast at the rate of two episodes per week. This was the first time that the series had ever been moved from its traditional Saturday evening slot, and the change was accepted only reluctantly by the production team.

Christopher H Bidmead had left the team after the expiry of his year's contract and a young writer named Antony Root, who had previously worked at the BBC's TV Drama Script Unit, was given a short attachment to *Doctor Who* as a replacement script editor. Root started work on the series in January 1981 and ultimately received a credit on three stories (and also a co-credit on *K-9 and Company*), although he commissioned none of them; his involvement was essentially confined to suggesting and performing rewrites and ensuring that scripts were ready in time for recording. Root later went on to a distinguished career as a TV and film producer. The new permanent script editor was Eric Saward, who was offered the post on the strength of his season nineteen story *The Visitation*. He joined the team in mid-April 1981, working alongside Root on *K-9 and Company* and on a number of other stories before assuming full responsibility around mid-way through the season's production.

The other important behind-the-scenes change for this season was the discontinuation of Barry Letts's role as the series' executive producer. This was decided upon in August 1981 as it was felt that John Nathan-Turner was by this point sufficiently well established as producer to render such supervision unnecessary.

CASTROVALVA

Writer: Christopher H Bidmead. **Director:** Fiona Cumming. **Designer:** Janet Budden. **Costumes:** Odile Dicks-Mireaux. **Make-Up:** Marion Richards. **Incidental Music:** Paddy Kingsland. **Visual Effects:** Simon McDonald. **Film Cameraman:** John Baker. **Film Editor:** Mike Houghton, Robin Jackman. **Studio Lighting:** Ron Bristow. **Studio Sound:** Laurie Taylor. **Production Assistant:** Olivia Cripps. **Assistant Floor Manager:** Renny Tasker.

	First UK TX	Scheduled TX	Actual TX	Duration	Viewers	Chart Pos.
Part One	04/01/82	18.55*	18.55	24'14"	9.1	54
Part Two	05/01/82	19.00	19.02	24'13"	8.6	84
Part Three	11/01/82	18.55	18.55	23'35"	10.2	47
Part Four	12/01/82	19.05	19.06	24'12"	10.4	46

* In Scotland the scheduled transmission time was 15.30

Plot: The newly regenerated Doctor escapes with his companions back to the TARDIS. Suffering from post-regeneration trauma, he only narrowly manages to save the ship from destruction as it plunges back to Event One, the hydrogen in-rush that preceded the creation of the universe. He then seeks sanctuary in the peaceful domain of Castrovalva, only to discover that it is an illusory, dimensionally paradoxical trap set for him by the Master with the unwilling aid of a kidnapped Adric. The Doctor eventually wins the day by enlisting the help of the Castrovalvan people who, although also part of the Master's creation, are nevertheless able to exercise free will.

Episode endings:
1. The TARDIS is heading back in time toward the hydrogen inrush that created the universe. The air is getting hotter and hotter and the ship starts to buck and shudder. The Master appears on the scanner screen and bids Tegan and Nyssa farewell forever.
2. Nyssa and Tegan are carrying the Doctor toward the city Castrovalva in the zero cabinet – a box made out of the doors of the TARDIS's now jettisoned zero room (a healing environment). They see Castrovalva perched on a rocky mountain ahead and hide the cabinet while they go to try to find a way in. When they return, they find blood on the ground, and the Doctor missing.
3. The Doctor, Tegan and Nyssa decide to leave Castrovalva. They traverse some walkways but arrive back in the main square from which they left. The Doctor is affected by the spatial disturbance and they go back to his room, intending to return him to the zero cabinet. When they get there, they discover that the cabinet has gone. The Doctor, seeing an impossibly fragmented view of Castrovalva through the window, realises that they are caught in a space/time trap.
4. The Doctor and his friends make their way back to the TARDIS. Tegan is disappointed that she was not, after all, responsible for piloting the TARDIS to Castrovalva – it was all down to the Master. The Doctor, contemplating his regeneration, comments that, whoever he feels like, it is absolutely splendid.

IT WAS MADE WHERE...?

OB Recording: 01.09.81-04.09.81.

Locations: Crowborough WT Station, Duddleswell (on B2026), nr Crowborough, East Sussex; Buckhurst Park, Withyham, East Sussex; Harrison's Rocks, Birchden Wood/Ayttons Wood, nr Groombridge, Sussex.

Studio Recording: 15.09.81-16.09.81 in TC3, 29.09.81-01.10.81 in TC6, 08.10.81 (gallery only) (studio unknown)

ADDITIONAL CREDITED CAST

The Master (Anthony Ainley), Head of Security (Dallas Cavell[1]), Ruther (Frank Wylie[2-4]), Shardovan (Derek Waring[3,4]), Mergrave (Michael Sheard[3,4]), Portreeve (Neil Toynay[3*]), Child (Souska John[3]).

* 'Neil Toynay' is an anagram of 'Tony Ainley'. This was the second time in the series' history that a pseudonym had been used for an actor in order to conceal a plot twist (the first instance having occurred on season two's *The Rescue*).

Note: Tom Baker appears in the pre-titles sequence, in the reprise from *Logopolis* Part Four, but uncredited.

THINGS TO WATCH OUT FOR

- This story marks the first use of another set of new opening and closing title sequences, similar to the previous season's and again designed by Sid Sutton but this time incorporating Peter Davison's face in place of Tom Baker's.
- The Doctor affixes a stick of Castrovalvan (and therefore presumably illusory) celery to his lapel.
- The newly-regenerated Doctor mentions several companions – including Jamie, Jo and the Brigadier – and several established monster races – including the Daleks, the Ogrons and the Ice Warriors. He also uses the phrase 'Reverse the polarity of the neutron flow', more commonly associated with the third Doctor.
- A smoke effect is overlaid on the picture during the scenes in the TARDIS as it approaches the Event One explosion.

THINGS YOU MIGHT NOT HAVE KNOWN

- Working title: *The Visitor*.
- For the first time, *Doctor Who* was transmitted not in a Saturday teatime slot but on Mondays and Tuesdays. This was to be the case for all the stories of season nineteen. For season twenty, the days would change to Tuesdays and Wednesdays (except for the first episode of *Arc of Infinity*, transmitted on a Monday). The anniversary special *The Five Doctors* was transmitted on a Friday. Then, for season twenty-one, the transmission days changed again to Thursdays and Fridays (except from *Resurrection of the Daleks*, the two episodes of which went out on consecutive Wednesdays).
- Sound effects for the jungle/forest in Parts Two, Three and Four were taken from a BBC effects record and were of a jungle in Sri Lanka at dawn in the year 1945. Other sound effects included a canary singing, a Tibetan horn, wind effects and an open fireplace.
- The story originally planned to launch the fifth Doctor on screen was *Project Zeta-Sigma* (working title: *Project '4G'*) by John Flanagan and Andrew McCulloch, which

would also have been the first of the season to be made. This was abandoned at a late stage, however, necessitating the commissioning of a hasty replacement and the rejigging of the season's production order.

- Although *Castrovalva* was the first transmitted story to feature Peter Davison as the Doctor, it was actually recorded fourth, after *Four to Doomsday*, *The Visitation* and *Kinda*.
- On 27 July 1981 the BBC's Head of Series and Serials, David Reid, sent a memo to producer John Nathan-Turner after reading through Christopher H Bidmead's initial scripts. He asked if a re-cap was going to be included to explain the change of Doctor, and also commented that the end of Part Three was unclear. Nathan-Turner replied that a re-cap was indeed going to be included at the start, and that the end of Part Three would be altered accordingly.
- The story was inspired in part by two prints by the Dutch artist Maurits Cornelis Escher (1898-1972) hanging in the office of the then Controller of BBC1, but the title was taken from that of an unrepresentative lithograph by the same artist of a castle set atop a mountainside. Works by Escher that more accurately represent the flavour of the story include 'Up and Down' (1947), 'House of Stairs' (1951), 'Relativity' (1953), 'Belvedere' (1958), 'Ascending and Descending' (1960) and 'Waterfall' (1961).
- After transmission of the first episode, Graeme McDonald, the head of Drama Group at the BBC, wrote to David Reid, Head of Drama, expressing his concern at the production standards. 'The discrepancy of production standards between the K9 show and last night's *Doctor Who* makes me think you should have a word with John Nathan-Turner about the latter. *Doctor Who* is too valuable a show to us to let its standard slip so dramatically,' he wrote. 'The spotlight the new Dr.Who puts on the show makes this halting start the more embarrassing. I suggest we will have to monitor John's scripts and choice of directors more carefully in the future.'

QUOTE, UNQUOTE

- **Tegan:** 'If ... My dad used to say that "if" was the most powerful word in the English language.'
- **Doctor:** 'I know it ... It's on the tip ... it's on the tip of my mind. The books are five hundred years old at least, but ...' **Shardovan:** [With realisation] 'The books are old, but they chronicle the rise of Castrovalva up to the present day.'
- **Shardovan:** 'You made us, man of evil. But we are free!'

ANALYSIS

'The nine-day *Doctor Who* story is with us,' wrote Peter G Lovelady in *Shada* 8 in 1981, 'with new times, new titles and a new Doctor.' The series' new twice-weekly transmission pattern undeniably had a very considerable impact on the way in which it was perceived by contemporary viewers. It meant that each story was effectively over in half the time that it would have been previously, and that the relative importance of the cliffhanger endings to odd-numbered episodes was diminished as the next instalment could be seen a mere twenty-four hours later, rather than the following week as had been traditional. Even more significantly, it meant that the season as a whole would be over and done with within the space of a mere three months, rather than six as in the recent past, giving it far less opportunity to make an impact and maintain *Doctor Who*'s profile as a familiar fixture on the British television landscape. This was just the first of a succession of scheduling changes that the series would suffer during the eighties – a problem with which it had never really been troubled in the past – arguably with very negative consequences in terms of its popularity and, ultimately, its longevity.

Castrovalva itself has been well received by most reviewers. 'Thankfully *Doctor Who* is a [series] that is always discovering and experimenting, but never more so than when the reign of a new Doctor begins,' commented Robert Craker in *TARDIS* Volume 7 Number 1 dated March/April 1982. 'Tom Baker's debut story was quite a disappointment, but *Castrovalva* was definitely not that. It was brim-full of original ideas and pleasant surprises.'

In fact, the ideas underlying the story, although original in *Doctor Who* terms, were largely inspired by the works of Dutch illustrator M C Escher, whose lithographs of impossible architecture and twisted geometry formed the basis for the design of the city of Castrovalva. (Escher actually created a picture called *Castrovalva*, showing a walled city atop a mountain). Although a bold endeavour on the production team's part, the challenge of replicating such illusions on screen was unfortunately an overly demanding one for the series to meet. The BBC's electronic effects technology was not really up to the task, and – although the visualisation of Castrovalva's ultimate demise is certainly passable, and quite an achievement for the time – it is no surprise to find that the Escher influences are confined for the most part to the story's plot and dialogue, with many references to 'recursive occlusion' and space folding back on itself. This concerned Ian K McLachlan, as he explained in the same issue of *TARDIS*: 'I wonder if it was not too cerebral for the audience. Would it not perhaps have been better to have started with a more traditional monster story to grab the casual viewer?'

Also problematic in terms of *Castrovalva*'s general appeal is the fact that much of the action of the first two episodes is confined to the Doctor's TARDIS, with the Doctor himself either acting bizarrely or being completely incapacitated. It is instructive to contrast this with the approach taken in previous 'post regeneration' stories. *Castrovalva* certainly lacks anything with the audience pulling power of the Daleks, as seen in Patrick Troughton's debut adventure; and while the Jon Pertwee and Tom Baker Doctors had both been seen to be incapacitated at the outset, there were at the same time other plot threads – involving UNIT with the Autons and the K1 robot respectively – running in parallel. In *Castrovalva*, on the other hand, the focus is exclusively on the plight of the Doctor and his companions.

Another factor not helping matters is that the story carries on directly from where *Logopolis* left off and cannot be fully appreciated without a knowledge of what has gone before – or at least of who the Master is and of what he hopes to achieve. (It is just as well that *Logopolis* was repeated in November/December 1981, giving viewers a chance to catch up.) This incarnation of the Doctor's evil nemesis is nothing if not persistent, and this gives rise to something of an anomaly in the plotting of *Castrovalva*. The Master had no way of knowing that the Doctor would survive his fall from the radio telescope at the end of *Logopolis*, and yet he is already prepared at the beginning of this sequel to kidnap Adric and trap him within a web of power. Using Adric's mathematical skills, he then causes the Doctor's TARDIS to travel back to the very start of the universe, where he fully expects the Doctor to be destroyed – hence the end of Part One. Even as the TARDIS veers away from Event One, however, Tegan discovers yet another trap – a reference to Castrovalva (a fictional construct by the Master) – planted in the TARDIS's

5 FIFTH DOCTOR

index file. This tends to suggest that the Master actually expects each of his plans to fail, arguably diminishing the threat posed by the character.

Things improve considerably in the second half of the story, when the Doctor and his companions finally reach Castrovalva. The Castrovalvan characters are well written and acted, and special praise must go to Anthony Ainley for his performance as the Portreeve, which is so convincing that many viewers at the time failed to spot that this was actually the Master in disguise – although admittedly many others found it obvious. The sets and costumes, too, are excellent, being both distinctive and very much in keeping with the slightly 'fairy tale' quality of the city.

Perhaps the greatest legacy of *Castrovalva* is that, although it was not the first of the Peter Davison stories to be made, it effectively sets the scene for the remainder of his era. This was noted by Alec Charles in *Aggedor* Issue 5 in 1983: '*Castrovalva* ... set down strict guidelines [including] the overdone Master and his rather too obvious disguises; the two "new" companions and the Doctor's reactions to them ("You, Tegan, have it in you to be a fine co-ordinator, keeping us all together during the healing time; Nyssa, of course, has the technical skills and understanding"); and, of course, the new Doctor.'

Davison is excellent as the Doctor throughout this adventure. He manages to bring his own identity to the character while at the same time giving nods to his predecessors – most obviously in the early scenes in which he does brief impressions of some of them – as the Doctor suffers 'regeneration trauma'. The literal unravelling of the fourth Doctor's trademark scarf is also a nice touch. On the downside, the regular outfit chosen for the new Doctor is simply awful. Following the trend set in the eighteenth season, it is very obviously a designed costume, almost a uniform, rather than – as had previously been the case – an eccentric collection of otherwise largely unremarkable clothes that one might conceivably be able to pick up in a charity shop or a jumble sale. The same approach is reflected in the new companions' similarly uniform-like costumes which, with rare exceptions, they wear in every story regardless of the circumstances. This 'costuming' of the regular characters removes a lot of their individuality and believability as people, and inevitably makes the Doctor in particular stand out from the crowd, whereas in the past he had been able to blend in.

All in all, though, *Castrovalva* makes a reasonable start to the fifth Doctor's era.

FOUR TO DOOMSDAY

Writer: Terence Dudley. **Director:** John Black. **Designer:** Tony Burrough. **Costumes:** Colin Lavers. **Make-Up:** Dorka Nieradzik. **Incidental Music:** Roger Limb. **Fight Arranger:** B H Barry. **Choreographer:** Sue Lefton. **Visual Effects:** Mickey Edwards. **Studio Lighting:** Don Babbage. **Studio Sound:** Alan Machin. **Production Assistant:** Jean Davis. **Assistant Floor Manager:** Val McCrimmon.

	First UK TX	Scheduled TX	Actual TX	Duration	Viewers	Chart Pos.
Part One	18/01/82	18.55	18.57	23'36"	8.4	66
Part Two	19/01/82	19.05	19.05	24'11"	8.8	61
Part Three	25/01/82	18.55	18.57	24'09"	8.9	63
Part Four	26/01/82	19.05	19.07	24'52"	9.4	53

Plot: The TARDIS arrives on board a huge spaceship where the Doctor and his companions encounter the frog-like Urbankans and a population of human androids. The androids are drawn from four different ethnic groups – Greek (led by Bigon), Chinese (led by Lin Futu), Mayan (led by Villagra) and Aboriginal Australian (led by Kurkutji) – and perform regular displays of dance and other rituals termed 'recreationals'. The Urbankans' leader, Monarch, aided by his ministers Persuasion and Enlightenment, is engaged in a complex scheme to plunder from Earth the raw materials needed to enable him to travel back in time and thereby confirm his belief in his own status as the universe's divine creator. Monarch has a poison that he intends to use to conquer humanity so that Earth can be repopulated with his androids. The Doctor, however, throws a canister of the poison at Monarch, causing him to shrink away to virtually nothing.

Episode endings:
1. The time travellers are astonished as a man and a woman appear wearing elegant green clothes identical to those earlier sketched by Tegan. The man introduces himself and his companion: they are the previously frog-like Persuasion and Enlightenment.
2. Bigon demonstrates to an astonished Doctor that within his chest and beneath his face there is just a mass of electronics. Holding up a printed circuit connected to his chest, he states: 'This is me.'
3. Adric is restrained as, on Persuasion's orders, the Doctor is forced to his knees and one of the Greek androids raises a sword to decapitate him.
4. The Doctor and his companions depart in the TARDIS. Once they are on their way, however, Nyssa suddenly collapses.

IT WAS MADE WHERE...?

Studio Recording: 13.04.81-15.04.81, 28.04.81-30.04.81 all in TC6

ADDITIONAL CREDITED CAST

Monarch (Stratford Johns), Persuasion (Paul Shelley), Enlightenment (Annie Lambert), Bigon (Philip Locke), Lin Futu (Burt Kwouk), Kurkutji (Illarrio Bisi Pedro[1,2,4]), Villagra (Nadia Hammam[1,2,4]).

THINGS TO WATCH OUT FOR

- Stratford Johns, best known for his starring role as Barlow in the BBC police series *Z Cars* and its *Softly, Softly* spin-offs, plays Monarch.
- The monopticons are floating, ball like security cameras aboard Monarch's ship.
- Urbanka is revealed to be in the solar system Inokshi in Galaxy 1489.
- Several facts about the Doctor are disclosed. He claims that he once took five wickets in a cricket match for New South Wales. It is discovered that he can withstand sub-zero temperatures for six minutes and can put himself into a trance which reduces the need for oxygen (possibly referring back to the season thirteen story *Terror of the Zygons*).
- Elaborate dance sequences were crafted for each of the main civilisations represented. The choreographer brought in to handle this aspect was Sue Lefton. A fight arranger, B. H. Barry, was also contracted to supervise a mock battle between two Trojan warriors.

THINGS YOU MIGHT NOT HAVE KNOWN

- Working title: *Day of Wrath*.
- *Four to Doomsday* replaced the abandoned *Project Zeta-Sigma* in the production schedule.
- The didgeridoo music played during the Aborigine recreationals was the signature tune of a BBC programme called *Quest Under Capricorn*, first transmitted in the early sixties.
- John Nathan-Turner requested that the space suits designed for the Doctor, Adric, Tegan and Nyssa be retained for possible future use following the end of production for this story.

QUOTE, UNQUOTE

- **The Doctor:** [On being introduced to Persuasion] 'Friendly, I hope?'
- **Monarch:** 'Conformity is the only freedom.'

ANALYSIS

Four to Doomsday is a visual treat, and in this respect at least can certainly be counted a success. 'I really enjoyed *Four to Doomsday* from start to finish,' wrote Ian K McLachlan in *TARDIS* Volume 7 Number 1 dated March/April 1982. 'I was really carried along by the story, being transported to that strange Urbankan vessel from the first shot. I thought the dance sequences were particularly good and showed just how adaptable a formula the programme [has]. The special effects too were among the best I can remember, from those black balls which really looked as though they had minds of their own, through to the shock revelation scene ... and the shrinking of Monarch. When you consider that the [spacewalk] sequence must have been done on a miniscule budget it is ... well ... even more amazing than the TARDIS. I was quite moved by it.' John C Harding, writing in *Shada* 8 in 1981, was equally admiring of the story's production values: 'The Urbankan ship was superb, especially the control room – aesthetically functional. It was believable, yet a good deal of "alienness" was acheived by having things of [familiar] design with very subtle changes: e.g. the oddly shaped monitor screens, which I loved. The impressively detailed corridors were superbly used by [John] Black to give a truly effective image of them being very long and intricate – actually leading from room to room, not just unconnected sets as it sometimes appears. I liked the original touch of the doors lighting up when they opened. Nice.'

The characterisation and on-screen realisation of Monarch and his fellow Urbankans is similarly impressive, as Harding pointed out: 'Monarch [was] a most intriguing character. It was not selfishness which motivated him in his evil task, but benevolence: he was [in his own mind] a god seeking to free his people from "the great tyranny in the universe – internal and external organs". Monarch's motivation clearly shows the aims of Terence Dudley in penning [the story]. He is pushing his ideas of the dangers of letting technology take over man, instead of being a tool, and his argument against the autocratic system of government – a poor man's mix of [George Orwell's] *1984* and [Aldous Huxley's] *Brave New World*. Monarch personifies these evils and the story shows his faults and his eventual downfall.'

Thomas Noonan, also writing in *TARDIS* Volume 7 Number 1, expressed disappointment with other aspects of the characterisation, and in particular with that of the Doctor himself: 'Davison's Doctor has grace, courtesy (with occasional firmness), thoughtfulness in managing his wards, quiet competence and technological efficiency. The hints of quick enthusiasm and energy are no more than result from the irresponsibility of privilege, not (as yet) the eccentricity of earlier Doctors. Altogether ... he seems to be [the] patrician ideal, basically a Tristan character. The emphasis on his "powers" is different, but doesn't help. The incidents involving his spacewalking without a spacesuit, and his taking a quick trance to avoid breathing, were ludicrous but so gratuitous that it seemed inappropriate to laugh, difficult to know *how* to respond at all. In fact, the whole spacewalk sequence, though visually charming in a puppet show manner, was on the verge of a comedy sketch, and at the point when Enlightenment cast the Doctor adrift looked like a parody of *Blake's 7* (maybe because of the lack of dialogue and the musical accompaniment). A major characteristic of the whole serial was the conflict between a temptation to laugh, and the suspicion that that wasn't the effect intended. To indulge that temptation too much would be harmful, but one could get a good deal of entertainment out of the story by indulging it slightly.'

Where the story falls down, unfortunately, is in its scripting. There are a number of major plot holes, and the recent departure of Christopher H Bidead from the script editor's post is readily apparent from the inclusion of some very dodgy science – especially in the aforementioned spacewalk sequence, where the Doctor somehow manages to survive for several minutes in the freezing vacuum of space without the benefit of a pressure suit. The central concepts are interesting, certainly, but – as becomes increasingly the case during this period of the series' history – style ultimately wins out over content. Nevertheless, *Four to Doomsday* remains an enjoyable adventure overall, as Noonan noted: 'It is quite common for *Doctor Who* stories to start suggestively and then become banal. What was unusual about *Four to Doomsday* was the extent of the gap between early promise and later decay in the plot and the fact that a continuing charm, especially of some characters and performances, diverted attention from the decay and from a more ominous weakness of character and uncertainty of tone, so that the whole offered a good deal of enjoyment in a roistering sort of way.'

KINDA

Writer: Christopher Bailey. **Director:** Peter Grimwade. **Designer:** Malcolm Thornton. **Costumes:** Barbara Kidd. **Make-Up:** Suzan Broad. **Incidental Music:** Peter Howell. **Visual Effects:** Peter Logan. **Studio Lighting:** Mike Jefferies. **Studio Sound:** Alan Machin. **Production Assistant:** Sue Plumb, Rosemary Parsons. **Assistant Floor Manager:** Val McCrimmon.

Note: Some material in Part Four of *Kinda* was recorded as a remount during the first studio session for *Earthshock*, using the crew of that story.

	First UK TX	Scheduled TX	Actual TX	Duration	Viewers	Chart Pos.
Part One	01/02/82	18.55	18.57	24'50"	8.4	78
Part Two	02/02/82	19.05	19.04	24'58"	9.4	45
Part Three	08/02/82	18.55	18.57	24'17"	8.5	67
Part Four	09/02/82	19.05	19.06	24'28"	8.9	56

Plot: The TARDIS visits the planet Deva Loka, where Nyssa remains behind in the ship to recover from a mild mental disorientation while the Doctor, Tegan and Adric explore. Tegan falls asleep under some wind chimes and becomes possessed by an evil force, a Mara. Also on Deva Loka is a survey team assessing the planet for colonisation, but three of their number have disappeared and the remainder – Sanders, his deputy Hindle and the scientist Todd – are encountering difficulties in their dealings with the outwardly primitive but telepathically gifted native people, the Kinda. Hindle becomes mentally unstable, but his mind is eventually cleared by a Kinda device called the Box of Jhana. Aided by the Kinda, the Doctor ultimately succeeds in banishing the Mara – which manifests itself in the form of a giant snake – by trapping it in a circle of mirrors.

Episode endings:
1. In the survey team's dome, Hindle turns his gun on the Doctor, Adric and Todd. Two of the silent male Kinda approach down the corridor, also aiming handguns at the trio. Todd argues that Hindle has no power to arrest them, but Hindle raves: 'You forget. I am now in command. I have the power of life and death over all of you!'
2. The Doctor, Sanders and Todd are locked in a cell with the Box of Jhana. Hindle, watching from a view screen in the dome's control room, orders the Doctor to open the Box, threatening to have him shot if he disobeys. Todd warns the Doctor that the Box could kill them, but he replies that the same could be said of Hindle. The Doctor's hands grasp the lid of the Box, and Todd screams in terror.
3. The Doctor realises that in order to thwart the Mara the Kinda's planned attack on the survey team's dome must be averted. He and Todd need the help of the wise old Kinda woman Panna to get them back to the dome through the forest. Todd runs into Panna's cave but finds the old woman sitting motionless. She calls the Doctor over. It appears that Panna is dead.
4. Todd tells the Doctor that Sanders intends to stay on Deva Loka but that it is a bit too green for her. As the Kinda arrive and look on, the Doctor bids farewell to Todd and follows his companions into the TARDIS, pausing on the threshold to note: 'I think paradise is a little too green for me, as well.'

IT WAS MADE WHERE...?

Studio Recording: 29.07.81-31.07.81, 12.08.81-14.08.81 all in TC8, 20.08.81 (gallery only) in TC8. Additional scenes recorded during the first studio recording of *Earthshock*, 10.11.81 in TC8.

ADDITIONAL CREDITED CAST

Sanders (Richard Todd), Todd (Nerys Hughes), Hindle (Simon Rouse), Anatta (Anna Wing[1]), Anicca (Roger Milner[1]), Dukkha (Jeffrey Stewart[1,2]), Aris (Adrian Mills), Panna (Mary Morris[2-4]), Karuna (Sarah Prince[2-4]), Trickster (Lee Cornes[3,4]).

POPULAR MYTHS

- Pop star Kate Bush wrote this story under a pseudonym. (She didn't.)
- Playwright Tom Stoppard wrote this story under a pseudonym. (He didn't.)

THINGS TO WATCH OUT FOR

- Highly experienced British film star Richard Todd plays Sanders.
- Nerys Hughes, better known for her starring roles in the BBC's *The Liver Birds* and *The District Nurse*, plays Todd.
- Adrian Mills, seen here as Aris, later became a television presenter, most notably on the BBC's consumer programme *That's Life*.
- The characters and situations that Tegan encounters in her own mind are deliberate distortions of events that she has recently experienced. For example, she encounters two characters (named Anatta (Anna Wing) and Anicca (Roger Milner) in the credits) playing draughts beside a strange metal structure, described in the script as a 'caravan', just as at the start of the story Adric and Nyssa were playing draughts beside the TARDIS. The stranger who taunts her is named on the closing credits as Dukkha – which apart from its Buddhist meaning is also a play on the word 'Doctor'.

THINGS YOU MIGHT NOT HAVE KNOWN

- Working title: *The Kinda*
- Christopher Bailey's script was heavily influenced by Buddhist teachings and philosophy. Many words and names are taken from Buddhism: Anatta meaning egolessness; Anicca meaning impermanence; Dukkha meaning pain, suffering, sorrow and misery; Panna meaning wisdom; Karuna meaning compassion; Jana or Jhana meaning meditation; and Mara meaning temptation.
- During recording it was realised that Part Four was running under length. Christopher Bailey was thus asked to provide some further material. The additional scenes featured Adric and Tegan discussing the situation while the Doctor and Todd try to persuade Hindle not to destroy the dome. They were recorded during the first studio session for *Earthshock*.
- The reason for Sarah Sutton's non-appearance in much of this story was that she had been contracted for only twenty-four of the season's twenty-six episodes and therefore had to drop out for the making of two episodes.
- The large snake prop was made by an external special effects company, Stephen Greenfield Construction.
- Barnaby's Picture Library supplied a transparency for the establishing shots of the forest. The photographer was Keith N Radford.
- The making of this story was featured in the media studies book *Doctor Who – The Unfolding Text* by John Tulloch and Manuel Alvarado, published by Macmillan in 1982.
- Peter Howell created the Mara's screech by running a violin bow down a cymbal and loading the sound into a Fairlight computer synthesiser. The sound of the wind chimes had previously been used in a movement of his track 'Through a Glass Darkly – A Lyrical Adventure' on side one of the album 'Through A Glass Darkly'.

QUOTE, UNQUOTE

- **Aris:** 'I am Aris! I have voice!'

- **Sanders:** 'Straight-down-the-line thinking, that's what this situation needs.'
- **The Doctor:** 'An apple a day keeps the … Ah.'
- **Karuna:** 'How many fathers do the "not we" have?' **The Doctor:** 'Well, on the whole, one!'

ANALYSIS

The highlights of this story are, in keeping with the trend of the time, its images and concepts – particularly the aspects of Buddhist philosophy with which writer Christopher Bailey has infused his scripts. 'Everyone knows that *Kinda* is about Buddhism,' asserted Cassandra May in *Matrix* Issue 51 dated summer 1995. 'The names of people and things – the Box of Jhana, Panna and Karuna, the Mara – are Buddhist names, and they have meanings within Buddhist philosophy that have relevance to the plot. The escape from the Wheel of Time is the essence of the Buddhist Nirvana.' As May went on to point out, however, Buddhism is not the only source from which Bailey took his inspiration: 'The terror and temptations that the Mara draws on are based around classic Freudian theories and phobias: the Oedipus complex, the intuitive feminine unconscious, the logical masculine conscious, rape and castration fantasies/phobias and the dangers of unleashed individuality.' Paul Cornell, writing in the Premiere Issue of *Dreamwatch* dated October 1994, also thought that the story's Buddhist influences have been overstated: 'A thousand repetitive articles about Buddhist imagery have muddied the waters by suggesting that there's a code to *Kinda*, that if you can understand what it's about, then it'll all click and you'll suddenly love it. That's untrue … The Buddhist articles also obscure the fact that the story is a Christian parable. Indeed, it elects not to be about any particular religion, inventing one of its own.' As Rion Deesold noted in *TARDIS* Volume 7 Number 1 dated March/April 1982: 'The more one thinks about the story the more [one] realises what there is to it.'

The downside to all this admirable conceptual and thematic depth is that little concession is made to the younger or more casual viewer in terms of plot exposition and clarity. Nicholas Setchfield, writing in *Axos* Issue 3 in 1982, was one of many who felt that 'like *Warriors' Gate*, it suffered from being just a shade too complex'. Even if one finds the story difficult to follow, however, there is much in *Kinda* to admire. One of the most notable aspects is the strong emphasis placed on the Mara-possessed Tegan. Particularly memorable are the dream sequences in Part One, where she encounters in the 'Dark Places' of her own mind the mysterious and sinister figures of Anicca, Anatta and Dukkha, and the later, erotically charged scene in which – in a clear parallel with the Garden of Eden story – she sits in a tree and drops apples on the Kinda male Aris below.

'Of course it is Tegan who is central to the plot,' noted Jim Sangster in *In-Vision* Issue Fifty-Seven dated May 1995, 'and it's obvious that the director Peter Grimwade relished the chance to play around with the traditional focus of attention, deliberately giving us only tantalising glimpses of the scenes in the Dark Places of the Inside and slowly building up to the real villain of the piece, the Mara. Trapped within her own dreams, Tegan finds herself forced to question her very existence ("You, my dear, can't possibly exist, so go away!"), experiencing a challenge to her sense of identity ("Sooner or later, you will agree to be me – this side of madness or the other"), and finally being mentally tortured into surrendering her body to the Mara's possession. In what is at base a rape scene in all but the actual act, Janet Fielding is given a chance to run the gamut of emotions as Tegan changes from bolshie Australian to terrified victim.'

On the production front, Deva Loka is one of the less convincing alien environments to be presented in *Doctor Who*, probably the worst aspect of all being the very plastic-looking tree from which the possessed Tegan drops her apples on Aris. The snake prop used to represent the Mara's ultimate manifestation has also been much criticised by reviewers – 'to wait four episodes to see the ultimate evil only to be confronted with a novelty bouncy castle is a major disappointment,' suggested Sangster – although, as *Doctor Who*'s visual effects go, it is actually not all that bad.

On the whole, the commendable intelligence and sophistication of Christopher Bailey's scripts, the deftness of Peter Grimwade's direction and the quality of the performances from a very strong cast – Janet Fielding being particularly outstanding – easily outweigh any less positive features that *Kinda* might possess. Rion Deesold, for one, was well satisfied, and felt that even its much-discussed complexity was no barrier to the story being understood: '*Doctor Who* is at last being presented to adults – never playing down to its audience. *Kinda* could be compared to last season's *Warriors' Gate* in that it was an unusual breed of adventure. While I enjoyed *Warriors' Gate*, I preferred *Kinda* which tied up virtually all the loose ends in the final episode and at a pace which could be easily followed.'

THE VISITATION

Writer: Eric Saward. **Director:** Peter Moffatt. **Designer:** Ken Starkey. **Costumes:** Odile Dicks-Mireaux. **Make-Up:** Carolyn Perry. **Incidental Music:** Paddy Kingsland. **Visual Effects:** Peter Wragg. **Film Cameraman:** Peter Chapman. **Film Editor:** Ken Bilton. **Studio Lighting:** Henry Barber. **Studio Sound:** Alan Machin. **Production Assistant:** Julia Randall. **Assistant Floor Manager:** Alison Symington.

	First UK TX	Scheduled TX	Actual TX	Duration	Viewers	Chart Pos.
Part One	15/02/82	18.55	18.57	24'11"	9.1	54
Part Two	16/02/82	19.05	19.06	24'26"	9.3	48
Part Three	22/02/82	18.55	18.58	24'24"	9.9	41
Part Four	23/02/82	19.05	19.05	23'32"	10.1	40

Plot: The Doctor attempts to take Tegan back to Heathrow Airport but the TARDIS arrives in the 17th Century instead of the 20th. The time travellers discover that a space capsule has crash-landed nearby and that its alien occupants, three Terileptil prison escapees, intend to wipe out all indigenous life on Earth by releasing rats infected with an enhanced strain of bubonic plague. The creatures are also using a sophisticated android to strike terror into the local villagers. Aided by itinerant thespian Richard Mace, the Doctor tracks the Terileptils to their base in Pudding Lane, London. The creatures are ultimately destroyed when a fire breaks out and the Terileptil leader's weapon explodes – also setting off the Great Fire of London.

Episode endings:

1.   The travellers investigate an apparently deserted manor house, where the Doctor finds a

fake wall at the bottom of a flight of steps. Nyssa goes to fetch Tegan and Adric, but when they get to the steps the Doctor has gone. The android closes and bolts a door behind the three friends, trapping them. Tegan calls out to the Doctor.

2. The Doctor and Mace go to speak to the local miller. When they get to his house, however, the man leaves in his horse and cart as though in a trance. They suddenly find themselves surrounded by villagers and sentenced to execution. They are forced to kneel with their heads bowed before a man who prepares to decapitate them with a scythe.

3. The Terileptil leader explains to the Doctor his plan to release rats infected with a genetically re-engineered plague virus. The Terileptil leaves the Doctor locked in a cell with Tegan and Mace, who are both now under the alien's control. The Doctor tries desperately to break through Tegan's conditioning, but she starts to open the rats' cage ...

4. The travellers leave in the TARDIS. Tegan is concerned about the fire that has broken out, but the Doctor knowingly comments that they should let it run its course. The sign on the wall outside the Terileptils' base reads 'Pudding Lane'.

IT WAS MADE WHERE...?

Ealing Filming: 01.05.81 on Stage 2
Location Recording: 05.05.81-08.05.81
Locations: Black Park, nr Iver, Slough; Tithe Barn, Hurley High Street, Hurley, Berks.
Studio Recording: 20.05.81-21.05.81 in TC3 and 03.06.81-05.06.81 in TC3

ADDITIONAL CREDITED CAST

Richard Mace (Michael Robbins), Android (Peter van Dissel), The Squire (John Savident[1]), Charles (Anthony Calf[1]), Ralph (John Baker[1]), Elizabeth (Valerie Fyfer[1]), Villager (Richard Hampton[1-3]), Miller (James Charlton), Terileptil (Michael Melia[2-4]), Poacher (Neil West[2,3]), Headman (Eric Dodson[3]).

THINGS TO WATCH OUT FOR

- There is a brilliantly written and directed 'prologue' in which the local Squire and his family are wiped out by the Terileptils and their robot.
- Continuity references are made back to *Kinda* when Tegan and Nyssa speak in the TARDIS in Part One: interesting, as *The Visitation* was actually made before *Kinda*.
- Part Three features the destruction of the sonic screwdriver, a remarkable tool used by the Doctor off and on since season five's *Fury from the Deep*.
- The three Terileptils have different colours featured on their costumes. The leader has a green tint, and the other two blue and red respectively.
- The Terileptil leader's mask was the first example in *Doctor Who* of an effect achieved with animatronics – the use of mechanically controlled components to achieve lifelike movement. Remote controlled by radio, the mouth moved, the lips curled and the gills on the side of the head opened and closed as the creature 'breathed'. The head was constructed by Peter Wragg of the BBC's Visual Effects Department, while the heads of the other two Terileptils, and all three bodies, were made by Richard Gregory of the specialist effects company Imagineering, who were to create many of the monsters and special props for the fifth Doctor stories.

- Working titles: *Invasion of the Plague Men*, *The Plague Rats*.
- The character Richard Mace had previously featured in three plays – *The Assassin* (1974), *Pegasus* (1975) and *The Nemesis Machine* (1976) – that Eric Saward had written for BBC Radio 4.
- The making of this story was the subject of Alan Road's book *Doctor Who – The Making of a Television Series* published by Andre Deutsch in 1982.
- The name Terileptil was derived by writer Eric Saward from 'territorial reptile'.
- Stock footage of fireworks exploding was used at the beginning of Part One to simulate the lights seen by Elizabeth when the Terileptils' capsule arrived on Earth.
- John Nathan-Turner sent a note to the BBC's presentation department around the time of this story's transmission requesting that if at all possible there should be no spoken trails over the end titles of *Doctor Who*.

QUOTE, UNQUOTE

- **Terileptil:** 'Where is this Doctor from?' **Tegan:** 'He's never told us. He likes to be mysterious, although he talks a lot about ... er ... Guildford. I think that's where he comes from.' **Terileptil:** 'You're being a very stupid woman.' **Tegan:** 'That isn't a very original observation.'
- **Nyssa:** 'We should wait for the Doctor. We can't take on the android by ourselves.' **Adric:** 'Why isn't he here? Why is he never around when you want him?'
- **Richard Mace:** 'I have appeared before some of the most hostile audiences in the world. Today I met death in a cellar. But I have never been so afraid until I met the man with the scythe.'

ANALYSIS

'*The Visitation*, for me, was television at its most magnificent,' enthused Mark Willis in *TARDIS* Volume 7 Number 2 dated May/June 1982. 'It was virtually flawless.' Willis was not the only person singing the story's praises. John Moran, for example, wrote in the same issue of *TARDIS*: '[It] was a hit for me simply because it was set in a certain period of the 17th Century when a national disaster occurred and this was one of the basic ingredients of the story – the Black Plague. It is a very subtle but very clever way of writing a *Doctor Who* story [to take] actual occurrences ... and [build] a story round [them].' Paul Dixon, another correspondent to the same magazine, commented: 'The sequences simply oozed with atmosphere – helped particularly by the fantastic music and chilling breathing noises of the aliens. The android cleverly interpreted by the manor owner as one of the creatures in armour was fairly good, but I disliked the decorated cricket gloves it wore.'

Producer John Nathan-Turner once suggested that *The Visitation*'s relatively high proportion of location filming – which is admittedly excellent – was the factor most responsible for its popularity amongst the series' fans. As these contemporary reviewers' comments would indicate, however, there is actually far more to it than that. Simply put, writer Eric Saward in his debut contribution to the series has come up with an archetypal pseudo-historical *Doctor Who* story, complete with a superb supporting character in the person of Richard Mace.

Not every review of the story has been so positive, however. 'In a recent issue of the satirical multimedia fanzine *Spot*,' reported Alex Roberts in *DWB* No. 127 dated June

1994, 'Sophie Street condemned *The Visitation* as a thinly veiled rip-off of all of *Four to Doomsday*'s best ideas: "space opera repeats itself as pseudo-history: for the first time as Bigon's Greek tragedy, for the second time as Richard Mace's farce". She argued that Saward's script had more similarities to Terence Dudley's than just the beheading cliffhanger: "For three green amphibian Urbankans read three green Terileptils; for synthetic ethnic minorities read villagers (both controlled by devices mounted at their wrists); for frogs read rats. The settings are starkly different, but not much else is."'

Roberts went on to dispute Street's observations: 'What she fails to acknowledge is the fact that *The Visitation* is not simply a set of superficial plot devices: the joy of the story lies in its characters, its dialogue and, in particular, that refreshingly old-fashioned setting. *The Visitation* is, after all, the first *Doctor Who* story to be set exclusively in the planet Earth's past since *Horror of Fang Rock* four years previously, and its 17th Century scenery is ... crucial in establishing not only *The Visitation*'s storyline but also its unique feel. Along with *The Time Warrior* and *The Masque of Mandragora*, it is one of the very few colour stories which comes anywhere near to exploiting the dramatic potential of its historical backdrop: *Pyramids of Mars* and *Horror of Fang Rock* (fine though they are) could have been set at virtually any time, in any isolated spot, in any corner of a TV studio, without necessitating much severe alteration to their storylines.'

Even the most highly acclaimed of stories can have their weaknesses, however, and here – as is often the case in the eighteenth and nineteenth seasons – the main problem is Matthew Waterhouse's peculiar performance as Adric. His irritatingly petulant delivery of much of his dialogue (such as in the scene where he bleats about the Doctor never being around when he is needed); his inability to show any convincing emotion (as evidenced at the point where he discovers to his 'delight' that Nyssa is still alive); his poor physical acting (examples including his obviously faked tripping over in the forest and his annoying trait of never seeming to know what to do with his hands); these and other factors combine to make one wish that he had never started travelling with the Doctor in the first place. In short, he is dreadful.

All in all, though, *The Visitation* is a very enjoyable story, and one of the highlights of the season.

BLACK ORCHID

Writer: Terence Dudley. **Director:** Ron Jones. **Designer:** Tony Burrough. **Costumes:** Rosalind Ebbutt. **Make-Up:** Lisa Westcott. **Incidental Music:** Roger Limb. **Choreographer:** Gary Downie. **Visual Effects:** Tony Auger. **Film Cameraman:** Peter Chapman. **Film Editor:** Mike Houghton. **Studio Lighting:** Fred Wright. **Studio Sound:** Alan Machin. **Production Assistant:** Juley Harding. **Assistant Floor Manager:** Val McCrimmon.

	First UK TX	Scheduled TX	Actual TX	Duration	Viewers	Chart Pos.
Part One	01/03/82	18.55	18.57	24'56"	9.9	57
Part Two	02/03/82	19.05	19.04	24'41"	10.1	55

Plot: The TARDIS arrives on Earth in 1925 where, due to a case of mistaken identity, the Doctor ends up playing in a local cricket match. The travellers then accept an invitation to a masked fancy dress ball, but events take on a more sinister tone as a number of murders are perpetrated at the country home of their host Lord Cranleigh. The Doctor comes under suspicion but the murderer is eventually revealed to be Cranleigh's brother George, who has been kept locked up in the house ever since returning in a deranged and disfigured state from an expedition up the Amazon to find the legendary black orchid. George mistakes Nyssa for his former fiancée Ann Talbot, who looks identical, and takes her up to the roof of the house. He is persuaded by the Doctor to let her go, but then falls from the roof to his death.

Episode endings:
1. The unknown figure wearing the Doctor's harlequin fancy dress costume grabs Ann – or is it Nyssa? – by the wrists. A passing servant comes to the girl's aid, but the harlequin grasps him about the throat and throws him violently to the floor. The girl faints, and the harlequin crosses to her and reaches out to put his hands around her neck ...
2. On returning from George's funeral, Lord Cranleigh, his mother Lady Cranleigh and Ann bid farewell to the time travellers outside the TARDIS. Tegan is carrying a large box containing their fancy dress costumes, which they have been allowed to keep, and Lady Cranleigh gives the Doctor a further gift: a leather-bound book. The Doctor thanks her and opens the first page. Opposite a photograph of the author is the legend: 'Black Orchid by George Cranleigh'.

IT WAS MADE WHERE...?

Location Recording: 05.10.81-09.10.81
Locations: Buckinghamshire Railway Centre, Quainton, Bucks; Quainton Road between Quainton and Waddesdon, Bucks; house and yard at 99 Quainton Road, Quainton, Bucks; Buckhurst Park, Withyham, East Sussex.
Studio Recording: 20.10.81-21.10.81 in TC3

ADDITIONAL CREDITED CAST

Ann (Sarah Sutton)*, Lady Cranleigh (Barbara Murray), Sir Robert Muir (Moray Watson), Lord Cranleigh (Michael Cochrane), Brewster (Brian Hawksley), Tanner (Timothy Block[1]), Latoni (Ahmed Khalil), The Unknown[1]/George Cranleigh[2] (Gareth Milne)**, Sergeant Markham (Ivor Salter[2]), Constable Cummings (Andrew Tourell[2]).

* Sarah Sutton was credited on both episodes as playing 'Nyssa/Ann'.
** Gareth Milne was credited as 'The Unknown' on Part One in order to conceal the murderer's identity, which would not be revealed until Part Two.

THINGS TO WATCH OUT FOR

- Actress Vanessa Paine doubles for Sarah Sutton in certain shots where Nyssa and Ann are seen together.
- Stock footage of a steam train was used in Part One to simulate the arrival of a real train at the station. The footage came from a programme called *God's Wonderful Railway*.
- The following period songs are played during the story: 'Lazy' by Irving Berlin, 'Show Me The Way To Go Home' by Irving King, 'Pasadena' by Warren,

'Charleston' by Mack-Johnson, 'Gentlemen Prefer Blondes' by Irving Berlin, 'Dinah' by Feldman, '5'2'' Eyes of Blue' by Henderson and 'When Erastus Plays His Old Kazoo' by Coslow-Fain-Spier.

THINGS YOU MIGHT NOT HAVE KNOWN

- Working title: *The Beast*.
- Other locations considered for this story but not ultimately used included: New Lodge, Drift Road, Windsor; Missenden Abbey, Great Missenden; Pennyhill Park, Bagshot, Surrey; Berkshire College of Agriculture, Burchett's Green, Berkshire; Taplow House Hotel, Berry Hill, Taplow, nr Maidenhead; Nether Winchendon, Aylesbury, Bucks.

QUOTE, UNQUOTE

- **Adric:** 'So what is a railway station?' **The Doctor:** 'Well, a place where one embarks and disembarks from compartments on wheels drawn along these rails by a steam engine – rarely on time.' **Nyssa:** 'What a very silly activity.' **The Doctor:** 'You think so? As a boy, I always wanted to drive one.'
- **Tegan:** 'It's fancy dress, isn't it?' **Lord Cranleigh:** 'Yes.' **Tegan:** 'Well, we haven't got any costumes.' **Sir Robert Muir:** 'Oh. I was just thinking how charming yours was.'

ANALYSIS

Black Orchid marks the very welcome return of the pure historical story – although, as David Richardson pointed out in *Skaro* Volume Two Number Five dated June 1982, it does not really have all that much in common with the classic historical stories of sixties *Doctor Who*: 'Instead of having an adventure set around a particular event in Earth's history, such as the fire of Rome, here we have a plot that could have occurred in the present day and been little different for it. Fortunately much of *Black Orchid* was spent creating the mood of the 1920s, with the railway station, cricket match, chauffeurs and "Worcester Talbots", such that, for the first episode at least, we were presented almost with a total party atmosphere, a leisurely trip back in time. The story of George Cranleigh need not have taken place in the 1920s, but the fact that it did made both episodes true masterpieces.'

The BBC has always excelled at making period drama, so it is perhaps no surprise to find that *Black Orchid* has uniformly high production values. In terms of style it has often been compared to an adaptation of one of Agatha Christie's classic crime novels, although Vanessa Bishop argued in *In-Vision* Issue Fifty-Nine dated August 1995 that such comparisons are rather misplaced:

'If by mentioning … Agatha Christie we mean a "whodunit", then this canny little two-parter has deceived us, because we never, at any point in the story, have to ask ourselves that question. From the opening moments we know exactly who the killer is – it's the character with the breathing problem in the jacquard sweater and the brogues; there's our murderer. There is an air of mystery, of course … we don't know the identity of the brogue-wearer and there's that foreign chap [Latoni] striking an immediate contrast with the very Englishness of the Cranleigh estate. But there's never any mystery to the murder, as we see the act committed …

'In some ways it's the *Doctor Who*iness that gets in the way of it all. The [series']

insistence on showing you everything robs you of the key element in a "whodunit". Each of the characters must appear to the viewer as equally innocent or equally guilty as each other. But no – the opening murder is committed when the house is all but empty; all the suspects are at the cricket match so all have perfect alibis. Instead of the Doctor's harlequin costume simply appearing at the dance, we see it being taken from his room by that fellow in the brogues, and instead of the Doctor producing an alibi of being lost in the corridors of Cranleigh Hall, which would seem as shaky to us as it does to his hosts, we actually see it.'

One very pleasing aspect of the story, and in particular its first episode, was noted by Paul West in *TARDIS* Volume 7 Number 2 dated May/June 1982: 'Peter Davison's zest for cricket was handled in this episode perhaps more effectively than in any other, when the traditional English cricketing scene was skilfully integrated with the gradual build up of menace at the manor. This was highlighted in a cunningly witty reference to "the master" – W G Grace, momentarily mistaken for the Doctor's old-time adversary.'

Another bonus is Sarah Sutton's dual role as Nyssa and Ann, which gives her a little more to do than usual. The 'double' idea has admittedly been done to death by this point but, as Mark Gillespie observed in the same issue of *TARDIS*, this is not a story that calls for any great originality: 'Oh look. Another double. Perhaps that was the only slightly less than credible part of *Black Orchid*, the rest of it being refreshingly inconsequential in the affairs of the universe. No planets saved, no invasions thwarted and no enslaved civilisations liberated, just a relatively small domestic problem centred around a family with a dreadful secret … Not the most obvious situation for a *Doctor Who* story, and in a season where the TARDIS crew save the Earth from all sorts of nasty fates, an easily forgettable one. *Black Orchid* however has a certain intriguing charm that is difficult to pin down but leaves a definite impression upon one's mind.'

The only pity is that the success of this experimental two-parter did not in the end lead on to further historical adventures in later seasons. '*Black Orchid* was an excursion,' wrote David Richardson, 'nothing more nor less. It lacked the depth of a true historical story, and could hardly be called a classic, but it was a greatly enjoyable mid-season break.'

EARTHSHOCK

Writer: Eric Saward. **Director:** Peter Grimwade. **Designer:** Bernard Lloyd-Jones. **Costumes:** Dinah Collin. **Make-Up:** Joan Stribling. **Incidental Music:** Malcolm Clarke. **Visual Effects:** Steve Bowman. **Film Cameraman:** Keith Hopper. **Film Editor:** Mike Houghton. **Studio Lighting:** Fred Wright. **Studio Sound:** Alan Machin. **Production Assistant:** Jane Ashford. **Assistant Floor Manager:** Nick Laughland.

	First UK TX	Scheduled TX	Actual TX	Duration	Viewers	Chart Pos.
Part One	08/03/82	18.55	18.56	24'22"	9.1	45
Part Two	09/03/82	19.05	19.06	24'23"	8.8	50
Part Three	15/03/82	18.55	18.58	24'24"	9.8	32
Part Four	16/03/82	19.05	19.03	24'28"	9.6	40

Plot: The TARDIS arrives on Earth in the 26th Century in a cave system containing numerous dinosaur fossils. The Doctor's party comes under suspicion from a military force, led by Lieutenant Scott, who are investigating the disappearance of a group of palaeontologists and geologists. They are all then attacked by androids – the true culprits – under the control of the Cybermen. The Doctor manages to deactivate a bomb intended by the Cybermen to destroy an imminent peace conference. He then follows the bomb's activating signal to an approaching space freighter, commanded by Captain Briggs, on board which it transpires that an army of Cybermen are concealed. An attempt by Adric to thwart the Cybermen's plans result in the freighter being inadvertently sent millions of years into the past, where it explodes and causes the extinction of the dinosaurs – and also the death of Adric. The Doctor destroys the Cyber Leader by forcing into its chest unit some gold fragments from a badge previously worn by Adric to signify his mathematical excellence.

Episode endings:
1. The Doctor, Tegan and Nyssa have been taken prisoner in the caves by Lieutenant Scott and his troops. They start to investigate a mysterious metal hatch but are forced to take cover when two black-clad androids suddenly appear and start firing bolts of energy at them from their hands. One of the androids scans the scene and relays the image to a group of Cybermen. The Cyber Leader gives the order: 'Destroy them! Destroy them at once!'
2. The Doctor and Adric are exploring the hold of the freighter when screams ring out. They hurry to the source and find the bodies of two slaughtered crewmen. The freighter's security officer, Ringway, steps up behind them. He states that they have been caught red handed, and that on this ship murderers are executed.
3. The Cybermen storm the bridge of the freighter and take control, completing the reactivation of their troops. The Cyber Leader proudly points out to the Doctor a view screen image of columns of marching Cybermen in the hold.
4. The Doctor, Tegan and Nyssa watch helplessly from the TARDIS as the freighter hurtles toward Earth. On board, a dying Cyberman damages the controls and Adric realises that he cannot prevent the impact. The boy stands solemnly, holding his dead brother's Outler belt. The freighter hits the Earth's atmosphere and there is a massive explosion. Tegan and Nyssa break down in tears, and the Doctor stands silently.

IT WAS MADE WHERE...?

Location Recording: 29.10.81
Location: Springwell Lock Quarry, off Springwell Lane, Rickmansworth, Herts.
Studio Recording: 10.11.81-12.11.81 in TC8, 24.11.81-26.11.81 in TC8

ADDITIONAL CREDITED CAST

Scott (James Warwick), Kyle (Clare Clifford), Walters (Steve Morley[1]), Snyder (Suzi Arden[1]), Mitchell (Ann Holloway[1]), First Trooper (Anne Clements[1]), Second Trooper (Mark Straker[1]), Cyber Leader (David Banks), Briggs (Beryl Reid[2-4]), Berger (June Bland[2-4]), Ringway (Alec Sabin[2,3]), Cyber Lieutenant (Mark Hardy[2-4]), First Crew Member (Mark Fletcher[2]), Second Crew Member (Christopher Whittingham[2]).

THINGS TO WATCH OUT FOR

- The Cybermen make a shock return at the end of Part One. Producer John Nathan-

Turner went to great lengths – including having the studio observation galleries closed for the duration of the recording, turning down the offer of a *Radio Times* cover feature on the story and crediting the Cyber Leader as simply 'Leader' and the Cyber Lieutenant as simply 'Lieutenant' in the *Radio Times* cast listing for the second episode (as *Doctor Who* was now being transmitted twice-weekly, only two episodes of each story featured a cast list along with the billing) – to try to ensure that the Cybermen's appearance in this story remained a total surprise to viewers.

- A sequence of clips from earlier stories is seen as the Cyber Leader discusses some of the Doctor's past encounters with the Cybermen. These are from: *The Tenth Planet* Episode 2, *The Wheel In Space* Episode 6 and *Revenge of the Cybermen* Part Three. All are shown in monochrome.
- Adric is killed at the end of the story. The closing titles for Part Four are rolled in silence over a picture of his broken badge for mathematical excellence. This is the first time since Episode Ten of *The War Games* in 1969 that the credits have been rolled as opposed to presented as static captions.
- Seven Cybermen and one Cyber Leader (distinguished by the tubes on the sides of his head being black rather than silver) were constructed by the Imagineering firm for this story

THINGS YOU MIGHT NOT HAVE KNOWN

- Working title: *Sentinel*. (The titles *Sentenial*, *Cenenal* and *Sentinal* also appear on BBC paperwork, but these are almost certainly simply misprints and misspellings.)
- Gareth Hunt was originally considered for the part of Scott.
- Following the story's transmission, letters of complaint were received from viewers concerned about seeing Cybermen with plastic bags over their heads, and also about the death of Adric.
- This story was a last minute replacement for Christopher Priest's *The Enemy Within*, which would also have seen Adric being killed off.

QUOTE, UNQUOTE

- **The Doctor:** 'Brave heart, Tegan.'
- **Cyber Lieutenant:** 'What is it?' **Cyber Leader:** 'A TARDIS.' **Cyber Lieutenant:** 'A Time Lord. But they're forbidden to interfere.' **Cyber Leader:** 'This one calls himself the Doctor and does nothing else but interfere.'
- **Tegan:** 'I'm just a mouth on legs.'
- **The Doctor:** 'Emotions have their uses.' **Cyber Leader:** 'They restrict and curtail the intellect, and logic of the mind.' **The Doctor:** 'They also enhance life. When did you last have the pleasure of smelling a flower, watching a sunset, eating a well-prepared meal?' **Cyber Leader:** 'These things are irrelevant.' **The Doctor:** 'For some people, small, beautiful events is what life is all about!'

ANALYSIS

It was perhaps only a matter of time before the new Doctor found himself up against one of the 'old favourite' monster races. Just as the Daleks had been used to help ease Patrick Troughton into the role and the Daleks (again) and the Cybermen had been dusted off for two of Tom Baker's first few stories, so the Cybermen were chosen by the production team to make a comeback in Peter Davison's debut season, after an absence of some seven years.

The opening episode of *Earthshock* is intentionally structured to misdirect viewers as to who the enemy might be, and is a masterpiece of suspense and terror. Director Peter Grimwade handles the cast and cameras with aplomb and wrings every scrap of tension from his gloomy underground tunnels, mysterious black-clad figures and unwary military team. 'The deadly black androids are terrifying – they flit about silently, in the darkness,' observed Ian Berriman in *DWB* No. 105 dated September 1992. 'They do nothing, they explain nothing, they just kill. They are clinical angels of death. In fact they're too good – despite their simplicity (a couple of body stockings and face masks can't have eaten into the budget much) they are much more impressive than the Cybermen. They are subtle, they are undetectable, and better still, they can run!' The moment of revelation, when the viewer finally learns who is behind the events unfolding on Earth, is one of *Doctor Who*'s all-time classic episode endings. 'After the strenuous efforts of the production office to avoid advance publicity [for the Cybermen's return],' wrote Peter Anghelides in *Shada* 10 dated May/June 1982, 'the ending of [Part One] was a real surprise – not the half-hearted "discovery" of *Death to the Daleks*, for example, or *The Sontaran Experiment*. The advantage of this revelation … is that it gives the viewer an omniscient overview of the events that are occurring. We are never in any doubt as to whose machinations are putting our heroes in danger, but we are made more fearful; we know the danger is there, but we know that our heroes don't know.'

The Cybermen featured here are altogether more effective than those seen in season twelve's *Revenge of the Cybermen*. They have been logically updated and streamlined, given a more 'eighties' look, and yet retain their aura of power and efficiency undiminished. The casting of David Banks as the Cyber Leader is particularly key to their success. Banks makes the part his own in a way that has not really been seen with one of the series' monsters since Michael Wisher gave his definitive performance as Davros back in *Genesis of the Daleks*.

General reaction to the story at the time of its original transmission verged on the rapturous. 'Clearly the classic of the season,' wrote Stephen Collins in *Zerinza* Issue 27 in 1982, '*Earthshock* is for me one of the best *Doctor Who* stories of all time, combining a fine script, an excellent monster, crisp direction and the daring step of wiping out a companion – all combined to produce an epic adventure.' In latter years the story has been reassessed in a less positive light by some reviewers, including Ian Berriman: 'As the name *Earthshock* suggests, it's a story which relies on shocks – surprises, twists – a typical Saward characteristic. This made it very exciting to watch at the time (which is, of course, what counts). The continual surprises stopped you from noticing how very little plot there was. On repeated viewing, however, the story's inadequacies stand out. When you know that the Cybermen are in it, that the dinosaurs get splatted by a space freighter, that Ringway is a traitor and that Adric cops it, what you're left with is a lot of bloody awful padding.'

Padded or not, the story as a whole stands up very well and is highly entertaining. Such deficiencies as there are in the plotting are really not all that noticeable. The icing on the cake comes at the end of Part Four when the annoying Adric is finally written out, and in a highly dramatic way that shows the level of brilliance to which *Doctor Who* could still ascend if the production team only put their minds to it. John Connors, writing in *TARDIS* Volume 7 Number 2 dated May/June 1982, was particularly affected by the youngster's departure: 'Matthew Waterhouse's … final scenes … and in [Part One] where he gives as good as he gets in the argument with Davison, [exemplify] his skill and acting ability. Although some … seem to dislike him … I found his approach original, clever and at all times interesting. He made Adric into a real rough diamond, far surpassing original character drafts, and I'm sure we'll see a lot more of Matthew in the years to come. I certainly hope so anyway. Adric will ultimately be remembered as a tragic hero – "I try so hard" [is] the quote which comes most to mind from his time. I shall certainly miss him.' No doubt many children in the audience will have shared these sentiments; and if nothing else Connors' comments do at least go to show that in *Doctor Who* there are no absolutes, and that even those aspects of the series that are greatly disliked by most reviewers are admired by some – a sentiment that might perhaps provide a crumb of comfort to all those involved in the making of the season's closing story …

TIME-FLIGHT

Writer: Peter Grimwade. **Director:** Ron Jones. **Designer:** Richard McManan-Smith. **Costumes:** Amy Roberts. **Make-Up:** Dorka Nieradzik. **Incidental Music:** Roger Limb. **Visual Effects:** Peter Logan. **Film Cameraman:** Peter Chapman. **Film Editor:** Mike Houghton. **Studio Lighting:** Eric Wallis. **Studio Sound:** Martin Ridout. **Production Assistant:** Joan Elliott. **Assistant Floor Manager:** Lynn Richards.

	First UK TX	Scheduled TX	Actual TX	Duration	Viewers	Chart Pos.
Part One	22/03/82	18.55	18.57	24'56"	10.0	26
Part Two	23/03/82	19.05	19.06	23'58"	8.5	48
Part Three	29/03/82	18.55	18.57	24'29"	8.9	46
Part Four	30/03/82	18.50	18.52	24'30"	8.1	64

Plot: The Doctor finally manages to deliver Tegan to Heathrow Airport, where he gets drawn into investigating the in-flight disappearance of a Concorde. Following the same flight path in another Concorde, with the TARDIS stowed in the hold, he discovers that it has been transported back millions of years into the past through a time corridor. On prehistoric Earth he and his friends encounter a genie-like figure named Kalid and his protoplasmic servants, the Plasmatons. Kalid turns out to be just the latest guise adopted by the Master, who is engaged in a complex scheme to try to gain control of a powerful alien gestalt called the Xeraphin and use it as a dynamorphic generator in his TARDIS. The Master's interference has caused the Xeraphin to become divided. Its evil side now intends to take over the universe, but the Doctor, Tegan and Nyssa are able to overcome it by combining their will power. The Master, tricked by the Doctor, ends up trapped on the Xeraphin's home planet Xeriphas. The Doctor and Nyssa make a quick departure in the TARDIS, apparently abandoning Tegan at Heathrow.

Episode endings:
1. Plasmatons suddenly materialise around the Doctor, and he is engulfed in protoplasmic matter.
2. Kalid collapses, apparently dead, and Professor Hayter, a Concorde passenger who has managed to resist the conditioning to which the others have succumbed, discovers on opening the base of a console that the source of the genie-like figure's power was mere electronics.

The Doctor is incredulous. Suddenly the Master rises from the floor, divesting himself of the remnants of his Kalid disguise and observing that the Doctor never does understand.

3. The Doctor realises that the Master has succeeded in transferring the Xeraphin to the centre of his TARDIS. He tells Nyssa and Tegan that his old adversary has finally defeated him.

4. Tegan arrives back from a nostalgic wander around Heathrow Airport just in time to see the TARDIS departing without her.

IT WAS MADE WHERE...?

Location Recording: 06.01.82-07.01.82, 11.01.82

Locations: Balcony, Terminal 1, Heathrow Airport, Hounslow, Middlesex; Roof Car Park, Terminal 3, Heathrow Airport, Hounslow, Middx; Concorde, BA Maintenance Area (Concorde Hangar), Heathrow Airport, Hounslow, Middx.

Studio Recording: 19.01.82-20.01.82 in TC8, 24.01.82 (studio unknown), 01.02.82-03.02.82 in TC8, 08.02.82 in TC6

ADDITIONAL CREDITED CAST

Captain Stapley (Richard Easton), Flight Engineeer Scobie (Keith Drinkel), First Officer Bilton (Michael Cashman), Horton (Peter Dahlsen[1,4]), Sheard (Peter McDermott[1,4]), Captain Urquhart (John Flint[1]), Andrews (Peter Cellier[1]), Angela Clifford (Judith Byfield[1-3]), Kalid (Leon Ny Taiy[1*]), Professor Hayter (Nigel Stock[2-4]), The Master (Anthony Ainley[2-4]), Adric (Matthew Waterhouse[2]), Anithon (Hugh Hayes[3]), Zarak (André Winterton[3]).

* 'Leon Ny Taiy' is an anagram of 'Tony Ainley' – another instance of a pseudonym being used for the actor in order to conceal the Master's presence in the story.

THINGS TO WATCH OUT FOR

- There are cameo appearances by Adric, the Melkur (from season eighteen's *The Keeper of Traken*) and a Terileptil (from *The Visitation*) in Part Two as images conjured up to try to dissuade Nyssa and Tegan from entering the inner sanctum presided over by Kalid.
- Well known actor Nigel Stock appears here as Professor Hayter. His many notable roles included the lead in the BBC's medical drama series *Owen MD*.
- Michael Cashman, now better known for his appearances in *EastEnders* and for his work as a gay rights activist, plays Concorde First Officer Bilton.
- The snake-like Plasmaton creature that threatens the Doctor in Part Three was a hand puppet. It was operated against a CSO background by Richard Gregory of the Imagineering company that supplied it.

THINGS YOU MIGHT NOT HAVE KNOWN

- Working title: *Zanadin*.
- David Reid, the BBC's Head of Series and Serials, sent a note to John Nathan-Turner after seeing the scripts. He commented: 'Be very careful with all the disintegrating bodies – it can be very frightening. Make sure it's not *too* frightening.' He added: 'Are you really going to be able to get Concordes to play around with?'
- Two of writer Peter Grimwade's original character names, Captains Irvine and

Rathbone, were changed before the story went into production as checks had revealed that there were real British Airways pilots with those names.
- On 25 January 1982, Grimwade was asked to write an additional seven minutes for Part Three as that episode was running under time.

QUOTE, UNQUOTE
- **Captain Stapley:** 'I thought you were going with the Doctor.' **Tegan:** 'So did I ...'

ANALYSIS

Time-Flight suffers from the same problem as many of the other stories of this period – a difficult-to-follow and hole-ridden plot. The Master's scheme is ridiculously convoluted and illogical; and Richard Walter, writing in *TARDIS* Volume 7 Number 2 dated May/June 1982, spotted another oddity: 'Why oh why did the Master disguise himself as Kalid when (a) the Doctor was nowhere near and (b) even if he had [been there was no apparent purpose served by] the disguise. While I find Anthony Ainley an excellent character actor ..., there is something lacking in the "new" Master. I tend to think that it is the scripts which do not seem to allow for the Master to be as ruthless as he used to be; and *Time-Flight* in particular gave little material for a good Master/Doctor adventure.'

Worse still, Peter Grimwade's scripts make totally unrealistic demands of the production. Consequently, after a quite promising start evoking memories of season four's airport-based *The Faceless Ones*, the whole thing goes badly downhill, as Simon M Lydiard observed in *Skaro* Volume Two Number Five dated June 1982:

'The early scenes at Heathrow Airport were some of the best Earth scenes [for many years]. With an unpretentious, almost documentary style of direction, Ron Jones evoked the "realistic" feel so typical of the later Troughton Earth-based stories and the early Pertwees. The location filming in and around Concorde was beautifully done and was one of the high points of the season ...

'However, despite its excellent beginnings, I was left feeling rather disappointed with this story ... Not only was it set in two completely different times, it was made in two completely different styles of production – the modern day Earth scenes being entirely convincing, whilst the prehistoric scenes looked rather false. In fact, once we arrived where the main part of the story was to take place the whole [thing] seemed to descend to another level.'

Scenes involving Concorde crash-landing on the barren plains of prehistoric Earth would be difficult enough for an epic cinema film to achieve convincingly, let alone a series with the modest resources of *Doctor Who*. Just how the production team ever thought that this story could be made to work is a total mystery. The realisation of its requirements was always going to be an uphill struggle, and in the final analysis the whole thing is a bit of a shambles. Particularly unsuccessful is the ill-conceived attempt to mix stock footage of Concorde aircraft with a studio-bound 'landscape'; and the Plasmatons must be just about the most poorly realised and uninspiring monsters ever to appear in the series. One of the story's few saving graces is the idea of the Xeraphin although, as Simon M Lydiard suggested, even this is not as well developed as it might be: 'The Xeraphin looked to me very much like something out of *Star Trek*, [but] the concept of a failing gestalt of good and evil was an interesting and reasonably effective one, though not enough was made of it ... But sadly, what *Time-Flight* really lacked was coherency.'

Richard Walter surely echoed the thoughts of many when he wrote: 'There is no doubt in my mind that *Time-Flight* was the worst story in an otherwise excellent twenty-six episode season.'

The apparent abandonment of Tegan at Heathrow was never intended to mark her last appearance in *Doctor Who*; the aim was simply to create a cliffhanger ending and thus help to maintain viewers' interest over the (now much longer than in the past) break between seasons – an idea also prompted in part by the use of a similar device in *Blake's 7*. Tegan would therefore return in the first story of the following year's run, which would again be overseen by producer John Nathan-Turner and script editor Eric Saward.

DOCTOR WHO SEASON TWENTY (1983)

Regular Cast:
The Doctor (Peter Davison)
Nyssa (Sarah Sutton) until *Terminus* Part Four
Tegan (Janet Fielding) from *Arc of Infinity* Part Two onwards
Turlough (Mark Strickson) from *Mawdryn Undead* Part One onwards

Regular Crew:
Producer: John Nathan-Turner.
Script Editor: Eric Saward.
Production Associate: June Collins on all stories, but uncredited on *Snakedance*, Angela Smith on *Snakedance*.
Title Music: Ron Grainer and the BBC Radiophonic Workshop, arranged by Peter Howell.
Special Sounds: Dick Mills.

The twice weekly transmission pattern introduced for season nineteen was retained for season twenty. Parts One and Two of the opening story went out on the Monday and Wednesday evenings respectively of the first week of January 1983 and then, in a late change of plan, the remaining episodes of the season followed on consecutive Tuesday and Wednesday evenings. In terms of its content, the new season maintained the generally high standard of production seen the previous year, although again many reviewers expressed reservations that style was tending to be given precedence over substance. This season as a whole also drew much more heavily than had previous ones on established *Doctor Who* mythology. There was indeed at least one element from the Doctor's past in every story – a fact that, after it was pointed out to him by fan Ian Levine, John Nathan-Turner used as part of his promotion of the series in its twentieth anniversary year. The celebratory tone was apparent right from the outset as the season got under way with a story that had strong links to the series' tenth anniversary back in 1973 …

ARC OF INFINITY

Writer: Johnny Byrne. **Director:** Ron Jones. **Designer:** Marjorie Pratt. **Costumes:** Dee Robson. **Make-Up:** Fran Needham. **Incidental Music:** Roger Limb. **Visual Effects:** Christopher Lawson. **Film Cameraman:** Fintan Sheehan. **Film Editor:** Bernard Ashby. **Studio Lighting:** Don Babbage. **Studio Sound:** Trevor Webster. **Production Assistant:** Diana Brookes. **Assistant Floor Manager:** Lynn Richards.

	First UK TX	Scheduled TX	Actual TX	Duration	Viewers	Chart Pos.
Part One	03/01/83	18.45	18.46	24'37"	7.2	74
Part Two	05/01/83	18.45	18.47	24'42"	7.3	66
Part Three	11/01/83	18.50	18.52	24'37"	6.9	89
Part Four	12/01/83	18.45	18.46	24'28"	7.2	82

Plot: An antimatter creature has crossed into normal space via a phenomenon known as the Arc of Infinity but needs to bond physically with a Time Lord in order to remain stable. A traitor on Gallifrey has chosen the Doctor as the victim. The High Council, headed by President Borusa, decides that the Doctor's life must be terminated in order to avoid this danger. Tegan meanwhile arrives in Amsterdam to visit her cousin, Colin Frazer, only to learn that he has disappeared. She enters a crypt in search of him and is captured by a hideous creature, the Ergon. On Gallifrey, the traitor is revealed as Councillor Hedin and his master as the legendary Time Lord figure Omega, who has been trapped for centuries in the universe of antimatter. Omega seizes control of the Matrix. The Doctor however is able to trace him to Amsterdam thanks to clues received via the Matrix from Tegan – who has been taken to Omega's TARDIS by the Ergon. Omega's body is turning into a replica of the Doctor's, but the bonding is incomplete and there will soon be a massive explosion as he reverts to antimatter. The Doctor, Nyssa and Tegan chase Omega through Amsterdam and eventually corner him. Omega wills his own destruction, but the Doctor fires the Ergon's matter converter at him and he fades harmlessly away.

Episode endings:
1. To Nyssa's horror, the Doctor is shot by Commander Maxil of the Chancellery Guard and falls motionless to the ground.
2. The Doctor is prepared for termination and the equipment activated. Nyssa and the members of the High Council watch as his body fades slowly away. Suddenly the room is bathed in a bright light and a negative image of the antimatter renegade briefly appears in the Doctor's place. Then the process is over and Maxil announces that judgment has been carried out. Nyssa looks accusingly at the Time Lords.
3. With Hedin exposed as the traitor and shot dead by the Castellan, the Doctor tells President Borusa that urgent action is needed if Omega is to be stopped. Nyssa then draws his attention to the screen behind him and he realises that it is too late: Omega controls the Matrix. A negative image of Omega dominates the Matrix screen.
4. Tegan tells the Doctor and Nyssa that she has been sacked from her job as an air hostess and that they are stuck with her. Nyssa gives her a delighted hug, but the Doctor appears less pleased ...

IT WAS MADE WHERE...?

Location Recording: 03.05.82–07.05.82
Locations: all locations are in Amsterdam, Holland: Schiphol Airport, arrivals hall; Muntplein (Mint Tower Square); flower market, Muntplein; Schiphol Airport runway; Bob's Youth Hostel and adjacent streets, NZ Voorburgwal 92; police station and adjacent streets, Lijnbaansgracht 219; Hoopman Bodega, Leidsplein 4; Vondelpark Youth Hostel, Zandpad 5; Amstelveld and adjacent streets; flower stall, Prinsengracht/Utrechtestraat; 'Huis Frankendael', Middenweg 72; Amstel Lock and adjacent streets (south of Skinny Bridge); Central Station forecourt (telephone); Dam Square; Damrak.
Studio Recording: 17.05.82–18.05.82, 31.05.82–02.06.82 all in TC1

ADDITIONAL CREDITED CAST

Lord President Borusa (Leonard Sachs), Councillor Hedin (Michael Gough[1-3]), The Renegade[1,2]/Omega[3,4] (Ian Collier)*, Commander Maxil (Colin Baker[1-3]), The Castellan (Paul Jerricho), Damon (Neil Daglish), Chancellor Thalia (Elspet Gray), Cardinal Zorac (Max Harvey), Robin Stuart (Andrew Boxer), Colin Frazer (Alastair Cumming), Talor (John D. Collins[1]), Hotel Receptionist (Maya Woolfe[1,4]), The Ergon (Malcolm Harvey), Second Receptionist (Guy Groen[4]).

* To preserve the initial mystery surrounding Omega's identity, the character was credited as 'The Renegade' for the first two episodes.

POPULAR MYTHS

- New regular costumes for Nyssa and Tegan are seen for the first time in this story. (Although Tegan's new costume makes its debut here, Nyssa's is not seen until the following story, *Snakedance*. This myth derives from the fact that numerous publicity photographs of the two actresses wearing their new costumes were taken during *Arc of Infinity*'s location shoot in Amsterdam.)

THINGS TO WATCH OUT FOR

- Future Doctor Colin Baker makes his *Doctor Who* debut as Maxil – and gets to shoot the current incumbent of the lead role in the closing scene of Part One.
- Ian Collier takes on the role of Omega, originally played by Stephen Thorne in season ten's *The Three Doctors*. Collier had appeared once before in the series, as Stuart Hyde in season nine's *The Time Monster*.
- Distinguished actor Michael Gough, who had previously played the Celestial Toymaker in the eponymous season three story and been married to Anneke Wills, alias the Doctor's companion Polly, appears here as the misguided traitor Hedin.
- Leonard Sachs, previously seen as Admiral de Coligny in season three's *The Massacre of St Bartholomew's Eve*, plays the latest incarnation of Borusa, now elevated to the position of Lord President.
- Producer John Nathan-Turner makes a Hitchcockian cameo appearance in the Amsterdam location scenes.

THINGS YOU MIGHT NOT HAVE KNOWN

- Working titles: *Time of Neman*, *Time of Omega*.

- Alastair Cumming, son of regular *Doctor Who* director Fiona Cumming and production manager Ian Fraser, plays Colin Frazer.
- The tune played on the barrel organ in Part Four of this story was sixteen seconds of a traditional piece called 'Canal Song'. The episode also featured one minute and ten seconds of an organ playing 'Tulips From Amsterdam'. Both pieces were recorded on location.
- The use of an overseas location attracted much interest from the British press with no fewer than five newspapers, as well as the Press Association, sending journalists to cover the filming.

QUOTE, UNQUOTE

- **Councillor Hedin:** [To Omega]: 'What we are, we owe to you.'

ANALYSIS

Arc of Infinity is a prime example of a story with very high production values but, ultimately, not much else in its favour. The location filming in Amsterdam; Omega's new costume; the new outfit and hairstyle for Tegan; the glitzy new designs for Gallifrey. It all looks very nice, but where's the substance? One could in fact argue that in this instance the production team's apparent determination to foreground the series' glossy visuals actually acts as a positive obstacle to the telling of a coherent and exciting story. This is true particularly of the extensive location sequences, which at times seem more appropriate to a travelogue than to a science-fiction drama series. 'The use of foreign locations in the [series] has always been a bone of contention within fandom,' observed Duncan Harvey in *DWB* No. 124 dated March 1994. 'While it is true that they prove that there is life beyond London and the Home Counties, in *Arc of Infinity* there is little justification for setting the story in Amsterdam. We are given a rather dubious explanation concerning the water pressure available to the fusion booster below sea level (which rather ignores the water pressure available in *any* city from the domestic water mains!), but one can't help but think that the money would have been better spent elsewhere. Worst of all is the gruesome way that we are introduced to the setting of Amsterdam. Director Ron Jones uses a blatantly unsubtle establishing shot which would not look out of place in an ITC film series, and when combined with the strains of "Tulips from Amsterdam" all that is missing is a Simon Templar style voice-over introduction ...'

The contrived idea of Tegan being abandoned by the Doctor at the end of the previous season precipitates the use of an even more artificial plot device to bring her back into the picture at the beginning of this one, as Gary Levy pointed out in *DWB* No. 1 dated August 1983: 'A major error was the way Tegan was reintroduced. What a coincidence that her cousin, whilst on holiday, should get involved in the evil plot being hatched by the Doctor's old enemy Omega! The only reason she was written out in *Time-Flight* was to keep viewers guessing if she had gone for good. If *Doctor Who* is to [be turned] into a sci-fi version of ... *Dallas* then at least do it in a believable fashion.'

Another problem with the scripts is that they place rather too much emphasis on the build-up to the surprise revelation of Omega's involvement at the end of Part Three. Although this is fine for the fans, who actually know who Omega is, it must fall very flat for the more casual viewer. It also means that the character's identity has to be rather clumsily disguised for most of the story. Ian K McLachlan, writing in

TARDIS Volume 8 Number 1 dated March 1983, thought that it was a mistake for the character to be brought back at all: 'After all, he was a classic villain. It would have been better to have let him rest in peace rather than have a feeble excuse for a reappearance. As somebody said: the villain of the tenth season becomes just another one of the twentieth.'

David Atkins, writing in the same issue of TARDIS, made some valid criticisms of the story's token monster: 'Although most of the costumes were splendid, with the Ergon we were treated to one of the most absurd sights ever seen in the [series]. He was really quite indescribable, although I've heard some humorous attempts varying from "a plucked chicken" to "a pantomime horse". The Doctor described it as one of Omega's less successful attempts at psycho-synthesis. I can't help but agree.'

There are however a few redeeming features to Arc of Infinity. Tegan's initial distance from the main action gives Nyssa a chance to shine, and her character is particularly well handled – perhaps not surprisingly, given that the writer is her creator Johnny Byrne. Omega is also well characterised, and Peter Davison gives an excellent performance in his dual role in the fourth episode. Some reviewers, indeed, have reacted very positively to the story. Douglas Potter, another of those who commented in TARDIS Volume 8 Number 1, was full of praise for it: 'Plot, scenery, locations, all merged with the most meticulous acting. Michael Gough was magnificent as the proud scheming Hedin and his scene ... with Leonard Sachs's Borusa shows how actors half their age cannot play a part with such care. Ian Collier's Omega was a sad pathetic figure, half wanting revenge and half rest. Omega's moment of happiness by the barrel organ in Amsterdam was very sad and brilliantly portrayed – ... Stephen Thorne was not missed. Peter Davison was at his brilliant best and I can give him the real tribute that I no longer miss Tom Baker.'

Arc of Infinity is not exactly a bad story but, as Ian K McLachlan concluded, it could have been much better: 'I am very fond of the three stories which are the roots of Arc of Infinity. The Three Doctors, The Deadly Assassin and The Invasion of Time. Indeed the first one is my favourite Pertwee story, the second two my favourite two Baker serials. So surely for me Arc of Infinity must be the best Davison story so far? I'm afraid not. Sequels don't have to be as good as the original story. They must be better. And certainly I felt that Arc of Infinity was a pale imitation of the other three. Oh I enjoyed it all right. I was enthralled as the episodes danced before my eyes. But at the end I was left with an empty feeling. The feeling that it should have been so much better. All the ingredients were there. But somehow they didn't gel.'

SNAKEDANCE

Writer: Christopher Bailey. **Director:** Fiona Cumming. **Designer:** Jan Spoczynski. **Costumes:** Ken Trew. **Make-Up:** Marion Richards. **Incidental Music:** Peter Howell. **Visual Effects:** Andy Lazell. **Film Cameraman:** John Baker. **Film Editor:** Alastair Mackay. **Studio Lighting:** Henry Barber. **Studio Sound:** Martin Ridout. **Production Assistant:** Rita Dunn. **Assistant Floor Manager:** Maggy Campbell.

	First UK TX	Scheduled TX	Actual TX	Duration	Viewers	Chart Pos.
Part One	18/01/83	18.50	18.50	24'26"	6.7	95
Part Two	19/01/83	18.45	18.47	24'35"	7.7	75
Part Three	25/01/83	18.50	18.50	24'29"	6.6	98
Part Four	26/01/83	18.45	18.44	24'29"	7.4	78

Plot: Tegan falls once more under the influence of the Mara and directs the TARDIS to the planet Manussa. There the Federator's son Lon and his mother Tanha are preparing for a ceremony to celebrate the banishment of the Mara five hundred years earlier. The Mara takes control of Lon and uses him and Tegan to obtain from Ambril, the Director of Historical Research, the 'great crystal' – the large blue stone that originally brought it into being by focusing energy from the minds of the planet's one-time inhabitants. The Mara now plans to use the crystal during the ceremony to bring about its return to corporeal existence. The Doctor and Nyssa, aided by Ambril's assistant Chela, locate Ambril's aged predecessor Dojjen, who predicted the Mara's rebirth before wandering off into the wilderness. The Doctor allows himself to be bitten by a snake in order to enter a state of mental commune with Dojjen, who tells him that fear is the only true venom and that in order to defeat the Mara he must find the still point within himself. The Doctor and his friends then return to the caves where the ceremony is being held. The Doctor, by concentrating his thoughts with the aid of a small replica of the great crystal, is able to find the still point and repel the Mara.

Episode endings:
1. Tegan collapses in the market square and is taken into a fortune teller's booth. The fortune teller removes from around the young woman's neck the dream inhibiting device that the Doctor earlier gave her. Tegan then succumbs to the Mara's influence and causes a snake skull to appear in the fortune teller's crystal ball. The skull gets bigger and bigger until the ball shatters.
2. The Mara-possessed Tegan and Lon take a carnival barker named Dugdale into a secret room behind a cave wall carved with snake images. Once inside, they link hands and order Dugdale to look at them. Although frightened, he eventually obeys and sees Tegan's eyes glowing red.
3. Chela rescues the Doctor and Nyssa from the cells, but they are recaptured by guards. The possessed Lon orders that they be killed. Nyssa screams.
4. Dojjen walks calmly away from his mountain refuge. In the caves, the Doctor assures a tearful Tegan that she is now free of the Mara forever.

IT WAS MADE WHERE...?

Ealing Filming: 31.03.82 on stage 2
Studio Recording: 12.04.82-14.04.82, 26.04.82-28.04.82 all in TC6, 29.09.82 (post dubbing only) (studio unknown)

ADDITIONAL CREDITED CAST

Ambril (John Carson), Tanha (Colette O'Neil), Dojjen (Preston Lockwood[1,3,4]), Lon (Martin Clunes), Dugdale (Brian Miller), Fortune Teller (Hilary Sesta[1,2]), Hawker (George Ballantine[1]), Chela (Johnathon Morris[2-4]), Puppeteer (Barry Smith[3]), Megaphone Man (Brian Grellis[4]).

THINGS TO WATCH OUT FOR

- A young Martin Clunes, now better known as one of the stars of the sitcom *Men Behaving Badly*, appears in an early television role as Lon.
- Brian Miller, whose wife Elisabeth Sladen had portrayed the Doctor's companion Sarah Jane Smith, portrays Dugdale.
- Johnathon Morris, later to star in the BBC sitcom *Bread*, appears as Chela.

THINGS YOU MIGHT NOT HAVE KNOWN

- The BBC designer for this production, Jan Spoczynski, wanted to have the studio settings made by an outside contractor but was initially refused permission. Then, at a very late date, it was decided that half the work should after all go outside. This resulted in a rushed job, with which Spoczynski was dissatisfied.
- For the scenes involving snakes, two garter snakes and one tree snake, all of them non-poisonous varieties, were hired from a specialist company called Janimals run by Jan Gray. For the scenes where the snakes are to bite Dojjen and the Doctor, a replica garter snake head was created by the Visual Effects Department.
- Writer Christopher Bailey provided a detailed design of what the carved picture on the cave wall, into which the Great Crystal would be inserted, was to look like.

QUOTE, UNQUOTE

- **The Doctor:** 'Dreams are important ... never underestimate them.'
- **Tegan:** 'Why am I so confused?' **Mara:** 'You're divided against yourself. A stranger in your own mind. You are pathetic. Look at me! I can make up your mind.' **Tegan:** 'No.' **Mara:** 'Why not? What are you afraid of? Just who do you think you are?'
- **Dojjen:** 'Fear is the only poison.'
- **The Doctor:** 'What is the snakedance?' **Dojjen:** 'This is. Here and now. The dance goes on. It is all the dance. Everywhere and always. So. Find the still point. Only then can the Mara be defeated.' **The Doctor:** 'The still point. The point of safety. But it's in the chamber somewhere. Where?' **Dojjen:** 'No. The still point is within yourself, nowhere else. To destroy the Mara you must find the still point.'

ANALYSIS

Sequels are always difficult things to pull off successfully as they risk disappointing those viewers who liked the original story and alienating those who didn't. In the case of *Snakedance*, John Connors was initially amongst the latter group but eventually found himself won over, as he explained in *TARDIS* Volume 8 Number 1 dated March 1983: 'I didn't like *Kinda* one iota – all plastic jungles, inflatable air-beds and the like – so when I heard about *Snakedance* I could hardly suppress a yawn. Another waste of time, I thought – an excuse to get surreal and pseudo-intellectual at everyone's expense, another glut of material for people to write reams of copy about.

'How wrong I was. *Snakedance* turned out to be a grade one strike. A rich vein of ideas and imagination netted together by a competent enthusiastic cast and an atmosphere steeped in mysticism, mystery and intrigue ... It made *Arc of Infinity* look like a cheap pantomime.'

Conners was spot on. *Snakedance* is one of the most consistently enjoyable stories of the fifth Doctor's era. This is due in large part to Christopher Bailey's excellent scripts, which differ from those for *Kinda* in that they not only present some sophisticated abstract ideas but also manage to combine these with a plot that is clear and easy for the viewer to understand. The major influence is once again Buddhism – which may well account for the similarities between this story and another, much earlier one that also drew heavily on that philosophy, as pointed out by Guy Clapperton in the same issue of *TARDIS*: 'If I were to start off a review by saying that the story involved a large blue crystal which had to be put into its rightful place in a cave, went on to say that the villain was manifested as something people have phobias about, and that the Doctor defeated it by overcoming fear, which adventure would I be talking about? In fact I am talking about *Snakedance*, but I could easily have been reviewing *Planet of the Spiders*. The basic plots are so similar, with the Doctor finding a mystical mentor (Dojjen or K'anpo, whichever you want), but even so, *Snakedance* stands up well on its own.'

Fiona Cumming's assured direction matches the quality of the writing, and the whole thing is visually flawless. 'Ms Cumming's direction, along with a script simply crammed with superb dialogue, has managed to produce [a story] which must surely be recognised as a classic,' argued Simon Lidyard in *Skaro* Volume 3 Number 4 in 1983. '*Snakedance* is very close to being the perfect *Doctor Who* story in that it combines brilliant televisual imagery and excitement with a powerful undercurrent of philosophy, unobtrusive to those with no interest in such things, but rich and fulfilling for those who do [appreciate it].'

Like *Kinda*, *Snakedance* is all the more enjoyable for the scope that it affords Janet Fielding to give one of the most chilling portrayals of alien possession ever seen in *Doctor Who*. Fielding seems so much more committed and convincing here than in her usual performance as Tegan; her withering stare, wicked grin and cajoling voice combining to convey a sense of almost demonic evil. In short, the actress proves that she can really deliver the goods, and it is actually rather a shame to see her reverting at the end of the story to the familiar, by now somewhat fake indignation of Tegan.

Good though *Snakedance* undoubtedly is, not everyone liked it. 'I must confess to finding it very boring indeed,' wrote Ian K McLachlan, again in *TARDIS*. 'When it was all over I thought to myself: "What on earth was the point of it all?" Nothing really had changed on the planet as a result of the adventure. Nobody had been changed to any extent by the Doctor's visit. If he hadn't arrived on Manussa then nothing at all would have happened. Indeed if he had left Tegan in Amsterdam then I wonder what would have happened? There were a lot of dialogues in this one, but little real revelation of character. It was all too obscure, and although religion interests me greatly, I got the impression that *Snakedance* was trying hard to be intellectual and failing ... It was well executed. The only thing I felt was lacking was a good story.'

This raises an important aspect of storytelling: that the characters should somehow be changed by their experiences. In *Snakedance*, most of the change is undergone by the Doctor and Tegan. The Doctor learns that some battles must be fought with peace and quietness (using the 'still point') while Tegan discovers what it feels like to want to kill and destroy for pleasure. It could be argued however that the political situation of Manussa would also be bound to change significantly as a result of the events depicted: Ambril learning that wealth does not always come from physical artefacts; Lon growing up to be a good and compassionate Federator; and the population in general finally coming to understand the purpose of the snakedancers and to recognise Dojjen not simply as an insane hermit but as a wise man who was actually telling the truth.

All things considered, *Snakedance* is a very special story indeed. In marked contrast to 'blockbusters' such as *Earthshock*, which tend to be all action and no thought, here we have a story that relies on thought more than action. It makes a refreshing change.

THE GUARDIAN TRILOGY

The third, fourth and fifth stories of the twentieth season were conceived by John Nathan-Turner and Eric Saward as a trilogy reintroducing the Black Guardian and his opposite number the White Guardian – characters devised by former producer Graham Williams as part of his concept for the Doctor's quest for the Key to Time, as seen in season sixteen. They would be played, as before, by Valentine Dyall and Cyril Luckham respectively.

Nathan-Turner decided that during the course of the Guardian trilogy Nyssa should make her exit from the series and a new regular be introduced to take her place. (He had actually considered having her written out during the course of the previous season, but this had been objected to by Peter Davison – who considered her the best-suited of the three companions to his Doctor – and so the producer had ultimately elected to have Adric killed off instead.) The new companion devised by Nathan-Turner was Turlough, a young man of mysterious background and suspect motivation who would be substituted for another schoolboy character already included in writer Peter Grimwade's story *Mawdryn Undead*. The actor chosen by Nathan-Turner to play Turlough after extensive auditions was Mark Strickson, who accepted the role in preference to an alternative one that he had been offered in the BBC's hospital-based drama serial *Angels*. His fair hair was died red for the part as Nathan-Turner thought that he would otherwise look too similar to Davison in long shot.

This trilogy was to be the last time that the awesomely powerful Guardians featured in *Doctor Who*.

MAWDRYN UNDEAD

Writer: Peter Grimwade. **Director:** Peter Moffatt. **Designer:** Stephen Scott. **Costumes:** Amy Roberts, Richard Croft. **Make-Up:** Sheelagh Wells, Carolyn Perry. **Incidental Music:** Paddy Kingsland. **Visual Effects:** Stuart Brisdon. **Film Cameraman:** Godfrey Johnson. **Film Editor:** Chris Woolley. **Studio Lighting:** Don Babbage. **Studio Sound:** Martin Ridout. **Production Assistant:** Valerie Letley. **Assistant Floor Manager:** Ian Tootle.

	First UK TX	Scheduled TX	Actual TX	Duration	Viewers	Chart Pos.
Part One	01/02/83	18.50	18.51	24'03"	6.5	103
Part Two	02/02/83	18.45	18.46	24'33"	7.5	83
Part Three	08/02/83	18.50	18.50	24'32"	7.4	84
Part Four	09/02/83	18.45	18.47	24'33"	7.7	78

Plot: The Black Guardian recruits a young man named Turlough to assassinate the Doctor. Although outwardly an ordinary pupil at a boys' private boarding school, Turlough is in fact an alien who believes that the Guardian will return him home if he succeeds. The TARDIS meanwhile has its instruments jammed by a mysterious signal and is forced to materialise on board a massive spaceship in a fixed orbit. The Doctor discovers that the signal – a beam to guide the ship's transmat capsule – is being transmitted from Earth. He travels down to the planet in the capsule, leaving Nyssa and Tegan in the TARDIS with the co-ordinates pre-set to follow. Things go wrong, however, as the Doctor arrives in 1983 but the TARDIS materialises in 1977. Tegan and Nyssa encounter a man with a badly burned body and think that this could be the Doctor. Tegan goes for medical aid and runs into the Doctor's old friend the Brigadier, now retired from UNIT and working as a maths teacher at the school. They join Nyssa and, at the mysterious stranger's urging, use the TARDIS to travel up to the spaceship. The stranger is actually Mawdryn, one of a group of alien mutants travelling endlessly in a state of perpetual regeneration brought upon themselves through the use of a stolen Time Lord device. The Doctor takes Turlough and the 1983 version of the Brigadier up to the ship in the transmat capsule. He reluctantly agrees to supply from his own body the energy needed to end the mutants' ordeal, even though this will mean the loss of his remaining regenerations. In the event, however, the energy comes not from the Doctor but from an explosion caused when the two Brigadiers meet.

Episode endings:
1. Turlough, responding to the Black Guardian's exhortations, picks up a large rock and prepares to smash it down on the back of the Doctor's head.
2. Tegan, Nyssa and the Brigadier enter the TARDIS control room. Mawdryn, now wearing the Doctor's old coat, turns to face them. The top of his skull is missing, revealing his pulsing brain. Nyssa screams.
3. The mutants take their places in the regeneration room and Mawdryn pleads with the Doctor to help them die by giving them his energy. The Doctor refuses, explaining to Tegan that if he does so it will be the end of him as a Time Lord.
4. The Doctor, Nyssa and Tegan deliver the 1983 version of the Brigadier back home. Turlough is in the TARDIS control room when they return. He asks if he can join them, and the Doctor comments that he already has. In space, Mawdryn's ship self-destructs.

IT WAS MADE WHERE...?

Location Filming: 24.08.82-27.08.82
Locations: Middlesex Polytechnic, Trent Park, Bramley Road, Cockfosters, London N14; 'obelisk' at Trent Park, Cockfosters.
Studio Recording: 08.09.82-09.09.82 in TC6, 22.09.82-24.09.82 in TC8

ADDITIONAL CREDITED CAST

The Brigadier (Nicholas Courtney), Black Guardian (Valentine Dyall), Headmaster (Angus MacKay[1,2]), Ibbotson (Stephen Garlick[1,2]), Doctor Runciman (Roger Hammond[1,4]), Matron (Sheila Gill[1]), Mawdryn (David Collings[2-4]), 1st Mutant (Peter Walmsley[3,4]), 2nd Mutant (Brian Darnley[3,4]).

THINGS TO WATCH OUT FOR

- The Doctor's reaction is remarkable when Nyssa enters the TARDIS control room in Part One. Presumably it is because of her new outfit ...
- When the Doctor 'unlocks' the Brigadier's memory in Part Two, it is revealed that

Sergeant Benton left the army in 1979 and now sells second hand cars and that Harry Sullivan was seconded to NATO to work on a secret project at Porton Down. Prior to a short sequence of clips, the Doctor mentions Jo Grant, Sarah Jane, Liz Shaw, Yeti and Colonel Lethbridge-Stewart. The clips are from the following episodes: *The Three Doctors* Episode Two, *The Web of Fear* Episode 1, *The Invasion* Episode Five, *The Claws of Axos* Episode Four, *Day of the Daleks* Episode Four, *Spearhead from Space* Episode 3, *Robot* Part Two, *Terror of the Zygons* Part Two and *Terror of the Zygons* Part Four.

THINGS YOU MIGHT NOT HAVE KNOWN

- Former producer Graham Williams, the creator of the Guardians, did not know about their return in this season and learned about it only years later during an on-stage interview at a *Doctor Who* convention.
- The effects of the Mutants' disease on Tegan and Nyssa were represented in two ways: first by ageing Janet Fielding and Sarah Sutton with make-up as the TARDIS travelled forwards in time; then by substituting two child actresses – Sian Pattenden for Tegan and Lucy Baker for Nyssa – as it travelled backwards in time.
- The record to which the Brigadier listens in his room is a track called 'Lilliburlero' from an LP called 'Bandstand'.
- Nick Gillard (stuntman and stunt arranger) doubled for Mark Strickson and Paul Heasman doubled for Stephen Garlick in the scene where the car crashes. The van driver was played by stuntman Mark McRide.
- Richard Sheekey doubled for Nicholas Courtney when the two Brigadiers were called to be in the same shot together and split screen effects could not be used.
- The Brigadier's moustache was retained in the BBC's 'wig store' for future use following the completion of this story.

QUOTE, UNQUOTE

- **Tegan:** 'Maybe the capsule's malfunctioned. I hate those transmat things. Like travelling in a food mixer and just as dangerous. I'd be afraid of coming out puréed.'
- **Mawdryn:** 'Perpetual regeneration.' **Nyssa:** 'Regeneration? You don't mean it's happening again?' **Mawdryn:** 'Life without end or form. Changing. Changing.'
- **The Brigadier:** 'Are we stuck on this ship?' **The Doctor:** 'I wonder … if I reverse the polarity of the neutron flow …'

ANALYSIS

Mawdryn Undead is arguably one of the most ambitious stories that *Doctor Who* ever attempted. It utilises the time travel aspect of the series to the full and tackles head on an idea that had been only toyed with before – that of an adventure taking place in two time zones, with events in the earlier one affecting those in the later one.

Considering that Ian K McLachlan disliked the excellent *Snakedance*, his reaction to *Mawdryn Undead* in *TARDIS* Volume 8 Number 1 dated March 1983 is interesting: 'For me it was the best Davison story to date. It had an unusual plot, the return of the good old Brigadier, the marvellous Valentine Dyall, … terrific … incidental music, a highly original plot, a set of very suspenseful episodes … I could go on. The magic of *Doctor Who* for me was embodied in *Mawdryn Undead*.'

A part of the story's appeal lies in its complexity. Not only has writer Peter Grimwade chosen to weave an intricate web of interaction between the two time zones, he has also been required by the production team to make this story the first part of the Guardian trilogy and to introduce a new companion for the Doctor in the person of Turlough. On top of all this, he has come up with Mawdryn and his band of shuffling mutants. These tragic characters are somewhat ill defined but, as Ian K McLachlan observed, have a unique motivation: 'For once the "baddies" didn't want to take over the Earth, but just wanted to die. A new idea in *Doctor Who*. But then Peter Grimwade doesn't write conventional scripts.'

Yet another element in the mix is the return of Nicholas Courtney as the Brigadier – a popular move with many of the series' fans. '*Mawdryn Undead* was definitely the best [of the Guardian trilogy],' commented Andrew Evans in *A Voyage Through 25 Years of Doctor Who* dated December 1988, 'due in no small part to the fact that it marked the return to the programme after eight years of Nicholas Courtney as the Brigadier. What was rather difficult to swallow, however, was that he is now teaching mathematics in a boys' public school! Not exactly what one would have predicted for the former UNIT commander. It would have made more sense if he had turned up in a military academy.'

The inclusion of the Brigadier actually gives rise to perhaps the most hotly debated and criticised aspect of the story – that the dates specified in it are completely at odds with the fairly well established time frame in which the UNIT adventures of the second, third and fourth Doctors' eras took place. To recap briefly, season six's *The Invasion* was set about four years after season five's *The Web of Fear*, which in turn was set some forty years after the same season's *The Abominable Snowmen*, which was stated to have taken place in 1935. This means that the date in *The Invasion* must have been about 1979, which implies that the third Doctor's sojourn on Earth must have occurred in the early eighties. Sarah Jane Smith actually states in season thirteen's *Pyramids of Mars* that she comes from 1980 which, making allowances for possible imprecision on her part, more or less ties in with this. According to *Mawdryn Undead*, however, the Brigadier has already retired from UNIT and taken up a new career as a maths teacher by 1977. Simply put, this doesn't add up, and is probably the biggest continuity gaffe ever made in the series. Almost every other apparent discrepancy in the Doctor's adventures can be rationally explained away, but – unless, perhaps, one entertains the idea that the stories take place in slightly different parallel universes – the dating of *Mawdryn Undead* remains an intractable anomaly.

It is nevertheless good to see the Brigadier making a return to the series, and Nicholas Courtney gives an excellent performance in his unusual dual role. Of the other members of the guest cast the most notable by far is David Collings, whose casting as Mawdryn was inspired. Especially memorable are the scenes in which the character is seen blackened and bloodied from his experiences in the transmat capsule – a tribute, too, to the artistry of the make-up team, as is the later scene in which Tegan and Nyssa are subjected to rapid ageing.

Some reviewers have found *Mawdryn Undead*'s undeniable complexity a bit much to take. Richard Patey, another of those writing in *TARDIS* Volume 8 Number 1, was puzzled: 'Why was Turlough on Earth? What is the full story behind the mutants? Why did they wear pizzas on their heads? I can only assume that all will be answered later in the series.' Most, however, have been far more complimentary about the story. Paul West was particularly generous in his praise in *Shada* 14 dated March/April 1983: '*Mawdryn Undead* was a superb story, with good sets, particularly the spaceship, good acting from the main cast as well and a very good script from Peter Grimwade (*Time-Flight* must have been an off day for him). Inevitably there are parts of it I could nit-pick at, notably Nyssa's and Tegan's failure to notice that Mawdryn's burnt body wasn't a bit like the Doctor's, but despite this I feel everything came together to make this, without doubt, a classic *Doctor Who* story.'

Despite the overloading of the scripts, the story does ultimately work and is never less than enjoyable. A tribute, perhaps, to Peter Grimwade's skills as a writer.

TERMINUS

Writer: Steve Gallagher. **Director:** Mary Ridge. **Designer:** Dick Coles. **Costumes:** Dee Robson. **Make-Up:** Joan Stribling. **Incidental Music:** Roger Limb. **Fight Arranger:** John Waller. **Visual Effects:** Peter Pegrum. **Film Cameraman:** Remi Adefarasin. **Film Editor:** Frances Parker. **Studio Lighting:** Sam Barclay. **Studio Sound:** Scott Talbott. **Production Assistant:** Rena Butterwick. **Assistant Floor Manager:** Polly Davidson, Adrian Heywood.

	First UK TX	Scheduled TX	Actual TX	Duration	Viewers	Chart Pos.
Part One	15/02/83*	18.55*	18.55	24'58"	6.8	86
Part Two	16/02/83	18.45	18.46	24'40"	7.5	75
Part Three	22/02/83	18.55	18.55	24'39"	6.5	97
Part Four	23/02/83	18.45	18.46	24'49"	7.4	80

* The first UK transmission of this episode was in Wales, when it was scheduled at 18:45 on 14/02/83.

Plot: The TARDIS attaches itself to a space liner after Turlough, still under the Black Guardian's influence, damages its controls. The Doctor and Nyssa meet two space pirates, Kari and Olvir, who have come on board the liner in search of plunder, while Tegan and Turlough get lost in the infrastructure. The liner docks with what appears to be a hulk floating in space. This is Terminus, which claims to offer a cure for lazar disease. It is crewed by a group of armoured slave workers, the Vanir, while the cure is administered by a huge dog-like creature known as the Garm. Nyssa, who has contracted the disease from sufferers transported aboard the liner, discovers that the cure – involving exposure to radiation – does actually work. The Doctor and Kari meanwhile learn that the ship, once capable of time travel, was responsible for the creation of the universe when an ejection of fuel from one of its engines caused the 'big bang'. Aided by Kari and the Garm, the Doctor is able to disconnect a still active but damaged engine that is on the point of exploding – something that could result in the universe's destruction.

Episode endings:
1. As lazars emerge from sealed compartments and jostle their way through the corridors of the liner, Olvir hysterically shouts that this is a leper ship and they are all going to die.
2. An armoured Vanir, Valgard, drops the staff with which he has been attempting to choke

Kari and turns his attention instead to the Doctor, grasping him about the throat and stating that he is going to kill him.

3. Turlough, on the Black Guardian's instructions, sabotages some equipment aboard Terminus. In the control room, the effects are seen by the Doctor and Kari: an automatic sequence has begun to jettison fuel from the damaged engine. The Doctor tells Kari: 'If we don't do something quickly, the whole universe will be destroyed.'

4. Nyssa decides to part company with the Doctor and remain with the Vanir to help them run Terminus as a proper hospital. Turlough meanwhile is given an ultimatum by the Black Guardian: this is his last chance to kill the Doctor.

IT WAS MADE WHERE...?

Ealing Filming: 29.09.82-30.09.82 on stage 3B
Studio Recording: 11.10.82-12.10.82 in TC6, 25.10.82-27.10.82 in TC8, 18.12.82 (remount) in TC1

ADDITIONAL CREDITED CAST

Kari (Liza Goddard), Olvir (Dominic Guard), Black Guardian (Valentine Dyall), Inga (Rachel Weaver[1,3]), Tannoy Voice (Martin Muncaster[1,2,4]), Eirak (Martin Potter[2-4]), Valgard (Andrew Burt[2-4]), Sigurd (Tim Munro[2-4]), Bor (Peter Benson[2-4]), The Garm (R. J. Bell[2-4]).

POPULAR MYTHS

• This story was originally to have featured the Ice Warriors. (It wasn't.)

THINGS TO WATCH OUT FOR

• The set design work by Dick Coles is excellent
• There were two drone robots constructed for the story, but only one was seen on screen.
• Nyssa has a moving departure scene.

THINGS YOU MIGHT NOT HAVE KNOWN

• Kari and Olvir were not originally intended to be seen wearing their space helmets, but this plan was changed when the story was recorded. As they had not been designed to be worn, the masks steamed up, making it difficult for the actors to see, speak and breathe. Small holes were drilled in the front of them to try to alleviate this problem.
• Following transmission, the production office received a letter from Peter Osborne, the Marketing Sales Manager of Tannoy Ltd, complaining about the use of the credit 'tannoy voice' for the voice of the ship's computer. He pointed out that 'tannoy' was not a generic term but a registered trade mark referring to products manufactured by Tannoy Ltd.
• A letter of complaint was also received from David Stevenson MD, a senior lecturer at the Liverpool school of tropical medicine, regarding the depiction of leprosy in the story.

QUOTE, UNQUOTE

• **Bor:** [On discovering that he is not dead.] 'It's a relief. I am hoping for something rather better on the other side.'

Terminus is a story that, in theory, has quite a lot going for it. The idea that the universe was created due to the actions of a time-travelling spaceship is an ingenious and appealing one, reflecting writer Steve Gallagher's hard science-fiction influences; the Vanir are interesting and impressively costumed characters; and the Garm is an unusual and well realised 'monster'. What really lets it down, however, is its shortage of incident, coupled with its unremittingly grim atmosphere. 'This was the most disappointing story of the season for me,' wrote Andrew Claderbank in *TARDIS* Volume 8 Number 2 dated June 1983, echoing the views of many. 'The first two episodes were so slow that they almost went backwards; I was continually willing something to happen – but nothing did.' Peter G Lovelady, commenting in *Shada* 14 dated March/April 1983, suggested that the problem lay in the scripts:

'Gallagher's splitting up of the main characters so early on was really a double-edged sword – it was fine in the first episode but it left Tegan and Turlough trapped in the ship for three more episodes with little to do except escape two stages of sterilisation by miraculous chance ...

'It is acceptable (even desirable) to pace the first and possibly the second episodes slowly: but we then expect some acceleration and revelation. This Gallagher failed to deliver, which points [toward it being] too [insubstantial] a story.'

Alec Charles, however, felt that the blame for the story's failure rested elsewhere, as he explained in *Aggedor* Issue 4 in 1983: 'I think what really let *Terminus* down was the production and terrible acting – note how the best bits [were] those which featured the regulars in the TARDIS. The script ... was simply superb – and its message was present, but not intrusive.'

Neil Sadler, writing in *Cloister Bell* 6/7 in 1983, expressed dissatisfaction with the story's characters, and more particularly with the performances of the guest cast: 'Liza [Goddard's Kari served] as a companion [substitute] character, although goodness knows with three companions wandering about I would hardly have thought this necessary, and Goddard's ... acting was very poor, especially in comparison to Nerys Hughes's Todd who performed a similar function in last year's *Kinda*. Dominic Guard was similarly disappointing as Olvir (loved that pony-tail!) and it seemed a wasted opportunity not to pair him off with Nyssa at the end, which would have been the sole reason for having him in the serial. [Amongst] the Vanir the two major characters, Eirak and Valgard, were acted totally without any effort or commitment by Martin Potter and Andrew Burt and only Bor, a minor character, was well acted by Peter Benson.'

Even the story's best features and most interesting concepts have drawn criticism from some reviewers. Peter G Lovelady, for example, disliked the idea of the 'big bang' starting as an explosion of fuel from one of Terminus's engines: 'Okay, so the Black Guardian said it's not impossible to go meddling with time, but sending bombs back into the past must surely break all the rules. And then the Doctor says the fuel was jettisoned into a *void* which becomes the universe. Since Terminus was already in a universe it can't possibly have created its own. In my opinion the idea was just needlessly hyperbolic.' Andrew Calderbank was similarly unimpressed by the Garm: 'I can think of no *Doctor Who* monster that has terrified me less than the Garm ... Lightbulb eyes bug me.'

It must say something for the impact of the rest of the story that *Terminus*'s most well-remembered incident is one in which Nyssa, for no apparent reason at all, suddenly removes her skirt. Guy Clapperton recalled this with amusement in *Aggedor* Issue 4 in 1983: '"So there I am in this spaceship at the centre of the universe surrounded by lepers – and suddenly nearly all my clothes fall off! But it's all done in the best possible taste!" Was that a quote from Kenny Everett or Sarah Sutton? As it happens, it's a quote from me, because I just made it up, but it could have been either. Nyssa's loss of costume was a cheap gimmick to get the lads watching what was otherwise a pretty drab story.'

'The climax to the story was non-existent,' wrote Neil Sadler, 'and the inclusion of the nonsense about the beginning and end of the universe was the work of a decidedly desperate author. The leaving of Nyssa and the end with the Black Guardian finished off the story on a high note but the rest ... was slow and completely unoriginal.'

Harsh words, perhaps, but on the whole *Terminus* does unfortunately deserve its poor reputation.

ENLIGHTENMENT

Writer: Barbara Clegg. **Director:** Fiona Cumming. **Designer:** Colin Green. **Costumes:** Dinah Collin. **Make-Up:** Jean Steward, Carolyn Perry. **Incidental Music:** Malcolm Clarke. **Visual Effects:** Mike Kelt. **Film Cameraman:** John Walker, Paul Hellings-Wheeler. **Film Editor:** Mitchell Boyd, Ian McKendrick. **Studio Lighting:** Fred Wright. **Studio Sound:** Martin Ridout. **Production Assistant:** Pat O'Leary. **Assistant Floor Manager:** Val McCrimmon, Ian Tootle.

	First UK TX	Scheduled TX	Actual TX	Duration	Viewers	Chart Pos.
Part One	01/03/83	18.55	18.55	24'12"	6.6	89
Part Two	02/03/83	18.45	18.46	24'23"	7.2	76
Part Three	08/03/83	18.55	18.55	24'38"	6.2	99
Part Four	09/03/83	18.45	18.46	24'34"	7.3	68

Plot: The White Guardian warns of impending danger and directs the TARDIS to what appears to be an Edwardian sailing yacht, the *SS Shadow*, but is actually one of a number of spaceships taking part in a race through the solar system, the prize being Enlightenment. The yacht's Captain Striker and his fellow officers are Eternals who feed off the thoughts and emotions of their kidnapped human crew – Ephemerals – in order to fill their own empty existences. Turlough attempts to escape the Black Guardian's influence by jumping into space but is rescued and taken on board the ship of Captain Wrack – another of the Eternals. Two of the other ships in the race are destroyed and Turlough discovers that this has been brought about by Wrack using a concentrated beam of mental energy with the aid of the Black Guardian. The Doctor boards Wrack's ship, finds her source of power and, with Turlough's help, ejects her and her number two, Mansell, into space. The Doctor and Turlough then pilot the ship into port – a glowing crystalline structure hanging in space – and, in doing so, win the race. The White Guardian offers a portion of Enlightenment to Turlough, while the Black Guardian demands that the boy give the Doctor over to him in exchange for a huge diamond within a glowing artifact – apparently the prize. Turlough makes his choice: he sweeps the crystal from the table straight toward the Black Guardian, who vanishes in flames. The boy is now free, as Enlightenment was not in fact the crystal but the choice.

Episode endings:

1. The time travellers make their way to the bridge of the *SS Shadow* where they discover that they are not on a yacht at all. They are on – literally – a space ship.

2. The Doctor and his friends are given spacesuits and taken out onto the deck of Striker's ship. Turlough hears the Black Guardian threatening him in his mind. Desperate to escape, he climbs over the deck railing and prepares to jump overboard. The Doctor shouts: 'No!'

3. The Doctor, Tegan and Striker's first mate Marriner accept an invitation to attend a party aboard Captain Wrack's ship. During the party, Wrack freezes Tegan in time and places in her tiara a red crystal that will act as a focus for her power and ensure the destruction of Striker's ship. Wrack laughs as she relishes the prospect of the Doctor's destruction.

4. The White Guardian fades from sight. Turlough wants to return to his home planet and the Doctor agrees to take him there.

IT WAS MADE WHERE...?

Ealing filming: 03.11.82-05.11.82 on Stage 3B
Model effects: 08.11.82-12.11.82 on Model Stage, BBC Visual Effects Workshop
Studio Recording: 17.01.83-18.01.83, 30.01.83-02.02.83 all in TC1, around 07.02.83 (gallery only) (studio unknown)

ADDITIONAL CREDITED CAST

Striker (Keith Barron), Black Guardian (Valentine Dyall), White Guardian (Cyril Luckham[1,4]), Marriner (Christopher Brown), Jackson (Tony Caunter[1-3]), Collier (Clive Kneller[1]), First Officer (James McClure[1,2]), Wrack (Lynda Baron[3,4]), Mansell (Leee John[3,4]).

THINGS TO WATCH OUT FOR

- Valentine Dyall and Cyril Luckham reprise their roles as the Black and White Guardians from the sixteenth season stories *The Ribos Operation* and *The Armageddon Factor* respectively.
- The Doctor swaps his stick of Castrovalvan celery for a stick of Eternal (and presumably therefore similarly illusory) celery.
- Leee John, who plays Mansell here, was the lead singer with the pop group Imagination at the time this story was recorded.

THINGS YOU MIGHT NOT HAVE KNOWN

- Working title: *The Enlighteners*. This was changed at the suggestion of the production team.
- Dolore Whiteman, who played Tegan's Aunt Vanessa in the fourth Doctor's final story *Logopolis*, was hired for a special photocall on 18 October 1982 to provide the photograph that Tegan finds in her cabin on *SS Shadow*.
- Striker and Mansell were originally to have been played by, respectively, Peter Sallis and David Rhule, who did actually start rehearsals, with recording scheduled for 16.11.82-17.11.82 and 30.11.82-02.12.82. The making of the story was then delayed by industrial action, however, and as they were unable to make the new dates Keith Barron and Leee John were brought in instead.
- The incidental music used for Wrack's party was originally written by Malcolm

Clarke for *Borges at 80* and can be found on the Radiophonic Workshop's 'Soundhouse' LP. The track is called 'The Milonga'.
- The story was found to be running short during rehearsals, so an additional one and a half minutes was written for Part One and an additional two minutes for Part Two.
- Striker's ship was unnamed in the original scripts, but a name had to be created for use on the crew's jerseys, uniforms and life belts.

- **Marriner:** [To Tegan] 'You won't try to run away again, will you? Please. You see, I find you fascinating … quite fascinating.'
- **Striker:** 'You are not an Ephemeral. You are a … a time dweller. You travel in time.' **The Doctor:** 'You're reading my thoughts.' **Striker:** 'You are a Time Lord. A lord of time. Are there lords in such a small domain?' **The Doctor:** 'And where do you function?' **Striker:** 'Eternity … the endless wastes of eternity.'
- **Striker:** 'Superior beings do not punish inferiors … We use them … kindly.'
- **White Guardian:** [Speaking of the Black Guardian.] 'Be vigilant, Doctor. Once you denied him the Key to Time, now you have thwarted him again. He will be waiting for the third encounter, and his power does not diminish. … While I exist, he exists also … until we are no longer needed.'

ANALYSIS

'*Enlightenment* was … the one story in the twentieth season that I could watch time and time again,' wrote Carole Noble in *TARDIS* Volume 8 Number 2 dated June 1983. 'There have not been many stories from *Doctor Who* I could make that comment about'. Martin Day, on the other hand, left readers of the same magazine in no doubt that he was distinctly unimpressed: 'I thought *Terminus* was one of the worst [John Nathan-Turner] productions, but … *Enlightenment* [was] ten times worse! This story was absolute rubbish, and I find it difficult [to find] words strong enough to describe it. The story ended up on a par with such tripe as *Destiny of the Daleks* and is the worst story I have ever had the displeasure to see, my viewing spanning from the Pertwee era … In fact, *Enlightenment* was so bad it made *The Horns of Nimon* seem worthy of an Oscar and was, to put it bluntly, the worst *Doctor Who* story *ever*!'

Viewed today, *Enlightenment* hardly seems the sort of story to attract such extremes of contrasting opinion. It is a well-made, entertaining diversion centring around the charming, almost whimsical notion of a race around the solar system by loftily powerful beings using spacecraft that look like sailing ships. It is this fantastic image that is the most memorable aspect of the story, as Justin Richards noted in *Aggedor* Issue 4 in 1983: 'We can share with Tegan the spectacle of the ships spread out across space at the end of Part [One], as she looks out from the deck of the *Shadow*; a scene repeated in all its impressive magnificence at the start of the [second] episode.' If the Eternals' ships had been merely sleek rockets, or even a motley collection of different craft (rather like an outer space version of *Wacky Races*), then the impact would have been nowhere near as great. As it is, a sense of grandeur is achieved and the concept is both bold and strangely beautiful.

The Eternals are fascinating characters, being creepy and frightening but at the same time rather sad and pathetic with their reliance on 'Ephemerals' to give substance to their otherwise barren lives. The biggest impression is made by Marriner, excellently portrayed by Christopher Brown. 'His performance did not falter at any point,' wrote Matthew Prince in *Cloister Bell* 6/7 in 1983. 'He was perhaps the most convincing of them all ... I could [almost] *feel* him searching the reluctant ... Tegan's mind, and his voice was perfect. His best scenes were with Tegan.' Keith Barron's reserved and thoughtful Striker also comes over well, and certainly far better than does Lynda Baron's hideously overacted Wrack, who is a total pantomime villain complete with leather boots and thigh-slapping enthusiasm. Even Wrack has had her admirers, however, including Gareth Roberts in *DWB* No. 111 dated March 1993: 'Lynda Baron's appearance as the curvaceous Captain Wrack ... is unquestionably the best thing about the story. Her delicious address to camera at the cliffhanger [at the end of Part Three] is her finest moment, although her delivery of the line "You are remarkable in other ways, Doctor, for an Ephemeral," deserves a mention. She's also a dirty cheat whose vacuum shield has a big ON and OFF switch obviously taken from the mind of a *Space: 1999* set designer. The Wrack scenes are also hugely entertaining, unlike some of the series' later forays into the dangerous domain of low camp.' Even the most generous of reviewers, though, would be hard pressed to find anything good to say about the performance of Leee John, lead singer of the eighties pop group Imagination, as Mansell; the only consolation is that he is mercifully left in the background for much of the story and given little to do.

The only really disappointing aspect of *Enlightenment* is that it provides a somewhat lame conclusion to the 'Guardian trilogy'. In the end, the whole thing apparently hangs on whether or not Turlough chooses to sell the Doctor out by taking a glowing crystal. The two Guardians are seen together for the first time – ruling out one possible interpretation of the end of *The Armageddon Factor*, that they are two aspects of the same entity – and the Black Guardian is ultimately banished in flames as Turlough rejects the crystal. But so what? What's to stop him simply trying again? And, perhaps most puzzling of all, why does each of the Guardians wear a dead bird on his head?

THE KING'S DEMONS

Writer: Terence Dudley. **Director:** Tony Virgo. **Designer:** Ken Ledsham. **Costumes:** Colin Lavers. **Make-Up:** Elizabeth Rowell, Frances Hannon. **Incidental Music:** Jonathan Gibbs, Peter Howell. **Lute Player:** Jacob Lindberg. **Fight Arranger:** John Waller. **Visual Effects:** Tony Harding. **Film Cameraman:** Remi Adefarasin. **Film Editor:** Mike Rowbotham. **Studio Lighting:** Peter Smee. **Studio Sound:** Martin Ridout. **Production Assistant:** Sue Upton. **Assistant Floor Manager:** Sue Hedden.

	First UK TX	Scheduled TX	Actual TX	Duration	Viewers	Chart Pos.
Part One	15/03/83	18.55	18.55	24'48"	5.8	107
Part Two	16/03/83	18.45	18.47	24'27"	7.2	66

Plot: The TARDIS materialises in 13th Century England during a joust held in the presence of King John. The King welcomes the Doctor, Tegan and Turlough as his 'demons', but his actions toward the family of his host Ranulf fitz William are decidedly hostile. The Doctor discovers that what appears to be the King is in fact a shape-changing android called Kamelion whom the

Master found on Xeriphas. The Master has disguised himself as the King's Champion, Sir Gilles Estram, and is using Kamelion in a plot to discredit the King and prevent the signing of the Magna Carta, thereby changing the course of history. The Doctor manages to wrest control of Kamelion away from the Master, exposing his arch enemy's scheme.

Episode endings:

1. Sir Gilles's face blurs and changes into the more familiar visage of the Master, who aims his tissue compression eliminator at the Doctor.
2. To Turlough's surprise and Tegan's dismay, the Doctor accepts Kamelion as a new travelling companion aboard the TARDIS. Tegan insists that she does not wish to be returned home, however, and the Doctor admits that the co-ordinates are already set for the Eye of Orion.

IT WAS MADE WHERE...?

Location Filming: 05.12.82-07.12.82
Location: Bodiam Castle, Bodiam, East Sussex.
Studio Recording: 19.12.82-20.12.82, 16.01.83 all in TC1

ADDITIONAL CREDITED CAST

The Master (Anthony Ainley), Ranulf (Frank Windsor), The King (Gerald Flood*), Isabella (Isla Blair), Hugh (Christopher Villiers), Sir Geoffrey (Michael J. Jackson), Jester (Peter Burroughs[1]).

* Gerald Flood also provided, uncredited, the voice of Kamelion in Part Two.
Note: In order to conceal the fact that the Master featured in this story the *Radio Times* credited him as Sir Gilles Estram played by James Stoker – 'Estram' being an anagram of 'Master' and 'James Stoker' being an anagram of 'Master's joke'.

THINGS TO WATCH OUT FOR

- This story's excellent guest cast includes: Frank Windsor, well known as Sergeant Watt in *Z Cars* and its *Softly, Softly* spin-offs; distinguished stage and television actress Isla Blair; and Gerald Flood, popular amongst telefantasy fans for his roles in early sixties ABC serials such as *Pathfinders in Space* and its sequels, amongst many other programmes.
- *The King's Demons* marks the debut appearance of short-lived new 'companion' Kamelion. Kamelion was a computer controlled, sound activated, animated robot created by software designer Mike Power and computer hardware expert Chris Padmore. Padmore was a colleague of freelance designer Richard Gregory, and during recording of *Earthshock*, for which Gregory had supplied the newly designed Cyberman costumes, Gregory approached John Nathan-Turner to see whether he would be interested in featuring the robot in the series. Nathan-Turner agreed. Unfortunately Kamelion's limitations quickly became apparent: a period of nearly two weeks was reportedly required to program in the speech for each episode; the robot was unable to walk; and it became subject to numerous internal BBC union demarcation issues. Unfortunately, Mike Power was killed in a boating accident shortly after it had been decided to include the robot in the series, and no-one else had the technical knowledge to build and maintain the software to run it. As a result,

Kamelion was effectively written out of the series until season twenty-one's *Planet of Fire*, when the Doctor destroyed it for good.

- The sword fight between the Doctor and the Master was performed by Peter Davison and Anthony Ainley themselves, with no stuntmen involved. The fight was choreographed by John Waller.
- The song in praise of war had lyrics by Terence Dudley and music by Peter Howell and was sung by Gerald Flood. Both verses featured in Part One, and the first was also sung in Part Two. The lyrics were as follows:

> We sing in praise of total war
> Against the Saracen we abhor
> To free the tomb of Christ the Lord
> We'll put the known world to the sword
>
> There is no glory greater than
> To serve with gold the son of Man
> No riches here on Earth shall see
> No scutage in Eternity

THINGS YOU MIGHT NOT HAVE KNOWN

- Working title: *The Android*.
- Part One of this story was promoted by the BBC as the sixth hundredth *Doctor Who* episode.
- Following the second episode of *The King's Demons*, a special advertising trailer was transmitted for the forthcoming *Doctor Who* celebration at Longleat House in Wiltshire. The trailer consisted of a voice-over and the following clips: Hartnell title sequence from *100,000 BC*; Troughton title sequence from *The Krotons*; first Pertwee title sequence from *Carnival of Monsters*; second Baker title sequence from *Logopolis*; Davison title sequence from *Castrovalva*; and the *Doctor Who* logo from the Davison title sequence. This was actually a compilation of two pre-existing trailers: one for *The Five Faces of Doctor Who* repeat season of 1981 and one for *Castrovalva*.
- Peter Howell was originally to have composed all the incidental music for this story but, due to commitments on the BBC's radiophonic drama *Inferno Revisited*, he was in the end able to complete only the lute music, which was played in studio by Jakob Lindberg. The rest of the story's incidental music was composed by Jonathan Gibbs, a newcomer to the Radiophonic Workshop staff. A musician named Tim Barry was hired to play the drums for this.
- The stuntmen in the joust scenes were Brian Bowes and Nick Wilkinson.

QUOTE, UNQUOTE

- **The King:** 'Do our demons come to visit us?'
- **Ranulf:** [Speaking of Sir Gilles Estram] 'He is said to be the best swordsman in France.' **The Doctor:** 'Well, fortunately, we are in England.'
- **The Master:** 'Oh my dear Doctor, you have been naïve.'

FIFTH DOCTOR

The closing story of the twentieth season is just as disappointing as the opening one, and for basically the same reason: it is another case of style being given precedence over content.

The period settings and costumes as usual look wonderful, and the excellent cast give uniformly good performances. The location work is also extremely effective and pleasant on the eye. 'It was a lovely production – the jousting, feasting and lute playing were all captivating,' commented Saul Nassé in *TARDIS* Volume 8 Number 2 dated June 1983. 'It was really rather a shame that there had to be a story, and the Master (*so* obvious with one glance!) rather intruded on the atmosphere ... These "historical" two-parters provide a welcome break from the other, more science-fictiony stories.'

This is the nub of the problem: the Master seems to have been shoe-horned into a story in which he does not really belong, and the rather feeble rationale offered for his presence is highly unconvincing. Why should the Master be interested in preventing the signing of the Magna Carta? Even the Doctor is moved to comment that this is small-time villainy by his standards, which is almost tantamount to giving an on-screen admission of the story's limitations. 'As always the Master had nothing to do,' complained Paul Dixon in the same issue of *TARDIS*, 'and once again we arrived when his plans were precisely nowhere, no grand plots, alliances with spectacular enemies or partially successful intergalactic schemes like the ones in *Frontier in Space*. To those people who will write the next Master stories a word in your ear about his plans: "Big is beautiful".' Robert Shearman, reviewing the story in *Cloister Bell* 6/7 in 1983, was also dissatisfied with the way in which the Master was presented: 'Why was the Master dressed up as Sir Gilles Estram (geddit?) [when, as in *Time-Flight*,] he had no reason [to disguise himself]? Once he had done that shimmering effect and changed into [his usual appearance] (how does he do that anyway, and if he can do it why can't the Doctor?) it didn't make much difference to the 13th Century characters. [And] why did Sir Gilles have such an abominable French accent?'

As with many of the earlier stories set in Earth's past, questions have been raised about the historical accuracy of *The King's Demons*. 'It is one thing to realise that Bad King John might not have been so bad after all,' noted Alec Charles, again in *TARDIS* Volume 8 Number 2. 'It is a totally different thing to claim that he wanted Magna Carta – and the Doctor's prattle about Magna Carta being at the base of our modern "democratic" system seems very unfounded. It appears that Terence Dudley skipped rather a lot of research work for this unrealistic two-parter. Magna Carta was in no way the long charter of general social liberties that the Doctor seems to think it was ... The presentation of the baron as being a good guy in *The King's Demons* is also far from realistic.' Guy Clapperton, however, offered a rather different opinion in *Shada* 15 dated May/June 1983: 'The Doctor's disagreement with the textbook view of King John was interesting, and the link with the theory at the time that John himself was a demon gave the whole thing a well-researched feel.'

On one level *The King's Demons* is just an introductory vehicle for Kamelion but, as the android is hardly one of the most welcome or successful additions ever made to the series, this isn't really enough to satisfy. 'The whole story just seemed to dissolve into chaos,' suggested Johnathan L Pinkney in *Aggedor* Issue 4 in 1983, 'with the introduction of Kamelion, a C-3PO look-, sound- and act-alike, and no doubt a would-be K9-like problem solver.'

Guy Clapperton, however, had some fair points to make in the story's defence: 'There will be many writers who will say that this story was a comedown after *Enlightenment* and should not have finished off the twentieth season of *Doctor Who*. In a way this statement is perfectly justified, but it must be borne in mind that *The King's Demons* was not intended as a big finish, it was a prelude to the next story – shelved due to an electricians' strike. This is made obvious by the unambitious plot and the fact that it was only two parts long. When ... these factors [are considered] the story stands up quite well as entertainment, although it can never have a place amongst the classics.'

Production of the latter half of the twentieth season had been badly affected by industrial action on the part of BBC electricians. This had disrupted a planned remount day for *Terminus* and the studio sessions for *Enlightenment*, necessitating rescheduling in order to complete them. The original intention of the production team had been that the season should conclude with an Eric Saward-written four-part anniversary story entitled *The Return*, featuring the Daleks and Davros. The net effect of all these earlier problems, however, was that there was no longer any studio time available for this story to be recorded. Consequently it had to be temporarily shelved (eventually to be revamped as *Resurrection of the Daleks* the following year), leaving the season to close prematurely with *The King's Demons*. This was not quite the end of *Doctor Who*'s twentieth anniversary celebrations on air, however, as later in the year it would be back again for a one-off special ...

TWENTIETH ANNIVERSARY SPECIAL

John Nathan-Turner started thinking as early as the summer of 1981 about the possibility of celebrating *Doctor Who*'s twentieth anniversary with a special story. His initial proposal was that the transmission of season twenty should be brought forward to the autumn of 1982, and that of season twenty-one to the autumn of 1983, so that such a story could be slotted into the running order of the latter to coincide with the anniversary date of 23 November. This was rejected by his superiors, but Controller of BBC1 Alan Hart suggested instead that a one-off ninety minute programme might be produced to mark the anniversary. As plans for this developed, Nathan-Turner and Eric Saward decided that they wanted a story featuring all five television Doctors to date as well as numerous companions and monsters. One early consideration was how to include the first Doctor, in view of the fact that William Hartnell had died in 1975. It was concluded that the best option would be to recast the part; the actor eventually chosen was Richard Hurndall, whom Nathan-Turner had seen in an episode of *Blake's 7* and considered to resemble Hartnell.

Robert Holmes was the production team's first choice of writer to script the special. He drafted some possible scenarios for their consideration and then worked on a scene breakdown under the title *The Six Doctors* (reflecting the fact that the version of the first Doctor seen here would have been revealed at the end to be an android duplicate constructed by the Cybermen). This was eventually abandoned, and in November 1982 Terrance Dicks was commissioned to script a replacement story under the new title *The Five Doctors*.

One difficulty faced by the production team and writer was that, while both Patrick Troughton and Jon Pertwee readily agreed to appear in the special, Tom Baker eventually turned down the invitation. To ensure that the fourth Doctor was still represented in the programme, Nathan-Turner arranged for the incorporation of some scenes from *Shada*, the seventeenth season story that had been abandoned part-completed due to industrial action and never transmitted.

Nathan-Turner was keen to have each Doctor accompanied by at least one of his original companions. The initial intention was to team Susan (Carole Ann Ford) with the first Doctor, Victoria (Deborah Watling) with the second, Jo (Katy Manning) with the third, Sarah (Elisabeth Sladen) with the fourth and, naturally enough, Tegan (Janet Fielding) and Turlough (Mark Strickson) with the fifth. Watling and Manning ultimately proved to be unavailable, however, so in the event Sarah was paired with the third Doctor and the Brigadier (Nicholas Courtney) with the second. Dicks also wrote in 'cameo appearances' by four other companions – Liz Shaw (Caroline John), Captain Yates (Richard Franklin), Jamie (Frazer Hines) and Zoe (Wendy Padbury) – who were confirmed only at a very late stage.

Nathan-Turner's initial choice of director for *The Five Doctors* was Waris Hussein, who had handled the series' first story, *100,000 BC*, back in 1963. Hussein turned the offer down, however, and Peter Moffatt was then given the assignment instead. Filming and studio recording for the special was carried out during March 1983.

Nathan-Turner had hoped that the special would be transmitted in the UK on the actual anniversary date, 23 November. This was not to be, however, as scheduling problems caused Hart to move it back to Friday 25 November, when it went out as a part of the annual *Children in Need* telethon fronted by presenter Terry Wogan. In some UK regions captions were run across the bottom of the screen during the transmission giving updates on the amounts of money pledged by viewers. *The Five Doctors* was actually premiered in Chicago, USA, on 23 November, making it the first *Doctor Who* story ever to receive its initial screening outside the UK.

THE FIVE DOCTORS

Producer: John Nathan-Turner. **Script Editor:** Eric Saward. **Production Associate:** June Collins. **Title Music:** Ron Grainer and the BBC Radiophonic Workshop, arranged by Peter Howell. **Special Sounds:** Dick Mills. **Writer:** Terrance Dicks. **Director:** Peter Moffatt. **Designer:** Malcolm Thornton. **Costumes:** Colin Lavers. **Make-Up:** Jill Hagger. **Incidental Music:** Peter Howell. **Visual Effects:** John Brace. **Film Cameraman:** John Baker. **Film Editor:** M A C Adams. **Studio Lighting:** Don Babbage. **Studio Sound:** Martin Ridout. **Production Assistant:** Jean Davis. **Assistant Floor Manager:** Pauline Seager.

First UK TX	Scheduled TX	Actual TX	Duration	Viewers	Chart Pos.
25/11/83	19.20	19.20	90'23"	7.7	54

Plot: The fifth Doctor and his past incarnations are taken out of time by a forbidden time scoop device. The fourth Doctor becomes trapped in the vortex but the others find themselves, together with a number of their old companions, in the Death Zone on their home planet Gallifrey, facing a Dalek, a Yeti, a quicksilver Raston Warrior Robot and numerous Cybermen. Also present is the Master, who has been summoned by the High Council of Time Lords to help the Doctor. It turns out that President Borusa is the mysterious operator of the time scoop. He aims to use the Doctors to breach the defences of the Dark Tower – Rassilon's tomb – so that he can enter there and claim immortality. When he does so, however, he is condemned by Rassilon to eternal existence in the form of a living statue.

Episode endings:

1. Chancellor Flavia entreats the Doctor to stay on Gallifrey and take up his duties as Lord President. The Doctor gives her full deputy powers until he returns, then leaves with Tegan and Turlough in the TARDIS. Tegan cannot believe that the Doctor prefers to go on the run in a rackety old TARDIS. The Doctor, however, smiles and observes that that is how it all started.

IT WAS MADE WHERE...?

Location Filming: 15.10.79, 19.10.79 (*Shada* footage), 05.03.83, 07.03.83-11.03.83, 13.03.83-15.03.83, 17.03.83

Locations: Plas Brondanw, Llanfrothen, Penrhyndeudraeth, Gwynedd; Carreg Y Foel Gron, off B4407, nr Ffestiniog; Manod Quarry, Cwt Y Bugail, Ffestiniog; Cwm Bychan, nr Llanbedr, Gwynedd; Tilehouse Lane, Upper Denham, Bucks; MOD/YMCA Hostel, Hayling Lane, off Tilehouse Lane, Upper Denham, Bucks; 2 West Common Road, Uxbridge, Middlesex; Bus Stop, 15 North Common Road, Uxbridge, Middx; The Blacks, River Cam, Cambridge (*Shada* footage); Blackmoor Head Yard, Cambridge (*Shada* footage).

Ealing Filming: 18.03.83 (Stage unknown)

Studio Recording: 29.03.83-31.03.83

CAST

The Doctor (Peter Davison, Jon Pertwee, Patrick Troughton, Richard Hurndall, Tom Baker, William Hartnell), Tegan (Janet Fielding), Turlough (Mark Strickson), Sarah Jane Smith (Elisabeth Sladen), Susan (Carole Ann Ford), The Brigadier (Nicholas Courtney), Romana (Lalla Ward), The Master (Anthony Ainley), Lord President Borusa (Philip Latham), Chancellor Flavia (Dinah Sheridan), The Castellan (Paul Jerricho), Cyber Leader (David Banks), Cyber Lieutenant (Mark Hardy), Rassilon (Richard Mathews), Jamie (Frazer Hines), Zoe (Wendy Padbury), Liz Shaw (Caroline John), Captain Yates (Richard Franklin), Crichton (David Savile), Voice of K9 (John Leeson), Dalek Voice (Roy Skelton), Dalek Operator (John Scott Martin), Commander (Stuart Blake), Technician (Stephen Meredith), Sergeant (Ray Float), Guard (John Tallents), Cyber Scout (William Kenton), Raston Robot (Keith Hodiak).

POPULAR MYTHS

• The story was originally to have featured Omega. (This was never the intention.)

THINGS TO WATCH OUT FOR

• A clip of William Hartnell as the Doctor, taken from season two's *The Dalek Invasion of Earth: Flashpoint*, is used as an opening pre-titles sequence.

- Making their debut here are a new TARDIS control console and interior set.
- Jamie, Zoe, Liz Shaw and Captain Yates as seen in this story are only phantoms who – in scenes highly reminiscent of one in season nineteen's *Time-Flight* – try to dissaude the second and third Doctors from progressing through the Tower.
- The closing title music mixes Delia Derbyshire's sixties arrangement with Peter Howell's eighties one. This special one-off version was also Howell's work.

THINGS YOU MIGHT NOT HAVE KNOWN

- Working title: *The Six Doctors*. The outline version with this title was written by Robert Holmes.

QUOTE, UNQUOTE

- **Crichton:** 'What the blazes is going on? Who was that strange little man?' **Sergeant:** 'The Doctor.' **Crichton:** 'Who?'
- **The Fifth Doctor:** 'Great chunks of my past, detatching themselves like melting icebergs.'
- **The Castellan:** 'I am innocent. I have never seen that casket before.' **Borusa:** 'Take him to security and discover the truth. Commander, you are authorised to use the mind probe.' **The Castellan:** 'What? No, not the mind probe!'
- **The Brigadier:** [To the Doctors] 'Splendid fellows ... all of you.'

ANALYSIS

The idea of a celebratory story featuring all the Doctors to date was a good one when used in season ten's *The Three Doctors*. All good ideas can be taken too far, however, and this is exactly what happened when John Nathan-Turner and Eric Saward decided to commission *The Five Doctors*. The basic approach adopted by writer Terrance Dicks is the same as in that earlier story, only this time there are two more Doctors to fit in and, at the production team's request, numerous companions and old adversaries as well. The end result is not as bad as it could have been, thanks mainly to the fact that Dicks's simple catch-all script allowed for last minute chopping and changing of characters, depending on which actors happened to be available, while still retaining basically the same plot. Even so, the story fairly groans at the seams with the inclusion of so many 'old favourites'.

Saul Gething, writing in *TARDIS* Volume 8 Number 4 dated January 1984, felt that it was only partly successful: 'If the Doctors managed to get a chance to "strut their stuff" then I'm afraid I can't say the same about the various companions. In my opinion the talents of the performers who played them were wasted. I mean, what were they called upon to do apart from tripping over the odd rock or maybe at the very most knocking the Master out? Not a lot ... Tegan and Turlough would have been sufficient for the purposes of the story ... without the rest of them ...' Guy Clapperton also felt the story was a little 'Doctor heavy', as he explained in the same issue of *TARDIS*: 'I couldn't help but wonder whether the Tom Baker footage was really necessary. Baker was conspicuous by his absence but then again that was hardly the fault of the production team. Nice to see Troughton and Pertwee back in action – bits of it were a real joy, such as the second Doctor's comment about Colonel Crichton – "Well, my replacement didn't look too promising either" – and Pertwee's description of Baker – "All teeth and curls?". Richard Hurndall was a perfectly adequate first Doctor in much the same way that Anthony Ainley is a good Master – we can't have the originals so there's no point criticising the newer versions for not being exactly as we remember them. Hurndall gave a good performance and the casual (particularly younger) viewer would be quite convinced that he was watching the first Doctor.'

Clapperton may well have been right in suggesting that the Hurndall version of the first Doctor would pass muster with the casual viewer, although anyone familiar with the William Hartnell version would quickly spot that there is actually little more than a passing similarity between the two (as the opening pre-titles clip of Hartnell only serves to emphasise). His comments about Anthony Ainley's Master, on the other hand, overlook the fact that there was never any need for him to have resembled Roger Delgado's original in the first place; just as the Doctor had acquired a new appearance and personality each time he regenerated, so too could the Master have done. At least, though, the Master is given something worthwhile to do in this story. Particularly memorable are the amusing scenes in which he tries, in vain, to convince one or other of the Doctors that he is for once actually trying to help him. Ainley's performance went down well with L Bradick, again writing in *TARDIS* Volume 8 Number 4: 'Thank goodness Anthony Ainley was given decent lines, so that he could prove that *Time-Flight* and *The King's Demons* were not his fault. In fact, in the scene where he enters the High Council room he reminded me very much of Roger Delgado.'

Aside from the Master, the main villains threatening the Doctors in their mission to reach the Dark Tower are the Cybermen. Andrew Ruddick, another of those expressing their views in *TARDIS*, disliked the way in which they were depicted: '[John Nathan-Turner] has severely dented the image of the Cybermen. It made me furious. They were portrayed as mindless robots instead of their usual cool calculating selves. A whole squad were left shattered by the [Raston Robot]. Then they fell for an obvious trick, being blasted down on the board in the Tower after the Master had enticed them to cross over. To add insult to injury even the Cyber Leader was caught off guard by the Master and destroyed. It was very sad to see the Cybermen's reputation tarnished.' Ian Kildin, writing in *Eye of Horus* Issue 5 dated March 1984, had a very different point of view: 'I know it sounds rather sadistic but I loved the way the Raston Robot dispatched the Cyber patrol; this was probably the most graphic scene of mass killing ever in *Doctor Who*. It was incredibly realistic, [and] the way the lances shot from the Robot's arms was a superb piece of visual effects ... I could only feel sorry for the Cybermen; they didn't stand a chance. They were also ruthlessly tricked by the Master; a trick resulting in the annihilation of another group. The time scoop must have brought at least three Cyber Leaders to the Death Zone.' Justin Richards also felt that the Cybermen were a welcome element in the story, as he explained in *Shada: A Special* dated December 1983: 'The Cybermen ... were at their best ... At last we got the impression that there were more than eight or nine of them altogether. The Raston Warrior Robot, which almost looked silly, actually featured tremendously impressively, scything down Cybermen with great panache.'

There is arguably little point in trying to analyse *The Five Doctors* in great detail as the whole thing was really just an excuse to get everyone together for a celebration. Some of the Doctors and companions undoubtedly fare better than others, however, as Tim Munro commented in *DWB* No. 80 dated August 1990: 'Pat Troughton stole the show ... and probably kept Joe Public watching with his hilarious rudeness to Crichton and his misbehaviour in the tomb. Nicholas Courtney was on top form, trudging through the

Death Zone with world-weary trepidation. Elisabeth Sladen effortlessly rose above bland lines to retain her "best companion" crown, and Jon Pertwee's infectious zest diverted attention from his woefully uncharacteristic dialogue. Sadly, Carole Ann Ford was not so lucky. Faced with no written character, she had to improvise from very routine lines. Thus we get no idea whatsoever of how Susan had matured in her life on Earth – it was like a middle-aged woman playing a teenager! Another opportunity wasted.'

Perhaps the biggest problem, given that the story is touted (and titled) as featuring all five Doctors, is that only four of them actually take part in the main action – and one of these is, unavoidably, played by an actor other than the original. 'My only dislike,' wrote David Hamilton, also in *Eye of Horus* Issue 5, 'was the fact that Tom Baker was not seen as much as … the other Doctors. Surely there was more of the unseen *Shada* material that could have been used?' Perhaps, but then the plot would have had to have been made even more convoluted to accommodate the scenes from *Shada* that were available. And it must be borne in mind that, at least during the initial stages of plotting and scripting, Dicks was proceeding on the assumption that Baker would actually be appearing.

The Five Doctors, as the only example of a story produced out of season as a one-off special to celebrate an anniversary, remains something of an anomaly. As a celebration it works, but as a serious entry in the *Doctor Who* canon it fails to stand up to scrutiny.

DOCTOR WHO SEASON TWENTY-ONE (1984)

Regular Cast:

The Doctor (Peter Davison) until *The Caves of Androzani* Part Four
The Doctor (Colin Baker) from *The Twin Dilemma* Part One onwards
Tegan (Janet Fielding) until *Resurrection of the Daleks* Part Two
Turlough (Mark Strickson) until *Planet of Fire* Part Four
Peri (Nicola Bryant) from *Planet of Fire* Part One onwards

Regular Crew:

Producer: John Nathan-Turner.
Script Editor: Eric Saward.
Production Associate: June Collins.
Title Music: Ron Grainer and the BBC Radiophonic Workshop, arranged by Peter Howell.
Special Sounds: Dick Mills.

Season twenty-one, which again had John Nathan-Turner as producer and Eric Saward as script editor throughout, continued the previous year's theme of drawing on popular elements from the series' past. These included Davros and the Daleks in a revamped version of the story postponed due to industrial action; the Master; and, rather more surprisingly, two related monster races that had both made their debuts over ten years earlier during the era of the third Doctor ...

WARRIORS OF THE DEEP

Writer: Johnny Byrne. **Director:** Pennant Roberts. **Designer:** Tony Burrough. **Costumes:** Judy Pepperdine. **Make-Up:** Jennifer Hughes. **Incidental Music:** Jonathan Gibbs. **Visual Effects:** Mat Irvine. **OB Cameraman:** John Baker. **Studio Lighting:** Peter Smee. **Studio Sound:** Martin Ridout. **Production Assistant:** Norma Flint. **Assistant Floor Manager:** Adrian Hayward.

	First UK TX	Scheduled TX	Actual TX	Duration	Viewers	Chart Pos.
Part One	05/01/84	18.40	18.41	24'48"	7.6	51
Part Two	06/01/84	18.40	18.41	24'04"	7.5	52
Part Three	12/01/84	18.40	18.41	24'02"	7.3	74
Part Four	13/01/84	18.40	18.41	24'25"	6.6	87

Plot: The Doctor, Tegan and Turlough arrive at an underwater Sea Base on Earth, where a scientific and military team led by Commander Vorshak are monitoring a rival power bloc. The team undergo regular missile launch test sequences to ensure that they are ready at all times to combat an attack. Three Silurians led by Icthar – the surviving members of a Silurian triad –

revive a colony of Sea Devil Warriors in order to invade the base and use its weapons to attack the opposing power bloc, thus provoking a global war that will allow the reptiles to conquer the Earth. The Doctor uses ultra-violet light to destroy the reptiles' giant electrified sea beast, the Myrka, and suggests using hexachromite gas to kill the remaining invaders. He then links his own brain into the base's computer to prevent the firing of the missiles.

Episode endings:
1. The Doctor is knocked from a walkway in a struggle with some Sea Base guards and falls into the water tank below. Tegan wants to stay and try to rescue him but Turlough urges her to flee, telling her that she must face the fact that the Doctor has drowned. The Doctor's body lies motionless in the water below.
2. The Doctor and Tegan are trapped in an airlock as the Myrka forces its way in and advances towards them. Tegan exclaims that the creature is going to kill them.
3. The Sea Devil leader Sauvix shoots down Nilson, a member of the Sea Base team who has been traitorously working for the opposing power bloc, and then turns his weapon on the Doctor and Tegan, telling them: 'Your turn.'
4. With Silurians and Sea Devils lying dead all around him and his companions, the Doctor grimly comments that there should have been another way.

IT WAS MADE WHERE...?

OB Recording: 28.06.83
Location: Royal Engineers Diving Establishment, McMullen Barracks, Marchwood, nr Southampton, Hants.
Shepperton (OB) Recording: 29.06.83-30.06.83 stage A (water tank)
Visual Effects: 04.07.83-07.07.83 at BBC Visual Effects Workshop
Studio Recording: 23.06.83-24.06.83, 13.07.83-15.07.83 all in TC6, 18.07.83-19.07.83 (voice redubbing only) (studio unknown)

ADDITIONAL CREDITED CAST

Vorshak (Tom Adams), Solow (Ingrid Pitt[1-3]), Nilson (Ian McCulloch[1-3]), Bulic (Nigel Humphreys), Maddox (Martin Neil[1-3]), Preston (Tara Ward), Icthar (Norman Comer), Karina (Nitza Saul[1,2]), Scibus (Stuart Blake), Tarpok (Vincent Brimble), Sauvix (Christopher Farries), Paroli (James Coombes[1-3]).

THINGS TO WATCH OUT FOR

- *Warriors of the Deep* boasts some excellent modelwork, including that of the Sentinel Six defence satellite encountered by the TARDIS in Part One; the Sea Base; and the Silurian vessel.
- Gareth Milne doubles – very convincingly – for Peter Davison in the underwater swimming sequence in Part Two.
- Ian McCulloch, well known for his role as Greg in Terry Nation's BBC series *Survivors*, appears here as Nilson.
- Horror film star Ingrid Pitt plays Solow. She had previously appeared in *Doctor Who* as Queen Galleia in season nine's *The Time Monster*.

- The Myrka was played by two actors, William Perrie and John Asquith, who also played the pantomime horse in the BBC children's programme *Rentaghost*.
- In Johnny Byrne's original scripts, Icthar was the only Silurian to be named. The other two Silurians were referred to simply as 'First Companion' and 'Second Companion'.

QUOTE, UNQUOTE

- **Tegan:** 'What year are we in?' **The Doctor:** 'Around two thousand and eighty-four.' **Tegan:** 'Little seems to have changed since my time.' **The Doctor:** 'Absolutely nothing, Tegan. There are still two power blocs, fingers poised to annihilate each other.'
- **The Doctor:** 'I sometimes wonder why I like the people of this miserable planet so much.'
- **The Doctor:** 'There should have been another way.'

ANALYSIS

Warriors of the Deep is a classic case of well written scripts being let down by inappropriate production. The basic premise of a future Earth where two superpowers are facing off against one another with their respective arsenals of nuclear weapons poised to fire is an intriguing one with a great deal of promise. An added bonus is that writer Johnny Byrne astutely avoids identifying the two power blocs in conventional 20th Century terms. The plotting is also good, and the return of the Silurians and the Sea Devils is in principle welcome. Unfortunately, much of this potential is simply thrown away.

One of the most serious flaws is that the spacious, generally floodlit sets of Sea Base 4 give the viewer no sense of its location and engender none of the tension that would have been created had they been cramped and dark as Byrne had intended. 'The sets are simple and it shows,' bemoaned Charles Sandford in *Capitol Spires* Issue 2 dated July 1993. 'The main problem is that they appear too sterile and brightly lit and fail to give the impression of being under the sea. Perhaps if the [whole thing] had [had subdued lighting] it would have come across with rather more atmosphere. Also the evidence of seeing views through portholes would have lent more credibility to the base being under the sea. The only sets that truly work [are the interiors of] the Silurian ship, which because of subdued lighting [look] believable.'

The other major failing in the production is the realisation of the monsters. The Myrka looks simply terrible, and the scenes in which various members of the cast try desperately but unsuccessfully to appear afraid of it as it lumbers towards them at nothing more than a snail's pace are either deeply embarrassing or highly amusing, depending on the viewer's disposition. The new costumes designed for the Silurians and the Sea Devils are also not a patch on the originals and fail to impress – particularly as they are not always properly fitted to the actors inside. 'The Silurians and especially the Sea Devils seemed to have been redesigned for the hell of it,' protested Saul Nassé in *TARDIS* Volume 9 Number 1 in 1984. 'The sight of that hatted Sea Devil standing in the background, its head practically horizontal, will haunt me forever. The faces were completely static, which compounded the total lack of credibility. In short, this story destroyed the image of the Sea Devils/Silurians and was an insult to the memory of [their creator] Malcolm Hulke.' Charles Sandford had similar reservations: 'The Silurian costumes were dreadful and [made the creatures look] like what they were: men in rubber suits. As for the Sea

Devils, they all appeared to have a permanent crick in the neck! Why they were redesigned is a mystery to me as the originals were far superior. And as for the Myrka – it was about as frightening as Dobbin the Horse from *Rentaghost*; a near black-out would be the only thing that would have made this creation anywhere near believable.'

Quite apart from the design changes, there is the unfortunate fact that the Silurians' third eye now nonsensically flashes in synchronisation with their speech, whereas previously it had acted as a ray tool. The Sea Devil voice is thankfully the same as in their debut story, but the Silurians now speak in a kind of electronic monotone that is nowhere near as distinctive or appropriate as the voice heard in *Doctor Who and the Silurians*. The creatures now have names, too, whereas in their original outings they did not, and they actually refer to themselves as 'Silurians' and 'Sea Devils', whereas previously these had been simply descriptive (and inaccurate) terms assigned to them by other characters. And then there are some rather curious dialogue references to what seems to be an unseen prior encounter between the Doctor and the reptiles. Actually, this is not such a bad idea in principle – there is, after all, no reason to assume that all the Doctor's adventures have been seen on screen (a fact since exploited to good effect in ranges of 'missing adventure' novels, audio plays and novellas) – but here disappointment sets in when one learns that the writer and production team really intended these references to be continuity links back to the earlier transmitted stories; they just botched them so badly that it is not apparent to the viewer. All this raises an interesting question: why did the production team think it worth bringing back old monsters in the first place if they were going to do so with such a lack of care and attention that it simply sullied viewers' memories of the originals?

The performances from the other members of *Warriors of the Deep*'s guest cast are all sadly lacking in conviction – in some cases, in fact, completely wooden – and just to add to the story's problems there are some quite bizarre touches of direction from Pennant Roberts, such as in the scene where he has Ingrid Pitt as Solow making an almost surreal Kung Fu-style attack on the Myrka. The final reaction can only be one of great disappointment, as summed up by Frank Band, also writing in *TARDIS* Volume 9 Number 1: 'I'm afraid I didn't like this story at all. The plot and the characters all had a lot of potential but, in my opinion, not nearly enough was made of them. The moral issues surrounding the Siluarians' right to the planet, the Doctor's position and the entrenchment of the two opposing power blocs were all underplayed. Indeed I'm sure that anyone who didn't know the plot of *Doctor Who and the Silurians* and *The Sea Devils* would have wondered why the Doctor was making such a fuss about not killing them. The Silurians and the Sea Devils should have aroused our sympathy by themselves, through their words and actions; instead the Doctor half-heartedly encouraged everyone to have some respect for them, while they singularly failed to provide a good reason why anyone should.'

THE AWAKENING

Writer: Eric Pringle. **Director:** Michael Owen Morris. **Designer:** Barry Newbery. **Costumes:** Jackie Southern. **Make-Up:** Ann Ailes. **Incidental Music:** Peter Howell. **Visual Effects:** Tony Harding. **Film Cameraman:** Paul Wheeler. **Film Editor:** M A C

Adams. **Studio Lighting:** Peter Catlett. **Studio Sound:** Martin Ridout. **Production Assistant:** Rosemary Parsons. **Assistant Floor Manager:** Marcus D F White.

	First UK TX	Scheduled TX	Actual TX	Duration	Viewers	Chart Pos.
Part One	19/01/84	18.40	18.41	25'18"	7.9	61
Part Two	20/01/84	18.40	18.41	24'47"	6.6	84

Plot: An alien war machine, the Malus, is affecting the inhabitants of the English country village of Little Hodcombe in 1984 so that a re-enactment of a Civil War battle turns into the real thing. The Malus's aim is to gather sufficient psychic energy to activate itself fully. The TARDIS travellers arrive to meet Tegan's grandfather – one of the villagers – but become involved in the machinations of Sir George Hutchinson, who is in thrall to the Malus. The battle in 1643 becomes linked through time to 1984 and Will Chandler, a youth from the earlier time, finds himself in the present day. The Malus is defeated when Will pushes Sir George to his death.

Episode endings:
1. In the village church, the Doctor tells Will and school teacher Jane Hampden of the origins of the Malus. Suddenly a section of plaster falls from the wall. The Doctor pulls more of the surrounding plaster away to reveal a giant, green-eyed roaring demonic face. The Doctor is engulfed in smoke that emerges from its mouth.
2. The TARDIS dematerialises from the church, which is consumed in a huge explosion as the Malus is destroyed. The Doctor promises to drop the villagers off home and return Will to his own time. Tegan, however, suggests staying to spend some time with her grandfather. Outnumbered, the Doctor agrees. Turlough fancies a cup of tea. Will declares this to be 'an evil brew', but the Doctor replies that he quite likes it.

IT WAS MADE WHERE...?

Location Filming: 19.07.83-22.07.83
Locations: ford at Tarrant Monkton, nr Blandford Forum, Dorset; St Bartholomew's Church, Shapwick, nr Wimborne Minster, Dorset; village cross, opposite Anchor Inn, Shapwick; meadow near church, Shapwick, Dorset; Bishops Court Farm, Shapwick, Dorset; village of Martin, nr Fordingbridge, Hants; Martin Down, nr Martin, Hants; stable at rear of Damers Cottage, Martin, nr Fordingbridge, Hants.
Studio Recording: 04.08.83-06.08.83 in TC6, 12.08.83 (gallery only) (studio unknown)

ADDITIONAL CREDITED CAST

Jane Hampden (Polly James), Sir George (Denis Lill), Colonel Wolsey (Glyn Houston), Joseph Willow (Jack Galloway), Will Chandler (Keith Jayne), Trooper (Christopher Saul), Andrew Verney (Frederick Hall[2]).

POPULAR MYTHS

- *The Awakening* was originally written as a four-part story featuring the Daleks. (It wasn't.)

THINGS TO WATCH OUT FOR

- Polly James, one of the stars of *The Liver Birds*, appears here as Jane Hampden.

5 FIFTH DOCTOR

- There is a bravura performance from Keith Jayne as Will Chandler – arguably one of the most convincing and memorable companions the Doctor never had.
- *The Awakening* provided the last credit on the series for its longest-serving set designer Barry Newbery, who had handled the first story back in 1963 and many others since.

THINGS YOU MIGHT NOT HAVE KNOWN

- Working title: *War Game*.
- This story was commissioned and scripted as a four part adventure, incorrectly rumoured to have featured the Daleks, and reworked into a two part story at a later date.
- Two drummers were hired to appear on screen during the preparations for the May Queen ceremony in Part Two. These were referred to in BBC documentation as Drummer Tuite and Drummer Cooney.
- The scene in which the trooper is beheaded was edited slightly for transmission as the recorded version was considered too horrific.
- The mentions of the Terileptils mining tinclavic on the planet Raaga were added by script editor Eric Saward as a reference back to his own season nineteen story *The Visitation*.
- The part of Sir John Hutchinson (later changed to Sir George) was originally offered to Clifford Rose on 4 July 1983, but he turned it down as he couldn't ride a horse. The role was subsequently offered to an actor named Charles Kay, whom director Michael Owen Morris knew from *Fall of Eagles*, and also to Anthony Valentine, but neither accepted.
- The part of Andrew Verney was originally offered to Maurice Denham, who would appear later in the season as Azmael in *The Twin Dilemma*.
- John Horton was originally scheduled to handle the visual effects for this story, but on 3 June 1983 producer John Nathan-Turner wrote to Michealjohn Harris, Head of Visual Effects, requesting that he be replaced as there had been a 'clash of personalities' between Horton and director Michael Owen Morris on a previous production unrelated to *Doctor Who*.
- This story was scripted to have included a scene in the TARDIS with Kamelion, but this was edited out of the final programme due to the episode overrunning.

QUOTE, UNQUOTE

- **Sir George:** 'The tradition must continue. Something is coming to our village. Something very wonderful and strange.'
- **Turlough:** 'We're running out of places to run.' **Tegan:** 'It's the story of our lives.'

ANALYSIS

Considering that *The Awakening* is only a two-part adventure there is an awful lot packed into it; and indeed it comes across as being one of the more substantial stories of the season. It falls firmly into the same pseudo-historical category as *The Time Meddler*, *The Time Warrior* and *The Visitation*, and is one of the best examples of this story type. 'From start to finish *The Awakening* positively reeked of class,' enthused Saul Nassé in *TARDIS* Volume 9 Number 1 in 1984. 'Whilst the script obviously had its roots in *The Dæmons*, it had plenty of new ideas, and stood up well against the classic. The look was terrific, apart from the initial model shot. The larger Malus was especially excellent: it conveyed more menace than an army of plastic Sea Devils. It was good having so much of the story on film, which almost guarantees that "real" feeling.'

The idea of the threat to the village being an alien war machine was a nice twist on the familiar 'alien invasion' scenario, as was the concept of the creature (if it can be properly described as such) being able to create links through time and mix up past and present so as to obtain enough psychic power to become fully active. The other guest characters in the story are also strong and well acted, and special praise must go to Keith Jayne, who manages to convey a kind of childlike innocence in his excellent portrayal of Will. 'Keith Jayne's Will Chandler and Polly James's Jane Hampden made for extremely amiable companions,' commented Mark Willis in *Zygon* Issue 1 dated August 1984, 'and did an effective job in eclipsing Fielding's and Strickson's regulars for this viewer. Given more screen time, I'm convinced Polly James would have been able to develop Jane to the admirable extent that her fellow ex-Liver Bird did … Todd in *Kinda*. Glyn Houston was an amiable Colonel Wolsey, and while both Denis Lill and Jack Galloway went notably OTT this never really endangered the production's success; Joseph Willow's "No recriminations", I'll-be-a-good-boy-now bit was rather strained, however.'

Another much-praised element of the story is its lavish visuals. 'The design of this story [was] excellent …,' wrote an uncredited reviewer in *Capitol Spires* Issue 1 dated spring 1993. 'The interior of the church [was] the pinnacle of excellence, but it should be mentioned that the other sets were [also] realistic and believable. My only gripe must be the Malus in the church, which was not as frightening or plausible as it could have been, … slightly letting the story down. The locations chosen were again superb and the village really echoed the storyline of a lazy summer afternoon.'

Given that the scripts called for the Malus to appear as a vast demonic face, the image seen on screen is actually a pretty fair representation of this. Also effective is the smaller Malus projection that manifests itself on a number of occasions, including at one point clinging to the interior wall of the TARDIS. *The Awakening* actually has quite a strong horror content, particularly for this period of the series' history. The projections of soldiers from the past are eerie and disturbing, good use being made of lighting and sound effects to give them a threatening appearance. The scene in which a trooper is beheaded by three of the phantoms is gruesome enough to make even the most hardened of viewers wince, and serves to emphasise just how dangerous the Malus is.

On the downside, the action is occasionally a little too rushed, and it seems rather implausible that the other villagers would simply go along with Sir George when he decides to have all roads to the village blocked off (this story's rather more prosaic equivalent of *The Dæmons'* heat barrier) and, more particularly, when he proposes to have Tegan burnt at the stake. The final scenes, with everyone bundled into the TARDIS, are also somewhat unsatisfactory. Once the TARDIS was a sanctuary, a safe haven, a home to the Doctor and his companions. Now it seems to be little more than a time and space taxi, ferrying all manner of people about in order to rescue them from danger and return them to their point of origin. These, though, are only minor flaws in an otherwise excellent story. Mark Willis summed things up well: '*The Awakening* was a fast-paced tale in which a lot of good television was crammed into fifty minutes. It may well have achieved even greater success had it been allowed three episodes, but … it is a production which [proves] that there will always be a place in *Doctor Who* for an Earth story in which history is heavily embroiled.'

FRONTIOS

Writer: Christopher H Bidmead. **Director:** Ron Jones. **Designer:** David Buckingham.
Costumes: Anushia Nieradzik. **Make-Up:** Jill Hagger. **Incidental Music:** Paddy
Kingsland. **Visual Effects:** Dave Havard. **Studio Lighting:** John Summers. **Studio
Sound:** Martin Ridout. **Production Assistant:** Valerie Letley. **Assistant Floor
Manager:** Joanna Guritz, Ed Stevenson.

	First UK TX	Scheduled TX	Actual TX	Duration	Viewers	Chart Pos.
Part One	26/01/84	18.40	18.41	24'39"	8.0	58
Part Two	27/01/84	18.40	18.41	24'35"	5.8	115
Part Three	02/02/84	18.40	18.40	24'30"	7.8	59
Part Four	03/02/84	18.40	18.42	24'26"	5.6	112

Plot: The TARDIS is dragged down to the surface of the planet Frontios and apparently
destroyed during a meteorite bombardment. The Doctor is forced to help the planet's human
colonists – refugees from a doomed future Earth – and eventually discovers that their problems
stem from an infestation of Tractators, burrowing insect-like creatures led by the intelligent
Gravis. The Tractators have been using gravitational force to cause regular meteorite
bombardments in order to keep the colonists weak so that they can prey on their bodies and
use them as components in their mining machines. Turlough knows of the creatures through a
deep seated racial memory from his own planet. He recalls that they can be rendered harmless
by separating the Gravis from the rest of the colony. The Doctor achieves this by tricking the
Gravis into reassembling the TARDIS around itself.

Episode endings:
1. The latest meteorite bombardment ends and the Doctor, Tegan and Turlough emerge from
   cover to find that where they left the TARDIS there is now only the ship's hat stand. The
   Doctor concludes that the TARDIS has been destroyed.
2. The Doctor watches from hiding as a group of Tractators gather round a young woman
   prisoner, Norna. He then sees Tegan approaching and warns her to keep away, but in
   doing so reveals his own presence. He is caught in a gravity force beam and drawn to
   stand next to Norna in the midst of the group of Tractators.
3. The Doctor and Tegan are surrounded by Tractators. A mining machine trundles into view
   and they see that the body of one of the colonists is trapped within it. Tegan thinks that she
   recognises the man's face and the Doctor realises that it is the colonists' original leader,
   Captain Revere.
4. The TARDIS has not long dematerialised from Frontios when an outside influence starts to
   affect it. The Doctor tells Tegan and Turlough that something is pulling them toward the centre
   of the universe. He does not know what it is, but anticipates that they are going to find out.

IT WAS MADE WHERE...?

Studio Recording: 24.08.83-26.08.83, 07.09.83-09.09.83 all in TC6, 14.09.83 (gallery
only) (studio unknown)

ADDITIONAL CREDITED CAST

Brazen (Peter Gilmore), Norna (Lesley Dunlop), Range (William Lucas), Plantagenet (Jeff Rawle), Cockerill (Maurice O'Connell), Orderly (Richard Ashley[1]), Gravis (John Gillett[2-4]), Tractators (George Campbell[2-4], Michael Malcolm[2-4], Stephen Speed[2-4], William Bowen[2-4], Hedi Khursandi[2-4]), Deputy (Alison Skilbeck[3]), Retrograde (Raymond Murtagh[3,4]).

Note: Captain Revere was played, uncredited, by John Beardmore.

POPULAR MYTHS

- This story was originally intended to feature Richard Hurndall in a black and white retrospective adventure remembered by Peter Davison's Doctor after hitting his head on the TARDIS control console. (It wasn't.)

THINGS TO WATCH OUT FOR

- Peter Gilmore, well known for his starring role as sea captain James Onedin in the BBC's period drama serial *The Onedin Line*, plays Brazen.
- Jeff Rawle, one of the stars of the Channel 4 comedy series *Drop the Dead Donkey*, is seen here in the very different role of the colony's deputy leader Plantagenet.
- The helmets worn by Brazen's guards were originally used in *Blake's 7*.

THINGS YOU MIGHT NOT HAVE KNOWN

- Working title: *The Wanderers*. The titles *Frontious*, *Frotious* and *The Frontios* also appear on BBC documentation, but these are almost certainly misprints or misspellings of *Frontios*.
- The transmission of the final episode was followed by a trailer of clips for the following story, *Resurrection of the Daleks*.
- The part of Range was originally to have been played by actor Peter Arne, but he was murdered at his home prior to the start of recording – an event that made front-page news in the London *Evening Standard* newspaper.
- The actors playing the Tractators were all trained dancers as the script called for the creatures to curl around people like woodlice. The design of the costumes did not allow for this movement, however. Between takes, the actors also had to be fed oxygen via a tube under the base of their costumes, as very little air could get inside.
- The original designer on this story was Barrie Dobbins. He was replaced by David Buckingham around the start of July 1983.
- On 6 March 1984, script editor Eric Saward wrote to Christopher H Bidmead to ask if he would be interested in writing another story featuring the Tractators and also the Master. His reply is unrecorded.

QUOTE, UNQUOTE

- **Turlough:** [Reading gleefully from the TARDIS log]: 'Fleeing from the imminence of a *catastrophic* collision with the Sun, refugees from the *doomed* planet Earth ...'
- **The Doctor:** [Speaking of the TARDIS.] 'As an invasion weapon, you'd have to agree that it's about as offensive as a chicken *vol-au-vent*.'

'There's something rather eerie about people being sucked down to their death in a mound of soil – drowning on dry land, or "Frontios [burying] its own dead" as somebody put it in this rather different-from-the-norm story … *Frontios* was a perfect example of a carefully structured story building (from a rather unconvincing opening scene) to paint a detailed picture of the last remnants of Earth's civilisation, marooned on Frontios after a mysterious crash caused by the (suspicious) blow-out of its guidance and pilot systems.'

This assessment by John Connors, writing in *Shada* 18 dated July 1984, hit the nail right on the head. *Frontios* is a very well written story by former script editor Christopher H Bidmead, and a quirky and unusual one too. In fact in some respects it departs perhaps just a shade too much from the norm, as Robert Byrne suggested in *TARDIS* Volume 9 Number 1 in 1984: 'The Doctor's constant worrying about breaking the laws of time seemed rather strange considering how he has ignored them in the past, and also when you remember that the Doctor isn't on very good terms with the Time Lords at the moment … I was also rather surprised at the Doctor's lack of concern when the TARDIS seemed to be destroyed.' Another rather unfortunate aspect of the story was highlighted by Christopher Denyer in the same issue of *TARDIS*: 'It bore many Bidmead hallmarks, particularly the abuse of the TARDIS (jettisoning rooms etc). I dislike this kind of treatment as it removes the air of magic surrounding the machine – the TARDIS is becoming like a clown's joke car.' These flaws aside (and it must be said that the sub-plot about the TARDIS's apparent destruction just doesn't work), Bidmead's writing on this occasion deserves nothing but praise – which is exactly what it got from Connors: 'It was the sheer quality of the script which held the story up, and apart from obvious shining one liners … there were some marvellous touches [in the dialogue], like Brazen's "They look to you" to Plantagenet – a small line which summed up a whole lot about the situation.'

The Tractators are interesting creations, as Daniel O'Mahony discussed in *Matrix* Issue 47, dated Autumn 1993: 'The gravitational power exercised by the Tractators is well handled, understated and rendered effectively through good visual effects. The scenes with the Gravis drawing together the fragments of the TARDIS with its own power are impressive but not overloaded and we're left to imagine the sheer energy the Tractators could generate collectively (which makes their plan to turn the planet into a giant spaceship less silly than it might appear). The power relationship between the Gravis and the ordinary Tractators is also understated and comes across well. It also contrasts neatly with the human colony. With the Gravis gone, the Tractators become disorganised and harmless. With Plantagenet believed dead, the colony becomes equally disorganised, degenerating into savagery and scavenging, though eventually producing new leaders from the ranks – Cockerill, for example. If [there are] any meanings to this story it's here: *Frontios* is about the relationships between leaders, followers and their societies, and what happens to those societies when the power base is removed. Revere, Plantagenet and Cockerill are human Gravises.'

A particularly welcome feature of the story's scripts is that they offer the three regulars some exceptionally strong material to work with. Peter Davison, Mark Strickson and Janet Fielding all rise to the occasion, giving excellent performances. 'What a Doctor!' enthused John Connors. 'I believe that this was Peter Davison's finest moment in the role as he truly found a niche to portray the Doctor [in]… Janet Fielding at last had a good springboard – nice to see [Tegan] more than usually positive … – whilst Mark

Strickson was a great laugh as [Turlough teased her over the destruction of the Earth] and just as [good] when facing the long-forgotten fears of the Tractators in [Part Three] with a disturbing zombie-like expression clouding his features.'

The story's guest cast are also highly impressive. The production is, as usual, very slick-looking, although certain aspects of it fail to convince – the Tractator costumes, for example, are rather too bulky and inflexible (albeit still better than many other monster costumes seen in *Doctor Who*) and the planetary landscape is rather too obviously studio-bound. The lighting, however, is outstanding, being very subtle and appropriate at a time in the series' history when something akin to floodlighting was unfortunately becoming more usual.

All things considered, *Frontios* is one of the strongest stories of the twenty-first season, and indeed of the fifth Doctor's era as a whole.

RESURRECTION OF THE DALEKS

Writer: Eric Saward. **Director:** Matthew Robinson. **Designer:** John Anderson. **Costumes:** Janet Tharby. **Make-Up:** Eileen Mair. **Incidental Music:** Malcolm Clarke. **Visual Effects:** Peter Wragg. **Film Cameraman:** Ian Punter. **Film Editor:** Dan Rae. **Studio Lighting:** Ron Bristow. **Studio Sound:** Scott Talbott. **Production Assistant:** Joy Sinclair. **Assistant Floor Manager:** Matthew Burge.

	First UK TX	Scheduled TX	Actual TX	Duration	Viewers	Chart Pos.
Part One	08/02/84	18.50	18.50	46'24"	7.3	73
Part Two	15/02/84	18.45	18.52	46'52"	8.0	53

Note: Although written and recorded as four standard length episodes, this story was re-edited before transmission into two double-length episodes. This was done in order to free up two of the transmission slots originally allocated to *Doctor Who* to be used for additional coverage of the winter Olympics.

Plot: The TARDIS becomes caught in a time corridor but the Doctor manages to free it and it then materialises in present day London within sight of Tower Bridge. Investigating some nearby warehouses, the travellers stumble into a trap that the Daleks have set for them. The Daleks also attack a space station orbiting Earth in the future. Their aim is to rescue their creator, Davros, who has been held there in suspended animation since his capture by humanity. They want him to help them find an antidote to an anti-Dalek virus created by the Movellans. In addition, the Daleks have constructed android duplicates and installed some of them in key positions of authority on Earth. They now intend to send duplicates of the Doctor and his companions to Gallifrey in order to assassinate the High Council of the Time Lords. These plans ultimately fail, however, as one of their duplicate humans, Stien, rebels and destroys the space station. Davros is unable to find a cure for the virus but has an escape pod ready in case of problems. Commander Lytton, an alien mercenary working for the Daleks, escapes to Earth. Tegan, sickened by all the killing she has seen, decides to remain on her home planet.

Episode endings:

1. The Doctor and Stien arrive on the Dalek ship in the TARDIS. The Doctor starts to call for Turlough but finds himself held at gunpoint by Stien, who admits that he serves the Daleks and is their agent.

2. In the aftermath of the climactic battle, Tegan elects not to travel on with the Doctor and runs off in tears. The Doctor and Turlough enter the TARDIS and leave. As the TARDIS dematerialises, Tegan returns. 'Brave heart, Tegan,' she says to herself. 'Doctor, I will miss you.'

IT WAS MADE WHERE...?

Location Filming: 11.09.83-12.09.83
Locations: Curlew Street, Bermondsey, London, SE1; Shad Thames, Bermondsey, London, SE1; Lafone Street, Bermondsey, London, SE1; Butler's Wharf, Bermondsey, London, SE1.
Studio Recording: 21.09.83-23.09.83, 05.10.83-07.10.83 all in TC8, 20.10.83 (gallery only) in TC6, 21.10.83 (gallery only) in TC1.

ADDITIONAL CREDITED CAST

Stien (Rodney Bewes), Styles (Rula Lenska), Colonel Archer (Del Henney), Lytton (Maurice Colbourne), Professor Laird (Chloe Ashcroft), Sergeant Calder (Philip McGough), Davros (Terry Molloy), Mercer (Jim Findley), Osborn (Sneh Gupta[1]), Trooper (Roger Davenport), Crewmembers (John Adam Baker[1], Linsey Turner), Galloway (William Sleigh[1]), Dalek Voices (Brian Miller, Royce Mills), Dalek Operators (John Scott Martin, Cy Town, Tony Starr, Toby Byrne), Kiston (Les Grantham[2]*).

* Also in Part One, but uncredited.

POPULAR MYTHS

- It was due to the success of the double-length episode format of this story that the BBC decided to adopt the same format for the whole of the following season. (It had already been decided before this that season twenty-two would consist of thirteen episodes of approximately forty-five minutes each.)

THINGS TO WATCH OUT FOR

- There is an impressive opening sequence in which two 'fake' policemen wipe out a group of escaping slaves, watched by a solitary old man.
- The 'Dalek' headgear worn by Lytton and his troops is somewhat daft.
- There is another sequence of clips from past stories as the Doctor's brain waves are drained by the Daleks' replication equipment in Part Two. These are as follows: Turlough (*Terminus*); Tegan (*Logopolis*); Nyssa (*Black Orchid*); Adric (*Warriors' Gate*); Romana II (*Warriors' Gate*); Romana I (*The Ribos Operation*); K9 (*Warriors' Gate*); Harry (*Terror of the Zygons*); fourth Doctor (*Pyramids of Mars*); Sarah (*Pyramids of Mars*); Jo (*The Mutants* (1972)); the Brigadier (*The Ambassadors of Death*); Liz Shaw (*Spearhead from Space*); third Doctor (*The Mutants* (1972)); Zoe (*The War Games*); Victoria (*The Enemy of the World*); Jamie (*The Enemy of the World*); the second Doctor (*The War Games*); Ben (*The Tenth Planet*); Polly (*The Tenth Planet*); Dodo (*The War Machines*); Sara (*The Daleks' Master Plan*); Katarina (publicity still); Steven (*The Time Meddler*); Vicki (*The Rescue*); Barbara (*The*

Mutants); Ian (*The Mutants*); Susan (*The Mutants*); and the first Doctor (*The Daleks' Master Plan*). A clip of Leela was inadvertently omitted.

- Rodney Bewes, well known as one of *The Likely Lads* in the BBC sitcom and its *Whatever Happened to the Likely Lads?* sequel, plays Stien.
- Rula Lenska, of Thames TV's *Rock Follies* fame, plays Styles – a rare example of a relatively major character in a story who never gets to meet the Doctor.
- Chloe Ashcroft, better known as a presenter of the BBC's pre-school children's programme *Play School*, appears here as Professor Laird.
- Les Grantham appears as Kiston, an engineer taken over by Davros. Grantham went on to star, under his full name Leslie Grantham, as 'Dirty' Den Watts in the BBC soap opera *EastEnders*.

THINGS YOU MIGHT NOT HAVE KNOWN

- Working title: *The Return*.
- The original four-episode edit of the story was sold overseas by BBC Enterprises, but some copies without full sound effects and music were inadvertently distributed instead of the completed versions. Part Two of that version had an additional sequence and a different cliffhanger ending.
- Davros's mask was sculpted by effects designer Stan Mitchell, who had also been responsible for the Silurian masks for *Warriors of the Deep*.
- This story had originally been planned to close the previous season (following directly on from *The King's Demons*) but had to be cancelled before production began due to disruption resulting from industrial action. The filming and studio dates for this original version were to have been as follows: Film: 04.01.83-05.01.83; Studio: 16.01.83-18.01.83 and 30.01.83-01.02.83.

QUOTE, UNQUOTE

- **Davros:** 'I have waited a long time for this. Once the Doctor is exterminated, I shall build a new race of Daleks. They will be even more deadly and I, Davros, shall be their leader! This time we shall triumph. My Daleks shall once more become the supreme beings!'
- **The Doctor:** 'Once before I held back from destroying the Daleks. It was a mistake I do not intend to repeat. Davros must die.'
- **Davros:** 'You hesitate Doctor. If I were you, I would be dead.' **The Doctor:** 'I lack your practice, Davros.' **Davros:** 'You are soft, like all Time Lords. You prefer to stand and watch. Action requires courage. Something you lack.'
- **Tegan:** 'I'm not coming with you.' **The Doctor:** 'I beg your pardon?' **Tegan:** 'I'm tired of it.' **The Doctor:** 'What's the matter?' **Tegan:** 'A lot of good people have died today. I'm sick of it.' **The Doctor:** 'You think I wanted it this way?' **Tegan:** 'No. It's just I don't think I can go on.' **The Doctor:** 'You want to stay on Earth?' **Tegan:** 'My aunt Vanessa said, when I became an air stewardess, if you stop enjoying it, give it up.' **The Doctor:** 'Tegan …' **Tegan:** 'It's stopped being fun, Doctor.'

ANALYSIS

Resurrection of the Daleks does for the Daleks what *Earthshock* did for the Cybermen. It updates the concept (but not the look in this case) by drawing extensively on past successes. As Simon Cheshire commented in *TARDIS* Volume 9 Number 1 in 1984: 'Eric Saward again showed that he can take all the best bits from the golden oldies and blend them with great skill into a serious piece of drama with never a dull moment and never a lapse in the dialogue. I suppose some people might criticise him for being derivative, but seeing as the last decent Dalek [story] was nine years ago I hardly think that matters.' Stephen Bell expressed similar sentiments in the same magazine: 'If *Destiny of the Daleks* was the story which disgraced the Doctor's most famous arch-enemies then *Resurrection of the Daleks* has surely redeemed them. After *Earthshock* it was difficult to see how Eric Saward could come up with a story as good, but he has succeeded in doing just that ... Almost everything about this story was first rate, but I would especially cite the hunt for the Dalek creature in the warehouse, the confrontation between the Doctor and Davros and the climactic battle and explosion ... Maurice Colbourne was superb as Lytton and the exchanges of dialogue between him and the Supreme Dalek were a delight.'

While there is nothing wrong in principle with the series drawing on its own past for inspiration – *The Awakening*'s homage to season eight's *The Dæmons* is a good case in point – the worrying thing about *Resurrection of the Daleks* is the sheer number of elements that it plunders from earlier stories. Stephen Birchard, also in *TARDIS* Volume 9 Number 1, listed some of the main examples: 'The Daleks' presence in London with an army of controlled humans is straight out of *The Dalek Invasion of Earth*; the Daleks' ability to time travel and [the fact that they] specifically want the Doctor [hail] from *The Chase*; Davros's wish to restore instinct is suggestive of *The Evil of the Daleks*, as is the Dalek civil war which occurred between the Daleks loyal to the Dalek Supreme and those loyal to Davros; *Day of the Daleks* [is] commemorated by the obligatory flashback sequence with the Doctor tied to the operating table; the Doctor's hesitation at killing Davros was a deliberate re-enactment of the similar scene in *Genesis of the Daleks*; and finally the war with the Movellans brought us bang up to date with *Destiny of the Daleks*.'

This almost slavish reliance on *Doctor Who*'s own mythology to provide the basis for new stories was to blight the series over the next couple of seasons; and although the seeds of it were sown a little earlier in stories such as *Earthshock*, *Arc of Infinity* and *Warriors of the Deep*, it is in *Resurrection of the Daleks* that it arguably takes root. Anyone trying to dissect the plot is left with a succession of excellent set pieces surrounded by a garbled mess. Inconsistencies and unanswered questions abound. How have the Daleks managed to create duplicates of the fifth Doctor, Tegan and Turlough when they have never met them before? Why does Stien behave – even when he is alone – in a manner that suggests he is a rebel when he is actually a Dalek agent? How does Davros come to have the nifty injection device that enables him to take over humans and Daleks with consummate ease? What exactly is the Daleks' plan? Why have they sent canisters of Movellan virus to Earth down a time corridor?

Perhaps the most disappointing aspect of the story is the reintroduction of Davros. Doug Smith, writing in *Shada* 18 dated July 1984, gave him a rather cool welcome: 'Davros's return was only to be expected, and it's unfortunate, in some respects, that we can't seem to have a Dalek story now without their creator appearing as well; a shame, also, that the production team left a possibility for the scientist's return [in a future story]. The new mask, presumably designed to take into account the effects of cryogenic suspension, came across far better [than might have been expected], partly because it responded to movement so realistically, but mainly due to Terry Molloy's portrayal. There's always a danger of overplaying megalomania, thus turning it [into] cliché, but in this case any such risk was carefully avoided. Although the differences in the mask were acceptable, the changes in Davros's chair were not; it certainly is a peculiar form of cryogenic suspension that can alter controls like that!' Molloy's performance is certainly an improvement on David Gooderson's in *Destiny of the Daleks* but still comes nowhere near to matching Michael Wisher's in *Genesis of the Daleks*. The depth that Wisher brought to the character has gone; he now comes across as a one-dimensional lunatic who rants a lot and sounds more and more like one of his own creations. Even the subtleties of Davros's original mask have been lost, and the third 'eye' is now bigger and more blatantly a flashing light bulb than before.

Another problem with the story is that the Doctor is scarcely involved in the main action. Alan Stevens, writing in *DWB* No. 119 dated November 1993, had some interesting thoughts to offer on this:

'Eric Saward has written a plotline for the Daleks that makes the Doctor's presence totally superfluous, and condemns him to the ignominious fate of either wandering around an abandoned warehouse prodding bits of paper with a stick, or lying on a sheet of bubble-wrap waiting for his brain to be sucked out.

'In fact the entire scenario concerning the Dalek duplicates seems to have just been one massive plot device, tacked on for the sole purpose of getting the Doctor out of the way … It is only in the last twenty-five minutes that the Doctor gets to perform any act of real significance – his decision to assassinate Davros so as to prevent him from saving the Dalek race from the Movellan virus … When the moment eventually comes to pull the trigger, the Doctor finds himself facing a *Genesis of the Daleks*-style moral dilemma, which results in him being unable to commit the double crime of murder and genocide …

'Unfortunately this scene is severely undermined when the Doctor is later seen first blowing up Daleks with high explosives and then, with the statement "Lunch has arrived", releasing the Movellan virus inside the warehouse so as to kill the rest of the Daleks [in] what must have been a very painful and horrific death. Ah yes, you all say, but surely the Daleks are so evil they deserve all they get? But if that's true why then couldn't [he] bring himself to kill their creator …? The only conclusion I can find is that perhaps he was unable to shoot because Davros is a humanoid, whereas the Daleks are amoeboid blobs, but if that's the case then that makes the fifth Doctor a racist whose morality is on a par with that of the Daleks themselves!'

This is a strong accusation, but the logic of Stevens' point is hard to refute.

Resurrection of the Daleks sadly marks a notable escalation of the trend in mid-eighties *Doctor Who* toward a concentration on action and set pieces (not to mention gratuitous continuity references) at the expense of telling good original stories. Although superficially entertaining, it does not bear close examination or repeated viewing – which is all the more sad considering that at the time of its original transmission the home video market was really taking off in a big way.

PLANET OF FIRE

Writer: Peter Grimwade. **Director:** Fiona Cumming. **Designer:** Malcolm Thornton. **Costumes:** John Peacock. **Make-Up:** Elizabeth Rowell. **Incidental Music:** Peter Howell. **Visual Effects:** Chris Lawson. **Film Cameraman:** John Walker. **Film Editor:**

Alastair Mitchell. **Studio Lighting:** John Summers. **Studio Sound:** Scott Talbott. **Production Assistant:** Claire Hughes Smith. **Assistant Floor Manager:** Robert Evans.

	First UK TX	Scheduled TX	Actual TX	Duration	Viewers	Chart Pos.
Part One	23/02/84	18.40	18.41	24'26"	7.4	71
Part Two	24/02/84	18.40	18.42	24'20"	6.1	102
Part Three	01/03/84	18.40	18.41	23'57"	7.4	67
Part Four	02/03/84	18.40	18.41	24'44"	7.0	74

Plot: On holiday in Lanzarote, a young American girl named Peri narrowly escapes drowning when she is rescued from the sea by Turlough and taken into the TARDIS to recover. The Doctor is on the island because the TARDIS has detected a mysterious signal being transmitted from an unknown artifact retrieved from the sea bed by Peri's stepfather, Howard Foster. The Master reasserts his control over Kamelion and gets it to bring the TARDIS, along with the Doctor, Turlough and Peri, to the planet Sarn, where he is hoping to use that world's supply of revitalising numismaton gas to restore his body – accidentally shrunken in an experiment with his tissue compression eliminator weapon – to its correct size. It transpires that amongst the Sarn natives, who worship a fire god named Logar, are political prisoners from Trion – Turlough's home world. Turlough too is revealed to be a political refugee. He meets his brother and later discovers that Trion has granted an amnesty to all political prisoners, enabling them to return home. The Master is apparently killed when a stream of numismaton gas in which he is bathing turns to a normal hot flame. The Doctor destroys Kamelion at the robot's own bidding as it has become completely unstable. Peri leaves with the Doctor.

Episode endings:
1. The TARDIS arrives on the planet Sarn and the Doctor and Turlough venture outside, leaving Peri in the control room with, apparently, her stepfather Howard Foster. The latter is really a disguised Kamelion, however, and after closing the TARDIS doors he transforms into an image of the Master. Peri asks who he is, and he replies: 'I am the Master, and you will obey me.'
2. The Kamelion-Master exhorts the people of Sarn to sacrifice the 'unbelievers' amongst them by throwing them into the flames of a furnace. The Doctor, who is one of those to be sacrificed, is seemingly powerless to prevent this.
3. Peri takes refuge in the Master's TARDIS. She sees a box on the floor and, lifting the lid, is shocked to find inside it the miniaturised form of the Master. He tells her: 'You escaped from my slave, but you will obey me – or die.'
4. The Doctor accedes to Peri's request to be allowed to travel with him and, as the TARDIS lurches violently in flight, welcomes her aboard.

IT WAS MADE WHERE...?
Location Filming: 14.10.83-15.10.83, 17.10.83-19.10.83
Locations: all on the island of Lanzarote: Papagayo Beach and bay; Mirador del Rio (high observation point); Quay and cafe at Orzola; Fire Mountain, Ridge, Asphalt Triangle, Cave of Doves, Valley of Tranquillity; Guides Cave, Steep Hill, High area near Camel Path, Volcano mouth, Yellow Area, Los Hornitos – all at Islote de Hilario, Montañas del Fuego.

Studio Recording: 26.10.83-27.10.83 in TC1, 09.11.83-11.11.83 in TC6

ADDITIONAL CREDITED CAST

Timanov (Peter Wyngarde), The Master (Anthony Ainley), Sorasta (Barbara Shelley), Amyand (James Bate), Professor Howard Foster (Dallas Adams), Voice of Kamelion (Gerald Flood[1,2]), Malkon (Edward Highmore), Roskal (Jonathan Caplan), Curt (Michael Bangerter[1]), Lookout (Simon Sutton[1,2]), Zuko (Max Arthur[2]), Lomand (John Alkin[4]).

THINGS TO WATCH OUT FOR

- Peter Wyngarde, better known as cult icon Jason King in the eponymous ITC series and its *Department S* forebear, appears here as the Sarn elder Timanov.
- The Doctor wears a variation on his usual costume, with different trousers and – initially – a waistcoat.
- Part One features some stock music composed by J Leach and produced by Alan Howe. This is from an LP called 'From Other Lands No. 12' published by Music de Wolfe Ltd, and the track used is band seven, 'Zapateado', from side one, 'Spain'.
- Part Three features a transparency of the Kouros Acropolis from the Sheridan Photo Library.
- Part Four features stock footage of erupting volcanoes and lava from Movietone (33.5 seconds) and Visnews (5 seconds).

THINGS YOU MIGHT NOT HAVE KNOWN

- Working title: *Planet of Fear*.
- Turlough's full name, rank and serial number are revealed as: Vizlor Turlough; Junior Ensign Commander; VTEC9/12/44.
- According to Peri's passport, she and Howard live on 45th Street, St Michelle, Pasadena, California. Her date of birth is 15 November, but the year is unreadable.
- The following beings were, according to Turlough, Trion agents keeping track of their prisoners: an agrarian commissioner on Vardon; a tax inspector on Derveg and – in Turlough's own case – an eccentric solicitor in Chancery Lane, London.

QUOTE, UNQUOTE

- **Kamelion-Master:** 'I am the Master!' **Peri:** 'I'm Perpugilliam Brown, and I can shout just as loud as you can!'
- **Timanov:** 'You will never understand, Amyand. Logar is everywhere. He cares for the faithful.'
- **Turlough:** 'I don't want to go, Doctor. I've learnt a lot from you.'
- **The Master:** [As he is engulfed in flames.] 'Doctor ... I'll plague you to the end of time for this. Help me! I'll give you anything in creation. Please! Would you show mercy to your own ... Aargh!'

ANALYSIS

As someone once rather cynically observed, *Planet of Fire* is not so much a story as a series of explanations. Peri is introduced; the Master is brought back for a further return appearance; Kamelion is destroyed; Turlough's background is at last revealed; and finally

Turlough is written out. This overloading of the scripts – which is even more extreme than that required of the luckless writer Peter Grimwade in his previous *Doctor Who* assignment, *Mawdryn Undead* – probably accounts in large part for the drubbing that the story has received from most reviewers. 'The worst story of the season so far,' wrote Robert Davis in *Skonnos* Issue 7 in 1984. '*Planet of Fire* had a lot to offer, and looking at what [it] had to include you would think this would be an action packed story. Suffice to say [you] would be sadly mistaken! The first three episodes were total padding, and could have been easily condensed down to a singe episode, making the story an acceptable two-parter.' These criticisms, although not untypical of those directed at the story, are far too harsh. Given all the imposed prerequisites, including the need to incorporate the Lanzarote location, the end result is by no means as bad as it might have been.

The plot involving the inhabitants of the volcanic planet Sarn is actually quite an interesting one even if, with all the other elements eating up screen time, it is rather less well developed than one might have liked. 'The breadth of the community on Sarn is enhanced by the supporting characters,' noted Jane Killick in *In-Vision* Issue 75 dated November 1997. 'Even those with only a small part in the story have distinct personalities. Roskal, for example, has few lines but those he does have demonstrate his interest in the technology left by the Trions and in learning how to use it. It is enough to show how the community has been held back by the old teachings, represented by Timanov, and how they have the capacity to advance. The Doctor says as much to Amyand, who has emerged as a character with strong leadership qualities. The story of the Sarns, therefore, is of a people ready to abandon their old, primitive ways and prosper in a new life away from the planet.'

Another point in this story's favour is that the location filming in Lanzarote is a lot more appropriate than was that in Amsterdam for *Arc of Infinity* – although it is perhaps a pity that it is used to represent both Sarn and Lanzarote itself, as it is immediately obvious to the viewer that the sequences have all been shot in the same place.

Tim Munro, writing in *TARDIS* Volume 9 Number 1 in 1984, drew attention to some other redeeming features: 'Turlough's origins were cleverly revealed and all tied up perfectly with the little we were told about him in *Mawdryn Undead*. The concept of the shrunken Master was inspired to say the least, as was the battle for control of Kamelion ... Mark Strickson was superb and I am furious that we've lost him so soon. What a waste! ... Anthony Ainley had possibly the worst dialogue in history but being Anthony Ainley he put in a great effort, made it believable and livened up an otherwise tedious story.'

In fact it is remarkable just how much more imposing and dangerous Anthony Ainley's Master (or strictly speaking the Kamelion-Master) seems when wearing an ordinary business suit in this story as opposed to his standard 'penguin' outfit. He really does put one in mind of Roger Delgado in these scenes, making all the more regrettable the production team's apparent determination 'to have him usually presented as something akin to a moustache-twirling pantomime villain. (Visitors to the studio for this story actually recall Ainley giving a very intense, serious performance during recording of one particular scene and receiving firm instructions from the control gallery to go 'more OTT' – i.e. over the top – for a retake.)

The other members of the guest cast all give good performances, although the distinguished Barbara Shelley is somewhat wasted in the minor role of Sorasta. Best of all is Peter Wyngarde as Timanov, as Steve Mercer agreed in *Shada* 18 dated July 1984: 'Top honours for this story must go ... to Peter Wyngarde, oozing faith, fire and fanaticism [in] a quite brilliant performance ... He, by himself, made the worshippers of Logar seem real, an authentic culture. His final scene, offered a chance of salvation and reconciliation by Amyand and rejecting it rather than his faith, was easily the most memorable of the whole story, although his first encounter with Kamelion and his successful plea for a "sign from Logar" in [Part One] ran it close. Quite simply, it was one of the most impressive performances I've ever seen in a *Doctor Who* story ... If only every guest star gave such good value.'

Nicola Bryant makes a good debut as Peri, helping to compensate for the viewer's disappointment at the loss of the excellent and rather underused Turlough. In fact, notwithstanding the light-hearted closing scene between the Doctor and Peri in the TARDIS, the story as a whole ends on a rather downbeat note. 'Generally speaking [it] left me feeling quite sad,' observed Robert Craker, again in *TARDIS* Volume 9 Number 1, 'after the Doctor's reluctant destruction of poor old Kamelion (to the delight of most fans, I dare say) who had been well used throughout ..., and finally the Doctor's refusal to help the trapped Master, leading to what would appear to be his final demise. At least, it was clear that the Doctor [thought he was] no more. It can't be though, can it? The final encounter between the two Time Lords would surely be something more momentous.'

THE CAVES OF ANDROZANI

Writer: Robert Holmes. **Director:** Graeme Harper. **Designer:** John Hurst. **Costumes:** Andrew Rose. **Make-Up:** Jan Nethercot, Shirley Stallard. **Incidental Music:** Roger Limb. **Visual Effects:** Jim Francis, Stuart Brisdon. **Film Cameraman:** John Walker. **Film Editor:** Roger Guertin. **Studio Lighting:** Don Babbage. **Studio Sound:** Scott Talbott. **Production Assistant:** Juley Harding. **Assistant Floor Manager:** Sue Hedden.

	First UK TX	Scheduled TX	Actual TX	Duration	Viewers	Chart Pos.
Part One	08/03/84	18.40	18.41	24'33"	6.9	66
Part Two	09/03/84	18.40	18.41	25'00"	6.6	75
Part Three	15/03/84	18.40	18.42	24'36"	7.8	62
Part Four	16/03/84	18.40	18.41	25'37"	7.8	62

Plot: The TARDIS arrives on Androzani Minor, the source of a life-prolonging drug refined from a substance called spectrox. Production of the drug is controlled by Sharaz Jek, a facially deformed madman in self imposed exile, who blames Morgus, a powerful industrialist on Androzani Major, for all his misfortunes. Jek is fighting government troops sent to liberate the drug. His weaponry is being supplied by gun-runners secretly employed by Morgus, who receives payment from Jek in refined spectrox. This gives Morgus a monopoly of the drug on Major. Jek becomes infatuated with Peri and saves her and the Doctor from being executed on Morgus's orders by government troops led by General Chellak. The two travellers escape after learning that they have contracted spectrox toxaemia, a fatal condition to which there is only one antidote – the milk from a queen bat, which the Doctor must obtain from the deep caves on Minor. Morgus, seeing his power base slipping away, travels to Minor. In a climactic battle, Morgus, Jek and all the soldiers are killed. With moments to spare, the Doctor carries Peri back to the TARDIS where he gives her all the milk that he has managed to collect. She recovers, but the Doctor has to regenerate to save his own life.

Episode endings:
1. The Doctor and Peri are brought before a military firing squad. General Chellak gives the order to fire, and the soldiers pump bullets into them.
2. The Doctor takes cover as Stotz and his band of gun runners are attacked by a ferocious magma beast. The creature then turns and approaches the rock behind which he is crouching …
3. The Doctor has been confined on the gun runners' ship but manages to break free and take over the controls, piloting it back toward Androzani Minor. Stotz and his men try to regain access to the bridge by cutting through the door. The planet looms large on the ship's view screen and the Doctor tells Stotz: 'I'm not going to let you stop me now!'
4. The Doctor collapses to the floor of the TARDIS control room and regenerates. The bewildered Peri wants to know what has happened. 'Change, my dear,' explains the new Doctor. 'And it seems not a moment too soon.'

IT WAS MADE WHERE...?

Location Filming: 15.11.83-17.11.83
Location: Masters Pit, Stokeford Heath, Gallows Hill, Wareham, Dorset.
Studio Recording: 15.12.83-17.12.83 in TC6, 11.01.84-12.01.84 in TC6

ADDITIONAL CREDITED CAST

Sharaz Jek (Christopher Gable), Morgus (John Normington), Salateen (Robert Glenister), Stotz (Maurice Roëves), Chellak (Martin Cochrane), Krelper (Roy Holder), Timmin (Barbara Kinghorn), President (David Neal[1-3]), The Doctor (Colin Baker[4]), Soldier (Ian Staples[4]), The Master (Anthony Ainley[4]), Adric (Matthew Waterhouse[4]), Nyssa (Sarah Sutton[4]), Tegan (Janet Fielding[4]), Turlough (Mark Strickson[4]), Voice of Kamelion (Gerald Flood[4]).

THINGS TO WATCH OUT FOR

- Brief, specially recorded cameos for all the fifth Doctor's companions and the Master are seen during the regeneration sequence in Part Four.
- The closing credits to Part Four feature the face of new Doctor Colin Baker and list him before Peter Davison.
- When the Doctor is in the control room of Stotz's ship, he apparently has a premonition of his coming regeneration when he sees the same patterns as at the story's conclusion.

THINGS YOU MIGHT NOT HAVE KNOWN

- Working title: *Chain Reaction*.
- One of the soldier extras was played by Steve Wickham, later to become Coordinator of the *Doctor Who* Appreciation Society.
- 'John Peyre' is credited for 'design effects' on Part Four. This is a misspelling of the name of Jean Peyre, a Frenchman who created the matte paintings for the shots where the Doctor travels down to obtain the bat's milk.

- **Peri:** 'Doctor, why do you wear a stick of celery in your lapel?' **The Doctor:** 'Does it offend you?' **Peri:** 'No, just curious.' **The Doctor:** 'Safety precaution. I'm allergic to certain gases in the praxis range of the spectrum.' **Peri:** 'Well how does the celery help?' **The Doctor:** 'If the gas is present, the celery turns purple.' **Peri:** 'And then what do you do?' **The Doctor:** 'I eat the celery. If nothing else I'm sure it's good for my teeth.'

- **Sharaz Jek:** 'We shall become the best of companions.' **The Doctor:** 'What do you say, Peri? We can go on nature walks, have picnics and jolly evenings round the camp fire.' **Sharaz Jek:** 'Don't mock me, Doctor. Beauty I must have, but you are dispensible.' **Doctor:** 'Thank you.' **Sharaz Jek:** 'You have the mouth of a prattling jackanapes … But your eyes … they tell a different story.'

'*The Caves of Androzani* [is] surely the best set of four episodes since John Nathan-Turner took over the reins of producer … The script, the acting, the direction (oh, that direction!) were all so perfect, that one wonders why there are so many people in the world who want to criticise the show.' So wrote Antony Dexter in *Shada* 18 dated July 1984, and many would agree with his sentiments. *The Caves of Androzani* is certainly one of the best *Doctor Who* stories ever made, if not *the* best. It is one of those rare cases of a production in which everything – scripting, direction, casting, acting, design, music, effects – seems to have gone almost exactly right, leading to an end product that is as close to perfection as the series ever got. 'More "scenes" stick in the memory from this one story than [from all the] others this season put together,' continued Dexter. 'the wonderful death of the President, the opening long-shot of the Doctor and Peri, the final fight of Jek, Morgus and Stotz, each dying so dramatically, and of course that splendid regeneration – easily the most interesting so far. So many good scenes, but my favourite was the one that most surprised me. One minute that sly but not unlikeable Salateen is bravely leading his troops, declaring their safety in the face of the enemy, the next minute, he's been blasted half way down the cave. Such shocks are few and far between, these days, and whenever they do crop up, it's a rare director who [resists the temptation] to glorify it – but here Harper just skipped over it, making the whole death casual – like some third rate extra had died. And that in turn made the whole incident far more effective than a long gaze at the dying body could ever have done.'

The story revolves around the characters of Sharaz Jek and Morgus, two people diametrically opposed to each other in every way. Initially it seems that perhaps Jek is the villain, and yet Morgus is far more calculating and cold, and it appears that the former has been driven insane by the perceived duplicity of the latter and by his subsequent enforced exile. The casting of these two roles was key to the success of the story and Graeme Harper, making his directorial debut on the series, got it exactly right, as Tim Westmacott agreed in *Zygon* Issue 1 dated August 1984:

'Christopher Gable and John Normington deserve great praise for bringing to life respectively an emotional character concealed in a leather mask and an unemotional one [for] whom a single raised eyebrow would indicate almost total loss of self-control. Jek was the archetypal *Phantom of the Opera* monster. [He appears] at first to be a callous murderer but gradually the layers are peeled away to reveal a pathetic individual who more than anything [wants] the company of people. When he says of Peri … "Oh, my exquisite child, how could I ever let you go?" we sympathise with her; but the moment he removes his mask and Peri screams at his scalded features, prompting him to leap under the table like a wounded dog, we immediately change our attitude to this "monster" who only wanted to be a man ...

'Morgus, on the other hand, evoked no sympathy ... As boss of the Sirius Conglomerate and controller of "the most valuable substance in the universe", he was only interested in profit. "The world will forever be in your debt", says his secretary Timmin, referring to his proposed peace mission to Androzani Minor. "Quite so," replies Morgus, thinking in terms of financial gain. He felt no qualms about assassinating the President, whom he believed told Chellak to fake the execution of the Doctor and Peri, in order to protect his interests. "It could have been worse – it could have been me," he tells Timmin, with a face as expressionless as someone more used to watching a monitor screen than talking to people.'

The gun runner characters are also interesting, and presented with a degree of gritty realism unusual for this period of the series' history. Maurice Roëves's Stotz, their cold and cruel leader, is particularly impressive. The scene in which he leaves his fellows in their ship, only to return a few moments later to gun them all down in cold blood, just so that he will not have to share the promised wealth of spectrox with them, is greatly shocking in its abruptness.

There is, unfortunately, one element of the production that is less than fully effective – namely the realisation of the magma monster. This creature, we are told, lives in the caves beneath the surface of Androzani Minor and emerges every so often to kill a few soldiers. When we get to see it, it is little more than a man-sized walking dragon with stubby arms. Not exactly a terrifying prospect, and Harper's valiant attempts to keep it in the shadows and reveal it only in quick cutaways are only partly successful in disguising its deficiencies. It is a pity, with hindsight, that this creature could not have been dropped from the story altogether, as it really adds nothing to the plot and makes for a rather lame conclusion to Part Two. This is doubly disappointing given that the cliffhanger endings to Parts One and Three rank among the best in the series' history. They are all the more impressive for the fact that they involve no cheating whatsoever on the part of the writer or director. When the Doctor and Peri face the firing squad at the end of Part One, what we see happen is what actually does happen – there is no cutting away at the last minute or re-editing of the beginning of the following episode to reveal that the soldiers did not in fact fire, or anything like that. Likewise the ending to Part Three is incredibly dramatic, with the music, sound effects and acting – particularly from Peter Davison – all building up to a nerve-shattering climax.

Keith Topping, reviewing the story in *DWB* No. 95 dated November 1991, wrote: 'It probably isn't the masterpiece that it is often made out to be, but it carries a quality that few stories ... can match and its slickness is also its salvation.' *The Caves of Androzani* is indeed slick. It is also entertaining and frightening and confronts some adult themes and issues with a frankness generally absent from most *Doctor Who* of this era.

To cap it all, the story ends with one of the best regeneration sequences in the series' history, ushering in the new Doctor. 'The last few seconds are notable,' observed Christopher Denyer in *TARDIS* Volume 9 Number 1 in 1984. 'In three curt lines, Colin Baker gives a strong indication of his Doctor's personality, and it bodes well for the future. The era of the fifth Doctor ended with a truly excellent, gripping adventure, and the era of the sixth Doctor has begun in fine style.'

The Sixth Doctor
(Colin Baker)
1984-1986

COLIN BAKER IS THE SIXTH DOCTOR

Colin Baker was born in 1943 and spent his earliest years in London with his mother while his father served in the armed forces. After the War, the family moved to Rochdale and he attended school in Manchester. It was here that – through a fellow pupil's mother, who was a casting director at Granada TV – he had his first experience of acting, taking a small role in a series called *My Wife's Sister*. He went on to attend St Bede's College in Manchester, where he took part in their annual productions of Gilbert and Sullivan operettas. Later he studied law and started out on a career as a solicitor. By this point however he had joined the North Manchester Amateur Dramatic Society and become hooked on acting, and at the age of twenty-three he decided to pursue this interest professionally. He won a place at the London Academy of Music and Dramatic Art (LAMDA), where he trained for three years. After leaving LAMDA, he took a temporary job as a taxi driver. Before long though he gained a part in a major BBC2 drama series, *The Roads to Freedom* (1970). This led to further TV roles, including two more for BBC2: Count Wenceslas Steinbock in Balzac's *Cousin Bette* (1971) and Prince Anatol Kuragin in a twenty part serialisation of Tolstoy's *War and Peace* (1972-73). He also took on a wide range of theatre work, including a number of Shakespearian roles.

In the mid-seventies Baker landed the role that would make him 'the man viewers love to hate' – the ruthless Paul Merroney in the BBC1 drama series *The Brothers*. This ended in 1976, however, and he then found that he was strongly typecast as a 'bad guy' on TV. For the next five years he worked almost exclusively in the theatre, appearing in everything from comedies to thrillers as well as more Shakespeare. His few television roles during this period included Bayban the Berserker in the *Blake's 7* episode *City on the Edge of the World* (1980) and Commander Maxil in the season twenty *Doctor Who* story *Arc of Infinity*. Shortly after this, he and John Nathan-Turner both happened to be guests at the same wedding, where he unwittingly impressed the producer with his ability to keep the others in their group entertained during the course of the afternoon. This later led to him being invited by Nathan-Turner to play the sixth Doctor. His accession to the role was announced in August 1983 and, reflecting the high level of public interest in *Doctor Who*, was even the subject of an item on the BBC's early evening news bulletin, which featured a clip of his appearance as Maxil. In a brief interview, he confirmed that he intended to stay with the series for some considerable time, even suggesting an intention to outdo the fourth Doctor's record seven year stint. Ultimately this was not to be, but Baker was nevertheless pleased to have had an opportunity to make his mark in such a popular institution: 'I wanted to honour the tradition that those other five guys had upheld so marvellously before. I just wanted to add another cherry to the cake.'

THE TWIN DILEMMA

Writer: Anthony Steven. **Director:** Peter Moffatt. **Designer:** Valerie Warrender. **Costumes:** Pat Godfrey. **Make-Up:** Denise Baron. **Incidental Music:** Malcolm Clarke. **Visual Effects:** Stuart Brisdon. **Film Cameraman:** John Baker, John Walker. **Film Editor:** Ian McKendrick. **Studio Lighting:** Don Babbage. **Studio Sound:** Scott Talbott. **Production Assistant:** Christine Fawcett. **Assistant Floor Manager:** Stephen Jeffery-Poulter, Beth Millward.

	First UK TX	Scheduled TX	Actual TX	Duration	Viewers	Chart Pos.
Part One	22/03/84	18.40	18.41	24'42"	7.6	66
Part Two	23/03/84	18.40	18.41	25'09"	7.4	71
Part Three	29/03/84	18.40	18.41	24'27"	7.0	59
Part Four	30/03/84	18.40	18.43	25'04"	6.3	67

Plot: A race of giant gastropods has taken over the planet Jaconda. Their leader, Mestor, now intends to cause an enormous explosion in order to spread his people's eggs throughout the galaxy, and he kidnaps juvenile twin geniuses from Earth to work out the necessary mathematical equations. Space fighters led by Lieutenant Hugo Lang are dispatched to get the twins back, but they come under attack and Lang is the sole survivor when his ship crashes on the asteroid Titan 3. The Doctor and Peri become involved and help Jaconda's elderly former ruler Professor Edgeworth, who is really a Time Lord named Azmael, to defeat Mestor and free the planet's bird-like indigenous people from the gastropods' reign of terror. Azmael, however, sacrifices his life in the process.

Episode endings:
1. The injured Hugo Lang suddenly raises himself from the floor of the TARDIS and aims a gun at the Doctor. Accusing the Time Lord of being responsible for the deaths of his whole command, he prepares to kill him.
2. Ignoring threats from Hugo, Peri activates the TARDIS scanner just in time to see the dome of the 'safe house' on Titan 3 destroyed in a huge explosion. Believing that the Doctor was still inside, she breaks down in tears.
3. Azmael has the Doctor restrained from going to rescue Peri from the gastropods. The Doctor is distraught at the prospect of his companion being killed.
4. The Doctor tells Peri: 'Whatever else happens, I am the Doctor – whether you like it or not!'

IT WAS MADE WHERE...?

Location filming: 07.02.84-08.02.84
Locations: Springwell Quarry, Springwell Lane, Rickmansworth, Herts; Gerrards Cross Sand and Gravel Quarry, Wapsey's Wood, Oxford Road, Gerrards Cross, Bucks.
Studio: 24.01.84-26.01.84 in TC8, 14.02.84-16.02.84 in TC3

ADDITIONAL CREDITED CAST

Edgeworth (Maurice Denham), Hugo Lang (Kevin McNally), Mestor (Edwin Richfield), Sylvest (Dennis Chinnery[1]), Noma (Barry Stanton), Drak (Oliver Smith),

6 SIXTH DOCTOR

Fabian (Helen Blatch[1]), Elena (Dione Inman[1]), Romulus (Gavin Conrad)*, Remus (Andrew Conrad), Chamberlain (Seymour Green[3,4]), Prisoner (Roger Nott[3]), Jocondan Guard (John Wilson[3]).

* Gavin Conrad's real name was Paul Conrad, but he could not be credited as such as there was another actor already working under that name.

POPULAR MYTHS

- The Edgeworth character was originally intended to be the first Doctor. (He wasn't.)

THINGS TO WATCH OUT FOR

- New opening and closing title sequences – somewhat gaudier versions of the previous ones, incorporating Colin Baker's face rather than Peter Davison's – make their debut on *The Twin Dilemma*. They were designed by Sid Sutton and Terry Handley.
- Distinguished actor Maurice Denham plays Edgeworth.
- Actor Edwin Richfield (Mestor) had previously appeared in *Doctor Who* playing Captain Hart in the 1972 story *The Sea Devils*.
- The Doctor uses the TARDIS's wardrobe room to look for a new set of clothes. Among the garments he picks up are the voluminous fur coat worn by the second Doctor in *The Five Doctors*, and a velvet jacket similar to those favoured by his third incarnation.
- A musical cue associated with Tegan is used when the Doctor recalls her in Part Two.
- Three Gastropod costumes were made for the story by Richard Gregory of the freelance effects firm Imagineering. The one for Mestor was more sophisticated than the other two, featuring an animated mouthpiece, and the mask was designed to be easily removable as the actor, Edwin Richfield, suffered from claustrophobia.

THINGS YOU MIGHT NOT HAVE KNOWN

- Fabian was originally envisaged as a male character, and the Jocondan Chamberlain as a female one.
- Eric Saward extensively re-wrote Anthony Steven's original scripts.
- One of the two Gastropod extras in Part Three was played by Steve Wickham, who had also appeared in *The Caves of Androzani* and who went on to become Coordinator of the *Doctor Who* Appreciation Society.
- The cat badge worn by the Doctor in his lapel for this story was hand-made and painted by Suzie Trevor, and purchased for the programme from a specialist badge shop in central London.
- Production of *The Twin Dilemma* was affected by industrial action at the BBC. It eventually went into the studio about a month later than intended and, unusually, the location filming was done not in advance of but between the two blocks of studio work.

QUOTE, UNQUOTE

- **The Doctor:** 'Well, look at me. I'm old, lacking in vigour, my mind's in turmoil. I no longer know if I'm coming, have gone, or even been. I'm falling to pieces. I no longer even have any clothes sense … Self-pity is all I have left.'
- **The Doctor:** 'In my time I have been threatened by experts!'
- **The Doctor:** 'The very core of my being is on fire with guilt and rage!'

The era of the sixth Doctor gets off to a truly dreadful start with a story that is at times almost painful to watch. One of the most disappointing things about it is the depiction of the new Doctor himself. Perhaps the best that can be said about this is that the idea of making him dangerously unstable was a brave attempt at a different approach. Sadly however his bizarre behaviour and outrageous mood-swings seem forced and artificial, and succeed only in alienating the viewer. The worst moment of all comes in the first episode where, in a violent fit, he tries to strangle Peri before eventually managing to compose himself. One can imagine viewers switching off in droves at this point, having become completely disillusioned with the series. Surprisingly, however, most contemporary fan reaction to Colin Baker's debut was cautiously optimistic. Simon Cheshire, for example, suggested in *TARDIS* Volume 9 Number 1 in 1984 that the Doctor was just about the only thing worth watching in the story: 'The sixth Doctor looks like turning out very well indeed – he has traces of his predecessors, yet he's sufficiently different to be an interesting and enjoyable character in his own right. If his neat blend of arrogant flippancy continues then I'm sure he'll be a firm favourite in years to come. Indeed his scenes with Peri were the only ones which really worked in this ropey escapade. The whole thing was just coloured-in *Flash Gordon*.' Tim Munro, writing in the same magazine, had rather more mixed views: 'I find it difficult to judge [Colin Baker] after so little a time, but what I've seen of him I've mostly liked. His arrogance and total self-obsession [are] very nice, and his attitude to Peri in the first episode was magnificent. On the other hand I don't like the move to a totally alien Doctor – a Doctor who does not comprehend compassion and who retains his alien values might as well go home and be President.'

A major problem with the sixth Doctor is the horrendous costume that he is required to wear. Continuing John Nathan-Turner's policy of giving his Doctors highly stylised, uniform-like outfits, this one was designed according to his remit to be 'totally tasteless'. Quite apart from the obvious fact that this makes the series' lead character look a complete joke, it also has the unfortunate effect in storytelling terms of precluding any possibility of him entering unobtrusively into a situation or being anything other than the centre of attention. A still further drawback is that it encourages, indeed almost requires, the series' designers to make all other aspects of the production look equally bright and gaudy, simply to compete. It would have been no good the costume designers giving Peri subtly hued outfits to wear, for example, as she would have simply faded into the background. So in *The Twin Dilemma* we have her sporting a blouse that appears to have been made out of deckchair material; and similarly Hugo Lang, who spends quite a bit of his time with the two regulars, acquires a jacket that seems to consist of sections of garishly coloured tinfoil.

Anthony Steven's scripts for *The Twin Dilemma*, apparently heavily rewritten by Eric Saward, leave much to be desired. Ian Clarke, also reviewing the story in *TARDIS* Volume 9 Number 1, highlighted some of their deficiencies: 'The general theme of a power to change matter by mathematics being misused and thus resulting in a threat to the universe is hardly original … Season twenty-one has contained some excellent dialogue, but not, I'm afraid, [in] this tale. It just seemed so full of clichés. I was most irritated by the scene in [Part Two] where Hugo, given the whole TARDIS to search for a small section of his gun, not only goes into the wardrobe but finds the precise piece of clothing in which it is hidden!'

It doesn't help matters, either, that Peter Moffatt's direction on this occasion is flat and uninteresting, and the whole production has a rather tacky, B-movie feel to it. The gastropods must be one of the series' most uninspired creations, as Andrew Martin observed in *Shada* 18 dated July 1984: 'Mestor, played by … Edwin Richfield, was a run-of-the-mill *Doctor Who* baddie, all threats, gurgling voice and hand-jiving …. The gastropods were a nice idea wasted. I've always advocated slugs as monsters in *Doctor Who* as I'm petrified of the damn things. But … wasn't there a case for making the monsters in this story a little less like ultra-cheap Tractators?' On the plus side, though, the bird-like Jocondans are quite effective, due in large part to Denise Baron's excellent make-up design. 'It would have been so easy to do them as boring humanoids,' noted Tim Munro, 'but thankfully the make-up people rose to the challenge.' The performances are equally varied, ranging from the praiseworthy – Maurice Denham as Azmael and Seymour Green as the Jocondan Chamberlain – to the lamentable – Gavin and Andrew Conrad as the twins and, jaw-droppingly atrocious, Helen Blatch as Fabian. Gary Russell, writing in *Zygon* Issue 1 dated August 1984, tried hard to look on the bright side:

'The bit where the Doctor challenges Mestor, then throws the bottle and fails to have any effect, is a great scene, followed shortly after by Azmael's death throes, where the Doctor [allows] the very humanity that he claimed not [to] possess [to] show through beautifully.

'The last episode … is actually the best of the four …, showing the Doctor finally waking up to the fact that he has changed and his new life is worth living. Thus he fights to save Peri, the twins, Joconda and even [the] to an extent … rather clichéd character of Hugo Lang (a very *Boys' Own Paper* name if ever there was one).

'Trying to find any other good points in this story is rather difficult. The leads made it worth watching [and] the costumes and make-up for the Jocondans were splendid, but let down by the characterisations – a shame that although they looked birdy the opportunity was missed to play them that way, as the Menoptra [were] played [as] insects back in 1965.'

In the end, one can only agree with Russell's conclusion that: '*The Twin Dilemma* was, apart from the acting of Baker and Bryant (and she became ropy occasionally), a silly waste of ninety minutes.'

Peter Davison, recalling advice he had received from Patrick Troughton that three years was the optimum length of time to play the Doctor, had decided at the end of season twenty that he would quit the series at the end of season twenty-one. In subsequent discussions he had indicated to John Nathan-Turner that he might, after all, be prepared to stay on for a fourth season, but this change of heart had come too late as action had already been put in hand to write him out. His imminent departure was announced in late July 1983 and, like his original appointment to the role, even received coverage on the BBC's main evening news programme.

Nathan-Turner had decided to break with recent precedent by making the new Doctor's debut story the last of the current season, rather than the first of the next. The main aim of this was to engage viewers' interest in the newcomer and so maintain their loyalty over the between-seasons break. Somewhat at odds with this, however, was the decision then taken by the production team to make the sixth Doctor unstable and, at least initially, unlikeable – an approach they adopted partly in order to keep their options open as to how the character would be portrayed in the longer term. So ended a season that had seen *Doctor Who* going through a number of significant developments – although arguably none as significant as those that lay in store during the remainder of the sixth Doctor's era …

DOCTOR WHO SEASON TWENTY-TWO (1985)

Regular Cast:
The Doctor (Colin Baker)
Peri (Nicola Bryant)

Regular Crew:
Producer: John Nathan-Turner.
Script Editor: Eric Saward.
Production Associate: June Collins on *Attack of the Cybermen*, Sue Anstruther on all stories except *Revelation of the Daleks*, Angela Smith on *Revelation of the Daleks*.
Title Music: Ron Grainer and the BBC Radiophonic Workshop, arranged by Peter Howell.
Special Sounds: Dick Mills.

Doctor Who's twenty-second season would not only show the new Doctor becoming noticeably more stable after his rather manic debut in *The Twin Dilemma* but would also see some important changes being made to the style and pacing of the stories themselves. These came about largely as a consequence of a decision taken by Controller of BBC1 Alan Hart to double the length of each episode, with a consequent halving from twenty-six to thirteen of the number of episodes per season. The new episode length was originally to have been fifty minutes but was eventually fixed at forty-five minutes after John Nathan-Turner pointed out that, with fewer title sequences required, a fifty minute episode would actually have demanded *more* than twice the usual programme content, increasing the strain on the series' budget and resources. In another respect, however, this season marked a return to tradition, as it saw the series back in a Saturday evening slot for the first time since Tom Baker's departure. It was also the first since season seventeen to have the same regular cast – Colin Baker and Nicola Bryant – throughout. There was, however, a major upheaval in the offing …

ATTACK OF THE CYBERMEN

Writer: Paula Moore. **Director:** Matthew Robinson. **Designer:** Marjorie Pratt. **Costumes:** Anushia Nieradzik. **Make-Up:** Linda McInnes. **Incidental Music:** Malcolm Clarke. **Visual Effects:** Chris Lawson. **Film Cameraman:** Godfrey Johnson. **Film Editor:** M A C Adams. **Studio Lighting:** Henry Barber. **Studio Sound:** Andrew Stacey. **Production Assistant:** Llinos Wyn Jones. **Assistant Floor Manager:** Pennie Bloomfield.

	First UK TX	Scheduled TX	Actual TX	Duration	Viewers	Chart Pos.
Part One	05/01/85	17.20	17.23	44'17"	8.9	71
Part Two	12/01/85	17.20	17.23	44'29"	7.2	104

Plot: The TARDIS is lured to Earth in 1985 by a distress call sent by Lytton, who has made contact with a group of Cybermen based in London's sewers. The Doctor and Peri are then captured and forced to take Lytton and the Cybermen in the TARDIS to the Cybermen's home planet Telos. The Cybermen have stolen a time vessel from another race and plan to change history by crashing Halley's comet into Earth and obliterating it before it can bring about the demise of their original home world, Mondas, in 1986. Lytton is in fact however a double agent employed by the Cryons – a species native to Telos. His mission is to capture the stolen time vessel, but he fails and is partially converted into a Cyberman. The Doctor is unable to save him, but manages to kill the Cyber Controller. The Cryon leader Flast sacrifices her own life and a huge explosion completely destroys the tombs.

Episode endings:
1. The Doctor, Peri and an undercover detective named Russell, who has been investigating Lytton's criminal activities on Earth, enter the TARDIS only to find that the Cybermen have got there before them. The Cyber Leader enters the ship and orders that Peri be destroyed at once. Peri screams.
2. The Doctor and Peri leave in the TARDIS. The Doctor feels that things haven't gone very well and, despite reassurance from Peri, reflects: 'I don't think I've ever misjudged anybody quite as badly as I did Lytton.'

IT WAS MADE WHERE...?

Location filming: 29.05.84-01.06.84
Locations: Dartmouth Castle Public House, corner of Glenthorne Road and Overstone Road, London, E6; London Scrapyard, 161 Becklow Road, London W12; Davis Road and alley, Acton, London, W12; Gerrards Cross Sand and Gravel Quarry, Wapsey's Wood, Oxford Road, Gerrards Cross, Bucks; Cameron Scrap Merchant, 36 Birkbeck Road, London, W3.
Model filming: 07.06.84-08.06.84 (studio unknown)
Studio: 21.06.84-22.06.84, 05.07.84-07.07.84 all in TC6, 13.07.84 (gallery only) in TC2

ADDITIONAL CREDITED CAST

Lytton (Maurice Colbourne), Griffiths (Brian Glover), Russell (Terry Molloy[1]*), Payne (James Beckett[1]), Cyber Leader (David Banks), Cyber Controller (Michael Kilgarriff), Bates (Michael Attwell), Stratton (Jonathan David), Cyber Lieutenant (Brian Orrell), Cyberman (John Ainley), Bill (Stephen Churchett[1]), David (Stephen Wale[1]), Rost (Sarah Berger[2]), Threst (Esther Freud[2]), Flast (Faith Brown[2]), Varne (Sarah Greene[2]).

* Also at the beginning of Part Two, in the reprise from Part One, but uncredited.

POPULAR MYTHS

• This story was written by Eric Saward and fan Ian Levine under a pseudonym. (It wasn't, although Paula Moore is indeed a pseudonym, for Paula Woolsey, who had previously worked in radio and was a friend of Saward. Several plot ideas were initially suggested by Levine however and, due to Moore's complete inexperience as a writer, Saward played a significant part in development and rewriting of the scripts.)
• This story replaced one called *The Opera of Doom* featuring Lightfoot and Jago,

Padmasambhava, Omega, the Master, the Rills and the Cybermen. (This was a rumour deliberately started by a group of fans as a practical joke and then printed as fact in the news magazine *DWB*.)

THINGS TO WATCH OUT FOR

- Faith Brown, better known as an impressionist and entertainer, plays the Cryon leader Flast.
- Television presenter Sarah Greene appears as Varne, one of the Cryons.
- Former wrestler Brian Glover, well known as the voice of the 'Tetley Tea Folk' in television commercials, plays Griffiths.
- Terry Molloy, better known to Doctor Who fans as the third actor to play Davros and to the general public as Mike Tucker in the long-running BBC radio serial The Archers, appears here as Russell.
- The TARDIS changes its exterior shape for the first time in the series' history. It takes on the appearance of a cupboard, then a pipe organ and then an ornamental gateway before reverting back to its normal police box shape.
- Maurice Colbourne reprises his role of Lytton from the season twenty story Resurrection of the Daleks.
- Michael Kilgarriff reprises his role as the Cyber Controller from the season five story The Tomb of the Cybermen. He had also appeared as an Ogron in the season ten story Frontier in Space and as the Robot in the season twelve story Robot.
- A version of part of Ron Grainer's Steptoe and Son theme is used when the TARDIS arrives in the junkyard. When the ship converts into its pipe organ form, an arrangement of Bach's Toccata and Fugue is heard.

THINGS YOU MIGHT NOT HAVE KNOWN

- Lytton is revealed to originate from the planet Riften 5, the fifteenth satellite in orbit around Vita in Star System 690.
- Actress and celebrity Koo Stark was originally to have appeared in this story as one of the Cryons but pulled out after a disagreement with the production team over publicity.
- Esther Freud (Threst) is the daughter of Lucian and great-granddaughter of Sigmund. She's now better known as a writer. Her first novel, Hideous Kinky, was filmed starring Kate Winslet.

QUOTE, UNQUOTE

- **The Doctor:** 'The TARDIS, when working properly, is capable of many amazing things. Not unlike myself.'
- **Russell:** 'Who are you?' **The Doctor:** 'I've already told you. I am known as the Doctor. I'm also a Time Lord from the planet Gallifrey in the constellation of Kasterborous.' **Russell:** 'You're bonkers.' **The Doctor:** 'That's debatable.'
- **Peri:** 'What is that terrible smell?' **Lytton:** 'Death.' **Griffiths:** 'Trust him to cheer everyone up.' **Peri:** 'What do you mean, death?' **Lytton:** 'The sour, rank odour of death is unmistakable.' **Peri:** 'They're not dead. The Cybermen are hibernating.' **The Doctor:** 'You know far more than you're saying.' **Lytton:** 'You'll find out, Doctor. All in good time.'

Attack of the Cybermen is one of the most horribly derivative stories that *Doctor Who* ever turned out. It seems that John Nathan-Turner and Eric Saward had by this point become completely preoccupied with making the series in a style that would appeal to a small number of dedicated fans and, with this aim in mind, had decided to cram in as many elements from and references to past stories as they possibly could. Indeed they had even starting using certain fans as unpaid continuity advisers. Unfortunately this totally backfired as not only did it represent a complete misunderstanding of what the great majority of fans really wanted – i.e. well told original stories in the series' traditional style – but, at least if the viewing figures are anything to go by, it also succeeded in alienating many members of the general viewing public.

The major 'blasts from the past' in *Attack of the Cybermen* include: 76 Totter's Lane (*100,000 BC*), Lytton (*Resurrection of the Daleks*), the Cybermen in the sewers of London (*The Invasion*), the cryogenic hibernation units on Telos (*The Tomb of the Cybermen*), the Cyber Controller (*The Tomb of the Cybermen* again) and Mondas's imminent destruction in 1986 (*The Tenth Planet*). Out of this jumble of elements emerges a strange and confused tale of the Cybermen trying to prevent Mondas from being destroyed in the past while their domination of Telos seems assured in the future. The question has to be asked: what is the point of it all? Like *Resurrection of the Daleks*, it may be superficially exciting but it does not stand up to considered scrutiny or repeated viewing. Quite apart from anything else, one has to wonder what motivated Nathan-Turner and Saward to commission such a story – season opener, return of the Cybermen, lots of continuity – from someone who had, by her own later admission, no previous professional writing experience whatsoever. Is it any wonder that the scripts needed a lot of work?

To add insult to injury, having decided to put in all these elements from past stories, they have so badly failed to do them justice that the only possible effect is actually to irritate those whom they hoped to please: the fans. Tim Westmacott, writing in *Queen Bat* Issue 1 in 1985, drew attention to a specific example of a problem that arose directly as a result of a slavish, and in this case particularly pointless, adherence to the series' past: 'I'm tempted to … ask whether the Controller's real purpose in maintaining the ice tombs was to keep a well-stocked larder that he would frequently nip into when no-one was looking. Only hard-core *Doctor Who* fans would be aware that Michael Kilgarriff played the original Cyber Controller from *The Tomb of the Cybermen*, yet it is also we *Doctor Who* fans who are most offended by the result. They should get actors to fit the costumes, not make Cyber-tents for the sake of an obscure point of continuity.' Not only does the Cyber Controller conspicuously lack the impressive sleekness of his debut appearance in *The Tomb of the Cyberman* but the tombs themselves also look totally different and, similarly, nowhere near as effective.

Again like *Resurrection of the Daleks*, however, *Attack of the Cybermen* does have some saving graces, including Matthew Robinson's polished direction. The scenes in the sewers where a black-painted Cyberman kills some workmen at the start of the story are marvellously eerie, for example, and the moment when the sewer wall slides back to reveal the Cyber Leader is also nicely handled. The location work for the scenes set on the surface of Telos is magnificent, too. In amongst all the continuity references there are even one or two new ideas in the scripts. The references to Halley's comet were nicely topical at the time of transmission, and the Cryons are well thought out and interesting aliens with suitably distinctive appearances and mannerisms. Lytton's return is also a welcome one and actor Maurice Colbourne manages to give a boost to every scene in which he appears – although the gratuitous incident in which the Cybermen crush his hands is unnecessarily nasty and gory.

There are, in fact, some reviewers who have responded very warmly to this story. Andrew Evans, for example, wrote in *Shada* 19 dated November 1985: 'It had plenty of action, excitement and humour, old monsters, lots of continuity for the fans and of course heralded the first full season of a new Doctor. Colin Baker was brilliant and took advantage of a witty and lively script to fulfil the promise he had shown in *The Twin Dilemma*, which didn't allow him too much scope. There were some wonderfully comic moments, for example in [Part One] where he searches the two policemen, [and] in [Part Two] when he vents his anger on the Time Lords like at the beginning of *The Brain of Morbius* ...

'The opening scenes with Lytton and his gang were very entertaining, and a bit like *Minder*. I was very pleased to see Maurice Colbourne again, and I think it's very healthy that [John Nathan-Turner] is at least generating some new continuity by bringing back recent characters ... The two policemen patrolling the junkyard harked back to the very beginning of [the series' first episode,] *An Unearthly Child*. I would rather the TARDIS hadn't changed shape, simply because it was pointless, ... but thought it was done quite tastefully.'

This is perhaps the best that could be said of the story as a whole: pointless, but quite tastefully done.

VENGEANCE ON VAROS

Writer: Philip Martin. **Director:** Ron Jones. **Designer:** Tony Snoaden. **Costumes:** Anne Hardinge. **Make-Up:** Cecile Hay-Arthur, Dorka Nieradzik. **Incidental Music:** Jonathan Gibbs. **Visual Effects:** Charles Jeanes. **Studio Lighting:** Dennis Channon. **Studio Sound:** Andy Stacey. **Production Assistant:** Jane Whittaker, Pat Greenland. **Assistant Floor Manager:** Sophie Neville.

	First UK TX	Scheduled TX	Actual TX	Duration	Viewers	Chart Pos.
Part One	19/01/85	17.20	17.22	44'42"	7.2	110
Part Two	26/01/85	17.20	17.21	44'43"	7.0	108

Plot: The Doctor visits the planet Varos to obtain supplies of a rare ore called zeiton 7, vital to the functioning of the TARDIS. Varos was once a colony for the criminally insane and the descendants of the original guards still rule, while the poverty-stricken people are kept entertained by screenings of public torture from the Punishment Dome. Their Governor has been trying to negotiate a better export price for zeiton ore from Sil, an envoy of the Galatron Mining Corporation, whose reptilian body is supported and kept cool by a mobile water tank. The Doctor and Peri meet two rebels, Jondar and Areta. Peri and Areta are captured and almost reshaped into beast-like creatures by Quillam, the Dome's sadistic commandant, but the Doctor saves them and tells the Governor the true value of zeiton 7. Quillam and Varos's Chief Officer, who are in the pay of the Corporation, try to kill the Doctor and the Governor but are themselves despatched. Sil plans an invasion of Varos by a force from his home world, Thoros-Beta, but the Corporation veto this and instruct him to buy the zeiton ore at any price.

Episode endings:
1. The Doctor wanders into a No-Options Kill Centre in the Punishment Dome and suffers an hallucination, believing himself to be dying of thirst in a desert. Eventually he collapses motionless to the floor. The Governor, supervising a video recording of his ordeal, waits for a moment and then tells Bax, the vision mixer: 'And cut it – now!' Sil laughs evilly as the screens in the control room go blank.
2. Varosian citizens Arak and Etta are left at a loss to know what to do as, following an announcement by the Governor that there are to be no more transmissions from the Punishment Dome, the screen in their apartment fills with static.

IT WAS MADE WHERE...?
Studio: 18.07.84-20.07.84, 31.07.84-02.08.84 all in TC6

ADDITIONAL CREDITED CAST
Governor (Martin Jarvis), Sil (Nabil Shaban), Quillam (Nicholas Chagrin), Jondar (Jason Connery), Chief Officer (Forbes Collins), Arak (Stephen Yardley), Etta (Sheila Reid), Areta (Geraldine Alexander), Bax (Graham Cull), Maldak (Owen Teale), Rondel (Keith Skinner[1]), Priest (Hugh Martin[2]).

POPULAR MYTHS
- The Doctor at one point in this story deliberately pushes two guards into an acid bath. (In a struggle with the Doctor, one of the guards accidentally falls into the acid bath and pulls the other in after him.)

THINGS TO WATCH OUT FOR
- Jason Connery, son of James Bond star Sean Connery and later to come to popularity as the lead in the HTV/Goldcrest series *Robin of Sherwood*, appears here as the rebel Jondar.
- Well known actor Martin Jarvis makes his third *Doctor Who* appearance – previously he had been Hilio in season two's *The Web Planet* and Butler in season eleven's *Invasion of the Dinosaurs*, while here he plays the Governor of Varos.
- For the sequence when the Doctor imagines himself to be dying in a desert, stock footage was obtained from the EMI picture library. Footage of a bluebottle was obtained from Oxford Scientific Films to represent the giant gee-jee fly.

THINGS YOU MIGHT NOT HAVE KNOWN
- The story originally intended for this slot was *Space Whale* by comics writer Patrick Mills.
- *Vengeance on Varos* started life as a four part storyline entitled *Domain*, featuring the fifth Doctor, Tegan and Nyssa. A later working title was *Planet of Fear*, which was ruled out as being too similar to the previous season's *Planet of Fire*. The final title was devised by writer Philip Martin from the 'V' logo that he had suggested in his scripts.
- The script dates this story to the latter half of the 23rd Century, although this is not confirmed on screen.

- The characters of Arak and Etta were late additions. Philip Martin had conceived them as silent observers, but Eric Saward decided that they should comment on the action, rather like a Greek chorus.
- Nabil Shaban was cast as Sil after director Ron Jones interviewed a number of dwarves and midgets for the role. Shaban suffers from a disease called osteogenesis imperfecta, as a result of which his legs are underdeveloped and he needs to use a wheelchair.
- It was originally intended that Sil would be partly submerged in his tank. This was too difficult to realise in the studio, however, so it was decided that he should instead be perched on a platform above it.
- The marsh minnows that Sil habitually munches during the story were chopped peaches dyed green.
- The story had to be slightly edited for timing reasons, with the result that a number of scenes were lost. As some of these were humorous in nature, the finished story ended up being rather bleaker than Philip Martin had intended.

QUOTE, UNQUOTE

- **The Doctor:** [Speaking of Sil]: 'I think he needs more than water, Peri, eh?'
- **Arak:** 'No more executions, torture, nothing.' **Etta:** 'It's all changed. We're free.' **Arak:** 'Are we?' **Etta:** 'Yes.' **Arak:** 'What shall we do?' **Etta:** 'Dunno.'

ANALYSIS

After the disappointments of *The Twin Dilemma* and *Attack of the Cybermen*, the sixth Doctor is at last given some good material in writer Philip Martin's debut contribution to the series.

Vengeance on Varos is, in the best traditions of *Doctor Who*, a story that works on more than one level. At its simplest it is a tense and mildly horrific monster story that can be enjoyed as a piece of pure escapism, but at the other end of the spectrum it is an intelligent and thought-provoking discourse on such weighty issues as video nasties, torture and the responsibilities of leadership. As Steve Redford put it in *Shada* 19 dated November 1985: '*Vengeance on Varos* was a story for today – topical, hard-hitting and made to make people think about the power of video and what it could become. Not only that, it was a good yarn skilfully told ...'

Martin's scripts are excellent – the stylised, almost Shakespearian dialogue of the Varosian characters being particularly noteworthy – and Ron Jones's direction is appropriately moody and atmospheric. Colin Baker gives a very strong performance as the Doctor in this story, and SteveRedford for one was impressed: 'I think Colin Baker has made a great Doctor. I've taken to him from the first appearance. He gives everything he's got. I love his style of humour, wry and sarcastic ... I also like the way the Doctor is always getting at Peri for her whining.' The regulars are backed up on this occasion by a fine cast of supporting players, only Jason Connery as Jondar falling slightly short of expectations. Laura Hedgecock, writing in *MLG Megazine* No. 12 dated March/April 1985, was particularly taken with the portrayal of the Governor: 'The Governor [was] played with disgusted resignation by Martin Jarvis – whose [understated] acting ... served as a perfect [contrast] to the repulsiveness of Sil, who is the first villain in *Doctor Who* history to actually make me cringe, with his reptilian-like laughing and that [disgusting], disturbing body.'

6 · SIXTH DOCTOR

Sil is indeed an unusual and amusing character, excellently brought to life by the ideally-cast Nabil Shaban. With his fractured speech, excitable manner and deliciously evil laugh he easily qualifies as the best original villain created during the sixth Doctor's era. Not surprisingly, he has won many plaudits. 'Sil was a wonderful creation,' asserted Steve Redford, 'even allowing for the similarity between him and the Collector from *The Sun Makers*. The mask and costume were very convincing, and made him look absolutely repulsive. All of this was added to by Nabil Shaban's excellent portrayal, so thoroughly evil. I liked the scene where Sil demands a mirror so he can make himself look at his best. Also at the end when the Doctor is leaving, and he calls for him, begging him to stay, the look on Sil's face is wonderful ...'

Another interesting feature of the story is the inclusion of the characters Arak and Etta, who serve as a sort of Greek chorus offering comment on the action as it unfolds. '[These characters] are the light relief from the seriousness of the situation,' wrote Laura Hedgecock, 'as well as showing how the inhabitants of Varos have come to accept their miserable existence without a shred of pity for the poor victims of their system.'

If there is one serious criticism that could be made of *Vengeance on Varos* it is that it is perhaps just a little too unremittingly grim in tone. David Owen, writing in *DWB* No. 113 dated May 1993, was particularly concerned about the Doctor's role in the proceedings: 'The Doctor has killed many times over the years, but his actions have always been governed by a kind of Hippocratic ideal to preserve as many lives as possible. Usually, it's [a] pretty clear cut choice – despatch a single villain if there's no other way of dealing with him, and in so doing safeguard the lives of millions of innocents. No ethical dilemma there, no raised eyebrows. If it can be done by turning the villain's evil/greed/ruthlessness/whatever against him, then all the more poetic. In this story, the concept of turning the enemy's sword against him is taken a little too literally. As the Doctor and co escape in Part One having rescued Jondar, the Doctor turns the random laser beam emitter back on the pursuing guards causing one of them to be vapourised. Why not just throw a chair or something into their paths? At the beginning of Part Two, the Doctor struggles with not one but two acid bath attendants, causing them both to do passable Disprin impersonations. He could just as easily have run away. To make matters worse he then makes a "joke" about it to himself *a la* James Bond. Finally, in the End Zone he constructs a deliberately fatal trap from a piece of string and some poisonous tendrils to despatch the Chief Officer and Quillam. In the words of his predecessor, "There should have been another way."'

Antony Howe, an outspoken critic of this era of the series' history, was even more damning in his condemnation of the story in *A Voyage Through 25 Years of Doctor Who* dated December 1988: '*Vengeance on Varos* had some initially interesting ideas but they were not developed and it quickly degenerated (e.g. turning Peri into a bird was ridiculous!). The direction was poor, and in over-exploiting violence the story failed as a social criticism of "video nasties" – it itself was a video nasty! Ripping off the film *1984*, this world was very unpleasant, the sets were drab and the characters were all back-stabbing creeps – even the personable Governor was really a vicious, ruthless, greedy tyrant. The new alien, Sil, was absurdly helpless and was amazingly stupid, so how did he become so powerful? Doctor Wholigan was at home here: he sneered at men dying in a vat of acid; organised an ambush which killed many people; and did nothing at the end to help anyone, leaving the video and torture equipment intact and not helping to free the people from the Governor's tyranny.'

Laura Hedgecock, on the other hand, found criticisms of the story's level of violence misplaced: 'The idea of a society which uses [torture] as its pleasure, to the point of public executions being marketable, is not a new one – the Roman Empire did it some time back and the film *Videodrome* recently revamped it to new extremes ... The violence on show was bound to raise some protest, and this it did, but I fail to see how a society which glorifies such violent sports as boxing and wrestling can complain when this odd behaviour is suddenly pointed out to them during a Saturday teatime. After all, there isn't that much difference between watching two men beat each other up and watching a man being tortured, except that, thankfully, here one was fact and one was fiction.'

Hedgecock did however have one complaint about the story: 'The climax of *Vengeance on Varos* came all too quickly for me. It was unfortunately abrupt and far too clichéd and simple. Okay, we all like happy endings, but things don't just happen like that. Within the space of ten minutes the Doctor kills off all the bad guys [and] saves Jondar and the Governor, and ... the whole of Sil's invading fleet simply give up and go home! Tidy as the ending was, I couldn't help but feel more than a little cheated by the story's conclusion.'

This is a valid point. Overall, however, *Vengeance on Varos* stands up well and rates as one of the highlights of the sixth Doctor's brief era.

THE MARK OF THE RANI

Writer: Pip and Jane Baker. **Director:** Sarah Hellings. **Designer:** Paul Trerise. **Costumes:** Dinah Collin. **Make-Up:** Catherine Davies. **Incidental Music:** Jonathan Gibbs. **Visual Effects:** David Barton. **Film Cameraman:** Kevin Rowley. **Film Editor:** Ray Wingrove. **Studio Lighting:** Don Babbage. **Studio Sound:** Keith Bowden. **Production Assistant:** Carolyn Mawdsley. **Assistant Floor Manager:** Penny Williams.

Note: Both episodes bore an additional credit reading 'The BBC wish to acknowledge the co-operation of the Ironbridge Gorge Museum.'

	First UK TX	Scheduled TX	Actual TX	Duration	Viewers	Chart Pos.
Part One	02/02/85	17.20	17.22	45'01"	6.3	111
Part Two	09/02/85	17.20	17.22	44'32"	7.3	84

Plot: The TARDIS arrives in Killingworth in 19th Century England, where the Master is plotting to kill some of the key figures of the industrial revolution. Also present is the Rani, a Time Lord biochemist who was cast out from Gallifrey and is now dictator of the planet Miasimia Goria. The Rani has altered the metabolism of Miasimia Goria's populace to heighten their awareness, but in the process has inadvertently lowered their ability to sleep. In order to correct this she has been drawing a fluid from the brains of humans at various points in Earth's history, unconcerned that this leaves them aggressive and unable to sleep themselves. Now she is adding to the unrest caused in England by the Luddites. She has also planted some land mines that turn people into trees. The Doctor sabotages the Rani's TARDIS and she and the Master are sent spinning into the vortex at the mercy of a rapidly growing tyrannosaurus rex embryo –

a specimen collected on one of her earlier visits to Earth.

Episode endings:
1. The Doctor, strapped to a trolley, is placed on top of a mine cart by a group of rowdy miners and pushed down a slope. The cart rattles along its rails, fast approaching the gaping entrance to the mine shaft.
2. The TARDIS dematerialises, leaving Lord Ravensworth and George Stephenson puzzled as to where the Doctor and Peri have gone. Lord Ravensworth comments: 'You know, I always said he was a strange sort of fellow.'

IT WAS MADE WHERE...?

Location filming: 22.10.84-02.11.84 and 12.11.84

Locations: Granville Colliery spoil heaps, Lodge Road, Donnington Wood, Donnington, Telford, Shropshire; Blists Hill Open Air Museum, Ironbridge Gorge, Shropshire; Coalport China Works, Coalport, Telford, Shropshire; Park Wood, Bury Street, Ruislip, Middx.

Studio: 18.11.84-20.11.84 in TC1, 28.11.84 (gallery only) (studio unknown)

ADDITIONAL CREDITED CAST

The Master (Anthony Ainley), The Rani (Kate O'Mara), Lord Ravensworth (Terence Alexander), Jack Ward (Peter Childs), Luke Ward (Gary Cady), Guard (Richard Steele), Tim Bass (William Ilkley), Edwin Green (Hus Levent[1]), Sam Rudge (Kevin White[1]), Drayman (Martin Whitby[1]), Young Woman (Sarah James[1]), Older Woman (Cordelia Ditton[1]), George Stephenson (Gawn Grainger[2]).

POPULAR MYTHS

- John Nathan-Turner cast Kate O'Mara as the Rani because of her starring role in the popular American soap opera *Dynasty*. (O'Mara had yet to begin work on *Dynasty* when she was cast as the Rani. She was however well known for her appearances in a number of UK soap operas, including for the BBC *The Brothers* – opposite Colin Baker – and *Triangle*.)

THINGS TO WATCH OUT FOR

- No explanation is given for the Master's escape from his apparent death at the end of the previous season's *Planet of Fire*.
- Popular actor Terence Alexander, best known for his role as Charlie Hungerford in the BBC's *Bergerac*, plays Lord Ravensworth.
- In this adventure viewers see the inside of the Doctor's patchwork coat, revealing the presence of three cat silhouettes sewn into the lining. Baker had arranged for this to be done – one cat for each story of the season so far.

THINGS YOU MIGHT NOT HAVE KNOWN

- Working titles: *Too Clever by Far*, *Enter the Rani*
- Nicola Bryant hurt her neck while on location for this story and had to wear a brace to hold it steady between takes.
- The Rani's chemically impregnated maggots were realised both with real maggots

(for the shots of them squirming) and with marzipan (for scenes where they had to be eaten by actors).

- The incidental music for this story was originally to have been provided by freelance composer John Lewis, but he died while working on it. His estate was paid a fee for the 12 minutes' worth of music he had already completed for Part One, and for the 20.5 minutes' worth he had completed for Part Two. None of this music was used on the transmitted story.

- **The Master:** [Speaking of the Doctor] 'He wears yellow trousers and a vulgarly coloured coat, but tread carefully – he's treacherous.'
- **The Rani:** [Speaking of the Master]: 'He'd get dizzy if he tried to walk in a straight line!'

Stories with a historical setting are something of a rarity in seventies and eighties *Doctor Who*, and *The Mark of the Rani* makes a very pleasant departure from the norm. In fact, with its inclusion of steam engine pioneer George Stephenson, it is the first story to feature a *bona fide* historical figure since season three's *The Gunfighters* (or possibly season six's *The Mind Robber*, if the Master of the Land of Fiction in that story is, as implied, real-life author Bracebridge Hemyng). This can only be a welcome development in a series that is supposed to revolve around time travel. The setting is very well realised, too, with some excellent location filming, and makes a nice contrast to the futuristic locales in which the other sixth Doctor stories take place. 'The undoubted star of the story was the 19th Century mining village at Blists Hill Open Air Museum in Ironbridge,' suggested Tim Westmacott in *Peladon* Issue Five dated autumn 1988. 'The sunlight seemed to induce a magic from the stone of the buildings and the all-embracing foliage that cast an air of tranquillity over everything. The beautifully simple but effective incidental music combined with the images to create a feeling of bygone times when life was hard, but simpler, with a calmness which drew strength and security from the absence of change; the calm before the storm of the encroaching industrial revolution which the Luddites were keen to preserve.'

The plot is a relatively leisurely and straightforward one, which also makes a refreshing change for this period of the series' history, although Westmacott felt that there were a number of elements within it that ought to have been developed further:

'The Rani's mission to collect brain fluid which promoted sleep would have carried more credibility if we had been given a glance of the planet she ruled ... in the state of chaos which prompted the trip. It would also have been nice to see her operating in various times of Earth's history and as a by-product being partially responsible for starting many of our wars.

'The other main disappointment was that after the mention of the forthcoming historic meeting of scientists such as Faraday, Telford, Brunel etc we didn't see a single one of them apart from George Stephenson. If they had appeared we could have seen in progress the Master's plan to change the course of history to his own purpose. This would have lent credence to what, [as in] *The King's Demons*, looked like a case of choosing the time and place for a story first and working out a reason for the presence of the Master as an afterthought.'

The most entertaining aspect of the story is the amusing interplay between the three outcast Time Lords – the Doctor, the Master and the Rani – who seem at times almost to forget the momentous events going on around them as they indulge in their own private feud. Simon Ferns, writing in *MLG Megazine* No. 12 dated March/April 1985, appreciated this, although he found certain aspects of it rather puzzling: 'Kate O'Mara was suitably impressive as the Rani, who overshadowed Ainley's Master ... The [use of the] Master's [tissue compression eliminator] was strange: it killed both [a] dog and [a] guard but left no shrunken bodies behind. Continuity was left behind, [though]. How could the Master believe the Doctor's TARDIS could be destroyed by pushing it down a mine shaft? ... Likewise it was difficult to believe the Master's and the Rani's haste to escape the collapsing pit shaft – or maybe later TARDIS models can be destroyed more easily? ... Throughout the story the Rani always seemed to be in far more control of the situation than the Master, which again seemed strange, as it was the Master who had set the whole thing up.'

The story's production values are excellent, and there are some notably good sets on display. 'The control room of the Rani's TARDIS really made me gasp,' confessed Westmacott. 'The predominant slate grey lit subtly by a glowing pink suggested perfectly the character of its owner, which was confirmed and consolidated by the silver studded black console at its heart ... I applaud the effort put into its design and construction.'

One aspect of the story much derided by reviewers is the idea of people being transformed into trees by the Rani's land mines. 'Those trees ... were very amusing,' asserted Ferns, 'especially when the Doctor ended up slung between them, but not when Peri was attacked by a limp-wristed one. Maybe this was a bright idea from the socially conscious [writers Pip and Jane Baker], who [during the course of the story warned] us against the destruction of the hedgerows, [about] not being a vegetarian and [about] the dangers of smoking cigarettes. Even the Doctor's speech about scientists having no conscience [smacked] of this feeling. The final solution was found through an "All Things Bright and Beautiful" [device], as it was Peri's valerian herbs that cured the Luddites and an overgrown tyrannosaurus rex that halted the Rani and the Master. Indeed nature versus man became [a recurring] theme within this story.'

Nicholas Setchfield, reviewing the story for *Shada* 19 dated November 1985, was left with a feeling of dissatisfaction: 'In all, ... *The Mark of the Rani* failed. It failed not in the sense that it was poorly produced – it wasn't, and its gloss made it shine brighter than many of its contemporaries, each episode nothing if not pleasant to watch. But it was hollow, vacuous, stagnant ... impressions not helped in the least by the annoyingly open-ended conclusion – hardly the most accurate of words – concerning the Rani and the Master ... A beginning was there, but where were the middle and the end? Nothing progressed, nothing was satisfactorily resolved. The Doctor simply tinkered with the Rani's control console and [the two renegades were] zapped by mistake into the farthest reaches of the universe ... The Master seemed entirely bereft of a convincing plan to dispose of the Doctor, apparently preferring now to let fate run its uneven course whilst his *grand vision* of disrupting history was ultimately inconsequential and finally wasted ... A pretty runaround in history it might have been – in all honesty, it really wasn't much else.'

THE TWO DOCTORS

Writer: Robert Holmes. **Director:** Peter Moffatt. **Designer:** Tony Burrough. **Costumes:** Jan Wright. **Make-Up:** Catherine Davies. **Incidental Music:** Peter Howell. **Visual Effects:** Steven Drewett. **Film Cameraman:** John Walker. **Film Editor:** Mike Robotham. **Studio Lighting:** Don Babbage. **Studio Sound:** Keith Bowden. **Production Assistant:** Patricia O'Leary. **Assistant Floor Manager:** Ilsa Rowe.

	First UK TX	Scheduled TX	Actual TX	Duration	Viewers	Chart Pos.
Part One	16/02/85	17.20	17.22	44'22"	6.6	92
Part Two	23/02/85	17.20	17.21	44'49"	6.0	90
Part Three	02/03/85	17.20	17.23	44'45"	6.9	66

Plot: The second Doctor and Jamie are sent by the Time Lords to space station Camera in order to put a stop to unauthorised time travel experiments being carried out there under the auspices of the head of projects, Dastari. Dastari has been biologically augmenting Androgums, a race of voracious gourmands, including the chatelaine Chessene who has secretly allied herself with Group Marshal Stike of the Ninth Sontaran Battle Group. The Sontarans raid the station, killing almost all aboard. They capture the second Doctor and take him to Earth, imprisoning him in a hacienda near the Spanish city of Seville. There Dastari, also in league with the Sontarans, plans to dissect him in order to find the Rassilon Imprimature – the symbiotic nuclei within a Time Lord's genes that are the key to time travel. The sixth Doctor and Peri rescue Jamie from the station and then follow the trail to Spain. The second Doctor is imprinted by Dastari with genes taken from Shockeye, the space station's Androgum chef, but the sixth Doctor rescues him and kills Shockeye. Chessene destroys the Sontarans and, reverting to base instincts, kills Dastari. She herself then dies through molecular disintegration when she attempts to time travel without the Imprimature.

Episode endings:
1. The sixth Doctor and Peri make their way through the infrastructure of the seemingly deserted space station. The Doctor attempts to disarm the station's computer but receives a defensive blast of vorum gas in the face and collapses unconscious just as Peri is attacked by a fierce humanoid creature.
2. Peri runs from the hacienda chased by Shockeye. She trips and falls, and Shockeye quickly looms over her, muttering with delight.
3. The sixth Doctor and Peri head off to their TARDIS. Peri hesitantly enquires if they are going fishing again and the Doctor tells her that they are not: from now on, it is a vegetarian diet for both of them.

IT WAS MADE WHERE...?

Location filming: 09.08.84-16.08.84
Locations: the following areas of Seville, Spain: Rio Guadiamar, SE521, between Gerena and Aznalcollar; Dehera Boyar hacienda, between Gerena and El Garrobo; Country Road between Gerena and El Garrobo; Seville Cathedral, Avenida de la Constitucion;

6 SIXTH DOCTOR

Santa Cruz streets; *Restaurant del Laurel*.
Studio: 30.08.84-31.08.84 in TC1, 13.09.84-14.09.84, 27.09.84-28.09.84 all in TC6, 04.10.84-05.10.84 (gallery only) (studio unkown)

ADDITIONAL CREDITED CAST

The Doctor (Patrick Troughton), Jamie (Frazer Hines), Shockeye (John Stratton), Chessene (Jacqueline Pearce), Dastari (Laurence Payne), Doña Arana (Aimee Delamain[1]), Oscar (James Saxon), Anita (Carmen Gomez), Varl (Tim Raynham), Technician (Nicholas Fawcett[1]), Stike (Clinton Greyn[2,3]).

THINGS TO WATCH OUT FOR

- The opening moments of the first episode, featuring the second Doctor and Jamie in the TARDIS, are in black and white – recalling the stories of the second Doctor's own era.
- Jacqueline Pearce, better known as the evil Servalan in the BBC science fiction series *Blake's 7*, appears here as Chessene.
- Director Peter Moffatt and costume designer Jan Wright are seen as customers sitting outside the *Bar Hosteria del Laurel* in Part Three.
- Laurence Payne, playing Dastari, had appeared in *Doctor Who* twice before: as Johnny Ringo in season three's *The Gunfighters* and as Morix in season eighteen's *The Leisure Hive*.
- Complementing Peter Howell's radiophonic incidental music are a number of pieces played on Spanish guitar by Les Thatcher.

THINGS YOU MIGHT NOT HAVE KNOWN

- Working titles: *The Kraglon Inheritance*, *The Androgum Inheritance*. Other rumoured working titles are *Parallax*, *The Seventh Augmentment* and *Creation*, but these do not appear in any known BBC documentation.
- 'Dastari' is an anagram of 'a TARDIS'.
- Producer John Nathan-Turner carried out some script editing duties on this story while Eric Saward was off-contract writing *Revelation of the Daleks*.
- The original location planned for *The Two Doctors* was New Orleans, USA. It was commissioned after another story intended to feature an American location, *Way Down Yonder* by Lesley Elizabeth Thomas (who was herself American), fell through. In the end, this idea proved financially unviable. John Nathan-Turner then suggested Venice, Italy, as an alternative, but this was ruled out as it was felt that there would be too many tourists who would disrupt shooting.
- The extremely high temperatures in Spain caused problems during the location filming, particularly for actors Clinton Greyn and Tim Raynham in their heavy Sontaran costumes and make-up.
- The role of Chessene was originally to have been played by character actress Elizabeth Spriggs, but she had to pull out shortly before production.
- The BBC Radio 4 schools' programme *Wavelength* on 20 September 1984 ran a feature on the making of this story, including recorded interviews with Colin Baker, Patrick Troughton, Nicola Bryant and members of the production team.

- **The Doctor:** 'What's the use of a good quotation if you can't change it?'
- **Shockeye:** '"The gratification of pleasure is the sole motive of action." Is that not our law?' **Chessene:** 'I still accept it, but there are pleasures other than the purely sensual.' **Shockeye:** 'For you, perhaps. Fortunately, I have not been augmented.' **Chessene:** 'Take care. Your purity could easily become insufferable.'
- **Peri:** 'What's that awful smell?' **The Doctor:** 'Mainly decaying food. And corpses.' **Peri:** 'Corpses?' **The Doctor:** 'That is the smell of death, Peri. Ancient must, heavy in the air. Fruit-soft flesh peeling from white bones. The unholy, unburiable smell of Armageddon. Nothing quite so evocative as one's sense of smell, is there?' **Peri:** 'I feel sick!'
- **Stike:** 'It is not easy being commander. The loneliness of supreme responsibility …'

ANALYSIS

The Two Doctors is a story that promises an awful lot but ultimately fails to deliver on just about every major count. The biggest problem, as in *Resurrection of the Daleks* and *Attack of the Cybermen* before it, is an over-reliance on the series' established mythology. The 'shopping list' of elements that the production team prevailed upon writer Robert Holmes to incorporate on this occasion included not only the second Doctor (as Patrick Troughton had enjoyed himself so much making *The Five Doctors* and John Nathan-Turner was keen to have another multiple Doctor story) but also his companion Jamie and, to provide the opposition, the Sontarans (which, although they were Holmes's own creations, he would have preferred not to use). On top of all this they also asked him to set part of the action in a foreign location (originally New Orleans in the USA and then, when this was discovered to be too expensive, Seville in Spain).

Not surprisingly, the resultant story is something of a mess. D Adams gave a fairly typical reaction to it in *TARDIS* Volume 10 Number 2 dated June 1985: 'This for me was the disappointment of the season … [It] was ludicrous, with a weak plot … The only element of the story that was fairly enjoyable was John Stratton's Shockeye. Patrick Troughton and Frazer Hines were wasted in a story that I think should never have been screened.' Nigel G Hilburd, writing in the same magazine, agreed: 'Although it could be entertaining in parts, the whole was disappointing. It was obviously meant to be a humorous story, but where was the storyline?' John Connors, reviewing the story in *MLG Magazine* No. 12 dated March/April 1985, put it rather more bluntly: 'Quite the worst excuse for an adventure we've had since, oh, about *Time-Flight* I think, full of boredom, padding, more boredom and a little bit more padding.'

The most scathing criticism, however, came from Antony Howe, writing in *A Voyage Through 25 Years of Doctor Who* dated December 1988: '*The Two Doctors* was a monumental bore. Chasing up and down corridors is now usual, but why waste money going to Seville just to run up and down alleyways? There is really stunning scenery in Spain, but we never saw it. The idea of the two Doctors meeting was unbelievable – it was absurd that the sixth Doctor had no memory of what had happened, and how could he possibly be affected by the Androgum conversion of the second Doctor? And why did the Sontarans need to learn about time travel when they could safely do that hundreds of years before? Vastly worse was the vicious nature of the story. The gore and violence … were [completely] avoidable [and] added nothing that could not have been cut by a ten minute rewrite. Shockeye did not have to kill and eat a blind helpless old woman, or

… eat a rat; Chessene did not need to lap up blood; Oscar did not need to be stabbed to death in the stomach; the Sontarans did not need to be burnt with acid, mutilated and blown up – all lovingly shown on screen! Worst of all was the murder of Shockeye … This was the death of *Doctor Who*.'

Justin Richards, writing in *DWB* No. 120 dated December 1993, thought that the presentation of the Sontarans was a factor in the story's favour: 'Robert Holmes's love of the Sontarans is obvious – Stike and Varl not only get some of the best lines, they are better defined and better acted than the haughty but emotionless Chessene, the manic Shockeye, or Dastari – who seems bored with the entire thing right from the start. Had the Sontarans been the main villains – or just survived the longest – this would have helped the final episode immeasurably.' Andrew Stirling-Brown, another reviewer in *TARDIS* Volume 10 Number 2, felt the opposite: 'My main grouch lay in the treatment of the monsters. The Sontarans got a raw deal, I thought; comic *Dad's Army/It Ain't Half Hot Mum*-style soldiers, quite unnecessary to the plot. Just convenient shock troops and chauffeurs for Dastari and the Androgums. In fact any monster would have done, they just happened to suit John Nathan-Turner's current "old comeback" policy.' One of the problems with the Sontarans in this story is that their costumes are not as effective as in the past; the loose-fitting collars have a tendency to flap about and completely spoil the illusion that the creatures have thick necks. Peter Moffatt's undramatic long-shot revelation of the creatures is also an extraordinarily poor piece of direction that doesn't exactly help them to make an impact.

By far the most interesting of the guest characters is Shockeye, marvellously played by John Stratton. His fawning manner and obsession with food are always entertaining, and the scenes of him with an Androgum-infected second Doctor in Part Three are very amusing – even though they again have little to do with the plot. In fact, the plot changes mid-way through the story when Chessene – played by Jacqueline Pearce in a manner that suggests she still thinks she is Servalan in *Blake's 7* – abruptly decides that she no longer wants the second Doctor's symbiotic nuclei removed (which was the whole point of kidnapping a Time Lord in the first place) but, bizarrely, wants him changed into an Androgum instead.

The Two Doctors is, unfortunately, fatally misconceived; another attempt to exploit *Doctor Who*'s past glories without offering anything new.

TIMELASH

Writer: Glen McCoy. **Director:** Pennant Roberts. **Designer:** Bob Cove. **Costumes:** Alun Hughes. **Make-Up:** Vanessa Poulton. **Incidental Music:** Liz Parker. **Visual Effects:** Kevin Molloy. **Studio Lighting:** Henry Barber. **Studio Sound:** Andy Stacey. **Production Assistant:** Jane Whittaker. **Assistant Floor Manager:** Abigail Sharp.

Note: Some material in Part Two of *Timelash* was recorded as a remount during the first studio session for *Revelation of the Daleks*, using the crew of that story.

	First UK TX	Scheduled TX	Actual TX	Duration	Viewers	Chart Pos.
Part One	09/03/85	17.20	17.23	45'00"	6.7	69
Part Two	16/03/85	17.20	17.21	44'36"	7.4	79

Plot: On the planet Karfel a high ranking official, Maylin Tekker, uses threats against Peri to force the Doctor to go to Earth and bring back a young woman called Vena who, while holding a precious amulet, has accidentally fallen into the Timelash – a time tunnel through which the planet's tyrannical ruler the Borad banishes all rebels. The Doctor also inadvertently brings back Herbert, a man from the 19th Century, who stows away aboard the TARDIS. The Borad was once a Karfelon scientist but accidentally sprayed himself with an unstable compound called mustakozene-80 while experimenting on a Morlox – a savage underground reptilian creature – and consequently became half-Karfelon, half-Morlox. The Borad plans to bring about the deaths of all the Karfelons by provoking a war with their neighbours, the Bandrils, and repopulate the planet with creatures such as himself, starting with Peri. The Doctor uses a kontron time crystal to defeat a clone of the Borad and makes peace with the Bandrils. He then defeats the real Borad by banishing him through the Timelash to 12th Century Scotland.

Episode endings:
1. Tekker tricks the Doctor into parting with the amulet and orders an android to throw the Time Lord into the Timelash. The android grasps the Doctor's neck and pushes him forward.
2. The danger over, the Doctor and Peri enter the TARDIS to take Herbert home. Herbert is still outside and the Doctor calls for him to hurry up. He shows Peri Herbert's calling card, which identifies him as H G Wells, the famous novelist.

IT WAS MADE WHERE...?
Studio: 04.12.84-06.12.84 in TC4, 19.12.84-21.12.84 in TC8, 29.12.84 (gallery only) (studio unknown), 30.01.85 in TC8

ADDITIONAL CREDITED CAST
Tekker (Paul Darrow), Mykros (Eric Deacon), Vena (Jeananne Crowley), Maylin Renis (Neil Hallett[1]), Borad (Robert Ashby), Kendron (David Ashton), Herbert (David Chandler), Brunner (Peter Robert Scott), Sezon (Dicken Ashworth), Katz (Tracy Louise Ward), Tyheer (Martin Gower[1]), Aram (Christine Kavanagh[1]), Gazak (Steven Mackintosh[1]), Old Man (Denis Carey), Android (Dean Hollingsworth), Guardolier (James Richardson), Bandril Ambassador (Martin Gower[2]*).

* Also in Part One but uncredited.

THINGS TO WATCH OUT FOR
- A major source of inspiration for this story were the works of novelist H G Wells. For instance, Vena and the Morlox take the places of Weena and the Morlocks (*The Time Machine*); the Borad is a hybrid creature (*The Island of Doctor Moreau*); and the Doctor becomes invisible when using the kontron crystal (*The Invisible Man*).
- Paul Darrow, better known as Avon in *Blake's 7*, plays Tekker.
- Denis Carey appears as the face of the Borad. He had previously played Professor Chronotis in the abandoned season seventeen story *Shada* and the Keeper in season

eighteen's *The Keeper of Traken*.

- A mural of the third Doctor's face is revealed behind a section of wall panelling in the Timelash control room; this painting, supposedly a legacy of a previous visit by the Doctor to the planet Karfelon, was actually the work of American fan artist Gail Bennett.
- A Bandril is seen only on a communications screen. The creature was realised as a hand-operated puppet.
- A photograph of Jo Grant (Katy Manning) is seen in a locket owned by Katz.

THINGS YOU MIGHT NOT HAVE KNOWN

- Writer Glen McCoy also worked as an ambulance driver.
- In early draft scripts, the Bandrils were called Gurdels and the character Aram was male rather than female.

QUOTE, UNQUOTE

- **Herbert:** 'Avaunt thee, foul fanged fiend.' **The Doctor:** 'I can assure you I'm not that long in the tooth, and neat blood brings me out in a rash.' **Herbert:** 'Back from where you came, spirit of the glass.' **The Doctor:** 'Not just yet, if you don't mind.'
- **Tekker:** 'The stories I've heard about you. The great Doctor, all knowing and all powerful. You're about as powerful as a burnt out android. Our ruler has finished with you once and for all.' … **The Doctor:** 'You're as warped as your dictator friend.' **Tekker:** 'Save your breath for the Timelash, Doctor. Most people depart with a scream.'
- **The Borad:** 'Choose your next words carefully, Doctor. They could be your last.'
- **The Doctor:** 'The waves of time wash us all clean.'

ANALYSIS

Timelash is not a popular story amongst *Doctor Who* fans. The following assessment by Antony Howe in *A Voyage Through 25 Years of Doctor Who* dated December 1988 is fairly representative: '*Timelash* was the cheapest production [of the season]. The tinsel sets were tawdry and the "seat-belts" on the TARDIS console were laughable. The actors [apparently] made little effort – Herbert was so bad I thought he might be Adric's elder brother, and why was Paul Darrow allowed to ham it up so outrageously? The squeaky-voiced, blue-faced android was painful. The ugly Jon Pertwee painting was an insult to a great Doctor … The plot was childish, and yet another alien wanted to marry Peri! The pseudo-science to explain the Borad's plan was trash, as was his magical escape after having been shot by [the Doctor] … As for the Doctor using the TARDIS as a missile deflector – yawn.'

It is difficult to disagree with any of these criticisms, and yet *Timelash* does have one thing going for it: in the midst of a season that has more than its fair share of derivative, incomprehensible and inappropriately violent stories, it stands out as being a reassuringly traditional *Doctor Who* adventure. Andy Lennard, writing in *MLG Megazine* No. 12 dated March/April 1985, found this extremely welcome: 'A simple tale, told simply, with a beginning and an end, full of traditional *Doctor Who* elements … This is why it succeeded. It made a refreshing change from the other stories of this season, especially as it had no old foes on show (well, none that we'd seen before, anyway).'

This last comment is a reference to the fact that the Doctor is revealed to have visited Karfel once before, during his third incarnation, when he was travelling with Jo Grant and one or more other unknown companions. This is a nice twist on the idea of the Doctor revisiting the scene of a past adventure – here he is doing just that, and yet the viewer knows nothing about the earlier encounter.

The story's 'monster' is conceived along tried-and-trusted lines: a misguided scientist, scarred by his own experimentation, enslaving a whole planet to his will so that he can destroy it and recreate its people in his own image. The Borad is effectively realised on screen by way of some good make-up (although it is a pity that the reptilian half of his face was not better aligned with the humanoid half so that the eyes were on the same level), and Robert Ashby steals all the acting honours with his brilliantly chilling vocalisation of evil.

Another character of note is Paul Darrow's Tekker. Apparently, despite director Pennant Roberts' attempts to dissuade him from doing so, Darrow insisted on approaching this part as an over the top pastiche of Olivier playing Shakespeare's King Richard. Andy Lennard liked the end result: 'If it cost a lot to hire Paul Darrow then, as far as I'm concerned, it was worth it. Okay, so he was over the top, but not enough to make you wince every time he spoke. His characterisation of Tekker was perfectly cold and evil, owing more than a little to the nastier side of Avon, just as Jacqueline Pearce became a cipher of Servalan in *The Two Doctors*. Darrow also got some of the best dialogue; an example being his farewell to the Doctor.' The trouble is that Darrow doesn't just speak his lines, he positively declaims them, and it is rather too obvious that he is having a whale of a time sending up this pompous, self-opinioned character.

The only other character to make any real impression (the remaining Karfelons being uniformly bland and lifeless) is Herbert. Some commentators have, admittedly, been harshly critical of David Chandler's performance in this role, describing it as inept and amateurish, but a more charitable view is that he does his best with the poor material he is afforded. Playing a young and boundlessly enthusiastic H G Wells was never going to be easy, and the character suffers through being given too much prominence. It might have been more effective to have had Wells as an older man realising that his works were perhaps not fictions after all.

Peter Owen, writing in *TARDIS* Volume 10 Number 2 dated June 1985, gave a nicely balanced summation: 'This was a good traditional story, if a little disposable, and a pleasant filler between the two much-vaunted epics of the season. The script was rather basic, and peppered with rather silly ideas, some of which came off well, and some of which did not. The Androids were quite dinky, but the Morlox were awful. The idea of the ten-second time lapse was never fully explained, and seemed superfluous anyway. On the other hand there was a nice thematic link in Part One with the various pendants – the Maylin's amulet is a symbol of the Borad's power, Peri's Saint Christopher (the patron saint of travellers) stresses the importance of travel, and the locket with Jo's face in it points to the importance of past events … On balance I think I preferred this to *The Two Doctors*, mostly because it was so unpretentious.'

REVELATION OF THE DALEKS

Writer: Eric Saward. **Director:** Graeme Harper. **Designer:** Alan Spalding. **Costumes:** Pat Godfrey. **Make-Up:** Dorka Nieradzik. **Incidental Music:** Roger Limb. **Visual**

Effects: John Brace. **Film Cameraman:** John Walker. **Film Editor:** Ray Wingrove. **Studio Lighting:** Don Babbage. **Studio Sound:** Andy Stacey. **Production Assistant:** Elizabeth Sherry. **Assistant Floor Manager:** Jo O'Leary.

	First UK TX	Scheduled TX	Actual TX	Duration	Viewers	Chart Pos.
Part One	23/03/85	17.20	17.22	44'31"	7.4	65
Part Two	30/03/85	17.20	17.22	45'26"	7.7	58

Plot: The Doctor and Peri arrive on the planet Necros where, in a facility called Tranquil Repose presided over by Mr Jobel and his assistant Tasambeker, the wealthy can have their newly-deceased bodies cryogenically frozen until such time as medical science can cure whatever killed them. The Doctor wishes to pay his last respects to his friend Professor Arthur Stengos, and also to assuage some nagging suspicions about the man's death. His suspicions prove justified, as it turns out that this is just a ruse to lure him into a trap. The Great Healer masterminding Tranquil Repose is Davros, who is using the organic material in the cryogenic storage units both as the raw material for the synthetic food that is Necros's biggest export and also to create a whole new army of Daleks with which to take control of the universe. Davros's plans are foiled when Daleks loyal to the Dalek Supreme arrive on Necros and take him prisoner. The Doctor suggests to the planet's inhabitants a new basis for their economy.

Episode endings:
1. The Doctor is shocked to find a giant carving of his own face on a huge gravestone in the Garden of Fond Memories on Necros. He believes this means that he will die here in his current incarnation. Peri cries out in alarm as suddenly the gravestone topples over and falls toward the Doctor, threatening to crush him.
2. The Doctor decides to take Peri on a holiday and prepares to tell her their intended destination.

IT WAS MADE WHERE...?
Location filming: 07.01.85-10.01.85
Locations: IBM UK HQ, Cosham, Portsmouth, Hants; Tangmere Aerodrome, Tangmere, West Sussex; Goodwood horse racing track; Halnaker, West Sussex.
Studio: 17.01.85-18.01.85 in TC1, 30.01.85-31.01.85 in TC8, 04.02.85 (gallery only) in TC5

ADDITIONAL CREDITED CAST
Kara (Eleanor Bron), Jobel (Clive Swift), D. J. (Alexei Sayle), Davros (Terry Molloy), Tasambeker (Jenny Tomasin), Orcini (William Gaunt), Bostock (John Ogwen), Grigory (Stephen Flynn), Natasha (Bridget Lynch-Blosse), Takis (Trevor Cooper), Lilt (Colin Spaull), Vogel (Hugh Walters), Head of Stengos (Alec Linstead[1]), Mutant (Ken Barker[1]), Dalek Voices (Roy Skelton, Royce Mills), Dalek Operators (John Scott Martin, Cy Town, Tony Starr, Toby Byrne), Computer Voice (Penelope Lee[2]).

THINGS TO WATCH OUT FOR
- Davros and his Daleks are seen for the first time to be able to hover some distance from the ground.
- This story features a transparent Dalek – an idea devised by the series' original story

editor, David Whitaker, for his 1964 novelisation of the creatures' debut story.

- Comedy performer Alexei Sayle appears in a semi-serious role as the DJ who broadcasts to the dead on Necros.
- William Gaunt, well remembered as Richard Barrett in the ITC series *The Champions* amongst many other notable roles, appears here as the noble mercenary Orcini.
- Distinguished actress Eleanor Bron, who had previously made a cameo appearance in season seventeen's *City of Death*, portrays Kara, who hires Orcini to assassinate Davros.
- A ten second stock shot of factory complexes used in Part One came from World Backgrounds.

THINGS YOU MIGHT NOT HAVE KNOWN

- The Tranquil Repose DJ played his captive, and largely unaware, audience the following tunes: 'Good Vibrations' (The Surfers), 'Whiter Shade of Pale' (Procul Harum), 'Hound Dog' (cover of Presley version), 'Blue Suede Shoes' (cover of Presley version), 'In the Mood' (The Ted Heath Orchestra), 'Moonlight Serenade' (The Ted Heath Orchestra) and 'Fire' (Jimi Hendrix Experience).

QUOTE, UNQUOTE

- **Orcini:** 'This is Bostock, my squire. I'm afraid the only philosophy practised by Bostock is to do as little about his personal hygiene as possible.' **Kara:** 'Not at all! The odour of nature has … charms all of its own …' **Orcini:** 'Yes, well, he may smell like rotting flesh, but he's an excellent squire.'
- **Peri:** [Being helped over a wall by the Doctor] 'Don't drop me.' **The Doctor:** 'Drop you! I'll be lucky to lift you, the amount you weigh.' **Peri:** 'Watch it, porky!'
- **Jobel:** [To Tasambeker] 'I would rather run away … with my mother!'

ANALYSIS

One of the most frustrating things about mid-eighties *Doctor Who* is its extreme inconsistency of tone and quality. Earlier periods of the series' history had had their ups and downs, of course, but within any given season the stories had all tended to be produced in a similar style and to be of a roughly comparable standard. In seasons twenty-one and twenty-two, on the other hand, they are all over the place. For every gritty classic like *The Caves of Androzani* there is a gaudy clunker like *The Twin Dilemma*, for every derivative travesty like *Attack of the Cybermen* an innovative triumph like *Vengeance on Varos*. *Revelation of the Daleks* is arguably so superior in almost every way to disappointments like *Attack of the Cybermen* and *The Two Doctors* that it is difficult to believe that they are all part of the same series, let alone the same season.

'It was splendid,' enthused Andrew Stirling-Brown in *TARDIS* Volume 10 Number 2 dated June 1985, 'Saward's intriguing script, Harper's captivating direction, Limb's atmospheric score … pure magic. The only story this season to have enough impact to keep me watching on the edge of my seat.' 'Has to go down as one of the best Dalek stories of all time,' agreed Danny Neill in the same magazine. 'The newly [redesigned] Daleks, better designed Davros/Great Healer, the soldier type Orcini and his comrade and even the DJ were brilliant.'

The two regulars, Colin Baker and Nicola Bryant, give outstanding performances here, and the positively stellar guest cast are uniformly excellent. Graeme Harper's stylish

6 SIXTH DOCTOR

and atmospheric direction is also superb, as John Pettigrew observed in *DWB* No. 113 dated May 1993:

'This director seems to have a genuine love for his job ... Jon Pertwee has been quoted as saying that Daleks are boring. With flat, run of the mill direction, they can come over as bland and ordinary. In *Revelation of the Daleks* they are shot from low down, from high up and [from] close up to portions of their frame. The effect is one of sheer menace, a larger than life image of alien terror.

'And it's not just the Daleks that are given a good visual presence. Harper doesn't content himself with normal head and shoulder shots. Here, we have cameras angled from above, suggesting security cameras. The scene where the Doctor and Peri scale the wall to Tranquil Repose is similarly given a different angle – Colin Baker is filmed from very low down as he struggles to push [Nicola Bryant] over. The result is a typical, average scene given a refreshing approach. Other neat touches of Harper's include panning from slightly low to slightly high during dialogue scenes, injecting life into the corridor scenes by using long shots and zooms and effective use of lighting ... The shadowy red lighting for the embryo tanks is a simple but convincing device. Hand-held cameras ... are employed for some scenes – notably Jobel's murder.'

Eric Saward's scripts provide, as Pettigrew put it, 'a brilliant mix of horror, pathos and irony'.

'*Revelation of the Daleks* handles the question of cannibalism with greater sensitivity than *The Two Doctors*,' noted Diane McGinn, also writing in *DWB* No. 113. 'Indeed, it's ironic that *The Two Doctors* does not, strictly speaking, feature cannibalism at all, but provoked a storm of criticism, while the implied consumption of human flesh on a massive scale in *Revelation of the Daleks* passed almost unremarked. What takes place off screen takes place out of mind, it would seem ... Rewatching *Revelation of the Daleks*, it is astonishing how close to the wind it sails, how adult is its general attitude. Grigory's drunkenness is obvious, and it doesn't do to dwell upon the images brought to mind by Jobel's comment about "cleaning out the preparation room with a toothbrush," but what about the sexual undercurrents which pervade the story, undercurrents of all types, even down to vague implications of necrophilia, not to mention the tiny moments of disgusting reality such as the nose-picking [by one of Jobel's attendants].'

The main source of inspiration relied upon on by Saward on this occasion is an unusual one: Evelyn Waugh's humorous novella *The Loved One*. McGinn thought this worked very successfully: '*Revelation of the Daleks* is not a typical *Doctor Who* story. The Doctor's role is far too small and it ends with its resolution still to come off screen. But, in that it is not typical, it epitomises the series at its best. It demonstrates how the series can surprise, how it can take a work of literature and reinterpret it, turning it upside down. It demonstrates that there are, genuinely, no limits to the subjects it can take within its stride, that its format is flexible enough to encompass anything.'

As McGinn observed, the Doctor does have rather less involvement in the main action here than would normally be the case; indeed he and Peri do not even reach Tranquil Repose until the end of Part One. This has contributed to a feeling amongst a minority of commentators that the story is slow and lacking in excitement. Another negative point that could be made is that it is a little disappointing to see the Daleks yet again having to share the limelight with Davros, whose elaborate plan to trap the Doctor seems somewhat far-fetched. 'Unfortunately ... wherever there are Daleks, now there is Davros, ...' noted Stephen Murphy, another contributor to *TARDIS* Volume 10 Number 2. 'I have never been overfond of Davros, and certainly don't think the character has merited so many appearances. Nice to see, though … the re-emergence of the "civil war" idea as in *The Evil of the Daleks* and *Resurrection of the Daleks*. The creations of Davros, however, have lost their dependence on him, and it would be nice to see a script that just featured Daleks.'

John Binns, writing in *Matrix* Issue 51 dated summer 1995, recognised that that there were complaints that could be levelled at the story, but considered that they would be misplaced: 'It would be possible to say that *Revelation of the Daleks* was very slow paced, that it was lacking in action, that it had only a minimal role for the Doctor and Peri, that the role of the Daleks was as little more than decoration. One could also point out that the story was not only laced with gratuitous horror, but had main and subsidiary plots which could easily be called unsuitable for a young audience. But using these points as criticism would, it seems, be missing the point somehow. While they would all be fairly damning to a normal *Doctor Who* story, the mere fact that all could be levelled at *Revelation of the Daleks* indicates that it was trying to do something [different].'

The great majority of commentators would agree with Diane McGinn when she wrote: '*Revelation of the Daleks* is perhaps the most successful story of the Colin Baker era – a story which can hold its head high amongst the greats of *Doctor Who*.'

Revelation of the Daleks was one of a number of stories in the twenty-second season to provoke criticism regarding the level of violence and horror in *Doctor Who* – and, unlike previous criticism of this kind, on this occasion it came as much from the series' fans and members of the general viewing public as from self-appointed TV watchdogs. Some commentators even suggested that this season marked a departure from the strong moral standpoint that had previously been one of *Doctor Who*'s most distinctive and popular features. The stories undoubtedly dealt with some unusually heavy themes, including video nasties, genetic experimentation and cannibalism, and also featured gory and disturbing scenes of torture, dismemberment and suffering. Even the Doctor's actions did not entirely escape reproach, attention being drawn to his shooting down of some Cybermen in *Attack of the Cybermen*, his engineering of the killing of Quillam and the Varosian Chief Officer in *Vengeance on Varos* and his asphyxiation of Shockeye in *The Two Doctors*. It was not only viewers, either, who had concerns about aspects of this season's content; some senior BBC executives also had serious reservations. As written and recorded, *Revelation of the Daleks* should have ended with the Doctor promising to take Peri to Blackpool. By the time its closing episode came to be transmitted, however, the series' very continuation was in doubt, and a freeze-frame ending was substituted with the word 'Blackpool' left unspoken on the Doctor's lips …

CANCELLATION!

At the end of February 1985, part way through transmission of *The Two Doctors*, the shock news hit the press that the BBC had decided to cancel *Doctor Who*'s twenty-third season. This provoked a storm of controversy over the months that followed, and Controller of BBC1 Michael Grade and Head of Series and Serials Jonathan Powell offered several different justifications for their decision. They claimed that the series had become too violent; that it had lost its appeal; that the production team had grown complacent; and that the forty-five minute episode format had proved unsuccessful, necessitating a return to the old twenty-five minute length (a decision announced by Powell in mid-April 1985). Their true motivation, however, appears to have been to help alleviate a financial crisis within the BBC. This was due firstly to the advent of the new soap opera *EastEnders*, of which there were to be 104 episodes made within the year, and secondly to a decision taken to bring forward by several months the launch of the BBC's daytime television service, to pre-empt ITV's rival effort. Further bad news lay in store for *Doctor Who* fans as an announcement was made in mid-December 1985 confirming a long-standing rumour that the new season, when it did eventually appear, would be only fourteen episodes long.

One thing to come out of the hiatus was the original *Doctor Who* radio serial *Slipback*, recorded in mid-June and broadcast between mid-July and early August on BBC Radio 4 as part of a new children's magazine programme entitled *Pirate Radio Four*. Its six ten-minute instalments, written by Eric Saward, told of the dangers encountered by the sixth Doctor and Peri (played as usual by Colin Baker and Nicola Bryant) on board a spaceship called the Vipod Mor, where the alien Captain Slarn (Valentine Dyall) threatened to unleash a deadly virus in a fit of pique.

Work on the original season twenty-three had been quite well-advanced before it was cancelled. Scripts for former producer Graham Williams's *The Nightmare Fair*, which was to have been the opening story, had already been distributed and director Matthew Robinson had been preparing to start filming at the beginning of April. In two forty-five-minute episodes, it was to have been set in Blackpool and to have seen the return of the Celestial Toymaker – played, as in his season three debut, by Michael Gough. The second two-parter was to have been *The Ultimate Evil*, written by Wally K Daly and directed by Fiona Cumming, telling of a scheme by the evil Dwarf Mordant to provoke a war between two neighbouring races. Another two-parter for which scripts had been drafted was Philip Martin's *Mission to Magnus*, featuring Sil and the Ice Warriors and due to be directed by Ron Jones. A Robert Holmes three-parter called *Yellow Fever and How to Cure It* was to have boasted location filming in Singapore and return appearances by the Autons, the Rani and possibly also the Master. Candidates for the two remaining two-part slots were Christopher H Bidmead's *In the Hollows of Time*, a Bill Pritchard submission (title unknown) and Michael Feeney Callan's *The Children of January*.

Following the cancellation, Holmes, Bidmead and Callan were asked to continue working on their stories, but to adapt them from forty-five minute to twenty-five minute episodes. Pip and Jane Baker were also commissioned in mid-March to write a four-parter called *Gallifrey*. Shortly after this, however, all these stories were abandoned as the production team decided that they needed to make a completely fresh start in their preparations for the 'new' twenty-third season.

DOCTOR WHO SEASON TWENTY-THREE [1986]

Regular Cast:
The Doctor (Colin Baker)
The Valeyard (Michael Jayston)
The Inquisitor (Lynda Bellingham)
Peri (Nicola Bryant) until Part Eight
Melanie (Bonnie Langford) from Part Nine onwards

Regular Crew:
Producer: John Nathan-Turner.
Script Editor: Eric Saward on Parts One to Eight and Thirteen. John Nathan-Turner uncredited on Parts Nine to Twelve and Fourteen.
Production Associate: Angela Smith on Parts One to Eight, Thirteen and Fourteen. June Collins on Parts Five to Eight uncredited and on Parts Nine to Twelve. Jenny Doe on Parts Nine to Twelve.
Title Music: Ron Grainer and the BBC Radiophonic Workshop, arranged by Dominic Glynn.
Special Sounds: Dick Mills.

It was Eric Saward who proposed that the 'new' twenty-third season should have a linking plot in which the Doctor was placed on trial by the Time Lords for his interference in other worlds – a reflection of the fact that *Doctor Who* itself was still effectively on trial at this point. John Nathan-Turner quickly approved this, and the two worked out a format for the story. Drawing inspiration from Dickens's *A Christmas Carol*, they decided to structure the plot so that the trial evidence came from three different stages of the Doctor's life – past, present and future – and everything was wrapped up in a fourth segment at the end. Two figures appearing throughout the season would be the Valeyard (prosecuting counsel) and the Inquisitor (judge), for whom the production team finalised detailed character outlines at the beginning of July 1985.

The writers originally chosen to script the season were Robert Holmes, Philip Martin, David Halliwell and Jack Trevor Story. The intention was that Holmes and Martin would each provide a four-part segment of evidence; that Halliwell and Story would contribute two episodes apiece of a further four-part segment; and that Holmes would then be responsible for the two-part conclusion. They were asked to avoid including anything overtly horrific in their scripts and to make the story fun and entertaining – an approach designed to meet Controller Michael Grade's wish, expressed in a short meeting with Nathan-Turner, for the series to become less violent and more humorous. Work progressed relatively smoothly on the segments assigned to Holmes and Martin but problems arose on those entrusted to Halliwell and Story, who were both eventually paid off. The production team commissioned a replacement third segment from Christopher H Bidmead, but this was also rejected. A further replacement was then commissioned from *Sapphire & Steel* creator P J Hammond, but this too came to nothing. Pip and Jane Baker were the next writers approached to fill the four-part gap, and their submission finally met with the production team's approval. Commissioned at the beginning of March 1986, the scripts had to be written within the space of a month in view of the shortage of time now remaining.

December 1985 had meanwhile seen an actress being cast by Nathan-Turner to play the new companion, Mel, who would be introduced part-way through the season. This was well-known entertainer Bonnie Langford, whose popularity with younger viewers was seen by the producer as having the potential to boost *Doctor Who*'s audience. Part Eight would be the last on which Nicola Bryant worked as she had reached a mutual agreement with the production team to leave at this point.

In early February 1986, Robert Holmes was commissioned as planned to provide the story's concluding two-part segment. Shortly after this, however, he fell seriously ill and found it increasingly difficult to work. Another complication arose at around this time when Saward decided to quit the production team and return to freelance writing, which left the series temporarily without a script editor. Holmes grew steadily weaker and died in mid-May 1986, having completed only a rough draft of the first episode of the closing segment and nothing at all beyond an initial outline of the second. Saward was then persuaded by Nathan-Turner to return to the project to take over where Holmes had left off. Subsequently however the two men had a major disagreement over the story's ending. The original idea apparently agreed between Saward and Nathan-Turner had been to close on a cliffhanger, with the Doctor and the Valeyard locked in mortal combat in the time vortex, but the producer later vetoed this on the grounds that it was too down-beat and would end the series on an inconclusive note if BBC management then decided to cancel it permanently. Incensed by Nathan-Turner's change of mind, Saward withdrew permission for his script to be used. The producer therefore brought in Pip and Jane Baker to write a completely new final episode as an emergency measure.

THE TRIAL OF A TIME LORD

Writer: Robert Holmes[1-4], [13], Philip Martin[5-8], Pip and Jane Baker[9-12,14]. **Director:** Nicholas Mallett[1-4], Ron Jones[5-8], Chris Clough[9-14]. **Designer:** John Anderson[1-4], Andrew Howe-Davies[5-8], Dinah Walker[9-12], Michael Trevor[13,14]. **Costumes:** Ken Trew[1-4], John Hearne[5-8], Andrew Rose[9-14]. **Make-Up:** Denise Baron[1-4], Dorka Nieradzik[5-8], Shaunna Harrison[9-14]. **Incidental Music:** Dominic Glynn[1-4,13,14], Richard Hartley[5-8], Malcolm Clarke[9-12]. **Visual Effects:** Mike Kelt[1-4], Peter Wragg[5-8], Kevin Molloy[9-14]. **OB Cameraman:** unknown. **Studio Lighting:** Mike Jefferies[1-4], Don Babbage[5-14]. **Studio Sound:** Brian Clark. **Production Assistant:** Joy Sinclair[1-4], Karen Jones[5-8], Jane Wellesley[9-14]. **Assistant Floor Manager:** Stephen Jeffery-Poulter[1-4], Sally Newman[1-4], Anna Price[5-8], Karen Little[9-14].

	First UK TX	Scheduled TX	Actual TX	Duration	Viewers	Chart Pos.
Part One	06/09/86	17.45	17.47	24'57"	4.9	69
Part Two	13/09/86	17.45	17.47	24'44"	4.9	75
Part Three	20/09/86	17.45	17.48	24'18"	3.9	98
Part Four	27/09/86	17.45	17.46	24'20"	3.7	97
Part Five	04/10/86	17.45	17.47	24'42"	4.8	76
Part Six	11/10/86	17.45	17.46	24'45"	4.6	87
Part Seven	18/10/86	17.45	17.47	24'33"	5.1	87
Part Eight	25/10/86	17.45	17.48	24'44"	5.0	84
Part Nine	01/11/86	17.45	17.47	24'56"	5.2	85
Part Ten	08/11/86	17.45	17.46	24'18"	4.6	93
Part Eleven	15/11/86	17.45	17.47	24'07"	5.3	86
Part Twelve	22/11/86	17.45	17.46	24'45"	5.2	89
Part Thirteen	29/11/86	17.20	17.20	24'42"	4.4	98
Part Fourteen	06/12/86	17.45	17.46	29'30"	5.6	80

Plot: The TARDIS is drawn to a space station where the Doctor is subjected to a Time Lord inquiry into his behaviour, presided over by an Inquisitor. The prosecuting counsel, the Valeyard, presents the first piece of his evidence, which consists of a recording played back on a screen linked to the Matrix. It concerns a visit by the Doctor and Peri to the desolate planet Ravolox, which turns out to be a future Earth, shifted light-years through space. The court watches as the pair get caught up in a conflict between the surface-dwelling Tribe of the Free, led by Queen Katryca, and the planet's other inhabitants, a group of subterranean technocrats and their robotic ruler Drathro. Two shady off-worlders, Glitz and Dibber, are meanwhile attempting to appropriate from Drathro some mysterious 'secrets' – details of which are censored from the Matrix record. The 'secrets' are eventually destroyed, along with Drathro, as a result of the Doctor's actions. The Valeyard's second segment of evidence relates to the planet Thoros-Beta. Here the Doctor and Peri meet their old adversary Sil and others of his Mentor race, whose leader Kiv is awaiting an operation from a scientist named Crozier to transplant his brain into another body. They also form an uneasy alliance with a kidnapped Krontep warrior, King Yrcanos, and encounter a group of resistance fighters. Peri is eventually chosen as the recipient of Kiv's consciousness and is apparently killed in an ensuing melee sanctioned by the Time Lords to prevent Crozier's work from disturbing the balance of nature. The distraught Doctor then gives the court his evidence for the defence. He chooses an incident from his own future, in which he and his companion Mel arrive on the space liner *Hyperion III* in response to a distress call. There they battle against and ultimately destroy a hostile race of alien plants, the Vervoids, while also helping to thwart a mutiny by the ship's security officer, Rudge. With the evidence complete, the Doctor learns that the Master has gained illicit access to the Matrix in his TARDIS. Glitz is now revealed to be the Master's associate and the 'secrets' to be information stolen from the Matrix. The Valeyard admits his identity as a distillation of the dark side of the Doctor's nature, somewhere between his twelfth and thirteenth incarnations, out to take control over his remaining lives. With the help of Mel, who along with Glitz has been brought to the space station by the Master, the Doctor defeats his future self – although, as they leave in the TARDIS with all charges in the trial having been dropped, it appears that the Valeyard has taken over the body of the Keeper of the Matrix and may not have been as completely vanquished as they had thought …

Episode endings:

1. The Valeyard suggests to the Inquisitor that what started out as a mere inquiry into the Doctor's behaviour should become a trial, and that if he is found guilty the sentence should be the termination of his life. The Doctor looks shocked.

2. The Doctor, Peri, Glitz, Dibber and the underground dweller Balazar are trapped between the advancing Tribe of the Free and Drathro's L1 robot. Peri asks what they should do and the Doctor replies: 'I don't know. I really think this could be the end.' The Doctor looks concerned.

3. The Doctor and Peri encounter Merdeen, one of Drathro's 'train guards', in the corridors of the underground complex. He tells them that he is hunting. When the Doctor enquires who his quarry is he replies: 'You'. He raises a crossbow weapon and fires.

4. In the Time Lord courtroom, the Doctor derides the evidence so far presented by the Valeyard. The Valeyard retorts that better is to come, and that when he has finished the court will demand the Doctor's life. The Doctor looks defiant.

5. The Doctor is strapped to an operating table in Crozier's laboratory and a metal helmet placed on his head. Sil instructs Crozier to use the equipment to extract from the Doctor the truth about his and Peri's earlier encounter with a sea creature called the Raak, which ended in the creature's death. Crozier warns that this could prove fatal, but Sil is unconcerned. The equipment is switched on and the Doctor convulses in agony.

6. King Yrcanos aims a gun at the Doctor, who has apparently allied himself with the Mentors, and tells him, 'Now Doctor, it is your turn to die.' The Doctor looks horrified.

7. Peri, Yrcanos, Yrcanos's squire the Lukoser and the resistance fighters are all shot down by the Mentors' guards, led by Frax. Watching these events on the Matrix screen in the Time Lord courtroom, the Doctor protests that he was not responsible. The Valeyard, however, replies: 'In your mind, perhaps not. But in reality it is somewhat different, Doctor.' The Doctor looks perturbed.

8. The distraught Doctor alleges that the Time Lords had an ulterior motive for taking him out of time and thus preventing him from saving Peri – and he has every intention of finding out what it is. The Doctor looks resolute.

9. A crewman named Edwardes takes Mel down to the hold of the *Hyperion III* and shows her a caged area, assigned to the agronomist Professor Lasky, in which a number of large

plant pods are growing. He offers to take her inside, but when he touches the gate he receives a fatal electric shock. Mel screams as electric sparks fly around the pods, causing one of them to break open and a strange growth to protrude.

10. The Doctor and Mel, wearing gas masks, enter a quarantined room on board the *Hyperion III* and find lying on a bench an unconscious woman with a horribly mutated face. The woman suddenly opens an eye and Mel screams. The Doctor looks astonished.

11. The Doctor tells the Commodore of the *Hyperion III* that his colleague on the bridge is steering the ship straight into the eye of the Black Hole of Tartarus. Professor Lasky is stunned by this news. The Doctor looks accusingly at the Commodore.

12. In the Time Lord courtroom the Doctor admits that his actions on board the *Hyperion III* resulted in the deaths of all the Vervoids. He justifies this by arguing that if even one of the creatures had reached the ship's destination, Earth, it would have meant the end of the human race. The Valeyard, however, asserts that the charge in the Doctor's trial must now be one of genocide. The Doctor looks shocked.

13. In the virtual reality of the Matrix, the Doctor finds himself on a beach. Hands emerge from the shingle beneath his feet and drag him down, threatening to pull him into the ground. The taunting voice of the Valeyard bids him goodbye. The Doctor shouts: 'No!'

14. Mel determines to subject the Doctor to a fitness regime, requiring him to drink carrot juice and use an exercise bike. They leave in the TARDIS, the Doctor sarcastically repeating: 'Carrot juice, carrot juice, carrot juice!' In the courtroom, the departing Inquisitor tells the Keeper to requisition anything he needs to effect repairs to the Matrix. The Keeper replies 'Yes, my lady.' When he turns, however, his face is that of the Valeyard. He chuckles evilly to himself.

IT WAS MADE WHERE...?

Parts One – Four
OB: 08.04.86-11.04.86
Locations: Butser Ancient Farm Project, Pidham Hill, Hants; Queen Elizabeth Country Park, Gravel Hill, Horndean, Hants.
Studio: 24.04.86-25.04.86 in TC6, 10.05.86-12.05.86 in TC3, 16.05.86 (gallery only) (studio unknown)

Parts Five – Eight
OB: 15.06.86-16.06.86
Location: Telscombe Cliffs, Peacehaven, East Sussex.
Studio: 27.05.86-29.05.86 in TC1, 11.06.86-13.06.86 (studio unknown), 18.06.86 (gallery only) (studio unknown)

Parts Nine – Twelve
Studio: 30.07.86-01.08.86 in TC3, 12.08.86-14.08.86 (studio unknown)

Parts Thirteen – Fourteen
OB: 23.06.86-24.06.86, 30.06.86-04.07.86
Locations: Gladstone Pottery Museum, Uttoxeter Road, Longton, Stoke on Trent, Staffs; Camber Sands, Camber, East Sussex.
Studio: 16.07.86-17.07.86 in TC1

6. SIXTH DOCTOR

Katryca (Joan Sims[1-4]), Glitz (Tony Selby[1-4,13,14]), Dibber (Glen Murphy[1-4]), Merdeen (Tom Chadbon[1-4]), Drathro (Roger Brierley[1-4]), Broken Tooth (David Rodigan[1-4]), Balazar (Adam Blackwood[1-4]), Grell (Timothy Walker[1-4]), Humker (Billy McColl[2-4]), Tandrell (Sion Tudor Owen[2-4]), King Yrcanos (Brian Blessed[5-8]), Sil (Nabil Shaban[5-8]), Kiv (Christopher Ryan[5-8]), Crozier (Patrick Ryecart[5-8]), Matrona Kani (Alibe Parsons[5-8]), Frax (Trevor Laird[5-8]), The Lukoser (Thomas Branch[5-8]), Tuza (Gordon Warnecke[7,8]), Mentor (Richard Harvey[8]), Professor Lasky (Honor Blackman[9-12]), Commodore (Michael Craig[9-12]), Rudge (Denys Hawthorne[9-12]), Janet (Yolande Palfrey[9-12]), Doland (Malcolm Tierney[9-12]), Bruchner (David Allister[9-12]), Grenville[9]/Enzu[10] (Tony Scoggo[9, 10]), Kimber (Arthur Hewlett[9,10*]), Edwardes (Simon Slater[9**]), Atza (Sam Howard[9-12]), Ortezo (Leon Davis[9-12]), Guard[9,11]/First Guard[10] (Hugh Beverton[9-11***]), Duty Officer (Mike Mungarvan[10]), Second Guard (Martin Weedon[10*]), Mutant[10]/Ruth Baxter[11,12] (Barbara Ward[10-12]), First Vervoid (Peppi Borza[11,12]), Second Vervoid (Bob Appleby[11,12]), The Master (Anthony Ainley[13,14]), Popplewick (Geoffrey Hughes[13,14]), Keeper of the Matrix (James Bree[13,14]).

* Also in Parts Eleven and Twelve as a corpse, but uncredited.
** Also in Part Ten, in the reprise from Part Nine, and in Parts Eleven and Twelve as a corpse, but uncredited.
*** Also in Part Twelve as a corpse, but uncredited.

- The working title of Parts Nine to Twelve was *Terror of the Vervoids*. (It was *The Ultimate Foe*. *Terror of the Vervoids* was a later invention, not used at the time of production. Writers Pip and Jane Baker prefer to refer to this segment as *The Vervoids*.)
- The working title of Parts Thirteen and Fourteen was *The Ultimate Foe*. (It was *Time Inc.*. *The Ultimate Foe* was, as mentioned above, the working title of Parts Nine to Twelve.)

- Many well-known actors appear in guest roles in this story. These include Lynda Bellingham, familiar to viewers as the 'Mum' in a long-running series of television commercials for Oxo stock cubes, appearing here as the Inquisitor; Michael Jayston, whose many television credits include roles in *Quiller* and *The Power Game*, looking suitably menacing as the Valeyard; comic actress Joan Sims, popular as one of the team from the *Carry On …* films series, portraying warrior queen Katryca; Glen Murphy, now better known for his starring role in the LWT fire service drama series *London's Burning*, playing Glitz's sidekick Dibber; larger-than-life actor Brian Blessed taking on the role of King Yrcanos; Christopher Ryan, who rose to prominence as one of *The Young Ones* in the BBC's pioneering alternative comedy series, heavily made-up and costumed as Kiv; and Honor Blackman, famous for her role as Cathy Gale in *The Avengers*, seen here as Professor Lasky.
- Merdeen is played by Tom Chadbon, who had previously appeared in *Doctor Who* as

the detective Duggan in the season seventeen story *City of Death*.

- The train guards' helmets were originally created for the troopers in the Cyberman adventure *Earthshock* during the fifth Doctor's era.
- The Doctor states in this adventure that he is 900 years old.
- It is revealed that Sabalom Glitz comes from Salostophus in Andromeda.
- Immediately prior to the transmission of Part Three, a narrative spoken by the BBC continuity announcer over a colour slide from the story gave a brief summary of events so far. The same was then done for all subsequent episodes in the season.
- In Part Three, when the Doctor is recovering from being captured by the service robot, his voice reverts for a moment to that of the fourth Doctor (achieved by Colin Baker doing an impression of Tom Baker) and calls Peri 'Sarah Jane'.
- The impressive opening model shot of the Time Lord space station was filmed at Peerless Studios using a computer-controlled camera rig. The forty-five second scene took a week to set up and shoot, working from 9 a.m. to 11 p.m., and another week to edit. The model itself was built by Visual Effects Department assistants working to designer Mike Kelt's drawings. It was assembled from six fibreglass sections, then embellished with detailed plastic components and dozens of lights. The full construction measured six feet in diameter.
- The then-new HARRY digital image manipulation process was used for the first time in *Doctor Who* to colour Thoros-Beta's sky and seas and to provide the image of Thoros-Alpha in the sky.
- Mel's surname, 'Bush', is not given on screen in this season.
- The model of the *Hyperion III* was designed by Kevin Molloy, who wanted to capture the feel of an art-deco ocean liner. It was three feet long and vacuum-formed in thermal plastic.
- Part Fourteen is almost half an hour long. When the first edit was completed it was discovered that it had considerably overrun, but John Nathan-Turner was able to gain permission for the series' slot to be extended by five minutes for the week of its transmission so that most of the recorded material could be retained.
- A brief clip of Peri is seen at the story's conclusion, when it is revealed that she has not in fact been killed but has escaped to become the consort of King Yrcanos.
- The stock barrel organ music used for the scenes featuring Popplewick's Fantasy Factory offices.was 'Can You Handle This?', composed by Ken Jones and Keith Grant and taken from an LP called *Hymns, Carols, Mechanical Instruments*.

THINGS YOU MIGHT NOT HAVE KNOWN

- Working titles: Parts One to Four: *The Mysterious Planet*; Parts Five to Eight: *The Planet of Sil*, *Mindwarp*; Parts Nine to Twelve: *The Ultimate Foe*; Parts Thirteen and Fourteen: *Time Inc.*.
- David Rodigan, who played Broken Tooth in this story, was better known as David 'Roots' Rodigan, a reggae music DJ on London's Capital Radio.
- Roger Brierley, the actor credited as Drathro, provided only the voice. He was originally to have been inside the costume as well, but found he could not work in such a confined space. Visual effects assistant Paul McGuiness stepped in and took his place.
- The food sludge in which Balazar gets covered in Part Four was made from mashed potato, water and food colouring.

6 SIXTH DOCTOR

- Drathro, the L1 robot and Sil all appeared on the BBC children's programme *Blue Peter* to publicise the season.
- It was originally proposed that much of the Mentors' dialogue would be spoken in their own alien language and translated by way of on-screen subtitles, but this idea was dropped as posing too many problems.
- The cat badges worn by Colin Baker during the season were designed and hand-painted from his own cats, Eric and Weeble, by Maggie Howard of Maggie's Moggies.

QUOTE, UNQUOTE

- **The Doctor:** [To Peri] 'Planets come and go. Stars perish. Matter disperses, coalesces, forms into other patterns, other worlds. Nothing can be eternal.'
- **King Yrcanos:** 'Today prudence shall be our watchword. Tomorrow we shall soak the land in blood!'
- **The Doctor:** [To the Time Lords] 'In all my travellings throughout the universe, I have battled against evil, against power-mad conspirators. I should have stayed here! The oldest civilisation, decadent, degenerate and rotten to the core! Power-mad conspirators, Daleks, Sontarans, Cybermen – they're still in the nursery compared to us! Ten million years of absolute power – that's what it takes to be really corrupt!'

ANALYSIS

A fourteen part *Doctor Who* story is not necessarily doomed to fail. Season three's *The Daleks' Master Plan* was only two episodes shorter, and that was superb. Sadly however *The Trial of a Time Lord*, although a brave attempt, falls a long way short of expectations.

Its inherent weakness stems largely from the production team's apparent inability to decide whether they were making a single epic-length story, as in the case of *The Daleks' Master Plan*, or a sequence of separate stories with a linking theme, in the manner of the Key to Time season. *The Trial of a Time Lord* was certainly presented and promoted to the general public as a single fourteen part story – it was billed as such on screen and in *Radio Times* – and yet in the behind-the-scenes information that Nathan-Turner and Saward provided and the interviews that they granted to fanzines, both gave the clear impression that they regarded it as ·consisting of four separate but linked stories corresponding to the four distinct segments of the Doctor's trial. This is reflected in the fact that most fan reviewers have actually treated the season in this piecemeal way, rather than assessing it on its merits as a whole. Each of the four segments certainly had its own individual working title – *The Mysterious Planet* for Parts One to Four, *Mindwarp* for Parts Five to Eight, *The Ultimate Foe* for Parts Nine to Twelve and *Time Inc* for Parts Thirteen and Fourteen – and their respective writers worked for the most part completely independently of each other.

It is telling that when Pip and Jane Baker were commissioned to provide a replacement script for the final episode, after Saward withdrew his, they had no idea how the story was originally supposed to end, despite having themselves written four of the earlier episodes, and nor indeed did they know how it had begun – they had to go and research this from scratch and try to put together a script that would successfully tie up all the loose ends. That they were only partially successful in achieving this aim is hardly surprising, and not something for which they can be held to blame. If the production team had been really serious about presenting a coherent fourteen-part story, with different writers responsible for different episodes, they should arguably have devised at the outset a detailed storyline for the whole thing, with a clear beginning, middle and end, so that each of the writers knew exactly where his or her contribution was supposed to fit into the overall picture. That they failed to do so, despite having had the luxury of the longest period ever available to any production team for the preparation of a season, can be seen as a damning indictment.

There are two valid points that could be made in their defence. First, they did at least start out with reasonably good intentions, convening a round-table meeting to discuss with the four writers originally envisaged as contributing to the season the general approach that they were required to take; it is just unfortunate that two of those four writers, David Halliwell and Jack Trevor Story, ultimately had their scripts rejected. Secondly, they could not have foreseen that one of the other writers, Robert Holmes, who set up the story in the opening segment and should have concluded it in the closing one, would sadly die before his task was completed. Presumably Holmes, if no-one else, had actually discussed the resolution with Saward and had a fair idea as to what it was supposed to be. These problems need not have been anywhere near as serious as they were, however, if the production had really embraced the idea of making a fourteen part epic in a wholehearted way, rather than taking the curious 'half way house' approach of treating it as a single story for some purposes but as four separate stories with a linking theme for others.

As it is, *The Trial of a Time Lord*, viewed as a whole, is simply a mess. Questions posed at the beginning remain unanswered at the end, and there is a distinct lack of internal logic and consistency. It is, for example, very difficult to believe that in the Time Lord legal system – or indeed in any reasonable legal system – the charge directed at the accused, and even the type of proceedings involved, could really be changed at a moment's notice seemingly on the whim of the prosecuting counsel. Quite apart from the obvious difficulties created by the aforementioned lack of coordination between all the different writers, there is the more fundamental problem that the overarching plot suggested by Saward and accepted by Nathan-Turner simply doesn't work. The idea of the Doctor being placed on trial by the Time Lords for his interference in the affairs of other planets is not exactly an original one to start with – season six's *The War Games* was the first to use it, and season fourteen's *The Deadly Assassin* also had the Doctor being placed on trial by his own people, albeit on a different charge – and stretched over fourteen episodes it leads to a seemingly endless succession of tedious courtroom scenes that very quickly try the viewer's patience. 'The trial sequences are astonishingly dull,' agreed Lance Parkin in *Matrix* Issue 49 dated spring 1994. 'The only courtroom drama in the history of television to lack any tension at all. The whole framing device is badly handled – the scripting is repetitive, the acting is lacklustre, technically it's poor: the set creaks, the vision and sound mixes to the main story are badly done, on one occasion you can hear someone clearly saying "Take six".'

The only way in which these scenes could perhaps have been rescued would have been to have had them acted out on a really impressive courtroom set with lots of visual interest and plenty of scope for variation of camera angles. The set seen in the transmitted story, however, is poorly designed, looking small and cramped and far too conventional in its general layout. This unimaginative interior is difficult to reconcile with the space station exterior and singularly fails to convey any impression of grandeur or sense of the Time Lords' power. In fact, most ordinary English county courts boast more impressive accommodation than this, and one almost wishes that all these linking trial scenes had actually been recorded on location rather than in studio – something that could have been quite easily justified in plot terms by having the whole trial set within the virtual reality of the Matrix. Another option would have been to have taken a cue from the trial scenes in *The War Games* and had the action played out entirely in a black void, with the protagonists revealed in pools of light and Matrix screens appearing around them as and when required. Not only would this have been far more effective than what was actually done, it would also no doubt have been far cheaper, freeing up money to be used on other aspects of the production.

In storytelling terms, too, the trial scenario is far from ideal. Admittedly it does lead to the rather amusing situation of the Doctor effectively sitting down to watch *Doctor Who* for fourteen weeks, passing comment on the action from time to time and making the occasional in-joke. ('I would appreciate it if these violent and repetitious scenes could be kept to a minimum,' he says at one point, in a clear reference to the criticisms aimed at the previous season; although things do perhaps get a little out of hand when he actually starts to deride the story and suggest that it is boring.) On the downside however there are many questions raised of the 'But shouldn't the Doctor already know what's going to happen next?' sort or, perhaps even more seriously, the 'Doesn't the fact that we are seeing evidence from the Doctor's future mean that he must be found not guilty?' or 'How can he take Mel with him in the TARDIS at the end when he's not even supposed to have met her yet?' variety. The plot device of the Doctor having lost his memory is all too obviously a ploy to try to get around some of these problems, and things go badly awry in the Thoros-Beta episodes, so that it is impossible to tell if the Doctor's apparent siding with the Mentors is a trick on his part, a consequence of someone tampering with the Matrix record or the result of mental instability brought on by Crozier's experiments. And just what exactly is the Valeyard trying to achieve? He is ultimately revealed to be a personification of the dark side of the Doctor's nature, somewhere between his twelfth and thirteenth incarnations (presumably analogous to the Watcher, the interim state between his fourth and fifth incarnations, as seen in season eighteen's *Logopolis*), and yet he spends much of the early part of the story calling for the accused's – i.e. his own – death, and then later reveals an ulterior motive of wanting somehow to take over all his remaining incarnations. This is just total nonsense.

Another problem with the overarching plot is that it is highly convoluted and, even more so than most *Doctor Who* of this period, draws very heavily on the series' own established mythology, making few concessions to the more casual viewer who might not be altogether *au fait* with the Time Lords, Gallifrey, the Matrix or even the Master. What's more, in order to stand any chance of following Parts Thirteen and Fourteen, one needs to be aware of things that are established in Parts One to Four, including relatively minor details such as the mysterious 'secrets' sought by Glitz and Dibber and the suspicious excising of certain material from the Matrix record (something that, incidentally, everyone in the court seems to understand the reason for except the accused, again calling into question the rationality of the Time Lord legal system). This too must count against the story's appeal to the more casual viewer; and certainly anyone coming to it late after missing a few episodes would be very hard pressed to pick up all the threads of the plot (although there was at least a brief voice-over recap given before the start of each of the later episodes on their original transmission). 'Who in their right minds is going to remember one small subplot for thirteen weeks and wait that long for a hurried explanation to be revealed?' asked Graeme Wood in *The MLG Magazine* Issue 21 dated spring 1987. 'Only a fan.'

Yet another problem, again stemming in part from the somewhat tedious nature of the trial scenario itself, is that this story has arguably the poorest collection of cliffhanger episode endings in the series' history. No fewer than ten of the fourteen episodes end in exactly the same way, on a close up of the Doctor expressing intense emotion of one sort or another. Admittedly this is nothing new for the sixth Doctor's era – even his debut story, *The Twin Dilemma*, had three out of four episodes ending in this way – but here it is particularly groan-inducing and lacking in dramatic impact. It must be a tribute of sorts to Colin Baker's acting ability that he is at least able to manage a slightly different expression each time (although when it comes to Part Ten, where his face is largely obscured by a gas mask, one has to hazard a guess), but this is all put into perspective by the really cracking cliffhanger at the end of Part Nine, which serves only to highlight just how inadequate the others are. If only they could all have been this good!

The story certainly begins well enough. The new Dominic Glynn arrangement of Ron Grainer's famous theme music is an improvement on the previous Peter Howell version, indeed probably the best of those used during the eighties, and puts the viewer in a good frame of mind to enjoy the opening episode. (A pity, though, that Nathan-Turner apparently never realised what almost everyone else did: that the original Delia Derbyshire arrangement was simply unbeatable and should never have been dropped in the first place.) The episode then gets under way in earnest with a breathtakingly superb model shot of the Time Lord space station – although, as Brian Willis noted in *Muck and Devastation* Issue Two dated May 1987, disillusion quickly sets in: 'The opening sequence of the first episode … cheered me up considerably; a lovely, smooth piece of effects work as we see the TARDIS being drawn by a tractor beam into a vast space station. I liked it a lot … which [was] just as well [as] we were to see an awful lot of it in the next fourteen weeks. And its subsequent appearances were to reinforce a nagging feeling that set in in [Part One]: that the whole sequence was purely gratuitous; nothing to do with the story at all. Why should the trial be held in a space station anyway? … Nobody seemed to mention the fact that they *were* in space, so for all the difference it made the whole thing might as well have been set on Gallifrey.'

One of the most pleasing things about the scenes set on Ravolox is that, as noted by Tim Collins in *DWB* Number 39 dated October 1986, the Doctor and Peri are shown to have a much better relationship than in the previous season: 'Colin [Baker] and Nicola [Bryant] were finally allowed to portray their characters as *people* who *liked* each other, who joked *with* rather than *at* each other, and who were chums – not simply fellow travellers. It was a joy to see Colin putting his arm around Nicola so often and to see them smiling at each other – such a relief from the constant whining, moaning and bickering that summarised their relationship throughout season twenty-two!'

The other characters in these Robert Holmes scripted episodes are rather variable, as Brian Willis pointed out:

'Glitz, played by Tony Selby, is the best thing about this [segment of the] story; a [typical] Holmes creation in the tradition of Vorg, Garron and Henry Gordon Jago. [He is] blessed with the blarney, and as trustworthy as a hyena …

'If Glitz is the best thing …, Katryca is the worst. She is supposed to be a warrior queen, not unlike Boadicea, yet Joan Sims plays her with all the ferocity of a menopausal Avon lady.'

The 'light relief' characters Humker and Tandrell, servants to Drathro, are even more poorly depicted, and the revelation that they have been selected for their role be virtue of being the two brightest students amongst the underground dwellers repeats an idea used by Holmes in his season six story *The Krotons*. In fact the most disappointing aspect of this segment of *The Trial of a Time Lord* is the uncharacteristically lacklustre quality of Holmes's scripts, as Willis suggested: 'This … was Robert Holmes's last completed contribution to the series. Holmes was probably *Doctor Who*'s best writer; he had a perfect understanding of all the elements that made it successful. The list of stories from [his] pen contains more classics than any one man has a right to … That's why it's so sad to see [this] as his swansong. It's not that it's … bad …; but there's a weariness to it, as though he was just clearing up a contractual obligation.'

The Thoros-Beta segment is a little better – although, as Peter Anghelides pointed out in *DWB* Number 40 dated November 1986, it still has its problems: 'I think … that the lack of depth in so many of the characterisations is because [writer] Philip Martin and [director] Ron Jones have failed to create a believable society. The power of Yrcanos, manifested in Brian Blessed's huge televisual presence, is thus undercut by our inability to visualise him as the head of an unseen army … There is no unseen population we can conceive of [here]. This is despite attempts to give shape to Yrcanos's personality by taking time out to muse about the afterlife, his powers of leadership and his plans for marrying. Such scenes …, far from punctuating a racy narrative with moments of reflective non-narrative, instead hold up an already flagging storyline. With such an absence of narrative depth, the voiced threat that all future life in the universe is endangered by Crozier's work becomes hugely melodramatic. At the one moment where we might be concerned for the effects of the work, [specifically] the convincing transmogrification of the character we have known for many weeks, the whole emphasis of the end of Peri's role in the series is thrown onto the Doctor and his trial. So long and thanks for all the fish, as Kiv might say.'

One very positive feature of these Philip Martin scripted episodes is the return of Sil, as David Brunt argued in *Muck and Devastation* Issue Two: 'Nabil Shaban as Sil, more restrained than in *Vengeance on Varos* and minus his superloo, was in fine form and conning everyone in sight, with one eye on the profits and one eye on the door to make a quick getaway in true conman style.' It is good too to be introduced to some other members of Sil's race, including his long-suffering leader Kiv; and in Part Eight there is a very nice interlude – apparently added by Eric Saward – involving an elderly Mentor with an amusingly world-weary attitude. The other characters in this segment of the story are, on the other hand, rather less memorable, even the usually excellent Patrick Ryecart failing to make much of an impression in the clichéd role of Crozier. 'The biggest disappointment for me was watching Tuza's great warrior army of half a dozen extras,' wrote David Brunt. 'Even Gordon Warnecke didn't help matters with a terrible performance. That these were the battle trained army of warriors that Yrcanos intended to attack the Mentors with was stretching credibility a bit far; if they could fall into a deep depression at the sight of a polystyrene rock fall then the sight of a Mentor would have driven them all mad.'

One of the most dramatic and impressive moments of the entire season comes toward the end of Part Eight, as Peter Anghelides described: 'Nicola Bryant's transformation was so alarmingly different when she became Kiv (additionally visualised by her baldness) that her exit from the series was horribly thrilling. Of the two stock options (marrying or killing her off), this is the one which seemed most appropriate, and which produced the best we've seen of the lead actress since *The Caves of Androzani*.' It is just a pity that this excellent and fitting final scene for Peri is completely undermined at the end of Part Fourteen when it is revealed that she did not in fact die after all but, unbelievably, went to live with King Yrcanos as his mate. As Nigel Griffiths put it in *Muck and Devastation* Issue Two: 'What a shame [John Nathan-Turner] decided to cop out on that brilliant exit.'

The most successful segment of the story as a whole is the third one, featuring the Vervoids. This is partly because the irritating courtroom scenes are kept to a minimum, allowing the story to flow rather better than during the other segments, but mainly because the scripts themselves are entertaining and quite easy to follow, complemented by Chris Clough's well paced and stylish direction. The 'whodunit' element could perhaps be considered rather unsatisfactory, leaving a few loose ends and unanswered questions, but on the other hand this is entirely in keeping with the Agatha Christie motif, Christie's own stories often being full of holes and highly implausible in their resolution. Reaction to the Vervoids themselves has been mixed. 'The Vervoids – the latest attempt to stick a guy in a wet suit and hope that no-one notices,' commented Michael James, also in *Muck and Devastation* Issue Two. 'The Costume Department overdid it a bit by gluing [what looked like] a cauliflower to the head of the suit and leaving the zips prominent [for] everyone [to see]. And as for giving them Geordie accents – that made them really memorable for me …' Other reviewers, however, have been more favourably disposed toward these creatures, praising imaginative design features such as the inclusion of the 'sting' in their hands and drawing attention to the tension generated by their lurking presence in the ship's ducting.

One problem becomes very apparent in the episodes set on board the *Hyperion III*, as Lance Parkin observed: 'Bonnie Langford is terrible … Can anyone find … a scene or a single line in which she is anything other than awful? She is a fine entertainer, quite a presence on the stage by all accounts, and she is clearly enthusiastic to be in *Doctor Who*, but none of that excuses the fact that she is totally miscast.' Langford is actually even less convincing in Parts Thirteen and Fourteen than she is in Parts Nine to Twelve, owing no doubt to the fact that she was still 'finding her feet' when they were recorded (bearing in mind that the episodes were made out of transmission sequence).

The best aspect of this last segment is that it contains some superb imagery in the scenes set in the Valeyard's fantasy domain within the Matrix. Chris Clough's direction is again excellent here and, after the relative disappointment of his opening episodes for the story, it's nice to be able to say that Robert Holmes's final credited script, that for Part Thirteen, is a good one. As the conclusion to a fourteen-part story, however, these episodes remain a severe let-down. 'The trial ends in confusion,' wrote Diane McGinn in *DWB* No. 118 dated October 1993, 'with a plethora of different schemes and explanations fighting each other in such a way that the viewer is left with no idea what was really going on.'

The only real saving grace of *The Trial of a Time Lord* is that it shows Colin Baker's Doctor in a rather better light than before, and makes one realise just how significant a contribution he could have made to the series had his era not been cut unexpectedly short. 'The major failing of Colin Baker's Doctor in my opinion,' wrote Nigel Griffiths, 'has been the lack of feeling that [he] has … shown. For instance on the planet Varos his companion was in the process of being converted into a bird and he did not immediately

6. SIXTH DOCTOR

attempt to stop it – reacting in a way that no other Doctor would have ... This led to the viewer not seeing [him] as a hero and [losing] interest in him. However during the trial Colin made the Doctor into a more appealing character, showing real sadness at the supposed death of Peri ... and real outrage at the activities of the Time Lords.'

Despite this, *The Trial of a Time Lord* can only be considered a monumental wasted opportunity; a grave disappointment for which the usual mitigating factors – lack of time and money – cannot, for once, be held to account.

Despite the changes made to the series' style and content in the wake of the cancellation of the original season twenty-three, Controller of BBC1 Michael Grade remained badly disposed toward *Doctor Who*. He did eventually give the go-ahead for a further season to be produced – but only on condition that a different actor was given the lead role. Colin Baker was in fact offered the chance to appear in the first four episodes of the twenty-fourth season in a story to explain the Doctor's regeneration, but he declined to do so, so *The Trial of a Time Lord* would unexpectedly stand as his last appearance in the series. The news that he would not be returning as the Doctor was broken to the general public in early December 1986. Many of the series' fans were incensed by the treatment that Baker had received from the BBC. There was however clearly no prospect of Grade reversing his decision, so another new Doctor would have to be cast to take *Doctor Who* into the late eighties. Nathan-Turner had acceded to his superiors' request to inform Baker of his ousting from the series only on the understanding that he himself would finally be allowed to move on to a different project, so it seemed that season twenty-four would find newcomers both in front of and behind the cameras ...

The Seventh Doctor
(Sylvester McCoy)
1987-1989

SYLVESTER McCOY IS THE SEVENTH DOCTOR

'Just for purely acting charms, it's a great role to play,' said Sylvester McCoy in a 1993 interview about his portrayal of the seventh Doctor. 'You're asked to call upon all sorts of acting in it, from kind of merry to mad, and all the various things in between.'

McCoy was born James Kent-Smith in Dunoon, Scotland, in 1943. His father had been killed in the War a couple of months earlier and, as his mother subsequently suffered from mental health problems, he was brought up mainly by his grandmother and aunts. He attended a local school and from there went on to Blair's College, a seminary in Aberdeen, where between the ages of twelve and sixteen he trained to be a priest. He eventually applied to join a Dominican order as a monk but was turned down as he was too young. He went instead to Dunoon Grammar School, where on getting to know his female fellow pupils he quickly abandoned the idea of becoming a priest or a monk. On finishing his education he moved to London, where his grammar school education won him immediate employment with an insurance company in the City. He trained in this job and continued in it until the age of twenty-seven, when he decided that it was not really for him. The pop music and theatre industries were booming at this time, and he felt that entertainment was an area that he would prefer to get into. He managed to obtain a job selling tickets and keeping the box office records at London's Roundhouse Theatre where, through a friendship with the actor Brian Murphy, he met director Ken Campbell and agreed to join him in a new venture called the Ken Campbell Roadshow. It was Campbell who subsequently devised the name Sylveste McCoy for a stuntman character in a show that they were performing, and he later decided to adopt this as his stage identity after a critic misunderstood it to be his real name. After several years the name evolved into its final form.

The stunts that McCoy undertook in Campbell's show included setting light to his head, putting ferrets down his trousers, exploding bombs on his chest and hammering nails up his nose, all of which earned him a reputation as an eccentric, daredevil performer. The show was a great success and went on to tour all over Europe. It also gave McCoy an opportunity to break into legitimate theatre, and he soon found himself being invited to appear in numerous plays and musicals. It was while he was starring at the National Theatre in *The Pied Piper*, a play written especially for him, that he heard that the BBC were looking for a new lead actor to replace Colin Baker in *Doctor Who*. He had applied for the job once before, when Peter Davison had relinquished the role, but had discovered that Baker had already been cast. Undaunted, he telephoned John Nathan-Turner to put himself forward once more. By a strange coincidence, moments after they had finished speaking, a BBC producer named Clive Doig, with whom McCoy had often worked, also telephoned Nathan-Turner to suggest that he would make a good Doctor. Nathan-Turner, although initially suspecting collusion, was sufficiently intrigued to go and see McCoy in *The Pied Piper* in January 1987. He was greatly impressed, and eventually offered McCoy the role of the seventh Doctor. 'Suddenly there I was,' recalled McCoy in a later interview, 'a lunatic actor, thrown into this extraordinary world, which for the most part I enjoyed enormously.'

The enduring image of McCoy's Doctor is of a lively fellow with dark wavy hair and a faint Scots accent, sporting a paisley-patterned scarf and a question-mark pullover and brolly. 'I definitely started off playing it for laughs,' he commented. 'I hadn't watched *Doctor Who* for years, but had memories of Patrick Troughton, Jon Pertwee and early Tom Baker. I remembered it as being humourous and so started out doing it like that. As it developed, my Doctor became very serious, but still with the comic element there. I was moving towards that in the end.'

DOCTOR WHO SEASON TWENTY-FOUR [1987]

Regular Cast:
The Doctor (Sylvester McCoy)
Melanie (Bonnie Langford)
Ace (Sophie Aldred) from *Dragonfire* Part One onwards

Regular Crew:
Producer: John Nathan-Turner.
Script Editor: Andrew Cartmel.
Production Associate: Ann Faggetter.
Title Music: Ron Grainer and the BBC Radiophonic Workshop, arranged by Keff McCulloch.
Special Sounds: Dick Mills.

After informing Colin Baker in October 1986 that his contract as the Doctor was not to be renewed, John Nathan-Turner went on extended leave over the winter, under the impression that this would mark the end of his time as producer of *Doctor Who*. On his return, however, he was told that he would have to remain in the job for the following season. Despite his stated reluctance to do so, he had no choice but to comply if he was to remain a staff producer at the BBC. A serious problem requiring immediate attention was the lack of any suitable scripts lined up for production. Nathan-Turner therefore, as a matter of urgency, set about finding a new script editor to succeed Eric Saward. Andrew Cartmel had been working for a computer company in Cambridge but had also attended some workshops at the BBC's Television Drama Script Unit and had got an agent on the strength of some unproduced scripts. After his agent, who knew Nathan-Turner, heard that a new script editor was required for *Doctor Who*, Cartmel travelled to London for an interview and was offered the job.

Meanwhile, recognising that time was running very short to get production of the new season under way, Nathan-Turner had already contacted Pip and Jane Baker and asked if they would consider writing the new Doctor's introductory story …

TIME AND THE RANI

Writer: Pip and Jane Baker. **Director:** Andrew Morgan. **Designer:** Geoff Powell. **Costumes:** Ken Trew. **Make-Up:** Lesley Rawstorne. **Incidental Music:** Keff McCulloch. **Visual Effects:** Colin Mapson. **OB Cameraman:** Alastair Mitchell, John Hawes. **Studio Lighting:** Henry Barber. **Studio Sound:** Brian Clark. **Production Assistant:** Joy Sinclair. **Assistant Floor Manager:** Joanna Newbery, Christopher Sandeman.

	First UK TX	Scheduled TX	Actual TX	Duration	Viewers	Chart Pos.
Part One	07/09/87	19.35	19.35	24'44"	5.1	71
Part Two	14/09/87	19.35	19.34	24'36"	4.2	85
Part Three	21/09/87	19.35	19.36	24'23"	4.3	81
Part Four	28/09/87	19.35	19.36	24'38"	4.9	86

Plot: The Rani has taken control of the planet Lakertya and forced the peaceful Lakertyans to build a rocket silo-cum-laboratory base into a cliff face. She is aided by the Tetraps, a race of bat-like creatures, and plans to fire a rocket loaded with loyhargil, a substance with the same properties as strange matter, at an asteroid completely composed of the latter. As a preliminary to this she has created a huge artificial brain and kidnapped a number of geniuses – including Pasteur and Einstein from Earth – to imbue it with the ability first to identify and then to calculate the correct way to create loyhargil for her in the laboratory. The newly-regenerated Doctor and Mel manage to stop her and the planet is saved. The Rani is captured by the Tetraps, who decide to take her as a prisoner back to their home world.

Episode endings:
1. Mel falls into one of the Rani's booby traps and is caught within a spinning globe. She screams as the globe bounces across the surface of Lakertya, every impact threatening to cause it to explode.
2. The Doctor seeks refuge from the Rani in the Tetraps' eyrie. The waking Tetraps surround him menacingly.
3. The Rani is triumphant as the huge brain that she has created starts to draw information from the Doctor's mind. The Doctor, forcibly linked to the equipment by way of a helmet-like device, lies helpless as the process continues.
4. Mel tells the Doctor that he will take a bit of getting used to, but he replies: 'I'll grow on you, Mel. I'll grow on you.' They enter the TARDIS and it dematerialises.

IT WAS MADE WHERE...?
OB Recording: 04.04.87-08.04.87
Locations: Cloford Quarry, Cloford, nr Frome, Somerset; Whatley Quarry, Whatley, nr Frome, Somerset; Westdown Quarry, nr Chantry, Frome, Somerset.
Studio Recording: 20.04.87-21.04.87 in TC8, 03.05.87-05.05.87 in TC1

ADDITIONAL CREDITED CAST
The Rani (Kate O'Mara), Ikona (Mark Greenstreet), Beyus (Donald Pickering), Sarn

(Karen Clegg[1]), Urak (Richard Gauntlett), Faroon (Wanda Ventham[2-4]), Lanisha (John Segal[3]), Special Voices (Peter Tuddenham[3,4], Jacki Webb[3,4]).

THINGS TO WATCH OUT FOR

- As usual at the start of a new Doctor's era, this story marks the debut of new opening and closing title sequences, accompanied – as on the previous two occasions – by a new theme music arrangement. For the first time, the new title sequences were created on a computer. The work was carried out by BBC graphic designer Oliver Elmes in collaboration with Gareth Edwards at CAL Video, a freelance computer graphics company. An early version of the new opening titles is erroneously featured at the beginning of Part Four of *Time and the Rani*, with Sylvester McCoy's face much less distinct than in the final version approved by John Nathan-Turner. (The final version is however substituted on the BBC video release of the story.)
- *Time and the Rani* features only the third pre-titles sequence in the series' history (the previous ones having been for season nineteen's *Castrovalva* and the twentieth anniversary special *The Five Doctors*). This sequence shows the TARDIS being attacked in space and crashing on Lakertya, where the Rani and Urak enter and the Doctor regenerates. The computer-generated images of the TARDIS in space were commissioned from CAL, as John Nathan-Turner had been impressed by their work on the new title sequences.
- 'Loyhargil' is an anagram of 'holy grail'.
- Wanda Ventham and Donald Pickering appear as Faroon and Beyus respectively. Ventham had previously featured in *Doctor Who* in season fifteen's *Image of the Fendahl* and Pickering had been seen in the first season's *The Keys of Marinus*. Both had also appeared in *The Faceless Ones* in season four.

THINGS YOU MIGHT NOT HAVE KNOWN

- Working title: *Strange Matter*.

QUOTE, UNQUOTE

- **The Doctor:** 'The more I know me, the less I like me.'
- **The Rani:** 'I've had enough of this drivel.'

ANALYSIS

Time and the Rani opens (like the fifth Doctor's debut story, *Castrovalva*) with a pre-titles sequence leading up to the Doctor's regeneration. Unfortunately this gets the Sylvester McCoy era off to a rather bad start as the viewer is given no indication of the reasons for this latest transformation of appearance or the circumstances that precipitated it. (Surely it could not have been caused simply by him falling from his exercise bike when the TARDIS was attacked by the Rani, as some commentators have suggested? While this could perhaps be seen as some sort of barbed comment aimed at the health and fitness industry, and would certainly justify the sixth Doctor's reluctance to submit to Mel's exercise regime, it would be too prosaic for words.) Even given the difficulties created by Colin Baker's unwillingness to return for a regeneration story, one would have thought that the writers and/or production team could have come up with something better than this. Still, it could have been worse, as Nigel Griffiths pointed out in *Muck and Devastation* Issue Three dated December 1987: 'The regeneration [effect] was weak but we must be thankful that there was one included, as simply having the new Doctor lying on the floor of the console room would have been very unsatisfying.'

The new opening titles designed by Oliver Elmes and realised by Gareth Edwards of CAL Video are quite spectacular, and certainly an improvement on the previous ones for which Sid Sutton was responsible, although still not in the same league as the pioneering work of Bernard Lodge. The new theme arrangement by Keff McCulloch is not too bad, either, although perhaps not as good as the Dominic Glynn one, and similarly not a patch on the original and still much-missed Delia Derbyshire version.

As for the story proper, this turns out to be a case of: nice production, shame about the scripts. Writers Pip and Jane Baker did admittedly have a problem in that they had no idea who would be playing the new Doctor or how he would be characterised – and, at least when they started work on the project, the series had no script editor for them to discuss things with, either – but this can be no excuse for the fact that they came up with a story that is totally uninvolving. *Time and the Rani* takes place on an alien planet with alien characters in an alien situation, and the viewer really has no-one to identify with and nothing to relate to. A story of this kind can sometimes be made to work if there is some other dimension to it – if it has an underlying moral message, for example, or if it serves as an allegory of a situation closer to home – or even if the characters are sufficiently three-dimensional and their circumstances sufficiently interesting. Here, however, the Bakers present a one-level plot with one-dimensional characters and, despite the suggestion of a wider universal significance to the Rani's plan, the viewer is tempted to ask: 'So what?'

All the least successful aspects of the writers' work on the sixth Doctor's era sadly resurface in this story, writ large. The idea of a group of 'great men' being gathered together for a meeting was just about plausible in season twenty-two's *The Mark of the Rani*, but here it is taken to ludicrous extremes with the notion of the Rani rounding up a gaggle of geniuses – including a number from Earth, naturally enough – and putting them to work on her pet project. Then there is the dreadful dialogue that the Bakers seem to delight in concocting for their characters. Perhaps the most notable example here is the Rani's explanation of what she is trying to achieve: 'In the aftermath of the explosion, helium-2 will fuse with the upper zones of the Lakertyan atmosphere to form a shell of chronons … In the same millisecond as the chronon shell is being formed, the hot-house effect of the gamma rays will cause the primate cortex of the brain to go into chain reaction, multiplying until the gap between shell and planet is filled'. Hmm …

Production-wise, though, this story does have a good deal going for it. Andrew Morgan's direction is competent and stylish, the OB location work is excellent and even the Tetraps are quite well realised – although, considering that they are supposed to have 360° vision, it is amazing how often people seem to be able to get past them or sneak up on them without being seen. Perhaps best of all are the visual effects, which must be considered some of the best ever presented in the series up to this point. The Rani's bubble traps are spectacularly good, and there is also some superb modelwork in evidence.

Another highlight is Kate O'Mara's performance as the Rani which, although undeniably camp and over the top, perfectly suits the mood of the piece and is never less than entertaining. She almost steals the show, in fact, and her impersonation of Bonnie Langford in the amusing sequence where the Rani fools the disorientated and drugged

Doctor into believing that she is Mel is wickedly perceptive. Few other actresses could cope so well with appalling lines like: 'I have the loyhargil – nothing can stop me now!'

Then there is the new Doctor himself. Paul Dumont, writing in *DWB* No. 48 dated October 1987, had mixed feelings: 'On the basis of his first few episodes, Sylvester McCoy is a far more interesting Doctor to watch than the previous two. He has a presence that Davison rarely had. Unfortunately he has inherited from Colin Baker a clowning, over the top pantomime aspect – dancing round the Rani's control panel with Mel, running away Scooby Doo-like from the Rani – and I was saddened to see him shove a Tetrap into a trap; I thought that the brutality had gone out with Colin Baker.' Nigel Griffiths, on the other hand, was wholly enthusiastic: 'Sylvester [McCoy] can be summed up best with one word – magic. From his early fumblings with the spoons through to his "I'll grow on you" to Mel at the end, he proved that he was an inspired choice. I loved the way [Colin Baker's] costume hung on him throughout the first episode … I've always found it strange that after, in a sense, dying, the newly regenerated Doctor always thinks first of changing his clothes – surely that wouldn't cross his mind straight away? With this one it didn't, and wasn't it a refreshing change!'

When the new Doctor's regular costume is eventually revealed it is, thankfully, a vast improvement on those worn by Peter Davison and Colin Baker. The only thing that really lets it down is the question-mark pattern on the pullover which – even more so than the question-marks on the shirt collars of the other eighties Doctors – is far too arch and self-aware.

Time and the Rani sees *Doctor Who* in a state of transition; although it introduces the seventh Doctor, it still has a great deal in common with the stories of the sixth Doctor's era. It would not be until new script editor Andrew Cartmel really started to make his mark that the Sylvester McCoy stories would begin to acquire a distinctive quality of their own.

PARADISE TOWERS

Writer: Stephen Wyatt. **Director:** Nicholas Mallett. **Designer:** Martin Collins. **Costumes:** Janet Tharby. **Make-Up:** Shaunna Harrison. **Incidental Music:** Keff McCulloch. **Visual Effects:** Simon Tayler. **OB Cameraman:** Alastair Mitchell, David Hunter. **Studio Lighting:** Henry Barber. **Studio Sound:** Brian Clark. **Production Assistant:** Frances Graham. **Assistant Floor Manager:** Val McCrimmon.

	First UK TX	Scheduled TX	Actual TX	Duration	Viewers	Chart Pos.
Part One	05/10/87	19.35	19.34	24'33"	4.5	88
Part Two	12/10/87	19.35	19.38	24'39"	5.2	84
Part Three	19/10/87	19.35	19.36	24'30"	5.0	79
Part Four	26/10/87	19.35	19.35	24'21"	5.0	93

Plot: Mel wants to go swimming so the Doctor takes her to a tower block called Paradise Towers where there is reputed to be a fantastic pool. When they arrive they discover that the place is far from being the superb leisure resort they had expected – it is run-down and dilapidated. The hallways are roamed by gangs of young girls known as Kangs; the apartments are inhabited by cannibalistic old ladies, the Rezzies; and the building is managed by a group of dictatorial caretakers, presided over by the Chief Caretaker. The latter is in thrall to the disembodied Great Architect Kroagnon, the building's creator, who is using giant cleaning machines systematically to kill all the occupants as he considers that they are spoiling his creation by living there. The Great Architect eventually manifests himself by taking over the Chief Caretaker's body, but the Doctor and Mel join forces with the Kangs, the Rezzies and Pex – the only young man left in the complex – to defeat him. Pex, however, is apparently killed in the struggle.

Episode endings:
1. The Chief Caretaker greets the Doctor and apparently believes him to be the Great Architect. The next moment, however, he tells the Deputy Chief to kill the Doctor.
2. Mel pays a second visit on some Rezzies named Tabby and Tilda. The two old ladies at first seem friendly, but then Tilda ensnares Mel in a crocheted shawl and Tabby threatens her with a toasting fork. Mel screams.
3. The Doctor and three Kangs – Blue Kang Leader, Bin Liner and Fire Escape – watch as the Chief Caretaker is 'processed' by Kroagnon, currently in the form of a large machine in Paradise Towers' basement. They turn to run, but one of the robot cleaners grabs the Doctor by his throat and starts to throttle him.
4. The fight against the Great Architect has resulted in everyone working together, assuring a better future. The Doctor and Mel say their goodbyes. They have been made honorary Kangs. They leave in the TARDIS, the wall beside which is marked with some red and blue 'wallscrawl' and the slogan 'Pex Lives'.

IT WAS MADE WHERE...?

OB Recording: 21.05.87-22.05.87
Location: Elmswell House, Nightingales Lane, Chalfont St Giles, Buckinghamshire.
Studio Recording: 04.06.87-05.06.87, 17.06.87-19.06.87 all in TC1

ADDITIONAL CREDITED CAST

Chief Caretaker (Richard Briers), Deputy Chief (Clive Merrison), Tilda (Brenda Bruce[1-3]), Tabby (Elizabeth Spriggs[1-3]), Fire Escape (Julie Brennon), Bin Liner (Annabel Yuresha), Pex (Howard Cooke), Blue Kang Leader (Catherine Cusack), Young Caretaker (Joseph Young[1]), Yellow Kang (Astra Sheridan[1]), Maddy (Judy Cornwell[2-4]), Video Commentary (Simon Coady[3]).

Note: The voice of the Great Architect in Parts Two and Three was provided by Richard Briers.

THINGS TO WATCH OUT FOR

- Guest star roles in this story are taken by well known actors Richard Briers, Brenda Bruce, Elizabeth Spriggs and Judy Cornwell.
- The caretakers' unusual salute consists of raising the horizontal palms of their hands to rest on their top lips.
- Julie Brennon, who played Fire Escape, was the then wife of former companion actor Mark Strickson.
- Catherine Cusack, playing the Blue Kang Leader, is the youngest daughter of Irish actor

Cyril Cusack, who was at one point considered for the role of the first Doctor in 1963.

- Annabel Yuresha, playing Bin Liner, is the daughter of Belinda Wright and Jelko Yuresha, who both danced regularly with the London Festival Ballet.
- For the scenes in the swimming pool where Mel is attacked by a robot, Bonnie Langford was doubled by stunt woman Ellie Bertram.

THINGS YOU MIGHT NOT HAVE KNOWN

- Working title: none, although the commissioning documents refer to the story as *Paradise Tower*.
- The part of the Deputy Chief Caretaker was originally offered to Edward Hardwick but he was unable to take it as he was working on a film.
- The incidental music composer originally assigned to *Paradise Towers* was David Snell. He completed a score for all four episodes but was informed by John Nathan-Turner in a letter dated 11 September 1987 that it was unsatisfactory. Nathan-Turner commented that while the original sample music that Snell had provided had been fine, the completed work tended in his view to detract from the action of the story rather than enhance it. Snell responded in a letter dated 18 September, expressing disappointment and commenting that, when he had completed the music for the first two episodes, director Nicholas Mallett had assured him that Nathan-Turner was very happy with it. Snell was willing to rewrite, free of charge, any sequences that Nathan-Turner disliked, but this offer was not taken up and instead Keff McCulloch was contracted at a very late stage to supply an alternative score.

QUOTE, UNQUOTE

- **Fire Escape:** 'Red Kang eye-spy says we can't go through usual carrydor. Blue Kangs out and lurking.' **Bin Liner:** 'And the yellow?' **Fire Escape:** 'No yellows. All unalive now.'
- **Bin Liner:** 'No Exit's not here.' **Fire Escape:** 'Where is she?' **Bin Liner:** 'Was on talkie-phone three before Caretakers attacked ...' **Fire Escape:** 'But now? ... Mayhaps No Exit's returned to Red Kang headquarters.' **Bin Liner:** 'Mayhaps ... or ...' **Fire Escape:** 'Or ...' **Bin Liner:** 'No Exit's unalive.' **Fire Escape:** 'Taken to the cleaners?' **Bin Liner:** 'Yes. Taken to the cleaners.'
- **Chief Caretaker/Great Architect:** 'Attention all robotic cleaners. Attention all robotic cleaners. At last Kroagnon can leave the basement prison they trapped his bodiless brain in. And return in this borrowed body to the corridors and lifts of his own creation. They buried me away because I wanted to stop them using the Tower. And now you and I will destroy them.'
- **Bin Liner:** 'Hail Pex. Hail the unalive who gave his life for the Tower. In life he was not a Kang, but in death he was brave and bold as a Kang should be.'

ANALYSIS

Paradise Towers is a story that promises a great deal but, as Paul Scoones discussed in *TSV* 50 dated February 1997, ultimately fails to deliver: 'In an attempt to portray a microcosm of society in a state of moral and social decay, *Paradise Towers* had a great deal more potential for examining social issues than was realised. Although the script is imaginative, it is far from flawless, and although there are touches of style and a few noteworthy performances, the overall impression is one of a missed opportunity for a much better story.'

Writer Stephen Wyatt's debut contribution to the series, based in part on J G Ballard's novel *High Rise*, does indeed have a lot to recommend it. On one level – as exemplified by the Kangs' unusual names and distinctive vocabulary – it has a pleasingly fresh and imaginative fantasy quality to it, but on another it does clearly have some more serious things to say about issues such as inner city living and social decline. The subject of urban architecture and its impact on the people who have to inhabit it was in fact quite a topical one in the UK at the time of the story's original transmission, owing to some controversial remarks made on the subject by Prince Charles, but opinions differ as to whether or not Wyatt was in any way influenced by this. It is similarly uncertain whether or not he intended the different groups of Kangs, with their signature colours of red, blue and yellow, to represent the country's three main political parties, which promote themselves using the same colours. The scenario he presents is actually somewhat reminiscent of that seen in Terry Gilliam's surreal 1985 film *Brazil*: a bizarre, pseudo-fascist society in which the authorities mindlessly enforce a welter of nonsensical rules and regulations – a case of bureaucracy gone quite literally mad.

The story has a quite poignant and moving ending, too, with the 'cowardly cutlet' Pex being the only one brave enough to stand up and fight alongside the Doctor and losing his life as a result (or apparently so, as Wyatt has said in interviews that the 'Pex Lives' graffito in the final shot is intended to hint that he might have survived after all). The only valid criticisms that could perhaps be made of Wyatt's scripts are that they are not as well plotted as they might be and contain one or two ideas that are not fully thought through. 'It should have been possible to have established a credible community created and defined by the surroundings they are obliged to inhabit,' wrote Peter Anghelides in *DWB* No. 49 dated November 1987. 'But the basic premise is never properly explored, and does not stand any real examination. Why should the original inhabitants have "trapped his bodiless [brain]" in the basement in order to prevent Kroagnon preventing them from using his Tower – why not kill him? Why allow Kroagnon enough technology in his prison to allow "corporelectroscopy" and rebirth? Why put him into a prison of which he himself says: "Nobody knows my Paradise Towers better than I do"?'

Where *Paradise Towers* really falls down, though, is in its translation from script to screen. All too often the production seems to be working against Wyatt's intentions rather than in sympathy with them. Pex, for example, was originally intended to be a hulking, heavily-muscled character – an Arnold Schwarzenegger type – so that his initially cowardly nature would make a surprising and amusing contrast, but director Nick Mallett completely undermined this by choosing Howard Cooke, an actor of average build, to play the part. Then there is the story's incidental music score, provided at the last minute by Keff McCulloch after the one supplied by the original composer, David Snell, was deemed unsuitable by the producer. This strident, rhythmic, very 'eighties' accompaniment is so inappropriate to the mood of the piece that one has to wonder if Snell's attempt could really have been any worse. While this can only remain a matter for speculation, it is undoubtedly the case that a more brooding, atmospheric score would have greatly enhanced the story's effectiveness.

It seems that director Nick Mallett decided to treat *Paradise Towers* as a whimsical, comic strip-style adventure. This is especially apparent in his handling of the excellent (if anything, overqualified) cast, whose spirited, mannered performances are constantly in danger of overstepping the thin dividing line between 'larger than life' and 'over the top'. In some cases this works well. 'Elizabeth Spriggs and Brenda Bruce provided delicious cameos as Tabby and Tilda before being dragged through an implausibly small hole in their kitchenette wall,' wrote Peter Anghelides, 'and (until the scales fell from her eyes in Part Four) one could sympathise with Judy Cornwell's Maddy too'. Annabel Yuresha also turns in a good performance as Bin Liner, making her the most engaging of all the Kangs. In most cases, however, the results are less successful. Bonnie Langford, in particular, does herself no favours in this story, as Paul Scoones observed: 'If *Paradise Towers* had never been made, Bonnie Langford's contribution to *Doctor Who* might be remembered with considerably greater fondness ... When [she is] forced to spend most of the adventure running up and down corridors with only [the] walking cliché [Pex] for company, the worst excesses of her acting are all too obvious. Langford is undoubtedly an accomplished and experienced entertainer, but she is clearly out of her depth in a serious dramatic role, dreadfully over-emphasising her lines and delivering them in [an] unchanging high-pitched breathless croak. Worse still, her bubbly enthusiasm is undaunted by the horrors she encounters. She seems to have little regard for what has come before in the story, and rarely conveys emotions appropriate to her character's situation.'

Richard Briers' outrageously overacted portrayal of the 'possessed' Chief Caretaker – which occasionally puts one in mind of the sick humour of George A Romero's zombie films, an effect no doubt unintended – is the least successful aspect of the whole story, turning the character into a laughing stock and completely negating any sense of menace that might otherwise have been present. Some commentators, however, have praised Briers' performance. Paul Scoones, for example, wrote: 'Briers deserves particular mention for [the scenes] in which he plays the Great Architect Kroagnon inhabiting the Chief Caretaker's body. Briers adopts jerky, puppet-like body movements and a slurred speech pattern which marvellously capture the sense of a creature operating an unfamiliar body.'

This unnerving observation may perhaps provide a clue as to why Mallett directed the story in the way that he did. Hitleresque fascists, street gangs, killer robots, animated cadavers and sweet little old ladies with cannibalistic tendencies are really the stuff of nightmares, and if treated in a totally serious and straightforward way could potentially have provoked a controversy even greater than that surrounding certain aspects of season twenty-two. Even with the more whimsical approach that Mallett adopted, the story still managed to attract criticism for its use of kitchen implements in a threatening context. It seems that in the era of the 'moral majority' there was a limit – and quite a strict one, at that – to what *Doctor Who* could get away with.

DELTA AND THE BANNERMEN

Writer: Malcolm Kohll. **Director:** Chris Clough. **Designer:** John Asbridge. **Costumes:** Richard Croft. **Make-Up:** Gillian Thomas. **Incidental Music:** Keff McCulloch. **Fight Arranger:** Roy Scammell. **Visual Effects:** Andy McVean. **Film Cameraman:** William Dudman. **OB Cameraman:** Alastair Mitchell, Chas Snare. **Production Assistant:** Rosemary Parsons. **Assistant Floor Manager:** Christopher Sandeman, Kim Wilcocks.

Note: There were some studio scenes recorded for the first episode during the studio sessions for *Dragonfire* and using that story's crew.

	First UK TX	Scheduled TX	Actual TX	Duration	Viewers	Chart Pos.
Part One	02/11/87	19.35	19.35	24'47"	5.3	90
Part Two	09/11/87	19.35	19.36	24'23"	5.1	93
Part Three	16/11/87	19.35	19.35	24'22"	5.4	87

Plot: A Chimeron queen called Delta, the last surviving member of her race, is being pursued by the evil Gavrok and his Bannermen, intent on a mission of genocide. Delta finds herself on board a space bus of tourists *en route* to Earth when it is knocked off course by an American satellite and ends up at a Welsh holiday camp in 1959. The Doctor and Mel, having won a holiday with the tourists, help Delta to evade the rampaging Bannermen long enough to allow her child to hatch from its egg and grow to maturity. She, her daughter and a young man named Billy – who sacrifices his humanity to be with her – then escape to start a new life and ensure the continuation of the Chimeron race.

Episode endings:
1. The Doctor and a young woman named Ray are held at gun point by an alien bounty hunter, Keillor, who has given away Delta's location to the Bannermen in return for a promised reward. The Doctor tells Keillor that he should let Ray go as she is of no use to him. He replies: 'I don't just kill for money. It's also something I enjoy.'
2. The Doctor confronts Gavrok and warns him that he will be brought to justice for his crimes. He demands the release of Mel and the holiday camp manager Burton, who have been held prisoner by the Bannermen, and starts to leave with them. The Bannermen prime their weapons for firing, and the Doctor worriedly speculates that he may have gone a little too far.
3. The American secret service agents Hawk and Weismuller are astonished as the TARDIS dematerialises. The mysterious beekeeper Goronwy glances up at the sky and gives a knowing smile and wink.

IT WAS MADE WHERE...?

OB Recording: 24.06.87-27.06.87, 29.06.87-04.07.87, 06.07.87-07.07.87
Locations: Springwell Lock Quarry, Rickmansworth, Buckinghamshire; Sutton Farm, Fort Road, nr Penarth, S. Glamorgan, Wales; Psygollyn Mawr, Hensol Forest, nr Welsh St. Donats, S. Glamorgan, Wales; Coed Y Wallas, Castle-Upon-Alun, S. Glamorgan, Wales; Majestic Holiday Camp, Barry Island, S. Glamorgan, Wales; Hanger 50, Llandow Industrial Estate, British Tissues Hangar, nr Nash, S. Glamorgan, Wales.
Studio Recording: 12.08.87 in TC3

ADDITIONAL CREDITED CAST

Gavrok (Don Henderson), Delta (Belinda Mayne), Weismuller (Stubby Kaye), Hawk (Morgan Deare), Tollmaster (Ken Dodd[1]), Burton (Richard Davies), Billy (David Kinder), Ray (Sara Griffiths), Murray (Johnny Dennis[1, 2]), Keillor (Brian Hibbard[1,2]), Chima (Tim Scott[1]), Bollitt (Anita Graham[1,2]), Adlon (Leslie Meadows[1,2]), The Lorells (Robin Aspland[1], Keff McCulloch[1], Justin Myers[1], Ralph Salmins[1]), Vocalists (Tracey Wilson, Jodie Wilson)*, Goronwy (Hugh Lloyd[2,3]), Vinny (Martyn Geraint[2]),

Callon (Clive Condon[2,3]), Arrex (Richard Mitchley[2,3]), Young Chimeron (Jessica McGough[2], Amy Osborn[2]), Chimeron Princess (Laura Collins[3], Carley Joseph[3]).

* The vocalists are seen on screen only in Part One; they are heard in Parts Two and Three in the story's incidental music.

THINGS TO WATCH OUT FOR

- Don Henderson, well known for his role as George Bulman in *The XYY Man* and its spin offs, and later for his co-starring role as Frank Kane in the BBC drama *The Paradise Club*, appears here as Gavrok.
- Guest appearances are made in this story by a number of popular actors better known for their comedy and variety work. These include Ken Dodd, Hugh Lloyd, Stubby Kaye and Richard Davies.
- This story marks the first appearance of the Doctor's distinctive question-mark handle umbrella.
- Sylvester McCoy can be seen wearing his spectacles – normally removed before recording – in some long shots of him riding a motor bike.

THINGS YOU MIGHT NOT HAVE KNOWN

- Working title: *The Flight of the Chimeron*.
- Keillor, the alien bounty hunter, is never referred to by name in the story's dialogue; his name is given only in the closing credits.
- The part of Ray was one of two considered to be potential companion characters. The final decision as to whether the one to be kept on would be Ray or Ace (from the next transmitted story, *Dragonfire*) depended partly on when Bonnie Langford decided to leave the series. Ultimately Langford stayed until the end of the season, and it was decided that Ace would be the character to become the new companion.
- Ray was originally to have been played by Lynn Gardner, but the actress was injured during a driving lesson and had to be replaced at short notice by Sarah Griffiths. By way of compensation, Gardner was given a speaking role in the following story, *Dragonfire*.
- The Lorells, the singing group seen in this story, were actually incidental music composer Keff McCulloch and sisters Tracey and Jodie Wilson, the former of whom was later to be married to McCulloch.
- Bob Gabriel, a director on the BBC's *EastEnders*, was originally slated to direct *Delta and the Bannermen* when his work on the soap opera was completed. It is unknown why he did not in the end take the assignment.

QUOTE, UNQUOTE

- **The Doctor:** 'Many a slap 'twixt a cup and a lap.'
- **Murray:** [Speaking of the crystal needed to power the Nostalgia Trips bus, of which he is the pilot] 'I'm trying to use mind power to make it grow faster … but I haven't had much luck.'
- **The Doctor:** 'Love has never been known for its rationality.'
- **Burton:** 'You are not the Happy Hearts Holiday Club from Bolton, but instead are spacemen in fear of an attack from some other spacemen?'

7 SEVENTH DOCTOR

ANALYSIS

Delta and the Bannermen is even more whimsical than the story that immediately preceded it, but in this case the scripts by Malcolm Kohll and the direction by Chris Clough are perfectly in tune with each other and the end result is much more successful. 'Even during the dark days of season twenty-three,' wrote Brian Willis in *Muck and Devastation* Issue Three dated December 1987, 'if somebody had told me that the next season (if there ever *was* such a thing) would feature such luminaries as Ken Dodd, Stubby Kaye and Hugh Lloyd, I would have laughed in that somebody's face. And if that somebody had then gone on to suggest that I would actually *enjoy* a story featuring the said personalities, I would probably have screamed with mirth. The very idea ... Actually, I rather liked *Delta and the Bannermen*.'

The story has a very 'fifties sci-fi' feel to it, recalling films of the *I Married a Monster from Outer Space* variety – an impression greatly enhanced by the setting of the main action in that very era and by more specific touches such as the use of period songs both in the performances of the holiday camp group, the Lorells, and in the incidental music score. The light-heartedness of the holiday camp atmosphere contrasts nicely with the grimness of the Bannermen's intentions and their genocidal hatred of the Chimerons.

'The whole thing had the air of a *Hi-de-Hi!* episode directed by James Cameron ...,' continued Willis. 'The casting was variable, ranging from Don Henderson (terrific – the man was born to eat raw meat and shoot comedians in the back), through ... Ken Dodd (not quite so terrific, but not in enough scenes to be embarrassing) to Stubby Kaye (who perpetually looked as if he'd wandered on [location] by mistake).

'So why did I like it? Two reasons. First, the whole story was kept moving at a breathless pace by ... Chris Clough. Whatever holes there were in the [plot], the speed of it all – from the battle on the Chimeron home planet [at] the beginning of [Part One] to the destruction of Gavrok in [Part Three] – kept you moving straight past them relentlessly. Secondly, [although the] script was not by any means a classic, ... it had an air of unashamed absurdity and – dare I say it – silliness that made it, in parts, extremely memorable. The idea of a group of extraterrestrial rock and roll fans on a trip to Disneyland but having to land at Barry Butlins instead because their bus-shaped spaceship has hit a US satellite is one that could have come from Douglas Adams.'

The story boasts a good collection of supporting characters, the most intriguing of which is the beekeeper Goronwy, well played by Hugh Lloyd, who seems so unfazed by all the strange events going on around him that some commentators have been led to suggest that he might actually be an alien, or even perhaps a Time Lord living in 'retirement' on Earth. The regulars also come over well in this story. Bonnie Langford seems much more comfortable than usual in the familiar holiday camp setting, and Sylvester McCoy is also by this point starting to settle into his role. 'For my money the seventh Doctor really came of age in this story,' wrote Mark Stammers in *The Frame* No. 5 dated February 1988. 'McCoy was in his element and so was his Doctor, and apart from a couple of duff lines I enjoyed his performance throughout. He was less manic than in the preceding tales; the misquotations were still there, but more in the background, as was the continual hat-doffing which had been so much a part of *Paradise Towers*.'

Delta and the Bannermen is another step in the right direction for the seventh Doctor and, all in all, a highly enjoyable romp.

DRAGONFIRE

Writer: Ian Briggs. **Director:** Chris Clough. **Designer:** John Asbridge. **Costumes:** Richard Croft. **Make-Up:** Gillian Thomas. **Incidental Music:** Dominic Glynn. **Visual Effects:** Andy McVean. **Studio Lighting:** Don Babbage. **Studio Sound:** Brian Clark. **Production Assistant:** Rosemary Parsons, Karen King. **Assistant Floor Manager:** Christopher Sandeman.

	First UK TX	Scheduled TX	Actual TX	Duration	Viewers	Chart Pos.
Part One	23/11/87	19.35	19.37	24'01"	5.5	80
Part Two	30/11/87	19.35	19.35	24'40"	5.0	96
Part Three	07/12/87	19.35	19.36	24'26"	4.7	94

Plot: The TARDIS materialises in Iceworld, a space trading colony on the dark side of the planet Svartos. The Doctor and Mel encounter Glitz and learn that he has come here to search for a supposed treasure guarded by a dragon. Also on Svartos is Kane, a – literally – cold-blooded criminal who has been imprisoned here by his own people from the planet Proamon. The Doctor and Mel, aided by Ace, a disaffected waitress, discover that the 'dragon' is a biomechanoid and the 'treasure' a power crystal held within its head. Kane is desperate to obtain the crystal and the Doctor uses it to bargain with him for Ace's freedom. It turns out that Iceworld is a huge spacecraft and the crystal the key that Kane needs in order to activate it. Iceworld takes off and Kane determines to return to Proamon and take revenge on his people. The Doctor however reveals that Proamon no longer exists. Kane despairingly opens a viewing port, allowing bright light to flood into the control room and causing himself to melt.

Episode endings:
1. Having lost Glitz in the tunnels beneath the surface of Svartos, the Doctor reaches a precipice bordered by safety railings. He climbs over the railings, hooks the handle of his umbrella over them and dangles precariously over the sheer drop, his hands slowly slipping down the umbrella's length.
2. The dragon's head opens to reveal a crystal crackling with energy. Kane, following events via a bug planted in Glitz's treasure map, is delighted: 'At last. After 3,000 years. The dragonfire shall be mine!'
3. Mel decides to stay on Iceworld with Glitz, and the Doctor agrees to take Ace with him in the TARDIS. The TARDIS dematerialises seen only by a little girl, Stellar.

IT WAS MADE WHERE...?
Studio Recording: 28.07.87-30.07.87 in TC1, 12.08.87-13.08.87 in TC3

ADDITIONAL CREDITED CAST
Glitz (Tony Selby), Kane (Edward Peel), Belazs (Patricia Quinn[1,2]), Kracauer (Tony Osoba[1,2]), Customer (Shirin Taylor[1,3]), Anderson (Ian Mackenzie[1,3]), McLuhan (Stephanie Fayerman[1,3]), Bazin (Stuart Organ[1,3]), Zed (Sean Blowers[1]), Pudovkin (Nigel Miles-Thomas[1,2]), The Creature (Leslie Meadows), Announcer (Lynn

Gardner[1,3]), Stellar (Miranda Borman[1,3]), Archivist (Daphne Oxenford[2]), Arnheim (Chris MacDonnell[2]).

THINGS TO WATCH OUT FOR

- Major sources of inspiration for this story included the 1939 MGM film *The Wizard of Oz* (the idea of Ace, real name Dorothy, being whisked off to Iceworld in a time storm) and Twentieth Century Fox's *Alien* saga (the ANT hunt in Part Three, and the appearance of the dragon), amongst others.
- Script editor Andrew Cartmel encouraged his writers to read the academic media studies textbook *Doctor Who – The Unfolding Text* by John Tulloch and Manuel Alvarado to help acquaint themselves with the series, and Ian Briggs actually used some short passages from that book in the dialogue of *Dragonfire*.
- Tony Osoba plays Kracauer. Osoba had appeared in *Doctor Who* previously as one of the android Movellans in *Destiny of the Daleks*. He was better known, however, for his appearances in the popular comedy programme *Porridge*.

THINGS YOU MIGHT NOT HAVE KNOWN

- Working titles: *Absolute Zero*, *The Pyramid's Treasure*, *Pyramid in Space*.
- Kane was originally to have been called Hess, but this was changed so as to avoid any suggestion that it was a reference to the Nazi war criminal Rudolph Hess.
- *Dragonfire* was promoted as being the one hundred and fiftieth transmitted *Doctor Who* story, but in fact it was only the one hundred and forty-seventh. The production team had arrived at their total by counting the previous year's season-long *The Trial of a Time Lord* as four stories.
- Glitz was added to the story at a relatively late stage in place of a similar character called Razorback in the original scripts.
- When it was decided that Ace would travel on with the Doctor and become the new companion, the production team requested that Ian Briggs sign a waiver of all rights in the character. This was done in order to avoid problems that had occurred on two occasions in the past with writers disputing the BBC's ownership of companion characters that they had claimed to have created in their stories.

QUOTE, UNQUOTE

- **Kane:** 'None of my mercenary force will be willing when I bring them out of cryosleep. The process causes complete loss of memory. With no memories they can have no past, no future, no will of their own, no purpose except to obey me. Through them I shall be invincible. My power shall be absolute.'
- **Ace:** 'Do you feel like arguing with a can of deodorant that registers nine on the Richter scale?'
- **Ace:** 'Melanie! Don't listen to her, she doesn't mean it. Doughnut, give him the treasure. I'm sixteen. I'm too young to be freeze-dried.'
- **Mel:** 'Oh all right, you win.' **The Doctor:** 'I do? I usually do.' **Mel:** 'I'm going now.' **The Doctor:** 'That's right, yes, you're going. You've gone for ages, you've already gone, you're still here, just arrived, haven't even met you yet. It all depends on who you are and how you look at it. Strange business, time.'
- **The Doctor:** 'Think about me when you're living your life, one day after another,

all in a neat pattern. Think about the homeless traveller in his old police box, his days like crazy paving.'

'By the standards of season twenty-four, *Dragonfire* was really quite good,' commented Tim Munro in *DWB* No. 51 dated January 1988. 'It was the only story which came anywhere near to recapturing the unique atmosphere of "real" *Doctor Who*, instead of the cosily bland pantomime which has characterised this season.'

What Munro had spotted was that *Doctor Who* had undergone a process of change during season twenty-four as new Doctor Sylvester McCoy and, perhaps more particularly, new script editor Andrew Cartmel had gradually got to grips with their respective jobs and started to make their presence felt. The stories had all been flawed in one way or another, but – with the possible exception of *Time and the Rani*, which was really a hang-over from the sixth Doctor's era – they had all nevertheless shown considerable potential and held out a great deal of hope for better things to come. *Doctor Who* 1987-style was more whimsical than ever before, and arguably aimed at a somewhat younger age group, but it was also fresh and imaginative and original, eschewing the increasing introspection and self-indulgence of the previous Doctor's era.

Not everyone liked this approach, however, and many commentators argued that the series had taken on the quality of a glitzy pantomime overloaded with inappropriate showbusiness 'guest stars' – almost a case of *Doctor Who* by numbers, on the mistaken assumption that if the supporting cast were famous enough then any deficiencies in plotting or direction could be overlooked. Munro developed this line of argument: '*Dragonfire* tried, albeit in vain, to break free of its sloppily produced confines by returning to the show's previous strengths of atmosphere, plot and credible characterisation. As a result there's a jarring clash between Ian Briggs's original basic story and detailed characters, John Nathan-Turner's pantomime production and Andrew Cartmel's increasingly obvious preference for reducing the show even further into fairytale. *Dragonfire* is a gaudy and silly pantomime, just like the rest of season twenty-four, but unlike the other stories one feels *it should have been far more than that*. This story actually had incredible potential, yet again destroyed by an incompetent production team.'

For an example of incompetent production one need look no further than the literal 'cliffhanger' ending to Part One, which must surely be the most ludicrous ever presented in *Doctor Who*. It could perhaps be seen as some kind of reductive, self-reflexive comment on the aspect of the series' format that requires the Doctor to get himself into serious danger once every twenty-five minutes, but in fact it is simply rubbish. To be fair, though, *Dragonfire* actually succeeds in a great many respects. One of the principal reasons for this is that all the cast seem to take their parts seriously. Edward Peel, in particular, turns in a superb performance as the villain of the piece, Kane. '[He is] one of the McCoy era's few half-decent villains,' commented Kenny Smith in *The Paisley Pattern Dr Who Annual* in 1993. '[He] … comes across rather well as the embittered exile, who has waited 3,000 years for revenge.'

Peel has real on-screen presence and electrifies every scene in which he appears. Kane is a well-conceived character, too, although David Brunt, writing in *Muck and Devastation* Issue Three dated December 1987, felt that he was a little unoriginal: '[A] "slightly" insane renegade, stronger than most people, with a low body temperature, exiled on a barren planet with his band of mercenaries … Surely that was the basic idea behind *Star Trek II: The Wrath of Khan*? [And was it just a] coincidence that the villain's name is Kane, not too dissimilar?'

The fact that Kane is not an entirely unsympathetic character – he can exist only at sub-zero temperatures, can kill with a touch and yet is embittered by the loss of his one true love – serves only to enhance his appeal, making him a memorable adversary for the Doctor. Particularly effective is a scene in which he tries to seduce Ace with the promise of power and she appears almost to succumb. His suicide scene is also a real high point, not only because of the added pathos it brings to the character but also because the visual effect of his face blistering and melting away in the sunlight is absolutely superb and, what's more, unusually horrific for this period of the series' history. True, it is similar to one seen at the end of Stephen Spielberg's 1981 feature film *Raiders of the Lost Ark*, but it was achieved in only a fraction of the time and with very little money, and nothing like it had ever been attempted before on British television. That it works so brilliantly is a real tribute to the talents of its uncredited freelance designers Susan Moore and Stephen Mansfield, who had also been responsible for the baby Chimeron in *Delta and the Bannermen* and would go on to create many other memorable creatures for the series over the course of the following two seasons.

The other particularly noteworthy aspect of *Dragonfire* is that it introduces a new companion, Ace, played by Sophie Aldred. Kenny Smith was none too impressed: 'Right from the word go, I found her irritating and obnoxious. [She] was supposed to be sixteen and … I found her antics very embarrassing … A bad start for [the character].' Mark Eldridge, writing in *DWB* No. 122 dated January 1994, expressed a similar opinion: 'Her constant yells of "Mega!", "Brill!", "Ace!" and "Wicked!" quickly begin to grate and it makes you wonder how the production team [thought] that a streetwise sixteen-year-old would go around saying any of these things.' These criticisms, however, are too harsh. While she admittedly fails to convey here the assurance and strength of personality that she would show in later stories, Aldred actually makes quite a good first impression in the role. And there is no doubt that she is a great improvement on Bonnie Langford, who thankfully bows out at the end of Part Three. Langford was just totally miscast in *Doctor Who*, and her brief tenure is looked upon by many as a major factor contributing toward the series' decline in popularity in the late eighties, as well as evidence of an apparent lack of awareness on the part of the production team as to how the series was being perceived by fans and general viewing public alike.

Season twenty-four had seen *Doctor Who* consigned back to a weekday evening slot, as during the fifth Doctor's era, although this time broadcast at the rate of only one episode per week opposite ITV's phenomenally popular soap opera *Coronation Street* – as would continue to be the case during the following two seasons. It had been something of a learning experience for the many newcomers who had joined the series, most of whom – including script editor Andrew Cartmel, writers Stephen Wyatt, Malcolm Kohll and Ian Briggs and companion actress Sophie Aldred – were either relatively or completely inexperienced in television work. It had also taken some time for Sylvester McCoy, in conjunction with the production team, to decide exactly how his Doctor ought to be portrayed, and this in turn had taken time to filter through to the scripts. The season had consequently been a somewhat flawed one in itself, but at the same time had laid down a solid foundation for the remainder of the seventh Doctor's era – as would quickly become apparent the following year.

DOCTOR WHO SEASON TWENTY-FIVE (1988-1989)

Regular Cast:

The Doctor (Sylvester McCoy)

Ace (Sophie Aldred)

Regular Crew:

Producer: John Nathan-Turner.

Script Editor: Andrew Cartmel.

Production Associate: June Collins on all stories. Hilary Barratt uncredited on *Remembrance of the Daleks*.

Title Music: Ron Grainer and the BBC Radiophonic Workshop, arranged by Keff McCulloch.

Special Sounds: Dick Mills.

Andrew Cartmel had time to take a more considered approach to the twenty-fifth season than he had to the twenty-fourth. After viewing a number of highly-regarded stories from the series' past, including season thirteen's *The Seeds of Doom* and season fourteen's *The Talons of Weng-Chiang*, he formed the view that the essentially serious and dramatic approach of earlier eras had been rather more effective than the relatively light-hearted and comedic one of Sylvester McCoy's first season. He discussed this with John Nathan-Turner and they decided that the departure of the somewhat lightweight character of Mel and the arrival of the strong, streetwise Ace should mark the start of a more general shift of emphasis back toward that more serious and dramatic style.

Another move that Cartmel was keen to make was to introduce a greater degree of mystery into the Doctor's character. He felt that over the years there had been too much revealed about the initially enigmatic time traveller's background, and that this had considerably lessened the appeal of the character. With Nathan-Turner's approval, he would therefore brief the writers of the twenty-fifth season to include in their stories some elements casting doubt on aspects of the Doctor's established history and on the true nature of his character. This was very much in line with McCoy's own thinking about the role. His initial instincts had been to interpret it in a humorous way – most of his previous acting experience having been in comedy – but as he had settled in he had realised that it would be better if he played it much straighter.

The first fruits of this revised approach were to be seen in the new season's opening story, which kicked off the series' twenty-fifth anniversary year with the return, once again, of the Doctor's oldest adversaries …

REMEMBRANCE OF THE DALEKS

Writer: Ben Aaronovitch. **Director:** Andrew Morgan. **Designer:** Martin Collins. **Costumes:** Ken Trew. **Make-Up:** Christine Greenwood. **Incidental Music:** Keff McCulloch. **Fight Arranger:** Tip Tipping. **Visual Effects:** Stuart Brisdon. **OB Cameraman:** Robin Sutherland, Barry Chaston. **Studio Lighting:** Henry Barber. **Studio Sound:** Scott Talbott. **Production Assistant:** Rosemary Parsons. **Assistant Floor Manager:** Val McCrimmon, Lynn Grant.

	First UK TX	Scheduled TX	Actual TX	Duration	Viewers	Chart Pos.
Part One	05/10/88	19.35	19.35	24'33"	5.5	78
Part Two	12/10/88	19.35	19.35	24'31"	5.8	78
Part Three	19/10/88	19.35	19.34	24'30"	5.1	91
Part Four	26/10/88	19.35	19.34	24'36"	5.0	96

Plot: The TARDIS arrives in London in November 1963, where the Doctor and Ace discover that two rival factions of Daleks – one loyal to the Dalek Emperor and one to the Dalek Supreme – are seeking the Hand of Omega, a powerful Time Lord device that the first Doctor hid there during an earlier sojourn on Earth. The Daleks are focusing their search around Coal Hill School – the school that the Doctor's grand-daughter Susan attended – while a military unit led by Group Captain Gilmore is attempting to resist their incursions. The Doctor tries to keep Gilmore and his team out of harm's way while the two Dalek factions battle each other for control of the Hand. The imperial Daleks eventually overpower those led by the Dalek Supreme and capture the device. The Dalek Emperor is revealed to be Davros, now with only the last vestiges of his humanoid form remaining. The Doctor begs him not to use the Hand, but is ignored. However, this is just the final ruse in a complex trap laid by the Time Lord to defeat his old adversaries. The Hand vaporises the creatures' home planet, Skaro, by turning its sun into a supernova, and then returns to destroy their forces orbiting Earth. The Doctor confronts the Dalek Supreme and causes it to self-destruct by convincing it that it is the sole surviving member of its race.

Episode endings:
1. The Doctor is trapped at the top of a flight of stairs leading from the basement of Coal Hill School as an imperial Dalek ascends behind him chanting that he is an enemy of the Daleks and will be exterminated.
2. Ace fumbles ineffectually with a rocket launcher weapon as three imperial Daleks surround her and prepare to exterminate.
3. A Dalek shuttle craft lands in the playground of Coal Hill School and the Doctor muses that he might have miscalculated
4. Ace asks the Doctor: 'We did good, didn't we?' He replies: 'Perhaps. Time will tell. It always does.'

IT WAS MADE WHERE...?

OB Recording: 04.04.88-09.04.88, 11.04.88-13.04.88

Locations: 12 Theed Street, Lambeth, London; Kew Bridge Steam Museum, Green Dragon Lane, Brentford, Middx; railway bridge, Windmill Walk, Lambeth, London; Willesden Lane Cemetery, Willesden Lane, London; bridge at Wulfstan Road/Brunel Road, Ealing, London; TA Hall, Horn Lane, Acton, London; John Nodes and Sons Ltd, 181 Ladbroke Grove, London; railway bridge, Old Oak Common Lane, North Acton, London; streets near Kendal Avenue, London; St John's School, Macbeth Street, Hammersmith, London; alley off Macbeth Street, Hammersmith, London.

Studio Recording: 16.04.88 (studio unknown), 24.04.88 (studio unknown), 27.04.88-29.04.88 in TC8

ADDITIONAL CREDITED CAST

Gilmore (Simon Williams), Mike (Dursley McLinden), Rachel (Pamela Salem), Allison (Karen Gledhill), Ratcliffe (George Sewell), Headmaster (Michael Sheard[1,2]), Harry (Harry Fowler[1,3]), The Girl (Jasmine Breaks), Embery (Peter Hamilton Dyer[1]), Dalek Operators (Hugh Spight[1-3], John Scott Martin[2-4], Tony Starr[2-4], Cy Town[2-4]), Voice (John Leeson[1-3]), Vicar (Peter Halliday[2]), John (Joseph Marcell[2]), Martin (William Thomas[2]), Kaufman (Derek Keller[2]), Emperor Dalek[3]/Davros[4] (Roy Tromelly[3]/Terry Molloy[4*]), Black Dalek Operator (Hugh Spight[4]), Voices[1-3]/Dalek Voices[4] (Roy Skelton, Brian Miller[2-4], Royce Mills[2-4]).

* Terry Molloy was credited as 'Roy Tromelly' – an anagram of his name – on Part Three so as to conceal from viewers the fact that Davros, a character he had played in the two previous Dalek stories, was within the Emperor's casing.

POPULAR MYTHS

- This story reveals for the first time that the Daleks are capable of ascending stairs. (Although this is the first time that a Dalek is actually *seen* to ascend a flight of stairs, there is a scene in season two's *The Chase: Journey into Terror* in which such an occurrence is clearly implied; and season twenty-two's *Revelation of the Daleks* shows that both the Daleks and Davros are capable of hovering above the ground.)

THINGS TO WATCH OUT FOR

- This story marks the fourth use in the series' history of a pre-titles sequence. This one shows the Dalek mothership approaching Earth, accompanied by soundtrack extracts from famous early sixties speeches by a number of prominent figures – John F Kennedy, General Charles de Gaulle, the Duke of Edinburgh, Martin Luther King and John F Kennedy (again).
- The Doctor again returns to the junkyard in Totter's Lane, as previously seen in the series' first story, *100,000 BC*, and in season twenty-two's *Attack of the Cybermen*. The owner's name is this time shown as being 'I M Forman', rather than 'I M Foreman', on the junkyard gates.
- The Doctor leaves a 'calling card' bearing a question-mark symbol.
- Simon Williams, one of the stars of LWT's *Upstairs, Downstairs*, appears here as Gilmore.
- Mentions of 'Bernard' and 'the British Rocket Group' are in-joke references to Bernard Quatermass and his team as seen in Nigel Kneale's seminal fifties serials.
- From this story onwards, *Doctor Who* was transmitted with NICAM stereo sound,

although – except for the 1996 television movie – only in the London region.

- The following records were used on the soundtrack for this story: 'Return to Sender' by Otis Blackwell and Winfield Scott, arranged by Keff McCulloch; 'Do You Want To Know A Secret' by the Beatles; 'Children's Favourites' by White, arranged by Keff McCulloch (this piece had also been used in *Delta and the Bannermen*); 'Apache' by Jerry Lordan, arranged by Keff McCulloch; 'Lollipop' by the Mudlarks; and 'A Taste of Honey' by the Beatles.
- Pamela Salem and Michael Sheard make return *Doctor Who* appearances in this story Salem had played a voice in *The Face of Evil* and Toos in *The Robots of Death*, both in season fourteen, while Sheard had clocked up an impressive five previous appearances, in *The Ark* (season one), *The Mind of Evil* (season eight), *Pyramids of Mars* (season thirteen), *The Invisible Enemy* (season fifteen) and *Castrovalva* (season nineteen).

THINGS YOU MIGHT NOT HAVE KNOWN

- Working title: *Nemesis of the Doctor*.
- A crane was hired to lower the Daleks' shuttle craft down into the playground of St John's School.
- Ratcliffe was originally to have been called Gummer. The part was originally offered to Stratford Johns.
- The following actors were considered for roles in this story: Neil Stacy, Ian Ogilvy (Gilmore), Peter Tilbury (headmaster), Mark McGann (Mike).

QUOTE, UNQUOTE

- **John:** 'If this sugar thing hadn't started, my great grandfather wouldn't have been kidnapped … and sold in Kingston. I'd have been an African!' **The Doctor:** 'See. Every large decision creates ripples.'
- **The Doctor:** [To Ace] 'Do you remember the Zygon gambit with the Loch Ness Monster? Or the Yeti in the Underground? Your species has an amazing capacity for self-deception.'
- **The Doctor:** 'Oi, Dalek! It's me, the Doctor! What's the matter, don't you recognise your mortal enemy?'

ANALYSIS

Remembrance of the Daleks gets the season off to a fine start. Ben Aaronovitch's excellent debut scripts for the series contain just enough continuity references to make things suitably nostalgic for the fans in this anniversary year, but not so many as to cause confusion for the general viewing public. It is not only continuity references that give this story its nostalgic flavour, either, as Aaronovitch's scripts, Andrew Morgan's superb direction and the designers' fine attention to period detail combine to capture perfectly the distinctive feel of the era in which the action takes place.

'Starting with [a] spectacularly-executed pre-titles sequence, the story moves along in a fast, tautly-directed blend of visual excitement and no-nonsense dialogue …,' noted Stephen O'Brien in *Peladon* Issue Five dated autumn 1988. 'Each episode is a masterly example of smooth, efficient writing.

'Aaronovitch's story is deceptively simple. On the one hand it is just a chase for the Hand of Omega between two Dalek factions. On the other, there are implications of racial tensions and the quest for racial purity that sow the seeds of more serious thought … This is the first story in recent years to deal with these issues in a way that is integral to the plot. The racial injustices on Skaro, with the eternal-seeming war between different races of Daleks, are mirrored in the 20th Century on Earth. In a marvellous acted scene, Ace discovers [a] "No Coloureds" sign in the window [of the house where she is staying], and *Doctor Who* makes one of its rare social statements. The choice of (the great) Martin Luther King's voice, amongst others, superimposed over [an image of] the Earth [in the pre-titles sequence] cannot be coincidence, as cannot the relevance of the Doctor's late night conversation with the black man [John] in the café – another beautifully underacted scene.'

The Daleks themselves are extremely impressive this time around, as an uncredited reviewer observed in *DWB* No. 117 dated September 1993: 'Far from being Davros's stooges of their last couple of [stories], they were evil, cunning, vicious, all by themselves (or so it seemed). Dignity was finally restored.'

'They don't move as well as they might on location,' commented Justin Richards in *DWB* 60 dated November 1988, 'but they always appear powerful and technologically sophisticated. This image is enhanced in the first episode by the Dalek's eye view effect, with its changing readout and cross-hairs. A shame that this is not used later as well. The Daleks' ability to climb stairs is an interesting addition to their abilities, and one that will be appreciated by everyone, not just the fans. It also disposes neatly of the usual criticisms of their obvious impotence in this respect.

'Two other new additions to the Dalek canon are the Emperor and the Special Weapons Dalek. The Emperor is not terribly impressive, though the secret of his contents is well guarded. The Special Weapons Dalek is more interesting. It is certainly powerful, although apparently blind! And why is it so dirty when its fellows are all spruced up for the occasion? The main problem is … that it is *too* powerful. Once [it is] wheeled into action, the Imperial Daleks easily triumph, having fared less well up to that point.'

There are many wonderful moments and images in *Remembrance of the Daleks*, some of which were highlighted by *DWB* No. 117's uncredited reviewer: 'The battle in the junkyard, the philosophical café scene, the Doctor's destruction of the Black Dalek by logic, the gunner Dalek, the creepy little girl, the Doctor's manipulation of the Hand of Omega … and, of course, the moment to end them all, the climax to [Part One when the Dalek ascends the flight of stairs].'

The story's supporting characters are all well written and played, and the regulars are likewise on top form here – although Stephen O'Brien felt that one of them fared much better than the other:

'Sylvester McCoy's performance I still find embarrassing and unconvincing. Sylv is at his best when in contemplative mood … but exceedingly inept at conveying outrage or anger. Sorry, I'm just not a … fan …

'For the first time in the [series'] history, the companion overshadows the Doctor. Sophie Aldred has made the role of Ace her own, and has sidestepped the usual stereotypical companion mould by being individualistic and strong in her performance. Although the script generates her character's actions, Soph as an actress is extremely good at bringing depth and a certain reality to the part. She is also very likeable, a characteristic not shared by her recent predecessors. Together, she and McCoy make a wonderful team, though I'm tempted to believe this is more to her credit than his.'

Dalek stories always have something of the sense of a 'special occasion' about them, and in this case it is fully justified. *Remembrance of the Daleks* is a delight from beginning to end and stands as one of the best examples of late eighties *Doctor Who*.

THE HAPPINESS PATROL

Writer: Graeme Curry. **Director:** Chris Clough. **Designer:** John Asbridge. **Costumes:** Richard Croft. **Make-Up:** Dorka Nieradzik. **Incidental Music:** Dominic Glynn. **Visual Effects:** Perry Brahan. **Studio Lighting:** Don Babbage. **Studio Sound:** Scott Talbott, Trevor Webster. **Production Assistant:** Jane Wellesley. **Assistant Floor Manager:** Lynn Grant.

	First UK TX	Scheduled TX	Actual TX	Duration	Viewers	Chart Pos.
Part One	02/11/88	19.35	19.35	24'51"	5.3	96
Part Two	09/11/88	19.35	19.35	24'48"	4.6	104
Part Three	16/11/88	19.35	19.35	24'25"	5.3	88

Plot: The TARDIS arrives on the planet Terra Alpha where the Doctor and Ace discover a society in which sadness is against the law – a law enforced with considerable zeal by the brightly uniformed Happiness Patrol. The planet is ruled over by Helen A with the aid of her companion Joseph C and her carnivorous pet Stigorax named Fifi. The penalty for those found guilty of unhappiness is to die in a stream of molten candy prepared by Helen A's executioner, the robotic Kandy Man, and his associate Gilbert M. The time travellers help to foment rebellion amongst the downtrodden population and the subterranean Pipe People – the planet's original inhabitants – and Helen A is overthrown. Joseph C and Gilbert M escape in a shuttle, while the Kandy Man is destroyed and Fifi killed. Helen A finally realises that happiness is nothing without the contrast of sadness.

Episode endings:
1. The Doctor and a blues musician named Earl Sigma are captured trying to flee the Kandy Kitchen. The Kandy Man tells them that he likes his volunteers to die with smiles on their faces.
2. The Doctor discovers that Ace will be appearing at the Happiness Patrol audition at the forum that night. A member of the Happiness Patrol arrives and paints a large 'R I P' over a poster of a previous forum attraction, a woman named Daphne S. The forum doorman comments that she obviously didn't go down too well.
3. Ace picks up a paint pot to finish off the job of restoring the TARDIS to its normal blue, it having earlier been repainted pink by the Happiness Patrol. She asks the Doctor if he is all right. He replies that happiness will prevail.

Studio Recording: 26.07.88-28.07.88 in TC3, 10.08.88-11.08.88 in TC8

ADDITIONAL CREDITED CAST

Helen A. (Sheila Hancock), Joseph C. (Ronald Fraser), Daisy K. (Georgina Hale), Priscilla P. (Rachel Bell), Gilbert M. (Harold Innocent), Trevor Sigma (John Normington), Susan Q. (Lesley Dunlop), Earl Sigma (Richard D. Sharp), Harold V. (Tim Barker[1]), Silas P. (Jonathan Burn[1]), Kandy Man (David John Pope), Killjoy (Mary Healey[1])*, Forum Doorman (Tim Scott[2,3]), Snipers** (Steve Swinscoe[2], Mark Carroll[2]), Wences (Philip Neve[2,3]), Wulfric (Ryan Freedman[2,3]), Newscaster (Annie Hulley[3]).

*Although identified only as 'Killjoy' in the closing credits to Part One, the character played by Mary Healey is named Daphne S, as confirmed by the poster at the conclusion of Part Two.
** The snipers were billed in *Radio Times*, but not on screen, as David S and Alex S.

POPULAR MYTHS

- Part Three of this story was originally intended to consist of animation rather than live action. (It wasn't.)

THINGS TO WATCH OUT FOR

- In the scenes set in the underground tunnels in Part Three the Kandy Man has no metal brace around his mouth. The brace was added to the costume following these initial recordings to try to disguise the features of the actor inside.

THINGS YOU MIGHT NOT HAVE KNOWN

- Working title: *The Crooked Smile*.
- The howl of Helen A's pet Stigorax Fifi was actually the modulated sound of director Chris Clough's own voice.
- Patricia Routledge and Jill Bennett were amongst the actresses considered for the role of Helen A; Prunella Ransome and Rosalind Ayres were amongst those considered for the role of Susan Q.
- The mouth organ was played not by Earl Sigma actor Richard D Sharp but, from out of vision, by musician Adam Burney.

QUOTE, UNQUOTE

- **Kandy Man:** 'You see, I make sweets. Not just any old sweets, but sweets that are so good, so delicious that sometimes, if I'm on form, the human physiology is not equipped to bear the pleasure. Tell them what I'm trying to say, Gilbert.' **Gilbert M.:** 'He makes sweets that kill people.'
- **Sniper 2:** 'Get back. Or he'll use the gun.' **The Doctor:** 'Yes, I imagine he will. You like guns, don't you?' **Sniper 1:** 'This is a specialised weapon. It's designed for roof duty. Designed for long range. I've never used one up close before.' **Sniper 2:** 'Let him go.' **Sniper 1:** 'No.' **The Doctor:** 'No. In fact … let him come a little closer.' **Sniper 1:** 'Stay where you are.' **The Doctor:** 'Why? Scared? Why should you be scared? You're the one with the gun.' **Sniper 1:** 'That's right.' **The Doctor:** 'And you like guns, don't you?' **Sniper 2:** 'He'll kill you.' **The Doctor:** 'Of course he will. That's what guns are for. Pull a trigger. End a life. Simple, isn't it?' **Sniper 1:** 'Yes.' **The Doctor:** 'Makes sense, doesn't it?' **Sniper 1:** 'Yes.' **The Doctor:** 'A life, killing life.' **Sniper 2:** 'Who are you?' **The Doctor:** 'Shut up. Why don't you do it then?

SEVENTH DOCTOR

Look me in the eye. Pull the trigger. End my life.' **Sniper 1:** 'No.' **The Doctor:** 'Why not?' **Sniper 1:** 'I can't.' **The Doctor:** 'Why not?' **Sniper 1:** 'I don't know.' **The Doctor:** 'You don't, do you. Throw away your gun.'

- **The Doctor:** 'I can hear the sound of empires toppling.'

The Happiness Patrol is, on the face of it, a colourful fantasy with a simple moral. As the Doctor puts it in Part Three: 'Happiness is nothing unless it exists side by side with sadness.' The scenario is in some ways similar to that of season four's *The Macra Terror*; both stories involve a human colony where the inhabitants are expected to be contented and cheery at all times – or else. However, whereas in *The Macra Terror* the penalty for dissent was brainwashing, or possibly being sent to work in the mines, on Terra Alpha things are rather simpler: disobedience of the rules brings a sentence of death. Happiness Patrols – gangs of brightly dressed women with big guns – roam the city killing or arresting anyone believed to be a 'killjoy'. There are formal executions at which attendance is compulsory, and labour camps where drones toil under the watchful eye of guards. Terra Alpha is, in short, not a nice place to live.

This is an interesting idea in itself, but on closer examination *The Happiness Patrol* can be seen to work on more complex levels too. What first-time writer Graeme Curry has given the viewer is, in essence, an Orwellian parable: a cautionary tale reflecting on the state of British society at the time of the story's original transmission. Many reviewers have spotted the fact that the planet's dictatorial ruler, Helen A, was intended by Curry to be a representation of one-time Prime Minister Margaret Thatcher, with Joseph C in the supporting role of her husband Dennis, but the allegory appears to go much deeper than that. The demoralised drones marching in silent protest against Helen A's harsh policies are the planet's 'working class', while the Pipe People – a literal underclass – are disenfranchised members of this 'happy' society, perhaps the equivalent of the poor and the unemployed in Thatcher's Britain (although some commentators have suggested that there is also a gay rights message here).

'The political parable was kept mercifully subtle,' suggested Jonathan Way in *DWB* 61 dated December 1988, 'and Sheila Hancock's take-off of Margaret Thatcher was a joy. I don't always think that layering of a story in this way works very well, but this case is an exception, and I enjoyed it.'

'As well as being a political allegory of Thatcher's Britain, *The Happiness Patrol* was ultimately a morality tale,' added Craig Hinton in *DWB* No. 65 dated May 1989. 'Helen A had attempted to set herself up as a paragon of efficiency and ruthlessness. Her marriage to Joseph C was clearly a frigid, loveless one. Yet there was a chink in her armour, and we had observed it throughout the three episodes. Once her empire had fallen, Helen A refused to accept that she was responsible. How could she compromise her infallibility and admit that she was wrong? Even the Doctor's impassioned speech failed to move her. Symbolically she was her own undoing. At the sight of a dying Fifi, her candy-covered shell cracked. Her soft centre revealed, Helen A rejoined the human race.'

The most contentious aspect of the story is undoubtedly the Kandy Man. This creature, creating lethal sweets in its brightly-lit Kandy Kitchen and taking a real pleasure in its job, is a masterpiece of design work and easily the story's most striking and memorable image. Actor David John Pope imbues it with great personality, too, and it comes across as part spoiled child and part scheming psychopath. Many reviewers, however, have found the whole idea of a robot made out of sweets unacceptably bizarre, and the Kandy Man's undoubted similarity to the Bertie Bassett marketing character, used for many years to promote a range of liquorice confectionery in the UK, has also been cited as a major failing. 'Nothing in the world could have prepared me for the sight of the Kandy Man,' commented Jonathan Way. 'Oh yes, I'd heard reports, mutterings of discontent from fans who had seen glimpses of the costume, but somehow my imagination could not rise to the challenge. But then, on 2 November, there it was – squeaky voice and all. A sight to challenge the Nimon as the series' all-time clanger.'

Director Chris Clough and his team apparently decided to avoid dwelling on the more sinister aspects of Graeme Curry's scripts and instead to present the story in a more light-hearted and whimsical vein. A conscious effort seems to have been made to avoid a naturalistic style – the sets and costumes, for instance, are obviously artificial and stagey – and in that sense *The Happiness Patrol* is rather akin to the previous season's *Paradise Towers*. Where it has the advantage over that earlier story, however, is in the strength and conviction of its performances. If *Doctor Who* is going to work, it has to be played for real; that didn't happen on *Paradise Towers*, but here, thankfully, it does. Best of all is Sheila Hancock, who gives a nicely understated portrayal of Helen A, although special mention must also go to the regulars, Sylvester McCoy and Sophie Aldred, who are by this point shaping up into a really excellent Doctor and companion team. Other less prominent characters, such as Earl Sigma, Susan Q and the Pipe People, are also well played, although sadly not as well developed as they might be – a fact no doubt attributable in part to the shortage of time available for characterisation in a three-part story.

The Happiness Patrol has sometimes been referred to as an 'oddball' story, and in many ways this is justified as it is certainly not what might be considered 'traditional' *Doctor Who*. Its experimental nature has won it many critics, but also many admirers; and if nothing else it proves that in its twenty-fifth anniversary year the series still had the capacity to provoke controversy, even amongst its staunchest supporters.

SILVER NEMESIS

Writer: Kevin Clarke. **Director:** Chris Clough. **Designer:** John Asbridge. **Costumes:** Richard Croft. **Make-Up:** Dorka Nieradzik. **Incidental Music:** Keff McCulloch. **Fight Arranger:** Paul Heasman, Nick Gillard. **Visual Effects:** Perry Brahan. **OB Cameraman:** Barry Chaston, Alan Jessop. **Production Assistant:** Jane Wellesley. **Assistant Floor Manager:** Lynn Grant, Jeremy Fry.

	First UK TX	Scheduled TX	Actual TX	Duration	Viewers	Chart Pos.
Part One	23/11/88	19.35	19.35	24'31"	6.1	76
Part Two	30/11/88	19.35	19.36	24'12"	5.2	94
Part Three	07/12/88	19.35	19.35	24'36"	5.2	98

Note: Parts Two and Three had their first transmission in New Zealand, as part of a compilation version of the whole story shown on 25 November 1988 to celebrate the series' anniversary.

Plot: The Doctor and Ace visit England in 1988, where three rival factions – the Cybermen, a group of Nazis and a 17th Century sorceress named Lady Peinforte – are attempting to gain control of a statue made of a living metal, validium, that was created by Rassilon as the ultimate defence for Gallifrey. The statue has three components – a bow, an arrow and the figure itself – that must be brought together in order for it to be activated. They have been separated since 1638 when, in order to foil the first attempt by Peinforte to seize it, the Doctor launched the figure into orbit in a powered asteroid. This asteroid has been approaching the Earth at twenty-five yearly intervals ever since, leaving a succession of disasters in its wake, and has now crash-landed near Windsor Castle. The Doctor plays the three factions off against one other and eventually appears to concede defeat to the Cyber Leader. However, this is just part of a carefully-laid trap, and the Cybermen's fleet is totally wiped out by the statue.

Episode endings:
1. A spaceship touches down near Windsor and the occupants emerge. Ace asks who they are, and the Doctor replies: 'Cybermen.'
2. The Doctor discovers on a scanner that there are thousands of previously-invisible Cyber warships waiting above the Earth.
3. Ace asks the Doctor: 'Who are you?' He smiles and puts a finger to his lips.

IT WAS MADE WHERE...?

OB Recording: 22.06.88-24.06.88, 26.06.88-02.07.88, 05.07.88
Locations: Greenwich Gas Works, Tunnel Avenue, nr Blackwall Tunnel, London; Arundel Castle Estate, Arundel, W. Sussex; streets in Arundel (High Street, Tarrant Street, London Road), W. Sussex; St Mary's, Bramber, nr Steyning, W. Sussex; 'Casa Del Mer', Marine Parade, Goring-by-Sea, W. Sussex; Black Jack's Mill Restaurant, Harefield, Uxbridge.

ADDITIONAL CREDITED CAST

De Flores (Anton Diffring), Lady Peinforte (Fiona Walker), Richard (Gerard Murphy), Mathematician (Leslie French), Karl (Metin Yenal), Security Guard (Martyn Read[1]), Cyber Leader (David Banks), Jazz Quartet (Courtney Pine[1] and Adrian Reid[1], Ernest Mothle[1], Frank Tontoh[1]), Cyber Lieutenant (Mark Hardy[2,3]), Skinheads (Chris Chering[2], Symond Lawes[2]), Cyberman (Brian Orrell[2, 3]), Mrs Remington (Dolores Gray[3]).

THINGS TO WATCH OUT FOR

- Celebrated British jazz artist Courtney Pine and his group appear as themselves in Part One, in a scene where the Doctor admits to a love for this form of music.
- There is a humorous scene in which the Doctor and Ace narrowly avoid bumping into the Queen and her corgis at Windsor Castle.
- Ace wears on her jacket an earring that she will not be seen to acquire until the following story, *The Greatest Show in the Galaxy* – a continuity error caused by a late change in the season's transmission order, made by John Nathan-Turner so that the first episode of *Silver Nemesis* would be seen on the actual twenty-fifth anniversary date.
- Anton Diffring, well known for his numerous roles as German officers in Second World War films, appears here as De Flores. The role was originally offered to Charles Gray (the note specifying 'no German accent required').

- Lady Peinforte's mathematician is played by Leslie French, one of the actors considered for the role of the first Doctor in 1963. The part was originally offered to Geoffrey Bayldon and then to Richard Vernon.
- The story features a brief guest appearance as American tourist Mrs Remington by 'golden age' Hollywood film star Dolores Gray. This character was originally written as a man called Milton P Remington
- There are a number of cameo appearances by well-known production staff and actors in this story. The tour guide showing visitors around Windsor Castle is director and producer Vere Lorrimer (who had not previously worked on the series) while those in his party include production assistant Ian Fraser, directors Fiona Cumming, Andrew Morgan and Peter Moffatt, actor Nicholas Courtney, writer Graeme Curry and production unit manager Kathleen Bidmead. Kevin Clarke, the writer of *Silver Nemesis*, is also seen as a tourist at the Castle, as one of the passers-by in Windsor as Lady Peinforte and Richard make their way through the streets and as a car driver who declines to stop and give Lady Peinforte a lift in Part Three.
- The part of Lady Peinforte was offered to, in order, Billie Whitelaw, Anna Massey, Penelope Wilton and Sarah Badel before eventually being accepted by Fiona Walker, who had made her television debut in *Doctor Who* as Kala in the season one story *The Keys of Marinus*.

THINGS YOU MIGHT NOT HAVE KNOWN

- Working title: *The Harbinger, Nemesis*.
- *Silver Nemesis* was the first in-season *Doctor Who* story to have some of its episodes premiered outside the UK; Parts Two and Three were first transmitted in New Zealand on 25 November. Previously, only the twentieth anniversary special *The Five Doctors* had been seen in another country – the USA – before it went out in its home territory.
- The gasworks location where some of the key scenes of this story were recorded subsequently became the site of the controversial Millennium Dome.
- Prince Edward was approached to play a non-speaking 'member of the Royal Family'. The Prince's equerry apparently wrote back stating that he would be too busy as he had just started working for Andrew Lloyd Webber's Really Useful Company.
- The music performed by Courtney Pine and his ensemble was recorded at Lime Grove Studios on 12 June 1988. The pieces played in Part One were called 'Pe Pi Po' and 'Adrian's Affair'. The piece played on Ace's ghettoblaster to jam the Cybermen's signals later in the story was by the same ensemble and called 'Frank's Quest'.

QUOTE, UNQUOTE

- **Lady Peinforte:** [To Richard, speaking of an animal in the Windsor Safari Park] 'The bear will not pursue us – such things happen only in the theatre.'
- **De Flores:** [To the Cyber Leader] 'I don't know if you are familiar with Wagner's 'Ring des Nibelungen'? Now we, we are the Supermen. But you, you are the Giants.'

ANALYSIS

'There's a difference between the postmodern approach to being hip to one's own textuality ...,' observed Nick Pegg in *Perigosto Stick* Issue Two dated August 1991, 'and simply fannying about with in-jokes and self-referentially sampling past reference points.

7 SEVENTH DOCTOR

From its title onwards, *Silver Nemesis* is so persistently, so systematically aware of itself that it's in constant danger of suffocating as it takes an ever-decreasing spiral route up its own tightly-clenched bottom.'

This is by no means the only problem with the 'official' twenty-fifth anniversary story, which is undoubtedly the weak link in an otherwise strong season. Another serious flaw was highlighted by Mark Stammers in *The Frame* No. 9 dated February 1989: 'It was clear from the beginning that there were far too many villains running around. Just Lady Peinforte and the Cybermen would have been enough, but with the Nazis included as well it meant that one group of baddies had either to stand around a bit, while the other two fought it out, or to get sidetracked into wandering around the countryside, attacking skinheads or taking a lift in Dolores Gray's car.'

'De Flores and his shock troops come off worst of all,' thought Pegg, 'serving no independent function in the action besides bringing the bow along in the first place – and that alone is hardly reason for their presence – and raising no textually meaningful assertions at all. The scene in which de Flores indulges in a Wagnerian evocation of himself and the Cybermen as, respectively, the Superman and the Giants ("Zey are *von*derfoll creatures!") is tacky, pretentious and very funny, and the oblique mention of Hitler as he implies that the Cybermen are the super-race that his one-time leader had prophesied, while presumably supposed to tie in with the Doctor's assertion that the Nemesis comet caused the annexing of Austria in 1938, is even sillier ...

'Lady Peinforte and particularly Richard do somewhat better ... There are moments here of genuine mysticism, [and] black magic is seen to work without any need for pseudo-scientific demystification ... For the most part, though, the success of these characters is down to the fact that Fiona Walker and Gerard Murphy – both fine classical actors – have clearly taken the decision to send the whole thing up outrageously. Fiona Walker in particular makes a meal of her more ludicrous speeches – "Thou art not in all wise so useless", "The silver creatures there do hold the Nemesis" and so on – which are in no wise like unto how people did bespeak in 1638, as it happeneth, forsooth.'

'As for the Cybermen,' added Stammers, 'they were back with yet another redesign and seemed a bit tougher than their recent predecessors, although they did go all weak at the knees at the very mention of the word "gold". And it was never explained why they felt they needed the Nemesis in the first place.'

Matters are not helped by Chris Clough's below-par direction, which looks distinctly rushed, and some rather illogical editing. *Silver Nemesis* is not a total disaster, however, and actually received some quite positive feedback at the time of its original transmission. Journalist Alan Coren, for example, wrote in the *Mail on Sunday* dated 27 November 1988:

'How simultaneously ancient and modern (which is to say magical and relevant) it was.

'Switching between an evil necromancer's bolt-hole in 1638 and an evil Nazi's bunker in 1988, the plot embraces not only the quasi-scientific hoo-ha of intergalactic ironmongery, time theory, cybernauts and ghastly new weaponry.

'It also has the traditional paraphernalia of ancient magicians and wicked Jacobean plotters and mystic totems, with the launching of the Fourth Reich thrown in.

'What's up Doc? Everything, and a rattling good everything, too.

'It also has the central strength it has enjoyed for a quarter of a century, Doctor Who himself. Here is that familar English figure, the heroic eccentric, rescued from the suspicion the English have of cleverness by an endearing, and thus humanising, barminess.'

A less complimentary press reaction was to be found in Nick Smurthwaite's review in *Stage and Television Today* dated 15 December 1988:

'It still looks cheap and amateurish. Worse than that, it looks tired and I found myself less than engaged by Sylvester McCoy's half-hearted Doctor.

'Most of the action seemed to be taking place in an aircraft hangar, with echoey acoustics to match. The ... Cybermen ... still manage to miss everyone when they take aim with their deadly laser guns, while the Doctor's current sidekick Ace ... scores a bull's eye every time with her catapult.'

This mixed response was echoed in contemporary fan opinion. Daniel Blythe was one of those who liked the story, as he explained in *DWB* No. 62 dated February 1989: '*Silver Nemesis*, for me, has been *the* highlight of the season so far. Like *Remembrance of the Daleks* there were a lot of loose ends, but here one got the impression that they were *meant* to be there! Together with some very good acting [and] scripting and some marvellous special effects, the story succeeded in entertaining, holding the attention and restoring the "mystery" of the Doctor.' Andrew Hardwick, writing in the same magazine, felt differently: 'After the seeds of a good story were planted in [Part One], *Silver Nemesis* tumbled heavily downhill. Interesting ideas like the mystery of Nemesis, a possible Fourth Reich and returning to the Doctor some degree of enigma were spoiled by sloppy execution. The main fault ... lies ... with the script – a mine of inconsistencies, bad characterisation and generally stupid plotting. Lady Peinforte and friend were totally unconvincing as basically simple people thrown into a completely alien world. Walking through the streets of Windsor? Hitching a ride? Come on!'

More recent fan reaction to the story has been almost uniformly negative. Tim Munro, writing in *DWB* No. 113 dated May 1993, was particularly damning: '*Silver Nemesis* ... is a loose conglomeration of unrelated events, haphazardly thrown together without regard for their relevance to each other. The result lacks even a semblance of cohesion and feels completely aimless, as if the cast and crew were just dashing around on location from one set-piece to the next. At its worst, *Silver Nemesis* gives the strong impression that it was improvised without any script at all. Its total lack of discernible plot or theme leaves the viewer infuriatingly dissatisfied, no wiser at the finish than at the start as to what it's all about, and it hasn't even the courtesy to provide food for thought, which might at least make its ambiguity forgiveable. A message can cover a multitude of sins.'

'Perhaps Kevin Clarke was a little too ambitious in trying to fit so many elements into just three episodes,' suggested Stammers. 'Here ... was a story that would have benefited greatly from being told in four or even six episodes. But I fear the days of seasons which can afford to accommodate six-parters are long past.' This can be seen, with hindsight, as an overly charitable summation; three episodes of *Silver Nemesis* is more than enough for most viewers, let alone six.

THE GREATEST SHOW IN THE GALAXY

Writer: Stephen Wyatt. **Director:** Alan Wareing. **Designer:** David Laskey. **Costumes:** Rosalind Ebbutt. **Make-Up:** Denise Baron. **Incidental Music:** Mark Ayres. **Visual Effects:** Steve Bowman. **OB Cameraman:** Barry Chaston, Alan Jessop. **Studio**

Lighting: Don Babbage, Henry Barber. **Studio Sound:** Scott Talbott. **Production Assistant:** Alexandra Todd. **Assistant Floor Manager:** David Tilley, Duncan McAlpine.

Note: None of this story was recorded in a studio as such; the scenes originally intended for its studio sessions, which had to be cancelled as a consequence of dangerous white asbestos being discovered inside Television Centre, were recorded inside a large tent erected in the car park of the BBC's Elstree Studios (home of the soap opera *EastEnders*). The crew, however, remained as it would have been in studio.

	First UK TX	Scheduled TX	Actual TX	Duration	Viewers	Chart Pos.
Part One	14/12/88	19.35	19.35	24'23"	5.0	86
Part Two	21/12/88	19.35	19.36	24'20"	5.3	99
Part Three	28/12/88	19.40	19.40	24'30"	4.8	108
Part Four	04/01/89	19.35	19.38	24'24"	6.6	79

Plot: The Doctor and Ace head for the Psychic Circus on the planet Segonax, where they meet a disparate group of fellow visitors including a pompous explorer named Captain Cook and his companion Mags and a biker known as Nord. The Circus itself is dominated by the sinister Chief Clown and his deadly troupe of robot clowns, who organise a talent contest in which all visitors take part. The audience consists of just a single strange family – mother, father and daughter – seated at the ringside. Although hindered by the treacherous Cook, the Doctor eventually discovers that the Circus hides a terrible secret: the family are in reality the Gods of Ragnarok, powerful creatures with an insatiable craving for entertainment who invariably destroy those who fail to please them. With Ace's help, the Doctor ends the Gods' influence here and returns the Circus to the control of its original hippie owners.

Episode endings:
1. Mags screams at what she sees in the Psychic Circus ring, but the sound is blotted out by a device held by the Ringmaster. Outside, the Doctor asks Ace to decide whether they are going in or not.
2. The Doctor and Mags find a tunnel leading to a deep pit at the bottom of which can be seen an eye like those depicted on some kites at the entrance to the Circus. They are disturbed by the Captain who comes up behind them with an escort of robot clowns. He has come to inform the Doctor that he is wanted: he is the next act due on in the ring.
3. In the ring, the Captain asks for the light of a 'devil moon' to be thrown on Mags. Under the light, Mags starts to change: she is a werewolf.
4. The Doctor and Ace leave the Circus in the control of Kingpin and Mags. Kingpin asks if the Doctor might stay, but he comments that he finds circuses a little sinister.

IT WAS MADE WHERE...?

OB Recording: 14.05.88-18.05.88, 06.06.88-10.06.88, 15.06.88-16.06.88, 18.06.88
Locations: Skinner's Road, Golden Pond and the Blue Lagoon, all at ECC Quarry (West Knighton Pit), Warmwell, Dorset; tent erected in car park of BBC Elstree Studios, Borehamwood, Hertfordshire; Borehamwood, Hertfordshire.

ADDITIONAL CREDITED CAST

The Captain (T.P. McKenna), Mags (Jessica Martin), Ringmaster (Ricco Ross), Stallslady (Peggy Mount[1,4]), Chief Clown (Ian Reddington), Morgana (Deborah Manship), Bellboy (Christopher Guard[1-3]), Whizzkid (Gian Sammarco[1-3]), Nord (Daniel Peacock[1,2]), Flowerchild (Dee Sadler[1]), Bus Conductor (Dean Hollingsworth[1,3,4*]), Deadbeat (Chris Jury[2-4]), Dad (David Ashford[2-4]**), Mum (Janet Hargreaves[2-4]**), Little Girl (Kathryn Ludlow[2-4]**).

* Dean Hollingsworth as Bus Conductor is credited on Part Three but does not appear.
** David Ashford and Janet Hargreaves played and voiced two of the Gods in Part Four. The third, however, was played (uncredited) by Lorne McCulloch rather than by Kathryn Ludlow and voiced (again uncredited) by director Alan Wareing.

THINGS TO WATCH OUT FOR

- Ace wears the fourth Doctor's scarf and Mel's top from *Paradise Towers* as she searches for her rucksack in Part One.
- An impressive cast for this story includes Chris Jury, better known for his appearances in *Lovejoy*; Ian Reddington before his regular starring role as market manager 'tricky Dicky' in *EastEnders*; Gian Sammarco fresh from starring as Adrian Mole in *The Secret Diaries of Adrian Mole*; impressionist Jessica Martin; and popular actors Daniel Peacock, T P McKenna and Peggy Mount.
- The Doctor performs some conjuring tricks in Part Four. Sylvester McCoy was coached in magic by Geoffrey Durham, otherwise known as the Great Soprendo, for these scenes.

THINGS YOU MIGHT NOT HAVE KNOWN

- Each of the masks for the robot clowns was different and each was designed by a different make-up assistant, overseen by designer Denise Baron.
- The Whizzkid, the unnamed character portrayed by Gian Sammarco, was a deliberate parody of the sort of fan that the production office perceived that *Doctor Who* attracted.
- Following completion of the story, incidental music composer Mark Ayres wrote to the head of BBC Records suggesting the release of a spin-off single called 'The Psychic Circus'. This track, inspired by the plot of the story but not featured within it, was written by Christopher Guard and performed by Guard, Ayres and other cast members. The track was apparently liked by Nathan-Turner, who gave his blessing to its release. The BBC was not interested, however, and so the project was abandoned.

QUOTE, UNQUOTE

- **Nord:** [To Ace] 'I told you, girl, to get lost. Or I'll do something 'orrible to your ears.'
- **Mum:** 'I don't think much of this, Father.' **Dad:** 'Nothing's happening, is it.' **Mum:** 'Not that I can see.' **Little Girl:** 'Mum, Mum!' **Mum:** 'What is it?' **Little Girl:** 'I'm bored.' **Dad:** 'There's no point in going on, dear. We're all bored. Something has to happen soon.'
- **Captain:** 'So you've always been interested in the psychic circus, have you?' **Whizzkid:** 'Well yes, of course. I've never been able to visit it before now, but I've

SEVENTH DOCTOR

got all sorts of souvenirs. Copies of all the advertising satellites that have ever been sent out. All the posters. I had a long correspondence with one of the founder members too, soon after it started. Although I never got to see the early days, I know it's not as good as it used to be, but I'm still terribly interested.'

ANALYSIS

The Greatest Show in the Galaxy is aptly named, coming at the end of a season that can be seen as the culmination of a trend of gradual improvement by way of which *Doctor Who* had effectively pulled itself out of its mid-eighties slump and – the disappointing *Silver Nemesis* notwithstanding – regained much of its former glory. 'Images from this story will be remembered by today's youngsters in a decade or two's time,' suggested Brian J Robb in the February 1989 edition of *Celestial Toyroom*. 'The clowns driving a silent hearse that glides across the landscape, dressed as undertakers; the tent, on a barren [landscape], with another [planet] hanging above; the robot repair room scenes, a triumph of lighting; the hippie bus; the painted smiles of the clowns watching as Mags undergoes a frightening transformation; and the revelation of the true nature of the Gods of Ragnarok, will all be recalled.'

Setting a story in and around a sinister circus was an excellent idea, and the clowns make creepy, unsettling villains. Special mention must go to Ian Reddington, who truly shines as the Chief Clown – something that is all the more remarkable for the fact that he has hardly any dialogue. His voice, when it is heard, is eerily light and breathy, and his ever-smiling face is never more sinister than when he gestures with a wave of his hand as visitors to the circus die horribly. Sometimes he seems almost inhuman, like one of his robot underlings, but his death scream when he is killed at the end of the story belies his cold, unfeeling exterior.

The cliffhanger ending to the first episode is a classic. As Mags screams at whatever horror she sees in the ring (and the viewer never actually witnesses any killing, only the aftermath) she is somehow silenced by the Ringmaster. Outside, meanwhile, the Doctor and Ace pause. Should they enter the Circus or not? The audience is screaming for Ace to refuse to walk into the lion's den, just as Mags is silently screaming at the horror that awaits them if they do. A superb sequence of images ends with Ace still trying to make up her mind.

Jessica Martin gives one of the best performances of the story, managing to convey just the right degree of innocence and youthfulness to preserve the surprise of Mags's true nature until the moment of revelation. The sequence at the end of Part Three in which she transforms into a slavering beast is classic *Doctor Who*, and the closing image of a drooling and fanged monster attacking the camera must surely have left many an impressionable youngster fearing to go to bed that night. Christopher Guard's Bellboy, Chris Jury's Deadbeat and T P McKenna's Captain are also well written and acted characters. Rather less impressive are Daniel Peacock as Nord and Gian Sammarco as Whizzkid, who fail to make the most of their admittedly limited roles. In fact one gets the distinct impression that these two characters were added to the story simply to make up the numbers, although many commentators have suggested that Whizzkid was also intended to serve as a parody of *Doctor Who* fans (which, if true, suggests an alarming misconception on the part of the writer and/or production team as to what the fans, or at least the vast majority of them, were really like).

Tension grows as the story develops with the discovery of a murderous robot bus conductor; the building up of uncertainty as to which of the visitors to the Circus will be next in the ring; and the introduction of an odd family – mother, father and daughter – who appear to be watching and marking each act out of ten. These latter characters seem to be equated by writer Stephen Wyatt with viewers at home, passing judgment on the story, and when seen in this light some of their lines are rather amusing. A good example comes in a scene where they comment that nothing seems to be happening, and that something needs to happen soon – neatly echoing the viewer's own feelings as, at this point, the action has fallen into something of a lull.

The pace soon picks up, though, and the story careers toward a somewhat confused finale. Captain Cook is somehow revived from the dead and the Doctor crosses some sort of time/space portal to find himself performing for the three Gods of Ragnarok.

Mark Stammers, writing in *The Frame* No. 9 dated February 1989, liked the story's on-screen presentation, and felt that it made a fitting end to the anniversary season:

'Overall, the story flowed well – a consequence of having some of the best direction of the season ... The design of the sets was also very good, and was complemented by excellent lighting which wasn't, for once, too harsh or strong. The tent corridors, although simple, worked very effectively. Here especially, the understated lighting added much to the overall impact. The design of the Gods and their amphitheatre was highly imaginative, too.

'Looking back, the anniversary season was one of variety. The production team continued their policy of trying out new ideas, and although not all of them succeeded, enough of them *did* to make it one of the best seasons for a number of years.'

The Greatest Show in the Galaxy continued the approach begun earlier in the season of depicting the Doctor as an enigmatic manipulator of events with a distinctly mysterious past. He visits the Psychic Circus having apparently guessed that it is a cover for the Gods of Ragnarok, whom he describes as old enemies – despite the fact that they have never before been mentioned in the series. Ace, meanwhile, is left to do much of the detective work and to handle most of the action scenes. These trends would be continued in the following season, when the Doctor – and the series as a whole – would become even darker in tone and an even greater emphasis would be placed on Ace. What no-one at the time could have known was that, after more than a quarter of a century of adventures, the series would soon be facing a very uncertain future.

DOCTOR WHO SEASON TWENTY-SIX (1989)

Regular Cast:
The Doctor (Sylvester McCoy)
Ace (Sophie Aldred)

Regular Crew:
Producer: John Nathan-Turner.
Script Editor: Andrew Cartmel.
Production Associate: June Collins.
Title Music: Ron Grainer and the BBC Radiophonic Workshop, arranged by Keff McCulloch.
Special Sounds: Dick Mills.

John Nathan-Turner had been content to remain as *Doctor Who*'s producer for the twenty-fifth anniversary season but had again asked his BBC superiors to make this his last year on the series. In the event, however, he was once more persuaded to stay on for a further season. Andrew Cartmel also remained on the production team, taking him into his third year as script editor. Season twenty-six would continue to show the Doctor acting in an increasingly enigmatic light, manipulating events from the background rather than taking centre stage, while Ace gained an ever greater share of the action. The Doctor's companion would in fact turn out to be effectively the pivotal character in three of the season's four stories, and – unusually – actress Sophie Aldred was given an opportunity at an early stage of the season's production to talk to the writers about the development of her character. This was a consequence of Cartmel's preferred approach of working with his writers as a team and involving them more closely in the production than would normally have been the case in the past. Ben Aaronovitch was particularly heavily involved in the development of the season, acting almost as an unofficial assistant script editor – and also contributed its first story.

BATTLEFIELD

Writer: Ben Aaronovitch. **Director:** Michael Kerrigan. **Designer:** Martin Collins. **Costumes:** Anushia Nieradzik. **Make-Up:** Juliette Mayer. **Incidental Music:** Keff McCulloch. **Fight Arranger:** Alf Joint. **Visual Effects:** Dave Bezkorowajny. **OB Cameraman:** Paul Harding, Alan Jessop. **Production Assistant:** Rosemary Parsons. **Assistant Floor Manager:** Matthew Purves, Julian Herne.

	First UK TX	Scheduled TX	Actual TX	Duration	Viewers	Chart Pos.
Part One	06/09/89	19.35	19.35	24'06"	3.1	102
Part Two	13/09/89	19.35	19.35	24'07"	3.9	91

Part Three	20/09/89	19.35	19.35	24'13"	3.6	95
Part Four	27/09/89	19.35	19.35	24'14"	4.0	89

Plot: The TARDIS materialises in the English countryside near the village of Carbury, where a nuclear missile convoy under the command of UNIT's Brigadier Winifred Bambera has run into difficulties. Lying on the bed of the nearby Lake Vortigern is a spaceship from another dimension containing the body of King Arthur, supposedly held in suspended animation, and his sword Excalibur. Ancelyn, a knight from the other dimension, arrives on Earth to aid the King but is followed by his rival Mordred and the latter's mother, a powerful sorceress named Morgaine. They all recognise the Doctor as Merlin – a fact that the Time Lord attributes to events in his own future. A battle breaks out between UNIT and Morgaine's men. Brigadier Lethbridge-Stewart has come out of retirement to assist in the crisis and ends up using silver bullets to kill the Destroyer – an awesomely powerful creature unshackled by Morgaine to devour the world – although he himself is almost killed in the process. Morgaine tries to fire the nuclear missile but is overcome by shock when the Doctor tells her that Arthur is in fact dead. She and her son are then taken prisoner by UNIT.

Episode endings:
1. The Doctor, Ace and a young woman named Shou Yuing find an armoured knight lying unconscious in a barn. This is Ancelyn who, when he wakes, greets the Doctor as Merlin. Brigadier Bambera arrives and orders them all to stay where they are. Mordred then storms into the barn with his knights and gives orders that all those present be killed.
2. In the spacecraft under the lake, Ace activates a defence mechanism and becomes trapped in a tank that rapidly fills with water. The Doctor tries to help her but is knocked unconscious by a defensive snake-like creature. Ace tries desperately but in vain to escape from the tank.
3. Morgaine decides to give Ace and Shou Yuing over to the Destroyer. A huge blue-faced demon appears in the room and the two young women look on in horror.
4. Ace, Shou Yuing, Bambera and the Brigadier's wife Doris set off for a drive in Bessie, leaving the Doctor and Ancelyn to spend some time with the Brigadier. The Brigadier asks Ancelyn if he is any good with a lawnmower, while the Doctor agrees to cook supper.

IT WAS MADE WHERE...?

OB Recording: 06.05.89-08.05.89, 11.05.89, 13.05.89-17.05.89
Locations: Fulmer Plant Park, Cherry Tree Lane, Fulmer, Bucks; Little Paston, Fulmer Common Road, Fulmer, Bucks; Black Park Country Park, Iver, Bucks; Dowager House, St Martin Without, Lincolnshire; Hambleton Old Hall, Upper Hambleton, Leicestershire; Hambleton Ridge, Upper Hambleton, Leicestershire; Rutland Water, Upper Hambleton, Leicestershire; Twyford Woods, Lincolnshire; Castle Cement, Pit Lane, Ketton, Lincolnshire; Memorial Cross, Upper Hambleton, Leicestershire; Church of St Andrew, Upper Hambleton, Leicestershire.
Studio Recording: 30.05.89-01.06.89 in TC3, 01.08.89-03.08.89 in TC3 (voice overdubbing by McCoy and Aldred takes place during this period), 13.08.89 (studio unknown)

Morgaine (Jean Marsh), Brigadier Lethbridge-Stewart (Nicholas Courtney), Peter Warmsly (James Ellis[1-3]), Brigadier Winifred Bambera (Angela Bruce), Mordred (Christopher Bowen), Ancelyn (Marcus Gilbert), Doris (Angela Douglas[1,4]), Pat Rowlinson (Noel Collins[1-3]), Elizabeth Rowlinson (June Bland[1-3]), Shou Yuing (Ling Tai), Sergeant Zbrigniev (Robert Jezek[1]), Flight Lieutenant Lavel (Dorota Rae[2,3]), Knight Commander (Stefan Schwartz[2-4]), Major Husak (Paul Tomany[3]), The Destroyer (Marek Anton[4*]).

* Also in Part Three, but uncredited.

POPULAR MYTHS

- The incidental music for this story was originally to have been provided by the rock group Hawkwind. (It wasn't.)

THINGS TO WATCH OUT FOR

- The Brigadier's wife Doris may be the same woman mentioned in a scene in season eleven's *Planet of the Spiders*.
- The Doctor pays for his drinks with a five pound piece – they are in the future, he tells Ace.
- The sequence where Ace becomes trapped in the water tank is notable as, during recording, the tank cracked, causing Sophie Aldred to sustain minor cuts to her hands and creating a major hazard as water flooded out onto the studio floor. The moment when the tank first cracked can be seen in Part Three as the Doctor struggles with the controls and Ace is lifted clear of the water. The full sequence was subsequently used in a studio safety video for the BBC.
- James Ellis, well remembered for his role as Lynch in *Z Cars*, appears here as archaeologist Peter Warmsly.
- Jean Marsh, former wife of third Doctor Jon Pertwee, makes her third *Doctor Who* appearance. In season two's *The Crusade* she was Princess Joanna; in season three's *The Daleks' Master Plan* she was Sara Kingdom; here she is Morgaine.

THINGS YOU MIGHT NOT HAVE KNOWN

- Working titles: *Nightfall*, *Storm Over Avallion*.
- Assistant floor manager Matthew Purves was the son of former companion actor Peter Purves.
- It was at one point intended that Brigadier Lethbridge-Stewart would be killed by the Destroyer at the end of this story, but this idea was abandoned before recording. The suggestion that the Brigadier might be killed off was nevertheless used by John Nathan-Turner as a publicity gimmick.

QUOTE, UNQUOTE

- **Brigadier Lethbridge-Stewart:** 'My blood and thunder days are long past.'
- **Shou Yuing:** 'Can someone tell me what on earth is going on?' **The Doctor:** 'Well if my hunch is right, the Earth could be at the centre of a war that doesn't even

belong to this dimension.'

- **The Destroyer:** 'Ah … little man. What do you want of me?' **Brigadier Lethbridge-Stewart:** 'Get off my world!' … **The Destroyer:** 'Pitiful. Can this world do no better than you as their champion?' **The Brigadier Lethbridge-Stewart:** 'Probably. I just do the best I can.'

ANALYSIS

Back in the days when each *Doctor Who* season consisted of half a dozen stories or more it was arguably not too great a cause for concern if the occasional four-parter happened to slip a little below par. In a season of only four stories, however, if one of them turns out to be a disappointment it is a much more serious problem. *Battlefield*, sadly, falls very much into this category. Although by no means the worst season opener the series ever had, it is decidedly lacklustre and a great disappointment after the same writer's excellent *Remembrance of the Daleks* the previous year.

It is perhaps surprising that *Doctor Who* had not previously delved into the world of Arthurian legend. Craig Hinton, writing in *DWB* No. 77 dated May 1990, felt that by the time it got round to doing so it was rather too late: '*Battlefield* was a concept ten years out of date. The admixture of popular mythology – be it Arthurian, Greek, Tolkienian – with the motifs of popular science-fiction – time portals, energy weapons *et al* – was innovative when first exploited in films such as *Hercules* or *Krull*, but now seems jaded and *passé*.'

The sight of Arthurian knights clanking around the countryside with swords and ray-guns, the destructive capabilities of which seem to be rather less than the average firework, is distinctly uninspiring – at times, in fact, almost laughable – and their poorly staged 'battles' are made to seem even more pointless when it is revealed that Morgaine has at her disposal, in the form of the Destroyer, a far more terrible weapon that could simply have wiped her opponents out with a gesture.

Jean Marsh actually steals the show as Morgaine. She may be typecast in this 'evil witch' type of role (having played similar characters in films such as *Return to Oz* and *Willow*), but she is undeniably very good at it. What really distinguishes Morgaine is that she has a certain depth of character and is not totally unsympathetic. Her battle against Arthur goes way back, and yet at the end she is genuinely sad when she learns that her worthy opponent (and, it would seem, one-time lover) has passed away. She kills a UNIT officer, Lavel, in a marvellously eerie and cold-blooded scene, and yet restores the sight of the previously blind pub landlady Elizabeth Rowlinson by way of payment for some drinks. This complex character deserved a little more screen time than she was allowed.

One of the main problems with the story is that there are simply too many characters, leaving insufficient scope for any of them to be fully developed. Even though some are packed off in Part Three when the area is evacuated, this still leaves Ancelyn, Bambera, Shou Yuing, Mordred, Morgaine, the Doctor, the Brigadier *and* the Destroyer all heading for a showdown. Aaronovitch does at least manage to pair some of the characters off quite successfully – the combination of Ancelyn and Bambera works best, although Ace and Shou Yuing also have some good interplay at times – but the whole thing could have been greatly improved if this overloading of characters had been avoided.

In production terms, the most impressive feature of *Battlefield* is undoubtedly the Destroyer – a superb creation, very well realised. 'He is a masterpiece of make-up, costume and effects,' wrote Justin Richards in *DWB* No. 71 dated November 1989.

'Well lit, well shot, and musically impressive, he has only two flaws. One is that he appears at the end of Part Three – the flagging story needed something earlier – and is killed mid-way through Part Four (rather easily, as it turns out) so we get little chance to appreciate the monster. The other problem is that the Destroyer is *too* impressive. He is about to destroy the world, and there is no doubt that he can. But as the fires blaze and the world around him begins to explode, the Destroyer seems uninvolved. He has only to be there for chaos to set in. Much more interesting visually would be to have him involved in it – hurling lightning bolts about and the like.'

Another point in the story's favour is the welcome return of UNIT in a revamped form, although it has to be said that Angela Bruce's Bambera isn't really in the same league as Nicholas Courtney's Lethbridge-Stewart. Courtney's final appearance in the series finds him in good form, and one can easily excuse the rather implausible plot device of the powers-that-be calling the Brigadier out of retirement to take charge of the crisis; this is a fitting way for the character to be remembered.

Much less successful is Keff McCulloch's incidental music which, far from enhancing the story's effectiveness, positively detracts from it. (An early edit of the story, minus music, was once shown at a *Doctor Who* convention, and many attendees were moved to comment just how much more dramatic and enjoyable it was *without* this impediment.)

Battlefield is not exactly a bad story but, as Nicholas Davies observed in *Stage and Television Today*, it could and should have been very much better:

'The new series kicked off with a sort of King Arthur story. In this, the knights of the round table materialise in more-or-less modern Britain, possibly to heed the call of a nation in need, although this is not clear, nor is the reason why the knights are armed with broad sword and laser-gun. Although the Doctor did mutter something about wars being waged in parallel dimensions of time.

'The Doctor is ably aided by his assistant Ace ... who is a lot trendier than the assistants of old, and she loves explosives, which can't be bad. But on the whole I find *Doctor Who* a bit much these days. It's been given a 7.30 p.m. slot but will have most appeal to the very young. What it needs is to grow up a bit. Forget spending on sets and costumes. All the Doctor needs is a good script and more blood and gore.'

GHOST LIGHT

Writer: Marc Platt. **Director:** Alan Wareing. **Designer:** Nick Somerville. **Costumes:** Ken Trew. **Make-Up:** Joan Stribling. **Incidental Music:** Mark Ayres. **Fight Arranger:** Paul Heasman. **Visual Effects:** Malcolm James. **Studio Lighting:** Henry Barber. **Studio Sound:** Scott Talbott, Keith Bowden. **Production Assistant:** Valerie Whiston. **Assistant Floor Manager:** Stephen Garwood.

	First UK TX	Scheduled TX	Actual TX	Duration	Viewers	Chart Pos.
Part One	04/10/89	19.35	19.34	24'17"	4.2	94
Part Two	11/10/89	19.35	19.34	24'18"	4.0	93
Part Three	18/10/89	19.35	19.35	24'17"	4.0	104

Plot: The Doctor brings Ace to Gabriel Chase, an old house that she once burnt down in her home town of Perivale. The year is 1883 and the house is presided over by Josiah Samuel Smith, who turns out to be the evolved form of an alien brought to Earth in a stone spaceship that is now in the basement. Others present include the explorer Redvers Fenn-Cooper, who has been driven mad by what he has seen there, and Nimrod, Smith's Neanderthal manservant. Smith intends to use Fenn-Cooper's unwitting help in a plot to kill Queen Victoria and restore the British Empire to its former glory. His plans are hampered by Control, a female alien whose life-cycle is in balance with his own. Ace inadvertently causes the release of the spaceship's true owner – a powerful alien being known as Light. Light originally came to Earth to compile a catalogue of its species but, on discovering that his catalogue has now been made obsolete by evolution, he decides to destroy all life on the planet. He disintegrates when the Doctor convinces him that evolution is irresistible and that he himself is constantly changing. Control has meanwhile evolved into a lady and Smith has reverted to an earlier, primitive form. They leave in the spaceship, along with Nimrod and Fenn-Cooper, heading for new adventures.

Episode endings:
1. Ace, panicked by her memories of the house, hurries downstairs. She sees an open lift and enters it. Mrs Pritchard, the housekeeper, sends the lift down. In the basement, Ace finds the stone spaceship. A curtain pulls back to reveal two husks, which lurch towards her. Ace backs away in alarm, while Control hisses 'Ratkin' at her from a cell.
2. With everyone assembled, the Doctor calls for the lift's current occupant to exit. There is a flash of blinding light and all but the Doctor and Ace shield their eyes.
3. Light disperses, but the Doctor comments that the house will remember. Ace has only one regret: she wishes she'd blown the house up rather than burning it down.

IT WAS MADE WHERE...?

OB Recording: 21.06.89
Location: Stanton Court, 11 Greenhill, Weymouth, Dorset.
Studio Recording: 18.07.89-19.07.89, 01.08.89-03.08.89 all in TC3

ADDITIONAL CREDITED CAST

Josiah (Ian Hogg), Mrs Pritchard (Sylvia Syms), Redvers Fenn-Cooper (Michael Cochrane), Control (Sharon Duce), Gwendoline (Katharine Schlesinger*), Reverend Ernest Matthews (John Nettleton[1,2]), Nimrod (Carl Forgione), Mrs Grose (Brenda Kempner[1,2]), Inspector Mackenzie (Frank Windsor[2,3]), Light (John Hallam[3]).

* On the closing credits of Parts One and Two Katharine Schlesinger's first name is misspelt 'Katherine'. (This has been changed to the correct spelling on the version of the story released on BBC video).

THINGS TO WATCH OUT FOR

- *Ghost Light* was the final *Doctor Who* story to be made by the BBC as part of the on-going series.
- The story has an excellent cast, including distinguished stage and screen actress Sylvia Syms.

7 SEVENTH DOCTOR

- A genuine period song is sung by Katharine Schlesinger at one point during the action. This is the highly appropriate 'That's the Way to the Zoo', composed by J F Mitchell. It was played out of vision by Alasdair Nicolson.
- There is a location-recorded establishing shot of Gabriel Chase. This was committed to tape during work on *Survival*.

THINGS YOU MIGHT NOT HAVE KNOWN

- Working titles: *The Beastiary*, *Life Cycle*.
- The very last *Doctor Who* scene to be recorded at the BBC was the one in which Mrs Pritchard and her daughter Gwendoline are turned to stone.

QUOTE, UNQUOTE

- **Ace:** 'Is this an asylum with the patients in charge?'
- **Gwendoline:** 'Sir, I think Mr Matthews is confused.' **The Doctor:** 'Never mind. I'll have him completely bewildered by the time I'm finished.'
- **Ace:** 'It's true isn't it. This is the house I told you about.' **The Doctor:** 'You were thirteen. You climbed over the wall for a dare.' **Ace:** 'That's your surprise isn't it? Bringing me back here.' **The Doctor:** 'Remind me what it was that you sensed when you entered this deserted house. An aura of intense evil?' **Ace:** 'Don't you have things you hate?' **The Doctor:** 'I can't stand burnt toast. I loathe bus stations. Terrible places. Full of lost luggage and lost souls.' **Ace:** 'I told you I never wanted to come back here again.' **The Doctor:** 'And then there's unrequited love. And tyranny. And cruelty.' **Ace:** 'Too right.' **The Doctor:** 'We all have a universe of our own terrors to face.' **Ace:** 'I face mine on my own terms.' **The Doctor:** 'But don't you want to know what happened here?' **Ace:** 'No!' **The Doctor:** 'You've learned something you didn't recognise when you were thirteen?' **Ace:** 'Like what?' **The Doctor:** 'The nature of the horror that you sensed here.' **Ace:** 'It's alien.'

ANALYSIS

Newcomer Marc Platt, only the second *Doctor Who* fan to have had one of his own stories accepted for production (the first, Andrew Smith, having been responsible for season eighteen's *Full Circle*), came up with arguably the most densely-written, multi-layered and challenging set of scripts that the series ever had. Even some of those who worked on the story later confessed that they had not entirely grasped what it was all about, and most reviewers have admitted to greater or lesser degrees of confusion.

'Maybe *Doctor Who* shouldn't give you the explanations on a plate,' commented Craig Hinton in *DWB* No. 77 dated May 1990. 'In all forms of drama it is more satisfying to infer than to have it rammed down your throat. And indeed, *Ghost Light* started off as an intellectual jigsaw puzzle that allowed the viewer to piece together the clues, one that would lead to a climax which would have been the final assembly, as the picture became clear.

'Somewhere – and I doubt that it was Platt's script – some of the vital information went missing. The result was a jigsaw puzzle without a picture on the box, and with some pieces absent. Without this, the climax vanished, to be replaced by a less than fulfilling *dénouement* that clarified nothing.'

Closer examination of the story, however, shows that all the supposedly 'missing pieces' are in fact present – if rather difficult to spot. This had been pointed out by Julian

Knott in *DWB* No. 72 dated December 1989: 'A script as well-balanced as it was well-packed into three episodes (with no discernible padding) deserves much praise. After a couple of viewings it becomes apparent that there is hardly a word wasted, and that many key words and phrases have been picked to convey a very specific meaning (such as the Doctor's remark that Ace's change of clothes into [those of] a "Victorian gentleman" is a "metamorphosis"). Every action has a reason, every occurrence an explanation. Even the standard defuse-the-bomb/stop-the-countdown "firestorm program" sequence at the end made enough sense in context, and succeeded in rounding the story off nicely. Even if some things are not made clear at the time they occur, then they are explained, or can be explained, at a later stage.'

Ghost Light is *Doctor Who* for the video age; a story that can be truly appreciated only after multiple viewings, as the subtleties and nuances contained within are legion.

'I found *Ghost Light* thoroughly enjoyable from beginning to end ...,' wrote Peter Darrington in the November 1989 edition of *Celestial Farmyard*. 'The whole production came across as a real piece of good BBC drama, of a standard *Doctor Who* has not managed to [reach] for a good few years.' Julian Knott was similarly lavish in his praise: 'Like only its most eminent of predecessors, *Ghost Light* is a *Doctor Who* masterpiece. Not only was it Sylvester McCoy's best *Doctor Who* story to date, it is one of the finest stories for many years.'

The story contains a number of fascinating and well-written characters, but there is one who stands head and shoulders above the rest: Ace. *Ghost Light* is very much Ace's story, proving that *Doctor Who*'s format is flexible enough to allow the companion character to be accorded as much time and attention as the Doctor himself. This approach was to typify and empower the series of original novels that started to be released once the television series had been effectively cancelled, and *Ghost Light* can be seen in many ways as the forerunner of and inspiration for those works.

The way the Doctor is depicted in this story, and to a certain extent in season twenty-six generally, has been rather more controversial. 'We are shown one of the most spiteful sides of the Doctor's character in the series' history,' asserted Craig Hinton. 'Learning that Ace is afraid of an old house in Perivale, [he] takes it upon himself to arrange her catharsis. How magnanimous of him. The poor girl is scared witless during the course of the Doctor's "psychoanalysis", while he merrily plots and manipulates ... Not quite the philanthropic traveller of old, is he?' Maybe not, but he is developing as a character, and learning to understand his travelling companion a little better into the bargain.

'For the last three weeks I have been enthralled, confused and disturbed by *Ghost Light*,' wrote Gareth Preston in the winter 1989 edition of *TARDIS*. 'Once again [*Doctor Who*] has demonstrated its flexibility and imagination with a highly original suspense story, laced with pithy comments on Victorian society ...

'The most important factor about this adventure is that it makes us think: about "Victorian values"; about the nature of life; about facing the bad parts of our past. In short, this story had depth. I really enjoyed it.'

Its undeniable complexity notwithstanding, it is difficult to fault *Ghost Light*. It provides an excellent illustration of the very positive way in which the series was developing under John Nathan-Turner's increasingly mature stewardship, with the inspired Andrew Cartmel as script editor, an imaginative and understanding team of writers working alongside him and a Doctor and companion partnership rich with possibilities. That this should turn out to be the final story produced as part of the ongoing series is very ironic. After a period in the mid-eighties when the BBC seemed almost to have lost the knack of making good *Doctor Who*, they had rediscovered it with a vengeance – only to throw it all away again.

THE CURSE OF FENRIC

Writer: Ian Briggs. **Director:** Nicholas Mallett. **Designer:** David Laskey. **Costumes:** Ken Trew. **Make-Up:** Denise Baron. **Incidental Music:** Mark Ayres. **Fight Arranger:** Tip Tipping. **Visual Effects:** Graham Brown. **OB Cameraman:** Paul Harding, Alan Jessop. **Production Assistant:** Winifred Hopkins. **Assistant Floor Manager:** Judy Corry.

	First UK TX	Scheduled TX	Actual TX	Duration	Viewers	Chart Pos.
Part One	25/10/89	19.35	19.34	24'23"	4.3	—
Part Two	01/11/89	19.35	19.34	24'09"	4.0	—
Part Three	08/11/89	19.35	19.34	24'11"	4.0	—
Part Four	15/11/89	19.35	19.35	24'16"	4.2	—

Plot: The TARDIS materialises at a secret naval base off the coast of Northumberland toward the end of the Second World War. Dr Judson, a scientist there, has created the Ultima Machine, an early computer designed to break German codes. The base's Commander Millington plans to let a Russian commando unit led by Captain Sorin steal the Machine's core, which he has booby-trapped with deadly toxin. Judson uses the Machine to translate some ancient runes from the crypt of the nearby St Judes church and this leads to the release of Fenric, an evil entity from the dawn of time whom the Doctor trapped seventeen centuries earlier in a Chinese flask by defeating it at chess. The flask was later stolen and buried at the church by Vikings. The base and church are attacked by Haemovores. These are humans who have been transformed into hideous vampiric creatures by the Ancient Haemovore – the last survivor of a pollution-ravaged future Earth, who has been brought back in time by Fenric. Fenric takes over Judson's body to challenge the Doctor to a rematch at chess, and Ace unwittingly helps it to win. Fenric, now in Sorin's body, reveals that Ace, Judson, Millington, Sorin and Wainwright, the vicar of St Judes, are all 'Wolves of Fenric' – pawns in its battle against the Doctor. It now plans to release the deadly toxin but the Doctor succeeds in turning the Ancient Haemovore against it and its host body is killed by the gas. The baby daughter of a young woman whom Ace helped to escape from the Haemovores is revealed to be her future mother.

Episode endings:
1. The Doctor and Ace find a Russian soldier lying dead on the beach. Suddenly they are surrounded by other Russian soldiers who aim their rifles at them. The Doctor looks perturbed.
2. The Ultima Machine runs out of control and Commander Millington declares: 'You're too late, Doctor!' The Doctor looks anxious.
3. Dr Judson rises from his wheelchair to stand behind the Doctor, his eyes glowing yellow – he is Fenric. He states: 'We play the contest again, Time Lord.' The Doctor looks worried.
4. Ace dives into the sea, then swims ashore and rejoins the Doctor. They see a sign on the

beach warning that there are 'Dangerous Undercurrents'. Ace asks the Doctor if this is the case, and he replies that it is not anymore. They walk away together.

IT WAS MADE WHERE...?

OB Recording: 03.04.89-08.04.89, 11.04.89-15.04.89, 18.04.89-20.04.89
Locations: Crowborough Training Camp, Crowborough, E. Sussex; St Lawrence's Parish Church, The Moor, Hawkhurst, Kent; Bedgebury Lower School, Lillesden, Hawkhurst, Kent; Roses Farm, Slip Way Hill, Hawkhurst, Kent; Yew Tree Farm, Slip Way Hill, Hawkhurst, Kent; Lulworth Cove, Weld Estate, Dorset.
Studio Recording: 01.08.89-03.08.89 in TC3 (voice overdubbing by McCoy and Aldred take place during this period)

ADDITIONAL CREDITED CAST

Dr. Judson (Dinsdale Landen), Commander Millington (Alfred Lynch), The Rev. Mr. Wainwright (Nicholas Parsons[1-3]), Miss Hardaker (Janet Henfrey[1-3]), Captain Sorin (Tomek Bork), Sgt. Prozorov (Peter Czajkowski[1-3]), Vershinin (Marek Anton), Petrossian (Mark Conrad[1]), Jean (Joann Kenny), Phyllis (Joanne Bell), Nurse Crane (Anne Reid), Kathleen Dudman (Cory Pulman), Baby (Aaron Hanley[1,3,4*]), Captain Bates (Stevan Rimkus), Sgt. Leigh (Marcus Hutton), Perkins (Christien Anholt[1-3]), Ancient Haemovore (Raymond Trickett[4]).

* Also in Part Two, but uncredited.

THINGS TO WATCH OUT FOR

- Nicholas Parsons, better known as the host of Anglia TV's game show *The Sale of the Century*, revives his earlier acting career in the role of Mr Wainwright, vicar of St Judes.
- Marek Anton, who occupied the Destroyer costume in *Battlefield*, is seen here in person as the Russian soldier Vershinin.
- There are a few anachronisms in the story, such as Commander Millington's moustache (Royal Navy officers were required to have either a full beard and moustache or else to be clean shaven) and a signpost indicating the way to Maiden's Point (all such signposts were taken down during the war, to hinder the enemy in the event of an invasion).

THINGS YOU MIGHT NOT HAVE KNOWN

- Working titles: *Wolf-Time*, *The Wolves of Fenric*.
- The baby – revealed to be Ace's mother – was in fact the son of the landlord and landlady of The Bush pub on Shepherd's Bush green, a few minutes' walk from the *Doctor Who* office and frequently visited by the production team.
- An edition of the BBC children's show *Take Two* on 19 April 1989 included an item on the making of *The Curse of Fenric*, then still under its working title *The Wolves of Fenric*. This was introduced by presenter Phillip Schofield and considered the question of what frightens children. After canvassing the views of members of the studio audience (all children), Schofield read out a script extract describing the death of vampires Jean and Phyllis. There then followed a short pre-recorded documentary looking at the development and realisation of this scene.

- Sylvester McCoy's sons Sam and Joe Kent-Smith make a cameo appearance in this story as Haemovores.

- **The Doctor:** [Reading a Norse inscription revealed on the wall of the church crypt] 'We hoped to return to the North Way, but the dark curse follows our dragon ship … The Wolves of Fenric shall return for their treasure, and then shall the dark evil rule eternally.'
- **Ace:** 'I'm not a little girl anymore.'
- **Ace:** 'There's a wind whipping up. I can feel it through my clothes …'

The Curse of Fenric is, in a sense, a traditional Doctor-versus-monsters story, suitably updated to fit the series' late eighties style. At the same time, however, it is very much more than that. Peter Anghelides, writing in *DWB* No. 73 dated January 1990, tried to pin it down: 'Was it a discourse on the morality of warfare – questioning the rights of the Allies to bomb Germany into submission fifty years after the event? Was it a lurid spy drama about double-crossing the Cold War enemy? Was it a vampire story of the first order? An eco-thriller cashing in on the green renaissance? An investigation of Ace's background? A traditional *Doctor Who* monster thrash? The culmination of the seventh Doctor's mysterious and omnipotent opposition to an unknown evil force? Well, actually, it was all of these. Blink and you'd miss one.'

The story is actually quite horrific in places – which is perhaps not altogether surprising when one realises that writer Ian Briggs has craftily borrowed many plot elements from John Carpenter's 1979 chiller *The Fog*, including an artifact being found concealed in the church wall, the vicar losing his faith, the church being stormed by grotesque creatures that emerge from the sea and the heroine being trapped on a high roof as the creatures try to reach her. This sort of borrowing is nothing new in *Doctor Who*, however, and is quite acceptable here – indeed, Briggs is to be congratulated on paying homage to such a fine source!

Another major inspiration for the story is Norse mythology, as Mary McLean noted in *Celestial Farmyard* Issue 4 dated February 1990: 'Great play is made of the myth of the wolf Fenric (or Fenrir, as he is also known …); it is when [this creature] breaks its bonds that the twilight of the gods shall be upon us. The Fenric wolf swallowed Odin, the father of the gods, and brought about the end of the world. The great battle of Ragnarok was fought. We have already met the Gods of Ragnarok in *The Greatest Show in the Galaxy*, though these would seem to exist in a different dimension. However, the connection is there for any interested parties to develop.'

An aspect of the story much commented upon by reviewers is the particular focus that it places on Ace. 'Briggs, the creator of Ace, develops her character beautifully,' wrote Mary McLean, 'and it is in this story that we really see [her] grow up. She is better able to cope with emotion, both her own and that of those around her. Her flirtation with the young sergeant in the third episode, buying time for the Doctor to free the Russian captain, shows us that she has come a long way since Dragonfire and she is no longer a tomboy but rather a young woman, coming to terms with her own sexuality … It's a nice touch that Ace creates her own future by sending her "gran" to [safety].'

This is another well directed story, too, with some highly atmospheric sequences and fine performances from a well chosen cast. 'The direction was Nicholas Mallett's best to date,' opined Gareth Negus in the Spring 1990 edition of *TARDIS*. 'Unobtrusive but with many effective sequences such as ... the attack on the church. This led into the best final episode since *The Caves of Androzani* Part Four. I was genuinely anxious to see what happened next, as more and more extras bit the dust; a sensation I haven't enjoyed with *Doctor Who* for ages.'

Justin Richards, writing in *TV Zone* Issue 4 dated March 1990, summed up the feelings of many: 'The excellent incidental music, the performances, the effects work, the transforming weather, the evocative scripting and the taut camerawork and editing all combine to produce what is a very atmospheric story. It is at once entertaining and frightening. It is stimulating and nerve-wracking. It is intellectual and a smashing adventure yarn.' *The Curse of Fenric* is, in short, a real gem of a story, and a major highlight of the McCoy era.

SURVIVAL

Writer: Rona Munro. **Director:** Alan Wareing. **Designer:** Nick Somerville. **Costumes:** Ken Trew. **Make-Up:** Joan Stribling. **Incidental Music:** Dominic Glynn. **Fight Arranger:** Paul Heasman, Tip Tipping. **Visual Effects:** Malcolm James. **OB Cameraman:** Paul Harding, Alan Jessop. **Production Assistant:** Valerie Whiston. **Assistant Floor Manager:** Stephen Garwood, Leigh Poole.

	First UK TX	Scheduled TX	Actual TX	Duration	Viewers	Chart Pos.
Part One	22/11/89	19.35	19.36	24'14"	5.0	89
Part Two	29/11/89	19.35	19.35	24'13"	4.8	96
Part Three	06/12/89	19.35	19.35	24'20"	5.0	91

Plot: The Doctor takes Ace to present day Perivale so that she can revisit old friends. Most of them however have been transported by cat-like Kitlings to the planet of the Cheetah People, a race with the power to teleport through space. Ace is transported and joins up with two of her friends, Midge and Shreela, and a boy named Derek. The Doctor follows and encounters the Master, who has drawn him into a trap to try to gain his help. This planet gradually transforms its inhabitants into Cheetah People – an influence to which the Master himself has fallen victim – while they in turn, through the savagery of their actions, cause the planet to move ever closer to total destruction. Midge is overcome by the planet's influence, and the Master uses him to teleport to Perivale. Ace, who has developed an affinity with a Cheetah woman called Karra, gains the same ability and takes the Doctor and the others back as well. The Master causes Midge's death and kills Karra, who has followed them all to Earth. Then, succumbing to the influence of the now-disintegrating Cheetah planet, he drags the Doctor back there. The Doctor refuses to fight him, however, and is transported back to Earth. He rejoins Ace, and they head off for new adventures.

Episode endings:
1. The Doctor and Sergeant Paterson, another of those transported from Perivale, find

themselves in the middle of a Cheetah camp. The Doctor pulls back the flap of a tent to find, seated inside, the Master. The Master's eyes glow yellow and he comments that the Doctor's arrival is an unexpected pleasure.

2. Ace falls under the planet's influence, her eyes glowing yellow. The Doctor looks perturbed.
3. The Doctor and Ace head back toward the TARDIS.

IT WAS MADE WHERE...?

OB Recording: 10.06.89-15.06.89, 18.06.89-23.06.89
Locations: 3 Medway Drive, Perivale, Ealing, London; Drayton Court Public House, The Avenue, Ealing, London; 4 The Avenue, Ealing, London; Motorcycles Unlimited, 2 Medway Parade, Perivale, Ealing, London; Londis Food Market, 20 Medway Parade, Perivale, Ealing, London; Sceptre Financial Services, 23 Medway Parade, Perivale, Ealing, London; 63 Medway Parade, Perivale, Ealing, London; balcony outside flats, 37/39 Medway Parade, Perivale, Ealing, London; children's play area, Ealing Central Sports Ground, Horsenden Lane South, Perivale, London; Colwyn Avenue, Perivale, Ealing, London; wall in Bleasdale Avenue, Perivale, Ealing, London; alley off Colwyn Avenue, Perivale, Ealing, London; 45 Woodhouse Avenue, Perivale, Ealing, London; EYJ Martial Arts Centre, North Ealing Sports Centre, Greenford Road, Sudbury Hill, London; notice board on Horsenden Hill, Perivale, London; Horsenden Hill, Perivale, London; ECC Quarry (West Knighton Pit), Warmwell, Dorset.
Studio Recording: 23.11.89 (studio unknown) (McCoy's "We've got work to do..." speech)

ADDITIONAL CREDITED CAST

The Master (Anthony Ainley), Paterson (Julian Holloway), Karra (Lisa Bowerman), Harvey (Norman Pace[1]), Len (Gareth Hale[1]), Midge (William Barton), Shreela (Sakuntala Ramanee), Derek (David John), Stuart (Sean Oliver[1]), Ange (Kate Eaton[1]), Woman (Kathleen Bidmead[1]), Squeak (Adele Silva[3]), Neighbour (Michelle Martin[3]).

THINGS TO WATCH OUT FOR

- There is a cameo appearance by comedy duo Hale and Pace, playing shopkeepers Harvey and Len.
- Stunt legend Eddie Kidd doubles for William Barton in a motor cycle crash scene in Part Three. This led to the series' regular stunt arranger Tip Tipping walking off the production, as Kidd was apparently not a member of the actors' union Equity.
- A poignant final monologue by Sylvester McCoy as the Doctor was over-dubbed after the story's completion, when it became apparent that the series would probably not be returning to production in the near future.

THINGS YOU MIGHT NOT HAVE KNOWN

- Working titles: *Cat Flap*, *Blood Hunt*.
- Hale and Pace swapped roles shortly before recording – Hale was originally to have played Harvey and Pace to have played Len.

QUOTE, UNQUOTE

- **The Doctor:** 'If we fight like animals, we'll die like animals!'
- **Ace:** 'I felt like I could run forever, like I could smell the wind and feel the grass

under my feet, and just run forever.' **The Doctor:** 'The planet's gone, but it lives on inside you, and it always will.'

- **The Doctor:** 'There are worlds out there where the sky is burning, where the sea's asleep and the rivers dream, people made of smoke and cities made of song. Somewhere there's danger, somewhere there's injustice and somewhere else the tea is getting cold. Come on, Ace, we've got work to do.'

Rona Munro's *Survival* is another very good story, which strikes just the right balance between genuinely funny off-beat humour and compelling drama. It is refreshing to see the Doctor back in a contemporary Earth setting in the Perivale scenes, while the parts of the story set on the Cheetah planet are equally impressive, having something of an epic, science-fantasy quality about them – particularly the final, near apocalyptic struggle between the Doctor and the Master (which could perhaps have gone on a little longer).

'The McCoy years are ... hugely charming once they get under way ...,' wrote Matthew Jones on an internet newsgroup in 1997. 'For me the finest moment is *Survival*. It slips from a gentle urban comedy thriller to something deeper, more sensual and more involving when our heroes reach the Cheetah planet. The moment where Ace feeds the Cheetah by the lake is so haunting, and her transformation had me on the edge of my seat. It's poetic, adult, feminine, and is everything the show ought to be about ... It also has that moment where the TARDIS materialises (in a single bound) in a suburban driveway. A hundred nights of prayer answered in a single television moment!'

The story revolves around the idea of evolution, which had also been a key theme of *Ghost Light* and, with its implication that the human race could eventually become Haemovores, *The Curse of Fenric*. 'Rona Munro's script is influenced heavily by Darwinian and Nietzschian concepts,' reckoned Nicholas Winters in *TSV* Issue 50 dated February 1997. 'It is a battle for survival (the oft-repeated line "survival of the fittest") where those who survive are those who are prepared to undergo change (to evolve). The Nietzschian element comes in with the idea of becoming what you are fighting against.'

The Cheetah People and their planet are certainly highly imaginative and original concepts; and although the former are less than brilliantly realised, looking rather too cuddly and unconvincing, the latter is well brought to the screen by all concerned, as Brian J Robb observed: 'Rona Munro has created ... a unique alien landscape ... The ideas in *Survival* hark back to some of the classic *Doctor Who* planets of the past – the link betwen the creatures and the doomed planet, and the "contamination" of the new arrivals ... are both cleverly used science-fiction ideas. The planet is as much a character in the drama as the leads.' The effectiveness of these scenes is greatly enhanced by the use of some superb electronic video effects – an aspect of the series' production that improved by leaps and bounds during the McCoy era. 'Despite the budgetary restrictions,' observed Nicholas Winters, 'the quarries in *Survival* finally feel like they are another planet, with the bizarre skyline occupied by an alien moon and streams of smoke from the volcanic breakdown of the planet. The Cheetah People's costumes are effective, as are the eyes and teeth of people "possessed" by the planet. Perhaps the only slight let-down is the ... animatronic cat, which from a distance looks suitably frightening and alien [but] close up ... looks [just like what it is].'

One of the most remarkable aspects of the story is the superb performance of Anthony

SEVENTH DOCTOR

Ainley, who at last gets to play the Master in the way that one suspects he really wanted to all along – deadly serious and implacably evil, but with occasional flashes of dark humour. He really is first rate here – and certainly looks much more imposing in his new costume – making the viewer regret all the more that so many of the earlier Master stories of the eighties were such wasted opportunities. 'For the first time …,' argued Winters, '[Ainley] gets to play a version of the Master that he, and not [Roger] Delgado, is more successful at. The animal and desperate nature of the Master shines through brilliantly in Ainley, something that may not have been possible with Delgado's gentleman villain.'

That *Doctor Who* had to come to an end at this point, at least as an on-going series, is deeply regrettable; that it went out on such a very high note is, however, something to be thankful for.

If a twenty-seventh season of *Doctor Who* had gone ahead as originally intended it is probable that John Nathan-Turner would have remained as the series' producer, although whether or not Andrew Cartmel would have continued as script editor is less certain. If Cartmel had stayed on, writers in the running to contribute stories would have included Ben Aaronovitch, Marc Platt, Robin Mukherjee, Charles Vincent and Cartmel himself. If he had not, then Aaronovitch and Platt would have been at the top of the shortlist of candidates to take over from him. The intention was that Sylvester McCoy would remain as the Doctor throughout the fourteen episode season, but that Sophie Aldred would make her exit as Ace after the first seven episodes (although she was under contract for eight) to be replaced by a new companion character. All these plans came to nothing, however, and a few months after the completion of work on season twenty-six the *Doctor Who* office was closed down altogether, with no new production in prospect.

INTO THE WILDERNESS

As rumours of *Doctor Who*'s possible demise began to spread during the course of 1989 concerned fans sought reassurances from the BBC. In response, a number of BBC executives, including new Head of Serials Peter Cregeen, indicated that there were no plans for the series to be axed and that they were confident that it would continue successfully throughout the nineties. While welcoming these encouraging statements, many fans remained doubtful that the BBC had been completely frank about its intentions. This scepticism would ultimately appear to have been justified as – aside from two radio serials, *The Paradise of Death* (recorded in 1993) and *Doctor Who and the Ghosts of N Space* (recorded in 1994 but not transmitted until 1996) and the brief two part skit *Dimensions in Time* (recorded in 1993 as part of the *Children in Need* telethon) – it would be over six years before *Doctor Who* would again return to production, and then in a very different form from the one that it had taken in the past. In the meantime, at least as far as new television adventures were concerned, the good Doctor was effectively in limbo…

The Eighth Doctor
(Paul McGann)
1996-?

THE TELEVISION MOVIE

In 1994, Philip David Segal – an Englishman working as a television producer under contract to Stephen Spielberg's Amblin company in the USA – was granted by BBC Enterprises the rights to make a new series of *Doctor Who*. The project was initially envisaged as a three-way co-production between Amblin, BBC Enterprises and Universal Television in the USA. Writer John Leekley was commissioned by Segal to put together a 'series bible' – a detailed document outlining the concept and its intended treatment – and the script for a movie-length pilot episode. Leekley's script, entitled simply *Doctor Who*, was completed in September 1994, but ultimately failed to find favour with the three co-producers. Robert de Laurentis was then commissioned to provide a replacement; his attempt, entitled *Dr Who?*, was completed in December 1994. Segal subsequently used this as a basis for pitching the idea to the Fox network, but they initially turned it down, believing that a series would be too expensive to produce. After Segal had entered into discussions with some other networks, however, the project was finally picked up by Trevor Walton of Fox's made-for-TV feature division. A new script was required and, although Segal's first choice of writer was Terrance Dicks, it was eventually commissioned from Matthew Jacobs, another Englishman who already had experience of working in American network television. Amblin dropped out of the picture in 1995 after Spielberg joined forces with former Disney executive Jeffrey Katzenberg and music mogul David Geffen in a new company called Dreamworks SKG, leaving Segal himself to produce the movie as a joint venture with Universal Television and BBC Worldwide (as BBC Enterprises had by this point been renamed).

PAUL McGANN IS THE EIGHTH DOCTOR

'I knew I'd have an effect on lots of people,' reflected Paul McGann in a 1996 interview, 'and especially on children. It is a responsibility. But I thought that if I was going to do telly, I may as well do the biggest telly. And there's no doubt the biggest telly is *Doctor Who*.'

McGann was born in Surrey in 1959 but grew up in Liverpool after his family moved there when he was a child. His father was a metallurgist and his mother a teacher. He began his acting career in the theatre before moving on to film and television work. His big break came in 1985 when he took the lead role of Percy Toplis in the BBC's production of Alan Bleasdale's controversial *The Monocled Mutineer*. Two years later he was one of the stars of the HandMade Films production *Withnail and I*, which quickly became a cult classic. He then pursued film work in Hollywood for a time but had only moderate success. His most notable role from this period came in Twentieth Century Fox's *Alien³* in 1992. Misfortune followed when a knee injury forced him to give up the lead role in ITV's *Sharpe* saga, but his career took off again when he landed a part in the film *The Three Musketeers*. This was followed by successes in, amongst others, the 1995 Irish famine drama *The Hanging Gale* – appearing alongside his three actor brothers Joe, Mark and Stephen – and *The One that Got Away*. He was always Philip Segal's first choice to play the eighth Doctor in the *Doctor Who* television movie and, although he was initially very reluctant to do so, he eventually came round to the idea. 'I can't say that it's a part I would always have wanted,' he admitted, 'but now I'm involved I find it fascinating ... and a really good laugh!'

DOCTOR WHO

Executive Producer: Philip David Segal, Alex Beaton. **Executive Producer for the BBC:** Jo Wright. **Producer:** Peter V Ware. **Co-Producer:** Matthew Jacobs. **Visual Effects Producer:** Tony Dow. **Title Music:** Ron Grainer and the BBC Radiophonic Workshop, arranged by John Debney and John Sponsler. **Writer:** Matthew Jacobs. **Director:** Geoffrey Sax. **Designer:** Richard Hudolin. **Costumes:** Jori Woodman. **Make-Up:** Joann Fowler. **Incidental Music:** John Debney, John Sponsler, Louis Serbe. **Fight Arranger:** J J Makaro, Fred Perron. **Film Cameraman:** Glen MacPherson. **Film Editor:** Patrick Lussier.

First UK TX	Scheduled TX	Actual TX	Duration	Viewers	Chart Pos.
27/05/96	20.30	20.29	84'39"	9.08	9

Note: The television movie was first transmitted in Canada on 12 May 1996.

Plot: The Master is apparently exterminated by the Daleks on Skaro, and the Doctor agrees to take his remains back to Gallifrey in the TARDIS. The Master is not really dead, however, but has transformed into a shapeless morphant creature. He causes the TARDIS to make an emergency landing on Earth, in the city of San Francisco, in the year 1999. The Doctor emerges from the ship to find himself in the midst of a street battle between rival gangs. He sustains gunshot wounds and, accompanied by young gang member Chang Lee, is taken to hospital for emergency treatment. Surgeon Dr Grace Holloway attempts to save his life but, failing to understand his alien physiology, actually causes his 'death'. The Doctor later regenerates into his eighth physical form. The Master has meanwhile taken over the body of an ambulance driver named Bruce. This is just a temporary measure until he can achieve his ultimate goal: to inhabit the Doctor's body. He gains access to the Doctor's TARDIS and, with lies and false promises, wins Chang Lee over to his side. The Doctor manages to convince Grace that he is the same man that she thought had died on her operating table, and that he is an alien Time Lord – albeit half human on his mother's side. Together they race against time to prevent the Master's scheme from bringing about the Earth's destruction at midnight on 31 December. They eventually succeed, and the Master is sucked into the Eye of Harmony within the TARDIS's cloister room. The Doctor bids farewell to Grace and Chang Lee – who ultimately saw the error of his ways – and departs in the TARDIS as the world celebrates the millennium.

Episode endings:
1. The new Doctor settles back in his armchair in the TARDIS control room to continue reading H G Wells's novel *The Time Machine*. The gramophone record that he is listening to suddenly gets stuck in a groove, as it did at the start of the adventure, and he exclaims: 'Oh no, not again!'

EIGHTH DOCTOR

IT WAS MADE WHERE...?

Location Filming: 15.01.96-19.01.96, 23.01.96-26.01.96, 29.01.96-30.01.96, 01.02.96-02.02.96, 05.02.96-08.02.96

Locations: alley between E Georgia/Union Street; 218 East Georgia; Venus Theatre; 221 Union Street; 222 Keefer Street; BC Children's Hospital, 4480 Oak Street; Golden Crown Centre, 211 E Georgia Street, Impark lot #420; 1998 Odgen Street; Plaza of Nations, B100 – 750 Pacific Blvd; Sun Yat Sen Garden, 578 Carrall Street; John Livingstone Park, Carrall Street/Keefer Street junction, nr GM Place; Carrall Street/Keefer Street junction, nr GM Place. All locations in Vancouver, British Columbia, Canada.

Studio Filming: 22.01.96, 31.01.96, 08.02.96-10.02.96, 12.02.96-15.02.96, 19.02.96-21.02.96 all at 8651 Eastlake Drive, Burnaby, BC, Canada.

CREDITED CAST

Starring: Paul McGann. Special Guest Star: Eric Roberts. Guest Starring: Daphne Ashbrook, Sylvester McCoy, Yee Jee Tso, John Novak, Michael David Simms. Wheeler (Catherine Lough), Curtis (Dolores Drake), Pete (William Sasko), Gareth (Jeremy Radick), Miranda (Eliza Roberts), Motorcycle Policeman (Bill Croft), Professor Wagg (Dave Hurtubise), Ted (Joel Wirkkunen), Security Man (Dee Jay Jackson), The Old Master (Gordon Tipple), News Anchor (Mi-Jung Lee), News Anchor (Joanna Piros).

Note: Paul McGann played the Doctor, Eric Roberts played the Master, Daphne Ashbrook played Dr Grace Holloway, Sylvester McCoy played the Old Doctor, Yee Jee Tso played Chang Lee, John Novak played Salinger and Michael David Simms played Dr Swift. The opening titles include the credit: 'Based on the original series broadcast on the BBC'. (This was removed from the version first transmitted in the UK, but without the loss of any footage.)

POPULAR MYTHS

- This movie had the working title *The Enemy Within*. (Executive producer Philip Segal suggested to fans that if they wanted a title for the movie other than just *Doctor Who*, they could refer to it as *Enemy Within*. However neither *Enemy Within* nor *The Enemy Within* was ever used as a working title during production.)

THINGS TO WATCH OUT FOR

- Sylvester McCoy gives a great, dignified performance in his last appearance as the seventh Doctor.
- The Doctor's sonic screwdriver returns.
- The UK transmission of the story featured a dedication after the closing credits to the actor Jon Pertwee, who had died seven days earlier on 20 May. The idea of dedicating the transmission in this way was suggested in a fax to Controller of BBC1 Alan Yentob by Kevin Davies, a freelance film maker who had directed the 1993 BBC documentary *30 Years in the TARDIS*. It was also suggested independently by executive producer Philip Segal.

- The movie was originally supposed to open with a voice-over monologue by the Master. This was actually recorded – hence the on-screen credit given to Gordon Tipple – but removed and replaced with a different monologue by the Doctor when the producers concluded as a result of test screenings that American viewers unfamiliar with *Doctor Who* needed an introduction that would more clearly explain the premise to them.
- The version of the move first transmitted on BBC1 on 27 May 1996 was edited, with over two minutes of the programme removed. The material edited out was as follows:
  - The Chinese youths continue to shoot at the car as it backs away.
  - The Chinese thugs open fire with automatic weapons and kill Chang Lee's two companions. Chang Lee stands terrified in front of them. Wind starts blowing around them.
  - Chang Lee reacts in horror as the thugs raise their guns to aim at him.
  - The thugs open fire on the TARDIS, which is unaffected by the hail of bullets.
  - Chang Lee emerges from behind the TARDIS and runs over to look at the bodies of his friends, then turns toward the fallen body of the Doctor.
  - Grace continues to operate on the Doctor. (This scene was drastically shortened and the music rearranged as a result. Grace's attempts to retrieve the probe and the efforts to revive the Doctor were significantly shortened; and Grace's mention of the probe still being stuck in the body and the Doctor's final scream were cut completely.)
  - Bruce's wife's neck snaps. (Only the sound effect of this was removed; the picture was retained intact.)
  - The Master twists Chang Lee's head.

It was also this version of the movie that was released on BBC video in the UK (although it was the complete version that was released in other countries, including Australia). The complete version was subsequently screened on BBC2, as part of a celebratory *Doctor Who* Night, and a near-complete version (missing only the 'Based on the original series broadcast on the BBC' credit) was released on BBC DVD in 2001.
- A twenty minute documentary, *The Making of Doctor Who – The Movie*, part of a programme called *Sci-Fi Buzz*, was shown by the Sci-Fi Channel on 25 May and on a number of other occasions over the next six months. This was based around the movie's 'electronic press kit'.

- **Dr Grace Holloway:** 'But you have no recollection of family?' **The Doctor:** 'No. No wait … I do. I remember. I'm with my father. We're lying back in the grass. It's a warm Gallifreyan night.' **Dr Grace Holloway:** 'Gallifreyan?' **The Doctor:** 'Gallifrey! Yes, this must be where I live. Now, where is that?' **Dr Grace Holloway:** 'I've never heard of it. What do you remember?' **The Doctor:** 'A meteor storm! And the sky above us was dancing with lights – purple, green, brilliant yellow … Yes!' **Dr Grace Holloway:** 'What?' **The Doctor:** 'These shoes! They fit perfectly. Yes!'
- **The Doctor:** 'Grace, I came back to life before your eyes. I held back death. Look,

EIGHTH DOCTOR

695

I can't make your dream come true forever, but I can make it come true today.'
- **Chang Lee:** [Laughing.] 'You kill me!' **The Master:** 'You want me to *kill* you?' **Chang Lee:** 'No, no! I mean, you make me laugh, man. You're a funny guy.' **The Master:** 'I'm glad one of us is amused.'
- **The Master:** 'I always dress for the occasion.'
- **The Doctor:** 'You want dominion over the living, yet all you do is kill!' **The Master:** 'Life is wasted on the living!'

ANALYSIS

Perhaps the most surprising aspect of the *Doctor Who* television movie is how true it remained to the spirit of the original BBC series. It could easily have been very different. One wonders how fans would have reacted to a movie in which the Doctor was the impressionable young grandson of the Time Lord President, his half-brother the Master was the Gallifreyan Minister of Defence and the Daleks looked like Cybermen – all of which ideas featured in the earlier, ultimately rejected versions of the script.

The movie as eventually made and transmitted actually went almost too far in the opposite direction. Executive producer Philip Segal – who in a number of interviews expressed strong criticism of the direction that *Doctor Who* took during the eighties and a determination to try to recapture its original essence – seemingly seized every possible opportunity to pay homage to the series' established mythology. He commissioned a totally accurate replica of the original police box; he had the TARDIS interior liberally bedecked with the seal of Rassilon; he gave the new Doctor a costume reminiscent of William Hartnell's and very much in keeping with the series' traditions; he reintroduced the sonic screwdriver; he approved script references to the Daleks, Skaro, the Time Lords, Gallifrey and other key elements of *Doctor Who* lore; he insisted on using a new arrangement of the original Ron Grainer-composed theme music (even though this meant paying huge royalties to its US publishers); he made sure that the story adhered as closely as possible to established continuity; and so on.

Of course this is not to deny that the movie constituted an Americanised version of *Doctor Who*. This was always going to be the case. In fact, in focusing on these essentially superficial trappings – or giving 'kisses to the past', as he often put it – Segal to some extent missed the point of what *really* constituted the original essence of *Doctor Who*.

The original point of the police box, for instance, was not that the Doctor's time/space machine should have a quirkily anachronistic and eccentric external appearance, but that it should look like a familiar, everyday object, thus challenging viewers' preconceptions and encouraging them not to take their surroundings for granted. In this respect, the 1988 feature film *Bill and Ted's Excellent Adventure*, with its use of a contemporary American phone booth as a time machine, was arguably more true to the original spirit of *Doctor Who* than was Segal's movie. Similarly, the original point of the various strange items carried by the Doctor in his pockets – the sonic screwdriver, the yo-yo, the jelly babies and so on – was to indicate his alien eccentricity and ingenuity and, more often than not, to solve a particular plot problem for the writers. In the movie, on the other hand, they appear to have been included almost gratuitously, simply because they were considered to be standard accoutrements of the Doctor's persona. If anything, they serve to indicate not his alien eccentricity but his *British* eccentricity. This is apparent from a very telling scene in which Grace and a jelly baby-wielding Doctor confront a motorcycle cop. 'He's British,' Grace tells the cop by way of explanation for the Doctor's strange behaviour. 'Yes, I suppose I am,' adds the Doctor – a significant comment that really makes very little sense within the fictional context of the series as opposed to the factual one (unless, that is, the Doctor – now established to be half human – had a British mother).

There are other ways in which the movie makes reference to supposed British eccentricities – a preoccupation that, perhaps needless to say, formed no part whatsoever of the BBC version of *Doctor Who*. Although it was by no means unknown for the Doctor to express a liking for tea in the original series – *The Awakening* comes immediately to mind in this regard – he certainly seems particularly partial to it in the movie, reflecting the standard US stereotype of the tea-obsessed Briton. It seems almost obligatory in US productions featuring a British actor to have one of the other characters at some point poking fun at his accent, and sure enough the movie has a scene in which Eric Roberts' Master is heard to do exactly that. And the Doctor's reference to the TARDIS having a 'cloaking device' certainly owes more to the quintessentially American *Star Trek* than to 'classic' *Doctor Who*, as does the whole notion of him being half human.

Opinions legitimately differ as to what does actually constitute the true essence of *Doctor Who*, but key elements often identified by commentators include: stories that work on more than one level, with deeper themes discernible beneath the superficial action and adventure; a greater emphasis on characterisation and well-plotted drama than on slick production and flashy special effects; and a scary, almost subversive quality that regularly sent kids scurrying behind the sofa and Mary Whitehouse complaining to the press. The television movie possesses none of these attributes. The story works on only one, relatively superficial level; characterisation is minimal and the plot full of gaping holes, while lavish attention is focused on the impressive visuals; and, although there are undoubtedly some scary scenes, the overall approach is more formulaic than subversive, with the inclusion of many stock elements of standard US action/adventure fare – a violent gun battle (typically pruned for UK transmission); a 'cartoon terrible' villain (to use Eric Roberts' own description of his incarnation of the Master); a youthful sidekick; a lengthy 'car chase' scene; a romantic involvement between the star and the leading lady; and so on. Some commentators have suggested that the movie was aimed at the same audience as *The X-Files* – 'the producers were clearly chasing *The X-Files* ... and wanted a slice of its success,' wrote Daniel O'Mahony in *Skaro* No. 13 dated summer 1997 – but if this was really the case then it went well wide of the mark, as the latter has a truly subversive quality and is one of the few American-produced genre series successfully to avoid most of the well-worn clichés.

The era of the original BBC series of which the movie is most reminiscent is, ironically enough, that of the eighties – the very era about which Segal has been so scathing in interviews. The emphasis on slick production rather than strong storytelling; the muddled plot; the poorly explained resolution; the numerous continuity references; the inclusion of familiar *Doctor Who* icons largely for nostalgia value; the use of a rearranged version of the Ron Grainer theme music: these are all features that the movie shares with eighties *Doctor Who*.

Ultimately, however, the movie should be judged not on the short-sighted basis of its degree of success in recapturing the original essence of *Doctor Who*, but on its own merits as an entertaining adventure updating the series' format for an international audience of the nineties. Viewed in this light, and notwithstanding misgivings about the coherence of its plot, it can only be judged a triumph. 'This production has surpassed my expectations and is one hundred percent what *Doctor Who* should be like in the 1990s,' enthused John Connors in *Skaro* No. 13. 'Pile-driving excitement, powerful drama, strange goings-on and a sense of humour ... If it doesn't end up in my all-time ... top ten, I shall be very surprised. Everyone involved in the conception, development and production of this deserves absolute praise and gratitude.'

There is a great deal to admire in the movie, including the stylish, imaginative direction by Geoffrey Sax. 'A lot of credit must ... go to [him] ...,' suggested Michael Evans in *Matrix* Issue 53 dated autumn 1996. '[His] merging of parallel scenes (the Doctor's regeneration versus the takeover of Bruce, or better still the Doctor finding his new costume while Chang Lee roots through the seventh Doctor's belongings) was lovely. His composition, such as the unshowy use of two half-faces during the turning of Lee, was the sign of a director who was interested in his material ... Notwithstanding the budget, Sax made this one of the best directed pieces of *Doctor Who* ever, and it was certainly the best lit; moody without just being dark, and making terrific and unusual use of colour.'

The movie has excellent production values all round, as Graham Howard pointed out in *TSV* 48 dated August 1996:

'One of the advantages of having a generous budget – as this movie did have – is that at last *Doctor Who* was able to showcase some stunning visuals and special effects. From the regeneration sequence (I loved the juxtaposition of [an] old *Frankenstein* movie with the Doctor's regeneration) to the climactic scenes at the end, it would seem that no expense was spared in providing an impressive visual look to the movie. The opening titles looked good, with a nineties feel to them, though [the theme music was] rather lacklustre ...

'Special mention must go to what was probably the most expensive of the [sets]: the new TARDIS interior. The idea of giving the TARDIS a Wellsian *The Time Machine* type feel in which old-world charm would contrast with a highly advanced technology initially appealed, [although] I now feel there was not enough contrast. While it is fine for the decor of the "living area" to be styled with an Edwardian feel, it would have been preferable for the TARDIS control systems to exhibit the more traditional trappings of an advanced technology – particularly the central control console – as opposed to the rather primitive appearance that was given.'

One particularly positive aspect of Matthew Jacobs' script is that it contains some great material for the Doctor, which has him acting very true to form: an incident where he threatens the motorcycle cop by turning a gun on *himself* – behaviour far removed from that of a typical American hero figure – is a wonderful example. His elegant, Byronesque costume and hair are also superb, and thankfully a complete departure from the uniform-like, question-mark-bedecked look of the eighties Doctors. Paul McGann himself is magnificent, turning in a stronger debut performance in the role than any of his predecessors bar Hartnell and making one long to see him in action again in further stories. 'Imagine this were a four part story to launch a new BBC series,' wrote Michael Haslett in *Skaro* No. 13. 'We'd be ready to make excuses for a new Doctor, reminding ourselves that it takes time to settle in the role, for an actor to find his feet and for a writer to find his actor. All the more remarkable, then, that McGann, a reluctant Time Lord if ever there was one, should immediately get a firm hold on what it is to be the Doctor. Evincing traits of toothy Tom Baker and potty Patrick Troughton but most of all something daringly unique to this eighth incarnation, McGann provided a crucial balance to the proceedings.'

Eric Roberts' Master, although very different from the Roger Delgado and Anthony Ainley versions, is also wonderful. Tim Munro, another contributor to *Skaro* No. 13, was highly impressed:

'Curiously enough, watching him makes one realise the vast mistake that was made with Ainley's Master, [specifically] that the actor was never allowed to put his own stamp on the part. So much of Ainley's portrayal was dictated by how the role was already perceived that he was usually left playing a crude caricature of [Delgado's original], rather than building his own interpretation. In contrast, Roberts plays the part entirely his own way, paying his dues to the past without being hidebound by it, and so ... brings to the role much that is fresh and uniquely his own, giving us a progression in the character – it's clearly the same man, but also a little different, which is exactly how regenerations should be handled.

'This Master retains the charm, wit, genius and guile of his predecessors, but he's also a far more unstable, unpredictable personality. Roberts' splendidly multifaceted portrayal gives us the most complex, disturbing version of the Master to date, capable of startlingly abrupt changes of manner, from silky charm and smooth self-control to outbursts of shocking, almost bestial physical violence and naked sadism ... From his shocking murder of Bruce's wife to the vicious kicking he gives the Doctor, this is the Master as truly, satanically evil and frightening as he's ever been played.'

Daphne Ashbrook's portrayal of Dr Grace Holloway is also excellent, as Michael Evans agreed: '[She] brought a real lightness of touch to her performance, successfully mixing comedy and drama, often in the same scene ... She even got to out-Doctor the Doctor, as Lalla [Ward] used to, and basically gave the impression that this was a role she loved playing. Her scenes with Paul McGann captured all that was good about the most successful Doctor-companion relationships, but redefined that relationship too into a mutual need and enjoyment of each other's company.'

The two most contentious aspects of the movie, in terms of *Doctor Who* continuity, are the fact that the Doctor kisses Grace – '[This] is completely (and I mean completely) out of character,' asserted Edwin Patterson in *TSV* 49 dated November 1996 – and that he reveals himself to be half human. Michael Evans, however, took issue with those who considered these developments inappropriate:

'A contrived love interest was quite definitely not what was presented ... Chaste yet genuinely affectionate, these kisses seemed perfectly natural within the Grace/eighth Doctor relationship. In this movie it would be unthinkable that, after coming through so much, the Doctor and Grace wouldn't share a farewell kiss. In fact, by comparison, it makes some previous partings, such as the Doctor's goodbye to Todd in *Kinda*, seem unnaturally hollow ... *Doctor Who* stories can no longer get away with having no emotional impact on the characters.

'Similarly, I have no problem whatsoever with the revelation of the Doctor being half human, as portrayed on screen. During the movie, it is presented variously as a fact, a revelation and a joke. [This means that it] begs more questions than it answers, and that is how it should be.'

If the movie has a central theme, it is that of regeneration and rebirth. The scene in which the new Doctor 'rises from the dead' and emerges from the hospital mortuary wrapped only in a shroud is a clear reference to the Biblical story of the resurrection of

Christ (the mortuary attendant actually cries out "Oh, God!" before collapsing); and this is carried through into the climactic scene in the TARDIS cloister room where the Master attaches to the Doctor's head a device that looks like a crown of thorns and effectively attempts to 'crucify' him above the Eye of Harmony.

Regrettably, as the movie ultimately failed to lead on to the hoped-for series, the Doctor's 'resurrection' proved to be a relatively short one. It was nevertheless extremely welcome and worthwhile. As Michael Evans put it: 'It was good to have him back, if only for one night.'

EPILOGUE

The *Doctor Who* television movie performed well in the UK, gaining over nine million viewers and some generally positive feedback. It did less well in the USA, however, where it was transmitted opposite some very strong competition, and in the end Fox failed to pick up the option for a series or even, as had also been mooted, one or more follow up movies. The rights to the series are believed to have reverted to the BBC at the end of 1997, leaving it arguably as much in limbo as it had been before the movie was ever made.

What the movie did achieve, however, and what may ultimately be seen as its greatest contribution to *Doctor Who*'s long and chequered history, was to give a fresh impetus to all the various 'spin-off' projects initiated in the series' absence – including, in particular, the ranges of original novels and, latterly, the Big Finish audio dramas, in which McGann has reprised his eighth Doctor role to great effect. With a new Doctor at the helm of a redesigned TARDIS, the creative minds behind these projects now have greater freedom than ever before to explore new fictional realms and dimensions, limited only by the extent of their own imaginations.

By the end of 2002, the eighth Doctor had already enjoyed over sixty original adventures in literary form, and a further ten in audio form.

It remains to be seen whether the Doctor will ever return for further original adventures on television.

APPENDIX A — DOCTOR WHO SPIN OFF

K·9 AND COMPANY

Producer: John Nathan-Turner. **Script Editors:** Eric Saward, Antony Root. **Production Associate:** Angela Smith. **Title Music:** Fiachra Trench and Ian Levine, arranged by Peter Howell. **Special Sounds:** Dick Mills. **Writer:** Terence Dudley. **Director:** John Black. **Designer:** Nigel Jones. **Costumes:** Ann Arnold. **Make-Up:** Susie Bancroft. **Incidental Music:** Peter Howell. **Visual Effects:** Mat Irvine. **Film Cameraman:** Michael Williams. **Film Editor:** Michael Lomas. **Studio Lighting:** Barry Hill. **Studio Sound:** David Hughes. **Production Managers:** Robert Gabriel, Matthew Kuipers. **Assistant Floor Manager:** Sue Hedden.

	First UK TX	Scheduled TX	Actual TX	Duration	Viewers	Chart Pos.
A Girl's Best Friend	28/12/81	17.45	17.46	49'56"	8.4	—

Plot: Sarah pays a Christmas visit to her Aunt Lavinia's house in the village of Moreton Harwood. She discovers that Lavinia, a noted scientist, has yet to return from a lecture tour of the USA. She does however meet Brendan – Lavinia's ward – and Commander Bill Pollock – her partner in a small market garden business. Also in the house, in a box sent to her by the Doctor, she finds K9. Brendan is kidnapped by a local coven of witches who want to sacrifice him to the goddess Hecate. Sarah, with K9's assistance, foils their plan and unmasks their leaders – Commander Pollock and local postmistress Lily Gregson.

IT WAS MADE WHERE...?

Location filming: 09.11.81, 12.11.81-17.11.81
Locations: Ruined church, North Woodchester, Gloucs; Crossroads, Sapperton, Gloucs; Barnsley House, Barnsley, Gloucs; Miserden Petrol Station, Miserden, Gloucs; Wishanger Farm, Wishanger, Gloucs; Miserden Park Estate, Miserden, Gloucs; St Andrew's Church, Miserden, Gloucs; Bisley, Gloucs; Daneway, Gloucs.
Studio: 29.11.81-30.11.81 in Studio A, BBC Pebble Mill, 01.12.81 in unknown studio, BBC Pebble Mill

CREDITED CAST

Sarah Jane Smith (Elisabeth Sladen), Voice of K9 (John Leeson), George Tracey (Colin Jeavons), Henry Tobias (John Quarmby), Sergeant Wilson (Nigel Gregory), Peter Tracey (Sean Chapman), Aunt Lavinia (Mary Wimbush), Juno Baker (Linda Polan), Brendan Richards (Ian Sears), Commander Pollock (Bill Fraser), Howard Baker (Neville Barber), Lilly Gregson (Gillian Martell), PC Carter (Stephen Oxley).

THINGS TO WATCH OUT FOR

- The bouncy title music was written and composed for the show by long-time *Doctor Who* fan, Ian Levine, along with his writing partner Fiachra Trench. Levine and Trench also wrote and produced the 1985 *Doctor Who* charity record 'Doctor in Distress'.

- K9 Mark III has been left for Sarah to find as a present by the Doctor.

THINGS YOU MIGHT NOT HAVE KNOWN

- Head of Drama, David Reid, expressed concern on reading the scripts for *K·9 and Company*. 'From experience I know that you'll get a lot of complaints the moment you start showing witchcraft rituals,' he wrote to Nathan-Turner on 5 October 1981. 'You'll probably get round robins from church congregations etc, and a lot of "disgusteds" who object to children seeing it etc. So, wherever possible, stick to the "thriller" elements of the story rather than the Black Arts.'

QUOTE, UNQUOTE

- **Lavinia (about Sarah)**: 'She's like a butterfly. Never in one place long enough to lick a stamp.'
- **Tracey**: 'You have always wanted to be let in.' **Peter**: 'No!' **Tracey**: 'You've been chosen.' **Peter**: 'No!' **Tracey**: 'You will be initiated tonight.' **Peter**: 'No!' **Tracey**: 'We must be complete for the solstice.' **Peter**: 'No!' **Tracey**: 'Then be sure you go like Vince Wilson to everlasting fire.'
- **Brendan**: 'Who is the Doctor?' **K9**: 'Affirmative.'

ANALYSIS

K·9 and Company was the only *bona fide* (or should that be *fido?*) *Doctor Who* spin-off ever to be produced for television (although there have since been a number of others in different media, including novels, audio dramas and comic strips). As such there was quite a lot riding on this pilot episode, *A Girl's Best Friend*, and expectations were high.

The spur for the commissioning of the pilot was the enormous popularity of K9, and more specifically the public outcry that followed producer John Nathan-Turner's decision to drop the robot dog from *Doctor Who*. It must have been apparent from the start, though, that K9 could not carry a whole series on its own, owing to its limitations in terms both of character and, more particularly, of practicality. The K9 prop was notoriously unreliable and time-consuming to work with and – John Leeson's excellent vocal contribution notwithstanding – afforded relatively little potential for dramatic interaction with other characters.

The obvious solution was to have one or more additional regulars working in partnership with K9 and carrying the weight of the dialogue and action. And who better to fulfil this function than one of the Doctor's other former companions, of the two-legged variety? It is interesting to speculate, for a moment, just how different this pilot episode – and any subsequent series – might have turned out had the companion selected for the role been, say, Leela or Romana. In the former case, viewers could have been presented with a series of adventures on the Time Lords' home planet, Gallifrey, following on from the events of the season fifteen story *The Invasion of Time*. In the latter case, the stories could have focused on the exploits of K9 and Romana in E-Space after they parted company with the Doctor at the end of season eighteen's *Warriors' Gate*, with plenty of scope for the depiction of unfamiliar worlds, alien civilisations, hi-tech hardware and monstrous adversaries.

As it was, the companion chosen to team up with K9 was Sarah Jane Smith, played by

Elisabeth Sladen. This was by no means a silly or surprising move, as Sarah was by some margin the most popular of all the Doctor's companions – certainly amongst *Doctor Who* fans, as confirmed by the results of numerous fanzine polls and surveys. What it did mean, though, given that Sarah was a late-20th Century English journalist, was that *K·9 and Company* would almost inevitably present Earth-bound stories with fewer overt science-fiction trappings than *Doctor Who*. The wisdom of this was later questioned by some – including K9's creators Bob Baker and Dave Martin and even Nathan-Turner himself. There was, however, no reason in principle why a series in this vein could not be made to work (the suggestion in Nathan-Turner's format document that its style might be more akin to that of *The Avengers* than of *Doctor Who* was interesting), and – as producers Derrick Sherwin and Peter Bryant realised as far back as the late 1960s, when they devised the Earth exile format for *Doctor Who*'s seventh season – the use of Earthly settings and characters places much less of a strain on the budget than the creation of far-flung planets and monsters.

The problem with *A Girl's Best Friend*, as numerous commentators have noted, is that the clichéd central plot idea of secret witchcraft rituals being carried out in a sleepy English village – a stock story type of British action-adventure series for many years – is put across with a distinct lack of flair and inventiveness, and certainly nowhere near as successfully as in *The Daemons* in season eight, *Image of the Fendahl* in season fifteen and *The Stones of Blood* in season sixteen of *Doctor Who* – probably its three closest antecedents in the parent series.

David McNay, reviewing the production for the Off The Telly website in 2000, was not impressed: 'Unfortunately this is a very badly written story … The whole sacrifice plot is rather quickly dealt with, and if you don't concentrate you might just miss it. The "poor harvest" rationale is briefly mentioned by K9 seconds before Sarah Jane asks him something else, and if you didn't hear it that time you might think [the coven are actually intent on] killing Brendan due to his annoying laugh and posture. In fact it's all rather *Scooby Doo*. All it's missing is a "Nice Lily Gregson from the post office! It was you all along!" and the allusion … would be complete.'

Another aspect of the production that McNay, and many others, greatly disliked was the opening title sequence: 'In what must have seemed like a good idea at the time, the producers have tried to recreate a *Hart to Hart*-style montage of Sarah Jane and K9 up to various activities. K9 is limited to trundling along a road, and Sarah Jane just sits outside a pub typing and sipping wine (as all good reporters do) before heading off for a jog. It looks terrible …'

Others have been even more hostile. 'The pilot is at times incredibly boring to watch and ultimately a great failure,' opined Tim Roll-Pickering in a review on the *Doctor Who* Ratings Guide website in 2002, 'and it's hard to escape asking the question: "What was the point of it all?"'

These damning comments are too harsh, however, as *A Girl's Best Friend* is not without its positive features. One thing agreed upon by almost every reviewer is that Elisabeth Sladen makes a very welcome return as Sarah and gives, as usual, a highly engaging performance. Fred Winn, writing in *Zerinza* Issue No. 23 dated May 1982, liked the way her character was handled: 'No longer a wide-eyed, compulsive screamer, Sarah is once again the incisive, resourceful journo with a mind able to grasp the inconsistencies surrounding the mysterious absence of her Aunt Lavinia.'

Winn, unlike some other reviewers, was also favourably disposed toward Sarah's new friend, Brendan: 'Brendan Richards is well played by Ian Sears. Unlike the dreary, self-opinioned, stumbling bumbler Adric, Brendan is a quiet, believable schoolboy, about to take his O Level exams.' It could indeed be said that all the story's main characters, including Bill Fraser's bluff Commander Pollack and Colin Jeavons's sinister, skulking George Tracey, are well-drawn and portrayed, and this must be counted one of its stongest points.

The production is a polished one, too, with good visuals, impressive yet suitably unobtrusive visual effects and evocative incidental music, and John Black's direction is as competent as ever. Terence Dudley's script also has its merits, as Jeremy Bentham noted in reviewing the special for *Doctor Who Monthly* No. 62 dated March 1982: 'One of the nice twists to the story was the way in which it avoided answering the fundamental question – does black magic live on in rural, Cotswold England? *K·9 and Company* suggested it might but hedged around giving clear evidence of demonic powers at work. Certainly there were midnight sacrifices offered to the unholy, but not once did either of the two officiating priests – disguised beneath beautiful caprician masks ... – display any supernatural powers. No lightning bolts from fingers or ghostly manifestations. Even those moments which seemed to present evidence were all explainable. Was Pollock lying about the thirteen second hailstorm which ruined Lavinia Smith's crops one year? Did Vince Wilson die by natural causes after all, despite the symbolic sight of a goat nearby? And what about the tractor that nearly drove Sarah into a fatal car crash? In *Planet of the Spiders* that self-same scene (even down to some of the camera shots) was indeed a pointer to supernatural powers, but in *K·9 and Company* ... who is to say?'

Bentham was, indeed, quite positive about the production as a whole, and about its potential to launch a full series of *K·9 and Company*: 'The characters are all there: K9, Sarah Jane with her legion of Fleet Street contacts, the globe-trotting Aunt Lavinia, and even young Brendan might prove an eventual worthy recruit to the company. The setting of Moreton Harwood with all its P G Wodehouse trappings would make an excellent base of operations, and the surrounding countryside has that picturesque attraction that drew so many to *All Creatures Great and Small*.'

As things transpired, of course, a full series was not to be, and in truth Bentham rather overstates the case for the defence. Perhaps the fairest way to sum up *A Girl's Best Friend* is to say that it was by no means a bad piece of festive-season family drama, just an unexceptional, and at times rather dull one – not what was needed to convince the powers-that-be at the BBC that *K·9 and Company* deserved a regular place in the programme schedules.

APPENDIX B — OTHER DOCTOR WHO PRODUCTIONS

Several *Doctor Who* sketches or segments have appeared on television within other productions. These are detailed below. We have not provided any critical analyses of these programmes as they made for educational, charitable or similar purposes, rather than as pieces of drama in their own right, and are not generally regarded as *bona fide* entries in the *Doctor Who* canon.

IN A FIX WITH SONTARANS

Writer: Eric Saward. **Director:** Marcus Mortimore. **Special Sound:** Dick Mills, BBC Radiophonic Workshop. **Lighting:** Peter Wesson. **Sound:** Richard Chamberlain. **Designer:** Gwen Evans. **Producer:** Roger Ordish.

	First UK TX	Scheduled TX	Actual TX	Duration	Viewers	Chart Pos.
A Fix With Sontarans	23/02/85	18.05*	—	8'46"	—	—

* This is the start time of *Jim'll Fix It*, not of the *Doctor Who* segment.

> **Plot:** The Doctor is making hurried adjustments to the TARDIS console when the ship's matter transporter activates and Tegan appears. The Doctor apologises to his former companion and asks for her help as there are two Sontarans on board with a vitrox bomb. Tegan reactivates the matter transporter and a young boy named Gareth Jenkins appears, dressed in a similar manner to the sixth Doctor. The newcomer offers to stay and help in repelling the Sontarans. The interior door to the console room explodes as two Sontarans enter. When Gareth is introduced to them, they explain that in the year 2001, a Sontaran attack on Earth will be defeated by a defence force led by a Gareth Jenkins. They plan to kill the boy now to ensure the future success of their invasion. The Doctor, however, knocks their gun away, Gareth activates the TARDIS energiser, and the Sontarans dissolve in a jet of smoke. The Doctor asks Gareth how he had the knowledge to operate the TARDIS. Gareth replies that he has seen the Doctor do it on the telly. Just then an image appears on the scanner. Tegan describes it as monstrous, and the Doctor agrees that it is revolting. It is Jimmy Savile.

IT WAS MADE WHERE...?

Studio: 20.02.85 (studio unknown)

CREDITED CAST

No cast were credited on screen.
The participants were: The Doctor (Colin Baker), Tegan (Janet Fielding), Gareth Jenkins (himself), Group Marshal Nathan (Clinton Greyn), Sontaran (Tim Raynham), Jimmy Savile (himself).

THINGS TO WATCH OUT FOR

- *In A Fix With Sontarans* was a one-part mini-story shown within the BBC1 light entertainment programme *Jim'll Fix It* – a series in which Jimmy Savile OBE made viewers' dreams come true. It is one of the rare examples of *Doctor Who* being featured within another BBC TV programme with the Doctor played in character and by the regular actor.
- Eight-year-old Gareth Jenkins had written in to *Jim'll Fix It* asking if he could see Colin Baker and go inside the TARDIS.
- Alongside Colin Baker as the Doctor, Janet Fielding reprised her role as Tegan, complete with the air-hostess uniform that she had worn in her earliest *Doctor Who* stories. Clinton Greyn and Tim Raynham played the Sontarans, as they had done also in *The Two Doctors*.

THINGS YOU MIGHT NOT HAVE KNOWN

- The sketch was originally to have featured Nicola Bryant playing Peri, but she was out of the country on holiday so the script was changed to incorporate Tegan instead.
- The name of the Sontaran Group Marshal was changed from Stern to Nathan by actor Clinton Greyn during recording. His subordinate, Turner, was not named on screen.

SEARCH OUT SPACE

Producer: Lambros Atteshlis. **Series Producer:** Robin Mudge. **Director:** Berry-Anne Billingsley. **Writers:** Lambros Atteshlis, Berry-Anne Billingsley. **Designer:** Peter Findley. **Visual Effects:** Mat Irvine. **Lighting:** John Collins. **Sound:** Dave Brinnicombe. **Production Assistants:** Eve Lucas, Andrea Hanus. **Assistant Floor Manager:** Crispin Avon.

	First UK TX	Scheduled TX	Actual TX	Duration	Viewers	Chart Pos.
The Ultimate Challenge	21/11/90	10.15	—	19'15"	—	—

BBC2 transmission – part of the 'Planet Earth' module of 'Search Out Science'.

> **Plot: The** Doctor is the host of a gameshow and the contestants are the viewer, Ace, K9 and, from the planet Glurk, Cedric. Cedric, Ace and K9 are given various questions to answer and several suggestions are given along the way.

IT WAS MADE WHERE...?

Studio Recording: 20.05.90 at BBC Model Stage, 25.05.90 at Ealing Film Studios
Location/OB: 14.05.90, 15.05.90, 18.05.90, 21.05.90
Locations: Avalon Travel Agency, Ealing, London; The Danish Kitchen, Ealing, London; foot tunnel nr. Shepherd's Bush Underground Station, London; Jodrell Bank Science Centre, Cheshire; concourse outside the Lloyds Building, Leadenhall Street, London.

CREDITED CAST

The Doctor (Sylvester McCoy), Cedric (Stephen Johnson), Ace (Sophie Aldred), Voice of K9 (John Leeson).

THINGS TO WATCH OUT FOR

- This one-off entry in the BBC schools series *Search Out Science* featured Sylvester McCoy as the Doctor and Sophie Aldred as Ace.
- The visual effects were created by Mat Irvine, who had worked on the *Doctor Who* series and who also had a fully operational K9 prop that he loaned to the production.
- The programme was the fifteenth and last in the unit 'Planet Earth'. The title in *Radio Times* and all paperwork is *Search Out Space*. The on-screen title *The Ultimate Challenge* applies to the linking device of the quiz show only, as opposed to all the sketches in the programme.
- The questions posed to the contestants (and, in brackets, the answers given) are as follows:

    The first challenge is for Cedric: what shape is the Earth? (He ponders and, with clues from Ace and K9, incorrectly decides that it is a cylinder.)
    The second challenge: what makes day and night? (Cedric suggests that a spinning light or a spinning Earth could cause the effect. There are additional clues from Ace and K9.)
    Third: what makes summer hot and winter cold? (Cedric postulates that in winter the Earth is further from the Sun than in summer. K9 thinks that in winter the Sun gives out less heat, or the heat is more concentrated.)
    Fourth: why does the Moon appear to change shape? (There are clues from Ace – she is reflected in a mirror, but is the light real or reflected? – and from Cedric – who explains that moonlight is really reflected sunlight.)
    Fifth: how would you find out how many days there are in a lunar month? (The Doctor presents a clue: a picture showing the phases of the Moon.)
    The Doctor introduces a new subject: the stars. Round one is called: 'who, how, where, why, what'.
    Who can see the stars in the daytime? (Ace can with a radio telescope.)
    When can you see stars with an ordinary telescope?
    How many stars are there?
    How would you count them?
    Cedric asks: where is K9? (K9 is floating in space. He has two questions: 'When can I come down?' and 'Which way is down?')
    The final question in this round comes from the Doctor: what is yellow or red or brown or black or orange or blue? (K9 comments that this is easy; it is a piece of metal when heated. The Doctor tells him that the answer is in the stars. K9 trundles off and finds large coloured discs on the ground. He realises that the colours represent stars at different stages of their life. He fails to get the answer and dematerialises. The Doctor rescues him from space using the TARDIS.)
    The Doctor poses the final question: the key to the universe is hidden somewhere in the universe, but where is it? Thirty seconds is allowed in which to answer. (K9 states that the task is hopeless – which is the correct answer.)

- Many of the sound effects used in the production were from *Doctor Who* itself. A section of the theme music from the *K-9 and Company* spin-off programme was also used.

DIMENSIONS IN TIME

Producer: John Nathan-Turner. **EastEnders Producer:** Leonard Lewis. **Children in Need Editor:** Nick Handel. **Title Music:** Ron Grainer, arranged by Cybertech. **Writers:** John Nathan-Turner, David Roden*. **Director:** Stuart Macdonald. **Designer:** Derek Evans. **Costumes:** Ken Trew. **Make-Up:** Leslie Smith. **Incidental Music:** Keff McCulloch. **Visual Effects:** Mike Tucker. **Cameramen:** Tommy Beier, Nigel Saunders. **Lighting:** Dave Wells, Alan Rixon. **Sound:** Peter Ball, Barry Bonner. **Production Manager:** Gary Downie. **Assistant Floor Manager:** Jenny Drewett.

*Only the two writers were credited on screen.

	First UK TX	Scheduled TX	Actual TX	Duration	Viewers	Chart Pos.
Part One	26/11/93	—	20.08	07'38"	13.8	15
Part Two	27/11/93	—	19.23	05'27"	13.6	10

Plot: The Rani tries to trap all the incarnations of the Doctor in a time loop in London's East End. When they start to suspect her plan, she releases a horde of monsters to attack them. The Doctor realises that the Rani is trying to transfer her time tunnel to Greenwich. With her store of genetic codes for every living thing, evolution will then be hers to control. The Doctor realises that the Rani's system will overload as she mistakenly traps Romana as well as the Doctor and pulls the Rani's TARDIS into the time tunnel. The trapped Doctors are freed.

Episode endings:
1. In Albert Square, the Rani and her menagerie of monsters confront the Doctor, Nyssa and Peri outside the Queen Vic public house.
2. With the Rani defeated, the Doctor and Ace leave in the TARDIS.

Studio: 21.09.93 at Fountain TV Studios, New Malden, Surrey.
Location OB: 22.09.93-24.09.93
Locations: Cutty Sark, Greenwich, London, SE10; Royal Naval College, Romney Road, Greenwich, London, SE10; National Maritime Museum/Queen's House, Romney Road, Greenwich, London, SE10; *EastEnders* backlot, BBC Elstree Centre, Clarendon Road, Borehamwood, Herts.

No cast were credited on screen.
The main participants were: The Rani (Kate O'Mara), Cyrian (Sam West), The Doctor (Tom Baker, Sylvester McCoy, Colin Baker, Jon Pertwee, Peter Davison), Ace (Sophie

Aldred), Sanjay Kapoor (Deepak Verma[1]), Gita Kapoor (Shobu Kapoor[1]), Mel (Bonnie Langford[1]), Pauline Fowler (Wendy Richard[1]), Kathy Beale (Gillian Taylforth[1]), Young Ian Beale (Tim Handel[1]), Susan Foreman (Carole Ann Ford[1]), Sharon Mitchell (Letitia Dean[1]), Sarah Jane Smith (Elisabeth Sladen[1]), Nyssa (Sarah Sutton), Peri (Nicola Bryant), Pat Butcher (Pam St Clement[1]), Liz Shaw (Caroline John[2]), Mandy Salter (Nicola Stapleton[2]), Big Ron (Ron Tarr*), Captain Yates (Richard Franklin[2]), Brigadier Lethbridge Stewart (Nicholas Courtney[2]), Ian Beale (Adam Woodyatt[2]), Phil Mitchell (Steve McFadden[2]), Grant Mitchell (Ross Kemp[2]), Romana (Lalla Ward[2]), Frank Butcher (Mike Reid[2]), Victoria Waterfield (Deborah Watling[2]), Leela (Louise Jameson[2]), Voice of K9 (John Leeson[2]).

* Not in broadcast version.

THINGS TO WATCH OUT FOR

- This was a two-part romp produced for the BBC's annual Children in Need telethon in 1993. It was intended to be watched through special polarised filter glasses to achieve a 3-D effect.
- The action is centred around the fictional Albert Square, setting for the BBC's soap opera *EastEnders*. Many of the then regular cast of *EastEnders* appear in their usual roles.
- The costumes for the monsters that invaded Albert Square were supplied from the BBC's own stock and from the private collections of a number of *Doctor Who* fans who made appearances in the show either as passers-by or wearing the costumes. One of the most prominent of these appearances was by Andrew Beech, former Coordinator of the *Doctor Who* Appreciation Society, who wore the ceremonial robes and collar of a Time Lord. Other monsters or characters glimpsed during the course of the action (and, noted in brackets, the *Doctor Who* stories in which they originally featured) were: Cyberman (Tony Kirke, David Miller) (various), Ogron (Derek Handley) (*Day of the Daleks, Frontier in Space*), Vanir (John Frank Rosenbaum) (*Terminus*), Tractator (operator: Martin Wilkie) (*Frontios*), Tetrap (operator: Martin Wilkie) (*Time and the Rani*), Zog (operator: Martin Wilkie) (from the stage play *The Ultimate Adventure*), Fifi the Stigorax (operator: Stephen Mansfield) (*The Happiness Patrol*), Vervoid (Anthony Clark) (*The Trial of a Time Lord*), Mutant (Paul Lunn) (*Mawdryn Undead*), the biomechanoid (operator: Martin Wilkie) (*Dragonfire*), Mentor (Philip Newman) (*The Trial of a Time Lord*), Argolin (Andy Hopkinson) (*The Leisure Hive*), D84 robot (Illona Macdonald) (*The Robots of Death*), Plasmaton (Tim Packham) (*Time-Flight*), Melkur (unknown) (*The Keeper of Traken*), Sea Devil (Mike Fillis) (*The Sea Devils*) and a Mogarian (Stephen Coates) (*The Trial of a Time Lord*).
- The first segment of the story was shown during the Children In Need telethon itself on the Friday evening, in a link up with presenter Noel Edmonds' fictional house at Crinkley Bottom. Jon Pertwee was introduced and 'watched' the story with Edmonds and the studio audience in the house. The second segment was shown during *Noel's House Party* on the Saturday evening, but no guests were present.
- The series' familiar theme music was re-arranged for the production by Mike Fillis (who played a Sea Devil) and Adrian Pack, who gave Nathan-Turner a demo tape during the recording on the Albert Square lot. Nathan-Turner had already approached both the Pet Shop Boys and Erasure to provide the theme but,

according to his later recollection, both groups had declined. Fillis and Pack eventually made their version of the theme commercially available on a CD entitled 'Cybertech' in 1994.

- Tara Ford, the daughter of Carole Ann Ford, also appears as an extra.

THINGS YOU MIGHT NOT HAVE KNOWN

- David Roden is a pen name for David Mansell.
- Between the first and second episodes, a telephone vote was held to determine which of two *EastEnders* characters – Mandy or Big Ron – would help the Doctor. The first check of the state of voting showed Mandy with 17,162 votes (57%) and Big Ron with 12,704 (43%). The final tally had Mandy with 22,484 votes (56%) and Big Ron with 17,044 votes (44%).
- To keep costs down, the set for the Rani's TARDIS control room was borrowed from Dominitemporal Services Ltd, the commercial arm of the *Doctor Who* Appreciation Society, who had recently had it constructed for a *Doctor Who* convention.
- The spacecraft exterior of the Rani's TARDIS was adapted from a model used in the BBV independent video *Summoned by Shadows* (which also starred Colin Baker and Nicola Bryant).
- The Rani's assistant was named Cyrian (an in-joke, as it was at one point hoped that distinguished actor Sir Ian McKellen would take the role) but this was not revealed in the final dialogue.
- A Dalek and Dalek troopers were originally intended to appear, but did not.

DOCTOR WHO AND THE CURSE OF FATAL DEATH

Writer: Steven Moffat. **Director:** John Henderson. **Designer:** Simon Kimmell. **Costumes:** Rebecca Hale. **Make-Up:** Jan Sewell. **Incidental Music Consultant:** Mark Ayres. **Visual Effects:** Andy McVean. **Director of Photography:** Chris Howard. **Sound Recordist:** John Midgley. **Production Manager:** Alison McPhail. **1st Assistant Director:** Tim Lewis. **2nd Assistant Director:** Sharon Ricketts. **Producer:** Sue Vertue. **Executive Producer:** Richard Curtis.

	First UK TX	Scheduled TX	Actual TX	Duration	Viewers	Chart Pos.
Part One	12/03/99	—	20:11	5'40"	9.8	6
Part Two	12/03/99	—	20:37	4'55"	9.4	6
Part Three	12/03/99	—	21:40	4'55"	5.8	6
Part Four	12/03/99	—	22:09	7'18"	8.7	6

Broadcast on BBC1 as part of 'Red Nose Day 1999: The Record Breaker' (19:00 on 12.03.99 to 01:00 on 13.03.99). Stereo transmission. Scheduled in *Radio Times* as a three-part story, with the episodes to be broadcast at, respectively, the following times: 20:00-20:10; 20:30-20:40 and 21:35-21:45. This was changed shortly before broadcast.

Plot: The Doctor asks the Master to meet him in a citadel on the planet Terserus, where he reveals that he intends to retire and settle down with his assistant Emma. The Master, however, has laid various traps for the Doctor. All of these the Doctor foils by travelling back in time and bribing the citadel's architect before the Master does so. The Master ends up bringing the Daleks to kill the Doctor, and they take him and Emma captive. The Master intends to use zectronic energy to rule the universe, but the Doctor destroys the beam locator and regenerates three times before dying. The Master and the Daleks renounce evil, but before they leave, the Doctor regenerates a final time into a female form. Emma is no longer interested in him, so the Doctor leaves with the Master.

Episode endings:
1. The Master prepares to pull the lever that will send the Doctor and Emma down into the sewers.
2. Running down some corridors, the Doctor ushers Emma into a room where they'll be safe. It's full of Daleks.
3. Hit by a blast of energy, the Doctor starts to regenerate.
4. The Master decides that he likes the new female incarnation of the Doctor and they leave arm in arm.

IT WAS MADE WHERE...?
Studio: 26.02.99-28.02.99 at Pinewood Studios, Iver, Bucks.

CREDITED CAST
No cast or crew were credited on transmission.
The main participants were: The Doctors (Rowan Atkinson, Richard E Grant[4], Jim Broadbent[4], Hugh Grant[4], Joanna Lumley[4]), Emma (Julia Sawalha), The Master (Jonathan Pryce), Stunts (Gabe Cronnelly[2]), Daleks' Voices (Roy Skelton[2-4], Dave Chapman[2-4]).

THINGS TO WATCH OUT FOR
- The Daleks and the TARDIS control room set and console were all obtained from fan Ashley Neal-Fuller, who had constructed them with a group of friends for an amateur *Doctor Who* film production called *Devious*.
- Jonathan Pryce gives a wonderfully over the top performance as the Master.
- Thanks credits are given on the closing titles to the following: Pinewood Studios, Comac Lighting, Positive Film & Television, Arri Media, The Mill, Willie's Wheels, VideoSonics (dubbing editors Glenn Calder and Philip Meehan), The Spot Co., Michael Samuelson Lighting, The Location Café, Ashley Neal-Fuller, Stephen Cranford, David Clarke, Chris Kirk (all helped supply Daleks and other materials and operated the Daleks also), Gary Gillatt, David Saunders and Andrew Beech.
- The original on-screen title was *Doctor Who and The Curse of Fatal Death*. This was changed for the video release, with the '*Doctor Who and*'portion being dropped.

THINGS YOU MIGHT NOT HAVE KNOWN
- The majority of the music and sound effects for this production were sourced by Mark Ayres from existing *Doctor Who* stories. Ayres did however compose three new cues for the production: two for the zectronic beam machine operation, and one to introduce Hugh Grant as the Doctor.

APPENDIX C - AVAILABILITY CHECKLIST

The following table details which *Doctor Who* episodes are currently held in the BBC's archives and which have been made commercially available to the public over the years in the form of videos, DVDs, novelisations, talking books, audio soundracks and script books. (Some stories have also been released on laserdisc, but these are not detailed below.) A great many of these items have now been deleted or withdrawn, and we have not therefore given ISBN or catalogue numbers or publishers for them. They may still be obtainable however from public libraries, second hand shops, specialist dealers etc. New items are still being released on a regular basis, and the table has been designed so that readers may keep it up to date themselves by blocking out the relevant boxes.

KEY

ARCH = Archive holding. Lists all episodes held in complete or near complete form in the BBC's archives. The following episodes made in colour are currently held only in black and white: *The Mind of Evil* – all; *Planet of the Daleks* – 3; *Invasion of the Dinosaurs* – 1 (*Invasion*). Complete soundtrack recordings are held for all episodes currently missing in their original form. Clips from some of these episodes are also held.

V = Video cassette releases. Some of these releases have presented edited versions of stories, and some extended versions. A number of stories have been released in more than one form. *100,000 BC* has appeared as *An Unearthly Child*, *The Mutants* (1963/64) as *The Daleks* and *Inside the Spaceship* as *The Edge of Destruction*. The surviving episodes from *The Crusade* were released on *The Hartnell Years* (third episode only) and as part of *The Crusade/The Space Museum* boxed set (first and third episodes, with a CD of the soundracks to the second and fourth); those from *The Celestial Toymaker* on *The Hartnell Years*; those from *The Abominable Snowmen*, *The Enemy of the World* and *The Space Pirates* on *The Troughton Years*; those from *The Daleks' Master Plan* and *The Evil of the Daleks* on *Daleks – The Early Years*; those from *The Moonbase* and *The Wheel in Space* on *Cybermen – The Early Years*; and that from *The Underwater Menace* in a package with those from *The Ice Warriors* (including a partial reconstruction and complete soundtrack CD of the second and third episodes of the latter). *The Chase* and *Remembrance of the Daleks* were released in a 'Dalek tin' boxed set; *The Trial of a Time Lord* was released in a 'TARDIS tin' boxed set. The Pilot Episode and *Inside the Spaceship* were released on a single tape. *Attack of the Cybermen* and *The Tenth Planet* (first three episodes, with a partial reconstruction and complete soundtrack CD of the fourth) were released in a 'Cyberman tin' boxed set. *Colony in Space* and *The Time Monster* were released in a 'Master tin' boxed set. The 'First Doctor' boxed set included *The Sensorites*, *The Time Meddler* and *The Gunfighters*. The stationers W H Smith have made available two exclusive boxed sets: a Dalek set and a Time Lord set, containing re-releases of a number of stories previously available on BBC video.

D = DVD releases. Some of these releases have presented the stories in edited or extended form only. All have included a variety of optional 'extras', including in some cases scenes deleted from the original broadcast versions. The six stories of the Key to Time season (*The Ribos Operation*, *The Pirate Planet*, *The Stones of Blood*, *The Androids of Tara*, *The Power of Kroll* and *The Armageddon Factor*) have been released as a six DVD boxed set and as individual DVDs, but in the USA only.

NOVELISATION = Novelisation and author. In this form *100,000 BC* has appeared as *An Unearthly Child*; *The Mutants* (1963/64) as *Doctor Who in an Exciting Adventure with the Daleks* and *The Daleks*; *Inside the Spaceship* as *The Edge of Destruction*; *The Web Planet* as *The Zarbi**; *The Crusade* as *The Crusaders*; *The Daleks' Master Plan* as *Mission to the Unknown* (first section) and *The Mutation of Time* (second section); *The Massacre of St Bartholomew's Eve* as *The Massacre*; *The Moonbase* as *The Cybermen*; *Spearhead from Space* as *The Auton Invasion*; *Doctor Who and the Silurians* as *The Cave Monsters**; *Colony in Space* as *The Doomsday Weapon*; *Frontier in Space* as *The Space War*; *Invasion of the Dinosaurs* as *The Dinosaur Invasion**; *Robot* as *The Giant Robot**; *Terror of the Zygons* as *The Loch Ness Monster**; *The Sun Makers* as *The Sunmakers*; and *The Trial of a Time Lord* as *The Mysterious Planet* (Parts One to Four), *Mindwarp* (Parts Five to Eight), *Terror of the Vervoids* (Parts Nine to Twelve) and *The Ultimate Foe* (Parts Thirteen and Fourteen). Those marked * have also appeared in editions under their television titles. Most novelisations have been published in hardback as well as paperback.

T = Talking book abridged version of novelisation, released on audio cassette.

A = Audio cassette or CD release of soundtrack recording (in some cases edited) with voice-over narration.

S = Script book. In this form *100,000 BC* has appeared as *The Tribe of Gum*, and *The Mutants* (1963/64) as *The Daleks*.

STORY TITLE	ARCH	V	D	NOVELISATION	T	A	S
100,000 BC	All	■	□	■ Terrance Dicks	□	□	■
The Mutants	All	■	□	■ David Whitaker	□	□	■
Inside the Spaceship	All	■	□	■ Nigel Robinson	□	□	□
Marco Polo	None	□	□	■ John Lucarotti	□	□	□
The Keys of Marinus	All	■	□	■ Philip Hinchcliffe	□	□	□
The Aztecs	All	■	■	■ John Lucarotti	□	□	□
The Sensorites	All	■	□	■ Nigel Robinson	□	□	□
The Reign of Terror	1-3, 6	□	□	■ Ian Marter	□	□	□
Planet of Giants	All	■	□	■ Terrance Dicks	□	□	□
The Dalek Invasion of Earth	All	■	□	■ Terrance Dicks	□	□	□
The Rescue	All	■	□	■ Ian Marter	□	□	□
The Romans	All	■	□	■ Donald Cotton	□	□	□
The Web Planet	All	■	□	■ Bill Strutton	□	□	□
The Crusade	1, 3	■	□	■ David Whitaker	□	□	■

STORY TITLE	ARCH	V	D	NOVELISATION	T	A	S
The Space Museum	All	■	□	■ Glyn Jones	□	□	□
The Chase	All	■	□	■ John Peel	□	□	□
The Time Meddler	All	■	□	■ Nigel Robinson	□	□	□
Galaxy 4	None	□	□	■ William Emms	□	■	■
Mission to the Unknown	None	□	□	■ John Peel	□	■	□
The Myth Makers	None	□	□	■ Donald Cotton	□	■	□
The Daleks' Master Plan	5, 10	■	□	■ John Peel	□	■	□
The Massacre of St Bartholomew's Eve	None	□	□	■ John Lucarotti	□	■	□
The Ark	All	■	□	■ Paul Erickson	□	□	□
The Celestial Toymaker	4	■	□	■ Gerry Davis/Alison Bingeman	□	■	□
The Gunfighters	All	■	□	■ Donald Cotton	□	□	□
The Savages	None	□	□	■ Ian Stuart Black	□	□	□
The War Machines	All	■	□	■ Ian Stuart Black	□	□	□
The Smugglers	None	□	□	■ Terrance Dicks	□	□	□
The Tenth Planet	1-3	■	□	■ Gerry Davis	□	□	□
The Power of the Daleks	None	□	□	■ John Peel	□	■	■
The Highlanders	None	□	□	■ Gerry Davis	□	■	□
The Underwater Menace	3	■	□	■ Nigel Robinson	□	□	□
The Moonbase	2, 4	■	□	■ Gerry Davis	□	□	□
The Macra Terror	None	□	□	■ Ian Stuart Black	□	□	□
The Faceless Ones	1, 3	□	□	■ Terrance Dicks	□	□	□
The Evil of the Daleks	2	■	□	■ John Peel	□	□	□
The Tomb of the Cybermen	All	■	■	■ Gerry Davis	□	□	■
The Abominable Snowmen	2	■	□	■ Terrance Dicks	□	□	□
The Ice Warriors	1, 4-6	■	□	■ Brian Hayles	□	□	□
The Enemy of the World	3	■	□	■ Ian Marter	□	□	□
The Web of Fear	1	□	□	■ Terrance Dicks	□	□	□
Fury from the Deep	None	□	□	■ Victor Pemberton	□	□	□
The Wheel in Space	3, 6	■	□	■ Terrance Dicks	□	□	□
The Dominators	All	■	□	■ Ian Marter	□	□	□
The Mind Robber	All	■	□	■ Peter Ling	□	□	□
The Invasion	2, 3, 5-8	■	□	■ Ian Marter	□	□	□
The Krotons	All	■	□	■ Terrance Dicks	□	□	□
The Seeds of Death	All	■	■	■ Terrance Dicks	□	□	□
The Space Pirates	2	■	□	■ Terrance Dicks	□	■	□
The War Games	All	■	□	■ Malcolm Hulke	□	□	□
Spearhead from Space	All	■	■	■ Terrance Dicks	□	□	□
Doctor Who and the Silurians	All	■	□	■ Malcolm Hulke	□	□	□
The Ambassadors of Death	All	■	□	■ Terrance Dicks	□	□	□
Inferno	All	■	□	■ Terrance Dicks	□	□	□
Terror of the Autons	All	■	□	■ Terrance Dicks	□	□	□
The Mind of Evil	All	■	□	■ Terrance Dicks	□	□	□
The Claws of Axos	All	■	□	■ Terrance Dicks	□	□	□
Colony in Space	All	■	□	■ Malcolm Hulke	□	□	□

STORY TITLE	ARCH	V	D	NOVELISATION	T	A	S
The Dæmons	All	■	□	■ Barry Letts	□	□	■
Day of the Daleks	All	■	□	■ Terrance Dicks	□	□	□
The Curse of Peladon	All	■	□	■ Brian Hayles	■	□	□
The Sea Devils	All	■	□	■ Malcolm Hulke	□	□	□
The Mutants	All	■	□	■ Terrance Dicks	□	□	□
The Time Monster	All	■	□	■ Terrance Dicks	□	□	□
The Three Doctors	All	■	■	■ Terrance Dicks	□	□	□
Carnival of Monsters	All	■	□	■ Terrance Dicks	□	□	□
Frontier in Space	All	■	□	■ Malcolm Hulke	□	□	□
Planet of the Daleks	All	■	□	■ Terrance Dicks	■	□	□
The Green Death	All	■	□	■ Malcolm Hulke	□	□	□
The Time Warrior	All	■	□	■ Terrance Dicks	□	□	□
Invasion of the Dinosaurs	All	□	□	■ Malcolm Hulke	□	□	□
Death to the Daleks	All	■	□	■ Terrance Dicks	□	□	□
The Monster of Peladon	All	■	□	■ Terrance Dicks	□	□	□
Planet of the Spiders	All	■	□	■ Terrance Dicks	□	□	□
Robot	All	■	□	■ Terrance Dicks	□	□	□
The Ark in Space	All	■	■	■ Ian Marter	□	□	□
The Sontaran Experiment	All	■	□	■ Ian Marter	□	□	□
Genesis of the Daleks	All	■	□	■ Terrance Dicks	□	■	□
Revenge of the Cybermen	All	■	□	■ Terrance Dicks	□	□	□
Terror of the Zygons	All	■	□	■ Terrance Dicks	□	□	□
Planet of Evil	All	■	□	■ Terrance Dicks	□	□	□
Pyramids of Mars	All	■	□	■ Terrance Dicks	□	□	□
The Android Invasion	All	■	□	■ Terrance Dicks	□	□	□
The Brain of Morbius	All	■	□	■ Terrance Dicks	□	□	□
The Seeds of Doom	All	■	□	■ Philip Hinchcliffe	□	□	□
The Masque of Mandragora	All	■	□	■ Philip Hinchcliffe	□	□	□
The Hand of Fear	All	■	□	■ Terrance Dicks	□	□	□
The Deadly Assassin	All	■	□	■ Terrance Dicks	□	□	□
The Face of Evil	All	■	□	■ Terrance Dicks	□	□	□
The Robots of Death	All	■	■	■ Terrance Dicks	□	□	□
The Talons of Weng-Chiang	All	■	■	■ Terrance Dicks	□	□	■
Horror of Fang Rock	All	■	□	■ Terrance Dicks	□	□	□
The Invisible Enemy	All	■	□	■ Terrance Dicks	□	□	□
Image of the Fendahl	All	■	□	■ Terrance Dicks	□	□	□
The Sun Makers	All	■	□	■ Terrance Dicks	□	□	□
Underworld	All	■	□	■ Terrance Dicks	□	□	□
The Invasion of Time	All	■	□	■ Terrance Dicks	□	□	□
The Ribos Operation	All	■	■	■ Ian Marter	□	□	□
The Pirate Planet	All	■	■	□	□	□	□
The Stones of Blood	All	■	■	■ Terrance Dicks	□	□	□
The Androids of Tara	All	■	■	■ Terrance Dicks	□	□	□
The Power of Kroll	All	■	■	■ Terrance Dicks	□	□	□
The Armageddon Factor	All	■	■	■ Terrance Dicks	□	□	□

STORY TITLE	ARCH	V	D	NOVELISATION	T	A	S
Destiny of the Daleks	All	■	□	■ Terrance Dicks	□	□	□
City of Death	All	■	□	□	□	□	□
The Creature from the Pit	All	■	□	■ David Fisher	□	□	□
Nightmare of Eden	All	■	□	■ Terrance Dicks	□	□	□
The Horns of Nimon	All	□	□	■ Terrance Dicks	□	□	□
The Leisure Hive	All	■	□	■ David Fisher	□	□	□
Meglos	All	■	□	■ Terrance Dicks	□	□	□
Full Circle	All	■	□	■ Andrew Smith	□	□	□
State of Decay	All	■	□	■ Terrance Dicks	■	□	□
Warriors' Gate	All	■	□	■ John Lydecker	□	□	□
The Keeper of Traken	All	■	□	■ Terrance Dicks	□	□	□
Logopolis	All	■	□	■ Christopher H Bidmead	□	□	□
Castrovalva	All	■	□	■ Christopher H Bidmead	□	□	□
Four to Doomsday	All	■	□	■ Terrance Dicks	□	□	□
Kinda	All	■	□	■ Terrance Dicks	■	□	□
The Visitation	All	■	□	■ Eric Saward	□	□	□
Black Orchid	All	■	□	■ Terence Dudley	□	□	□
Earthshock	All	■	□	■ Ian Marter	□	□	□
Time-Flight	All	■	□	■ Peter Grimwade	□	□	□
Arc of Infinity	All	■	□	■ Terrance Dicks	□	□	□
Snakedance	All	■	□	■ Terrance Dicks	□	□	□
Mawdryn Undead	All	■	□	■ Peter Grimwade	□	□	□
Terminus	All	■	□	■ John Lydecker	□	□	□
Enlightenment	All	■	□	■ Barbara Clegg	□	□	□
The King's Demons	All	■	□	■ Terence Dudley	□	□	□
The Five Doctors	All	■	■	■ Terrance Dicks	□	□	□
Warriors of the Deep	All	■	□	■ Terrance Dicks	■	□	□
The Awakening	All	■	□	■ Eric Pringle	□	□	□
Frontios	All	■	□	■ Christopher H Bidmead	□	□	□
Resurrection of the Daleks	All	■	■	□	□	□	□
Planet of Fire	All	■	□	■ Peter Grimwade	□	□	□
The Caves of Androzani	All	■	□	■ Terrance Dicks	□	□	□
The Twin Dilemma	All	■	□	■ Eric Saward	□	□	□
Attack of the Cybermen	All	■	□	■ Eric Saward	■	□	□
Vengeance on Varos	All	■	■	■ Philip Martin	■	□	□
The Mark of the Rani	All	■	□	■ Pip and Jane Baker	□	□	□
The Two Doctors	All	■	□	■ Robert Holmes	□	□	□
Timelash	All	■	□	■ Glen McCoy	□	□	□
Revelation of the Daleks	All	■	□	□	□	□	□
The Trial of a Time Lord (1-4)	All	■	□	■ Terrance Dicks	□	□	□
The Trial of a Time Lord (5-8)	All	■	□	■ Philip Martin	□	□	□
The Trial of a Time Lord (9-12)	All	■	□	■ Pip and Jane Baker	□	□	□
The Trial of a Time Lord (13-14)	All	■	□	■ Pip and Jane Baker	□	□	□
Time and the Rani	All	■	□	■ Pip and Jane Baker	□	□	□
Paradise Towers	All	■	□	■ Stephen Wyatt	□	□	□

STORY TITLE	ARCH	V	D	NOVELISATION	T	A	S
Delta and the Bannermen	All	■	□	■ Malcolm Kohll	□	□	□
Dragonfire	All	■	□	■ Ian Briggs	□	□	□
Remembrance of the Daleks	All	■	■	■ Ben Aaronovitch	□	□	□
The Happiness Patrol	All	■	□	■ Graeme Curry	□	□	□
Silver Nemesis	All	■	□	■ Kevin Clarke	□	□	□
The Greatest Show in the Galaxy	All	■	□	■ Stephen Wyatt	□	□	□
Battlefield	All	■	□	■ Marc Platt	□	□	□
Ghost Light	All	■	□	■ Marc Platt	□	□	■
The Curse of Fenric	All	■	□	■ Ian Briggs	□	□	□
Survival	All	■	□	■ Rona Munro	□	□	□
Doctor Who	All	■	■	■ Gary Russell	■	□	■
K9 and Company	All	■	□	■ Terence Dudley	□	□	□
In A Fix With Sontarans	All	□	□	□	□	□	□
Search Out Space	All	□	□	□	□	□	□
Dimensions in Time	All	□	□	□	□	□	□
Doctor Who and The Curse of Fatal Death	All	■	□	□	□	□	□

INDEX BY TITLE

INDEX BY NAME

Page numbers in italics denote entries in the episode cast and crew listings.

Attwell, Michael *191, 604*
Auger, Tony *536*
Avon, Crispin *706*
Avon, Roger *7, 108*
Ayres, Mark *671,* 673, *680, 684, 710,* 711
Ayres, Rosalind 665
Babbage, Don *510, 526, 548, 555, 570, 593, 599,*
 611, 615, 622, 629, 655, 664, 672
Bacon, Norman *501*
Badcoe, Brian *342*
Badel, Sarah 669
Badger, Peter *60*
Bailey, Christopher *529,* 531, 532, 533, *551,* 553
Bailey, Edmund *251*
Bailey, John *47, 176, 486*
Bailie, David *417*
Baker, Bob *280,* 282, *306,* 309, *316, 366,* 368, *405,*
 407, *424, 427,* 430, *438,* 440, *465, 482,* 484, 703
Baker, Chris 394
Baker, Colin 300, 361, *549,* 549, *575, 594,* 594,
 596, 598, 600, 601, 602, *603,* 603, 607, 609,
 612, 616, 623, 624, 626, *627,* 633, 634, 637,
 639-640, 643, 645, 647, *705, 706, 708,* 710
Baker, George *501,* 501
Baker, Jane *611,* 614, 626, 628, *629,* 634, 643, *644,* 646
Baker, John *175, 271, 285,* 304, *316, 402, 522, 534,*
 551, 570, 575, 523, 571, 599
Baker, John Adam *586*
Baker, Jules *282*
Baker, Lucy *557*
Baker, Pip *611,* 614, 626, 628, *629,* 634, 643, *644,* 646
Baker, Tom *353, 358, 359,* 361, 362, 363, *378,*
 385, 388, 390, 395, 399, *401,* 401, 405, *414,*
 416, *424,* 424, 445, 446, *447,* 448, 452, 453,
 455, *470,* 470, 474-475, 478, 485, 487, 490,
 491, 494, 495, 499, 502, 503, 505, 514, 515,
 516, 517, 523, 525, 570, 572, 574, *708*
Baldock, Peter *414*
Bale, Terry *51, 300*
Ball, Peter *708*
Ballantine, George *552*
Balsdon, J R *354*
Bancroft, Susie *701*
Bangerter, Michael *591*
Banks Stewart, Robert *378,* 381, 394, *396,* 398,
 399, 400, *419,* 492
Banks, David *540,* 542, *571, 604, 668*
Baraker, Gabor *36, 77*
Barber, Henry *513, 533, 551, 603, 618, 644, 647,*
 660, 672, 680
Barber, Neville *312, 701*
Barclay, Richard *35*
Barclay, Sam *18, 559*
Barker, Hugh *35, 166*
Barker, Ken *622*
Barker, Tim 665
Barkworth, Peter *191,* 193

Barlow, Tim *472, 472*
Barnes, Larry 421
Barnes, Richard *483*
Barnikel, Philip *186, 194, 199*
Baron, David *188*
Baron, Denise *599, 602, 629, 671,* 673, *684*
Baron, Lynda *124,* 126, 127, *563,* 565
Barr, Patrick *162*
Barrard, John *51,* 54
Barratt, Hilary *659*
Barratt, Reginald *57*
Barrett, Joan *306, 310*
Barrett, Ray *65,* 67
Barrington, Albert *108*
Barrington, Michael *397*
Barron, Keith *563,* 563, 565
Barron, Ray *397*
Barrs, Johnny *277*
Barry, Anna *295*
Barry, B H *218, 526,* 527
Barry, Brendan *256*
Barry, Christopher *26,* 28-29, 34, *64,* 66, *67,* 69,
 70, 85, *128, 148, 288,* 290, 291, *306,* 308, 309,
 310, 312, *360,* 361, *392,* 394, *470, 479,* 480, 482
Barry, Morris *161,* 163, 165, *183,* 184, 186, *213,*
 217, *480,* 480
Barry, Tim *567*
Bartlett, Bobi *222,* 226, *227, 231,* 276
Bartlett, Peter *186*
Barton, David *611*
Barton, Keith *492*
Barton, Paul *256*
Barton, William *688,* 688
Baskcomb, John *272*
Bate, James *591*
Bateman, Geoffrey *483*
Bates, Leslie *36, 114*
Bateson, Timothy *449,* 449
Bathurst, Peter *150, 281*
Baugh, Martin *186, 190,* 192, *194, 199, 203, 206,*
 213, 216, *218*
Baverstock, Donald 14, 16, 17, 33
Baxter, Lois *460*
Baxter, Trevor *421,* 422
Bay, John *78*
Bayldon, Geoffrey *480,* 480, 481, 669
Bayler, Terence *118, 241*
Bayly, Johnson *214*
BBC Radiophonic Workshop 16, *18, 21, 55, 95,*
 137, 171, *182,* 189, *206,* 208, *213, 249, 270,*
 280, *294, 316,* 316, *336,* 348, *359, 378, 401,*
 424, 447, 470, 491, 494, *521, 547, 570, 575, 603,*
 627, 643, 659, 676, 693, 705
Beacham, Rod *200*
Beale, Richard *118, 125, 167, 332*
Bear, Jeremy *306, 396*
Beardmore, John *583*

Cult TV Guides from Telos

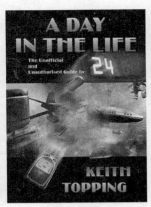

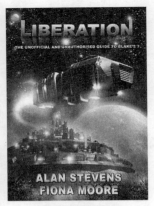

BEYOND THE GATE
The Unofficial and
Unauthorised Guide to
Stargate SG-1
BY KEITH TOPPING

A DAY IN THE LIFE
The Unofficial and
Unauthorised Guide to
24
BY KEITH TOPPING

LIBERATION:
The Unofficial and
Unauthorised Guide to
Blake's 7
BY ALAN STEVENS
& FIONA MOORE

Beyond the Gate is an indispensable unofficial and unauthorised guide to the *Stargate* universe. Author Keith Topping breaks down each of the series' 100-plus episodes, analysing the elements and recurring themes that make it so popular.
288pp. A5 paperback original   £9.99 UK $17.95 US $24.95 CAN

A Day in the Life chronicles the critically acclaimed first season of the innovative TV thriller, *24*. Author Keith Topping offers his distinctive breakdown of each episode, with behind-the-scenes details and examples of when the show's logic went off course.
192pp. A5 paperback original   £9.99 UK $17.95 US $24.95 CAN

The publication of *Liberation: The Unofficial and Unauthorised Guide to Blake's 7* coincides with the 25th anniversary of *Blake's 7*. The book offers analyses of every episode, examination of key episodes from their genesis to the final version, and excerpts from original scripts and interviews with people involved in the production.
250pp. (approx.) A5 paperback original   £9.99 UK $19.95 US $24.95 CAN
Signed and numbered limited ed. hardback   £30 UK $59.95 US $64.95 CAN

Available from **Telos Orders, Beech House, Chapel Lane, Moulton, Cheshire, CW9 8PQ, England**. Please add the following p&p to the prices above: Single title ordered: UK: £2.50; Europe: £4.00; USA/Canada: £7.50; Rest of World: £8.50. Two or more titles ordered: UK: £4.00; Europe: £5.00; USA/Canada: £10.00; Rest of World: £11.00. Please make cheques (in pounds sterling only) payable to **Telos Publishing Ltd**. All Telos titles can also be ordered online by credit card.
Visit **www.telos.co.uk** for more information.